S0-ANQ-364

THE LEGEND OF SLEEPY HOLLOW

AND OTHER STORIES

THE LEGEND OF SLEEPY HOLLOW

AND OTHER STORIES

WASHINGTON IRVING

FALL RIVER PRESS

New York

FALL RIVER PRESS

New York

An Imprint of Sterling Publishing
1166 Avenue of the Americas
New York, NY 10036

The texts used in this volume were all published as volumes in the author's revised edition of *The Works of Washington Irving*:
The Sketch Book. New York: George P. Putnam, 1850.
Tales of a Traveller. New York: George P. Putnam, 1849.
Wolfert's Roost and Other Papers. New York: George P. Putnam, 1864.

The Fell Types are digitally reproduced by Igino Marini.
www.iginomarini.com

ISBN 978-1-4351-6067-5

Manufactured in the United States of America

4 6 8 10 9 7 5 3

www.sterlingpublishing.com

Contents

The Sketch Book

Tales of a Traveller

PART I

STRANGE STORIES BY A NERVOUS GENTLEMAN

PART II

BUCKTHORNE AND HIS FRIENDS

Part III

The Italian Banditti

Part IV

The Money-Diggers

Wolfert's Roost and Other Papers

Introduction

IN 1815, WASHINGTON IRVING TRAVELED TO ENGLAND ON A MISSION TO RESCUE HIS FAMily's trading company, which had suffered disastrous reversals during the War of 1812. His to failure keep the business from dissolving in bankruptcy two years later proved a great boon to American literature. Freed of business responsibilities, and faced with virtually no prospects of employment, Irving determined to pursue a writing career and began fleshing out themes and ideas that he had jotted down in notebooks between 1815 and 1818. The stories and essays that he produced were published in seven installments in the United States between 1819 and 1820 under the title *The Sketch Book*, and attributed to Geoffrey Crayon, Gent. *The Sketch Book* met with critical and popular acclaim in the United States and abroad, and it secured Irving a permanent place in American letters.

It's not surprising that Irving would produce a landmark of American literature while living as an expatriate from the United States, as he was arguably the most American of the new nation's authors. Born on April 3, 1783, just five days after the truce that ended America's war of independence from Great Britain, and named after American war hero George Washington, Irving was the youngest child of a prosperous Manhattan-based family, deeply invested in the merchant trade. He began studying law in 1799, and eventually passed the bar, but his heart was always in writing. Between 1802 and 1803, New York's *Morning Chronicle* published nine satirical letter-essays that he had written as Jonathan Oldstyle, Gent., the first of several pseudonyms that he would employ. Irving continued on this satirical bent, writing most of the miscellaneous pieces that were collected *Salmagundi; or, the Whim-Whams and Opinions of Launcelot Langstaff, Esq. & Others* (1807-1808). His masterpiece in this vein, *A History of New-York, from the Beginning of the World to the End of the Dutch Dynasty* (1809) by Diedrich Knickerbocker, is a burlesque of New York history featuring caricatures of contemporary celebrities and politicians.

The Sketch Book, published under his Geoffrey Crayon, Gent. pseudonym,was Irving's first book after *A History of New-York*, and it is remembered today almost exclusively for the publication of "Rip Van Winkle" and "The Legend of Sleepy Hollow," stories inspired by his travels as a teenager to New York's Catskill Mountains and Hudson River Valley. While those stories are acknowledged classics of American folklore, their singling out obscures Irving's achievement in the volume. Both tales are embedded, along with other stories, in a framework of sketches on life in America, England, and the European continent, all rich with local color and history. It's not clear whether Irving distinguished these stories from his sketches, but it's worth noting that at the time they were published works of fiction were almost entirely of novel length. *The Sketch Book* heralds the emergence of the short story as a literary form in its own right, sprung from the same sources of inspiration that informed Irving's essays.

Most collections that Irving was to publish would be mixes of short stories and sketches so fancifully told that they are hard to distinguish from fiction. *Tales of a Traveller* (1824), another Geoffrey Crayon work, appeared two years after a collection of more than fifty linked stories and essays that Irving published as *Bracebridge Hall* (1822), and its contents are similarly structured. Irving grouped its tales and sketches into four story cycles, one of them related by the same "nervous gentleman" who makes an appearance in *Bracebridge Hall.* Two of the book's best-known tales have achieved renown independent of their story cycles. "The Adventure of the German Student" is Irving's nod to the gothic horror tradition, a popular literary form for much of the preceding half-century. "The Devil and Tom Walker" is a dark satire on avarice and greed in American business dealings, and among the first deal-with-a-devil stories, now a staple of weird fiction. Like "Rip Van Winkle" and "The Legend of Sleepy Hollow," these stories show Irving's flare for fantasy, a thread that would eventually wind through the short stories of Edgar Allan Poe, Nathaniel Hawthorne, and other American writers who followed in his footsteps.

By the time Irving collected the stories and sketches published in *Wolfert's Roost and Other Papers*, he was back living in America, having served as Minister to Spain during the presidency of John Tyler and seen his collected works enshrined in a sixteen-volume set. The contents of this volume show the same storytelling dexterity and vivacity on display in Irving's earlier collections, especially "Guests of Gibbet Island," one of Irving's greatest blends of humor and supernatural horror.

Today, Irving is remembered in literary circles as the first American writer to make a living from his writing and the author who pioneered the short-story form. To the casual reader, however, he will always be remembered as the author of "The Legend of Sleepy Hollow," a tale of supernatural shenanigans in old New York that continues to inspire adaptations for the screen and other media nearly two centuries after it was published. *The Legend of Sleepy Hollow and Other Stories* commemorates this tale as a masterpiece of American mythmaking and celebrates the storytelling magic that was Washington Irving's special gift.

THE SKETCH BOOK

The Author's Account of Himself

I am of this mind with Homer, that as the snaile that crept out of her shel was turned eftsoons into a toad, and thereby was forced to make a stoole to sit on; so the traveller that stragleth from his owne country is in a short time transformed into so monstrous a shape, that he is faine to alter his mansion with his manners, and to live where he can, not where he would.

LYLY'S *EUPHUES*

I WAS ALWAYS FOND OF VISITING NEW SCENES, AND OBSERVING STRANGE characters and manners. Even when a mere child I began my travels, and made many tours of discovery into foreign parts and unknown regions of my native city, to the frequent alarm of my parents, and the emolument of the town-crier. As I grew into boyhood, I extended the range of my observations. My holiday afternoons were spent in rambles about the surrounding country. I made myself familiar with all its places famous in history or fable. I knew every spot where a murder or robbery had been committed, or a ghost seen. I visited the neighboring villages, and added greatly to my stock of knowledge, by noting their habits and customs, and conversing with their sages and great men. I even journeyed one long summers day to the summit of the most distant hill, whence I stretched my eye over many a mile of terra incognita, and was astonished to find how vast a globe I inhabited.

This rambling propensity strengthened with my years. Books of voyages and travels became my passion, and in devouring their contents, I neglected the regular exercises of the school. How wistfully would I wander about the pier-heads in fine weather, and watch the parting ships, bound to distant climes—with what longing eyes would I gaze after their lessening sails, and waft myself in imagination to the ends of the earth!

Further reading and thinking, though they brought this vague inclination into more reasonable bounds, only served to make it more decided. I visited various parts of my own country; and had I been merely a lover of fine scenery, I should have felt little desire to seek elsewhere its gratification: for on no country have the charms of nature been more prodigally lavished. Her mighty lakes, like oceans of liquid silver; her mountains, with their bright aerial tints; her valleys, teeming with wild fertility; her tremendous cataracts, thundering in their solitudes; her boundless plains, waving with spontaneous verdure; her broad deep rivers, rolling in solemn silence to the ocean; her trackless forests, where vegetation puts forth all its magnificence; her skies, kindling with the magic of summer clouds and glorious sunshine;—no, never need an American look beyond his own country for the sublime and beautiful of natural scenery.

But Europe held forth the charms of storied and poetical association. There were to be seen the masterpieces of art, the refinements of highly-cultivated society, the quaint peculiarities of ancient and local custom. My native country was full of youthful promise: Europe was rich in the accumulated treasures of age. Her very ruins told the history of times gone by, and every mouldering stone was a chronicle. I longed to wander over the scenes of renowned achievement—to tread, as it were, in the footsteps of antiquity—to loiter about the ruined castle—to meditate on the falling tower—to escape, in short, from the common-place realities of the present and lose myself among the shadowy grandeurs of the past.

I had, beside all this, an earnest desire to see the great men of the earth. We have, it is true, our great men in America: not a city but has an ample share of them. I have mingled among them in my time, and been almost withered by the shade into which they cast me; for there is nothing so baleful to a small man as the shade of a great one, particularly the great man of a city. But I was anxious to see the great men of Europe; for I had read in the works of various philosophers, that all animals degenerated in America, and man among the number. A great man of Europe, thought I, must therefore be as superior to a great man of America, as a peak of the Alps to a highland of the Hudson; and in this idea I was confirmed, by observing the comparative importance and swelling magnitude of many English travelers among us, who, I was assured, were very little people in their own country. I will visit this land of wonders, thought I, and see the gigantic race from which I am degenerated.

It has been either my good or evil lot to have my roving passion gratified. I have wandered through different countries, and witnessed many of the shifting scenes of life. I cannot say that I have studied them with the eye of a philosopher; but rather with the sauntering gaze with which humble lovers of the picturesque stroll from the window of one print-shop to another; caught, sometimes by the delineations of beauty, sometimes by the distortions of caricature, and sometimes by the loveliness of landscape. As it is the fashion for modern tourists to travel pencil in hand, and bring home their portfolios filled with sketches, I am disposed to get up a few for the entertainment of my friends. When, however, I look over the hints and memorandums I have taken down for the purpose, my heart almost fails me at finding how my idle humor has led me aside from the great objects studied by every regular traveler who would make a book. I fear I shall give equal disappointment with an unlucky landscape painter, who had traveled on the continent but, following the bent of his vagrant inclination, had sketched in nooks, and corners, and by-places. His sketch-book was accordingly crowded with cottages, and landscapes, and obscure ruins; but he had neglected to paint St Peter's, or the Coliseum; the cascade of Terni, or the bay of Naples; and had not a single glacier or volcano in his whole collection.

The Voyage

Ships, ships, I will descrie you
Amidst the main,
I will come and try you,
What you are protecting,
And projecting,
What's your end and aim.
One goes abroad for merchandise and trading,
Another stays to keep his country from invading,
A third is coming home with rich and wealthy lading.
Halloo! my fancie, whither wilt thon go?

OLD POEM

TO AN AMERICAN VISITING EUROPE, THE LONG VOYAGE HE HAS TO MAKE is an excellent preparative. The temporary absence of worldly scenes and employments produces a state of mind peculiarly fitted to receive new and vivid impressions. The vast space of waters that separates the hemispheres is like a blank page in existence. There is no gradual transition by which, as in Europe, the features and population of one country blend almost imperceptibly with those of another. From the moment you lose sight of the land you have left, all is vacancy until you step on the opposite shore, and are launched at once into the bustle and novelties of another world.

In traveling by land there is a continuity of scene, and a connected succession of persons and incidents, that carry on the story of life, and lessen the effect of absence and separation. We drag, it is true, a "lengthening chain" at each remove of our pilgrimage; but the chain is unbroken: we can trace it back link by link; and we feel that the last still grapples us to home. But a wide sea voyage severs us at once. It makes us conscious of being cast loose from the secure anchorage of settled life, and sent adrift upon a doubtful world. It interposes a gulf, not merely imaginary, but real, between us and our homes—a gulf subject to tempest, and fear, and uncertainty, rendering distance palpable, and return precarious.

Such, at least, was the case with myself. As I saw the last blue line of my native land fade away like a cloud in the horizon, it seemed as if I had closed one volume of the world and its concerns, and had time for meditation, before I opened another. That land, too, now vanishing from my view, which contained all most dear to me in life; what vicissitudes might occur in it—what changes might take place in me, before I should visit it again! Who can tell, when he sets forth to wander, whither he may be driven by the uncertain currents of existence; or when he may return; or whether it may ever be his lot to revisit the scenes of his childhood?

I said that at sea all is vacancy; I should correct the expression. To one given to day-dreaming, and fond of losing himself in reveries, a sea voyage is full of subjects for meditation; but then they are the wonders of the deep, and of the air, and rather tend to abstract the mind from worldly themes. I delighted to loll over the quarter-railing, or climb to the main-top, of a calm day, and muse for hours together on the tranquil bosom of a summer's sea; to gaze upon the piles of golden clouds just peering above the horizon, fancy them some fairy realms, and people them with a creation of my own;—to watch the gentle undulating billows, rolling their silver volumes, as if to die away on those happy shores.

There was a delicious sensation of mingled security and awe with which I looked down, from my giddy height, on the monsters of the deep at their uncouth gambols. Shoals of porpoises tumbling about the bow of the ship; the grampus slowly heaving his huge form above the surface; or the ravenous shark, darting, like a spectre, through the blue waters. My imagination would conjure up all that I had heard or read of the watery world beneath me; of the finny herds that roam its fathomless valleys; of the shapeless monsters that lurk among the very foundations of the earth; and of those wild phantasms that swell the tales of fishermen and sailors.

Sometimes a distant sail, gliding along the edge of the ocean, would be another theme of idle speculation. How interesting this fragment of a world, hastening to rejoin the great mass of existence! What a glorious monument of human invention; which has in a manner triumphed over wind and wave; has brought the ends of the world into communion; has established an interchange of blessings, pouring into the sterile regions of the north all the luxuries of the south; has diffused the light of knowledge and the charities of cultivated life; and has thus bound together those scattered portions of the human race, between which nature seemed to have thrown an insurmountable barrier.

We one day descried some shapeless object drifting at a distance. At sea, every thing that breaks the monotony of the surrounding expanse attracts attention. It proved to be the must of a ship that must have been completely wrecked; for there were the remains of handkerchiefs, by which some of the crew had fastened themselves to this spar, to prevent their being washed off by the waves. There was no trace by which the name of the ship could be ascertained. The wreck had evidently drifted about for many months; clusters of shell-fish had fastened about it, and long sea-weeds flaunted at its sides. But where, thought I, is the crew? Their struggle has long been over— they have gone down amidst the roar of the tempest—their bones lie whitening among the caverns of the deep. Silence, oblivion, like the waves, have closed over them, and no one can tell the story of their end. What sighs have been wafted after that ship! what prayers offered up at the deserted fireside of home! How often has the mistress, the wife, the mother, pored over the daily news, to catch some casual intelligence of this rover of the deep! How has expectation darkened into anxiety—anxiety into dread—and dread into despair! Alas! not one memento may ever return for love to cherish. All that may ever be known, is, that she sailed from her port, and was never heard of more!"

The sight of this wreck, as usual, gave rise to many dismal anecdotes. This was particularly the case in the evening, when the weather, which had hitherto been fair, began to look wild and threatening, and gave indications of one of those sudden storms which will sometimes break in upon the serenity of a summer voyage. As we sat round the dull light of a lamp in the cabin, that made the gloom more ghastly, every one had his tale of shipwreck and disaster. I was particularly struck with a short one related by the captain.

"As I was once sailing," said he, "in a fine stout ship across the banks of Newfoundland, one of those heavy fogs which prevail in those parts rendered it impossible for us to see far ahead even in the daytime; but at night the weather was so thick that we could not distinguish any object at twice the length of the ship. I kept lights at the mast-head, and a constant watch forward to look out for fishing smacks, which are accustomed to lie at anchor on the banks. The wind was blowing a smacking breeze, and we were going at a great rate through the water. Suddenly the watch gave the alarm of 'a sail ahead!'—it was scarcely uttered before we were upon her. She was a small schooner, at anchor, with her broadside towards us. The crew were all asleep, and had neglected to hoist a light. We struck her just amid-ships. The force, the size, and weight of our vessel bore her down below the waves; we passed over her and were hurried on our course. As the crashing wreck was sinking beneath us, I had a glimpse of two or three half-naked wretches rushing from her cabin; they just started from their beds to be swallowed shrieking by the waves. I heard their drowning cry mingling with the wind. The blast that bore it to our ears swept us out of all farther hearing. I shall never forget that cry! It was some time before we could put the ship about, she was under such headway. We returned, as nearly as we could guess, to the place where the smack had anchored. We cruised about for several hours in the dense fog. We fired signal guns, and listened if we might hear the halloo of any survivors: but all was silent—we never saw or heard any thing of them more."

I confess these stories, for a time, put an end to all my fine fancies. The storm increased with the night. The sea was lashed into tremendous confusion. There was a fearful, sullen sound of rushing waves, and broken surges. Deep called unto deep. At times the black volume of clouds over head seemed rent asunder by flashes of lightning which quivered along the foaming billows, and made the succeeding darkness doubly terrible. The thunders bellowed over the wild waste of waters, and were echoed and prolonged by the mountain waves. As I saw the ship staggering and plunging among these roaring caverns, it seemed miraculous that she regained her balance, or preserved her buoyancy. Her yards would dip into the water: her bow was almost buried beneath the waves. Sometimes an impending surge appeared ready to overwhelm her, and nothing but a dexterous movement of the helm preserved her from the shock.

When I retired to my cabin, the awful scene still followed me. The whistling of the wind through the rigging sounded like funereal wailings. The creaking of the masts, the straining and groaning of bulk-heads, as the ship labored in the weltering sea, were frightful. As I heard the waves rushing along the sides of the ship, and roaring in my very ear, it seemed as if Death were raging round this floating prison, seeking for his prey: the mere starting of a nail, the yawning of a seam, might give him entrance.

A fine day, however, with a tranquil sea and favoring breeze, soon put all these dismal reflections to flight. It is impossible to resist the gladdening influence of fine weather and fair wind at sea. When the ship is decked out in all her canvas, every sail swelled, and careering gayly over the curling waves, how lofty, how gallant she appears—how she seems to lord it over the deep!

I might fill a volume with the reveries of a sea voyage, for with me it is almost a continual reverie—but it is time to get to shore.

It was a fine sunny morning when the thrilling cry of "land!" was given from the mast-head. None but those who have experienced it can form an idea of the delicious throng of sensations which rush into an American's bosom, when he first comes in sight of Europe. There is a volume of associations with the very name. It is the land of promises teeming with every thing of which his childhood has heard, or on which his studious years have pondered.

From that time until the moment of arrival, it was all feverish excitement. The ships of war, that prowled like guardian giants along the coast; the headlands of Ireland, stretching out into the channel; the Welsh mountains, towering into the clouds; all were objects of intense interest As we sailed up the Mersey, I reconnoitred the shores with a telescope. My eye dwelt with delight on neat cottages, with their trim shrubberies and green grass plots. I saw the mouldering ruin of an abbey overrun with ivy, and the taper spire of a village church rising from the brow of a neighboring hill—all were characteristic of England.

The tide and wind were so favorable that the ship was enabled to come at once to the pier. It was thronged with people; some, idle lookers-on, others, eager expectants of friends or relatives. I could distinguish the merchant to whom the ship was consigned. I knew him by his calculating brow and restless air. His hands were thrust into his pockets; he was whistling thoughtfully, and walking to and fro, a small space having been accorded him by the crowd, in deference to his temporary importance. There were repeated cheerings and salutations interchanged between the shore and the ship, as friends happened to recognize each other. I particularly noticed one young woman of humble dress, but interesting demeanor. She was leaning forward from among the crowd; her eye hurried over the ship as it neared the shore, to catch some wished-for countenance. She seemed disappointed and agitated; when I heard a faint voice call her name. It was from a poor sailor who had been ill all the voyage, and had excited the sympathy of every one on board. When the weather was fine, his messmates had spread a mattress for him on deck in the shade, but of late his illness had so increased, that he had taken to his hammock, and only breathed a wish that he might see his wife before he died. He had been helped on deck as we came up the river, and was now leaning against the shrouds, with a countenance so wasted, so pale, so ghastly, that it was no wonder even the eye of affection did not recognize him. But at the sound of his voice, her eye darted on his features; it read, at once, a whole volume of sorrow; she clasped her hands, uttered a faint shriek, and stood wringing them in silent agony.

All now was hurry and bustle. The meetings of acquaintances—the greetings of friends—the consultations of men of business. I alone was solitary and idle. I had no friend to meet, no cheering to receive. I stepped upon the land of my forefathers—but felt that I was a stranger in the land.

Roscoe

—In the service of mankind to be
A guardian god below; still to employ
The mind's brave ardor in heroic aims,
Such as may raise us o'er the groveling herd,
And make us shine for ever—that is life.

THOMSON

One of the first places to which a stranger is taken in Liverpool is the Athenæum. It is established on a liberal and judicious plan; it contains a good library, and spacious reading-room, and is the great literary resort of the place. Go there at what hour you may, you are sure to find it filled with grave-looking personages, deeply absorbed in the study of newspapers.

As I was once visiting this haunt of the learned, my attention was attracted to a person just entering the room. He was advanced in life, tall, and of a form that might once have been commanding, but it was a little bowed by time—perhaps by care. He had a noble Roman style of countenance; a head that would have pleased a painter; and though some slight furrows on his brow showed that wasting thought had been busy there, yet his eye still beamed with the fire of a poetic soul. There was something in his whole appearance that indicated a being of a different order from the bustling race around him.

I inquired his name, and was informed that it was Roscoe. I drew back with an involuntary feeling of veneration. This, then, was an author of celebrity; this was one of those men, whose voices have gone forth to the ends of the earth; with whose minds I have communed even in the solitudes of America. Accustomed, as we are in our country, to know European writers only by their works, we cannot conceive of them, as of other men, engrossed by trivial or sordid pursuits, and jostling with the crowd of common minds in the dusty paths of life. They pass before our imaginations like superior beings, radiant with the emanations of their genius, and surrounded by a halo of literary glory.

To find, therefore, the elegant historian of the Medici, mingling among the busy sons of traffic, at first shocked my poetical ideas; but it is from the very circumstances and situation in which he has been placed, that Mr. Roscoe derives his highest claims to admiration. It is interesting to notice how some minds seem almost to create themselves, springing up under every disadvantage, and working their solitary but irresistible way through a thousand obstacles. Nature seems to delight in disappointing the assiduities of art, with which it would rear legitimate dullness to maturity; and to glory in the vigor and luxuriance of her chance productions. She scatters the seeds of genius to the winds, and though some may perish among the stony places of the world, and some be choked by the thorns and brambles of early adversity, yet others will now and then strike root even in the clefts of the rock, struggle bravely up into sunshine, and spread over their sterile birthplace all the beauties of vegetation.

Such has been the case with Mr. Roscoe. Born in a place apparently ungenial to the growth of literary talent; in the very market-place of trade; without fortune, family connections, or patronage; self-prompted, self-sustained, and almost self-taught, he has conquered every obstacle, achieved his way to eminence, and, having become one of the ornaments of the nation, has tamed the whole force of his talents and influence to advance and embellish his native town.

Indeed, it is this last trait in his character which has given him the greatest interest in my eyes, and induced me particularly to point him out to my countrymen. Eminent as are his literary merits, he is but one among the many distinguished authors of this intellectual nation. They, however, in general, live but for their own fame, or their own pleasures. Their private history presents no lesson to the world, or, perhaps, a humiliating one of human frailty and inconsistency. At best, they are prone to steal away from the bustle and commonplace of busy existence; to indulge in the selfishness of lettered ease; and to revel in scenes of mental, but exclusive enjoyment.

Mr. Roscoe, on the contrary, has claimed none of the accorded privileges of talent. He has shut himself up in no garden of thought, nor elysium of fancy; but has gone forth into the highways and thoroughfares of life; he has planted bowers by the way-side, for the refreshment of the pilgrim and the sojourner, and has opened pure fountains, where the laboring man may turn aside from the dust and heat of the day, and drink of the living streams of knowledge. There is a "daily beauty in his life," on which mankind may meditate and grow better. It exhibits no lofty and almost useless, because inimitable, example of excellence; but presents a picture of active, yet simple and imitable virtues, which are within every man's reach, but which, unfortunately, are not exercised by many, or this world would be a paradise.

But his private life is peculiarly worthy the attention of the citizens of our young and busy country, where literature and the elegant arts must grow up side by side with the coarser plants of daily necessity; and must depend for their culture, not on the exclusive devotion of time and wealth, nor the quickening rays of titled patronage, but on hours and seasons snatched from the pursuit of worldly interests, by intelligent and public-spirited individuals.

He has shown how much may be done for a place in hours of leisure by one master spirit, and how completely it can give its own impress to surrounding objects. Like his own Lorenzo De' Medici, on whom he seems to have fixed his eye as on a pure model of antiquity, he has interwoven the history of his life with the history of his native town, and has made the foundations of its fame the monuments of his virtues. Wherever you go in Liverpool, you perceive traces of his footsteps in all that is elegant and liberal. He found the tide of wealth flowing merely in the channels of traffick; he has diverted from it invigorating rills to refresh the garden of literature. By his own example and constant exertions he has effected that union of commerce and the intellectual pursuits, so eloquently recommended in one of his latest writings:[1] and has practically proved how beautifully they may be brought to harmonize, and to benefit each other. The noble institutions for literary and scientific purposes, which reflect such credit on Liverpool, and are giving such an impulse to the public mind, have mostly been originated, and have all been effectively promoted, by Mr. Roscoe; and when we consider the rapidly increasing opulence and magnitude of that town, which promises to vie in commercial importance with the metropolis, it will be perceived that in awakening an ambition of mental improvement among its inhabitants, he has effected a great benefit to the cause of British literature.

In America, we know Mr. Roscoe only as the author—in Liverpool he is spoken of as the banker; and I was told of his having been unfortunate in business. I could not

---

1. Address on the opening of the Liverpool Institution.

pity him, as I heard some rich men do. I considered him far above the reach of my pity. Those who live only for the world, and in the world, may be cast down by the frowns of adversity; but a man like Roscoe is not to be overcome by the reverses of fortune. They do but drive him in upon the resources of his own mind; to the superior society of his own thoughts; which the best of men are apt sometimes to neglect, and to roam abroad in search of less worthy associates. He is independent of the world around him. He lives with antiquity and posterity; with antiquity, in the sweet communion of studious retirement; and with posterity, in the generous aspirings after future renown. The solitude of such a mind is its state of highest enjoyment. It is then visited by those elevated meditations which are the proper aliment of noble souls, and are, like manna, sent from heaven, in the wilderness of this world.

While my feelings were yet alive on the subject, it was my fortune to light on further traces of Mr. Roscoe. I was riding out with a gentleman, to view the environs of Liverpool, when he turned off, through a gate, into some ornamented grounds. After riding a short distance, we came to a spacious mansion of freestone, built in the Grecian style. It was not in the purest taste, yet it had an air of elegance, and the situation was delightful. A fine lawn sloped away from it, studded with clumps of trees, so disposed as to break a soft fertile country into a variety of landscapes. The Mersey was seen winding a broad quiet sheet of water through an expanse of green meadow-land; while the Welsh mountains, blended with clouds, and melting into distance, bordered the horizon.

This was Roscoe's favorite residence during the days of his prosperity. It had been the seat of elegant hospitality and literary retirement. The house was now silent and deserted. I saw the windows of the study, which looked out upon the soft scenery I have mentioned. The windows were closed—the library was gone. Two or three ill-favored beings were loitering about the place, whom my fancy pictured into retainers of the law. It was like visiting some classic fountain, that had once welled its pure waters in a sacred shade, but finding it dry and dusty, with the lizard and the toad brooding over the shattered marbles.

I inquired after the fate of Mr. Roscoe's library, which had consisted of scarce and foreign books, from many of which he had drawn the materials for his Italian histories. It had passed under the hammer of the auctioneer, and was dispersed about the country. The good people of the vicinity thronged like wreckers to get some part of the noble vessel that had been driven on shore. Did such a scene admit of ludicrous associations, we might imagine something whimsical in this strange irruption in the regions of learning. Pigmies rummaging the armory of a giant, and contending for the possession of weapons which they could not wield. We might picture to ourselves some knot of speculators, debating with calculating brow over the quaint binding and illuminated margin of an obsolete author; of the air of intense, but baffled sagacity, with which some successful purchaser attempted to dive into the black-letter bargain he had secured.

It is a beautiful incident in the story of Mr. Roscoe's misfortunes, and one which cannot fail to interest the studious mind, that the parting with his books seems to have touched upon his tenderest feelings, and to have been the only circumstance that could provoke the notice of his muse. The scholar only knows how dear these silent, yet eloquent, companions of pure thoughts and innocent hours become in the seasons of adversity. When all that is worldly turns to dross around us, these only retain their steady value. When friends grow cold, and the converse of intimates languishes into vapid civility and commonplace, these only continue the unaltered countenance of happier days, and cheer us with that true friendship which never deceived hope, nor deserted sorrow.

I do not wish to censure; but, surely, if the people of Liverpool had been properly sensible of what was due to Mr. Roscoe and themselves, his library would never have been sold. Good worldly reasons may, doubtless, be given for the circumstance, which it would be difficult to combat with others that might seem merely fanciful; but it certainly appears to me such an opportunity as seldom occurs, of cheering a noble mind struggling under misfortunes, by one of the most delicate, but most expressive tokens of public sympathy. It is difficult, however, to estimate a man of genius properly who is daily before our eyes. He becomes mingled and confounded with other men. His great qualities lose their novelty, we become too familiar with the common materials which form the basis even of the loftiest character. Some of Mr. Roscoe's townsmen may regard him merely as a man of business; others as a politician; all find him engaged like themselves in ordinary occupations, and surpassed, perhaps, by themselves on some points of worldly wisdom. Even that amiable and unostentatious simplicity of character, which give the nameless grace to real excellence, may cause him to be undervalued by some coarse minds, who do not know that true worth is always void of glare and pretension. But the man of letters, who speaks of Liverpool, speaks of it as the residence of Roscoe.—The intelligent traveler who visits it inquires where Roscoe is to be seen.—He is the literary landmark of the place, indicating its existence to the distant scholar.—He is, like Pompey's column at Alexandria, towering alone in classic dignity.

The following sonnet, addressed by Mr. Roscoe to his books on parting with them, is alluded to in the preceding article. If any thing can add effect to the pure feeling and elevated thought here displayed, it is the conviction, that the whole is no effusion of fancy, but a faithful transcript from the writer's heart.

TO MY BOOKS

As one who, destined from his friends to part,
Regrets his loss, but hopes again erewhile
To share their converse and enjoy their smile,
And tempers as he may affliction's dart;

Thus, loved associates, chiefs of elder art,
Teachers of wisdom, who could once beguile
My tedious hours, and lighten every toil,
I now resign you; nor with fainting heart;

For pass a few short years, or days, or hours,
And happier seasons may their dawn unfold,
And all your sacred fellowship restore:
When, freed from earth, unlimited its powers,
Mind shall with mind direct communion hold,
And kindred spirits meet to part no more.

The Wife

The treasures of the deep are not so precious
As are the conceal'd comforts of a man
Locked up in woman's love. I scent the air
Of blessings, when I come but near the house.
What a delicious breath marriage sends forth . . .
The violet bed's not sweeter.

MIDDLETON

I HAVE OFTEN HAD OCCASION TO REMARK THE FORTITUDE WITH WHICH women sustain the most oyerwhelming reverses of fortune. Those disasters which break down the spirit of a man, and prostrate him in the dust, seem to call forth all the energies of the softer sex, and give such intrepidity and elevation to their character, that at times it approaches to sublimity. Nothing can be more touching than to behold a soft and tender female, who had been all weakness and dependence, and alive to every trivial roughness, while treading the prosperous paths of life, suddenly rising in mental force to be the comforter and support of her husband under misfortune, and abiding, with unshrinking firmness, the bitterest blasts of adversity.

As the vine, which has long twined its graceful foliage about the oak, and been lifted by it into sunshine, will, when the hardy plant is rifted by the thunderbolt, cling round it with its caressing tendrils, and bind up its shattered boughs; so is it beautifully ordered by Providence, that woman, who is the mere dependent and ornament of man in his happier hours, should be his stay and solace when smitten with sudden calamity; winding herself into the rugged recesses of his nature, tenderly supporting the drooping head, and binding up the broken heart.

I was once congratulating a friend, who had around him a blooming family, knit together in the strongest affection. "I can wish you no better lot," said he, with enthusiasm, "than to have a wife and children. If you are prosperous, there they are to share your prosperity; if otherwise, there they are to comfort you." And, indeed, I have observed that a married man falling into misfortune is more apt to retrieve his situation in the world than a single one; partly because he is more stimulated to exertion by the necessities of the helpless and beloved beings who depend upon him for subsistence; but chiefly because his spirits are soothed and relieved by domestic endearments, and his self-respect kept alive by finding, that though all abroad is darkness and humiliation, yet there is still a little world of love at home, of which he is the monarch. Whereas a single man is apt to run to waste and self-neglect; to fancy himself lonely and abandoned, and his heart to fall to ruin like some deserted mansion, for want of an inhabitant.

These observations call to mind a little domestic story, of which I was once a witness. My intimate friend, Leslie, had married a beautiful and accomplished girl, who had been brought up in the midst of fashionable life. She had, it is true, no fortune, but that of my friend was ample; and he delighted in the anticipation of indulging her in every elegant pursuit, and administering to those delicate tastes and fancies that spread a kind of witchery about the sex.—"Her life," said he, "shall be like a fairy tale."

The very difference in their characters produced an harmonious combination: he was of a romantic and somewhat serious cast; she was all life and gladness. I have often noticed the mute rapture with which he would gaze upon her in company, of which her sprightly powers made her the delight; and how, in the midst of applause, her eye would still turn to him, as if there alone she sought favor and acceptance. When leaning on his arm, her slender form contrasted finely with his tall manly person. The fond confiding air with which she looked up to him seemed to call forth a flush of triumphant pride and cherishing tenderness, as if he doted on his lovely burden for its very helplessness. Never did a couple set forward on the flowery path of early and well-suited marriage with a fairer prospect of felicity.

It was the misfortune of my friend, however, to have embarked his property in large speculations; and he had not been married many months, when, by a succession of sudden disasters, it was swept from him, and he found himself reduced almost to penury. For a time he kept his situation to himself, and went about with a haggard countenance, and a breaking heart. His life was but a protracted agony; and what rendered it more insupportable was the necessity of keeping up a smile in the presence of his wife; for he could not bring himself to overwhelm her with the news. She saw, however, with the quick eyes of affection, that all was not well with him. She marked his altered looks and stifled sighs, and was not to be deceived by his sickly and vapid attempts at cheerfulness. She tasked all her sprightly powers and tender blandishments to win him back to happiness; but she only drove the arrow deeper into his soul. The more he saw cause to love her, the more torturing was the thought that he was soon to make her wretched. A little while, thought he, and the smile will vanish from that cheek—the song will die away from those lips—the lustre of those eyes will be quenched with sorrow; and the happy heart, which now beats lightly in that bosom, will be weighed down like mine, by the cares and miseries of the world.

At length he came to me one day, and related his whole situation in a tone of the deepest despair. When I heard him through I inquired, "Does your wife know all this?"—At the question he burst into an agony of tears. "For God's sake!" cried he, "if you have any pity on me, don't mention my wife; it is the thought of her that drives me almost to madness!"

"And why not?" said I. "She must know it sooner or later: you cannot keep it long from her, and the intelligence may break upon her in a more startling manner, than if imparted by yourself; for the accents of those we love soften the harshest tidings. Besides, you are depriving yourself of the comforts of her sympathy; and not merely that, but also endangering the only bond that can keep hearts together—an unreserved community of thought and feeling. She will soon perceive that something is secretly preying upon your mind; and true love will not brook reserve; it feels undervalued and outraged, when even the sorrows of those it loves are concealed from it."

Oh, but, my friend! to think what a blow I am to give to all her future prospects—how I am to strike her very soul to the earth, by telling her that her husband is a beggar! that she is to forego all the elegancies of life—all the pleasures of society—to shrink with me into indigence and obscurity! To tell her that I have dragged her down from the sphere in which she might have continued to move in constant brightness—the light of every eye—the admiration of every heart!—How can she bear poverty? she has been brought up in all the refinements of opulence. How can she bear neglect? she has been the idol of society. Oh I it will break her heart—it will break her heart!—"

I saw his grief was eloquent and I let it have its flow; for sorrow relieves itself by words. When his paroxysm had subsided, and he had relapsed into moody silence, I resumed the subject gently, and urged him to break his situation at once to his wife. He shook his head mournfully; but positively.

"But how are you to keep it from her? It is necessary she should know it, that you may take the steps proper to the alteration of your circumstances. You must change your style of living—nay," observing a pang to pass across his countenance, "don't let that afflict you. I am sure you have never placed your happiness in outward show—you have yet friends, warm friends, who will not think the worse of you for being leas splendidly lodged: and surely it does not require a palace to be happy with Mary—"

"I could be happy with her," cried he, convulsively, "in a hovel!—I could go down with her into poverty and the dust!—I could—I could—God bless her!—God bless her!" cried he, bursting into a transport of grief and tenderness.

"And believe me, my friend," said I, stepping up, and grasping him warmly by the hand, "believe me she can be the same with you. Ay, more: it will be a source of pride and triumph to her—it will call forth all the latent energies and fervent sympathies of her nature; for she will rejoice to prove that she loves you for yourself. There is in every true woman's heart a spark of heavenly fire, which lies dormant in the broad daylight of prosperity; but which kindles up, and beams and blazes in the dark hour of adversity. No man knows what the wife of his bosom is—no man knows what a ministering angel she is—until he has gone with her through the fiery trials of this world."

There was something in the earnestness of my manner, and the figurative style of my language, that caught the excited imagination of Leslie. I knew the auditor I had to deal with; and following up the impression I had made, I finished by persuading him to go home and unburden his sad heart to his wife.

I must confess, notwithstanding all I had said, I felt some little solitude for the result. Who can calculate on the fortitude of one whose whole life has been a round of pleasures? Her gay spirits might revolt at the dark downward path of low humility suddenly pointed out before her, and might cling to the sunny regions in which they had hitherto reveled. Besides, ruin in fashionable life is accompanied by so many galling mortifications, to which in other ranks it is a stranger.—In short, I could not meet Leslie the next morning without trepidation. He had made the disclosure.

"And how did she bear it?"

"Like an angel! It seemed rather to be a relief to her mind, for she threw her arms round my neck, and asked if this was all that had lately made me unhappy—But, poor girl," added he, "she cannot realize the change we must undergo. She has no idea of poverty but in the abstract; she has only read of it in poetry, where it is allied to love. She feels as yet no privation; she suffers no loss of accustomed conveniencies nor elegancies. When we come practically to experience its sordid cares, its paltry wants, its petty humiliations—then will be the real trial."

"But," said I, "now that you have got over the severest task, that of breaking it to her, the sooner you let the world into the secret the better. The disclosure may be mortifying; but then it is a single misery, and soon over: whereas you otherwise suffer it, in anticipation, every hour in the day. It is not poverty so much as pretence, that harasses a ruined man—the struggle between a proud mind and an empty purse—the keeping up a hollow show that must soon come to an end. Have the courage to appear poor, and you disarm poverty of its sharpest sting." On this point I found Leslie perfectly prepared. He had no false pride himself, and as to his wife, she was only anxious to conform to their altered fortunes.

Some days afterwards he called upon me in the evening. He had disposed of his dwelling house, and taken a small cottage in the country, a few miles from town. He had been busied all day in sending out furniture. The new establishment required few articles, and those of the simplest kind. All the splendid furniture of his late residence had been sold, excepting his wife's harp. That, he said, was too closely associated with the idea of herself; it belonged to the little story of their loves; for some of the sweetest moments of their courtship were those when he had leaned over that instrument, and listened to the melting tones of her voice. I could not but smile at this instance of romantic gallantry in a doting husband.

He was now going out to the cottage, where his wife had been all day superintending its arrangement. My feelings had become strongly interested in the progress of this family story, and, as it was a fine evening, I offered to accompany him.

He was wearied with the fatigues of the day, and, as he walked out, fell into a fit of gloomy musing.

"Poor Mary!" at length broke, with a heavy sigh, from his lips.

"And what of her?" asked I: "has anything happened to her?"

"What," said he, darting an impatient glance, "is it nothing to be reduced to this paltry situation—to be caged in a miserable cottage—to be obliged to toil almost in the menial concerns of her wretched habitation?"

"Has she then repined at the change?"

"Repined! she has been nothing but sweetness and good humor. Indeed, she seems in better spirits than I have over known her; she has been to me all love, and tenderness, and comfort!"

"Admirable girl!" exclaimed I, "You call yourself poor, my friend; you never were so rich—you never knew the boundless treasures of excellence you possess in that woman."

"Oh! but, my friend, if this first meeting at the cottage were over, I think I could then be comfortable. But this is her first day of real experience; she has been introduced into a humble dwelling—she has been employed all day in arranging its miserable equipments—she has, for the first time, known the fatigues of domestic employment—she has, for the first time, looked round her on a home destitute of every thing elegant,—almost of every thing convenient; and may now be sitting down, exhausted and spiritless, brooding over a prospect of future poverty."

There was a degree of probability in this picture that I could not gainsay, so we walked on in silence.

After turning from the main road up a narrow lane, so thickly shaded with forest trees as to give it a complete air of seclusion, we came in sight of the cottage. It was humble enough in its appearance for the most pastoral poet; and yet it had a pleasing rural look. A wild vine had overrun one end with a profusion of foliage; a few trees threw their branches gracefully over it; and I observed several pots of flowers tastefully disposed about the door, and on the grassplot in front. A small wicket gate opened upon a footpath that wound through some shrubbery to the door. Just as we approached, we heard the sound of music—Leslie grasped my arm; we paused and listened. It was Mary's voice singing, in a style of the most touching simplicity, a little air of which her husband was peculiarly fond.

I felt Leslie's hand tremble on my arm. He stepped forward to hear more distinctly. His step made a noise on the gravel walk. A bright beautiful face glanced out at the window, and vanished—a light footstep was heard—and Mary came tripping forth to meet us: she was in a pretty rural dress of white; a few wild flowers were twisted in her fine hair; a fresh bloom was on her cheek; her whole countenance beamed with smiles—I had never seen her look so lovely.

"My dear George," cried she, " I am so glad you are come! I have been watching and watching for you; and running down the lane, and looking out for you. I've set out a table under a beautiful tree behind the cottage; and I've been gathering some of the most delicious strawberries, for I know you are fond of them—and we have such excellent cream—and every thing is so sweet and still here— Oh!" said she, putting her arm within his, and looking up brightly in his face, "Oh, we shall be so happy!"

Poor Leslie was overcome. He caught her to his bosom—he folded his arms round her—he kissed her again and again—he could not speak, but the tears gushed into his eyes; and he often assured me, that though the world has since gone prosperously with him, and his life has, indeed, been a happy one, yet never has he experienced a moment of more exquisite felicity.

Rip Van Winkle

A Posthumous Writing of Diedrich Knickerbocker

By Woden, God of Saxons,
From when comes Wensday, that is Wodensday.
Truth is a thing that ever will I keep
Unto thylike day in which I creep into
My sepulchre—

CARTWRIGHT

[THE FOLLOWING TALE WAS FOUND AMONG THE PAPERS OF THE LATE DIEDRICH Knickerbocker, an old gentleman of New-York, who was very curious in the Dutch history of the province, and the manners of the descendants from its primitive settlers. His historical researches, however, did not lie so much among books as among men; for the former are lamentably scanty on his favorite topics; whereas he found the old burghers, and still more their wives, rich in that legendary lore, so invaluable to true history. Whenever, therefore, he happened upon a genuine Dutch family, snugly shut up in its low-roofed farmhouse, under a spreading sycamore, he looked upon it as a little clasped volume of black-letter, and studied it with the zeal of a book-worm.

The result of all these researches was a history of the province during the reign of the Dutch governors, which he published some years since. There have been various opinions as to the literary character of his work, and, to tell the truth, it is not a whit better than it should be. Its chief merit is its scrupulous accuracy, which indeed was a little questioned, on its first appearance, but has since been completely established; and it is now admitted into all historical collections, as a book of unquestionable authority.

The old gentleman died shortly after the publication of his work, and now that he is dead and gone, it cannot do much harm to his memory to say, that his time might have been much better employed in weightier labors. He, however, was apt to ride his hobby his own way; and though it did now and then kick up the dust a little in the eyes of his neighbors, and grieve the spirit of some friends, for whom he felt the truest deference and affection; yet his errors and follies are remembered "more in sorrow than in anger," and it begins to be suspected, that he never intended to injure or offend. But however his memory may be appreciated by critics, it is still held dear by many folk, whose good opinion is well worth having; particularly by certain biscuit-bakers, who have gone so far as to imprint his likeness on their new-year cakes; and have thus given him a chance for immortality, almost equal to the being stamped on a Waterloo Medal, or a Queen Anne's farthing.]

WHOEVER HAS MADE A VOYAGE UP THE HUDSON MUST REMEMBER the Kaatskill mountains. They are a dismembered branch of the great Appalachian family, and are seen away to the west of the river, swelling up to a noble height, and lording it over the surrounding country. Every change of season, every change of weather, indeed every hour of the day, produces some change in the magical hues and shapes of these mountains, and they are regarded by all the good wives, far and near, as perfect barometers. When the weather is fair and settled, they are clothed in blue and purple, and print their bold outlines on the clear evening sky; but sometimes, when the rest of the landscape is cloudless, they will gather a hood of gray vapors about their summits, which, in the last rays of the setting sun, will glow and light up like a crown of glory.

At the foot of these fairy mountains, the voyager may have descried the light smoke curling up from a village, whose shingle-roofs gleam among the trees, just where the blue tints of the upland melt away into the fresh green of the nearer landscape. It is a little village, of great antiquity, having been founded by some of the Dutch colonists, in the early times of the province, just about the beginning of the government of the good Peter Stuyvesant, (may he rest in peace!) and there were some of the houses of the original settlers standing within a few years, built of small yellow bricks brought from Holland, having latticed windows and gable fronts, surmounted with weather-cocks.

In that same village, and in one of these very houses which, to tell the precise truth, was sadly time-worn and weather-beaten), there lived many years since, while the country was yet a province of Great Britain, a simple good-natured fellow, of the name of Rip Van Winkle. He was a descendant of the Van Winkles who figured so gallantly in the chivalrous days of Peter Stuyvesant, and accompanied him to the siege of Fort Christina. He inherited, however, but little of the martial character of his ancestors. I have observed that he was a simple good-natured man; he was, moreover, a kind neighbor, and an obedient hen-pecked husband. Indeed, to the latter circumstance might be owing that meekness of spirit which gained him such universal popularity; for those men are most apt to be obsequious and conciliating abroad, who are under the discipline of shrews at home. Their tempers, doubtless, are rendered pliant and malleable in the fiery furnace of domestic tribulation, and a curtain lecture is worth all the sermons in the world for teaching the virtues of patience and long-suffering. A termagant wife may, therefore, in some respects, be considered a tolerable blessing; and if so, Rip Van Winkle was thrice blessed.

Certain it is, that he was a great favorite among all the good wives of the village, who, as usual with the amiable sex, took his part in all family squabbles; and never failed, whenever they talked those matters over in their evening gossipings, to lay all the blame on Dame Van Winkle. The children of the village, too, would shout with joy whenever he approached. He assisted at their sports, made their playthings, taught them to fly kites and shoot marbles, and told them long stories of ghosts, witches, and Indians. Whenever he went dodging about the village, he was surrounded by a troop of them, hanging on his skirts, clambering on his back, and playing a thousand tricks on him with impunity; and not a dog would bark at him throughout the neighborhood.

The great error in Rip's composition was an insuperable aversion to all kinds of profitable labor. It could not be from the want of assiduity or perseverance; for he would sit on a wet rock, with a rod as long and heavy as a Tartar's lance, and fish all day without a murmur, even though he should not be encouraged by a single nibble. He would carry a fowling-piece on his shoulder for hours together, trudging through woods and swamps, and up hill and down dale, to shoot a few squirrels or wild pigeons. He would never refuse to assist a neighbor even in the roughest toil, and was a foremost man at all country frolics for husking Indian com, or building stone-fences; the women of the village, too, used to employ him to run their errands, and to do such little odd jobs as their less obliging husbands would not do for them. In a word Rip was ready to attend to any body's business but his own; but as to doing family duty, and keeping his farm in order, he found it impossible.

In fact, he declared it was of no use to work on his farm; it was the most pestilent little piece of ground in the whole country; every thing about it went wrong, and would go wrong, in spite of him. His fences were continually falling to pieces; his cow would either go astray, or get among the cabbages; weeds were sure to grow quicker in his fields than any where else; the rain always made a point of setting in just as he had some out-door work to do; so that though his patrimonial estate had dwindled away under his management, acre by acre, until there was little more left than a mere patch of Indian com and potatoes, yet it was the worst conditioned farm in the neighborhood.

His children, too, were as ragged and wild as if they belonged to nobody. His son Rip, an urchin begotten in his own likeness, promised to inherit the habits, with the old clothes of his father. He was generally seen trooping like a colt at his mother's heels, equipped in a pair of his father's cast-off galligaskins, which he had much ado to hold up with one hand as a fine lady does her train in bad weather.

Rip Van Winkle, however, was one of those happy mortals, of foolish, well-oiled dispositions, who take the world easy, eat white bread or brown, whichever can be got with least thought or trouble, and would rather starve on a penny than work for a pound. If left to himself, he would have whistled life away in perfect contentment; but his wife kept continually dinning in his ears about his idleness, his carelessness, and the ruin he was bringing on his family. Morning, noon, and night, her tongue was incessantly going, and every thing he said or did was sure to produce a torrent of household eloquence. Rip had but one way of replying to all lectures of the kind, and that, by frequent use had grown into a habit. He shrugged his shoulders, shook his head, cast up his eyes, but said nothing. This, however, always provoked a fresh volley from his wife; so that he was fain to draw off his forces, and take to the outside of the house—the only side which, in truth, belongs to a hen-pecked husband.

Rip's sole domestic adherent was his dog Wolf, who was as much hen-pecked as his master; for Dame Van Winkle regarded them as companions in idleness, and even looked upon Wolf with an evil eye, as the cause of his master's going so often astray. True it is, in all points of spirit befitting an honorable dog, he was as courageous an animal as ever scoured the woods—but what courage can withstand the ever-during and all-besetting terrors of a woman's tongue? The moment Wolf entered the house his crest fell, his tail drooped to the ground or curled between his legs, he sneaked about with a gallows air, casting many a sidelong glance at Dame Van Winkle, and at the least flourish of a broomstick or ladle, he would fly to the door with yelping precipitation.

Times grew worse and worse with Rip Van Winkle as years of matrimony rolled on; a tart temper never mellows with age, and a sharp tongue is the only edged tool that grows keener with constant use. For a long while he used to console himself, when driven from home, by frequenting a kind of perpetual dub of the sages, philosophers, and other idle personages of the village; which held its sessions on a bench before a small inn, designated by a rubicund portrait of His Majesty George the Third. Here they used to sit in the shade through a long lazy summer's day, talking listlessly over village gossip, or telling endless sleepy stories about nothing. But it would hare been worth any statesman's money to have heard the profound discussions that sometimes took place, when by chance an old newspaper fell into their hands from some passing traveler. How solemnly they would listen to the contents, as drawled out by Derrick Van Bummel, the schoolmaster, a dapper learned little man, who was not to be daunted by the most gigantic word in the dictionary; and how sagely they would deliberate upon public events some months after they had taken place.

The opinions of this junto were completely controlled by Nicholas Vedder, a patriarch of the village and landlord of the inn, at the door of which he took his seat from morning till night, just moving sufficiently to avoid the sun and keep in the shade of a large tree; so that the neighbors could tell the hour by his movements as accurately as by a sun-dial. It is true he was rarely heard to speak, but smoked his pipe incessantly. His adherents, however (for every great man has his adherents), perfectly understood him, and knew how to gather his opinions. When any thing that was read or related displeased him, he was observed to smoke his pipe vehemently, and to send forth short, frequent and angry puffs; but when pleased, he would inhale the smoke slowly and tranquilly, and emit it in light and placid clouds; and sometimes, taking the pipe from his mouth, and letting the fragrant vapor curl about his nose, would gravely nod his head in token of perfect approbation.

From even this strong-hold the unlucky Rip was at length routed by his termagant wife, who would suddenly break in upon the tranquillity of the assemblage and call the members all to naught; nor was that august personage, Nicholas Vedder himself sacred from the daring tongue of this terrible virago, who charged him outright with encouraging her husband in habits of idleness.

Poor Rip was at last reduced almost to despair; and his only alternative, to escape from the labor of the farm and clamor of his wife, was to take gun in hand and stroll away into the woods. Here he would sometimes seat himself at the foot of a tree, and share the contents of his wallet with Wolf, with whom he sympathized as a fellow sufferer in persecution. "Poor Wolf," he would say, thy mistress leads thee a dog's life of it; but never mind, my lad, whilst I live thou shalt never want a friend to stand by thee!" Wolf would wag his tail, look wistfully in his master's face, and if dogs can feel pity, I verily believe he reciprocated the sentiment with all his heart.

In a long ramble of the kind on a fine autumnal day, Rip had unconsciously scrambled to one of the highest parts of the Kaatskill mountains. He was after his favorite sport of squirrel shooting, and the still solitudes had echoed and re-echoed with the reports of his gun. Panting and fatigued, he threw himself, late in the afternoon, on a green knoll, covered with mountain herbage, that crowned the brow of a precipice. From an opening between the trees he could overlook all the lower country for many a mile of rich woodland. He saw at a distance the lordly Hudson, far, far below him, moving on its silent but majestic course, with the reflection of a purple cloud, or the sail of a lagging bark, here and there sleeping on its glassy bosom, and at last losing itself in the blue highlands.

On the other side he looked down into a deep mountain glen wild, lonely, and shagged, the bottom filled with fragments from the impending cliffs, and scarcely lighted by the reflected rays of the setting sun. For some time Rip lay musing on this scene; evening was gradually advancing; the mountains began to throw their long blue shadows over the valleys; he saw that it would be dark long before he could reach the village, and he heaved a heavy sigh when he thought of encountering the terrors of Dame Van Winkle.

As he was about to descend, he heard a voice from a distance, hallooing, "Rip Van Winkle! Rip Van Winkle!" He looked round, but could see nothing but a crow winging its solitary flight across the mountain. He thought his fancy must have deceived him, and turned again to descend, when he heard the same crying through the still evening air; "Rip Van Winkle! Rip Van Winkle!"—at the same time Wolf bristled up his back, and giving a low growl, skulked to his master's side, looking fearfully down into the glen. Rip now felt a vague apprehension stealing over him; he looked anxiously in the same direction, and perceived a strange figure slowly toiling up the rocks, and bending under the weight of something he carried on his back. He was surprised to see any human being in this lonely and unfrequented place, but supposing it to be some one of the neighborhood in need of his assistance, he hastened down to yield it.

On nearer approach he was still more surprised at the singularity of the stranger's appearance. He was a short square-built old fellow, with thick bushy hair, and a grizzled beard. His dress was of the antique Dutch fashion—a cloth jerkin strapped round the waist—several pair of breeches, the outer one of ample volume, decorated with rows of buttons down the sides, and bunches at the knees. He bore on his shoulder a stout keg, that seemed full of liquor, and made signs for Rip to approach and assist him with the load. Though rather shy and distrustful of this new acquaintance. Rip complied with his usual alacrity; and mutually relieving each other, they clambered up a narrow gully, apparently the dry bed of a mountain torrent As they ascended, Rip every now and then heard long rolling peals, like distant thunder, that seemed to issue out of a deep ravine, or rather cleft, between lofty rocks, toward which their rugged path conducted. He paused for an instant, but supposing it to be the muttering of one of those transient thunder-showers which often take place in mountain heights, he proceeded. Passing through the ravine, they came to a hollow, like a small amphitheatre, surrounded by perpendicular precipices, over the brinks of which impending trees shot their branches, so that you only caught glimpses of the azure sky and the bright evening cloud. During he whole time Rip and his companion had labored on in silence; for though the former marveled greatly what could be the object of carrying a keg of liquor up this wild mountain, yet there was something strange and incomprehensible about the unknown, that inspired awe and checked familiarity.

On entering the amphitheatre, new objects of wonder presented themselves. On a level spot in the centre was a company of odd-looking personages playing at nine-pins. They were dressed in a quaint outlandish fashion; some wore short doublets, others jerkins, with long knives in their belts, and most of them had enormous breeches, of similar style with that of the guide's. Their visages, too, were peculiar: one had a large head, broad face, and small piggish eyes: the face of another seemed to consist entirely of nose, and was surmounted by a white sugar-loaf hat, set off with a little red cock's tail. They all had beards, of various shapes and colors. There was one who seemed to be the commander. He was a stout old gentleman, with a weather-beaten countenance; he wore a laced doublet, broad belt and hanger, high crowned hat and feather, red stockings, and high-heeled shoes, with roses in them. The whole group reminded Rip of the figures in an old Flemish painting, in the parlor of Dominie Van Shaick, the village parson, and which had been brought over from Holland at the time of the settlement.

What seemed particularly odd to Rip was, that though these folks were evidently amusing themselves, yet they maintained the gravest faces, the most mysterious silence, and were, withal, the most melancholy party of pleasure he had ever witnessed. Nothing interrupted the stillness of the scene but the noise of the balls, which, whenever they were rolled, echoed along the mountains like rumbling peals of thunder.

As Rip and his companion approached them, they suddenly desisted from their play, and stared at him with such fixed statue-like gaze and such strange, uncouth, lack-lustre countenances, that his heart tamed within him, and his knees smote together. His companion now emptied the contents of the keg into large flagons, and made signs to him to wait upon the company. He obeyed with fear and trembling; they quaffed the liquor in profound silence, and then returned to their game.

By degrees Rip's awe and apprehension subsided. He even ventured, when no eye was fixed upon him, to taste the beverage, which he found had much of the flavor of excellent Hollands. He was naturally a thirsty soul, and was soon tempted to repeat the draught. One taste provoked another; and he reiterated his visits to the flagon so often that at length his senses were overpowered, his eyes swam in his head, his head gradually declined, and he fell into a deep sleep.

On waking, he found himself on the green knoll whence he had first seen the old man of the glen. He rubbed his eyes—it was a bright sunny morning. The birds were hopping and twittering among the bushes, and the eagle was wheeling aloft, and breasting the pure mountain breeze. "Surely," thought Rip, "I have not slept here all night." He recalled the occurrences before he fell asleep. The strange man with a keg of liquor—the mountain ravine—the wild retreat among the rocks—the wobegone party at nine-pins—the flagon—"Oh! that flagon! that wicked flagon!" thought Rip—"what excuse shall I make to Dame Van Winkle!"

He looked round for his gun, but in place of the clean well-oiled fowling-piece, he found an old firelock lying by him, the barrel incrusted with rust, the lock falling off, and the stock worm-eaten. He now suspected that the grave roysters of the mountain had put a trick upon him, and, having dosed him with liquor, had robbed him of his gun. Wolf, too, had disappeared, but he might have strayed away after a squirrel or partridge. He whistled after him and shouted his name, but all in vain; the echoes repeated his whistle and shout, but no dog was to be seen.

He determined to revisit the scene of the last evenings gambol, and if he met with any of the party, to demand his dog and gun. As he rose to walk, he found himself stiff in the joints, and wanting in his usual activity. "These mountain beds do not agree with me," thought Rip, "and if this frolic should lay me up with a fit of the rheumatism, I shall have a blessed time with Dame Van Winkle." With some difficulty he got down into the glen: he found the gully up which he and his companion had ascended the preceding evening; but to his astonishment a mountain stream was now foaming down it, leaping from rock to rock, and filling the glen with babbling murmurs. He, however, made shift to scramble up its sides, working his toilsome way through thickets of birch, sassafras, and witch-hazel, and sometimes tripped up or entangled by the wild grapevines that twisted their coils or tendrils from tree to tree, and spread a kind of network in his path.

At length he reached to where the ravine had opened through the cliffs to the amphitheatre; but no traces of such opening remained. The rocks presented a high impenetrable wall, over which the torrent came tumbling in a sheet of feathery foam, and fell into a broad deep basin, black from the shadows of the surrounding forest. Here, then, poor Rip was brought to a stand. He again called and whistled after his dog; he was only answered by the cawing of a flock of idle crows, sporting high in air about a dry tree that overhung a sunny precipice; and who, secure in their elevation, seemed to look down and scoff at the poor man's perplexities. What was to be done? the morning was passing away, and Rip felt famished for want of his breakfast. He grieved to give up his dog and gun; he dreaded to meet his wife; but it would not do to starve among the mountains. He shook his head, shouldered the rusty firelock, and, with a heart full of trouble and anxiety, turned his steps homeward.

As he approached the village he met a number of people, but none whom he knew, which somewhat surprised him, for he had thought himself acquainted with every one in the country round. Their dress, too, was of a different fashion from that to which he was accustomed. They all stared at him with equal marks of surprise, and whenever they cast their eyes upon him, invariably stroked their chins. The constant recurrence of this gesture induced Rip, involuntarily, to do the same, when, to his astonishment, he found his beard had grown a foot long!

He had now entered the skirts of the village. A troop of strange children ran at his heels, hooting after him, and pointing at his gray beard. The dogs, too, not one of which he recognized for an old acquaintance, barked at him as he passed. The very village was altered; it was larger and more populous. There were rows of houses which he had never seen before, and those which had been his familiar haunts had disappeared. Strange names were over the doors—strange faces at the windows—every thing was strange. His mind now misgave him; he began to doubt whether both he and the world around him were not bewitched. Surely this was his native village, which he had left but the day before. There stood the Kaatskill mountains—there ran the silver Hudson at a distance—there was every hill and dale precisely as it had always been—Rip was sorely perplexed—"That flagon last night," thought he, "has addled my poor head sadly!"

It was with some difficulty that he found the way to his own house, which he approached with silent awe, expecting every moment to hear the shrill voice of Dame Van Winkle. He found the house gone to decay—the roof fallen in, the windows shattered, and the doors off the hinges. A half-starved dog that looked like Wolf was skulking about it Rip called him by name, but the cur snarled, showed his teeth, and passed on. This was an unkind cut indeed—"My very dog," sighed poor Rip, "has forgotten me!"

He entered the house, which, to tell the truth, Dame Van Winkle had always kept in neat order. It was empty, forlorn, and apparently abandoned. This desolateness overcame all his connubial fears—he called loudly for his wife and children—the lonely chambers rang for a moment with his voice, and then all again was silence.

He now hurried forth, and hastened to his old resort, the village inn—but it too was gone. A large rickety wooden building stood in its place, with great gaping windows, some of them broken and mended with old hats and petticoats, and over the door was painted, "The Union Hotel, by Jonathan Doolittle." Instead of the great tree that used to shelter the quiet little Dutch inn of yore, there now was reared a tall naked pole, with something on the top that looked like a red night-cap, and from it was fluttering a flag, on which was a singular assemblage of stars and stripes—all this was strange and incomprehensible. He recognized on the sign, however, the ruby face of King George, under which he had smoked so many a peaceful pipe; but even this was singularly metamorphosed. The red coat was changed for one of blue and buff, a sword was held in the hand instead of a sceptre, the head was decorated with a cocked hat, and underneath was painted in large characters, GENERAL WASHINGTON.

There was, as usual, a crowd of folk about the door, but none that Rip recollected. The very character of the people seemed changed. There was a busy, bustling, disputatious tone about it, instead of the accustomed phlegm and drowsy tranquillity. He looked in vain for the sage Nicholas Vedder, with his broad face, double chin, and fair long pipe, uttering clouds of tobacco-smoke instead of idle speeches; or Van Bummel, the schoolmaster, doling forth the contents of an ancient newspaper. In place of these, a lean, bilious-looking fellow, with his pockets full of handbills, was haranguing vehemently about rights of citizens—elections—members of congress—liberty—Bunker's Hill—heroes of seventy-six—and other words, which were a perfect Babylonish jargon to the bewildered Van Winkle.

The appearance of Rip, with his long grizzled beard, his rusty fowling-piece, his uncouth dress, and an army of women and children at his heels, soon attracted the attention of the tavern politicians. They crowded round him, eyeing him from head to foot with great curiosity. The orator bustled up to him, and, drawing him partly aside, inquired on which side he voted?" Rip stared in vacant stupidity. Another short but busy little fellow pulled him by the arm, and, rising on tiptoe, inquired in his ear, "Whether he was Federal or Democrat?" Rip was equally at a loss to comprehend the question; when a knowing, self-important old gentleman, in a sharp cocked hat, made his way through the crowd, putting them to the right and left with his elbows as he passed, and planting himself before Van Winkle, with one arm akimbo, the other resting on his cane, his keen eyes and sharp hat penetrating, as it were, into his very soul, demanded in an austere tone, "what brought him to the election with a gun on his shoulder, and a mob at his heels, and whether he meant to breed a riot in the village?"—"Alas! gentlemen," cried Rip, somewhat dismayed, "I am a poor quiet man, a native of the place, and a loyal subject of the king, God bless him!"

Here a general shout burst from the by-standers—"A tory! a tory! a spy! a refugee! hustle him! away with him!" It was with great difficulty that the self-important man in the cocked hat restored order; and, having assumed a tenfold austerity of brow, demanded again of the unknown culprit, what he came there for, and whom he was seeking? The poor man humbly assured him that he meant no harm, but merely came there in search of some of his neighbors, who used to keep about the tavern.

"Well—who are they?—name them."

Rip bethought himself a moment, and inquired, "Where's Nicholas Vedder?"

There was a silence for a little while, when an old man replied, in a thin piping voice, "Nicholas Vedder! why, he is dead and gone these eighteen years! There was a wooden tombstone in the church-yard that used to tell all about him, but that's rotten and gone too."

"Where's Brom Dutcher?"

"Oh, he went off to the army in the beginning of the war; some say he was killed at the storming of Stony Point—others say he was drowned in a squall at the foot of Antony's Nose. I don't know—he never came back again."

"Where's Van Bummel, the schoolmaster?"

"He went off to the wars too, was a great militia general, and is now in congress."

Rip's heart died away at hearing of these sad changes in his home and friends, and finding himself thus alone in the world. Every answer puzzled him too, by treating of such enormous lapses of time, and of matters which he could not understand: war—congress—Stony Point;—he had no courage to ask after any more friends, but cried out in despair, Does nobody here know Rip Van Winkle?"

"Oh, Rip Van Winkle!" exclaimed two or three, "Oh, to be sure! that's Rip Van Winkle yonder, leaning against the tree."

Rip looked, and beheld a precise counterpart of himself, as he went up the mountain: apparently as lazy, and certainly as ragged. The poor fellow was now completely confounded. He doubted his own identity, and whether he was himself or another man. In the midst of his bewilderment, the man in the cocked hat demanded who he was, and what was his name?

"God knows," exclaimed he, at his wit's end; "I'm not myself—I'm somebody else—that's me yonder—no—that's somebody else got into my shoes—I was myself last night, but I fell asleep on the mountain, and they've changed my gun, and every thing's changed, and I'm changed, and I can't tell what's my name, or who I am!"

The by-standers began now to look at each other, nod, wink significantly, and tap their fingers against their foreheads. There was a whisper, also, about securing the gun, and keeping the old fellow from doing mischief, at the very suggestion of which the self-important man in the cocked hat retired with some precipitation. At this critical moment a fresh comely woman pressed through the throng to get a peep at the gray-bearded man. She had a chubby child in her arms, which, frightened at his looks, began to cry. "Hush, Rip," cried she, "hush, you little fool; the old man won't hurt you." The name of the child, the air of the mother, the tone of her voice, all awakened a train of recollections in his mind. "What is your name, my good woman?" asked he.

"Judith Gardenier."

"And your fathers name?"

"Ah, poor man, Rip Yan Winkle was his name, but it's twenty years since he went away from home with his gun, and never has been heard of since—his dog came home without him; but whether he shot himself, or was carried away by the Indians, nobody can tell. I was then but a little girl."

Rip had but one question more to ask; but he put it with a faltering voice:

"Where's your mother?"

"Oh, she too had died but a short time since; she broke a blood-vessel in a fit of passion at a New-England pedler."

There was a drop of comfort, at least, in this intelligence. The honest man could contain himself no longer. He caught his daughter and her child in his arms. "I am your father!" cried he—"Young Rip Van Winkle once—old Rip Van Winkle now!—Does nobody know poor Rip Van Winkle?"

All stood amazed, until an old woman tottering out from among the crowd, put her hand to her brow, and peering under it in his face for a moment, exclaimed, "Sure enough! it is Rip Van Winkle—it is himself! Welcome home again, old neighbor—Why, where have you been these twenty long years?"

Rip's story was soon told, for the whole twenty years had been to him but as one night. The neighbors stared when they heard it; some were seen to wink at each other, and put their tongues in their cheeks: and the self-important man in the cocked hat, who, when the alarm was over, had returned to the field, screwed down the corners of his mouth, and shook his head—upon which there was a general shaking of the head throughout the assemblage.

It was determined, however, to take the opinion of old Peter Vanderdonk, who was seen slowly advancing up the road. He was a descendant of the historian of that name, who wrote one of the earliest accounts of the province. Peter was the most ancient inhabitant of the village, and well versed in all the wonderful events and traditions of the neighborhood. He recollected Rip at once, and corroborated his story in the most satisfactory manner. He assured the company that it was a fact, handed down from his ancestor the historian, that the Kaatskill mountains had always been haunted by strange beings. That it was affirmed that the great Hendrick Hudson, the first discoverer of the river and country, kept a kind of vigil there every twenty years, with his crew of the Half-moon; being permitted in this way to revisit the scenes of his enterprise, and keep a guardian eye upon the river, and the great city called by his name. That his father had once seen them in their old Dutch dresses playing at ninepins in a hollow of the mountain; and that he himself had heard, one summer afternoon, the sound of their balls, like distant peals of thunder.

To make a long story short, the company broke up, and returned to the more important concerns of the election. Rip's daughter took him home to live with her; she had a snug, well-furnished house, and a stout cheery farmer for a husband, whom Rip recollected for one of the urchins that used to climb upon his back. As to Rip's son and heir, who was the ditto of himself, seen leaning against the tree, he was employed to work on the farm; but evinced an hereditary disposition to attend to any thing else but his business.

Rip now resumed his old walks and habits; he soon found many of his former cronies though all rather the worse for the wear and tear of time; and preferred making friends among the rising generation, with whom he soon grew into great favor.

Having nothing to do at home, and being arrived at that happy age when a man can be idle with impunity, he took his place once more on the bench at the inn door, and was reverenced as one of the patriarchs of the village, and a chronicle of the old times "before the war." It was some time before he could get into the regular track of gossip, or could be made to comprehend the strange events that had taken place during his torpor. How that there had been a revolutionary war—that the country had thrown off the yoke of old England—and that, instead of being a subject of his Majesty George the Third, he was now a free citizen of the United States. Rip, in fact, was no politician; the changes of states and empires made but little impression on him; but there was one species of despotism under which he had long groaned, and that was—petticoat government. Happily that was at an end; he had got his neck out of the yoke of matrimony, and could go in and out whenever he pleased, without dreading the tyranny of Dame Van Winkle. Whenever her name was mentioned, however, he shook his head, shrugged his shoulders, and cast up his eyes; which might pass either for an expression of resignation to his fate, or joy at his deliverance.

He used to tell his story to every stranger that arrived at Mr. Doolittle's hotel. He was observed, at first, to vary on some points every time he told it, which was, doubtless, owing to his having so recently awaked. It at last settled down precisely to the tale I have related, and not a man, woman, or child in the neighborhood, but knew it by heart. Some always pretended to doubt the reality of it, and insisted that Rip had been out of his head, and that this was one point on which he always remained flighty. The old Dutch inhabitants, however, almost universally gave it full credit Even to this day they never hear a thunderstorm of a summer afternoon about the Kaatskill, but they say Hendrick Hudson and his crew are at their game of nine-pins; and it is a common wish of all henpecked husbands in the neighborhood, when life hangs heavy on their hands, that they might have a quieting draught out of Rip Van Winkle's flagon.

NOTE

The foregoing Tale, one would suspect, had been suggested to Mr. Knickerbocker by a little German superstition about the Emperor Frederick *der Rothbart*, and the Kypphaüser mountain: the subjoined note, however, which he had appended to the tale, shows that it is an absolute fact, narrated with his usual fidelity:

"The story of Rip Van Winkle may seem incredible to many, but nevertheless I give it my full belief, for I know the vicinity of our old Dutch settlements to have been very subject to marvelous events and appearances. Indeed, I have heard many stranger stories than this, in the villages along the Hudson; all of which were too well authenticated to admit of a doubt. I have even talked with Rip Van Winkle myself, who, when last I saw him, was a very venerable old man, and so perfectly rational and consistent on every other point, that I think no conscientious person could refuse to take this into the bargain; nay, I have seen a certificate on the subject taken before a country justice, and signed with a cross, in the justice's own handwriting. The story, therefore, is beyond the possibility of doubt.

D. K."

POSTSCRIPT

The following are traveling notes from a memorandum-book of Mr. Knickerbocker:

The Kaatsberg, or Catskill Mountains, have always been a region full of fable. The Indians considered them the abode of spirits, who influenced the weather, spreading sunshine or clouds over the landscape, and sending good or bad hunting seasons. They were ruled by an old squaw spirit, said to be their mother. She dwelt on the highest peak of the Catskills, and had charge of the doors of day and night to open and shut them at the proper hour. She hung up the new moons in the skies, and cut up the old ones into stars. In times of drought, if properly propitiated, she would spin light summer clouds out of cobwebs and morning dew, and send them off from the crest of the mountain, flake after flake, like flakes of carded cotton, to float in the air: until, dissolved by the heat of the sun, they would fall in gentle showers, causing the grass to spring, the fruits to ripen, and the corn to grow an inch an hour. If diseased, however, she would brew up clouds black as ink, sitting in the midst of them like a bottle-bellied spider in the midst of its web; and when these clouds broke, wo betide the valleys!

In old times, say the Indian traditions, there was a kind of Manitou or Spirit, who kept about the wildest recesses of the Catskill Mountains and took a mischievous pleasure in wreaking all kinds of evils and vexations upon the red men. Sometimes he would assume the form of a bear, a panther, or a deer, lead the bewildered hunter a weary chase through tangled forests and among ragged rocks; and then spring off with a load ho! ho! leaving him aghast on the brink of a beetling precipice or raging torrent.

The favorite abode of this Manitou is still shown. It is a great rock or cliff on the loneliest part of the mountains, and, from the flowering vines which clamber about it, and the wild flowers which abound in its neighborhood, is known by the name of the Garden Rock. Near the foot of it is a small lake, the haunt of the solitary bittern, with water-snakes basking in the sun on the leaves of the pond-lilies, which lie on the surface. This place was held in great awe by the Indians, insomuch that the boldest hunter would not pursue his game within its precincts. Once upon a time, however, a hunter who had lost his way, penetrated to the garden rock, where he beheld a number of gourds placed in the crotches of trees. One of these he seized and made off with it, but in the hurry of his retreat he let it fall among the rocks, when a great stream gushed forth, which washed him away and swept him down precipices, where he was dashed to pieces, and the stream made its way to the Hudson and continues to flow to the present day; being the identical stream known by the name of the Kaaters-kill.

English Writers on America

Methinks I see in my mind a noble and puissant nation, rousing herself like a strong mare after sleep, and shaking her invincible locks: methinks I see her as an eagle, mewing her might youth, and kindling her endazzled eyes at the full mid-day beam.

MILTON ON THE LIBERTY OF THE PRESS

IT IS WITH FEELINGS OF DEEP REGRET THAT I OBSERVE THE LITERARY animosity daily growing up between England and America. Great curiosity has been awakened of late with respect to the United States, and the London press has teemed with volumes of travels through the Republic; but they seem intended to diffuse error rather than knowledge; and so successful have they been, that, notwithstanding the constant intercourse between the nations, there is no people concerning whom the great mass of the British public have less pure information, or entertain more numerous prejudices.

English travelers are the best and the worst in the world. Where no motives of pride or interest intervene, none can equal them for profound and philosophical views of society, or faithful and graphical descriptions of external objects; but when either the interest or reputation of their own country comes in collision with that of another, they go to the opposite extreme, and forget their usual probity and candor, in the indulgence of splenetic remark, and an illiberal spirit of ridicule.

Hence, their travels are more honest and accurate, the more remote the country described. I would place implicit confidence in an Englishman's description of the regions beyond the cataracts of the Nile; of unknown islands in the Yellow Sea; of the interior of India; or of any other tract which other travelers might be apt to picture out with the illusions of their fancies; but I would cautiously receive his account of his immediate neighbors, and of those nations with which he is in habits of most frequent intercourse. However I might be disposed to trust his probity, I dare not trust his prejudices.

It has also been the peculiar lot of our country to be visited by the worst kind of English travelers. While men of philosophical spirit and cultivated minds have been sent from England to ransack the poles, to penetrate the deserts, and to study the manners and customs of barbarous nations, with which she can have no permanent intercourse of profit or pleasure; it has been left to the broken-down tradesman, the scheming adventurer, the wandering mechanic, the Manchester and Birmingham agent, to be her oracles respecting America. From such sources she is content to receive her information respecting a country in a singular state of moral and physical development; a country in which one of the greatest political experiments in the history of the world is now performing; and which presents the most profound and momentous studies to the statesman and the philosopher.

That such men should give prejudicial accounts of America is not a matter of surprise. The themes it offers for contemplation are too vast and elevated for their capacities. The national character is yet in a state of fermentation; it may have its frothiness and sediment, but its ingredients are sound and wholesome; it has already given proofs of powerful and generous qualities; and the whole promises to settle down into something substantially excellent. But the causes which are operating to strengthen and ennoble it, and its daily indication of admirable properties, are all lost upon these purblind observers; who are only affected by the little asperities incident to its present situation. They are capable of judging only of the surface of things; of those matters which come in contact with their private interests and personal gratifications. They miss some of the snug conveniences and petty comforts which belong to an old, highly-finished, and over-populous state of society; where the ranks of useful labor are crowded, and many earn a painful and servile subsistence by studying the very caprices of appetite and self-indulgence. These minor comforts, however, are all-important in the estimation of narrow minds; which either do not perceive, or will not acknowledge, that they are more than counterbalanced among us by great and generally diffused blessings.

They may, perhaps, have been disappointed in some unreasonable expectation of sudden gain. They may have pictured America to themselves an El Dorado, where gold and silver abounded, and the natives were lacking in sagacity; and where they were to become strangely and suddenly rich, in some unforeseen, but easy manner. The same weakness of mind that indulges absurd expectations produces petulance in disappointment. Such persons become embittered against the country on finding that there, as every where else, a man must sow before he can reap; must win wealth by industry and talent; and must contend with the common difficulties of nature, and the shrewdness of an intelligent and enterprising people.

Perhaps, through mistaken, or ill-directed hospitality, or from the prompt disposition to cheer and countenance the stranger, prevalent among my countrymen, they may have been treated with unwonted respect in America; and having been accustomed all their lives to consider themselves below the surface of good society, and brought up in a servile feeling of inferiority, they become arrogant on the common boon of civility: they attribute to the lowliness of others their own elevation; and underrate a society where there are no artificial distinctions, and where, by any chance, such individuals as themselves can rise to consequence.

One would suppose, however, that information coming from such sources, on a subject where the truth is so desirable, would be received with caution by the censors of the press; that the motives of these men, their veracity, their opportunities of inquiry and observation, and their capacities for judging correctly, would be rigorously scrutinized before their evidence was admitted, in such sweeping extent, against a kindred nation. The very reverse, however, is the case, and it furnishes a striking instance of human inconsistency. Nothing can surpass the vigilance with which English critics will examine the credibility of the traveler who publishes an account of some distant, and comparatively unimportant, country. How warily will they compare the measurements of a pyramid, or the descriptions of a ruin; and how sternly will they censure any inaccuracy in these contributions of merely curious knowledge: while they will receive, with eagerness and unhesitating faith, the gross misrepresentations of coarse and obscure writers, concerning a country with which their own is placed in the most important and delicate relations. Nay, they will even make these apocryphal volumes text-books, on which to enlarge with a zeal and an ability worthy of a more generous cause.

I shall not, however, dwell on this irksome and hackneyed topic; nor should I have adverted to it, but for the undue interest apparently taken in it by my countrymen, and certain injurious effects which I apprehended it might produce upon the national feeling. We attach too much consequence to these attacks. They cannot do us any essential injury. The tissue of misrepresentations attempted to be woven round us are like cobwebs woven round the limbs of an infant giant. Our country continually outgrows them. One falsehood after another falls off of itself. We have but to live on, and every day we live a whole volume of refutation. All the writers of England united, if we could for a moment suppose their great minds stooping to so unworthy a combination, could not conceal our rapidly-growing importance, and matchless prosperity. They could not conceal that these are owing, not merely to physical and local, but also to moral causes—to the political liberty, the general diffusion of knowledge, the prevalence of sound moral and religious principles, which give force and sustained energy to the character of a people; and which, in fact, have been the acknowledged and wonderful supporters of their own national power and glory.

But why are we so exquisitely alive to the aspersions of England? Why do we suffer ourselves to be so affected by the contumely she has endeavored to cast upon us? It is not in the opinion of England alone that honor lives, and reputation has its being. The world at large is the arbiter of a nation's fame; with its thousand eyes it witnesses a nation's deeds, and from their collective testimony is national glory or national disgrace established.

For ourselves, therefore, it is comparatively of but little importance whether England does us justice or not; it is, perhaps, of far more importance to herself. She is instilling anger and resentment into the bosom of a youthful nation, to grow with its growth and strengthen with its strength. If in America, as some of her writers are laboring to convince her, she is hereafter to find an invidious rival, and a gigantic foe, she may thank those very writers for having provoked rivalship and irritated hostility. Every one knows the all-pervading influence of literature at the present day, and how much the opinions and passions of mankind are under its control. The mere contests of the sword are temporary; their wounds are but in the flesh, and it is the pride of the generous to forgive and forget them; but the slanders of the pen pierce to the heart; they rankle longest in the noblest spirits; they dwell ever present in the mind, and render it morbidly sensitive to the most trifling collision. It is but seldom that any one overt act produces hostilities between two nations; there exists, most commonly, a previous jealousy and ill-will; a predisposition to take offence. Trace these to their cause, and how often will they be found to originate in the mischievous effusions of mercenary writers; who, secure in their closets, and for ignominious bread, concoct and circulate the venom that is to inflame the generous and the brave.

I am not laying too much stress upon this point; for it applies most emphatically to our particular case. Over no nation does this press hold a more absolute control than over the people of America; for the universal education of the poorest classes makes every individual a reader. There is nothing published in England on the subject of our country that does not circulate through every part of it. There is not a calumny dropped from English pen, nor an unworthy sarcasm uttered by an English statesman, that does not go to blight good-will, and add to the mass of latent resentment. Possessing, then, as England does the fountain-head whence the literature of the language flows, how completely is it in her power, and how truly is it her duty, to make it the medium of amiable and magnanimous feeling—a stream where the two nations might meet together, and drink in peace and kindness. Should she, however, persist in turning it to waters of bitterness, the tune may come when she may repent her folly. The present friendship of America may be of but little moment to her; but the future destinies of that country do not admit of a doubt; over those of England there lower some shadows of uncertainty. Should, then, a day of gloom arrive; should those reverses overtake her, from which the proudest empires have not been exempt; she may look back with regret at her infatuation, in repulsing from her side a nation she might have grappled to her bosom, and thus destroying her only chance for real friendship beyond the boundaries of her own dominions.

There is a general impression in England, that the people of the United States are inimical to the parent country. It is one of the errors which have been diligently propagated by designing writers. There is, doubtless, considerable political hostility, and a general soreness at the illiberality of the English press; but, generally speaking, the prepossessions of the people are strongly in favor of England. Indeed, at one time, they amounted, in many parts of the Union, to an absurd degree of bigotry. The bare name of Englishman was a passport to the confidence and hospitality of every family, and too often gave a transient currency to the worthless and the ungrateful. Throughout the country there was something of enthusiasm connected with the idea of England. We looked to it with a hallowed feeling of tenderness and veneration, as the land of oar forefathers—the august repository of the monuments and antiquities of our race—the birthplace and mausoleum of the sages and heroes of our paternal history. After our own country, there was none in whose glory we more delighted—none whose good opinion we were more anxious to possess—none toward which our hearts yearned with such throbbings of warm consanguinity. Even during the late war, whenever there was the least opportunity for kind feelings to spring forth, it was the delight of the generous spirits of our country to show that, in the midst of hostilities, they still kept alive the sparks of future friendship.

Is all this to be at an end? Is this golden band of kindred sympathies, so rare between nations, to be broken for ever?—Perhaps it is for the best—it may dispel an illusion which might have kept us in mental vassalage; which might have interfered occasionally with our true interests, and prevented the growth of proper national pride. But it is hard to give up the kindred tie! and there are feelings dearer than interest—closer to the heart than pride—that will still make us cast back a look of regret, as we wander farther and farther from the paternal roof, and lament the waywardness of the parent that would repel the affections of the child.

Short-sighted and injudicious, however, as the conduct of England may be in this system of aspersion, recrimination on our part would be equally ill-judged. I speak not of a prompt and spirited vindication of our country, nor the keenest castigation of her slanderers—but I allude to a disposition to retaliate in kind; to retort sarcasm, and inspire prejudice; which seems to be spreading widely among our writers. Let us guard particularly against such a temper, for it would double the evil instead of redressing the wrong. Nothing is so easy and inviting as the retort of abuse and sarcasm; but it is a paltry and an unprofitable contest. It is the alternative of a morbid mind, fretted into petulance, rather than warmed into indignation. If England is willing to permit the mean jealousies of trade, or the rancorous animosities of politics, to deprave the integrity of her press, and poison the fountain of public opinion, let us beware of her example. She may deem it her interest to diffuse error, and engender antipathy, for the purpose of checking emigration; we have no purpose of the kind to serve. Neither have we any spirit of national jealousy to gratify, for as yet, in all our rivalships with England, we are the rising and the gaining party. There can be no end to answer, therefore, but the gratification of resentment—a mere spirit of retaliation; and even that is impotent. Our retorts are never republished in England; they fall short, therefore, of their aim; but they foster a querulous and peevish temper among our writers; they sour the sweet flow of our early literature, and sow thorns and brambles among its blossoms. What is still worse, they circulate through our own country, and, as far as they have effect, excite virulent national prejudices. This last is the evil most especially to be deprecated. Governed, as we are, entirely by public opinion, the utmost care should be taken to preserve the purity of the public mind. Knowledge is power, and truth is knowledge; whoever, therefore, knowingly propagates a prejudice, willfully saps the foundation of his country's strength.

The members of a republic, above all other men, should be candid and dispassionate. They are, individually, portions of the sovereign mind and sovereign will, and should be enabled to come to all questions of national concern with calm and unbiased judgments. From the peculiar nature of our relations with England, we must have more frequent questions of a difficult and delicate character with her than with any other nation; questions that affect the most acute and excitable feelings; and as, in the adjusting of these, our national measures most ultimately be determined by popular sentiment, we cannot be too anxiously attentive to purify it from all latent passion or prepossession.

Opening, too, as we do, an asylum for strangers from every portion of the earth, we should receive all with impartiality. It should be our pride to exhibit an example of one nation, at least, destitute of national antipathies, and exercising not merely the overt acts of hospitality, but those more rare and noble courtesies which spring from liberality of opinion.

What have we to do with national prejudices? They are the inveterate diseases of old countries, contracted in rude and ignorant ages, when nations knew but little of each other, and looked beyond their own boundaries with distrust and hostility. We, on the contrary, have sprung into national existence in an enlightened and philosophic age, when the different parts of the habitable world, and the various branches of the human family, have been indefatigably studied and made known to each other; and we forego the advantages of our birth, if we do not shake off the national prejudices, as we would the local superstitions of the old world.

But above all let us not be influenced by any angry feelings, so far as to shut our eyes to the perception of what is really excellent and amiable in the English character. We are a young people, necessarily an imitative one, and must take our examples and models, in a great degree, from the existing nations of Europe. There is no country more worthy of our study than England. The spirit of her constitution is most analogous to ours. The manners of her people—their intellectual activity—their freedom of opinion—their habits of thinking on those subjects which concern the dearest interests and most sacred charities of private life, are all congenial to the American character; and, in fact, are all intrinsically excellent; for it is in the moral feeling of the people that the deep foundations of British prosperity are laid; and however the superstructure may be time-worn, or overrun by abuses, there must be something solid in the basis, admirable in the materials, and stable in the structure of an edifice, that so long has towered unshaken amidst the tempests of the world.

Let it be the pride of our writers, therefore, discarding all feelings of irritation, and disdaining to retaliate the illiberality of British authors, to speak of the English nation without prejudice, and with determined candor. While they rebuke the indiscriminating bigotry with which some of our countrymen admire and imitate every thing English, merely because it is English, let them frankly point out what is really worthy of approbation. We may thus place England before us as a perpetual volume of reference, wherein are recorded sound deductions from ages of experience; and while we avoid the errors and absurdities which may have crept into the page, we may draw thence golden maxims of practical wisdom, wherewith to strengthen and to embellish our national character.

Rural Life in England

> Oh! friendly to the best pursuits of man,
> Friendly to thought, to virtue, and to peace,
> Domestic life in rural pleasures past!
>
> COWPER

THE STRANGER WHO WOULD FORM A CORRECT OPINION OF THE ENGLISH character must not confine his observations to the metropolis. He must go forth into the country; he must sojourn in villages and hamlets; he must visit castles, villas, farm-houses, cottages; he must wander through parks and gardens; along hedges and green lanes; he must loiter about country churches; attend wakes and fairs, and other rural festivals; and cope with the people in all their conditions, and all their habits and humors.

In some countries the large cities absorb the wealth and fashion of the nation; they are the only fixed abodes of elegant and intelligent society, and the country is inhabited almost entirely by boorish peasantry. In England, on the contrary, the metropolis is a mere gathering-place, or general rendezvous, of the polite classes, where they devote a small portion of the year to a hurry of gayety and dissipation, and, having indulged this kind of carnival, return again to the apparently more congenial habits of rural life. The various orders of society are therefore diffused over the whole surface of the kingdom, and the most retired neighborhoods afford specimens of the different ranks.

The English, in fact, are strongly gifted with the rural feeling. They possess a quick sensibility to the beauties of nature, and a keen relish for the pleasures and employments of the country. This passion seems inherent in them. Even the inhabitants of cities, born and brought up among brick walls and bustling streets, enter with facility into rural habits, and evince a tact for rural occupation. The merchant has his snug retreat in the vicinity of the metropolis, where he often displays as much pride and zeal in the cultivation of his flower-garden, and the maturing of his fruits, as he does in the conduct of his business, and the success of a commercial enterprise. Even those less fortunate individuals, who are doomed to pass their lives in the midst of din and traffic, contrive to have something that shall remind them of the green aspect of nature. In the most dark and dingy quarters of the city, the drawing-room window resembles frequently a bank of flowers; every spot capable of vegetation has its grassplot and flower-bed; and every square its mimic park, laid out with picturesque taste, and gleaming with refreshing verdure.

Those who see the Englishman only in town are apt to form an unfavorable opinion of his social character. He is either absorbed in business, or distracted by the thousand engagements that dissipate time, thought, and feeling, in this huge metropolis. He has, therefore, too commonly a look of hurry and abstraction. Wherever he happens to be, he is on the point of going some where else; at the moment he is talking on one subject, his mind is wandering to another; and while paying a friendly visit, he is calculating how he shall economize time so as to pay the other visits allotted in the morning. An immense metropolis, like London, is calculated to make men selfish and uninteresting. In their casual and transient meetings, they can but deal briefly in commonplaces. They present but the cold superficies of character—its rich and genial qualities have no time to be warmed into a flow.

It is in the country that the Englishman gives scope to his natural feelings. He breaks loose gladly from the cold formalities and negative civilities of town; throws off his habits of shy reserve, and becomes joyous and free-hearted. He manages to collect round him all the conveniences and elegancies of polite life, and to banish its restraints. His country-seat abounds with every requisite, either for studious retirement, tasteful gratification, or rural exercise. Books, paintings, music, horses, dogs, and sporting implements of all kinds, are at hand. He puts no constraint either upon his guests or himself, but in the true spirit of hospitality provides the means of enjoyment, and leaves every one to partake according to his inclination.

The taste of the English in the cultivation of land, and in what is called landscape gardening, is unrivaled. They have studied nature intently, and discover an exquisite sense of her beautiful forms and harmonious combinations. Those charms, which in other countries she lavishes in wild solitudes, are here assembled round the haunts of domestic life. They seem to have caught her coy and furtive graces, and spread them, like witchery, about their rural abodes.

Nothing can be more imposing than the magnificence of English park scenery. Vast lawns that extend like sheets of vivid green, with here and there clumps of gigantic trees, heaping up rich piles of foliage: the solemn pomp of groves and woodland glades, with the deer trooping in silent herds across them; the hare, bounding away to the covert; or the pheasant, suddenly bursting upon the wing: the brook, taught to wind in natural meanderings, or expand into a glassy lake: the sequestered pool, reflecting the quivering trees, with the yellow leaf sleeping on its bosom, and the trout roaming fearlessly about its limpid waters; while some rustic temple or sylvan statue, grown green and dank with age, gives an air of classic sanctity to the seclusion.

These are but a few of the features of park scenery; but what most delights me, is the creative talent with which the English decorate the unostentatious abodes of middle life. The rudest habitation, the most unpromising and scanty portion of land, in the hands of an Englishman of taste, becomes a little paradise. With a nicely discriminating eye, he seizes at once upon its capabilities, and pictures in his mind the future landscape. The sterile spot grows into loveliness under his hand; and yet the operations of art which produce the effect are scarcely to be perceived. The cherishing and training of some trees; the cautious pruning of others; the nice distribution of flowers and plants of tender and graceful foliage; the introduction of a green slope of velvet turf; the partial opening to a peep of blue distance, or silver gleam of water: all these are managed with a delicate tact, a pervading yet quiet assiduity, like the magic touchings with which a painter finishes up a favorite picture.

The residence of people of fortune and refinement in the country has diffused a degree of taste and elegance in rural economy, that descends to the lowest class. The very laborer, with his thatched cottage and narrow slip of ground, attends to their embellishment. The trim hedge, the grassplot before the door, the little flower-bed bordered with snug box, the woodbine trained up against the wall, and hanging its blossoms about the lattice, the pot of flowers in the window, the holly, providently planted about the house, to cheat winter of its dreariness, and to throw in a semblance of green summer to cheer the fireside: all these bespeak the influence of taste, flowing down from high sources, and pervading the lowest levels of the public mind. If ever Love, as poets sing, delights to visit a cottage, it must be the cottage of an English peasant.

The fondness for rural life among the higher classes of the English has had a great and salutary effect upon the national character. I do not know a finer race of men than the English gentlemen. Instead of the softness and effeminacy which characterize the men of rank in most countries, they exhibit a union of elegance and strength, a robustness of frame and freshness of complexion, which I am inclined to attribute to their living so much in the open air, and pursuing so eagerly the invigorating recreations of the country. These hardy exercises produce also a healthful tone of mind and spirits, and a manliness and simplicity of manners, which even the follies and dissipations of the town cannot easily pervert, and can never entirely destroy. In the country, too, the different orders of society seem to approach more freely, to be more disposed to blend and operate favorably upon each other. The distinctions between them do not appear to be so marked and impassable as in the cities. The manner in which property has been distributed into small estates and farms has established a regular gradation from the nobleman, through the classes of gentry, small landed proprietors, and substantial farmers, down to the laboring peasantry; and while it has thus banded the extremes of society together, has infused into each intermediate rank a spirit of independence. This, it must be confessed, is not so universally the case at present as it was formerly; the larger estates having, in late years of distress, absorbed the smaller, and, in some parts of the country, almost annihilated the sturdy race of small farmers. These, however, I believe, are but casual breaks in the general system I have mentioned.

In rural occupation there is nothing mean and debasing. It leads a man forth among scenes of natural grandeur and beauty; it leaves him to the workings of his own mind, operated upon by the purest and most elevating of external influences. Such a man may be simple and rough, but he cannot be vulgar. The man of refinement, therefore, finds nothing revolting in an intercourse with the lower orders in rural life, as he does when he casually mingles with the lower orders of cities. He lays aside his distance and reserve, and is glad to wave the distinctions of rank, and to enter into the honest, heartfelt enjoyments of common life. Indeed the very amusements of the country bring men more and more together; and the sound of hound and horn blend all feelings into harmony. I believe this is one great reason why the nobility and gentry are more popular among the inferior orders in England than they are in any other country; and why the latter have endured so many excessive pressures and extremities, without repining more generally at the unequal distribution of fortune and privilege.

To this mingling of cultivated and rustic society may also be attributed the rural feeling that runs through British literature; the frequent use of illustrations from rural life; those incomparable descriptions of nature that abound in the British poets, that have continued down from "the Flower and the Leaf" of Chaucer, and have brought into our closets all the freshness and fragrance of the dewy landscape. The pastoral writers of other countries appear as if they had paid nature an occasional visit and become acquainted with her general charms; but the British poets have lived and reveled with her—they have wooed her in her most secret haunts—they have watched her minutest caprices. A spray could not tremble in the breeze—a leaf could not rustle to the ground—a diamond drop could not patter in the stream—a fragrance could not exhale from the humble violet, nor a daisy unfold its crimson tints to the morning, but it has been noticed by these impassioned and delicate observers, and wrought up into some beautiful morality.

The effect of this devotion of elegant minds to rural occupations has been wonderful on the face of the country. A great part of the island is rather level, and would be monotonous, were it not for the charms of culture: but it is studded and gemmed, as it were, with castles and palaces, and embroidered with parks and gardens. It does not abound in grand and sublime prospects, but rather in little home scenes of rural repose and sheltered quiet. Every antique farm-house and moss-grown cottage is a picture: and as the roads are continually winding, and the view is shut in by groves and hedges, the eye is delighted by a continual succession of small landscapes of captivating loveliness.

The great charm, however, of English scenery is the moral feeling that seems to pervade it. It is associated in the mind with ideas of order, of quiet, of sober well-established principles, of hoary usage and reverend custom. Every thing seems to be the growth of ages of regular and peaceful existence. The old church of remote architecture, with its low massive portal; its gothic tower; its windows rich with tracery and painted glass, in scrupulous preservation; its stately monuments of warriors and worthies of the olden time, ancestors of the present lords of the soil; its tombstone, recording successive generations of sturdy yeomanry, whose progeny still plough the same fields, and kneel at the same altar—the parsonage, a quaint irregular pile, partly antiquated, but repaired and altered in the tastes of various ages and occupants—the stile and footpath leading from the churchyard, across pleasant fields, and along shady hedge-rows, according to an immemorial right, of way—the neighboring village, with its venerable cottages, its public green sheltered by trees, under which the forefathers of the present race have sported—the antique family mansion, standing apart in some little rural domain, but looking down with a protecting air on the surrounding scene: all these common features of English lands evince a calm and settled security, and hereditary transmission of homebred virtues and local attachments, that speak deeply and touchingly tor the moral character of the nation.

It is a pleasing sight of a Sunday morning, when the bell is sending its sober melody across the quiet fields, to behold the peasantry in the best finery, with ruddy faces and modest cheerfulness, thronging tranquilly along the green lanes to church; but it is still more pleasing to see them in the evenings, gathering about their cottage doors, and appearing to exult in the humble comforts and embellishments which their own hands have spread around them.

It is this sweet home-feeling, this settled repose of affection in the domestic scene, that is, after all, the parent of the steadiest virtues and purest enjoyments; and I cannot dose these desultory remarks better, than by quoting the words of a modern English poet, who has depicted it with remarkable felicity:

Through each gradation, from the castled hall,
The city dome, the villa crown'd with shade,
But chief from modest mansions numberless,
In town or hamlet, shelt'ring middle life,
Down to the cottaged vale, and straw-roof'd shed;
This western isle hath long been famed for scenes
Where bliss domestic finds a dwelling-place;
Domestic bliss, that, like a harmless dove,
(Honor and sweet endearment keeping guard,)
Can centre in a little quiet nest
All that desire would fly for through the earth;
That can, the world eluding, be itself
A world enjoy'd; that wants no witnesses
But its own sharers, and approving heaven;
That, like a flower deep hid in rocky cleft.
Smiles, though 'tis looking only at the sky.[1]

1. From a Poem on the death of the Princess Charlotte, by the Reverend Rann Kennedy, A. M.

The Broken Heart

I never heard
Of any true affection, but 'twas nipt
With care, that, like the caterpillar, eats
The leaves of the spring's sweetest book, the rose.
MIDDLETON

IT IS A COMMON PRACTICE WITH THOSE WHO HAVE OUTLIVED THE susceptibility of early feeling, or have been brought up in the gay heartlessness of dissipated life, to laugh at all love stories, and to treat the tales of romantic passion as mere fictions of novelists and poets. My observations on human nature have induced me to think otherwise. They have convinced me, that however the surface of the character may be chilled and frozen by the cares of the world, or cultivated into mere smiles by the arts of society, still there are dormant fires lurking in the depths of the coldest bosom, which, when once enkindled, become impetuous, and are sometimes desolating in their effects. Indeed, I am a true believer in the blind deity, and go to the full extent of his doctrines. Shall I confess it?—I believe in broken hearts, and the possibility of dying of disappointed love. I do not, however, consider it a malady often fatal to my own sex; but I firmly believe that it withers down many a lovely woman into an early grave.

Man is the creature of interest and ambition. His nature leads him forth into the struggle and bustle of the world. Love is but the embellishment of his early life, or a song piped in the intervals of the acts. He seeks for fame, for fortune, for space in the world's thought, and dominion over his fellow-men. But a woman's whole life is a history of the affections. The heart is her world: it is there her ambition strives for empire; it is there her avarice seeks for hidden treasures. She sends forth her sympathies on adventure; she embarks her whole soul in the traffic of affection; and if shipwrecked, her case is hopeless—for it is a bankruptcy of the heart

To a man the disappointment of love may occasion some bitter pangs: it wounds some feelings of tenderness—it blasts some prospects of felicity; but he is an active being—he may dissipate his thoughts in the whirl of varied occupation, or may plunge into the tide of pleasure; or, if the scene of disappointment be too full of painful associations, he can shift his abode at will, and taking as it were the wings of the morning, can "fly to the uttermost parts of the earth, and be at rest."

But woman's is comparatively a fixed, a secluded, and meditative life. She is more the companion of her own thoughts and feelings; and if they are turned to ministers of sorrow, where shall she look for consolation? Her lot is to be wooed and won; and if unhappy in her love, her heart is like some fortress that has been captured, and sacked, and abandoned, and left desolate.

How many bright eyes grow dim—how many soft cheeks grow pale—how many lovely forms fade away into the tomb, and none can tell the cause that blighted their loveliness! As the dove will clasp its wings to its side, and cover and conceal the arrow that is preying on its vitals, so is it the nature of woman to hide from the world the pangs of wounded affection. The love of a delicate female is always shy and silent. Even when fortunate, she scarcely breathes it to herself; but when otherwise she buries it in the recesses of her bosom, and there lets it cower and brood among the ruins of her peace. With her the desire of the heart has failed. The great charm of existence is at an end. She neglects all the cheerful exercises which gladden the spirits, quicken the pulses, and send the tide of life in healthful currents through the veins. Her rest is broken—the sweet refreshment of sleep is poisoned by melancholy dreams—"dry sorrow drinks her blood," until her enfeebled frame sinks under the slightest external injury. Look for her, after a little while, and you find friendship weeping over her untimely grave, and wondering that one, who but lately glowed with all the radiance of health and beauty, should so speedily be brought down to "darkness and the worm." You will be told of some wintry chill, some casual indisposition, that laid her low;—but no one knows of the mental malady which previously sapped her strength, and made her so easy a prey to the spoiler.

She is like some tender tree, the pride and beauty of the grove; graceful in its form, bright in its foliage, but with the worm preying at its heart. We find it suddenly withering, when it should be most fresh and luxuriant. We see it drooping its branches to the earth, and shedding leaf by leaf, until, wasted and perished away, it falls even in the stillness of the forest; and as we muse over the beautiful ruin, we strive in vain to recollect the blast or thunderbolt that could have smitten it with decay.

I have seen many instances of women running to waste and self-neglect, and disappearing gradually from the earth, almost as if they had been exhaled to heaven; and have repeatedly fancied that I could trace their death through the various declensions of consumption, cold, debility, languor, melancholy, until I reached the first symptom of disappointed love. But an instance of the kind was lately told to me; the circumstances are well known in the country where they happened, and I shall but give them in the manner in which they were related.

Every one must recollect the tragical story of young E——, the Irish patriot; it was too touching to be soon forgotten. During the troubles in Ireland, he was tried, condemned, and executed, on a charge of treason. His fate made a deep impression on public sympathy. He was so young—so intelligent—so generous—so brave—so every thing that we are apt to like in a young man. His conduct under trial, too, was so lofty and intrepid. The noble indignation with which he repelled the charge of treason against his country—the eloquent vindication of his name—and his pathetic appeal to posterity, in the hopeless hour of condemnation—all these entered deeply into every generous bosom, and even his enemies lamented the stern policy that dictated his execution.

But there was one heart, whose anguish it would be impossible to describe. In happier days and fairer fortunes, he had won the affections of a beautiful and interesting girl, the daughter of a late celebrated Irish barrister. She loved him with the disinterested fervor of a woman's first and early love. When every worldly maxim arrayed itself against him; when blasted in fortune, and disgrace and danger darkened around his name, she loved him the more ardently for his very sufferings. If, then, his fate could awaken the sympathy even of his foes, what must have been the agony of her, whose whole soul was occupied by his image! Let those tell who have had the portals of the tomb suddenly closed between them and the being they most loved on earth—who have sat at its threshold, as one shut out in a cold and lonely world, whence all that was most lovely and loving had departed.

But then the horrors of such a grave! so frightful, so dishonored! three was nothing for memory to dwell on that could soothe the pang of separation—none of those tender though melancholy circumstances, which endear the parting scene—nothing to melt sorrow into those blessed tears, sent like the dews of heaven, to revive the heart in the parting hour of anguish.

To render her widowed situation more desolate, she had incurred her father's displeasure by her unfortunate attachment, and was an exile from the paternal roof. But could the sympathy and kind offices of friends have reached a spirit so shocked and driven in by horror, she would have experienced no want of consolation, for the Irish are a people of quick and generous sensibilities. The most delicate and cherishing attentions were paid her by families of wealth and distinction. She was led into society, and they tried by all kinds of occupation and amusement to dissipate her grief, and wean her from the tragical story of her loves. But it was all in vain. There are some strokes of calamity which scathe and scorch the soul—which penetrate to the vital seat of happiness—and blast it never again to put forth bud or blossom. She never objected to frequent the haunts of pleasure, but was as much alone there as in the depths of solitude; walking about in a sad reverie, apparently unconscious of the world around her. She carried with her an inward woe that mocked at all the blandishments of friendship, and "heeded not the song of the charmer, charm he never so wisely."

The person who told me her story had seen her at a masquerade. There can be no exhibition of far-gone wretchedness more striking and painful than to meet it in such a scene. To find it wandering like a spectre, lonely and joyless, where all around is gay—to see it dressed out in the trappings of mirth, and looking so wan and wobegone, as if it had tried in vain to cheat the poor heart into a momentary forgetfulness of sorrow. After strolling through the splendid rooms and giddy crowd with an air of utter abstraction, she sat herself down on the steps of an orchestra, and, looking about for some time with a vacant air, that showed her insensibility to the garish scene, she began, with the capriciousness of a sickly heart, to warble a little plaintive air. She had an exquisite voice; but on this occasion it was so simple, so touching, it breathed forth such a soul of wretchedness, that she drew a crowd mute and silent around her, and melted every one into tears.

The story of one so true and tender could not but excite great interest in a country remarkable for enthusiasm. It completely won the heart of a brave officer, who paid his addresses to her, and thought that one so true to the dead could not but prove affectionate to the living. She declined his attentions, for her thoughts were irrevocably engrossed by the memory of her former lover. He, however, persisted in his suit. He solicited not her tenderness, but her esteem. He was assisted by her conviction of his worth, and her sense of her own destitute and dependent situation, for she was existing on the kindness of friends. In a word, he at length succeeded in gaining her hand, though with the solemn assurance, that her heart was unalterably another's.

He took her with him to Sicily, hoping that a change of scene might wear out the remembrance of early woes. She was an amiable and exemplary wife, and made an effort to be a happy one; but nothing could cure the silent and devouring melancholy that had entered into her very soul. She wasted away in a slow, but hopeless decline, and at length sunk into the grave, the victim of a broken heart.

It was on her that Moore, the distinguished Irish poet, composed the following lines:

She is far from the land where her young hero sleeps,
And lovers around her are sighing:
But coldly she turns from their gaze, and weeps,
For her heart in his grave is lying.

She sings the wild songs of her dear native plains,
Every note which he loved awaking—
Ah! little they think, who delight in her strains,
How the heart of the minstrel is breaking!

He had lived for his love—for his country he died,
They were all that to life had entwined him—
Nor soon shall the tears of his country be dried,
Nor long will his love stay behind him!

Oh! make her a grave where the sunbeams rest,
When they promise a glorious morrow;
They shine o'er her sleep, like a smile from the west,
From her own loved island of sorrow!

The Art of Book-making

If that severe doom of Synesius be true—"It is a greater offence to steal dead men's labor than their clothes," what shall become of most writers?

BURTON'S *ANATOMY OF MELANCHOLY*

I HAVE OFTEN WONDERED AT THE EXTREME FECUNDITY OF THE PRESS, AND how it comes to pass that so many heads, on which nature seemed to have inflicted the curse of barrenness, should teem with voluminous productions. As a man travels on, however, in the journey of life, his objects of wonder daily diminish, and he is continually finding out some very simple cause for some great matter of marvel. Thus have I chanced, in my peregrinations about this great metropolis, to blunder upon a scene which unfolded to me some of the mysteries of the book-making craft, and at once put an end to my astonishment.

I was one summer's day loitering through the great saloons of the British Museum, with that listlessness with which one is apt to saunter about a museum in warm weather; sometimes lolling over the glass cases of minerals, sometimes studying the hieroglyphics on an Egyptian mummy, and sometimes trying, with nearly equal success, to comprehend the allegorical paintings on the lofty ceilings. Whilst I was gazing about in this idle way, my attention was attracted to a distant door, at the end of a suit of apartments. It was closed, but every now and then it would open, and some strange-favored being, generally clothed in black, would steal forth, and glide through the rooms, without noticing any of the surrounding objects. There was an air of mystery about this that piqued my languid curiosity, and I determined to attempt the passage of that strait, and to explore the unknown regions beyond. The door yielded to my hand, with that facility with which the portals of enchanted castles yield to the adventurous knight-errant. I found myself in a spacious chamber, surrounded with great cases of venerable books. Above the cases, and just under the cornice, were arranged a great number of black-looking portraits of ancient authors. About the room were placed long tables, with stands for reading and writing, at which sat many pale, studious personages, poring intently over dusty volumes, rummaging among mouldy manuscripts, and taking copious notes of their contents. A hushed stillness reigned through this mysterious apartment, excepting that you might hear the racing of pens over sheets of paper, or occasionally, the deep sigh of one of these sages, as he shifted his position to turn over the page of an old folio; doubtless arising from that hollowness and flatulency incident to learned research.

Now and then one of these personages would write something on a small slip of paper, and ring a bell, whereupon a familiar would appear, take the paper in profound silence, glide out of the room, and return shortly loaded with ponderous tomes, upon which the other would fall tooth and nail with famished voracity. I had no longer a doubt that I had happened upon a body of magi, deeply engaged in the study of occult sciences. The scene reminded me of an old Arabian tale, of a philosopher shut up in an enchanted library, in the bosom of a mountain, which opened only once a year; where he made the spirits of the place bring him books of all kinds of dark knowledge, so that at the end of the year, when the magic portal once more swung open on its hinges, he issued forth so versed in forbidden lore, as to be able to soar above the heads of the multitude, and to control the powers of nature.

My curiosity being now fully aroused, I whispered to one of the familiars, as he was about to leave the room, and begged an interpretation of the strange scene before me. A few words were sufficient for the purpose. I found that these mysterious personages, whom I had mistaken for magi, were principally authors, and in the very act of manufacturing books. I was, in fact, in the reading-room of the great British Library—an immense collection of volumes of all ages and languages, many of which are now forgotten, and most of which are seldom read: one of these sequestered pools of obsolete literature, to which modern authors repair, and draw buckets full of classic lore, or "pure English, undefiled," wherewith to swell their own scanty rills of thought.

Being now in possession of the secret, I sat down in a corner, and watched the process of this book manufactory. I noticed one lean, bilious-looking wight, who sought none but the most worm-eaten volumes, printed in black-letter. He was evidently constructing some work of profound erudition, that would be purchased by every man who wished to be thought learned, placed upon a conspicuous shelf of his library, or laid open upon his table; but never read. I observed him, now and then, draw a large fragment of biscuit out of his pocket, and gnaw; whether it was his dinner, or whether he was endeavoring to keep off that exhaustion of the stomach produced by much pondering over dry works, I leave to harder students than myself to determine.

There was one dapper little gentleman in bright-colored clothes, with a chirping, gossiping expression of countenance, who had all the appearance of an author on good terms with his bookseller. After considering him attentively, I recognized in him a diligent getter-up of miscellaneous works, which bustled off well with the trade. I was curious to see how he manufactured his wares. He made more stir and show of business than any of the others; dipping into various books, fluttering over the leaves of manuscripts, taking a morsel out of one, a morsel out of another, "line upon line, precept upon precept, here a little and there a little." The contents of his book seemed to be as heterogeneous as those of the witches' caldron in Macbeth. It was here a finger and there a thumb, toe of frog and blind-worm's sting, with his own gossip poured in like "baboon's blood," to make the medley "slab and good."

After all, thought I, may not this pilfering disposition be implanted in authors for wise purposes; may it not be the way in which Providence has taken care that the seeds of knowledge and wisdom shall be preserved from age to age, in spite of the inevitable decay of the works in which they were first produced? We see that nature has wisely, though whimsically, provided for the conveyance of seeds from clime to clime, in the maws of certain birds; so that animals which, in themselves, are little better than carrion, and apparently the lawless plunderers of the orchard and the cornfield, are, in fact, nature's carriers to disperse and perpetuate her blessings. In like manner, the beauties and fine thoughts of ancient and obsolete authors are caught up by these flights of predatory writers, and cast forth again to flourish and bear fruit in a remote and distant tract of time. Many of their works, also, undergo a kind of metempsychosis, and spring up under new forms. What was formerly a ponderous history revives in the shape of a romance—an old legend changes into a modern play—and a sober philosophical treatise famishes the body for a whole series of bouncing and sparkling essays. Thus it is in the clearing of our American woodlands; where we burn down a forest of stately pines, a progeny of dwarf oaks start up in their place: and we never see the prostrate trunk of a tree mouldering into soil, but it gives birth to a whole tribe of fungi.

Let us not, then, lament over the decay and oblivion into which ancient writers descend; they do but submit to the great law of nature, which declares that all sublunary shapes of matter shall be limited in their duration, but which decrees, also, that their elements shall never perish. Generation after generation, both in animal and vegetable life, passes away, but the vital principle is transmitted to posterity, and the species continue to flourish. Thus, also, do authors beget authors, and having produced a numerous progeny, in a good old age they sleep with their fathers, that is to say, with the authors who preceded them—and from whom they had stolen.

Whilst I was indulging in these rambling fancies, I had leaned my head against a pile of reverend folios. Whether it was owing to the soporific emanations from these works; or to the profound quiet of the room; or to the lassitude arising from much wandering; or to an unlucky habit of napping at improper times and places, with which I am grievously afflicted, so it was, that I fell into a doze. Still, however, my imagination continued busy, and indeed the same scene remained before my mind's eye, only a little changed in some of the details. I dreamt that the chamber was still decorated with the portraits of ancient authors, but that the number was increased. The long tables had disappeared, and, in place of the sage magi, I beheld a ragged, threadbare throng, such as may be seen plying about the great repository of cast-off clothes, Monmouth-street. Whenever they seized upon a book, by one of those incongruities common to dreams, methought it turned into a garment of foreign or antique fashion, with which they proceeded to equip themselves. I noticed, however, that no one pretended to clothe himself from any particular suit, but took a sleeve from one, a cape from another, a skirt from a third, thus decking himself out piecemeal, while some of his original rags would peep out from among his borrowed finery.

There was a portly, rosy, well-fed parson, whom I observed ogling several mouldy polemical writers through an eye-glass. He soon contrived to slip on the voluminous mantle of one of the old fathers, and, having purloined the gray beard of another, endeavored to look exceedingly wise; but the smirking commonplace of his countenance set at naught all the trappings of wisdom. One sickly-looking gentleman was busied embroidering a very flimsy garment with gold thread drawn out of several old court-dresses of the reign of Queen Elizabeth. Another had trimmed himself magnificently from an illuminated manuscript, had stuck a nosegay in his bosom, culled from "The Paradise of Daintie Devices" and having put Sir Philip Sidney's hat on one side of his head, strutted off with an exquisite air of vulgar elegance. A third, who was but of puny dimensions, had bolstered himself out bravely with the spoils from several obscure tracts of philosophy, so that he had a very imposing front; but he was lamentably tattered in rear, and I perceived that he had patched his small-clothes with scraps of parchment from a Latin author.

There were some well-dressed gentlemen, it is true, who only helped themselves to a gem or so, which sparkled among their own ornaments, without eclipsing them. Some, too, seemed to contemplate the costumes of the old writers, merely to imbibe their principles of taste, and to catch their air and spirit; but I grieve to say, that too many were apt to array themselves from top to toe, in the patchwork manner I have mentioned. I shall not omit to speak of one genius, in drab breeches and gaiters, and an Arcadian hat, who had a violent propensity to the pastoral, but whose rural wanderings had been confined to the classic haunts of Primrose Hill, and the solitudes of the Regent's Park. He had decked himself in wreaths and ribands from all the old pastoral poets, and, hanging his head on one side, went about with a fantastical lack-a-daisical air, "babbling about green fields" But the personage that most struck my attention was a pragmatical old gentleman, in clerical robes, with a remarkably large and square, but bald head. He entered the room wheezing and puffing, elbowed his way through the throng, with a look of sturdy self-confidence, and having laid hands upon a thick Greek quarto, clapped it upon his head, and swept majestically away in a formidable frizzled wig.

In the height of this literary masquerade, a cry suddenly resounded from every side, of "Thieves! Thieves!" I looked, and lo! the portraits about the wall became animated! The old authors thrust out, first a head, then a shoulder, from the canvas, looked down curiously, for an instant, upon the motley throng, and then descended with fury in their eyes, to claim their rifled property. The scene of scampering and hubbub that ensued baffles all description. The unhappy culprits endeavored in vain to escape with plunder. On one side might be seen half a dozen old monks, stripping a modern professor; on another, there was sad devastation carried into the ranks of modern dramatic writers. Beaumont and Fletcher, side by side, raged round the field like Castor and Pollux, and sturdy Ben Jonson enacted more wonders than when a volunteer with the army in Flanders. As to the dapper little compiler of farragos, mentioned some time since, he had arrayed himself in as many patches and colors as Harlequin, and there was as fierce a contention of claimants about him, as about the dead body of Patroclus. I was grieved to see many men, to whom I had been accustomed to look up with awe and reverence, fain to steal off with scarce a rag to cover their nakedness. Just then my eye was caught by the pragmatical old gentleman in the Greek grizzled wig, who was scrambling away in sore affright with half a score of authors in full cry after him! They were close upon his haunches: in a twinkling off went his wig; at every turn some strip of raiment was peeled away; until in a few moments, from his domineering pomp, he shrunk into a little, pursy, "chopped bald shot," and made his exit with only a few tags and rags fluttering at his back.

There was something so ludicrous in the catastrophe of this learned Theban, that I burst into an immoderate fit of laughter, which broke the whole illusion. The tumult and the scuffle were at an end. The chamber resumed its usual appearance. The old authors shrunk back into their picture-frames, and hung in shadowy solemnity along the walls. In short, I found myself wide awake in my comer, with the whole assemblage of bookworms gazing at me with astonishment. Nothing of the dream had been real but my burst of laughter, a sound never before heard in that grave sanctuary, and so abhorrent to the ears of wisdom, as to electrify the fraternity.

The librarian now stepped up to me, and demanded whether I had a card of admission. At first I did not comprehend him, but I soon found that the library was a kind of literary "preserve," subject to game-laws, and that no one must presume to hunt there without special license and permission. In a word, I stood convicted of being an arrant poacher, and was glad to make a precipitate retreat, lest I should have a whole pack of authors let loose upon me.

A Royal Poet

Though your body be confined,
And soft love a prisoner bound,
Yet the beauty of your mind
Neither check nor chain hath found.
Look nobly, then, and dare
Even the fetters that your wear.

FLETCHER

On a soft sunny morning, in the genial month of May, I made an excursion to Windsor Castle. It is a place of storied and poetical associations. The very external aspect of the proud old pile is enough to inspire high thought. It rears its irregular walls and massive towers, like a mural crown, round the brow of a lofty ridge, waves its royal banner in the clouds, and looks down, with a lordly air, upon the surrounding world.

On this morning the weather was of that voluptuous vernal kind, which calls forth all the latent romance of a man's temperament, filling his mind with music, and disposing him to quote poetry and dream of beauty. In wandering through the magnificent saloons and long echoing galleries of the castle, I passed with indifference by whole rows of portraits of warriors and statesmen, but lingered in the chamber, where hang the likenesses of the beauties which graced the gay court of Charles the Second; and as I gazed upon them, depicted with amorous, half-disheveled tresses, and the sleepy eye of love, I blessed the pencil of Sir Peter Lely, which had thus enabled me to bask in the reflected rays of beauty. In traversing also the "large green courts," with sunshine beaming on the gray walls, and glancing along the velvet turf, my mind was engrossed with the image of the tender, the gallant, but hapless Surry, and his account of his loitering about them in his stripling days, when enamored of the Lady Geraldine—

With eyes cast up unto the maiden's tower,
With easie sighs, such as men draw in love.

In this mood of mere poetical susceptibility, I visited the ancient Keep of the Castle, where James the First of Scotland, the pride and theme of Scottish poets and historians, was for many years of his youth detained a prisoner of state. It is a large gray tower, that has stood the brunt of ages, and is still in good preservation. It stands on a mound, which elevates it above the other parts of the castle, and a great flight of steps leads to the interior. In the armory, a gothic hall, furnished with weapons of various kinds and ages, I was shown a coat of armor hanging against the wall, which had once belonged to James. Hence I was conducted up a staircase to a suit of apartments of faded magnificence, hung with storied tapestry, which formed his prison, and the scene of that passionate and fanciful amour, which has woven into the web of his story the magical hues of poetry and fiction.

The whole history of this amiable but unfortunate prince is highly romantic At the tender age of eleven he was sent from home by his father, Robert III, and destined for the French court, to be reared under the eye of the French monarch, secure from the treachery and danger that surrounded the royal house of Scotland. It was his mishap in the course of his voyage to fall into the hands of the English, and he was detained prisoner by Henry IV, notwithstanding that a truce existed between the two countries.

The intelligence of his capture, coming in the train of many sorrows and disasters, proved fatal to his unhappy father. "The news," we are told, "was brought to him while at supper, and did so overwhelm him with grief, that he was almost ready to give up the ghost into the hands of the servant that attended him. But being carried to his bed-chamber, he abstained from all food, and in three days died of hunger and grief, at Bothesay."[1]

James was detained in captivity above eighteen years; but thou deprived of personal liberty, he was treated with the respect due to his rank. Care was taken to instruct him in all the branches of useful knowledge cultivated at that period, and to give him those mental and personal accomplishments deemed proper for a prince. Perhaps, in this respect, his imprisonment was an advantage, as it enabled him to apply

1. Buchanan

himself the more exclusively to his improvement, and quietly to imbibe that rich fund of knowledge, and to cherish those elegant tastes, which have given such a lustre to his memory. The picture drawn of him in early life, by the Scottish historians, is highly captivating, and seems rather the description of a hero of romance, than of a character in real history. He was well learnt, we are told, "to fight with the sword, to joust, to tournay, to wrestle, to sing and dance; he was an expert mediciner, right crafty in playing both of lute and harp, and sundry other instruments of music and was expert in grammar, oratory, and poetry."[2]

With this combination of manly and delicate accomplishments, fitting him to shine both in active and elegant life, and calculated to give him an intense relish for joyous existence, it must have been a severe trial, in an age of bustle and chivalry, to pass the spring-time of his years in monotonous captivity. It was the good fortune of James, however, to be gifted with a powerful poetic fancy, and to be visited in his prison by the choicest inspirations of the muse. Some minds corrode and grow inactive under the loss of personal liberty; others grow morbid and irritable; but it is the nature of the poet to become tender and imaginative in the loneliness of confinement. He banquets upon the honey of his own thoughts, and, like the captive bird, pours forth his soul in melody.

> Have you not seen the nightingale,
> A pilgrim cooped into a cage,
> How doth she chant her wonted tale,
> In that her lonely hermitage!
> Even there her charming melody doth prove
> That all her boughs are trees, her cage a grove.[3]

Indeed, it is the divine attribute of the imagination, that it is irrepressible, unconfinable; that when the real world is shut out, it can create a world for itself, and with a necromantic power, can conjure up glorious shapes and forms, and brilliant visions, to make solitude populous and irradiate the gloom of the dungeon. Such was the world of pomp and pageant that lived round Tasso in his dismal cell at Ferrara, when he conceived the splendid scenes of his Jerusalem; and we may consider the "King's

2. Ballenden's Translation of Hector Boyce.

3. Roger L'Estrange.

Quair," composed by James, during his captivity at Windsor, as another of those beautiful breakings-forth of the soul from the restraint and gloom of the prison house.

The subject of the poem is his love for the Lady Jane Beaufort, daughter of the Earl of Somerset, and a princess of the blood royal of England, of whom he became enamored in the course of his captivity. What gives it a peculiar value, is that it may be considered a transcript of the royal bard's true feelings, and the story of his real, loves and fortunes. It is not often that sovereigns write poetry, or that poets deal in fact. It is gratifying to the pride of a common man, to find a monarch thus suing, as it were, for admission into his closet, and seeking to win his favor by administering to his pleasures. It is a proof of the honest equality of intellectual competition, which strips off all the trappings of factitious dignity, brings the candidate down to a level with his fellow men, and obliges him to depend on his own native powers for distinction. It is curious, too, to get at the history of a monarch's heart, and to find the simple affections of human nature throbbing under the ermine. But James had learnt to be a poet before he was a king: he was schooled in adversity, and reared in the company of his own thoughts. Monarchs have seldom time to parley with their hearts, or to meditate their minds into poetry; and had James been brought up amidst the adulation and gayety of a court, we should never, in all probability, have had such a poem as the Quair.

I have been particularly interested by those parts of the poem which breathe his immediate thoughts concerning his situation, or which are connected with the apartment in the tower. They have thus a personal and local charm, and are given with such circumstantial truth, as to make the reader present with the captive in his prison, and the companion of his meditations.

Such is the account which he gives of his weariness of spirit, and of the incident which first suggested the idea of writing the poem. It was the still midwatch of a clear moonlight night; the stars, he says, were twinkling as fire in the high vault of heaven; and "Cynthia rinsing her golden locks in Aquarius." He lay in bed wakeful and restless, and took a hook to beguile the tedious hours. The book he chose was Boetius' Consolations of Philosophy, a work popular among the writers of that day, and which had been translated by his great prototype Chaucer. From the high eulogium in which he indulges, it is evident this was one of his favorite volumes while in prison: and indeed it is an admirable text-book for meditation under adversity. It is the legacy of a noble and enduring spirit, purified by sorrow and suffering, bequeathing to its successors in calamity the maxims of sweet morality, and the trains of eloquent but simple reasoning, by which it was enabled to bear up against the various ills of life. It is a talisman, which the unfortunate may treasure up in his bosom, or, like the good King James, lay upon his nightly pillow.

After closing the volume, he turns its contents over in his mind, and gradually falls into a fit of musing on the fickleness of fortune, the vicissitudes of his own life, and the evils that had overtaken him even in his tender youth. Suddenly he hears the bell ringing to matins; but its sound, chiming in with his melancholy fancies, seems to him like a voice exhorting him to write his story. In the spirit of poetic errantry he determines to comply with this intimation: he therefore takes pen in hand, makes with it a sign of the cross to implore a benediction, and sallies forth into the fairy land of poetry. There is something extremely fanciful in all this, and it is interesting as furnishing a striking and beautiful instance of the simple manner in which whole trains of poetical thought are sometimes awakened, and literary enterprises suggested to the mind.

In the course of his poem he more than once bewails the peculiar hardness of his fate; thus doomed to lonely and inactive life, and shut up from the freedom and pleasure of the world, in which the meanest animal indulges unrestrained. There is a sweetness, however, in his very complaints; they are the lamentations of an amiable and social spirit at being denied the indulgence of its kind and generous propensities; there is nothing in them harsh nor exaggerated; they flow with a natural and touching pathos, and are perhaps rendered more touching by their simple brevity. They contrast finely with those elaborate and iterated repinings, which we sometimes meet with in poetry;—the effusions of morbid minds sickening under miseries of their own creating, and venting their bitterness upon an unoffending world. James speaks of his privations with acute sensibility, but having mentioned them passes on, as if his manly mind disdained to brood over unavoidable calamities. When such a spirit breaks forth into complaint, however brief, we are aware how great must be the suffering that extorts the murmur. We sympathize with James, a romantic, active, and accomplished prince, cut off in the lustihood of youth from all the enterprise, the noble uses, and vigorous delights of life; as we do with Milton, alive to all the beauties of nature and glories of art, when he breathes forth brief, but deep-toned lamentations over his perpetual blindness.

Had not James evinced a deficiency of poetic artifice, we might almost have suspected that these lowerings of gloomy reflection were meant as preparative to the brightest scene of his story; and to contrast with that refulgence of light and loveliness, that exhilarating accompaniment of bird and song, and foliage and flower, and all the revel of the year, with which he ushers in the lady of his heart It is this scene, in particular, which throws all the magic of romance about the old castle keep. He had risen, he says, at daybreak, according to custom, to escape from the dreary meditations of a sleepless pillow. "Bewailing in his chamber thus alone," despairing of all joy and remedy, "fortified of thought and wobegone," he had wandered to the window, to indulge the captive's miserable solace of gazing wistfully upon the world from which he is excluded. The window looked forth upon a small garden which lay at the foot of the tower. It was a quiet, sheltered spot, adorned with arbors and green alleys, and protected from the passing gaze by trees and hawthorn hedges.

Now was there made, fast by the tower's wall,
A garden faire, and in the corners set
An arbour green with wandis long and small
Railed about, and so with leaves beset
Was all the place and hawthorn hedges knet,
That lyf[4] was none, walkyng there forbye
That might within scarce any wight espye.

So thick the branches and the leves grene,
Beshaded all the alleys that there were,
And midst of every arbour might be sene
The sharpe, grene, swete juniper,
Growing so fair, with branches here and there,
That as it seemed to a lyf without,
The boughs did spread the arbour all about.

And on the small grene twistis[5] set
The lytel swete nightingales, and sung
So loud and clear, the hymnis consecrate
Of lovis use, now soft, now loud among,
That all the garden and the wallis rung
Right of their song—

4. Person.

5. Small boughs or twigs. *Note.*—The language of the quotations is generally modernized.

It was the month of May, when everything was in bloom; and he interprets the song of the nightingale into the language of his enamored feeling:

> Worship, all ye that lovers be, this May,
> For of your bliss the kalends are begun,
> And sing with us, away, winter, away,
> Come, summer, come, the sweet season and sun.

As he gazes on the scene, and listens to the notes of the birds, he gradually relapses into one of those tender and undefinable reveries, which fill the youthful bosom in this delicious season. He wonders what this love may be, of which he has so often read, and which thus seems breathed forth in the quickening breath of May, and melting all nature into ecstasy and song. If it really be so great a felicity, and if it be a boon thus generally dispensed to the most insignificant beings, why is he alone cut off from its enjoyments?

> Oft would I think, O Lord, what may this be,
> That love is of such noble myght and kynde?
> Loving his folks, and such prosperitee
> Is it of him, as we in books do find:
> May he oure hertes setten[6] and unbynd:
> Hath he upon oar hertes such maistrye?
> Or is all this bat feynit fimtasye?
>
> For giff he be of so grete excellence,
> That he of every wight hath care and charge.
> What haye I gilt[7] to him, or done offense,
> That I an thral'd, and birdis go at large?

In the midst of his musing, as he casts his eye downward, he beholds "the fairest and the freshest young floure" that ever he had seen. It is the lovely Lady Jane, walking in the garden to enjoy the beauty of that "fresh May morrowe." Breaking thus suddenly

6. Incline.

7. What injury have I done, etc.

upon his sight, in the moment of loneliness and excited susceptibility, she at once captivates the fancy of the romantic prince, and becomes the object of his wandering wishes, the sovereign of his ideal world.

There is, in this charming scene, an evident resemblance to the early part of Chaucer's Knight's Tale; where Palamon and Arcite fall in love with Emilia, whom they see walking in the garden of their prison. Perhaps the similarity of the actual fact to the incident which he had read in Chaucer may have induced James to dwell on it in his poem. His description of the Lady Jane is given in the picturesque and minute manner of his master; and being doubtless taken from the life, is a perfect portrait of a beauty of that day. He dwells, with the fondness of a lover, on every article of her apparel, from the net of pearl, splendent with emeralds and sapphires, that confined her golden hair, even to the "goodly chaine of small orfeverye"[8] about her neck, whereby there hung a ruby in shape of a heart, that seemed, he says, like a spark of fire burning upon her white bosom. Her dress of white tissue was looped up to enable her to walk with more freedom. She was accompanied by two female attendants, and about her sported a little hound decorated with bells; probably the small Italian hound of exquisite symmetry, which was a parlor favorite and pet among the fashionable dames of ancient times. James closes his description by a burst of general eulogium:

> In her was youth, beauty, with humble port,
> Bounty, richesse, and womanly feature;
> God better knows than my pen can report,
> Wisdom, largesse,[9] estate,[10] and cunning[11] sure.
> In every point so guided her measure,
> In word, in deed, in shape, in countenance,
> That nature might no more her child advance.

The departure of the Lady Jane from the garden puts an end to this transient riot of the heart With her departs the amorous illusion that had shed a temporary charm over

8. Wrought gold.

9. Dignity.

10. Bounty.

11. Discretion.

the scene of his captivity, and he relapses into loneliness, now rendered tenfold more intolerable by this passing beam of unattainable beauty. Through the long and weary day he repines at his unhappy lot, and when evening approaches, and Phœbus, as he beautifully expresses it, had "bade farewell to every leaf and flower," he still lingers at the window, and, laying his head upon the cold stone, gives vent to a mingled flow of love and sorrow, until, gradually lulled by the mute melancholy of the twilight hour, he lapses, half sleeping, half swoon," into a vision, which occupies the remainder of the poem, and in which is allegorically shadowed out the history of his passion.

When he wakes from his trance, he rises from his stony pillow, and, pacing his apartment, full of dreary reflections, questions his spirit whither it has been wandering; whether, indeed, all that has passed before his dreaming fancy has been conjured up by preceding circumstances; or whether it is a vision, intended to comfort and assure him in his despondency. If the latter, he prays that some token may be sent to confirm the promise of happier days, given him in his slumbers. Suddenly, a turtle dove, of the purest whiteness, comes flying in at the window, and alights upon his hand, bearing in her bill a branch of red gilliflower, on the leaves of which is written, in letters of gold, the following sentence:

> Awake! awake! I bring, lover, I bring
> The newis glad that blissful is, and sure
> Of thy comfort; now laugh, and play, and sing,
> For in the heaven decretit is thy cure.

He receives the branch with mingled hope and dread; reads it with rapture: and this, he says, was the first token of his succeeding happiness. Whether this is a mere poetic fiction, or whether the Lady Jane did actually send him a token of her favor in this romantic way, remains to be determined according to the faith or fancy of the reader. He concludes his poem, by intimating that the promise conveyed in the vision and by the flower is fulfilled, by his being restored to liberty, and made happy in the possession of the sovereign of his heart.

Such is the poetical account given by James of his love adventures in Windsor Castle. How much of it is absolute fact, and how much the embellishment of fancy, it is fruitless to conjecture: let us not, however, reject every romantic incident as incompatible with real life; but let us sometimes take a poet at his word. I have noticed merely those parts of the poem immediately connected with the tower, and have passed over a large part, written in the allegorical vein, so much cultivated at that day. The language, of course, is quaint and antiquated, so that the beauty of many of its golden phrases will scarcely be perceived at the present day; but it is impossible not to be charmed with the genuine sentiment, the delightful artlessness and urbanity, which prevail throughout it. The descriptions of nature too, with which it is embellished, are given with a truth, a discrimination, and a freshness, worthy of the most cultivated periods of the art.

As an amatory poem, it is edifying in these days of coarser thinking, to notice the nature, refinement, and exquisite delicacy which pervade it; banishing every gross thought or immodest expression, and presenting female loveliness, clothed in all its chivalrous attributes of almost supernatural purity and grace.

James flourished nearly about the time of Chaucer and Gower, and was evidently an admirer and studier of their writings. Indeed, in one of his stanzas he acknowledges them as his masters; and, in some parts of his poem, we find traces of similarity to their productions, more especially to those of Chaucer. There are always, however, general features of resemblance in the works of contemporary authors, which are not so much borrowed from each other as from the times. Writers, like bees, toll their sweets in the wide world; they incorporate with their own conceptions the anecdotes and thoughts current in society; and thus each generation has some features in common, characteristic of the age in which it lived.

James belongs to one of the most brilliant eras of our literary history, and establishes the claims of his country to a participation in its primitive honors. Whilst a small cluster of English writers are constantly cited as the fathers of our verse, the name of their great Scottish compeer is apt to be passed over in silence; but he is evidently worthy of being enrolled in that little constellation of remote but never-failing luminaries, who shine in the highest firmament of literature, and who, like morning stars, sang together at the bright dawning of British poesy.

Such of my readers as may not be familiar with Scottish history (though the manner in which it has of late been woven with captivating fiction has made it a universal study) may be curious to learn something of the subsequent history of James, and the fortunes of his love. His passion for the Lady Jane, as it was the solace of his captivity, so it facilitated his release, it being imagined by the court that a connexion with the blood royal of England would attach him to its own interests. He was ultimately restored to his liberty and crown, having previously espoused the Lady Jane, who accompanied him to Scotland, and made him a most tender and devoted wife.

He found his kingdom in great confusion, the feudal chieftains having taken advantage of the troubles and irregularities of a long interregnum to strengthen themselves in their possessions, and place themselves above the power of the laws. James sought to found the basis of his power in the affections of his people. He attached the lower orders to him by the reformation of abuses, the temperate and equable administration of justice, the encouragement of the arts of peace, and the promotion of every thing that could diffuse comfort, competency, and innocent enjoyment through the humblest ranks of society. He mingled occasionally among the common people in disguise; visited their firesides; entered into their cares, their pursuits, and their amusements; informed himself of the mechanical arts, and how they could best be patronized and improved; and was thus an all-pervading spirit, watching with a benevolent eye over the meanest of his subjects. Having in this generous manner made himself strong in the hearts of the common people, he turned himself to curb the power of the factious nobility; to strip them of those dangerous immunities which they had usurped; to punish such as had been guilty of flagrant offences; and to bring the whole into proper obedience to the crown. For some time they bore this with outward submission, but with secret impatience and brooding resentment. A conspiracy was at length formed against his life, at the head of which was his own uncle, Robert Stewart, Earl of Athol, who, being too old himself for the perpetration of the deed of blood, instigated his grandson Sir Robert Stewart, together with Sir Robert Graham, and others of less note, to commit the deed. They broke into his bedchamber at the Dominican Convent near Perth, where he was residing, and barbarously murdered him by oft-repeated wounds. His faithful queen, rushing to throw her tender body between him and the sword, was twice wounded in the ineffectual attempt to shield him from the assassin; and it was not until she had been forcibly torn from his person, that the murder was accomplished.

It was the recollection of this romantic tale of former times, and of the golden little poem which had its birthplace in this tower, that made me visit the old pile with more than common interest The suit of armor hanging up in the hall, richly gilt and embellished, as if to figure in the tournay, brought the image of the gallant and romantic prince vividly before my imagination. I paced the deserted chambers where he had composed his poem; I leaned upon the window, and endeavored to persuade myself it was the very one where he had been visited by his vision; I looked out upon the spot where he had first seen the Lady Jane. It was the same genial and joyous month; the birds were again vying with each other in strains of liquid melody; every thing was bursting into vegetation, and budding forth the tender promise of the year. Time, which delights to obliterate the sterner memorials of human pride, seems to have passed lightly over this little scene of poetry and love, and to have withheld his desolating hand. Several centuries have gone by, yet the garden still flourishes at the foot of the tower. It occupies what was once the moat of the keep; and though some parts have been separated by dividing walls, yet others have still their arbors and shaded walks, as in the days of James, and the whole is sheltered, blooming, and retired. There is a charm about a spot that has been printed by the footsteps of departed beauty, and consecrated by the inspirations of the poet, which is heightened, rather than impaired, by the lapse of ages. It is, indeed, the gift of poetry to hallow every place in which it moves; to breathe around nature an odor more exquisite than the perfume of the rose, and to shed over it a tint more magical than the blush of morning.

Others may dwell on the illustrious deeds of James as a warrior and a legislator; but I have delighted to view him merely as the companion of his fellow-men, the benefactor of the human heart, stooping from his high estate to sow the sweet flowers of poetry and song in the paths of common life. He was the first to cultivate the vigorous and hardy plant of Scottish genius, which has since become so prolific of the most wholesome and highly-flavored fruit. He carried with him into the sterner regions of the north all the fertilizing arts of southern refinement. He did every thing in his power to win his countrymen to the gay, the elegant, and gentle arts, which soften and refine the character of a people, and wreathe a grace round the loftiness of a proud and warlike spirit. He wrote many poems, which, unfortunately for the fullness of his fame, are now lost to the world; one, which is still preserved, called "Christ's Kirk of the Green," shows how diligently he had made himself acquainted with the rustic sports and pastimes, which constitute such a source of kind and social feeling among the Scottish peasantry; and with what simple and happy humor he could enter into their enjoyments. He contributed greatly to improve the national music; and traces of his tender sentiment, and elegant taste, are said to exist in those witching airs, still piped among the wild mountains and lonely glens of Scotland. He has thus connected his image with whatever is most gracious an endearing in the national character; he has embalmed his memory in song, and floated his name to after ages in the rich streams of Scottish melody. The recollection of these things was kindling at my heart as I paced the silent scene of his imprisonment I have visited Vaucluse with as much enthusiasm as a pilgrim would visit the shrine at Loretto; but I have never felt more poetical devotion than when contemplating the old tower and the little garden at Windsor, and musing over the romantic loves of the Lady Jane and the Royal Poet of Scotland.

The Country Church

A gentleman!
What, o' the woolpack? Or the sugar-chest?
Or lists of velvet? Which is't, pound, or yard,
You vend your gentry by?

BEGGAR'S BUSH

THERE ARE FEW PLACES MORE FAVORABLE TO THE STUDY OF CHARACTER than an English country church. I was once passing a few weeks at the seat of a friend, who resided in the vicinity of one, the appearance of which particularly struck my fancy. It was one of those rich morsels of quaint antiquity which give such a peculiar charm to English landscape. It stood in the midst of a country filled with ancient families, and contained, within its cold and silent aisles, the congregated dust of many noble generations. The interior walls were incrusted with monuments of every age and style. The light streamed through windows dimmed with armorial bearings, richly emblazoned in stained glass. In various parts of the church were tombs of knights, and high-born dames, of gorgeous workmanship, with their effigies in colored marble. On every side the eye was struck with some instance of aspiring mortality; some haughty memorial which human pride had erected over its kindred dust, in this temple of the most humble of all religions.

The congregation was composed of the neighboring people of rank, who sat in pews, sumptuously lined and cushioned, furnished with richly-gilded prayer-books, and decorated with their arms upon the pew doors; of the villagers and peasantry, who filled the back seats, and a small gallery beside the organ; and of the poor of the parish, who were ranged on benches in the aisles.

The service was performed by a snuffling well-fed vicar, who had a snug dwelling near the church. He was a privileged guest at all the tables of the neighborhood, and had been the keenest fox-hunter in the country; until age and good living had disabled him from doing any thing more than ride to see the hounds throw off, and make one at the hunting dinner.

Under the ministry of such a pastor, I found it impossible to get into the train of thought suitable to the time and place: so, having, like many other feeble Christians, compromised with my conscience, by laying the sin of my own delinquency at another person's threshold, I occupied myself by making observations on my neighbors.

I was as yet a stranger in England, and curious to notice the manners of its fashionable classes. I found, as usual, that there was the least pretension where there was the most acknowledged title to respect. I was particularly struck, for instance, with the family of a nobleman of high rank, consisting of several sons and daughters. Nothing could be more simple and unassuming than their appearance. They generally came to church in the plainest equipage, and often on foot. The young ladies would stop and converse in the kindest manner with the peasantry, caress the children, and listen to the stories of the humble cottagers. Their countenances were open and beautifully fair, with an expression of high refinement but, at the same time, a frank cheerfulness, and an engaging affability. Their brothers were tall, and elegantly formed. They were dressed fashionably, but simply; with strict neatness and propriety, but without any mannerism or foppishness. Their whole demeanor was easy and natural, with that lofty grace, and noble frankness, which bespeak freeborn souls that have never been checked in their growth by feelings of inferiority. There is a healthful hardiness about real dignity, that never dreads contact and communion with others, however humble. It is only spurious pride that is morbid and sensitive, and shrinks from every touch. I was pleased to see the manner in which they would converse with the peasantry about those rural concerns and field-sports, in which the gentlemen of this country so much delight. In these conversations there was neither haughtiness on the one part, nor servility on the other; and you were only reminded of the difference of rank by the habitual respect of the peasant.

In contrast to these was the family of a wealthy citizen, who had amassed a vast fortune; and, having purchased the estate and mansion of a ruined nobleman in the neighborhood, was endeavoring to assume all the style and dignity of an hereditary lord of the soil. The family always came to church *en prince*. They were rolled majestically along in a carriage emblazoned with arms. The crest glittered in silver radiance from every part of the harness where a crest could possibly be placed. A fat coachman, in a three-cornered hat, richly laced, and a flaxen wig, curling dose round his rosy face, was seated on the box, with a sleek Danish dog beside him. Two footmen, in gorgeous liveries, with huge bouquets, and gold-headed canes, lolled behind. The carriage rose and sunk on its long springs with peculiar stateliness of motion. The very horses champed their bits, arched their necks, and glanced their eyes more proudly than common horses; either because they had caught a little of the family feeling, or were reined up more tightly than ordinary.

I could not but admire the style with which this splendid pageant was brought up to the gate of the church-yard. There was a vast effect produced at the turning of an angle of the wall;—a great smacking of the whip, straining and scrambling of horses, glistening of harness, and flashing of wheels through gravel. This was the moment of triumph and vainglory to the coachman. The horses were urged and checked until they were fretted into a foam. They threw out their feet in a prancing trot, dashing about pebbles at every step. The crowd of villagers sauntering quietly to church, opened precipitately to the right and left, gaping in vacant admiration. On reaching the gate, the horses were pulled up with a suddenness that produced an immediate stop, and almost threw them on their haunches.

There was an extraordinary hurry of the footman to alight, pull down the steps, and prepare every thing for the descent on earth of this august family. The old citizen first emerged his round red face from out the door, looking about him with the pompous air of a man accustomed to rule on 'Change, and shake the Stock Market with a nod. His consort, a fine, fleshy, comfortable dame, followed him. There seemed, I must confess, but little pride in her composition. She was the picture of broad, honest, vulgar enjoyment. The world went well with her; and she liked the world. She had fine clothes, a fine house, a fine carriage, fine children, every thing was fine about her: it was nothing but driving about, and visiting and feasting. Life was to her a perpetual revel; it was one long Lord Mayor's day.

Two daughters succeeded to this goodly couple. They certainly were handsome; but had a supercilious air, that chilled admiration, and disposed the spectator to be critical. They were ultra-fashionable in dress; and, though no one could deny the richness of their decorations, yet their appropriateness might be questioned amidst the simplicity of a country church. They descended loftily from the carriage, and moved up the line of peasantry with a step that seemed dainty of the soil it trod on. They cast an excursive glance around, that passed coldly over the burly faces of the peasantry, until they met the eyes of the nobleman's family, when their countenances immediately brightened into smiles, and they made the most profound and elegant courtesies, which were returned in a manner that showed they were but slight acquaintances.

I must not forget the two sons of this aspiring citizen, who came to church in a dashing curricle, with outriders. They were arrayed in the extremity of the mode, with all that pedantry of dress which marks the man of questionable pretensions to style. They kept entirely by themselves, eyeing every one askance that came near them, as if measuring his claims to respectability; yet they were without conversation, except the exchange of an occasional cant phrase. They even moved artificially; for their bodies, in compliance with the caprice of the day, had been disciplined into the absence of all ease and freedom. Art had done every thing to accomplish them as men of fashion, but nature had denied them the nameless grace. They were vulgarly shaped, like men formed for the common purposes of life, and had that air of supercilious assumption which is never seen in the true gentleman.

I have been rather minute in drawing the pictures of these two families, because I considered them specimens of what is often to be met with in this country—the unpretending great, and the arrogant little. I have no respect for titled rank, unless it be accompanied with true nobility of soul; but I have remarked in all countries where artificial distinctions exist, that the very highest classes are always the most courteous and unassuming. Those who are well assured of their own standing are least apt to trespass on that of others: whereas nothing is so offensive as the aspirings of vulgarity, which thinks to elevate itself by humiliating its neighbor.

As I have brought these families, into contrast, I must notice their behavior in church. That of the nobleman's family was quiet, serious, and attentive. Not that they appeared to have any fervor of devotion, but rather a respect for sacred things, and sacred places, inseparable from good breeding. The others, on the contrary, were in a perpetual flutter and whisper; they betrayed a continual consciousness of finery, and a sorry ambition of being the wonders of a rural congregation.

The old gentleman was the only one really attentive to the service. He took the whole burden of family devotion upon himself, standing bolt upright, and uttering the responses with a loud voice that might be heard all over the church. It was evident that he was one of those thorough church and king men, who connect the idea of devotion and loyalty; who consider the Deity, somehow or other, of the government party, and religion "a very excellent sort of thing, that ought to be countenanced and kept up."

When he joined so loudly in the service, it seemed more by way of example to the lower orders, to show them that, though so great and wealthy, he was not above being religious; as I have seen a turtle-fed alderman swallow publicly a basin of charity soup, smacking his lips at every monthful, and pronouncing it "excellent food for the poor."

When the service was at an end, I was curious to witness the several exits of my groups. The young noblemen and their sisters, as the day was fine, preferred strolling home across the fields, chatting with the country people as they went. The others departed as they came, in grand parade. Again were the equipages wheeled up to the gate. There was again the smacking of whips, the clattering of hoofs, and the glittering of harness. The horses started off almost at a bound; the villagers again hurried to right and left; the wheels threw up a cloud of dust; and the aspiring family was rapt out of sight in a whirlwind.

The Widow and Her Son

> Pittie old age, within whose silver haires
> Honour and revrence evermore have rain'd.
>
> MARLOWE'S *TAMBURLAINE.*

THOSE WHO ARE IN THE HABIT OF REMARKING SUCH MATTERS MOST HAVE noticed the passive quiet of an English landscape on Sunday. The clacking of the mill, the regularly recurring stroke of the flail, the din of the blacksmith's hammer, the whistling of the ploughman, the rattling of the cart, and all other sounds of rural labor are suspended. The very farm-dogs bark less frequently, being less disturbed by passing travelers. At such times I have almost fancied the winds sunk into quiet, and that the sunny landscape, with its fresh green tints melting into blue haze, enjoyed the hallowed calm.

> Sweet day, so pure, so calm, so bright,
> The bridal of the earth and sky.

Well was it ordained that the day of devotion should be a day of rest. The holy repose which reigns over the face of nature, has its moral influence; every restless passion is charmed down, and we feel the natural religion of the soul gently springing up within us. For my part, there are feelings that visit me, in a country church, amid the beautiful serenity of nature, which I experience no where else; and if not a more religious, I think I am a better man on Sunday than on any other day of the seven.

During my recent residence in the country I used frequently to attend at the old village church. Its shadowy aisles; its mouldering monuments; its dark oaken paneling, all reverend with the gloom of departed years, seemed to fit it for the haunt of solemn meditation; but being in a wealthy aristocratic neighborhood, the glitter of fashion penetrated even into the sanctuary; and I felt myself continually thrown back upon the world by the frigidity and pomp of the poor worms around me. The only being in the whole congregation who appeared thoroughly to feel the humble and prostrate piety of a true Christian was a poor decrepit old woman, bending under the weight of years and infirmities. She bore the traces of something better than abject poverty. The lingerings of decent pride were visible in her appearance. Her dress, though humble in the extreme, was scrupulously dean. Some trivial respect, too, had been awarded her, for she did not take her seat among the village poor, but sat alone on the steps of the altar. She seemed to have survived all love, all friendship, all society; and to have nothing left her but the hopes of heaven. When I saw her feebly rising and bending her aged form in prayer; habitually conning her prayer-book, which her palsied hand and failing eyes would not permit her to read, but which she evidently knew by heart; I felt persuaded that the faltering voice of that poor woman arose to heaven far before the responses of the clerk, the swell of the organ, or the chanting of the choir.

I am fond of loitering about country churches, and this was so delightfully situated, that it frequently attracted me. It stood on a knoll, round which a small stream made a beautiful bend, and then wound its way through a long reach of soft meadow scenery. The church was surrounded by yew-trees which seemed almost coeval with itself. Its tall Gothic spire shot up lightly from among them, with rooks and crows generally wheeling about it. I was seated there one still sunny morning, watching two laborers who were digging a grave. They had chosen one of the most remote and neglected corners of the church-yard; where, from the number of nameless graves around, it would appear that the indigent and friendless were huddled into the earth. I was told that the new-made grave was for the only son of a poor widow. While I was meditating on the distinctions of worldly rank, which extend thus down into the very dust, the toll of the bell announced the approach of the funeral. They were the obsequies of poverty, with which pride had nothing to do. A coffin of the plainest materials, without pall or other covering, was borne by some of the villagers. The sexton walked before with an air of cold indifference. There were no mock mourners m the trappings of affected woe; but there was one real mourner who feebly tottered after the corpse. It was the aged mother of the deceased—the poor old woman whom I had seen seated on the steps of the altar. She was supported by a humble friend, who was endeavoring to comfort her. A few of the neighboring poor had joined the train, and some children of the village were running hand in hand, now shouting with unthinking mirth, and now pausing to gaze, with childish curiosity, on the grief of the mourner.

As the funeral train approached the grave, the parson issued from the church porch, arrayed in the surplice, with prayer-book in hand, and attended by the clerk. The service, however, was a mere act of charity. The deceased had been destitute, and the survivor was penniless. It was shuffled through, therefore, in form, but coldly and unfeelingly. The well-fed priest moved but a few steps from the church door; his voice could scarcely be heard at the grave; and never did I hear the funeral service, that sublime and touching ceremony, turned into such a frigid mummery of words.

I approached the grave. The coffin was placed on the ground. On it were inscribed the name and age of the deceased—"George Somers, aged 26 years." The poor mother had been assisted to kneel down at the head of it. Her withered hands were clasped, as if in prayer, but I could perceive by a feeble rocking of the body, and a convulsive motion of the lips, that she was gazing on the last relics of her son, with the yearnings of a mother's heart.

Preparations were made to deposit the coffin in the earth. There was that bustling stir which breaks so harshly on the feelings of grief and affection; directions given in the cold tones of business; the striking of spades into sand and gravel; which, at the grave of those we love, is, of all sounds, the most withering. The bustle around seemed to waken the mother from a wretched reverie. She raised her glazed eyes, and looked about with a faint wildness. As the men approached with cords to lower the coffin into the grave, she wrung her hands, and broke into an agony of grief. The poor woman who attended her took her by the arm, endeavoring to raise her from the earth, and to whisper something like consolation—"Nay, now—nay, now—don't take it so sorely to heart." She could only shake her head and wring her hands, as one not to be comforted.

As they lowered the body into the earth, the creaking of the cords seemed to agonize her; but when, on some accidental obstruction, there was a justling of the coffin, all the tenderness of the mother burst forth; as if any harm could come to him who was far beyond the reach of worldly suffering.

I could see no more—my heart swelled into my throat—my eyes filled with tears—I felt as if I were acting a barbarous part in standing by and gazing idly on this scene of maternal anguish. I wandered to another part of the church-yard, where I remained until the funeral train had dispersed.

When I saw the mother slowly and painfully quitting the grave, leaving behind her the remains of all that was dear to her on earth, and returning to silence and destitution, my heart ached for her. What, thought I, are the distresses of the rich! they have friends to soothe—pleasures to beguile—a world to divert and dissipate their griefs. What are the sorrows of the young! Their growing minds soon close above the wound—their elastic spirits soon rise beneath the pressure—their green and ductile affections soon twine round new objects. But the sorrows of the poor, who have no outward appliances to soothe—the sorrows of the aged, with whom life at best is but a wintry day, and who can look for no after-growth of joy—the sorrows of a widow, aged, solitary, destitute, mourning over an only son, the last solace of her years; these are indeed sorrows which make us feel the impotency of consolation.

It was some time before I left the church-yard. On my way homeward I met with the woman who had acted as comforter: she was just returning from accompanying the mother to her lonely habitation, and I drew from her some particulars connected with the affecting scene I had witnessed.

The parents of the deceased had resided in the village from childhood. They had inhabited one of the neatest cottages, and by various rural occupations, and the assistance of a small garden had supported themselves creditably and comfortably and led a happy and a blameless life. They had one son, who had grown up to be the staff and pride of their age.—"Oh, sir!" said the good woman, "he was such a comely lad, so sweet-tempered, so kind to every one around him, so dutiful to his parents! It did one's heart good to see him of a Sunday, dressed out in his best, so tall, so straight, so cheery, supporting his old mother to church—for she was always fonder of leaning on George's arm, than on her goodman's; and, poor soul, she might well be proud of him, for a finer lad there was not in the country round."

Unfortunately, the son was tempted, during a year of scarcity and agricultural hardship, to enter into the service of one of the small craft that plied on a neighboring river. He had not been long in this employ when he was entrapped by a press-gang, and carried off to sea. His parents received tidings of his seizure, but beyond that they could learn nothing. It was the loss of their main prop. The father, who was already infirm, grew heartless and melancholy, and sunk into his grave. The widow, left lonely in her age and feebleness, could no longer support herself, and came upon the parish. Still there was a kind feeling toward her throughout the village, and a certain respect as being one of the oldest inhabitants. As no one applied for the cottage, in which she had passed so many happy days, she was permitted to remain in it, where she lived solitary and almost helpless. The few wants of nature were chiefly supplied from the scanty productions of her little garden, which the neighbors would now and then cultivate for her. It was but a few days before the time at which these circumstances were told me, that she was gathering some vegetables for her repast, when she heard the cottage door which faced the garden suddenly opened. A stranger came out, and seemed to be looking eagerly and wildly around. He was dressed in seaman's clothes, was emaciated and ghostly pale, and bore the air of one broken by sickness and hardships. He saw her, and hastened towards her, but his steps were faint and faltering; he sank on his knees before her, and sobbed like a child. The poor woman gazed upon him with a vacant and wandering eye—"Oh my dear, dear mother! don't you know your son? your poor boy George?" It was indeed the wreck of her once noble lad, who, shattered by wounds, by sickness and foreign imprisonment, had, at length, dragged his wasted limbs homeward, to repose among the scenes of his childhood.

I will not attempt to detail the particulars of such a meeting, where joy and sorrow were so completely blended: still he was alive! he was come home! he might yet live to comfort and cherish her old age! Nature, however, was exhausted in him; and if any thing had been wanting to finish the work of fate, the desolation of his native cottage would have been sufficient. He stretched himself on the pallet on which his widowed mother had passed many a sleepless night, and he never rose from it again.

The villagers, when they heard that George Somers had returned, crowded to see him, offering every comfort and assistance that their humble means afforded. He was too weak, however, to talk—he could only look his thanks. His mother was his constant attendant; and he seemed unwilling to be helped by any other hand.

There is something in sickness that breaks down the pride of manhood; that softens the heart, and brings it back to the feelings of infancy. Who that has languished, even in advanced life, in sickness and despondency; who that has pined on a weary bed in the neglect and loneliness of a foreign land; but has thought on the mother "that looked on his childhood," that smoothed his pillow, and administered to his helplessness? Oh! there is an enduring tenderness in the love of a mother to her son that transcends all other affections of the heart It Is neither to be chilled by selfishness, nor daunted by danger, nor weakened by worthlessness, nor stifled by ingratitude. She will sacrifice every comfort to his convenience; she will surrender every pleasure to his enjoyment; she will glory in his fame, and exult in his prosperity; and, if misfortune overtake him, he will be the dearer to her from misfortune; and if disgrace settle upon his name, she will still love and cherish him in spite of his disgrace; and if all the world beside cast him off, she will be all the world to him.

Poor George Somers had known what it was to be in sickness, and none to soothe—lonely and in prison, and none to visit him. He could not endure his mother from his sight; if she moved away, his eye would follow her. She would sit for hours by his bed, watching him as he slept. Sometimes he would start from a feverish dream, and look anxiously up until he saw her bending over him; when he would take her hand, lay it on his bosom, and fall asleep with the tranquillity of a child. In this way he died.

My first impulse on hearing this humble tale of affliction was to visit the cottage of the mourner, and administer pecuniary assistance, and, if possible, comfort. I found, however, on inquiry, that the good feelings of the villagers had prompted them to do every thing that the case admitted: and as the poor know best how to console each other's sorrows, I did not venture to intrude.

The next Sunday I was at the village church; when, to my surprise, I saw the poor old woman tottering down the use to her accustomed seat on the steps of the altar.

She had made an effort to put on something like mourning for her son; and nothing could be more touching than this struggle between pious affection and utter poverty: a black riband or so—a faded black handkerchief, and one or two more such humble attempts to express by outward signs that grief which passes show. When I looked round upon the storied monuments, the stately hatchments, the cold marble pomp, with which grandeur mourned magnificently over departed pride, and turned to this poor widow, bowed down by age and sorrow, at the altar of her God, and offering up the prayers and praises of a pious, though a broken heart, I felt that this living monument of real grief was worth them all.

I related her story to some of the wealthy members of the congregation, and they were moved by it. They exerted themselves to render her situation more comfortable, and to lighten her afflictions. It was, however, but smoothing a few steps to the grave. In the course of a Sunday or two after, she was missed from her usual seat at church, and before I left the neighborhood, I heard, with a feeling of satisfaction, that she had quietly breathed her last, and had gone to rejoin those she loved, in that world where sorrow is never known, and friends are never parted.

A Sunday in London

In a preceding paper I have spoken of an English Sunday in the country, and its tranquilizing effect upon the landscape; but where is its sacred influence more strikingly apparent than in the very heart of that great Babel, London? On this sacred day, the gigantic monster is charmed into repose. The intolerable din and struggle of the week are at an end. The shops are shut. The fires of forges and manufactories are extinguished; and the sun, no longer obscured by murky clouds of smoke, pours down a sober yellow radiance into the quiet streets. The few pedestrians we meet, instead of hurrying forward with anxious countenances, move leisurely along; their brows are smoothed from the wrinkles of business and care; they have put on their Sunday looks, and Sunday manners, with their Sunday clothes, and are cleansed in mind as well as in person.

And now the melodious clangor of bells from church towers summons their several flocks to the fold. Forth issues from his mansion the family of the decent tradesman, the small children in the advance; then the citizen and his comely spouse, followed by the grown-up daughters, with small morocco-bound prayer-books laid in the folds of their pocket-handkerchiefs. The housemaid looks after them from the window, admiring the finery of the family, and receiving, perhaps, a nod and smile from her young mistresses, at whose toilet she has assisted.

Now rumbles along the carriage of some magnate of the city, peradventure an alderman or a sheriff; and now the patter of many feet announces a procession of charity scholars, in uniforms of antique cut, and each with a prayer-book under his arm.

The ring of bells is at an end; the rambling of the carriage has ceased; the pattering of feet is heard no more; the flocks are folded in ancient churches, cramped up in by-lanes and corners of the crowded city, where the vigilant beadle keeps watch, like the shepherd's dog, round the threshold of the sanctuary. For a time every thing is hushed; but soon is heard the deep, pervading sound of the organ, rolling and vibrating through the empty lanes and courts; and the sweet chanting of the choir making them resound with melody and praise. Never have I been more sensible of the sanctifying effect of church music, than when I have heard it thus poured forth, like a river of joy, through the inmost recesses of this great metropolis, elevating it, as it were, from all the sordid pollutions of the week; and bearing the poor world-worn soul on a tide of triumphant harmony to heaven.

The morning service is at an end. The streets are again alive with the congregations returning to their homes, but soon again relapse into silence. Now comes on the Sunday dinner, which, to the city tradesman, is a meal of some importance. There is more leisure for social enjoyment at the board. Members of the family can now gather together, who are separated by the laborious occupations of the week. A school-boy may be permitted on that day to come to the paternal home; an old friend of the family takes his accustomed Sunday seat at the board, tells over his well-known stories, and rejoices young and old with his well-known jokes.

On Sunday afternoon the city pours forth its legions to breathe the fresh air and enjoy the sunshine of the parks and rural environs. Satirists may say what they please about the rural enjoyments of a London citizen on Sunday, but to me there is something delightful in beholding the poor prisoner of the crowded and dusty city enabled thus to come forth once a week and throw him upon the green bosom of nature. He is like a child restored to the mother's breast; and they who first spread out these noble parks and magnificent pleasure-grounds which surround this metropolis, have done at least as much for its health and morality, as if they had expended the amount of cost in hospitals, prisons, and penitentiaries.

The Boar's Head Tavern, Eastcheap

A Shakspearian Research

> A tavern is the rendezvous, the exchange, the staple of good fellows. I have heard my great-grandfather tell, how his great-grandfather should say, that it was an old proverb when his great-grandfather was a child, that "it was a good wind that blew a man to the wise."
>
> MOTHER BOMBIE

IT IS A PIOUS CUSTOM, IN SOME CATHOLIC COUNTRIES, TO HONOR THE MEMORY of saints by votive lights burnt before their pictures. The popularity of a saint, therefore, may be known by the number of these offerings. One, perhaps, is left to moulder in the darkness of his little chapel; another may have a solitary lamp to throw its blinking rays athwart his effigy; while the whole blaze of adoration is lavished at the shrine of some beatified father of renown. The wealthy devotee brings his huge luminary of wax; the eager zealot his seven-branched candlestick, and even the mendicant pilgrim is by no means satisfied that sufficient light is thrown upon the deceased, unless he hangs up his little lamp of smoking oil. The consequence is, that in the eagerness to enlighten, they are often apt to obscure; and I have occasionally seen an unlucky saint almost smoked out of countenance by the officiousness of his followers.

In like manner has it fared with the immortal Shakspeare. Every writer considers it his bounden duty to light up some portion of his character or works, and to rescue some merit from oblivion. The commentator, opulent in words, produces vast tomes of dissertations; the common herd of editors send up mists of obscurity from their notes at the bottom of each page; and every casual scribbler brings his farthing rushlight of eulogy or research, to swell the cloud of incense and of smoke.

As I honor all established usages of my brethren of the quill, I thought it but proper to contribute my mite of homage to the memory of the illustrious bard. I was for some time, however, sorely puzzled in what way I should discharge this duty. I found myself anticipated in every attempt at a new reading; every doubtful line had been explained a dozen different ways, and perplexed beyond the reach of elucidation; and as to fine passages, they had all been amply praised by previous admirers; nay, so completely had the bard, of late, been overlarded with panegyric by a great German critic, that it was difficult now to find even a fault that had not been argued into a beauty.

In this perplexity, I was one morning turning over his pages, when I casually opened upon the comic scenes of Henry IV, and was, in a moment, completely lost in the madcap revelry of the Boar's Head Tavern. So vividly and naturally are these scenes of humor depicted, and with such force and consistency are the characters sustained, that they become mingled up in the mind with the facts and personages of real life. To few readers does it occur, that these are all ideal creations of a poet's brain, and that, in sober truth, no such knot of merry roysters ever enlivened the dull neighborhood of Eastcheap.

For my part, I love to give myself up to the illusions of poetry. A hero of fiction that never existed is just as valuable to me as a hero of history that existed a thousand years since: and, if I may be excused such an insensibility to the common ties of human nature, I would not give up fat Jack for half the great men of ancient chronicle. What have the heroes of yore done for me, or men like me? They have conquered countries of which I do not enjoy an acre; or they have gained laurels of which I do not inherit a leaf; or they have furnished examples of hair-brained prowess, which I have neither the opportunity nor the inclination to follow. But, old Jack Falstaff!—kind Jack Falstaff!—sweet Jack Falstaff!—has enlarged the boundaries of human enjoyment; he has added vast regions of wit and good humor, in which the poorest man may revel; and has bequeathed a never-failing inheritance of jolly laughter, to make mankind merrier and better to the latest posterity.

A thought suddenly struck me: "I will make a pilgrimage to Eastcheap," said I, closing the book, "and see if the old Boar's Head Tavern still exists. Who knows but I may light upon some legendary traces of Dame Quickly and her guests; at any rate, there will be a kindred pleasure, in treading the halls once vocal with their mirth, to that the toper enjoys in smelling to the empty cask once filled with generous wine."

The resolution was no sooner formed than put in execution. I forbear to treat of the various adventures and wonders I encountered in my travels; of the haunted regions of Cock Lane; of the faded glories of Little Britain, and the parts adjacent; what perils I ran in Cateaton-street and old Jewry; of the renowned Guildhall and its two stunted giants, the pride and wonder of the city, and the terror of all unlucky urchins; and how I visited London Stone, and struck my staff upon it, in imitation of that arch rebel, Jack Cade.

Let it suffice to say, that I at length arrived in merry Eastcheap, that ancient region of wit and wassail, where the very names of the streets relished of good cheer, as Pudding Lane bears testimony even at the present day. For Eastcheap, says old Stowe, "was always famous for its convivial doings. The cookes cried hot ribbes of beef roasted, pies well baked, and other victuals: there was clattering of pewter pots, harpe, pipe, and sawtrie." Alas! how sadly is the scene changed since the roarings days of Falstaff and old Stowe! The madcap royster has given place to the plodding tradesman; the clattering of pots and the sound of harpe and sawtrie," to the din of carts and the accursed dinging of the dustman's bell; and no song is heard, save, haply, the strain of some siren from Billingsgate, chanting the eulogy of deceased mackerel.

I sought, in vain, for the ancient abode of Dame Quickly. The only relic of it is a boar's head, carved in relief in stone, which formerly served as the sign, but at present is built into the parting line of two houses, which stand on the site of the renowned old tavern.

For the history of this little abode of good fellowship, I was referred to a tallow-chandler's widow, opposite, who had been born and brought up on the spot, and was looked up to as the indisputable chronicler of the neighborhood. I found her seated in a little back parlor, the window of which looked out upon a yard about eight feet square, laid out as a flower-garden; while a glass door opposite afforded a distant peep of the street, through a vista of soap and tallow candles: the two views, which comprised, in all probability, her prospects in life, and the little world in which she had lived, and moved, and had her being, for the better part of a century.

To be versed in the history of Eastcheap great and little, from London Stone even unto the Monument, was, doubtless, in her opinion, to be acquainted with the history of the universe. Yet, with all this, she possessed the simplicity of true wisdom, and that liberal communicative disposition, which I have generally remarked in intelligent old ladies, knowing in the concerns of their neighborhood.

Her information, however, did not extend far back into antiquity. She could throw no light upon the history of the Boar's Head, from the time that Dame Quickly espoused the valiant Pistol, until the great fire of London, when it was unfortunately burnt down. It was soon rebuilt, and continued to flourish under the old name and sign, until a dying landlord, struck with remorse for double scores, bad measures, and other iniquities, which are incident to the sinful race of publicans, endeavored to make his peace with heaven, by bequeathing the tavern to St. Michael's Church, Crooked Lane, toward the supporting of a chaplain. For some time the vestry meetings were regularly held there; but it was observed that the old Boar never held up his head under church government. He gradually declined, and finally gave his last gasp about thirty years since. The tavern was then turned into shops; but she informed me that a picture of it was still preserved in St Michael's Church, which stood just in the rear. To get a sight of this picture was now my determination; so, having informed myself of the abode of the sexton, I took my leave of the venerable chronicler of Eastcheap, my visit having doubtless raised greatly her opinion of her legendary lore, and furnished an important incident in the history of her life.

It cost me some difficulty, and much curious inquiry, to ferret out the humble hanger-on to the church. I had to explore Crooked Lane, and divers little alleys, and elbows, and dark passages with which this old city is perforated, like an ancient cheese, or a worm-eaten chest of drawers. At length I traced him to a corner of a small court, surrounded by lofty houses, where the inhabitants enjoy about as much of the face of heaven, as a community of frogs at the bottom of a well. The sexton was a meek, acquiescing little man, of a bowing, lowly habit: yet he had a pleasant twinkling in his eye, and, if encouraged, would now and then hazard a small pleasantry; such as a man of his low estate might venture to make in the company of high churchwardens, and other mighty men of the earth. I found him in company with the deputy organist, seated apart, like Milton's angels, discoursing, no doubt, on high doctrinal points, and setting the affairs of the church over a friendly pot of ale—for the lower classes of English seldom deliberate on any weighty matter without the assistance of a cool tankard to clear their understandings. I arrived at the moment when they had finished their ale and their argument, and were about to repair to the church to put it in order; so, having made known my wishes, I received their gracious permission to accompany them.

The church of St Michael's, Crooked Lane, standing a short distance from Billingsgate, is enriched with the tombs of many fishmongers of renown; and as every profession has its galaxy of glory, and its constellation of great men, I presume the monument of a mighty fishmonger of the olden tune is regarded with as much reverence by succeeding generations of the craft, as poets feel on contemplating the tomb of Virgil, or soldiers the monument of a Marlborough or Turenne.

I cannot but turn aside, while thus speaking of illustrious men, to observe that St. Michael's, Crooked Lane, contains also the ashes of that doughty champion, William Walworth, knight, who so manfully clove down the sturdy wight, Wat Tyler, in Smithfield; a hero worthy of honorable blazon, as almost the only Lord Mayor on record famous for deeds of arms:—the sovereigns of Cockney being generally renowned as the most pacific of all potentates.[1]

Adjoining the church, in a small cemetery, immediately under the back window of what was once the Boards Head, stands the tombstone of Robert Preston, whilom drawer at the tavern. It is now nearly a century since this trusty drawer of good liquor closed his bustling career, and was thus quietly deposited within call of his customers. As I was clearing away the weeds from his epitaph, the little sexton drew me on one

---

1. The following was the ancient inscription on the monument of this worthy; which, unhappily, was destroyed in the great conflagration.

> Hereunder lyth a man of Fame,
> William Walworth callyd by name;
> Fishmonger he was in lyfftime here,
> And twise Lord Maior, as in books appere;
> Who, with courage stoat and manly myght.
> Slew Jack Straw in Kyng Richard's sight.
> For which act done, and trew entent,
> The Kyng made him knyght incontinent;
> And gave him armes, as here you see,
> To declare his fact and chivaldrie.
> He left this lyff the yere of our God
> Thirteen hundred fourscore and three odd.

An error in the foregoing inscription has been corrected by the venerable Stowe. "Whereas," saith he, "'it hath been far spread abroad by vulgar opinion, that the rebel smitten down so manfully by Sir William Walworth, the then worthy Lord Maior, was named Jack Straw, and not Wat Tyler, I thought good to reconcile this rash-conceived doubt by such testimony as I find in ancient and good records. The principal leaders, or captains, of the commons, were Wat Tyler, as the first man the second was John, or Jack, Straw, etc., etc."

STOWE'S LONDON

side with a mysterious air, and informed me in a low voice, that once upon a time, on a dark wintry night, when the wind was unruly, howling, and whistling, banging about doors and windows, and twirling weathercocks, so that the living were frightened out of their beds, and even the dead could not sleep quietly in their graves, the ghost of honest Preston, which happened to be airing itself in the church-yard, was attracted by the well-known call of "waiter" from the Boar's Head, and made its sudden appearance in the midst of a roaring club, just as the parish clerk was singing a stave from the "mirre garland of Captain Death"; to the discomfiture of sundry train-band captains, and the conversion of an infidel attorney, who became a zealous Christian on the spot, and was never known to twist the truth afterwards, except in the way of business.

I beg it may be remembered, that I do not pledge myself for the authenticity of this anecdote; though it is well known that the church-yards and by-corners of this old metropolis are very much infested with perturbed spirits; and every one must have heard of the Cock Lane ghost, and the apparition that guards the regalia in the Tower, which has frightened so many bold sentinels almost out of their wits.

Be all this as it may, this Robert Preston seems to have been a worthy successor to the nimble-tongued Francis, who attended upon the revels of Prince Hal; to have been equally prompt with his "anon, anon, sir"; and to have transcended his predecessor in honesty; for Falstaff, the veracity of whose taste no man will venture to impeach, flatly accuses Francis of putting lime in his sack; whereas honest Preston's epitaph lauds him for the sobriety of his conduct, the soundness of his wine, and the fairness of his measure.[2] The worthy dignitaries of the church, however, did not appear much capti-

---

2. As this inscription is rife with excellent morality, I transcribe it for the admonition of delinquent tapsters. It is, no doubt, the production of some choice spirit, who once frequented the Boar's Head.

> Bacchus, to give the toping world surprise,
> Produced one sober son, and here he lies.
> Though rear'd among full hogsheads, he defy'd
> The charms of wine, and every one beside.
> O reader, if to justice thou'rt inclined,
> Keep honest Preston daily in thy mind.
> He drew good wine, took care to fill his pots,
> Had sundry virtues that excused his faults.
> You that on Bacchus have the like dependance,
> Pray copy Bob in measure and attendance.

vated by the sober virtues of the tapster; the deputy organist, who had a moist look out of the eye, made some shrewd remark on the abstemiousness of a man brought up among full hogsheads; and the little sexton corroborated his opinion by a significant wink, and a dubious shake of the head.

Thus far my researches, though they threw much light on the history of tapsters, fishmongers, and Lord Mayors, yet disappointed me in the great object of my quest, the picture of the Boar's Head Tavern. No such painting was to be found in the church of St. Michael. "Marry and amen!" said I, "here endeth my research!" So I was giving the matter up, with the air of a baffled antiquary, when my friend the sexton, perceiving me to be curious in every thing relative to the old tavern, offered to show me the choice vessels of the vestry, which had been handed down from remote times, when the parish meetings were held at the Boar's Head. These were deposited in the parish club-room which had been transferred, on the decline of the ancient establishment, to a tavern in the neighborhood.

A few steps brought us to the house, which stands No. 12 Miles Lane, bearing the title of The Mason's Arms, and is kept by Master Edward Honeyball, the "bully-rock" of the establishment. It is one of those little taverns which abound in the heart of the city, and from the centre of gossip and intelligence of the neighborhood. We entered the bar-room, which was narrow and darkling; for in these close lanes but few rays of reflected light are enabled to struggle down to the inhabitants, whose broad day is at best but a tolerable twilight. The room was partitioned into boxes, each containing a table spread with a clean white cloth, ready for dinner. This showed that the guests were of the good old stamp, and divided their day equally, for it was but just one o'clock. At the lower end of the room was a clear coal fire, before which a breast of lamb was roasting. A row of bright brass candlesticks and pewter mugs glistened along the mantle-piece, and an old-fashioned clock ticked in one corner. There was something primitive in this medley of kitchen, parlor, and hall, that carried me back to earlier times, and pleased me. The place, indeed, was humble, but every thing had that look of order and neatness, which bespeaks the superintendence of a notable English housewife. A group of amphibious-looking beings, who might be either fishermen or sailors, were regaling themselves in one of the boxes. As I was a visitor of rather higher pretensions, I was ushered into a little misshapen back-room, having at least nine corners. It was lighted by a sky-light, furnished with antiquated leathern chairs, and ornamented with the portrait of a fat pig. It was evidently appropriated to particular customers, and I found a shabby gentleman, in a red nose and oil-doth hat, seated in one corner, meditating on a half-empty pot of porter.

The old sexton had taken the landlady aside, and with an air of profound importance imparted to her my errand. Dame Honeyball was a likely, plump, bustling little woman, and no bad substitute for that paragon of hostesses, Dame Quickly. She seemed delighted with an opportunity to oblige; and hurrying up stairs to the archives of her house, where the precious vessels of the parish club were deposited, she returned, smiling and courtesying, with them in her hands.

The first she presented me was a japanned iron tobacco-box, of gigantic size, out of which, I was told, the vestry had smoked at their stated meetings, since time immemorial; and which was never suffered to be profaned by vulgar hands, or used on common occasions. I received it with becoming reverence; but what was my delight, at beholding on its cover the identical painting of which I was in quest! There was displayed the outside of the Boar's Head Tavern, and before the door was to be seen the whole convivial group, at table, in full revel; pictured with that wonderful fidelity and force, with which the portraits of renowned generals and commodores are illustrated on tobacco-boxes, for the benefit of posterity. Lest, however, there should be any mistake, the cunning limner had warily inscribed the names of Prince Hal and Falstaff on the bottoms of their chairs.

On the inside of the cover was an inscription, nearly obliterated, recording that this box was the gift of Sir Richard Gore, for the use of the vestry meetings at the Boar's Head Tavern, and that it was "repaired and beautified by his successor, Mr. John Packard, 1767." Such is a faithful description of this august and venerable relic; and I question whether the learned Scriblerius contemplated his Roman shield, or the Knights of the Round Table the long-sought san-greal, with more exultation.

While I was meditating on it with enraptured gaze, Dame Honeyball, who was highly gratified by the interest it excited, put in my hands a drinking cup or goblet, which also belonged to the vestry, and was descended from the old Boar's Head. It bore the inscription of having been the gift of Francis Wythers, knight, and was held, she told me, in exceeding great value, being considered very "antyke." This last opinion was strengthened by the shabby gentleman in the red nose and oil-cloth hat, and whom I strongly suspected of being a lineal descendant from the valiant Bardolph. He suddenly aroused from his meditation on the pot of porter, and, casting a knowing look at the goblet, exclaimed, "Ay, ay! the head don't ache now that made that there article!"

The great importance attached to this memento of ancient revelry by modern churchwardens at first puzzled me; but there is nothing sharpens the apprehension so much as antiquarian research; for I immediately perceived that this could be no other than the identical "parcel-gilt goblet" on which Falstaff made his loving, but faithless vow to Dame Quickly; and which would, of course, be treasured up with care among the regalia of her domains, as a testimony of that solemn contract.[3]

Mine hostess, indeed, gave me a long history how the goblet had been handed down from generation to generation. She also entertained me with many particulars concerning the worthy vestrymen who have seated themselves thus quietly on the stools of the ancient roysters of Eastcheap, and, like so many commentators, utter clouds of smoke in honor of Shakspeare. These I forbear to relate, lest my readers should not be as curious in these matters as myself. Suffice it to say, the neighbors, one and all, about Eastcheap, believe that Falstaff and his merry crew actually lived and reveled there. Nay, there are several legendary anecdotes concerning him still extant among the oldest frequenters of the Mason's Arms, which they give as transmitted down from their forefathers; and Mr. M'Kash, an Irish hairdresser, whose shop stands on the site of the old Boar's Head, has several dry jokes of Fat Jack's, not laid down in the books, with which he makes his customers ready to die of laughter.

I now turned to my friend the sexton to make some further inquiries, but I found him sunk in pensive meditation. His head had declined a little on one side; a deep sigh heaved from the very bottom of his stomach; and, though I could not see a tear trembling in his eye, yet a moisture was evidently stealing from a corner of his mouth. I followed the direction of his eye through the door which stood open, and found it fixed wistfully on the savory breast of lamb, roasting in dripping richness before the fire.

I now called to mind that, in the eagerness of my recondite investigation, I was keeping the poor man from his dinner. My bowels yearned with sympathy, and, putting in his hand a small token of my gratitude and goodness, I departed, with a hearty benediction on him, Dame Honeyball, and the Parish Club of Crooked Lane;—not forgetting my shabby, but sententious friend, in the oil-cloth hat and copper nose.

---

3. Thou didst swear to me upon a *parcel-gilt goblet*, sitting in my Dolphin chamber, at the round table, by a sea-coal fire, on Wednesday, in Whitsunweek, when the prince broke thy head for likening his lather to a singing man at Windsor; thou didst swear to me then, as I was washing thy wound, to marry me, and make me my lady, thy wife. Canst thou deny it?—*Henry IV. Part 2.*

Thus have I given a "tedious brief" account of this interesting research, for which, if it prove too short and unsatisfactory, I can only plead my inexperience in this branch of literature, so deservedly popular at the present day. I am aware that a more skillful illustrator of the immortal bard would have swelled the materials I have touched upon, to a good merchantable bulk; comprising the biographies of William Walworth, Jack Straw, and Robert Preston; some notice of the eminent fishmongers of St. Michael's; the history of Eastcheap, great and little; private anecdotes of Dame Honeyball, and her pretty daughter, whom I have not even mentioned; to say nothing of a damsel tending the breast of lamb, (and whom, by the way, I remarked to be a comely lass, with a neat foot and ankle;)—the whole enlivened by the riots of Wat Tyler, and illuminated by the great fire of London.

All this I leave, as a rich mine, to be worked by future commentators; nor do I despair of seeing the tobacco-box, and the "parcel-gilt goblet," which I have thus brought to light, the subjects of future engravings, and almost as fruitful of voluminous dissertations and disputes as the shield of Achilles, or the far-famed Portland vase.

The Mutability of Literature

A Colloquy in Westminster Abbey

I know that all beneath the moon decays,
And what by mortals in this world is brought,
In time's great period shall return to nought.
I know that all the muse's heavenly lays,
With toil of sprite which are so dearly bought,
As idle sounds, of few or noe are sought
That there is nothing lighter than mere praise.

Drummond of Hawthornden

There are certain half-dreaming moods of mind, in which we naturally steal away from noise and glare, and seek some quiet haunt, where we may indulge our reveries and build our air castles undisturbed. In such a mood I was loitering about the old gray cloisters of Westminster Abbey, enjoying that luxury of wandering thought which one is apt to dignify with the name of reflection; when suddenly an interruption of madcap boys from Westminster School, playing at foot-ball, broke in upon the monastic stillness of the place, making the vaulted passages and mouldering tombs echo with their merriment. I sought to take refuge from their noise by penetrating still deeper into the solitudes of the pile, and applied to one of the vergers for admission to the library. He conducted me through a portal rich with the crumbling sculpture of former ages, which opened upon a gloomy passage leading to the chapter-house and the chamber in which doomsday book is deposited. Just within the passage is a small door on the left. To this the verger applied a key; it was double locked, and opened with some difficulty, as if seldom used. We now ascended a dark narrow staircase, and, passing through a second door, entered the library.

I found myself in a lofty antique hall, the roof supported by massive joists of old English oak. It was soberly lighted by a row of gothic windows at a considerable height from the floor, and which apparently opened upon the roofs of the cloisters. An ancient picture of some reverend dignitary of the church in his robes hung over the fireplace. Around the hall and in a small gallery were the books, arranged in carved oaken cases. They consisted principally of old polemical writers, and were much more worn by time than use. In the centre of the library was a solitary table with two or three books on it, an inkstand without ink, and a few pens parched by long disuse. The place seemed fitted for quiet study and profound meditation. It was buried deep among the massive walls of the abbey, and shut up from the tumult of the world. I could only hear now and then the shouts of the school-boys faintly swelling from the cloisters, and the sound of a bell tolling for prayers, echoing soberly along the roofs of the abbey. By degrees the shouts of merriment grew fainter and fainter, and at length died away; the bell ceased to toll, and a profound silence reigned through the dusky hall.

I had taken down a little thick quarto, curiously bound in parchment, with brass clasps, and seated myself at the table in a venerable elbow-chair. Instead of reading, however, I was beguiled by the solemn monastic air, and lifeless quiet of the place, into a train of musing. As I looked around upon the old volumes in their mouldering covers, thus ranged on the shelves, and apparently never disturbed in their repose, I could not but consider the library a kind of literary catacomb, where authors, like mummies, are piously entombed, and left to blacken and moulder in dusty oblivion.

How much, thought I, has each of these volumes, now thrust aside with such indifference, cost some aching head! how many weary days! how many sleepless nights! How have their authors buried themselves in the solitude of cells and cloisters; shut themselves up from the face of man, and the still more blessed face of nature; and devoted themselves to painful research and intense reflection! And all for what? to occupy an inch of dusty shelf—to have the title of their works read now and then in a future age, by some drowsy churchman or casual straggler like myself; and in another age to be lost, even to remembrance. Such is the amount of this boasted immortality. A mere temporary rumor, a local sound; like the tone of that bell which has just tolled among these towers, filling the ear for a moment—lingering transiently in echo— and then passing away like a thing that was not!

While I sat half murmuring, half meditating these unprofitable speculations with my head resting on my hand, I was thrumming with the other hand upon the quarto, until I accidentally loosened the clasps; when, to my utter astonishment, the little book gave two or three yawns, like one awaking from a deep sleep; then a husky hem; and at length began to talk. At first its voice was very hoarse and broken, being much troubled by a cobweb which some studious spider had woven across it; and having probably contracted a cold from long exposure to the chills and damps of the abbey. In a short time, however, it became more distinct, and I soon found it an exceedingly fluent conversable little tome. Its language, to be sure, was rather quaint and obsolete, and its pronunciation, what, in the present day, would be deemed barbarous; but I shall endeavor, as far as I am able, to render it in modern parlance.

It began with railings about the neglect of the world—about merit being suffered to languish in obscurity, and other such commonplace topics of literary repining, and complained bitterly that it had not been opened for more than two centuries. That the dean only looked now and then into the library, sometimes took down a volume or two, trifled with them for a few moments, and then returned them to their shelves. "What a plague do they mean," said the little quarto, which I began to perceive was somewhat choleric, "what a plague do they mean by keeping several thousand volumes of us shut up here, and watched by a set of old vergers, like so many beauties in a harem, merely to be looked at now and then by the dean? Books were written to give pleasure and to be enjoyed; and I would have a rule passed that the dean should pay each of us a visit at least once a year; or if he is not equal to the task, let them once in a while turn loose the whole school of Westminster among us, that at any rate we may now and then have an airing."

"Softly, my worthy friend," replied I, "you are not aware how much better you are off than most books of your generation. By being stored away in this ancient library, you are like the treasured remains of those saints and monarchs, which lie enshrined in the adjoining chapels; while the remains of your contemporary mortals, left to the ordinary course of nature, have long since returned to dust."

"Sir," said the little tome, ruffling his leaves and looking big, "I was written for all the world, not for the bookworms of an abbey. I was intended to circulate from hand to hand, like other great contemporary works; but here have I been clasped up for more than two centuries, and might have silently fallen a prey to these worms that are playing the very vengeance with my intestines, if you had not by chance given me an opportunity of uttering a few last words before I go to pieces."

"My good friend," rejoined I, "had you been left to the circulation of which you speak, you would long ere this have been no more. To judge from your physiognomy, you are now well stricken in years: very few of your contemporaries can be at present in existence; and those few owe their longevity to being immured like yourself in old libraries; which, suffer me to add, instead of likening to harems, you might more properly and gratefully have compared to those infirmaries attached to religious establishments, for the benefit of the old and decrepit, and where, by quiet fostering and no employment, they often endure to an amazingly good-for-nothing old age. You talk of your contemporaries as if in circulation—where do we meet with their works? what do we hear of Robert Groteste, of Lincoln? No one could have toiled harder than he for immortality. He is said to have written nearly two hundred volumes. He built, as it were, a pyramid of books to perpetuate his name: but, alas! the pyramid has long since fallen, and only a few fragments are scattered in various libraries, where they are scarcely disturbed even by the antiquarian. What do we hear of Giraldus Cambrensis, the historian, antiquary, philosopher, theologian, and poet? He declined two bishoprics, that he might shut himself up and write for posterity; but posterity never inquires after his labors. What of Henry of Huntingdon, who, besides a learned history of England, wrote a treatise on the contempt of the world, which the world has revenged by forgetting him? What is quoted of Joseph of Exeter, styled the miracle of his age in classical composition? Of his three great heroic poems one is lost for ever, excepting a mere fragment; the others are known only to a few of the curious in literature; and as to his love verses and epigrams, they have entirely disappeared. What is in current use of John Wallis, the Franciscan, who acquired the name of the tree of life? Of William of Malmsbury;—of Simeon of Durham;—of Benedict of Peterborough;—of John Hanvill of St. Albans;—of—"

"Prithee, friend," cried the quarto, in a testy tone, how old do you think me? You are talking of authors that lived long before my time, and wrote either in Latin or French, so that they in a manner expatriated themselves, and deserved to be forgotten;[1] but I, sir, was ushered into the world from the press of the renowned Wynkyn de Worde. I was written in my own native tongue at a time when the language had become fixed; and indeed I was considered a model of pure and elegant English."

---

1. In Latin and French hath many soueraine wittes had great delyte to endite, and have many noble thinges fulfilde, but certes there ben some that speaken their poisye in French, of which speche the Frenchmen have as good a fantasye as we have in hearying of Frenchmen's Englishe.

—*Chaucer's Testament of Love.*

(I should observe that these remarks were couched in such intolerably antiquated terms, that I have had infinite difficulty in rendering them into modern phraseology.)

"I cry your mercy," said I, "for mistaking your age; but it matters little: almost all the writers of your time have likewise passed into forgetfulness; and De Worde's publications are mere literary rarities among book-collectors. The purity and stability of language, too, on which you found your claims to perpetuity, have been the fallacious dependence of authors of every age, even back to the times of the worthy Robert of Gloucester, who wrote his history in rhymes of mongrel Saxon.[2] Even now many talk of Spenser's 'well of pure English undefiled,' as if the language ever sprang from a well or fountain-head, and was not rather a mere confluence of various tongues, perpetually subject to changes and intermixtures. It is this which has made English literature so extremely mutable, and the reputation built upon it so fleeting. Unless thought can be committed to something more permanent and unchangeable than such a medium, even thought must share the fate of every thing else, and fall into decay. This should serve as a check upon the vanity and exultation of the most popular writer. He finds the language in which he has embarked his fame gradually altering, and subject to the dilapidations of time and the caprice of fashion. He looks back and beholds the early authors of his country, once the favorites of their day, supplanted by modern writers. A few short ages have covered them with obscurity, and their merits can only be relished by the quaint taste of the bookworm. And such, he anticipates, will be the fate of his own work, which, however it may be admired in its day, and held up as a model of purity, will in the course of years grow antiquated and obsolete; until it shall become almost as unintelligible in its native land as an Egyptian obelisk, or one of those Runic inscriptions said to exist in the deserts of Tartary. I declare," added I, with some emotion, "when I contemplate a modern library, filled with new works, in all the bravery of rich gilding and binding, I feel disposed to sit down and weep; like the good Xerxes, when he surveyed his army, pranked out in all the splendor of military array, and reflected that in one hundred years not one of them would be in existence!"

---

2. Holinshed, in his Chronicle, observes, "afterwards, also, by deligent travell of Geffry Chaucer and of John Gowre, in the time of Richard the Second, and after them of John Scogan and John Lydgate, monke of Berne, our said toong was brought to an excellent passe, notwithstanding that it never came unto the type of perfection until the time of Queen Elizabeth, wherein John Jewell, Bishop of Sarum, John Fox, and sundrie learned and excellent writers, hare fully accomplished the ornature of the same, to their great praise and immortal commendation."

"Ah," said the little quarto, with a heavy sigh, "I see how it is; these modern scribblers have superseded all the good old authors. I suppose nothing is read now-a-days but Sir Philip Sydney's Arcadia, Sackville's stately plays, and Mirror for Magistrates, or the fine-spun euphuisms of the 'unparalleled John Lyly.'"

"There you are again mistaken," said I; "the writers whom you suppose in vogue, because they happened to be so when you were last in circulation, have long since had their day. Sir Philip Sydney's Arcadia, the immortality of which was so fondly predicted by his admirers,[3] and which, in truth, is full of noble thoughts, delicate images, and graceful turns of language, is now scarcely ever mentioned. Sackville has strutted into obscurity; and even Lyly, though his writings were once the delight of a court, and apparently perpetuated by a proverb, is now scarcely known even by name. A whole crowd of authors who wrote and wrangled at the time, have likewise gone down, with all their writings and their controversies. Wave after wave of succeeding literature has rolled over them, until they are buried so deep, that it is only now and then that some industrious diver after fragments of antiquity brings up a specimen for the gratification of the curious.

"For my part," I continued, "I consider this mutability of language a wise precaution of Providence for the benefit of the world at large, and of authors in particular. To reason from analogy, we daily behold the varied and beautiful tribes of vegetables springing up, flourishing, adorning the fields for a short time, and then fading into dust, to make way for their successors. Were not this the case, the fecundity of nature would be a grievance instead of a blessing. The earth would groan with rank and excessive vegetation, and its surface become a tangled wilderness. In like manner the works of genius and learning decline, and make way for subsequent productions. Language gradually varies, and with it fade away the writings of authors who have flourished their allotted time; otherwise, the creative powers of genius would overstock the world, and the mind would be completely bewildered in the endless mazes of literature. Formerly there were some restraints on this excessive multiplication. Works had to be transcribed by hand, which was a slow and laborious operation; they were

3. Live ever sweete booke; the simple image of his gentle witt, and the golden pillar of his noble courage; and ever notify unto the world that thy writer was the secretary of eloquence, the breath of the muses, the honey bee of the daintyest flowers of witt and arte, the pith of morale and intellectual virtues, the arme of Bellona in the field, the tonge of Suada in the chamber, the sprite of Practise in ease, and the paragon of excellency in print.—*Harvey Pierce's Supererogation.*

written either on parchment, which was expensive, so that one work was often erased to make way for another; or on papyrus, which was fragile and extremely perishable. Authorship was a limited and unprofitable craft, pursued chiefly by monks in the leisure and solitude of their cloisters. The accumulation of manuscripts was slow and costly, and confined almost entirely to monasteries. To these circumstances it may, in some measure, be owing that we have not been inundated by the intellect of antiquity; that the fountains of thought have not been broken up, and modern genius drowned in the deluge. But the inventions of paper and the press have put an end to all these restraints. They have made every one a writer, and enabled every mind to pour itself into print, and diffuse itself over the whole intellectual world. The consequences are alarming. The stream of literature has swollen into a torrent—augmented into a river—expanded into a sea. A few centuries since, five or six hundred manuscripts constituted a great library; but what would you say to libraries such as actually exist, containing three or four hundred thousand volumes; legions of authors at the same time busy; and the press going on with fearfully increasing activity, to double and quadruple the number? Unless some unforeseen mortality should break out among the progeny of the muse, now that she has become so prolific, I tremble for posterity. I fear the mere fluctuation of language will not be sufficient. Criticism may do much. It increases with the increase of literature, and resembles one of those salutary checks on population spoken of by economists. All possible encouragement, therefore, should be given to the growth of critics, good or bad. But I fear all will be in vain; let criticism do what it may, writers will write, printers will print, and the world will inevitably be overstocked with good books. It will soon be the employment of a lifetime merely to learn their names. Many a man of passable information, at the present day, reads scarcely anything but reviews; and before long a man of erudition will be little better than a mere walking catalogue."

"My very good sir," said the little quarto, yawning most drearily in my face, "excuse my interrupting you, but I perceive you are rather given to prose. I would ask the fate of an author who was making some noise just as I left the world. His reputation, however, was considered quite temporary. The learned shook their heads at him, for he was a poor half-educated varlet, that knew little of Latin, and nothing of Greek, and had been obliged to run the country for deer-stealing. I think his name was Shakspeare. I presume he soon sunk into oblivion."

"On the contrary," said I, "it is owing to that very man that the literature of his period has experienced a duration beyond the ordinary term of English literature.

There rise authors now and then, who seem proof against the mutability of language, because they have rooted themselves in the unchanging principles of human nature. They are like gigantic trees that we sometimes see on the banks of a stream; which, by their vast and deep roots, penetrating through the mere surface, and laying hold on the very foundations of the earth, preserve the soil around them from being swept away by the ever-flowing current, and hold up many a neighboring plant, and, perhaps, worthless weed, to perpetuity. Such is the case with Shakspeare, whom we behold defying the encroachments of time, retaining in modern use the language and literature of his day, and giving duration to many an indifferent author, merely from having flourished in his vicinity. But even he, I grieve to say, is gradually assuming the tint of age, and his whole form is overrun by a profusion of commentators, who, like clambering vines and creepers, almost bury the noble plant that upholds them."

Here the little quarto began to heave his sides and chuckle, until at length he broke out in a plethoric fit of laughter that had well nigh choked him, by reason of his excessive corpulency. "Mighty well!" cried he, as soon as he could recover breath, "mighty well! and so you would persuade me that the literature of an age is to be perpetuated by a vagabond deer-stealer! by a man without learning; by a poet, forsooth—a poet!" And here he wheezed forth another fit of laughter.

I confess that I felt somewhat nettled at this rudeness, which, however, I pardoned on account of his having flourished in a less polished age. I determined, nevertheless, not to give up my point.

"Yes," resumed I, positively, "a poet; for of all writers he has the best chance for immortality. Others may write from the head, but he writes from the heart, and the heart will always understand him. He is the faithful portrayer of nature, whose features are always the same, and always interesting. Prose writers are voluminous and unwieldy; their pages are crowded with commonplaces, and their thoughts expanded into tediousness. But with the true poet everything is terse, touching, or brilliant. He gives the choicest thoughts in the choicest language. He illustrates them by every thing that he sees most striking in nature and art. He enriches them by pictures of human life, such as it is passing before him. His writings, therefore, contain the spirit, the aroma, if I may use the phrase, of the age in which he lives. They are caskets which inclose within a small compass the wealth of the language—its family jewels, which are thus transmitted in a portable form to posterity. The setting may occasionally be antiquated, and require now and then to be renewed, as in the case of Chaucer; but the brilliancy and intrinsic value of the gems continue unaltered. Cast a look back over the long reach of literary history. What vast valleys of dullness, filled with monkish legends and academical controversies! what bogs of theological speculations! what dreary wastes of metaphysics! Here and there only do we behold the heaven-illumined bards, elevated like beacons on their widely-separate heights, to transmit the pure light of poetical intelligence from age to age."[4]

I was just about to launch forth into eulogiums upon the poets of the day, when the sudden opening of the door caused me to turn my head. It was the verger, who came to inform me that it was time to close the library. I sought to have a parting word with the quarto, but the worthy little tome was silent; the clasps were closed: and it looked perfectly unconscious of all that had passed. I have been to the library two or three times since, and have endeavored to draw it into further conversation, but in vain; and whether all this rambling colloquy actually took place, or whether it was another of those odd day-dreams to which I am subject, I have never to this moment been able to discover.

---

4. Thorow earth and waters deepe,
  The pen by skill doth passe:
And featly nyps the worldes abase,
  And shoes as in a glasse,
The vertu and the vice
  Of every wight alyve;
The honey comb that bee doth make
  Is not so sweet in hyve.
As are the golden leves
  That drop from poet's head!
Which doth surmount our common talke
  As farre as dross doth lead.
Churchyard

Rural Funerals

Here's a few flowers! but about midnight more:
The herbs that have on them cold dew o' the night;
Are strewings fitt'st for graves—
You were as flowers now wither'd; even so
These herblets shall, which we upon you strow.

CYMBELINE

AMONG THE BEAUTIFUL AND SIMPLE-HEARTED CUSTOMS OF RURAL LIFE which still linger in some parts of England, are those of strewing flowers before the funerals, and planting them at the graves of departed friends. These, it is said, are the remains of some of the rites of the primitive church; but they are of still higher antiquity, having been observed among the Greeks and Romans, and frequently mentioned by their writers, and were, no doubt, the spontaneous tributes of unlettered affection, originating long before art had tasked itself to modulate sorrow into song, or story it on the monument. They are now only to be met with in the most distant and retired places of the kingdom, where fashion and innovation have not been able to throng in, and trample out all the curious and interesting traces of the olden time.

In Glamorganshire, we are told, the bed whereon the corpse lies is covered with flowers, a custom alluded to in one of the wild and plaintive ditties of Ophelia:

White his shroud as the mountain snow,
Larded all with sweet flowers;
Which be-wept to the grave did go,
With true love showers.

There is also a most delicate and beautiful rite observed in some of the remote villages of the south, at the funeral of a female who has died young and unmarried. A chaplet of white flowers is borne before the corpse by a young girl nearest in age, size, and resemblance, and is afterwards hung up in the church over the accustomed seat of the deceased. These chaplets are sometimes made of white paper, in imitation of flowers, and inside of them is generally a pair of white gloves. They are intended as emblems of the purity of the deceased, and the crown of glory which she has received in heaven.

In some parts of the country, also, the dead are carried to the grave with the singing of psalms and hymns: a kind of triumph, "to show," says Bourne, "that they have finished their course with joy, and are become conquerors." This, I am informed, is observed in some of the northern counties, particularly in Northumberland, and it has a pleasing, though melancholy effect, to hear, of a still evening, in some lonely country scene, the mournful melody of a funeral dirge swelling from a distance, and to see the train slowly moving along the landscape.

Thus, thus, and thus, we compass round
Thy harmlesse and unhaunted ground,
And as we sing thy dirge, we will
The dafodill
And other flowers lay upon
The altar of our love, thy stone.

HERRICK

There is also a solemn respect paid by the traveler to the passing funeral in these sequestered places; for such spectacle occurring among the quiet abodes of nature, sink deep into the soul. As the mourning train approaches, he pauses, uncovered, to let it go by; he then follows silently in the rear; sometimes quite to the grave, at other times for a few hundred yards, and, having paid this tribute of respect to the deceased, turns and resumes his journey.

The rich vein of melancholy which runs through the English character, and gives it some of its most touching and ennobling graces, is finely evidenced in these pathetic customs, and in the solicitude shown by the common people for an honored and a peaceful grave. The humblest peasant, whatever may be his lowly lot while living, is anxious that some little respect may be paid to his remains. Sir Thomas Overbury, describing the "faire and happy milkmaid," observes, "thus lives she, and all her care is, that she may die in the spring time, to have store of flowers stucke upon her windingsheet." The poets, too, who always breathe the feeling of a nation, continually advert to this fond solitude about the grave. In "The Maid's Tragedy," by Beaumont and Fletcher, there is a beautiful instance of the kind, describing the capricious melancholy of a broken-hearted girl:

> When she sees a bank
> Stuck full of flowers, she, with a sigh, will tell
> Her servants, what a pretty place it were
> To bury lovers in; and make her maids
> Pluck 'em, and strew her over like a cone.

The custom of decorating graves was once universally prevalent: osiers were carefully bent over them to keep the turf uninjured, and about them were planted evergreens and flowers. We adorn their graves," says Evelyn, in his Sylva, "with flowers and redolent plants, just emblems of the life of man, which has been compared in Holy Scriptures to those fading beauties, whose roots being buried in dishonor, rise again in glory." This usage has now become extremely rare in England; but it may still be met with in the church-yards of retired villages, among the Welsh mountains; and I recollect an instance of it at the small town of Ruthen, which lies at the head of the beautiful vale of Clewyd. I have been told also by a friend, who was present at the funeral of a young girl in Glamorganshire, that the female attendants had their aprons full of flowers, which, as soon as the body was interred, they stuck about the grave.

He noticed several graves which had been decorated in the same manner. As the flowers had been merely stuck in the ground, and not planted, they had soon withered, and might be seen in various states of decay; some drooping, others quite perished. They were afterwards to be supplanted by holly, rosemary, and other evergreens; which on some graves had grown to great luxuriance, and overshadowed the tombstones.

There was formerly a melancholy fancifulness in the arrangement of these rustic offerings, that had something in it truly poetical. The rose was sometimes blended with the lily, to form a general emblem of frail mortality. This sweet flower," said Evelyn, "borne on a branch set with thorns, and accompanied with the lily, are natural hieroglyphics of our fugitive, umbratile, anxious, and transitory life, which, making so fair a show for a time, is not yet without its thorns and crosses." The nature and color of the flowers, and of the ribands with which they were tied, had often a particular reference to the qualities or story of the deceased, or were expressive of the feelings of the mourner. In an old poem, entitled "Corydon's Doleful Knell," a lover specifies the decorations he intends to use:

A garland shall be framed
    By art and nature's skill.
Of sundry-colored flowers,
    In token of good-will.

And sundry-color'd ribands
    On it I will bestow;
But chiefly blacke and yellowe
    With her to grave shall go.

I'll deck her tomb with flowers.
    The rarest ever seen;
And with my tears as showers,
    I'll keep them fresh and green.

The white rose, we are told, was planted at the grave of a virgin; her chaplet was tied with white ribands, in token of her spotless innocence; though sometimes black ribands were intermingled, to bespeak the grief of the survivors. The red rose was occasionally used in remembrance of such as had been remarkable for benevolence; but roses in general were appropriated to the graves of lovers. Evelyn tells us that the custom was not altogether extinct in his time, near his dwelling in the county of Surrey, "where the maidens yearly planted and decked the graves of their defunct sweethearts with rose-bushes." And Camden likewise remarks, in his Britannia: "Here is also a certain custom, observed time out of mind, of planting rose-trees upon the graves, especially by the young men and maids who have lost their loves; so that this churchyard is now full of them."

When the deceased had been unhappy in their loves, emblems of a more gloomy character were used, such as the yew and cypress; and if flowers were strewn, they were of the most melancholy colors. Thus, in poems by Thomas Stanley, Esq. (published in 1651), is the following stanza:

Yet strew
Upon my dismall grave
Such offerings as yon have,
Forsaken cypresse and sad yewe;
For kinder flowers can take no birth
Or growth from such unhappy earth.

In "The Maid's Tragedy," a pathetic little air is introduced, illustrative of this mode of decorating the funerals of females who had been disappointed in love:

Lay a garland on my hearse.
Of the dismall yew.
Maidens, willow branches wear.
Say I died true.

My love was false, but I was firm,
From my hour of birth,
Upon my buried body lie
Lightly, gentle earth.

The natural effect of sorrow over the dead is to refine and elevate the mind; and we have a proof of it in the purity of sentiment and the unaffected elegance of thought which pervaded the whole of these funeral observances. Thus, it was an especial precaution, that none but sweet-scented evergreens and flowers should be employed. The intention seems to have been to soften the horrors of the tomb, to beguile the mind from brooding over the disgraces of perishing mortality, and to associate the memory of the deceased with the most delicate and beautiful objects in nature. There is a dismal process going on in the grave, ere dust can return to its kindred dust, which the imagination shrinks from contemplating; and we seek still to think of the form we have loved, with those refined associations which it awakened when blooming before us in youth and beauty. "Lay her i' the earth," says Laertes, of his virgin sister,

And from her fair and unpolluted flesh
May violets spring!

Herrick, also, in his "Dirge of Jephtha," pours forth a fragrant flow of poetical thought and image, which in a manner embalms the dead in the recollections of the living.

Sleep in thy peace, thy bed of spice,
And make this place all Paradise:
May sweets grow here! and smoke from hence
Fat frankincense.
Let balme and cassia send their scent
From out thy maiden monument.

* * * * *

May all shie maids at wonted hours
Come forth to strew thy tombe with flowers!
May virgins, when they come to mourn,
Male incense burn
Upon thine altar! then return
And leave thee sleeping in thine urn.

I might crowd my pages with extracts from the older British poets, who wrote when these rites were more prevalent, and delighted frequently to allude to them; but I have already quoted more than is necessary. I cannot however refrain from giving a passage from Shakspeare, even though it should appear trite; which illustrates the emblematical meaning often conveyed in these floral tributes; and at the same time possesses that magic of language and appositeness of imagery for which he stands preeminent.

With fairest flowers,
Whilst summer lasts, and I live here, Fidele,
I'll sweeten thy sad grave; thou shalt not lack
The flower that's like thy face, pale primrose; nor
The azured harebell, like thy veins; no, nor
The leaf of eglantine; whom not to slander,
Outsweeten'd not thy breath.

There is certainly something more affecting in these prompt and spontaneous offerings of nature, than in the most costly monuments of art; the hand strews the flower while the heart is warm, and the tear falls on the grave as affection is binding the osier round the sod; but pathos expires under the slow labor of the chisel, and is chilled among the cold conceits of sculptured marble.

It is greatly to be regretted, that a custom so truly elegant and touching has disappeared from general use, and exists only in the most remote and insignificant villages. But it seems as if poetical custom always shuns the walks of cultivated society. In proportion as people grow polite they cease to be poetical. They talk of poetry, but they have learnt to check its free impulses, to distrust its sallying emotions, and to supply its most affecting and picturesque usages, by studied form and pompous ceremonial. Few pageants can be more stately and frigid than an English funeral in town. It is made up of show and gloomy parade; mourning carriages, mourning horses, mourning plumes, and hireling mourners, who make a mockery of grief. "There is a grave digged," says Jeremy Taylor, "and a solemn mourning, and a great talk in the neighborhood, and when the daies are finished, they shall be, and they shall be remembered no more." The associate in the gay and crowded city is soon forgotten; the hurrying succession of new intimates and new pleasures effaces him from our minds, and the very scenes and circles in which he moved are incessantly fluctuating. But funerals in the country are solemnly impressive. The stroke of death makes a wider space in the village circle, and is an awful event in the tranquil uniformity of rural life. The passing bell tolls its knell in every ear; it steals with its pervading melancholy over hill and vale, and saddens all the landscape.

The fixed and unchanging features of the country also perpetuate the memory of the friend with whom we once enjoyed them; who was the companion of our most retired walks, and gave animation to every lonely scene. His idea is associated with every charm of nature; we hear his voice in the echo which he once delighted to awaken; his spirit haunts the grove which he once frequented; we think of him in the wild upland solitude, or amidst the pensive beauty of the valley. In the freshness of joyous morning, we remember his beaming smiles and bounding gayety; and when sober evening returns with its gathering shadows and subduing quiet, we call to mind many a twilight hour of gentle talk and sweet-souled melancholy.

Each lonely place shall him restore
For him the tear be duly shed;
Beloved, till life can charm no more;
And mourn'd till pity's self be dead

Another cause that perpetuates the memory of the deceased in the country is that the grave is more immediately in sight of the survivors. They pass it on their way to prayer, it meets their eyes when their hearts are softened by the exercises of devotion; they linger about it on the Sabbath, when the mind is disengaged from worldly cares, and most disposed to turn aside from present pleasures and present loves, and to sit down among the solemn mementos of the past. In North Wales the peasantry kneel and pray over the graves of their deceased friends for several Sundays after the interment; and where the tender rite of strewing and planting flowers is still practised, it is always renewed on Easter, Whitsuntide, and other festivals, when the season brings the companion of former festivity more vividly to mind. It is also invariably performed by the nearest relatives and friends; no menials nor hirelings are employed; and if a neighbor yields assistance, it would be deemed an insult to offer compensation.

I have dwelt upon this beautiful rural custom, because, as it is one of the last, so is it one of the holiest offices of love. The grave is the ordeal of true affection. It is there that the divine passion of the soul manifests its superiority to the instinctive impulse of mere animal attachment. The latter must be continually refreshed and kept alive by the presence of its object; but the love that is seated in the soul can live on long remembrance. The mere inclinations of sense languish and decline with the charms which excited them, and turn with shuddering disgust from the dismal precincts of the tomb; but it is thence that truly spiritual affection rises, purified from every sensual desire, and returns, like a holy flame, to illumine and sanctify the heart of the survivor.

The sorrow for the dead is the only sorrow from which we refuse to be divorced. Every other wound we seek to heal—every other affliction to forget; but this wound we consider it a duty to keep open—this affliction we cherish and brood over in solitude. Where is the mother who would willingly forget the infant that perished like a blossom from her arms, though every recollection is a pang? Where is the child that would willingly forget the most tender of parents, though to remember be but to lament? Who, even in the hour of agony, would forget the friend over whom he mourns? Who, even when the tomb is closing upon the remains of her he most loved; when he feels his heart, as it were, crushed in the closing of its portal; would accept of consolation that must be bought by forgetfulness?—No, the love which survives the tomb is one of the noblest attributes of the soul. If it has its woes, it has likewise its delights; and when the overwhelming burst of grief is calmed into the gentle tear of recollection; when the sudden anguish and the convulsive agony over the present ruins of all that we most loved, is softened away into pensive meditation on all that it was in the days of its loveliness—who would root out such a sorrow from the heart? Though it may sometimes throw a passing cloud over the bright hour of gayety, or spread a deeper sadness over the hour of gloom, yet who would exchange it, even for the song of pleasure, or the burst of revelry? No, there is a voice from the tomb sweeter than song. There is a remembrance of the dead to which we turn even from the charms of the living. Oh the grave!—the grave!—It buries every error—covers every defect—extinguishes every resentment! From its peaceful bosom spring none but fond regrets and tender recollections. Who can look down upon the grave even of an enemy, and not feel a compunctious throb, that he should ever have warred with the poor handful of earth that lies mouldering before him!

But the grave of those we loved—what a place for meditation! There it is that we call up in long review the whole history of virtue and gentleness, and the thousand endearments lavished upon us almost unheeded in the daily intercourse of intimacy—there it is that we dwell upon the tenderness, the solemn, awful tenderness of the parting scene. The bed of death, with all its stifled griefs—its noiseless attendance—its mute, watchful assiduities. The last testimonies of expiring love! The feeble, fluttering, thrilling—oh! how thrilling!—pressure of the hand! The faint, faltering accents, struggling in death to give one more assurance of affection! The last fond look of the glazing eye, turning upon us even from the threshold of existence!

Ay, go to the grave of buried love, and meditate! There settle the account with thy conscience for every past benefit unrequited—every past endearment unregarded, of that departed being, who can never—never—never return to be soothed by thy contrition!

If thou art a child, and hast ever added a sorrow to the soul, or a furrow to the silvered brow of an affectionate parent—if thou art a husband, and hast ever caused the fond bosom that ventured its whole happiness in thy arms to doubt one moment of thy kindness or thy truth—if thou art a friend, and hast ever wronged, in thought, or word, or deed, the spirit that generously confided in thee—if thou art a lover, and hast ever given one unmerited pang to that true heart which now lies cold and still beneath the feet;—then be sure that every unkind look, every ungracious word, every ungentle action, will come thronging back upon thy memory, and knocking dolefully at thy soul—then be sure that thou wilt lie down sorrowing and repentant on the grave, and utter the unheard groan, and pour the unavailing tear; more deep, more bitter, because unheard and unavailing.

Then weave thy chaplet of flowers, and strew the beauties of nature about the grave; console thy broken spirit, if thou canst, with these tender, yet futile tributes of regret; but take warning by the bitterness of this thy contrite affliction over the dead, and henceforth be more faithful and affectionate in the discharge of thy duties to the living.

In writing the preceding article, it was not intended to give a full detail of the funeral customs of the English peasantry, but merely to furnish a few hints and quotations illustrative of particular rites, to be appended, by way of note, to another paper, which has been withheld. The article swelled insensibly into its present form, and this is mentioned as an apology for so brief and casual a notice of these usages, after they have been amply and learnedly investigated in other works.

I must observe, also that I am well aware that this custom of adorning graves with flowers prevails in other countries besides England. Indeed, in some it is much more general, and is observed even by the rich and fashionable; but it is then apt to lose its simplicity, and to degenerate into affectation. Bright, in his travels in Lower Hungary, tells of monuments of marble, and recesses formed for retirement, with seats placed among bowers of greenhouse plants; and that the graves generally are covered with the gayest flowers of the season. He gives a casual picture of filial piety, which I cannot but describe; for I trust it is as useful as it is delightful, to illustrate the amiable virtues of the sex. "When I was at Berlin," says he, "I followed the celebrated Iffland to the grave. Mingled with some pomp, you might trace much real feeling. In the midst of the ceremony, my attention was attracted by a young woman, who stood on a mound of earth, newly covered with turf, which she anxiously protected from the feet of the passing crowd. It was the tomb of her parent; and the figure of this affectionate daughter presented a monument more striking than the most costly work of art."

I will barely add an instance of sepulchral decoration that I once met with among the mountains of Switzerland. It was at the village of Gersau, which stands on the borders of the Lake of Lucern, at the foot of Mount Rigi. It was once the capital of a miniature republic, shut up between the Alps and the Lake, and accessible on the land side only by foot-paths. The whole force of the republic did not exceed six hundred fighting men; and a few miles of circumference, scooped out as it were from the bosom of the mountains, comprised its territory. The village of Gersau seemed separated from the rest of the world, and retained the golden simplicity of a purer age. It had a small church, with a burying-ground adjoining. At the heads of the graves were placed crosses of wood or iron. On some were affixed miniatures, rudely executed, but evidently attempts at likenesses of the deceased. On the crosses were hung chaplets of flowers, some withering, others fresh, as if occasionally renewed. I paused with interest at this scene; I felt that I was at the source of poetical description, for these were the beautiful but unaffected offerings of the heart which poets are fain to record. In a gayer and more populous place, I should have suspected them to have been suggested by factitious sentiment, derived from books; but the good people of Gersau knew little of books; there was not a novel nor a love poem in the village; and I question whether any peasant of the place dreamt, while he was twining a fresh chaplet for the grave of his mistress, that he was fulfilling one of the most fanciful rites of poetical devotion, and that he was practically a poet.

The Inn Kitchen

Shall I not take mine ease in mine inn?
FALSTAFF

During a journey I once made through the Netherlands, I had arrived one evening at the *Pomme d'Or,* the principal inn of a small Flemish village. It was after the hour of the *table d'hôte,* so that I was obliged to make a solitary supper from relics of its ampler board. The weather was chilly; I was seated alone in one end of a great gloomy dining-room, and, my repast being over, I had the prospect before me of a long dull evening without any visible means of enlivening it. I summoned mine host, and requested something to read; he brought me the whole literary stock of his household, a Dutch family Bible, an almanac in the same language, and a number of old Paris newspapers. As I sat dozing over one of the latter, reading old news and stale criticisms, my ear was now and then struck with bursts of laughter which seemed to proceed from the kitchen. Every one that traveled on the continent must know how favorite a resort the kitchen of a country inn is to the middle and inferior order of travelers; particularly in that equivocal kind of weather, when a fire becomes agreeable toward evening. I threw aside the newspaper, and explored my way to the kitchen, to take a peep at the group that appeared to be so merry. It was composed partly of travelers who had arrived some hours before in a diligence, and partly of the usual attendants and hangers-on of inns. They were seated round a great burnished stove, that might have been mistaken for an altar, at which they were worshiping. It was covered with various kitchen vessels of resplendent brightness; among which steamed and hissed a huge copper tea-kettle. A large lamp threw a strong mass of light upon the group, bringing out many odd features in strong relief. Its yellow rays partially illumined the spacious kitchen, dying duskily away into remote corners; except where they settled in mellow radiance on the broad side of a flitch of bacon, or were reflected back from well-scoured utensils, that gleamed from the midst of obscurity. A strapping Flemish lass, with long golden pendants in her ears, and a necklace with a golden heart suspended to it, was the presiding priestess of the temple.

Many of the company were furnished with pipes, and most of them with some kind of evening potation. I found their mirth was occasioned by anecdotes, which a little swarthy Frenchman, with a dry weazen face and large whiskers, was giving of his love adventures; at the end of each of which there was one of those bursts of honest unceremonious laughter, in which a man indulges in that temple of true liberty, an inn.

As I had no better mode of getting through a tedious blustering evening, I took my seat near the stove, and listened to a variety of travelers' tales, some very extravagant, and most very dull. All of them, however, have faded from my treacherous memory except one, which I will endeavor to relate. I fear, however, it derived its chief zest from the manner in which it was told, and the peculiar air and appearance of the narrator. He was a corpulent old Swiss, who had the look of a veteran traveler. He was dressed in a tarnished green traveling-jacket, with a broad belt round his waist, and a pair of overalls, with buttons from the hips to the ankles. He was of a full rubicund countenance, with a double chin, aquiline nose, and a pleasant twinkling eye. His hair was light, and curled from under an old green velvet traveling-cap stuck on one side of his head. He was interrupted more than once by the arrival of guests, or the remarks of his auditors; and paused now and then to replenish his pipe; at which times he had generally a roguish leer, and a sly joke for the buxom kitchen-maid.

I wish my readers could imagine the old fellow lolling in a huge arm-chair, one arm akimbo, the other holding a curiously twisted tobacco pipe, formed of genuine *écume de mer,* decorated with silver chain and silken tassel—his head cocked on one side, and a whimsical cut of the eye occasionally, as he related the following story.

The Spectre Bridegroom

A Traveler's Tale[1]

He tha: supper for is dight,
He lyes full cold, I trow, this night!
Yestreen to chamber I him led,
This night Gray-Steel has made his bed.
SIR EGER, SIR GRAHAME, AND SIR GRAY-STEEL

On the summit of one of the heights of the Odenwald, a wild and romantic tract of Upper Germany, that lies not far from the confluence of the Main and the Rhine, there stood, many, many years since, the Castle of the Baron Von Landshort. It is now quite fallen to decay, and almost buried among beech trees and dark firs; above which, however, its old watch-tower may still be seen struggling, like the former possessor I have mentioned, to carry a high head, and look down upon the neighboring country.

The baron was a dry branch of the great family of Katzenellenbogen,[2] and inherited the relics of the property, and all the pride of his ancestors. Though the warlike disposition of his predecessors had much impaired the family possessions, yet the baron still endeavored to keep up some show of former state. The times were peaceable, and the German nobles, in general, had abandoned their inconvenient old castles, perched

---

1. The erudite reader, well versed in good-for-nothing lore, will perceive that the above Tale must have been suggested to the old Swiss by a little French anecdote, a circumstance said to have taken place at Paris.

2. i.e., CAT'S-ELBOW. The name of a family of those parts very powerful in former times. The appellation, we are told, was given in compliment to a peerless dame of the family, celebrated for her fine arm.

like eagles' nests among the mountains, and had built more convenient residences in the valleys: still the baron remained proudly drawn up in his little fortress, cherishing, with hereditary inveteracy, all the old family feuds; so that he was on ill terms with some of his nearest neighbors, on account of disputes that had happened between their great-great-grandfathers.

The baron had but one child, a daughter; but nature, when she grants but one child, always compensates by making it a prodigy; and so it was with the daughter of the baron. All the nurses, gossips, and country cousins, assured her father that she had not her equal for beauty in all Germany; and who should know better than they? She had, moreover, been brought up with great care under the superintendence of two maiden aunts, who had spent some years of their early life at one of the little German courts, and were skilled in all the branches of knowledge necessary to the education of a fine lady. Under their instructions she became a miracle of accomplishments. By the time she was eighteen, she could embroider to admiration, and had worked whole histories of the saints in tapestry, with such strength of expression in their countenances, that they looked like so many souls in purgatory. She could read without great difficulty, and had spelled her way through several church legends, and almost all the chivalric wonders of the Heldenbuch. She had even made considerable proficiency in writing; could sign her own name without missing a letter, and so legibly that her aunts could read it without spectacles. She excelled in making little elegant good-for-nothing lady-like nicknacks of all kinds; was versed in the most abstruse dancing of the day; played a number of airs on the harp and guitar; and knew all the tender ballads of the Minnielieders by heart.

Her aunts, too, having been great flirts and coquettes in their younger days, were admirably calculated to be vigilant guardians and strict censors of the conduct of their niece; for there is no duenna so rigidly prudent, and inexorably decorous, as a superannuated coquette. She was rarely suffered out of their sight; never went beyond the domains of the castle, unless well attended, or rather well watched; had continual lectures read to her about strict decorum and implicit obedience; and, as to the men—pah!—she was taught to hold them at such a distance, and in such absolute distrust, that, unless properly authorized, she would not have cast a glance upon the handsomest cavalier in the world—no, not if he were even dying at her feet.

The good effects of this system were wonderfully apparent. The young lady was a pattern of docility and correctness. While others were wasting their sweetness in the glare of the world, and liable to be plucked and thrown aside by every hand; she was coyly blooming into fresh and lovely womanhood under the protection of those immaculate spinsters, like a rose-bud blushing forth among guardian thorns. Her aunts looked upon her with pride and exultation, and vaunted that though all the other young ladies in the world might go astray, yet, thank Heaven, nothing of the kind could happen to the heiress of Katzenellenbogen.

But, however scantily the Baron Yon Landshort might be provided with children, his household was by no means a small one; for Providence had enriched him with abundance of poor relations. They, one and all, possessed the affectionate disposition common to humble relatives; were wonderfully attached to the baron, and took every possible occasion to come in swarms and enliven the castle. All family festivals were commemorated by these good people at the baron's expense; and when they were filled with good cheer, they would declare that there was nothing on earth so delightful as these family meetings, these jubilees of the heart.

The baron, though a small man, had a large soul, and it swelled with satisfaction at the consciousness of being the greatest man in the little world about him. He loved to tell long stories about the stark old warriors whose portraits looked grimly down from the walls around, and he found no listeners equal to those who fed at his expense. He was much given to the marvelous, and a firm believer in all those supernatural tales with which every mountain and valley in Germany abounds. The faith of his guests exceeded even his own: they listened to every tale of wonder with open eyes and mouth, and never failed to be astonished, even though repeated for the hundredth time. Thus lived the Baron Von Landshort, the oracle of his table, the absolute monarch of his little territory, and happy, above all things, in the persuasion that he was the wisest man of the age.

At the time of which my story treats, there was a great family gathering at the castle, on an affair of the utmost importance: it was to receive the destined bridegroom of the baron's daughter. A negotiation had been carried on between the father and an old nobleman of Bavaria, to unite the dignity of their houses by the marriage of their children. The preliminaries had been conducted with proper punctilio. The young people were betrothed without seeing each other; and the time was appointed for the marriage ceremony. The young Count Von Altenburg had been recalled from the army for the purpose, and was actually on his way to the baron's to receive his bride. Missives had even been received from him, from Wurtzburg, where he was accidentally detained, mentioning the day and hour when be might be expected to arrive.

The castle was in a tumult of preparation to give him a suitable welcome. The fair bride had been decked out with uncommon care. The two aunts had superintended her toilet, and quarreled the whole morning about every article of her dress. The young lady had taken advantage of their contest to follow the bent of her own taste; and fortunately it was a good one. She looked as lovely as youthful bridegroom could desire; and the flutter of expectation heightened the lustre of her charms.

The suffusions that mantled her face and neck, the gentle heaving of the bosom, the eye now and then lost in reverie, a betrayed the soft tumult that was going on in her little heart. The aunts were continually hovering around her; for maiden aunts are apt to take great interest in affairs of this nature. They were giving her a world of staid counsel how to deport herself, what to say, and in what manner to receive the expected lover.

The baron was no less busied in preparations. He had, in truth, nothing exactly to do: but be was naturally a fuming bustling little man, and could not remain passive when all the world was in a hurry. He worried from top to bottom of the castle with an air of infinite anxiety; he continually called the servants from their work to exhort them to be diligent; and buzzed about every hall and chamber, as idly restless and importunate as a blue-bottle fly on a warm summer's day.

In the meantime the failed calf had been killed; the forests had rung with the clamor of the huntsmen; the kitchen was crowded with good cheer; the cellars had yielded up whole oceans of *Rhein-wein* and *Ferne-wein*; and even the great Heidelburg tun had been laid under contribution. Every thing was ready to receive the distinguished guest with *Saus und Braus* in the true spirit of German hospitality—but the guest delayed to make his appearance. Hour rolled after hour. The sun, that had poured his downward rays upon the rich forest of the Odenwald, now just gleamed along the summits of the mountains. The baron mounted the highest tower, and strained his eyes in hopes of catching a distant sight of the count and his attendants. Once he thought he beheld them; the sound of horns came floating from the valley, prolonged by the mountain echoes. A number of horsemen were seen far below, slowly advancing along the road; but when they had nearly reached the foot of the mountain, they suddenly struck off in a different direction. The last ray of sunshine departed—the bats began to flit by in the twilight—the road grew dimmer and dimmer to the view; and nothing appeared stirring in it, but now and then a peasant lagging homeward from his labor.

While the old castle of Landshort was in this state of perplexity, a very interesting scene was transacting in a different part of the Odenwald.

The young Count Von Altenburg was tranquilly pursuing his route in that sober jog-trot way, in which a man travels toward matrimony when his friends have taken all the trouble and uncertainly of courtship off his hands, and a bride is waiting for him, as certainly as a dinner at the end of his journey. He had encountered, at Wurtzburg, a youthful companion in arms, with whom he had seen some service on the frontiers; Herman Von Starkenfaust, one of the stoutest hands, and worthiest hearts, of German chivalry, who was now returning from the army. His father's castle was not far distant from the old fortress of Landshort, although an hereditary feud rendered the families hostile, and strangers to each other.

In the warm-hearted moment of recognition, the young friends related all their past adventures and fortunes, and the count gave the whole history of his intended nuptials with a young lady whom he had never seen, but of whose charms he had received the most enrapturing descriptions.

As the route of the friends lay in the same direction, they agreed to perform the rest of their journey together; and, that they might do it the more leisurely, set off from Wurtzburg at an early hour, the count having given directions for his retinue to follow and overtake him.

They beguiled their wayfaring with recollections of the military scenes and adventures; but the count was apt to be little tedious, now and then, about the reputed charms of his bride, and the felicity that awaited him.

In this way they had entered among the mountains of the Odenwald, and were traversing one of its most lonely and thickly wooded passes. It is well known that the forests of Germany have always been as much infested by robbers as its castles by spectres; and, at this time, the former were particularly numerous, from the hordes of disbanded soldiers wandering about the country. It will not appear extraordinary, therefore, that the cavaliers were attacked by a gang of these stragglers, in the midst of the forest. They defended themselves with bravery, but were nearly overpowered, when the count's retinue arrived to their assistance. At sight of them the robbers fled, but not until the count had received a mortal wound. He was slowly and carefully conveyed back to the city of Wurtzburg, and a friar summoned from a neighboring convent, who was famous for his skill in administering to both soul and body; but half of his skill was superfluous; the moments of the unfortunate count were numbered.

With his dying breath he entreated his friend to repair instantly to the castle of Landshort, and explain the fatal cause of his not keeping his appointment with his bride. Though not the most ardent of lovers, he was one of the most punctilious of men, and appeared earnestly solicitous that his mission should be speedily and courteously executed. "Unless this is done," said he, "I shall not sleep quietly in my grave!" He repeated these last words with peculiar solemnity. A request, at a moment so impressive, admitted no hesitation. Starkenfaust endeavored to soothe him to calmness; promised faithfully to execute his wish, and gave him his hand in solemn pledge. The dying man pressed it in acknowledgment, but soon lapsed into delirium—raved about his bride—his engagements—his plighted word; ordered his horse, that he might ride to the castle of Landshort; and expired in the fancied act of vaulting into the saddle.

Starkenfaust bestowed a sigh and a soldier's tear on the untimely fate of his comrade; and then pondered on the awkward mission he had undertaken. His heart was heavy, and his head perplexed; for he was to present himself an unbidden guest among hostile people, and to damp their festivity with tidings fatal to their hopes. Still there were certain whisperings of curiosity in his bosom to see this far-famed beauty of Katzenellenbogen, so cautiously shut up from the world; for he was a passionate admirer of the sex, and there was a dash of eccentricity and enterprise in his character that made him fond of all singular adventure.

Previous to his departure he made all due arrangements with the holy fraternity of the convent for the funeral solemnities of his friend, who was to be buried in the cathedral of Wurtzburg, near some of his illustrious relatives; and the mourning retinue of the count took charge of his remains.

It is now high time that we should return to the ancient family of Katzenellenbogen, who were impatient for their guest, and still more for their dinner; and to the worthy little baron, whom we left airing himself on the watch-tower.

Night closed in, but still no guest arrived. The baron descended from the tower in despair. The banquet, which had been delayed from hour to hour, could no longer be postponed. The meats were already overdone; the cook in an agony; and the whole household had the look of a garrison that had been reduced by famine. The baron was obliged reluctantly to give orders for the feast without the presence of the guest. All were seated at table, and just on the point of commencing, when the sound of a horn from without the gate gave notice of the approach of a stranger. Another long blast filled the old courts of the castle with its echoes, and was answered by the warder from the walls. The baron hastened to receive his future son-in-law.

The drawbridge had been let down, and the stranger was before the gate. He was a tall gallant cavalier, mounted on a black steed. His countenance was pale, but he had a beaming, romantic eye, and an air of stately melancholy. The baron was a little mortified that he should have come in this simple, solitary style. His dignity for a moment was ruffled, and he felt disposed to consider it a want of proper respect for the important occasion, and the important family with which he was to be connected. He pacified himself, however, with the conclusion, that it must have been youthful impatience which had induced him thus to spur on sooner than his attendants.

"I am sorry," said the stranger, "to break in upon you thus unseasonably—"

Here the baron interrupted him with a world of compliments and greetings; for, to tell the truth, he prided himself upon his courtesy and eloquence. The stranger attempted, once or twice, to stem the torrent of words, but in vain, so he bowed his head and suffered it to flow on. By the time the baron had come to a pause, they had reached the inner court of the castle; and the stranger was again about to speak, when he was once more interrupted by the appearance of the female part of the family, leading forth the shrinking and blushing bride. He gazed on her for a moment as one entranced; it seemed as if his whole soul beamed forth in the gaze, and rested upon that lovely form. One of the maiden aunts whispered something in her ear; she made an effort to speak; her moist blue eye was timidly raised; gave a shy glance of inquiry on the stranger; and was cast again to the ground. The words died away; but there was a sweet smile playing about her lips, and a soft dimpling of the cheek that showed her glance had not been unsatisfactory. It was impossible for a girl of the fond age of eighteen, highly predisposed for love and matrimony, not to be pleased with so gallant a cavalier.

The late hour at which the guest had arrived left no time for parley. The baron was peremptory, and deferred all particular conversation until the morning, and led the way to the untasted banquet.

It was served up in the great hall of the castle. Around the walls hung the hard-favored portraits of the heroes of the house of Katzenellenbogen, and the trophies which they had gained in the field and in the chase. Hacked corslets, splintered jousting spears, and tattered banners, were mingled with the spoils of sylvan warfare; the jaws of the wolf, and the tusks of the boar, grinned horribly among cross-bows and battle-axes, and a huge pair of antlers branched immediately aver the head of the youthful bridegroom.

The cavalier took but little notice of the company or the entertainment. He scarcely tasted the banquet, but seemed absorbed in admiration of his bride. He conversed in a low tone that could not be overheard—for the language of love is never loud; but where is the female ear so dull that it cannot catch the softest whisper of the lover? There was a mingled tenderness and gravity in his manner, that appeared to have a powerful effect upon the young lady. Her color came and went as she listened with deep attention. Now and then she made some blushing reply, and when his eye was turned away, she would steal a sidelong glance at his romantic countenance, and heave a gentle sigh of tender happiness. It was evident that the young couple were completely enamored. The aunts, who were deeply versed in the mysteries of the heart, declared that they had fallen in love with each other at first sight.

The feast went on merrily, or at least noisily, for the guests were all blessed with those keen appetites that attend upon light purses and mountain air. The baron told his best and longest stories, and never had he told them so well, or with such great effect. If there was any thing marvelous, his auditors were lost in astonishment; and if any thing facetious, they were sure to laugh exactly in the right place. The baron, it is true, like most great men, was too dignified to utter any joke but a dull one; it was always enforced, however, by a bumper of excellent Hockheimer; and even a dull joke, at one's own table, served up with jolly old wine, is irresistible. Many good things were said by poorer and keener wits, that would not bear repeating, except on similar occasions; many sly speeches whispered in ladies' ears, that almost convulsed them with suppressed laughter; and a song or two roared out by a poor, but merry and broad-faced cousin of the baron, that absolutely made the maiden aunts hold up their fans.

Amidst all this revelry, the stranger guest maintained a most singular and unseasonable gravity. His countenance assumed a deeper cast of dejection as the evening advanced; and, strange as it may appear, even the baron's jokes seemed only to render him the more melancholy. At times he was lost in thought, and at times there was a perturbed and restless wandering of the eye that bespoke a mind but ill at ease. His conversations with the bride became more and more earnest and mysterious. Lowering clouds began to steal over the fair serenity of her brow, and tremors to run through her tender frame.

All this could not escape the notice of the company. Their gayety was chilled by the unaccountable gloom of the bridegroom; their spirits were infected; whispers and glances were interchanged, accompanied by shrugs and dubious shakes of the head.

The song and the laugh grew less and less frequent; there were dreary pauses in the conversation, which were at length succeeded by wild tales and supernatural legends. One dismal story produced another still more dismal, and the baron nearly frightened some of the ladies into hysterics with the history of the goblin horseman that carried away the fair Leonora; a dreadful story, which has since been put into excellent verse, and is read and believed by all the world.

The bridegroom listened to this tale with profound attention. He kept his eyes steadily fixed on the baron, and, as the story drew to a close, began gradually to rise from his seat, growing taller and taller, until, in the baron's entranced eye, he seemed almost to tower into a giant. The moment the tale was finished, he heaved a deep sigh, and took a solemn farewell of the company. They were all amazement. The baron was perfectly thunder-struck.

"What! going to leave the castle at midnight? why, every thing was prepared for his reception; a chamber was ready for him if he wished to retire."

The stranger shook his head mournfully and mysteriously; "I must lay my head in a different chamber to-night!"

There was something in this reply, and the tone in which it was uttered, that made the baron's heart misgive him; but he rallied his forces, and repeated his hospitable entreaties.

The stranger shook his head silently, but positively, at every offer; and, waving his farewell to the company, stalked slowly out of the hall. The maiden aunts were absolutely petrified—the bride hung her head, and a tear stole to her eye.

The baron followed the stranger to the great court of the castle, where the black charger stood pawing the earth, and snorting with impatience.—When they had reached the portal, whose deep archway was dimly lighted by a cresset, the stranger paused, and addressed the baron in a hollow tone of voice, which the vaulted roof rendered still more sepulchral.

"Now that we are alone," said he, "I will impart to you the reason of my going. I have a solemn, an indispensable engagement—"

"Why," said the baron, "cannot you send some one in your place?"

"It admits of no substitute—I must attend it in person—I must away to Wurtzburg cathedral—"

"Ay," said the baron, plucking up spirit, "but not until to-morrow—to-morrow you shall take your bride there."

"No! no!" replied the stranger, with tenfold solemnity, "my engagement is with no bride—the worms! the worms expect me! I am a dead man—I have been slain by robbers—my body lies at Wurtzburg—at midnight I am to be buried—the grave is waiting for me—I must keep my appointment!"

He sprang on his black charger, dashed over the drawbridge, and the clattering of his horse's hoofs was lost in the whistling of the night blast.

The baron returned to the hall in the utmost consternation, and related what had passed. Two ladies fainted outright, others sickened at the idea of having banqueted with a spectre. It was the opinion of some, that this might be the wild huntsman, famous in German legend. Some talked of mountain sprites, of wood-demons, and of other supernatural beings, with which the good people of Germany have been so grievously harassed since time immemorial. One of the poor relations ventured to suggest that it might be some sportive evasion of the young cavalier, and that the very gloominess of the caprice seemed to accord with so melancholy a personage. This, however, drew on him the indignation of the whole company, and especially of the baron, who looked upon him as little better than an infidel; so that he was fain to at abjure his heresy as speedily as possible, and come into the faith of the true believers.

But whatever may have been the doubts entertained, they were completely put to an end by the arrival, next day, of regular missives, confirming the intelligence of the young count's murder, and his interment in Wurtzburg cathedral.

The dismay at the castle may well be imagined. The baron shut himself up in his chamber. The guests, who had come to rejoice with him, could not think of abandoning him in his distress. They wandered about the courts, or collected in groups in the hall, shaking their heads and shrugging their shoulders, at the troubles of so good a man; and sat longer than ever at table, and ate and drank more stoutly than ever, by way of keeping up their spirits. But the situation of the widowed bride most pitiable. To have lost a husband before she had even embraced him—and such a husband! if the very spectre could be so gracious and noble, what must have been the living man? She filled the house with lamentations.

On the night of the second day of her widowhood she had retired to her chamber, accompanied by one of her aunts, who insisted on sleeping with her. The aunt, who was one of the best tellers of ghost stories in all Germany, had just been recounting one of her longest, and had fallen asleep in the very midst of it. The chamber was remote, and overlooked a small garden. The niece lay pensively gazing at the beams of the rising moon, as they trembled on the leaves of an aspen-tree before the lattice. The castle clock had just tolled midnight, when a soft strain of music stole up from the garden. She rose hastily from her bed, and stepped lightly to the window. A tall figure stood among the shadows of the trees. As it raised its head, a beam of moonlight fell upon the countenance. Heaven and earth! she beheld the Spectre Bridegroom! A loud shriek at that moment burst upon her ear, and her aunt, who had been awakened by the music, and had followed her silently to the window, fell into her arms. When she looked again, the spectre had disappeared.

Of the two females, the aunt now required the most soothing, for she was perfectly beside herself with terror. As to the young lady, there was something, even in the spectre of her lover, that seemed endearing. There was still the semblance of manly beauty; and though the shadow of a man is but little calculated to satisfy the affections of a love-sick girl, yet, where the substance is not to be had, even that is consoling. The aunt declared she would never sleep in that chamber again; the niece, for once, was refractory, and declared as strongly that she would sleep in no other in the castle: the consequence was, that she had to sleep in it alone: but she drew a promise from her aunt not to relate the story of the spectre, lest she should be denied the only melancholy pleasure left her on earth—that of inhabiting the chamber over which the guardian shade of her lover kept its nightly vigils.

How long the good old lady would have observed this promise is uncertain, for she dearly loved to talk of the marvelous, and there is a triumph in being the first to tell a frightful story; it is, however, still quoted in the neighborhood, as a memorable instance of female secrecy, that she kept it to herself for a whole week; when she was suddenly absolved from all further restraint, by intelligence brought to the breakfast table one morning that the young lady was not to be found. Her room was empty—the bed had not been slept in—the window was open, and the bird had flown!

The astonishment and concern with which the intelligence was received, can only be imagined by those who have witnessed the agitation which the mishaps of a great man cause among his friends. Even the poor relations paused for a moment from the indefatigable labors of the trencher; when the aunt, who had at first been struck speechless, wrung her hands, and shrieked out, "The goblin! the goblin! she's carried away by the goblin!"

In a few words she related the fearful scene of the garden, and concluded that the spectre must have carried off his bride. Two of the domestics corroborated the opinion, for they had heard the clattering of a horse's hoofs down the mountain about night, and had no doubt that it was the spectre on his black charger, bearing her away to the tomb. All present were struck with the direful probability; for events of the kind are extremely common in Germany, as many well authenticated histories bear witness.

What a lamentable situation was that of the poor baron! What a heart-rending dilemma for a fond father, and a member of the great family of Katzenellenbogen! His only daughter had either been rapt away to the grave, or he was to have some wood-demon for a son-in-law, and, perchance, a troop of goblin grandchildren. As usual, he was completely bewildered, and all the castle in an uproar. The men were ordered to take horse, and scour every road and path and glen of the Odenwald. The baron himself had just drawn on his jack-boots, girded on his sword, and was about to mount his steed to sally forth on the doubtful quest, when he was brought to a pause by a new apparition. A lady was seen approaching the castle, mounted on a palfrey, attended by a cavalier on horseback. She galloped the gate, sprang from her horse, and falling at the baron's feet, embraced his knees. It was his lost daughter, and her companion—the Spectre Bridegroom! The baron was astounded. He looked at his daughter, then at the spectre, and almost doubted the evidence of his senses. The latter, too, was wonderfully improved in his appearance since his visit to the world of spirits. His dress was splendid, and set off a noble figure of manly symmetry. He was no longer pale and melancholy. His fine countenance was flushed with the glow of youth, and joy rioted in his large dark eye.

The mystery was soon cleared up. The cavalier (for, in truth, as you must have known all the while, he was no goblin) announced himself as Sir Herman Von Starkenfaust. He related his adventure with the young count. He told how he had hastened to the castle to deliver the unwelcome tidings, but that the eloquence of the baron had interrupted him in every attempt to tell his tale. How the sight of the bride had completely captivated him, and that to pass a few hours near her, he had tacitly suffered the mistake to continue. How he had been sorely perplexed in what way to make a decent retreat, until the baron's goblin stories had suggested his eccentric exit. How, fearing the feudal hostility of the family, he had repeated his visits by stealth—had haunted the garden beneath the young lady's window—had wooed—had won—had borne away in triumph—and, in a word, had wedded the fair.

Under any other circumstances the baron would have been inflexible, for he was tenacious of paternal authority, and devoutly obstinate in all family feuds; but he loved his daughter; he had lamented her as lost; he rejoiced to find her still alive; and, though her husband was of a hostile house, yet, thank Heaven, he was not a goblin. There was something, it must be acknowledged, that did not exactly accord with his notions of strict veracity, in the joke the knight had passed upon him of his being a dead man; but several old friends present, who had served in the wars, assured him that every stratagem was excusable in love, and that the cavalier was entitled to especial privilege, having lately served as a trooper.

Matters, therefore, were happily arranged. The baron pardoned the young couple on the spot. The revels at the castle were resumed. The poor relations overwhelmed this new member of the family with loving kindness; he was so gallant, so generous—and so rich. The aunts, it is true, were somewhat scandalized that their system of strict seclusion, and passive obedience should be so badly exemplified, but attributed it all to their negligence in not having the windows grated. One of them was particularly mortified at having her marvelous story marred, and that the only spectre she had ever seen should turn out a counterfeit; but the niece seemed perfectly happy at having found him substantial flesh and blood—and so the story ends.

Westminster Abbey

When I behold, with deep astonishment,
To famous Westminster how there resorte
Living in brasse or stoney monument,
The princes and the worthies of all sorte;
Doe not I see reformed nobilitie,
Without contempt, or pride, or ostentation,
And looke upon offenselesse majesty,
Naked of pomp or earthly domination?
And how a play-game of a painted stone
Contents the quiet now and silent sprites,
Whome all the world which late they stood upon
Could not content nor quench their appetites.
Life is a frost of cold felicitie,
And death the thaw of all our vanitie.

CHRISTOLERO'S EPIGRAMS, BY T.B. 1508

ON ONE OF THOSE SOBER AND RATHER MELANCHOLY DAYS IN THE LATTER part of Autumn, when the shadows of morning and evening almost mingle together, and throw a gloom over the decline of the year, I passed several hours in rambling about Westminster Abbey. There was something congenial to the season in the mournful magnificence of the old pile; and, as I passed its threshold, seemed like stepping back into the regions of antiquity and, losing myself among the shades of former ages.

I entered from the inner court of Westminster School, through a long, low, vaulted passage, that had an almost subterranean look, being dimly lighted in one part by circular perforations in the massive walls. Through this dark avenue I had a distant view of the cloisters, with the figure of an old verger, in his black gown, moving along their shadowy vaults, and seeming like a spectre from one of the neighboring tombs. The approach to the abbey through these gloomy monastic remains prepares the mind for its solemn contemplation. The cloisters still retain something of the quiet and seclusion of former days. The gray walls are discolored by damps, and crumbling with age; a coat of hoary moss has gathered over the inscriptions of the mural monuments, and obscured the death's heads, and other funereal emblems. The sharp touches of the chisel are gone from the rich tracery of the arches; the roses which adorned the key-stones have lost their leafy beauty; every thing bears marks of the gradual dilapidations of time, which yet has something touching and pleasing in its very decay.

The sun was pouring down a yellow autumnal ray into the square of the cloisters; beaming upon a scanty plot of grass in the centre, and lighting up an angle of the vaulted passage with a kind of dusky splendor. From between the arcades, the eye glanced up to a bit of blue sky or a passing cloud; and beheld the sun-gilt pinnacles of the abbey towering into the azure heaven.

As I paced the cloisters, sometimes contemplating this mingled picture of glory and decay, and sometimes endeavoring to decipher the inscriptions on the tombstones, which formed the pavement beneath my feet, my eye was attracted to three figures, rudely carved in relief, but nearly worn away by the footsteps of many generations. They were the effigies of three of the early abbots; the epitaphs were entirely effaced; the names alone remained, having no doubt been renewed in later times. (Vitalis. Abbas. 1082, and Gislebertus Crispinus. Abbas. 1114, and Laurentius. Abbas. 1176.) I remained some little while, musing over these casual relics of antiquity, thus left like wrecks upon this distant shore of time, telling no tale but that such beings had been and had perished; teaching no moral but the futility of that pride which hopes still to exact homage in its ashes, and to live in an inscription. A little longer, and even these faint records will be obliterated, and the monument will cease to be a memorial. Whilst I was yet looking down upon these gravestones, I was roused by the sound of the abbey clock, reverberating from buttress to buttress, and echoing among the cloisters. It is almost startling to hear this warning of departed time sounding among the tombs, and telling the lapse of the hour, which, like a billow, has rolled us onward towards the grave. I pursued my walk to an arched door opening to the interior of the abbey. On entering here, the magnitude of the building breaks fully upon the mind, contrasted with the vaults of the cloisters. The eyes gaze with wonder at clustered columns of gigantic dimensions, with arches springing from them to such an amazing height; and man wandering about their bases, shrunk into insignificance in comparison with his own handiwork. The spaciousness and gloom of this vast edifice produce a profound and mysterious awe. We step cautiously and softly about, as if fearful of disturbing the hallowed silence of the tomb; while every footfall whispers along the walls, and chatters among the sepulchres, making us more sensible of the quiet we have interrupted.

It seems as if the awful nature of the place presses down upon the soul, and hushes the beholder into noiseless reverence. We feel that we are surrounded by the congregated bones of the great men of past times, who have filled history with their deeds, and the earth with their renown.

And yet it almost provokes a smile at the vanity of human ambition, to see how they are crowded together and jostled in the dust; what parsimony is observed in doling out a scanty nook, a gloomy corner, a little portion of earth, to those, whom, when alive, kingdoms could not satisfy; and how many shapes, and forms, and artifices, are devised to catch the casual notice of the passenger, and save from forgetfulness, for a few short years, a name which once aspired to occupy ages of the world's thought and admiration.

I passed some time in Poet's Corner, which occupies an end of one of the transepts or cross aisles of the abbey. The monuments are generally simple; for the lives of literary men afford no striking themes for the sculptor. Shakspeare and Addison have statues erected to their memories; but the greater part have busts, medallions, and sometimes mere inscriptions. Notwithstanding the simplicity of these memorials, I have always observed that the visitors to the abbey remained longest about them. A kinder and fonder feeling takes place of that cold curiosity or vague admiration with which they gaze on the splendid monuments of the great and the heroic. They linger about these as about the tombs of friends and companions; for indeed there is something of companionship between the author and the reader. Other men are known to posterity only through the medium of history, which is continually growing faint and obscure: but the intercourse between the author and his fellow-men is ever new, active, and immediate. He has lived for them more than for himself; he has sacrificed surrounding enjoyments, and shut himself up from the delights of social life, that he might the more intimately commune with distant minds and distant ages. Well may the world cherish his renown; for it has been purchased, not by deeds of violence and blood, but by the diligent dispensation of pleasure. Well may posterity be grateful to his memory; for he has left it an inheritance, not of empty names and sounding actions, but whole treasures of wisdom, bright gems of thought, and golden veins of language.

From Poet's Corner I continued my stroll towards that part of the abbey which contains the sepulchres of the kings. I wandered among what once were chapels, but which are now occupied by the tombs and monuments of the great. At every turn I met with some illustrious name; or the cognizance of some powerful house renowned in history. As the eye darts into these dusky chambers of death, it catches glimpses of quaint effigies; some kneeling in niches, as if in devotion; others stretched upon the tombs, with hands piously pressed together: warriors in armor, as if reposing after battle; prelates with crosiers and mitres; and nobles in robes and coronets, lying as it were in state. In glancing over this scene, so strangely populous, yet where every form is so still and silent, it seems almost as if we were treading a mansion of that fabled city, where every being had been suddenly transmuted into stone.

I paused to contemplate a tomb on which lay the effigy of a knight in complete armor. A large buckler was on one arm, the hands were pressed together in supplication upon the breast: the face was almost covered by the morion; the legs were crossed, in token of the warrior's having been engaged in the holy war. It was the tomb of a crusader; of one of those military enthusiasts, who so strangely mingled religion and romance, and whose exploits form the connecting link between fact and fiction; between the history and the fairy tale. There is something extremely picturesque in the tombs of these adventurers, decorated as they are with rude armorial bearings and gothic sculpture. They comport with the antiquated chapels in which they are generally found; and in considering them, the imagination is apt to kindle with the legendary associations, the romantic fiction, the chivalrous pomp and pageantry, which poetry has spread over the wars for the sepulchre of Christ. They are the relics of times utterly gone by; of beings passed from recollection; of customs and manners with which ours have no affinity. They are like objects from some strange and distant land, of which we have no certain knowledge, and about which all our conceptions are vague and visionary. There is something extremely solemn and awful in those effigies on gothic tombs, extended as if in the sleep of death, or in the supplication of the dying hour. They have an effect infinitely more impressive on my feelings than the fanciful attitudes, the over-wrought conceits, and allegorical groups, which abound on modern monuments. I have been struck, also, with the superiority of many of the old sepulchral inscriptions. There was a noble way, in former times, of saying things simply, and yet saying them proudly; and I do not know an epitaph that breathes a loftier consciousness of family worth and honorable lineage, than one which affirms, of a noble house, that "all the brothers were brave, and all the sisters virtuous."

In the opposite transept to Poet's Comer stands a monument which is among the most renowned achievements of modern art; but which to me appears horrible rather than sublime. It is the tomb of Mrs. Nightingale, by Roubillac. The bottom of the monument is represented as throwing open its marble doors, and a sheeted skeleton is starting forth. The shroud is falling from his fleshless frame as he launches his dart at his victim. She is sinking into her affrighted husband's arms, who strives, with vain and frantic effort, to avert the blow. The whole is executed with terrible truth and spirit; we almost fancy we hear the gibbering yell of triumph bursting from the distended jaws of the spectre.—But why should we thus seek to clothe death with unnecessary terrors, and to spread horrors round the tomb of those we love? The grave should be surrounded by every thing that inspire tenderness and veneration for the dead; or that might win the living to virtue. It is the place, not of disgust and dismay, but of sorrow and meditation.

While wandering about these gloomy vaults and silent aisles, studying the records of the dead, the sound of busy existence from without occasionally reaches the ear;—the rumbling of the passing equipage; the murmur of the multitude; or perhaps the light laugh of pleasure. The contrast is striking with death-like repose around: and it has a strange effect upon the feelings, thus to hear the surges of active life hurrying along, and beating against the very walls of the sepulchre.

I continued in this way to move from tomb to tomb, and from chapel to chapel. The day was gradually wearing away; the distant tread of loiterers about the abbey grew less and less frequent; the sweet-tongued bell was summoning to evening prayers; and I saw at a distance the choristers, in their white surplices, crossing the aisle and entering the choir. I stood before the entrance to Henry the Seventh's chapel. A flight of steps lead up to it, through a deep and gloomy, but magnificent arch. Great gates of brass, richly and delicately wrought, turn heavily upon their hinges, as if proudly reluctant to admit the feet of common mortals into this most gorgeous of sepulchres.

On entering, the eye is astonished by the pomp of architecture, and the elaborate beauty of sculptured detail. The very walls are wrought into universal ornament, incrusted with tracery, and scooped into niches, crowded with the statues of saints and martyrs. Stone seems, by the cunning labor of the chisel, to have been robbed of its weight and density, suspended aloft, as if by magic, and the fretted roof achieved with the wonderful minuteness and airy security of a cobweb.

Along the sides of the chapel are the lofty stalls of the Knights of the Bath, richly carved of oak, though with the grotesque decorations of Gothic architecture. On the pinnacles of the stalls are affixed the helmets and crests of the knights, with their scarfs and swords; and above them are suspended their banners, emblazoned with armorial bearings, and contrasting the splendor of gold and purple and crimson, with the cold gray fretwork of the roof. In the midst of this grand mausoleum stands the sepulchre of its founder,—his effigy, with that of his queen, extended on a sumptuous tomb, and the whole surrounded by a superbly-wrought brazen railing.

There is a sad dreariness in this magnificence; this strange mixture of tombs and trophies; these emblems of living and aspiring ambition, close beside mementos which show the dust and oblivion in which all must sooner or later terminate. Nothing impresses the mind with a deeper feeling of loneliness, than to tread the silent and deserted scene of former throng and pageant. On looking round on the vacant stalls of the knights and their esquires, and on the rows of dusty but gorgeous banners that were once borne before them, my imagination conjured up the scene when this hall was bright with the valor and beauty of the land; glittering with the splendor of jeweled rank and military array; alive with the tread of many feet and the hum of an admiring multitude. All had passed away; the silence of death had settled again upon the place, interrupted only by the casual chirping of birds, which had found their way into the chapel, and built their nests among its friezes and pendants—sure signs of solitariness and desertion.

When I read the names inscribed on the banners, they were those of men scattered far and wide about the world; some tossing upon distant seas; some under arms in distant lands; some mingling in the busy intrigues of courts and cabinets; all seeking to deserve one more distinction in this mansion of shadowy honors: the melancholy reward of a monument.

Two small aisles on each side of this chapel present a touching instance of the equality of the grave; which brings down the oppressor to a level with the oppressed, and mingles the dust of the bitterest enemies together. In one is the sepulchre of the haughty Elizabeth; in the others is that of her victim, the lovely and unfortunate Mary. Not an hour in the day but some ejaculation of pity is uttered over the fate of the latter, mingled with indignation at her oppressor. The walls of Elizabeth's sepulchre continually echo with the sighs of sympathy heaved at the grave of her rival.

A peculiar melancholy reigns over the aisle where Mary lies buried. The light struggles dimly through windows darkened by dust. The greater part of the place is in deep shadow, and the walls are stained and tinted by time and weather. A marble figure of Mary is stretched upon the tomb, round which is an iron railing, much corroded, bearing her national emblem—the thistle. I was weary with wandering, and sat down to rest myself by this monument, revolving in my mind the chequered and disastrous story of poor Mary.

The sound of casual footsteps had ceased from the abbey. I could only hear, now and then, the distant voice of the priest repeating the evening service, and the faint responses of the choir; these paused for a time, and all was hushed. The stillness, the desertion and obscurity that were gradually prevailing around, gave a deeper and more solemn interest to the place:

> For in the silent grave no conversation,
> No joyful tread of friends, no voice of lovers,
> No careful father's counsel—nothing's heard,
> For nothing is, but all oblivion.
> Dust, and an endless darkness.

Suddenly the notes of the deep-laboring organ burst upon the ear, falling with doubled and redoubled intensity, and rolling, as it were, huge billows of sound. How well do their volume and grandeur accord with this mighty building! With what pomp do they swell through its vast vaults, and breathe their awful harmony through these caves of death, and make the silent sepulchre vocal!—And now they rise in triumphant acclamation, heaving higher and higher their accordant notes, and piling sound on sound.—And now they pause, and the soft voices of the choir break out into sweet gushes of melody; they soar aloft, and warble along the roof, and seem to play about these lofty vaults like the pure airs of heaven. Again the pealing organ heaves its thrilling thunders, compressing air into music, and rolling it forth upon the soul. What long-drawn cadences! What solemn sweeping concords! It grows more and more dense and powerful—it fills the vast pile, and seems to jar the very walls—the ear is stunned—the senses are overwhelmed. And now it is winding up in full jubilee—it is rising from the earth to heaven—the very soul seems rapt away and floated upwards on this swelling tide of harmony!

I sat for some time lost in that kind of reverie which a strain of music is apt sometimes to inspire: the shadows of evening were gradually thickening round me; the monuments began to cast deeper and deeper gloom; and the distant clock again gave token of the slowly waning day.

I rose and prepared to leave the abbey. As I descended the flight of steps which lead into the body of the building, my eye was caught by the shrine of Edward the Confessor, and I ascended the small staircase that conducts to it, to take from thence a general survey of this wilderness of tombs. The shrine is elevated upon a kind of platform, and close around it are the sepulchres of various kings and queens. From this eminence the eye looks down between pillars and funeral trophies to the chapels and chambers below, crowded with tombs; where warriors, prelates, courtiers, and statesmen, lie mouldering in their "beds of darkness." Close by me stood the great chair of coronation, rudely carved of oak, in the barbarous taste of a remote and gothic age. The scene seemed almost as if contrived, with theatrical artifice, to produce an effect upon the beholder. Here was a type of the beginning and the end of human pomp and power; here it was literally but a step from the throne to the sepulchre. Would not one think that these incongruous mementos had been gathered together as a lesson to living greatness?—to show it, even in the moment of its proudest exaltation, the neglect and dishonor to which it must soon arrive; how soon that crown which encircles its brow must pass away, and it must lie down in the dust and disgraces of the tomb, and be trampled upon by the feet of the meanest of the multitude. For, strange to tell, even the grave is here no longer a sanctuary. There is a shocking levity in some natures, which leads them to sport with awful and hallowed things; and there are base minds, which delight to revenge on the illustrious dead the abject homage and groveling servility which they pay to the living. The coffin of Edward the Confessor has been broken open, and his remains despoiled of their funereal ornaments; the sceptre has been stolen from the hand of the imperious Elizabeth, and the effigy of Henry the Fifth lies headless. Not a royal monument but bears some proof how false and fugitive is the homage of mankind. Some are plundered; some mutilated; some covered with ribaldry and insult—all more or less outraged and dishonored!

The last beams of day were now faintly streaming through the painted windows in the high vaults above me; the lower parts of the abbey were already wrapped in the obscurity of twilight. The chapels and aisles grew darker and darker. The effigies of the kings faded into shadows; the marble figures of the monuments assumed strange shapes in the uncertain light; the evening breeze crept through the aisles like the cold breath of the grave; and even the distant footfall of a verger, traversing the Poet's Corner, had something strange and dreary in its sound. I slowly retraced my morning's walk, and as I passed out at the portal of the cloisters, the door, closing with a jarring noise behind me, filled the whole building with echoes.

I endeavored to form some arrangement in my mind of the objects I had been contemplating, but found they were already fallen into indistinctness and confusion. Names, inscriptions, trophies, had all become confounded in my recollection, though I had scarcely taken my foot from off the threshold. What, thought I, is this vast assemblage of sepulchres but a treasury of humiliation; a huge pile of reiterated homilies on the emptiness of renown, and the certainly of oblivion! It is, indeed, the empire of death; his great shadowy palace, where he sits in state, mocking at the relics of human glory, and spreading dust and forgetfulness on the monuments of princes. How idle a boast, after all, is the immortality of a name! Time is ever silently turning over his pages; we are too much engrossed by the story of the present, to think of the characters and anecdotes that gave interest to the past; and each age is a volume thrown aside to be speedily forgotten. The idol of to-day pushes the hero of yesterday out of our recollection; and will, in turn, be supplanted by his successor of to-morrow. "Our fathers," says Sir Thomas Brown, "find their graves in our short memories, and sadly tell us how we may be buried in our survivors." History fades into fable; fact becomes clouded with doubt and controversy; the inscription moulders from the tablet; the statue falls from the pedestal. Columns, arches, pyramids, what are they but heaps of sand; and their epitaphs, but characters written in the dust? What is the security of a tomb, or the perpetuity of an embalmment? The remains of Alexander the Great have been scattered to the wind, and his empty sarcophagus is now the mere curiosity of a museum. "The Egyptian mummies, which Cambyses or time hath spared, avarice now consumeth; Mizraim cures wounds, and Pharaoh is sold for balsams."[1]

What then is to insure this pile which now towers above me from sharing the fate of mightier mausoleums? The time must come when its gilded vaults, which now

1. Sir T. Brown.

spring so loftily, shall lie in rubbish beneath the feet; when, instead of the sound of melody and praise, the wind shall whistle through the broken arches, and the owl hoot from the shattered tower—when the garish sunbeam shall break into these gloomy mansions of death, and the ivy twine round the fallen column; and the fox-glove hang its blossoms about the nameless urn, as if in mockery of the dead. Thus man passes away; his name perishes from record and recollection; his history is as a tale that is told, and his very monument becomes a ruin.

NOTES CONCERNING WESTMINSTER ABBEY

Toward the end of the sixth century, when Britain, under the dominion of the Saxons, was in a state of barbarism and idolatry, Pope Gregory the Great, struck with the beauty of some Anglo-Saxon youths exposed for sale in the market-place at Rome, conceived a fancy for the race, and determined to send missionaries to preach the gospel among these comely but benighted islanders. He was encouraged to this by learning that Ethelbert, king of Kent, and the most potent of the Anglo-Saxon princes, had married Bertha, a Christian princess, only daughter of the king of Paris, and that she was allowed by stipulation the full exercise of her religion.

The shrewd pontiff knew the influence of the sex in matters of religious faith. He forthwith dispatched Augustine, a Roman monk, with forty associates, to the court of Ethelbert at Canterbury, to effect the conversion of the king and to obtain through him a foothold in the island.

Ethelbert received them warily, and held a conference in the open air; being distrustful of foreign priestcraft, and fearful of spells and magic. They ultimately succeeded in making him as good a Christian as his wife; the conversion of the king of course produced the conversion of his loyal subjects. The zeal and success of Augustine were rewarded by his being made archbishop of Canterbury, and being endowed with authority over all the British churches.

One of the most prominent converts was Segebert or Sebert, king of the East Saxons, a nephew of Ethelbert. He reigned at London, of which Mellitus, one of the Roman monks who had come over with Augustine was made bishop.

Sebert, in 605, in his religious zeal, founded a monastery by the river side to the west of the city, on the ruins of a temple of Apollo, being, in fact, the origin of the present pile of Westminster Abbey. Great preparations were made for the consecration of the church, which was to be dedicated to St. Peter. On the morning of the appointed day, Mellitus, the bishop, proceeded with great pomp and solemnity to perform the ceremony. On approaching the edifice he was met by a fisherman, who informed him that it was needless to proceed, as the ceremony was over. The bishop stared with surprise, when the fisherman went on to relate, that the night before, as he was in his boat on the Thames, St. Peter appeared to him, and told him that he intended to consecrate the church himself, that very night. The apostle accordingly went into the church, which suddenly became illuminated. The ceremony was performed in sumptuous style, accompanied by strains of heavenly music and clouds of fragrant incense. After this, the apostle came into the boat and ordered the fisherman to cast his net. He did so, and had a miraculous draught of fishes; one of which he was commanded to present to the bishop, and to signify to him that the apostle had relieved him from the necessity of consecrating the church.

Mellitus was a wary man, slow of belief, and required confirmation of the fisherman's tale. He opened the church doors, and beheld wax candles, crosses, holy water; oil sprinkled in various places, and various other traces of a grand ceremonial. If he had still any lingering doubts, they were completely removed on the fisherman's producing the identical fish which he had been ordered by the apostle to present to him. To resist this would have been to resist ocular demonstration. The good bishop accordingly was convinced that the church had actually been consecrated by St. Peter in person; so he reverently abstained from proceeding further in the business.

The foregoing tradition is said to be the reason why King Edward the Confessor chose this place as the site of a religious house which he meant to endow. He pulled down the old church and built another in its place in 1045. In this his remains were deposited in a magnificent shrine.

The sacred edifice again underwent modifications, if not a reconstruction, by Henry III, in 1220, and began to assume its present appearance.

Under Henry VIII it lost its conventional character, that monarch turning the monks away, and seizing upon the revenues.

RELICS OF EDWARD THE CONFESSOR

A curious narrative was printed in 1668, by one of the choristers of the cathedral, who appears to have been the Paul Pry of the sacred edifice, giving an account of his rummaging among the bones of Edward the Confessor, after they had quietly reposed in their sepulchre upwards of six hundred years, and of his drawing forth the crucifix and golden chain of the deceased monarch. During eighteen years that he had officiated in the choir, it had been a common tradition, he says, among his brother choristers and the gray-headed servants of the abbey, that the body of King Edward was deposited in a kind of chest or coffin, which was indistinctly seen in the upper part of the shrine erected to his memory. None of the abbey gossips, however, had ventured upon a nearer inspection, until the worthy narrator, to gratify his curiosity, mounted to the coffin by the aid of a ladder, and found it to be made of wood, apparently very strong and firm, being secured by bands of iron.

Subsequently, in 1685, on taking down the scaffolding used in the coronation of James II, the coffin was found to be broken, a hole appearing in the lid, probably made, through accident, by the workmen. No one ventured, however, to meddle with the sacred depository of royal dust, until, several weeks afterwards, the circumstance came to the knowledge of the aforesaid chorister. He forthwith repaired to the abbey in company with two friends, of congenial tastes, who were desirous of inspecting the tombs. Procuring a ladder, he again mounted to the coffin, and found, as had been represented, a hole in the lid about six inches long and four inches broad, just in front of the left breast. Thrusting in his hand, and groping among the bones, he drew from underneath the shoulder a crucifix, richly adorned and enameled, affixed to a gold chain twenty-four inches long. These he showed to his inquisitive friends, who were equally surprised with himself.

"At the time," says he, "when I took the cross and chain out of the coffin, *I drew the head to the hole and viewed it,* being very sound and firm, with the upper and nether jaws whole and full of teeth, and a list of gold above an inch broad, in the nature of a coronet, surrounding the temples. There was also in the coffin, white linen and gold-colored flowered silk, that looked indifferent fresh; but the least stress put thereto showed it was well nigh perished. There were all his bones, and much dust likewise, which I left as I found."

It is difficult to conceive a more grotesque lesson to human pride than the skull of Edward the Confessor thus irreverently pulled about in its coffin by a prying chorister, and brought to grin face to face with him through a hole in the lid!

Having satisfied his curiosity, the chorister put the crucifix and chain back again into the coffin, and sought the dean, to apprise him of his discovery. The dean not being accessible at the time, and fearing that the "holy treasure" might be taken away by other hands, he got a brother chorister to accompany him to the shrine about two or three hours afterwards, and in his presence again drew forth the relics. These he afterwards delivered on his knees to King James. The king subsequently had the old coffin inclosed in a new one of great strength: "each plank being two inches thick and cramped together with large iron wedges, where it now remains (1688) as a testimony of his pious care, that no abuse might be offered to the sacred ashes therein reposited."

As the history of this shrine is full of moral, I subjoin a description of it in modern times. "The solitary and forlorn shrine," says a British writer, "now stands a mere skeleton of what it was. A few faint traces of its sparkling decorations inlaid on solid mortar catches the rays of the sun, for ever set on its splendor. . . . Only two of the spiral pillars remain. The wooden Ionic top is much broken, and covered with dust. The mosaic is picked away in every part within reach; only the lozenges of about a foot square and five circular pieces of the rich marble remain."—*Malcolm, Lond. rediv.*

INSCRIPTION ON A MONUMENT ALLUDED TO IN THE SKETCH

Here lyes the Loyal Duke of Newcastle, and his Dutchess his second wife, by whom he had no issue. Her name was Margaret Lucas, youngest sister to the Lord Lucas of Colchester, a noble family; for all the brothers were valiant, and all the sisters virtuous. This Dutchess was a wise, witty, and learned lady, which her many Bookes do well testify: she was a most virtuous, and loving and careful wife, and was with her lord all the time of his banishment and miseries, and when he came home, never parted from him in his solitary retirements.

* * *

In the winter time, when the days are short, the service in the afternoon is performed by the light of tapers. The effect is fine of the choir partially lighted op, while the main body of the cathedral and the transepts are in profound and cavernous darkness. The white dresses of the choristers gleam amidst the deep brown of the oaken slats and canopies; the partial illumination makes enormous shadows from columns and screens, and darting into the surrounding gloom, catches here and there upon a sepulchral decoration, or monumental effigy. The swelling notes of the organ accord well with the scene.

When the service is over the dean is lighted to his dwelling, in the old conventual part of the pile, by the boys of the choir, in their white dresses, bearing tapers, and the procession passes through the abbey and along the shadowy cloisters, lighting up angles and arches and grim sepulchral monuments, and leaving all behind in darkness.

* * *

On entering the cloisters at night from what is called the Dean's Yard, the eye ranging through a dark vaulted passage catches a distant view of a white marble figure reclining on a tomb, on which a strong glare thrown by a gas light has quite a spectral effect. It is a mural monument of one of the Pultneys.

The cloisters are well worth visiting by moonlight, when the moon is in the full.

Christmas

But is old, old, good old Christmas gone? Nothing but the hair of his good, gray, old head and beard left? Well, I will have that, seeing I cannot have more of him.

Hue and Cry after Christmas

A man might then behold
At Christmas, in each hall
Good fires to curb the cold,
And meat for great and small.
The neighbors were friendly bidden,
And all had welcome true.
The poor from the gates were not chidden,
When this old cap was new.

Old Song

Nothing in England exercises a more delightful spell over my imagination, than the lingerings of the holiday customs and rural games of former times. They recall the pictures my fancy used to draw in the May morning of life, when as yet I only knew the world through books, and believed it to be all that poets had painted it; and they bring with them the flavor of those honest days of yore, in which, perhaps, with equal fallacy, I am apt to think the world was more homebred, social, and joyous than at present. I regret to say that they are daily growing more and more faint, being gradually worn away by time, but still more obliterated by modern fashion. They resemble those picturesque morsels of gothic architecture, which we see crumbling in various parts of the country, partly dilapidated by the waste of ages, and partly lost in the additions and alterations of latter days. Poetry, however, clings with cherishing fondness about the rural game and holiday revel, from which it has derived so many of its themes—as the ivy winds its rich foliage about the gothic arch and mouldering tower, gratefully repaying their support, by clasping together their tottering remains, and, as it were, embalming them in verdure.

Of all the old festivals, however, that of Christmas awakens the strongest and most heartfelt associations. There is a tone of solemn and sacred feeling that blends with our conviviality, and lifts the spirit to a state of hallowed and elevated enjoyment. The services of the church about this season are extremely tender and inspiring. They dwell on the beautiful story of the origin of our faith, and the pastoral scenes that accompanied its announcement. They gradually increase in fervor and pathos during the season of Advent, until they break forth in full jubilee on the morning that brought peace and good-will to men. I do not know a grander effect of music on the moral feelings, than to hear the full choir and the pealing organ performing a Christmas anthem in a cathedral, and filling every part of the vast pile with triumphant harmony.

It is a beautiful arrangement, also, derived from days of yore, that this festival, which commemorates the announcement of the religion of peace and love, has been made the season for gathering together of family connections, and drawing closer again those bands of kindred hearts, which the cares and pleasures and sorrows of the world are continually operating to cast loose; of calling back the children of a family, who have launched forth in life, and wandered widely asunder, once more to assemble about the paternal hearth, that rallying place of the affections, there to grow young and loving again among the endearing mementos of childhood.

There is something in the very season of the year that gives a charm to the festivity of Christmas. At other times we derive a great portion of our pleasures from the mere beauties of nature. Our feelings sally forth and dissipate themselves over the sunny landscape, and we "live abroad and every where." The song of the bird, the murmur of the stream, the breathing fragrance of spring, the soft voluptuousness of summer, the golden pomp of autumn; earth with its mantle of refreshing green, and heaven with its deep delicious blue and its cloudy magnificence, all fill us with mute but exquisite delight, and we revel in the luxury of mere sensation. But in the depth of winter, when nature lies despoiled of every charm, and wrapped in her shroud of sheeted snow, we turn for our gratifications to moral sources. The dreariness and desolation of the landscape, the short gloomy days and darksome nights, while they circumscribe our wanderings, shut in our feelings also from rambling abroad, and make us more keenly disposed for the pleasure of the social circle. Our thoughts are more concentrated; our friendly sympathies more aroused. We feel more sensibly the charm of each other's society, and are brought more closely together by dependence on each other for enjoyment. Heart calleth unto heart; and we draw our pleasures from the deep wells of loving-kindness, which lie in the quiet recesses of our bosoms; and which, when resorted to, furnish forth the pure element of domestic felicity.

The pitchy gloom without makes the heart dilate on entering the room filled with the glow and warmth of the evening fire. The ruddy blaze diffuses an artificial summer and sunshine through the room, and lights up each countenance in a kindlier welcome. Where does the honest face of hospitality expand into a broader and more cordial smile—where is the shy glance of love more sweetly eloquent—than by the winter fireside? and as the hollow blast of wintry wind rushes through the hall, claps the distant door, whistles about the casement, and rumbles down the chimney, what can be more grateful than that feeling of sober and sheltered security, with which we look round upon the comfortable chamber and the scene of domestic hilarity?

The English, from the great prevalence of rural habit throughout every class of society, have always been fond of those festivals and holidays which agreeably interrupt the stillness of country life; and they were, in former days, particularly observant of the religious and social rites of Christmas. It is inspiring to read even the dry details which some antiquaries have given of the quaint humors, the burlesque pageants, the complete abandonment to mirth and good-fellowship, with which this festival was celebrated. It seemed to throw open every door, and unlock every heart. It brought the peasant and the peer together, and blended all ranks in one warm generous flow of joy and kindness. The old halls of castles and manor-houses resounded with the harp and the Christmas carol, and their ample boards groaned under the weight of hospitality. Even the poorest cottage welcomed the festive season with green decorations of bay and holly—the cheerful fire glanced its rays through the lattice, inviting the passengers to raise the latch, and join the gossip knot huddled round the hearth, beguiling the long evening with legendary jokes and oft-told Christmas tales.

One of the least pleasing effects of modern refinement is the havoc it has made among the hearty old holiday customs. It has completely taken off the sharp touchings and spirited reliefs of these embellishments of life, and has worn down society into a more smooth and polished, but certainly a less characteristic surface. Many of the games and ceremonials of Christmas have entirely disappeared, and, like the sherris sack of old Falstaff, are become matters of speculation and dispute among commentators. They flourished in times full of spirit and lustihood, when men enjoyed life roughly, but heartily and vigorously; times wild and picturesque, which have furnished poetry with its richest materials, and the drama with its most attractive variety of characters and manners. The world has become more worldly. There is more of dissipation, and less of enjoyment. Pleasure has expanded into a broader, but a shallower stream; and has forsaken many of those deep and quiet channels where it flowed sweetly through the calm bosom of domestic life. Society has acquired a more enlightened and elegant tone; but it has lost many of its strong local peculiarities, its home-bred feelings, its honest fireside delights. The traditionary customs of golden-hearted antiquity, its feudal hospitalities, and lordly wassailings, have passed away with the baronial castles and stately manor-houses in which they were celebrated. They comported with the shadowy hall, the great oaken gallery, and the tapestried parlor, but are unfitted to the light showy saloons and gay drawing-rooms of the modern villa.

Shorn, however, as it is, of its ancient and festive honors, Christmas is still a period of delightful excitement in England. It is gratifying to see that home feeling completely aroused which holds so powerful a place in every English bosom. The preparations making on every side for the social board that is again to unite friends and kindred; the presents of good cheer passing and repassing, those tokens of regard, and quickeners of kind feelings; the evergreens distributed about houses and churches, emblems of peace and gladness; all these have the most pleasing effect in producing fond associations, and kindling benevolent sympathies. Even the sound of the Waits, rude as may be their minstrelsy, breaks upon the mid-watches of a winter night with the effect of perfect harmony. As I have been awakened by them in that still and solemn hour, "when deep sleep falleth upon man," I have listened with a hushed delight, and, connecting them with the sacred and joyous occasion, have almost fancied them into another celestial choir, announcing peace and good-will to mankind.

How delightfully the imagination, when wrought upon by these moral influences, turns every thing to melody and beauty! The very crowing of the cock, heard sometimes in the profound repose of the country, "telling the night watches to his feathery dames," was thought by the common people to announce the approach of this sacred festival:

Some say that ever 'gainst that season comes
Wherein our Saviour's birth is celebrated,
This bird of dawning singeth all night long;
And then, they say, no spirit dares stir abroad;
The nights are wholesome—then no planets strike.
No fairy takes, no witch hath power to charm,
So hallow'd and so gracious is the time.

Amidst the general call to happiness, the bustle of the spirits, and stir of the affections, which prevail at this period, what bosom can remain insensible? It is, indeed, the season of regenerated feeling—the season for kindling, not merely the fire of hospitality in the hall, but the genial flame of charity in the heart.

The scene of early love again rises green to memory beyond the sterile waste of years; and the idea of home, fraught with the fragrance of home-dwelling joys, reanimates the drooping spirit; as the Arabian breeze will sometimes waft the freshness of the distant fields to the weary pilgrim of the desert.

Stranger and sojourner as I am in the land—though for me no social hearth may blaze, no hospitable roof throw open its doors, nor the warm grasp of friendship welcome me at the threshold—yet I feel the influence of the season beaming into my soul from the happy looks of those around me. Surely happiness is reflective, like the light of heaven; and every countenance, bright with smiles, and glowing with innocent enjoyment, is a mirror transmitting to others the rays of a supreme and ever-shining benevolence. He who can turn churlishly away from contemplating the felicity of his fellow beings, and can sit down darkling and repining in his loneliness when all around is joyful, may have his moments of strong excitement and selfish gratification, but he wants the genial and social sympathies which constitute the charm of a merry Christmas.

The Stage Coach

Omne bené
Sine pœnâ
Tempus est ludendi.
Venit hora
Abeque morâ
Libros deponendi.
OLD HOLIDAY SCHOOL SONG

IN THE PRECEDING PAPER I HAVE MADE SOME GENERAL OBSERVATIONS ON the Christmas festivities of England, and am tempted to illustrate them by some anecdotes of a Christmas passed in the country; in perusing which I would most courteously invite my reader to lay aside the austerity of wisdom, and to put on that genuine holiday spirit which is tolerant of folly, and anxious only for amusement.

In the course of a December tour in Yorkshire, I rode for a long distance in one of the public coaches, on the day preceding Christmas. The coach was crowded, both inside and out, with passengers, who, by their talk, seemed principally bound to the mansions of relations or friends, to eat the Christmas dinner. It was loaded also with hampers of game, and baskets and boxes of delicacies; and hares hung dangling their long ears about the coachman's box, presents from distant friends for the impending feast. I had three fine rosy-cheeked school-boys for my fellow passengers inside, full of the buxom health and manly spirit which I have observed in the children of this country. They were returning home for the holidays in high glee, and promising themselves a world of enjoyment. It was delightful to hear the gigantic plans of the little rogues, and the impracticable feats they were to perform during their six weeks' emancipation from the abhorred thraldom of book, birch, and pedagogue. They were full of anticipations of the meeting with the family and household, down to the very cat and dog; and of the joy they were to give their little sisters by the presents with which their pockets were crammed; but the meeting to which they seemed to look forward with the greatest impatience was with Bantam, which I found to be a pony, and, according to their talk, possessed of more virtues than any steed since the days of Bucephalus. How he could trot! how he could run! and then such leaps as he would take—there was not a hedge in the whole country that he could not clear.

They were under the particular guardianship of the coachman, to whom, whenever an opportunity presented, they addressed a host of questions, and pronounced him one of the best fellows in the world. Indeed, I could not but notice the more than ordinary air of bustle and importance of the coachman, who wore his hat a little on one side, and had a large bunch of Christmas greens stuck in the button-hole of his coat. He is always a personage full of mighty care and business, but he is particularly so during this season, having so many commissions to execute in consequence of the great interchange of presents. And here, perhaps, it may not be unacceptable to my untraveled readers, to have a sketch that may serve as a general representation of this very numerous and important class of functionaries, who have a dress, a manner, a language, an air, peculiar to themselves, and prevalent throughout the fraternity; so that, wherever an English stage-coachman may be seen, he cannot be mistaken for one of any other craft or mystery.

He has commonly a broad, full face, curiously mottled with red, as if the blood had been forced by hard feeding into every vessel of the skin; he is swelled into jolly dimensions by frequent potations of malt liquors, and his bulk is still further increased by a multiplicity of coats, in which he is buried like a cauliflower, the upper one reaching to his heels. He wears a broad-brimmed, low-crowned hat; a huge roll of colored handkerchief about his neck, knowingly knotted and tucked in at the bosom; and has in summer time a large bouquet of flowers in his button-hole; the present, most probably, of some enamored country lass. His waistcoat is commonly of some bright color, striped, and his smallclothes extend far below the knees, to meet a pair of jockey boots which reach about half way up his legs.

All this costume is maintained with much precision; he has a pride in having his clothes of excellent materials; and, notwithstanding the seeming grossness of his appearance, there is still discernible that neatness and propriety of person, which is almost inherent in an Englishman. He enjoys great consequence and consideration along the road; has frequent conferences with the village housewives, who look upon him as a man of great trust and dependence; and he seems to have a good understanding with every bright-eyed country lass. The moment he arrives where the horses are to be changed, he throws down the reins with something of an air, and abandons the cattle to the care of the ostler; his duty being merely to drive from one stage to another. When off the box, his hands are thrust into the pockets of his great coat, and he rolls about the inn yard with an air of the most absolute lordliness. Here he is generally surrounded by an admiring throng of ostlers, stable-boys, shoeblacks, and those nameless hangers-on, that infest inns and taverns, and run errands, and do all kind of odd jobs, for the privilege of battening on the drippings of the kitchen and the leakage of the taproom. These all look up to him as to an oracle; treasure up his cant phrases; echo his opinions about horses and other topics of jockey lore; and above all, endeavor to imitate his air and carriage. Every ragamuffin that has a coat to his back, thrusts his hands in the pockets, rolls in his gait, talks slang, and is an embryo Coachey.

Perhaps it might be owing to the pleasing serenity that reigned in my own mind, that I fancied I saw cheerfulness in every countenance throughout the journey. A stage coach, however, carries animation always with it, and puts the world in motion as it whirls along. The horn, sounded at the entrance of a village, produces a general bustle. Some hasten forth to meet friends; some with bundles and bandboxes to secure places, and in the hurry of the moment can hardly take leave of the group that accompanies them. In the meantime, the coachman has a world of small commissions to execute. Sometimes he delivers a hare or pheasant; sometimes jerks a small parcel or newspaper to the door of a public house; and sometimes, with knowing leer and words of sly import, hands to some half-blushing, half-laughing housemaid an odd-shaped billet-doux from some rustic admirer. As the coach rattles through the village, every one runs to the window, and you have glances on every side of fresh country faces and blooming giggling girls. At the corners are assembled juntos of village idlers and wise men, who take their stations there for the important purpose of seeing company pass; but the sagest knot is generally at the blacksmith's, to whom the passing of the coach is an event fruitful of much speculation. The smith, with the horse's heel in his lap, pauses as the vehicle whirls by; the cyclops round the anvil suspend their ringing hammers, and suffer the iron to grow cool; and the sooty spectre, in brown paper cap, laboring at the bellows, leans on the handle for a moment, and permits the asthmatic engine to heave a long-drawn sigh, while he glares through the murky smoke and sulphureous gleams of the smithy.

Perhaps the impending holiday might have given a more than usual animation to the country, for it seemed to me as if every body was in good looks and good spirits. Game, poultry, and other luxuries of the table, were in brisk circulation in the villages; the grocers', butchers' and fruiterers' shops were thronged with customers. The housewives were stirring briskly about, putting their dwellings in order; and the glossy branches of holly with their bright-red berries, began to appear at the windows. The scene brought to mind an old writer's account of Christmas preparations:—"Now capons and hens, besides turkeys, geese, and ducks, with beef and mutton—must all die—for in twelve days a multitude of people will not be fed with a little. Now plums and spice, sugar and honey, square it among pies and broth. Now or never must music be in tune, for the youth must dance and sing to get them a heat, while the aged sit by the fire. The country maid leaves half her market, and must be sent again, if she forgets a pack of cards on Christmas eve. Great is the contention of holly and ivy, whether master or dame wears the breeches. Dice and cards benefit the butler; and if the cook do not lack wit, he will sweetly lick his fingers."

I was roused from this fit of luxurious meditation, by a shout from my little traveling companions. They had been looking out of the coach windows for the last few miles, recognizing every tree and cottage as they approached home, and now there was a general burst of joy—"There's John! and there's old Carlo! and there's Bantam!" cried the happy little rogues, clapping their hands.

At the end of a lane there was an old sober looking servant in livery, waiting for them; he was accompanied by a superannuated pointer, and by the redoubtable Bantam, a little old rat of a pony, with a shaggy mane and long rusty tail, who stood dozing quietly by the road-side, little dreaming of the bustling times that awaited him.

I was pleased to see the fondness with which the little fellows leaped about the steady old footman, and hugged the pointer; who wriggled his whole body for joy. But Bantam was the great object of interest; all wanted to mount at once, and it was with some difficulty that John arranged that they should ride by turns, and the eldest should ride first.

Off they set at last; one on the pony, with the dog bounding and barking before him, and the others holding John's hands; both talking at once, and overpowering him with questions about home, and with school anecdotes. I looked after them with a feeling in which I do not know whether pleasure or melancholy predominated; for I was reminded of those days when, like them, I had neither known care nor sorrow, and a holiday was the summit of earthly felicity. We stopped a few moments afterwards to water the horses, and on resuming our route, a turn of the road brought us in sight of a neat country seat. I could just distinguish the forms of a lady and two young girls in the portico, and I saw my little comrades, with Bantam, Carlo, and old John, trooping along the carriage road. I leaned out of the coach window, in hopes of witnessing the happy meeting, but a grove of trees shut it from my sight.

In the evening we reached a village where I had determined to pass the night. As we drove into the great gateway of the inn, I saw on one side the light of a rousing kitchen fire beaming through a window. I entered, and admired, for the hundredth time, that picture of convenience, neatness, and broad honest enjoyment, the kitchen of an English inn. It was of spacious dimensions, hung round with copper and tin vessels highly polished, and decorated here and there with a Christmas green. Hams, tongues, and flitches of bacon, were suspended from the ceiling; a smoke-jack made its ceaseless clanking beside the fireplace, and a clock ticked in one comer. A well-scoured deal table extended along one side of the kitchen, with a cold round of beef, and other hearty viands, upon it, over which two foaming tankards of ale seemed mounting guard. Travelers of inferior order were preparing to attack this stout repast, while others sat smoking and gossiping over their ale on two high-backed oaken settles beside the fire. Trim housemaids were hurrying backwards and forwards under the directions of a fresh bustling landlady; but still seizing an occasional moment to exchange a flippant word, and have a rallying laugh, with the group round the fire. The scene completely realized Poor Robin's humble idea of the comforts of mid-winter:

> Now trees their leafy hats do bare
> To reverence Winter's silvery hair;
> A handsome hostess, merry host,
> A pot of ale now and a toast,
> Tobacco and a good coal fire,
> Are things this season doth require.[1]

I had not been long at the inn when a post-chaise drove up to the door. A young gentleman stept out, and by the light of the lamps I caught a glimpse of a countenance

---

1. Poor Robin's Almanac, 1684.

which I thought I knew. I moved forward to get a nearer view, when his eye caught mine. I was not mistaken; it was Frank Bracebridge, a sprightly good-humored young fellow, with whom I had once traveled on the continent. Our meeting was extremely cordial, for the countenance of an old fellow-traveler always brings up the recollection of a thousand pleasant scenes, odd adventures, and excellent jokes. To discuss all these in a transient interview at an inn was impossible; and finding that I was not pressed for time, and was merely making a tour of observation, he insisted that I should give him a day or two at his father's country seat, to which he was going to pass the holidays, and which lay at a few miles distance. "It is better than eating a solitary Christmas dinner at an inn," said he, "and I can assure you of a hearty welcome in something of the old-fashioned style." His reasoning was cogent, and I must confess the preparation I had seen for universal festivity and social enjoyment had made me feel a little impatient of my loneliness. I closed, therefore, at once, with his invitation; the chaise drove up to the door, and in a few moments I was on my way to the family mansion of the Bracebridges.

Christmas Eve

Saint Francis and Saint Benedight
Bless this house from wicked wight;
From the night-mare and the goblin,
That is hight good fellow Robin;
Keep it from all evil spirits,
Fairies, weasels, rats, and ferrets:
From curfew time
To the next prime
CARTWRIGHT

IT WAS A BRILLIANT MOONLIGHT NIGHT, BUT EXTREMELY COLD; OUR CHAISE whirled rapidly over the frozen ground; the postboy smacked his whip incessantly, and a part of the time his horses were on a gallop. "He knows where he is going," said my companion, laughing, "and is eager to arrive in time for some of the merriment and good cheer of the servants' hall. My father, you must know, is a bigoted devotee of the old school, and prides himself upon keeping up something of old English hospitality. He is a tolerable specimen of what you will rarely meet with now-a-days in its purity, the old English country gentleman; for our men of fortune spend so much of their time in town, and fashion is carried so much into the country, that the strong rich peculiarities of ancient rural life are almost polished away. My father, however, from early years, took honest Peacham[1] for his text-book, instead of Chesterfield; he determined in his own mind, that there was no condition more

1. Peacham's Complete Gentleman, 1622.

truly honorable and enviable than that of a country gentleman on his paternal lands, and therefore passes the whole of his time on his estate. He is a strenuous advocate for the revival of the old rural games and holiday observances, and is deeply read in the writers, ancient and modern, who have treated on the subject. Indeed, his favorite range of reading is among the authors who flourished at least two centuries since; who, he insists, wrote and thought more like true Englishmen than any of their successors. He even regrets sometimes that he had not been born a few centuries earlier, when England was itself, and had its peculiar manners and customs. As he lives at some distance from the main road, in rather a lonely part of the country, without any rival gentry near him, he has that most enviable of all blessings to an Englishman, an opportunity of indulging the bent of his own humor without molestation. Being representative of the oldest family in the neighborhood, and a great part of the peasantry being his tenants, he is much looked up to, and, in general, is known simply by the appellation of 'The Squire'; a title which has been accorded to the head of the family since time immemorial. I think it best to give you these hints about my worthy old father, to prepare you for any eccentricities that might otherwise appear absurd."

We had passed for some time along the wall of a park, and at length the chaise stopped at the gate. It was in a heavy magnificent old style, of iron bars, fancifully wrought at top into flourishes and flowers. The huge square columns that supported the gate were surmounted by the family crest. Close adjoining was the porter's lodge, sheltered under dark fir-trees, and almost buried in shrubbery.

The postboy rang a large porter's belly which resounded through the still frosty air, and was answered by the distant barking of dogs, with which the mansion-house seemed garrisoned. An old woman immediately appeared at the gate. As the moonlight fell strongly upon her, I had a full view of a little primitive dame, dressed very much in the antique taste, with a neat kerchief and stomacher, and her silver hair peeping from under a cap of snowy whiteness. She came curtseying forth, with many expressions of simple joy at seeing her young master. Her husband, it seemed, was up at the house keeping Christmas eve in the servants' hall; they could not do without him, as he was the best hand at a song and story in the household.

My friend proposed that we should alight and walk through the park to the hall, which was at no great distance, while the chaise should follow on. Our road wound through a noble avenue of trees, among the naked branches of which the moon glittered as she rolled through the deep vault of a cloudless sky. The lawn beyond was sheeted with a slight covering of snow, which here and there sparkled as the moonbeams caught a frosty crystal; and at a distance might be seen a thin transparent vapor, stealing up from the low grounds and threatening gradually to shroud the landscape.

My companion looked around him with transport:—"How often," said he, "have I scampered up this avenue, on returning home on school vacations! How often have I played under these trees when a boy! I feel a degree of filial reverence for them, as we look up to those who have cherished us in childhood. My father was always scrupulous in exacting our holidays, and having us around him on family festivals. He used to direct and superintend our games with the strictness that some parents do the studies of their children. He was very particular that we should play the old English games according to their original form; and consulted old books for precedent and authority for every 'merrie disport'; yet I assure you there never was pedantry so delightful. It was the policy of the good old gentleman to make his children feel that home was the happiest place in the world; and I value this delicious home-feeling as one of the choicest gifts a parent could bestow."

We were interrupted by the clamor of a troop of dogs of all sorts and sizes, "mongrel, puppy, whelp and hound, and curs of low degree," that, disturbed by the ring of the porter's bell and the rattling of the chaise, came bounding, open-mouthed, across the lawn.

—The little dogs and all,
Tray, Blanch, and Sweetheart, see, they bark at me!

cried Bracebridge, laughing. At the sound of his voice, the bark was changed into a yelp of delight, and in a moment he was surrounded and almost overpowered by the caresses of the faithful animals.

We had now come in full view of the old family mansion, partly thrown in deep shadow, and partly lit up by the cold moonshine. It was an irregular building, of some magnitude, and seemed to be of the architecture of different periods. One wing was evidently very ancient, with heavy stone-shafted bow windows jutting out and overrun with ivy, from among the foliage of which the small diamond-shaped panes of glass glittered with the moonbeams. The rest of the house was in the French taste of Charles the Second's time, having been repaired and altered, as my friend told me, by one of his ancestors, who returned with that monarch at the Restoration. The grounds about the house were laid out in the old formal manner of artificial flower-beds, clipped shrubberies, raised terraces, and heavy stone balustrades, ornamented with urns, a leaden statue or two, and a jet of water. The old gentleman, I was told, was extremely careful to preserve this obsolete finery in all its original state. He admired this fashion in gardening; it had an air of magnificence, was courtly and noble, and befitting good old family style. The boasted imitation of nature in modern gardening had sprung up with modern republican notions, but did not suit a monarchical government; it smacked of the leveling system.—I could not help smiling at this introduction of politics into gardening, though I expressed some apprehension that I should find the old gentleman rather intolerant in his creed.—Frank assured me, however, that it was almost the only instance in which he had ever heard his father meddle with politics; and he believed that he had got this notion from a member of parliament who once passed a few weeks with him. The squire was glad of any argument to defend his clipped yew-trees and formal terraces, which had been occasionally attacked by modern landscape gardeners.

As we approached the house, we heard the sound of music, and now and then a burst of laughter, from one end of the building. This, Bracebridge said, must proceed from the servants' hall, where a great deal of revelry was permitted, and even encouraged, by the squire, throughout the twelve days of Christmas, provided every thing was done conformably to ancient usage. Here were kept up the old games of hoodman blind, shoe the wild mare, hot cockles, steal the white loaf, bob apple, and snap dragon: the Yule clog and Christmas candle were regularly burnt, and the mistletoe, with its white berries, hung up, to the imminent peril of all the pretty housemaids.[2]

So intent were the servants upon their sports, that we had to ring repeatedly before we could make ourselves heard. On our arrival being announced, the squire came out to receive us, accompanied by his two other sons; one a young officer in

---

2. The mistletoe is still hung up in farmhouses and kitchens at Christmas; and the young men have the privilege of kissing the girls under it, plucking each time a berry from the bush. When the berries are all picked, the privilege ceases.

the army, home on leave of absence; the other an Oxonian, just from the university. The squire was a fine healthy-looking old gentleman, with silver hair curling lightly round an open florid countenance; in which the physiognomist, with the advantage, like myself, of a previous hint or two, might discover a singular mixture of whim and benevolence.

The family meeting was warm and affectionate: as the evening was far advanced, the squire would not permit us to change our traveling dresses, but ushered us at once to the company, which was assembled in a large old-fashioned hall. It was composed of different branches of a numerous family connection, where there were the usual proportion of old uncles and aunts, comfortable married dames, superannuated spinsters, blooming country cousins, half-fledged striplings, and bright-eyed boarding-school hoydens. They were variously occupied; some at a round game of cards; others conversing around the fireplace; at one end of the hall was a group of the young folks, some nearly grown up, others of a more tender and budding age, fully engrossed by a merry game; and a profusion of wooden horses, penny trumpets, and tattered dolls, about the floor, showed traces of a troop of little fairy beings, who, having frolicked through a happy day, had been carried off to slumber through a peaceful night.

While the mutual greetings were going on between young Bracebridge and his relatives, I had time to scan the apartment. I have called it a hall, for so it had certainly been in old times, and the squire had evidently endeavored to restore it to something of its primitive state. Over the heavy projecting fireplace was suspended a picture of a warrior in armor, standing by a white horse, and on the opposite wall hung a helmet, buckler, and lance. At one end an enormous pair of antlers were inserted in the wall, the branches serving as hooks on which to suspend hats, whips, and spurs; and in the corners of the apartment were fowling-pieces, fishing-rods, and other sporting implements. The furniture was of the cumbrous workmanship of former days, though some articles of modern convenience had been added, and the oaken floor had been carpeted; so that the whole presented an odd mixture of parlor and hall.

The grate had been removed from the wide overwhelming fireplace, to make way for a fire of wood, in the midst of which was an enormous log glowing and blazing, and sending forth a vast volume of light and heat: this I understood was the Yule clog, which the squire was particular in having brought in and illumined on a Christmas eve, according to ancient custom.[3]

It was really delightful to see the old squire seated in his hereditary elbow chair, by the hospitable fireside of his ancestors, and looking around him like the sun of a system, beaming warmth and gladness to every heart. Even the very dog that lay stretched at his feet, as he lazily shifted his position and yawned, would look fondly up in his master's face, wag his tail against the floor, and stretch himself again to sleep, confident of kindness and protection. There is an emanation from the heart in genuine hospitality which cannot be described, but is immediately felt, and puts the stranger at once at his ease. I had not been seated many minutes by the comfortable hearth of the worthy old cavalier, before I found myself as much at home as if I had been one of the family.

Supper was announced shortly after our arrival. It was served up in a spacious oaken chamber, the panels of which shone with wax, and around which were several family portraits decorated with holly and ivy. Besides the accustomed lights, two great wax tapers, called Christmas candles, wreathed with greens, were placed on a highly polished beaufet among the family plate. The table was abundantly spread with substantial fare; but the squire made his supper of frumenty, a dish made of wheat cakes boiled in milk, with rich spices, being a standing dish in old times for Christmas eve. I was happy to find my old friend, minced pie, in the retinue of the feast; and

---

3. The *Yule clog* is a great log of wood, sometimes the root of a tree, brought into the house with great ceremony, on Christmas eve, laid in the fireplace, and lighted with the brand of last year's clog. While it lasted, there was great drinking, singing, and telling of tales. Sometimes it was accompanied by Christmas candles; but in the cottages the only light was from the ruddy blaze of the great wood fire. The Yule clog was to burn all night; if it went out, it was considered a sign of ill luck.

Herrick mentions it in one of his songs:—

Come, bring with a noise,
My merrie, merrie boyes,
The Christmas log to the firing;
While my good dame, she
Bids ye all be free,
And drink to your hearts desiring.

The Yule clog is still burnt in many farmhouses and kitchens in England, particularly in the north, and there are several superstitions connected with it among the peasantry. If a squinting person come to the house while it is burning, or a person barefooted, it is considered an ill omen. The brand remaining from the Yule clog is carefully put away to light the next year's Christmas fire.

finding him to be perfectly orthodox, and that I need not be ashamed of my predilection, I greeted him with all the warmth wherewith we usually greet an old and very genteel acquaintance.

The mirth of the company was greatly promoted by the humors of an eccentric personage whom Mr. Bracebridge always addressed with the quaint appellation of Master Simon. He was a tight brisk little man, with the air of an arrant old bachelor. His nose was shaped like the bill of a parrot; his face slightly pitted with the small-pox, with a dry perpetual bloom on it, like a frostbitten leaf in autumn. He had an eye of great quickness and vivacity, with a drollery and lurking waggery of expression that was irresistible. He was evidently the wit of the family, dealing very much in sly jokes and innuendoes with the ladies, and making infinite merriment by harpings upon old themes; which, unfortunately, my ignorance of the family chronicles did not permit me to enjoy. It seemed to be his great delight during supper to keep a young girl next him in a continual agony of stifled laughter, in spite of her awe of the reproving looks of her mother, who sat opposite. Indeed, he was the idol of the younger part of the company, who laughed at every thing he said or did, and at every turn of his countenance. I could not wonder at it; for he must have been a miracle of accomplishments in their eyes. He could imitate Punch and Judy; make an old woman of his hand, with the assistance of a burnt cork and pocket-handkerchief; and cut an orange into such a ludicrous caricature, that the young folks were ready to die with laughing.

I was let briefly into his history by Frank Bracebridge. He was an old bachelor, of a small independent income, which, by careful management, was sufficient for all his wants. He revolved through the family system like a vagrant comet in its orbit; sometimes visiting one branch, and sometimes another quite remote; as is often the case with gentlemen of extensive connections and small fortunes in England. He had a chirping buoyant disposition, always enjoying the present moment; and his frequent change of scene and company prevented his acquiring those rusty unaccommodating habits, with which old bachelors are so uncharitably charged. He was a complete family chronicle, being versed in the genealogy, history, and intermarriages of the whole house of Bracebridge, which made him a great favorite with the old folks; he was a beau of all the elder ladies and superannuated spinsters, among whom he was habitually considered rather a young fellow, and he was master of the revels among the children; so that there was not a more popular being in the sphere in which he moved than Mr. Simon Bracebridge. Of late years, he had resided almost entirely with the squire, to whom he had become a factotum, and whom he particularly delighted by jumping with his humor in respect to old times, and by having a scrap of an old song to suit every occasion. We had presently a specimen of his last-mentioned talent, for no sooner was supper removed, and spiced wines and other beverages peculiar to the season introduced, than Master Simon was called on for a good old Christmas song. He bethought himself for a moment, and then, with a sparkle of the eye, and a voice that was by no means bad, excepting that it ran occasionally into a falsetto, like the notes of a split reed, he quavered forth a quaint old ditty.

Now Christmas is come,
Let us beat up the drum,
And call all our neighbors together,
And when they appear,
Let us make them such cheer,
As will keep out the wind and the weather, etc.

The supper had disposed every one to gayety, and an old harper was summoned from the servants' hall, where he had been strumming all the evening, and to all appearance comforting himself with some of the squire's home-brewed. He was a kind of hanger-on, I was told, of the establishment, and, though ostensibly a resident of the village, was oftener to be found in the squire's kitchen than his own home, the old gentleman being fond of the sound of "harp in hall."

The dance, like most dances after supper, was a merry one; some of the older folks joined in it, and the squire himself figured down several couple with a partner, with whom he affirmed he had danced at every Christmas for nearly half a century. Master Simon, who seemed to be a kind of connecting link between the old times and the new, and to be withal a little antiquated in the taste of his accomplishments, evidently piqued himself on his dancing, and was endeavoring to gain credit by the heel and toe, rigadoon, and other graces of the ancient school; but he had unluckily assorted himself with a little romping girl from boarding-school, who, by her wild vivacity, kept him continually on the stretch, and defeated all his sober attempts at elegance:—such are the ill-assorted matches to which antique gentlemen are unfortunately prone!

The young Oxonian, on the contrary, had led out one of his maiden aunts, on whom the rogue played a thousand little knaveries with impunity; he was full of practical jokes, and his delight was to tease his aunts and cousins; yet, like all madcap youngsters, he was a universal favorite among the women. The most interesting couple in the dance was the young officer and a ward of the squire's, a beautiful blushing girl of seventeen. From several shy glances which I had noticed in the course of the evening, I suspected there was a little kindness growing up between them; and, indeed, the young soldier was just the hero to captivate a romantic girl. He was tall, slender, and handsome, and, like most young British officers of late years, had picked up various small accomplishments on the continent—he could talk French and Italian—draw landscapes, sing very tolerably—dance divinely; but, above all, he had been wounded at Waterloo:—what girl of seventeen, well read in poetry and romance, could resist such a mirror of chivalry and perfection!

The moment the dance was over, he caught up a guitar, and, lolling against the old marble fireplace, in an attitude which I am half inclined to suspect was studied, began the little French air of the Troubadour. The squire, however, exclaimed against having any thing on Christmas eve but good old English; upon which the young minstrel, casting up his eye for a moment, as if in an effort of memory, strode into another strain, and, with a charming air of gallantry, gave Herrick's "Night-Piece to Julia":

Her eyes the glow-worm lend thee,
The shooting stars attend thee,
    And the elves also,
    Whose little eyes glow
Like the sparks of fire, befriend thee.

No Will o' the Wisp mislight thee;
Nor snake nor slow-worm bite thee;
    But on, on thy way,
    Not making a stay,
Since ghost there is none to affright thee.

Then let not the dark thee cumber;
What though the moon does slumber,
    The stars of the night
    Will lend thee their light,
Like tapers clear without number.

Then, Julia, let me woo thee,
Thus, thus to come unto me,
And when I shall meet
Thy silvery feet,
My soul I'll pour into thee.

The song might or might not have been intended in compliment to the fair Julia, for so I found his partner was called; she, however, was certainly unconscious of any such application, for she never looked at the singer, but kept her eyes cast upon the floor. Her face was suffused, it is true, with a beautiful blush, and there was a gentle heaving of the bosom, but all that was doubtless caused by the exercise of the dance; indeed, so great was her indifference, that she amused herself with plucking to pieces a choice bouquet of hot-house flowers, and by the time the song was concluded the nosegay lay in ruins on the floor.

The party now broke up for the night with the kind-hearted old custom of shaking hands. As I passed through the hall, on my way to my chamber, the dying embers of the Yule clog still sent forth a dusky glow, and had it not been the season when "no spirit dares stir abroad," I should have been half tempted to steal from my room at midnight, and peep whether the fairies might not be at their revels about the hearth.

My chamber was in the old part of the mansion, the ponderous furniture of which might have been fabricated in the days of the giants. The room was panneled, with cornices of heavy carved work, in which flowers and grotesque faces were strangely intermingled; and a row of black-looking portraits stared mournfully at me from the walls. The bed was of rich though faded damask, with a lofty tester, and stood in a niche opposite a bow window. I had scarcely got into bed when a strain of music seemed to break forth in the air just below the window. I listened, and found it proceeded from a band, which I concluded to be the waits from some neighboring village. They went round the house, playing under the windows. I drew aside the curtains to hear them more distinctly. The moonbeams fell through the upper part of the casement, partially lighting up the antiquated apartment. The sounds, as they receded, became more soft and aerial, and seemed to accord with the quiet and moonlight. I listened and listened—they became more and more tender and remote, and, as they gradually died away, my head sunk upon the pillow, and I fell asleep.

Christmas Day

Dark and dull night, flie hence away,
And give the honor to this day
That sees December turn'd to May.

* * * * *

Why does the chilling winter's morne
Smile like a field beset with corn?
Or smell like to a meade new-shorne,
Thus on the sudden?—Come and see
The cause why things thus fragrant be

HERRICK

WHEN I WOKE THE NEXT MORNING, IT SEEMED AS IF ALL THE EVENTS of the preceding evening had been a dream, and nothing but the identity of the ancient chamber convinced me of their reality. While I lay musing on my pillow, I heard the sound of little feet pattering outside of the door, and a whispering consultation. Presently a choir of small voices chanted forth an old Christmas carol, the burden of which was—

Rejoice, our Saviour he was born
On Christmas day in the morning.

I rose softly, slipt on my clothes, opened the door suddenly, and beheld one of the most beautiful little fairy groups that a painter could imagine. It consisted of a boy and two girls, the eldest not more than six, and lovely as seraphs. They were going the rounds of the house, and singing at every chamber door; but my sudden appearance frightened them into mute bashfulness. They remained for a moment playing on their lips with their fingers, and now and then stealing a shy glance, from under their eyebrows, until, as if by one impulse, they scampered away, and as they turned an angle of the gallery, I heard them laughing in triumph at their escape.

Every thing conspired to produce kind and happy feelings in this strong-hold of old-fashioned hospitality. The window of my chamber looked out upon what in summer would have been a beautiful landscape. There was a sloping lawn, a fine stream winding at the foot of it, and a tract of park beyond, with noble clumps of trees, and herds of deer. At a distance was a neat hamlet, with the smoke from the cottage chimneys hanging over it; and a church with its dark spire in strong relief against the clear cold sky. The house was surrounded with evergreens, according to the English custom, which would have given almost an appearance of summer; but the morning was extremely frosty; the light vapor of the preceding evening had been precipitated by the cold, and covered all the trees and every blade of grass with its fine crystalizations. The rays of a bright morning sun had a dazzling effect among the glittering foliage. A robin, perched upon the top of a mountain ash that hung its clusters of red berries just before my window, was basking himself in the sunshine, and piping a few querulous notes; and a peacock was displaying all the glories of his train, and strutting with the pride and gravity of a Spanish grandee, on the terrace walk below.

I had scarcely dressed myself, when a servant appeared to invite me to family prayers. He showed me the way to a small chapel in the old wing of the house, where I found the principal part of the family already assembled in a kind of gallery, furnished with cushions, hassocks, and large prayer-books; the servants were seated on benches below. The old gentleman read prayers from a desk in front of the gallery, and Master Simon acted as clerk, and made the responses; and I must do him the justice to say that he acquitted himself with great gravity and decorum.

The service was followed by a Christmas carol, which Mr. Bracebridge himself had constructed from a poem of his favorite author, Herrick; and it had been adapted to an old church melody by Master Simon. As there were several good voices among the household, the effect was extremely pleasing; but I was particularly gratified by the exaltation of heart, and sudden sally of grateful feeling, with which the worthy squire delivered one stanza; his eye glistening, and his voice rambling out of all the bounds of time and tune:

'Tis thou that crown'st my glittering hearth
With guiltlesse mirth,
And givest me Waasaile bowles to drink
Spiced to the brink:
Lord, 'tis thy plenty-dropping hand
That soiles my land:
And giv'st me for my bushell sowne,
Twice ten for one.

I afterwards understood that early morning service was read on every Sunday and saint's day throughout the year, either by Mr. Bracebridge or by some member of the family. It was once almost universally the case at the seats of the nobility and gentry of England, and it is much to be regretted that the custom is falling into neglect; for the dullest observer must be sensible of the order and serenity prevalent in those households, where the occasional exercise of a beautiful form of worship in the morning gives, as it were, the key-note to every temper for the day, and attunes every spirit to harmony.

Our breakfast consisted of what the squire denominated true old English fare. He indulged in some bitter lamentations over modern breakfasts of tea and toast, which he censured as among the causes of modern effeminacy and weak nerves, and the decline of old English heartiness; and though he admitted them to his table to suit the palates of his guests, yet there was a brave display of cold meats, wine, and ale, on the sideboard.

After breakfast I walked about the grounds with Frank Bracebridge and Master Simon, or Mr. Simon, as he was called by every body but the squire. We were escorted by a number of gentlemanlike dogs, that seemed loungers about the establishment; from the frisking spaniel to the steady old stag-hound; the last of which was of a race that had been in the family time out of mind: they were all obedient to a dog-whistle which hung to Master Simon's button-hole, and in the midst of their gambols would glance an eye occasionally upon a small switch he carried in his hand.

The old mansion had a still more venerable look in the yellow sunshine than by pale moonlight; and I could not but feel the force of the squire's idea, that the formal terraces, heavily moulded balustrades, and clipped yew-trees, carried with them an air of proud aristocracy. There appeared to be an unusual number of peacocks about the place, and I was making some remarks upon what I termed a flock of them, that were basking under a sunny wall, when I was gently corrected in my phraseology by Master Simon, who told me that, according to the most ancient and approved treatise on hunting, I must say a *muster* of peacocks. "In the same way," added he, with a slight air of pedantry, "we say a flight of doves or swallows, a bevy of quails, a herd of deer, of wrens, or cranes, a skulk of foxes, or a building of rooks." He went on to inform me that, according to Sir Anthony Fitzherbert, we ought to ascribe to this bird "both understanding and glory; for, being praised, he will presently set up his tail, chiefly against the sun, to the intent you may the better behold the beauty thereof. But at the fall of the leaf, when his tail falleth, he will mourn and hide himself in corners, till his tail come again as it was."

I could not help smiling at this display of small erudition on so whimsical a subject; but I found that the peacocks were birds of some consequence at the hall; for Frank Bracebridge informed me that they were great favorites with his father, who was extremely careful to keep up the breed; partly because they belonged to chivalry, and were in great request at the stately banquets of the olden time; and partly because they had a pomp and magnificence about them, highly becoming an old family mansion. Nothing, he was accustomed to say, had an air of greater state and dignity than a peacock perched upon an antique stone balustrade.

Master Simon had now to hurry off, having an appointment at the parish church with the village choristers, who were to perform some music of his selection. There was something extremely agreeable in the cheerful flow of animal spirits of the little man; and I confess I had been somewhat surprised at his apt quotations from authors who certainly were not in the range of every-day reading. I mentioned this last circumstance to Frank Bracebridge, who told me with a smile that Master Simon's whole stock of erudition was confined to some half a dozen old authors, which the squire had put into his hands, and which he read over and over, whenever he had a studious fit; as he sometimes had on a rainy day, or a long winter evening. Sir Anthony Fitzherbert's Book of Husbandry; Markham's Country Contentments; the Tretyse of Hunting, by Sir Thomas Cockayne, Knight; Isaac Walton's Angler, and two or three more such ancient worthies of the pen, were his standard authorities; and, like all men who know but a few books, he looked up to them with a kind of idolatry, and quoted them on all occasions. As to his songs, they were chiefly picked out of old books in the squire's library, and adapted to tunes that were popular among the choice spirits of the last century. His practical application of scraps of literature, however, had caused him to be looked upon as a prodigy of book knowledge by all the grooms, huntsmen, and small sportsmen of the neighborhood.

While we were talking we heard the distant toll of the village bell, and I was told that the squire was a little particular in having his household at church on a Christmas morning; considering it a day of pouring out of thanks and rejoicing; for, as old Tusser observed,

> At Christmas be merry, *and thankful withal,*
> And feast thy poor neighbors, the great with the small.

"If you are disposed to go to church," said Frank Bracebridge, "I can promise you a specimen of my cousin Simon's musical achievements. As the church is destitute of an organ, he has formed a band from the village amateurs, and established a musical club for their improvement; he has also sorted a choir, as he sorted my father's pack of hounds, according to the directions of Jervaise Markham, in his Country Contentments: for the bass he has sought out all the 'deep, solemn mouths,' and for the tenor the 'loud-ringing mouths,' among the country bumpkins; and for 'sweet mouths,' he has culled with curious taste among the prettiest lasses in the neighborhood; though these last, he affirms, are the most difficult to keep in tune; your pretty female singer being exceedingly wayward and capricious, and very liable to accident."

As the morning, though frosty, was remarkably fine and dear, the most of the family walked to the church, which was a very old building of gray stone, and stood near a village, about half a mile from the park gate. Adjoining it was a low snug parsonage, which seemed coeval with the church. The front of it was perfectly matted with a yew-tree, that had been trained against its walls, through the dense foliage of which, apertures had been formed to admit light into the small antique lattices. As we passed this sheltered nest, the parson issued forth and preceded us.

I had expected to see a sleek well-conditioned pastor, such as is often found in a snug living in the vicinity of a rich patron's table, but I was disappointed. The parson was a little, meagre, black-looking man, with a grizzled wig that was too wide, and stood off from each ear; so that his head seemed to have shrunk away within it, like a dried filbert in its shell. He wore a rusty coat, with great skirts, and pockets that would have held the church Bible and prayer book: and his small legs seemed still smaller, from being planted in large shoes, decorated with enormous buckles.

I was informed by Frank Bracebridge, that the parson had been a chum of his father's at Oxford, and had received this living shortly after the latter had come to his estate. He was a complete black-letter hunter, and would scarcely read a work printed in the Roman character. The editions of Caxton and Wynkin de Worde were his delight; and he was indefatigable in his researches after such old English writers as have fallen into oblivion from their worthlessness. In deference, perhaps, to the notions of Mr. Bracebridge, he had made diligent investigations into the festive rites and holiday customs of former times; and had been as zealous in the inquiry as if he had been a boon companion; but it was merely with that plodding spirit with which men of adust temperament follow up any track of study, merely because it is denominated learning; indifferent to its intrinsic nature, whether it be the illustration of the wisdom, or of the ribaldry and obscenity of antiquity. He had pored over these old volumes so intensely, that they seemed to have been reflected into his countenance; which, if the face be indeed an index of the mind, might be compared to a title-page of black-letter.

On reaching the church porch, we found the parson rebuking the gray-headed sexton for having used mistletoe among the greens with which the church was decorated. It was, he observed, an unholy plant, profaned by having been used by the Druids in their mystic ceremonies; and though it might be innocently employed in the festive ornamenting of halls and kitchens, yet it had been deemed by the Fathers of the Church as unhallowed, and totally unfit for sacred purposes. So tenacious was he on this point, that the poor sexton was obliged to strip down a great part of the humble trophies of his taste, before the parson would consent to enter upon the service of the day.

The interior of the church was venerable but simple; on the walls were several mural monuments of the Bracebridges, and just beside the altar was a tomb of ancient workmanship, on which lay the effigy of a warrior in armor, with his legs crossed, a sign of his having been a crusader. I was told it was one of the family who had signalized himself in the Holy Land, and the same whose picture hung over the fireplace in the hall.

During service, Master Simon stood up in the pew, and repeated the responses very audibly; evincing that kind of ceremonious devotion punctually observed by a gentleman of the old school, and a man of old family connections. I observed too that he turned over the leaves of a folio prayer-book with something of a flourish; possibly to show off an enormous seal-ring which enriched one of his fingers, and which had the look of a family relic. But he was evidently most solicitous about the musical part of the service, keeping his eye fixed intently on the choir, and beating time with much gesticulation and emphasis.

The orchestra was in a small gallery, and presented a most whimsical grouping of heads, piled one above the other, among which I particularly noticed that of the village tailor, a pale fellow with a retreating forehead and chin, who played on the clarinet, and seemed to have blown his face to a point; and there was another, a short pursy man, stooping and laboring at a bass-viol, so as to show nothing but the top of a round bald head, like the egg of an ostrich. There were two or three pretty faces among the female singers, to which the keen air of a frosty morning had given a bright rosy tint; but the gentlemen choristers had evidently been chosen, like old Cremona fiddles, more for tone than looks; and as several had to sing from the same book, there were clusterings of odd physiognomies, not unlike those groups of cherubs we sometimes see on country tombstones.

The usual services of the choir were managed tolerably well, the vocal parts generally lagging a little behind the instrumental, and some loitering fiddler now and then making up for lost time by traveling over a passage with prodigious celerity, and clearing more bars than the keenest fox-hunter to be in at the death. But the great trial was an anthem that had been prepared and arranged by Master Simon, and on which he had founded great expectation. Unluckily there was a blunder at the very outset; the musicians became flurried; Master Simon was in a fever; every thing went on lamely and irregularly until they came to a chorus beginning "Now let us sing with one accord," which seemed to be a signal for parting company: all became discord and confusion; each shifted for himself, and got to the end as well, or, rather, as soon as he could, excepting one old chorister in a pair of horn spectacles, bestriding and pinching a long sonorous nose; who happened to stand a little apart, and, being wrapped up in his own melody, kept on a quavering course, wriggling his head, ogling his book, and winding all up by a nasal solo of at least three bars duration.

The parson gave us a most erudite sermon on the rites and ceremonies of Christmas, and the propriety of observing it not merely as a day of thanksgiving, but of rejoicing; supporting the correctness of his opinions by the earliest usages of the church, and enforcing them by the authorities of Theophilus of Cesarea, St. Cyprian, St. Chrysostom, St. Augustine, and a cloud more of saints and fathers, from whom he made copious quotations. I was a little at a loss to perceive the necessity of such a mighty army of forces to maintain a point which no one present seemed inclined to dispute; but I soon found that the good man had a legion of ideal adversaries to contend with; having, in the course of his researches on the subject of Christmas, got completely embroiled in the sectarian controversies of the Revolution, when the Puritans made such a fierce assault upon the ceremonies of the church, and poor old Christmas was driven out of the land by proclamation of Parliament.[1] The worthy parson lived but with times past, and knew but little of the present.

Shut up among worm-eaten tomes in the retirement of his antiquated little study, the pages of old times were to him as the gazettes of the day; while the era of the Revolution was mere modern history. He forgot that nearly two centuries had elapsed since the fiery persecution of poor mince-pie throughout the land; when plum porridge was denounced as "mere popery," and roast beef as anti-christian; and that Christmas had been brought in again triumphantly with the merry court of King Charles at the Restoration. He kindled into warmth with the ardor of his contest, and the host of imaginary foes with whom he had to combat; he had a stubborn conflict with old Prynne and two or three other forgotten champions of the Round Heads, on the subject of Christmas festivity; and concluded by urging his hearers, in the most solemn and affecting manner, to stand to the traditional customs of their fathers, and feast and make merry on this joyful anniversary of the Church.

I have seldom known a sermon attended apparently with more immediate effects; for on leaving the church the congregation seemed one and all possessed with the gayety of spirit so earnestly enjoined by their pastor. The elder folks gathered in knots in the church-yard, greeting and shaking hands; and the children ran about crying

---

1. From the "Flying Eagle," a small Gazette, published December 24th, 1652—"The House spent much time this day about the business of the Navy, for settling the affairs at sea, and before they rose, were presented with a terrible remonstrance against Christmas day, grounded upon divine Scriptures, 2 Cor. v. 16. 1 Cor. xv. 14. 17; and in honor of the Lord's Day, grounded upon these Scriptures, John xx. 1. Rev. i. 10. Psalms cxviii. 24. Lev. xxiii. 7. 11. Mark xv. 8. Psalms lxxxiv. 10, in which Christmas is called Anti-christ's masse, and those Masse-mongers and Papists who observe it, etc. In consequence of which parliament spent some time in consultation about the abolition of Christmas day, passed orders to that effect, and resolved to sit on the following day, which was commonly called Christmas day."

Ule! Ule! and repeating some uncouth rhymes,[2] which the parson, who had joined us, informed me had been handed down from days of yore. The villagers doffed their hats to the squire as he passed, giving him the good wishes of the season with every appearance of heartfelt sincerity, and were invited by him to the hall, to take something to keep out the cold of the weather; and I heard blessings uttered by several of the poor, which convinced me that, in the midst of his enjoyments, the worthy old cavalier had not forgotten the true Christmas virtue of charity.

On our way homeward his heart seemed overflowed with generous and happy feelings. As we passed over a rising ground which commanded something of a prospect, the sounds of rustic merriment now and then reached our ears: the squire paused for a few moments, and looked around with an air of inexpressible benignity. The beauty of the day was of itself sufficient to inspire philanthropy. Notwithstanding the frostiness of the morning, the sun in his cloudless journey had acquired sufficient power to melt away the thin covering of snow from every southern declivity, and to bring out the living green which adorns an English landscape even in mid-winter. Large tracts of smiling verdure contrasted with the dazzling whiteness of the shaded slopes and hollows. Every sheltered bank, on which the broad rays rested, yielded its silver rill of cold and limpid water, glittering through the dripping grass; and sent up slight exhalations to contribute to the thin haze that hung just above the surface of the earth. There was something truly cheering in this triumph of warmth and verdure over the frosty thraldom of winter; it was, as the squire observed, an emblem of Christmas hospitality, breaking through the chills of ceremony and selfishness, and thawing every heart into a flow. He pointed with pleasure to the indications of good cheer reeking from the chimneys of the comfortable farmhouses, and low thatched cottages. "I love," said he, "to see this day well kept by rich and poor; it is a great thing to have one day in the year, at least, when you are sure of being welcome wherever you go, and of having, as it were, the world all thrown open to you; and I am almost disposed to join with Poor Robin, in his malediction on every churlish enemy to this honest festival:

---

2. "Ule! Ule!
Three puddings in a pule;
Crack nuts and cry ule!"

Those who at Christmas do repine,
And would fain hence dispatch him,
May they with old Duke Humphry dine,
Or else may Squire Ketch catch 'em.

The squire went on to lament the deplorable decay of the games and amusements which were once prevalent at this season among the lower orders, and countenanced by the higher; when the old halls of castles and manor-houses were thrown open at daylight; when the tables were covered with brawn, and beef, and humming ale; when the harp and the carol resounded all day long, and when rich and poor were alike welcome to enter and make merry.[3] "Our old games and local customs," said he, "had a great effect in making the peasant fond of his home, and the promotion of them by the gentry made him fond of his lord. They made the times merrier, and kinder, and better, and I can truly say, with one of our old poets:

I like them well—the carious preciseness
And all-pretended gravity of those
That seek to banish hence these harmless sports,
Have thrust away much ancient honesty.

"The nation," continued he, "is altered; we have almost lost our simple true-hearted peasantry. They have broken asunder from the higher classes, and seem to think their interests are separate. They have become too knowing, and begin to read newspapers, listen to ale-house politicians, and talk of reform. I think one mode to keep them in good humor in these hard times would be for the nobility and gentry to pass more time on their estates, mingle more among the country people, and set the merry old English games going again."

Such was the good squire's project for mitigating public discontent: and indeed, he had once attempted to put his doctrine in practice, and a few years before had kept

---

3. "An English gentleman, at the opening of the great day, i.e. on Christmas day in the morning, had all his tenants and neighbors enter his hall by daybreak. The strong beer was broached, and the black-jacks went plentifully about with toast, sugar and nutmeg, and good Cheshire cheese. The Hackin (the great sausage) must be boiled by daybreak, or else two young men must take the maiden (i.e. the cook) by the arms, and run her round the market-place till she is shamed of her laziness."—*Round about our Sea-Coal Fire.*

open house during the holidays in the old style. The country people, however, did not understand how to play their parts in the scene of hospitality; many uncouth circumstances occurred; the manor was overrun by all the vagrants of the country, and more beggars drawn into the neighborhood in one week than the parish officers could get rid of in a year. Since then, he had contented himself with inviting the decent part of the neighboring peasantry to call at the hall on Christmas day, and with distributing beef, and bread, and ale, among the poor, that they might make merry in their own dwellings.

We had not been long home when the sound of music was heard from a distance. A band of country lads, without coats, their shirt sleeves fancifully tied with ribands, their hats decorated with greens, and clubs in their hands, was seen advancing up the avenue, followed by a large number of villagers and peasantry. They stopped before the hall door, where the music struck up a peculiar air, and the lads performed a curious and intricate dance, advancing, retreating, and striking their clubs together, keeping exact time to the music; while one, whimsically crowned with a fox's skin, the tail of which flaunted down his back, kept capering round the skirts of the dance, and rattling a Christmas box with many antic gesticulations.

The squire eyed this fanciful exhibition with great interest and delight, and gave me a full account of its origin, which he traced to the times when the Romans held possession of the island; plainly proving that this was a lineal descendant of the sword dance of the ancients. "It was now," he said, "nearly extinct, but he had accidentally met with traces of it in the neighborhood, and had encouraged its revival; though, to tell the truth, it was too apt to be followed up by the rough cudgel play, and broken heads in the evening."

After the dance was concluded, the whole party was entertained with brawn and beef, and stout home-brewed. The squire himself mingled among the rustics, and was received with awkward demonstrations of deference and regard. It is true I perceived two or three of the younger peasants, as they were raising their tankards to their mouths, when the squire's back was turned, making something of a grimace, and giving each other the wink; but the moment they caught my eye they pulled grave faces, and were exceedingly demure. With Master Simon, however, they all seemed more at their ease. His varied occupations and amusements had made him well known throughout the neighborhood. He was a visitor at every farmhouse and cottage; gossiped with the farmers and their wives; romped with their daughters; and, like that type of a vagrant bachelor, the bumblebee, tolled the sweets from all the rosy lips of the country round.

The bashfulness of the guests soon gave way before good cheer and affability. There is something genuine and affectionate in the gayety of the lower orders, when it is excited by the bounty and familiarity of those above them; the warm glow of gratitude enters into their mirth, and a kind word or a small pleasantry frankly uttered by a patron, gladdens the heart of the dependent more than oil and wine. When the squire had retired, the merriment increased, and there was much joking and laughter, particularly between Master Simon and a hale, ruddy-faced, white-headed farmer, who appeared to be the wit of the village; for I observed all his companions to wait with open months for his retorts, and burst into a gratuitous laugh before they could well understand them.

The whole house indeed seemed abandoned to merriment: as I passed to my room to dress for dinner, I heard the sound of music in a small court, and looking through a window that commanded it, I perceived a band of wandering musicians, with pandean pipes and tambourine; a pretty coquettish housemaid was dancing a jig with a smart country lad, while several of the other servants were looking on. In the midst of her sport the girl caught a glimpse of my face at the window, and, coloring up, ran off with an air of roguish affected confusion.

The Christmas Dinner

Lo, now is come our joyful'st feast!
　　Let every man be jolly,
Eache roome with yvie leaves is drest,
　　And every post with holly.
Now all our neighbours' chimneys smoke,
　　And Christmas blocks are burning;
Their ovens they with bak't meats choke
　　And all their spits are turning.
　　　　Without the door let sorrow lie,
　　　　And if, for cold, it hap to die,
　　　　Wee'le bury it in a Christmas pye,
　　　　And evermore be merry.

WITHERS' JUVENILIA

I HAD FINISHED MY TOILET, AND WAS LOITERING WITH FRANK BRACEBRIDGE in the library, when we heard a distant thwacking sound, which he informed me was a signal for the serving up of the dinner. The squire kept up old customs in kitchen as well as hall; and the rolling-pin, struck upon the dresser by the cook, summoned the servants to carry in the meats.

Jut in this nick the cook knock'd thrice,
And all the waiters in a trice
　　His summons did obey;
Each serving man, with dish in hand,
March'd boldly up, like our train band,
　　Presented and away.[1]

---

1. Sir John Suckling.

The dinner was served up in the great hall, where the squire always held his Christmas banquet. A blazing crackling fire of logs had been heaped on to warm the spacious apartment, and the flame went sparkling and wreathing up the wide-mouthed chimney. The great picture of the crusader and his white horse had been profusely decorated with greens for the occasion; and holly and ivy had likewise been wreathed round the helmet and weapons on the opposite wall, which I understood were the arms of the same warrior. I must own, by the by, I had strong doubts about the authenticity of the painting and armor as having belonged to the crusader, they certainly having the stamp of more recent days; but I was told that the painting had been so considered time out of mind; and that, as to the armor, it had been found in a lumber-room, and elevated to its present situation by the squire, who at once determined it to be the armor of the family hero; and as he was absolute authority on all such subjects in his own household, the matter had passed into current acceptation. A sideboard was set out just under this chivalric trophy, on which was a display of plate that might have vied (at least in variety) with Belshazzar's parade of the vessels of the temple: "flagons, cans, cups, beakers, goblets, basins, and ewers"; the gorgeous utensils of good companionship that had gradually accumulated through many generations of jovial housekeepers. Before these stood the two Yule candles, beaming like two stars of the first magnitude; other lights were distributed in branches, and the whole array glittered like a firmament of silver.

We were ushered into this banqueting scene with the sound of minstrelsy, the old harper being seated on a stool beside the fireplace, and twanging his instrument with a vast deal more power than melody. Never did Christmas board display a more goodly and gracious assemblage of countenances; those who were not handsome were, at least, happy; and happiness is a rare improver of your hard-favored visage. I always consider an old English family as well worth studying as a collection of Holbein portraits or Albert Durer's prints. There is much antiquarian lore to be acquired; much knowledge of the physiognomies of former times. Perhaps it may be from having continually before their eyes those rows of old family portraits, with which the mansions of this country are stocked; certain it is, that the quaint features of antiquity are often most faithfully perpetuated in these ancient lines; and I have traced an old family nose through a whole picture gallery, legitimately handed down from generation to generation, almost from the time of the Conquest. Something of the kind was to be observed in the worthy company around me. Many of their faces had evidently originated in a gothic age, and been merely copied by succeeding generations; and there was one little girl in particular, of staid demeanor, with a high Roman nose, and an antique vinegar aspect, who was a great favorite of the squire's, being, as he said, a Bracebridge all over, and the very counterpart of one of his ancestors who figured in the court of Henry VIII.

The parson said grace, which was not a short familiar one, such as is commonly addressed to the Deity in these unceremonious, days; but a long, courtly, well-worded one of the ancient school. There was now a pause, as if something was expected; when suddenly the butler entered the hall with some degree of bustle: he was attended by a servant on each side with a large wax-light, and bore a silver dish, on which was an enormous pig's head, decorated with rosemary, with a lemon in its mouth, which was placed with great formality at the head of the table. The moment this pageant made its appearance, the harper struck up a flourish; at the conclusion of which the young Oxonian, on receiving a hint from the squire, gave, with an air of the most comic gravity, an old carol, the first verse of which was as follows:

Caput apri defero
Reddens landes Domino.
The boar's head in hand bring I,
With garlands gay and rosemary.
I pray you all synge merily
Qui estis in convivio.

Though prepared to witness many of these little eccentricities, from being apprised of the peculiar hobby of mine host; yet, I confess, the parade with which so odd a dish was introduced somewhat perplexed me, until I gathered from the conversation of the squire and the parson, that it was meant to represent the bringing in of the boar's head; a dish formerly served up with much ceremony and the sound of minstrelsy and song, at great tables, on Christmas day. "I like the old custom," said the squire, "not merely because it is stately and pleasing in itself, but because it was observed at the college at Oxford at which I was educated. When I hear the old song chanted, it brings to mind the time when I was young and gamesome—and the noble old college hall—and my fellow students loitering about in their black gowns; many of whom, poor lads, are now in their graves!"

The parson, however, whose mind was not haunted by such associations, and who was always more taken up with the text than the sentiment, objected to the Oxonian's version of the carol; which he affirmed was different from that sung at college. He went on, with the dry perseverance of a commentator, to give the college reading, accompanied by sundry annotations; addressing himself at first to the company at large; but finding their attention gradually diverted to other talk and other objects, he lowered his tone as his number of auditors diminished, until he concluded his remarks in an under voice, to a fat-headed old gentleman next him, who was silently engaged in the discussion of a huge plateful of turkey.[2]

The table was literally loaded with good cheer, and presented an epitome of country abundance, in this season of overflowing larders. A distinguished post was allotted to "ancient sirloin," as mine host termed it; being, as he added, "the standard of old English hospitality, and a joint of goodly presence, and full of expectation." There were several dishes quaintly decorated, and which had evidently something traditional in their embellishments; but about which, as I did not like to appear over-curious, I asked no questions.

I could not, however, but notice a pie, magnificently decorated with peacock's feathers, in imitation of the tail of that bird, which overshadowed a considerable tract of the table. This, the squire confessed, with some little hesitation, was a pheasant pie, though a peacock pie was certainly the most authentical; but there had been such a

---

2. The old ceremony of serving up the boar's head on Christmas day is still observed in the hall of Queen's College, Oxford. I was favored by the parson with a copy of the carol as now sung, and as it may be acceptable to such of my readers as are curious in these grave and learned matters, I give it entire.

The boar's head in hand bear I,
Bedeck'd with bays and rosemary;
And I pray you, my masters, be merry
Quot estis in conviyio.
Caput apri defero,
Reddens laudes domino.

The boar's head, as I understand,
Is the rarest dish in all this land,
Which thus bedeck'd with a gay garland
Let us servire cantico.
Caput apri defero, etc.

mortality among the peacocks this season, that he could not prevail upon himself to have one killed.[3]

Our steward hath provided this
In honor of the King of Bliss,
Which on this day to be served is
In Reginensi Atrio.
Caput apri defero,
etc., etc., etc.

It would be tedious, perhaps, to my wiser readers, who may not have that foolish fondness for odd and obsolete things to which I am a little given, were I to mention the other make-shifts of this worthy old humorist, by which he was endeavoring to follow up, though at humble distance, the quaint customs of antiquity. I was pleased, however, to see the respect shown to his whims by his children and relatives; who, indeed, entered readily into the full spirit of them, and seemed all well versed in their parts; having doubtless been present at many a rehearsal. I was amused, too, at the air of profound gravity with which the butler and other servants executed the duties assigned them, however eccentric. They had an old-fashioned look; having, for the most part, been brought up in the household, and grown into keeping with the antiquated mansion, and the humors of its lord; and most probably looked upon all his whimsical regulations as the established laws of honorable housekeeping.

When the cloth was removed, the butler brought in a huge silver vessel of rare and curious workmanship, which he placed before the squire. Its appearance was hailed with

---

3. The peacock was anciently in great demand for stately entertainments. Sometimes it was made into a pie, at one end of which the head appeared above the crust in all its plumage, with the beak richly gilt; at the other end the tail was displayed. Such pies were served up at the solemn banquets of chivalry, when knights-errant pledged themselves to undertake any perilous enterprise, whence came the ancient oath, used by Justice Shallow, "by cock and pie."

The peacock was also an important dish for the Christmas feast; and Massinger, in his City Madam, gives some idea of the extravagance with which this, as well as other dishes, was prepared for the gorgeous revels of the olden times:—

Men may talk of Country Christmasses,
Their thirty pound butter'd eggs, their pies of carps' tongues
Their pheasants drench'd with ambergris; *the carcases of three fat wethers bruised for gravy to make sauce for a single peacock!*

acclamation; being the Wassail Bowl, so renowned in Christmas festivity. The contents had been prepared by the squire himself; for it was a beverage in the skillful mixture of which he particularly prided himself: alleging that it was too abstruse and complex for the comprehension of an ordinary servant. It was a potation, indeed, that might well make the heart of a toper leap within him; being composed of the richest and raciest wines, highly spiced and sweetened, with roasted apples bobbing about the surface.[4]

The old gentleman's whole countenance beamed with a serene look of indwelling delight, as he stirred this mighty bowl. Having raised it to his lips, with a hearty wish of a merry Christmas to all present, he sent it brimming round the board, for every one to follow his example, according to the primitive style; pronouncing it "the ancient fountain of good feeling, where all hearts met together."[5]

There was much laughing and rallying as the honest emblem of Christmas joviality circulated, and was kissed rather coyly by the ladies. When it reached Master Simon, he raised it in both hands, and with the air of a boon companion struck up an old Wassail chanson:

The brown bowle,
The merry brown bowle,
As it goes round-about-a,
Fill
Still,
Let the world say what it will,
And drink your fill all out-a.

---

4. The Wassail Bowl was sometimes composed of ale instead of wine; with nutmeg, sugar, toast, ginger, and roasted crabs; in this way the nut-brown beverage is still prepared in some old families, and round the hearths of substantial farmers at Christmas. It is also called Lamb's Wool, and is celebrated by Herrick in his Twelfth Night:

Next crowne the bowle full
With gentle Lamb's Wool;
Add sugar, nutmeg, and ginger,
With store of ale too;
And thus ye must doe
To make the Wassaile a swinger.

5. "The custom of drinking out of the same cup gave place to each having his cup. When the steward came to the doore with the Wassel, he was to cry three times, *Wassel, Wassel, Wassel,* and then the chappell (chaplein) was to answer with a song."—ARCHÆOLOGIA.

The deep canne,
The merry deep canne,
As thou dost freely quaff-a,
Sing
Fling,
Be as merry as a king,
And sound a lusty langh-a.[6]

Much of the conversation during dinner turned upon family topics, to which I was a stranger. There was, however, a great deal of rallying of Master Simon about some gay widow, with whom he was accused of having a flirtation. This attack was commenced by the ladies; but it was continued throughout the dinner by the fat-headed old gentleman next the parson, with the persevering assiduity of a slow hound; being one of those long-winded jokers, who, though rather dull at starting game, are unrivaled for their talents in hunting it down. At every pause in the general conversation, he renewed his bantering in pretty much the same terms; winking hard at me with both eyes, whenever he gave Master Simon what he considered a home thrust. The latter, indeed, seemed fond of being teased on the subject, as old bachelors are apt to be; and he took occasion to inform me, in an under tone, that the lady in question was a prodigiously fine woman, and drove her own curricle.

The dinner-time passed away in this flow of innocent hilarity, and, though the old hall may have resounded in its time with many a scene of broader rout and revel, yet I doubt whether it ever witnessed more honest and genuine enjoyment. How easy it is for one benevolent being to diffuse pleasure around him; and how truly is a kind heart a fountain of gladness, making every thing in its vicinity to freshen into smiles! the joyous disposition of the worthy squire was perfectly contagious; he was happy himself, and disposed to make all the world happy; and the little eccentricities of his humor did but season, in a manner, the sweetness of his philanthropy.

When the ladies had retired, the conversation, as usual, became still more animated; many good things were broached which had been thought of during dinner, but which would not exactly do for a lady's ear; and though I cannot positively affirm

---

6. From Poor Robin's Almanac.

that there was much wit uttered, yet I have certainly heard many contests of rare wit produce much less laughter. Wit, after all, is a mighty tart, pungent ingredient, and much too acid for some stomachs; but honest good humor is the oil and wine of a merry meeting, and there is no jovial companionship equal to that where the jokes are rather small, and the laughter abundant.

The squire told several long stories of early college pranks and adventures, in some of which the parson had been a sharer; though in looking at the latter, it required some effort of imagination to figure such a little dark anatomy of a man into the perpetrator of a madcap gambol. Indeed, the two college chums presented pictures of what men may be made by their different lots in life. The squire had left the university to live lustily on his paternal domains, in the vigorous enjoyment of prosperity and sunshine, and had flourished on to a hearty and florid old age; whilst the poor parson, on the contrary, had dried and withered away, among dusty tomes, in the silence and shadows of his study. Still there seemed to be a spark of almost extinguished fire, feebly glimmering in the bottom of his soul; and as the squire hinted at a sly story of the parson and a pretty milk-maid, whom they once met on the banks of the Isis, the old gentleman made an "alphabet of faces," which, as far as I could decipher his physiognomy, I verily believe was indicative of laughter;—indeed, I have rarely met with an old gentleman that took absolute offence at the imputed gallantries of his youth.

I found the tide of wine and wassail fast gaining on the dry land of sober judgment. The company grew merrier and louder as their jokes grew duller. Master Simon was in as chirping a humor as a grasshopper filled with dew; his old songs grew of a warmer complexion, and he began to talk maudlin about the widow. He even gave a long song about the wooing of a widow, which he informed me he had gathered from an excellent black-letter work, entitled "Cupid's Solicitor for Love," containing store of good advice for bachelors, and which he promised to lend me: the first verse was to this effect:

He that will woo a widow must not dally,
He must make hay while the sun doth shine;
He must not stand with her, shall I, shall I,
But boldly say, Widow, thou must be mine,

This song inspired the fat-headed old gentleman, who made several attempts to tell a rather broad story out of Joe Miller, that was pat to the purpose; but he always stuck in the middle, every body recollecting the latter part excepting himself. The parson, too, began to show the effects of good cheer, having gradually settled down into a dose, and his wig sitting most suspiciously on one side. Just at this juncture we were summoned to the drawing-room, and, I suspect, at the private instigation of mine host, whose joviality seemed always tempered with a proper love of decorum.

After the dinner table was removed, the hall was given up to the younger members of the family, who, prompted to all kind of noisy mirth by the Oxonian and Master Simon, made its old walls ring with their merriment, as they played at romping games. I delight in witnessing the gambols of children, and particularly at this happy holiday season, and could not help stealing out of the drawing-room on hearing one of their peals of laughter. I found them at the game of blindman's-buff. Master Simon, who was the leader of their revels, and seemed on all occasions to fulfill the office of that ancient potentate, the Lord of Misrule,[7] was blinded in the midst of the hall. The little beings were as busy about him as the mock fairies about Falstaff; pinching him, plucking at the skirts of his coat, and tickling him with straws. One fine blue-eyed girl of about thirteen, with her flaxen hair all in beautiful confusion, her frolic face in a glow, her frock half torn off her shoulders, a complete picture of a romp, was the chief tormentor; and, from the slyness with which Master Simon avoided the smaller game, and hemmed this wild little nymph in corners, and obliged her to jump shrieking over chairs, I suspected the rogue of being not a whit more blinded than was convenient.

When I returned to the drawing-room, I found the company seated round the fire, listening to the parson, who was deeply ensconced in a high-backed oaken chair, the work of some cunning artificer of yore, which had been brought from the library for his particular accommodation. From this venerable piece of furniture, with which his shadowy figure and dark weazen face so admirably accorded, he was dealing out strange accounts of the popular superstitions and legends of the surrounding country, with which he had become acquainted in the course of his antiquarian researches. I am half inclined to think that the old gentleman was himself somewhat tinctured with superstition, as men are very apt to be who live a recluse and studious life in

---

7. At Christmasse there was in the Kinge's house, wheresoever hee was lodged, a lorde of misrule, or mayster of merie disportes, and the like had ye in the house of every nobleman of honor, or good worshippe, were he spirituaall or temporall.—STOWE.

a sequestered part of the country, and pore over black-letter tracts, so often filled with the marvelous and supernatural. He gave us several anecdotes of the fancies of the neighboring peasantry, concerning the effigy of the crusader, which lay on the tomb by the church altar. As it was the only monument of the kind in that part of the country, it had always been regarded with feelings of superstition by the good wives of the village. It was said to get up from the tomb and walk the rounds of the churchyard in stormy nights, particularly when it thundered; and one old woman, whose cottage bordered on the church-yard, had seen it through the windows of the church, when the moon shone, slowly pacing up and down the aisles. It was the belief that some wrong had been left unredressed by the deceased, or some treasure hidden, which kept the spirit in a state of trouble and restlessness. Some talked of gold and jewels buried in the tomb, over which the spectre kept watch; and there was a story current of a sexton in old times who endeavored to break his way to the coffin at night, but, just as he reached it, received a violent blow from the marble hand of the effigy, which stretched him senseless on the pavement. These tales were often laughed at by some of the sturdier among the rustics, yet when night came on, there were many of the stoutest unbelievers that were shy of venturing alone in the footpath that led across the church-yard.

From these and other anecdotes that followed, the crusader appeared to be the favorite hero of ghost stories throughout the vicinity. His picture, which hung up in the hall, was thought by the servants to have something supernatural about it; for they remarked that, in whatever part of the hall you went, the eyes of the warrior were still fixed on you. The old porter's wife too, at the lodge, who had been born and brought up in the family, and was a great gossip among the maid servants, affirmed, that in her young days she had often heard say, that on Midsummer eve, when it was well known all kinds of ghosts, goblins, and fairies become visible and walk abroad, the crusader used to mount his horse, come down from his picture, ride about the house, down the avenue, and so to the church to visit the tomb; on which occasion the church door most civilly swung open of itself; not that he needed it; for he rode through closed gates and even stone walls, and had been seen by one of the dairy-maids to pass between two bars of the great park gate, making himself as thin as a sheet of paper.

All these superstitions I found had been very much countenanced by the squire, who, though not superstitious himself, was very fond of seeing others so. He listened to every goblin tale of the neighboring gossips with infinite gravity, and held the porter's wife in high favor on account of her talent for the marvelous. He was himself a great reader of old legends and romances, and often lamented that he could not believe in them; for a superstitious person, he thought, must live in a kind of fairy land.

Whilst we were all attention to the parson's stories, our ears were suddenly assailed by a burst of heterogeneous sounds from the hall, in which were mingled something like the clang of rude minstrelsy, with the uproar of many small voices and girlish laughter. The door suddenly flew open, and a train came trooping into the room, that might almost have been mistaken for the breaking up of the court of Fairy. That indefatigable spirit, Master Simon, in the faithful discharge of his duties as lord of misrule, had conceived the idea of a Christmas mummery or masking; and having called in to his assistance the Oxonian and the young officer, who were equally ripe for any thing that should occasion romping and merriment, they had carried it into instant effect. The old housekeeper had been consulted; the antique clothes-presses and wardrobes rummaged and made to yield up the relics of finery that had not seen the light for several generations; the younger part of the company had been privately convened from the parlor and hall, and the whole had been bedizened out, into a burlesque imitation of an antique mask.[8]

Master Simon led the van, as "Ancient Christmas," quaintly appareled in a ruff, a short cloak, which had very much the aspect of one of the old housekeeper's petticoats, and a hat that might have served for a village steeple, and must indubitably have figured in the days of the Covenanters. From under this his nose curved boldly forth, flushed with a frost-bitten bloom, that seemed the very trophy of a December blast. He was accompanied by the blue-eyed romp, dished up as "Dame Mince Pie," in the venerable magnificence of a faded brocade, long stomacher, peaked hat, and high-heeled shoes. The young officer appeared as Robin Hood, in a sporting dress of Kendal green, and a foraging cap with a gold tassel.

The costume, to be sure, did not bear testimony to deep research, and there was an evident eye to the picturesque, natural to a young gallant in the presence of his

---

8. Maskings or mummeries were favorite sports at Christmas in old times; and the wardrobes at halls and manor-houses were often laid under contribution to furnish dresses and fantastic designings. I strongly suspect Master Simon to have taken the idea of his from Ben Jonson's Masque of Christmas.

mistress. The fair Julia hung on his arm in a pretty rustic dress, as "Maid Marian." The rest of the train had been metamorphosed in various ways; the girls trussed up in the finery of the ancient belles of the Bracebridge line, and the striplings bewhiskered with burnt cork, and gravely clad in broad skirts, hanging sleeves, and full-bottomed wigs, to represent the character of Roast Beef, Plum Pudding, and other worthies celebrated in ancient maskings. The whole was under the control of the Oxonian, in the appropriate character of Misrule; and I observed that he exercised rather a mischievous sway with his wand over the smaller personages of the pageant.

The irruption of this motley crew, with beat of drum, according to ancient custom, was the consummation of uproar and merriment. Master Simon covered himself with glory by the stateliness with which, as Ancient Christmas, he walked a minuet with the peerless, though giggling, Dame Mince Pie. It was followed by a dance of all the characters, which, from its medley of costumes, seemed as though the old family portraits had skipped down from their frames to join in the sport. Different centuries were figuring at cross hands and right and left; the dark ages were cutting pirouettes and rigadoons; and the days of Queen Bess jiggling merrily down the middle, through a line of succeeding generations.

The worthy squire contemplated these fantastic sports, and this resurrection of his old wardrobe, with the simple relish of childish delight. He stood chuckling and rubbing his hands, and scarcely hearing a word the parson said, notwithstanding that the latter was discoursing most authentically on the ancient and stately dance at the Paon, or peacock, from which he conceived the minuet to be derived.[9] For my part I was in a continual excitement from the varied scenes of whim and innocent gayety passing before me. It was inspiring to see wild-eyed frolic and warm-hearted hospitality breaking out from among the chills and glooms of winter, and old age throwing off his apathy, and catching once more the freshness of youthful enjoyment. I felt also an interest in the scene, from the consideration that these fleeting customs were posting fast into oblivion, and that this was, perhaps, the only family in England in which the whole of them was still punctiliously observed. There was a quaintness, too, mingled

---

9. Sir John Hawkins, speaking of the dance called the Pavon, from pavo, a peacock, says, "It is a grave and majestic dance; the method of dancing it anciently was by gentlemen dressed with caps and swords, by those of the long robe in their gowns, by the peers in their mantles, and by the ladies in gowns with long trains, the motion whereof, in dancing, resembled that of a peacock."—*History of Music*.

with all this revelry, that gave it a peculiar zest: it was suited to the time and place; and as the old manor-house almost reeled with mirth and wassail, it seemed echoing back the joviality of long departed years.[10]

But enough of Christmas and its gambols; it is time for me to pause in this garrulity. Methinks I hear the questions asked by my graver readers, "To what purpose is all this—how is the world to be made wiser by this talk?" Alas! is there not wisdom enough extant for the instruction of the world? And if not, are there not thousands of abler pens laboring for its improvement!—It is so much pleasanter to please than to instruct—to play the companion rather than the preceptor.

What, after all, is the mite of wisdom that I could throw into the mass of knowledge; or how am I sure that my sagest deductions may be safe guides for the opinions of others? But in writing to amuse, if I fail, the only evil is in my own disappointment. If, however, I can by any lucky chance, in these days of evil, rub out one wrinkle from the brow of care, or beguile the heavy heart of one moment of sorrow; if I can now and then penetrate through the gathering film of misanthropy, prompt a benevolent view of human nature, and make my reader more in good humor with his fellow beings and himself, surely surely, I shall not then have written entirely in vain.

---

10. At the time of the first publication of this paper, the picture of an old-fashioned Christmas in the country was pronounced by some as out of date. The author had afterwards an opportunity of witnessing almost all the customs above described, existing in unexpected vigor in the skirts of Derbyrshire and Yorkshire, where he passed the Christmas holidays. The reader will find some notice of them in the author's account of his sojourn at Newstead Abbey.

London Antiques

—I do walk
Methinks like Guido Vaux, with my dark lanthorn,
Stealing to set the town o' fire; i' th' country
I should be taken for William o' the Wisp,
Or Robin Goodfellow.

FLETCHER

I AM SOMEWHAT OF AN ANTIQUITY HUNTER, AND AM FOND OF EXPLORING London in quest of the relics of old times. These are principally to be found in the depths of the city, swallowed up and almost lost in a wilderness of brick and mortar; but deriving poetical and romantic interest from the commonplace prosaic world around them. I was struck with an instance of the kind in the course of a recent summer ramble into the city; for the city is only to be explored to advantage in summer time, when free from the smoke and fog, and rain and mud of winter. I had been buffeting for some time against the current of population setting through Fleet-street. The warm weather had unstrung my nerves, and made me sensitive to every jar and jostle and discordant sound. The flesh was weary, the spirit faint, and I was getting out of humor with the bustling busy throng through which I had to struggle, when in a fit of desperation I tore my way through the crowd, plunged into a by lane, and after passing through several obscure nooks and angles, emerged into a quaint and quiet court with a grassplot in the centre, overhung by elms, and kept perpetually fresh and green by a fountain with its sparkling jet of water. A student with book in hand was seated on a stone bench, partly reading, partly meditating on the movements of two or three trim nursery maids with their infant charges.

I was like an Arab who had suddenly come upon an oasis amid the panting sterility of the desert. By degrees the quiet and coolness of the place soothed my nerves and refreshed my spirit. I pursued my walk, and came, hard by, to a very ancient chapel, with a low-browed Saxon portal of massive and rich architecture. The interior was circular and lofty, and lighted from above. Around were monumental tombs of ancient date, on which were extended the marble effigies of warriors in armor. Some had the hands devoutly crossed upon the breast; others grasped the pommel of the sword, menacing hostility even in the tomb!—while the crossed legs of several indicated soldiers of the Faith who had been on crusades to the Holy Land.

I was, in fact, in the chapel of the Knights Templars, strangely situated in the very centre of sordid traffic; and I do not know a more impressive lesson for the man of the world than thus suddenly to tarn aside from the highway of busy money-seeking life, and sit down among these shadowy sepulchres, where all is twilight, dust, and forgetfulness.

In a subsequent tour of observation, I encountered another of these relics of a "foregone world" locked up in the heart of the city. I had been wandering for some time through dull monotonous streets, destitute of any thing to strike the eye or excite the imagination, when I beheld before me a gothic gateway of mouldering antiquity. It opened into a spacious quadrangle forming the court-yard of a stately gothic pile, the portal of which stood invitingly open.

It was apparently a public edifice, and as I was antiquity hunting, I ventured in, though with dubious steps. Meeting no one either to oppose or rebuke my intrusion, I continued on until I found myself in a great hall, with a lofty arched roof and oaken gallery, all of gothic architecture. At one end of the hall was an enormous fireplace, with wooden settles on each side; at the other end was a raised platform, or dais, the seat of state, above which was the portrait of a man in antique garb, with a long robe, a ruff, and a venerable gray beard.

The whole establishment had an air of monastic quiet and seclusion, and what gave it a mysterious charm, was, that I had not met with a human being since I had passed the threshold.

Encouraged by this loneliness, I seated myself in a recess of a large bow window, which admitted a broad flood of yellow sunshine, checkered here and there by tints from panes of colored glass; while an open casement let in the soft summer air. Here leaning my head on my hand, and my arm on an old oaken table, I indulged in a sort of reverie about what might have been the ancient uses of this edifice. It had evidently been of monastic origin; perhaps one of those collegiate establishments built of yore for the promotion of learning, where the patient monk, in the ample solitude of the cloister, added page to page and volume to volume, emulating in the productions of his brain the magnitude of the pile he inhabited.

As I was seated in this musing mood, a small panneled door m an arch at the upper end of the hall was opened, and a number of gray-headed old men, clad in long black cloaks, came forth one by one; proceeding in that manner through the hall, without uttering a word, each turning a pale face on me as he passed, and disappearing through a door at the lower end.

I was singularly struck with their appearance; their black cloaks and antiquated air comported with the style of this most venerable and mysterious pile. It was as if the ghosts of the departed years, about which I had been musing, were passing in review before me. Pleasing myself with such fancies, I set out, in the spirit of romance, to explore what I pictured to myself a realm of shadows, existing in the very centre of substantial realities.

My ramble led me through a labyrinth of interior courts and corridors and dilapidated cloisters, for the main edifice had many additions and dependences, built at various times and in various styles; in one open space a number of boys, who evidently belonged to the establishment, were at their sports; but every where I observed those mysterious old gray men in black mantles, sometimes sauntering alone, sometimes conversing in groups: they appeared to be the pervading genii of the place. I now called to mind what I had read of certain colleges in old times, where judicial astrology, geomancy, necromancy, and other forbidden and magical sciences were taught. Was this an establishment of the kind, and were these black-cloaked old men really professors of the black art?

These surmises were passing through my mind as my eye glanced into a chamber, hung round with all kinds of strange and uncouth objects; implements of savage warfare; strange idols and stuffed alligators; bottled serpents and monsters decorated the mantelpiece; while on the high tester of an old-fashioned bedstead grinned a human skull, flanked on each side by a dried cat.

I approached to regard more narrowly this mystic chamber, which seemed a fitting laboratory for a necromancer, when I was startled at beholding a human countenance staring at me from a dusky corner. It was that of a small, shriveled old man, with thin cheeks, bright eyes, and gray wiry projecting eyebrows. I at first doubted whether it were not a mummy curiously preserved, but it moved, and I saw that it was alive. It was another of these black-cloaked old men, and, as I regarded his quaint physiognomy, his obsolete garb, and the hideous and sinister objects by which he was surrounded, I began to persuade myself that I had come upon the arch mago, who ruled over this magical fraternity.

Seeing me pausing before the door, he rose and invited me to enter. I obeyed, with singular hardihood, for how did I know whether a wave of his wand might not metamorphose me into some strange monster, or conjure me into one of the bottles on his mantelpiece? He proved, however, to be any thing but a conjurer, and his simple garrulity soon dispelled all the magic and mystery with which I had enveloped this antiquated pile and its no less antiquated inhabitants.

It appeared that I had made my way into the centre of an ancient asylum for superannuated tradesmen and decayed householders, with which was connected a school for a limited number of boys. It was founded upwards of two centuries since on an old monastic establishment, and retained somewhat of the conventual air and character. The shadowy line of old men in black mantles who had passed before me in the hall, and whom I had elevated into magi, turned out to be the pensioners returning from morning service in the chapel.

John Hallum, the little collector of curiosities whom I had made the arch magician, had been for six years a resident of the place, and had decorated this final nestling place of his old age with relics and rarities picked up in the course of his life. According to his own account, he had been somewhat of a traveler; having once been in France, and very near making a visit to Holland. He regretted not having visited the latter country, "as then he might have said he had been there."—He was evidently a traveler of the simple kind.

He was aristocratical too in his notions; keeping aloof, as I found, from the ordinary run of pensioners. His chief associates were a blind man who spoke Latin and Greek, of both which languages Hallum was profoundly ignorant; and a broken-down gentleman who had run through a fortune of forty thousand pounds left him by his father, and ten thousand pounds, the marriage portion of his wife. Little Hallum seemed to consider it an indubitable sign of gentle blood as well as of lofty spirit to be able to squander such enormous sums.

P. S. The picturesque remnant of old times into which I have thus beguiled the reader is what is called the Charter House, originally the Chartreuse. It was founded in 1611, on the remains of an ancient convent, by Sir Thomas Sutton, being one of those noble charities set on foot by individual munificence, and kept up with the quaintness and sanctity of ancient times amidst the modern changes and innovations of London. Here eighty broken-down men, who have seen better days, are provided, in their old age, with food, clothing, fuel, and a yearly allowance for private expenses. They dine together as did the monks of old, in the hall which had been the refectory of the original convent. Attached to the establishment is a school for forty-four boys.

Stow, whose work I have consulted on the subject, speaking of the obligations of the gray-headed pensioners, says, "They are not to intermeddle with any business touching the affairs of the hospital, but to attend only to the service of God, and take thankfully what is provided for them, without muttering, murmuring, or grudging. None to wear weapon, long hair, colored boots, spurs or colored shoes, feathers in their hats, or any ruffian-like or unseemly apparel, but such as becomes hospital men to wear." "And in truth," adds Stow, "happy are they that are so taken from the cares and sorrows of the world, and fixed in so good a place as these old men are; having nothing to care for, but the good of their souls, to serve God and to live in brotherly love."

* * *

For the amusement of such as have been interested by the preceding sketch, taken down from my own observation, and who may wish to know a little more about the mysteries of London, I subjoin a modicum of local history, put into my hands by an odd-looking old gentleman in a small brown wig and a snuff-colored coat, with whom I became acquainted shortly after my visit to the Charter House. I confess I was a little dubious at first, whether it was not one of those apocryphal tales often passed off upon inquiring travelers like myself; and which have brought our general character for veracity into such unmerited reproach. On making proper inquiries, however, I have received the most satisfactory assurances of the author's probity; and, indeed, have been told that he is actually engaged in a full and particular account of the very interesting region in which he resides; of which the following may be considered merely as a foretaste.

Little Britain

What I write is most true. . . . I have a whole booke of cases lying by me, which if I should sette foorth, some grave auntients (within the hearing of Bow bell) would be out of charity with me.

NASHE

IN THE CENTRE OF THE GREAT CITY OF LONDON LIES A SMALL NEIGHBORHOOD, consisting of a cluster of narrow streets and courts, of very venerable and debilitated houses, which goes by the name of LITTLE BRITAIN. Christ Church School and St. Bartholomew's Hospital bound it on the west; Smithfield and Long Lane on the north; Aldersgate Street, like an arm of the sea, divides it from the eastern part of the city; whilst the yawning gulf of Bull-and-Mouth Street separates it from Butcher Lane, and the regions of Newgate. Over this little territory, thus bounded and designated, the great dome of St. Paul's, swelling above the intervening houses of Paternoster Row, Amen Corner, and Ave-Maria Lane, looks down with an air of motherly protection.

This quarter derives its appellation from having been, in ancient times, the residence of the Dukes of Brittany. As London increased, however, rank and fashion rolled off to the west, and trade, creeping on at their heels, took possession of their deserted abodes. For some time Little Britain became the great mart of learning, and was peopled by the busy and prolific race of booksellers: these also gradually deserted it, and, emigrating beyond the great strait of Newgate Street, settled down in Paternoster Row and St. Paul's Church-Yard, where they continue to increase and multiply even at the present day.

But though thus fallen into decline, Little Britain still bears traces of its former splendor. There are several houses ready to tumble down, the fronts of which are magnificently enriched with old oaken carvings of hideous faces, unknown birds, beasts, and fishes; and fruits and flowers which it would perplex a naturalist to classify. There are also, in Aldersgate Street, certain remains of what were once spacious and lordly family mansions, but which have in latter days been subdivided into several tenements. Here may often be found the family of a petty tradesman, with its trumpery furniture, burrowing among the relics of antiquated finery, in great rambling time-stained apartments, with fretted ceilings, gilded cornices, and enormous marble fireplaces. The lanes and courts also contain many smaller houses, not on so grand a scale, but, like your small ancient gentry, sturdily maintaining their claims to equal antiquity. These have their gable ends to the street; great bow windows, with diamond panes set in lead, grotesque carvings, and low arched door-ways.[1]

In this most venerable and sheltered little nest have I passed several quiet years of existence, comfortably lodged in the second floor of one of the smallest but oldest edifices. My sitting-room is an old wainscoted chamber, with small panels, and set off with a miscellaneous array of furniture. I have a particular respect for three or four high-backed claw-footed chairs, covered with tarnished brocade, which bear the marks of having seen better days, and have doubtless figured in some of the old palaces of Little Britain. They seem to me to keep together, and to look down with sovereign contempt upon their leathern-bottomed neighbors; as I have seen decayed gentry carry a high head among the plebeian society with which they were reduced to associate. The whole front of my sitting-room is taken up with a bow window; on the panes of which are recorded the names of previous occupants for many generations, mingled with scraps of very indifferent gentleman-like poetry, written in characters which I can scarcely decipher, and which extol the charms of many a beauty of Little Britain, who has long, long since bloomed, faded, and passed away. As I am an idle personage, with no apparent occupation, and pay my bill regularly every week, I am looked upon as the only independent gentleman of the neighborhood, and, being curious to learn the internal state of a community so apparently shut up within itself, I have managed to work my way into all the concerns and secrets of the place.

Little Britain may truly be called the heart's core of the city, the stronghold of true John Bullism. It is a fragment of London as it was in its better days, with its antiquated folks and fashions. Here flourish in great preservation many of the holiday games and customs of yore. The inhabitants most religiously eat pancakes on Shrove Tuesday, hot cross-buns on Good Friday, and roast goose at Michaelmas; they send love-letters on Valentine's Day, burn the Pope on the Fifth of November, and kiss all

---

1. It is evident that the author of this interesting communication has included, in his general title of Little Britain, many of those little lanes and courts that belong immediately to Cloth Fair.

the girls under the mistletoe at Christmas. Roast beef and plum-pudding are also held in superstitious veneration, and port and sherry maintain their grounds as the only true English wines, all others being considered vile outlandish beverages.

Little Britain has its long catalogue of city wonders, which its inhabitants consider the wonders of the world; such as the great bell of St. Paul's, which sours all the beer when it tolls; the figures that strike the hours at St. Dunstan's clock; the Monument; the lions in the Tower; and the wooden giants in Guild-hall. They still believe in dreams and fortune-telling, and an old woman that lives in Bull-and-Mouth Street makes a tolerable subsistence by detecting stolen goods, and promising the girls good husbands. They are apt to be rendered uncomfortable by comets and eclipses; and if a dog howls dolefully at night, it is looked upon as a sure sign of a death in the place. There are even many ghost stories current, particularly concerning the old mansion-houses; in several of which it is said strange sights are sometimes seen. Lords and ladies, the former in full-bottomed wigs, hanging sleeves, and swords, the latter in lappets, stays, hoops, and brocade, have been seen walking up and down the great waste chambers, on moonlight nights; and are supposed to be the shades of the ancient proprietors in their court-dresses.

Little Britain has likewise its sages and great men. One of the most important of the former is a tall, dry old gentleman, of the name of Skryme, who keeps a small apothecary's shop. He has a cadaverous countenance, full of cavities, and projections, with a brown circle round each eye, like a pair of horn spectacles. He is much thought of by the old women, who consider him as a kind of conjurer, because he has two or three stuffed alligators hanging up in his shop, and several snakes in bottles. He is a great reader of almanacs and newspapers, and is much given to pore over alarming accounts of plots, conspiracies, fires, earthquakes, and volcanic eruptions; which last phenomena he considers as signs of the times. He has always some dismal tale of the kind to deal out to his customers, with their doses; and thus at the same time puts both soul and body into an uproar. He is a great believer in omens and predictions; and has the prophecies of Robert Nixon and Mother Shipton by heart. No man can make so much out of an eclipse, or even an unusually dark day; and he shook the tail of the last comet over the heads of his customers and disciples until they were nearly frightened out of their wits. He has lately got hold of a popular legend or prophecy, on which he has been unusually eloquent. There has been a saying current among the ancient sibyls, who treasure up these things, that when the grasshopper on the top of the Exchange shook hands with the dragon on the top of Bow Church steeple, fearful events would take place. This strange conjunction, it seems, has as strangely come to pass. The same architect has been engaged lately on the repairs of the cupola of the Exchange and the steeple of Bow Church; and, fearful to relate, the dragon and the grasshopper actually lie, cheek by jole, in the yard of his workshop.

"Others," as Mr. Skryme is accustomed to say, "may go star-gazing, and look for conjunctions in the heavens, but here is a conjunction on the earth, near at home, and under our own eyes, which surpasses all the signs and calculations of astrologers." Since these portentous weather-cocks have thus laid their heads together, wonderful events had already occurred. The good old king, notwithstanding that he had lived eighty-two years, had all at once given up the ghost; another king had mounted the throne; a royal duke had died suddenly—another, in France, had been murdered; there had been radical meetings in all parts of the kingdom; the bloody scenes at Manchester; the great plot in Cato Street;—and, above all, the queen had returned to England! All these sinister events are recounted by Mr. Skryme with a mysterious look, and a dismal shake of the head; and being taken with his drugs, and associated in the minds of his auditors with stuffed-sea-monsters, bottled serpents, and his own visage, which is a title-page of tribulation, they have spread great gloom through the minds of the people of Little Britain. They shake their heads whenever they go by Bow Church, and observe that they never expected any good to come of taking down that steeple, which in old times told nothing but glad tidings, as the history of Whittington and his Cat bears witness.

The rival oracle of Little Britain is a substantial cheesemonger, who lives in a fragment of one of the old family mansions, and is as magnificently lodged as a round-bellied mite in the midst of one of his own Cheshires. Indeed, he is a man of no little standing and importance; and his renown extends through Huggin Lane and Lad Lane, and even unto Aldermanbury. His opinion is very much taken in affairs of state, having read the Sunday papers for the last half century, together with the Gentleman's Magazine, Rapin's History of England, and the Naval Chronicle. His head is stored with invaluable maxims which have borne the test of time and use for centuries. It is his firm opinion that "it is a moral impossible," so long as England is true to herself, that anything can shake her: and he has much to say on the subject of the national debt; which, somehow or other, he proves to be a great national bulwark and blessing. He passed the greater part of his life in the purlieus of Little Britain, until of late years, when, having become rich, and grown into the dignity of a Sunday cane, he begins to take his pleasure and see the world. He has therefore made several excursions to Hampstead, Highgate, and other neighboring towns, where he has passed whole afternoons in looking back upon the metropolis through a telescope and endeavoring to descry the steeple of St. Bartholomew's. Not a stage-coachman of Bull-and-Mouth Street but touches his hat as he passes; and he is considered quite a patron at the coach-office of the Goose and Gridiron, St. Paul's Churchyard. His family have been very urgent for him to make an expedition to Margate, but he has great doubts of those new gimcracks, the steamboats, and indeed thinks himself too advanced in life to undertake sea-voyages.

Little Britain has occasionally its factions and divisions, and party spirit ran very high at one time, in consequence of two rival "Burial Societies" being set up in the place. One held its meeting at the Swan and Horse Shoe, and was patronized by the cheesemonger; the other at the Cock and Crown, under the auspices of the apothecary: it is needless to say that the latter was the most flourishing. I have passed an evening or two at each, and have acquired much valuable information, as to the best mode of being buried, the comparative merits of churchyards, together with divers hints on the subject of patent-iron coffins. I have heard the question discussed in all its bearings as to the legality of prohibiting the latter on account of their durability. The feuds occasioned by these societies have happily died of late; but they were for a long time prevailing themes of controversy, the people of Little Britain being extremely solicitous of funeral honors and of lying comfortably in their graves.

Besides these two funeral societies there is a third of quite a different cast, which tends to throw the sunshine of good-humor over the whole neighborhood. It meets once a week at a little old-fashioned house, kept by a jolly publican of the name of Wagstaff, and bearing for insignia a resplendent half-moon, with a most seductive bunch of grapes. The whole edifice is covered with inscriptions to catch the eye of the thirsty wayfarer; such as "Truman, Hanbury, and Co.'s Entire," "Wine, Rum, and Brandy Vaults," "Old Tom, Rum and Compounds," etc. This indeed has been a temple of Bacchus and Momus from time immemorial. It has always been in the family of the Wagstaffs, so that its history is tolerably preserved by the present landlord. It was much frequented by the gallants and cavalieros of the reign of Elizabeth, and was looked into now and then by the wits of Charles the Second's day. But what Wagstaff principally prides himself upon is, that Henry the Eighth, in one of his nocturnal rambles, broke the head of one of his ancestors with his famous walking-staff. This however is considered as rather a dubious and vainglorious boast of the landlord.

The club which now holds its weekly sessions here goes by the name of "the Roaring Lads of Little Britain." They abound in old catches, glees, and choice stories that are traditional in the place, and not to be met with in any other part of the metropolis. There is a mad-cap undertaker who is inimitable at a merry song, but the life of the club, and indeed the prime wit of Little Britain, is bully Wagstaff himself. His ancestors were all wags before him, and he has inherited with the inn a large stock of songs and jokes, which go with it from generation to generation as heirlooms. He is a dapper little fellow, with bandy legs and pot belly, a red face, with a moist merry eye, and a little shock of gray hair behind. At the opening of every club night he is called in to sing his "Confession of Faith," which is the famous old drinking trowl from Gammer Gurton's Needle. He sings it, to be sure, with many variations, as he received it from his father's lips; for it has been a standing favorite at the Half-Moon and Bunch of Grapes ever since it was written; nay, he affirms that his predecessors have often had the honor of singing it before the nobility and gentry at Christmas mummeries, when Little Britain was in all its glory.[2]

---

2. As mine host of the Half-Moon's Confession of Faith may not be familiar to the majority of readers, and as it is a specimen of the current songs of Little Britain, I subjoin it in its original orthography. I would observe, that the whole club always join in the chorus with a fearful thumping on the table and clattering of pewter pots.

I cannot eate but lytle meate,
  My stomacke is not good,
But sure I thinke that I can drinke
  With him that weares a hood.
Though I go bare, take ye no care,
  I nothing am a colde,
  I stuff my skyn so full within,
  Of joly good ale and olde.
Chorus. Backe and syde go bare, go bare,
  Both foote and hand go colde,
But belly, God send thee good ale ynoughe,
  Whether it be new or olde.

I have no rost, but a nut brawne toste
  And a crab laid in the fyre;
A little breade shall do me steade,
  Much breade I not desyre.
No frost nor snow, nor winde, I trowe,
  Can hurte mee, if I wolde,
I am so wrapt and throwly lapt
  Of joly good ale and olde.
Chorus. Backe and syde go bare, go bare, etc.

It would do one's heart good to hear, on a club night, the shouts of merriment, the snatches of song, and now and then the choral bursts of half a dozen discordant voices, which issue from this jovial mansion. At such times the street is lined with listeners, who enjoy a delight equal to that of gazing into a confectioner's window, or snuffing up the steams of a cook-shop.

There are two annual events which produce great stir and sensation in Little Britain; these are St. Bartholomew's Fair, and the Lord Mayor's Day. During the time of the fair, which is held in the adjoining regions of Smithfield, there is nothing going on but gossiping and gadding about. The late quiet streets of Little Britain are overrun with an irruption of strange figures and faces; every tavern is a scene of rout and revel. The fiddle and the song are heard from the tap-room, morning, noon, and night; and at each window may be seen some group of boon companions, with half-shut eyes, hats on one side, pipe in mouth, and tankard in hand, fondling, and prosing, and singing maudlin songs over their liquor. Even the sober decorum of private families, which I must say is rigidly kept up at other times among my neighbors, is no proof against this Saturnalia. There is no such thing as keeping maid-servants within doors. Their brains are absolutely set madding with Punch and the Puppet Show; the Flying Horses; Signior Polito; the Fire-Eater; the celebrated Mr. Paap; and the Irish Giant. The children too lavish all their holiday money in toys

---

And Tyb my wife, that, as her lyfe,
Loveth well good ale to seeke,
Full oft drynkes shee, tyll ye may see,
The teares run downe her cheeke.
Then doth shee trowle to me the bowle,
Even as a mault-worme sholde,
And sayth, sweete harte, I took my parte
Of this jolly good ale and olde.
Chorus. Backe and syde go bare, go bare, etc.

Now let them drynke, tyll they nod and winke,
Even as goode fellowes sholde doe,
They shall not mysse to have the blisse,
Good ale doth bring men to;
And all poore soules that have scowred bowles,
Or have them lustily trolde,
God save the lyves of them and their wives,
Whether they be yonge or olde.
Chorus. Backe and syde go bare, go bare, etc.

and gilt gingerbread, and fill the house with the Lilliputian din of drums, trumpets, and penny-whistles.

But the Lord Mayor's Day is the great anniversary. The Lord Mayor is looked up to by the inhabitants of Little Britain as the greatest potentate upon earth; his gilt coach with six horses as the summit of human splendor; and his procession, with all the Sheriffs and Aldermen in his train, as the grandest of earthly pageants. How they exult in the idea, that the King himself dare not enter the city, without first knocking at the gate of Temple Bar, and asking permission of the Lord Mayor: for if he did, heaven and earth! there is no knowing what might be the consequence. The man in armor who rides before the Lord Mayor, and is the city champion, has orders to cut down every body that offends against the dignity of the city; and then there is the little man with a velvet porringer on his head, who sits at the window of the state coach, and holds the city sword, as long as a pike-staff—Odd's blood! If he once draws that sword, Majesty itself is not safe!

Under the protection of this mighty potentate, therefore, the good people of Little Britain sleep in peace. Temple Bar is an effectual barrier against all interior foes; and as to foreign invasion, the Lord Mayor has but to throw himself into the Tower, call in the train bands, and put the standing army of Beef-eaters under arms, and he may bid defiance to the world!

Thus wrapped up in its own concerns, its own habits, and its own opinions, Little Britain has long flourished as a sound heart to this great fungous metropolis. I have pleased myself with considering it as a chosen spot, where the principles of sturdy John Bullism were garnered up, like seed corn, to renew the national character, when it had run to waste and degeneracy. I have rejoiced also in the general spirit of harmony that prevailed throughout it; for though there might now and then be a few clashes of opinion between the adherents of the cheesemonger and the apothecary, and an occasional feud between the burial societies, yet these were but transient clouds, and soon passed away. The neighbors met with good-will, parted with a shake of the hand, and never abused each other except behind their backs.

I could give rare descriptions of snug junketing parties at which I have been present; where we played at All-Fours, Pope-Joan, Tom-come-tickle-me, and other choice old games; and where we sometimes had a good old English country dance to the tune of Sir Roger de Coverley. Once a year also the neighbors would gather together and go on a gypsy party to Epping Forest. It would have done any man's heart good to see the merriment that took place here as we banqueted on the grass under the trees. How we made the woods ring with bursts of laughter at the songs of little Wagstaff and the merry undertaker! After dinner, too, the young folks would play at blindman's-buff and hide-and-seek; and it was amusing to see them tangled among the briers, and to hear a fine romping girl now and then squeak from among the bushes. The elder folks would gather round the cheesemonger and the apothecary, to hear them talk politics, for they generally brought out a newspaper in their pockets, to pass away time in the country. They would now and then, to be sure, get a little warm in argument; but their disputes were always adjusted by reference to a worthy old umbrella maker in a double chin, who, never exactly comprehending the subject, managed somehow or other to decide in favor of both parties.

All empires, however, says some philosopher or historian, are doomed to changes and revolutions. Luxury and innovation creep in; factions arise; and families now and then spring up, whose ambition and intrigues throw the whole system into confusion. Thus in letter days has the tranquillity of Little Britain been grievously disturbed, and its golden simplicity of manners threatened with total subversion, by the aspiring family of a retired butcher.

The family of the Lambs had long been among the most thriving and popular in the neighborhood: the Miss Lambs were the belles of Little Britain, and every body was pleased when Old Lamb had made money enough to shut up shop, and put his name on a brass plate on his door. In an evil hour, however, one of the Miss Lambs had the honor of being a lady in attendance on the Lady Mayoress, at her grand annual ball, on which occasion she wore three towering ostrich feathers on her head. The family never got over it; they were immediately smitten with a passion for high life; set up a one-horse carriage, put a bit of gold lace round the errand-boy's hat, and have been the talk and detestation of the whole neighborhood ever since. They could no longer be induced to play at Pope-Joan or blindman's-buff; they could endure no dances but quadrilles, which nobody had ever heard of in Little Britain; and they took to reading novels, talking bad French, and playing upon the piano. Their brother too, who had been articled to an attorney, set up for a dandy and a critic, characters hitherto unknown in these parts; and he confounded the worthy folks exceedingly by talking about Kean, the opera, and the Edinburgh Review.

What was still worse, the Lambs gave a grand ball, to which they neglected to invite any of their old neighbors; but they had a great deal of genteel company from Theobald's Road, Red-lion Square, and other parts towards the west. There were several beaux of their brother's acquaintance from Gray's Inn Lane and Hatton Garden; and not less than three Aldermen's ladies with their daughters. This was not to be forgotten or forgiven. All Little Britain was in an uproar with the smacking of whips, the lashing of miserable horses, and the rattling and jingling of hackney coaches. The gossips of the neighborhood might be seen popping their night-caps out at every window, watching the crazy vehicles rumble by; and there was a knot of virulent old cronies, that kept a look-out from a house just opposite the retired butcher's, and scanned and criticised every one that knocked at the door.

This dance was a cause of almost open war, and the whole neighborhood declared they would have nothing more to say to the Lambs. It is true that Mrs. Lamb, when she had no engagements with her quality acquaintance, would give little humdrum tea junketings to some of her old cronies, "quite," as she would say, "in a friendly way"; and it is equally true that her invitations were always accepted, in spite of all previous vows to the contrary. Nay, the good ladies would sit and be delighted with the music of the Miss Lambs, who would condescend to strum an Irish melody for them on the piano; and they would listen with wonderful interest to Mrs. Lamb's anecdotes of Alderman Plunket's family, of Portsoken-ward, and the Miss Timberlakes, the rich heiresses of Crutched-Friars; but then they relieved their consciences, and averted the reproaches of their confederates, by canvassing at the next gossiping convocation everything that had passed, and pulling the Lambs and their rout all to pieces.

The only one of the family that could not be made fashionable was the retired butcher himself. Honest Lamb, in spite of the meekness of his name, was a rough, hearty old fellow, with the voice of a lion, a head of black hair like a shoe-brush, and a broad face mottled like his own beef. It was in vain that the daughters always spoke of him as "the old gentleman," addressed him as "papa," in tones of infinite softness, and endeavored to coax him into a dressing-gown and slippers, and other gentlemanly habits. Do what they might, there was no keeping down the butcher. His sturdy nature would break through all their glozings. He had a hearty vulgar good humor that was irrepressible. His very jokes made his sensitive daughters shudder; and he persisted in wearing his blue cotton coat of a morning, dining at two o'clock, and having a "bit of sausage with his tea."

He was doomed, however, to share the unpopularity of his family. He found his old comrades gradually growing cold and civil to him; no longer laughing at his jokes; and now and then throwing out a fling at "some people," and a hint about "quality binding." This both nettled and perplexed the honest butcher; and his wife and daughters, with the consummate policy of the shrewder sex, taking advantage of the circumstance, at length prevailed upon him to give up his afternoon's pipe and tankard at Wagstaff's; to sit after dinner by himself and take his pint of port—a liquor he detested—and to nod in his chair in solitary and dismal gentility.

The Miss Lambs might now be seen flaunting along the streets in French bonnets, with unknown beaux; and talking and laughing so loud that it distressed the nerves of every good lady within hearing. They even went so far as to attempt patronage, and actually induced a French dancing-master to set up in the neighborhood; but the worthy folks of Little Britain took fire at it, and did so persecute the poor Gaul, that he was fain to pack up fiddle and dancing-pumps, and decamp with such precipitation, that he absolutely forgot to pay for his lodgings.

I had flattered myself, at first, with the idea that all this fiery indignation on the part of the community was merely the overflowing of their zeal for good old English manners, and their horror of innovation; and I applauded the silent contempt they were so vociferous in expressing, for upstart pride, French fashions, and the Miss Lambs. But I grieve to say that I soon perceived the infection had taken hold; and that my neighbors, after condemning, were beginning to follow their example. I overheard my landlady importuning her husband to let their daughters have one quarter at French and music, and that they might take a few lessons in quadrille. I even saw, in the course of a few Sundays, no less than five French bonnets, precisely like those of the Miss Lambs, parading about Little Britain.

I still had my hopes that all this folly would gradually die away; that the Lambs might move out of the neighborhood; might die, or might run away with attorneys' apprentices; and that quiet and simplicity might be again restored to the community. But unluckily a rival power arose. An opulent oilman died, and left a widow with a large jointure and a family of buxom daughters. The young ladies had long been repining in secret at the parsimony of a prudent father, which kept down all their elegant aspirings. Their ambition, being now no longer restrained, broke out into a blaze, and they openly took the field against the family of the butcher. It is true that the Lambs, having had the first start, had naturally an advantage of them in the fashionable career. They could speak a little bad French, play the piano, dance quadrilles, and had formed high acquaintances; but the Trotters were not to be distanced. When the Lambs appeared with two feathers in their hats, the Miss Trotters mounted four, and of twice as fine colors. If the Lambs gave a dance, the Trotters were sure not to be behindhand: and though they might not boast of as good company, yet they had double the number, and were twice as merry.

The whole community has at length divided itself into fashionable factions, under the banners of these two families. The old games of Pope-Joan and Tom-come-tickle-me are entirely discarded; there is no such thing as getting up an honest country dance; and on my attempting to kiss a young lady under the mistletoe last Christmas, I was indignantly repulsed; the Miss Lambs having pronounced it "shocking vulgar." Bitter rivalry has also broken out as to the most fashionable part of Little Britain; the Lambs standing up for the dignity of Cross-Keys Square, and the Trotters for the vicinity of St. Bartholomew's.

Thus is this little territory torn by factions and internal dissensions, like the great empire whose name it bears; and what will be the result would puzzle the apothecary himself, with all his talent at prognostics, to determine; though I apprehend that it will terminate in the total downfall of genuine John Bullism.

The immediate effects are extremely unpleasant to me. Being a single man, and, as I observed before, rather an idle good-for-nothing personage, I have been considered the only gentleman by profession in the place. I stand therefore in high favor with both parties, and have to hear all their cabinet counsels and mutual backbitings. As I am too civil not to agree with the ladies on all occasions, I have committed myself most horribly with both parties, by abusing their opponents. I might manage to reconcile this to my conscience, which is a truly accommodating one, but I cannot to my apprehension—if the Lambs and Trotters ever come to a reconciliation, and compare notes, I am ruined!

I have determined, therefore, to beat a retreat in time, and am actually looking out for some other nest in this great city, where old English manners are still kept up; where French is neither eaten, drunk, danced, nor spoken; and where there are no fashionable families of retired tradesmen. This found, I will, like a veteran rat, hasten away before I have an old house about my ears; bid a long, though a sorrowful adieu to my present abode, and leave the rival factions of the Lambs and the Trotters to divide the distracted empire of LITTLE BRITAIN.

Stratford-On-Avon

Thou soft-flowing Avon, by thy silver stream
Of things more than mortal sweet Shakespeare would dream;
The fairies by moonlight dance round his green bed,
For hallow'd the turf is which pillow'd his head.

GARRICK

TO A HOMELESS MAN, WHO HAS NO SPOT ON THIS WIDE WORLD WHICH HE can truly call his own, there is a momentary feeling of something like independence and territorial consequence when, after a weary day's travel, he kicks off his boots, thrusts his feet into slippers, and stretches himself before an inn fire. Let the world without go as it may; let kingdoms rise or fall, so long as he has the wherewithal to pay his bill, he is, for the time being, the very monarch of all he surveys. The arm-chair is his throne, the poker his sceptre, and the little parlor, some twelve feet square, his undisputed empire. It is a morsel of certainty, snatched from the midst of the uncertainties of life; it is a sunny moment gleaming out kindly on a cloudy day: and he who has advanced some way on the pilgrimage of existence knows the importance of husbanding even morsels and moments of enjoyment. "Shall I not take mine ease in mine inn?" thought I, as I gave the fire a stir, lolled back in my elbow-chair, and cast a complacent look about the little parlor of the Red Horse, at Stratford-on-Avon.

The words of sweet Shakspeare were just passing through my mind as the clock struck midnight from the tower of the church in which he lies buried. There was a gentle tap at the door, and a pretty chambermaid, putting in her smiling face, inquired, with a hesitating air, whether I had rung. I understood it as a modest hint that it was time to retire. My dream of absolute dominion was at an end; so abdicating my throne, like a prudent potentate, to avoid being deposed, and putting the Stratford

Guide-Book under my arm as a pillow companion, I went to bed, and dreamt all night of Shakspeare, the jubilee, and David Garrick.

The next morning was one of those quickening mornings which we sometimes have in early spring; for it was about the middle of March. The chills of a long winter had suddenly given way; the north wind had spent its last gasp; and a mild air came stealing from the west, breathing the breath of life into nature, and wooing every bud and flower to burst forth into fragrance and beauty.

I had come to Stratford on a poetical pilgrimage. My first visit was to the house where Shakspeare was born, and where, according to tradition, he was brought up to his father's craft of wool-combing. It is a small mean-looking edifice of wood and plaster, a true nestling-place of genius, which seems to delight in hatching its offspring in by-corners. The walls of its squalid chambers are covered with names and inscriptions in every language, by pilgrims of all nations, ranks, and conditions, from the prince to the peasant; and present a simple, but striking instance of the spontaneous and universal homage of mankind to the great poet of nature.

The house is shown by a garrulous old lady, in a frosty red face, lighted up by a cold blue anxious eye, and garnished with artificial locks of flaxen hair curling from under an exceedingly dirty cap. She was peculiarly assiduous in exhibiting the relics with which this, like all other celebrated shrines, abounds. There was the shattered stock of the very matchlock with which Shakspeare shot the deer, on his poaching exploits. There, too, was his tobacco-box; which proves that he was a rival smoker of Sir Walter Raleigh: the sword also with which he played Hamlet; and the identical lantern with which Friar Laurence discovered Romeo and Juliet at the tomb! There was an ample supply also of Shakspeare's mulberry-tree, which seems to have as extraordinary powers of self-multiplication as the wood of the true cross; of which there is enough extant to build a ship of the line.

The most favorite object of curiosity, however, is Shakspeare's chair. It stands in the chimney nook of a small gloomy chamber, just behind what was his father's shop. Here he may many a time have sat when a boy, watching the slowly revolving spit with all the longing of an urchin; or of an evening, listening to the cronies and gossips of Stratford, dealing forth churchyard tales and legendary anecdotes of the troublesome times of England. In this chair it is the custom of every one that visits the house to sit: whether this be done with the hope of imbibing any of the inspiration of the bard I am at a loss to say, I merely mention the fact; and mine hostess privately assured me that, though built of solid oak, such was the fervent zeal of devotees, that the chair had to be new bottomed at least once in three years. It is worthy of notice also, in the history of this extraordinary chair, that it partakes something of the volatile nature of the Santa Casa of Loretto, or the flying chair of the Arabian enchanter; for though sold some few years since to a northern princess, yet, strange to tell, it has found its way back again to the old chimney corner.

I am always of easy faith in such matters, and am ever willing to be deceived, where the deceit is pleasant and costs nothing. I am therefore a ready believer in relics, legends, and local anecdotes of goblins and great men; and would advise all travelers who travel for their gratification to be the same. What is it to us, whether these stories be true or false, so long as we can persuade ourselves into the belief of them, and enjoy all the charm of the reality? There is nothing like resolute good-humored credulity in these matters; and on this occasion I went even so far as willingly to believe the claims of mine hostess to a lineal descent from the poet, when, unluckily for my faith, she put into my hands a play of her own composition, which set all belief in her own consanguinity at defiance.

From the birthplace of Shakspeare a few paces brought me to his grave. He lies buried in the chancel of the parish church, a large and venerable pile, mouldering with age, but richly ornamented. It stands on the banks of the Avon, on an embowered point, and separated by adjoining gardens from the suburbs of the town. Its situation is quiet and retired: the river runs murmuring at the foot of the church-yard, and the elms which grow upon its banks droop their branches into its clear bosom. An avenue of limes, the boughs of which are curiously interlaced, so as to form in summer an arched way of foliage, leads up from the gate of the yard to the church porch. The graves are overgrown with grass; the gray tombstones, some of them nearly sunk into the earth, are half covered with moss, which has likewise tinted the reverend old building. Small birds have built their nests among the cornices and fissures of the walls, and keep up a continual flutter and chirping; and rooks are sailing and cawing about its lofty gray spire.

In the course of my rambles I met with the gray-headed sexton, Edmonds, and accompanied him home to get the key of the church. He had lived in Stratford, man and boy, for eighty years, and seemed still to consider himself a vigorous man, with the trivial exception that he had nearly lost the use of his legs for a few years past. His dwelling was a cottage, looking out upon the Avon and its bordering meadows; and was a picture of that neatness, order, and comfort, which pervade the humblest dwellings in this country. A low whitewashed room with a stone floor carefully scrubbed, served for parlor, kitchen, and hall. Rows of pewter and earthen dishes glittered along the dresser. On an old oaken table, well rubbed and polished, lay the family Bible and prayer-book, and the drawer contained the family library, composed of about half a score of well-thumbed volumes. An ancient clock, that important article of cottage furniture, ticked on the opposite side of the room; with a bright warming-pan hanging on one side of it, and the old man's horn-handled Sunday cane on the other. The fireplace, as usual, was wide and deep enough to admit a gossip knot within its jambs. In one corner sat the old man's granddaughter sewing, a pretty blue-eyed girl,—and in the opposite corner was a superannuated crony, whom he addressed by the name of John Ange, and who, I found, had been his companion from childhood. They had played together in infancy; they had worked together in manhood; they were now tottering about and gossiping away the evening of life; and in a short time they will probably be buried together in the neighboring church-yard. It is not often that we see two streams of existence running thus evenly and tranquilly side by side; it is only in such quiet "bosom scenes" of life that they are to be met with.

I had hoped to gather some traditionary anecdotes of the bard from these ancient chroniclers; but they had nothing new to impart. The long interval during which Shakspeare's writings lay in comparative neglect has spread its shadow over his history; and it is his good or evil lot that scarcely anything remains to his biographers but a scanty handful of conjectures.

The sexton and his companion had been employed as carpenters on the preparations for the celebrated Stratford Jubilee, and they remembered Garrick, the prime mover of the fête, who superintended the arrangements, and who, according to the sexton, was "a short punch man, very lively and bustling." John Ange had assisted also in cutting down Shakspeare's mulberry tree, of which he had a morsel in his pocket for sale; no doubt a sovereign quickener of literary conception.

I was grieved to hear these two worthy wights speak very dubiously of the eloquent dame who shows the Shakspeare house. John Ange shook his head when I mentioned her valuable and inexhaustible collection of relics, particularly her remains of the mulberry tree; and the old sexton even expressed a doubt as to Shakspeare having been born in her house. I soon discovered that he looked upon her mansion with an evil eye, as a rival to the poet's tomb; the latter having comparatively but few visitors. Thus it is that historians differ at the very outset, and mere pebbles make the stream of truth diverge into different channels even at the fountain head.

We approached the church through the avenue of limes, and entered by a gothic porch, highly ornamented, with carved doors of massive oak. The interior is spacious, and the architecture and embellishments superior to those of most country churches. There are several ancient monuments of nobility and gentry, over some of which hang funeral escutcheons, and banners dropping piecemeal from the walls. The tomb of Shakspeare is in the chancel. The place is solemn and sepulchral. Tall elms wave before the pointed windows, and the Avon, which runs at a short distance from the walls, keeps up a low perpetual murmur. A flat stone marks the spot where the bard is buried. There are four lines inscribed on it, said to have been written by himself, and which have in them something extremely awful. If they are indeed his own, they show that solicitude about the quiet of the grave, which seems natural to fine sensibilities and thoughtful minds.

Good friend, for Jesus' sake, forbeare
To dig the dust enclosed here.
Blessed be he that spares these stones,
And curst be he that moves my bones.

Just over the grave, in a niche of the wall, is a bust of Shakspeare, put up shortly after his death and considered as a resemblance. The aspect is pleasant and serene, with a finely-arched forehead; and I thought I could read in it clear indications of that cheerful, social disposition, by which he was as much characterized among his contemporaries as by the vastness of his genius. The inscription mentions his age at the time of his decease—fifty-three years; an untimely death for the world: for what fruit might not have been expected from the golden autumn of such a mind, sheltered as it was from the stormy vicissitudes of life, and flourishing in the sunshine of popular and royal favor.

The inscription on the tombstone has not been without its effect. It has prevented the removal of his remains from the bosom of his native place to Westminster Abbey, which was at one time contemplated. A few years since also, as some laborers were digging to make an adjoining vault, the earth caved in, so as to leave a vacant space almost like an arch, through which one might have reached into his grave. No one, however, presumed to meddle with his remains so awfully guarded by a malediction;

and lest any of the idle or the curious, or any collector of relics, should be tempted to commit depredations, the old sexton kept watch over the place for two days, until the vault was finished and the aperture closed again. He told me that he had made bold to look in at the hole, but could see neither coffin nor bones; nothing but dust. It was something, I thought, to have seen the dust of Shakspeare.

Next to this grave are those of his wife, his favorite daughter, Mrs. Hall, and others of his family. On a tomb close by, also, is a full-length effigy of his old friend John Combe, of usurious memory; on whom he is said to have written a ludicrous epitaph. There are other monuments around, but the mind refuses to dwell on anything that is not connected with Shakspeare. His idea pervades the place; the whole pile seems but as his mausoleum. The feelings, no longer checked and thwarted by doubt, here indulge in perfect confidence: other traces of him may be false or dubious, but here is palpable evidence and absolute certainty. As I trod the sounding pavement there was something intense and thrilling in the idea, that, in very truth, the remains of Shakspeare were mouldering beneath my feet. It was a long time before I could prevail upon myself to leave the place; and as I passed through the churchyard, I plucked a branch from one of the yew trees, the only relic that I have brought from Stratford.

I had now visited the usual objects of a pilgrim's devotion, but I had a desire to see the old family seat of the Lucys, at Charlecot, and to ramble through the park where Shakspeare, in company with some of the roisterers of Stratford, committed his youthful offence of deer-stealing. In this hare-brained exploit we are told that he was taken prisoner, and carried to the keeper's lodge, where he remained all night in doleful captivity. When brought into the presence of Sir Thomas Lucy, his treatment must have been galling and humiliating; for it so wrought upon his spirit as to produce a rough pasquinade, which was affixed to the park gate at Charlecot.[1]

---

1 The following is the only stanza extant of this lampoon:—

> A parliament member, a justice of peace,
> At home a poor scarecrow, at London an asse,
> If lowsie is Lucy, as some volke miscalle it,
> Then Lucy is lowsie, whatever befall it,
> He thinks himself great;
> Yet an asse in his state,
> We allow by his ears but with asses to mate,
> If Lucy is lowsie, as some volke miscalle it,
> Then sing lowsie Lucy whatever befall it.

This flagitious attack upon the dignity of the knight so incensed him, that he applied to a lawyer at Warwick to put the severity of the laws in force against the rhyming deer-stalker. Shakspeare did not wait to brave the united puissance of a knight of the shire and a country attorney. He forthwith abandoned the pleasant banks of the Avon and his paternal trade; wandered away to London; became a hanger-on to the theatres; then an actor; and, finally, wrote for the stage; and thus, through the persecution of Sir Thomas Lucy, Stratford lost an indifferent wool-comber, and the world gained an immortal poet. He retained, however, for a long time, a sense of the harsh treatment of the Lord of Charlecot, and revenged himself in his writings; but in the sportive way of a good-natured mind. Sir Thomas is said to be the original of Justice Shallow, and the satire is slyly fixed upon him by the justice's armorial bearings, which, like those of the knight, had white luces[2] in the quarterings.

Various attempts have been made by his biographers to soften and explain away this early transgression of the poet; but I look upon it as one of those thoughtless exploits natural to his situation and turn of mind. Shakspeare, when young, had doubtless all the wildness and irregularity of an ardent, undisciplined, and undirected genius. The poetic temperament has naturally something in it of the vagabond. When left to itself it runs loosely and wildly, and delights in every thing eccentric and licentious. It is often a turn-up of a die, in the gambling freaks of fate, whether a natural genius shall turn out a great rogue or a great poet; and had not Shakspeare's mind fortunately taken a literary bias, he might have as daringly transcended all civil, as he has all dramatic laws.

I have little doubt that, in early life, when running, like an unbroken colt, about the neighborhood of Stratford, he was to be found in the company of all kinds of odd anomalous characters; that he associated with all the madcaps of the place, and was one of those unlucky urchins, at mention of whom old men shake their heads, and predict that they will one day come to the gallows. To him the poaching in Sir Thomas Lucy's park was doubtless like a foray to a Scottish knight, and struck his eager, and, as yet untamed, imagination as something delightfully adventurous.[3]

---

2 The luce is a pike or jack, and abounds in the Avon about Charlecot.

3 A proof of Shakspeare's random habits and associates in his youthful days may be found in a traditionary anecdote, picked up at Stratford by the elder Ireland, and mentioned in his "Picturesque Views on the Avon."

About seven miles from Stratford lies the thirsty little market town of Bedford, famous for its ale. Two societies of the village yeomanry used to meet, under the appellation of the Bedford topers, and

The old mansion of Charlecot and its surrounding park still remain in the possession of the Lucy family, and are peculiarly interesting, from being connected with this whimsical but eventful circumstance in the scanty history of the bard. As the house stood at little more than three miles' distance from Stratford, I resolved to pay it a pedestrian visit, that I might stroll leisurely through some of those scenes from which Shakspeare must have derived his earliest ideas of rural imagery.

The country was yet naked and leafless; but English scenery is always verdant, and the sudden change in the temperature of the weather was surprising in its quickening effects upon the landscape. It was inspiring and animating to witness this first awakening of spring; to feel its warm breath stealing over the senses; to see the moist mellow earth beginning to put forth the green sprout and the tender blade: and the trees and shrubs, in their reviving tints and bursting buds, giving the promise of returning foliage and flower. The cold snow-drop, that little borderer on the skirts of winter, was to be seen with its chaste white blossoms in the small gardens before the cottages. The bleating of the new-dropt lambs was faintly heard from the fields. The sparrow twittered about the thatched eaves and budding hedges; the robin threw a livelier note into his late querulous wintry strain; and the lark, springing up from the reeking bosom of the meadow, towered away into the bright fleecy cloud, pouring forth torrents of melody. As I watched the little songster mounting up higher and higher, until his body was a mere speck on the white bosom of the cloud, while the

---

to challenge the lovers of good ale of the neighboring villages to a contest of drinking. Among others, the people of Stratford were called out to prove the strength of their heads; and in the number of the champions was Shakspeare, who, in spite of the proverb that "they who drink beer will think beer," was as true to his ale as Falstaff to his sack. The chivalry of Stratford was staggered at the first onset, and sounded a retreat while they had yet legs to carry them off the field. They had scarcely marched a mile when, their legs failing them, they were forced to lie down under a crab-tree, where they passed the night. It was still standing, and goes by the name of Shakspeare's tree.

In the morning his companions awaked the bard, and proposed returning to Bedford, but he declined, saying he had enough, having drank with

> Piping Pebworth, Dancing Marston,
> Haunted Hilbro', Hungry Grafton,
> Dudging Exhall, Papist Wicksford,
> Beggarly Broom, and Drunken Bedford.

"The villages here alluded to," says Ireland, "still bear the epithets thus given them: the people of Pebworth, are still famed for their skill on the pipe and tabor; Hilborough is now called Haunted Hilborough; and Grafton is famous for the poverty of its soil."

ear was still filled with his music, it called to mind Shakspeare's exquisite little song in Cymbeline:

> Hark! hark! the lark at heav'n's gate sings,
> And Phoebus 'gins arise,
> His steeds to water at those springs,
> On chaliced flowers that lies.
>
> And winking mary-buds begin
> To ope their golden eyes;
> With every thing that pretty bin,
> My lady sweet arise!

Indeed the whole country about here is poetic ground: everything is associated with the idea of Shakspeare. Every old cottage that I saw, I fancied into some resort of his boyhood, where he had acquired his intimate knowledge of rustic life and manners, and heard those legendary tales and wild superstitions which he has woven like witchcraft into his dramas. For in his time, we are told, it was a popular amusement in winter evenings "to sit round the fire, and tell merry tales of errant knights, queens, lovers, lords, ladies, giants, dwarfs, thieves, cheaters, witches, fairies, goblins, and friars."[4]

My route for a part of the way lay in sight of the Avon, which made a variety of the most fancy doublings and windings through a wide and fertile valley; sometimes glittering from among willows, which fringed its borders; sometimes disappearing among groves, or beneath green banks; and sometimes rambling out into full view, and making an azure sweep round a slope of meadow-land. This beautiful bosom of country is called the Vale of the Red Horse. A distant line of undulating blue hills seems to be its boundary, whilst all the soft intervening landscape lies in a manner enchained in the silver links of the Avon.

After pursuing the road for about three miles, I turned off into a footpath, which led along the borders of fields, and under hedgerows to a private gate of the park; there

---

4. Scot, in his "Discoverie of Witchcraft," enumerates a host of these fireside fancies: "And they have so fraid us with bull-beggars, spirits, witches, urchins, elves, hags, fairies, satyrs, pans, faunes, syrens, kit with the can sticke, tritons, centaurs, dwarfes, giantes, imps, calcars, conjurors, nymphes, changelings, incubus, Robin-goodfellow, the spoorne, the mare, the man in the oke, the hell-waine, the fier drake, the puckle, Tom Thombe, hobgoblins, Tom Tumbler, boneless, and such other bugs, that we were afraid of our own shadowes."

was a stile, however, for the benefit of the pedestrian; there being a public right of way through the grounds. I delight in these hospitable estates, in which every one has a kind of property—at least as far as the footpath is concerned. It in some measure reconciles a poor man to his lot, and, what is more, to the better lot of his neighbor, thus to have parks and pleasure-grounds thrown open for his recreation. He breathes the pure air as freely, and lolls as luxuriously under the shade, as the lord of the soil; and if he has not the privilege of calling all that he sees his own, he has not, at the same time, the trouble of paying for it, and keeping it in order.

I now found myself among noble avenues of oaks and elms, whose vast size bespoke the growth of centuries. The wind sounded solemnly among their branches, and the rooks cawed from their hereditary nests in the tree tops. The eye ranged through a long lessening vista, with nothing to interrupt the view but a distant statue; and a vagrant deer stalking like a shadow across the opening.

There is something about these stately old avenues that has the effect of gothic architecture, not merely from the pretended similarity of form, but from their bearing the evidence of long duration, and of having had their origin in a period of time with which we associate ideas of romantic grandeur. They betoken also the long-settled dignity, and proudly-concentrated independence of an ancient family; and I have heard a worthy but aristocratic old friend observe, when speaking of the sumptuous palaces of modern gentry, that "money could do much with stone and mortar, but, thank Heaven, there was no such thing as suddenly building up an avenue of oaks."

It was from wandering in early life among this rich scenery, and about the romantic solitudes of the adjoining park of Fullbroke, which then formed a part of the Lucy estate, that some of Shakspeare's commentators have supposed he derived his noble forest meditations of Jaques, and the enchanting woodland pictures in "As you like it." It is in lonely wanderings through such scenes, that the mind drinks deep but quiet draughts of inspiration, and becomes intensely sensible of the beauty and majesty of nature. The imagination kindles into reverie and rapture; vague but exquisite images and ideas keep breaking upon it; and we revel in a mute and almost incommunicable luxury of thought. It was in some such mood, and perhaps under one of those very trees before me, which threw their broad shades over the grassy banks and quivering waters of the Avon, that the poet's fancy may have sallied forth into that little song which breathes the very soul of a rural voluptuary:

Under the green wood tree,
Who loves to lie with me,
And tune his merry throat
Unto the sweet bird's note,
Come hither, come hither, come hither.
Here shall he see
No enemy,
But winter and rough weather.

I had now come in sight of the house. It is a large building of brick, with stone quoins, and is in the gothic style of Queen Elizabeth's day, having been built in the first year of her reign. The exterior remains very nearly in its original state, and may be considered a fair specimen of the residence of a wealthy country gentleman of those days. A great gateway opens from the park into a kind of court-yard in front of the house, ornamented with a grassplot, shrubs, and flower-beds. The gateway is in imitation of the ancient barbacan; being a kind of out-post, and flanked by towers; though evidently for mere ornament, instead of defence. The front of the house is completely in the old style; with stone-shafted casements, a great bow-window of heavy stone-work, and a portal with armorial bearings over it, carved in stone. At each corner of the building is an octagon tower, surmounted by a gilt ball and weather-cock.

The Avon, which winds through the park, makes a bend just at the foot of a gently-sloping bank which sweeps down from the rear of the house. Large herds of deer were feeding or reposing upon its borders; and swans were sailing majestically upon its bosom. As I contemplated the venerable old mansion, I called to mind Falstaff's encomium on Justice Shallow's abode, and the affected indifference and real vanity of the latter:

Falstaff. You have a goodly dwelling and a rich.

Shallow. Barren, barren, barren; beggars all, beggars all, Sir John:—marry, good air.

Whatever may have been the joviality of the old mansion in the days of Shakspeare, it had now an air of stillness and solitude. The great iron gateway that opened into the court-yard was locked; there was no show of servants bustling about the place; the deer gazed quietly at me as I passed, being no longer harried by the moss-troopers of

Stratford. The only sign of domestic life that I met with was a white cat, stealing with wary look and stealthy pace towards the stables, as if on some nefarious expedition. I must not omit to mention the carcass of a scoundrel crow which I saw suspended against the barn wall, as it shows that the Lucys still inherit that lordly abhorrence of poachers, and maintain that rigorous exercise of territorial power which was so strenuously manifested in the case of the bard.

After prowling about for some time, I at length found my way to a lateral portal, which was the every-day entrance to the mansion. I was courteously received by a worthy old housekeeper, who, with the civility and communicativeness of her order, showed me the interior of the house. The greater part has undergone alterations, and been adapted to modern tastes and modes of living: there is a fine old oaken staircase; and the great hall, that noble feature in an ancient manor-house, still retains much of the appearance it must have had in the days of Shakspeare. The ceiling is arched and lofty; and at one end is a gallery in which stands an organ. The weapons and trophies of the chase, which formerly adorned the hall of a country gentleman, have made way for family portraits. There is a wide, hospitable fireplace, calculated for an ample old-fashioned wood fire, formerly the rallying-place of winter festivity. On the opposite side of the hall is the huge gothic bow-window, with stone shafts, which looks out upon the court-yard. Here are emblazoned in stained glass the armorial bearings of the Lucy family for many generations, some being dated in 1558. I was delighted to observe in the quarterings the three *white luces*, by which the character of Sir Thomas was first identified with that of Justice Shallow. They are mentioned in the first scene of the Merry Wives of Windsor, where the justice, is in a rage with Falstaff for having "beaten his men, killed his deer, and broken into his lodge." The poet had no doubt the offences of himself and his comrades in mind at the time, and we may suppose the family pride and vindictive threats of the puissant Shallow to be a caricature of the pompous indignation of Sir Thomas.

> *Shallow.* Sir Hugh, persuade me not: I will make a Star-Chamber matter of it; if he were twenty John Falstaffs, he shall not abuse Sir Robert Shallow, Esq.
>
> *Slender.* In the county of Gloster, justice of peace and *coram*.
>
> *Shallow.* Ay, cousin Slender, and *custalorum*.
>
> *Slender.* Ay, and *ratolorum* too, and a gentleman born, master parson; who writes himself *Armigero* in any bill, warrant, quittance, or obligation,

Armigero.

Shallow. Ay, that I do; and have done any time these three hundred years.

Slender. All his successors gone before him have done't, and all his ancestors that come after him may; they may give the dozen *white luces* in their coat.

*****

Shallow. The council shall hear it; it is a riot.

Evans. It is not meet the council hear of a riot; there is no fear of Got in a riot; the council, hear you, shall desire to hear the fear of Got, and not to hear a riot; take your vizaments in that.

Shallow. Ha! o' my life, if I were young again, the sword should end it!

Near the window thus emblazoned hung a portrait, by Sir Peter Lely, of one of the Lucy family, a great beauty of the time of Charles the Second: the old housekeeper shook her head as she pointed to the picture, and informed me that this lady had been sadly addicted to cards, and had gambled away a great portion of the family estate, among which was that part of the park where Shakspeare and his comrades had killed the deer. The lands thus lost had not been entirely regained by the family even at the present day. It is but justice to this recreant dame to confess that she had a surpassingly fine hand and arm.

The picture which most attracted my attention was a great painting over the fireplace, containing likenesses of Sir Thomas Lucy and his family, who inhabited the hall in the latter part of Shakspeare's lifetime. I at first thought that it was the vindictive knight himself but the housekeeper assured me that it was his son; the only likeness extant of the former being an effigy upon his tomb in the church of the neighboring hamlet of Charlecot.[5] The picture gives a lively idea of the costume and manners of the

---

5. This effigy is in white marble, and represents the Knight in complete armor. Near him lies the effigy of his wife, and on her tomb is the following inscription; which, if really composed by her husband, places him quite above the intellectual level of Master Shallow:

Here lyeth the Lady Joyce Lucy wife of Sir Thomas Lucy of Charlecot in ye county of Warwick, Knight, Daughter and heir of Thomas Acton of Sutton in ye county of Worcester Esquire who departed out of this wretched world to her heavenly kingdom ye 10 day of February in ye yeare of our Lord God 1595 and of her age 60 and three. All the time of her lyfe a true and faythful servant of her good God, never detected of any cryme or vice. In religion most sounde, in love to her husband most faythful and true. In friendship most constant; to what in trust was committed unto her most secret. In wisdom excelling. In governing of her house, bringing up of youth in ye fear of God that did converse with her moste rare and singular. A great maintayner of hospitality. Greatly esteemed of her betters;

time. Sir Thomas is dressed in ruff and doublet, white shoes with roses in them; and has a peaked yellow, or, as Master Slender would say, "a cane-colored beard." His lady is seated on the opposite side of the picture, in wide ruff and long stomacher, and the children have a most venerable stiffness and formality of dress. Hounds and spaniels are mingled in the family group; a hawk is seated on his perch in the foreground, and one of the children holds a bow;—all intimating the knight's skill in hunting, hawking, and archery—so indispensable to an accomplished gentleman in those days.[6]

I regretted to find that the ancient furniture of the hall had disappeared; for I had hoped to meet with the stately elbow-chair of carved oak, in which the country squire of former days was wont to sway the sceptre of empire over his rural domains; and in which it might be presumed the redoubted Sir Thomas sat enthroned in awful state when the recreant Shakspeare was brought before him. As I like to deck out pictures for my own entertainment, I pleased myself with the idea that this very hall had been the scene of the unlucky bard's examination on the morning after his captivity in the lodge. I fancied to myself the rural potentate surrounded by his body-guard of butler, pages, and blue-coated serving-men with their badges; while the luckless culprit was brought in, forlorn and chopfallen, in the custody of gamekeepers, huntsmen, and whippers-in, and followed by a rabble rout of country clowns. I fancied bright faces of curious housemaids peeping from the half-opened doors; while from the gallery the fair daughters of the knight leaned gracefully forward, eyeing the youthful prisoner with that pity "that dwells in womanhood."—Who would have thought that this poor varlet, thus trembling before the brief authority of a country squire, and the sport of rustic boors, was soon to become the delight of princes, the theme of all tongues and ages, the dictator to the human mind, and was to confer immortality on his oppressor by a caricature and a lampoon!

---

misliked of none unless of the envyous. When all is spoken that can be saide a woman so garnished with virtue as not to be bettered and hardly to be equalled by any. As shee lived most virtuously so shee died most Godly. Set downe by him yt best did knowe what hath byn written to be true.

Thomas Lucye.

6. Bishop Earle, speaking of the country gentleman of his time, observes, "his housekeeping is seen much in the different families of dogs, and serving-men attendant on their kennels; and the deepness of their throats is the depth of his discourse. A hawk he esteems the true burden of nobility, and is exceedingly ambitious to seem delighted with the sport, and have his fist gloved with his jesses." And Gilpin, in his description of a Mr. Hastings, remarks, "he kept all sorts of hounds that run buck, fox, hare, otter, and badger; and had hawks of all kinds both long and short winged. His great hall was commonly strewed with marrow-bones, and full of hawk perches, hounds, spaniels, and terriers. On a broad hearth, paved with brick, lay some of the choicest terriers, hounds, and spaniels."

I was now invited by the butler to walk into the garden, and I felt inclined to visit the orchard and harbor where the justice treated Sir John Falstaff and Cousin Silence "to a last year's pippin of his own grafting, with a dish of caraways"; but I had already spent so much of the day in my ramblings that I was obliged to give up any further investigations. When about to take my leave I was gratified by the civil entreaties of the housekeeper and butler, that I would take some refreshment: an instance of good old hospitality which, I grieve to say, we castle-hunters seldom meet with in modern days. I make no doubt it is a virtue which the present representative of the Lucys inherits from his ancestors; for Shakspeare, even in his caricature, makes Justice Shallow importunate in this respect, as witness his pressing instances to Falstaff:

> By cock and pye, Sir, you shall not away to-night . . . I will not excuse you; you shall not be excused; excuses shall not be admitted; there is no excuse shall serve; you shall not be excused . . . Some pigeons, Davy; a couple of short-legged hens; a joint of mutton; and any pretty little tiny kickshaws, tell William Cook.

I now bade a reluctant farewell to the old hall. My mind had become so completely possessed by the imaginary scenes and characters connected with it, that I seemed to be actually living among them. Every thing brought them as it were before my eyes; and as the door of the dining-room opened I almost expected to hear the feeble voice of Master Silence quavering forth his favorite ditty:

> 'Tis merry in hall, when beards wag all,
> And welcome merry shrove-tide!

On returning to my inn I could not but reflect on the singular gift of the poet; to be able thus to spread the magic of his mind over the very face of nature; to give to things and places a charm and character not their own, and to turn this "working-day world" into a perfect fairy land. He is indeed the true enchanter, whose spell operates, not upon the senses, but upon the imagination and the heart. Under the wizard influence of Shakspeare I had been walking all day in a complete delusion. I had surveyed the landscape through the prism of poetry, which tinged every object with the hues of the rainbow. I had been surrounded with fancied beings; with mere airy nothings, conjured up by poetic power; yet which, to me, had all the charm of reality. I had heard Jaques soliloquize beneath his oak: had beheld the fair Rosalind and her companion adventuring through the woodlands; and, above all, had been once more present in spirit with fat Jack Falstaff and his contemporaries, from the august Justice Shallow, down to the gentle Master Slender and the sweet Anne Page. Ten thousand honors and blessings on the bard who has thus gilded the dull realities of life with innocent illusions; who has spread exquisite and unbought pleasures in my chequered path; and beguiled my spirit in many a lonely hour, with all the cordial and cheerful sympathies of social life!

As I crossed the bridge over the Avon on my return, I paused to contemplate the distant church in which the poet lies buried, and could not but exult in the malediction, which has kept his ashes undisturbed in its quiet and hallowed vaults. What honor could his name have derived from being mingled in dusty companionship with the epitaphs and escutcheons and venal eulogiums of a titled multitude? What would a crowded corner in Westminster Abbey have been, compared with this reverend pile, which seems to stand in beautiful loneliness as his sole mausoleum! The solicitude about the grave may be but the offspring of an overwrought sensibility; but human nature is made up of foibles and prejudices; and its best and tenderest affections are mingled with these factitious feelings. He who has sought renown about the world, and has reaped a full harvest of worldly favor, will find, after all, that there is no love, no admiration, no applause, so sweet to the soul as that which springs up in his native place. It is there that he seeks to be gathered in peace and honor among his kindred and his early friends. And when the weary heart and failing head begin to warn him that the evening of life is drawing on, he turns as fondly as does the infant to the mother's arms, to sink to sleep in the bosom of the scene of his childhood.

How would it have cheered the spirit of the youthful bard, when, wandering forth in disgrace upon a doubtful world, he cast back a heavy look upon his paternal home, could he have foreseen that, before many years, he should return to it covered with renown; that his name should become the boast and glory of his native place; that his ashes should be religiously guarded as its most precious treasure; and that its lessening spire, on which his eyes were fixed in tearful contemplation, should one day become the beacon, towering amidst the gentle landscape, to guide the literary pilgrim of every nation to his tomb!

Traits of Indian Character

I appeal to any white man if ever he entered Logan's cabin hungry, and he gave him not to eat; if ever he came cold and naked, and he clothed him not.

SPEECH OF AN INDIAN CHIEF

THERE IS SOMETHING IN THE CHARACTER AND HABITS OF THE NORTH American savage, taken in connection with the scenery over which he is accustomed to range, its vast lakes, boundless forests, majestic rivers, and trackless plains, that is, to my mind, wonderfully striking and sublime. He is formed for the wilderness, as the Arab is for the desert. His nature is stern, simple, and enduring; fitted to grapple with difficulties, and to support privations. There seems but little soil in his heart for the support of the kindly virtues; and yet, if we would but take the trouble to penetrate through that proud stoicism and habitual taciturnity, which lock up his character from casual observation, we should find him linked to his fellow-man of civilized life by more of those sympathies and affections than are usually ascribed to him.

It has been the lot of the unfortunate aborigines of America, in the early periods of colonization, to be doubly wronged by the white men. They have been dispossessed of their hereditary possessions by mercenary and frequently wanton warfare: and their characters have been traduced by bigoted and interested writers. The colonist often treated them like beasts of the forest; and the author has endeavored to justify him in his outrages. The former found it easier to exterminate than to civilize; the latter to vilify than to discriminate. The appellations of savage and pagan were deemed sufficient to sanction the hostilities of both; and thus the poor wanderers of the forest were persecuted and defamed, not because they were guilty, but because they were ignorant.

The rights of the savage have seldom been properly appreciated or respected by the white man. In peace he has too often been the dupe of artful traffic; in war he has been regarded as a ferocious animal, whose life or death was a question of mere precaution and convenience. Man is cruelly wasteful of life when his own safety is endangered, and he is sheltered by impunity; and little mercy is to be expected from him, when he feels the sting of the reptile and is conscious of the power to destroy.

The same prejudices, which were indulged thus early, exist in common circulation at the present day. Certain learned societies have, it is true, with laudable diligence, endeavored to investigate and record the real characters and manners of the Indian tribes; the American government, too, has wisely and humanely exerted itself to inculcate a friendly and forbearing spirit towards them, and to protect them from fraud and injustice.[1] The current opinion of the Indian character, however, is too apt to be formed from the miserable hordes which infest the frontiers, and hang on the skirts of the settlements. These are too commonly composed of degenerate beings, corrupted and enfeebled by the vices of society, without being benefited by its civilization. That proud independence, which formed the main pillar of savage virtue, has been shaken down, and the whole moral fabric lies in ruins. Their spirits are humiliated and debased by a sense of inferiority, and their native courage cowed and daunted by the superior knowledge and power of their enlightened neighbors. Society has advanced upon them like one of those withering airs that will sometimes breed desolation over a whole region of fertility. It has enervated their strength, multiplied their diseases, and superinduced upon their original barbarity the low vices of artificial life. It has given them a thousand superfluous wants, whilst it has diminished their means of mere existence. It has driven before it the animals of the chase, who fly from the sound of the axe and the smoke of the settlement, and seek refuge in the depths of remoter forests and yet untrodden wilds. Thus do we too often find the Indians on our frontiers to be the mere wrecks and remnants of once powerful tribes, who have lingered in the vicinity of the settlements, and sunk into precarious and vagabond existence. Poverty, repining and hopeless poverty, a canker of the mind unknown in savage life, corrodes their spirits, and blights every free and noble quality of their natures. They become drunken, indolent, feeble, thievish, and pusillanimous. They loiter like vagrants about

1. The American government has been indefatigable in its exertions to ameliorate the situation of the Indians, and to introduce among them the arts of civilization, and civil and religious knowledge. To protect them from the frauds of the white traders, no purchase of land from them by individuals is permitted; nor is any person allowed to receive lands from them as a present, without the express sanction of government. These precautions are strictly enforced.

the settlements, among spacious dwellings replete with elaborate comforts, which only render them sensible of the comparative wretchedness of their own condition. Luxury spreads its ample board before their eyes; but they are excluded from the banquet. Plenty revels over the fields, but they are starving in the midst of its abundance: the whole wilderness has blossomed into a garden; but they feel as reptiles that infest it.

How different was their state while yet the undisputed lords of the soil! Their wants were few, and the means of gratification within their reach. They saw every one round them sharing the same lot, enduring the same hardships, feeding on the same aliments, arrayed in the same rude garments. No roof then rose, but was open to the homeless stranger; no smoke curled among the trees, but he was welcome to sit down by its fire and join the hunter in his repast. "For," says an old historian of New England, "their life is so void of care, and they are so loving also, that they make use of those things they enjoy as common goods, and are therein so compassionate, that rather than one should starve through want, they would starve all; thus they pass their time merrily, not regarding our pomp, but are better content with their own, which some men esteem so meanly of." Such were the Indians whilst in the pride and energy of their primitive natures: they resembled those wild plants, which thrive best in the shades of the forest, but shrink from the hand of cultivation, and perish beneath the influence of the sun.

In discussing the savage character, writers have been too prone to indulge in vulgar prejudice and passionate exaggeration, instead of the candid temper of true philosophy. They have not sufficiently considered the peculiar circumstances in which the Indians have been placed, and the peculiar principles under which they have been educated. No being acts more rigidly from rule than the Indian. His whole conduct is regulated according to some general maxims early implanted in his mind. The moral laws that govern him are, to be sure, but few; but then he conforms to them all;—the white man abounds in laws of religion, morals, and manners, but how many does he violate?

A frequent ground of accusation against the Indians is their disregard of treaties, and the treachery and wantonness with which, in time of apparent peace, they will suddenly fly to hostilities. The intercourse of the white men with the Indians, however, is too apt to be cold, distrustful, oppressive, and insulting. They seldom treat them with that confidence and frankness which are indispensable to real friendship; nor is sufficient caution observed not to offend against those feelings of pride or superstition, which often prompt the Indian to hostility quicker than mere considerations of interest. The solitary savage feels silently, but acutely. His sensibilities are not diffused over so wide a surface as those of the white man; but they run in steadier and deeper channels. His pride, his affections, his superstitions, are all directed towards fewer objects; but the wounds inflicted on them are proportionably severe, and furnish motives of hostility which we cannot sufficiently appreciate. Where a community is also limited in number, and forms one great patriarchal family, as in an Indian tribe, the injury of an individual is the injury of the whole; and the sentiment of vengeance is almost instantaneously diffused. One council fire is sufficient for the discussion and arrangement of a plan of hostilities. Here all the fighting men and sages assemble. Eloquence and superstition combine to inflame the minds of the warriors. The orator awakens their martial ardor, and they are wrought up to a kind of religious desperation, by the visions of the prophet and the dreamer.

An instance of one of those sudden exasperations, arising from a motive peculiar to the Indian character, is extant in an old record of the early settlement of Massachusetts. The planters of Plymouth had defaced the monuments of the dead at Passonagessit, and had plundered the grave of the Sachem's mother of some skins with which it had been decorated. The Indians are remarkable for the reverence which they entertain for the sepulchres of their kindred. Tribes that have passed generations exiled from the abodes of their ancestors, when by chance they have been traveling in the vicinity, have been known to turn aside from the highway, and, guided by wonderfully accurate tradition, have crossed the country for miles to some tumulus, buried perhaps in woods, where the bones of their tribe were anciently deposited; and there have passed hours in silent meditation. Influenced by this sublime and holy feeling, the Sachem, whose mother's tomb had been violated, gathered his men together, and addressed them in the following beautifully simple and pathetic harangue; a curious specimen of Indian eloquence, and an affecting instance of filial piety in a savage.

"When last the glorious light of all the sky was underneath this globe, and birds grew silent, I began to settle, as my custom is, to take repose. Before mine eyes were fast closed, methought I saw a vision, at which my spirit was much troubled; and trembling at that doleful sight, a spirit cried aloud, 'Behold, my son, whom I have cherished, see the breasts that gave thee suck, the hands that lapped thee warm, and fed thee oft. Canst thou forget to take revenge of those wild people who have defaced my monument in a despiteful manner, disdaining our antiquities and honorable customs? See, now, the Sachem's grave lies like the common people, defaced by an ignoble race.

Thy mother doth complain, and implores thy aid against this thievish people, who have newly intruded on our land. If this be suffered, I shall not rest quiet in my everlasting habitation.' This said, the spirit vanished, and I, all in a sweat, not able scarce to speak, began to get some strength, and recollect my spirits that were fled, and determined to demand your counsel and assistance."

I have adduced this anecdote at some length, as it tends to show how these sudden acts of hostility, which have been attributed to caprice and perfidy, may often arise from deep and generous motives, which our inattention to Indian character and customs prevents our properly appreciating.

Another ground of violent outcry against the Indians is their barbarity to the vanquished. This had its origin partly in policy and partly in superstition. The tribes, though sometimes called nations, were never so formidable in their numbers, but that the loss of several warriors was sensibly felt; this was particularly the case when they had been frequently engaged in warfare; and many an instance occurs in Indian history, where a tribe, that had long been formidable to its neighbors has been broken up and driven away, by the capture and massacre of its principal fighting men. There was a strong temptation, therefore, to the victor to be merciless; not so much to gratify any cruel revenge, as to provide for future security. The Indians had also the superstitious belief, frequent among barbarous nations, and prevalent also among the ancients, that the manes of their friends who had fallen in battle were soothed by the blood of the captives. The prisoners, however, who are not thus sacrificed, are adopted into their families in the place of the slain, and are treated with the confidence and affection of relatives and friends; nay, so hospitable and tender is their entertainment, that when the alternative is offered them, they will often prefer to remain with their adopted brethren, rather than return to the home and the friends of their youth.

The cruelty of the Indians towards their prisoners has been heightened since the colonization of the whites. What was formerly a compliance with policy and superstition, has been exasperated into a gratification of vengeance. They cannot but be sensible that the white men are the usurpers of their ancient dominion, the cause of their degradation, and the gradual destroyers of their race. They go forth to battle, smarting with injuries and indignities which they have individually suffered, and they are driven to madness and despair by the wide-spreading desolation, and the overwhelming ruin of European warfare. The whites have too frequently set them an example of violence, by burning their villages, and laying waste their slender means of subsistence: and yet they wonder that savages do not show moderation and magnanimity towards those who have left them nothing but mere existence and wretchedness.

We stigmatize the Indians, also, as cowardly and treacherous, because they use stratagem in warfare, in preference to open force; but in this they are fully justified by their rude code of honor. They are early taught that stratagem is praiseworthy; the bravest warrior thinks it no disgrace to lurk in silence, and take every advantage of his foe: he triumphs in the superior craft and sagacity by which he has been enabled to surprise and destroy an enemy. Indeed, man is naturally more prone to subtilty than open valor, owing to his physical weakness in comparison with other animals. They are endowed with natural weapons of defence: with horns, with tusks, with hoofs, and talons; but man has to depend on his superior sagacity. In all his encounters with these, his proper enemies, he resorts to stratagem; and when he perversely turns his hostility against his fellow-man, he at first continues the same subtle mode of warfare.

The natural principle of war is to do the most harm to our enemy with the least harm to ourselves; and this of course is to be effected by stratagem. That chivalrous courage which induces us to despise the suggestions of prudence, and to rush in the face of certain danger, is the offspring of society, and produced by education. It is honorable, because it is in fact the triumph of lofty sentiment over an instinctive repugnance to pain, and over those yearnings after personal ease and security, which society has condemned as ignoble. It is kept alive by pride and the fear of shame; and thus the dread of real evil is overcome by the superior dread of an evil which exists but in the imagination. It has been cherished and stimulated also by various means. It has been the theme of spirit-stirring song and chivalrous story. The poet and minstrel have delighted to shed round it the splendors of fiction; and even the historian has forgotten the sober gravity of narration, and broken forth into enthusiasm and rhapsody in its praise. Triumphs and gorgeous pageants have been its reward: monuments, on which art has exhausted its skill, and opulence its treasures, have been erected to perpetuate a nation's gratitude and admiration. Thus artificially excited, courage has risen to an extraordinary and factitious degree of heroism: and, arrayed in all the glorious "pomp and circumstance of war," this turbulent quality has even been able to eclipse many of those quiet, but invaluable virtues, which silently ennoble the human character, and swell the tide of human happiness.

But if courage intrinsically consists in the defiance of danger and pain, the life of the Indian is a continual exhibition of it. He lives in a state of perpetual hostility and risk. Peril and adventure are congenial to his nature; or rather seem necessary to arouse his faculties and to give an interest to his existence. Surrounded by hostile tribes, whose mode of warfare is by ambush and surprisal, he is always prepared for fight, and lives with his weapons in his hands. As the ship careers in fearful singleness through the solitudes of ocean;—as the bird mingles among clouds and storms, and wings its way, a mere speck, across the pathless fields of air;—so the Indian holds his course, silent, solitary, but undaunted, through the boundless bosom of the wilderness. His expeditions may vie in distance and danger with the pilgrimage of the devotee, or the crusade of the knight-errant. He traverses vast forests, exposed to the hazards of lonely sickness, of lurking enemies, and pining famine. Stormy lakes, those great inland seas, are no obstacles to his wanderings: in his light canoe of bark he sports, like a feather, on their waves, and darts with the swiftness of an arrow, down the roaring rapids of the rivers. His very subsistence is snatched from the midst of toil and peril. He gains his food by the hardships and dangers of the chase: he wraps himself in the spoils of the bear, the panther, and the buffalo, and sleeps among the thunders of the cataract.

No hero of ancient or modern days can surpass the Indian in his lofty contempt of death, and the fortitude with which he sustains his cruelest affliction. Indeed, we here behold him rising superior to the white man, in consequence of his peculiar education. The latter rushes to glorious death at the cannon's mouth; the former calmly contemplates its approach, and triumphantly endures it, amidst the varied torments of surrounding foes and the protracted agonies of fire. He even takes a pride in taunting his persecutors, and provoking their ingenuity of torture; and as the devouring flames prey on his very vitals, and the flesh shrinks from the sinews, he raises his last song of triumph, breathing the defiance of an unconquered heart, and invoking the spirits of his fathers to witness that he dies without a groan.

Notwithstanding the obloquy with which the early historians have overshadowed the characters of the unfortunate natives, some bright gleams occasionally break through, which throw a degree of melancholy lustre on their memories. Facts are occasionally to be met with in the rude annals of the eastern provinces, which, though recorded with the coloring of prejudice and bigotry, yet speak for themselves; and will be dwelt on with applause and sympathy, when prejudice shall have passed away.

In one of the homely narratives of the Indian wars in New England, there is a touching account of the desolation carried into the tribe of the Pequod Indians. Humanity shrinks from the cold-blooded detail of indiscriminate butchery. In one place we read of the surprisal of an Indian fort in the night, when the wigwams were wrapped in flames, and the miserable inhabitants shot down and slain in attempting to escape, "all being despatched and ended in the course of an hour." After a series of similar transactions "our soldiers," as the historian piously observes, "being resolved by God's assistance to make a final destruction of them," the unhappy savages being hunted from their homes, and fortresses and pursued with fire and sword, a scanty, but gallant band, the sad remnant of the Pequod warriors, with their wives and children, took refuge in a swamp.

Burning with indignation, and rendered sullen by despair; with hearts bursting with grief at the destruction of their tribe, and spirits galled and sore at the fancied ignominy of their defeat, they refused to ask their lives at the hands of an insulting foe, and preferred death to submission.

As the night drew on they were surrounded in their dismal retreat, so as to render escape impracticable. Thus situated, their enemy "plied them with shot all the time, by which means many were killed and buried in the mire." In the darkness and fog that preceded the dawn of day some few broke through the besiegers and escaped into the woods: "the rest were left to the conquerors, of which many were killed in the swamp, like sullen dogs who would rather, in their self-willedness and madness, sit still and be shot through, or cut to pieces," than implore for mercy. When the day broke upon this handful of forlorn but dauntless spirits, the soldiers, we are told, entering the swamp, "saw several heaps of them sitting close together, upon whom they discharged their pieces, laden with ten or twelve pistol bullets at a time, putting the muzzles of the pieces under the boughs, within a few yards of them; so as, besides those that were found dead, many more were killed and sunk into the mire, and never were minded more by friend or foe."

Can any one read this plain unvarnished tale, without admiring the stern resolution, the unbending pride, the loftiness of spirit, that seemed to nerve the hearts of these self-taught heroes and to raise them above the instinctive feelings of human nature? When the Gauls laid waste the city of Rome, they found the senators clothed in their robes, and seated with stern tranquillity in their curule chairs; in this manner they suffered death without resistance or even supplication. Such conduct was, in them, applauded as noble and magnanimous; in the hapless Indian it was reviled as obstinate and sullen. How truly are we the dupes of show and circumstance! How different is virtue clothed in purple and enthroned in state, from virtue, naked and destitute, and perishing obscurely in a wilderness!

But I forbear to dwell on these gloomy pictures. The eastern tribes have long since disappeared; the forests that sheltered them have been laid low, and scarce any traces remain of them in the thickly-settled states of New England, excepting here and there the Indian name of a village or a stream. And such must, sooner or later, be the fate of those other tribes which skirt the frontiers, and have occasionally been inveigled from their forests to mingle in the wars of white men. In a little while, and they will go the way that their brethren have gone before. The few hordes which still linger about the shores of Huron, and Superior and the tributary streams of the Mississippi, will share the fate of those tribes that once spread over Massachusetts and Connecticut, and lorded it along the proud banks of the Hudson; of that gigantic race said to have existed on the borders of the Susquehanna; and of those various nations that flourished about the Potomac and the Rappahannock, and that peopled the forests of the vast valley of Shenandoah. They will vanish like a vapor from the face of the earth; their very history will be lost in forgetfulness; and "the places that now know them will know them no more for ever." Or if, perchance, some dubious memorial of them should survive, it may be in the romantic dreams of the poet, to people in imagination his glades and groves, like the fauns and satyrs and sylvan deities of antiquity. But should he venture upon the dark story of their wrongs and wretchedness; should he tell how they were invaded, corrupted, despoiled, driven from their native abodes and the sepulchres of their fathers, hunted like wild beasts about the earth, and sent down with violence and butchery to the grave, posterity will either turn with horror and incredulity from the tale or blush with indignation at the inhumanity of their forefathers.—"We are driven back," said an old warrior, "until we can retreat no farther—our hatchets are broken, our bows are snapped, our fires are nearly extinguished—a little longer and the white man will cease to persecute us—for we shall cease to exist!"

Philip of Pokanoket

An Indian Memoir

As monumental bronze unchanged his look:
A soul that pity touch'd, but never shook:
Train'd from his tree-rock'd cradle to his bier,
The fierce extremes of good and ill to brook
Impassive—fearing but the shame of fear—
A stoic of the woods—a man without a tear.

CAMPBELL

IT IS TO BE REGRETTED THAT THOSE EARLY WRITERS, WHO TREATED OF THE discovery and settlement of America, have not given us more particular and candid accounts of the remarkable characters that flourished in savage life. The scanty anecdotes which have reached us are full of peculiarity and interest; they furnish us with nearer glimpses of human nature, and show what man is in a comparatively primitive state, and what he owes to civilization. There is something of the charm of discovery in lighting upon these wild and unexplored tracts of human nature; in witnessing, as it were, the native growth of moral sentiment, and perceiving those generous and romantic qualities which have been artificially cultivated by society, vegetating in spontaneous hardihood and rude magnificence.

In civilized life, where the happiness, and indeed almost the existence, of man depends so much upon the opinion of his fellow-men, he is constantly acting a studied part. The bold and peculiar traits of native character are refined away, or softened down by the levelling influence of what is termed good-breeding; and he practises so many petty deceptions, and affects so many generous sentiments, for the purposes of popularity, that it is difficult to distinguish his real from his artificial character. The

Indian, on the contrary, free from the restraints and refinements of polished life, and, in a great degree, a solitary and independent being, obeys the impulses of his inclination or the dictates of his judgment; and thus the attributes of his nature, being freely indulged, grow singly great and striking. Society is like a lawn, where every roughness is smoothed, every bramble eradicated, and where the eye is delighted by the smiling verdure of a velvet surface; he, however, who would study nature in its wildness and variety, must plunge into the forest, must explore the glen, must stem the torrent, and dare the precipice.

These reflections arose on casually looking through a volume of early colonial history, wherein are recorded, with great bitterness, the outrages of the Indians, and their wars with the settlers of New England. It is painful to perceive, even from these partial narratives, how the footsteps of civilization may be traced in the blood of the aborigines; how easily the colonists were moved to hostility by the lust of conquest; how merciless and exterminating was their warfare. The imagination shrinks at the idea of how many intellectual beings were hunted from the earth, how many brave and noble hearts, of nature's sterling coinage, were broken down and trampled in the dust!

Such was the fate of PHILIP OF POKANOKET, an Indian warrior, whose name was once a terror throughout Massachusetts and Connecticut. He was the most distinguished of a number of contemporary Sachems who reigned over the Pequods, the Narragansets, the Wampanoags, and the other eastern tribes, at the time of the first settlement of New England; a band of native untaught heroes, who made the most generous struggle of which human nature is capable; fighting to the last gasp in the cause of their country, without a hope of victory or a thought of renown. Worthy of an age of poetry, and fit subjects for local story and romantic fiction, they have left scarcely any authentic traces on the page of history, but stalk, like gigantic shadows, in the dim twilight of tradition.[1]

When the pilgrims, as the Plymouth settlers are called by their descendants, first took refuge on the shores of the New World, from the religious persecutions of the Old, their situation was to the last degree gloomy and disheartening. Few in number, and that number rapidly perishing away through sickness and hardships; surrounded by a howling wilderness and savage tribes; exposed to the rigors of an almost arctic

---

1. While correcting the proof sheets of this article, the author is informed that a celebrated English poet has nearly finished an heroic poem on the story of Philip of Pokanoket.

winter, and the vicissitudes of an ever-shifting climate; their minds were filled with doleful forebodings, and nothing preserved them from sinking into despondency but the strong excitement of religious enthusiasm. In this forlorn situation they were visited by Massasoit, chief Sagamore of the Wampanoags, a powerful chief, who reigned over a great extent of country. Instead of taking advantage of the scanty number of the strangers, and expelling them from his territories, into which they had intruded, he seemed at once to conceive for them a generous friendship, and extended towards them the rites of primitive hospitality. He came early in the spring to their settlement of New Plymouth, attended by a mere handful of followers; entered into a solemn league of peace and amity; sold them a portion of the soil, and promised to secure for them the good-will of his savage allies. Whatever may be said of Indian perfidy, it is certain that the integrity and good faith of Massasoit have never been impeached. He continued a firm and magnanimous friend of the white men; suffering them to extend their possessions, and to strengthen themselves in the land; and betraying no jealousy of their increasing power and prosperity. Shortly before his death he came once more to New Plymouth, with his son Alexander, for the purpose of renewing the covenant of peace, and of securing it to his posterity.

At this conference he endeavored to protect the religion of his forefathers from the encroaching zeal of the missionaries; and stipulated that no further attempt should be made to draw off his people from their ancient faith; but, finding the English obstinately opposed to any such condition, he mildly relinquished the demand. Almost the last act of his life was to bring his two sons, Alexander and Philip (as they had been named by the English), to the residence of a principal settler, recommending mutual kindness and confidence; and entreating that the same love and amity which had existed between the white men and himself might be continued afterwards with his children. The good old Sachem died in peace, and was happily gathered to his fathers before sorrow came upon his tribe; his children remained behind to experience the ingratitude of white men.

His eldest son, Alexander, succeeded him. He was of a quick and impetuous temper, and proudly tenacious of his hereditary rights and dignity. The intrusive policy and dictatorial conduct of the strangers excited his indignation; and he beheld with uneasiness their exterminating wars with the neighboring tribes. He was doomed soon to incur their hostility, being accused of plotting with the Narragansets to rise against the English and drive them from the land. It is impossible to say whether this accusation was warranted by facts, or was grounded on mere suspicions. It is evident, however, by the violent and overbearing measures of the settlers, that they had by this time begun to feel conscious of the rapid increase of their power, and to grow harsh and inconsiderate in their treatment of the natives. They dispatched an armed force to seize upon Alexander, and to bring him before their courts. He was traced to his woodland haunts, and surprised at a hunting house, where he was reposing with a band of his followers, unarmed, after the toils of the chase. The suddenness of his arrest, and the outrage offered to his sovereign dignity, so preyed upon the irascible feelings of this proud savage, as to throw him into a raging fever. He was permitted to return home on condition of sending his son as a pledge for his re-appearance; but the blow he had received was fatal, and before he reached his home he fell a victim to the agonies of a wounded spirit.

The successor of Alexander was Metamocet, or King Philip, as he was called by the settlers, on account of his lofty spirit and ambitious temper. These, together with his well-known energy and enterprise, had rendered him an object of great jealousy and apprehension, and he was accused of having always cherished a secret and implacable hostility towards the whites. Such may very probably, and very naturally, have been the case. He considered them as originally but mere intruders into the country, who had presumed upon indulgence, and were extending an influence baneful to savage life. He saw the whole race of his countrymen melting before them from the face of the earth; their territories slipping from their hands, and their tribes becoming feeble, scattered, and dependent. It may be said that the soil was originally purchased by the settlers; but who does not know the nature of Indian purchases, in the early periods of colonization? The Europeans always made thrifty bargains through their superior adroitness in traffic; and they gained vast accessions of territory by easily provoked hostilities. An uncultivated savage is never a nice inquirer into the refinements of law, by which an injury may be gradually and legally inflicted. Leading facts are all by which he judges; and it was enough for Philip to know that before the intrusion of the Europeans his countrymen were lords of the soil, and that now they were becoming vagabonds in the land of their fathers.

But whatever may have been his feelings of general hostility, and his particular indignation at the treatment of his brother, he suppressed them for the present, renewed the contract with the settlers, and resided peaceably for many years at Pokanoket, or, as it was called by the English, Mount Hope,[2] the ancient seat of dominion of his tribe. Suspicions, however, which were at first but vague and indefinite, began to acquire form and substance; and he was at length charged with attempting to instigate the various Eastern tribes to rise at once, and, by a simultaneous effort, to throw off the yoke of their oppressors. It is difficult at this distant period to assign the proper credit due to these early accusations against the Indians. There was a proneness to suspicion, and an aptness to acts of violence, on the part of the whites, that gave weight and importance to every idle tale. Informers abounded where talebearing met with countenance and reward; and the sword was readily unsheathed when its success was certain, and it carved out empire.

The only positive evidence on record against Philip is the accusation of one Sausaman, a renegado Indian, whose natural cunning had been quickened by a partial education which he had received among the settlers. He changed his faith and his allegiance two or three times, with a facility that evinced the looseness of his principles. He had acted for some time as Philip's confidential secretary and counsellor, and had enjoyed his bounty and protection. Finding, however, that the clouds of adversity were gathering round his patron, he abandoned his service and went over to the whites; and, in order to gain their favor, charged his former benefactor with plotting against their safety. A rigorous investigation took place. Philip and several of his subjects submitted to be examined, but nothing was proved against them. The settlers, however, had now gone too far to retract; they had previously determined that Philip was a dangerous neighbor; they had publicly evinced their distrust, and had done enough to insure his hostility; according, therefore, to the usual mode of reasoning in these cases, his destruction had become necessary to their security. Sausaman, the treacherous informer, was shortly afterwards found dead, in a pond, having fallen a victim to the vengeance of his tribe. Three Indians, one of whom was a friend and counsellor of Philip, were apprehended and tried, and, on the testimony of one very questionable witness, were condemned and executed as murderers.

This treatment of his subjects, and ignominious punishment of his friend, outraged the pride and exasperated the passions of Philip. The bolt which had fallen thus at his

2. Now Bristol, Rhode Island.

very feet awakened him to the gathering storm, and he determined to trust himself no longer in the power of the white men. The fate of his insulted and broken-hearted brother still rankled in his mind; and he had a further warning in the tragical story of Miantonimo, a great Sachem of the Narragansets, who, after manfully facing his accusers before a tribunal of the colonists, exculpating himself from a charge of conspiracy, and receiving assurances of amity, had been perfidiously despatched at their instigation. Philip, therefore, gathered his fighting men about him; persuaded all strangers that he could to join his cause; sent the women and children to the Narragansetts for safety; and wherever he appeared, was continually surrounded by armed warriors.

When the two parties were thus in a state of distrust and irritation, the least spark was sufficient to set them in a flame. The Indians, having weapons in their hands, grew mischievous, and committed various petty depredations. In one of their maraudings a warrior was fired on and killed by a settler. This was the signal for open hostilities; the Indians pressed to revenge the death of their comrade, and the alarm of war resounded through the Plymouth colony.

In the early chronicles of these dark and melancholy times we meet with many indications of the diseased state of the public mind. The gloom of religious abstraction, and the wildness of their situation, among trackless forests and savage tribes, had disposed the colonists to superstitious fancies, and had filled their imaginations with the frightful chimeras of witchcraft and spectrology. They were much given also to a belief in omens. The troubles with Philip and his Indians were preceded, we are told, by a variety of those awful warnings which forerun great and public calamities. The perfect form of an Indian bow appeared in the air at New Plymouth, which was looked upon by the inhabitants as a "prodigious apparition." At Hadley, Northampton, and other towns in their neighborhood "was heard the report of a great piece of ordnance, with a shaking of the earth and a considerable echo."[3] Others were alarmed on a still sunshiny morning by the discharge of guns and muskets; bullets seemed to whistle past them, and the noise of drums resounded in the air, seeming to pass away to the westward; others fancied that they heard the galloping of horses over their heads; and certain monstrous births, which took place about the time, filled the superstitious in some towns with doleful forebodings. Many of these portentous sights and sounds may

---

3. The Rev. Increase Mather's History.

be ascribed to natural phenomena: to the northern lights which occur vividly in those latitudes; the meteors which explode in the air; the casual rushing of a blast through the top branches of the forest; the crash of fallen trees or disrupted rocks; and to those other uncouth sounds and echoes which will sometimes strike the ear so strangely amidst the profound stillness of woodland solitudes. These may have startled some melancholy imaginations, may have been exaggerated by the love for the marvellous, and listened to with that avidity with which we devour whatever is fearful and mysterious. The universal currency of these superstitious fancies, and the grave record made of them by one of the learned men of the day, are strongly characteristic of the times.

The nature of the contest that ensued was such as too often distinguishes the warfare between civilized men and savages. On the part of the whites it was conducted with superior skill and success; but with a wastefulness of the blood, and a disregard of the natural rights of their antagonists: on the part of the Indians it was waged with the desperation of men fearless of death, and who had nothing to expect from peace, but humiliation, dependence, and decay.

The events of the war are transmitted to us by a worthy clergyman of the time; who dwells with horror and indignation on every hostile act of the Indians, however justifiable, whilst he mentions with applause the most sanguinary atrocities of the whites. Philip is reviled as a murderer and a traitor, without considering that he was a true born prince, gallantly fighting at the head of his subjects to avenge the wrongs of his family; to retrieve the tottering power of his line; and to deliver his native land from the oppression of usurping strangers.

The project of a wide and simultaneous revolt, if such had really been formed, was worthy of a capacious mind, and, had it not been prematurely discovered, might have been overwhelming in its consequences. The war that actually broke out was but a war of detail, a mere succession of casual exploits and unconnected enterprises. Still it sets forth the military genius and daring prowess of Philip; and wherever, in the prejudiced and passionate narrations that have been given of it, we can arrive at simple facts, we find him displaying a vigorous mind, a fertility of expedients, a contempt of suffering and hardship, and an unconquerable resolution, that command our sympathy and applause.

Driven from his paternal domains at Mount Hope, he threw himself into the depths of those vast and trackless forests that skirted the settlements, and were almost impervious to anything but a wild beast, or an Indian. Here he gathered together his forces, like the storm accumulating its stores of mischief in the bosom of the thunder cloud, and would suddenly emerge at a time and place least expected, carrying havoc and dismay into the villages. There were now and then indications of these impending ravages, that filled the minds of the colonists with awe and apprehension. The report of a distant gun would perhaps be heard from the solitary woodland, where there was known to be no white man; the cattle which had been wandering in the woods would sometimes return home wounded; or an Indian or two would be seen lurking about the skirts of the forests, and suddenly disappearing; as the lightning will sometimes be seen playing silently about the edge of the cloud that is brewing up the tempest.

Though sometimes pursued and even surrounded by the settlers, yet Philip as often escaped almost miraculously from their toils, and, plunging into the wilderness, would be lost to all search or inquiry, until he again emerged at some far distant quarter, laying the country desolate. Among his strong-holds, were the great swamps or morasses, which extend in some parts of New England; composed of loose bogs of deep black mud; perplexed with thickets, brambles, rank weeds, the shattered and mouldering trunks of fallen trees, overshadowed by lugubrious hemlocks. The uncertain footing and the tangled mazes of these shaggy wilds, rendered them almost impracticable to the white man, though the Indian could thrid their labyrinths with the agility of a deer. Into one of these, the great swamp of Pocasset Neck, was Philip once driven with a band of his followers. The English did not dare to pursue him, fearing to venture into these dark and frightful recesses, where they might perish in fens and miry pits, or be shot down by lurking foes. They therefore invested the entrance to the Neck, and began to build a fort, with the thought of starving out the foe; but Philip and his warriors wafted themselves on a raft over an arm of the sea, in the dead of night, leaving the women and children behind; and escaped away to the westward, kindling the flames of war among the tribes of Massachusetts and the Nipmuck country, and threatening the colony of Connecticut.

In this way Philip became a theme of universal apprehension. The mystery in which he was enveloped exaggerated his real terrors. He was an evil that walked in darkness; whose coming none could foresee, and against which none knew when to be on the alert. The whole country abounded with rumors and alarms. Philip seemed almost possessed of ubiquity; for, in whatever part of the widely-extended frontier an irruption from the forest took place, Philip was said to be its leader. Many superstitious notions also were circulated concerning him. He was said to deal in necromancy, and to be attended by an old Indian witch or prophetess, whom he consulted, and who assisted him by her charms and incantations. This, indeed, was frequently the case with Indian chiefs; either through their own credulity, or to act upon that of their followers: and the influence of the prophet and the dreamer over Indian superstition has been fully evidenced in recent instances of savage warfare.

At the time that Philip effected his escape from Pocasset, his fortunes were in a desperate condition. His forces had been thinned by repeated fights, and he had lost almost the whole of his resources. In this time of adversity he found a faithful friend in Canonchet, chief Sachem of all the Narragansets. He was the son and heir of Miantonimo, the great Sachem, who, as already mentioned, after an honorable acquittal of the charge of conspiracy, had been privately put to death at the perfidious instigations of the settlers. "He was the heir," says the old chronicler, "of all his father's pride and insolence, as well as of his malice towards the English";—he certainly was the heir of his insults and injuries, and the legitimate avenger of his murder. Though he had forborne to take an active part in this hopeless war, yet he received Philip and his broken forces with open arms; and gave them the most generous countenance and support. This at once drew upon him the hostility of the English; and it was determined to strike a signal blow that should involve both the Sachems in one common ruin. A great force was, therefore, gathered together from Massachusetts, Plymouth, and Connecticut, and was sent into the Narraganset country in the depth of winter, when the swamps, being frozen and leafless, could be traversed with comparative facility, and would no longer afford dark and impenetrable fastnesses to the Indians.

Apprehensive of attack, Canonchet had conveyed the greater part of his stores, together with the old, the infirm, the women and children of his tribe, to a strong fortress; where he and Philip had likewise drawn up the flower of their forces. This fortress, deemed by the Indians impregnable, was situated upon a rising mound or kind of island, of five or six acres, in the midst of a swamp; it was constructed with a degree of judgment and skill vastly superior to what is usually displayed in Indian fortification, and indicative of the martial genius of these two chieftains.

Guided by a renegado Indian, the English penetrated, through December snows, to this strong-hold and came upon the garrison by surprise. The fight was fierce and tumultuous. The assailants were repulsed in their first attack, and several of their bravest officers were shot down in the act of storming the fortress, sword in hand. The assault was renewed with greater success. A lodgment was effected. The Indians were driven from one post to another. They disputed their ground inch by inch, fighting with the fury of despair. Most of their veterans were cut to pieces; and after a long and bloody battle, Philip and Canonchet, with a handful of surviving warriors, retreated from the fort, and took refuge in the thickets of the surrounding forest.

The victors set fire to the wigwams and the fort; the whole was soon in a blaze; many of the old men, the women and the children perished in the flames. This last outrage overcame even the stoicism of the savage. The neighboring woods resounded with the yells of rage and despair, uttered by the fugitive warriors, as they beheld the destruction of their dwellings, and heard the agonizing cries of their wives and offspring. "The burning of the wigwams," says a contemporary writer, "the shrieks and cries of the women and children, and the yelling of the warriors, exhibited a most horrible and affecting scene, so that it greatly moved some of the soldiers." The same writer cautiously adds, "they were in *much doubt* then, and afterwards seriously inquired, whether burning their enemies alive could be consistent with humanity, and the benevolent principles of the gospel."[4]

The fate of the brave and generous Canonchet is worthy of particular mention: the last scene of his life is one of the noblest instances on record of Indian magnanimity.

Broken down in his power and resources by this signal defeat, yet faithful to his ally, and to the hapless cause which he had espoused, he rejected all overtures of peace, offered on condition of betraying Philip and his followers, and declared that "he would fight it out to the last man, rather than become a servant to the English." His home being destroyed; his country harassed and laid waste by the incursions of the conquerors; he was obliged to wander away to the banks of the Connecticut; where he formed a rallying point to the whole body of western Indians and laid waste several of the English settlements.

Early in the spring he departed on a hazardous expedition, with only thirty chosen men, to penetrate to Seaconck, in the vicinity of Mount Hope, and to procure seed corn to plant for the sustenance of his troops. This little band of adventurers had passed safely through the Pequod country, and were in the centre of the Narraganset, resting at some wigwams near Pautucket river, when an alarm was given of an approaching enemy.—Having but seven men by him at the time, Canonchet despatched two of them to the top of a neighboring hill, to bring intelligence of the foe.

---

4. MS. of the Rev. W. Ruggles.

Panic-struck by the appearance of a troop of English and Indians rapidly advancing, they fled in breathless terror past their chieftain, without stopping to inform him of the danger. Canonchet sent another scout, who did the same. He then sent two more, one of whom, hurrying back in confusion and affright, told him that the whole British army was at hand. Canonchet saw there was no choice but immediate flight. He attempted to escape round the hill, but was perceived and hotly pursued by the hostile Indians and a few of the fleetest of the English. Finding the swiftest pursuer close upon his heels, he threw off, first his blanket, then his silver-laced coat and belt of peag, by which his enemies knew him to be Canonchet, and redoubled the eagerness of pursuit.

At length, in dashing through the river, his foot slipped upon a stone, and he fell so deep as to wet his gun. This accident so struck him with despair, that, as he afterwards confessed, "his heart and his bowels turned within him, and he became like a rotten stick, void of strength."

To such a degree was he unnerved, that, being seized by a Pequod Indian within a short distance of the river, he made no resistance, though a man of great vigor of body and boldness of heart. But on being made prisoner the whole pride of his spirit arose within him; and from that moment, we find, in the anecdotes given by his enemies, nothing but repeated flashes of elevated and prince-like heroism. Being questioned by one of the English who first came up with him, and who had not attained his twenty second year, the proud-hearted warrior, looking with lofty contempt upon his youthful countenance, replied, "You are a child—you cannot understand matters of war—let your brother or your chief come—him will I answer."

Though repeated offers were made to him of his life, on condition of submitting with his nation to the English, yet he rejected them with disdain, and refused to send any proposals of the kind to the great body of his subjects; saying, that he knew none of them would comply. Being reproached with his breach of faith towards the whites; his boast that he would not deliver up a Wampanoag nor the paring of a Wampanoag's nail; and his threat that he would burn the English alive in their houses; he disdained to justify himself, haughtily answering that others were as forward for the war as himself, and "he desired to hear no more thereof."

So noble and unshaken a spirit, so true a fidelity to his cause and his friend, might have touched the feelings of the generous and the brave; but Canonchet was an Indian; a being towards whom war had no courtesy, humanity no law, religion no compassion—he was condemned to die. The last words of his that are recorded, are worthy the greatness of his soul. When sentence of death was passed upon him, he observed "that he liked it well, for he should die before his heart was soft, or he had spoken any thing unworthy of himself." His enemies gave him the death of a soldier, for he was shot at Stoningham, by three young Sachems of his own rank.

The defeat at the Narraganset fortress, and the death of Canonchet, were fatal blows to the fortunes of King Philip. He made an ineffectual attempt to raise a head of war, by stirring up the Mohawks to take arms; but, though possessed of the native talents of a statesman, his arts were counteracted by the superior arts of his enlightened enemies, and the terror of their warlike skill began to subdue the resolution of the neighboring tribes. The unfortunate chieftain saw himself daily stripped of power, and his ranks rapidly thinning around him. Some were suborned by the whites; others fell victims to hunger and fatigue, and to the frequent attacks by which they were harassed. His stores were all captured; his chosen friends were swept away from before his eyes; his uncle was shot down by his side; his sister was carried into captivity; and in one of his narrow escapes he was compelled to leave his beloved wife and only son to the mercy of the enemy. "His ruin," says the historian, "being thus gradually carried on, his misery was not prevented, but augmented thereby; being himself made acquainted with the sense and experimental feeling of the captivity of his children, loss of friends, slaughter of his subjects, bereavement of all family relations, and being stripped of all outward comforts, before his own life should be taken away."

To fill up the measure of his misfortunes, his own followers began to plot against his life, that by sacrificing him they might purchase dishonorable safety. Through treachery a number of his faithful adherents, the subjects of Wetamoe, an Indian princess of Pocasset, a near kinswoman and confederate of Philip, were betrayed into the hands of the enemy. Wetamoe was among them at the time, and attempted to make her escape by crossing a neighboring river: either exhausted by swimming, or starved with cold and hunger, she was found dead and naked near the water side. But persecution ceased not at the grave. Even death, the refuge of the wretched, where the wicked commonly cease from troubling, was no protection to this outcast female, whose great crime was affectionate fidelity to her kinsman and her friend. Her corpse was the object of unmanly and dastardly vengeance; the head was severed from the body and set upon a pole, and was thus exposed at Taunton, to the view of her captive subjects. They immediately recognized the features of their unfortunate queen, and were so affected at this barbarous spectacle, that we are told they broke forth into the "most horrid and diabolical lamentations."

However Philip had borne up against the complicated miseries and misfortunes that surrounded him, the treachery of his followers seemed to wring his heart and reduce him to despondency. It is said that "he never rejoiced afterwards, nor had success in any of his designs." The spring of hope was broken—the ardor of enterprise was extinguished—he looked around, and all was danger and darkness; there was no eye to pity, nor any arm that could bring deliverance. With a scanty band of followers, who still remained true to his desperate fortunes, the unhappy Philip wandered back to the vicinity of Mount Hope, the ancient dwelling of his fathers. Here he lurked about, like a spectre, among the scenes of former power and prosperity, now bereft of home, of family and friend. There needs no better picture of his destitute and piteous situation, than that furnished by the homely pen of the chronicler, who is unwarily enlisting the feelings of the reader in favor of the hapless warrior whom he reviles. "Philip," he says, "like a savage wild beast, having been hunted by the English forces through the woods, above a hundred miles backward and forward, at last was driven to his own den upon Mount Hope, where he retired, with a few of his best friends, into a swamp, which proved but a prison to keep him fast till the messengers of death came by divine permission to execute vengeance upon him."

Even in this last refuge of desperation and despair, a sullen grandeur gathers round his memory. We picture him to ourselves seated among his care-worn followers, brooding in silence over his blasted fortunes, and acquiring a savage sublimity from the wildness and dreariness of his lurking place. Defeated, but not dismayed—crushed to the earth, but not humiliated—he seemed to grow more haughty beneath disaster, and to experience a fierce satisfaction in draining the last dregs of bitterness. Little minds are tamed and subdued by misfortune; but great minds rise above it. The very idea of submission awakened the fury of Philip, and he smote to death one of his followers, who proposed an expedient of peace. The brother of the victim made his escape, and in revenge betrayed the retreat of his chieftain. A body of white men and Indians were immediately despatched to the swamp where Philip lay crouched, glaring with fury and despair. Before he was aware of their approach, they had begun to surround him. In a little while he saw five of his trustiest followers laid dead at his feet; all resistance was vain; he rushed forth from his covert, and made a headlong attempt to escape, but was shot through the heart by a renegado Indian of his own nation.

Such is the scanty story of the brave, but unfortunate King Philip; persecuted while living, slandered and dishonored when dead. If, however, we consider even the prejudiced anecdotes furnished us by his enemies, we may perceive in them traces of amiable and lofty character sufficient to awaken sympathy for his fate, and respect for his memory. We find that, amidst all the harassing cares and ferocious passions of constant warfare, he was alive to the softer feelings of connubial love and paternal tenderness, and to the generous sentiment of friendship. The captivity of his "beloved wife and only son" are mentioned with exultation as causing him poignant misery: the death of any near friend is triumphantly recorded as a new blow on his sensibilities; but the treachery and desertion of many of his followers, in whose affections he had confided, is said to have desolated his heart, and to have bereaved him of all further comfort. He was a patriot attached to his native soil—a prince true to his subjects, and indignant of their wrongs—a soldier, daring in battle, firm in adversity, patient of fatigue, of hunger, of every variety of bodily suffering, and ready to perish in the cause he had espoused. Proud of heart, and with an untamable love of natural liberty, he preferred to enjoy it among the beasts of the forests or in the dismal and famished recesses of swamps and morasses, rather than bow his haughty spirit to submission, and live dependent and despised in the ease and luxury of the settlements. With heroic qualities and bold achievements that would have graced a civilized warrior, and have rendered him the theme of the poet and the historian; he lived a wanderer and a fugitive in his native land, and went down, like a lonely bark foundering amid darkness and tempest—without a pitying eye to weep his fall, or a friendly hand to record his struggle.

John Bull

An old song, made by an aged old pate,
Of an old worshipful gentleman who had a great estate,
That kept a brave old house at a bountiful rate,
And an old porter to relieve the poor at his gate.
With an old study fill'd full of learned old books,
With an old reverend chaplain, you might know him by his looks,
With an old buttery-hatch worn quite off the hooks,
And an old kitchen that maintained half-a-dozen old cooks.
Like an old courtier, etc.

OLD SONG

THERE IS NO SPECIES OF HUMOR IN WHICH THE ENGLISH MORE EXCEL than that which consists in caricaturing and giving ludicrous appellations, or nicknames. In this way they have whimsically designated, not merely individuals, but nations; and, in their fondness for pushing a joke, they have not spared even themselves. One would think that, in personifying itself, a nation would be apt to picture something grand, heroic, and imposing; but it is characteristic of the peculiar humor of the English, and of their love for what is blunt, comic, and familiar, that they have embodied their national oddities in the figure of a sturdy, corpulent old fellow, with a three-cornered hat, red waistcoat, leather breeches, and stout oaken cudgel. Thus they have taken a singular delight in exhibiting their most private foibles in a laughable point of view; and have been so successful in their delineations, that there is scarcely a being in actual existence more absolutely present to the public mind than that eccentric personage, John Bull.

Perhaps the continual contemplation of the character thus drawn of them has contributed to fix it upon the nation; and thus to give reality to what at first may have been painted in a great measure from the imagination. Men are apt to acquire peculiarities that are continually ascribed to them. The common orders of English seem wonderfully captivated with the *beau ideal* which they have formed of John Bull, and endeavor to act up to the broad caricature that is perpetually before their eyes. Unluckily, they sometimes make their boasted Bull-ism an apology for their prejudice or grossness; and this I have especially noticed among those truly homebred and genuine sons of the soil who have never migrated beyond the sound of Bow-bells. If one of these should be a little uncouth in speech, and apt to utter impertinent truths, he confesses that he is a real John Bull, and always speaks his mind. If he now and then flies into an unreasonable burst of passion about trifles, he observes, that John Bull is a choleric old blade, but then his passion is over in a moment, and he bears no malice. If he betrays a coarseness of taste, and an insensibility to foreign refinements, he thanks heaven for his ignorance—he is a plain John Bull, and has no relish for frippery and nick-nacks. His very proneness to be gulled by strangers, and to pay extravagantly for absurdities, is excused under the plea of munificence—for John is always more generous than wise.

Thus, under the name of John Bull, he will contrive to argue every fault into a merit, and will frankly convict himself of being the honestest fellow in existence.

However little, therefore, the character may have suited in the first instance, it has gradually adapted itself to the nation, or rather they have adapted themselves to each other; and a stranger who wishes to study English peculiarities, may gather much valuable information from the innumerable portraits of John Bull, as exhibited in the windows of the caricature-shops. Still, however, he is one of those fertile humorists, that are continually throwing out new portraits, and presenting different aspects from different points of view; and, often as he has been described, I cannot resist the temptation to give a slight sketch of him, such as he has met my eye.

John Bull, to all appearance, is a plain downright matter-of-fact fellow, with much less of poetry about him than rich prose. There is little of romance in his nature, but a vast deal of strong natural feeling. He excels in humor more than in wit; is jolly rather than gay; melancholy rather than morose; can easily be moved to a sudden tear, or surprised into a broad laugh; but he loathes sentiment, and has no turn for light pleasantry. He is a boon companion, if you allow him to have his humor, and to talk about himself; and he will stand by a friend in a quarrel, with life and purse, however soundly he may be cudgeled.

In this last respect, to tell the truth, he has a propensity to be somewhat too ready. He is a busy-minded personage, who thinks not merely for himself and family, but for all the country round, and is most generously disposed to be every body's champion. He is continually volunteering his services to settle his neighbor's affairs, and takes it in great dudgeon if they engage in any matter of consequence without asking his advice; though he seldom engages in any friendly office of the kind without finishing by getting into a squabble with all parties, and then railing bitterly at their ingratitude. He unluckily took lessons in his youth in the noble science of defence, and having accomplished himself in the use of his limbs and his weapons, and become a perfect master at boxing and cudgel-play, he has had a troublesome life of it ever since. He cannot hear of a quarrel between the most distant of his neighbors, but he begins incontinently to fumble with the head of his cudgel, and consider whether his interest or honor does not require that he should meddle in the broil. Indeed he has extended his relations of pride and policy so completely over the whole country, that no event can take place, without infringing some of his finely-spun rights and dignities. Couched in his little domain, with these filaments stretching forth in every direction, he is like some choleric, bottle-bellied old spider, who has woven his web over a whole chamber, so that a fly cannot buzz, nor a breeze blow, without startling his repose, and causing him to sally forth wrathfully from his den.

Though really a good-hearted, good-tempered old fellow at bottom, yet he is singularly fond of being in the midst of contention. It is one of his peculiarities, however, that he only relishes the beginning of an affray; he always goes into a fight with alacrity, but comes out of it grumbling even when victorious; and though no one fights with more obstinacy to carry a contested point, yet, when the battle is over, and he comes to the reconciliation, he is so much taken up with the mere shaking of hands, that he is apt to let his antagonist pocket all that they have been quarrelling about. It is not, therefore, fighting that he ought so much to be on his guard against, as making friends. It is difficult to cudgel him out of a farthing; but put him in a good humor, and you may bargain him out of all the money in his pocket. He is like a stout ship, which will weather the roughest storm uninjured, but roll its masts overboard in the succeeding calm.

He is a little fond of playing the magnifico abroad; of pulling out a long purse; flinging his money bravely about at boxing matches, horse races, cock-fights, and carrying a high head among "gentlemen of the fancy"; but immediately after one of these fits of extravagance he will be taken with violent qualms of economy; stop short at the most trivial expenditure; talk desperately of being ruined and brought upon the parish; and, in such moods, will not pay the smallest tradesman's bill, without violent altercation. He is, in fact, the most punctual and discontented paymaster in the world, drawing his coin out of his breeches pocket with infinite reluctance; paying to the uttermost farthing, but accompanying every guinea with a growl.

With all his talk of economy, however, he is a bountiful provider, and a hospitable housekeeper. His economy is of a whimsical kind, its chief object being to devise how he may afford to be extravagant; for he will begrudge himself a beef-steak and pint of port one day, that he may roast an ox whole, broach a hogshead of ale, and treat all his neighbors on the next.

His domestic establishment is enormously expensive: not so much from any great outward parade, as from the great consumption of solid beef and pudding; the vast number of followers he feeds and clothes; and his singular disposition to pay hugely for small services. He is a most kind and indulgent master, and, provided his servants humor his peculiarities, flatter his vanity a little now and then, and do not peculate grossly on him before his face, they may manage him to perfection. Every thing that lives on him seems to thrive and grow fat. His house-servants are well paid, and pampered, and have little to do. His horses are sleek and lazy, and prance slowly before his state carriage; and his house-dogs sleep quietly about the door, and will hardly bark at a house-breaker.

His family mansion is an old castellated manor-house, gray with age, and of a most venerable, though weather-beaten appearance. It has been built upon no regular plan, but is a vast accumulation of parts, erected in various tastes and ages. The centre bears evident traces of Saxon architecture, and is as solid as ponderous stone and old English oak can make it. Like all the relics of that style, it is full of obscure passages, intricate mazes, and dusty chambers; and though these have been partially lighted up in modern days, yet there are many places where you must still grope in the dark. Additions have been made to the original edifice from time to time, and great alterations have taken place; towers and battlements have been erected during wars and tumults: wings built in time of peace; and out-houses, lodges, and offices, run up according to the whim or convenience of different generations, until it has become one of the most spacious, rambling tenements imaginable. An entire wing is taken up with the family chapel, a reverend pile, that must have been exceedingly sumptuous, and, indeed, in spite of having been altered and simplified at various periods, has still a look of solemn religious pomp. Its walls within are storied with the monuments of

John's ancestors; and it is snugly fitted up with soft cushions and well-lined chairs, where such of his family as are inclined to church services may doze comfortably in the discharge of their duties.

To keep up this chapel has cost John much money; but he is staunch in his religion, and piqued in his zeal, from the circumstance that many dissenting chapels have been erected in his vicinity, and several of his neighbors, with whom he has had quarrels, are strong papists.

To do the duties of the chapel he maintains, at a large expense, a pious and portly family chaplain. He is a most learned and decorous personage, and a truly well-bred Christian, who always backs the old gentleman in his opinions, winks discreetly at his little peccadilloes, rebukes the children when refractory, and is of great use in exhorting the tenants to read their Bibles, say their prayers, and, above all, to pay their rents punctually, and without grumbling.

The family apartments are in a very antiquated taste, somewhat heavy, and often inconvenient, but full of the solemn magnificence of former times; fitted up with rich, though faded tapestry, unwieldy furniture, and loads of massy gorgeous old plate. The vast fireplaces, ample kitchens, extensive cellars, and sumptuous banqueting halls, all speak of the roaring hospitality of days of yore, of which the modern festivity at the manor-house is but a shadow. There are, however, complete suites of rooms apparently deserted and time-worn; and towers and turrets that are tottering to decay; so that in high winds there is danger of their tumbling about the ears of the household.

John has frequently been advised to have the old edifice thoroughly overhauled; and to have some of the useless parts pulled down, and the others strengthened with their materials; but the old gentleman always grows testy on this subject. He swears the house is an excellent house—that it is tight and weather proof, and not to be shaken by tempests—that it has stood for several hundred years, and, therefore, is not likely to tumble down now—that as to its being inconvenient, his family is accustomed to the inconveniences, and would not be comfortable without them—that as to its unwieldy size and irregular construction, these result from its being the growth of centuries, and being improved by the wisdom of every generation—that an old family, like his, requires a large house to dwell in; new, upstart families may live in modern cottages and snug boxes; but an old English family should inhabit an old English manor-house. If you point out any part of the building as superfluous, he insists that it is material to the strength or decoration of the rest, and the harmony of the whole; and swears that the parts are so built into each other, that if you pull down one, you run the risk of having the whole about your ears.

The secret of the matter is, that John has a great disposition to protect and patronize. He thinks it indispensable to the dignity of an ancient and honorable family, to be bounteous in its appointments, and to be eaten up by dependents; and so, partly from pride, and partly from kind-heartedness, he makes it a rule always to give shelter and maintenance to his superannuated servants.

The consequence is, that, like many other venerable family establishments, his manor is incumbered by old retainers whom he cannot turn off, and an old style which he cannot lay down. His mansion is like a great hospital of invalids, and, with all its magnitude, is not a whit too large for its inhabitants. Not a nook or corner but is of use in housing some useless personage. Groups of veteran beef-eaters, gouty pensioners, and retired heroes of the buttery and the larder, are seen lolling about its ways, crawling over its lawns, dozing under its trees, or sunning themselves upon the benches at its doors. Every office and out-house is garrisoned by these supernumeraries and their families; for they are amazingly prolific, and when they die off, are sure to leave John a legacy of hungry mouths to be provided for. A mattock cannot be struck against the most mouldering tumble-down tower, but out pops, from some cranny or loop-hole, the gray pate of some superannuated hanger-on, who has lived at John's expense all his life, and makes the most grievous outcry at their pulling down the roof from over the head of a worn-out servant of the family. This is an appeal that John's honest heart never can withstand; so that a man, who has faithfully eaten his beef and pudding all his life, is sure to be rewarded with a pipe and tankard in his old days.

A great part of his park, also, is turned into paddocks, where his broken-down chargers are turned loose to graze undisturbed for the remainder of their existence—a worthy example of grateful recollection, which if some of his neighbors were to imitate, would not be to their discredit. Indeed, it is one of his great pleasures to point out these old steeds to his visitors, to dwell on their good qualities, extol their past services, and boast, with some little vainglory, of the perilous adventures and hardy exploits through which they have carried him.

He is given, however, to indulge his veneration for family usages, and family encumbrances, to a whimsical extent. His manor is infested by gangs of gipsies; yet he will not suffer them to be driven off, because they have infested the place time out of mind, and been regular poachers upon every generation of the family. He will scarcely permit a dry branch to be lopped from the great trees that surround the house, lest it should molest the rooks, that have bred there for centuries. Owls have taken possession of the dovecote; but they are hereditary owls, and must not be disturbed. Swallows have nearly choked up every chimney with their nests; martins build in every frieze and cornice; crows flutter about the towers, and perch on every weather-cock; and old gray-headed rats may be seen in every quarter of the house, running in and out of their holes undauntedly in broad daylight. In short, John has such a reverence for every thing that has been long in the family, that he will not hear even of abuses being reformed, because they are good old family abuses.

All these whims and habits have concurred woefully to drain the old gentleman's purse; and as he prides himself on punctuality in money matters, and wishes to maintain his credit in the neighborhood, they have caused him great perplexity in meeting his engagements. This, too, has been increased by the altercations and heart-burnings which are continually taking place in his family. His children have been brought up to different callings, and are of different ways of thinking; and as they have always been allowed to speak their minds freely, they do not fail to exercise the privilege most clamorously in the present posture of his affairs. Some stand up for the honor of the race, and are clear that the old establishment should be kept up in all its state, whatever may be the cost; others, who are more prudent and considerate, entreat the old gentleman to retrench his expenses, and to put his whole system of housekeeping on a more moderate footing. He has, indeed, at times, seemed inclined to listen to their opinions, but their wholesome advice has been completely defeated by the obstreperous conduct of one of his sons. This is a noisy rattle-pated fellow, of rather low habits, who neglects his business to frequent ale-houses—is the orator of village clubs, and a complete oracle among the poorest of his father's tenants. No sooner does he hear any of his brothers mention reform or retrenchment, than up he jumps, takes the words out of their mouths, and roars out for an overturn. When his tongue is once going nothing can stop it. He rants about the room; hectors the old man about his spendthrift practices; ridicules his tastes and pursuits; insists that he shall turn the old servants out of doors; give the broken-down horses to the hounds; send the fat chaplain packing, and take a field-preacher in his place—nay, that the whole family mansion shall be leveled with the ground, and a plain one of brick and mortar built in its place. He rails at every social entertainment and family festivity, and skulks away growling to the ale-house whenever an equipage drives up to the door. Though constantly complaining of the emptiness of his purse, yet he scruples not to spend all his pocket-money in these tavern convocations, and even runs up scores for the liquor over which he preaches about his father's extravagance.

It may readily be imagined how little such thwarting agrees with the old cavalier's fiery temperament. He has become so irritable, from repeated crossings, that the mere mention of retrenchment or reform is a signal for a brawl between him and the tavern oracle. As the latter is too sturdy and refractory for paternal discipline, having grown out of all fear of the cudgel, they have frequent scenes of wordy warfare, which at times run so high, that John is fain to call in the aid of his son Tom, an officer who has served abroad, but is at present living at home, on half-pay. This last is sure to stand by the old gentleman, right or wrong; likes nothing so much as a rocketing, roistering life; and is ready at a wink or nod, to out sabre, and flourish it over the orator's head, if he dares to array himself against parental authority.

These family dissensions, as usual, have got abroad, and are rare food for scandal in John's neighborhood. People begin to look wise, and shake their heads, whenever his affairs are mentioned. They all "hope that matters are not so bad with him as represented; but when a man's own children begin to rail at his extravagance, things must be badly managed. They understand he is mortgaged over head and ears, and is continually dabbling with money lenders. He is certainly an open-handed old gentleman, but they fear he has lived too fast; indeed, they never knew any good come of this fondness for hunting, racing, reveling, and prize-fighting. In short, Mr. Bull's estate is a very fine one, and has been in the family a long while; but, for all that, they have known many finer estates come to the hammer."

What is worst of all, is the effect which these pecuniary embarrassments and domestic feuds have had on the poor man himself. Instead of that jolly round corporation, and smug rosy face, which he used to present, he has of late become as shriveled and shrunk as a frost-bitten apple. His scarlet gold-laced waistcoat, which bellied out so bravely in those prosperous days when he sailed before the wind, now hangs loosely about him like a mainsail in a calm. His leather breeches are all in folds and wrinkles, and apparently have much ado to hold up the boots that yawn on both sides of his once sturdy legs.

Instead of strutting about as formerly, with his three-cornered hat on one side; flourishing his cudgel, and bringing it down every moment with a hearty thump upon the ground; looking every one sturdily in the face, and trolling out a stave of a catch or a drinking-song; he now goes about whistling thoughtfully to himself, with his head drooping down, his cudgel tucked under his arm, and his hands thrust to the bottom of his breeches pockets, which are evidently empty.

Such is the plight of honest John Bull at present; yet for all this the old fellow's spirit is as tall and as gallant as ever. If you drop the least expression of sympathy or concern, he takes fire in an instant; swears that he is the richest and stoutest fellow in the country; talks of laying out large sums to adorn his house or buy another estate; and with a valiant swagger and grasping of his cudgel, longs exceedingly to have another bout at quarter-staff.

Though there may be something rather whimsical in all this, yet I confess I cannot look upon John's situation without strong feelings of interest. With all his odd humors and obstinate prejudices, he is a sterling-hearted old blade. He may not be so wonderfully fine a fellow as he thinks himself, but he is at least twice as good as his neighbors represent him. His virtues are all his own; all plain, homebred, and unaffected. His very faults smack of the raciness of his good qualities. His extravagance savors of his generosity; his quarrelsomeness of his courage; his credulity of his open faith; his vanity of his pride; and his bluntness of his sincerity. They are all the redundancies of a rich and liberal character. He is like his own oak, rough without, but sound and solid within; whose bark abounds with excrescences in proportion to the growth and grandeur of the timber; and whose branches make a fearful groaning and murmuring in the least storm, from their very magnitude and luxuriance. There is something, too, in the appearance of his old family mansion that is extremely poetical and picturesque; and, as long as it can be rendered comfortably habitable, I should almost tremble to see it meddled with, during the present conflict of tastes and opinions. Some of his advisers are no doubt good architects, that might be of service; but many, I fear, are mere levelers, who, when they had once got to work with their mattocks on this venerable edifice, would never stop until they had brought it to the ground, and perhaps buried themselves among the ruins. All that I wish is, that John's present troubles may teach him more prudence in future. That he may cease to distress his mind about other people's affairs; that he may give up the fruitless attempt to promote the good of his neighbors, and the peace and happiness of the world, by dint of the cudgel; that he may remain quietly at home; gradually get his house into repair; cultivate his rich estate according to his fancy; husband his income—if he thinks proper; bring his unruly children into order—if he can; renew the jovial scenes of ancient prosperity; and long enjoy, on his paternal lands, a green, an honorable, and a merry old age.

The Pride of the Village

May no wolfe howle; no screech owle stir
A wing about thy sepulchre!
No boysterous winds or stormes come hither,
To starve or wither
Thy soft sweet earth! but, like a spring,
Love kept it ever flourishing.

HERRICK

IN THE COURSE OF AN EXCURSION THROUGH ONE OF THE REMOTE COUNTIES of England, I had struck into one of those cross roads that lead through the more secluded parts of the country, and stopped one afternoon at a village, the situation of which was beautifully rural and retired. There was an air of primitive simplicity about its inhabitants, not to be found in the villages which lie on the great coach-roads. I determined to pass the night there, and, having taken an early dinner, strolled out to enjoy the neighboring scenery.

My ramble, as is usually the case with travelers, soon led me to the church, which stood at a little distance from the village. Indeed, it was an object of some curiosity, its old tower being completely overrun with ivy, so that only here and there a jutting buttress, an angle of gray wall, or a fantastically carved ornament, peered through the verdant covering. It was a lovely evening. The early part of the day had been dark and showery, but in the afternoon it had cleared up; and though sullen clouds still hung over head, yet there was a broad tract of golden sky in the west, from which the setting sun gleamed through the dripping leaves, and lit up all nature into a melancholy smile. It seemed like the parting hour of a good Christian, smiling on the sins and sorrows of the world, and giving, in the serenity of his decline, an assurance that he will rise again in glory.

I had seated myself on a half-sunken tombstone, and was musing, as one is apt to do at this sober-thoughted hour, on past scenes and early friends—on those who were distant and those who were dead—and indulging in that kind of melancholy fancying, which has in it something sweeter even than pleasure. Every now and then the stroke of a bell from the neighboring tower fell on my ear; its tones were in unison with the scene, and, instead of jarring, chimed in with my feelings; and it was some time before I recollected that it must be tolling the knell of some new tenant of the tomb.

Presently I saw a funeral train moving across the village green; it wound slowly along a lane; was lost, and reappeared through the breaks of the hedges, until it passed the place where I was sitting. The pall was supported by young girls, dressed in white; and another, about the age of seventeen, walked before, bearing a chaplet of white flowers; a token that the deceased was a young and unmarried female. The corpse was followed by the parents. They were a venerable couple of the better order of peasantry. The father seemed to repress his feelings; but his fixed eye, contracted brow, and deeply-furrowed face, showed the struggle that was passing within. His wife hung on his arm, and wept aloud with the convulsive bursts of a mother's sorrow.

I followed the funeral into the church. The bier was placed in the centre aisle, and the chaplet of white flowers, with a pair of white gloves, was hung over the seat which the deceased had occupied.

Every one knows the soul-subduing pathos of the funeral service; for who is so fortunate as never to have followed some one he has loved to the tomb? But when performed over the remains of innocence and beauty, thus laid low in the bloom of existence—what can be more affecting? At that simple, but most solemn consignment of the body to the grave—"Earth to earth—ashes to ashes—dust to dust!"—the tears of the youthful companions of the deceased flowed unrestrained. The father still seemed to struggle with his feelings, and to comfort himself with the assurance that the dead are blessed which die in the Lord; but the mother only thought of her child as a flower of the field cut down and withered in the midst of its sweetness; she was like Rachel, "mourning over her children, and would not be comforted."

On returning to the inn, I learnt the whole story of the deceased. It was a simple one, and such as has often been told. She had been the beauty and pride of the village. Her father had once been an opulent farmer, but was reduced in circumstances. This was an only child, and brought up entirely at home, in the simplicity of rural life. She had been the pupil of the village pastor, the favorite lamb of his little flock. The good man watched over her education with paternal care; it was limited, and suitable to the sphere in which she was to move; for he only sought to make her an ornament to her station in life, not to raise her above it. The tenderness and indulgence of her parents, and the exemption from all ordinary occupations, had fostered a natural grace and delicacy of character, that accorded with the fragile loveliness of her form. She appeared like some tender plant of the garden, blooming accidentally amid the hardier natives of the fields.

The superiority of her charms was felt and acknowledged by her companions, but without envy; for it was surpassed by the unassuming gentleness and winning kindness of her manners. It might be truly said of her:

> This is the prettiest low-born lass, that ever
> Ran on the green-sward; nothing she does or seems,
> But smacks of something greater than herself;
> Too noble for this place.

The village was one of those sequestered spots, which still retain some vestiges of old English customs. It had its rural festivals and holiday pastimes, and still kept up some faint observance of the once popular rites of May. These, indeed, had been promoted by its present pastor, who was a lover of old customs, and one of those simple Christians that think their mission fulfilled by promoting joy on earth and good-will among mankind. Under his auspices the May-pole stood from year to year in the centre of the village green; on May-day it was decorated with garlands and streamers; and a queen or lady of the May was appointed, as in former times, to preside at the sports, and distribute the prizes and rewards. The picturesque situation of the village, and the fancifulness of its rustic fêtes, would often attract the notice of casual visitors. Among these, on one May-day, was a young officer, whose regiment had been recently quartered in the neighborhood. He was charmed with the native taste that pervaded this village pageant; but, above all, with the dawning loveliness of the queen of May. It was the village favorite, who was crowned with flowers, and blushing and smiling in all the beautiful confusion of girlish diffidence and delight. The artlessness of rural habits enabled him readily to make her acquaintance; he gradually won his way into her intimacy; and paid his court to her in that unthinking way in which young officers are too apt to trifle with rustic simplicity.

There was nothing in his advances to startle or alarm. He never even talked of love: but there are modes of making it more eloquent than language, and which convey it subtilely and irresistibly to the heart. The beam of the eye, the tone of voice, the thousand tendernesses which emanate from every word, and look, and action—these form the true eloquence of love, and can always be felt and understood, but never described. Can we wonder that they should readily win a heart, young, guileless, and susceptible? As to her, she loved almost unconsciously; she scarcely inquired what was the growing passion that was absorbing every thought and feeling, or what were to be its consequences. She, indeed, looked not to the future. When present, his looks and words occupied her whole attention; when absent, she thought but of what had passed at their recent interview. She would wander with him through the green lanes and rural scenes of the vicinity. He taught her to see new beauties in nature; he talked in the language of polite and cultivated life, and breathed into her ear the witcheries of romance and poetry.

Perhaps there could not have been a passion, between the sexes, more pure than this innocent girl's. The gallant figure of her youthful admirer, and the splendor of his military attire, might at first have charmed her eye; but it was not these that had captivated her heart. Her attachment had something in it of idolatry. She looked up to him as to a being of a superior order. She felt in his society the enthusiasm of a mind naturally delicate and poetical, and now first awakened to a keen perception of the beautiful and grand. Of the sordid distinctions of rank and fortune she thought nothing; it was the difference of intellect, of demeanor, of manners, from those of the rustic society to which she had been accustomed, that elevated him in her opinion. She would listen to him with charmed ear and downcast look of mute delight, and her cheek would mantle with enthusiasm; or if ever she ventured a shy glance of timid admiration, it was as quickly withdrawn, and she would sigh and blush at the idea of her comparative unworthiness.

Her lover was equally impassioned; but his passion was mingled with feelings of a coarser nature. He had begun the connection in levity; for he had often heard his brother officers boast of their village conquests, and thought some triumph of the kind necessary to his reputation as a man of spirit. But he was too full of youthful fervor. His heart had not yet been rendered sufficiently cold and selfish by a wandering and a dissipated life: it caught fire from the very flame it sought to kindle; and before he was aware of the nature of his situation, he became really in love.

What was he to do? There were the old obstacles which so incessantly occur in these heedless attachments. His rank in life—the prejudices of titled connections—his dependence upon a proud and unyielding father—all forbad him to think of matrimony:—but when he looked down upon this innocent being, so tender and confiding, there was a purity in her manners, a blamelessness in her life, and a beseeching modesty in her looks, that awed down every licentious feeling. In vain did he try to fortify himself by a thousand heartless examples of men of fashion; and to chill the glow of generous sentiment, with that cold derisive levity with which he had heard them talk of female virtue: whenever he came into her presence, she was still surrounded by that mysterious but impassive charm of virgin purity in whose hallowed sphere no guilty thought can live.

The sudden arrival of orders for the regiment to repair to the continent completed the confusion of his mind. He remained for a short time in a state of the most painful irresolution; he hesitated to communicate the tidings, until the day for marching was at hand; when he gave her the intelligence in the course of an evening ramble.

The idea of parting had never before occurred to her. It broke in at once upon her dream of felicity; she looked upon it as a sudden and insurmountable evil, and wept with the guileless simplicity of a child. He drew her to his bosom, and kissed the tears from her soft cheek; nor did he meet with a repulse, for there are moments of mingled sorrow and tenderness, which hallow the caresses of affection. He was naturally impetuous; and the sight of beauty, apparently yielding in his arms, the confidence of his power over her, and the dread of losing her for ever, all conspired to overwhelm his better feelings—he ventured to propose that she should leave her home, and be the companion of his fortunes.

He was quite a novice in seduction, and blushed and faltered at his own baseness; but so innocent of mind was his intended victim, that she was at first at a loss to comprehend his meaning; and why she should leave her native village, and the humble roof of her parents. When at last the nature of his proposal flashed upon her pure mind, the effect was withering. She did not weep—she did not break forth into reproach—she said not a word—but she shrunk back aghast as from a viper; gave him a look of anguish that pierced to his very soul; and, clasping her hands in agony, fled, as if for refuge, to her father's cottage.

The officer retired, confounded, humiliated, and repentant. It is uncertain what might have been the result of the conflict of his feelings, had not his thoughts been diverted by the bustle of departure. New scenes, new pleasures, and new companions, soon dissipated his self-reproach, and stifled his tenderness; yet, amidst the stir of camps, the revelries of garrisons, the array of armies, and even the din of battles, his thoughts would sometimes steal back to the scenes of rural quiet and village simplicity—the white cottage—the footpath along the silver brook and up the hawthorn hedge, and the little village maid loitering along it, leaning on his arm, and listening to him with eyes beaming with unconscious affection.

The shock which the poor girl had received, in the destruction of all her ideal world, had indeed been cruel. Faintings and hysterics had at first shaken her tender frame, and were succeeded by a settled and pining melancholy. She had beheld from her window the march of the departing troops. She had seen her faithless lover borne off, as if in triumph, amidst the sound of drum and trumpet, and the pomp of arms. She strained a last aching gaze after him, as the morning sun glittered about his figure, and his plume waved in the breeze; he passed away like a bright vision from her sight, and left her all in darkness.

It would be trite to dwell on the particulars of her after story. It was, like other tales of love, melancholy. She avoided society, and wandered out alone in the walks she had most frequented with her lover. She sought, like the stricken deer, to weep in silence and loneliness, and brood over the barbed sorrow that rankled in her soul. Sometimes she would be seen late of an evening sitting in the porch of the village church; and the milk-maids, returning from the fields, would now and then overhear her singing some plaintive ditty in the hawthorn walk. She became fervent in her devotions at church; and as the old people saw her approach, so wasted away, yet with a hectic gloom, and that hallowed air which melancholy diffuses round the form, they would make way for her, as for something spiritual, and looking after her, would shake their heads in gloomy foreboding.

She felt a conviction that she was hastening to the tomb, but looked forward to it as a place of rest. The silver cord that had bound her to existence was loosed, and there seemed to be no more pleasure under the sun. If ever her gentle bosom had entertained resentment against her lover, it was extinguished. She was incapable of angry passions; and in a moment of saddened tenderness, she penned him a farewell letter. It was couched in the simplest language, but touching from its very simplicity. She told him that she was dying, and did not conceal from him that his conduct was the cause. She even depicted the sufferings which she had experienced; but concluded with saying, that she could not die in peace, until she had sent him her forgiveness and her blessing.

By degrees her strength declined, that she could no longer leave the cottage. She could only totter to the window, where, propped up in her chair, it was her enjoyment to sit all day and look out upon the landscape. Still she uttered no complaint, nor imparted to any one the malady that was preying on her heart. She never even mentioned her lover's name; but would lay her head on her mother's bosom and weep in silence. Her poor parents hung, in mute anxiety, over this fading blossom of their hopes, still flattering themselves that it might again revive to freshness, and that the bright unearthly bloom which sometimes flushed her cheek might be the promise of returning health.

In this way she was seated between them one Sunday afternoon; her hands were clasped in theirs, the lattice was thrown open, and the soft air that stole in brought with it the fragrance of the clustering honeysuckle which her own hands had trained round the window.

Her father had just been reading a chapter in the Bible: it spoke of the vanity of worldly things, and of the joys of heaven: it seemed to have diffused comfort and serenity through her bosom. Her eye was fixed on the distant village church: the bell had tolled for the evening service; the last villager was lagging into the porch; and every thing had sunk into that hallowed stillness peculiar to the day of rest. Her parents were gazing on her with yearning hearts. Sickness and sorrow, which pass so roughly over some faces, had given to hers the expression of a seraph's. A tear trembled in her soft blue eye.—Was she thinking of her faithless lover?—or were her thoughts wandering to that distant church-yard, into whose bosom she might soon be gathered?

Suddenly the clang of hoofs was heard—a horseman galloped to the cottage—he dismounted before the window—the poor girl gave a faint exclamation, and sunk back in her chair: it was her repentant lover! He rushed into the house, and flew to clasp her to his bosom; but her wasted form—her deathlike countenance—so wan, yet so lovely in its desolation,—smote him to the soul, and he threw himself in agony at her feet. She was too faint to rise—she attempted to extend her trembling hand—her lips moved as if she spoke, but no word was articulated—she looked down upon him with a smile of unutterable tenderness, and closed her eyes forever!

Such are the particulars which I gathered of this village story. They are but scanty, and I am conscious have little novelty to recommend them. In the present rage also for strange incident and high-seasoned narrative, they may appear trite and insignificant, but they interested me strongly at the time; and, taken in connection with the affecting ceremony which I had just witnessed, left a deeper impression on my mind than many circumstances of a more striking nature. I have passed through the place since, and visited the church again, from a better motive than mere curiosity. It was a wintry evening; the trees were stripped of their foliage; the church-yard looked naked and mournful, and the wind rustled coldly through the dry grass. Evergreens, however, had been planted about the grave of the village favorite, and osiers were bent over it to keep the turf uninjured.

The church-door was open, and I stepped in. There hung the chaplet of flowers and the gloves, as on the day of the funeral: the flowers were withered, it is true, but care seemed to have been taken that no dust should soil their whiteness. I have seen many monuments, where art has exhausted its powers to awaken the sympathy of the spectator, but I have met with none that spoke more touchingly to my heart, than this simple but delicate memento of departed innocence.

The Angler

This day dame Nature seem'd in love,
The lusty sap began to move,
Fresh juice did stir th' embracing vines,
And birds had drawn their valentines.
The jealous trout that low did lie,
Rose at a well-dissembled flie.
There stood my friend, with patient skill,
Attending of his trembling quill.

SIR H. WOTTON

IT IS SAID THAT MANY AN UNLUCKY URCHIN IS INDUCED TO RUN AWAY FROM his family, and betake himself to a seafaring life, from reading the history of Robinson Crusoe; and I suspect that, in like manner, many of those worthy gentlemen who are given to haunt the sides of pastoral streams with angle-rods in hand, may trace the origin of their passion to the seductive pages of honest Izaak Walton. I recollect studying his "Complete Angler" several years since, in company with a knot of friends in America, and moreover that we were all completely bitten with the angling mania. It was early in the year; but as soon as the weather was auspicious, and that the spring began to melt into the verge of summer, we took rod in hand and sallied into the country, as stark mad as was ever Don Quixote from reading books of chivalry.

One of our party had equalled the Don in the fulness of his equipments: being attired cap-a-pie for the enterprise. He wore a broad-skirted fustian coat, perplexed with half a hundred pockets; a pair of stout shoes, and leathern gaiters; a basket slung on one side for fish; a patent rod, a landing net, and a score of other inconveniences, only to be found in the true angler's armory. Thus harnessed for the field, he was as great a matter of stare and wonderment among the country folk, who had never seen a regular angler, as was the steel-clad hero of La Mancha among the goatherds of the Sierra Morena.

Our first essay was along a mountain brook, among the Highlands of the Hudson; a most unfortunate place for the execution of those piscatory tactics which had been invented along the velvet margins of quiet English rivulets. It was one of those wild streams that lavish, among our romantic solitudes, unheeded beauties, enough to fill the sketch book of a hunter of the picturesque. Sometimes it would leap down rocky shelves, making small cascades, over which the trees threw their broad balancing sprays, and long nameless weeds hung in fringes from the impending banks, dripping with diamond drops. Sometimes it would brawl and fret along a ravine in the matted shade of a forest, filling it with murmurs; and after this termagant career, would steal forth into open day with the most placid, demure face imaginable; as I have seen some pestilent shrew of a housewife, after filling her home with uproar and ill-humor, come dimpling out of doors, swimming and curtseying, and smiling upon all the world.

How smoothly would this vagrant brook glide, at such times, through some bosom of green meadow-land among the mountains; where the quiet was only interrupted by the occasional tinkling of a bell from the lazy cattle among the clover, or the sound of a woodcutter's axe from the neighboring forest.

For my part, I was always a bungler at all kinds of sport that required either patience or adroitness, and had not angled above half an hour before I had completely "satisfied the sentiment," and convinced myself of the truth of Izaak Walton's opinion, that angling is something like poetry—a man must be born to it. I hooked myself instead of the fish; tangled my line in every tree; lost my bait; broke my rod; until I gave up the attempt in despair, and passed the day under the trees reading old Izaak; satisfied that it was his fascinating vein of honest simplicity and rural feeling that had bewitched me, and not the passion for angling. My companions, however, were more persevering in their delusion. I have them at this moment before my eyes, stealing along the border of the brook, where it lay open to the day, or was merely fringed by shrubs and bushes. I see the bittern rising with hollow scream as they break in upon his rarely-invaded haunt; the kingfisher watching them suspiciously from his dry tree that overhangs the deep black mill-pond in the gorge of the hills; the tortoise letting himself slip sideways from off the stone or log on which he is sunning himself; and the panic-struck frog plumping in headlong as they approach, and spreading an alarm throughout the watery world around.

I recollect also, that, after toiling and watching and creeping about for the greater parter part of a day, with scarcely any success in spite of all our admirable apparatus, a lubberly country urchin came down from the hills with a rod made from a branch of a tree, a few yards of twine, and, as Heaven shall help me! I believe a crooked pin for a hook, baited with a vile earthworm—and in half an hour caught more fish than we had nibbles throughout the day!

But, above all, I recollect the "good, honest, wholesome, hungry" repast which we made under a beech-tree, just by a spring of pure sweet water that stole out of the side of a hill; and how, when it was over, one of the party read old Izaak Walton's scene with the milkmaid, while I lay on the grass and built castles in a bright pile of clouds, until I fell asleep. All this may appear like mere egotism; yet I cannot refrain from uttering these recollections, which are passing like a strain of music over my mind, and have been called up by an agreeable scene which I witnessed not long since.

In the morning's stroll along the banks of the Alun, a beautiful little stream which flows down from the Welsh hills and throws itself into the Dee, my attention was attracted to a group seated on the margin. On approaching, I found it to consist of a veteran angler and two rustic disciples. The former was an old fellow with a wooden leg, with clothes very much but very carefully patched, betokening poverty, honestly come by, and decently maintained. His face bore the marks of former storms, but present fair weather; its furrows had been worn into an habitual smile; his iron-gray locks hung about his ears, and he had altogether the good-humored air of a constitutional philosopher who was disposed to take the world as it went. One of his companions was a ragged wight, with the skulking look of an arrant poacher, and I'll warrant could find his way to any gentleman's fish-pond in the neighborhood in the darkest night. The other was a tall, awkward, country lad, with a lounging gait, and apparently somewhat of a rustic beau. The old man was busy in examining the maw of a trout which he had just killed, to discover by its contents what insects were seasonable for bait, and was lecturing on the subject to his companions, who appeared to listen with infinite deference. I have a kind feeling towards all "brothers of the angle," ever since I read Izaak Walton. They are men, he affirms, of a "mild, sweet, and peaceable spirit"; and my esteem for them has been increased since I met with an old "Tretyse of fishing with the Angle," in which are set forth many of the maxims of their inoffensive fraternity. "Take good hede," sayeth this honest little tretyse, "that in going about your disportes ye open no man's gates but that ye shet them again. Also ye shall not use this forsayd crafti disport for no covetousness to the encreasing and sparing of your money only, but principally for your solace, and to cause the helth of your body and specyally of your soule."[1]

I thought that I could perceive in the veteran angler before me an exemplification of what I had read; and there was a cheerful contentedness in his looks that quite drew me towards him. I could not but remark the gallant manner in which he stumped from one part of the brook to another, waving his rod in the air, to keep the line from dragging on the ground, or catching among the bushes; and the adroitness with which he would throw his fly to any particular place; sometimes skimming it lightly along a little rapid; sometimes casting it into one of those dark holes made by a twisted root or overhanging bank, in which the large trout are apt to lurk. In the meanwhile he was giving instructions to his two disciples; showing them the manner in which they should handle their rods, fix their flies, and play them along the surface of the stream. The scene brought to my mind the instructions of the sage Piscator to his scholar. The country around was of that pastoral kind which Walton is fond of describing. It was a part of the great plain of Cheshire, close by the beautiful vale of Gessford, and just where the inferior Welsh hills begin to swell up from among fresh-smelling meadows. The day, too, like that recorded in his work, was mild and sunshiny, with now and then a soft-dropping shower, that sowed the whole earth with diamonds.

I soon fell into conversation with the old angler, and was so much entertained that, under pretext of receiving instructions in his art, I kept company with him almost the whole day; wandering along the banks of the stream, and listening to his talk. He was very communicative, having all the easy garrulity of cheerful old age; and I fancy was a little flattered by having an opportunity of displaying his piscatory lore; for who does not like now and then to play the sage?

He had been much of a rambler in his day, and had passed some years of his youth in America, particularly in Savannah, where he had entered into trade and had been ruined by the indiscretion of a partner. He had afterwards experienced many ups and

---

1. From this same treatise, it would appear that angling is a more industrious and devout employment than it is generally considered.—"For when ye purpose to go on your disportes in fishynge ye will not desyre greatlye many persons with you, which might let you of your game. And that ye may serve God devoutly in saying effectually your customable prayers. And thus doying, ye shall eschew and also avoyde many vices, as ydelness, which is principall cause to induce man to many other vices, as it is right well known."

downs in life, until he got into the navy, where his leg was carried away by a cannon ball, at the battle of Camperdown. This was the only stroke of real good fortune he had ever experienced, for it got him a pension, which, together with some small paternal property, brought him in a revenue of nearly forty pounds. On this he retired to his native village, where he lived quietly and independently; and devoted the remainder of his life to the "noble art of angling."

I found that he had read Izaak Walton attentively, and he seemed to have imbibed all his simple frankness and prevalent good humor. Though he had been sorely buffeted about the world, he was satisfied that the world, in itself, was good and beautiful. Though he had been as roughly used in different countries as a poor sheep that is fleeced by every hedge and thicket, yet he spoke of every nation with candor and kindness, appearing to look only on the good side of things: and, above all, he was almost the only man I had ever met with who had been an unfortunate adventurer in America, and had honesty and magnanimity enough to take the fault to his own door, and not to curse the country. The lad that was receiving his instructions, I learnt, was the son and heir apparent of a fat old widow who kept the village inn, and of course a youth of some expectation, and much courted by the idle gentleman-like personages of the place. In taking him under his care, therefore, the old man had probably an eye to a privileged corner in the tap-room, and an occasional cup of cheerful ale free of expense.

There is certainly something in angling, if we could forget, which anglers are apt to do, the cruelties and tortures inflicted on worms and insects, that tends to produce a gentleness of spirit, and a pure serenity of mind. As the English are methodical even in their recreations, and are the most scientific of sportsmen, it has been reduced among them to perfect rule and system. Indeed, it is an amusement peculiarly adapted to the mild and highly-cultivated scenery of England, where every roughness has been softened away from the landscape. It is delightful to saunter along those limpid streams which wander, like veins of silver, through the bosom of this beautiful country; leading one through a diversity of small home scenery; sometimes winding through ornamented grounds; sometimes brimming along through rich pasturage, where the fresh green is mingled with sweet-smelling flowers; sometimes venturing in sight of villages and hamlets, and then running capriciously away into shady retirements. The sweetness and serenity of nature, and the quiet watchfulness of the sport, gradually bring on pleasant fits of musing; which are now and then agreeably interrupted by the song of a bird, the distant whistle of the peasant, or perhaps the vagary of some fish, leaping out of the still water, and skimming transiently about its glassy surface. "When I would beget content," says Izaak Walton, "and increase confidence in the power and wisdom and providence of Almighty God, I will walk the meadows by some gliding stream, and there contemplate the lilies that take no care, and those very many other little living creatures that are not only created, but feed (man knows not how) by the goodness of the God of nature, and therefore trust in him."

I cannot forbear to give another quotation from one of those ancient champions of angling, which breathes the same innocent and happy spirit:

> Let me live harmlessly, and near the brink
> Of Trent or Avon have a dwelling-place,
> Where I may see my quill, or cork, down sink,
> With eager bite of pike, or bleak, or dace;
> And on the world and my Creator think:
> Whilst some men strive ill-gotten goods t' embrace:
> And others spend their time in base excess
> Of wine, or worse, in war, or wantonness.
> Let them that will, these pastimes still pursue,
> And on such pleasing fancies feed their fill;
> So I the fields and meadows green may view,
> And daily by fresh rivers walk at will,
> Among the daisies and the violets blue,
> Red hyacinth and yellow daffodil.[2]

On parting with the old angler I inquired after his place of abode, and happening to be in the neighborhood of the village a few evenings afterwards, I had the curiosity to seek him out. I found him living in a small cottage, containing only one room, but a perfect curiosity in its method and arrangement. It was on the skirts of the village, on a green bank, a little back from the road, with a small garden in front, stocked with kitchen herbs, and adorned with a few flowers. The whole front of the cottage was overrun with a honeysuckle. On the top was a ship for a weather-cock. The interior was fitted up in a truly nautical style, his ideas of comfort and convenience having been

---

2. J. Davors.

acquired on the berth-deck of a man-of-war. A hammock was slung from the ceiling, which, in the daytime, was lashed up so as to take but little room. From the centre of the chamber hung a model of a ship, of his own workmanship. Two or three chairs, a table, and a large sea-chest, formed the principal movables. About the wall were stuck up naval ballads, such as Admiral Hosier's Ghost, All in the Downs, and Tom Bowling, intermingled with pictures of sea-fights, among which the battle of Camperdown held a distinguished place. The mantel-piece was decorated with sea-shells; over which hung a quadrant, flanked by two wood-cuts of most bitter-looking naval commanders. His implements for angling were carefully disposed on nails and hooks about the room. On a shelf was arranged his library, containing a work on angling, much worn, a Bible covered with canvas, an odd volume or two of voyages, a nautical almanac, and a book of songs.

His family consisted of a large black cat with one eye, and a parrot which he had caught and tamed, and educated himself, in the course of one of his voyages; and which uttered a variety of sea phrases with the hoarse brattling tone of a veteran boatswain. The establishment reminded me of that of the renowned Robinson Crusoe; it was kept in neat order, everything being "stowed away" with the regularity of a ship of war; and he informed me that he "scoured the deck every morning, and swept it between meals."

I found him seated on a bench before the door, smoking his pipe in the soft evening sunshine. His cat was purring soberly on the threshold, and his parrot describing some strange evolutions in an iron ring that swung in the centre of his cage. He had been angling all day, and gave me a history of his sport with as much minuteness as a general would talk over a campaign; being particularly animated in relating the manner in which he had taken a large trout, which had completely tasked all his skill and wariness, and which he had sent as a trophy to mine hostess of the inn.

How comforting it is to see a cheerful and contented old age; and to behold a poor fellow, like this, after being tempest-tost through life, safely moored in a snug and quiet harbor in the evening of his days! His happiness, however, sprung from within himself, and was independent of external circumstances; for he had that inexhaustible good nature, which is the most precious gift of Heaven; spreading itself like oil over the troubled sea of thought, and keeping the mind smooth and equable in the roughest weather.

On inquiring further about him, I learnt that he was a universal favorite in the village, and the oracle of the tap-room; where he delighted the rustics with his songs, and, like Sinbad, astonished them with his stories of strange lands, and shipwrecks, and sea-fights. He was much noticed too by gentlemen sportsmen of the neighborhood; had taught several of them the art of angling; and was a privileged visitor to their kitchens. The whole tenor of his life was quiet and inoffensive, being principally passed about the neighboring streams, when the weather and season were favorable; and at other times he employed himself at home, preparing his fishing tackle for the next campaign, or manufacturing rods, nets, and flies, for his patrons and pupils among the gentry.

He was a regular attendant at church on Sundays, though he generally fell asleep during the sermon. He had made it his particular request that when he died he should be buried in a green spot, which he could see from his seat in church, and which he had marked out ever since he was a boy, and had thought of when far from home on the raging sea, in danger of being food for the fishes—it was the spot where his father and mother had been buried.

I have done, for I fear that my reader is growing weary; but I could not refrain from drawing the picture of this worthy "brother of the angle"; who has made me more than ever in love with the theory, though I fear I shall never be adroit in the practice of his art: and I will conclude this rambling sketch in the words of honest Izaak Walton, by craving the blessing of St. Peter's master upon my reader, "and upon all that are true lovers of virtue; and dare trust in his providence; and be quiet; and go a angling."

The Legend of Sleepy Hollow

Found Among the Papers of the Late Diedrich Knickerbocker

A pleasing land of drowsy head it was,
Of dreams that wave before the half-shut eye,
And of gay castles in the clouds that pass,
For ever flushing round a summer sky.
CASTLE OF INDOLENCE

IN THE BOSOM OF ONE OF THOSE SPACIOUS COVES WHICH INDENT THE EASTERN shore of the Hudson, at that broad expansion of the river denominated by the ancient Dutch navigators the Tappan Zee, and where they always prudently shortened sail, and implored the protection of St. Nicholas when they crossed, there lies a small market-town or rural port, which by some is called Greensburgh, but which is more generally and properly known by the name of Tarry Town. This name was given, we are told, in former days by the good housewives of the adjacent country, from the inveterate propensity of their husbands to linger about the village tavern on market days. Be that as it may, I do not vouch for the fact, but merely advert to it, for the sake of being precise and authentic. Not far from this village, perhaps about two miles, there is a little valley, or rather lap of land, among high hills, which is one of the quietest places in the whole world. A small brook glides through it, with just murmur enough to lull one to repose; and the occasional whistle of a quail, or tapping of a woodpecker, is almost the only sound that ever breaks in upon the uniform tranquillity.

I recollect that, when a stripling, my first exploit in squirrel-shooting was in a grove of tall walnut-trees that shades one side of the valley. I had wandered into it at noon time, when all nature is peculiarly quiet, and was startled by the roar of my own gun, as it broke the Sabbath stillness around, and was prolonged and reverberated by the angry echoes. If ever I should wish for a retreat, whither I might steal from the world and its distractions, and dream quietly away the remnant of a troubled life, I know of none more promising than this little valley.

From the listless repose of the place, and the peculiar character of its inhabitants, who are descendants from the original Dutch settlers, this sequestered glen has long been known by the name of SLEEPY HOLLOW, and its rustic lads are called the Sleepy Hollow Boys throughout all the neighboring country. A drowsy, dreamy influence seems to hang over the land, and to pervade the very atmosphere. Some say that the place was bewitched by a high German doctor, during the early days of the settlement; others, that an old Indian chief, the prophet or wizard of his tribe, held his powwows there before the country was discovered by Master Hendrick Hudson. Certain it is, the place still continues under the sway of some witching power, that holds a spell over the minds of the good people, causing them to walk in a continual reverie. They are given to all kinds of marvelous beliefs; are subject to trances and visions; and frequently see strange sights, and hear music and voices in the air. The whole neighborhood abounds with local tales, haunted spots, and twilight superstitions; stars shoot and meteors glare oftener across the valley than in any other part of the country, and the nightmare, with her whole nine fold, seems to make it the favorite scene of her gambols.

The dominant spirit, however, that haunts this enchanted region, and seems to be commander-in-chief of all the powers of the air, is the apparition of a figure on horseback without a head. It is said by some to be the ghost of a Hessian trooper, whose head had been carried away by a cannon-ball, in some nameless battle during the revolutionary war; and who is ever and anon seen by the country folk, hurrying along in the gloom of night, as if on the wings of the wind. His haunts are not confined to the valley, but extend at times to the adjacent roads, and especially to the vicinity of a church at no great distance. Indeed, certain of the most authentic historians of those parts, who have been careful in collecting and collating the floating facts concerning this spectre, allege that the body of the trooper, having been buried in the church-yard, the ghost rides forth to the scene of battle in nightly quest of his head; and that the rushing speed with which he sometimes passes along the Hollow, like a midnight blast, is owing to his being belated, and in a hurry to get back to the church-yard before daybreak.

Such is the general purport of this legendary superstition, which has furnished materials for many a wild story in that region of shadows; and the spectre is known, at all the country firesides, by the name of the Headless Horseman of Sleepy Hollow.

It is remarkable that the visionary propensity I have mentioned is not confined to the native inhabitants of the valley, but is unconsciously imbibed by every one who resides there for a time. However wide awake they may have been before they entered that sleepy region, they are sure, in a little time, to inhale the witching influence of the air, and begin to grow imaginative—to dream dreams, and see apparitions.

I mention this peaceful spot with all possible laud; for it is in such little retired Dutch valleys, found here and there embosomed in the great state of New-York, that population, manners, and customs, remain fixed; while the great torrent of migration and improvement, which is making such incessant changes in other parts of this restless country, sweeps by them unobserved. They are like those little nooks of still water which border a rapid stream; where we may see the straw and bubble riding quietly at anchor, or slowly revolving in their mimic harbor, undisturbed by the rush of the passing current. Though many years have elapsed since I trod the drowsy shades of Sleepy Hollow, yet I question whether I should not still find the same trees and the same families vegetating in its sheltered bosom.

In this by-place of nature there abode, in a remote period of American history, that is to say, some thirty years since, a worthy wight of the name of Ichabod Crane; who sojourned, or, as he expressed it, "tarried," in Sleepy Hollow for the purpose of instructing the children of the vicinity. He was a native of Connecticut; a state which supplies the Union with pioneers for the mind as well as for the forest, and sends forth yearly its legions of frontier woodmen and country schoolmasters. The cognomen of Crane was not inapplicable to his person. He was tall, but exceedingly lank, with narrow shoulders, long arms and legs, hands that dangled a mile out of his sleeves, feet that might have served for shovels, and his whole frame most loosely hung together. His head was small, and flat at top, with huge ears, large green glassy eyes, and a long snipe nose, so that it looked like a weather-cock, perched upon his spindle neck, to tell which way the wind blew. To see him striding along the profile of a hill on a windy day, with his clothes bagging and fluttering about him, one might have mistaken him for the genius of famine descending upon the earth, or some scarecrow eloped from a cornfield.

His school-house was a low building of one large room, rudely constructed of logs; the windows partly glazed, and partly patched with leaves of old copy-books.

It was most ingeniously secured at vacant hours, by a withe twisted in the handle of the door, and stakes set against the window-shutters; so that, though a thief might get in with perfect ease, he would find some embarrassment in getting out; an idea most probably borrowed by the architect, Yost Van Houten, from the mystery of an eel-pot. The school-house stood in a rather lonely but pleasant situation, just at the foot of a woody hill, with a brook running close by, and a formidable birch tree growing at one end of it. From hence the low murmur of his pupils' voices, conning over their lessons, might be heard in a drowsy summer's day, like the hum of a bee-hive; interrupted now and then by the authoritative voice of the master, in the tone of menace or command; or, peradventure, by the appalling sound of the birch, as he urged some tardy loiterer along the flowery path of knowledge. Truth to say, he was a conscientious man, and ever bore in mind the golden maxim, "Spare the rod and spoil the child."—Ichabod Crane's scholars certainly were not spoiled.

I would not have it imagined, however, that he was one of those cruel potentates of the school, who joy in the smart of their subjects; on the contrary, he administered justice with discrimination rather than severity; taking the burthen off the backs of the weak, and laying it on those of the strong. Your mere puny stripling, that winced at the least flourish of the rod, was passed by with indulgence; but the claims of justice were satisfied by inflicting a double portion on some little, tough, wrong-headed, broad-skirted Dutch urchin, who sulked and swelled and grew dogged and sullen beneath the birch. All this he called "doing his duty by their parents"; and he never inflicted a chastisement without following it by the assurance, so consolatory to the smarting urchin, that "he would remember it and thank him for it the longest day he had to live."

When school hours were over, he was even the companion and playmate of the larger boys; and on holiday afternoons would convoy some of the smaller ones home, who happened to have pretty sisters, or good housewives for mothers, noted for the comforts of the cupboard. Indeed it behooved him to keep on good terms with his pupils. The revenue arising from his school was small, and would have been scarcely sufficient to furnish him with daily bread, for he was a huge feeder, and though lank, had the dilating powers of an anaconda; but to help out his maintenance, he was, according to country custom in those parts, boarded and lodged at the houses of the farmers, whose children he instructed. With these he lived successively a week at a time; thus going the rounds of the neighborhood, with all his worldly effects tied up in a cotton handkerchief.

That all this might not be too onerous on the purses of his rustic patrons, who are apt to consider the costs of schooling a grievous burden, and schoolmasters as mere drones, he had various ways of rendering himself both useful and agreeable. He assisted the farmers occasionally in the lighter labors of their farms; helped to make hay; mended the fences; took the horses to water; drove the cows from pasture; and cut wood for the winter fire. He laid aside, too, all the dominant dignity and absolute sway with which he lorded it in his little empire, the school, and became wonderfully gentle and ingratiating. He found favor in the eyes of the mothers by petting the children, particularly the youngest; and like the lion bold, which whilom so magnanimously the lamb did hold, he would sit with a child on one knee, and rock a cradle with his foot for whole hours together.

In addition to his other vocations, he was the singing-master of the neighborhood, and picked up many bright shillings by instructing the young folks in psalmody. It was a matter of no little vanity to him, on Sundays, to take his station in front of the church gallery, with a band of chosen singers; where, in his own mind, he completely carried away the palm from the parson. Certain it is, his voice resounded far above all the rest of the congregation; and there are peculiar quavers still to be heard in that church, and which may even be heard half a mile off, quite to the opposite side of the mill-pond, on a still Sunday morning, which are said to be legitimately descended from the nose of Ichabod Crane. Thus, by divers little make-shifts in that ingenious way which is commonly denominated "by hook and by crook," the worthy pedagogue got on tolerably enough, and was thought, by all who understood nothing of the labor of headwork, to have a wonderfully easy life of it.

The schoolmaster is generally a man of some importance in the female circle of a rural neighborhood; being considered a kind of idle gentleman-like personage, of vastly superior taste and accomplishments to the rough country swains, and, indeed, inferior in learning only to the parson. His appearance, therefore, is apt to occasion some little stir at the tea-table of a farmhouse, and the addition of a supernumerary dish of cakes or sweetmeats, or, peradventure, the parade of a silver tea-pot. Our man of letters, therefore, was peculiarly happy in the smiles of all the country damsels. How he would figure among them in the church-yard, between services on Sundays! gathering grapes for them from the wild vines that overrun the surrounding trees; reciting for their amusement all the epitaphs on the tombstones; or sauntering, with a whole bevy of them, along the banks of the adjacent mill-pond; while the more bashful country bumpkins hung sheepishly back, envying his superior elegance and address.

From his half itinerant life, also, he was a kind of traveling gazette, carrying the whole budget of local gossip from house to house; so that his appearance was always greeted with satisfaction. He was, moreover, esteemed by the women as a man of great erudition, for he had read several books quite through, and was a perfect master of Cotton Mather's History of New England Witchcraft, in which, by the way, he most firmly and potently believed.

He was, in fact, an odd mixture of small shrewdness and simple credulity. His appetite for the marvelous, and his powers of digesting it, were equally extraordinary; and both had been increased by his residence in this spell-bound region. No tale was too gross or monstrous for his capacious swallow. It was often his delight, after his school was dismissed in the afternoon, to stretch himself on the rich bed of clover, bordering the little brook that whimpered by his school-house, and there con over old Mather's direful tales, until the gathering dusk of the evening made the printed page a mere mist before his eyes. Then, as he wended his way by swamp and stream and awful woodland, to the farmhouse where he happened to be quartered, every sound of nature, at that witching hour, fluttered his excited imagination: the moan of the whip-poor-will[1] from the hill-side; the boding cry of the tree-toad, that harbinger of storm; the dreary hooting of the screech-owl or the sudden rustling in the thicket of birds frightened from their roost. The fire-flies, too, which sparkled most vividly in the darkest places, now and then startled him, as one of uncommon brightness would stream across his path; and if, by chance, a huge blockhead of a beetle came winging his blundering flight against him, the poor varlet was ready to give up the ghost, with the idea that he was struck with a witch's token. His only resource on such occasions, either to drown thought or drive away evil spirits, was to sing psalm tunes;—and the good people of Sleepy Hollow, as they sat by their doors of an evening, were often filled with awe, at hearing his nasal melody, "in linked sweetness long drawn out," floating from the distant hill, or along the dusky road.

Another of his sources of fearful pleasure was, to pass long winter evenings with the old Dutch wives, as they sat spinning by the fire, with a row of apples roasting and spluttering along the hearth, and listen to their marvelous tales of ghosts and goblins, and haunted fields, and haunted brooks, and haunted bridges, and haunted houses, and

---

1. The whip-poor-will is a bird which is only heard at night. It receives its name from its note, which is thought to resemble those words.

particularly of the headless horseman, or Galloping Hessian of the Hollow, as they sometimes called him. He would delight them equally by his anecdotes of witchcraft, and of the direful omens and portentous sights and sounds in the air, which prevailed in the earlier times of Connecticut; and would frighten them wofully with speculations upon comets and shooting stars; and with the alarming fact that the world did absolutely turn round, and that they were half the time topsy-turvy!

But if there was a pleasure in all this, while snugly cuddling in the chimney corner of a chamber that was all of a ruddy glow from the crackling wood fire, and where, of course, no spectre dared to show its face, it was dearly purchased by the terrors of his subsequent walk homewards. What fearful shapes and shadows beset his path amidst the dim and ghastly glare of a snowy night!—With what wistful look did he eye every trembling ray of light streaming across the waste fields from some distant window!—How often was he appalled by some shrub covered with snow, which, like a sheeted spectre, beset his very path!—How often did he shrink with curdling awe at the sound of his own steps on the frosty crust beneath his feet; and dread to look over his shoulder, lest he should behold some uncouth being tramping close behind him!—and how often was he thrown into complete dismay by some rushing blast, howling among the trees, in the idea that it was the Galloping Hessian on one of his nightly scourings!

All these, however, were mere terrors of the night, phantoms of the mind that walk in darkness; and though he had seen many spectres in his time, and been more than once beset by Satan in divers shapes, in his lonely perambulations, yet daylight put an end to all these evils; and he would have passed a pleasant life of it, in despite of the devil and all his works, if his path had not been crossed by a being that causes more perplexity to mortal man than ghosts, goblins, and the whole race of witches put together, and that was—a woman.

Among the musical disciples who assembled, one evening in each week, to receive his instructions in psalmody, was Katrina Van Tassel, the daughter and only child of a substantial Dutch farmer. She was a blooming lass of fresh eighteen; plump as a partridge; ripe and melting and rosy-cheeked as one of her father's peaches, and universally famed, not merely for her beauty, but her vast expectations. She was withal a little of a coquette, as might be perceived even in her dress, which was a mixture of ancient and modern fashions, as most suited to set off her charms. She wore the ornaments of pure yellow gold, which her great-great-grandmother had brought over from Saardam; the tempting stomacher of the olden time; and withal a provokingly short petticoat, to display the prettiest foot and ankle in the country round.

Ichabod Crane had a soft and foolish heart towards the sex; and it is not to be wondered at, that so tempting a morsel soon found favor in his eyes; more especially after he had visited her in her paternal mansion. Old Baltus Van Tassel was a perfect picture of a thriving, contented, liberal-hearted farmer. He seldom, it is true, sent either his eyes or his thoughts beyond the boundaries of his own farm; but within those every thing was snug, happy, and well-conditioned. He was satisfied with his wealth, but not proud of it; and piqued himself upon the hearty abundance, rather than the style in which he lived. His stronghold was situated on the banks of the Hudson, in one of those green, sheltered, fertile nooks in which the Dutch farmers are so fond of nestling. A great elm-tree spread its broad branches over it; at the foot of which bubbled up a spring of the softest and sweetest water, in a little well, formed of a barrel; and then stole sparkling away through the grass, to a neighboring brook, that bubbled along among alders and dwarf willows. Hard by the farmhouse was a vast barn, that might have served for a church; every window and crevice of which seemed bursting forth with the treasures of the farm; the flail was busily resounding within it from morning to night; swallows and martins skimmed twittering about the eaves; and rows of pigeons, some with one eye turned up, as if watching the weather, some with their heads under their wings, or buried in their bosoms, and others, swelling, and cooing, and bowing about their dames, were enjoying the sunshine on the roof. Sleek unwieldy porkers were grunting in the repose and abundance of their pens; whence sallied forth, now and then, troops of sucking pigs, as if to snuff the air. A stately squadron of snowy geese were riding in an adjoining pond, convoying whole fleets of ducks; regiments of turkeys were gobbling through the farm-yard, and guinea fowls fretting about it, like ill-tempered housewives, with their peevish discontented cry. Before the barn door strutted the gallant cock, that pattern of a husband, a warrior, and a fine gentleman, clapping his burnished wings, and crowing in the pride and gladness of his heart—sometimes tearing up the earth with his feet, and then generously calling his ever-hungry family of wives and children to enjoy the rich morsel which he had discovered.

The pedagogue's mouth watered, as he looked upon this sumptuous promise of luxurious winter fare. In his devouring mind's eye, he pictured to himself every roasting-pig running about with a pudding in his belly, and an apple in his mouth; the pigeons were snugly put to bed in a comfortable pie, and tucked in with a coverlet of crust; the geese were swimming in their own gravy; and the ducks pairing cosily in dishes, like snug married couples, with a decent competency of onion sauce. In the porkers he saw carved out the future sleek side of bacon, and juicy relishing ham; not a turkey but he beheld daintily trussed up, with its gizzard under its wing, and, peradventure, a necklace of savory sausages; and even bright chanticleer himself lay sprawling on his back, in a side-dish, with uplifted claws, as if craving that quarter which his chivalrous spirit disdained to ask while living.

As the enraptured Ichabod fancied all this, and as he rolled his great green eyes over the fat meadow-lands, the rich fields of wheat, of rye, of buckwheat, and Indian corn, and the orchards burthened with ruddy fruit, which surrounded the warm tenement of Van Tassel, his heart yearned after the damsel who was to inherit these domains, and his imagination expanded with the idea, how they might be readily turned into cash, and the money invested in immense tracts of wild land, and shingle palaces in the wilderness. Nay, his busy fancy already realized his hopes, and presented to him the blooming Katrina, with a whole family of children, mounted on the top of a wagon loaded with household trumpery, with pots and kettles dangling beneath; and he beheld himself bestriding a pacing mare, with a colt at her heels, setting out for Kentucky, Tennessee, or the Lord knows where.

When he entered the house the conquest of his heart was complete. It was one of those spacious farmhouses, with high-ridged, but lowly-sloping roofs, built in the style handed down from the first Dutch settlers; the low projecting eaves forming a piazza along the front, capable of being closed up in bad weather. Under this were hung flails, harness, various utensils of husbandry, and nets for fishing in the neighboring river. Benches were built along the sides for summer use; and a great spinning-wheel at one end, and a churn at the other, showed the various uses to which this important porch might be devoted. From this piazza the wondering Ichabod entered the hall, which formed the centre of the mansion and the place of usual residence. Here, rows of resplendent pewter, ranged on a long dresser, dazzled his eyes. In one corner stood a huge bag of wool ready to be spun; in another a quantity of linsey-woolsey just from the loom; ears of Indian corn, and strings of dried apples and peaches, hung in gay festoons along the walls, mingled with the gaud of red peppers; and a door left ajar gave him a peep into the best parlor, where the claw-footed chairs, and dark mahogany tables, shone like mirrors; andirons, with their accompanying shovel and tongs, glistened from their covert of asparagus tops; mock oranges and conch-shells decorated the mantel-piece;

strings of various-colored birds' eggs were suspended above it; a great ostrich egg was hung from the centre of the room, and a corner cupboard, knowingly left open, displayed immense treasures of old silver and well-mended china.

From the moment Ichabod laid his eyes upon these regions of delight, the peace of his mind was at an end, and his only study was how to gain the affections of the peerless daughter of Van Tassel. In this enterprise, however, he had more real difficulties than generally fell to the lot of a knight-errant of yore, who seldom had anything but giants, enchanters, fiery dragons, and such-like easily conquered adversaries to contend with, and had to make his way merely through gates of iron and brass, and walls of adamant, to the castle keep, where the lady of his heart was confined; all which he achieved as easily as a man would carve his way to the centre of a Christmas pie; and then the lady gave him her hand as a matter of course. Ichabod, on the contrary, had to win his way to the heart of a country coquette, beset with a labyrinth of whims and caprices, which were for ever presenting new difficulties and impediments; and he had to encounter a host of fearful adversaries of real flesh and blood, the numerous rustic admirers, who beset every portal to her heart; keeping a watchful and angry eye upon each other, but ready to fly out in the common cause against any new competitor.

Among these the most formidable was a burly, roaring, roystering blade, of the name of Abraham, or, according to the Dutch abbreviation, Brom Van Brunt, the hero of the country round, which rang with his feats of strength and hardihood. He was broad-shouldered and double-jointed, with short curly black hair, and a bluff, but not unpleasant countenance, having a mingled air of fun and arrogance. From his Herculean frame and great powers of limb, he had received the nickname of BROM BONES, by which he was universally known. He was famed for great knowledge and skill in horsemanship, being as dexterous on horseback as a Tartar. He was foremost at all races and cock-fights; and, with the ascendancy which bodily strength acquires in rustic life, was the umpire in all disputes, setting his hat on one side, and giving his decisions with an air and tone admitting of no gainsay or appeal. He was always ready for either a fight or a frolic; but had more mischief than ill-will in his composition; and with all his overbearing roughness there was a strong dash of waggish good humor at bottom. He had three or four boon companions, who regarded him as their model, and at the head of whom he scoured the country, attending every scene of feud or merriment for miles around. In cold weather he was distinguished by a fur cap, surmounted with a flaunting fox's tail; and when the folks at a country gathering descried this well-known crest at a distance, whisking about among a squad of hard riders, they always stood by for a squall. Sometimes his crew would be heard dashing along past the farmhouses at midnight with hoop and halloo, like a troop of Don Cossacks; and the old dames, startled out of their sleep, would listen for a moment till the hurry-scurry had clattered by, and then exclaim, "Ay, there goes Brom Bones and his gang!" The neighbors looked upon him with a mixture of awe, admiration, and good will; and when any madcap prank, or rustic brawl, occurred in the vicinity, always shook their heads, and warranted Brom Bones was at the bottom of it.

This rantipole hero had for some time singled out the blooming Katrina for the object of his uncouth gallantries, and, though his amorous toyings were something like the gentle caresses and endearments of a bear, yet it was whispered that she did not altogether discourage his hopes. Certain it is, his advances were signals for rival candidates to retire, who felt no inclination to cross a lion in his amours; insomuch, that when his horse was seen tied to Van Tassel's paling, on a Sunday night, a sure sign that his master was courting, or, as it is termed, "sparking," within, all other suitors passed by in despair, and carried the war into other quarters.

Such was the formidable rival with whom Ichabod Crane had to contend, and, considering all things, a stouter man than he would have shrunk from the competition, and a wiser man would have despaired. He had, however, a happy mixture of pliability and perseverance in his nature; he was in form and spirit like a supple-jack—yielding, but tough; though he bent, he never broke; and though he bowed beneath the slightest pressure, yet, the moment it was away—jerk! he was as erect, and carried his head as high as ever.

To have taken the field openly against his rival would have been madness; for he was not man to be thwarted in his amours, any more than that stormy lover, Achilles. Ichabod, therefore, made his advances in a quiet and gently-insinuating manner. Under cover of his character of singing-master, he made frequent visits at the farmhouse; not that he had anything to apprehend from the meddlesome interference of parents, which is so often a stumbling-block in the path of lovers. Balt Van Tassel was an easy indulgent soul; he loved his daughter better even than his pipe, and, like a reasonable man and an excellent father, let her have her way in every thing. His notable little wife, too, had enough to do to attend to her housekeeping and manage her poultry; for, as she sagely observed, ducks and geese are foolish things, and must be looked after, but girls can take care of themselves. Thus while the busy dame bustled about the house, or plied her spinning-wheel at one end of the piazza, honest Balt would sit smoking his evening pipe at the other, watching the achievements of a little wooden warrior who, armed with a sword in each hand, was most valiantly fighting the wind on the pinnacle of the barn. In the meantime, Ichabod would carry on his suit with the daughter by the side of the spring under the great elm, or sauntering along in the twilight, that hour so favorable to the lover's eloquence.

I profess not to know how women's hearts are wooed and won. To me they have always been matters of riddle and admiration. Some seem to have but one vulnerable point, or door of access; while others have a thousand avenues, and may be captured in a thousand different ways. It is a great triumph of skill to gain the former, but still greater proof of generalship to maintain possession of the latter, for the man must battle for his fortress at every door and window. He who wins a thousand common hearts is therefore entitled to some renown; but he who keeps undisputed sway over the heart of a coquette, is indeed a hero. Certain it is, this was not the case with the redoubtable Brom Bones; and from the moment Ichabod Crane made his advances, the interests of the former evidently declined; his horse was no longer seen tied at the palings on Sunday nights, and a deadly feud gradually arose between him and the preceptor of Sleepy Hollow.

Brom, who had a degree of rough chivalry in his nature, would fain have carried matters to open warfare, and have settled their pretensions to the lady according to the mode of those most concise and simple reasoners, the knights-errant of yore—by single combat; but Ichabod was too conscious of the superior might of his adversary to enter the lists against him: he had overheard a boast of Bones, that he would "double the schoolmaster up and lay him on a shelf of his own school-house"; and he was too wary to give him an opportunity. There was something extremely provoking in this obstinately pacific system; it left Brom no alternative but to draw upon the funds of rustic waggery in his disposition, and to play off boorish practical jokes upon his rival. Ichabod became the object of whimsical persecution to Bones, and his gang of rough riders. They harried his hitherto peaceful domains; smoked out his singing school, by stopping up the chimney; broke into the school-house at night, in spite of its formidable fastenings of withe and window stakes, and turned everything topsy-turvy: so that the poor schoolmaster began to think all the witches in the country held their meetings there. But, what was still more annoying, Brom took all opportunities of turning him into ridicule in presence of his mistress, and had a scoundrel dog whom he taught to whine in the most ludicrous manner, and introduced as a rival of Ichabod's to instruct her in psalmody.

In this way matters went on for some time, without producing any material effect on the relative situation of the contending powers. On a fine autumnal afternoon, Ichabod, in pensive mood, sat enthroned on the lofty stool whence he usually watched all the concerns of his little literary realm. In his hand he swayed a ferule, that sceptre of despotic power; the birch of justice reposed on three nails, behind the throne, a constant terror to evil doers; while on the desk before him might be seen sundry contraband articles and prohibited weapons, detected upon the persons of idle urchins; such as half-munched apples, popguns, whirligigs, fly-cages, and whole legions of rampant little paper game-cocks. Apparently there had been some appalling act of justice recently inflicted, for his scholars were all busily intent upon their books, or slyly whispering behind them with one eye kept upon the master; and a kind of buzzing stillness reigned throughout the school-room. It was suddenly interrupted by the appearance of a negro, in tow-cloth jacket and trowsers, a round-crowned fragment of a hat, like the cap of Mercury, and mounted on the back of a ragged, wild, half-broken colt, which he managed with a rope by way of halter. He came clattering up to the school door with an invitation to Ichabod to attend a merry-making or "quilting frolic," to be held that evening at Mynheer Van Tassel's; and, having delivered his message with that air of importance, and effort at fine language, which a negro is apt to display on petty embassies of the kind, he dashed over the brook, and was seen scampering away up the hollow, full of the importance and hurry of his mission.

All was now bustle and hubbub in the late quiet school-room. The scholars were hurried through their lessons without stopping at trifles; those who were nimble skipped over half with impunity, and those who were tardy, had a smart application now and then in the rear, to quicken their speed, or help them over a tall word. Books were flung aside without being put away on the shelves, inkstands were overturned, benches thrown down, and the whole school was turned loose an hour before the usual time, bursting forth like a legion of young imps, yelping and racketing about the green, in joy at their early emancipation.

The gallant Ichabod now spent at least an extra half hour at his toilet, brushing and furbishing up his best, and indeed only suit of rusty black, and arranging his locks by a bit of broken looking-glass, that hung up in the school-house. That he might make his appearance before his mistress in the true style of a cavalier, he borrowed a horse from the farmer with whom he was domiciliated, a choleric old Dutchman, of the name of Hans Van Ripper, and, thus gallantly mounted, issued forth like a knight-errant in quest of adventures. But it is meet I should, in the true spirit of romantic story, give some account of the looks and equipments of my hero and his steed. The animal he bestrode was a broken-down plough-horse, that had outlived almost everything but his viciousness. He was gaunt and shagged, with a ewe neck and a head like a hammer; his rusty mane and tail were tangled and knotted with burrs; one eye had lost its pupil, and was glaring and spectral; but the other had the gleam of a genuine devil in it. Still, he must have had fire and mettle in his day, if we may judge from the name he bore of Gunpowder. He had, in fact, been a favorite steed of his master's, the choleric Van Ripper, who was a furious rider, and had infused, very probably, some of his own spirit into the animal; for, old and broken down as he looked, there was more of the lurking devil in him than in any young filly in the country.

Ichabod was a suitable figure for such a steed. He rode with short stirrups, which brought his knees nearly up to the pommel of the saddle; his sharp elbows stuck out like grasshoppers'; he carried his whip perpendicularly in his hand, like a sceptre, and, as his horse jogged on, the motion of his arms was not unlike the flapping of a pair of wings. A small wool hat rested on the top of his nose, for so his scanty strip of forehead might be called; and the skirts of his black coat fluttered out almost to the horse's tail. Such was the appearance of Ichabod and his steed, as they shambled out of the gate of Hans Van Ripper, and it was altogether such an apparition as is seldom to be met with in broad daylight.

It was, as I have said, a fine autumnal day, the sky was clear and serene, and nature wore that rich and golden livery which we always associate with the idea of abundance. The forests had put on their sober brown and yellow, while some trees of the tenderer kind had been nipped by the frosts into brilliant dyes of orange, purple, and scarlet. Streaming files of wild ducks began to make their appearance high in the air; the bark of the squirrel might be heard from the groves of beech and hickory nuts, and the pensive whistle of the quail at intervals from the neighboring stubble-field.

The small birds were taking their farewell banquets. In the fulness of their revelry, they fluttered, chirping and frolicking, from bush to bush, and tree to tree, capricious from the very profusion and variety around them. There was the honest cock-robin, the favorite game of stripling sportsmen, with its loud querulous note; and the twittering blackbirds flying in sable clouds; and the golden-winged woodpecker, with his crimson crest, his broad black gorget, and splendid plumage; and the cedar bird, with its red-tipt wings and yellow-tipt tail, and its little monteiro cap of feathers; and the blue jay, that noisy coxcomb, in his gay light-blue coat and white under clothes, screaming and chattering, bobbing and nodding and bowing, and pretending to be on good terms with every songster of the grove.

As Ichabod jogged slowly on his way, his eye, ever open to every symptom of culinary abundance, ranged with delight over the treasures of jolly zutumn. On all sides he beheld vast store of apples; some hanging in oppressive opulence on the trees; some gathered into baskets and barrels for the market; others heaped up in rich piles for the cider-press. Farther on he beheld great fields of Indian corn, with its golden ears peeping from their leafy coverts, and holding out the promise of cakes and hasty pudding; and the yellow pumpkins lying beneath them, turning up their fair round bellies to the sun, and giving ample prospects of the most luxurious of pies; and anon he passed the fragrant buckwheat fields, breathing the odor of the bee-hive, and as he beheld them, soft anticipations stole over his mind of dainty slapjacks, well buttered, and garnished with honey or treacle, by the delicate little dimpled hand of Katrina Van Tassel.

Thus feeding his mind with many sweet thoughts and "sugared suppositions," he journeyed along the sides of a range of hills which look out upon some of the goodliest scenes of the mighty Hudson. The sun gradually wheeled his broad disk down into the west. The wide bosom of the Tappan Zee lay motionless and glassy, excepting that here and there a gentle undulation waved and prolonged the blue shadow of the distant mountain. A few amber clouds floated in the sky, without a breath of air to move them. The horizon was of a fine golden tint, changing gradually into a pure apple green, and from that into the deep blue of the mid-heaven. A slanting ray lingered on the woody crests of the precipices that overhung some parts of the river, giving greater depth to the dark-gray and purple of their rocky sides. A sloop was loitering in the distance, dropping slowly down with the tide, her sail hanging uselessly against the mast; and as the reflection of the sky gleamed along the still water, it seemed as if the vessel was suspended in the air.

It was toward evening that Ichabod arrived at the castle of the Heer Van Tassel, which he found thronged with the pride and flower of the adjacent country. Old farmers, a spare leathern-faced race, in homespun coats and breeches, blue stockings, huge shoes, and magnificent pewter buckles. Their brisk withered little dames, in close crimped caps, long-waisted shortgowns, homespun petticoats, with scissors and pincushions, and gay calico pockets hanging on the outside. Buxom lasses, almost as antiquated as their mothers, excepting where a straw hat, a fine riband, or perhaps a white frock, gave symptoms of city innovation. The sons, in short square-skirted coats with rows of stupendous brass buttons, and their hair generally queued in the fashion of the times, especially if they could procure an eel-skin for the purpose, it being esteemed, throughout the country, as a potent nourisher and strengthener of the hair.

Brom Bones, however, was the hero of the scene, having come to the gathering on his favorite steed Daredevil, a creature, like himself, full of metal and mischief, and which no one but himself could manage. He was, in fact, noted for preferring vicious animals, given to all kinds of tricks, which kept the rider in constant risk of his neck, for he held a tractable well-broken horse as unworthy of a lad of spirit.

Fain would I pause to dwell upon the world of charms that burst upon the enraptured gaze of my hero, as he entered the state parlor of Van Tassel's mansion. Not those of the bevy of buxom lasses, with their luxurious display of red and white; but the ample charms of a genuine Dutch country tea-table, in the sumptuous time of autumn. Such heaped-up platters of cakes of various and almost indescribable kinds, known only to experienced Dutch housewives! There was the doughty dough-nut, the tenderer oly koek, and the crisp and crumbling cruller; sweet cakes and short cakes, ginger cakes and honey cakes, and the whole family of cakes. And then there were apple pies and peach pies and pumpkin pies; besides slices of ham and smoked beef; and moreover delectable dishes of preserved plums, and peaches, and pears, and quinces; not to mention broiled shad and roasted chickens; together with bowls of milk and cream, all mingled higgledy-piggledy, pretty much as I have enumerated them, with the motherly tea-pot sending up its clouds of vapor from the midst—Heaven bless the mark! I want breath and time to discuss this banquet as it deserves, and am too eager to get on with my story. Happily, Ichabod Crane was not in so great a hurry as his historian, but did ample justice to every dainty.

He was a kind and thankful creature, whose heart dilated in proportion as his skin was filled with good cheer; and whose spirits rose with eating as some men's do with drink. He could not help, too, rolling his large eyes round him as he ate, and chuckling with the possibility that he might one day be lord of all this scene of almost unimaginable luxury and splendor. Then, he thought, how soon he'd turn his back upon the old school-house; snap his fingers in the face of Hans Van Ripper, and every other niggardly patron, and kick any itinerant pedagogue out of doors that should dare to call him comrade!

Old Baltus Van Tassel moved about among his guests with a face dilated with content and good humor, round and jolly as the harvest moon. His hospitable attentions were brief, but expressive, being confined to a shake of the hand, a slap on the shoulder, a loud laugh, and a pressing invitation to "fall to, and help themselves."

And now the sound of the music from the common room, or hall, summoned to the dance. The musician was an old gray-headed negro, who had been the itinerant orchestra of the neighborhood for more than half a century. His instrument was as old and battered as himself. The greater part of the time he scraped on two or three strings, accompanying every movement of the bow with a motion of the head; bowing almost to the ground, and stamping with his foot whenever a fresh couple were to start.

Ichabod prided himself upon his dancing as much as upon his vocal powers. Not a limb, not a fibre about him was idle; and to have seen his loosely hung frame in full motion, and clattering about the room, you would have thought Saint Vitus himself, that blessed patron of the dance, was figuring before you in person. He was the admiration of all the negroes; who, having gathered, of all ages and sizes, from the farm and the neighborhood, stood forming a pyramid of shining black faces at every door and window, gazing with delight at the scene, rolling their white eyeballs, and showing grinning rows of ivory from ear to ear. How could the flogger of urchins be otherwise than animated and joyous? the lady of his heart was his partner in the dance, and smiling graciously in reply to all his amorous oglings; while Brom Bones, sorely smitten with love and jealousy, sat brooding by himself in one corner.

When the dance was at an end, Ichabod was attracted to a knot of the sager folks, who, with old Van Tassel, sat smoking at one end of the piazza, gossiping over former times, and drawing out long stories about the war.

This neighborhood, at the time of which I am speaking, was one of those highly favored places which abound with chronicle and great men. The British and American line had run near it during the war; it had therefore been the scene of marauding and infested with refugees, cow-boys, and all kinds of border chivalry. Just sufficient time had elapsed to enable each story-teller to dress up his tale with a little becoming fiction, and, in the indistinctness of his recollection, to make himself the hero of every exploit.

There was the story of Doffue Martling, a large blue-bearded Dutchman, who had nearly taken a British frigate with an old iron nine-pounder from a mud breastwork, only that his gun burst at the sixth discharge. And there was an old gentleman who shall be nameless, being too rich a mynheer to be lightly mentioned, who, in the battle of Whiteplains, being an excellent master of defence, parried a musket ball with a small sword, insomuch that he absolutely felt it whiz round the blade, and glance off at the hilt: in proof of which, he was ready at any time to show the sword, with the hilt a little bent. There were several more that had been equally great in the field, not one of whom but was persuaded that he had a considerable hand in bringing the war to a happy termination.

But all these were nothing to the tales of ghosts and apparitions that succeeded. The neighborhood is rich in legendary treasures of the kind. Local tales and superstitions thrive best in these sheltered long-settled retreats; but are trampled under foot by the shifting throng that forms the population of most of our country places. Besides, there is no encouragement for ghosts in most of our villages, for they have scarcely had time to finish their first nap, and turn themselves in their graves, before their surviving friends have traveled away from the neighborhood; so that when they turn out at night to walk their rounds, they have no acquaintance left to call upon. This is perhaps the reason why we so seldom hear of ghosts except in our long-established Dutch communities.

The immediate causes however, of the prevalence of supernatural stories in these parts, was doubtless owing to the vicinity of Sleepy Hollow. There was a contagion in the very air that blew from that haunted region; it breathed forth an atmosphere of dreams and fancies infecting all the land. Several of the Sleepy Hollow people were present at Van Tassel's, and, as usual, were doling out their wild and wonderful legends. Many dismal tales were told about funeral trains, and mourning cries and wailings heard and seen about the great tree where the unfortunate Major André was taken, and which stood in the neighborhood. Some mention was made also of the woman in white, that haunted the dark glen at Raven Rock, and was often heard to shriek on winter nights before a storm, having perished there in the snow. The chief part of the stories, however, turned upon the favorite spectre of Sleepy Hollow, the headless horseman, who had been heard several times of late, patrolling the country; and, it was said, tethered his horse nightly among the graves in the church-yard.

The sequestered situation of this church seems always to have made it a favorite haunt of troubled spirits. It stands on a knoll, surrounded by locust-trees and lofty elms, from among which its decent whitewashed walls shine modestly forth, like

Christian purity, beaming through the shades of retirement. A gentle slope descends from it to a silver sheet of water, bordered by high trees, between which, peeps may be caught at the blue hills of the Hudson. To look upon its grass-grown yard, where the sunbeams seem to sleep so quietly, one would think that there at least the dead might rest in peace. On one side of the church extends a wide woody dell, along which raves a large brook among broken rocks and trunks of fallen trees. Over a deep black part of the stream, not far from the church, was formerly thrown a wooden bridge; the road that led to it, and the bridge itself, were thickly shaded by overhanging trees, which cast a gloom about it, even in the daytime; but occasioned a fearful darkness at night. Such was one of the favorite haunts of the headless horseman; and the place where he was most frequently encountered. The tale was told of old Brouwer, a most heretical disbeliever in ghosts, how he met the horseman returning from his foray into Sleepy Hollow, and was obliged to get up behind him; how they galloped over bush and brake, over hill and swamp, until they reached the bridge; when the horseman suddenly turned into a skeleton, threw old Brouwer into the brook, and sprang away over the tree-tops with a clap of thunder.

This story was immediately matched by a thrice marvelous adventure of Brom Bones, who made light of the galloping Hessian as an arrant jockey. He affirmed that, on returning one night from the neighboring village of Sing-Sing, he had been overtaken by this midnight trooper; that he had offered to race with him for a bowl of punch, and should have won it too, for Daredevil beat the goblin horse all hollow, but just as they came to the church bridge, the Hessian bolted, and vanished in a flash of fire.

All these tales, told in that drowsy undertone with which men talk in the dark, the countenances of the listeners only now and then receiving a casual gleam from the glare of a pipe, sank deep in the mind of Ichabod. He repaid them in kind with large extracts from his invaluable author, Cotton Mather, and added many marvelous events that had taken place in his native state of Connecticut, and fearful sights which he had seen in his nightly walks about Sleepy Hollow.

The revel now gradually broke up. The old farmers gathered together their families in their wagons, and were heard for some time rattling along the hollow roads, and over the distant hills. Some of the damsels mounted on pillions behind their favorite swains, and their light-hearted laughter, mingling with the clatter of hoofs, echoed along the silent woodlands, sounding fainter and fainter until they gradually died away—and the late scene of noise and frolic was all silent and deserted. Ichabod only lingered behind, according to the custom of country lovers, to have a tête-à-tête with the heiress, fully convinced that he was now on the high road to success. What passed at this interview I will not pretend to say, for in fact I do not know. Something, however, I fear me, must have gone wrong, for he certainly sallied forth, after no very great interval, with an air quite desolate and chop-fallen.—Oh these women! these women! Could that girl have been playing off any of her coquettish tricks?—Was her encouragement of the poor pedagogue all a mere sham to secure her conquest of his rival?—Heaven only knows, not I!—Let it suffice to say, Ichabod stole forth with the air of one who had been sacking a hen-roost, rather than a fair lady's heart. Without looking to the right or left to notice the scene of rural wealth, on which he had so often gloated, he went straight to the stable, and with several hearty cuffs and kicks, roused his steed most uncourteously from the comfortable quarters in which he was soundly sleeping, dreaming of mountains of corn and oats, and whole valleys of timothy and clover.

It was the very witching time of night that Ichabod, heavy-hearted and crestfallen, pursued his travel homewards, along the sides of the lofty hills which rise above Tarry Town, and which he had traversed so cheerily in the afternoon. The hour was as dismal as himself. Far below him, the Tappan Zee spread its dusky and indistinct waste of waters, with here and there the tall mast of a sloop, riding quietly at anchor under the land. In the dead hush of midnight, he could even hear the barking of the watchdog from the opposite shore of the Hudson; but it was so vague and faint as only to give an idea of his distance from this faithful companion of man. Now and then, too, the long-drawn crowing of a cock, accidentally awakened, would sound far, far off, from some farmhouse away among the hills—but it was like a dreaming sound in his ear. No signs of life occurred near him, but occasionally the melancholy chirp of a cricket, or perhaps the guttural twang of a bull-frog, from a neighboring marsh, as if sleeping uncomfortably, and turning suddenly in his bed.

All the stories of ghosts and goblins that he had heard in the afternoon, now came crowding upon his recollection. The night grew darker and darker; the stars seemed to sink deeper in the sky, and driving clouds occasionally had them from his sight. He had never felt so lonely and dismal. He was, moreover, approaching the very place where many of the scenes of the ghost stories had been laid. In the centre of the road stood an enormous tulip-tree, which towered like a giant above all the other trees of the neighborhood, and formed a kind of landmark. Its limbs were gnarled, and fantastic, large enough to form trunks for ordinary trees, twisting down almost to the earth, and rising again into the air. It was connected with the tragical story of the unfortunate André, who had been taken prisoner hard by; and was universally known by the name of Major André's tree. The common people regarded it with a mixture of respect and superstition, partly out of sympathy for the fate of its ill-starred namesake, and partly from the tales of strange sights, and doleful lamentations told concerning it.

As Ichabod approached this fearful tree, he began to whistle: he thought his whistle was answered—it was but a blast sweeping sharply through the dry branches. As he approached a little nearer, he thought he saw something white, hanging in the midst of the tree—he paused and ceased whistling; but on looking more narrowly, perceived that it was a place where the tree had been scathed by lightning, and the white wood laid bare. Suddenly he heard a groan—his teeth chattered and his knees smote against the saddle: it was but the rubbing of one huge bough upon another, as they were swayed about by the breeze. He passed the tree in safety, but new perils lay before him.

About two hundred yards from the tree a small brook crossed the road, and ran into a marshy and thickly-wooded glen, known by the name of Wiley's swamp. A few rough logs, laid side by side, served for a bridge over this stream. On that side of the road where the brook entered the wood, a group of oaks and chestnuts, matted thick with wild grape-vines, threw a cavernous gloom over it. To pass this bridge was the severest trial. It was at this identical spot that the unfortunate André was captured, and under the covert of those chestnuts and vines were the sturdy yeomen concealed who surprised him. This has ever since been considered a haunted stream, and fearful are the feelings of the schoolboy who has to pass it alone after dark.

As he approached the stream, his heart began to thump; he summoned up, however, all his resolution, gave his horse half a score of kicks in the ribs, and attempted to dash briskly across the bridge; but instead of starting forward, the perverse old animal made a lateral movement, and ran broadside against the fence. Ichabod, whose fears increased with the delay, jerked the reins on the other side, and kicked lustily with the contrary foot: it was all in vain; his steed started, it is true, but it was only to plunge to the opposite side of the road into a thicket of brambles and alder bushes. The schoolmaster now bestowed both whip and heel upon the starveling ribs of old Gunpowder, who dashed forward, snuffing and snorting, but came to a stand just by the bridge, with a suddenness that had nearly sent his rider sprawling over his head. Just at this moment a plashy tramp by the side of the bridge caught the sensitive ear of Ichabod. In the dark shadow of the grove, on the margin of the brook, he beheld something huge, misshapen, black and towering. It stirred not, but seemed gathered up in the gloom, like some gigantic monster ready to spring upon the traveler.

The hair of the affrighted pedagogue rose upon his head with terror. What was to be done? To turn and fly was now too late; and besides, what chance was there of escaping ghost or goblin, if such it was, which could ride upon the wings of the wind? Summoning up, therefore, a show of courage, he demanded in stammering accents—"Who are you?" He received no reply. He repeated his demand in a still more agitated voice. Still there was no answer. Once more he cudgelled the sides of the inflexible Gunpowder, and, shutting his eyes, broke forth with involuntary fervor into a psalm tune. Just then the shadowy object of alarm put itself in motion, and, with a scramble and a bound, stood at once in the middle of the road. Though the night was dark and dismal, yet the form of the unknown might now in some degree be ascertained. He appeared to be a horseman of large dimensions, and mounted on a black horse of powerful frame. He made no offer of molestation or sociability, but kept aloof on one side of the road, jogging along on the blind side of old Gunpowder, who had now got over his fright and waywardness.

Ichabod, who had no relish for this strange midnight companion, and bethought himself of the adventure of Brom Bones with the Galloping Hessian, now quickened his steed, in hopes of leaving him behind. The stranger, however, quickened his horse to an equal pace. Ichabod pulled up, and fell into a walk, thinking to lag behind—the other did the same. His heart began to sink within him; he endeavored to resume his psalm tune, but his parched tongue clove to the roof of his mouth, and he could not utter a stave. There was something in the moody and dogged silence of this pertinacious companion, that was mysterious and appalling. It was soon fearfully accounted for. On mounting a rising ground, which brought the figure of his fellow-traveller in relief against the sky, gigantic in height, and muffled in a cloak, Ichabod was horror-struck, on perceiving that he was headless!—but his horror was still more increased, on observing that the head, which should have rested on his shoulders, was carried before him on the pommel of the saddle: his terror rose to desperation; he rained a shower of kicks and blows upon Gunpowder, hoping by a sudden movement, to give his companion the slip—but the spectre started full jump with him. Away then they dashed, through thick and thin; stones flying, and sparks flashing, at every bound. Ichabod's flimsy garments fluttered in the air, as he stretched his long lank body away over his horse's head, in the eagerness of his flight.

They had now reached the road which turns off to Sleepy Hollow; but Gunpowder, who seemed possessed with a demon, instead of keeping up it, made an opposite turn, and plunged headlong down hill to the left. This road leads through a sandy hollow, shaded by trees for about a quarter of a mile, where it crosses the bridge famous in goblin story, and just beyond swells the green knoll on which stands the whitewashed church.

As yet the panic of the steed had given his unskillful rider an apparent advantage in the chase; but just as he had got half way through the hollow, the girths of the saddle gave way, and he felt it slipping from under him. He seized it by the pommel, and endeavored to hold it firm, but in vain; and had just time to save himself by clasping old Gunpowder round the neck, when the saddle fell to the earth, and he heard it trampled under foot by his pursuer. For a moment the terror of Hans Van Ripper's wrath passed across his mind—for it was his Sunday saddle; but this was no time for petty fears; the goblin was hard on his haunches; and (unskilled rider that he was!) he had much ado to maintain his seat, sometimes slipping on one side, sometimes on another, and sometimes jolted on the high ridge of his horse's back bone, with a violence that he verily feared would cleave him asunder.

An opening in the trees now cheered him with the hopes that the church bridge was at hand. The wavering reflection of a silver star in the bosom of the brook told him that he was not mistaken. He saw the walls of the church dimly glaring under the trees beyond. He recollected the place where Brom Bones' ghostly competitor had disappeared. "If I can but reach that bridge," thought Ichabod, "I am safe." Just then he heard the black steed panting and blowing close behind him; he even fancied that he felt his hot breath. Another convulsive kick in the ribs, and old Gunpowder sprang upon the bridge; he thundered over the resounding planks; he gained the opposite side; and now Ichabod cast a look behind to see if his pursuer should vanish, according to rule, in a flash of fire and brimstone. Just then he saw the goblin rising in his stirrups, and in the very act of hurling his head at him. Ichabod endeavored to dodge the horrible missile, but too late. It encountered his cranium with a tremendous crash—he was tumbled headlong into the dust, and Gunpowder, the black steed, and the goblin rider, passed by like a whirlwind.

The next morning the old horse was found without his saddle, and with the bridle under his feet, soberly cropping the grass at his master's gate. Ichabod did not make his appearance at breakfast—dinner-hour came, but no Ichabod. The boys assembled at the school-house, and strolled idly about the banks of the brook; but no schoolmaster. Hans Van Ripper now began to feel some uneasiness about the fate of poor Ichabod, and his saddle. An inquiry was set on foot, and after diligent investigation they came upon his traces. In one part of the road leading to the church was found the saddle trampled in the dirt; the tracks of horses' hoofs deeply dented in the road, and evidently at furious speed, were traced to the bridge, beyond which, on the bank of a broad part of the brook, where the water ran deep and black, was found the hat of the unfortunate Ichabod, and close beside it a shattered pumpkin.

The brook was searched, but the body of the schoolmaster was not to be discovered. Hans Van Ripper, as executor of his estate, examined the bundle which contained all his worldly effects. They consisted of two shirts and a half; two stocks for the neck; a pair or two of worsted stockings; an old pair of corduroy small-clothes; a rusty razor; a book of psalm tunes, full of dog's ears; and a broken pitch-pipe. As to the books and furniture of the school-house, they belonged to the community, excepting Cotton Mather's History of Witchcraft, a New England Almanac, and a book of dreams and fortune-telling; in which last was a sheet of foolscap much scribbled and blotted in several fruitless attempts to make a copy of verses in honor of the heiress of Van Tassel. These magic books and the poetic scrawl were forthwith consigned to the flames by Hans Van Ripper; who from that time forward determined to send his children no more to school; observing that he never knew any good come of this same reading and writing. Whatever money the schoolmaster possessed, and he had received his quarter's pay but a day or two before, he must have had about his person at the time of his disappearance.

The mysterious event caused much speculation at the church on the following Sunday. Knots of gazers and gossips were collected in the church-yard, at the bridge, and at the spot where the hat and pumpkin had been found. The stories of Brouwer, of Bones, and a whole budget of others, were called to mind; and when they had diligently considered them all, and compared them with the symptoms of the present case, they shook their heads, and came to the conclusion that Ichabod had been carried off by the galloping Hessian. As he was a bachelor, and in nobody's debt, nobody troubled his head any more about him: the school was removed to a different quarter of the hollow, and another pedagogue reigned in his stead.

It is true, an old farmer, who had been down to New-York on a visit several years after, and from whom this account of the ghostly adventure was received, brought home the intelligence that Ichabod Crane was still alive; that he had left the neighborhood, partly through fear of the goblin and Hans Van Ripper, and partly in mortification at having been suddenly dismissed by the heiress; that he had changed his quarters to a distant part of the country; had kept school and studied law at the same time; had been admitted to the bar, turned politician, electioneered, written for the newspapers, and finally had been made a justice of the Ten Pound Court. Brom Bones too, who shortly after his rival's disappearance conducted the blooming Katrina in triumph to the altar, was observed to look exceedingly knowing whenever the story of Ichabod was related, and always burst into a hearty laugh at the mention of the pumpkin; which led some to suspect that he knew more about the matter than he chose to tell.

The old country wives, however, who are the best judges of these matters, maintain to this day that Ichabod was spirited away by supernatural means; and it is a favorite story often told about the neighborhood round the winter evening fire. The bridge became more than ever an object of superstitious awe, and that may be the reason why the road has been altered of late years, so as to approach the church by the border of the mill-pond. The school-house, being deserted, soon fell to decay, and was reported to be haunted by the ghost of the unfortunate pedagogue; and the plough-boy, loitering homeward of a still summer evening, has often fancied his voice at a distance, chanting a melancholy psalm tune among the tranquil solitudes of Sleepy Hollow.

POSTSCRIPT, FOUND IN THE HANDWRITING OF MR. KNICKERBOCKER

The preceding Tale is given, almost in the precise words in which I heard it related at a Corporation meeting of the ancient city of Manhattoes, at which were present many of its sagest and most illustrious burghers. The narrator was a pleasant, shabby, gentlemanly old fellow, in pepper-and-salt clothes, with a sadly humorous face; and one whom I strongly suspected of being poor;—he made such efforts to be entertaining. When his story was concluded, there was much laughter and approbation, particularly from two or three deputy aldermen, who had been asleep the greater part of the time. There was, however, one tall, dry-looking old gentleman, with beetling eyebrows, who maintained a grave and rather severe face throughout: now and then folding his arms, inclining his head, and looking down upon the floor, as if turning a doubt over in his mind. He was one of your wary men, who never laugh, but upon good grounds—when they have reason and the law on their side. When the mirth of the rest of the company had subsided, and silence was restored, he leaned one arm on the elbow of his chair, and, sticking the other a-kimbo, demanded, with a slight but exceedingly sage motion of the head, and contraction of the brow, what was the moral of the story and what it went to prove?

The story-teller, who was just putting a glass of wine to his lips, as a refreshment after his toils, paused for a moment, looked at his inquirer with an air of infinite deference, and, lowering the glass slowly to the table, observed, that the story was intended most logically to prove:—

"That there is no situation in life but has its advantages and pleasures—provided we will but take a joke as we find it:

"That, therefore, he that runs races with goblin troopers is likely to have rough riding of it.

"Ergo, for a country schoolmaster to be refused the hand of a Dutch heiress, is a certain step to high preferment in the state."

The cautious old gentleman knit his brows tenfold closer after this explanation, being sorely puzzled by the ratiocination of the syllogism; while, methought, the one in pepper-and-salt eyed him with something of a triumphant leer. At length, he observed, that all this was very well, but still he thought the story a little on the extravagant—there were one or two points on which he had his doubts.

"Faith, sir," replied the story-teller, "as to that matter, I don't believe one-half of it myself."

D. K.

L'Envoy[1]

Go, little booke, God send thee good passage,
And specially let this be thy prayere,
Unto them all that thee will read or hear,
Where thou art wrong, after their help to call,
Thee to correct in any part or all.
CHAUCER'S *BELLE DAME SANS MERCIE*

IN CONCLUDING A SECOND VOLUME OF THE SKETCH BOOK, THE AUTHOR cannot but express his deep sense of the indulgence with which his first has been received, and of the liberal disposition that has been evinced to treat him with kindness as a stranger. Even the critics, whatever may be said of them by others, he has found to be a singularly gentle and good-natured race; it is true that each has in turn objected to some one or two articles, and that these individual exceptions, taken in the aggregate, would amount almost to a total condemnation of his work; but then he has been consoled by observing, that what one has particularly censured, another has as particularly praised; and thus, the encomiums being set off against the objections, he finds his work, upon the whole, commended far beyond its deserts.

He is aware that he runs a risk of forfeiting much of this kind favor by not following the counsel that has been liberally bestowed upon him; for where abundance of valuable advice is given gratis, it may seem a man's own fault if he should go astray. He only can say, in his vindication, that he faithfully determined, for a time, to govern himself in his second volume by the opinions passed upon his first; but he was soon brought to a stand by the contrariety of excellent counsel. One kindly advised him to avoid the ludicrous; another to shun the pathetic; a third assured him that he was tolerable at description, but cautioned him to leave narrative alone; while a fourth declared that he had a very pretty

1. Closing the second volume of the London edition.

knack at turning a story, and was really entertaining when in a pensive mood, but was grievously mistaken if he imagined himself to possess a spirit of humor.

Thus perplexed by the advice of his friends, who each in turn closed some particular path, but left him all the world beside to range in, he found that to follow all their counsels would, in fact, be to stand still. He remained for a time sadly embarrassed; when, all at once, the thought struck him to ramble on as he had begun; that his work being miscellaneous and written for different humors, it could not be expected that any one would be pleased with the whole; but that if it should contain something to suit each reader, his end would be completely answered. Few guests sit down to a varied table with an equal appetite for every dish. One has an elegant horror of a roasted pig; another holds a curry or a devil in utter abomination; a third cannot tolerate the ancient flavor of venison and wild-fowl; and a fourth, of truly masculine stomach, looks with sovereign contempt on those knick-knacks, here and there dished up for the ladies. Thus each article is in condemned in its turn; and yet, amidst this variety of appetites seldom does a dish go away from the table without being tasted and relished by some one or other of the guests.

With these considerations he ventures to serve up this second volume in the same heterogeneous way with his first; simply requesting the reader, if he should find here and there something to please him, to rest assured that it was written expressly for intelligent readers like himself; but entreating him, should he find anything to dislike, to tolerate it, as one of those articles which the author has been obliged to write for readers of a less refined taste.

To be serious.—The author is conscious of the numerous faults and imperfections of his work; and well aware how little he is disciplined and accomplished in the arts of authorship. His deficiencies are also increased by a diffidence arising from his peculiar situation. He finds himself writing in a strange land, and appearing before a public which he has been accustomed from childhood, to regard with the highest feelings of awe and reverence. He is full of solicitude to deserve their approbation, yet finds that very solicitude continually embarrassing his powers, and depriving him of that ease and confidence which are necessary to successful exertion. Still, the kindness with which he is treated encourages him to go on, hoping that in time he may acquire a steadier footing; and thus he proceeds, half venturing, half shrinking, surprised at his own good-fortune, and wondering at his own temerity.

TALES OF A TRAVELLER

To the Reader

WORTHY AND DEAR READER!—HAST THOU EVER BEEN WAYLAID IN the midst of a pleasant tour by some treacherous malady: thy heels tripped up, and thou left to count the tedious minutes as they passed, in the solitude of an inn chamber? If thou hast, thou wilt be able to pity me. Behold me, interrupted in the course of my journeying up the fair banks of the Rhine, and laid up by indisposition in this old frontier town of Mentz. I have worn out every source of amusement. I know the sound of every clock that strikes, and bell that rings, in the place. I know to a second when to listen for the first tap of the Prussian drum, as it summons the garrison to parade, or at what hour to expect the distant sound of the Austrian military band. All these have grown wearisome to me; and even the well-known step of my doctor, as he slowly paces the corridor, with healing in the creak of his shoes, no longer affords an agreeable interruption to the monotony of my apartment.

For a time I attempted to beguile the weary hours, by studying German under the tuition of mine host's pretty little daughter, Katrine; but I soon found even German had not power to charm a languid ear, and that the conjugating of *ich liebe* might be powerless, however rosy the lips which uttered it.

I tried to read, but my mind would not fix itself. I turned over volume after volume, but threw them by with distaste; "Well, then," said I at length, in despair, "if I cannot read a book, I will write one." Never was there a more lucky idea; it at once gave me occupation and amusement. The writing of a book was considered in old times as an enterprise of toil and difficulty, insomuch that the most trifling lucubration was denominated a "work," and the world talked with awe and reverence of "the labors of the learned." These matters are better understood now-a-days.

Thanks to the improvements in all kind of manufactures, the art of book-making has been made familiar to the meanest capacity. Every body is an author. The scribbling of a quarto is the mere pastime of the idle; the young gentleman throws off his brace of duodecimos in the intervals of the sporting season, and the young lady produces her set of volumes with the same facility that her great-grandmother worked a set of chair-bottoms.

The idea having struck me, therefore, to write a book, the reader will easily perceive that the execution of it was no difficult matter. I rummaged my portfolio, and cast about, in my recollection, for those floating materials which a man naturally collects in travelling; and here I have arranged them in this little work.

As I know this to be a story-telling and a story-reading age, and that the world is fond of being taught by apologue, I have digested the instruction I would convey into a number of tales. They may not possess the power of amusement, which the tales told by many of my contemporaries possess; but then I value myself on the sound moral which each of them contains. This may not be apparent at first, but the reader will be sure to find it out in the end. I am for curing the world by gentle alternatives, not by violent doses; indeed, the patient should never be conscious that he is taking a dose. I have learnt this much from my experience under the hands of the worthy Hippocrates of Mentz.

I am not, therefore, for those barefaced tales which carry their moral on the surface, staring one in the face; they are enough to deter the squeamish reader. On the contrary, I have often hid my moral from sight, and disguised it as much as possible by sweets and spices, so that while the simple reader is listening with open mouth to a ghost or a love story, he may have a bolus of sound morality popped down his throat, and be never the wiser for the fraud.

As the public is apt to be curious about the sources whence an author draws his stories, doubtless that it may know how far to put faith in them, I would observe, that the Adventure of the German Student, or rather the latter part of it, is founded on an anecdote related to me as existing somewhere in French; and, indeed, I have been told, since writing it, that an ingenious tale has been founded on it by an English writer; but I have never met with either the former or the latter in print. Some of the circumstances in the Adventure of the Mysterious Picture, and in the Story of the Young Italian, are vague recollections of anecdotes related to me some years since; but from what source derived, I do not know. The Adventure of the Young Painter among the banditti is taken almost entirely from an authentic narrative in manuscript.

As to the other tales contained in this work, and indeed to my tales generally, I can make but one observation; I am an old traveller; I have read somewhat, heard and seen more, and dreamt more than all. My brain is filled, therefore, with all kinds of odds and ends. In travelling, these heterogeneous matters have become shaken up in my mind, as the articles are apt to be in an ill-packed travelling trunk; so that when I attempt to draw forth a fact, I cannot determine whether I have read, heard, or dreamt it; and I am always at a loss to know how much to believe of my own stories.

These matters being premised, fall to, worthy reader, with good appetite; and, above all, with good humor, to what is here set before thee. If the tales I have furnished should prove to be bad, they will at least be found short; so that no one will be wearied long on the same theme. "Variety is charming," as some poet observes.

There is a certain relief in change, even though it be from bad to worse! As I have often found in travelling in a stage-coach, that it is often a comfort to shift one's position, and be bruised in a new place.

Ever thine,

GEOFFREY CRAYON

Dated from the HOTEL DE DARMSTADT,
ci-devant HOTEL DE PARIS,
MENTZ, *otherwise called* MAYENCE

PART I

Strange Stories by a Nervous Gentleman

I'll tell you more, there was a fish taken,
A monstrous fish, with a sword by's side, a long sword,
A pike in's neck, and a gun in's nose, a huge gun,
And letters of mart in 's mouth from the Duke of Florence.

Cleanthes.—This is a monstrous lie.

Tony.— I do confess it.

Do you think I'd tell you truths?

FLETCHER'S *WIFE FOR A MONTH*

The Great Unknown

THE FOLLOWING ADVENTURES WERE RELATED TO ME BY THE SAME nervous gentleman who told me the romantic tale of the Stout Gentleman, published in *Bracebridge Hall*. It is very singular, that although I expressly stated that story to have been told to me, and described the very person who told it, still it has been received as an adventure that happened to myself. Now I protest I never met with any adventure of the kind. I should not have grieved at this, had it not been intimated by the author of Waverley, in an introduction to his novel of Peveril of the Peak, that he was himself the stout gentleman alluded to. I have ever since been importuned by questions and letters from gentlemen, and particularly from ladies without number, touching what I had seen of the Great Unknown.

Now all this is extremely tantalizing. It is like being congratulated on the high prize when one has drawn a blank; for I have just as great a desire as any one of the public to penetrate the mystery of that very singular personage, whose voice fills every corner of the world, without any one being able to tell whence it comes.

My friend, the nervous gentleman, also, who is a man of very shy, retired habits, complains that he has been excessively annoyed in consequence of its getting about in his neighborhood that he is the fortunate personage. Insomuch, that he has become a character of considerable notoriety in two or three country towns, and has been repeatedly teased to exhibit himself at blue-stocking parties, for no other reason than that of being "the gentleman who has had a glimpse of the author of Waverley."

Indeed the poor man has grown ten times as nervous as ever, since he has discovered, on such good authority, who the stout gentleman was; and will never forgive himself for not having made a more resolute effort to get a full sight of him. He has anxiously endeavored to call up a recollection of what he saw of that portly personage; and has ever since kept a curious eye on all gentlemen of more than ordinary dimensions, whom he has seen getting into stage-coaches. All in vain! The features he had caught a glimpse of seem common to the whole race of stout gentlemen, and the Great Unknown remains as great an unknown as ever.

* * *

Having premised these circumstances, I will now let the nervous gentleman proceed with his stories.

The Hunting Dinner

I WAS ONCE AT A HUNTING DINNER, GIVEN BY A WORTHY FOX-HUNTING OLD Baronet, who kept bachelor's hall in jovial style, in an ancient rook-haunted family mansion, in one of the middle counties. He had been a devoted admirer of the fair sex in his younger days; but, having travelled much, studied the sex in various countries with distinguished success, and returned home profoundly instructed, as he supposed, in the ways of woman, and a perfect master of the art of pleasing, had the mortification of being jilted by a little boarding-school girl, who was scarcely versed in the accidence of love.

The Baronet was completely overcome by such an incredible defeat; retired from the world in disgust; put himself under the government of his housekeeper; and took to fox-hunting like a perfect Nimrod. Whatever poets may say to the contrary, a man will grow out of love as he grows old; and a pack of fox-hounds may chase out of his heart even the memory of a boarding-school goddess. The Baronet was, when I saw him, as merry and mellow an old bachelor as ever followed a hound; and the love he had once felt for one woman had spread itself over the whole sex; so that there was not a pretty face in the whole country round but came in for a share.

The dinner was prolonged till a late hour; for our host having no ladies in his household to summon us to the drawing-room, the bottle maintained its true bachelor sway, unrivalled by its potent enemy the tea-kettle. The old hall in which we dined echoed to bursts of robustious fox-hunting merriment, that made the ancient antlers shake on the walls. By degrees, however, the wine and the wassail of mine host began to operate upon bodies already a little jaded by the chase. The choice spirits which flashed up at the beginning of the dinner, sparkled for a time, then gradually went out one after another, or only emitted now and then a faint gleam from the socket. Some of the briskest talkers, who had given tongue so bravely at the first burst, fell fast asleep; and none kept on their way but certain of those long-winded prosers, who, like short-legged hounds, worry on unnoticed at the bottom of conversation, but are sure to be in at the death. Even these at length subsided into silence; and scarcely any thing was heard but the nasal communications of two or three veteran masticators, who having been silent while awake, were indemnifying the company in their sleep.

At length the announcement of tea and coffee in the cedar-parlor roused all hands from this temporary torpor. Every one awoke marvellously renovated, and while sipping the refreshing beverage out of the Baronet's old-fashioned hereditary china, began to think of departing for their several homes. But here a sudden difficulty arose. While we had been prolonging our repast, a heavy winter storm had set in, with snow, rain, and sleet, driven by such bitter blasts of wind, that they threatened to penetrate to the very bone.

"It's all in vain," said our hospitable host, "to think of putting one's head out of doors in such weather. So, gentlemen, I hold you my guests for this night at least, and will have your quarters prepared accordingly."

The unruly weather, which became more and more tempestuous, rendered the hospitable suggestion unanswerable. The only question was, whether such an unexpected accession of company to an already crowded house would not put the housekeeper to her trumps to accommodate them.

"Pshaw," cried mine host, "did you ever know a bachelor's hall that was not elastic, and able to accommodate twice as many as it could hold?" So, out of a good-humored pique, the house-keeper was summoned to a consultation before us all. The old lady appeared in her gala suit of faded brocade, which rustled with flurry and agitation; for, in spite of our host's bravado, she was a little perplexed. But in a bachelor's house, and with bachelor guests, these matters are readily managed. There is no lady of the house to stand upon squeamish points about lodging gentlemen in odd holes and corners, and exposing the shabby parts of the establishment. A bachelor's housekeeper is used to shifts and emergencies; so, after much worrying to and fro, and divers consultations about the red-room, and the blue-room, and the chintz-room, and the damask-room, and the little room with the bow-window, the matter was finally arranged.

When all this was done, we were once more summoned to the standing rural amusement of eating. The time that had been consumed in dozing after dinner, and in the refreshment and consultation of the cedar-parlor, was sufficient, in the opinion of the rosy-faced butler, to engender a reasonable appetite for supper. A slight repast had, therefore, been tricked up from the residue of dinner, consisting of a cold sirloin of beef, hashed venison, a devilled leg of a turkey or so, and a few other of those light articles taken by country gentlemen to insure sound sleep and heavy snoring.

The nap after dinner had brightened up every one's wit; and a great deal of excellent humor was expended upon the perplexities of mine host and his housekeeper, by certain married gentlemen of the company, who considered themselves privileged in joking with a bachelor's establishment. From this the banter turned as to what quarters each would find, on being thus suddenly billeted in so antiquated a mansion.

"By my soul," said an Irish captain of dragoons, one of the most merry and boisterous of the party, "by my soul but I should not be surprised if some of those good-looking gentlefolks that hang along the walls should walk about the rooms of this stormy night; or if I should find the ghost of one of those long-waisted ladies turning into my bed in mistake for her grave in the church-yard."

"Do you believe in ghosts, then?" said a thin hatchet-faced gentleman, with projecting eyes like a lobster.

I had remarked this last personage during dinner time for one of those incessant questioners, who have a craving, unhealthy appetite in conversation. He never seemed satisfied with the whole of a story; never laughed when others laughed; but always put the joke to the question. He never could enjoy the kernel of the nut, but pestered himself to get more out of the shell. "Do you believe in ghosts, then?" said the inquisitive gentleman.

"Faith, but I do," replied the jovial Irishman. "I was brought up in the fear and belief of them. We had a Benshee in our own family, honey."

"A Benshee, and what's that?" cried the questioner.

"Why, an old lady ghost that tends upon your real Milesian families, and waits at their window to let them know when some of them are to die."

"A mighty pleasant piece of information!" cried an elderly gentleman with a knowing look, and with a flexible nose, to which he could give a whimsical twist when he wished to be waggish.

"By my soul, but I'd have you to know it's a piece of distinction to be waited on by a Benshee. It's a proof that one has pure blood in one's veins. But i'faith, now we are talking of ghosts, there never was a house or a night better fitted than the present for a ghost adventure. Pray, Sir John, haven't you such a thing as a haunted chamber to put a guest in?"

"Perhaps," said the Baronet, smiling, "I might accommodate you even on that point."

"Oh, I should like it of all things, my jewel. Some dark oaken room, with ugly, wobegone portraits, that stare dismally at one; and about which the housekeeper has a power of delightful stories of love and murder. And then a dim lamp, a table with a rusty sword across it, and a spectre all in white, to draw aside one's curtains at midnight—"

"In truth," said an old gentleman at one end of the table, "you put me in mind of an anecdote—"

"Oh, a ghost story! a ghost story!" was vociferated round the board, every one edging his chair a little nearer.

The attention of the whole company was now turned upon the speaker. He was an old gentleman, one side of whose face was no match for the other. The eyelid drooped and hung down like an unhinged window-shutter. Indeed, the whole side of his head was dilapidated, and seemed like the wing of a house shut up and haunted. I'll warrant that side was well stuffed with ghost stories.

There was a universal demand for the tale.

"Nay," said the old gentleman, "it's a mere anecdote, and a very common-place one; but such as it is you shall have it. It is a story that I once heard my uncle tell as having happened to himself. He was a man very apt to meet with strange adventures. I have heard him tell of others much more singular."

"What kind of a man was your uncle?" said the questioning gentleman.

"Why, he was rather a dry, shrewd kind of body; a great traveller, and fond of telling his adventures."

"Pray, how old might he have been when that happened."

"When what happened?" cried the gentleman with the flexible nose, impatiently. "Egad, you have not given any thing a chance to happen. Come, never mind our uncle's age; let us have his adventures."

The inquisitive gentleman being for the moment silenced, the old gentleman with the haunted head proceeded.

The Adventure of My Uncle

Many years since, some time before the French Revolution, my uncle passed several months at Paris. The English and French were on better terms in those days than at present, and mingled cordially in society. The English went abroad to spend money then, and the French were always ready to help them: they go abroad to save money at present, and that they can do without French assistance. Perhaps the travelling English were fewer and choicer than at present, when the whole nation has broke loose and inundated the continent. At any rate, they circulated more readily and currently in foreign society, and my uncle, during his residence in Paris, made many very intimate acquaintances among the French noblesse.

Some time afterwards, he was making a journey in the winter time in that part of Normandy called the Pays de Caux, when, as evening was closing in, he perceived the turrets of an ancient chateau rising out of the trees of its walled park; each turret with its high conical roof of gray slate, like a candle with an extinguisher on it.

"To whom does that chateau belong, friend?" cried my uncle to a meagre but fiery postilion, who, with tremendous jack-boots and cocked hat, was floundering on before him.

"To Monseigneur the Marquis de ——," said the postilion, touching his hat, partly out of respect to my uncle, and partly out of reverence to the noble name pronounced.

My uncle recollected the Marquis for a particular friend in Paris, who had often expressed a wish to see him at his paternal chateau. My uncle was an old traveller, one who knew well how to turn things to account. He revolved for a few moments in his mind how agreeable it would be to his friend the Marquis to be surprised in this sociable way by a pop visit; and how much more agreeable to himself to get into snug quarters in a chateau, and have a relish of the Marquis's well-known kitchen, and a smack of his superior Champagne and Burgundy, rather than put up with the miserable lodgment and miserable fare of a provincial inn. In a few minutes, therefore, the meagre postilion was cracking his whip like a very devil, or like a true Frenchman, up the long straight avenue that led to the chateau.

You have no doubt all seen French chateaus, as every body travels in France now-a-days. This was one of the oldest; standing naked and alone in the midst of a desert of gravel walks and cold stone terraces; with a cold-looking formal garden, cut into angles and rhomboids; and a cold leafless park, divided geometrically by straight alleys; and two or three cold-looking noseless statues; and fountains spouting cold water enough to make one's teeth chatter. At least such was the feeling they imparted on the wintry day of my uncle's visit; though, in hot summer weather, I'll warrant there was glare enough to scorch one's eyes out.

The smacking of the postilion's whip, which grew more and more intense the nearer they approached, frightened a flight of pigeons out of a dove-cot, and rooks out of the roofs, and finally a crew of servants out of the chateau, with the Marquis at their head. He was enchanted to see my uncle, for his chateau, like the house of our worthy host, had not many more guests at the time than it could accommodate. So he kissed my uncle on each cheek, after the French fashion, and ushered him into the castle.

The Marquis did the honors of the house with the urbanity of his country. In fact, he was proud of his old family chateau, for part of it was extremely old. There was a tower and chapel which had been built almost before the memory of man; but the rest was more modern, the castle having been nearly demolished during the wars of the league. The Marquis dwelt upon this event with great satisfaction, and seemed really to entertain a grateful feeling towards Henry the Fourth, for having thought his paternal mansion worth battering down. He had many stories to tell of the prowess of his ancestors; and several skull-caps, helmets, and cross-bows, and divers huge boots, and buff jerkins, to show, which had been worn by the leaguers. Above all, there was a two-handled sword, which he could hardly wield, but which he displayed, as a proof that there had been giants in his family.

In truth, he was but a small descendant from such great warriors. When you looked at their bluff visages and brawny limbs, as depicted in their portraits, and then at the little Marquis, with his spindle shanks, and his sallow lantern visage, flanked with a pair of powdered ear-locks, or *aîles de pigeon*, that seemed ready to fly away with it, you could hardly believe him to be of the same race. But when you looked at the eyes that sparkled out like a beetle's from each side of his hooked nose, you saw at once that he inherited all the fiery spirit of his forefathers. In fact, a Frenchman's spirit never exhales, however his body may dwindle. It rather rarefies, and grows more inflammable, as the earthy particles diminish; and I have seen valor enough in a little fiery-hearted French dwarf to have furnished out a tolerable giant.

When once the Marquis, as was his wont, put on one of the old helmets stuck up in his hall, though his head no more filled it than a dry pea its peascod, yet his eyes flashed from the bottom of the iron cavern with the brilliancy of carbuncles; and when he poised the ponderous two-handled sword of his ancestors, you would have thought you saw the doughty little David wielding the sword of Goliath, which was unto him like a weaver's beam.

However, gentlemen, I am dwelling too long on this description of the Marquis and his chateau, but you must excuse me; he was an old friend of my uncle; and whenever my uncle told the story, he was always fond of talking a great deal about his host—Poor little Marquis! He was one of that handful of gallant courtiers who made such a devoted but hopeless stand in the cause of their sovereign, in the chateau of the Tuileries, against the irruption of the mob on the sad tenth of August. He displayed the valor of a preux French chevalier to the last; flourishing feebly his little court sword with a *ça-ça*! in face of a whole legion of *sans culottes*; but was pinned to the wall like a butterfly, by the pike of a poissarde, and his heroic soul was borne up to heaven on his *aîles de pigeon*.

But all this has nothing to do with my story. To the point then. When the hour arrived for retiring for the night, my uncle was shown to his room in a venerable old tower. It was the oldest part of the chateau, and had in ancient times been the donjon or strong-hold; of course the chamber was none of the best. The Marquis had put him there, however, because he knew him to be a traveller of taste, and fond of antiquities; and also because the better apartments were already occupied. Indeed, he perfectly reconciled my uncle to his quarters by mentioning the great personages who had once inhabited them, all of whom were, in some way or other, connected with the family. If you would take his word for it, John Baliol, or as he called him, Jean de Bailleul, had died of chagrin in this very chamber, on hearing of the success of his rival, Robert the Bruce, at the battle of Bannockburn. And when he added that the Duke de Guise had slept in it, my uncle was fain to felicitate himself on being honored with such distinguished quarters.

The night was shrewd and windy, and the chamber none of the warmest. An old long-faced, long-bodied servant, in quaint livery, who attended upon my uncle, threw down an armful of wood beside the fireplace, gave a queer look about the room, and then wished him *bon repos* with a grimace and a shrug that would have been suspicious from any other than an old French servant.

The chamber had indeed a wild crazy look, enough to strike any one who had read romances with apprehension and foreboding. The windows were high and narrow, and had once been loop-holes, but had been rudely enlarged, as well as the extreme thickness of the walls would permit; and the ill-fitted casements rattled to every breeze. You would have thought, on a windy night, some of the old leaguers were tramping and clanking about the apartment in their huge boots and rattling spurs. A door which stood ajar, and, like a true French door, would stand ajar in spite of every reason and effort to the contrary, opened upon a long dark corridor, that led the Lord knows whither, and seemed just made for ghosts to air themselves in, when they turned out of their graves at midnight. The wind would spring up into a hoarse murmur through this passage, and creak the door to and fro, as if some dubious ghost were balancing in its mind whether to come in or not. In a word, it was precisely the kind of comfortless apartment that a ghost, if ghost there were in the chateau, would single out for its favorite lounge.

My uncle, however, though a man accustomed to meet with strange adventures, apprehended none at the time. He made several attempts to shut the door, but in vain. Not that he apprehended any thing, for he was too old a traveller to be daunted by a wild-looking apartment; but the night, as I have said, was cold and gusty, and the wind howled about the old turret pretty much as it does round this old mansion at this moment; and the breeze from the long dark corridor came in as damp and chilly as if from a dungeon. My uncle, therefore, since he could not close the door, threw a quantity of wood on the fire, which soon sent up a flame in the great wide-mouthed chimney that illumined the whole chamber; and made the shadow of the tongs on the opposite wall look like a long-legged giant. My uncle now clambered on the top of the half score of mattresses which form a French bed, and which stood in a deep recess; then tucking himself snugly in, and burying himself up to the chin in the bed-clothes, he lay looking at the fire, and listening to the wind, and thinking how knowingly he had come over his friend the Marquis for a night's lodging—and so he fell asleep.

He had not taken above half of his first nap when he was awakened by the clock of the chateau, in the turret over his chamber, which struck midnight. It was just such an old clock as ghosts are fond of. It had a deep, dismal tone, and struck so slowly and tediously that my uncle thought it would never have done. He counted and counted till he was confident he counted thirteen, and then it stopped.

The fire had burnt low, and the blaze of the last fagot was almost expiring, burning in small blue flames, which now and then lengthened up into little white gleams. My uncle lay with his eyes half closed, and his nightcap drawn almost down to his nose. His fancy was already wandering, and began to mingle up the present scene with the crater of Vesuvius, the French Opera, the Coliseum at Rome, Dolly's chop-house in London, and all the farrago of noted places with which the brain of a traveller is crammed:—in a word, he was just falling asleep.

Suddenly he was roused by the sound of footsteps, slowly pacing along the corridor. My uncle, as I have often heard him say himself, was a man not easily frightened. So he lay quiet, supposing this some other guest, or some servant on his way to bed. The footsteps, however, approached the door; the door gently opened; whether of its own accord, or whether pushed open, my uncle could not distinguish: a figure all in white glided in. It was a female, tall and stately, and of a commanding air. Her dress was of an ancient fashion, ample in volume, and sweeping the floor. She walked up to the fireplace, without regarding my uncle, who raised his nightcap with one hand, and stared earnestly at her. She remained for some time standing by the fire, which, flashing up at intervals, cast blue and white gleams of light, that enabled my uncle to remark her appearance minutely.

Her face was ghastly pale, and perhaps rendered still more so by the bluish light of the fire. It possessed beauty, but its beauty was saddened by care and anxiety. There was the look of one accustomed to trouble, but of one whom trouble could not cast down nor subdue; for there was still the predominating air of proud unconquerable resolution. Such at least was the opinion formed by my uncle, and he considered himself a great physiognomist.

The figure remained, as I said, for some time by the fire, putting out first one hand, then the other; then each foot alternately, as if warming itself; for your ghosts, if ghost it really was, are apt to be cold. My uncle, furthermore, remarked that it wore high-heeled shoes, after an ancient fashion, with paste or diamond buckles, that sparkled as though they were alive. At length the figure turned gently round, casting a glassy look about the apartment, which, as it passed over my uncle, made his blood run cold, and chilled the very marrow in his bones. It then stretched its arms towards heaven, clasped its hands, and wringing them in a supplicating manner, glided slowly out of the room.

My uncle lay for some time meditating on this visitation, for (as he remarked when he told me the story) though a man of firmness, he was also a man of reflection, and did not reject a thing because it was out of the regular course of events. However, being, as I have before said, a great traveller, and accustomed to strange adventures, he drew his nightcap resolutely over his eyes, turned his back to the door, hoisted the bed-clothes high over his shoulders, and gradually fell asleep.

How long he slept he could not say, when he was awakened by the voice of some one at his bed-side. He turned round, and beheld the old French servant, with his ear-locks in tight buckles on each side of a long lantern face, on which habit had deeply wrinkled an everlasting smile. He made a thousand grimaces, and asked a thousand pardons for disturbing Monsieur, but the morning was considerably advanced. While my uncle was dressing, he called vaguely to mind the visitor of the preceding night. He asked the ancient domestic what lady was in the habit of rambling about this part of the chateau at night. The old valet shrugged his shoulders as high as his head, laid one hand on his bosom, threw open the other with every finger extended, made a most whimsical grimace which he meant to be complimentary, and replied, that it was not for him to know any thing of *les bonnes fortunes* of Monsieur.

My uncle saw there was nothing satisfactory to be learnt in this quarter.—After breakfast, he was walking with the Marquis through the modern apartments of the chateau, sliding over the well-waxed floors of silken saloons, amidst furniture rich in gilding and brocade, until they came to a long picture-gallery, containing many portraits, some in oil and some in chalks.

Here was an ample field for the eloquence of his host, who had all the pride of a nobleman of the *ancien régime*. There was not a grand name in Normandy, and hardly one in France, which was not, in some way or other, connected with his house. My uncle stood listening with inward impatience, resting sometimes on one leg, sometimes on the other, as the little Marquis descanted, with his usual fire and vivacity, on the achievements of his ancestors, whose portraits hung along the wall; from the martial deeds of the stern warriors in steel, to the gallantries and intrigues of the blue-eyed gentlemen, with fair smiling faces, powdered ear-locks, laced ruffles, and pink and blue silk coats and breeches;—not forgetting the conquests of the lovely shepherdesses, with hooped petticoats and waists no thicker than an hour-glass, who appeared ruling over their sheep and their swains, with dainty crooks decorated with fluttering ribands.

In the midst of his friend's discourse, my uncle was startled on beholding a full-length portrait, the very counterpart of his visitor of the preceding night.

"Methinks," said he, pointing to it, "I have seen the original of this portrait."

"Pardonnez moi," replied the Marquis politely, "that can hardly be, as the lady has been dead more than a hundred years. That was the beautiful Duchess de Longueville, who figured during the minority of Louis the Fourteenth."

"And was there any thing remarkable in her history?"

Never was question more unlucky. The little Marquis immediately threw himself into the attitude of a man about to tell a long story. In fact, my uncle had pulled upon himself the whole history of the civil war of the Fronde, in which the beautiful Duchess had played so distinguished a part. Turenne, Coligni, Mazarine, were called up from their graves to grace his narration; nor were the affairs of the Barricadoes, nor the chivalry of the Port Cocheres forgotten. My uncle began to wish himself a thousand leagues off from the Marquis and his merciless memory, when suddenly the little man's recollections took a more interesting turn. He was relating the imprisonment of the Duke de Longueville with the Princes Condé and Conti in the chateau of Vincennes, and the ineffectual efforts of the Duchess to rouse the sturdy Normans to their rescue. He had come to that part where she was invested by the royal forces in the Castle of Dieppe.

"The spirit of the Duchess," proceeded the Marquis, "rose from her trials. It was astonishing to see so delicate and beautiful a being buffet so resolutely with hardships. She determined on a desperate means of escape. You may have seen the chateau in which she was mewed up; an old ragged wart of an edifice, standing on the knuckle of a hill, just above the rusty little town of Dieppe. One dark unruly night she issued secretly out of a small postern gate of the castle, which the enemy had neglected to guard. The postern gate is there to this very day; opening upon a narrow bridge over a deep fosse between the castle and the brow of the hill. She was followed by her female attendants, a few domestics, and some gallant cavaliers, who still remained faithful to her fortunes. Her object was to gain a small port about two leagues distant, where she had privately provided a vessel for her escape in case of emergency.

"The little band of fugitives were obliged to perform the distance on foot. When they arrived at the port the wind was high and stormy, the tide contrary, the vessel anchored far off in the road, and no means of getting on board but by a fishing shallop which lay tossing like a cockle-shell on the edge of the surf. The Duchess determined to risk the attempt. The seamen endeavored to dissuade her, but the imminence of her danger on shore, and the magnanimity of her spirit, urged her on. She had to be borne to the shallop in the arms of a mariner. Such was the violence of the winds and waves that he faltered, lost his foothold, and let his precious burden fall into the sea.

"The Duchess was nearly drowned, but partly through her own struggles, partly by the exertions of the seamen, she got to land. As soon as she had a little recovered strength, she insisted on renewing the attempt. The storm, however, had by this time become so violent as to set all efforts at defiance. To delay, was to be discovered and taken prisoner. As the only resource left, she procured horses, mounted with her female attendants, *en croupe*, behind the gallant gentlemen who accompanied her, and scoured the country to seek some temporary asylum.

"While the Duchess," continued the Marquis, laying his forefinger on my uncle's breast to arouse his flagging attention,—"while the Duchess, poor lady, was wandering amid the tempest in this disconsolate manner, she arrived at this chateau. Her approach caused some uneasiness; for the clattering of a troop of horse at dead of night up the avenue of a lonely chateau, in those unsettled times, and in a troubled part of the country, was enough to occasion alarm.

"A tall, broad-shouldered chasseur, armed to the teeth, galloped ahead, and announced the name of the visitor. All uneasiness was dispelled. The household turned out with flambeaux to receive her, and never did torches gleam on a more weather-beaten, travel-stained band than came tramping into the court. Such pale, care-worn faces, such bedraggled dresses, as the poor Duchess and her females presented, each seated behind her cavalier: while the half-drenched, half-drowsy pages and attendants seemed ready to fall from their horses with sleep and fatigue.

"The Duchess was received with a hearty welcome by my ancestor. She was ushered into the hall of the chateau, and the fires soon crackled and blazed, to cheer herself and her train; and every spit and stew-pan was put in requisition to prepare ample refreshment for the wayfarers.

"She had a right to our hospitalities," continued the Marquis, drawing himself up with a slight degree of stateliness, "for she was related to our family. I'll tell you how it was. Her father, Henry de Bourbon, Prince of Condé—"

"But, did the Duchess pass the night in the chateau?" said my uncle rather abruptly, terrified at the idea of getting involved in one of the Marquis's genealogical discussions.

"Oh, as to the Duchess, she was put into the very apartment you occupied last night, which at that time was a kind of state apartment. Her followers were quartered in the chambers opening upon the neighboring corridor, and her favorite page slept in an adjoining closet. Up and down the corridor walked the great chasseur who had announced her arrival, and who acted as a kind of sentinel or guard. He was a dark, stern, powerful-looking fellow; and as the light of a lamp in the corridor fell upon his deeply-marked face and sinewy form, he seemed capable of defending the castle with his single arm.

"It was a rough, rude night; about this time of the year—apropos!—now I think of it, last night was the anniversary of her visit. I may well remember the precise date, for it was a night not to be forgotten by our house. There is a singular tradition concerning it in our family." Here the Marquis hesitated, and a cloud seemed to gather about his bushy eyebrows. "There is a tradition—that a strange occurrence took place that night—A strange, mysterious, inexplicable occurrence—" Here he checked himself, and paused.

"Did it relate to that lady?" inquired my uncle eagerly.

"It was past the hour of midnight," resumed the Marquis,—"when the whole chateau— "Here he paused again. My uncle made a movement of anxious curiosity.

"Excuse me," said the Marquis, a slight blush streaking his sallow visage. "There are some circumstances connected with our family history which I do not like to relate. That was a rude period. A time of great crimes among great men: for you know high blood, when it runs wrong, will not run tamely, like blood of the *canaille*—poor lady!—But I have a little family pride, that—excuse me—we will change the subject, if you please—"

My uncle's curiosity was piqued. The pompous and magnificent introduction had led him to expect something wonderful in the story to which it served as a kind of avenue. He had no idea of being cheated out of it by a sudden fit of unreasonable squeamishness. Besides, being a traveller in quest of information, he considered it his duty to inquire into every thing.

The Marquis, however, evaded every question.—"Well," said my uncle, a little petulantly, "whatever you may think of it, I saw that lady last night."

The Marquis stepped back and gazed at him with surprise.

"She paid me a visit in my bed-chamber."

The Marquis pulled out his snuff-box with a shrug and a smile; taking this no doubt for an awkward piece of English pleasantry, which politeness required him to be charmed with.

My uncle went on gravely, however, and related the whole circumstance. The Marquis heard him through with profound attention, holding his snuff-box unopened in his hand. When the story was finished, he tapped on the lid of his box deliberately, took a long, sonorous pinch of snuff—

"Bah!" said the Marquis, and walked towards the other end of the gallery.—

Here the narrator paused. The company waited for some time for him to resume his narration; but he continued silent.

"Well," said the inquisitive gentleman—"and what did your uncle say then?"

"Nothing," replied the other.

"And what did the Marquis say farther?"

"Nothing."

"And is that all?"

"That is all," said the narrator, filling a glass of wine.

"I surmise," said the shrewd old gentleman with the waggish nose,—"I surmise the ghost must have been the old housekeeper walking her rounds to see that all was right."

"Bah!" said the narrator. "My uncle was too much accustomed to strange sights not to know a ghost from a housekeeper."

There was a murmur round the table half of merriment, half of disappointment. I was inclined to think the old gentleman had really an afterpart of his story in reserve; but he sipped his wine and said nothing more; and there was an odd expression about his dilapidated countenance which left me in doubt whether he were in drollery or earnest.

"Egad," said the knowing gentleman, with the flexible nose, "this story of your uncle puts me in mind of one that used to be told of an aunt of mine, by the mother's side; though I don't know that it will bear a comparison, as the good lady was not so prone to meet with strange adventures. But any rate you shall have it."

The Adventure of My Aunt

MY AUNT WAS A LADY OF LARGE FRAME, STRONG MIND, AND GREAT resolution: she was what might be termed a very manly woman. My uncle was a thin, puny little man, very meek and acquiescent, and no match for my aunt. It was observed that he dwindled and dwindled gradually away, from the day of his marriage. His wife's powerful mind was too much for him; it wore him out. My aunt, however, took all possible care of him; had half the doctors in town to prescribe for him; made him take all their prescriptions, and dosed him with physic enough to cure a whole hospital. All was in vain. My uncle grew worse and worse the more dosing and nursing he underwent, until in the end he added another to the long list of matrimonial victims who have been killed with kindness.

"And was it his ghost that appeared to her?" asked the inquisitive gentleman, who had questioned the former story-teller.

"You shall hear," replied the narrator. My aunt took on mightily for the death of her poor dear husband. Perhaps she felt some compunction at having given him so much physic, and nursed him into the grave. At any rate, she did all that a widow could do to honor his memory. She spared no expense in either the quantity or quality of her mourning weeds; wore a miniature of him about her neck as large as a little sun-dial, and had a full-length portrait of him always hanging in her bed-chamber. All the world extolled her conduct to the skies; and it was determined that a woman who behaved so well to the memory of one husband deserved soon to get another.

It was not long after this that she went to take up her residence in an old country-seat in Derbyshire, which had long been in the care of merely a steward and housekeeper. She took most of her servants with her, intending to make it her principal abode. The house stood in a lonely, wild part of the country, among the gray Derbyshire hills, with a murderer hanging in chains on a bleak height in full view.

The servants from town were half frightened out of their wits at the idea of living in such a dismal, pagan-looking place; especially when they got together in the servants' hall in the evening, and compared notes on all the hobgoblin stories picked up in the course of the day. They were afraid to venture alone about the gloomy, black-looking chambers. My lady's maid, who was troubled with nerves, declared she could never sleep alone in such a "gashly rummaging old building;" and the footman, who was a kind-hearted young fellow, did all in his power to cheer her up.

My aunt was struck with the lonely appearance of the house. Before going to bed, therefore, she examined well the fastnesses of the doors and windows; locked up the plate with her own hands, and carried the keys, together with a little box of money and jewels, to her own room; for she was a notable woman, and always saw to all things herself. Having put the keys under her pillow, and dismissed her maid, she sat by her toilet arranging her hair; for being, in spite of her grief for my uncle, rather a buxom widow, she was somewhat particular about her person. She sat for a little while looking at her face in the glass, first on one side, then on the other, as ladies are apt to do when they would ascertain whether they have been in good looks; for a roistering country squire of the neighborhood, with whom she had flirted when a girl, had called that day to welcome her to the country.

All of a sudden she thought she heard something move behind her. She looked hastily round, but there was nothing to be seen. Nothing but the grimly painted portrait of her poor dear man, hanging against the wall.

She gave a heavy sigh to his memory, as she was accustomed to do whenever she spoke of him in company, and then went on adjusting her night-dress, and thinking of the squire. Her sigh was re-echoed, or answered by a long-drawn breath. She looked round again, but no one was to be seen. She ascribed these sounds to the wind oozing through the rat-holes of the old mansion, and proceeded leisurely to put her hair in papers, when, all at once, she thought she perceived one of the eyes of the portrait move.

"The back of her head being towards it!" said the story-teller with the ruined head,—"good!"

"Yes, sir!" replied dryly the narrator, "her back being towards the portrait, but her eyes fixed on its reflection in the glass." Well, as I was saying, she perceived one of the eyes of the portrait move. So strange a circumstance, as you may well suppose, gave her a sudden shock. To assure herself of the fact, she put one hand to her forehead as if rubbing it; peeped through her fingers, and moved the candle with the other hand. The light of the taper gleamed on the eye, and was reflected from it. She was sure it moved. Nay more, it seemed to give her a wink, as she had sometimes known her husband to do when living! It struck a momentary chill to her heart; for she was a lone woman, and felt herself fearfully situated.

The chill was but transient. My aunt, who was almost as resolute a personage as your uncle, sir, (turning to the old story-teller,) became instantly calm and collected. She went on adjusting her dress. She even hummed an air, and did not make a single false note. She casually overturned a dressing-box; took a candle and picked up the articles one by one from the floor; pursued a rolling pincushion that was making the best of its way under the bed; then opened the door; looked for an instant into the corridor, as if in doubt whether to go; and then walked quietly out.

She hastened down stairs, ordered the servants to arm themselves with the weapons first at hand, placed herself at their head, and returned almost immediately.

Her hastily-levied army presented a formidable force. The steward had a rusty blunderbuss, the coachman a loaded whip, the footman a pair of horse-pistols, the cook a huge chopping-knife, and the butler a bottle in each hand. My aunt led the van with a red-hot poker, and in my opinion, she was the most formidable of the party. The waiting-maid, who dreaded to stay alone in the servants' hall, brought up the rear, smelling to a broken bottle of volatile salts, and expressing her terror of the ghostesses. "Ghosts!" said my aunt, resolutely. "I'll singe their whiskers for them!"

They entered the chamber. All was still and undisturbed as when she had left it. They approached the portrait of my uncle.

"Pull down that picture!" cried my aunt. A heavy groan, and a sound like the chattering of teeth, issued from the portrait. The servants shrunk back; the maid uttered a faint shriek, and clung to the footman for support.

"Instantly!" added my aunt, with a stamp of the foot.

The picture was pulled down, and from a recess behind it, in which had formerly stood a clock, they hauled forth a round-shouldered, black-bearded varlet, with a knife as long as my arm, but trembling all over like an aspen-leaf.

"Well, and who was he? No ghost, I suppose," said the inquisitive gentleman.

"A Knight of the Post," replied the narrator, "who had been smitten with the worth of the wealthy widow; or rather a marauding Tarquin, who had stolen into her chamber to violate her purse, and rifle her strong-box, when all the house should be asleep. In plain terms," continued he, "the vagabond was a loose idle fellow of the neighborhood, who had once been a servant in the house, and had been employed to assist in arranging it for the reception of its mistress. He confessed that he had contrived this hiding-place for his nefarious purposes, and had borrowed an eye from the portrait by way of a reconnoitering hole."

"And what did they do with him?—did they hang him?" resumed the questioner.

"Hang him!—how could they?" exclaimed a beetle-browed barrister, with a hawk's nose. "The offence was not capital. No robbery, no assault had been committed. No forcible entry or breaking into the premises—"

"My aunt," said the narrator, "was a woman of spirit, and apt to take the law in her own hands. She had her own notions of cleanliness also. She ordered the fellow to be drawn through the horse-pond, to cleanse away all offences, and then to be well rubbed down with an oaken towel."

"And what became of him afterwards?" said the inquisitive gentleman.

"I do not exactly know. I believe he was sent on a voyage of improvement to Botany Bay."

"And your aunt," said the inquisitive gentleman; "I'll warrant she took care to make her maid sleep in the room with her after that."

"No, sir, she did better; she gave her hand shortly after to the roistering squire; for she used to observe, that it was a dismal thing for a woman to sleep alone in the country."

"She was right," observed the inquisitive gentleman, nodding sagaciously; "but I am sorry they did not hang that fellow."

It was agreed on all hands that the last narrator had brought his tale to the most satisfactory conclusion, though a country clergyman present, regretted that the uncle and aunt, who figured in the different stories, had not been married together; they certainly would have been well matched.

"But I don't see, after all," said the inquisitive gentleman, "that there was any ghost in this last story."

"Oh! If it's ghosts you want, honey," cried the Irish Captain of Dragoons,—"if it's ghosts you want, you shall have a whole regiment of them. And since these gentlemen have given the adventures of their uncles and aunts, faith, and I'll even give you a chapter out of my own family history."

The Bold Dragoon:

or The Adventure of My Grandfather

My grandfather was a bold dragoon, for it's a profession, d'ye see, that has run in the family. All my forefathers have been dragoons, and died on the field of honor, except myself, and I hope my posterity may be able to say the same; however, I don't mean to be vainglorious. Well, my grandfather, as I said, was a bold dragoon, and had served in the Low Countries. In fact, he was one of that very army, which, according to my uncle Toby, swore so terribly in Flanders. He could swear a good stick himself; and moreover was the very man that introduced the doctrine Corporal Trim mentions of radical heat and radical moisture; or, in other words, the mode of keeping out the damps of ditch-water by burnt brandy. Be that as it may, it's nothing to the purport of my story. I only tell it to show you that my grandfather was a man not easily to be humbugged. He had seen service, or, according to his own phrase, he had seen the devil—and that's saying every thing.

Well, gentlemen, my grandfather was on his way to England, for which he intended to embark from Ostend—bad luck to the place! for one where I was kept by storms and head-winds for three long days, and the devil of a jolly companion or pretty face to comfort me. Well, as I was saying, my grandfather was on his way to England, or rather to Ostend—no matter which, it's all the same. So one evening, towards nightfall, he rode jollily into Bruges.—Very like you all know Bruges, gentlemen; a queer old-fashioned Flemish town, once, they say, a great place for trade and money-making in old times, when the Mynheers were in their glory; but almost as large and as empty as an Irishman's pocket at the present day.—Well, gentlemen, it was at the time of the annual fair. All Bruges was crowded; and the canals swarmed with Dutch boats, and the streets swarmed with Dutch merchants; and there was hardly any getting along for goods, wares, and merchandises, and peasants in big breeches, and women in half a score of petticoats.

My grandfather rode jollily along, in his easy slashing way, for he was a saucy, sunshiny fellow—staring about him at the motley crowd, and the old houses with gable ends to the street, and storks' nests in the chimneys; winking at the yafrows who showed their faces at the windows, and joking the women right and left in the street; all of whom laughed, and took it in amazing good part; for though he did not know a word of the language, yet he had always a knack of making himself understood among the women.

Well, gentlemen, it being the time of the annual fair, all the town was crowded, every inn and tavern full, and my grandfather applied in vain from one to the other for admittance. At length he rode up to an old rickety inn that looked ready to fall to pieces, and which all the rats would have run away from, if they could have found room in any other house to put their heads. It was just such a queer building as you see in Dutch pictures, with a tall roof that reached up into the clouds, and as many garrets, one over the other, as the seven heavens of Mahomet. Nothing had saved it from tumbling down but a stork's nest on the chimney, which always brings good luck to a house in the Low Countries; and at the very time of my grandfather's arrival, there were two of these long-legged birds of grace standing like ghosts on the chimney-top. Faith, but they've kept the house on its legs to this very day, for you may see it any time you pass through Bruges, as it stands there yet, only it is turned into a brewery of strong Flemish beer,—at least it was so when I came that way after the battle of Waterloo.

My grandfather eyed the house curiously as he approached. It might not have altogether struck his fancy, had he not seen in large letters over the door,

HEER VERKOOPT MAN GOEDEN DRANK.

My grandfather had learnt enough of the language to know that the sign promised good liquor. "This is the house for me," said he, stopping short before the door.

The sudden appearance of a dashing dragoon was an event in an old inn, frequented only by the peaceful sons of traffic. A rich burgher of Antwerp, a stately ample man in a broad Flemish hat, and who was the great man and great patron of the establishment, sat smoking a clean long pipe on one side of the door; a fat little distiller of Geneva, from Schiedam, sat smoking on the other; and the bottle-nosed host stood in the door, and the comely hostess, in crimped cap, beside him; and the hostess's daughter, a plump Flanders lass, with long gold pendants in her ears, was at a side window.

"Humph!" said the rich burgher of Antwerp, with a sulky glance at the stranger.

"De duyvel!" said the fat little distiller of Schiedam.

The landlord saw, with the quick glance of a publican, that the new guest was not at all to the taste of the old ones; and, to tell the truth, he did not like my grandfather's saucy eye. He shook his head. "Not a garret in the house but was full."

"Not a garret!" echoed the landlady.

"Not a garret!" echoed the daughter.

The burgher of Antwerp, and the little distiller of Schiedam, continued to smoke their pipes sullenly, eyeing the enemy askance from under their broad hats, but said nothing.

My grandfather was not a man to be browbeaten. He threw the reins on his horse's neck, cocked his head on one side, stuck one arm akimbo,—"Faith and troth!" said he, "but I'll sleep in this house this very night."—As he said this he gave a slap on his thigh, by way of emphasis—the slap went to the landlady's heart.

He followed up the vow by jumping off his horse, and making his way past the staring Mynheers into the public room.—May be you've been in the bar-room of an old Flemish inn—faith, but a handsome chamber it was as you'd wish to see; with a brick floor, and a great fireplace, with the whole Bible history in glazed tiles; and then the mantel-piece, pitching itself head foremost out of the wall, with a whole regiment of cracked teapots and earthen jugs paraded on it; not to mention half a dozen great Delft platters, hung about the room by way of pictures; and the little bar in one corner, and the bouncing bar-maid inside of it, with a red calico cap and yellow ear-drops.

My grandfather snapped his fingers over his head, as he cast an eye round the room—"Faith, this is the very house I've been looking after," said he.

There was some further show of resistance on the part of the garrison; but my grandfather was an old soldier, and an Irishman to boot, and not easily repulsed, especially after he had got into the fortress. So he blarneyed the landlord, kissed the landlord's wife, tickled the landlord's daughter, chucked the bar-maid under the chin; and it was agreed on all hands that it would be a thousand pities, and a burning shame into the bargain, to turn such a bold dragoon into the streets. So they laid their heads together, that is to say, my grandfather and the landlady, and it was at length agreed to accommodate him with an old chamber that had been for some time shut up.

"Some say it's haunted," whispered the landlord's daughter; "but you are a bold dragoon, and I dare say don't fear ghosts."

"The devil a bit!" said my grandfather, pinching her plump cheek. "But if I should be troubled by ghosts, I've been to the Red Sea in my time, and have a pleasant way of laying them, my darling."

And then he whispered something to the girl which made her laugh, and give him a good-humored box on the ear. In short, there was nobody knew better how to make his way among the petticoats than my grandfather.

In a little while, as was his usual way, he took complete possession of the house, swaggering all over it; into the stable to look after his horse, into the kitchen to look after his supper. He had something to say or do with every one; smoked with the Dutchmen, drank with the Germans, slapped the landlord on the shoulder, romped with his daughter and the bar-maid:—never, since the days of Alley Croaker, had such a rattling blade been seen. The landlord stared at him with astonishment; the landlord's daughter hung her head and giggled whenever he came near; and as he swaggered along the corridor, with his sword trailing by his side, the maids looked after him, and whispered to one another, "What a proper man!"

At supper, my grandfather took command of the table-d'hôte as though he had been at home; helped every body, not forgetting himself; talked with every one, whether he understood their language or not; and made his way into the intimacy of the rich burgher of Antwerp, who had never been known to be sociable with any one during his life. In fact, he revolutionized the whole establishment, and gave it such a rouse that the very house reeled with it. He outsat every one at table excepting the little fat distiller of Schiedam, who sat soaking a long time before he broke forth; but when he did, he was a very devil incarnate. He took a violent affection for my grandfather; so they sat drinking and smoking, and telling stories, and singing Dutch and Irish songs, without understanding a word each other said, until the little Hollander was fairly swamped with his own gin and water, and carried off to bed, whooping and hickuping, and trolling the burden of a Low Dutch love-song.

Well, gentlemen, my grandfather was shown to his quarters up a large staircase, composed of loads of hewn timber; and through long rigmarole passages, hung with blackened paintings of fish, and fruit, and game, and country frolics, and huge kitchens, and portly burgomasters, such as you see about old-fashioned Flemish inns, till at length he arrived at his room.

An old-times chamber it was, sure enough, and crowded with all kinds of trumpery. It looked like an infirmary for decayed and superannuated furniture, where every thing diseased or disabled was sent to nurse or to be forgotten. Or rather it might be taken for a general congress of old legitimate movables, where every kind and country had a representative. No two chairs were alike. Such high backs and low backs, and leather bottoms, and worsted bottoms, and straw bottoms, and no bottoms; and cracked marble tables with curiously carved legs, holding balls in their claws, as though they were going to play at nine-pins.

My grandfather made a bow to the motley assemblage as he entered, and, having undressed himself, placed his light in the fireplace, asking pardon of the tongs, which seemed to be making love to the shovel in the chimney-corner, and whispering soft nonsense in its ear.

The rest of the guests were by this time sound asleep, for your Mynheers are huge sleepers. The housemaids, one by one, crept up yawning to their attics; and not a female head in the inn was laid on a pillow that night without dreaming of the bold dragoon.

My grandfather, for his part, got into bed, and drew over him one of those great bags of down, under which they smother a man in the Low Countries; and there he lay, melting between two feather beds, like an anchovy sandwich between two slices of toast and butter. He was a warm complexioned man, and this smothering played the very deuce with him. So, sure enough, in a little time it seemed as if a legion of imps were twitching at him, and all the blood in his veins was in a fever heat.

He lay still, however, until all the house was quiet, excepting the snoring of the Mynheers from the different chambers; who answered one another in all kinds of tones and cadences, like so many bull-frogs in a swamp. The quieter the house became, the more unquiet became my grandfather. He waxed warmer and warmer, until at length the bed became too hot to hold him.

"May be the maid had warmed it too much?" said the curious gentleman, inquiringly.

"I rather think the contrary," replied the Irishman. "But, be that as it may, it grew too hot for my grandfather."

"Faith, there's no standing this any longer," says he. So he jumped out of bed and went strolling about the house.

"What for?" said the inquisitive gentleman.

"Why to cool himself, to be sure—or perhaps to find a more comfortable bed—or perhaps—But no matter what he went for—he never mentioned—and there 's no use in taking up our time in conjecturing."

Well, my grandfather had been for some time absent from his room, and was returning, perfectly cool, when just as he reached the door he heard a strange noise within. He paused and listened. It seemed as if some one were trying to hum a tune in defiance of the asthma. He recollected the report of the room being haunted; but he was no believer in ghosts, so he pushed the door gently open and peeped in.

Egad, gentlemen, there was a gambol carrying on within enough to have astonished St. Anthony himself. By the light of the fire he saw a pale weazen-faced fellow, in a long flannel gown and a tall white night-cap with a tassel to it, who sat by the fire with a bellows under his arm by way of bagpipe, from which he forced the asthmatical music that had bothered my grandfather. As he played, too, he kept twitching about with a thousand queer contortions, nodding his head, and bobbing about his tasselled night-cap.

My grandfather thought this very odd and mighty presumptuous, and was about to demand what business he had to play his wind instrument in another gentleman's quarters, when a new cause of astonishment met his eye. From the opposite side of the room a long-backed, bandy-legged chair covered with leather, and studded all over in a coxcombical fashion with little brass nails, got suddenly into motion, thrust out first a claw-foot, then a crooked arm, and at length, making a leg, sidled gracefully up to an easy chair of tarnished brocade, with a hole in its bottom, and led it gallantly out in a ghostly minuet about the floor.

The musician now played fiercer and fiercer, and bobbed his head and his night-cap about like mad. By degrees the dancing mania seemed to seize upon all the other pieces of furniture. The antique, long-bodied chairs paired off in couples and led down a country dance; a three-legged stool danced a hornpipe, though horribly puzzled by its supernumerary limb; while the amorous tongs seized the shovel round the waist, and whirled it about the room in a German waltz. In short all the movables got in motion: pirouetting hands across, right and left, like so many devils; all except a great clothes-press, which kept courtesying and courtesying in a corner, like a dowager, in exquisite time to the music; being rather too corpulent to dance, or, perhaps at a loss for a partner.

My grandfather concluded the latter to be the reason; so being, like a true Irishman, devoted to the sex, and at all times ready for a frolic, he bounced into the room, called to the musician to strike up Paddy O'Rafferty, capered up to the clothes-press, and seized upon the two handles to lead her out:—when—whirr! the whole revel was at an end. The chairs, tables, tongs and shovel, slunk in an instant as quietly into their places as if nothing had happened, and the musician vanished up the chimney, leaving the bellows behind him in his hurry. My grandfather found himself seated in the middle of the floor with the clothes-press sprawling before him, and the two handles jerked off, and in his hands.

"Then, after all, this was a mere dream!" said the inquisitive gentleman.

"The divil a bit of a dream!" replied the Irishman. "There never was a truer fact in this world. Faith, I should have liked to see any man tell my grandfather it was a dream."

Well, gentlemen, as the clothes-press was a mighty heavy body, and my grandfather likewise, particularly in rear, you may easily suppose that two such heavy bodies coming to the ground would make a bit of a noise. Faith, the old mansion shook as though it had mistaken it for an earthquake. The whole garrison was alarmed. The landlord, who slept below, hurried up with a candle to inquire the cause, but with all his haste his daughter had arrived at the scene of uproar before him. The landlord was followed by the landlady, who was followed by the bouncing bar-maid, who was followed by the simpering chamber-maids, all holding together, as well as they could, such garments as they had first laid hands on; but all in a terrible hurry to see what the deuce was to pay in the chamber of the bold dragoon.

My grandfather related the marvellous scene he had witnessed, and the broken handles of the prostrate clothes-press bore testimony to the fact. There was no contesting such evidence; particularly with a lad of my grandfather's complexion, who seemed able to make good every word either with sword or shillelah. So the landlord scratched his head and looked silly, as he was apt to do when puzzled. The landlady scratched—no, she did not scratch her head, but she knit her brow, and did not seem half pleased with the explanation. But the landlady's daughter corroborated it by recollecting that the last person who had dwelt in that chamber was a famous juggler who had died of St. Vitus's dance, and had no doubt infected all the furniture.

This set all things to rights, particularly when the chamber-maids declared that they had all witnessed strange carryings on in that room; and as they declared this upon their honors," there could not remain a doubt upon the subject.

"And did your grandfather go to bed again in that room?" said the inquisitive gentleman.

"That's more than I can tell. Where he passed the rest of the night was a secret he never disclosed. In fact, though he had seen much service, he was but indifferently acquainted with geography, and apt to make blunders in his travels about inns at night, which it would have puzzled him sadly to account for in the morning."

"Was he ever apt to walk in his sleep?" said the knowing old gentleman.

"Never that I heard of."

There was a little pause after this rigmarole Irish romance, when the old gentleman with the haunted head observed, that the stories hitherto related had rather a burlesque tendency. "I recollect an adventure, however," added he, "which I heard of during a residence at Paris, for the truth of which I can undertake to vouch, and which is of a very grave and singular nature."

The Adventure of the German Student

On a stormy night, in the tempestuous times of the French revolution, a young German was returning to his lodgings, at a late hour, across the old part of Paris. The lightning gleamed, and the loud daps of thunder rattled through the lofty narrow streets—but I should first tell you something about this young German.

Gottfried Wolfgang was a young man of good family. He had studied for some time at Gottingen, but being of a visionary and enthusiastic character, he had wandered into those wild and speculative doctrines which have so often bewildered German students. His secluded life, his intense application, and the singular nature of his studies, had an effect on both mind and body. His health was impaired; his imagination diseased. He had been indulging in fanciful speculations on spiritual essences, until, like Swedenborg, he had an ideal world of his own around him. He took up a notion, I do not know from what cause, that there was an evil influence hanging over him; an evil genius or spirit seeking to ensnare him and ensure his perdition. Such an idea working on his melancholy temperament, produced the most gloomy effects. He became haggard and desponding. His friends discovered the mental malady preying upon him, and determined that the best cure was a change of scene; he was sent, therefore, to finish his studies amidst the splendors and gayeties of Paris.

Wolfgang arrived at Paris at the breaking out of the revolution. The popular delirium at first caught his enthusiastic mind, and he was captivated by the political and philosophical theories of the day: but the scenes of blood which followed shocked his sensitive nature; disgusted him with society and the world, and made him more than ever a recluse. He shut himself up in a solitary apartment in the Pays Latin, the quarter of students. There, in a gloomy street not far from the monastic walls of the

Sorbonne, he pursued his favorite speculations. Sometimes he spent hours together in the great libraries of Paris, those catacombs of departed authors, rummaging among their hoards of dusty and obsolete works in quest of food for his unhealthy appetite. He was, in a manner, a literary ghoul, feeding in the charnel-house of decayed literature.

Wolfgang, though solitary and recluse, was of an ardent temperament, but for a time it operated merely upon his imagination. He was too shy and ignorant of the world to make any advances to the fair, but he was a passionate admirer of female beauty, and in his lonely chamber would often lose himself in reveries on forms and faces which he had seen, and his fancy would deck out images of loveliness far surpassing the reality.

While his mind was in this excited and sublimated state, a dream produced an extraordinary effect upon him. It was of a female face of transcendent beauty. So strong was the impression made, that he dreamt of it again and again. It haunted his thoughts by day, his slumbers by night; in fine, he became passionately enamoured of this shadow of a dream. This lasted so long that it became one of those fixed ideas which haunt the minds of melancholy men, and are at times mistaken for madness.

Such was Gottfried Wolfgang, and such his situation at the time I mentioned. He was returning home late one stormy night, through some of the old and gloomy streets of the *Marais*, the ancient part of Paris. The loud claps of thunder rattled among the high houses of the narrow streets. He came to the Place de Grève, the square where public executions are performed. The lightning quivered about the pinnacles of the ancient Hôtel de Ville, and shed flickering gleams over the open space in front. As Wolfgang was crossing the square, he shrank back with horror at finding himself close by the guillotine. It was the height of the reign of terror, when this dreadful instrument of death stood ever ready, and its scaffold was continually running with the blood of the virtuous and the brave. It had that very day been actively employed in the work of carnage, and there it stood in grim array, amidst a silent and sleeping city, waiting for fresh victims.

Wolfgang's heart sickened within him, and he was turning shuddering from the horrible engine, when he beheld a shadowy form, cowering as it were at the foot of the steps which led up to the scaffold. A succession of vivid flashes of lightning revealed it more distinctly. It was a female figure, dressed in black. She was seated on one of the lower steps of the scaffold, leaning forward, her face hid in her lap; and her long dishevelled tresses hanging to the ground, streaming with the rain which fell in torrents. Wolfgang paused. There was something awful in this solitary monument of wo. The female had the appearance of being above the common order. He knew the times to be full of vicissitude, and that many a fair head, which had once been pillowed on down, now wandered houseless. Perhaps this was some poor mourner whom the dreadful axe had rendered desolate, and who sat here heart-broken on the strand of existence, from which all that was dear to her had been launched into eternity.

He approached, and addressed her in the accents of sympathy. She raised her head and gazed wildly at him. What was his astonishment at beholding, by the bright glare of the lightning, the very face which had haunted him in his dreams. It was pale and disconsolate, but ravishingly beautiful.

Trembling with violent and conflicting emotions, Wolfgang again accosted her. He spoke something of her being exposed at such an hour of the night, and to the fury of such a storm, and offered to conduct her to her friends. She pointed to the guillotine with a gesture of dreadful signification.

"I have no friend on earth!" said she.

"But you have a home," said Wolfgang.

"Yes—in the grave!"

The heart of the student melted at the words.

"If a stranger dare make an offer," said he, "without danger of being misunderstood, I would offer my humble dwelling as a shelter; myself as a devoted friend. I am friendless myself in Paris, and a stranger in the land; but if my life could be of service, it is at your disposal, and should be sacrificed before harm or indignity should come to you."

There was an honest earnestness in the young man's manner that had its effect. His foreign accent, too, was in his favor; it showed him not to be a hackneyed inhabitant of Paris. Indeed, there is an eloquence in true enthusiasm that is not to be doubted. The homeless stranger confided herself implicitly to the protection of the student.

He supported her faltering steps across the Pont Neuf, and by the place where the statue of Henry the Fourth had been overthrown by the populace. The storm had abated, and the thunder rumbled at a distance. All Paris was quiet; that great volcano of human passion slumbered for a while, to gather fresh strength for the next day's eruption. The student conducted his charge through the ancient streets of the Pays Latin, and by the dusky walls of the Sorbonne, to the great dingy hotel which he inhabited. The old portress who admitted them stared with surprise at the unusual sight of the melancholy Wolfgang with a female companion.

On entering his apartment, the student, for the first time, blushed at the scantiness and indifference of his dwelling. He had but one chamber—an old-fashioned saloon—heavily carved, and fantastically furnished with the remains of former magnificence, for it was one of those hotels in the quarter of the Luxembourg palace which had once belonged to nobility. It was lumbered with books and papers, and all the usual apparatus of a student, and his bed stood in a recess at one end.

When lights were brought, and Wolfgang had a better opportunity of contemplating the stranger, he was more than ever intoxicated by her beauty. Her face was pale, but of a dazzling fairness, set off by a profusion of raven hair that hung clustering about it. Her eyes were large and brilliant, with a singular expression approaching almost to wildness. As far as her black dress permitted her shape to be seen, it was of perfect symmetry. Her whole appearance was highly striking, though she was dressed in the simplest style. The only thing approaching to an ornament which she wore, was a broad black band round her neck, clasped by diamonds.

The perplexity now commenced with the student how to dispose of the helpless being thus thrown upon his protection. He thought of abandoning his chamber to her, and seeking shelter for himself elsewhere. Still he was so fascinated by her charms, there seemed to be such a spell upon his thoughts and senses, that he could not tear himself from her presence. Her manner, too, was singular and unaccountable. She spoke no more of the guillotine. Her grief had abated. The attentions of the student had first won her confidence, and then, apparently, her heart. She was evidently an enthusiast like himself, and enthusiasts soon understand each other.

In the infatuation of the moment, Wolfgang avowed his passion for her. He told her the story of his mysterious dream, and how she had possessed his heart before he had even seen her. She was strangely affected by his recital, and acknowledged to have felt an impulse towards him equally unaccountable. It was the time for wild theory and wild actions. Old prejudices and superstitions were done away; every thing was under the sway of the "Goddess of Reason." Among other rubbish of the old times, the forms and ceremonies of marriage began to be considered superfluous bonds for honorable minds. Social compacts were the vogue. Wolfgang was too much of a theorist not to be tainted by the liberal doctrines of the day.

"Why should we separate?" said he: "our hearts are united; in the eye of reason and honor we are as one. What need is there of sordid forms to bind high souls together?"

The stranger listened with emotion: she had evidently received illumination at the same school.

"You have no home nor family," continued he; "let me be every thing to you, or rather let us be every thing to one another. If form is necessary, form shall be observed—there is my hand. I pledge myself to you for ever."

"For ever?" said the stranger, solemnly.

"For ever!" repeated Wolfgang.

The stranger clasped the hand extended to her. "Then I am yours," murmured she, and sank upon his bosom.

The next morning the student left his bride sleeping, and sallied forth at an early hour to seek more spacious apartments, suitable to the change in his situation. When he returned, he found the stranger lying with her head hanging over the bed, and one arm thrown over it. He spoke to her, but received no reply. He advanced to awaken her from her uneasy posture. On taking her hand, it was cold—there was no pulsation—her face was pallid and ghastly.—In a word—she was a corpse.

Horrified and frantic, he alarmed the house. A scene of confusion ensued. The police was summoned. As the officer of police entered the room, he started back on beholding the corpse.

"Great heaven!" cried he, "how did this woman come here?"

"Do you know any thing about her?" said Wolfgang, eagerly.

"Do I?" exclaimed the police officer: "she was guillotined yesterday."

He stepped forward; undid the black collar round the neck of the corpse, and the head rolled on the floor!

The student burst into a frenzy. "The fiend! the fiend has gained possession of me!" shrieked he: "I am lost for ever."

They tried to soothe him, but in vain. He was possessed with the frightful belief that an evil spirit had reanimated the dead body to ensnare him. He went distracted, and died in a mad-house.

Here the old gentleman with the haunted head finished his narrative.

"And is this really a fact?" said the inquisitive gentleman.

"A fact not to be doubted," replied the other. "I had it from the best authority. The student told it me himself. I saw him in a mad-house at Paris."

The Adventure of the Mysterious Picture

As one story of the kind produces another, and as all the company seemed fully engrossed by the subject, and disposed to bring their relatives and ancestors upon the scene, there is no knowing how many more strange adventures we might have heard, had not a corpulent old fox-hunter, who had slept soundly through the whole, now suddenly awakened, with a loud and long-drawn yawn. The sound broke the charm: the ghosts took to flight, as though it had been cock-crowing, and there was a universal move for bed.

"And now for the haunted chamber," said the Irish Captain, taking his candle.

"Ay, who's to be the hero of the night?" said the gentleman with the ruined head.

"That we shall see in the morning," said the old gentleman with the nose: "whoever looks pale and grizzly will have seen the ghost."

"Well, gentlemen," said the Baronet, "there's many a true thing said in jest—in fact, one of you will sleep in the room to-night—"

"What—a haunted room?—a haunted room?—I claim the adventure—and I—and I—and I," said a dozen guests, talking and laughing at the same time.

"No, no," said mine host, "there is a secret about one of my rooms on which I feel disposed to try an experiment: so, gentlemen, none of you shall know who has the haunted chamber until circumstances reveal it. I will not even know it myself, but will leave it to chance and the allotment of the housekeeper. At the same time, if it will be any satisfaction to you, I will observe, for the honor of my paternal mansion, that there's scarcely a chamber in it but is well worthy of being haunted."

We now separated for the night, and each went to his allotted room. Mine was in one wing of the building, and I could not but smile at its resemblance in style to those eventful apartments described in the tales of the supper-table. It was spacious and gloomy, decorated with lampblack portraits; a bed of ancient damask, with a tester sufficiently lofty to grace a couch of state, and a number of massive pieces of old-fashioned furniture. I drew a great claw-footed arm-chair before the wide fireplace; stirred up the fire; sat looking into it, and musing upon the odd stories I had heard, until, partly overcome by the fatigue of the day's hunting, and partly by the wine and wassail of mine host, I fell asleep in my chair.

The uneasiness of my position made my slumber troubled, and laid me at the mercy of all kinds of wild and fearful dreams. Now it was that my perfidious dinner and supper rose in rebellion against my peace. I was hag-ridden by a fat saddle of mutton; a plum-pudding weighed like lead upon my conscience; the merry-thought of a capon filled me with horrible suggestions; and a deviled-leg of a turkey stalked in all kinds of diabolical shapes through my imagination. In short, I had a violent fit of the nightmare. Some strange indefinite evil seemed hanging over me which I could not avert; something terrible and loathsome oppressed me which I could not shake off. I was conscious of being asleep, and strove to rouse myself, but every effort redoubled the evil; until gasping, struggling, almost strangling, I suddenly sprang bolt upright in my chair, and awoke.

The light on the mantel-piece had burnt low, and the wick was divided; there was a great winding-sheet made by the dripping wax on the side towards me. The disordered taper emitted a broad flaring flame, and threw a strong light on a painting over the fireplace which I had not hitherto observed. It consisted merely of a head, or rather a face, staring full upon me, with an expression that was startling. It was without a frame, and at the first glance I could hardly persuade myself that it was not a real face thrusting itself out of the dark oaken panel. I sat in my chair gazing at it, and the more I gazed, the more it disquieted me. I had never before been affected in the same way by any painting. The emotions it caused were strange and indefinite. They were something like what I have heard ascribed to the eyes of the basilisk, or like that mysterious influence in reptiles termed fascination. I passed my hand over my eyes several times, as if seeking instinctively to brush away the illusion—in vain. They instantly reverted to the picture, and its chilling, creeping influence over my flesh and blood was redoubled. I looked round the room on other pictures, either to divert my attention, or to see whether the same effect would be produced by them. Some of them were grim enough to produce the effect, if the mere grimness of the painting produced it.—No such thing—my eye passed over them all with perfect indifference, but the moment it reverted to this visage over the fireplace, it was as if an electric shock darted through me. The other pictures were dim and faded, but this one protruded from a plain background in the strongest relief, and with wonderful truth of coloring. The expression was that of agony—the agony of intense bodily pain; but a menace scowled upon the brow, and a few sprinklings of blood added to its ghastliness. Yet it was not all these characteristics; it was some horror of the mind, some inscrutable antipathy awakened by this picture, which harrowed up my feelings.

I tried to persuade myself that this was chimerical; that my brain was confused by the fumes of mine host's good cheer, and in some measure by the odd stories about paintings which had been told at supper. I determined to shake off these vapors of the mind; rose from my chair; walked about the room; snapped my fingers; rallied myself; laughed aloud.—It was a forced laugh, and the echo of it in the old chamber jarred upon my ear.—I walked to the window, and tried to discern the landscape through the glass. It was pitch darkness, and a howling storm without; and as I heard the wind moan among the trees, I caught a reflection of this accursed visage in the pane of glass, as though it were staring through the window at me. Even the reflection of it was thrilling.

How was this vile nervous fit, for such I now persuaded myself it was, to be conquered? I determined to force myself not to look at the painting, but to undress quickly and get into bed.—I began to undress, but in spite of every effort I could not keep myself from stealing a glance every now and then at the picture; and a glance was sufficient to distress me. Even when my back was turned to it, the idea of this strange face behind me, peeping over my shoulder, was insupportable. I threw off my clothes and hurried into bed, but still this visage gazed upon me. I had a full view of it in my bed, and for some time could not take my eyes from it. I had grown nervous to a dismal degree. I put out the light, and tried to force myself to sleep—all in vain. The fire gleaming up a little threw an uncertain light about the room, leaving, however, the region of the picture in deep shadow. What, thought I, if this be the chamber about which mine host spoke as having a mystery reigning over it? I had taken his words merely as spoken in jest; might they have a real import: I looked around. The faintly lighted apartment had all the qualifications requisite for a haunted chamber. It began in my infected imagination to assume strange appearances—the old portraits turned paler and paler, and blacker and blacker; the streaks of light and shadow thrown among the quaint articles of furniture gave them more singular shapes and characters.—There was a huge dark clothes-press of antique form, gorgeous in brass and lustrous with wax, that began to grow oppressive to me.

"Am I then," thought I, "indeed the hero of the haunted room? Is there really a spell laid upon me, or is this all some contrivance of mine host to raise a laugh at my expense?" The idea of being hag-ridden by my own fancy all night, and then bantered on my haggard looks the next day, was intolerable; but the very idea was sufficient to produce the effect, and to render me still more nervous.—"Pish," said I, "it can be no such thing. How could my worthy host imagine that I, or any man, would be so worried by a mere picture? It is my own diseased imagination that torments me."

I turned in bed, and shifted from side to side to try to fall asleep; but all in vain; when one cannot get asleep by lying quiet, it is seldom that tossing about will effect the purpose. The fire gradually went out, and left the room in darkness. Still I had the idea of that inexplicable countenance gazing and keeping watch upon me through the gloom—nay, what was worse, the very darkness seemed to magnify its terrors. It was like having an unseen enemy hanging about one in the night. Instead of having one picture now to worry me, I had a hundred. I fancied it in every direction—"There it is," thought I, "and there! and there! with its horrible and mysterious expression still gazing and gazing on me! No—if I must suffer the strange and dismal influence, it were better face a single foe than thus be haunted by a thousand images of it."

Whoever has been in a state of nervous agitation, must know that the longer it continues the more uncontrollable it grows. The very air of the chamber seemed at length infected by the baleful presence of this picture. I fancied it hovering over me. I almost felt the fearful visage from the wall approaching my face—it seemed breathing upon me. "This is not to be borne," said I, at length, springing out of bed: "I can stand this no longer—I shall only tumble and toss about here all night; make a very spectre of myself, and become the hero of the haunted chamber in good earnest. Whatever be the ill consequences, I'll quit this cursed room and seek a night's rest elsewhere—they can but laugh at me, at all events, and they'll be sure to have the laugh upon me if I pass a sleepless night, and show them a haggard and wobegone visage in the morning."

All this was half-muttered to myself as I hastily slipped on my clothes, which having done, I groped my way out of the room, and down stairs to the drawing-room. Here, after tumbling over two or three pieces of furniture, I made out to reach a sofa, and stretching myself upon it, determined to bivouac there for the night. The moment I found myself out of the neighborhood of that strange picture, it seemed as if the charm were broken. All its influence was at an end. I felt assured that it was confined to its own dreary chamber, for I had, with a sort of instinctive caution, turned the key when I closed the door, I soon calmed down, therefore, into a state of tranquillity; from that into a drowsiness, and, finally, into a deep sleep; out of which I did not awake until the housemaid, with her besom and her matin song, came to put the room in order. She stared at finding me stretched upon the sofa, but I presume circumstances of the kind were not uncommon after hunting-dinners in her master's bachelor establishment, for she went on with her song and her work, and took no further heed of me.

I had an unconquerable repugnance to return to my chamber; so I found my way to the butler's quarters, made my toilet in the best way circumstances would permit, and was among the first to appear at the breakfast-table. Our breakfast was a substantial fox-hunter's repast, and the company generally assembled at it. When ample justice had been done to the tea, coffee, cold meats, and humming ale, for all these were furnished in abundance, according to the tastes of the different guests, the conversation began to break out with all the liveliness and freshness of morning mirth.

"But who is the hero of the haunted chamber—who has seen the ghost last night?" said the inquisitive gentleman, rolling his lobster eyes about the table.

The question set every tongue in motion; a vast deal of bantering, criticising of countenances, of mutual accusation and retort, took place. Some had drunk deep, and some were unshaven; so that there were suspicious faces enough in the assembly. I alone could not enter with ease and vivacity into the joke—I felt tongue-tied, embarrassed. A recollection of what I had seen and felt the preceding night still haunted my mind. It seemed as if the mysterious picture still held a thrall upon me. I thought also that our host's eye was turned on me with an air of curiosity. In short, I was conscious that I was the hero of the night, and felt as if every one might read it in my looks. The joke, however, passed over, and no suspicion seemed to attach to me. I was just congratulating myself on my escape, when a servant came in saying, that the gentleman who had slept on the sofa in the drawing-room had left his watch under one of the pillows. My repeater was in his hand.

"What!" said the inquisitive gentleman, "did any gentleman sleep on the sofa?"

"Soho! soho! a hare—a hare!" cried the old gentleman with the flexible nose.

I could not avoid acknowledging the watch, and was rising in great confusion, when a boisterous old squire who sat beside me exclaimed, slapping me on the shoulder, "'Sblood, lad, thou art the man as has seen the ghost!"

The attention of the company was immediately turned to me: if my facc had been pale the moment before, it now glowed almost to burning. I tried to laugh, but could only make a grimace, and found the muscles of my face twitching at sixes and sevens, and totally out of all control.

It takes but little to raise a laugh among a set of fox-hunters; there was a world of merriment and joking on the subject, and as I never relished a joke overmuch when it was at my own expense, I began to feel a little nettled. I tried to look cool and calm, and to restrain my pique; but the coolness and calmness of a man in a passion are confounded treacherous.

"Gentlemen," said I, with a slight cocking of the chin, and a bad attempt at a smile, "this is all very pleasant—ha! ha!—very pleasant—but I'd have you know, I am as little superstitious as any of you—ha! ha!—and as to any thing like timidity—you may smile, gentlemen, but I trust there 's no one here means to insinuate, that—as to a room's being haunted—I repeat, gentlemen, (growing a little warm at seeing a cursed grin breaking out round me,) as to a room's being haunted, I have as little faith in such silly stories as any one. But, since you put the matter home to me, I will say that I have met with something in my room strange and inexplicable to me. (A shout of laughter.) Gentlemen, I am serious; I know well what I am saying; I am calm, gentle-men, (striking my fist upon the table,) by Heaven, I am calm. I am neither trifling, nor do I wish to be trifled with. (The laughter of the company suppressed, and with ludicrous attempts at gravity.) There is a picture in the room in which I was put last night, that has had an effect upon me the most singular and incomprehensible."

"A picture?" said the old gentleman with the haunted head. "A picture!" cried the narrator with the nose. "A picture! a picture!" echoed several voices. Here there was an ungovernable peal of laughter. I could not contain myself. I started up from my seat; looked round on the company with fiery indignation; thrust both of my hands into my pockets, and strode up to one of the windows as though I would have walked through it. I stopped short, looked out upon the landscape without distinguishing a feature of it, and felt my gorge rising almost to suffocation.

Mine host saw it was time to interfere. He had maintained an air of gravity through the whole of the scene; and now stepped forth, as if to shelter me from the overwhelming merriment of my companions.

"Gentlemen," said he, "I dislike to spoil sport, but you have had your laugh, and the joke of the haunted chamber has been enjoyed. I must now take the part of my guest. I must not only vindicate him from your pleasantries, but I must reconcile him to himself; for I suspect he is a little out of humor with his own feelings; and, above all, I must crave his pardon for having made him the subject of a kind of experiment. Yes, gentlemen, there is something strange and peculiar in the chamber to which our friend was shown last night; there is a picture in my house, which possesses a singular and mysterious influence, and with which there is connected a very curious story. It is a picture to which I attach a value from a variety of circumstances; and though I have often been tempted to destroy it, from the odd and uncomfortable sensations which it produces in every one that beholds it, yet I have never been able to prevail upon myself to make the sacrifice. It is a picture I never like to look upon myself, and which is held in awe by all my servants. I have therefore banished it to a room but rarely used, and should have had it covered last night, had not the nature of our conversation, and the whimsical talk about a haunted chamber, tempted me to let it remain, by way of experiment, to see whether a stranger, totally unacquainted with its story, would be affected by it."

The words of the Baronet had turned every thought into a different channel. All were anxious to hear the story of the mysterious picture; and, for myself, so strangely were my feelings interested, that I forgot to feel piqued at the experiment which my host had made upon my nerves, and joined eagerly in the general entreaty. As the morning was stormy, and denied all egress, my host was glad of any means of entertaining his company; so, drawing his arm-chair towards the fire, he began.—

The Adventure of the Mysterious Stranger

MANY YEARS SINCE, WHEN I WAS A YOUNG MAN, AND HAD JUST LEFT Oxford, I was sent on the grand tour to finish my education. I believe my parents had tried in vain to inoculate me with wisdom; so they sent me to mingle with society, in hopes that I might take it the natural way. Such, at least, appears the reason for which nine-tenths of our youngsters are sent abroad. In the course of my tour I remained some time at Venice. The romantic character of that place delighted me; I was very much amused by the air of adventure and intrigue prevalent in this region of masks and gondolas; and I was exceedingly smitten by a pair of languishing black eyes, that played upon my heart from under an Italian mantle; so I persuaded myself that I was lingering at Venice to study men and manners; at least I persuaded my friends so, and that answered all my purposes.

I was a little prone to be struck by peculiarities in character and conduct, and my imagination was so full of romantic associations with Italy, that I was always on the look-out for adventure. Every thing chimed in with such a humor in this old mermaid of a city. My suit of apartments were in a proud, melancholy palace on the grand canal, formerly the residence of a magnifico, and sumptuous with the traces of decayed grandeur. My gondolier was one of the shrewdest of his class, active, merry, intelligent, and, like his brethren, secret as the grave; that is to say, secret to all the world except his master. I had not had him a week before he put me behind all the curtains in Venice. I liked the silence and mystery of the place, and when I sometimes saw from my window a black gondola gliding mysteriously along in the dusk of the evening, with nothing visible but its little glimmering lantern, I would jump into my own zendeletta, and give a signal for pursuit—"But I am running away from my subject with the recollection of youthful follies," said the Baronet, checking himself. "Let us come to the point."

Among my familiar resorts was a cassino under the arcades on one side of the grand square of St. Mark. Here I used frequently to lounge and take my ice, on those warm summer nights, when in Italy every body lives abroad until morning. I was seated here one evening, when a group of Italians took their seat at a table on the opposite side of the saloon. Their conversation was gay and animated, and carried on with Italian vivacity and gesticulation. I remarked among them one young man, however, who appeared to take no share, and find no enjoyment in the conversation, though he seemed to force himself to attend to it. He was tall and slender, and of extremely prepossessing appearance. His features were fine, though emaciated. He had a profusion of black glossy hair, that curled lightly about his head, and contrasted with the extreme paleness of his countenance. His brow was haggard; deep furrows seemed to have been ploughed into his visage by care, not by age, for he was evidently in the prime of youth. His eye was full of expression and fire, but wild and unsteady. He seemed to be tormented by some strange fancy or apprehension. In spite of every effort to fix his attention on the conversation of his companions, I noticed that every now and then he would turn his head slowly round, give a glance over his shoulder, and then withdraw it with a sudden jerk, as if something painful met his eye. This was repeated at intervals of about a minute, and he appeared hardly to have recovered from one shock, before I saw him slowly preparing to encounter another.

After sitting some time in the cassino, the party paid for the refreshment they had taken, and departed. The young man was the last to leave the saloon, and I remarked him glancing behind him in the same way, just as he passed out of the door. I could not resist the impulse to rise and follow him; for I was at an age when a romantic feeling of curiosity is easily awakened. The party walked slowly down the arcades, talking and laughing as they went. They crossed the Piazetta, but paused in the middle of it to enjoy the scene. It was one of those moonlight nights, so brilliant and clear in the pure atmosphere of Italy. The moonbeams streamed on the tall tower of St. Mark, and lighted up the magnificent front and swelling domes of the cathedral. The party expressed their delight in animated terms. I kept my eye upon the young man. He alone seemed abstracted and self-occupied. I noticed the same singular and, as it were, furtive glance over the shoulder, which had attracted my attention in the cassino. The party moved on, and I followed; they passed along the walk called the Broglio, turned the corner of the Ducal Palace, and getting into a gondola, glided swiftly away.

The countenance and conduct of this young man dwelt upon my mind, and interested me exceedingly. I met him a day or two afterwards in a gallery of paintings. He was evidently a connoisseur, for he always singled out the most masterly productions, and the few remarks drawn from him by his companions showed an intimate acquaintance with the art. His own taste, however, ran on singular extremes. On Salvator Rosa, in his most savage and solitary scenes; on Raphael, Titian, and Correggio, in their softest delineations of female beauty; on these he would occasionally gaze with transient enthusiasm. But this seemed only a momentary forgetfulness. Still would recur that cautious glance behind, and always quickly withdrawn, as though something terrible met his view.

I encountered him frequently afterwards at the theatre, at balls, at concerts; at the promenades in the gardens of San Georgia; at the grotesque exhibitions in the square of St. Mark; among the throng of merchants on the exchange by the Rialto. He seemed, in fact, to seek crowds; to hunt after bustle and amusement; yet never to take any interest in either the business or the gayety of the scene. Ever an air of painful thought, of wretched abstraction; and ever that strange and recurring movement of glancing fearfully over the shoulder. I did not know at first but this might be caused by apprehension of arrest; or, perhaps, from dread of assassination. But if so, why should he go thus continually abroad; why expose himself at all times and in all places?

I became anxious to know this stranger. I was drawn to him by that romantic sympathy which sometimes draws young men towards each other. His melancholy threw a charm about him, no doubt heightened by the touching expression of his countenance, and the manly graces of his person; for manly beauty has its effect even upon men. I had an Englishman's habitual diffidence and awkwardness to contend with; but from frequently meeting him in the cassinos, I gradually edged myself into his acquaintance. I had no reserve on his part to contend with. He seemed, on the contrary, to court society; and, in fact, to seek any thing rather than be alone.

When he found that I really took an interest in him, he threw himself entirely on my friendship. He clung to me like a drowning man. He would walk with me for hours up and down the place of St. Mark—or would sit, until night was far advanced, in my apartments. He took rooms under the same roof with me; and his constant request was that I would permit him, when it did not incommode me, to sit by me in my saloon. It was not that he seemed to take a particular delight in my conversation, but rather that he craved the vicinity of a human being; and, above all, of a being that sympathized with him. "I have often heard," said he, "of the sincerity of Englishmen—thank God I have one at length for a friend!"

Yet he never seemed disposed to avail himself of my sympathy other than by mere companionship. He never sought to unbosom himself to me: there appeared to be a settled corroding anguish in his bosom that neither could be soothed "by silence nor by speaking."

A devouring melancholy preyed upon his heart, and seemed to be drying up the very blood in his veins. It was not a soft melancholy, the disease of the affections, but a parching, withering agony. I could see at times that his mouth was dry and feverish; he panted rather than breathed; his eyes were bloodshot; his cheeks pale and livid; with now and then faint streaks of red athwart them, baleful gleams of the fire that was consuming his heart. As my arm was within his, I felt him press it at times with a convulsive motion to his side; his hands would clinch themselves involuntarily, and a kind of shudder would run through his frame.

I reasoned with him about his melancholy, sought to draw from him the cause; he shrunk from all confiding: "Do not seek to know it," said he, "you could not relieve it if you knew it; you would not even seek to relieve it. On the contrary, I should lose your sympathy, and that," said he, pressing my hand convulsively, "that I feel has become too dear to me to risk."

I endeavored to awaken hope within him. He was young; life had a thousand pleasures in store for him; there was a healthy reaction in the youthful heart; it medicines all its own wounds—"Come, come," said I, "there is no grief so great that youth cannot outgrow it."—"No! no!" said he, clinching his teeth, and striking repeatedly, with the energy of despair, on his bosom—"it is here! here! deep rooted; draining my heart's blood. It grows and grows, while my heart withers and withers. I have a dreadful monitor that gives me no repose—that follows me step by step—and will follow me step by step, until it pushes me into my grave!"

As he said this he involuntarily gave one of those fearful glances over his shoulder, and shrunk back with more than usual horror. I could not resist the temptation to allude to this movement, which I supposed to be some mere malady of the nerves. The moment I mentioned it, his face became crimsoned and convulsed; he grasped me by both hands —

"For God's sake," exclaimed he, with a piercing voice, "never allude to that again.—Let us avoid this subject, my friend; you cannot relieve me, indeed you cannot relieve me, but you may add to the torments I suffer.—At some future day you shall know all."

I never resumed the subject; for however much my curiosity might be roused, I felt too true a compassion for his sufferings to increase them by my intrusion. I sought various ways to divert his mind, and to arouse him from the constant meditations in which he was plunged. He saw my efforts, and seconded them as far as in his power, for there was nothing moody or wayward in his nature. On the contrary, there was something frank, generous, unassuming in his whole deportment. All the sentiments he uttered were noble and lofty. He claimed no indulgence, asked no toleration, but seemed content to carry his load of misery in silence, and only sought to carry it by my side. There was a mute beseeching manner about him, as if he craved companionship as a charitable boon; and a tacit thankfulness in his looks, as if he felt grateful to me for not repulsing him.

I felt this melancholy to be infectious. It stole over my spirits; interfered with all my gay pursuits, and gradually saddened my life; yet I could not prevail upon myself to shake off a being who seemed to hang upon me for support. In truth, the generous traits of character which beamed through all his gloom penetrated to my heart. His bounty was lavish and open-handed: his charity melting and spontaneous; not confined to mere donations, which humiliate as much as they relieve. The tone of his voice, the beam of his eye, enhanced every gift, and surprised the poor suppliant with that rarest and sweetest of charities, the charity not merely of the hand, but of the heart. Indeed his liberality seemed to have something in it of self-abasement and expiation. He, in a manner, humbled himself before the mendicant. "What right have I to ease and affluence"—would he murmur to himself—"when innocence wanders in misery and rags?"

The carnival time arrived. I hoped the gay scenes then presented might have some cheering effect. I mingled with him in the motley throng that crowded the place of St. Mark. We frequented operas, masquerades, balls—all in vain. The evil kept growing on him. He became more and more haggard and agitated. Often, after we have returned from one of these scenes of revelry, I have entered his room and found him lying on his face on the sofa; his hands clinched in his fine hair, and his whole countenance bearing traces of the convulsions of his mind.

The carnival passed away; the time of Lent succeeded; passion week arrived; we attended one evening a solemn service in one of the churches, in the course of which a grand piece of vocal and instrumental music was performed, relating to the death of our Saviour.

I had remarked that he was always powerfully affected by music; on this occasion he was so in an extraordinary degree. As the pealing notes swelled through the lofty aisles; he seemed to kindle with fervor; his eyes rolled upwards, until nothing but the whites were visible; his hands were clasped together, until the fingers were deeply imprinted in the flesh. When the music expressed the dying agony, his face gradually sank upon his knees; and at the touching words resounding through the church, "*Jesu mori*," sobs burst from him uncontrolled—I had never seen him weep before. His had always been agony rather than sorrow. I augured well from the circumstance, and let him weep on uninterrupted. When the service was ended, we left the church. He hung on my arm as we walked homewards with something of a softer and more subdued manner, instead of that nervous agitation I had been accustomed to witness. He alluded to the service we had heard. "Music," said he, "is indeed the voice of heaven; never before have I felt more impressed by the story of the atonement of our Saviour.—Yes, my friend," said he, clasping his hands with a kind of transport, "I know that my Redeemer liveth!"

"We parted for the night. His room was not far from mine, and I heard him for some time busied in it. I fell asleep, but was awakened before daylight. The young man stood by my bedside, dressed for travelling. He held a sealed packet and a large parcel in his hand, which he laid on the table.

"Farewell, my friend," said he, "I am about to set forth on a long journey; but, before I go, I leave with you these remembrances. In this packet you will find the particulars of my story.—When you read them I shall be far away; do not remember me with aversion.—You have been indeed a friend to me.—You have poured oil into a broken heart, but you could not heal it.—Farewell! let me kiss your hand—I am unworthy to embrace you." He sank on his knees—seized my hand in despite of my efforts to the contrary, and covered it with kisses. I was so surprised by all the scene, that I had not been able to say a word.—"But we shall meet again," said I hastily, as I saw him hurrying towards the door. "Never, never, in this world !" said he solemnly.—He sprang once more to my bedside—seized my hand, pressed it to his heart and to his lips, and rushed out of the room.

Here the Baronet paused. He seemed lost in thought, and sat looking upon the floor, and drumming with his fingers on the arm of his chair.

And did this mysterious personage return?" said the inquisitive gentleman.

Never!" replied the Baronet, with a pensive shake of the head—"I never saw him again."

"And pray what has all this to do with the picture?" inquired the old gentleman with the nose.

"True," said the questioner—"is it the portrait of that crack-brained Italian?"

No," said the Baronet, dryly, not half liking the appellation given to his hero—"but this picture was inclosed in the parcel he left with me. The sealed packet contained its explanation. There was a request on the outside that I would not open it until six months had elapsed. I kept my promise in spite of my curiosity. I have a translation of it by me, and had meant to read it, by way of accounting for the mystery of the chamber; but I fear I have already detained the company too long."

Here there was a general wish expressed to have the manuscript read, particularly on the part of the inquisitive gentleman; so the worthy Baronet drew out a fairly-written manuscript, and, wiping his spectacles, read aloud the following story.—

The Story of the Young Italian

I WAS BORN AT NAPLES. MY PARENTS, THOUGH OF NOBLE RANK, WERE LIMITED in fortune, or rather, my father was ostentatious beyond his means, and expended so much on his palace, his equipage, and his retinue, that he was continually straitened in his pecuniary circumstances. I was a younger son, and looked upon with indifference by my father, who, from a principle of family pride, wished to leave all his property to my elder brother. I showed, when quite a child, an extreme sensibility. Every thing affected me violently. While yet an infant in my mother's arms, and before I had learnt to talk, I could be wrought upon to a wonderful degree of anguish or delight by the power of music. As I grew older, my feelings remained equally acute, and I was easily transported into paroxysms of pleasure or rage. It was the amusement of my relations and of the domestics to play upon this irritable temperament. I was moved to tears, tickled to laughter, provoked to fury, for the entertainment of company, who were amused by such a tempest of mighty passion in a pigmy frame—they little thought, or perhaps little heeded the dangerous sensibilities they were fostering. I thus became a little creature of passion before reason was developed. In a short time I grew too old to be a plaything, and then I became a torment. The tricks and passions I had been teased into became irksome, and I was disliked by my teachers for the very lessons they had taught me. My mother died; and my power as a spoiled child was at an end. There was no longer any necessity to humor or tolerate me, for there was nothing to be gained by it, as I was no favorite of my father. I therefore experienced the fate of a spoiled child in such a situation, and was neglected, or noticed only to be crossed and contradicted. Such was the early treatment of a heart, which, if I can judge of it at all, was naturally disposed to the extremes of tenderness and affection.

My father, as I have already said, never liked me—in fact, he never understood me; he looked upon me as wilful and wayward, as deficient in natural affection.—It was the stateliness of his own manner, the loftiness and grandeur of his own look, which had repelled me from his arms. I always pictured him to myself as I had seen him, clad in his senatorial robes, rustling with pomp and pride. The magnificence of his person daunted my young imagination. I could never approach him with the confiding affection of a child.

My father's feelings were wrapped up in my elder brother. He was to be the inheritor of the family title and the family dignity, and every thing was sacrificed to him—I, as well as every thing else. It was determined to devote me to the church, that so my humors and myself might be removed out of the way, either of tasking my father's time and trouble, or interfering with the interests of my brother. At an early age, therefore, before my mind had dawned upon the world and its delights, or known any thing of it beyond the precincts of my father's palace, I was sent to a convent, the superior of which was my uncle, and was confided entirely to his care.

My uncle was a man totally estranged from the world: he had never relished, for he had never tasted its pleasures; and he regarded rigid self-denial as the great basis of Christian virtue. He considered every one's temperament like his own; or at least he made them conform to it. His character and habits had an influence over the fraternity of which he was superior—a more gloomy, saturnine set of beings were never assembled together. The convent, too, was calculated to awaken sad and solitary thoughts. It was situated in a gloomy gorge of those mountains away south of Vesuvius. All distant views were shut out by sterile volcanic heights. A mountain-stream raved beneath its walls, and eagles screamed about its turrets.

I had been sent to this place at so tender an age as soon to lose all distinct recollection of the scenes I had left behind. As my mind expanded, therefore, it formed its idea of the world from the convent and its vicinity, and a dreary world it appeared to me. An early tinge of melancholy was thus infused into my character; and the dismal stories of the monks, about devils and evil spirits, with which they affrighted my young imagination, gave me a tendency to superstition which I could never effectually shake off. They took the same delight to work upon my ardent feelings, that had been so mischievously executed by my father's household. I can recollect the horrors with which they fed my heated fancy during an eruption of Vesuvius. We were distant from that volcano, with mountains between us; but its convulsive throes shook the solid foundations of nature. Earthquakes threatened to topple down our convent towers. A lurid, baleful light hung in the heavens at night, and showers of ashes, borne by the wind, fell in our narrow valley. The monks talked of the earth being honey-combed beneath us; of streams of molten lava raging through its veins; of caverns of sulphurous flames roaring in the centre, the abodes of demons and the damned; of fiery gulfs ready to yawn beneath our feet. All these tales were told to the doleful accompaniment of the mountain's thunders, whose low bellowing made the walls of our convent vibrate.

One of the monks had been a painter, but had retired from the world, and embraced this dismal life in expiation of some crime. He was a melancholy man, who pursued his art in the solitude of his cell, but made it a source of penance to him. His employment was to portray, either on canvas or in waxen models, the human face and human form, in the agonies of death, and in all the stages of dissolution and decay. The fearful mysteries of the charnel-house were unfolded in his labors; the loathsome banquet of the beetle and the worm. I turn with shuddering even from the recollection of his works, yet, at the time, my strong but ill-directed imagination seized with ardor upon his instructions in his art. Any thing was a variety from the dry studies and monotonous duties of the cloister. In a little while I became expert with my pencil, and my gloomy productions were thought worthy of decorating some of the altars of the chapel.

In this dismal way was a creature of feeling and fancy brought up. Every thing genial and amiable in my nature was repressed, and nothing brought out but what was unprofitable and ungracious. I was ardent in my temperament; quick, mercurial, impetuous, formed to be a creature all love and adoration; but a leaden hand was laid on all my finer qualities. I was taught nothing but fear and hatred. I hated my uncle. I hated the monks. I hated the convent in which I was immured. I hated the world; and I almost hated myself for being, as I supposed, so hating and hateful an animal.

When I had nearly attained the age of sixteen, I was suffered, on one occasion, to accompany one of the brethren on a mission to a distant part of the country. We soon left behind us the gloomy valley in which I had been pent up for so many years, and after a short journey among the mountains, emerged upon the voluptuous landscape that spreads itself about the Bay of Naples. Heavens! how transported was I, when I stretched my gaze over a vast reach of delicious sunny country, gay with groves and vineyards: with Vesuvius rearing its forked summit to my right; the blue Mediterranean to my left, with its enchanting coast, studded with shining towns and sumptuous villas; and Naples, my native Naples, gleaming far, far in the distance.

Good God! was this the lovely world from which I had been excluded! I had reached that age when the sensibilities are in all their bloom and freshness. Mine had been checked and chilled. They now burst forth with the suddenness of a retarded spring-time. My heart, hitherto unnaturally shrunk up, expanded into a riot of vague but delicious emotions. The beauty of nature intoxicated—bewildered me. The song of the peasants; their cheerful looks; their happy avocations; the picturesque gayety of their dresses; their rustic music; their dances; all broke upon me like witchcraft. My soul responded to the music, my heart danced in my bosom. All the men appeared amiable, all the women lovely.

I returned to the convent, that is to say, my body returned, but my heart and soul never entered there again. I could not forget this glimpse of a beautiful and a happy world—a world so suited to my natural character. I had felt so happy while in it; so different a being from what I felt myself when in the convent—that tomb of the living. I contrasted the countenances of the beings I had seen, full of fire and freshness and enjoyment, with the pallid, leaden, lack-lustre visages of the monks; the dance with the droning chant of the chapel. I had before found the exercises of the cloister wearisome, they now became intolerable. The dull round of duties wore away my spirit; my nerves became irritated by the fretful tinkling of the convent-bell, evermore dinging among the mountain echoes, evermore calling me from my repose at night, my pencil by day, to attend to some tedious and mechanical ceremony of devotion.

I was not of a nature to meditate long without putting my thoughts into action. My spirit had been suddenly aroused, and was now all awake within me. I watched an opportunity, fled from the convent, and made my way on foot to Naples. As I entered its gay and crowded streets, and beheld the variety and stir of life around me, the luxury of palaces, the splendor of equipages, and the pantomimic animation of the motley populace, I seemed as if awakened to a world of enchantment, and solemnly vowed that nothing should force me back to the monotony of the cloister.

I had to inquire my way to my father's palace, for I had been so young on leaving it that I knew not its situation. I found some difficulty in getting admitted to my father's presence; for the domestics scarcely knew that there was such a being as myself in existence, and my monastic dress did not operate in my favor. Even my father entertained no recollection of my person. I told him my name, threw myself at his feet, implored his forgiveness, and entreated that I might not be sent back to the convent.

He received me with the condescension of a patron, rather than the fondness of a parent; listened patiently, but coldly, to my tale of monastic grievances and disgusts, and promised to think what else could be done for me. This coldness blighted and drove back all the frank affection of my nature, that was ready to spring forth at the least warmth of parental kindness. All my early feelings towards my father revived. I again looked up to him as the stately magnificent being that had daunted my childish imagination, and felt as if I had no pretensions to his sympathies. My brother engrossed all his care and love; he inherited his nature, and carried himself towards me with a protecting rather than a fraternal air. It wounded my pride, which was great. I could brook condescension from my father, for I looked up to him with awe, as a superior being; but I could not brook patronage from a brother, who I felt was intellectually my inferior. The servants perceived that I was an unwelcome intruder in the paternal mansion, and, menial-like, they treated me with neglect. Thus baffled at every point, my affections outraged wherever they would attach themselves, I became sullen, silent, and desponding. My feelings, driven back upon myself, entered and preyed upon my own heart. I remained for some days an unwelcome guest rather than a restored son in my father's house. I was doomed never to be properly known there. I was made, by wrong treatment, strange even to myself, and they judged of me from my strangeness.

I was startled one day at the sight of one of the monks of my convent gliding out of my father's room. He saw me, but pretended not to notice me, and this very hypocrisy made me suspect something. I had become sore and susceptible in my feelings, every thing inflicted a wound on them. In this state of mind, I was treated with marked disrespect by a pampered minion, the favorite servant of my father. All the pride and passion of my nature rose in an instant, and I struck him to the earth. My father was passing by; he stopped not to inquire the reason, nor indeed could he read the long course of mental sufferings which were the real cause. He rebuked me with anger and scorn; summoning all the haughtiness of his nature and grandeur of his look to give weight to the contumely with which he treated me. I felt that I had not deserved it. I felt that I was not appreciated. I felt that I had that within me which merited better treatment. My heart swelled against a father's injustice. I broke through my habitual awe of him—I replied to him with impatience. My hot spirit flushed in my cheek and kindled in my eye; but my sensitive heart swelled as quickly, and before I had half vented my passion, I felt it suffocated and quenched in my tears. My father was astonished and incensed at this turning of the worm, and ordered me to my chamber. I retired in silence, choking with contending emotions.

I had not been long there when I overheard voices in an adjoining apartment. It was a consultation between my father and the monk, about the means of getting me back quietly to the convent. My resolution was taken. I had no longer a home nor a father. That very night I left the paternal roof. I got on board a vessel about making sail from the harbor, and abandoned myself to the wide world. No matter to what port she steered; any part of so beautiful a world was better than my convent. No matter where I was cast by fortune; any place would be more a home to me than the home I had left behind. The vessel was bound to Genoa. We arrived there after a voyage of a few days.

As I entered the harbor between the moles which embrace it, and beheld the amphitheatre of palaces, and churches, and splendid gardens, rising one above another, I felt at once its title to the appellation of Genoa the Superb. I landed on the mole an utter stranger, without knowing what to do, or whither to direct my steps. No matter: I was released from the thraldom of the convent and the humiliations of home. When I traversed the Strada Balbi and the Strada Nuova, those streets of palaces, and gazed at the wonders of architecture around me; when I wandered at close of day amid a gay throng of the brilliant and the beautiful, through the green alleys of the Aqua Verde, or among the colonnades and terraces of the magnificent Doria gardens; I thought it impossible to be ever otherwise than happy in Genoa.

A few days sufficed to show me my mistake. My scanty purse was exhausted, and for the first time in my life I experienced the sordid distress of penury. I had never known the want of money, and had never adverted to the possibility of such an evil. I was ignorant of the world and all its ways; and when first the idea of destitution came over my mind, its effect was withering. I was wandering penniless through the streets which no longer delighted my eyes, when chance led my steps into the magnificent church of the Annunciata.

A celebrated painter of the day was at that moment superintending the placing of one of his pictures over an altar. The proficiency which I had acquired in his art during my residence in the convent, had made me an enthusiastic amateur. I was struck, at the first glance, with the painting. It was the face of a Madonna. So innocent, so lovely, such a divine expression of maternal tenderness! I lost, for the moment, all recollection of myself in the enthusiasm of my art. I clasped my hands together, and uttered an ejaculation of delight. The painter perceived my emotion. He was flattered and gratified by it. My air and manner pleased him, and he accosted me. I felt too much the want of friendship to repel the advances of a stranger; and there was something in this one so benevolent and winning, that in a moment he gained my confidence.

I told him my story and my situation, concealing only my name and rank. He appeared strongly interested by my recital, invited me to his house, and from that time I became his favorite pupil. He thought he perceived in me extraordinary talents for the art, and his encomiums awakened all my ardor. What a blissful period of my existence was it that I passed beneath his roof! Another being seemed created within me; or rather, all that was amiable and excellent was drawn out. I was as recluse as ever I had been at the convent, but how different was my seclusion! My time was spent in storing my mind with lofty and poetical ideas; in meditating on all that was striking and noble in history and fiction; in studying and tracing all that was sublime and beautiful in nature. I was always a visionary, imaginative being, but now my reveries and imaginings all elevated me to rapture. I looked up to my master as to a benevolent genius that had opened to me a region of enchantment. He was not a native of Genoa, but had been drawn thither by the solicitations of several of the nobility, and had resided there but a few years, for the completion of certain works. His health was delicate, and he had to confide much of the filling up of his designs to the pencils of his scholars. He considered me as particularly happy in delineating the human countenance; in seizing upon characteristic though fleeting expressions, and fixing them powerfully upon my canvas. I was employed continually, therefore, in sketching faces, and often, when some particular grace or beauty of expression was wanted in a countenance, it was intrusted to my pencil. My benefactor was fond of bringing me forward; and partly, perhaps, through my actual skill, and partly through his partial praises, I began to be noted for the expressions of my countenances.

Among the various works which he had undertaken, was an historical piece for one of the palaces of Genoa, in which were to be introduced the likenesses of several of the family. Among these was one intrusted to my pencil. It was that of a young girl, as yet in a convent for her education. She came out for the purpose of sitting for the picture. I first saw her in an apartment of one of the sumptuous palaces of Genoa. She stood before a casement that looked out upon the bay; a stream of vernal sunshine fell upon her, and shed a kind of glory round her, as it lit up the rich crimson chamber. She was but sixteen years of age—and oh, how lovely! The scene broke upon me like a mere vision of spring and youth and beauty. I could have fallen down and worshipped her. She was like one of those fictions of poets and painters, when they would express the beau ideal that haunts their minds with shapes of indescribable perfection. I was permitted to sketch her countenance in various positions, and I fondly protracted the study that was undoing me. The more I gazed on her, the more I became enamoured; there was something almost painful in my intense admiration. I was but nineteen years of age, shy, diffident, and inexperienced. I was treated with attention by her mother; for my youth and my enthusiasm in my art had won favor for me; and I am inclined to think something in my air and manner inspired interest and respect. Still the kindness with which I was treated could not dispel the embarrassment into which my own imagination threw me when in presence of this lovely being. It elevated her into something almost more than mortal. She seemed too exquisite for earthly me; too delicate and exalted for human attainment. As I sat tracing her charms on my canvas, with my eyes occasionally riveted on her features, I drank in delicious poison that made me giddy. My heart alternately gushed with tenderness, and ached with despair. Now I became more than ever sensible of the violent fires that had lain dormant at the bottom of my soul. You who are born in a more temperate climate, and under a cooler sky, have little idea of the violence of passion in our southern bosoms.

A few days finished my task. Bianca returned to her convent, but her image remained indelibly impressed upon my heart. It dwelt in my imagination; it became my pervading idea of beauty. It had an effect even upon my pencil. I became noted for my felicity in depicting female loveliness: it was but because I multiplied the image of Bianca. I soothed and yet fed my fancy by introducing her in all the productions of my master. I have stood, with delight, in one of the chapels of the Annunciata, and heard the crowd extol the seraphic beauty of a saint which I had painted. I have seen them bow down in adoration before the painting; they were bowing before the loveliness of Bianca.

I existed in this kind of dream, I might almost say delirium, for upwards of a year. Such is the tenacity of my imagination, that the image formed in it continued in all its power and freshness. Indeed, I was a solitary, meditative being, much given to reverie, and apt to foster ideas which had once taken strong possession of me. I was roused from this fond, melancholy, delicious dream by the death of my worthy benefactor. I cannot describe the pangs his death occasioned me. It left me alone, and almost broken-hearted. He bequeathed to me his little property, which, from the liberality of his disposition, and his expensive style of living, was indeed but small; and he most particularly recommended me, in dying, to the protection of a nobleman who had been his patron.

The latter was a man who passed for munificent. He was a lover and an encourager of the arts, and evidently wished to be thought so. He fancied he saw in me indications of future excellence; my pencil had already attracted attention; he took me at once under his protection. Seeing that I was overwhelmed with grief, and incapable of exerting myself in the mansion of my late benefactor, he invited me to sojourn for a time at a villa which he possessed on the border of the sea, in the picturesque neighborhood of Sestri di Ponente.

I found at the villa the count's only son, Filippo. He was nearly of my age; prepossessing in his appearance, and fascinating in his manners; he attached himself to me, and seemed to court my good opinion. I thought there was something of profession in his kindness, and of caprice in his disposition; but I had nothing else near me to attach myself to, and my heart felt the need of something to repose upon. His education had been neglected; he looked upon me as his superior in mental powers and acquirements, and tacitly acknowledged my superiority. I felt that I was his equal in birth, and that gave independence to my manners, which had its effect. The caprice and tyranny I saw sometimes exercised on others, over whom he had power, were never manifested towards me. We became intimate friends and frequent companions. Still I loved to be alone, and to indulge in the reveries of my own imagination among the scenery by which I was surrounded.

The villa commanded a wide view of the Mediterranean, and of the picturesque Ligurian coast. It stood alone in the midst of ornamented grounds, finely decorated with statues and fountains, and laid out into groves and alleys and shady lawns. Every thing was assembled here that could gratify the taste, or agreeably occupy the mind. Soothed by the tranquillity of this elegant retreat, the turbulence of my feelings gradually subsided, and blending with the romantic spell which still reigned over my imagination, produced a soft, voluptuous melancholy.

I had not been long under the roof of the count, when our solitude was enlivened by another inhabitant. It was a daughter of a relative of the count, who had lately died in reduced circumstances, bequeathing this only child to his protection. I had heard much of her beauty from Filippo, but my fancy had become so engrossed by one idea of beauty, as not to admit of any other. We were in the central saloon of the villa when she arrived. She was still in mourning, and approached, leaning on the count's arm. As they ascended the marble portico, I was struck by the elegance of her figure and movement, by the grace with which the *mezzaro* the bewitching vail of Genoa, was folded about her slender form. They entered. Heavens! what was my surprise when I beheld Bianca before me! It was herself; pale with grief, but still more matured in loveliness than when I had last beheld her. The time that had elapsed had developed the graces of her person, and the sorrow she had undergone had diffused over her countenance an irresistible tenderness.

She blushed and trembled at seeing me, and tears rushed into her eyes, for she remembered in whose company she had been accustomed to behold me. For my part, I cannot express what were my emotions. By degrees I overcame the extreme shyness that had formerly paralyzed me in her presence. We were drawn together by sympathy of situation. We had each lost our best friend in the world; we were each, in some measure, thrown upon the kindness of others. When I came to know her intellectually, all my ideal picturings of her were confirmed. Her newness to the world, her delightful susceptibility to every thing beautiful and agreeable in nature, reminded me of my own emotions when first I escaped from the convent. Her rectitude of thinking delighted my judgment; the sweetness of her nature wrapped itself round my heart; and then her young, and tender, and budding loveliness, sent a delicious madness to my brain.

I gazed upon her with a kind of idolatry, as something more than mortal; and I felt humiliated at the idea of my comparative unworthiness. Yet she was mortal; and one of mortality's most susceptible and loving compounds;—for she loved me!

How first I discovered the transporting truth I cannot recollect. I believe it stole upon me by degrees as a wonder past hope or belief. We were both at such a tender and loving age; in constant intercourse with each other; mingling in the same elegant pursuits;—for music, poetry, and painting, were our mutual delights; and we were almost separated from society among lovely and romantic scenery. Is it strange that two young hearts, thus brought together, should readily twine round each other?

Oh, gods! what a dream—a transient dream of unalloyed delight, then passed over my soul! then it was that the world around me was indeed a paradise; for I had woman—lovely, delicious woman, to share it with me! How often have I rambled along the picturesque shores of Sestri, or climbed its wild mountains, with the coast gemmed with villas, and the blue sea far below me, and the slender Faro of Genoa on its romantic promontory in the distance; and as I sustained the faltering steps of Bianca, have thought there could no unhappiness enter into so beautiful a world! How often have we listened together to the nightingale, as it poured forth its rich notes among the moonlight bowers of the garden, and have wondered that poets could ever have fancied any thing melancholy in its song! Why, oh why is this budding season of life and tenderness so transient! why is this rosy cloud of love, that sheds such a glow over the morning of our days, so prone to brew up into the whirlwind and the storm!

I was the first to awaken from this blissful delirium of the affections. I had gained Bianca's heart, what was I to do with it? I had no wealth nor prospect to entitle me to her hand; was I to take advantage of her ignorance of the world, of her confiding affection, and draw her down to my own poverty? Was this requiting the hospitality of the count? was this requiting the love of Bianca?

Now first I began to feel that even successful love may have its bitterness. A corroding care gathered about my heart. I moved about the palace like a guilty being. I felt as if I had abused its hospitality, as if I were a thief within its walls. I could no longer look with unembarrassed mien in the countenance of the count. I accused myself of perfidy to him, and I thought he read it in my looks, and began to distrust and despise me. His manner had always been ostentatious and condescending; it now appeared cold and haughty. Filippo, too, became reserved and distant; or at least I suspected him to be so. Heavens! was this the mere coinage of my brain? Was I to become suspicious of all the world? A poor, surmising wretch; watching looks and gestures; and torturing myself with misconstructions? Or, if true, was I to remain beneath a roof where I was merely tolerated, and linger there on sufferance? "This is not to be endured!" exclaimed I: "I will tear myself from this state of self-abasement—I will break through this fascination, and fly—Fly!—Whither?—from the world? for where is the world when I leave Bianca behind me?"

My spirit was naturally proud, and swelled within me at the idea of being looked upon with contumely. Many times I was on the point of declaring my family and rank, and asserting my equality in the presence of Bianca, when I thought her relations assumed an air of superiority. But the feeling was transient. I considered myself discarded and condemned by my family; and had solemnly vowed never to own relationship to them until they themselves should claim it.

The struggle of my mind preyed upon my happiness and my health. It seemed as if the uncertainty of being loved would be less intolerable than thus to be assured of it, and yet not dare to enjoy the conviction. I was no longer the enraptured admirer of Bianca; I no longer hung in ecstasy on the tones of her voice, nor drank in with insatiate gaze the beauty of her countenance. Her very smiles ceased to delight me, for I felt culpable in having won them.

She could not but be sensible of the change in me, and inquired the cause with her usual frankness and simplicity. I could not evade the inquiry, for my heart was full to aching. I told her all the conflict of my soul; my devouring passion, my bitter self-upbraiding. "Yes," said I, "I am unworthy of you. I am an offcast from my family—a wanderer—a nameless, homeless wanderer—with nothing but poverty for my portion; and yet I have dared to love you—have dared to aspire to your love."

My agitation moved her to tears, but she saw nothing in my situation so hopeless as I had depicted it. Brought up in a convent, she knew nothing of the world—its wants—its cares: and indeed what woman is a worldly casuist in matters of the heart? Nay more, she kindled into a sweet enthusiasm when she spoke of my fortunes and myself. We had dwelt together on the works of the famous masters. I had related to her their histories; the high reputation, the influence, the magnificence to which they had attained. The companions of princes, the favorites of kings, the pride and boast of nations. All this she applied to me. Her love saw nothing in all their great productions that I was not able to achieve; and when I beheld the lovely creature glow with fervor, and her whole countenance radiant with visions of my glory, I was snatched up for the moment into the heaven of her own imagination.

I am dwelling too long upon this part of my story; yet I cannot help lingering over a period of my life, on which, with all its cares and conflicts, I look back with fondness, for as yet my soul was unstained by a crime. I do not know what might have been the result of this struggle between pride, delicacy, and passion, had I not read in a Neapolitan gazette, an account of the sudden death of my brother. It was accompanied by an earnest inquiry for intelligence concerning me, and a prayer, should this meet my eye, that I would hasten to Naples to comfort an infirm and afflicted father.

I was naturally of an affectionate disposition, but my brother had never been as a brother to me. I had long considered myself as disconnected from him, and his death caused me but little emotion. The thoughts of my father, infirm and suffering, touched me however to the quick; and when I thought of him, that lofty magnificent being, now bowed down and desolate, and suing to me for comfort, all my resentment for past neglect was subdued, and a glow of filial affection was awakened within me.

The predominant feeling, however, that overpowered all others, was transport at the sudden change in my whole fortunes. A home, a name, rank, wealth, awaited me; and love painted a still more rapturous prospect in the distance. I hastened to Bianca, and threw myself at her feet. "Oh, Bianca!" exclaimed I, "at length I can claim you for my own. I am no longer a nameless adventurer, a neglected, rejected outcast. Look—read—behold the tidings that restore me to my name and to myself!"

I will not dwell on the scene that ensued. Bianca rejoiced in the reverse of my situation, because she saw it lightened my heart of a load of care; for her own part, she had loved me for myself, and had never doubted that my own merits would command both fame and fortune.

I now felt all my native pride buoyant within me. I no longer walked with my eyes bent to the dust; hope elevated them to the skies—my soul was lit up with fresh fires, and beamed from my countenance.

I wished to impart the change in my circumstances to the count; to let him know who and what I was—and to make formal proposals for the hand of Bianca; but he was absent on a distant estate. I opened my whole soul to Filippo. Now first I told him of my passion, of the doubts and fears that had distracted me, and of the tidings that had suddenly dispelled them. He over-whelmed me with congratulations, and with the warmest expressions of sympathy; I embraced him in the fulness of my heart;—I felt compunctions for having suspected him of coldness, and asked him forgiveness for ever having doubted his friendship.

Nothing is so warm and enthusiastic as a sudden expansion of the heart between young men. Filippo entered into our concerns with the most eager interest. He was our confidant and counsellor. It was determined that I should hasten at once to Naples, to re-establish myself in my father's affections, and my paternal home; and the moment the reconciliation was effected, and my father's consent insured, I should return and demand Bianca of the count. Filippo engaged to secure his father's acquiescence; indeed he undertook to watch over our interests, and to be the channel through which we might correspond.

My parting with Bianca was tender—delicious—agonizing. It was in a little pavilion of the garden which had been one of our favorite resorts. How often and often did I return to have one more adieu, to have her look once more on in speechless emotion; to enjoy once more the rapturous sight of those tears streaming down her lovely cheeks; to seize once more on that delicate hand, the frankly accorded pledge of love, and cover it with tears and kisses! Heavens! there is a delight even in the parting agony of two lovers, worth a thousand tame pleasures of the world. I have her at this moment before my eyes, at the window of the pavilion, putting aside the vines which clustered about the casement, her form beaming forth in virgin light, her countenance all tears and smiles, sending a thousand and a thousand adieus after me, as hesitating, in a delirium of fondness and agitation, I faltered my way down the avenue.

As the bark bore me out of the harbor of Genoa, how eagerly my eye stretched along the coast of Sestri till it discovered the villa gleaming from among trees at the foot of the mountain. As long as day lasted I gazed and gazed upon it, till it lessened and lessened to a mere white speck in the distance; and still my intense and fixed gaze discerned it, when all other objects of the coast had blended into indistinct confusion, or were lost in the evening gloom.

On arriving at Naples, I hastened to my paternal home. My heart yearned for the long- withheld blessing of a father's love. As I entered the proud portal of the ancestral palace, my emotions were so great, that I could not speak. No one knew me; the servants gazed at me with curiosity and surprise. A few years of intellectual elevation and development had made a prodigious change in the poor fugitive stripling from the convent. Still, that no one should know me in my rightful home was overpowering. I felt like the prodigal son returned. I was a stranger in the house of my father. I burst into tears and wept aloud. When I made myself known, however, all was changed. I, who had once been almost repulsed from its walls, and forced to fly as an exile, was welcomed back with acclamation, with servility. One of the servants hastened to prepare my father for my reception; my eagerness to receive the paternal embrace was so great, that I could not await his return, but hurried after him. What a spectacle met my eyes as I entered the chamber! My father, whom I had left in the pride of vigorous age, whose noble and majestic bearing had so awed my young imagination, was bowed down and withered into decrepitude. A paralysis had ravaged his stately form, and left it a shaking ruin. He sat propped up in his chair, with pale, relaxed visage, and glassy wandering eye. His intellects had evidently shared in the ravages of his frame. The servant was endeavoring to make him comprehend that a visitor was at hand. I tottered up to him, and sank at his feet. All his past coldness and neglect were forgotten in his present sufferings. I remembered only that he was my parent, and that I had deserted him. I clasped his knee: my voice was almost filled with convulsive sobs. "Pardon—pardon! oh! my father!" was all that I could utter. His apprehension seemed slowly to return to him. He gazed at me for some moments with a vague, inquiring look; a convulsive tremor quivered about his lips; he feebly extended a shaking hand; laid it upon my head, and burst into an infantine flow of tears.

From that moment he would scarcely spare me from his sight. I appeared the only object that his heart responded to in the world; all else was as a blank to him. He had almost lost the power of speech, and the reasoning faculty seemed at an end. He was mute and passive, excepting that fits of childlike weeping would sometimes come over him without any immediate cause. If I left the room at any time, his eye was incessantly fixed on the door till my return, and on my entrance there was another gush of tears.

To talk with him of my concerns, in this ruined state of mind, would have been worse than useless; to have left him for ever so short a time would have been cruel, unnatural. Here then was a new trial for my affections. I wrote to Bianca an account of my return, and of my actual situation, painting in colors vivid, for they were true, the torments I suffered at our being thus separated; for the youthful lover every day of absence is an age of love lost. I inclosed the letter in one to Filippo, who was the channel of our correspondence. I received a reply from him full of friendship and sympathy; from Bianca, full assurances of affection and constancy. Week after week, month after month elapsed, without making any change in my circumstances. The vital flame which had seemed nearly extinct when first I met my father, kept fluttering on without any apparent diminution. I watched him constantly, faithfully, I had almost said patiently. I knew that his death alone would set me free—yet I never at any moment wished it. I felt too glad to be able to make any atonement for past disobedience; and denied as I had been all endearments of relationship in my early days, my heart yearned towards a father, who in his age and helplessness had thrown himself entirely on me for comfort.

My passion for Bianca gained daily more force from absence: by constant meditation it wore itself a deeper and deeper channel. I made no new friends nor acquaintances; sought none of the pleasures of Naples, which my rank and fortune threw open to me. Mine was a heart that confined itself to few objects, but dwelt upon them with the intenser passion. To sit by my father, administer to his wants, and to meditate on Bianca in the silence of his chamber, was my constant habit. Sometimes I amused myself with my pencil, in portraying the image ever present to my imagination. I transferred to canvas every look and smile of hers that dwelt in my heart. I showed them to my father, in hopes of awakening an interest in his bosom for the mere shadow of my love; but he was too far sunk in intellect to take any notice of them. When I received a letter from Bianca, it was a new source of solitary luxury. Her letters, it is true, were less and less frequent, but they were always full of assurances of unabated affection. They breathed not the frank and innocent warmth with which she expressed herself in conversation, but I accounted for it from the embarrassment which inexperienced minds have often to express themselves upon paper. Filippo assured me of her unaltered constancy. They both lamented, in the strongest terms, our continued separation, though they did justice to the filial piety that kept me by my father's side.

Nearly two years elapsed in this protracted exile. To me they were so many ages. Ardent and impetuous by nature, I scarcely know how I should have supported so long an absence, had I not felt assured that the faith of Bianca was equal to my own. At length my father died. Life went from him almost imperceptibly. I hung over him in mute affliction, and watched the expiring spasms of nature. His last faltering accents whispered repeatedly a blessing on me. Alas! how has it been fulfilled!

When I had paid due honors to his remains, and laid them in the tomb of our ancestors, I arranged briefly my affairs, put them in a posture to be easily at my command from a distance, and embarked once more with a bounding heart for Genoa.

Our voyage was propitious, and oh! what was my rapture, when first, in the dawn of morning, I saw the shadowy summits of the Apennines rising almost like clouds above the horizon! The sweet breath of summer just moved us over the long wavering billows that were rolling us on towards Genoa. By degrees the coast of Sestri rose like a creation of enchantment from the silver bosom of the deep. I beheld the line of villages and palaces studding its borders. My eye reverted to a well-known point, and at length, from the confusion of distant objects, it singled out the villa which contained Bianca. It was a mere speck in the landscape, but glimmering from afar, the polar star of my heart.

Again I gazed at it for a livelong summer's day, but oh! how different the emotions between departure and return. It now kept growing and growing, instead of lessening and lessening on my sight. My heart seemed to dilate with it. I looked at it through a telescope. I gradually defined one feature after another. The balconies of the central saloon where first I met Bianca beneath its roof; the terrace where we so often had passed the delightful summer evenings; the awning which shaded her chamber window; I almost fancied I saw her form beneath it. Could she but know her lover was in the bark whose white sail now gleamed on the sunny bosom of the sea! My fond impatience increased as we neared the coast; the ship seemed to lag lazily over the billows; I could almost have sprang into the sea, and swam to the desired shore.

The shadows of evening gradually shrouded the scene; but the moon arose in all her fulness and beauty, and shed the tender light so dear to lovers, over the romantic coast of Sestri. My soul was bathed in unutterable tenderness. I anticipated the heavenly evenings I should pass in once more wandering with Bianca by the light of that blessed moon.

It was late at night before we entered the harbor. As early next morning as I could get released from the formalities of landing, I threw myself on horseback, and hastened to the villa. As I galloped round the rocky promontory on which stands the Faro, and saw the coast of Sestri opening upon me, a thousand anxieties and doubts suddenly sprang up in my bosom. There is something fearful in returning to those we love, while yet uncertain what ills or changes absence may have effected. The turbulence of my agitation shook my very frame. I spurred my horse to redoubled speed; he was covered with foam when we both arrived panting at the gateway that opened to the grounds around the villa. I left my horse at a cottage, and walked through the grounds, that I might regain tranquillity for the approaching interview. I chid myself for having suffered mere doubts and surmises thus suddenly to overcome me; but I was always prone to be carried away by gusts of the feelings.

On entering the garden, every thing bore the same look as when I had left it; and this unchanged aspect of things reassured me. There were the alleys in which I had so often walked with Bianca, as we listened to the song of the nightingale; the same shades under which we had so often sat during the noontide heat. There were the same flowers of which she was fond; and which appeared still to be under the ministry of her hand. Every thing looked and breathed of Bianca; hope and joy flushed in my bosom at every step. I passed a little arbor, in which we had often sat and read together—a book and glove lay on the bench—It was Bianca's glove; it was a volume of the Metastasio I had given her. The glove lay in my favorite passage. I clasped them to my heart with rapture. "All is safe!" exclaimed I; "she loves me, she is still my own!"

I bounded lightly along the avenue, down which I had faltered so slowly at my departure. I beheld her favorite pavilion, which had witnessed our parting scene. The window was open, with the same vine clambering about it, precisely as when she waved and wept me an adieu. O how transporting was the contrast in my situation! As I passed near the pavilion, I heard the tones of a female voice: they thrilled through me with an appeal to my heart not to be mistaken. Before I could think, I *felt* they were Bianca's. For an instant I paused, overpowered with agitation. I feared to break so suddenly upon her. I softly ascended the steps of the pavilion. The door was open. I saw Bianca seated at a table; her back was towards me; she was warbling a soft melancholy air, and was occupied in drawing. A glance sufficed to show me that she was copying one of my own paintings. I gazed on her for a moment in a delicious tumult of emotions. She paused in her singing: a heavy sigh, almost a sob followed. I could no longer contain myself. "Bianca!" exclaimed I, in a half-smothered voice. She started at the sound, brushed back the ringlets that hung clustering about her face, darted a glance at me, uttered a piercing shriek, and would have fallen to the earth, had I not caught her in my arms.

"Bianca! my own Bianca!" exclaimed I, folding her to my bosom; my voice stifled in sobs of convulsive joy. She lay in my arms without sense or motion. Alarmed at the effects of my precipitation, I scarce knew what to do. I tried by a thousand endearing words to call her back to consciousness. She slowly recovered, and half opening her eyes, "Where am I?" murmured she faintly. " Here!" exclaimed I, pressing her to my bosom, "here—close to the heart that adores you—in the arms of your faithful Ottavio!" "Oh no! no! no!" shrieked she, starting into sudden life and terror—"away! away! leave me! leave me!"

She tore herself from my arms; rushed to a corner of the saloon, and covered her face with her hands, as if the very sight of me were baleful. I was thunderstruck. I could not believe my senses. I followed her, trembling, confounded. I endeavored to take her hand; but she shrunk from my very touch with horror.

"Good heavens, Bianca!" exclaimed I, "what is the meaning of this? Is this my reception after so long an absence? Is this the love you professed for me?"

At the mention of love, a shuddering ran through her. She turned to me a face wild with anguish: "No more of that—no more of that!" gasped she: "talk not to me of love—I—I—am married!"

I reeled as if I had received a mortal blow—a sickness struck to my very heart. I caught at a window-frame for support. For a moment or two every thing was chaos around me. When I recovered, I beheld Bianca lying on a sofa, her face buried in the pillow, and sobbing convulsively. Indignation for her fickleness for a moment overpowered every other feeling.

"Faithless—perjured!" cried I, striding across the room. But another glance at that beautiful being in distress, checked all my wrath. Anger could not dwell together with her idea in my soul.

"Oh! Bianca," exclaimed I, in anguish, "could I have dreamt of this? Could I have suspected you would have been false to me?"

She raised her face all streaming with tears, all disordered with emotion, and gave me one appealing look. "False to you!—They told me you were dead!"

"What," said I, "in spite of our constant correspondence?"

She gazed wildly at me: "Correspondence! what correspondence!"

"Have you not repeatedly received and replied to my letters?"

She clasped her hands with solemnity and fervor. "As I hope for mercy—never!"

A horrible surmise shot through my brain. "Who told you I was dead?"

"It was reported that the ship in which you embarked for Naples perished at sea."

"But who told you the report?"

She paused for an instant, and trembled:—"Filippo!"

"May the God of heaven curse him!" cried I, extending my clinched fists aloft.

"O do not curse him, do not curse him!" exclaimed she, "he is—he is—my husband!"

This was all that was wanting to unfold the perfidy that had heen practised upon me. My blood boiled like liquid fire in my veins. I gasped with rage too great for utterance—I remained for a time bewildered by the whirl of horrible thoughts that rushed through my mind. The poor victim of deception before me thought it was with her I was incensed. She faintly murmured forth her exculpation. I will not dwell upon it. I saw in it more than she meant to reveal. I saw with a glance how both of us had been betrayed.

" 'Tis well," muttered I to myself in smothered accents of concentrated fury. "He shall render an account of all this."

Bianca overheard me. New terror flashed in her countenance. "For mercy's sake, do not meet him!—say nothing of what has passed—for my sake say nothing to him—I only shall be the sufferer!"

A new suspicion darted across my mind,—"What!" exclaimed I, "do you then *fear* him? is he *unkind* to you? Tell me," reiterated I, grasping her hand, and looking her eagerly in the face, "tell me—*dares* he to use you harshly?"

"No! no! no!" cried she, faltering and embarrassed—but the glance at her face had told me volumes. I saw in her pallid and wasted features, in the prompt terror and subdued agony of her eye, a whole history of a mind broken down by tyranny. Great God! and was this beauteous flower snatched from me to be thus trampled upon? The idea roused me to madness. I clinched my teeth and my hands; I foamed at the mouth; every passion seemed to have resolved itself into the fury that like a lava boiled within my heart. Bianca shrunk from me in speechless affright. As I strode by the window, my eye darted down the alley. Fatal moment! I beheld Filippo at a distance! my brain was in delirium—I sprang from the pavilion, and was before him with the quickness of lightning. He saw me as I came rushing upon him—he turned pale, looked wildly to right and left, as if he would have fled, and trembling, drew his sword.

"Wretch!" cried I, "well may you draw your weapon!"

I spoke not another word—I snatched forth a stiletto, put by the sword which trembled in his hand, and buried my poniard in his bosom. He fell with the blow, but my rage was unsated. I sprang upon him with the blood-thirsty feeling of a tiger; redoubled my blows; mangled him in my frenzy, grasped him by the throat, until, with reiterated wounds and strangling convulsions, he expired in my grasp. I remained glaring on the countenance, horrible in death, that seemed to stare back with its protruded eyes upon me. Piercing shrieks roused me from my delirium. I looked round, and beheld Bianca flying distractedly towards us. My brain whirled—I waited not to meet her; but fled from the scene of horror. I fled forth from the garden like another Cain,—a hell within my bosom, and a curse upon my head. I fled without knowing whither, almost without knowing why. My only idea was to get farther and farther from the horrors I had left behind; as if I could throw space between myself and my conscience. I fled to the Apennines, and wandered for days and days among their savage heights. How I existed, I cannot tell—what rocks and precipices I braved, and how I braved them, I know not. I kept on and on, trying to out-travel the curse that clung to me. Alas! the shrieks of Bianca rung for ever in my ears. The horrible countenance of my victim was for ever before my eyes. The blood of Filippo cried to me from the ground. Rocks, trees, and torrents, all resounded with my crime. Then it was I felt how much more insupportable is the anguish of remorse than every other mental pang. Oh! could I but have cast off this crime that festered in my heart—could I but have regained the innocence that reigned in my breast as I entered the garden at Sestri—could I but have restored my victim to life, I felt as if I could look on with transport, even though Bianca were in his arms.

By degrees this frenzied fever of remorse settled into a permanent malady of the mind—into one of the most horrible that ever poor wretch was cursed with. Wherever I went, the countenance of him I had slain appeared to follow me. Whenever I turned my head, I beheld it behind me, hideous with the contortions of the dying moment. I have tried in every way to escape from this horrible phantom, but in vain. I know not whether it be an illusion of the mind, the consequence of my dismal education at the convent, or whether a phantom really sent by Heaven to punish me, but there it ever is—at all times—in all places. Nor has time nor habit had any effect in familiarizing me with its terrors. I have travelled from place to place—plunged into amusements—tried dissipation and distraction of every kind—all —all in vain. I once had recourse to my pencil, as a desperate experiment. I painted an exact resemblance of this phantom face. I placed it before me, in hopes that by constantly contemplating the copy, I might diminish the effect of the original. But I only doubled instead of diminishing the misery. Such is the curse that has clung to my footsteps—that has made my life a burden, but the thought of death terrible. God knows what I have suffered—what days and days, and nights and nights of sleepless torment—what a never-dying worm has preyed upon my heart—what an unquenchable fire has burned within my brain! He knows the wrongs that wrought upon my poor weak nature; that converted the tenderest of affections into the deadliest of fury. He knows best whether a frail erring creature has expiated by long-enduring torture and measureless remorse the crime of a moment of madness. Often, often have I prostrated myself in the dust, and implored that he would give me a sign of his forgiveness, and let me die.—

Thus far had I written some time since. I had meant to leave this record of misery and crime with you, to be read when I should be no more.

My prayer to Heaven has at length been heard. You were witness to my emotions last evening at the church, when the vaulted temple resounded with the words of atonement and redemption. I heard a voice speaking to me from the midst of the music; I heard it rising above the pealing of the organ and the voices of the choir—it spoke to me in tones of celestial melody —it promised mercy and forgiveness, but demanded from me full expiation. I go to make it. To-morrow I shall be on my way to Genoa, to surrender myself to justice. You who have pitied my sufferings, who have poured the balm of sympathy into my wounds, do not shrink from my memory with abhorrence now that you know my story. Recollect, that when you read of my crime I shall have atoned for it with my blood!

When the Baronet had finished, there was a universal desire expressed to see the painting of this frightful visage. After much entreaty the Baronet consented, on condition that they should only visit it one by one. He called his housekeeper, and gave her charge to conduct the gentlemen, singly, to the chamber. They all returned varying in their stories. Some affected in one way, some in another; some more, some less; but all agreeing that there was a certain something about the painting that had a very odd effect upon the feelings.

I stood in a deep bow-window with the Baronet, and could not help expressing my wonder. "After all," said I, "there are certain mysteries in our nature, certain inscrutable impulses and influences, which warrant one in being superstitious. Who can account for so many persons of different characters being thus strangely affected by a mere painting?"

"And especially when not one of them has seen it?" said the Baronet, with a smile.

"How!" exclaimed I, "not seen it?"

"Not one of them!" replied he, laying his finger on his lips, in sign of secrecy. "I saw that some of them were in a bantering vein, and did not choose that the memento of the poor Italian should be made a jest of. So I gave the housekeeper a hint to show them all to a different chamber!"

* * *

Thus end the stories of the Nervous Gentleman.

PART II

Buckthorne and His Friends

This world is the best that we live in.
To lend, or to spend, or to give in;
But to beg, or to borrow, or get a man's own,
'Tis the very worst world, sir, that ever was known.

LINES FROM AN INN WINDOW

Literary Life

Among other subjects of a traveller's curiosity, I had at one time a great craving after anecdotes of literary life; and being at London, one of the most noted places for the production of books, I was excessively anxious to know something of the animals which produced them. Chance fortunately threw me in the way of a literary man by the name of Buckthorne, an eccentric personage, who had lived much in the metropolis, and could give me the natural history of every odd animal to be met with in that wilderness of men. He readily imparted to me some useful hints upon the subject of my inquiry.

"The literary world," said he, "is made up of little confederacies, each looking upon its own members as the lights of the universe; and considering all others as mere transient meteors, doomed soon to fall and be forgotten, while its own luminaries are to shine steadily on to immortality."

"And pray," said I, "how is a man to get a peep into those confederacies you speak of? I presume an intercourse with authors is a kind of intellectual exchange, where one must bring his commodities to barter, and always give a *quid pro quo.*"

"Pooh, pooh! how you mistake," said Buckthorne, smiling; "you must never think to become popular among wits by shining. They go into society to shine themselves, not to admire the brilliancy of others. I once thought as you do, and never went into literary society without studying my part beforehand; the consequence was, that I soon got the name of an intolerable proser, and should in a little while have been completely excommunicated, had I not changed my plan of operations. No, sir, no character succeeds so well among wits as that of a good listener; or if ever you are eloquent, let it be when *tête-à-tête* with an author, and then in praise of his own works, or, what is nearly as acceptable, in disparagement of the works of his contemporaries. If ever he speaks favorably of the productions of a particular friend, dissent boldly from him; pronounce his friend to be a blockhead; never fear his being vexed; much as people speak of the irritability of authors, I never found one to take offence at such contradictions. No, no, sir, authors are particularly candid in admitting the faults of their friends.

"Indeed, I would advise you to be extremely sparing of remarks on all modern works, except to make sarcastic observations on the most distinguished writers of the day."

"Faith," said I, "I'll praise none that have not been dead for at least half a century."

"Even then," observed Mr. Buckthorne, "I would advise you to be rather cautious; for you must know that many old writers have been enlisted under the banners of different sects, and their merits have become as completely topics of party discussion as the merits of living statesmen and politicians. Nay, there have been whole periods of literature absolutely taboo'd, to use a South Sea phrase. It is, for example, as much as a man's critical reputation is worth in some circles, to say a word in praise of any of the writers of the reign of Charles the Second, or even of Queen Anne, they being all declared Frenchmen in disguise."

"And pray," said I, "when am I then to know that I am on safe grounds, being totally unacquainted with the literary landmarks, and the boundary line of fashionable taste."

"Oh!" replied he, "there is fortunately one tract of literature which forms a kind of neutral ground, on which all the literary meet amicably, and run riot in the excess of their good humor; and this is in the reigns of Elizabeth and James. Here you may praise away at random. Here it is "cut and come again;" and the more obscure the author, and the more quaint and crabbed his style, the more your admiration will smack of the real relish of the connoisseur; whose taste, like that of an epicure, is always for game that has an antiquated flavor.

"But," continued he, "as you seem anxious to know something of literary society, I will take an opportunity to introduce you to some coterie, where the talents of the day are assembled. I cannot promise you, however, that they will all be of the first order. Somehow or other, our great geniuses are not gregarious; they do not go in flocks, but fly singly in general society. They prefer mingling like common men with the multitude, and are apt to carry nothing of the author about them but the reputation. It is only the inferior orders that herd together, acquire strength and importance by their confederacies, and bear all the distinctive characteristics of their species."

A Literary Dinner

A FEW DAYS AFTER THIS CONVERSATION WITH MR. BUCKTHORNE, HE called upon me, and took me with him to a regular literary dinner. It was given by a great bookseller, or rather a company of booksellers, whose firm surpassed in length that of Shadrach, Meshech, and Abednego.

I was surprised to find between twenty and thirty guests assembled, most of whom I had never seen before. Mr. Buckthorne explained this to me, by informing me that this was a business dinner, or kind of field-day, which the house gave about twice a year to its authors. It is true they did occasionally give snug dinners to three or four literary men at a time; but then these were generally select authors, favorites of the public, such as had arrived at their sixth or seventh editions. "There are," said he, "certain geographical boundaries in the land of literature, and you may judge tolerably well of an author's popularity by the wine his bookseller gives him. An author crosses the port line about the third edition, and gets into claret; and when he has reached the sixth or seventh, he may revel in Champagne and Burgundy."

"And pray," said I, "how far may these gentlemen have reached that I see around me; are any of these claret drinkers?"

"Not exactly, not exactly. You find at these great dinners the common steady run of authors, one or two edition men; or if any others are invited, they are aware that it is a kind of republican meeting.—You understand me—a meeting of the republic of letters; and that they must expect nothing but plain substantial fare."

These hints enabled me to comprehend more fully the arrangement of the table. The two ends were occupied by two partners of the house; and the host seemed to have adopted Addison's idea as to the literary precedence of his guests. A popular poet had the post of honor; opposite to whom was a hot-pressed traveller in quarto with plates. A grave-looking antiquarian, who had produced several solid works, that were much quoted and little read, was treated with great respect, and seated next to a neat dressy gentleman in black, who had written a thin, genteel, hot-pressed octavo on political economy, that was getting into fashion. Several three-volumed duodecimo men, of fair currency, were placed about the centre of the table; while the lower end was taken up with small poets, translators, and authors who had not as yet risen into much notoriety.

The conversation during dinner was by fits and starts; breaking out here and there in various parts of the table in small flashes, and ending in smoke. The poet, who had the confidence of a man on good terms with the world, and independent of his bookseller, was very gay and brilliant, and said many clever things which set the partner next him in a roar, and delighted all the company. The other partner, however, maintained his sedateness, and kept carving on, with the air of a thorough man of business, intent upon the occupation of the moment. His gravity was explained to me by my friend Buckthorne. He informed me that the concerns of the house were admirably distributed among the partners. "Thus, for instance," said he, "the grave gentleman is the carving partner, who attends to the joints; and the other is the laughing partner, who attends to the jokes."

The general conversation was chiefly carried on at the upper end of the table, as the authors there seemed to possess the greatest courage of the tongue. As to the crew at the lower end, if they did not make much figure in talking, they did in eating. Never was there a more determined, inveterate, thoroughly sustained attack on the trencher than by this phalanx of masticators. When the cloth was removed, and the wine began to circulate, they grew very merry and jocose among themselves. Their jokes, however, if by chance any of them reached the upper end of the table, seldom produced much effect. Even the laughing partner did not think it necessary to honor them with a smile; which my neighbor Buckthorne accounted for, by informing me that there was a certain degree of popularity to be obtained before a bookseller could afford to laugh at an author's jokes.

Among this crew of questionable gentlemen thus seated below the salt, my eye singled out one in particular. He was rather shabbily dressed; though he had evidently made the most of a rusty black coat, and wore his shirt-frill plaited and puffed out voluminously at the bosom. His face was dusky, but florid, perhaps a little too florid, particularly about the nose; though the rosy hue gave the greater lustre to a twinkling black eye. He had a little the look of a boon companion, with that dash of the poor devil in it which gives an inexpressibly mellow tone to a man's humor. I had seldom seen a face of richer promise; but never was promise so ill kept. He said nothing, ate and drank with the keen appetite of a garreteer, and scarcely stopped to laugh, even at the good jokes from the upper end of the table. I inquired who he was. Buckthorne looked at him attentively: "Gad," said he, "I have seen that face before, but where I cannot recollect. He cannot be an author of any note. I suppose some writer of sermons, or grinder of foreign travels."

After dinner we retired to another room to take tea and coffee, where we were reinforced by a cloud of inferior guests,—authors of small volumes in boards, and pamphlets stitched in blue paper. These had not as yet arrived to the importance of a dinner invitation, but were invited occasionally to pass the evening in a friendly way. They were very respectful to the partners, and, indeed, seemed to stand a little in awe of them; but they paid devoted court to the lady of the house, and were extravagantly fond of the children. Some few, who did not feel confidence enough to make such advances, stood shyly off in corners, talking to one another; or turned over the portfolios of prints which they had not seen above five thousand times, or moused over the music on the forte-piano.

The poet and the thin octavo gentleman were the persons most current and at their ease in the drawing-room; being men evidently of circulation in the West End. They got on each side of the lady of the house, and paid her a thousand compliments and civilities, at some of which I thought she would have expired with delight. Every thing they said and did had the odor of fashionable life. I looked round in vain for the poor devil author in the rusty black coat; he had disappeared immediately after leaving the table, having a dread, no doubt, of the glaring light of a drawing-room. Finding nothing further to interest my attention, I took my departure soon after coffee had been served, leaving the poet, and the thin, genteel hot-pressed octavo gentleman, masters of the field.

The Club of Queer Fellows

I think it was the very next evening that, in coming out of Covent Garden Theatre with my eccentric friend Buckthorne, he proposed to give me another peep at life and character. Finding me willing for any research of the kind, he took me through a variety of the narrow courts and lanes about Covent Garden, until we stopped before a tavern from which we heard the bursts of merriment of a jovial party. There would be a loud peal of laughter, then an interval, then another peal, as if a prime wag were telling a story. After a little while there was a song, and at the close of each stanza a hearty roar, and a vehement thumping on the table.

"This is the place," whispered Buckthorne; "it is the club of queer fellows, a great resort of the small wits, third-rate actors, and newspaper critics of the theatres. Any one can go in on paying a sixpence at the bar for the use of the club."

We entered, therefore, without ceremony, and took our seats at a lone table in a dusky corner of the room. The club was assembled round a table, on which stood beverages of various kinds, according to the tastes of the individuals. The members were a set of queer fellows indeed; but what was my surprise on recognizing, in the prime wit of the meeting, the poor-devil author whom I had remarked at the booksellers' dinner for his promising face and his complete taciturnity. Matters, however, were entirely changed with him. There he was a mere cipher; here he was lord of the ascendant, the choice spirit, the dominant genius. He sat at the head of the table with his hat on, and an eye beaming even more luminously than his nose. He had a quip and a fillip for every one, and a good thing on every occasion. Nothing could be said or done without eliciting a spark from him: and I solemnly declare I have heard much worse wit even from noblemen. His jokes, it must be confessed, were rather wet, but they suited the circle over which he presided. The company were in that maudlin mood, when a little wit goes a great way. Every time he opened his lips there was sure to be a roar; and even sometimes before he had time to speak.

We were fortunate enough to enter in time for a glee composed by him expressly for the club, and which he sang with two boon companions, who would have been worthy subjects for Hogarth's pencil. As they were each provided with a written copy, I was enabled to procure the reading of it.

Merrily, merrily push round the glass,
And merrily troll the glee,
For he who won't drink till he wink, is an ass.
So, neighbor, I drink to thee.

Merrily, merrily fuddle thy nose.
Until it right rosy shall be;
For a jolly red nose, I speak under the rose,
Is a sign of good company.

We waited until the party broke up, and no one but the wit remained. He sat at the table with his legs stretched under it, and wide apart; his hands in his breeches pockets; his head drooped upon his breast; and gazing with lacklustre countenance on an empty tankard. His gayety was gone, his fire completely quenched.

My companion approached, and startled him from his fit of brown study, introducing himself on the strength of their having dined together at the booksellers'.

"By the way," said he, "it seems to me I have seen you before; your face is surely that of an old acquaintance, though for the life of me I cannot tell where I have known you."

"Very likely," replied he, with a smile; "many of my old friends have forgotten me. Though, to tell the truth, my memory in this instance is as bad as your own. If, however, it will assist your recollection in any way, my name is Thomas Dribble, at your service."

"What! Tom Dribble, who was at old Birchell's school in Warwickshire?"

"The same," said the other, coolly.

"Why, then, we are old schoolmates, though it's no wonder you don't recollect me. I was your junior by several years; don't you recollect little Jack Buckthorne?"

Here there ensued a scene of a school-fellow recognition, and a world of talk about old school times and school pranks. Mr. Dribble ended by observing, with a heavy sigh, "that times were sadly changed since those days."

"Faith, Mr. Dribble," said I, "you seem quite a different man here from what you were at dinner. I had no idea that you had so much stuff in you. There you were all silence, but here you absolutely keep the table in a roar."

"Ah! my dear sir," replied he, with a shake of the head, and a shrug of the shoulder, "I am a mere glow-worm. I never shine by daylight. Besides, it's a hard thing for a poor devil of an author to shine at the table of a rich bookseller. Who do you think would laugh at any thing I could say, when I had some of the current wits of the day about me? But here, though a poor devil, I am among still poorer devils than myself; men who look up to me as a man of letters, and a belle-esprit, and all my jokes pass as sterling gold from the mint."

"You surely do yourself injustice, sir," said I; "I have certainly heard more good things from you this evening, than from any of those beaux-esprits by whom you appear to have been so daunted."

"Ah, sir! but they have luck on their side: they are in the fashion—there's nothing like being in fashion. A man that has once got his character up for a wit is always sure of a laugh, say what he may. He may utter as much nonsense as he pleases, and all will pass current. No one stops to question the coin of a rich man; but a poor devil cannot pass off either a joke or a guinea, without its being examined on both sides. Wit and coin are always doubted with a threadbare coat."

"For my part," continued he, giving his hat a twitch a little more on one side,—"for my part, I hate your fine dinners; there's nothing, sir, like the freedom of a chop-house. I'd rather any time, have my steak and tankard among my own set, than drink claret and eat venison with your cursed civil, elegant company, who never laugh at a good joke from a poor devil for fear of its being vulgar. A good joke grows in a wet soil; it flourishes in low places, but withers on your d——d high, dry grounds. I once kept high company, sir, until I nearly ruined myself; I grew so dull, and vapid, and genteel. Nothing saved me but being arrested by my landlady, and thrown into prison; where a course of catch-clubs, eightpenny ale, and poor devil company, manured my mind, and brought it back to itself again."

As it was now growing late, we parted for the evening, though I felt anxious to know more of this practical philosopher. I was glad, therefore, when Buckthorne proposed to have another meeting, to talk over old school times, and inquired his schoolmate's address. The latter seemed at first a little shy of naming his lodgings; but suddenly, assuming an air of hardihood—"Green-arbor court, sir," exclaimed he—"Number —in Green-arbor court. You must know the place. Classic ground, sir, classic ground! It was there Goldsmith wrote his Vicar of Wakefield—I always like to live in literary haunts."

I was amused with this whimsical apology for shabby quarters. On our way homeward, Buckthorne assured me that this Dribble had been the prime wit and great wag of the school in their boyish days, and one of those unlucky urchins denominated bright geniuses. As he perceived me curious respecting his old schoolmate, he promised to take me with him in his proposed visit to Green-arbor court.

A few mornings afterward he called upon me, and we set forth on our expedition. He led me through a variety of singular alleys, and courts, and blind passages; for he appeared to be perfectly versed in all the intricate geography of the metropolis. At length we came out upon Fleet-market, and traversing it, turned up a narrow street to the bottom of a long steep flight of stone steps, called Break-neck-stairs. These, he told me, led up to Green-arbor court, and that down them poor Goldsmith might many a time have risked his neck. When we entered the court, I could not but smile to think in what out-of-the-way corners genius produces her bantlings! And the muses, those capricious dames, who, forsooth, so often refuse to visit palaces, and deny a single smile to votaries in splendid studies, and gilded drawing-rooms,—what holes and burrows will they frequent to lavish their favors on some ragged disciple!

This Green-arbor court I found to be a small square, surrounded by tall and miserable houses, the very intestines of which seemed turned inside out, to judge from the old garments and frippery fluttering from every window. It appeared to be a region of washerwomen, and lines were stretched about the little square, on which clothes were dangling to dry.

Just as we entered the square, a scuffle took place between two viragos about a disputed right to a wash-tub, and immediately the whole community was in a hubbub. Heads in mob-caps popped out of every window, and such a clamor of tongues ensued, that I was fain to stop my ears. Every amazon took part with one or other of the disputants, and brandished her arms, dripping with soap-suds, and fired away from her window as from the embrazure of a fortress; while the swarms of children nestled and cradled in every procreant chamber of this hive, waking with the noise, set up their shrill pipes to swell the general concert.

Poor Goldsmith! what a time must he have had of it, with his quiet disposition and nervous habits, penned up in this den of noise and vulgarity! How strange, that while every sight and sound was sufficient to embitter the heart, and fill it with misanthropy, his pen should be dropping the honey of Hybla! Yet it is more than probable that he drew many of his inimitable pictures of low life from the scenes which surrounded him in this abode. The circumstance of Mrs. Tibbs being obliged to wash her husband's two shirts in a neighbor's house, who refused to lend her wash-tub, may have been no sport of fancy, but a fact passing under his own eye. His landlady may have sat for the picture, and Beau Tibbs' scanty wardrobe have been a *fac-simile* of his own.

It was with some difficulty that we found our way to Dribble's lodgings. They were up two pair of stairs, in a room that looked upon the court, and when we entered, he was seated on the edge of his bed, writing at a broken table. He received us, however, with a free, open, poor-devil air, that was irresistible. It is true he did at first appear slightly confused; buttoned up his waistcoat a little higher, and tucked in a stray frill of linen. But he re-collected himself in an instant; gave a half swagger, half leer, as he stepped forth to receive us; drew a three-legged stool for Mr. Buckthorne; pointed me to a lumbering old damask chair, that looked like a dethroned monarch in exile; and bade us welcome to his garret.

We soon got engaged in conversation. Buckthorne and he had much to say about early school scenes; and as nothing opens a man's heart more than recollections of the kind, we soon drew from him a brief outline of his literary career.

The Poor-Devil Author

I BEGAN LIFE UNLUCKILY BY BEING THE WAG AND BRIGHT FELLOW AT SCHOOL; and I had the further misfortune of becoming the great genius of my native village. My father was a country attorney, and intended I should succeed him in business; but I had too much genius to study, and he was too fond of my genius to force it into the traces; so I fell into bad company, and took to bad habits. Do not mistake me. I mean that I fell into the company of village literati, and village blues, and took to writing village poetry.

It was quite the fashion in the village to be literary. There was a little knot of choice spirits of us, who assembled frequently together, formed ourselves into a Literary, Scientific, and Philosophical Society, and fancied ourselves the most learned Philos in existence. Every one had a great character assigned him, suggested by some casual habit or affectation. One heavy fellow drank an enormous quantity of tea, rolled in his arm-chair, talked sententiously, pronounced dogmatically, and was considered a second Dr. Johnson; another, who happened to be a curate, uttered coarse jokes, wrote doggerel rhymes, and was the Swift of our association. Thus we had also our Popes, and Goldsmiths, and Addisons; and a blue-stocking lady, whose drawing-room we frequented, who corresponded about nothing with all the world, and wrote letters with the stiffness and formality of a printed book, was cried up as another Mrs. Montagu. I was, by common consent, the juvenile prodigy, the poetical youth, the great genius, the pride and hope of the village, through whom it was to become one day as celebrated as Stratford on Avon.

My father died, and left me his blessing and his business. His blessing brought no money into my pocket; and as to his business, it soon deserted me; for I was busy writing poetry, and could not attend to law, and my clients, though they had great respect for my talents, had no faith in a poetical attorney.

I lost my business, therefore, spent my money, and finished my poem. It was the Pleasures of Melancholy, and was cried up to the skies by the whole circle. The Pleasures of Imagination, the Pleasures of Hope, and the Pleasures of Memory, though each had placed its author in the first rank of poets, were blank prose in comparison. Our Mrs. Montagu would cry over it from beginning to end. It was pronounced by all the members of the Literary, Scientific, and Philosophical Society, the greatest poem of the age, and all anticipated the noise it would make in the great world. There was not a doubt but the London booksellers would be mad after it, and the only fear of my friends was, that I would make a sacrifice by selling it too cheap. Every time they talked the matter over, they increased the price. They reckoned up the great sums given for the poems of certain popular writers, and determined that mine was worth more than all put together, and ought to be paid for accordingly. For my part, I was modest in my expectations, and determined that I would be satisfied with a thousand guineas. So I put my poem in my pocket, and set off for London.

My journey was joyous. My heart was light as my purse, and my head full of anticipations of fame and fortune. With what swelling pride did I cast my eyes upon old London from the heights of Highgate! I was like a general, looking down upon a place he expects to conquer. The great metropolis lay stretched before me, buried under a home-made cloud of murky smoke, that wrapped it from the brightness of a sunny day, and formed for it a kind of artificial bad weather. At the outskirts of the city, away to the west, the smoke gradually decreased until all was clear and sunny, and the view stretched uninterrupted to the blue line of the Kentish hills.

My eye turned fondly to where the mighty cupola of St. Paul swelled dimly through this misty chaos, and I pictured to myself the solemn realm of learning that lies about its base. How soon should the Pleasures of Melancholy throw this world of booksellers and printers into a bustle of business and delight! How soon should I hear my name repeated by printers' devils throughout Paternoster-row, and Angel-court, and Ave-Maria-lane, until Amen-corner should echo back the sound!

Arrived in town, I repaired at once to the most fashionable publisher. Every new author patronizes him of course. In fact, it had been determined in the village circle that he should be the fortunate man. I cannot tell you how vaingloriously I walked the streets. My head was in the clouds. I felt the airs of heaven playing about it, and fancied it already encircled by a halo of literary glory. As I passed by the windows of bookshops, I anticipated the time when my work would be shining among the hot-pressed wonders of the day; and my face, scratched on copper, or cut on wood, figuring in fellowship with those of Scott, and Byron, and Moore.

When I applied at the publisher's house, there was something in the loftiness of my air, and the dinginess of my dress, that struck the clerks with reverence. They doubtless took me for some person of consequence; probably a digger of Greek roots, or a penetrater of pyramids. A proud man in a dirty shirt is always an imposing character in the world of letters; one must feel intellectually secure before he can venture to dress shabbily; none but a great genius, or a great scholar, dares to be dirty; so I was ushered at once to the sanctum sanctorum of this high priest of Minerva.

The publishing of books is a very different affair now-a-days from what it was in the time of Bernard Lintot. I found the publisher a fashionably-dressed man, in an elegant drawing-room, furnished with sofas and portraits of celebrated authors, and cases of splendidly-bound books. He was writing letters at an elegant table. This was transacting business in style. The place seemed suited to the magnificent publications that issued from it. I rejoiced at the choice I had made of a publisher, for I always liked to encourage men of taste and spirit.

I stepped up to the table with the lofty poetical port I had been accustomed to maintain in our village circle; though I threw in it something of a patronizing air, such as one feels when about to make a man's fortune. The publisher paused with his pen in hand, and seemed waiting in mute suspense to know what was to be announced by so singular an apparition.

I put him at his ease in a moment, for I felt that I had but to come, see, and conquer. I made known my name, and the name of my poem; produced my precious roll of blotted manuscript; laid it on the table with an emphasis; and told him at once, to save time, and come directly to the point, the price was one thousand guineas.

I had given him no time to speak, nor did he seem so inclined. He continued looking at me for a moment with an air of whimsical perplexity; scanned me from head to foot; looked down at the manuscript, then up again at me, then pointed to a chair; and whistling softly to himself, went on writing his letter.

I sat for some time waiting his reply, supposing he was making up his mind; but he only paused occasionally to take a fresh dip of ink, to stroke his chin, or the tip of his nose, and then resumed his writing. It was evident his mind was intently occupied upon some other subject; but I had no idea that any other subject should be attended to, and my poem lie unnoticed on the table. I had supposed that every thing would make way for the Pleasures of Melancholy.

My gorge at length rose within me. I took up my manuscript, thrust it into my pocket, and walked out of the room; making some noise as I went out, to let my departure be heard. The publisher, however, was too much buried in minor concerns to notice it. I was suffered to walk down stairs without being called back. I sallied forth into the street, but no clerk was sent after me; nor did the publisher call after me from the drawing-room window. I have been told since, that he considered me either a madman or a fool. I leave you to judge how much he was in the wrong in his opinion.

When I turned the corner my crest fell. I cooled down in my pride and my expectations, and reduced my terms with the next bookseller to whom I applied. I had no better success; nor with a third, nor with a fourth. I then desired the booksellers to make an offer themselves; but the deuce an offer would they make. They told me poetry was a mere drug; every body wrote poetry; the market was overstocked with it. And then they said, the title of my poem was not taking; that pleasures of all kinds were worn threadbare, nothing but horrors did now-a-days, and even those were almost worn out. Tales of Pirates, Robbers, and bloody Turks, might answer tolerably well; but then they must come from some established well-known name, or the public would not look at them.

At last I offered to leave my poem with a bookseller, to read it, and judge for himself. "Why, really, my dear Mr. ——a—a—I forget your name," said he, casting an eye at my rusty coat and shabby gaiters, "really, sir, we are so pressed with business just now, and have so many manuscripts on hand to read, that we have not time to look at any new productions; but if you can call again in a week or two, or say the middle of next month, we may be able to look over your writings, and give you an answer. Don't forget, the month after next; good morning, sir; happy to see you any time you are passing this way." So saying, he bowed me out in the civilest way imaginable. In short, sir, instead of an eager competition to secure my poem, I could not even get it read! In the meantime I was harassed by letters from my friends, wanting to know when the work was to appear; who was to be my publisher; but above all things, warning me not to let it go too cheap.

There was but one alternative left. I determined to publish the poem myself; and to have my triumph over the booksellers, when it should become the fashion of the day. I accordingly published the Pleasures of Melancholy, and ruined myself. Excepting the copies sent to the reviews, and to my friends in the country, not one, I believe, ever left the bookseller's warehouse.

The printer's bill drained my purse, and the only notice that was taken of my work, was contained in the advertisements paid for by myself.

I could have borne all this, and have attributed it, as usual, to the mismanagement of the publisher, or the want of taste in the public; and could have made the usual appeal to posterity; but my village friends would not let me rest in quiet. They were picturing me to themselves feasting with the great, communing with the literary, and in the high career of fortune and renown. Every little while, some one would call on me with a letter of introduction from the village circle, recommending him to my attentions, and requesting that I would make him known in society; with a hint, that an introduction to a celebrated literary nobleman would be extremely agreeable. I determined, therefore, to change my lodgings, drop my correspondence, and disappear altogether from the view of my village admirers. Besides, I was anxious to make one more poetic attempt. I was by no means disheartened by the failure of my first. My poem was evidently too didactic. The public was wise enough. It no longer read for instruction. "They want horrors, do they?" said I: "I'faith! then they shall have enough of them." So I looked out for some quiet, retired place, where I might be out of reach of my friends, and have leisure to cook up some delectable dish of poetical "hell-broth."

I had some difficulty in finding a place to my mind, when chance threw me in the way of Canonbury Castle. It is an ancient brick tower, hard by "merry Islington;" the remains of a hunting-seat of Queen Elizabeth, where she took the pleasure of the country when the neighborhood was all woodland. What gave it particular interest in my eyes was the circumstance that it had been the residence of a poet.

It was here Goldsmith resided when he wrote his Deserted Village. I was shown the very apartment. It was a relic of the original style of the castle, with paneled wainscots and Gothic windows. I was pleased with its air of antiquity, and with its having been the residence of poor Goldy.

"Goldsmith was a pretty poet," said I to myself, "a very pretty poet, though rather of the old school. He did not think and feel so strongly as is the fashion now-a-days; but had he lived in these times of hot hearts and hot heads, he would no doubt have written quite differently."

In a few days I was quietly established in my new quarters; my books all arranged; my writing-desk placed by a window looking out into the fields; and I felt as snug as

Robinson Crusoe, when he had finished his bower. For several days I enjoyed all the novelty of change and the charms which grace new lodgings, before one has found out their defects. I rambled about the fields where I fancied Goldsmith had rambled. I explored merry Islington; ate my solitary dinner at the Black Bull, which, according to tradition, was a country-seat of Sir Walter Raleigh; and would sit and sip my wine, and muse on old times, in a quaint old room, where many a council had been held.

All this did very well for a few days. I was stimulated by novelty; inspired by the associations awakened in my mind by these curious haunts; and began to think I felt the spirit of composition stirring within me. But Sunday came, and with it the whole city world, swarming about Canonbury Castle. I could not open my window but I was stunned with shouts and noises from the cricket-ground; the late quiet road beneath my window was alive with the tread of feet and clack of tongues; and, to complete my misery, I found that my quiet retreat was absolutely a "show house," the tower and its contents being shown to strangers at sixpence a head.

There was a perpetual tramping up stairs of citizens and their families, to look about the country from the top of the tower, and to take a peep at the city through the telescope, to try if they could discern their own chimneys. And then, in the midst of a vein of thought, or a moment of inspiration, I was interrupted, and all my ideas put to flight, by my intolerable landlady's tapping at the door, and asking me if I would "just please to let a lady and gentleman come in, to take a look at Mr. Goldsmith's room." If you know any thing of what an author's study is, and what an author is himself, you must know that there was no standing this. I put a positive interdict on my room's being exhibited; but then it was shown when I was absent, and my papers put in confusion; and, on returning home one day, I absolutely found a cursed tradesman and his daughters gaping over my manuscripts, and my landlady in a panic at my appearance. I tried to make out a little longer, by taking the key in my pocket; but it would not do. I overheard mine hostess one day telling some of her customers on the stairs, that the room was occupied by an author, who was always in a tantrum if interrupted; and I immediately perceived, by a slight noise at the door, that they were peeping at me through the key-hole. By the head of Apollo, but this was quite too much! With all my eagerness for fame, and my ambition of the stare of the million, I had no idea of being exhibited by retail, at sixpence a head, and that through a key-hole. So I bid adieu to Canonbury Castle, merry Islington, and the haunts of poor Goldsmith, without having advanced a single line in my labors.

My next quarters were at a small, whitewashed cottage, which stands not far from Hampstead, just on the brow of a hill; looking over Chalk Farm and Camden Town, remarkable for the rival houses of Mother Red Cap and Mother Black Cap; and so across Crackscull Common to the distant city.

The cottage was in nowise remarkable in itself; but I regarded it with reverence, for it had been the asylum of a persecuted author. Hither poor Steele had retreated, and lain perdu, when persecuted by creditors and bailiffs—those immemorial plagues of authors and free-spirited gentlemen; and here he had written many numbers of the Spectator. It was hence, too, that he had dispatched those little notes to his lady, so full of affection and whimsicality, in which the fond husband, the careless gentleman, and the shifting spendthrift, were so oddly blended. I thought, as I first eyed the window of his apartment, that I could sit within it and write volumes.

No such thing! It was haymaking season, and, as ill-luck would have it, immediately opposite the cottage was a little ale-house, with the sign of the Load of Hay. Whether it was there in Steele's time, I cannot say; but it set all attempts at conception or inspiration at defiance. It was the resort of all the Irish haymakers who mow the broad fields in the neighborhood; and of drovers and teamsters who travel that road. Here they would gather in the endless summer twilight, or by the light of the harvest moon, and sit round a table at the door; and tipple, and laugh, and quarrel, and fight, and sing drowsy songs, and dawdle away the hours, until the deep solemn notes of St. Paul's clock would warn the varlets home.

In the daytime I was still less able to write. It was broad summer. The haymakers were at work in the fields, and the perfume of the new-mown hay brought with it the recollection of my native fields. So, instead of remaining in my room to write, I went wandering about Primrose Hill, and Hampstead Heights, and Shepherd's Fields, and all those Arcadian scenes so celebrated by London bards. I cannot tell you how many delicious hours I have passed, lying on the cocks of new-mown hay, on the pleasant slopes of some of those hills, inhaling the fragrance of the fields, while the summer-fly buzzed about me, or the grasshopper leaped into my bosom; and how I have gazed with half-shut eye upon the smoky mass of London, and listened to the distant sound of its population, and pitied the poor sons of earth, toiling in its bowels, like Gnomes in the "dark gold mine."

People may say what they please about cockney pastorals, but, after all, there is a vast deal of rural beauty about the western vicinity of London; and any one that has looked down upon the valley of West End, with its soft bosom of green pasturage lying open to the south, and dotted with cattle; the steeple of Hampstead rising among rich groves on the brow of the hill; and the learned height of Harrow in the distance; will confess that never has he seen a more absolutely rural landscape in the vicinity of a great metropolis.

Still, however, I found myself not a whit the better off for my frequent change of lodgings; and I began to discover, that in literature, as in trade, the old proverb holds good, "a rolling stone gathers no moss."

The tranquil beauty of the country played the very vengeance with me. I could not mount my fancy into the termagant vein. I could not conceive, amidst the smiling landscape, a scene of blood and murder; and the smug citizens in breeches and gaiters put all ideas of heroes and bandits out of my brain. I could think of nothing but dulcet subjects, "the Pleasures of Spring"—"the Pleasures of Solitude"—"the Pleasures of Tranquillity"—"the Pleasures of Sentiment"—nothing but pleasures; and I had the painful experience of "the Pleasures of Melancholy" too strongly in my recollection to be beguiled by them.

Chance at length befriended me. I had frequently, in my ramblings, loitered about Hampstead Hill, which is a kind of Parnassus of the metropolis. At such times I occasionally took my dinner at Jack Straw's Castle. It is a country inn so named: the very spot where that notorious rebel and his followers held their council of war. It is a favorite resort of citizens when rurally inclined, as it commands fine fresh air, and a good view of the city. I sat one day in the public room of this inn, ruminating over a beefsteak and a pint of port, when my imagination kindled up with ancient and heroic images. I had long wanted a theme and a hero; both suddenly broke upon my mind. I determined to write a poem on the history of Jack Straw. I was so full of my subject, that I was fearful of being anticipated. I wondered that none of the poets of the day, in their search after ruffian heroes, had never thought of Jack Straw. I went to work pell-mell, blotted several sheets of paper with choice floating thoughts, and battles, and descriptions, to be ready at a moment's warning. In a few days' time, I sketched out the skeleton of my poem, and nothing was wanting but to give it flesh and blood. I used to take my manuscript, and stroll about Caen-wood, and read aloud; and would dine at the Castle, by way of keeping up the vein of thought.

I was there one day, at rather a late hour, in the public room. There was no other company, but one man, who sat enjoying his pint of port at a window, and noticing the passers by. He was dressed in a green shooting-coat. His countenance was strongly marked: he had a hooked nose; a romantic eye, excepting that it had something of a squint; and altogether, as I thought, a poetical style of head. I was quite taken with the man, for you must know I am a little of a physiognomist; I set him down at once for either a poet or a philosopher.

As I like to make new acquaintances, considering every man a volume of human nature, I soon fell into conversation with the stranger, who, I was pleased to find, was by no means difficult of access. After I had dined, I joined him at the window, and we became so sociable that I proposed a bottle of wine together, to which he most cheerfully assented.

I was too full of my poem to keep long quiet on the subject, and began to talk about the origin of the tavern, and the history of Jack Straw. I found my new acquaintance to be perfectly at home on the topic, and to jump exactly with my humor in every respect. I became elevated by the wine and the conversation. In the fulness of an author's feelings, I told him of my projected poem, and repeated some passages, and he was in raptures. He was evidently of a strong poetical turn.

"Sir," said he, filling my glass at the same time, "our poets don't look at home. I don't see why we need go out of old England for robbers and rebels to write about. I like your Jack Straw, sir,—he 's a home-made hero. I like him, sir—I like him exceedingly. He 's English to the backbone—damme—Give me honest old England after all! Them's my sentiments, sir."

"I honor your sentiment," cried I, zealously; "it is exactly my own. An English ruffian is as good a ruffian for poetry as any in Italy, or Germany, or the Archipelago; but it is hard to make our poets think so."

"More shame for them!" replied the man in green. "What a plague would they have? What have we to do with their Archipelagos of Italy and Germany? Haven't we heaths and commons and highways on our own little island—ay, and stout fellows to pad the hoof over them too? Stick to home, I say,—them's my sentiments.—Come, sir, my service to you—I agree with you perfectly."

"Poets, in old times, had right notions on this subject," continued I; "witness the fine old ballads about Robin Hood, Allan a'Dale, and other stanch blades of yore."

"Right, sir, right," interrupted he; "Robin Hood! he was the lad to cry stand! to a man, and never to flinch."

"Ah, sir," said I, "they had famous bands of robbers in the good old times; those were glorious poetical days. The merry crew of Sherwood Forest, who led such a roving picturesque life 'under the greenwood tree.' I have often wished to visit their haunts, and tread the scenes of the exploits of Friar Tuck, and Clymm of the Clough, and Sir William of Cloudeslie."

"Nay, sir," said the gentleman in green, "we have had several very pretty gangs since their day. Those gallant dogs that kept about the great heaths in the neighborhood of London, about Bagshot, and Hounslow and Blackheath, for instance. Come, sir, my service to you. You don't drink."

"I suppose," cried I, emptying my glass, "I suppose you have heard of the famous Turpin, who was born in this very village of Hampstead, and who used to lurk with his gang in Epping Forest about a hundred years since?"

"Have I?" cried he, "to be sure I have! A hearty old blade that. Sound as pitch. Old Turpentine! as we used to call him. A famous fine fellow, sir."

"Well, sir," continued I, "I have visited Waltham Abbey and Chingford Church merely from the stories I heard when a boy of his exploits there, and I have searched Epping Forest for the cavern where he used to conceal himself. You must know," added I, "that I am a sort of amateur of highwaymen. They were dashing, daring fellows: the best apologies that we had for the knights-errant of yore. Ah, sir! the country has been sinking gradually into tameness and commonplace. We are losing the old English spirit. The bold knights of the Post have all dwindled down into lurking footpads and sneaking pickpockets; there's no such thing as a dashing, gentleman-like robbery committed now-a-days on the King's highway: a man may roll from one end of England to the other in a drowsy coach, or jingling post-chaise, without any other adventure than that of being occasionally overturned, sleeping in damp sheets, or having an ill-cooked dinner. We hear no more of public coaches being stopped and robbed by a well-mounted gang of resolute fellows, with pistols in their hands, and crapes over their faces. What a pretty poetical incident was it, for example, in domestic life, for a family carriage, on its way to a country seat, to be attacked about dark; the old gentleman eased of his purse and watch, the ladies of their necklaces and earings, by a politely spoken highwayman on a blood mare, who afterwards leaped the hedge and galloped across the country, to the admiration of Miss Caroline, the daughter, who would write a long and romantic account of the adventure to her friend, Miss Juliana, in town. Ah, sir! we meet with nothing of such incidents now-a-days."

"That, sir," said my companion, taking advantage of a pause, when I stopped to recover breath, and to take a glass of wine which he had just poured out, "that, sir, craving your pardon, is not owing to any want of old English pluck. It is the effect of this cursed system of banking. People do not travel with bags of gold as they did formerly. They have post notes, and drafts on bankers. To rob a coach is like catching a crow, where you have nothing but carrion flesh and feathers for your pains. But a coach in old times, sir, was as rich as a Spanish galleon. It turned out the yellow boys bravely. And a private carriage was a cool hundred or two at least."

I cannot express how much I was delighted with the sallies of my new acquaintance. He told me that he often frequented the Castle, and would be glad to know more of me; and I promised myself many a pleasant afternoon with him, when I should read him my poem as it proceeded, and benefit by his remarks; for it was evident he had the true poetical feeling.

"Come, sir," said he, pushing the bottle: "Damme, I like you! you're a man after my own heart. I'm cursed slow in making new acquaintances. One must be on the reserve, you know. But when I meet with a man of your kidney, damme, my heart jumps at once to him. Them's my sentiments, sir. Come, sir, here's Jack Straw's health! I presume one can drink it now-a-days without treason!"

"With all my heart," said I gayly, "and Dick Turpin's into the bargain!"

"Ah, sir," said the man in green, "those are the kind of men for poetry. The Newgate Calendar, sir! the Newgate Calendar is your only reading! There's the place to look for bold deeds and dashing fellows."

We were so much pleased with each other that we sat until a late hour. I insisted on paying the bill, for both my purse and my heart were full, and I agreed that he should pay the score at our next meeting. As the coaches had all gone that ran between Hampstead and London, we had to return on foot. He was so delighted with the idea of my poem, that he could talk of nothing else. He made me repeat such passages as I could remember; and though I did it in a very mangled manner, having a wretched memory, yet he was in raptures.

Every now and then he would break out with some scrap which he would misquote most terribly, would rub his hands and exclaim, "By Jupiter, that's fine, that's noble! Damme, sir, if I can conceive how you hit upon such ideas!"

I must confess I did not always relish his misquotations, which sometimes made absolute nonsense of the passages; but what author stands upon trifles when he is praised?

Never had I spent a more delightful evening. I did not perceive how the time flew. I could not bear to separate, but continued walking on, arm in arm, with him, past my lodgings, through Camden Town, and across Crackskull Common, talking the whole way about my poem.

When we were half way across the common, he interrupted me in the midst of a quotation, by telling me that this had been a famous place for footpads, and was still occasionally infested by them; and that a man had recently been shot there in attempting to defend himself.—"The more fool he!" cried I; "a man is an idiot to risk life, or even limb, to save a paltry purse of money. It's quite a different case from that of a duel, where one's honor is concerned. For my part," added I, "I should never think of making resistance against one of those desperadoes."

"Say you so?" cried my friend in green, turning suddenly upon me, and putting a pistol to my breast; "why, then, have at you, my lad!—come—disburse! empty! unsack!"

In a word, I found that the muse had played me another of her tricks, and had betrayed me into the hands of a footpad. There was no time to parley; he made me turn my pockets inside out; and hearing the sound of distant footsteps, he made one fell swoop upon purse, watch, and all; gave me a thwack over my unlucky pate that laid me sprawling on the ground, and scampered away with his booty.

I saw no more of my friend in green until a year or two afterwards; when I caught a sight of his poetical countenance among a crew of scapegraces heavily ironed, who were on the way for transportation. He recognized me at once, tipped me an impudent wink, and asked me how I came on with the history of Jack Straw's Castle.

The catastrophe at Crackskull Common put an end to my summer's campaign. I was cured of my poetical enthusiasm for rebels, robbers, and highwaymen. I was put out of conceit of my subject, and, what was worse, I was lightened of my purse, in which was almost every farthing I had in the world. So I abandoned Sir Richard Steele's cottage in despair, and crept into less celebrated, though no less poetical and airy lodgings in a garret in town.

I now determined to cultivate the society of the literary, and to enroll myself in the fraternity of authorship. It is by the constant collision of mind, thought I, that authors strike out the sparks of genius, and kindle up with glorious conceptions. Poetry is evidently a contagious complaint. I will keep company with poets; who knows but I may catch it as others have done?

I found no difficulty in making a circle of literary acquaintances, not having the sin of success lying at my door: indeed the failure of my poem was a kind of recommendation to their favor. It is true my new friends were not of the most brilliant names in literature; but then if you would take their words for it, they were like the prophets of old, men of whom the world was not worthy; and who were to live in future ages, when the ephemeral favorites of the day should be forgotten.

I soon discovered, however, that the more I mingled in literary society, the less I felt capable of writing; that poetry was not so catching as I imagined; and that in familiar life there was often nothing less poetical than a poet. Besides, I wanted the esprit du corps to turn these literary fellowships to any account. I could not bring myself to enlist in any particular sect. I saw something to like in them all, but found that would never do, for that the tacit condition on which a man enters into one of these sects is, that he abuses all the rest.

I perceived that there were little knots of authors who lived with, and for, and by one another. They considered themselves the salt of the earth. They fostered and kept up a conventional vein of thinking and talking, and joking on all subjects; and they cried each other up to the skies. Each sect had its particular creed; and set up certain authors as divinities, and fell down and worshipped them; and considered every one who did not worship them, or who worshipped any other, as a heretic and an infidel.

In quoting the writers of the day, I generally found them extolling names of which I had scarcely heard, and talking slightingly of others who were the favorites of the public. If I mentioned any recent work from the pen of a first-rate author, they had not read it; they had not time to read all that was spawned from the press; he wrote too much to write well;—and then they would break out into raptures about some Mr. Timson, or Tomson, or Jackson, whose works were neglected at the present day, but who was to be the wonder and delight of posterity! Alas! what heavy debts is this neglectful world daily accumulating on the shoulders of poor posterity!

But, above all, it was edifying to hear with what contempt they would talk of the great. Ye gods! how immeasurably the great are despised by the small fry of literature! It is true, an exception was now and then made of some nobleman, with whom, perhaps, they had casually shaken hands at an election, or hob or nobbed at a public dinner, and was pronounced a "devilish good fellow," and "no humbug;" but, in general, it was enough for a man to have a title, to be the object of their sovereign disdain: you have no idea how poetically and philosophically they would talk of nobility.

For my part this affected me but little; for though I had no bitterness against the great, and did not think the worse of a man for having innocently been born to a title, yet I did not feel my-self at present called upon to resent the indignities poured upon them by the little. But the hostility to the great writers of the day went sore against the grain with me. I could not enter into such feuds, nor participate in such animosities. I had not become author sufficiently to hate other authors. I could still find pleasure in the novelties of the press, and could find it in my heart to praise a contemporary, even though he were successful. Indeed I was miscellaneous in my taste, and could not confine it to any age or growth of writers. I could turn with delight from the glowing pages of Byron to the cool and polished raillery of Pope; and after wandering among the sacred groves of Paradise Lost, I could give myself up to voluptuous abandonment in the enchanted bowers of Lalla Rookh.

"I would have my authors," said I, "as various as my wines, and, in relishing the strong and the racy, would never decry the sparkling and exhilarating. Port and sherry are excellent stand-by's, and so is Madeira; but claret and Burgundy may be drunk now and then without disparagement to one 's palate, and Champagne is a beverage by no means to be despised."

Such was the tirade I uttered one day when a little flushed with ale at a literary club. I uttered it, too, with something of a flourish, for I thought my simile a clever one. Unluckily, my auditors were men who drank beer and hated Pope; so my figure about wines went for nothing, and my critical toleration was looked upon as downright heterodoxy. In a word, I soon became like a freethinker in religion, an outlaw from every sect, and fair game for all. Such are the melancholy consequences of not hating in literature.

I see you are growing weary, so I will be brief with the residue of my literary career. I will not detain you with a detail of my various attempts to get astride of Pegasus; of the poems I have written which were never printed, the plays I have presented which were never performed, and the tracts I have published which were never purchased. It seemed as if booksellers, managers, and the very public, had entered into a conspiracy to starve me. Still I could not prevail upon myself to give up the trial, nor abandon those dreams of renown in which I had indulged. How should I be able to look the literary circle of my native village in the face, if I were so completely to falsify their predictions? For some time longer, therefore, I continued to write for fame, and was, of course, the most miserable dog in existence, besides being in continual risk of starvation. I accumulated loads of literary treasure on my shelves—loads which were to be treasures to posterity; but, alas! they put not a penny into my purse. What was all this wealth to my present necessities? I could not patch my elbows with an ode; nor satisfy my hunger with blank verse. "Shall a man fill his belly with the east wind?" says the proverb. He may as well do so as with poetry.

I have many a time strolled sorrowfully along, with a sad heart and an empty stomach, about five o'clock, and looked wistfully down the areas in the west end of the town, and seen through the kitchen windows the fires gleaming, and the joints of meat turning on the spits and dripping with gravy, and the cook-maids beating up puddings, or trussing turkeys, and felt for the moment that if I could but have the run of one of those kitchens, Apollo and the Muses might have the hungry heights of Parnassus for me. Oh, sir! talk of meditations among the tombs—they are nothing so melancholy as the meditations of a poor devil without penny in pouch, along a line of kitchen-windows towards dinner-time.

At length, when almost reduced to famine and despair, the idea all at once entered my head, that perhaps I was not so clever a fellow as the village and myself had supposed. It was the salvation of me. The moment the idea popped into my brain it brought conviction and comfort with it. I awoke as from a dream —I gave up immortal fame to those who could live on air; took to writing for mere bread; and have ever since had a very tolerable life of it. There is no man of letters so much at his ease, sir, as he who has no character to gain or lose. I had to train myself to it a little, and to clip my wings short at first, or they would have carried me up into poetry in spite of myself. So I determined to begin by the opposite extreme, and abandoning the higher regions of the craft, I came plump down to the lowest, and turned creeper.

"Creeper! and pray what is that?" said I.

"Oh, sir, I see you are ignorant of the language of the craft; a creeper is one who furnishes the newspapers with paragraphs at so much a line; and who goes about in quest of misfortunes; attends the Bow-street Office; the Courts of Justice, and every other den of mischief and iniquity. We are paid at the rate of a penny a line, and as we can sell the same paragraph to almost every paper, we sometimes pick up a very decent day's work. Now and then the Muse is unkind, or the day uncommonly quiet, and then we rather starve; and sometimes the unconscionable editors will clip our paragraphs when they are a little too rhetorical, and snip off two-pence or three-pence at a go. I have many a time had my pot of porter snipped off of my dinner in this way, and have had to dine with dry lips. However, I cannot complain. I rose gradually in the lower ranks of the craft, and am now, I think, in the most comfortable region of literature."

"And pray," said I, "what may you be at present?"

"At present," said he, "I am a regular job-writer, and turn my hand to any thing. I work up the writings of others at so much a sheet; turn off translations; write second-rate articles to fill up reviews and magazines; compile travels and voyages, and furnish theatrical criticisms for the newspapers. All this authorship, you perceive, is anonymous; it gives me no reputation except among the trade; where I am considered an author of all work, and am always sure of employ. That's the only reputation I want. I sleep soundly, without dread of duns or critics, and leave immortal fame to those that choose to fret and fight about it. Take my word for it, the only happy author in this world is he who is below the care of reputation."

Notoriety

When we had emerged from the literary nest of honest Dribble, and had passed safely through the dangers of Break-neck-stairs, and the labyrinths of Fleet-market, Buckthorne indulged in many comments upon the peep into literary life which he had furnished me.

I expressed my surprise at finding it so different a world from what I had imagined. "It is always so," said he, "with strangers. The land of literature is a fairy land to those who view it from a distance, but, like all other landscapes, the charm fades on a nearer approach, and the thorns and briers become visible. The republic of letters is the most factious and discordant of all republics, ancient or modern."

"Yet," said I, smiling, "you would not have me take honest Dribble's experience as a view of the land. He is but a mousing owl; a mere groundling. We should have quite a different strain from one of those fortunate authors whom we see sporting about the empyreal heights of fashion, like swallows in the blue sky of a summer's day."

"Perhaps we might," replied he, "but I doubt it. I doubt whether if any one, even of the most successful, were to tell his actual feelings, you would not find the truth of friend Dribble's philosophy with respect to reputation. One you would find carrying a gay face to the world, while some vulture critic was preying upon his very liver. Another, who was simple enough to mistake fashion for fame, you would find watching countenances, and cultivating invitations, more ambitious to figure in the *beau monde* than the world of letters, and apt to be rendered wretched by the neglect of an illiterate peer, or a dissipated duchess. Those who were rising to fame, you would find tormented with anxiety to get higher; and those who had gained the summit, in constant apprehension of a decline.

"Even those who are indifferent to the buzz of notoriety, and the farce of fashion, are not much better off, being incessantly harassed by intrusions on their leisure, and interruptions of their pursuits; for, whatever may be his feelings, when once an author is launched into notoriety, he must go the rounds until the idle curiosity of the day is satisfied, and he is thrown aside to make way for some new caprice. Upon the whole, I do not know but he is most fortunate who engages in the whirl through ambition, however tormenting; as it is doubly irksome to be obliged to join in the game without being interested in the stake.

"There is a constant demand in the fashionable world for novelty; every nine days must have its wonder, no matter of what kind. At one time it is an author; at another a fire-eater; at another a composer, an Indian juggler, or an Indian chief; a man from the North Pole or the Pyramids; each figures through his brief term of notoriety, and then makes way for the succeeding wonder. You must know that we have oddity fanciers among our ladies of rank, who collect about them all kinds of remarkable beings; fiddlers, statesmen, singers, warriors, artists, philosophers, actors, and poets; every kind of personage, in short, who is noted for something peculiar; so that their routs are like fancy balls, where every one comes 'in character.'

"I have had infinite amusement at these parties in noticing how industriously every one was playing a part, and acting out of his natural line. There is not a more complete game at cross purposes than the intercourse of the literary and the great. The fine gentleman is always anxious to be thought a wit, and the wit a fine gentleman.

I have noticed a lord endeavoring to look wise and talk learnedly with a man of letters, who was aiming at a fashionable air, and the tone of a man who had lived about town. The peer quoted a score or two of learned authors, with whom he would fain be thought intimate, while the author talked of Sir John this, and Sir Harry that, and extolled the Burgundy he had drunk at Lord Such-a-one's. Each seemed to forget that he could only be interesting to the other in his proper character. Had the peer been merely a man of erudition, the author would never have listened to his prosing; and had the author known all the nobility in the Court Calendar, it would have given him no interest in the eyes of the peer.

"In the same way I have seen a fine lady, remarkable for beauty, weary a philosopher with flimsy metaphysics, while the philosopher put on an awkward air of gallantry, played with her fan, and prattled bout the Opera. I have heard a sentimental poet talk very stupidly with a statesman about the national debt: and on joining a knot of scientific old gentlemen conversing in a corner, expecting to hear the discussion of some valuable discovery, I found they were only amusing themselves with a fat story."

A Practical Philosopher

THE ANECDOTES I HAD HEARD OF BUCKTHORNE'S EARLY SCHOOLMATE, together with a variety of peculiarities which I had remarked in himself, gave me a strong curiosity to know something of his own history. I am a traveller of the good old school, and am fond of the custom laid down in books, according to which, whenever travellers met, they sat down forthwith, and gave a history of themselves and their adventures. This Buckthorne, too, was a man much to my taste; he had seen the world, and mingled with society, yet retained the strong eccentricities of a man who had lived much alone. There was a careless dash of good-humor about him which pleased me exceedingly; and at times an odd tinge of melancholy mingled with his humor, and gave it an additional zest. He was apt to run into long speculations upon society and manners, and to indulge in whimsical views of human nature; yet there was nothing ill-tempered in his satire. It ran more upon the follies than the vices of mankind; and even the follies of his fellow-man were treated with the leniency of one who felt himself to be but frail. He had evidently been a little chilled and buffeted by fortune, without being soured thereby: as some fruits become mellower and more generous in their flavor from having been bruised and frost-bitten.

I have always had a great relish for the conversation of practical philosophers of this stamp, who have profited by the "sweet uses" of adversity without imbibing its bitterness; who have learnt to estimate the world rightly, yet good-humoredly; and who, while they perceive the truth of the saying, that "all is vanity," are yet able to do so without vexation of spirit.

Such a man was Buckthorne. In general a laughing philosopher; and if at any time a shade of sadness stole across his brow, it was but transient; like a summer cloud, which soon goes by, and freshens and revives the fields over which it passes.

I was walking with him one day in Kensington Gardens—for he was a knowing epicure in all the cheap pleasures and rural haunts within reach of the metropolis. It was a delightful warm morning in spring; and he was in the happy mood of a pastoral citizen, when just turned loose into grass and sunshine. He had been watching a lark which, rising from a bed of daisies and yellow-cups, had sung his way up to a bright snowy cloud floating in the deep blue sky.

"Of all birds," said he, "I should like to be a lark. He revels in the brightest time of the day, in the happiest season of the year, among fresh meadows and opening flowers; and when he has sated himself with the sweetness of earth, he wings his flight up to heaven as if he would drink in the melody of the morning stars. Hark to that note! How it comes trilling down upon the ear! What a stream of music, note falling over note in delicious cadence! Who would trouble his head about operas and concerts when he could walk in the fields and hear such music for nothing? These are the enjoyments which set riches at scorn, and make even a poor man independent:

> I care not, Fortune, what you do deny:
> You cannot rob me of free nature's grace;
> You cannot shut the windows of the sky,
> Through which Aurora shows her bright'ning face;
> You cannot bar my constant feet to trace
> The woods and lawns by living streams at eve—

"Sir, there are homilies in nature's works worth all the wisdom of the schools, if we could but read them rightly, and one of the pleasantest lessons I ever received in time of trouble, was from hearing the notes of a lark."

I profited by this communicative vein to intimate to Buckthorne a wish to know something of the events of his life, which I fancied must have been an eventful one.

He smiled when I expressed my desire. "I have no great story," said he, "to relate. A mere tissue of errors and follies. But, such as it is, you shall have one epoch of it, by which you may judge of the rest." And so, without any further prelude, he gave me the following anecdotes of his early adventures.

Buckthorne:

or the Young Man of Great Expectations

I WAS BORN TO VERY LITTLE PROPERTY, BUT TO GREAT EXPECTATIONS—WHICH is, perhaps, one of the most unlucky fortunes a man can be born to. My father was a country gentleman, the last of a very ancient and honorable, but decayed family, and resided in an old hunting-lodge in Warwickshire. He was a keen sportsman, and lived to the extent of his moderate income, so that I had little to expect from that quarter; but then I had a rich uncle by the mother's side, a penurious, accumulating curmudgeon, who it was confidently expected would make me his heir, because he was an old bachelor, because I was named after him, and because he hated all the world except myself.

He was, in fact, an inveterate hater, a miser even in misanthropy, and hoarded up a grudge as he did a guinea. Thus, though my mother was an only sister, he had never forgiven her marriage with my father, against whom he had a cold, still, immovable pique, which had lain at the bottom of his heart, like a stone in a well, ever since they had been schoolboys together. My mother, however, considered me as the intermediate being that was to bring every thing again into harmony, for she looked upon me as a prodigy—God bless her! my heart overflows whenever I recall her tenderness. She was the most excellent, the most indulgent of mothers. I was her only child: it was a pity she had no more, for she had fondness of heart enough to have spoiled a dozen!

I was sent at an early age to a public school, sorely against my mother's wishes; but my father insisted that it was the only way to make boys hardy. The school was kept by a conscientious prig of the ancient system, who did his duty by the boys intrusted to his care: that is to say, we were flogged soundly when we did not get our lessons. We were put in classes, and thus flogged on in droves along the highways of knowledge, in much the same manner as cattle are driven to market; where those that are heavy in gait, or short in leg, have to suffer for the superior alertness or longer limbs of their companions.

For my part, I confess it with shame, I was an incorrigible laggard. I have always had the poetical feeling, that is to say, I have always been an idle fellow, and prone to play the vagabond. I used to get away from my books and school whenever I could, and ramble about the fields. I was surrounded by seductions for such a temperament. The schoolhouse was an old-fashioned whitewashed mansion, of wood and plaster, standing on the skirts of a beautiful village: close by it was the venerable church, with a tall Gothic spire; before it spread a lovely green valley, with a little stream glistening along through willow groves; while a line of blue hills bounding the landscape gave rise to many a summer-day-dream as to the fairy land that lay beyond.

In spite of all the scourgings I suffered at that school to make me love my book, I cannot but look back upon the place with fondness. Indeed, I considered this frequent flagellation as the common lot of humanity, and the regular mode in which scholars were made.

My kind mother used to lament over my details of the sore trials I underwent in the cause of learning; but my father turned a deaf ear to her expostulations. He had been flogged through school himself, and swore there was no other way of making a man of parts; though, let me speak it with all due reverence, my father was but an indifferent illustration of his theory, for he was considered a grievous blockhead.

My poetical temperament evinced itself at a very early period. The village church was attended every Sunday by a neighboring squire, the lord of the manor, whose park stretched quite to the village, and whose spacious country-seat seemed to take the church under its protection. Indeed, you would have thought the church had been consecrated to him instead of to the Deity. The parish clerk bowed low before him, and the vergers humbled themselves unto the dust in his presence. He always entered a little late, and with some stir; striking his cane emphatically on the ground, swaying his hat in his hand, and looking loftily to the right and left as he walked slowly up the aisle; and the parson, who always ate his Sunday dinner with him, never commenced service until he appeared. He sat with his family in a large pew, gorgeously lined, humbling himself devoutly on velvet cushions, and reading lessons of meekness and lowliness of spirit out of splendid gold and morocco prayer-books. Whenever the parson spoke of the difficulty of a rich man's entering the kingdom of heaven, the eyes of the congregation would turn towards the "grand pew," and I thought the squire seemed pleased with the application.

The pomp of this pew, and the aristocratical air of the family, struck my imagination wonderfully; and I fell desperately in love with a little daughter of the squire's, about twelve years of age. This freak of fancy made me more truant from my studies than ever. I used to stroll about the squire's park, and lurk near the house, to catch glimpses of this little damsel at the windows, or playing about the lawn, or walking out with her governess.

I had not enterprise nor impudence enough to venture from my concealment. Indeed I felt like an arrant poacher, until I read one or two of Ovid's Metamorphoses, when I pictured myself as some sylvan deity, and she a coy wood-nymph of whom I was in pursuit. There is something extremely delicious in these early awakenings of the tender passion. I can feel even at this moment the throbbing of my boyish bosom, whenever by chance I caught a glimpse of her white frock fluttering among the shrubbery. I carried about in my bosom a volume of Waller, which I had purloined from my mother's library; and I applied to my little fair one all the compliments lavished upon Sacharissa.

At length I danced with her at a school-ball. I was so awkward a booby, that I dared scarcely speak to her; I was filled with awe and embarrassment in her presence; but I was so inspired, that my poetical temperament for the first time broke out in verse, and I fabricated some glowing rhymes, in which I be-rhymed the little lady under the favorite name of Sacharissa. I slipped the verses, trembling and blushing, into her hand the next Sunday as she came out of church. The little prude handed them to her mamma; the mamma handed them to the squire; the squire, who had no soul for poetry, sent them in dudgeon to the schoolmaster; and the schoolmaster, with a barbarity worthy of the dark ages, gave me a sound and peculiarly humiliating flogging for thus trespassing upon Parnassus. This was a sad outset for a votary of the muse; it ought to have cured me of my passion for poetry; but it only confirmed it, for I felt the spirit of a martyr rising within me. What was as well, perhaps, it cured me of my passion for the young lady; for I felt so indignant at the ignominious horsing I had incurred in celebrating her charms, that I could not hold up my head in church. Fortunately for my wounded sensibility, the Midsummer holidays came on, and I returned home. My mother, as usual, inquired into all my school concerns, my little pleasures, and cares, and sorrows; for boyhood has its share of the one as well as of the other. I told her all, and she was indignant at the treatment I had experienced. She fired up at the arrogance of the squire, and the prudery of the daughter; and as to the schoolmaster, she wondered where was the use of having schoolmasters, and why boys could not remain at home, and be educated by tutors, under the eye of their mothers. She asked to see the verses I had written, and she was delighted with them; for, to confess the truth, she had a pretty taste in poetry. She even showed them to the parson's wife, who protested they were charming; and the parson's three daughters insisted on each having a copy of them.

All this was exceedingly balsamic, and I was still more consoled and encouraged, when the young ladies, who were the blue-stockings of the neighborhood, and had read Dr. Johnson's Lives quite through, assured my mother that great geniuses never studied, but were always idle; upon which I began to surmise that I was myself something out of the common run. My father, however, was of a very different opinion; for when my mother, in the pride of her heart, showed him my copy of verses, he threw them out of the window, asking her "if she meant to make a ballad-monger of the boy?" But he was a careless, common thinking man, and I cannot say that I ever loved him much; my mother absorbed all my filial affection.

I used occasionally, on holidays, to be sent on short visits to the uncle who was to make me his heir; they thought it would keep me in his mind, and render him fond of me. He was a withered, anxious-looking old fellow, and lived in a desolate old country-seat, which he suffered to go to ruin from absolute niggardliness. He kept but one man-servant, who had lived, or rather starved, with him for years. No woman was allowed to sleep in the house. A daughter of the old servant lived by the gate, in what had been a porter's lodge, and was permitted to come into the house about an hour each day, to make the beds, and cook a morsel of provisions. The park that surrounded the house was all run wild: the trees were grown out of shape; the fish-ponds stagnant; the urns and statues fallen from their pedestals, and buried among the rank grass. The hares and pheasants were so little molested, except by poachers, that they bred in great abundance, and sported about the rough lawns and weedy avenues. To guard the premises, and frighten off robbers, of whom he was somewhat apprehensive, and visitors, of whom he was in almost equal awe, my uncle kept two or three bloodhounds, who were always prowling round the house, and were the dread of the neighboring peasantry. They were gaunt and half starved, seemed ready to devour one from mere hunger, and were an effectual check on any stranger's approach to this wizard castle.

Such was my uncle's house, which I used to visit now and then during the holidays. I was, as I before said, the old man's favorite; that is to say, he did not hate me so much as he did the rest of the world. I had been apprized of his character, and cautioned to cultivate his good will; but I was too young and careless to be a courtier, and, indeed, have never been sufficiently studious of my interests to let them govern my feelings. However, we jogged on very well together, and as my visits cost him almost nothing, they did not seem to be very unwelcome. I brought with me my fishing-rod, and half supplied the table from the fish-ponds.

Our meals were solitary and unsocial. My uncle rarely spoke; he pointed to whatever he wanted, and the servant perfectly understood him. Indeed, his man John, or Iron John, as he was called in the neighborhood, was a counterpart of his master. He was a tall, bony old fellow, with a dry wig, that seemed made of cow's tail, and a face as tough as though it had been made of cow's hide. He was generally clad in a long, patched livery coat, taken out of the wardrobe of the house, and which bagged loosely about him, having evidently belonged to some corpulent predecessor, in the more plenteous days of the mansion. From long habits of taciturnity the hinges of his jaws seemed to have grown absolutely rusty, and it cost him as much effort to set them ajar, and to let out a tolerable sentence, as it would have done to set open the iron gates of the park, and let out the old family carriage, that was dropping to pieces in the coach-house.

I cannot say, however, but that I was for some time amused with my uncle's peculiarities. Even the very desolateness of the establishment had something in it that hit my fancy. When the weather was fine, I used to amuse myself in a solitary way, by rambling about the park, and coursing like a colt across its lawns. The hares and pheasants seemed to stare with surprise to see a human being walking these forbidden grounds by daylight. Sometimes I amused myself by jerking stones, or shooting at birds with a bow and arrows, for to have used a gun would have been treason. Now and then my path was crossed by a little red-headed, ragged-tailed urchin, the son of the woman at the lodge, who ran wild about the premises. I tried to draw him into familiarity, and to make a companion of him, but he seemed to have imbibed the strange unsociable character of every thing around him, and always kept aloof; so I considered him as another Orson, and amused myself with shooting at him with my bow and arrows, and he would hold up his breeches with one hand, and scamper away like a deer.

There was something in all this loneliness and wildness strangely pleasing to me. The great stables, empty and weather-broken, with the names of favorite horses over the vacant stalls; the windows bricked and boarded up; the broken roofs, garrisoned by rooks and jackdaws, all had a singularly forlorn appearance. One would have concluded the house to be totally uninhabited, were it not for a little thread of blue smoke, which now and then curled up like a corkscrew, from the centre of one of the wide chimneys, where my uncle's starveling meal was cooking.

My uncle's room was in a remote corner of the building, strongly secured, and generally locked. I was never admitted into this strong-hold, where the old man would remain for the greater part of the time, drawn up, like a veteran spider, in the citadel of his web. The rest of the mansion, however, was open to me, and I wandered about it unconstrained. The damp and rain which beat in through the broken windows, crumbled the paper from the walls, mouldered the pictures, and gradually destroyed the furniture. I loved to roam about the wide waste chambers in bad weather, and listen to the howling of the wind, and the banging about of the doors and window-shutters. I pleased myself with the idea how completely, when I came to the estate, I would renovate all things, and make the old building ring with merriment, till it was astonished at its own jocundity.

The chamber which I occupied on these visits, had been my mother's when a girl. There was still the toilet-table of her own adorning, the landscapes of her own drawing. She had never seen it since her marriage, but would often ask me, if every thing was still the same. All was just the same, for I loved that chamber on her account, and had taken pains to put every thing in order, and to mend all the flaws in the windows with my own hands. I anticipated the time when I should once more welcome her to the house of her fathers, and restore her to this little nestling place of her childhood.

At length my evil genius, or what, perhaps, is the same thing, the Muse, inspired me with the notion of rhyming again. My uncle, who never went to church, used on Sundays to read chapters out of the Bible; and Iron John, the woman from the lodge, and myself, were his congregation. It seemed to be all one to him what he read, so long as it was something from the Bible. Sometimes, therefore, it would be the Song of Solomon, and this withered anatomy would read about being "stayed with flagons, and comforted with apples, for he was sick of love." Sometimes he would hobble, with spectacles on nose, through whole chapters of hard Hebrew names in Deuteronomy, at which the poor woman would sigh and groan, as if wonderfully moved. His favorite book, however, was "The Pilgrim's Progress;" and when he came to that part which treats of Doubting Castle and Giant Despair, I thought invariably of him and his desolate old country-seat. So much did the idea amuse me, that I took to scribbling about it under the trees in the park; and in a few days had made some progress in a poem, in which I had given a description of the place, under the name of Doubting Castle, and personified my uncle as Giant Despair.

I lost my poem somewhere about the house, and I soon suspected that my uncle had found it, as he harshly intimated to me that I could return home, and that I need not come and see him again till he should send for me.

Just about this time my mother died. I cannot dwell upon the circumstance. My heart, careless and wayward as it is, gushes with the recollection. Her death was an event that perhaps gave a turn to all my after fortunes. With her died all that made home attractive. I had no longer any body whom I was ambitious to please, or fearful to offend. My father was a good kind of man in his way, but he had bad maxims in education, and we differed in material points. It makes a vast difference in opinion about the utility of the rod, which end happens to fall to one's share. I never could be brought into my father's way of thinking on the subject.

I now, therefore, began to grow very impatient of remaining at school, to be flogged for things that I did not like. I longed for variety, especially now that I had not my uncle's house to resort to, by way of diversifying the dulness of school, with the dreariness of his country-seat.

I was now almost seventeen, tall for my age, and full of idle fancies. I had a roving, inextinguishable desire to see different kinds of life, and different orders of society; and this vagrant humor had been fostered in me by Tom Dribble, the prime wag and great genius of the school, who had all the rambling propensities of a poet.

I used to sit at my desk in the school, on a fine summer's day, and instead of studying the book which lay open before me, my eye was gazing through the window on the green fields and blue hills. How I envied the happy groups seated on the tops of stage-coaches, chatting, and joking, and laughing, as they were whirled by the school-house on their way to the metropolis. Even the wagoners, trudging along beside their ponderous teams, and traversing the kingdom from one end to the other, were objects of envy to me: I fancied to myself what adventures they must experience, and what odd scenes of life they must witness. All this was, doubtless, the poetical temperament working within me, and tempting me forth into a world of its own creation, which I mistook for the world of real life.

While my mother lived, this strong propensity to rove was counteracted by the stronger attractions of home, and by the powerful ties of affection which drew me to her side; but now that she was gone, the attraction had ceased; the ties were severed.

I had no longer an anchorage-ground for my heart, but was at the mercy of every vagrant impulse. Nothing but the narrow allowance on which my father kept me, and the consequent penury of my purse, prevented me from mounting the top of a stage-coach, and launching myself adrift on the great ocean of life.

Just about this time the village was agitated for a day or two, by the passing through of several caravans, containing wild beasts, and other spectacles for a great fair annually held at a neighboring town.

I had never seen a fair of any consequence, and my curiosity was powerfully awakened by this bustle of preparation. I gazed with respect and wonder at the vagrant personages who accompanied these caravans. I loitered about the village inn, listening with curiosity and delight to the slang talk and cant jokes of the showmen and their followers; and I felt an eager desire to witness this fair, which my fancy decked out as something wonderfully fine.

A holiday afternoon presented, when I could be absent from noon until evening. A wagon was going from the village to the fair; I could not resist the temptation, nor the eloquence of Tom Dribble, who was a truant to the very heart's core. We hired seats, and set off full of boyish expectation. I promised myself that I would but take a peep at the land of promise, and hasten back again before my absence should be noticed.

Heavens! how happy I was on arriving at the fair! How I was enchanted with the world of fun and pageantry around me! The humors of Punch, the feats of the equestrians, the magical tricks of the conjurors! But what principally caught my attention was an itinerant theatre, where a tragedy, pantomime, and farce, were all acted in the course of half an hour; and more of the dramatis personae murdered, than at either Drury Lane or Covent Garden in the course of a whole evening. I have since seen many a play performed by the best actors in the world, but never have I derived half the delight from any that I did from this first representation.

There was a ferocious tyrant in a skullcap like an inverted porringer, and a dress of red baize, magnificently embroidered with gilt leather; with his face so bewhiskered, and his eyebrows so knit and expanded with burnt cork, that he made my heart quake within me, as he stamped about the little stage. I was enraptured too with the surpassing beauty of a distressed damsel in faded pink silk, and dirty white muslin, whom he held in cruel captivity by way of gaining her affections, and who wept, and wrung her hands, and flourished a ragged white handkerchief from the top of an impregnable tower of the size of a bandbox.

Even after I had come out from the play, I could not tear myself from the vicinity of the theatre, but lingered, gazing and wondering, and laughing at the dramatis personae as they per-formed their antics, or danced upon a stage in front of the booth, to decoy a new set of spectators.

I was so bewildered by the scene, and so lost in the crowd of sensations that kept swarming upon me, that I was like one entranced. I lost my companion, Tom Dribble, in a tumult and scuffle that took place near one of the shows; but I was too much occupied in mind to think long about him. I strolled about until dark, when the fair was lighted up, and a new scene of magic opened upon me. The illumination of the tents and booths, the brilliant effect of the stages decorated with lamps, with dramatic groups flaunting about them in gaudy dresses, contrasted splendidly with the surrounding darkness; while the uproar of drums, trumpets, fiddles, hautboys, and cymbals, mingled with the harangues of the showmen, the squeaking of Punch, and the shouts and laughter of the crowd, all united to complete my giddy distraction.

Time flew without my perceiving it. When I came to myself and thought of the school, I hastened to return. I inquired for the wagon in which I had come: it had been gone for hours! I asked the time: it was almost midnight! A sudden quaking seized me. How was I to get back to school? I was too weary to make the journey on foot, and I knew not where to apply for a conveyance. Even if I should find one, could I venture to disturb the schoolhouse long after midnight—to arouse that sleeping lion the usher in the very midst of his night's rest?—the idea was too dreadful for a delinquent schoolboy. All the horrors of return rushed upon me. My absence must long before this have been remarked;—and absent for a whole night!—a deed of darkness not easily to be expiated. The rod of the pedagogue budded forth into tenfold terrors before my affrighted fancy. I pictured to myself punishment and humiliation in every variety of form, and my heart sickened at the picture. Alas! how often are the petty ills of boyhood as painful to our tender natures, as are the sterner evils of manhood to our robuster minds.

I wandered about among the booths, and I might have derived a lesson from my actual feelings, how much the charms of this world depend upon ourselves; for I no longer saw any thing gay or delightful in the revelry around me. At length I lay down, wearied and perplexed, behind one of the large tents, and, covering myself with the margin of the tent cloth, to keep off the night chill, I soon fell asleep.

I had not slept long, when I was awakened by the noise of merriment within an adjoining booth. It was the itinerant theatre, rudely constructed of boards and canvas.

I peeped through an aperture, and saw the whole dramatis personae, tragedy, comedy, and pantomime, all refreshing themselves after the final dismissal of their auditors. They were merry and gamesome, and made the flimsy theatre ring with their laughter. I was astonished to see the tragedy tyrant in red baize and fierce whiskers, who had made my heart quake as he strutted about the boards, now trans-formed into a fat, good-humored fellow; the beaming porringer laid aside from his brow, and his jolly face washed from all the terrors of burnt cork. I was delighted, too, to see the distressed damsel, in faded silk and dirty muslin, who had trembled under his tyranny, and afflicted me so much by her sorrows, now seated familiarly on his knee, and quaffing from the same tankard. Harlequin lay asleep on one of the benches; and monks, satyrs, and vestal virgins, were grouped together, laughing outrageously at a broad story told by an unhappy count, who had been barbarously murdered in the tragedy.

This was, indeed, novelty to me. It was a peep into another planet. I gazed and listened with intense curiosity and enjoyment. They had a thousand odd stories and jokes about the events of the day, and burlesque descriptions and mimickings of the spectators who had been admiring them. Their conversation was full of allusions to their adventures at different places where they had exhibited; the characters they had met with in different villages; and the ludicrous difficulties in which they had occasionally been involved. All past cares and troubles were now turned, by these thoughtless beings, into matter of merriment, and made to contribute to the gayety of the moment. They had been moving from fair to fair about the kingdom, and were the next morning to set out on their way to London. My resolution was taken. I stole from my nest, and crept through a hedge into a neighboring field, where I went to work to make a tatterdemalion of myself. I tore my clothes; soiled them with dirt; begrimed my face and hands, and crawling near one of the booths, purloined an old hat, and left my new one in its place. It was an honest theft, and I hope may not hereafter rise up in judgment against me.

I now ventured to the scene of merry-making, and presenting myself before the dramatic corps, offered myself as a volunteer. I felt terribly agitated and abashed, for never before "stood I in such a presence." I had addressed myself to the manager of the company. He was a fat man, dressed in dirty white, with a red sash fringed with tinsel swathed round his body; his face was smeared with paint, and a majestic plume towered from an old spangled black bonnet. He was the Jupiter Tonans of this Olympus, and was surrounded by the inferior gods and goddesses of his court. He sat on the end of a bench, by a table, with one arm akimbo, and the other extended to the handle of a tankard, which he had slowly set down from his lips, as he surveyed me from head to foot. It was a moment of awful scrutiny; and I fancied the groups around all watching as in silent suspense, and waiting for the imperial nod.

He questioned me as to who I was; what were my qualifications; and what terms I expected. I passed myself off for a discharged servant from a gentleman's family; and as, happily, one does not require a special recommendation to get admitted into bad company, the questions on that head were easily satisfied. As to my accomplishments, I could spout a little poetry, and knew several scenes of plays, which I had learnt at school exhibitions, I could dance ——. That was enough. No further questions were asked me as to accomplishments; it was the very thing they wanted; and as I asked no wages but merely meat and drink, and safe conduct about the world, a bargain was struck in a moment.

Behold me, therefore, transformed on a sudden from a gentleman student to a dancing buffoon; for such, in fact, was the character in which I made my debut. I was one of those who formed the groups in the dramas, and was principally employed on the stage in front of the booth to attract company. I was equipped as a satyr, in a dress of drab frieze that fitted to my shape, with a great laughing mask, ornamented with huge ears and short horns. I was pleased with the disguise, because it kept me from the danger of being discovered, whilst we were in that part of the country; and as I had merely to dance and make antics, the character was favorable to a debutant—being almost on a par with Simon Smug's part of the lion, which required nothing but roaring.

I cannot tell you how happy I was at this sudden change in my situation. I felt no degradation, for I had seen too little of society to be thoughtful about the difference of rank; and a boy of sixteen is seldom aristocratical. I had given up no friend, for there seemed to be no one in the world that cared for me now that my poor mother was dead; I had given up no pleasure, for my pleasure was to ramble about and indulge the flow of a poetical imagination, and I now enjoyed it in perfection. There is no life so truly poetical as that of a dancing buffoon.

It may be said that all this argued grovelling inclinations. I do not think so. Not that I mean to vindicate myself in any great degree: I know too well what a whimsical compound I am. But in this instance I was seduced by no love of low company, nor disposition to indulge in low vices. I have always despised the brutally vulgar, and had a disgust at vice, whether in high or low life. I was governed merely by a sudden and thoughtless impulse. I had no idea of resorting to this profession as a mode of life, or of attaching myself to these people, as my future class of society. I thought merely of a temporary gratification to my curiosity, and an indulgence of my humors. I had already a strong relish for the peculiarities of character and the varieties of situation, and I have always been fond of the comedy of life, and desirous of seeing it through all its shifting scenes.

In mingling, therefore, among mountebanks and buffoons, I was protected by the very vivacity of imagination which had led me among them; I moved about, enveloped, as it were, in a protecting delusion, which my fancy spread around me. I assimilated to these people only as they struck me poetically; their whimsical ways and a certain picturesqueness in their mode of life entertained me; but I was neither amused nor corrupted by their vices. In short, I mingled among them, as Prince Hal did among his graceless associates, merely to gratify my humor.

I did not investigate my motives in this manner, at the time, for I was too careless and thoughtless to reason about the matter; but I do so now, when I look back with trembling to think of the ordeal to which I unthinkingly exposed myself, and the manner in which I passed through it. Nothing, I am convinced, but the poetical temperament, that hurried me into the scrape, brought me out of it without my becoming an arrant vagabond.

Full of the enjoyment of the moment, giddy with the wildness of animal spirits, so rapturous in a boy, I capered, I danced, I played a thousand fantastic tricks about the stage, in the villages in which we exhibited; and I was universally pronounced the most agreeable monster that had ever been seen in those parts. My disappearance from school had awakened my father's anxiety; for I one day heard a description of myself cried before the very booth in which I was exhibiting, with the offer of a reward for any intelligence of me. I had no great scruple about letting my father suffer a little uneasiness on my account; it would punish him for past indifference, and would make him value me the more when he found me again.

I have wondered that some of my comrades did not recognize me in the stray sheep that was cried; but they were all, no doubt, occupied by their own concerns. They were all laboring seriously in their antic vocation; for folly was a mere trade with most of them, and they often grinned and capered with heavy hearts. With me, on the contrary, it was all real. I acted *con amore,* and rattled and laughed from the irrepressible gayety of my spirits. It is true that, now and then, I started and looked grave on receiving a sudden thwack from the wooden sword of Harlequin in the course of my gambols, as it brought to mind the birch of my schoolmaster. But I soon got accustomed to it, and bore all the cuffing, mid kicking, and tumbling about, which form the practical wit of your itinerant pantomime, with a good humor that made me a prodigious favorite.

The country campaign of the troop was soon at an end, and we set off for the metropolis, to perform at the fairs which are held in its vicinity. The greater part of our theatrical property was sent on direct, to be in a state of preparation for the opening of the fairs; while a detachment of the company travelled slowly on, foraging among the villages. I was amused with the desultory, hap-hazard kind of life we led; here to-day and gone to-morrow. Sometimes revelling in ale-houses, sometimes feasting under hedges in the green fields. When audiences were crowded, and business profitable, we fared well; and when otherwise, we fared scantily, consoled ourselves, and made up with anticipations of the next day's success.

At length the increasing frequency of coaches hurrying past us, covered with passengers; the increasing number of carriages, carts, wagons, gigs, droves of cattle and flocks of sheep, all thronging the road; the snug country boxes with trim flower-gardens, twelve feet square, and their trees twelve feet high, all powdered with dust, and the innumerable seminaries for young ladies and gentlemen situated along the road for the benefit of country air and rural retirement; all these insignia announced that the mighty London was at hand. The hurry, and the crowd, and the bustle, and the noise, and the dust, increased as we proceeded, until I saw the great cloud of smoke hanging in the air, like a canopy of state, over this queen of cities.

In this way, then, did I enter the metropolis, a strolling vagabond, on the top of a caravan, with a crew of vagabonds about me; but I was as happy as a prince; for, like Prince Hal, I felt myself superior to my situation, and knew that I could at any time cast it off, and emerge into my proper sphere.

How my eyes sparkled as we passed Hyde Park Corner, and I saw splendid equipages rolling by; with powdered footmen behind, in rich liveries, with fine nosegays, and gold-headed canes; and with lovely women within, so sumptuously dressed, and so surpassingly fair! I was always extremely sensible to female beauty, and here I saw it in all its powers of fascination: for whatever may be said of "beauty unadorned," there is something almost awful in female loveliness decked out in jewelled state. The swanlike neck encircled with diamonds; the raven locks clustered with pearls; the ruby glowing on the snowy bosom, are objects which I could never contemplate without emotion; and a dazzling white arm clasped with bracelets, and taper, transparent fingers, laden with sparkling rings, are to me irresistible.

My very eyes ached as I gazed at the high and courtly beauty before me. It surpassed all that my imagination had conceived of the sex. I shrank, for a moment, into shame at the company in which I was placed, and repined at the vast distance that seemed to intervene between me and these magnificent beings.

I forbear to give a detail of the happy life I led about the skirts of the metropolis, playing at the various fairs held there during the latter part of spring, and the beginning of summer. This continued change from place to place, and scene to scene, fed my imagination with novelties, and kept my spirits in a perpetual state of excitement. As I was tall of my age, I aspired, at one time, to play heroes in tragedy; but, after two or three trials, I was pronounced by the manager totally unfit for the line; and our first tragic actress, who was a large woman, and held a small hero in abhorrence, confirmed his decision.

The fact is, I had attempted to give point to language which had no point, and nature to scenes which had no nature. They said I did not fill out my characters; and they were right. The characters had all been prepared for a different sort of man. Our tragedy hero was a round, robustious fellow, with an amazing voice; who stamped and slapped his breast until his wig shook again; and who roared and bellowed out his bombast until every phrase swelled upon the ear like the sound of a kettle-drum. I might as well have attempted to fill out his clothes as his characters. When we had a dialogue together, I was nothing before him, with my slender voice and discriminating manner. I might as well have attempted to parry a cudgel with a small-sword. If he found me in any way gaining ground upon him, he would take refuge in his mighty voice, and throw his tones like peals of thunder at me, until they were drowned in the still louder thunders of applause from the audience.

To tell the truth, I suspect that I was not shown fair play, and that there was management at the bottom; for without vanity I think I was a better actor than he. As I had not embarked in the vagabond line through ambition, I did not repine at lack of preferment; but I was grieved to find that a vagrant life was not without its cares and anxieties; and that jealousies, intrigues, and mad ambition, were to be found even among vagabonds.

Indeed, as I became more familiar with my situation, and the delusions of fancy gradually faded away, I began to find that my associates were not the happy careless creatures I had at first imagined them. They were jealous of each other's talents; they quarrelled about parts, the same as the actors on the grand theatres; they quarrelled about dresses; and there was one robe of yellow silk, trimmed with red, and a head-dress of three rumpled ostrich-feathers, which were continually setting the ladies of the company by the ears. Even those who had attained the highest honors were not more happy than the rest; for Mr. Flimsey himself, our first tragedian, and apparently a jovial good-humored fellow, confessed to me one day, in the fulness of his heart, that he was a miserable man. He had a brother-in-law, a relative by marriage, though not by blood, who was manager of a theatre in a small country town. And this same brother ("a little more than kin but less than kind") looked down upon him, and treated him with contumely, because, forsooth, he was but a strolling player. I tried to console him with the thoughts of the vast applause he daily received, but it was all in vain. He declared that it gave him no delight, and that he should never be a happy man, until the name of Flimsey rivalled the name of Crimp.

How little do those before the scenes know of what passes behind! how little can they judge, from the countenances of actors, of what is passing in their hearts! I have known two lovers quarrel like cats behind the scenes, who were, the moment after, to fly into each other's embraces. And I have dreaded, when our Belvidera was to take her farewell kiss of her Jaffier, lest she should bite a piece out of his cheek. Our tragedian was a rough joker off the stage; our prime clown the most peevish mortal living. The latter used to go about snapping and snarling, with a broad laugh painted on his countenance; and I can assure you, that whatever may be said of the gravity of a monkey, or the melancholy of a gibed cat, there is no more melancholy creature in existence than a mountebank off duty.

The only thing in which all parties agreed, was to backbite the manager, and cabal against his regulations. This, however, I have since discovered to be a common trait of human nature, and to take place in all communities. It would seem to be the main business of man to repine at government. In all situations of life into which I have looked, I have found mankind divided into two grand parties: those who ride, and those who are ridden. The great struggle of life seems to be which shall keep in the saddle. This, it appears to me, is the fundamental principle of politics whether in great or little life. However, I do not mean to moralize—but one cannot always sink the philosopher.

Well, then, to return to myself, it was determined, as I said, that I was not fit for tragedy, and, unluckily, as my study was bad, having a very poor memory, I was pronounced unfit for comedy also; besides, the line of young gentlemen was already engrossed by an actor with whom I could not pretend to enter into competition, he having filled it for almost half a century. I came down again, therefore, to pantomime. In consequence, however, of the good offices of the manager's lady, who had taken a liking to me, I was promoted from the part of the satyr to that of the lover; and with my face patched and painted, a huge cravat of paper, a steeple-crowned hat, and dangling long-skirted sky-blue coat, was metamorphosed into the lover of Columbine. My part did not call for much of the tender and sentimental. I had merely to pursue the fugitive fair one; to have a door now and then slammed in my face; to run my head occasionally against a post; to tumble and roll about with Pantaloon and the Clown; and to endure the hearty thwacks of Harlequin's wooden sword.

As ill luck would have it, my poetical temperament began to ferment within me, and to work out new troubles. The inflammatory air of a great metropolis, added to the rural scenes in which the fairs were held, such as Greenwich Park, Epping Forest, and the lovely valley of the West End, had a powerful effect upon me. While in Greenwich Park, I was witness to the old holiday games of running down hill, and kissing in the ring; and then the firmament of blooming faces and blue eyes that would be turned towards me, as I was playing antics on the stage; all these set my young blood and my poetical vein in full flow. In short, I played the character to the life, and became desperately enamoured of Columbine. She was a trim, well-made, tempting girl, with a roguish dimpling face, and fine chestnut hair clustering all about it. The moment I got fairly smitten, there was an end to all playing. I was such a creature of fancy and feeling, that I could not put on a pretended, when I was powerfully affected by a real emotion. I could not sport with a fiction that came so near to the fact. I became too natural in my acting to succeed. And then, what a situation for a lover! I was a mere stripling, and she played with my passion; for girls soon grow more adroit and knowing in these matters than your awkward youngsters. What agonies had I to suffer! Every time that she danced in front of the booth, and made such liberal displays of her charms, I was in torment. To complete my misery, I had a real rival in Harlequin, an active, vigorous, knowing varlet, of six-and-twenty. What had a raw, inexperienced youngster like me to hope from such a competition?

I had still, however, some advantages in my favor. In spite of my change of life, I retained that indescribable something which always distinguishes the gentleman; that something which dwells in a man's air and deportment, and not in his clothes; and which is as difficult for a gentleman to put off, as for a vulgar fellow to put on. The company generally felt it, and used to call me Little Gentleman Jack. The girl felt it too, and, in spite of her predilection for my powerful rival, she liked to flirt with me. This only aggravated my troubles, by increasing my passion, and awakening the jealousy of her party-colored lover.

Alas! think what I suffered at being obliged to keep up an ineffectual chase after my Columbine through whole pantomimes; to see her carried off in the vigorous arms of the happy Harlequin; and to be obliged, instead of snatching her from him, to tumble sprawling with Pantaloon and the Clown, and bear the infernal and degrading thwacks of my rival's weapon of lath, which, may heaven confound him! (excuse my passion,) the villain laid on with a malicious good-will: nay, I could absolutely hear him chuckle and laugh beneath his accursed mask—I beg pardon for growing a little warm in my narrative—I wish to be cool, but these recollections will sometimes agitate me. I have heard and read of many desperate and deplorable situations of lovers, but none, I think, in which true love was ever exposed to so severe and peculiar a trial.

This could not last long; flesh and blood, at least such flesh and blood as mine, could not bear it. I had repeated heart-burnings and quarrels with my rival, in which he treated me with the mortifying forbearance of a man towards a child. Had he quarrelled outright with me, I could have stomached it, at least I should have known what part to take; but to be humored and treated as a child in the presence of my mistress, when I felt all the bantam spirit of a little man swelling within me—Gods! it was insufferable!

At length, we were exhibiting one day at West End fair, which was at that time a very fashionable resort, and often beleaguered with gay equipages from town. Among the spectators that filled the first row of our little canvas theatre one afternoon, when I had to figure in a pantomime, were a number of young ladies from a boarding-school, with their governess. Guess my confusion, when, in the midst of my antics, I beheld among the number my quondam flame; her whom I had berhymed at school, her for whose charms I had smarted so severely, the cruel Sacharissa! What was worse, I fancied she recollected me, and was repeating the story of my humiliating flagellation, for I saw her whispering to her companions and her governess. I lost all consciousness of the part I was acting, and of the place where I was. I felt shrunk to nothing, and could have crept into a rat-hole—unluckily, none was open to receive me. Before I could recover from my confusion, I was tumbled over by Pantaloon and the clown, and I felt the sword of Harlequin making vigorous assaults in a manner most degrading to my dignity.

Heaven and earth! was I again to suffer martyrdom in this ignominious manner, in the knowledge and even before the very eyes of this most beautiful, but most disdainful of fair ones? All my long-smothered wrath broke out at once; the dormant feelings of the gentleman arose within me. Stung to the quick by intolerable mortification, I sprang on my feet in an instant; leaped upon Harlequin like a young tiger; tore off his mask; buffeted him in the face; and soon shed more blood on the stage, than had been spilt upon it during a whole tragic campaign of battles and murders.

As soon as Harlequin recovered from his surprise, he returned my assault with interest. I was nothing in his hands. I was game, to be sure, for I was a gentleman; but he had the clownish advantage of bone and muscle. I felt as if I could have fought even unto the death; and I was likely to do so, for he was, according to the boxing phrase, "putting my head into chancery," when the gentle Columbine flew to my assistance. God bless the women! they are always on the side of the weak and the oppressed!

The battle now became general; the dramatis personae ranged on either side. The manager interposed in vain; in vain were his spangled black bonnet and towering white feathers seen whisking about, and nodding, and bobbing in the thickest of the fight. Warriors, ladies, priests, satyrs, kings, queens, gods, and goddesses, all joined pell-mell in the affray; never, since the conflict under the walls of Troy, had there been such a chance-medley warfare of combatants, human and divine. The audience applauded, the ladies shrieked, and fled from the theatre; and a scene of discord ensued that baffles all description.

Nothing but the interference of the peace-officers restored some degree of order. The havoc, however, among dresses and decorations, put an end to all further acting for that day. The battle over, the next thing was to inquire why it was begun; a common question among politicians after a bloody and unprofitable war, and one not always easy to be answered. It was soon traced to me, and my unaccountable transport of passion, which they could only attribute to my having *run a muck*. The manager was judge and jury, and plaintiff into the bargain; and in such cases justice is always speedily administered. He came out of the fight as sublime a wreck as the Santissima Trinidada. His gallant plumes, which once towered aloft, were drooping about his ears; his robe of state hung in ribands from his back, and but ill concealed the ravages he had suffered in the rear. He had received kicks and cuffs from all sides during the tumult; for every one took the opportunity of slyly gratifying some lurking grudge on his fat carcass. He was a discreet man, and did not choose to declare war with all his company, so he swore all those kicks and cuffs had been given by me, and I let him enjoy the opinion. Some wounds he bore, however, which wore the incontestable traces of a woman's warfare: his sleek rosy cheek was scored by trickling furrows, which were ascribed to the nails of my intrepid and devoted Columbine. The ire of the monarch was not to be appeased; he had suffered in his person, and he had suffered in his purse; his dignity, too, had been insulted, and that went for something; for dignity is always more irascible, the more petty the potentate. He wreaked his wrath upon the beginners of the affray, and Columbine and myself were discharged, at once, from the company.

Figure me, then, to yourself, a stripling of little more than sixteen, a gentleman by birth, a vagabond by trade, turned adrift upon the world, making the best of my way through the crowd of West End fair; my mountebank dress fluttering in rags about me; the weeping Columbine hanging upon my arm, in splendid but tattered finery; the tears coursing one by one down her face, carrying off the red paint in torrents, and literally "preying upon her damask cheek."

The crowd made way for us as we passed, and hooted in our rear. I felt the ridicule of my situation, but had too much gallantry to desert this fair one, who had sacrificed every thing for me. Having wandered through the fair, we emerged, like another Adam and Eve, into unknown regions, and "had the world before us, where to choose." Never was a more disconsolate pair seen in the soft valley of West End. The luckless Columbine cast many a lingering look at the fair, which seemed to put on a more than usual splendor: its tents, and booths, and party-colored groups, all brightening in the sunshine, and gleaming among the trees; and its gay flags and streamers fluttering in the light summer airs. With a heavy sigh she would lean on my arm and proceed. I had no hope nor consolation to give her; but she had linked herself to my fortunes, and she was too much of a woman to desert me.

Pensive and silent, then, we traversed the beautiful fields which lie behind Hampstead, and wandered on, until the fiddle, and the hautboy, and the shout, and the laugh, were swallowed up in the deep sound of the big bass-drum, and even that died away into a distant rumble. We passed along the pleasant, sequestered walk of Nightingale-lane. For a pair of lovers, what scene could be more propitious?—But such a pair of lovers! Not a nightingale sang to soothe us: the very gipsies, who were encamped there during the fair, made no offer to tell the fortunes of such an ill-omened couple, whose fortunes, I suppose, they thought too legibly written to need an interpreter; and the gipsy children crawled into their cabins, and peeped out fearfully at us as we went by. For a moment I paused, and was almost tempted to turn gipsy, but the poetical feeling, for the present, was fully satisfied, and I passed on. Thus we travelled and travelled, like a prince and princess in a nursery tale, until we had traversed a part of Hampstead Heath, and arrived in the vicinity of Jack Straw's Castle. Here, wearied and dispirited, we seated ourselves on the margin of the hill, hard by the very milestone where Whittington of yore heard the Bow-bells ring out the presage of his future greatness. Alas! no bell rung an invitation to us, as we looked disconsolately upon the distant city. Old London seemed to wrap itself unsociably in its mantle of brown smoke, and to offer no encouragement to such a couple of tatterdemalions.

For once, at least, the usual course of the pantomime was reversed, Harlequin was jilted, and the lover had carried off Columbine in good earnest. But what was I to do with her? I could not take her in my hand, return to my father, throw myself on my knees, and crave his forgiveness and blessing, according to dramatic usage. The very dogs would have chased such a draggled-tailed beauty from the grounds.

In the midst of my doleful dumps, some one tapped me on the shoulder, and, looking up, I saw a couple of rough sturdy fellows standing behind me. Not knowing what to expect, I jumped on my legs, and was preparing again to make battle, but was tripped up and secured in a twinkling.

"Come, come, young master," said one of the fellows, in a gruff but good-humored tone, "don't let's have any of your tantrums; one would have thought you had had swing enough for this bout. Come; it's high time to leave off harlequinading, and go home to your father."

In fact, I had fallen into the hands of remorseless men. The cruel Sacharissa had proclaimed who I was, and that a reward had been offered throughout the country for any tidings of me; and they had seen a description of me which had been inserted in the public papers. Those harpies, therefore, for the mere sake of filthy lucre, were resolved to deliver me over into the hands of my father, and the clutches of my pedagogue.

In vain I swore I would not leave my faithful and afflicted Columbine. In vain I tore myself from their grasp, and flew to her; and vowed to protect her; and wiped the tears from her cheek, and with them a whole blush that might have vied with the carnation for brilliancy. My persecutors were inflexible; they even seemed to exult in our distress; and to enjoy this theatrical display of dirt, and finery, and tribulation. I was carried off in despair, leaving my Columbine destitute in the wide world; but many a look of agony did I cast back at her as she stood gazing piteously after me from the brink of Hampstead Hill; so forlorn, so fine, so ragged, so bedraggled, yet so beautiful.

Thus ended my first peep into the world. I returned home, rich in good-for-nothing experience, and dreading the reward I was to receive for my improvement. My reception, however, was quite different from what I had expected. My father had a spice of the devil in him, and did not seem to like me the worse for my freak, which he termed "sowing my wild oats." He happened to have some of his sporting friends to dine the very day of my return; they made me tell some of my adventures, and laughed heartily at them.

One old fellow, with an outrageously red nose, took to me hugely. I heard him whisper to my father that I was a lad of mettle, and might make something clever; to which my father replied, that I had good points, but was an ill-broken whelp, and required a great deal of the whip. Perhaps this very conversation raised me a little in his esteem, for I found the red-nosed old gentleman was a veteran fox-hunter of the neighborhood, for whose opinion my father had vast deference. Indeed, I believe he would have pardoned any thing in me more readily than poetry, which he called a cursed, sneaking, puling, housekeeping employment, the bane of all fine manhood. He swore it was unworthy of a youngster of my expectations, who was one day to have so great an estate, and would be able to keep horses and hounds, and hire poets to write songs for him into the bargain.

I had now satisfied, for a time, my roving propensity. I had exhausted the poetical feeling. I had been heartily buffeted out of my love for theatrical display. I felt humiliated by my exposure, and willing to hide my head any where for a season, so that I might be out of the way of the ridicule of the world; for I found folks not altogether so indulgent abroad as they were at my father's table. I could not stay at home; the house was intolerably doleful now that my mother was no longer there to cherish me. Every thing around spoke mournfully of her. The little flower-garden in which she delighted was all in disorder and overrun with weeds. I attempted for a day or two to arrange it, but my heart grew heavier and heavier as I labored. Every little broken-down flower, that I had seen her rear so tenderly, seemed to plead in mute eloquence to my feelings. There was a favorite honeysuckle which I had seen her often training with assiduity, and had heard her say it would be the pride of her garden. I found it grovelling along the ground, tangled and wild, and twining round every worthless weed; and it struck me as an emblem of myself, a mere scatterling, running to waste and uselessness. I could work no longer in the garden.

My father sent me to pay a visit to my uncle, by way of keeping the old gentleman in mind of me. I was received, as usual, without any expression of discontent, which we always considered equivalent to a hearty welcome. Whether he had ever heard of my strolling freak or not, I could not discover, he and his man were both so taciturn. I spent a day or two roaming about the dreary mansion and neglected park, and felt at one time, I believe, a touch of poetry, for I was tempted to drown myself in a fish-pond; I rebuked the evil spirit, however, and it left me. I found the same red-headed boy running wild about the park, but I felt in no humor to hunt him at present. On the contrary, I tried to coax him to me, and to make friends with him; but the young savage was untamable.

When I returned from my uncle's, I remained at home for some time, for my father was disposed, he said, to make a man of me. He took me out hunting with him, and I became a great favorite of the red-nosed squire, because I rode at every thing, never refused the boldest leap, and was always sure to be in at the death. I used often, however, to offend my father at hunting-dinners, by taking the wrong side in politics. My father was amazingly ignorant, so ignorant, in fact, as not to know that he knew nothing. He was stanch, however, to church and king, and full of old-fashioned prejudices. Now I had picked up a little knowledge in politics and religion during my rambles with the strollers, and found myself capable of setting him right as to many of his antiquated notions. I felt it my duty to do so; we were apt, therefore, to differ occasionally in the political discussions which sometimes arose at those hunting-dinners.

I was at that age when a man knows least, and is most vain of his knowledge, and when he is extremely tenacious in defending his opinion upon subjects about which he knows nothing. My father was a hard man for any one to argue with, for he never knew when he was refuted. I sometimes posed him a little, but then he had one argument that always settled the question; he would threaten to knock me down. I believe he at last grew tired of me, because I both outtalked and outrode him. The red-nosed squire, too, got out of conceit with me, because in the heat of the chase, I rode over him one day as he and his horse lay sprawling in the dirt: so I found myself getting into disgrace with all the world, and would have got heartily out of humor with myself, had I not been kept in tolerable self-conceit by the parson's three daughters.

They were the same who had admired my poetry on a former occasion, when it had brought me into disgrace at school; and I had ever since retained an exalted idea of their judgment. Indeed, they were young ladies not merely of taste but of science. Their education had been superintended by their mother, who was a blue-stocking.

They knew enough of botany to tell the technical names of all the flowers in the garden, and all their secret concerns into the bargain. They knew music too, not mere common-place music, but Rossini and Mozart, and they sang Moore's Irish Melodies to perfection. They had pretty little work-tables, covered with all kinds of objects of taste; specimens of lava, and painted eggs, and work-boxes, painted and varnished by themselves. They excelled in knotting and netting, and painted in water-colors; and made feather fans, and fire-screens, and worked in silks and worsteds; and talked French and Italian, and knew Shakspeare by heart. They even knew something of geology and mineralogy; and went about the neighborhood knocking stones to pieces, to the great admiration and perplexity of the country folk.

I am a little too minute, perhaps, in detailing their accomplishments, but I wish to let you see that these were not common-place young ladies, but had pretensions quite above the ordinary run. It was some consolation to me, therefore, to find favor in such eyes. Indeed, they had always marked me out for a genius, and considered my late vagrant freak as fresh proof of the fact. They observed that Shakspeare himself had been a mere pickle in his youth; that he had stolen a deer, as every one knew, and kept loose company, and consorted with actors: so I comforted myself marvellously with the idea of having so decided a Shakspearian trait in my character.

The youngest of the three, however, was my grand consolation. She was a pale, sentimental girl, with long "hyacinthine" ringlets hanging about her face. She wrote poetry herself, and we kept up a poetical correspondence. She had a taste for the drama, too, and I taught her how to act several of the scenes in Romeo and Juliet. I used to rehearse the garden scene under her lattice, which looked out from among woodbine and honeysuckles into the churchyard. I began to think her amazingly pretty as well as clever, and I believe I should have finished by falling in love with her, had not her father discovered our theatrical studies. He was a studious, abstracted man, generally too much absorbed in his learned and religious labors to notice the little foibles of his daughters, and perhaps blinded by a father's fondness; but he unexpectedly put his head out of his study-window one day in the midst of a scene, and put a stop to our rehearsals. He had a vast deal of that prosaic good sense which I for ever found a stumbling-block in my poetical path. My rambling freak had not struck the good man as poetically as it had his daughters. He drew his comparison from a different manual. He looked upon me as a prodigal son, and doubted whether I should ever arrive at the happy catastrophe of the fatted calf.

I fancy some intimation was given to my father of this new breaking out of my poetical temperament, for he suddenly intimated that it was high time I should prepare for the university. I dreaded a return to the school whence I had eloped: the ridicule of my fellow-scholars, and the glance from the squire's pew, would have been worse than death to me. I was fortunately spared the humiliation. My father sent me to board with a country clergyman, who had three or four boys under his care. I went to him joyfully, for I had often heard my mother mention him with esteem. In fact he had been an admirer of hers in his younger days, though too humble in fortune and modest in pretensions to aspire to her hand; but he had ever retained a tender regard for her. He was a good man; a worthy specimen of that valuable body of our country clergy who silently and unostentatiously do a vast deal of good; who are, as it were, woven into the whole system of rural life, and operate upon it with the steady yet unobtrusive influence of temperate piety and learned good sense. He lived in a small village not far from Warwick, one of those little communities where the scanty flock is, in a manner, folded into the bosom of the pastor. The venerable church, in its grass-grown cemetery, was one of those rural temples scattered about our country as if to sanctify the land.

I have the worthy pastor before my mind's eye at this moment, with his mild benevolent countenance, rendered still more venerable by his silver hairs. I have him before me, as I saw him on my arrival, seated in the embowered porch of his small parsonage, with a flower-garden before it, and his pupils gathered round him like his children. I shall never forget his reception of me, for I believe he thought of my poor mother at the time, and his heart yearned towards her child. His eye glistened when he received me at the door, and he took me into his arms as the adopted child of his affections. Never had I been so fortunately placed. He was one of those excellent members of our church, who help out their narrow salaries by instructing a few gentlemen's sons. I am convinced those little seminaries are among the best nurseries of talent and virtue in the land. Both heart and mind are cultivated and improved. The preceptor is the companion and the friend of his pupils. His sacred character gives him dignity in their eyes, and his solemn functions produce that elevation of mind and sobriety of conduct necessary to those who are to teach youth to think and act worthily.

I speak from my own random observation and experience; but I think I speak correctly. At any rate, I can trace much of what is good in my own heterogeneous compound to the short time I was under the instruction of that good man. He entered into the cares and occupations and amusements of his pupils; and won his way into our confidence, and studied our hearts and minds more intently than we did our books.

He soon sounded the depth of my character. I had become, as I have already hinted, a little liberal in my notions, and apt to philosophize on both politics and religion; having seen something of men and things, and learnt, from my fellow-philosophers, the strollers, to despise all vulgar prejudices. He did not attempt to cast down my vainglory, nor to question my right view of things; he merely instilled into my mind a little information on these topics; though in a quiet unobtrusive way, that never ruffled a feather of my self-conceit. I was astonished to find what a change a little knowledge makes in one's mode of viewing matters; and how different a subject is when one thinks, or when one only talks about it. I conceived a vast deference for my teacher, and was ambitious of his good opinion. In my zeal to make a favorable impression, I presented him with a whole ream of my poetry. He read it attentively, smiled, and pressed my hand when he returned it to me, but said nothing. The next day he set me at mathematics.

Somehow or other the process of teaching seemed robbed by him of all its austerity. I was not conscious that he thwarted an inclination or opposed a wish; but I felt that, for the time, my inclinations were entirely changed. I became fond of study, and zealous to improve myself. I made tolerable advances in studies which I had before considered as unattainable, and I wondered at my own proficiency. I thought, too, I astonished my preceptor; for I often caught his eyes fixed upon me with a peculiar expression. I suspect, since, that he was pensively tracing in my countenance the early lineaments of my mother.

Education was not apportioned by him into tasks, and enjoined as a labor, to be abandoned with joy the moment the hour of study was expired. We had, it is true, our allotted hours of occupation, to give us habits of method, and of the distribution of time; but they were made pleasant to us, and our feelings were enlisted in the cause. When they were over, education still went on. It pervaded all our relaxations and amusements. There was a steady march of improvement. Much of his instruction was given during pleasant rambles, or when seated on the margin of the Avon; and information received in that way, often makes a deeper impression than when acquired by poring over books. I have many of the pure and eloquent precepts that flowed from his lips associated in my mind with lovely scenes in nature, which make the recollection of them indescribably delightful.

I do not pretend to say that any miracle was effected with me. After all said and done, I was but a weak disciple. My poetical temperament still wrought within me and wrestled hard with wisdom, and, I fear, maintained the mastery. I found mathematics an intolerable task in fine weather. I would be prone to forget my problems, to watch the birds hopping about the windows, or the bees humming about the honeysuckles; and whenever I could steal away, I would wander about the grassy borders of the Avon, and excuse this truant propensity to myself with the idea that I was treading classic ground, over which Shakspeare had wandered. What luxurious idleness have I indulged, as I lay under the trees and watched the silver waves rippling through the arches of the broken bridge, and laving the rocky bases of old Warwick Castle; and how often have I thought of sweet Shakspeare, and in my boyish enthusiasm have kissed the waves which had washed his native village.

My good preceptor would often accompany me in these desultory rambles. He sought to get hold of this vagrant mood of mind and turn it to some account. He endeavored to teach me to mingle thought with mere sensation; to moralize on the scenes around; and to make the beauties of nature administer to the understanding and the heart. He endeavored to direct my imagination to high and noble objects, and to fill it with lofty images. In a word, he did all he could to make the best of a poetical temperament, and to counteract the mischief which had been done to me by my great expectations.

Had I been earlier put under the care of the good pastor, or remained with him a longer time, I really believe he would have made something of me. He had already brought a great deal of what had been flogged into me into tolerable order, and had weeded out much of the unprofitable wisdom which had sprung up in my vagabondizing. I already began to find that with all my genius a little study would be no disadvantage to me; and, in spite of my vagrant freaks, I began to doubt my being a second Shakspeare.

Just as I was making these precious discoveries, the good parson died. It was a melancholy day throughout the neighborhood. He had his little flock of scholars, his children, as he used to call us, gathered round him in his dying moments; and he gave us the parting advice of a father, now that he had to leave us, and we were to be separated from each other, and scattered about in the world. He took me by the hand, and talked with me earnestly and affectionately, and called to mind my mother, and used her name to enforce his dying exhortations, for I rather think he considered me the most erring and heedless of his flock. He held my hand in his, long after he had done speaking, and kept his eye fixed on me tenderly and almost piteously: his lips moved as if he were silently praying for me; and he died away, still holding me by the hand.

There was not a dry eye in the church when the funeral service was read from the pulpit from which he had so often preached. When the body was committed to the earth, our little band gathered round it, and watched the coffin as it was lowered into the grave. The parishioners looked at us with sympathy; for we were mourners not merely in dress but in heart. We lingered about the grave, and clung to one another for a time, weeping and speechless, and then parted, like a band of brothers parting from the paternal hearth, never to assemble there again.

How had the gentle spirit of that good man sweetened our natures, and linked our young hearts together by the kindest ties! I have always had a throb of pleasure at meeting with an old schoolmate, even though one of my truant associates; but whenever, in the course of my life, I have encountered one of that little flock with which I was folded on the banks of the Avon, it has been with a gush of affection, and a glow of virtue, that for the moment have made me a better man.

I was now sent to Oxford, and was wonderfully impressed on first entering it as a student. Learning here puts on all its majesty. It is lodged in palaces; it is sanctified by the sacred ceremonies of religion; it has a pomp and circumstance which powerfully affect the imagination. Such, at least, it had in my eyes, thoughtless as I was. My previous studies with the worthy pastor had prepared me to regard it with deference and awe. He had been educated here, and always spoke of the University with filial fondness and classic veneration. When I beheld the clustering spires and pinnacles of this most august of cities rising from the plain, I hailed them in my enthusiasm as the points of a diadem, which the nation had placed upon the brows of science.

For a time old Oxford was full of enjoyment for me. There was a charm about its monastic buildings; its great Gothic quadrangles; its solemn halls, and shadowy cloisters. I delighted, in the evenings, to get in places surrounded by the colleges, where all modern buildings were screened from the sight; and to see the professors and students sweeping along in the dusk in their antiquated caps and gowns. I seemed for a time to be transported among the people and edifices of the old times. I was a frequent attendant, also, of the evening service in the New College Hall; to hear the fine organ, and the choir swelling an anthem in that solemn building, where painting, music, and architecture, are in such admirable unison.

A favorite haunt, too, was the beautiful walk bordered by lofty elms along the river, behind the gray walls of Magdalen College, which goes by the name of Addison's Walk, from being his favorite resort when an Oxford student. I became also a lounger in the Bodleian library, and a great dipper into books, though I cannot say that I studied them; in fact, being no longer under direction or control, I was gradually relapsing into mere indulgence of the fancy. Still this would have been pleasant and harmless enough, and I might have awakened from mere literary dreaming to something better. The chances were in my favor, for the riotous times of the University were past. The days of hard drinking were at an end. The old feuds of "Town and Gown," like the civil wars of the White and Red Rose, had died away; and student and citizen slept in peace and whole skins, without risk of being summoned in the night to bloody brawl. It had become the fashion to study at the University, and the odds were always in favor of my following the fashion. Unluckily, however, I fell in company with a special knot of young fellows, of lively parts and ready wit, who had lived occasionally upon town, and become initiated into the *Fancy*. They voted study to be the toil of dull minds, by which they slowly crept up the hill, while genius arrived at it at a bound. I felt ashamed to play the owl among such gay birds; so I threw by my books, and became a man of spirit.

As my father made me a tolerable allowance, notwithstanding the narrowness of his income, having an eye always to my great expectations, I was enabled to appear to advantage among my companions. I cultivated all kinds of sport and exercises. I was one of the most expert oarsmen that rowed on the Isis. I boxed, fenced, angled, shot, and hunted, and my rooms in college were always decorated with whips of all kinds, spurs, fowling-pieces, fishing-rods, foils, and boxing-gloves. A pair of leather breeches would seem to be throwing one leg out of the half-open drawers, and empty bottles lumbered the bottom of every closet.

My father came to see me at college when I was in the height of my career. He asked me how I came on with my studies, and what kind of hunting there was in the neighborhood. He examined my various sporting apparatus with a curious eye; wanted to know if any of the professors were fox-hunters, and whether they were generally good shots, for he suspected their studying so much must be hurtful to the sight. We had a day's shooting together: I delighted him with my skill, and astonished him by my learned disquisitions on horse-flesh, and on Manton's guns; so, upon the whole, he departed highly satisfied with my improvement at college.

I do not know how it is, but I cannot be idle long without getting in love. I had not been a very long time a man of spirit, therefore, before I became deeply enamoured of a shopkeeper's daughter in the High-street, who, in fact, was the admiration of many of the students. I wrote several sonnets in praise of her, and spent half of my pocket money at the shop, in buying articles which I did not want, that I might have an opportunity of speaking to her. Her father, a severe-looking old gentleman, with bright silver buckles, and a crisp-curled wig, kept a strict guard on her, as the fathers generally do upon their daughters in Oxford, and well they may. I tried to get into his good graces, and to be sociable with him, but all in vain. I said several good things in his shop, but he never laughed: he had no relish for wit and humor. He was one of those dry old gentlemen who keep youngsters at bay. He had already brought up two or three daughters, and was experienced in the ways of students. He was as knowing and wary as a gray old badger that has often been hunted. To see him on Sunday, so stiff and starched in his demeanor, so precise in his dress, with his daughter under his arm, was enough to deter all graceless youngsters from approaching.

I managed, however, in spite of his vigilance, to have several conversations with the daughter, as I cheapened articles in the shop. I made terrible long bargains, and examined the articles over and over before I purchased. In the mean time, I would convey a sonnet or an acrostic under cover of a piece of cambric, or slipped into a pair of stockings; I would whisper soft nonsense into her ear as I haggled about the price; and would squeeze her hand tenderly as I received my half-pence of change in a bit of whity-brown paper. Let this serve as a hint to all haberdashers who have pretty daughters for shop-girls, and young students for customers. I do not know whether my words and looks were very eloquent, but my poetry was irresistible; for, to tell the truth, the girl had some literary taste, and was seldom without a book from the circulating library.

By the divine power of poetry, therefore, which is so potent with the lovely sex, did I subdue the heart of this fair little haberdasher. We carried on a sentimental correspondence for a time across the counter, and I supplied her with rhyme by the stockingfull. At length I prevailed on her to grant an assignation. But how was this to be effected? Her father kept her always under his eye; she never walked out alone; and the house was locked up the moment that the shop was shut. All these difficulties served but to give zest to the adventure. I proposed that the assignation should be in her own chamber, into which I would climb at night. The plan was irresistible.—A cruel father, a secret lover, and a clandestine meeting! All the little girl's studies from the circulating library seemed about to be realized.

But what had I in view in making this assignation? Indeed, I know not. I had no evil intentions, nor can I say that I had any good ones. I liked the girl, and wanted to have an opportunity of seeing more of her; and the assignation was made, as I have done many things else, heedlessly and without forethought. I asked myself a few questions of the kind, after all my arrangements were made, but the answers were very unsatisfactory. "Am I to ruin this poor thoughtless girl?" said I to myself. "No!" was the prompt and indignant answer. "Am I to run away with her?"—"Whither, and to what purpose?"—"Well, then, am I to marry her?"—"Poh! a man of my expectations marry a shopkeeper's daughter?" "What then am I to do with her?" "Hum—why—let me get into the chamber first, and then consider"—and so the self-examination ended.

Well, sir, "come what come might," I stole under cover of the darkness to the dwelling of my dulcinea. All was quiet. At the concerted signal her window was gently opened. It was just above the projecting bow-window of her father's shop, which assisted me in mounting. The house was low, and I was enabled to scale the fortress with tolerable ease. I clambered with a beating heart; I reached the casement; I hoisted my body half into the chamber; and was welcomed, not by the embraces of my expecting fair one, but by the grasp of the crabbed-looking old father in the crisp-curled wig.

I extricated myself from his clutches, and endeavored to make my retreat; but I was confounded by his cries of thieves! and robbers! I was bothered too by his Sunday cane, which was amazingly busy about my head as I descended, and against which my hat was but a poor protection. Never before had I an idea of the activity of an old man's arm, and the hardness of the knob of an ivory-headed cane. In my hurry and confusion I missed my footing, and fell sprawling on the pavement. I was immediately surrounded by myrmidons, who, I doubt not, were on the watch for me. Indeed, I was in no situation to escape, for I had sprained my ankle in the fall, and could not stand. I was seized as a housebreaker; and to exonerate myself of a greater crime, I had to accuse myself of a less. I made known who I was, and why I came there. Alas! the varlets knew it already, and were only amusing themselves at my expense. My perfidious muse had been playing me one of her slippery tricks. The old curmudgeon of a father had found my sonnets and acrostics hid away in holes and corners of his shop; he had no taste for poetry like his daughter, and had instituted a rigorous though silent observation. He had moused upon our letters, detected our plans, and prepared every thing for my reception. Thus was I ever doomed to be led into scrapes by the muse. Let no man henceforth carry on a secret amour in poetry!

The old man's ire was in some measure appeased by the pommeling of my head and the anguish of my sprain; so he did not put me to death on the spot. He was even humane enough to furnish a shutter, on which I was carried back to college like a wounded warrior. The porter was roused to admit me. The college gate was thrown open for my entry. The affair was blazed about the next morning, and became the joke of the college from the buttery to the hall.

I had leisure to repent during several weeks' confinement by my sprain, which I passed in translating Boethius's Consolations of Philosophy. I received a most tender and ill-spelled letter from my mistress, who had been sent to a relation in Coventry. She protested her innocence of my misfortune, and vowed to be true to me "till deth." I took no notice of the letter, for I was cured, for the present, both of love and poetry. Women, however, are more constant in their attachments than men, whatever philosophers may say to the contrary. I am assured that she actually remained faithful to her vow for several months; but she had to deal with a cruel father, whose heart was as hard as the knob of his cane. He was not to be touched by tears nor poetry, but absolutely compelled her to marry a reputable young tradesman, who made her a happy woman in spite of herself, and of all the rules of romance; and what is more, the mother of several children. They are at this very day a thriving couple, and keep a snug corner shop, just opposite the figure of Peeping Tom, at Coventry.

I will not fatigue you by any more details of my studies at Oxford; though they were not always as severe as these, nor did I always pay as dear for my lessons. To be brief, then, I lived on in my usual miscellaneous manner, gradually getting knowledge of good and evil, until I had attained my twenty-first year. I had scarcely come of age when I heard of the sudden death of my father. The shock was severe, for though he had never treated me with much kindness, still he was my father, and at his death, I felt alone in the world.

I returned home, and found myself the solitary master of the paternal mansion. A crowd of gloomy feelings came thronging upon me. It was a place that always sobered me, and brought me to reflection; now especially, it looked so deserted and melancholy.

I entered the little breakfasting-room. There were my father's whip and spurs, hanging by the fireplace; the Stud-Book, Sporting Magazine, and Racing Calendar, his only reading. His favorite spaniel lay on the hearth-rug. The poor animal, who had never before noticed me, now came fondling about me, licked my hand, then looked round the room, whined, wagged his tail slightly, and gazed wistfully in my face. I felt the full force of the appeal. "Poor Dash," said I, "we are both alone in the world, with nobody to care for us, and will take care of one another."—The dog never quitted me afterwards.

I could not go into my mother's room—my heart swelled when I passed within sight of the door. Her portrait hung in the parlor, just over the place where she used to sit. As I cast my eyes on it, I thought it looked at me with tenderness, and I burst into tears. I was a careless dog, it is true, hardened a little, perhaps, by living in public schools, and buffeting about among strangers, who cared nothing for me; but the recollection of a mother's tenderness was overcoming.

I was not of an age or a temperament to be long depressed. There was a reaction in my system, that always brought me up again after every pressure; and, indeed, my spirits were most buoyant after a temporary prostration. I settled the concerns of the estate as soon as possible; realized my property, which was not very considerable, but which appeared a vast deal to me, having a poetical eye, that magnified every thing; and finding myself, at the end of a few months, free of all further business or restraint, I determined to go to London and enjoy myself. Why should I not?—I was young, animated, joyous; had plenty of funds for present pleasures, and my uncle's estate in the perspective. Let those mope at college, and pore over books, thought I, who have their way to make in the world; it would be ridiculous drudgery in a youth of my expectations.

Away to London, therefore, I rattled in a tandem, determined to take the town gayly. I passed through several of the villages where I had played the Jack Pudding a few years before; and I visited the scenes of many of my adventures and follies, merely from that feeling of melancholy pleasure which we have in stepping again the footprints of foregone existence, even when they have passed among weeds and briers. I made a circuit in the latter part of my journey, so as to take in West End and Hampstead, the scenes of my last dramatic exploit, and of the battle royal of the booth. As I drove along the ridge of Hampstead Hill, by Jack Straw's Castle, I paused at the spot where Columbine and I had sat down so disconsolately in our ragged finery, and had looked dubiously on London. I almost expected to see her again, standing on the hill's brink, "like Niobe, all tears";—mournful as Babylon in ruins!

"Poor Columbine!" said I, with a heavy sigh, "thou wert a gallant, generous girl—a true woman; faithful to the distressed, and ready to sacrifice thyself in the cause of worthless man!"

I tried to whistle off the recollection of her, for there was always something of self-reproach with it. I drove gayly along the road, enjoying the stare of hostlers and stable-boys, as I managed my horses knowingly down the steep street of Hampstead; when, just at the skirts of the village, one of the traces of my leader came loose. I pulled up, and as the animal was restive, and my servant a bungler, I called for assistance to the robustious master of a snug ale-house, who stood at his door with a tankard in his hand. He came readily to assist me, followed by his wife, with her bosom half open, a child in her arms, and two more at her heels. I stared for a moment, as if doubting my eyes. I could not be mistaken; in the fat, beer-blown landlord of the ale-house, I recollected my old rival Harlequin, and in his slattern spouse, the once trim and dimpling Columbine.

The change of my looks from youth to manhood, and the change in my circumstances, prevented them from recognizing me. They could not suspect in the dashing young buck, fashionably dressed and driving his own equipage, the painted beau, with old peaked hat, and long, flimsy, sky-blue coat. My heart yearned with kindness towards Columbine, and I was glad to see her establishment a thriving one. As soon as the harness was adjusted, I tossed a small purse of gold into her ample bosom; and then, pretending to give my horses a hearty cut of the whip, I made the lash curl with a whistling about the sleek sides of ancient Harlequin. The horses dashed off like lightning, and I was whirled out of sight before either of the parties could get over their surprise at my liberal donations. I have always considered this as one of the greatest proofs of my poetical genius; it was distributing poetical justice in perfection.

I now entered London en cavalier, and became a blood upon town. I took fashionable lodgings, in the West End; employed the first tailor; frequented the regular lounges; gambled a little; lost my money good-humoredly, and gained a number of fashionable, good-for-nothing acquaintances. I gained some reputation also for a man of science, having become an expert boxer in the course of my studies at Oxford. I was distinguished, therefore, among the gentlemen of the Fancy; became hand and glove with certain boxing noblemen, and was the admiration of the Fives Court. A gentleman's science, however, is apt to get him into sad scrapes; he is too prone to play the knight-errant, and to pick up quarrels which less scientific gentlemen would quietly avoid. I undertook one day to punish the insolence of a porter. He was a Hercules of a fellow, but then I was so secure in my science! I gained the victory of course. The porter pocketed his humiliation, bound up his broken head, and went about his business as unconcernedly as though nothing had happened; while I went to bed with my victory, and did not dare to show my battered face for a fortnight: by which I discovered that a gentleman may have the worst of the battle even when victorious.

I am naturally a philosopher, and no one can moralize better after a misfortune has taken place; so I lay on my bed and moralized on this sorry ambition, which levels the gentleman with the clown, I know it is the opinion of many sages, who have thought deeply on these matters, that the noble science of boxing keeps up the bull-dog courage of the nation; and far be it from me to decry the advantage of becoming a nation of bull-dogs; but I now saw clearly that it was calculated to keep up the breed of English ruffians. "What is the Fives Court," said I to myself, as I turned uncomfortably in bed, "but a college of scoundrelism, where every bully-ruffian in the land may gain a fellowship? What is the slang language of the Fancy but a jargon by which fools and knaves commune and understand each other, and enjoy a kind of superiority over the uninitiated? What is a boxing match but an arena, where the noble and the illustrious are jostled into familiarity with the infamous and the vulgar? What, in fact, is the Fancy itself, but a chain of easy communication, extending from the peer down to the pickpocket, through the medium of which a man of rank may find he has shaken hands, at three removes, with the murderer on the gibbet?—

"Enough!" ejaculated I, thoroughly convinced through the force of my philosophy, and the pain of my bruises—"I'll have nothing more to do with the Fancy." So when I had recovered from my victory, I turned my attention to softer themes, and became a devoted admirer of the ladies. Had I had more industry and ambition in my nature, I might have worked my way to the very height of fashion, as I saw many laborious gentlemen doing around me. But it is a toilsome, an anxious, and an unhappy life; there are few beings so sleepless and miserable as your cultivators of fashionable smiles. I was quite content with that kind of society which forms the frontiers of fashion, and may be easily taken possession of. I found it a light, easy, productive soil. I had but to go about and sow visiting cards, and I reaped a whole harvest of invitations. Indeed, my figure and address were by no means against me. It was whispered, too, among the young ladies, that I was prodigiously clever, and wrote poetry; and the old ladies had ascertained that I was a young gentleman of good family, handsome fortune, and "great expectations."

I now was carried away by the hurry of gay life, so intoxicating to a young man, and which a man of poetical temperament enjoys so highly on his first tasting of it; that rapid variety of sensations; that whirl of brilliant objects; that succession of pungent pleasures! I had no time for thought. I only felt. I never attempted to write poetry; my poetry seemed all to go off by transpiration. I lived poetry; it was all a poetical dream to me. A mere sensualist knows nothing of the delights of a splendid metropolis. He lives in a round of animal gratifications and heartless habits. But to a young man of poetical feelings, it is an ideal world, a scene of enchantment and delusion; his imagination is in perpetual excitement, and gives a spiritual zest to every pleasure.

A season of town-life, however, somewhat sobered me of my intoxication; or rather I was rendered more serious by one of my old complaints—I fell in love. It was with a very pretty, though a very haughty fair one, who had come to London under the care of an old maiden aunt to enjoy the pleasures of a winter in town, and to get married. There was not a doubt of her commanding a choice of lovers; for she had long been the belle of a little cathedral city, and one of the poets of the place had absolutely celebrated her beauty in a copy of Latin verses. The most extravagant anticipations were formed by her friends of the sensation she would produce. It was feared by some that she might be precipitate in her choice, and take up with some inferior title. The aunt was determined nothing should gain her under a lord.

Alas! with all her charms, the young lady lacked the one thing needful—she had no money. So she waited in vain for duke, marquis, or earl, to throw himself at her feet. As the season waned, so did the lady's expectations; when, just towards the close, I made my advances.

I was most favorably received by both the young lady and her aunt. It is true, I had no title; but then such great expectations! A marked preference was immediately shown me over two rivals, the younger son of a needy baronet, and a captain of dragoons on half-pay. I did not absolutely take the field in form, for I was determined not to be precipitate; but I drove my equipage frequently through the street in which she lived, and was always sure to see her at the window, generally with a book in her hand. I resumed my knack at rhyming, and sent her a long copy of verses; anonymously, to be sure, but she knew my handwriting. Both aunt and niece, however, displayed the most delightful ignorance on the subject. The young lady showed them to me; wondered who they could be written by; and declared there was nothing in this world she loved so much as poetry; while the maiden aunt would put her pinching spectacles on her nose, and read them, with blunders in sense and sound, excruciating to an author's ears; protesting there was nothing equal to them in the whole Elegant Extracts.

The fashionable season closed without my adventuring to make a declaration, though I certainly had encouragement. I was not perfectly sure that I had effected a lodgment in the young lady's heart; and, to tell the truth, the aunt overdid her part, and was a little too extravagant in her liking of me. I knew that maiden aunts were not apt to be captivated by the mere personal merits of their nieces' admirers; and I wanted to ascertain how much of all this favor I owed to driving an equipage, and having great expectations.

I had received many hints how charming their native place was during the summer months; what pleasant society they had; and what beautiful drives about the neighborhood. They had not, therefore, returned home long, before I made my appearance in dashing style, driving down the principal street. The very next morning I was seen at prayers, seated in the same pew with the reigning belle. Questions were whispered about the aisles, after service, "Who is he?" and "What is he?" And the replies were as usual, "A young gentleman of good family and fortune, and great expectations."

I was much struck with the peculiarities of this reverend little place. A cathedral, with its dependencies and regulations, presents a picture of other times, and of a different order of things.

It is a rich relic of a more poetical age. There still linger about it the silence and solemnity of the cloister. In the present instance especially, where the cathedral was large, and the town small, its influence was the more apparent. The solemn pomp of the service, performed twice a day, with the grand intonations of the organ, and the voices of the choir swelling through the magnificent pile, diffused, as it were, a perpetual Sabbath over the place. This routine of solemn ceremony continually going on, independent, as it were, of the world; this daily offering of melody and praise, ascending like incense from the altar, had a powerful effect upon my imagination.

The aunt introduced me to her coterie, formed of families connected with the cathedral, and others of moderate fortune, but high respectability, who had nestled themselves under the wings of the cathedral to enjoy good society at moderate expense. It was a highly aristocratical little circle; scrupulous in its intercourse with others, and jealously cautious about admitting any thing common or unclean.

It seemed as if the courtesies of the old school had taken refuge here. There were continual interchanges of civilities, and of small presents of fruits and delicacies, and of complimentary crow-quill billets; for in a quiet, well-bred community like this, living entirely at ease, little duties, and little amusements, and little civilities, fill up the day. I have seen, in the midst of a warm day, a corpulent, powdered footman, issuing from the iron gateway of a stately mansion, and traversing the little place with an air of mighty import, bearing a small tart on a large silver salver.

Their evening amusements were sober and primitive. They assembled at a moderate hour; the young ladies played music, and the old ladies whist; and at an early hour they dispersed. There was no parade on these social occasions. Two or three old sedan chairs were in constant activity, though the greater part made their exit in clogs and pattens, with a footman or waiting-maid carrying a lantern in advance; and long before midnight the clank of pattens and gleam of lanterns about the quiet little place told that the evening party had dissolved.

Still I did not feel myself altogether so much at my ease as I had anticipated, considering the smallness of the place. I found it very different from other country places, and that it was not so easy to make a dash there. Sinner that I was! the very dignity and decorum of the little community was rebuking to me. I feared my past idleness and folly would rise in judgment against me. I stood in awe of the dignitaries of the cathedral, whom I saw mingling familiarly in society. I became nervous on this point. The creak of a prebendary's shoes sounding from one end of a quiet street to the other, was appalling to me; and the sight of a shovel hat was sufficient at any time to check me in the midst of my boldest poetical soarings.

And then the good aunt could not be quiet, but would cry me up for a genius, and extol my poetry to every one. So long as she confined this to the ladies it did well enough, because they were able to feel and appreciate poetry of the new romantic school. Nothing would content the good lady, however, but she must read my verses to a prebendary, who had long been the undoubted critic of the place. He was a thin, delicate old gentleman, of mild, polished manners, steeped to the lips in classic lore, and not easily put in a heat by any hot-blooded poetry of the day. He listened to my most fervid thoughts and fervid words without a glow; shook his head with a smile, and condemned them as not being according to Horace, as not being legitimate poetry.

Several old ladies, who had heretofore been my admirers, shook their heads at hearing this; they could not think of praising any poetry that was not according to Horace; and as to any thing illegitimate, it was not to be countenanced in good society.

Thanks to my stars, however, I had youth and novelty on my side: so the young ladies persisted in admiring my poetry in despite of Horace and illegitimacy.

I consoled myself with the good opinion of the young ladies, whom I had always found to be the best judges of poetry. As to these old scholars, said I, they are apt to be chilled by being steeped in the cold fountains of the classics. Still I felt that I was losing ground, and that it was necessary to bring matters to a point. Just at this time there was a public ball, attended by the best society of the place, and by the gentry of the neighborhood: I took great pains with my toilet on the occasion, and I had never looked better. I had determined that night to make my grand assault on the heart of the young lady, to battle it with all my forces, and the next morning to demand a surrender in due form.

I entered the ballroom amidst a buzz and flutter, which generally took place among the young ladies on my appearance. I was in fine spirits; for, to tell the truth, I had exhilarated myself by a cheerful glass of wine on the occasion. I talked, and rattled, and said a thousand silly things, slap-dash, with all the confidence of a man sure of his auditors,—and every thing had its effect.

In the midst of my triumph I observed a little knot gathering together in the upper part of the room. By degrees it increased. A tittering broke out there, and glances were cast round at me, and then there would be fresh tittering. Some of the young ladies would hurry away to distant parts of the room, and whisper to their friends. Wherever they went, there was still this tittering and glancing at me. I did not know what to make of all this. I looked at myself from head to foot, and peeped at my back in a glass, to see if any thing was odd about my person; any awkward exposure, any whimsical tag hanging out:—no—every thing was right—I was a perfect picture. I determined that it must be some choice saying of mine that was bandied about in this knot of merry beauties, and I determined to enjoy one of my good things in the rebound. I stepped gently, therefore, up the room, smiling at every one as I passed, who, I must say, all smiled and tittered in return. I approached the group, smirking and perking my chin, like a man who is full of pleasant feeling, and sure of being well received. The cluster of little belles opened as I advanced.

Heavens and earth! whom should I perceive in the midst of them but my early and tormenting flame, the everlasting Sacharissa! She was grown, it is true, into the full beauty of womanhood; but showed, by the provoking merriment of her countenance, that she perfectly recollected me, and the ridiculous flagellations of which she had twice been the cause.

I saw at once the exterminating cloud of ridicule bursting over me. My crest fell. The flame of love went suddenly out, or was extinguished by overwhelming shame. How I got down the room I know not: I fancied every one tittering at me. Just as I reached the door, I caught a glance of my mistress and her aunt listening to the whispers of Sacharissa, the old lady raising her hands and eyes, and the face of the young one lighted up, as I imagined, with scorn ineffable. I paused to see no more, but made two steps from the top of the stairs to the bottom. The next morning, before sunrise, I beat a retreat, and did not feel the blushes cool from my tingling cheeks, until I had lost sight of the old towers of the cathedral.

I now returned to town thoughtful and crest-fallen. My money was nearly spent, for I had lived freely and without calculation. The dream of love was over, and the reign of pleasure at an end. I determined to retrench while I had yet a trifle left: so selling my equipage and horses for half their value, I quietly put the money in my pocket, and turned pedestrian. I had not a doubt that, with my great expectations, I could at any time raise funds, either on usury or by borrowing; but I was principled against both, and resolved by strict economy, to make my slender purse hold out until my uncle should give up the ghost, or rather the estate. I staid at home, therefore, and read, and would have written, but I had already suffered too much from my poetical productions, which had generally involved me in some ridiculous scrape. I gradually acquired a rusty look, and had a straitened money-borrowing air, upon which the world began to shy me. I have never felt disposed to quarrel with the world for its conduct: it has always used me well. When I have been flush and gay, and disposed for society, it has caressed me; and when I have been pinched and reduced, and wished to be alone, why, it has left me alone; and what more could a man desire? Take my word for it, this world is a more obliging world than people generally represent it.

Well, sir, in the midst of my retrenchment, my retirement, and my studiousness, I received news that my uncle was dangerously ill. I hastened on the wings of an heir's affections to receive his dying breath and his last testament. I found him attended by his faithful valet, old Iron John; by the woman who occasionally worked about the house, and by the foxy-headed boy, young Orson, whom I had occasionally hunted about the park. Iron John gasped a kind of asthmatical salutation as I entered the room, and received me with something almost like a smile of welcome. The woman sat blubbering at the foot of the bed; and the foxy-headed Orson, who had now grown up to be a lubberly lout, stood gazing in stupid vacancy at a distance.

My uncle lay stretched upon his back. The chamber was without fire, or any of the comforts of a sick room. The cobwebs flaunted from the ceiling. The tester was covered with dust, and the curtains were tattered. From underneath the bed peeped out one end of his strong box. Against the wainscot were suspended rusty blunderbusses, horse-pistols, and a cut-and-thrust sword, with which he had fortified his room to defend his life and treasure. He had employed no physician during his illness; and from the scanty relics lying on the table, seemed almost to have denied to himself the assistance of a cook.

When I entered the room, he vas lying motionless; his eyes fixed and his mouth open: at the first look I thought him a corpse. The noise of my entrance made him turn his head. At the sight of me a ghastly smile came over his face, and his glazing eye gleamed with satisfaction. It was the only smile he had ever given me, and it went to my heart. "Poor old man!" thought I, "why should you force me to leave you thus desolate, when I see that my presence has the power to cheer you?"

"Nephew," said he, after several efforts, and in a low gasping voice—"I am glad you are come. I shall now die with satisfaction. Look," said he, raising his withered hand, and pointing—"look in that box on the table: you will find that I have not forgotten you."

I pressed his hand to my heart, and the tears stood in my eyes. I sat down by his bedside and watched him, but he never spoke again. My presence, however, gave him evident satisfaction; for every now and then, as he looked at me, a vague smile would come over his visage, and he would feebly point to the sealed box on the table. As the day wore away, his life appeared to wear away with it. Towards sunset his hand sank on the bed, and lay motionless, his eyes grew glazed, his mouth remained open, and thus he gradually died.

I could not but feel shocked at this absolute extinction of my kindred. I dropped a tear of real sorrow over this strange old man, who had thus reserved the smile of kindness to his death-bed; like an evening sun after a gloomy day, just shining out to set in darkness. Leaving the corpse in charge of the domestics, I retired for the night.

It was a rough night. The winds seemed as if singing my uncle's requiem about the mansion, and the bloodhounds howled without as if they knew of the death of their old master. Iron John almost grudged me the tallow candle to burn in my apartment, and light up its dreariness, so accustomed had he been to starveling economy. I could not sleep. The recollection of my uncle's dying scene, and the dreary sounds about the house affected my mind. These, however, were succeeded by plans for the future, and I lay awake the greater part of the night, indulging the poetical anticipation how soon I should make these old walls ring with cheerful life, and restore the hospitality of my mother's ancestors.

My uncle's funeral was decent, but private. I knew that nobody respected his memory, and I was determined none should be summoned to sneer over his funeral, and make merry at his grave. He was buried in the church of the neighboring village, though it was not the burying-place of his race; but he had expressly enjoined that he should not be buried with his family: he had quarrelled with most of them when living, and he carried his resentments even into the grave.

I defrayed the expenses of his funeral out of my own purse, that I might have done with the undertakers at once, and clear the ill-omened birds from the premises. I invited the parson of the parish, and the lawyer from the village, to attend at the house the next morning, and hear the reading of the will. I treated them to an excellent breakfast, a profusion that had not been seen at the house for many a year. As soon as the breakfast things were removed, I summoned Iron John, the woman, and the boy, for I was particular in having every one present and proceeding regularly. The box was placed on the table—all was silence—I broke the seal—raised the lid, and beheld—not the will—but my accursed poem of Doubting Castle and Giant Despair!

Could any mortal have conceived that this old withered man, so taciturn, and apparently so lost to feeling, could have treasured up for years the thoughtless pleasantry of a boy, to punish him with such cruel ingenuity? I now could account for his dying smile, the only one he had ever given me. He had been a grave man all his life; it was strange that he should die in the enjoyment of a joke, and it was hard that that joke should be at my expense.

The lawyer and the parson seemed at a loss to comprehend the matter. "Here must be some mistake," said the lawyer; "there is no will here."

"Oh!" said Iron John, creaking forth his rusty jaws, "if it is a will you are looking for, I believe I can find one."

He retired with the same singular smile with which he had greeted me on my arrival, and which I now apprehended boded me no good. In a little while he returned with a will perfect at all points, properly signed and sealed, and witnessed and worded with horrible correctness; in which the deceased left large legacies to Iron John and his daughter, and the residue of his fortune to the foxy-headed boy; who, to my utter astonishment, was his son by this very woman; he having married her privately, and, as I verily believe, for no other purpose than to have an heir, and so balk my father and his issue of the inheritance. There was one little proviso, in which he mentioned, that, having discovered his nephew to have a pretty turn for poetry, he presumed he had no occasion for wealth; he recommended him, however, to the patronage of his heir, and requested that he might have a garret, rent-free, in Doubting Castle.

Grave Reflections of a Disappointed Man

MR. BUCKTHORNE HAD PAUSED AT THE DEATH OF HIS UNCLE, AND THE downfall of his great expectations, which formed, as he said, an epoch in his history; and it was not until some little time afterwards, and in a very sober mood, that he resumed his party-colored narrative.

After leaving the remains of my defunct uncle, said he, when the gate closed between me and what was once to have been mine, I felt thrust out naked into the world, and completely abandoned to fortune. What was to become of me? I had been brought up to nothing but expectations, and they had all been disappointed. I had no relations to look to for counsel or assistance. The world seemed all to have died away from me. Wave after wave of relationship had ebbed off, and I was left a mere hulk upon the strand. I am not apt to be greatly cast down, but at this time I felt sadly disheartened. I could not realize my situation, nor form a conjecture how I was to get forward. I was now to endeavor to make money. The idea was new and strange to me. It was like being asked to discover the philosopher's stone. I had never thought about money otherwise than to put my hand into my pocket and find it; or if there were none there, to wait until a new supply came from home. I had considered life as a mere space of time to be filled up with enjoyments; but to have it portioned out into long hours and days of toil, merely that I might gain bread to give me strength to toil on—to labor but for the purpose of perpetuating a life of labor, was new and appalling to me. This may appear a very simple matter to some; but it will be understood by every unlucky wight in my predicament; who has had the misfortune of being born to great expectations.

I passed several days in rambling about the scenes of my boyhood; partly because I absolutely did not know what to do with myself, and partly because I did not know that I should ever see them again. I clung to them as one clings to a wreck, though he knows he must eventually cast himself loose and swim for his life. I sat down on a little hill within sight of my paternal home, but I did not venture to approach it, for I felt compunction at the thoughtlessness with which I had dissipated my patrimony; yet was I to blame, when I had the rich possessions of my curmudgeon of an uncle in expectation?

The new possessor of the place was making great alterations. The house was almost rebuilt. The trees which stood about it were cut down; my mother's flower-garden was thrown into a lawn—all was undergoing a change. I turned my back upon it with a sigh, and rambled to another part of the country.

How thoughtful a little adversity makes one! As I came within sight of the school-house where I had so often been flogged in the cause of wisdom, you would hardly have recognized the truant boy, who, but a few years since, had eloped so heedlessly from its walls. I leaned over the paling of the play-ground, and watched the scholars at their games, and looked to see if there might not be some urchin among them like I was once, full of gay dreams about life and the world. The play-ground seemed smaller than when I used to sport about it. The house and park too, of the neighboring squire, the father of the cruel Sacharissa, had shrunk in size and diminished in magnificence. The distant hills no longer appeared so far off, and, alas! no longer awaked ideas of a fairy land beyond.

As I was rambling pensively through a neighboring meadow, in which I had many a time gathered primroses, I met the very pedagogue who had been the tyrant and dread of my boyhood. I had sometimes vowed to myself, when suffering under his rod, that I would have my revenge if ever I met him when I had grown to be a man. The time had come; but I had no disposition to keep my vow. The few years which had matured me into a vigorous man had shrunk him into decrepitude. He appeared to have had a paralytic, stroke. I looked at him, and wondered that this poor helpless mortal could have been an object of terror to me; that I should have watched with anxiety the glance of that failing eye, or dreaded the power of that trembling hand. He tottered feebly along the path, and had some difficulty in getting over a stile. I ran and assisted him. He looked at me with surprise, but did not recognize me, and made a low bow of humility and thanks. I had no disposition to make myself known, for I felt that I had nothing to boast of. The pains he had taken, and the pains he had inflicted, had been equally useless. His repeated predictions were fully verified, and I felt that little Jack Buckthorne, the idle boy, had grown to be a very good-for-nothing man.

This is all very comfortless detail; but as I have told you of my follies, it is meet that I show you how for once I was schooled for them. The most thoughtless of mortals will some time or other have his day of gloom, when he will be compelled to reflect.

I felt on this occasion as if I had a kind of penance to perform and I made a pilgrimage in expiation of my past levity. Having passed a night at Leamington, I set off by a private path, which leads up a hill through a grove and across quiet fields, till I came to the small village, or rather hamlet, of Lenington. I sought the village church. It is an old low edifice of gray stone, on the brow of a small hill, looking over fertile fields, towards where the proud towers of Warwick castle lift themselves against the distant horizon.

A part of the churchyard is shaded by large trees. Under one of them my mother lay buried. You have no doubt thought me a light, heartless being. I thought myself so; but there are moments of adversity which let us into some feelings of our nature to which we might otherwise remain perpetual strangers.

I sought my mother's grave; the weeds were already matted over it, and the tombstone was half hid among nettles. I cleared them away, and they stung my hands; but I was heedless of the pain, for my heart ached too severely. I sat down on the grave, and read over and over again the epitaph on the stone.

It was simple,—but it was true. I had written it myself. I had tried to write a poetical epitaph, but in vain; my feelings refused to utter themselves in rhyme. My heart had gradually been filling during my lonely wanderings; it was now charged to the brim, and overflowed. I sank upon the grave, and buried my face in the tall grass, and wept like a child. Yes, I wept in man-hood upon the grave, as I had in infancy upon the bosom of my mother! Alas! how little do we appreciate a mother's tenderness while living! how heedless are we in youth of all her anxieties and kindness! But when she is dead and gone; when the cares and coldness of the world come withering to our hearts; when we find how hard it is to meet with true sympathy; how few love us for ourselves; how few will befriend us in our misfortunes; then it is that we think of the mother we have lost. It is true I had always loved my mother, even in my most heedless days; but I felt how inconsiderate and ineffectual had been my love. My heart melted as I retraced the days of infancy, when I was led by a mother's hand, and rocked to sleep in a mother's arms, and was without care or sorrow. "O my mother!" exclaimed I, burying my face again in the grass of the grave; "O that I were once more by your side; sleeping never to wake again on the cares and troubles of this world."

I am not naturally of a morbid temperament, and the violence of my emotion gradually exhausted itself. It was a hearty, honesty natural discharge of grief which had been slowly accumulating, and gave me wonderful relief. I rose from the grave as if I had been offering up a sacrifice, and I felt as if that sacrifice had been accepted.

I sat down again on the grass, and plucked, one by one, the weeds from her grave: the tears trickled more slowly down my cheeks, and ceased to be bitter. It was a comfort to think that she had died before sorrow and poverty came upon her child, and that all his great expectations were blasted.

I leaned my cheek upon my hand, and looked upon the landscape. Its quiet beauty soothed me. The whistle of a peasant from an adjoining field came cheerily to my ear. I seemed to respire hope and comfort with the free air that whispered through the leaves, and played lightly with my hair, and dried the tears upon my cheek. A lark, rising from the field before me, and leaving as it were a stream of song behind him as he rose, lifted my fancy with him. He hovered in the air just above the place where the towers of Warwick castle marked the horizon, and seemed as if fluttering with delight at his own melody. "Surely," thought I, "if there was such a thing as transmigration of souls, this might be taken for some poet let loose from earth, but still revelling in song, and caroling about fair fields and lordly towers."

At this moment the long-forgotten feeling of poetry rose within me. A thought sprang at once into my mind.—"I will become an author!" said I. "I have hitherto indulged in poetry as a pleasure, and it has brought me nothing but pain; let me try what it will do when I cultivate it with devotion as a pursuit."

The resolution thus suddenly aroused within me heaved a load from off my heart. I felt a confidence in it from the very place where it was formed. It seemed as though my mother's spirit whispered it to me from the grave. "I will henceforth," said I, "endeavor to be all that she fondly imagined me. I will endeavor to act as if she were witness of my actions; I will endeavor to acquit myself in such a manner that, when I revisit her grave, there may at least be no compunctious bitterness with my tears."

I bowed down and kissed the turf in solemn attestation of my vow. I plucked some primroses that were growing there, and laid them next my heart. I left the churchyard with my spirit once more lifted up, and set out a third time for London in the character of an author.—

Here my companion made a pause, and I waited in anxious suspense, hoping to have a whole volume of literary life unfolded to me. He seemed, however, to have sunk into a fit of pensive musing, and when, after some time, I gently roused him by a question or two as to his literary career,

"No," said he smiling, "over that part of my story I wish to leave a cloud. Let the mysteries of the craft rest sacred for me. Let those who have never ventured into the republic of letters still look upon it as a fairy land. Let them suppose the author the very being they picture him from his works—I am not the man to mar their illusion. I am not the man to hint, while one is admiring the silken web of Persia, that it has been spun from the entrails of a miserable worm."

"Well," said I, "if you will tell me nothing of your literary history, let me know at least if you have had any farther intelligence from Doubting Castle."

"Willingly," replied he, "though I have but little to communicate."

The Booby Squire

A LONG TIME ELAPSED, SAID BUCKTHORNE, WITHOUT MY RECEIVING ANY accounts of my cousin and his estate. Indeed, I felt so much soreness on the subject, that I wished if possible to shut it from my thoughts. At length chance took me to that part of the country, and I could not refrain from making some inquiries.

I learnt that my cousin had grown up ignorant, self-willed, and clownish. His ignorance and clownishness had prevented his mingling with the neighboring gentry: in spite of his great fortune, he had been unsuccessful in an attempt to gain the hand of the daughter of the parson, and had at length shrunk into the limits of such a society as a mere man of wealth can gather in a country neighborhood.

He kept horses and hounds, and a roaring table, at which were collected the loose livers of the country round, and the shabby gentlemen of a village in the vicinity. When he could get no other company, he would smoke and drink with his own servants, who in turn fleeced and despised him. Still, with all his apparent prodigality, he had a leaven of the old man in him, which showed that he was his trueborn son. He lived far within his income, was vulgar in his expenses, and penurious in many points wherein a gentleman would be extravagant. His house-servants were obliged occasionally to work on his estate, and part of the pleasure-grounds were ploughed up and devoted to husbandry.

His table, though plentiful, was coarse; his liquors were strong and bad; and more ale and whisky were expended in his establishment than generous wine. He was loud and arrogant at his own table, and exacted a rich man's homage from his vulgar and obsequious guests.

As to Iron John, his old grandfather, he had grown impatient of the tight hand his own grandson kept over him, and quarrelled with him soon after he came to the estate. The old man had retired to the neighboring village, where he lived on the legacy of his late master, in a small cottage, and was as seldom seen out of it as a rat out of his hole in daylight.

The cub, like Caliban, seemed to have an instinctive attachment to his mother. She resided with him, but, from long habit, she acted more as a servant than as a mistress of the mansion; for she toiled in all the domestic drudgery, and was oftener in the kitchen than the parlor. Such was the information which I collected of my rival cousin, who had so unexpectedly elbowed me out of all my expectations.

I now felt an irresistible hankering to pay a visit to this scene of my boyhood, and to get a peep at the odd kind of life that was passing within the mansion of my maternal ancestors. I deter-mined to do so in disguise. My booby cousin had never seen enough of me to be very familiar with my countenance, and a few years make great difference between youth and manhood. I understood he was a breeder of cattle, and proud of his stock; I dressed myself therefore as a substantial farmer, and with the assistance of a red scratch that came low down on my forehead, made a complete change in my physiognomy.

It was past three o'clock when I arrived at the gate of the park, and was admitted by an old woman who was washing in a dilapidated building which had once been a porter's lodge. I advanced up the remains of a noble avenue, many of the trees of which had been cut down and sold for timber. The grounds were in scarcely better keeping than during my uncle's lifetime. The grass was overgrown with weeds, and the trees wanted pruning and clearing of dead branches. Cattle were grazing about the lawns, and ducks and geese swimming in the fish-ponds. The road to the house bore very few traces of carriage-wheels, as my cousin received few visitors but such as came on foot or horseback, and never used a carriage himself. Once, indeed, as I was told, he had the old family carriage drawn out from among the dust and cobwebs of the coach-house, and furbished up, and driven, with his mother, to the village church, to take formal possession of the family pew; but there was such hooting and laughing after them, as they passed through the village, and such giggling and bantering about the church-door, that the pageant had never made a reappearance.

As I approached the house, a legion of whelps sallied out, barking at me, accompanied by the low howling, rather than barking, of two old worn out bloodhounds, which I recognized for the ancient lifeguards of my uncle. The house had still a neglected random appearance, though much altered for the better since my last visit. Several of the windows were broken and patched up with boards, and others had been bricked up to save taxes. I observed smoke, however, rising from the chimneys, a phenomenon rarely witnessed in the ancient establishment. On passing that part of the house where the dining-room was situated, I heard the sound of boisterous merriment, where three or four voices were talking at once, and oaths and laughter were horribly mingled.

The uproar of the dogs had brought a servant to the door, a tall hard-fisted country clown, with a livery coat put over the under garments of a ploughman. I requested to see the master of the house, but was told that he was at dinner with some "gem-men" of the neighborhood. I made known my business, and sent in to know if I might talk with the master about his cattle, for I felt a great desire to have a peep at him in his orgies.

Word was returned that he was engaged with company, and could not attend to business, but that if I would step in and take a drink of something, I was heartily welcome. I accordingly entered the hall, where whips and hats of all kinds and shapes were lying on an oaken table; two or three clownish servants were lounging about; every thing had a look of confusion and carelessness.

The apartments through which I passed had the same air of departed gentility and sluttish housekeeping. The once rich curtains were faded and dusty, the furniture greased and tarnished. On entering the dining-room I found a number of odd, vulgar-looking, rustic gentlemen seated round a table, on which were bottles, decanters, tankards, pipes, and tobacco. Several dogs were lying about the room, or sitting and watching their masters, and one was gnawing a bone under a side-table. The master of the feast sat at the head of the board. He was greatly altered. He had grown thick-set and rather gummy, with a fiery foxy head of hair. There was a singular mixture of foolishness, arrogance, and conceit, in his countenance. He was dressed in a vulgarly fine style, with leather breeches, a red waistcoat, and green coat, and was evidently, like his guests, a little flushed with drinking. The whole company stared at me with a whimsical muzzy look, like men whose senses were a little obfuscated by beer rather than wine.

My cousin, (God forgive me! the appellation sticks in my throat,) my cousin invited me with awkward civility, or, as he intended it, condescension, to sit to the table and drink. We talked, as usual, about the weather, the crops, politics, and hard times. My cousin was a loud politician, and evidently accustomed to talk without contradiction at his own table. He was amazingly loyal, and talked of standing by the throne to the last guinea, "as every gentleman of fortune should do." The village excise-man, who was half asleep, could just ejaculate "very true" to every thing he said. The conversation turned upon cattle; he boasted of his breed, his mode of crossing it, and of the general management of his estate. This unluckily drew on a history of the place and of the family. He spoke of my late uncle with the greatest irreverence, which I could easily forgive. He mentioned my name, and my blood began to boil. He described my frequent visits to my uncle, when I was a lad, and I found the varlet, even at that time, imp as he was, had known that he was to inherit the estate. He described the scene of my uncle's death, and the opening of the will, with a degree of coarse humor that I had not expected from him; and, vexed as I was, I could not help joining in the laugh, for I have always relished a joke, even though made at my own expense. He went on to speak of my various pursuits, my strolling freak, and that somewhat nettled me; at length he talked of my parents. He ridiculed my father; I stomached even that, though with great difficulty. He mentioned my mother with a sneer, and in an instant he lay sprawling at my feet.

Here a tumult succeeded: the table was nearly overturned; bottles, glasses, and tankards, rolled crashing and clattering about the floor. The company seized hold of both of us, to keep us from doing any further mischief. I struggled to get loose, for I was boiling with fury. My cousin defied me to strip and fight him on the lawn. I agreed, for I felt the strength of a giant in me, and I longed to pommel him soundly.

Away then we were borne. A ring was formed. I had a second assigned me in true boxing style. My cousin, as he advanced to fight, said something about his generosity in showing me such fair play, when I had made such an unprovoked attack upon him at his own table. "Stop there," cried I, in a rage. "Unprovoked? know that I am John Buckthorne, and you have insulted the memory of my mother."

The lout was suddenly struck by what I said: he drew back, and thought for a moment.

"Nay, damn it," said he, "that's too much—that's clean another thing—I've a mother myself—and no one shall speak ill of her, bad as she is."

He paused again: nature seemed to have a rough struggle in his rude bosom.

"Damn it, cousin," cried he, "I'm sorry for what I said. "Thou'st served me right in knocking me down, and I like thee the better for it. Here's my hand: come and live with me, and damn me but the best room in the house, and the best horse in the stable, shall be at thy service."

I declare to you I was strongly moved at this instance of nature breaking her way through such a lump of flesh. I forgave the fellow in a moment his two heinous crimes, of having been born in wedlock, and inheriting my estate. I shook the hand he offered me, to convince him that I bore him no ill-will; and then making my way through the gaping crowd of toadeaters, bade adieu to my uncle's domains for ever.—This is the last I have seen or heard of my cousin, or of the domestic concerns of Doubting Castle.

The Strolling Manager

As I was walking one morning with Buckthorne near one of the principal theatres, he directed my attention to a group of those equivocal beings that may often be seen hovering about the stage-doors of theatres. They were marvellously ill-favored in their attire, their coats buttoned up to their chins; yet they wore their hats smartly on one side, and had a certain knowing, dirty-gentlemanlike air, which is common to the subalterns of the drama. Buckthorne knew them well by early experience.

"These," said he, "are the ghosts of departed kings and heroes; fellows who sway sceptres and truncheons; command kingdoms and armies; and after giving away realms and treasures over night, have scarce a shilling to pay for a breakfast in the morning. Yet the y have the true vagabond abhorrence of all useful and industrious employment; and they have their pleasures too; one of which is to lounge in this way in the sunshine, at the stage-door, during rehearsals, and make hackneyed theatrical jokes on all passers-by. Nothing is more traditional and legitimate than the stage. Old scenery, old clothes, old sentiments, old ranting, and old jokes, are handed down from generation to generation; and will probably continue to be so until time shall be no more. Every hanger-on of a theatre becomes a wag by inheritance, and flourishes about at tap-rooms and sixpenny dubs with the property jokes of the green-room."

While amusing ourselves with reconnoitering this group, we noticed one in particular who appeared to be the oracle. He was a weatherbeaten veteran, a little bronzed by time and beer, who had no doubt grown gray in the parts of robbers, cardinals, Roman senators, and walking noblemen.

"There is something in the set of that hat, and the turn of that physiognomy, extremely familiar to me," said Buckthorne. He looked a little closer.—"I cannot be mistaken, that must be my old brother of the truncheon, Flimsey, the tragic hero of the Strolling Company."

It was he in fact. The poor fellow showed evident signs that times went hard with him, he was so finely and shabbily dressed. His coat was somewhat threadbare, and of the Lord Townley cut; single-breasted, and scarcely capable of meeting in front of his body, which, from long intimacy, had acquired the symmetry and robustness of a beer barrel. He wore a pair of dingy-white stockinet pantaloons, which had much ado to reach his waistcoat; a great quantity of dirty cravat; and a pair of old russet-colored tragedy boots.

When his companions had dispersed, Buckthorne drew him aside, and made himself known to him. The tragic veteran could scarcely recognise him, or believe that he was really his quondam associate, "little Gentleman Jack." Buckthorne invited him to a neighboring coffee-house to talk over old times; and in the course of a little while we were put in possession of his history in brief.

He had continued to act the heroes in the strolling company for some time after Buckthorne had left it, or rather had been driven from it so abruptly. At length the manager died, and the troop was thrown into confusion. Every one aspired to the crown, every one was for taking the lead; and the manager's widow, although a tragedy queen, and a brimstone to boot, pronounced it utterly impossible for a woman to keep any control over such a set of tempestuous rascallions.

"Upon this hint, I spoke," said Flimsey. I stepped forward, and offered my services in the most effectual way. They were accepted. In a week's time I married the widow, and succeeded to the throne. "The funeral baked meats did coldly furnish forth the marriage table," as Hamlet says. But the ghost of my predecessor never haunted me; and I inherited crowns, sceptres, bowls, daggers, and all the stage trappings and trumpery, not omitting the widow, without the least molestation.

I now led a flourishing life of it; for our company was pretty strong and attractive, and as my wife and I took the heavy parts of tragedy, it was a great saving to the treasury. We carried off the palm from all the rival shows at country fairs; and I assure you we have even drawn full houses, and been applauded by the critics at Batlemy Fair itself, though we had Astley's troop, the Irish giant, and "the death of Nelson" in wax-work, to contend against.

I soon began to experience, however, the cares of command. I discovered that there were cabals breaking out in the company, headed by the clown, who you may recollect was a terribly peevish, fractious fellow, and always in ill-humor. I had a great mind to turn him off at once, but I could not do without him, for there was not a droller scoundrel on the stage. His very shape was comic, for he had but to turn his back upon the audience, and all the ladies were ready to die with laughing. He felt his importance, and took advantage of it. He would keep the audience in a continual roar, and then come behind the soles, and fret and fume, and play the very devil. I excused a great deal in him, however, knowing that comic actors are a little prone to this infirmity of temper.

I had another trouble of a nearer and dearer nature to struggle with, which was the affection of my wife. As ill-luck would have it, she took it into her head to be very fond of me, and became intolerably jealous. I could not keep a pretty girl in the company, and hardly dared embrace an ugly one, even when my part required it. I have known her reduce a fine lady to tatters, "to very rags," as Hamlet says, in an instant, and destroy one of the very best dresses in the wardrobe, merely because she saw me kiss her at the side scenes; though I give you my honor it was done merely by way of rehearsal.

This was doubly annoying, because I have a natural liking to pretty faces, and wish to have them about me; and because they are indispensable to the success of a company at a fair, where one has to vie with so many rival theatres. But when once a jealous wife gets a freak in her head, there's no use in talking of interest or any thing else. Egad, sir, I have more than once trembled when, during a fit of her tantrums, she was playing high tragedy, and flourishing her tin dagger on the stage, lest she should give way to her humor, and stab some fancied rival in good earnest.

I went on better, however, than could be expected, considering the weakness of my flesh, and the violence of my rib. I had not a much worse time of it than old Jupiter, whose spouse was continually ferreting out some new intrigue, and making the heavens almost too hot to hold him.

At length, as luck would have it, we were performing at a country fair, when I understood the theatre of a neighboring town to be vacant. I had always been desirous to be enrolled in a settled company, and the height of my desire was to get on a par with a brother-in-law, who was manager of a regular theatre, and who had looked down upon me. Here was an opportunity not to be neglected. I concluded an agreement with the proprietors, and in a few days opened the theatre with great eclat.

Behold me now at the summit of my ambition, "the high top-gallant of my joy," as Romeo says. No longer a chieftain of a wandering tribe, but a monarch of a Intimate throne, and entitled to call even the great potentates of Covent Garden and Drury Lane cousins. You, no doubt, think my happiness complete. Alas, sir! I was one of the most uncomfortable dogs living. No one knows, who has not tried, the miser of a manager; but above all of a country manager. No one can conceive the contentions and quarrels within doors, the oppressions and vexations from without. I was pestered with the bloods and loungers of a country town, who infested my green-room, and played the mischief among my actresses. But there was no shaking them off. It would have been ruin to affront them; for though troublesome friends, they would have been dangerous enemies. Then there were the village critics and villa amateurs, who were continually tormenting me with advice, and getting into a passion if I would not take it; especially the village doctor and the village attorney, who had both been to London occasionally, and knew what acting should be.

I had also to manage as arrant a crew of scapegraces as ever were collected together within the walls of a theatre. I had been obliged to combine my original troop with some of the former troop of the theatre, who were favorites of the public. Here was a mixture that produced perpetual ferment. They were till the time either fighting or frolicking with each other, and I scarcely know which mood was least troublesome. If they quarrelled, every thing went wrong; and if they were friends, they were continually playing off some prank upon each other, or upon me; for I had unhappily acquired among them the character of an easy, good-natured fellow—the worst character that a manager can possess.

Their waggery at times drove me almost crazy; for there is noting so vexatious as the hackneyed tricks and hoaxes and pleasantries of a veteran band of theatrical vagabonds. I relished than well enough, it is true, while I was merely one of the company, but as manager I found them destestable. They were incessantly bringing some disgrace upon the theatre by their tavern frolicks and their pranks about the country town. All my lectures about the importance of keeping up the dignity of the profession and the respectability of the company were in vain. The villains could not sympathize with the delicate feelings of a man in station. They even trifled with the seriousness of stage business. I have had the whole piece interrupted, and a crowded audience of at least twenty-five pounds kept waiting, because the actors had hid away the breeches of Rosalind; and have known Hamlet to stalk solemnly on to deliver his soliloquy, with a dish-clout pinned to his skirts. Such are the baleful consequences of a manager's getting a character for good-nature.

I was intolerably annoyed, too, by the great actors who came down starring, as it is called, from London. Of all baneful influences, keep me from that of a London star.

A first-rate actress going the rounds of the country theatres is as bad as a blazing comet whisking about the heavens, and shaking fire and plagues and discords from its tail.

The moment one of these "heavenly bodies" appeared in my horizon, I was sure to be in hot water. My theatre was overrun by provincial dandies, copper-washed counterfeits of Bond-street loungers, who are always proud to be in the train of an actress from town, and anxious to be thought on exceeding good terms with her. It was really a relief to me when some random young nobleman would come in pursuit of the bait, and awe all this small fry at a distance. I have always felt myself more at ease with a nobleman than with the dandy of a country town.

And then the injuries I suffered in my personal dignity and my managerial authority from the visits of these great London actors! 'Sblood, sir, I was no longer master of myself on my throne. I was hectored and lectured in my own green-room, and made an absolute nincompoop on my own stage. There is no tyrant so absolute and capricious as a London star at a country theatre. I dreaded the sight of all of them, and yet if I did not engage them, I was sure of having the public clamorous against me. They drew full houses, and appeared to be making my fortune; but they swallowed up all the profits by their insatiable demands. They were absolute tape-worms to my little theatre; the more it took in the poorer it grew. They were sure to leave me with an exhausted public, empty benches, and a score or two of affronts to settle among the town's folk, in consequence of misunderstandings about the taking of places.

But the worst thing I had to undergo in my managerial career was patronage. Oh, sir! of all things deliver me from the patronage of the great people of a country town. It was my ruin. You must know that this town, though small, was filled with feuds, and parties, and great folks; being a busy little trading and manufacturing town. The mischief was that their greatness was of a kind not to be settled by reference to the court calendar, or college of heraldry; it was therefore the most quarrelsome kind of greatness in existence. You smile, sir, but let me tell you there are no feuds more furious than the frontier feuds which take place in these "debatable lands" of gentility. The most violent dispute that I ever knew in high life was one which occurred at a country town, on a question of precedence between the ladies of a manufacturer of pins and a manufacturer of needles.

At the town where I was situated there were perpetual altercations of the kind. The head manufacturer's lady, for instance, was at daggers-drawings with the head shopkeeper's, and both ware too rich and had too many friends to be treated lightly.

The doctor's and lawyer's ladies held their heads still higher; but they in their turn were kept in check by the wife of a country banker, who kept her own carriage; while a masculine widow of cracked character and second-hand fashion, who lived in a large house, and claimed to be in some way related to nobility, looked down upon them all. To be sure, her manners were not over elegant, nor her fortune over large; but then, sir, her blood—oh, her blood carried it all hollow; there was no withstanding a woman with such blood in her veins.

After all, her claims to high connexion were questioned, and she had frequent battles for precedence at balls and assemblies with some of the sturdy dames of the neighborhood, who stood upon their wealth and their virtue; but then she had two dashing daughters, who dressed as fine as dragons, had as high blood as their mother, and seconded her in every thing; so they carried their point with high heads, and every body hated, abused, and stood in awe of the Fantadlins.

Such was the state of the fashionable world in this self-important little town. Unluckily, I was not as well acquainted with its politics as I should have been. I had found myself a stranger and in great perplexities during my first season; I determined therefore, to put myself under the patronage of some powerful same, and thus to take the field with the prejudices of the public in my favor. I cast round my thoughts for the purpose, and in an evil hour they fell upon Mrs. Fantadlin. No one seemed to me to have a more absolute sway in the world of fashion. I had always noticed that her party slammed the box-door the loudest at the theatre; had most beaus attending on them, and talked and laughed loudest during the performance; and then the Miss Fantadlins wore always more feathers and flowers than any other ladies; and used quizzing-glasses incessantly. The first evening of my theatre's re-opening, therefore, was announced in staring capitals on the play-bills, as under the patronage of "The Honorable Mrs. Fantadlin."

Sir, the whole community flew to arms! the banker's wife felt her dignity grievously insulted at not having the preference; her husband being high bailiff and the richest man in the place. She immediately issued invitations for a large party, for the night of the performance, and asked many a lady to it whom she never had noticed before. Presume to patronize the theatre! Insufferable! And then for me to dare to term her "The Honorable!" What claim had she to the title forsooth! The fashionable world had long groaned under the tyranny of the Fantadlins, and were glad to make a common cause against this new instance of assumption. Those, too, who had never before been noticed by the banker's lady were ready to enlist in any quarrel for the honor of her acquaintance. All minor fends were forgotten. The doctor's lady and the lawyer's lady met together, and the manufacturer's lady and the shopkeeper's lady kissed each other; and all, headed by the bankers lady, voted the theatre a *bore*, and determined to encourage nothing but the Indian Jugglers and Mr. Walker's Eidouranion.

Alas for poor Pillgarlick! I knew little the mischief that was brewing against me. My box-book remained blank; the evening arrived; but no audience. The music struck up to a tolerable pit and gallery, but no fashionables! I peeped anxiously from behind the curtain, but the time passed away; the play was retarded until pit and gallery became furious; and I had to raise the curtain, and play my greatest part in tragedy to "a beggarly account of empty boxes."

It is true the Fantadlins came late, as was their custom, and entered like a tempest, with a flutter of feathers and red shawls; but they were evidently disconcerted at finding they had no one to admire and envy them, and were enraged at this glaring defection of their fashionable followers. All the beau-monde were engaged at the banker's lady's rout. They remained for some time in solitary and uncomfortable state, and though they had the theatre almost to themselves, yet, for the first time, they talked in whispers. They left the house at the end of the first piece, and I never saw them afterwards.

Such was the rock on which I split. I never got over the patronage of the Fantadlin family. My house was deserted; my actors grew discontented because they were ill paid; my door became a hammering place for every bailiff in the country; and my wife became more and more shrewish and tormenting the more I wanted comfort.

I tried for a time the usual consolation of a harassed and henpecked man; I took to the bottle, and tried to tipple away my cares, but in vain. I don't mean to decry the bottle; it is no doubt an excellent remedy in many cases, but it did not answer in mine. It cracked my voice, coppered my nose, but neither improved my wife nor my affairs. My establishment became a scene of confusion and peculation. I was considered a ruined man, and of course fair game for every one to pluck at, as every one plunders a sinking ship. Day after day some of the troop deserted, and, like deserting soldiers, carried off their arms and accoutrements with them. In this manner my wardrobe took legs and walked away, my finery strolled all over the country, my swords and daggers glittered in every barn, until, at last, my tailor made "one fell swoop," and carried off three dress-coats, half a dozen doublets, and nineteen pair of flesh-colored pantaloons.

This was the "be all and the end all" of my fortune. I no longer hesitated what to do. Egad, thought I, since stealing is the order of the day, I'll steal too; so I secretly gathered together the jewels of my wardrobe, packed up a hero's dress in a handkerchief, slung it on the end of a tragedy sword, and quietly stole off at dead of night, "the bell then beating one," leaving my queen and kingdom to the mercy of my rebellious subjects, and my merciless foes the bumbailiffs.

Such, sir, was the "end of all my greatness." I was heartily cured of all passion for governing, and returned once more into the ranks. I had for some time the usual run of an actor's life: I played in various country theatres, at fairs, and in barns; sometimes hard pushed, sometimes flush, until, on one occasion, I came within an ace of making my fortune, and becoming one of the wonders of the age.

I was playing the part of Richard the Third in a country barn, and in my best style; for, to tell the truth, I was a little in liquor, and the critics of the company always observed that I played with most effect when I had a glass too much. There was a thunder of applause when I came to that part where Richard cries for "a horse! a horse!" My cracked voice had always a wonderful effect here; it was like two voices run into one; you would have thought two men had been calling for a horse, or that Richard had called for two horses. And when I flung the taunt at Richmond, "Richard is *hoarse* with calling thee to arms," I thought the barn would have come down about my ears with the raptures of the audience.

The very next morning a person waited upon me at my lodgings. I saw at once he was a gentleman by his dress; for he had a large brooch in his bosom, thick rings on his fingers, and used a quizzing-glass. And a gentleman he proved to be; for I soon ascertained that he was a kept author, or kind of literary tailor to one of the great London theatres; one who worked under the manager's directions, and cut up and cut down plays, and patched and pieced, and new faced, and turned them inside out; in short, he was one of the readiest and greatest writers of the day.

He was now on a foraging excursion in quest of something that might be got up for a prodigy. The theatre, it seems, was in desperate condition—nothing but a miracle could save it. He had seen me act Richard the night before, and had pitched upon me for that miracle. I had a remarkable bluster in my style and swagger in my gait. I certainly differed from all other heroes of the barn: so the thought struck the agent to bring me out as a theatrical wonder, as the restorer of natural and legitimate acting, as this only one who could understand and act Shakspeare rightly.

When he opened his plan I shrunk from it with becoming modesty, for well as I thought of myself, I doubted my competency to such an undertaking.

I hinted at my imperfect knowledge of Shakspeare, having played his characters only after mutilated copies, interlarded with a great deal of my own talk by way of helping memory or heightening the effect

"So much the better," cried the gentleman with rings on his fingers; "so much the better. New readings, sir!—new readings! Don't study a line—let us have Shakspeare after your own fashion."

"But then my voice was cracked; it could not fill a London theatre."

"So much the better! so much the better! The public is tired of intonation—the *ore rotundo* has had its day. No, sir, your cracked voice is the very thing—spit and splutter, and snap and snarl, and 'play the very dog' about the stage, and you'll be the making of us."

"But then,"—I could not help blushing to the end of my very nose as I said it, but I was determined to be candid;—"but then," added I, there is one awkward circumstance; I have an unlucky habit—my misfortunes, and the exposures to which one is subjected in country barns, have obliged me now and then to—to—take a drop of something comfortable—and so—and so—."

"What! you drink?" cried the agent eagerly.

I bowed my head in blushing acknowledgment.

"So much the better! so much the better! The irregularities of genius! A sober fellow is commonplace. The public like an actor that drinks. Give me your hand sir. You're the very man to make a dash with."

I still hung back with lingering diffidence, declaring myself unworthy of such praise.

"'Sblood, man," cried he, "no praise at all. You don't imagine *I* think you a wonder; I only want the public to think so. Nothing is so easy as to gull the public, if you only set up a prodigy. Common talent any body can measure by common rule; but a prodigy sets all rule and measurement at defiance."

These words opened my eyes in an instant: we now came to a proper understanding, less flattering, it is true, to my vanity, but much more satisfactory to my judgment.

It was agreed that I should make my appearance before a London audience, as a dramatic sun just bursting from behind the clouds: one that was to banish all the lesser lights and false fires of the stage. Every precaution was to be taken to possess the public mind at every avenue. The pit was to be packed with sturdy clappers; the newspapers secured by vehement puffers; every theatrical resort to be haunted by hireling talkers. In a word, every engine of theatrical humbug was to be put in action. Wherever I differed from former actors, it was to be maintained that I was right and they were wrong. If I ranted, it was to be pure passion; if I were vulgar, it was to be pronounced a familiar touch of nature; if I made any queer blunder, it was to be a new reading. If my voice cracked, or I got out in my part, I was only to bounce, and grin, and snarl at the audience, and make any horrible grimace that came into my head, and my admirers were to call it "a great point," and to fall back and shout and yell with rapture.

"In short," said the gentleman with the quizzing-glass, "strike out boldly and bravely: no matter how or what you do, so that it be but odd and strange. If you do but escape pelting the first night, your fortune and the fortune of the theatre is made."

I set off for London, therefore, in company with the kept author, full of new plans and new hopes. I was to be the restorer of Shakspeare and Nature, and the legitimate drama; my very swagger was to be heroic, and my cracked voice the standard of elocution. Alas, sir, my usual luck attended me: before I arrived at the metropolis a rival wonder had appeared; a woman who could dance the slack rope, and run up a cord from the stage to the gallery with fireworks all round her. She was seized on by the manager with avidity. She was the saving of the great national theatre for the season. Nothing was talked of but Madame Saqui's fireworks and flesh-colored pantaloons; and Nature, Shakspeare, the legitimate drama, and poor Pillgarlick, were completely left in the lurch.

When Madame Saqui's performance grew stale, other wonders succeeded: horses, and harlequinades, and mummery of all kinds; until another dramatic prodigy was brought forward to play the very game for which I had been intended. I called upon the kept author for an explanation, but he was deeply engaged in writing a melo-drama or a pantomime, and was extremely testy on being interrupted in his studies. However, as the theatre was in some measure pledged to provide for me, the manager acted, according to the usual phrase, "like a man of honor," and I received an appointment in the corps. It had been a turn of a die whether I should be Alexander the Great or Alexander the coppersmith—the latter carried it. I could not be put at the head of the drama, so I was put at the tail of it. In other words, I was enrolled among the number of what are called *useful men*; those who enact soldiers, senators, and Banquo's shadowy line. I was perfectly satisfied with my lot; for I have always been a bit of a philosopher. If my situation was not splendid, it at least was secure; and in fact I have seen half a dozen prodigies appear, dazzle, burst like bubbles and pass away, and yet here I am, snug, unenvied and unmolested, at the foot of the profession.

You may smile; but let me tell you, we "useful men" are the only comfortable actors on the stage. We are safe from hisses, and below the hope of applause. We fear not the success of rivals, now dread the critic's pen. So long as we get the words of our parts, and they are not often many, it is all we care for. We have our own merriment, our own friends, and our own admirers—for every actor has his friends and admirers, from the highest to the lowest. The first-rate actor dines with the noble amateur, and entertains a fashionable table with scraps and songs and theatrical slip-slop. The second-rate actors have their second-rate friends and admirers, with whom they likewise spout tragedy and talk slip-slop—and so down even to us; who have our friends and admirers among spruce clerks and aspiring apprentices—who treat us to a dinner now and then, and enjoy at tenth hand the same scraps and songs and slip-slop that have been served up by our more fortunate brethren at the tables of the great.

I now, for the first time in my theatrical life, experience what true pleasure is. I have known enough of notoriety to pity the poor devils who are called favorites of the public. I would rather be a kitten in the arms of a spoiled child, to be one moment patted and pampered and the next moment thumped over the head with the spoon. I smile to see our leading actors fretting themselves with envy and jealousy about a trumpery renown, questionable in its quality, and uncertain in its duration. I laugh, too, though of course in my sleeve, at the bustle and importance, and trouble and perplexities of our manager—who is harassing himself to death in the hopeless effort to please every body.

I have found among my fellow subalterns two or three quondam managers, who like myself have wielded the sceptres of country theatres, and we have many a sly joke together at the expense of the manager and the public. Sometimes, too we meet, like deposed and exiled kings, talk over the events of our respective reigns, moralize over a tankard of ale, and laugh at the humbug of the great and little world; which, I take it, is the essence of practical philosophy.

Thus end the anecdotes of Buckthorne and his friends. It grieves me much that I could not procure from him further particulars of his history, and especially of that part of it which passed in town. He had evidently seen much of literary life; and, as he had never risen to eminence in letters, and yet was free from the gall of disappointment, I had hoped to gain some candid intelligence concerning his contemporaries. The testimony of such an honest chronicler would have been particularly valuable at the present time; when, owing to the extreme fecundity of the press, and the thousand anecdotes, criticisms, and biographical sketches that are daily poured forth concerning public characters it is extremely difficult to get at any truth concerning

He was always, however, excessively reserved and fastidious on this point, at which I very much wondered, authors in general appearing to think each other fair game, and being ready to serve each other up for the amusement of the public.

A few mornings after hearing the history of the ex-manager, I was surprised by a visit from Buckthorne before I was out of bed. He was dressed for travelling.

"Give me joy! give me joy!" said he, rubbing his hands with the utmost glee, "my great expectations are realized!"

I gazed at him with a look of wonder and inquiry.

"My booby cousin is dead!" cried he; "may he rest in peace! he nearly broke his neck in a fall from his horse in a fox-chase. By good luck, he lived long enough to make his will. He has made me his heir, partly out of an odd feeling of retributive justice, and partly because, as he says, none of his own family nor friends know how to enjoy such an estate. I'm off to the country to take possession. I've done with authorship. That for the critics!" said he, snapping his finger. "Come down to Doubting Castle, when I get settled, and, egad, I'll give you a rouse." So saying, he shook me heartily by the hand, and bounded off in high spirits.

A long time elapsed before I heard from him again. Indeed, it was but lately that I received a letter, written in the happiest of moods. He was getting the estate in fine order; every thing went to his wishes; and what was more, he was married to Sacharissa, who it seems had always entertained an ardent though secret attachment for him, which he fortunately discovered just after coming to his estate.

"I find," said he, "you are a little given to the sin of authorship, which I renounce: if the anecdotes I have given you of my story are of any interest, you may make use of them; but come down to Doubting Castle, and see how we live, and I'll give you my whole London life over a social glass; and a rattling history it shall be about authors and reviewers."

If ever I visit Doubting Castle and get the history he promises, the public shall be sure to hear of it.

PART III

The Italian Banditti

The Inn at Terracina

CRACK! CRACK! CRACK! CRACK! CRACK!

"Here comes the estafette from Naples," said mine host of the inn at Terracina; "bring out the relay."

The estafette came galloping up the road according to custom, brandishing over his head a short-handled whip, with a long, knotted lash, every smack of which made a report like a pistol. He was a tight, square-set young fellow, in the usual uniform: a smart blue coat, ornamented with facings and gold lace, but so short behind as to reach scarcely below his waistband, and cocked up not unlike the tail of a wren; a cocked hat edged with gold lace; a pair of stiff riding-boots; but, instead of the usual leathern breeches, he had a fragment of a pair of drawers, that scarcely furnished an apology for modesty to hide behind.

The estafette galloped up to the door, and jumped from his horse.

"A glass of rosolio, a fresh horse, and a pair of breeches," said he, "and quickly, *per l'amor di Dio*, I am behind my time, and must be off!"

"San Gennaro!" replied the host; "why, where hast thou left thy garment?"

"Among the robbers between this and Fondi."

"What, rob an estafette! I never heard of such folly. What could they hope to get from thee?"

"My leather breeches!" replied the estafette. "They were bran new, and shone like gold, and hit the fancy of the captain."

"Well, these fellows grow worse and worse. To meddle with an estafette! and that merely for the sake of a pair of leather breeches!"

The robbing of the government messenger seemed to strike the host with more astonishment than any other enormity that had taken place on the road; and, indeed, it was the first time so wanton an outrage had been committed; the robbers generally taking care not to meddle with any thing belonging to government.

The estafette was by this time equipped, for he had not lost an instant in making his preparations while talking. The relay was ready; the rosolio tossed off; he grasped the reins and the stirrup.

"Were there many robbers in the band?" said a handsome, dark young man, stepping forward from the door of the inn.

"As formidable a band as ever I saw," said the estafette, springing into the saddle.

"Are they cruel to travellers?" said a beautiful young Venetian lady, who had been hanging on the gentleman's arm.

"Cruel, signora!" echoed the estafette, giving a glance at the lady as he put spurs to his horse. "Corpo di Bacco! They stiletto all the men; and, as to the women—" Crack! crack! crack! crack! crack!—The last words were drowned in the smacking of the whip, and away galloped the estafette along the road to the Pontine marshes.

"Holy Virgin!" ejaculated the fair Venetian, "what will become of us!"

The inn of which we are speaking stands just outside the walls of Terracina, under a vast precipitous height of rocks, crowned with the rains of the castle of Theodric the Goth. The situation of Terracina is remarkable. It is a little, ancient, lazy Italian town, on the frontiers of the Roman territory. There seems to be an idle pause in every thing about the place. The Mediterranean spreads before it—that sea without flux or reflux. The port is without a sail, excepting that once in a while a solitary felucca may be seen disgorging its holy cargo of baccala, or codfish, the meagre provision for the quaresima, or Lent. The inhabitants are apparently a listless, heedless race, as people of soft sunny climates are apt to be; but under this passive, indolent exterior are said to lurk dangerous qualities. They are supposed by many to be little better than the banditti of the neighboring mountains, and indeed to hold a secret correspondence with them. The solitary watchtowers, erected here and there along the coast, speak of pirates and corsairs that hover about these shores; while the low huts, as stations for soldiers, which dot the distant road, as it winds up through an olive grove, intimate that in the ascent there is danger for the traveller, and facility for the bandit. Indeed, it is between this town and Fondi that the road to Naples is most infested by banditti. It has several winding and solitary places, where the robbers are enabled to see the traveller from a distance, from the brows of hills or impending precipices, and to lie in wait for him at lonely and difficult passes.

The Italian robbers are a desperate class of men, that have almost formed themselves into an order of society. They wear a kind of uniform, or rather costume, which openly designates their profession. This is probably done to diminish its skulking, lawless character, and to give it something of a military air in the eyes of the common people; or, perhaps, to catch by outward show and finery the fancies of the young men of the villages, and thus to gain recruits. Their dresses are often very rich and picturesque. They wear jackets and breeches of bright colors, sometimes gayly embroidered; their breasts are covered with medals and relics; their hats are broad-brimmed, with conical crowns, decorated with feathers, or variously-colored ribands; their hair is sometimes gathered in silk nets; they wear a kind of sandal of cloth or leather, bound round the legs with thongs, and extremely flexible, to enable them to scramble with ease and celerity among the mountain precipices; a broad belt of cloth, or a sash of silk net, is stuck full of pistols and stilettos; a carbine is slung at the back; while about them is generally thrown, in a negligent manner, a great dingy mantle, which serves as a protection in storms, or a bed in their bivouacs among the mountains.

They range over a great extent of wild country, along the chain of Apennines, bordering on different states; they know all the difficult passes, the short cuts for retreat, and the impracticable forests of the mountain summits, where no force dare follow them. They are secure of the good-will of the inhabitants of those regions, a poor and semi-barbarous race, whom they never disturb and often enrich. Indeed, they are considered as a sort of illegitimate heroes among the mountain villages, and in certain frontier towns where they dispose of their plunder. Thus countenanced, and sheltered, and secure in the fastnesses of their mountains, the robbers have set the weak police of the Italian states at defiance. It is in vain that their names and descriptions are posted on the doors of country churches, and rewards offered for them, alive or dead; the villagers are either too much awed by the terrible instances of vengeance inflicted by the brigands or have too good an understanding with them to be their betrayers. It is true they are now and then hunted and shot down like beasts of prey by the *gens-d'armes*, their heads put in iron cages, and stuck upon posts by the road-side, or their limbs hung up to blacken in the trees near the places where they have committed their atrocities; but these ghastly spectacles only serve to make some dreary pass of the road still more dreary, and to dismay the traveller, without deterring the bandit.

At the time that the estafette made his sudden appearance almost in *cuerpo*, as has been mentioned, the audacity of the robbers had risen to an unparalleled height. They had laid villas under contribution they had sent messages into country towns to tradesmen and rich burghers, demanding supplies of money, of clothing, or even of luxuries, with menaces of vengeance in case of refusal. They had their spies and emissaries in every town, village, and inn, along the principal roads, to give them notice of the movements and quality of travellers. They had plundered carriages, carried people of rank and fortune into the mountains, and obliged them to write for heavy ransoms, and had committed outrages on females who had fallen into their hands.

Such was briefly the state of the robbers, or rather such was the account of the rumors prevalent concerning them, when the scene took place at the inn of Terracina. The dark handsome young man, and the Venetian lady, incidentally mentioned, had arrived early that afternoon in a private carriage drawn by mules, and attended by a single servant. They had been recently married, were spending the honeymoon in travelling through these delicious countries, and were on their way to visit a rich aunt of the bride at Naples.

The lady was young, and tender, and timid. The stories she had heard along the road had filled her with apprehension, not more for herself than for her husband; for though she had been married almost a month, she still loved him almost to idolatry. When she reached Terracina, the rumors of the road had increased to an alarming magnitude; and the sight of two robbers' skulls, grinning in iron cages, on each side of the old gateway of the town, brought her to a pause. Her husband had tried in vain to reassure her; they had lingered all the afternoon at the inn, until it was too late to think of starting that evening, and the parting words of the estafette completed her affright.

"Let us return to Rome," said she, putting her arm within her husband's, and drawing towards him as if for protection.—"Let us return to Rome, and give up this visit to Naples."

"And give up the visit to your aunt too?" said the husband.

"Nay—what is my aunt in comparison with your safely?" said she, looking up tenderly in his face.

There was something in her tone and manner that showed she really was thinking more of her husband's safety at the moment than of her own; and being so recently married, and a match of pure affection too, it is very possible that she was: at least her husband thought so. Indeed any one who has heard the sweet musical tone of a Venetian voice, and the melting tenderness of a Venetian phrase, and felt the soil witchery of a Venetian eye, would not wonder at the husband's believing whatever they professed. He clasped the white hand that had been laid within his, put his arm round her slender waist, and drawing her fondly to his bosom, "This night, at least," said he, "we will pass at Terracina."

Crack! crack! crack! crack! Crack! Another apparition of the road attracted the attention of mine host and his guests. From the direction of the Pontine marshes, a carriage, drawn by half dozen horses, came driving at a furious rate; the postilions smacking their whips like mad, as is the case when conscious of the greatness or of the munificence of their fare. It was a landaulet with a servant mounted on the dickey. The compact, highly-finished, yet proudly simple construction of the carriage; the quantity of neat, well-arranged trunks and conveniences; the loads of box-coats on the dickey; the fresh, burly, bluff-looking face of the master at the window; and the ruddy, round-headed servant, in close-cropped hair, short coat, drab breeches, and long gaiters, all proclaimed at once that this was the equipage of an Englishman.

"Horses to Fondi," said the Englishman, as the landlord came bowing to the carriage door.

"Would not his Excellenza alight, and take some refreshments?"

"No—he did not mean to eat until he got to Fondi."

"But the horses will be some time in getting ready."

"Ah! that's always the way; nothing but delay in this cursed country."

"If his Excellenza would only walk into the house—"

"No, no, no!—I tell you no!—I want nothing but horses, and as quick as possible. John, see that the horses are got ready, and don't let us be kept here an hour or two. Tell him if we're delayed over the time, I'll lodge a complaint with the post-master."

John touched his hat, and set off to obey his master's orders with the taciturn obedience of an English servant.

In the meantime the Englishman got out of the carriage, and walked up and down before the inn with his hands in his pockets, taking no notice of the crowd of idlers who were gazing at him and his equipage. He was tall, stout, and well made; dressed with neatness and precision; wore a travelling cap of the color of gingerbread; and had rather an unhappy expression about the corners of his mouth: partly from not having yet made his dinner, and partly from not having been able to get on at a greater rate than seven miles an hour. Not that he had any other cause for haste than an Englishman's usual hurry to get to the end of a journey; or, to use the regular phrase, "to get on." Perhaps too he was a little sore from having been fleeced at every stage.

After some time, the servant returned from the stable with a look of some perplexity.

"Are the horses ready, John?"

"No, sir—I never saw such a place. There's no getting any thing done. I think your honor had better step into the house and get something to eat; it will be a long while before we get to Fundy."

"D—n the house—it's a mere trick—I'll not eat any thing, just to spite them," said the Englishman, still more crusty at the prospect of being so long without his dinner.

"They say your honor's very wrong," said John, "to set off at this late hour. The road's full of highwaymen."

"Mere tales to get custom."

"The estafette which passed us was stopped by a whole gang," said John, increasing his emphasis with each additional piece of information.

"I don't believe a word of it."

"They robbed him of his breeches," said John, giving at the same time a hitch to his own waistband.

"All humbug!"

Here the dark handsome young man stepped forward, and addressing the Englishman, very politely, in broken English, invited him to partake of a repast he was about to make.

"Thank'ee," said the Englishman, thrusting his hands deeper into his pockets, and casting a slight side-glance of suspicion at the young man, as if he thought, from his civility, he must have a design upon his purse.

"We shall be most happy, if you will do us the favor," said the lady in her soft Venetian dialect. There was a sweetness in her accents that was most persuasive. The Englishman cast a look upon her countenance; her beauty was still more eloquent. His features instantly relaxed. He made a polite bow. "With great pleasure, Signora," said he.

In short, the eagerness to "get on" was suddenly slackened; the determination to famish himself as far as Fondi, by way of punishing the landlord, was abandoned; John chose an apartment in the inn for his master's reception; and preparations were made to remain there until morning.

The carriage was unpacked of such of its contents as were indispensable for the night. There was the usual parade of trunks and writing-desks, and portfolios and dressing-boxes, and those other oppressive conveniences which burden a comfortable man. The observant loiterers about the inn-door, wrapped up in great dirt-colored cloaks, with only a hawk's eye uncovered, made many remarks to each other on this quantity of luggage that seemed enough for an army. The domestics of the inn talked with wonder of the splendid dressing-case, with its gold and silver furniture, that was spread out on the toilet-table, and the bag of gold that chinked as it was taken out of the trunk. The strange *Milor's* wealth, and the treasures he carried about him, were the talk, that evening, over all Terracina.

The Englishman took some time to make his ablutions and arrange his dress for table; and, after considerable labor and effort in putting himself at his ease, made his appearance, with stiff white cravat, his clothes free from the least speck of dust, and adjusted with precision. He made a civil bow on entering, in the unprofessing English way, which the fair Venetian, accustomed to the complimentary salutations of the continent, considered extremely cold.

The supper, as it was termed by the Italian, or dinner, as the Englishman called it, was now served: heaven and earth, and the waters under the earth, had been moved to furnish it; for there were birds of the air, and beasts of the field, and fish of the sea. The Englishman's servant, too, had turned the kitchen topsy-turvy in his zeal to cook his master a beefsteak; and made his appearance, loaded with ketchup, and soy, and Cayenne pepper, and Harvey sauce, and a bottle of port wine, from that warehouse, the carriage, in which his master seemed desirous of carrying England about the world with him. Indeed the repast was one of those Italian farragoes which require a little qualifying. The tureen of soup was a black sea, with livers, and limbs, and fragments of all kinds of birds and beasts floating like wrecks about it. A meagre winged animal, which my host called a delicate chicken, had evidently died of a consumption. The macaroni was smoked. The beefsteak was tough buffalo's flesh. There was what appeared to be a dish of stewed eels, of which the Englishman ate with great relish; but had nearly refunded them when told that they were vipers, caught among the rocks of Terracina, and esteemed a great delicacy.

Nothing, however, conquers a traveller's spleen sooner than eating, whatever may be the cookery; and nothing brings him into good humor with his company sooner than eating together: the Englishman, therefore, had not half finished his repast and his bottle, before he began to think the Venetian a very tolerable fellow for a foreigner, and his wife almost handsome enough to be an Englishwoman.

In the course of the repast, the usual topics of travellers were discussed, and among others, the reports of robbers, which harassed the mind of the fair Venetian.

The landlord and waiter dipped into the conversation with that familiarity permitted on the continent, and served up so many bloody tales as they served up the dishes, that they almost frightened away the poor lady's appetite.

The Englishman, who had a national antipathy to every thing technically called "humbug," listened to them all with a certain screw of the mouth, expressive of incredulity. There was the well-known story of the school of Terracina, captured by the robbers; and one of the scholars coolly massacred, in order to bring the parents to terms for the ransom of the rest. And another, of a gentleman of Rome, who received his son's ear in a letter, with information, that his son would be remitted to him in this way, by instalments, until he paid the required ransom.

The fair Venetian shuddered as she heard these tales; and the landlord, like a true narrator of the terrible, doubled the dose when he saw how it operated. He was just proceeding to relate the misfortunes of a great English lord and his family, when the Englishman, tired of his volubility, interrupted him, and pronounced these accounts to be mere travellers' tales, or the exaggerations of ignorant peasants and designing innkeepers. The landlord was indignant at the doubt levelled at his stories, and the innuendo levelled at his cloth; he cited, in corroboration, half a dozen tales still more terrible.

"I don't believe a word of them," said the Englishman.

"But the robbers have been tried and executed!"

"All a farce!"

"But their heads are stuck up along the road!"

"Old skulls accumulated during a century."

"The landlord muttered to himself as he went out at the door, "San Gennaro! quanto sono singolari questi Inglesi!"

A fresh hubbub outside of the inn announced the arrival of more travellers; and, from the variety of voices, or rather of clamors, the clattering of hoofs, the rattling of wheels, and the general uproar both within and without, the arrival seemed to be numerous.

It was, in fact, the procaccio and its convoy; a kind of can van which sets out on certain days for the transportation of merchandise, with an escort of soldiery to protect it from the robbers. Travellers avail themselves of its protection, and a long file of carriages generally accompany it.

A considerable time elapsed before either landlord or waiter returned; being hurried hither and thither by that tempest of noise and bustle, which takes place in an

Italian inn on the arrival of any considerable accession of custom. When mine host reappeared, there was a smile of triumph on his countenance.

"Perhaps," said he, as he cleared the table; "perhaps the signor has not heard of what has happened?"

"What?" said the Englishman, dryly.

"Why, the procaccio has brought accounts of fresh exploits of the robbers."

"Pish!"

"There's more news of the English Milor and his family," said the host exultingly.

"An English lord? What English lord?"

"Milor Popkin."

"Lord Popkins? I never heard of such a title!"

"O sicuro! a great nobleman, who passed through here lately with mi ladi and her daughters. A magnifico, one of the grand counsellors of London, an almanno!"

"Almanno—almanno?—tut—he means alderman."

"Sicuro—Aldermanno Popkin, and the Principessa Popkin, and the Signorine Popkin?" said mine host, triumphantly.

He now put himself into an attitude, and would have launched into a full detail, had he not been thwarted by the Englishman, who seemed determined neither to credit nor indulge him in his stories, but dryly motioned for him to clear away the table.

An Italian tongue, however, is not easily checked; that of mine host continued to wag with increasing volubility, as he conveyed the relics of the repast out of the room; and the last that could be distinguished of his voice, as it died away along the corridor, was the iteration of the favorite word, Popkin—Popkin—Popkin—pop—pop—pop.

The arrival of the procaccio had, indeed, filled the house with stories, as it had with guests. The Englishman and his companions walked after supper up and down the large ball, or common room of the inn, which ran through the centre of the building. It was spacious and somewhat dirty, with tables placed in various parts, at which groups of travellers were seated; while others strolled about, waiting, in famished impatience, for their evening's meal.

It was a heterogeneous assemblage of people of all ranks and countries, who had arrived in all kinds of vehicles. Though distinct knots of travellers, yet the travelling together, under one common escort, had jumbled them into a certain degree of companionship on the road; besides, on the continent travellers are always familiar, and nothing is more motley than the groups which gather casually together in sociable conversation in the public rooms of inns.

The formidable number, and formidable guard of the procaccio had prevented any molestation from banditti; but every party of travellers had its tales of wonder, and one carriage vied with another in its budget of assertions and surmises. Fierce whiskered faces had been seen peering over the rocks; carbines and stilettos gleaming from among the bushes; suspicious-looking fellows, with flapped hats, and scowling eyes, had occasionally reconnoitred a straggling carriage, but had disappeared on seeing the guard.

The fair Venetian listened to all these stories with that avidity with which we always pamper any feeling of alarm; even the Englishman began to feel interested in the common topic, and desirous of getting more correct information than mere flying reports. Conquering, therefore, that shyness which is prone to keep an Englishman solitary in crowds, he approached one of the talking groups, the oracle of which was a tall, thin Italian, with long aquiline nose, a high forehead, and lively prominent eye, beaming from under a green velvet travelling cap, with gold tassel. He was of Rome, a surgeon by profession, a poet by choice, and something of an improvisatore.

In the present instance, however, he was talking in plain prose but holding forth with the fluency of one who talks well, and likes to exert his talent. A question or two from the Englishman drew copious replies; for an Englishman sociable among strangers is regarded as a phenomenon on the continent and always treated with attention for the rarity's sake. The improvisatore gave much the same account of the banditti that I have already furnished.

"But why does not the police exert itself, and root them out?" demanded the Englishman.

"Because the police is too weak, and the banditti are too strong," replied the other. "To root them out would be a more difficult task than you imagine. They are connected and almost identified with the mountain peasantry and the people of the villages. The numerous bands have an understanding with each other, and with the country round. A gendarme cannot stir without their being aware of it. They have their scouts every where, who lurk about towns, villages, and inns, mingle in every crowd, and pervade every place of resort. I should not be surprised if some one should be supervising us at this moment."

The fair Venetian looked round fearfully, and turned pale.

Here the improvisatore was interrupted by a lively Neapolitan lawyer.

"By the way," said he, "I recollect a little adventure of a learned doctor, a friend of mine, which happened in this very neighborhood; not far from the ruins of Theodric's Castle, which are on the top of those great rocky heights above the town."

A wish was, of course, expressed to hear the adventure of the doctor by ail excepting the improvisatore, who, being fond of talking and of hearing himself talk, and accustomed, moreover, to harangue without interruption, looked rather annoyed at being checked when in full career. The Neapolitan, however, took no notice of his chagrin, but related the following anecdote.

The Adventure of the Little Antiquary

My friend, the Doctor, was a thorough antiquary; a little rusty, musty old fellow, always groping among ruins. He relished a building as you Englishmen relish a cheese,—the more mouldy and crumbling it was, the more it suited his taste. A shell of an old nameless temple, or the cracked walls of a broken-down amphitheatre, would throw him into raptures; and he took more delight in these crusts and cheese-parings of antiquity, than in the best-conditioned modern palaces.

He was a curious collector of coins also, and had just gained an accession of wealth that almost turned his brain. He had picked up, for instance, several Roman Consulars, half a Roman As, two Funics, which had doubtless belonged to the soldiers of Hannibal, having been found on the very spot where they had encamped among the Apennines. He had, moreover, one Samnite, struck after the Social War, and a Philistis, a queen that never existed; but above all, he valued himself upon a coin, indescribable to any but the initiated in these matters, bearing a cross on one side, and a pegasus on the other, and which, by some antiquarian logic, the little man adduced as an historical document, illustrating the progress of Christianity.

All these precious coins he carried about him in a leathern purse, buried deep in a pocket of his little black breeches.

The last maggot he had taken into his brain, was to hunt after the ancient cities of the Pelasgi, which are said to exist to this day among the mountains of the Abruzzi; but about which a singular degree of obscurity prevails.[1] He had made many discoveries

1. Among the many fond speculations of antiquaries is that of the existence of traces of the ancient Pelasgian cities in the Apennines; and many a wistful eye is cast by the traveller, versed in antiquarian

concerning them, and had recorded a great many valuable notes and memorandums on the subject, in a voluminous book, which he always carried about with him; either for the purpose of frequent reference, or through fear lest the precious document should fall into the hands of brother antiquaries. He had, therefore, a large pocket in the skirt of his coat, where he bore about this inestimable tome, banging against his rear as he walked.

Thus heavily laden with the spoils of antiquity, the good little man, during a sojourn at Terracina, mounted one day the rocky cliffs which overhang the town, to visit the castle of Theodric. He was groping about the ruins towards the hour of sunset, buried in his reflections, his wits no doubt wool-gathering among the Goths and Romans, when he heard footsteps behind him.

He turned, and beheld five or six young fellows, of rough, saucy demeanor, clad in a singular manner, half peasant, half huntsman, with carbines in their hands. Their whole appearance and carriage left him no doubt into what company he had fallen.

The Doctor was a feeble little man, poor in look, and poorer in purse. He had but little gold or silver to be robbed of; but then he had his curious ancient coin in his breeches pocket. He had, moreover, certain other valuables, such as an old silver

---

lore, at the richly-wooded mountains of the Abruzzi, as a forbidden fairy land of research. These spots, so beautiful, yet so inaccessible, from the rudeness of their inhabitants and the hordes of banditti which infest them, are a region of fable to the learned. Sometimes a wealthy virtuoso, whose purse and whose consequence could command a military escort, has penetrated to some individual point among the mountains; and sometimes a wandering artist or student, under protection of poverty or insignificance, has brought away some vague account, only calculated to give a keener edge to curiosity and conjecture.

By those who maintain the existence of the Pelasgian cities, it is affirmed, that the formation of the different kingdoms in the Peloponnesus gradually caused the expulsion thence of the Pelasgi; but that their great migration may be dated from the finishing the wall round Acropolis, and that at this period they came to Italy. To these, in the spirit of theory, they would ascribe the introduction of the elegant arts into the country. It is evident, however, that, as barbarians flying before the first dawn of civilization, they could bring little with them superior to the inventions of the aborigines, and nothing that would have survived to the antiquarian through such a lapse of ages. It would appear more probable, that these cities, improperly termed Pelasgian, were coeval with many that have been discovered. The romantic Aricia, built by Hippolytus before the siege of Troy, and the poetic Tibur, Æsculate and Proenes, built by Telegonus after the dispersion of the Greeks;—these, lying contiguous to inhabited and cultivated spots, have been discovered. There are others, too, on the ruins of which the later and more civilized Grecian colonists have ingrafted themselves, and which have become known by their merits or their medals. But that there are many still undiscovered, imbedded in the Abrazzi, it is the delight of the antiquarians to fancy. Strange that such a virgin soil for research, such an unknown realm of knowledge, should at this day remain in the very centre of hackneyed Italy!

watch, thick as a turnip, with figures on it large enough for a dock; and a set of seals at the end of a steel chain, dangling half way down to his knees. All these were of precious esteem, being family relics. He had also a seal-ring, a veritable antique intaglio, that covered half his knuckles. It was a Venus, which the old man almost worshipped with the zeal of a voluptuary. But what he most valued was his inestimable collection of hints relative to the Pelasgian cities, which he would gladly have given all the money in his pocket to have had safe at the bottom of his trunk in Terracina.

However, he plucked up a stout heart, at least as stout a heart as he could, seeing that he was but a puny little man at the best of times. So he wished the hunters a "buon giorno." They returned his salutation, giving the old gentleman a sociable slap on the back that made his heart leap into his throat.

They fell into conversation, and walked for some time together among the heights, the Doctor wishing them all the while at the bottom of the crater of Vesuvius. At length they came to a small osteria on the mountain, where they proposed to enter and have a cup of wine together: the Doctor consented, though he would as soon have been invited to drink hemlock.

One of the gang remained sentinel at the door; the others swaggered into the house, stood their guns in the corner of the room, and each drawing a pistol or stiletto out of his belt, laid it upon the table. They now drew benches round the board, called lustily for wine, and, hailing the Doctor as though he had been a boon companion of long standing, insisted upon his sitting down and making merry.

The worthy man complied with forced grimace, but with fear and trembling; sitting uneasily on the edge of his chair; eyeing ruefully the black-muzzled pistols, and cold, naked stilettos; and supping down heartburn with every drop of liquor. His new comrades, however, pushed the bottle bravely, and plied him vigorously. They sang, they laughed; told excellent stories of their robberies and combats, mingled with many ruffian jokes; and the little Doctor was fain to laugh at all their cut-throat pleasantries, though his heart was dying away at the very bottom of his bosom.

By their own account, they were young men from the villages, who had recently taken up this line of life out of the wild caprice of youth. They talked of their murderous exploits as a sports-man talks of his amusements: to shoot down a traveller seemed of little more consequence to them than to shoot a hare. They spoke with rapture of the glorious roving life they led, free as birds; here to-day, gone to-morrow; ranging the forests, climbing the rocks, scouring the valleys; the world their own wherever they could lay hold of it; full purses—merry companions—pretty women. The little antiquary got fuddled with their talk and their wine, for they did not spare bumpers. He half forgot his fears, his seal-ring, and his family-watch; even the treatise on the Pelasgian cities, which was warming under him, for a time faded from his memory in the glowing picture that they drew. He declares that he no longer wonders at the prevalence of this robber mania among the mountains; for he felt at the time, that, had he been a young man, and a strong man, and had there been no danger of the galleys in the background, he should have been half tempted himself to turn bandit.

At length the hour of separating arrived. The Doctor was suddenly called to himself and his fears by seeing the robbers resume their weapons. He now quaked for his valuables, and, above all, for his antiquarian treatise. He endeavored, however, to look cool and unconcerned; and drew from out his deep pocket a long, lank, leathern purse, far gone in consumption, at the bottom of which a few coin chinked with the trembling of his hand.

The chief of the party observed his movement, and laying his hand upon the antiquary's shoulder, "Harkee! Signor Dottore!" said he, "we have drunk together as friends and comrades; let us part as such. We understand you. We know who and what you are, for we know who every body is that sleeps at Terracina, or that puts foot upon the road. You are a rich man, but you carry all your wealth in your head: we cannot get at it, and we should not know what to do with it if we could. I see you are uneasy about your ring; but don't worry yourself, it is not worth taking; you think it an antique, but it's a counterfeit—a mere sham."

Here the ire of the antiquary rose: the Doctor forgot himself in his zeal for the character of his ring. Heaven and earth! his Venus a sham! Had they pronounced the wife of his bosom "no better than she should be," he could not have been more indignant. He fired up in vindication of his intaglio.

"Nay, nay," continued the robber, "we have no time to dispute about it; value it as you please. Come, you're a brave little old signor—one more cup of wine, and we'll pay the reckoning. No compliments—you shall not pay a grain—you are our guest—I insist upon it. So—now make the best of your way back to Terracina; it's growing late. Buono viaggio! And harkee! take care how you wander among these mountains,—you may not always fall into such good company."

They shouldered their guns; sprang gayly up the rocks; and the little Doctor hobbled back to Terracina, rejoicing that the robbers had left his watch, his coins, and his treatise, unmolested; but still indignant that they should have pronounced his Venus an impostor.

The improvisatore had shown many symptoms of impatience during this recital. He saw his theme in danger of being taken out of his hands, which to an able talker is always a grievance, but to an improvisatore is an absolute calamity: and then for it to be taken away by a Neapolitan, was still more vexatious; the inhabitants of the different Italian states having an implacable jealousy of each other in all things, great and small. He took advantage of the first pause of the Neapolitan to catch hold again of the thread of the conversation.

"As I observed before," said he, "the prowlings of the banditti are so extensive; they are so much in league with one another, and so interwoven with various ranks of society—"

"For that matter," said the Neapolitan, "I have heard that your government has had some understanding with those gentry; or, at least, has winked at their misdeeds."

"My government?" said the Roman, impatiently.

"Ay, they say that Cardinal Gonsalvi—"

"Hush!" said the Roman, holding up his finger, and rolling his large eyes about the room.

"Nay, I only repeat what I heard commonly rumored in Rome," replied the Neapolitan, sturdily. "It was openly said, that the cardinal had been up to the mountains, and had an interview with some of the chiefs. And I have been told, moreover, that while honest people have been kicking their heels in the cardinal's antechamber waiting by the hour for admittance, one of those stiletto-looking fellows has elbowed his way through the crowd, and entered without ceremony into the cardinal's presence."

"I know," observed the improvisatore, "that there have been such reports, and it is not impossible that government may have made use of these men at particular periods: such as at the time of your late abortive revolution, when your carbonari were so busy with their machinations all over the country. The information which such men could collect, who were familiar, not merely with the recesses and secret places of the mountains, but also with the dark and dangerous recesses of society; who knew every suspicious character, and all his movements and all his lurkings; in a word, who knew all that was plotting in a world of mischief;—the utility of such men as instruments in the hands of government was too obvious to be overlooked; and Cardinal Gonsalvi, as a politic statesman, may, perhaps, have made use of them. Besides, he knew that, with all their atrocities, the robbers were always respectful towards the church, and devout in their religion."

"Religion! religion!" echoed the Englishman.

"Yes, religion," repeated the Roman. "They have each their patron saint. They will cross themselves and say their prayers, whenever, in their mountain haunts, they hear the matin or the Ave-Maria bells sounding from the valleys; and will often descend from their retreats, and run imminent risks to visit some favorite shrine. I recollect an instance in point.

"I was one evening in the village of Frascati, which stands on the beautiful brow of a hill rising from the Campagna, just below the Abruzzi mountains. The people, as is usual in fine evenings in our Italian towns and villages, were recreating themselves in the open air, and chatting in groups in the public square. While I was conversing with a knot of friends, I noticed a tall fellow, wrapped in a great mantle, passing across the square, but skulking along in the dusk, as if anxious to avoid observation. The people drew back as he passed. It was whispered to me that he was a notorious bandit."

"But why was he not immediately seized?" said the Englishman.

"Because it was nobody's business; because nobody wished to incur the vengeance of his comrades; because there were not sufficient gendarmes near to insure security against the number of desperadoes he might have at hand; because the gendarmes might not have received particular instructions with respect to him, and might not feel disposed to engage in a hazardous conflict without compulsion. In short, I might give you a thousand reasons rising out of the state of our government and manners, not one of which after all might appear satisfactory."

The Englishman shrugged his shoulders with an air of contempt.

"I have been told," added the Roman, rather quickly, "that even in your metropolis of London, notorious thieves, well known to the police as such, walk the streets at noonday in search of their prey, and are not molested unless caught in the very act of robbery."

The Englishman gave another shrug, but with a different expression.

"Well, sir, I fixed my eye on this daring wolf, thus prowling through the fold, and saw him enter a church. I was curious to witness his devotion. You know our spacious magnificent churches. The one in which he entered was vast, and shrouded in the dusk of evening. At the extremity of the long aisles a couple of tapers feebly glimmered on the grand altar. In one of the side chapels was a votive candle placed before the image of a saint. Before this image the robber had prostrated himself. His mantle partly falling off from his shoulders as he knelt, revealed a form of Herculean strength; a stiletto and pistol glittered in his belt; and the light falling on his countenance, showed features not unhandsome, but strongly and fiercely characterized. As he prayed, he became vehemently agitated; his lips quivered; sighs and murmurs, almost groans, burst from him; he beat his breast with violence; then clasped his hands and wrung them convulsively, as he extended them towards the image. Never had I seen such a terrific picture of remorse. I felt fearful of being discovered watching him, and withdrew. Shortly afterwards, I saw him issue from the church wrapped in his mantle. He re-crossed the square, and no doubt returned to the mountains with a disburdened conscience, ready to incur a fresh arrear of crime."

Here the Neapolitan was about to get hold of the conversation, and had just preluded with the ominous remark, "That puts me in mind of a circumstance," when the improvisatore, too adroit to suffer himself to be again superseded, went on, pretending not to hear the interruption.

"Among the many circumstances connected with the banditti, which serve to render the traveller uneasy and insecure, is the understanding which they sometimes have with innkeepers. Many an isolated inn among the lonely parts of the Roman territories, and especially about the mountains, are of a dangerous and perfidious character. They are places where the banditti gather information, and where the unwary traveller, remote from hearing or assistance, is betrayed to the midnight dagger. The robberies committed at such inns are often accompanied by the most atrocious murders; for it is only by the complete extermination of their victims that the assassins can escape detection. I recollect an adventure," added he, "which occurred at one of these solitary mountain inns, which, as you all seem in a mood for robber anecdotes, may not be uninteresting."

Having secured the attention and awakened the curiosity of the by-standers, he paused for a moment, rolled up his large eyes as improvisatori are apt to do when they would recollect an impromptu, and then related with great dramatic effect the following story, which had, doubtless, by well prepared and digested beforehand.

The Belated Travellers

IT WAS LATE ONE EVENING THAT A CARRIAGE, DRAWN BY MULES, SLOWLY toiled its way up one of the passes of the Apennines. It was through one of the wildest defiles, where a hamlet occurred only at distant intervals, perched on the summit of some rocky height, or the white towers of a convent peeped out from among the thick mountain foliage. The carriage was of ancient and ponderous construction. Its faded embellishments spoke of former splendor, but its crazy springs and axle-trees creaked out the tale of present decline. Within was seated a tall, thin old gentleman, in a kind of military travelling dress, and a foraging cap trimmed with fur, though the gray locks which stole from under it hinted that his fighting days were over. Beside him was a pale, beautiful girl of eighteen, dressed in something of a northern or Polish costume. One servant was seated in front, a rusty, crusty-looking fellow, with a scar across his face, an orange-tawny *schnur-bart*, or pair of mustaches, bristling from under his nose, and altogether the air of an old soldier.

It was, in fact, the equipage of a Polish nobleman; a wreck of one of those princely families once of almost oriental magnificence, but broken down and impoverished by the disasters of Poland. The Count, like many other generous spirits, had been found guilty of the crime of patriotism, and was, in a manner, an exile from his country. He had resided for some time in the first cities of Italy, for the education of his daughter, in whom all his cares and pleasures were now centred. He had taken her into society, where her beauty and her accomplishments gained her many admirers; and had she not been the daughter of a poor broken-down Polish nobleman, it is more than probable many would have contended for her hand. Suddenly, however, her health became delicate and drooping; her gayety fled with the roses of her cheek, and she sank into silence and debility. The old Count saw the change with the solicitude of a parent. "We must try a change of air and scene," said he; and in a few days the old family carriage was rumbling among the Apennines.

Their only attendant was the veteran Caspar, who had been born in the family, and grown rusty in its service. He had followed his master in all his fortunes; had fought by his side; had stood over him when fallen in battle; and had received, in his defence, the sabre-cut which added such grimness to his countenance. He was now his valet, his steward, his butler, his factotum. The only being that rivalled his master in his affections was his youthful mistress. She had grown up under his eye, he had led her by the hand when she was a child, and he now looked upon her with the fondness of a parent. Nay, he even took the freedom of a parent in giving his blunt opinion on all matters which he thought were for her good; and felt a parent's vanity at seeing her gazed at and admired.

The evening was thickening; they had been for some time passing through narrow gorges of the mountains, along the edges of a tumbling stream. The scenery was lonely and savage. The rocks often beetled over the road, with flocks of white goats browsing on their brinks, and gazing down upon the travellers. They had between two and three leagues yet to go before they could reach any village; yet the muleteer, Pietro, a tippling old fellow, who had refreshed himself at the last halting-place with a more than ordinary quantity of wine, sat singing and talking alternately to his mules, and suffering them to lag on at a snail's pace, in spite of the frequent entreaties of the Count and maledictions of Caspar.

The clouds began to roll in heavy masses among the mountains, shrouding their summits from view. The air was damp and chilly. The Count's solicitude on his daughter's account overcame his usual patience. He leaned from the carriage, and called to old Pietro in an angry tone:

"Forward!" said he. "It will be midnight before we arrive at our inn."

"Yonder it is, Signor," said the muleteer.

"Where?" demanded the Count.

"Yonder," said Pietro, pointing to a desolate pile about a quarter of a league distant.

"That the place?—why, it looks more like a ruin than an inn. I thought we were to put up for the night at a comfortable village." Here Pietro uttered a string of piteous exclamations and ejaculations, such as are ever at the tip of the tongue of a delinquent muleteer. "Such roads! and such mountains! and then his poor animals were wayworn, and leg-weary; they would fall lame; they would never be able to reach the village. And then what could his Excellenza wish for better than the inn; a perfect castello—a palazza—and such people!—and such a larder!—and such beds!—His Excellenza might fare as sumptuously, and sleep as soundly there as a prince!"

The Count was easily persuaded, for he was anxious to get his daughter out of the night air; so in a little while the old carriage rattled and jingled into the great gateway of the inn.

The building did certainly in some measure answer to the muleteer's description. It was large enough for either castle or palace; built in a strong, but simple and almost rude style; with a great quantity of waste room. It had in fact been, in former times, a hunting-seat of one of the Italian princes. There was space enough within its walls and out-buildings to have accommodated a little army. A scanty household seemed now to people this dreary mansion. The faces that presented themselves on the arrival of the travellers were begrimed with dirt, and scowling in their expression. They all knew old Pietro, however, and gave him a welcome as he entered, singing and talking, and almost whooping, into the gateway.

The hostess of the inn waited herself on the Count and his daughter, to show them the apartments. They were conducted through a long gloomy corridor, and then through a suite of chambers opening into each other, with lofty ceilings, and great beams extending across them. Every thing, however, had a wretched, squalid look. The walls were damp and bare, excepting that here and there hung some great painting, large enough for a chapel, and blackened out of all distinction.

They chose two bedrooms, one within another; the inner one for the daughter. The bedsteads were massive and misshapen; but on examining the beds so vaunted by old Pietro, they found them stuffed with fibres of hemp knotted in great lumps. The Count shrugged his shoulders, but there was no choice left.

The chilliness of the apartments crept to their bones; and they were glad to return to a common chamber, or kind of hall, where was a fire burning in a huge cavern, miscalled a chimney. A quantity of green wood, just thrown on, puffed out volumes of smoke. The room corresponded to the rest of the mansion. The floor was paved and dirty. A great oaken table stood in the centre, immovable from its size and weight.

The only thing that contradicted this prevalent air of indigence was the dress of the hostess. She was a slattern of course; yet her garments, though dirty and negligent, were of costly materials. She wore several rings of great value on her fingers, and jewels in her ears, and round her neck was a string of large pearls, to which was attached a sparkling crucifix. She had the remains of beauty, yet there was something in the expression of her countenance that inspired the young lady with singular aversion. She was officious and obsequious in her attentions, and both the Count and his daughter felt relieved, when she consigned them to the care of a dark, sullen-looking servant-maid, and went off to superintend the supper.

Caspar was indignant at the muleteer for having, either through negligence or design, subjected his master and mistress to such quarters; and vowed by his mustaches to have revenge on the old varlet the moment they were safe out from among the mountains. He kept up a continual quarrel with the sulky servant-maid, which only served to increase the sinister expression with which she regarded the travellers, from under her strong dark eyebrows.

As to the Count, he was a good-humored passive traveller. Perhaps real misfortunes had subdued his spirit, and rendered him tolerant of many of those petty evils which make prosperous men miserable. He drew a large broken arm-chair to the fireside for his daughter, and another for himself, and seizing an enormous pair of tongs, endeavored to re-arrange the wood so as to produce a blaze. His efforts, however, were only repaid by thicker puffs of smoke, which almost overcame the good gentleman's patience. He would draw back, cast a look upon his delicate daughter, then upon the cheerless, squalid apartment, and shrugging his shoulders, would give a fresh stir to the fire.

Of all the miseries of a comfortless inn, however, there is none greater than sulky attendance: the good Count for some time bore the smoke in silence, rather than address himself to the scowling servant-maid. At length he was compelled to beg for drier firewood. The woman retired muttering. On re-entering the room hastily, with an armful of fagots, her foot slipped; she fell, and striking her head against the corner of a chair, cut her temple severely.

The blow stunned her for a time, and the wound bled profusely. When she recovered, she found the Count's daughter administering to her wound, and binding it up with her own handkerchief. It was such an attention as any woman of ordinary feeling would have yielded; but perhaps there was something in the appearance of the lovely being who bent over her, or in the tones of her voice, that touched the heart of the woman, unused to be ministered to by such hands. Certain it is, she was strongly affected. She caught the delicate hand of the Polonaise, and dressed it fervently to her lips:

"May San Francesco watch over you, Signora!" exclaimed she.

A new arrival broke the stillness of the inn. It was a Spanish Princess with a numerous retinue. The courtyard was in an uproar; the house in a bustle. The landlady hurried to attend such distinguished guests: and the poor Count and his daughter, and their supper, were for a moment forgotten. The veteran Caspar muttered Polish maledictions enough to agonize an Italian ear; but it was impossible to convince the hostess of the superiority of his old master and young mistress to the whole nobility of Spain.

The noise of the arrival had attracted the daughter to the window just as the new-comers had alighted. A young cavalier sprang out of the carriage, and handed out the Princess. The latter was a little shrivelled old lady, with a face of parchment and sparkling black eye; she was richly and gayly dressed, and walked with the assistance of a golden-headed cane as high as herself. The young man was tall and elegantly formed. The Count's daughter shrunk back at sight of him, though the deep frame of the window screened her from observation. She gave a heavy sigh as she closed the casement. What that sigh meant I cannot say. Perhaps it was at the contrast between the splendid equipage of the Princess, and the crazy rheumatic-looking old vehicle of her father, which stood hard by. Whatever might be the reason, the young lady closed the casement with a sigh. She returned to her chair,—a slight shivering passed over her delicate frame: she leaned her elbow on the arm of the chair, rested her pale cheek in the palm of her hand, and looked mournfully into the fire.

The Count thought she appeared paler than usual.

"Does any thing ail thee, my child?" said he.

"Nothing, dear father!" replied she, laying her hand within his, and looking up smiling in his face; but as she said so, a treacherous tear rose suddenly to her eye, and she turned away her head.

"The air of the window has chilled thee," said the Count, fondly, "but a good night's rest will make all well again."

The supper table was at length laid, and the supper about to be served, when the hostess appeared, with her usual obsequiousness, apologizing for showing in the new-comers; but the night air was cold, and there was no other chamber in the inn with a fire in it. She had scarcely made the apology when the Princess entered, leaning on the arm of the elegant young man.

The Count immediately recognized her for a lady whom he had met frequently in society, both at Rome and Naples; and at whose conversaziones, in fact, he had constantly been invited. The cavalier, too, was her nephew and heir, who had been greatly admired in the gay circles both for his merits and prospects, and who had once been on a visit at the same time with his daughter and himself at the villa of a nobleman near Naples. Report had recently affianced him to a rich Spanish heiress.

The meeting was agreeable to both the Count and the Princess. The former was a gentleman of the old school, courteous in the extreme; the Princess had been a belle in her youth, and a woman of fashion all her life, and liked to be attended to.

The young man approached the daughter, and began something of a complimentary observation; but his manner was embarrassed, and his compliment ended in an indistinct murmur; while the daughter bowed without looking up, moved her lips without articulating a word, and sank again into her chair, where she sat gazing into the fire, with a thousand varying expressions passing over her countenance.

This singular greeting of the young people was not perceived by the old ones, who were occupied at the time with their own courteous salutations. It was arranged that they should sup together; and as the Princess travelled with her own cook, a very tolerable supper soon smoked upon the board. This, too, was assisted by choice wines, and liquors, and delicate confitures brought from one of her carriages; for she was a veteran epicure, and curious in her relish for the good things of this world. She was, in fact, a vivacious little old lady, who mingled the woman of dissipation with the devotee. She was actually on her way to Loretto to expiate a long life of gallantries and peccadilloes by a rich offering at the holy shrine. She was, to be sure, rather a luxurious penitent, and a contrast to the primitive pilgrims, with scrip and staff, and cockle-shell; but then it would be unreasonable to expect such self-denial from people of fashion; and there was not a doubt of the ample efficacy of the rich crucifixes, and golden vessels, and jeweled ornaments, which she was bearing to the treasury of the blessed Virgin.

The Princess and the Count chatted much during supper about the scenes and society in which they had mingled, and did not notice that they had all the conversation to themselves: the young people were silent and constrained. The daughter ate nothing, in spite of the politeness of the Princess, who continually pressed her to taste of one or other of the delicacies. The Count shook his head.

"She is not well this evening," said he. "I thought she would have fainted just now as she was looking out of the window at your carriage on its arrival."

A crimson glow flushed to the very temples of the daughter; but she leaned over her plate, and her tresses cast a shade over her countenance.

When supper was over, they drew their chairs about the great fireplace. The flame and smoke had subsided, and a heap of glowing embers diffused a grateful warmth. A guitar, which had been brought from the Count's carriage, leaned against the wall; the Princess perceived it: "Can we not have a little music before parting for the night?" demanded she.

The Count was proud of his daughter's accomplishment, and joined in the request. The young man made an effort of politeness, and taking up the guitar, presented it, though in an embarrassed manner, to the fair musician. She would have declined it, but was too much confused to do so; indeed, she was so nervous and agitated, that she dared not trust her voice to make an excuse. She touched the instrument with a faltering hand, and, after preluding a little, accompanied herself in several Polish airs. Her father's eyes glistened as he sat gazing on her. Even the crusty Caspar lingered in the room, partly through a fondness for the music of his native country, but chiefly through his pride in the musician. Indeed, the melody of the voice, and the delicacy of the touch, were enough to have charmed more fastidious ears. The little Princess nodded her head and tapped her hand to the music, though exceedingly out of time; while the nephew sat buried in profound contemplation of a black picture on the opposite wall.

"And now," said the Count, patting her cheek fondly, "one more favor. Let the Princess hear that little Spanish air you were so fond of. You can't think," added he, "what a proficiency she has made in your language; though she has been a sad girl and neglected it of late."

The color flushed the pale cheek of the daughter. She hesitated, murmured something; but with sudden effort, collected herself, struck the guitar boldly, and began. It was a Spanish romance, with something of love and melancholy in it. She gave the first stanza with great expression, for the tremulous melting tones of her voice went to the heart; but her articulation failed, her lip quivered, the song died away, and she burst into tears.

The Count folded her tenderly in his arms. "Thou art not well, my child," said he, "and I am tasking thee cruelly. Retire to thy chamber, and God bless thee!" She bowed to the company without raising her eyes, and glided out of the room.

The Count shook his head as the door closed. "Something is the matter with that child," said he, "which I cannot divine. She has lost all health and spirits lately. She was always a tender flower, and I had much pains to rear her. Excuse a father's foolishness," continued he, "but I have seen much trouble in my family; and this poor girl is all that is now left to me; and she used to be so lively—"

"Maybe she's in love!" said the little Princess, with a shrewd nod of the head.

"Impossible!" replied the good Count artlessly. "She has never mentioned a word of such a thing to me."

How little did the worthy gentleman dream of the thousand cares, and griefs, and mighty love concerns which agitate a virgin heart, and which a timid girl scarcely breathes unto herself.

The nephew of the Princess rose abruptly and walked about the room.

When she found herself alone in her chamber, the feelings of the young lady, so long restrained, broke forth with violence. She opened the casement that the cool air might blow upon her throbbing temples. Perhaps there was some little pride or pique mingled with her emotions; though her gentle nature did not seem calculated to harbor any such angry inmate.

"He saw me weep!" said she with a sudden mantling of the cheek, and a swelling of the throat,—"but no matter!—no matter!"

And so saying, she threw her white arms across the window-frame, buried her face in them, and abandoned herself to an agony of tears. She remained lost in a reverie, until the sound of her father's and Caspar's voices in the adjoining room gave token that the party had retired for the night, The lights gleaming from window to window, showed that they were conducting the Princess to her apartments, which were in the opposite wing of the inn; and she distinctly saw the figure of the nephew as he passed one of the casements.

She heaved a deep heart-drawn sigh, and was about to close the lattice, when her attention was caught by words spoken below her window by two persons who had just turned an angle of the building.

"But what will become of the poor young lady?" said a voice which she recognized for that of the servant-woman.

"Pooh! she must take her chance," was the reply from old Pietro.

"But cannot she be spared?" asked the other entreatingly; "she's so kind-hearted!"

"Cospetto! what has got into thee?" replied the other petulantly: "would you mar the whole business for the sake of a silly girl?" By this time they had got so far from the window that the Polonaise could hear nothing further.

There was something in this fragment of conversation calculated to alarm. Did it relate to herself?—and if so, what was this impending danger from which it was entreated that she might be spared? She was several times on the point of tapping at her father's door, to tell him what she had heard; but she might have been mistaken; she might have heard indistinctly; the conversation might have alluded to some one else; at any rate, it was too indefinite to lead to any conclusion. While in this state of irresolution, she was startled by a low knocking against the wainscot in a remote part of her gloomy chamber. On holding up the light, she beheld a small door there, which she had not before remarked. It was bolted on the inside. She advanced, and demanded who knocked, and was answered in the voice of the female domestic. On opening the door, the woman stood before it pale and agitated. She entered softly, laying her finger on her lips in sign of caution and secrecy.

"Fly!" said she: "leave this house instantly, or you are lost!"

The young lady, trembling with alarm, demanded an explanation.

"I have no time," replied the woman, "I dare not—I shall be missed if I linger here—but fly instantly, or you are lost."

"And leave my father?"

"Where is he?"

"In the adjoining chamber."

"Call him, then, but lose no time."

The young lady knocked at her father's door. He was not yet retired to bed. She hurried into his room, and told him of the fearful warnings she had received. The Count returned with her into her chamber, followed by Caspar. His questions soon drew the truth out of the embarrassed answers of the woman. The inn was beset by robbers. They were to be introduced after midnight, when the attendants of the Princess and the rest of the travellers were sleeping, and would be an easy prey.

"But we can barricade the inn, we can defend ourselves," said the Count.

"What! when the people of the inn are in league with the banditti?"

"How then are we to escape? Can we not order out the carriage and depart?"

"San Francesco! for what? To give the alarm that the plot is discovered? That would make the robbers desperate, and bring them on you at once. They have had notice of the rich booty in the inn, and will not easily let it escape them."

"But how else are we to get off?"

"There is a horse behind the inn," said the woman, "from which the man has just dismounted who has been to summon the aid of part of the band at a distance."

"One horse; and there are three of us!" said the Count.

"And the Spanish Princess!" cried the daughter anxiously—"How can she be extricated from the danger?"

"Diavolo! what is she to me?" said the woman in sudden passion. "It is *you* I come to save, and you will betray me, and we shall all be lost! Hark!" continued she, "I am called—I shall be discovered—one word more. This door leads by a staircase to the courtyard. Under the shed, in the rear of the yard, is a small door leading out to the fields. You will find a horse there; mount it; make a circuit under the shadow of a ridge of rocks that you will see; proceed cautiously and quietly until you cross a brook, and find yourself on the road just where there are three white crosses nailed against a tree; then put your horse to his speed, and make the best of your way to the village—but recollect, my life is in your hands—say nothing of what you have heard or seen, whatever may happen at this inn."

The woman hurried away. A short and agitated consultation took place between the Count, his daughter, and the veteran Caspar. The young lady seemed to have lost all apprehension for herself in her solicitude for the safety of the Princess. "To fly in selfish silence, and leave her to be massacred!"—A shuddering seized her at the very thought. The gallantry of the Count, too, revolted at the idea. He could not consent to turn his back upon a party of helpless travellers, and leave them in ignorance of the danger which hung over them.

"But what is to become of the young lady," said Caspar, "if the alarm is given, and the inn thrown in a tumult? What may happen to her in a chance-medley affray?"

Here the feelings of the father were roused; he looked upon his lovely, helpless child, and trembled at the chance of her falling into the hands of ruffians.

The daughter, however, thought nothing of herself. "The Princess! the Princess!—only let the Princess know her danger." She was willing to share it with her.

At length Caspar interfered with the zeal of a faithful old servant. No time was to be lost—the first thing was to get the young lady out of danger. "Mount the horse," said he to the Count, "take her behind you, and fly! Make for the village, rouse the inhabitants, and send assistance. Leave me here to give the alarm to the Princess and her people. I am an old soldier, and I think we shall be able to stand siege until you send us aid."

The daughter would again have insisted on staying with the Princess—

"For what?" said old Caspar bluntly. "You could do no good—you would be in the way;—we should have to take care of you instead of ourselves."

There was no answering these objections; the Count seized his pistols, and taking his daughter under his arm, moved towards the staircase. The young lady paused, stepped back, and said, faltering with agitation—"There is a young cavalier with the Princess—her nephew—perhaps he may—"

"I understand you, Mademoiselle," replied old Caspar with a significant nod; "not a hair of his head shall suffer harm if I can help it!"

The young lady blushed deeper than ever; she had not anticipated being so thoroughly understood by the blunt old servant.

"That is not what I mean," said she, hesitating. She would have added something, or made some explanation, but the moments were precious, and her father hurried her away.

They found their way through the courtyard to the small postern gate where the horse stood, fastened to a ring in the wall. The Count mounted, took his daughter behind him, and they proceeded as quietly as possible in the direction which the woman had pointed out. Many a fearful and anxious look did the daughter cast back upon the gloomy pile; the lights which had feebly twinkled through the dusky casements were one by one disappearing, a sign that the inmates were gradually sinking to repose; and she trembled with impatience, lest succor should not arrive until that repose had been fatally interrupted.

They passed silently and safely along the skirts of the rocks, protected from observation by their overhanging shadows. They crossed the brook, and reached the place where three white crosses nailed against a tree told of some murder that had been committed there. Just as they had reached this ill-omened spot they beheld several men in the gloom coming down a craggy defile among the rocks.

"Who goes there?" exclaimed a voice. The Count put spurs to his horse, but one of the men sprang forward and seized the bridle. The horse started back, and reared, and had not the young lady clung to her father, she would have been thrown off. The Count leaned forward, put a pistol to the very head of the ruffian, and fired. The latter fell dead. The horse sprang forward. Two or three shots were fired which whistled by the fugitives, but only served to augment their speed. They reached the village in safety.

The whole place was soon roused; but such was the awe in which the banditti were held, that the inhabitants shrunk at the idea of encountering them. A desperate band had for some time infested that pass through the mountains, and the inn had long been suspected of being one of those horrible places where the unsuspicious wayfarer is entrapped and silently disposed of. The rich ornaments worn by the slattern hostess of the inn had excited heavy suspicions. Several instances had occurred of small parties of travellers disappearing mysteriously on that road, who, it was supposed at first, had been carried off by the robbers for the purpose of ransom, but who had never been heard of more. Such were the tales buzzed in the ears of the Count by the villagers, as he endeavored to rouse them to the rescue of the Princess and her train from their perilous situation. The daughter seconded the exertions of her father with all the eloquence of prayers, and tears, and beauty. Every moment that elapsed increased her anxiety until it became agonizing. Fortunately there was a body of gendarmes resting at the village. A number of the young villagers volunteered to accompany them, and the little army was put in motion. The Count having deposited his daughter in a place of safety, was too much of the old soldier not to hasten to the scene of danger. It would be difficult to paint the anxious dotation of the young lady while awaiting the result.

The party arrived at the inn just in time. The robbers, finding their plans discovered, and the travellers prepared for their reception, had become open and furious in their attack. The Princess's party had barricaded themselves in one suite of apartments, and repulsed the robbers from the doors and windows. Caspar had shown the generalship of a veteran, and the nephew of the Princess the dashing valor of a young soldier. Their ammunition, however, was nearly exhausted, and they would have found it difficult to hold out much longer, when a discharge from the musketry of the gendarmes gave them the joyful tidings of succor.

A fierce fight ensued, for part of the robbers were surprised in the inn, and had to stand siege in their turn; while their comrades made desperate attempts to relieve them from under cover of the neighboring rocks and thickets.

I cannot pretend to give a minute account of the fight, as I have heard it related in a variety of ways. Suffice it to say, the robbers were defeated; several of them killed, and several taken prisoners; which last, together with the people of the inn, were either executed or sent to the galleys.

I picked up these particulars in the course of a journey which I made some time after the event had taken place. I passed by the very inn. It was then dismantled, excepting one wing, in which a body of gendarmes was stationed. They pointed out to me the shot-holes in the window-frames, the walls, and the panels of the doors. There were a number of withered limbs dangling from the branches of a neighboring tree, and blackening in the air, which I was told were the limbs of the robbers who had been slain, and the culprits who had been executed. The whole place had a dismal, wild, forlorn look.

"Were any of the Princess's party killed?" inquired the Englishman.

"As far as I can recollect, there were two or three."

"Not the nephew, I trust?" said the fair Venetian.

"Oh no: he hastened with the Count to relieve the anxiety of the daughter by the assurances of victory. The young lady had been sustained throughout the interval of suspense by the very intensity of her feelings! The moment she saw her father returning in safety, accompanied by the nephew of the Princess, she uttered a cry of rapture, and fainted. Happily, however, she soon recovered, and what is more, was married shortly afterwards to the young cavalier, and the whole party accompanied the old Princess in her pilgrimage to Loretto, where her votive offerings may still be seen in the treasury of the Santa Casa."

It would be tedious to follow the devious course of the conversation as it wound through a maze of stories of the kind, until it was taken up by two other travellers who had come under convoy of the procaccio: Mr. Hobbs and Mr. Dobbs, a linen-draper and a green-grocer, just returning from a hasty tour in Greece and the Holy Land. They were full of the story of Alderman Popkins. They were astonished that the robbers should dare to molest a man of his importance on 'Change, he being an eminent dry-salter of Throgmorton-street, and a magistrate to boot.

In fact, the story of the Popkins family was but too true. It was attested by too many present to be for a moment doubted; and from the contradictory and concordant testimony of half a score, all eager to relate it, and all talking at the same time, the Englishman was enabled to gather the following particulars.

The Adventure of the Popkins Family

IT WAS BUT A FEW DAYS BEFORE, THAT THE CARRIAGE OF ALDERMAN POPKINS had driven up to the inn of Terracina. Those who have seen an English family-carriage on the continent must have remarked the sensation it produces. It is an epitome of England; a little morsel of the old island rolling about the world. Every thing about it compact, snug, finished, and fitting. The wheels turning on patent axles without rattling; the body, hanging so well on its springs, yielding to every motion, yet protecting from every shock; the ruddy faces gaping from the windows—sometimes of a portly old citizen, sometimes of a voluminous dowager, and sometimes of a fine fresh hoyden just from boarding-school. And then the dickeys loaded with well-dressed servants, beef-fed and bluff; looking down from their heights with contempt on all the world around; profoundly ignorant of the country and the people, and devoutly certain that every thing not English must be wrong.

Such was the carriage of Alderman Popkins as it made its appearance at Terracina. The courier who had preceded it to order horses, and who was a Neapolitan, had given a magnificent account of the richness and greatness of his master; blundering with an Italian's splendor of imagination about the Alderman's titles and dignities. The host had added his usual share of exaggeration; so that by the time the Alderman drove up to the door, he was a Milor—Magnifico—Principe—the Lord knows what!

The Alderman was advised to take an escort to Fondi and Itri, but he refused. It was as much as a man's life was worth, he said, to stop him on the king's highway: he would complain of it to the ambassador at Naples; he would make a national affair of it. The Principessa Popkins, a fresh, motherly dame, seemed perfectly secure in the protection of her husband, so omnipotent a man in the city. The Signorines Popkins, two fine bouncing girls, looked to their brother Tom, who had taken lessons in boxing;

and as to the dandy himself, he swore no scaramouch of an Italian robber would dare to meddle with an Englishman. The landlord shrugged his shoulders, and turned out the palms of his hands with a true Italian grimace, and the carriage of Milor Popkins rolled on.

They passed through several very suspicious places without any molestation. The Misses Popkins, who were very romantic, and had learnt to draw in water-colors, were enchanted with the savage scenery around; it was so like what they had read in Mrs. Radcliffe's romances; they should like of all things to make sketches. At length the carriage arrived at a place where the road wound up a long hill. Mrs. Popkins had sunk into a sleep; the young ladies were lost in the "Loves of the Angels"; and the dandy was hectoring the postilions from the coach-box. The Alderman got out, as he said, to stretch his legs up the hill. It was a long, winding ascent, and obliged him every now and then to stop and blow and wipe his forehead, with many a pish! and phew! being rather pursy and short of wind. As the carriage, however, was far behind him, and moved slowly under the weight of so many well-stuffed trunks and well-stuffed travellers, he had plenty of time to walk at leisure.

On a jutting point of a rock that overhung the road, nearly at the summit of the hill, just where the road began again to descend, he saw a solitary man seated, who appeared to be tending goats. Alderman Popkins was one of your shrewd travellers who always like to be picking up small information along the road; so he thought he'd just scramble up to the honest man, and have a little talk with him by way of learning the news and getting a lesson in Italian. As he drew near to the peasant, he did not half like his looks. He was partly reclining on the rocks, wrapped in the usual long mantle, which, with his slouched hat, only left a part of a swarthy visage, with a keen black eye, a beetle brow, and a fierce mustache to be seen. He had whistled several times to his dog, which was roving about the side of the hill. As the Alderman approached, he arose and greeted him. When standing erect, he seemed almost gigantic, at least in the eyes of Alderman Popkins, who, however, being a short man, might be deceived.

The latter would gladly now have been back in the carriage, or even on 'Change in London; for he was by no means well pleased with his company. However, he determined to put the best face on matters, and was beginning a conversation about the state of the weather, the baddishness of the crops, and the price of goats in that part of the country, when he heard a violent screaming. He ran to the edge of the rock, and looking over, beheld his carriage surrounded by robbers. One held down the fat footman, another had the dandy by his starched cravat, with a pistol to his head; one was rummaging a portmanteau, another rummaging the Principessa's pockets; while the two Misses Popkins were screaming from each window of the carriage, and their waiting-maid squalling from the dickey.

Alderman Popkins felt all the ire of the parent and the magistrate roused within him. He grasped his cane, and was on the point of scrambling down the rocks either to assault the robbers or to read the riot act, when he was suddenly seized by the arm. It was by his friend the goatherd, whose cloak falling open, discovered a belt stuck full of pistols and stilettos. In short, he found himself in the clutches of the captain of the band, who had stationed himself on the rock to look out for travellers and to give notice to his men.

A sad ransacking took place. Trunks were turned inside out, and all the finery and frippery of the Popkins family scattered about the road. Such a chaos of Venice beads and Roman mosaics, and Paris bonnets of the young ladies, mingled with the Alderman's nightcaps and lambs'-wool stockings, and the dandy's hair-brushes, stays, and starched cravats.

The gentlemen were eased of their purses and their watches, the ladies of their jewels; and the whole party were on the point of being carried up into the mountain, when fortunately the appearance of soldiers at a distance obliged the robbers to make off with the spoils they had secured, and leave the Popkins family to gather together the remnants of their effects, and make the best of their way to Fondi.

When safe arrived, the Alderman made a terrible blustering at the inn; threatened to complain to the ambassador at Naples, and was ready to shake his cane at the whole country. The dandy had many stories to tell of his scuffles with the brigands, who overpowered him merely by numbers. As to the Misses Popkins, they were quite delighted with the adventure, and were occupied the whole evening in writing it in their journals. They declared the captain of the band to be a most romantic-looking man, they dared to say some unfortunate lover or exiled noble-man; and several of the band to be very handsome young men—"quite picturesque!"

"In verity," said mine host of Terracina, "they say the captain of the band is *un gallant uomo*."

"A gallant man!" said the Englishman, indignantly: "I'd have your gallant man hanged like a dog!"

"To dare to meddle with Englishmen!" said Mr. Hobbs.

"And such a family as the Popkinses?" said Mr. Dobbs.

"They ought to come upon the county for damages!" said Mr. Hobbs.

"Our ambassador should make a complaint to the government of Naples," said Mr. Dobbs.

"They should be obliged to drive these rascals out of the country," said Hobbs.

"And if they did not, we should declare war against them," said Dobbs.

"Pish!—humbug!" muttered the Englishman to himself, and walked away.

The Englishman had been a little wearied by this story, and by the ultra zeal of his countrymen, and was glad when a summons to their supper relieved him from the crowd of travellers. He walked out with his Venetian friends and a young Frenchman of an interesting demeanor, who had become sociable with them in the course of the conversation. They directed their steps towards the sea, which was lit up by the rising moon.

As they strolled along the beach they came to where a party of soldiers were stationed in a circle. They were guarding a number of galley slaves, who were permitted to refresh themselves in the evening breeze, and sport and roll upon the sand.

The Frenchman paused, and pointed to the group of wretches at their sports. "It is difficult," said he, "to conceive a more frightful mass of crime than is here collected. Many of these have probably been robbers, such as you have heard described. Such is, too often, the career of crime in this country. The parricide, the fratricide, the infanticide, the miscreant of every kind, first flies from justice and turns mountain bandit; and then, when wearied of a life of danger, becomes traitor to his brother desperadoes; betrays them to punishment, and thus buys a commutation of his own sentence from death to the galleys; happy in the privilege of wallowing on the shore an hour a day, in this mere state of animal enjoyment."

The fair Venetian shuddered as she cast a look at the horde of wretches at their evening amusement. "They seemed," she said, "like so many serpents writhing together." And yet the idea that some of them had been robbers, those formidable beings that haunted her imagination, made her still cast another fearful glance, as we contemplate some terrible beast of prey, with a degree of awe and horror, even though caged and chained.

The conversation reverted to the tales of banditti which they had heard at the inn. The Englishman condemned some of them as fabrications, others as exaggerations. As to the story of the improvisatore, he pronounced it a mere piece of romance, originating in the heated brain of the narrator.

"And yet," said the Frenchman, "there is so much romance about the real life of those beings, and about the singular country they infest, that it is hard to tell what to reject on the ground of improbability. I have had an adventure happen to myself which gave me an opportunity of getting some insight into their manners and habits, which I found altogether out of the common run of existence."

There was an air of mingled frankness and modesty about the Frenchman which had gained the good will of the whole party, not even excepting the Englishman. They all eagerly inquired after the particulars of the circumstances he alluded to, and as they strolled slowly up and down the sea-shore, he related the following adventure.

The Painter's Adventure

I AM AN HISTORICAL PAINTER BY PROFESSION, AND RESIDED FOR SOME TIME IN the family of a foreign Prince at his villa, about fifteen miles from Rome, among some of the most interesting scenery of Italy. It is situated on the heights of ancient Tusculum. In its neighborhood are the ruins of the villas of Cicero, Scylla, Lucullus, Rufinus, and other illustrious Romans, who sought refuge here occasionally from their toils, in the bosom of a soft and luxurious repose. From the midst of delightful bowers, refreshed by the pure mountain breeze, the eye looks over a romantic landscape full of poetical and historical associations. The Albanian mountains; Tivoli, once the favorite residence of Horace and Mecænas; the vast, deserted, melancholy Campagna, with the Tiber winding through it, and St Peter's dome swelling in the midst, the monument, as it were, over the grave of ancient Rome.

I assisted the Prince in researches which he was making among the classic ruins of his vicinity: his exertions were highly successful. Many wrecks of admirable statues and fragments of exquisite sculpture were dug up; monuments of the taste and magnificence that reigned in the ancient Tusculan abodes. He had studded his villa and its grounds with statues, relievos, vases, and sarcophagi, thus retrieved from the bosom of the earth.

The mode of life pursued at the villa was delightfully serene, diversified by interesting occupations and elegant leisure. Every one passed the day according to his pleasure or pursuits; and we all assembled in a cheerful dinner party at sunset.

It was on the fourth of November, a beautiful serene day, that we had assembled in the saloon at the sound of the first dinner-bell. The family were surprised at the absence of the Prince's confessor. They waited for him in vain, and at length placed themselves at table. They at first attributed his absence to his having prolonged his customary walk; and the early part of the dinner passed without any uneasiness. When the dessert was served, however, without his making his appearance, they began to feel anxious. They feared he might have been taken ill in some alley of the woods, or might have fallen into the hands of robbers. Not far from the villa, with the interval of a small valley, rose the mountains of the Abruzzi, the strong-hold of banditti. Indeed, the neighborhood had for some time past been infested by them; and Barbone, a notorious bandit chief, had often been met prowling about the solitudes of Tusculum. The daring enterprises of these ruffians were well known: the objects of their cupidity or vengeance were insecure even in palaces. As yet they had respected the possessions of the Prince; but the idea of such dangerous spirits hovering about the neighborhood was sufficient to occasion alarm.

The fears of the company increased as evening closed in. The Prince ordered out forest guards and domestics with flam-beaux to search for the confessor. They had not departed long when a slight noise was heard in the corridor of the ground-floor. The family were dining on the first floor, and the remaining domestics were occupied in attendance. There was no one on the ground-floor at this moment but the housekeeper, the laundress, and three field laborers, who were resting themselves, and conversing with the women.

I heard the noise from below, and presuming it to be occasioned by the return of the absentee, I left the table and hastened down stairs, eager to gain intelligence that might relieve the anxiety of the Prince and Princess. I had scarcely reached the last step, when I beheld before me a man dressed as a bandit; a carbine in his hand, and a stiletto and pistols in his belt his countenance had a mingled expression of ferocity and trepidation: he sprang upon me, and exclaimed exultingly, "Ecco il principe!"

I saw at once into what hands I had fallen, but endeavored to summon up coolness and presence of mind. A glance towards the lower end of the corridor showed me several ruffians, clothed and armed in the same manner with the one who had seized me. They were guarding the two females with the field laborers. The robber, who held me firmly by the collar, demanded repeatedly whether or not I were the Prince: his object evidently was to carry off the Prince, and extort an immense ransom. He was enraged at receiving none but vague replies, for I felt the importance of misleading him.

A sudden thought struck me how I might extricate myself from his clutches. I was unarmed, it is true, but I was vigorous. His companions were at a distance. By a sudden exertion I might wrest myself from him, and spring up the staircase, whither he would not dare to follow me singly. The idea was put in practice as soon as conceived.

The ruffian's throat was bare; with my right hand I seized him by it, with my left hand I grasped the arm which held the carbine. The suddenness of my attack took him completely unawares, and the strangling nature of my grasp paralyzed him. He choked and faltered. I felt his hand relaxing its hold, and was on the point of jerking myself away, and darting up the staircase, before he could recover himself, when I was suddenly seized by some one from behind.

I had to let go my grasp. The bandit, once released, fell upon me with fury, and gave me several blows with the butt end of his carbine, one of which wounded me severely in the forehead and covered me with blood. He took advantage of my being stunned to rifle me of my watch, and whatever valuables I had about my person.

When I recovered from the effect of the blow, I heard the voice of the chief of the banditti, who exclaimed—"Quello e il principe; siamo contente; andiamo!" (It is the Prince; enough; let us be off.) The band immediately closed round me and dragged me out of the palace, bearing off the three laborers likewise.

I had no hat on, and the blood flowed from my wound; I managed to stanch it, however, with my pocket-handkerchief, which I bound round my forehead. The captain of the band conducted me in triumph, supposing me to be the Prince. We had gone some distance before he learnt his mistake from one of the laborers. His rage was terrible. It was too late to return to the villa and endeavor to retrieve his error, for by this time the alarm must have been given, and every one in arms. He darted at me a ferocious look—swore I had deceived him, and caused him to miss his fortune—and told me to prepare for death. The rest of the robbers were equally furious. I saw their hands upon their poniards, and I knew that death was seldom an empty threat with these ruffians. The laborers saw the peril into which their information had betrayed me, and eagerly assured the captain that I was a man for whom the Prince would pay a great ransom. This produced a pause. For my part, I cannot say that I had been much dismayed by their menaces. I mean not to make any boast of courage; but I have been so schooled to hardship during the late revolutions; and have beheld death around me in so many perilous and disastrous scenes, that I have become in some measure callous to its terrors. The frequent hazard of life makes a man at length as reckless of it as a gambler of his money. To their threat of death, I replied, "that the sooner it was executed the better." This reply seemed to astonish the captain; and the prospect of ransom held out by the laborers had no doubt, a still greater effect on him. He considered for a moment, assumed a calmer manner, and made a sign to his companions, who had remained waiting for my death-warrant. "Forward!" said he; "we will see about this matter by and by!"

We descended rapidly towards the road of La Molara, which leads to Rocca Priori. In the midst of this road is a solitary inn. The captain ordered the troop to halt at the distance of a pistol-shot from it, and enjoined profound silence. He approached the threshold alone, with noiseless steps. He examined the outside of the door very narrowly, and then returning precipitately, made a sign for the troop to continue its march in silence. It has since been ascertained, that this was one of those infamous inns which are the secret resorts of banditti. The innkeeper had an understanding with the captain as he most probably had with the chiefs of the different bands. When any of the patroles and gens-d'armes were quartered at his house, the brigands were warned of it by a preconcerted signal on the door; when there was no such signal, they might enter with safety, and he sure of welcome.

After pursuing our road a little further, we struck off towards the woody mountains which envelope Rocca Priori. Our march was long and painful; with many circuits and windings: at length we clambered a steep ascent, covered with a thick forest; and when we had reached the centre, I was told to seat myself on the ground. No sooner had I done so than, at a sign from their chief, the robbers surrounded me, and spreading their great cloaks from one to the other, formed a kind of pavilion of mantles, to which their bodies might be said to serve as columns. The captain then struck a light, and a flambeau was lit immediately. The mantles were extended to prevent the light of the flambeau from being seen through the forest. Anxious as was my situation, I could not look round upon this screen of dusky drapery, relieved by the bright colors of the robbers' garments, the gleaming of their weapons, and the variety of strong marked countenances, lit up by the flambeau, without admiring the picturesque effect of the scene. It was quite theatrical.

The captain now held an inkhorn, and giving me pen and paper, ordered me to write what he should dictate. I obeyed. It was a demand, couched in the style of robber eloquence, "that the Prince should send three thousand dollars for my ransom; or that my death should be the consequence of a refusal."

I knew enough of the desperate character of these beings to feel assured this was not an idle menace. Their only mode of insuring attention to their demands is to make the infliction of the penalty inevitable. I saw at once, however, that the demand was preposterous, and made in improper language.

I told the captain so, and assured him that so extravagant a sum would never be granted.—"That I was neither a friend nor relative of the Prince, but a mere artist, employed to execute certain paintings. That I had nothing to offer as a ransom, but the price of my labors; if this were not sufficient, my life was at their disposal; it was a thing on which I set but little value."

I was the more hardy in my reply, because I saw that coolness and hardihood had an effect upon the robbers. It is true, as I finished speaking, the captain laid his hand upon his stiletto; but he restrained himself, and snatching the letter, folded it, and ordered me in a peremptory tone to address it to the Prince. He then dispatched one of the laborers with it to Tusculum, who promised to return with all possible speed.

The robbers now prepared themselves for sleep, and I was told that I might do the same. They spread their great cloaks on the ground, and lay down around me. One was stationed at a little distance to keep watch, and was relieved every two hours. The strangeness and wildness of this mountain bivouac among lawless beings, whose hands seemed ever ready to grasp the stiletto, and with whom life was so trivial and insecure, was enough to banish repose. The coldness of the earth, and of the dew, however, had a still greater effect than mental causes in disturbing my rest. The airs wafted to these mountains from the distant Mediterranean, diffused a great chilliness as the night advanced. An expedient suggested itself. I called one of my fellow-prisoners, the laborers, and made him lie down be-side me. Whenever one of my limbs became chilled, I approached it to the robust limb of my neighbor, and borrowed some of his warmth. In this way I was able to obtain a little sleep.

Day at length dawned, and I was roused from my slumber by the voice of the chieftain. He desired me to rise and follow him. I obeyed. On considering his physiognomy attentively it appeared a little softened. He even assisted me in scrambling up the steep forest, among rocks and brambles. Habit had made him a vigorous mountaineer; but I found it excessively toilsome to climb these rugged heights. We arrived at length at the summit of the mountain.

Here it was that I felt all the enthusiasm of my art suddenly awakened; and I forgot in an instant all my perils and fatigues at this magnificent view of the sunrise in the midst of the mountains of the Abruzzi, It was on these heights that Hannibal first pitched his camp, and pointed out Rome to his followers. The eye embraces a vast extent of country. The minor height of Tusculum, with its villas and its sacred ruins, lie below; the Sabine hills and the Albanian mountains stretch on either hand; and beyond Tusculum and Frascati spreads out the immense Campagna, with its lines of tombs, and here and there a broken aqueduct stretching across it, and the towers and domes of the eternal city in the midst.

Fancy this scene lit up by the glories of a rising sun, and bursting upon my sight as I looked forth from among the majestic forests of the Abruzzi. Fancy, too, the savage foreground, made still more savage by groups of banditti, armed and dressed in their wild picturesque manner, and you will not wonder that the enthusiasm of a painter for a moment overpowered all his other feelings.

The banditti were astonished at my admiration of a scene which familiarity had made so common in their eyes. I took advantage of their halting at this spot, drew forth a quire of drawing-paper, and began to sketch the features of the landscape. The height on which I was seated was wild and solitary, separated from the ridge of Tusculum by a valley nearly three miles wide, though the distance appeared less from the purity of the atmosphere. This height was one of the favorite retreats of the banditti, commanding a look-out over the country; while at the same time it was covered with forests, and distant from the populous haunts of men.

While I was sketching, my attention was called off for a moment by the cries of birds, and the bleatings of sheep. I looked around, but could see nothing of the animals which uttered them. They were repeated, and appeared to come from the summits of the trees. On looking more narrowly, I perceived six of the robbers perched in the tops of oaks, which grew on the breezy crest of the mountain, and commanded an uninterrupted prospect. They were keeping a look-out like so many vultures; casting their eyes into the depths of the valley below us; communicating with each other by signs, or holding discourse in sounds which might be mistaken by the wayfarer for the cries of hawks and crows, or the bleating of the mountain flocks. After they had reconnoitered the neighborhood, and finished their singular discourse, they descended from their airy perch, and returned to their prisoners. The captain posted three of them at three naked sides of the mountain, while he remained to guard us with what appeared his most trusty companion.

I had my book of sketches in my hand; he requested to see it, and after having run his eye over it, expressed himself convinced of the truth of my assertion that I was a painter. I thought I saw a gleam of good feeling dawning in him, and determined to avail myself of it. I knew that the worst of men have their good points and their accessible sides, if one would but study them carefully. Indeed, there is a singular mixture in the character of the Italian robber. With reckless ferocity he often mingles traits of kindness and good-humor. He is not always radically bad; but driven to his course of life by some unpremeditated crime, the effect of those sudden bursts of passion to which the Italian temperament is prone. This has compelled him to take to the mountains, or, as it is technically termed among them, "andare in campagna." He has become a robber by profession; but, like a soldier, when not in action he can lay aside his weapon and his fierceness, and become like other men.

I took occasion, from the observations of the captain on my sketchings, to fall into conversation with him, and found him sociable and communicative. By degrees I became completely at my ease with him. I had fancied I perceived about him a degree of self-love, which I determined to make use of. I assumed an air of careless frankness, and told him, that, as an artist, I pretended to the power of judging of the physiognomy; that I thought I perceived something in his features and demeanor which announced him worthy of higher fortunes; that he was not formed to exercise the profession to which he had abandoned himself; that he had talents and qualities fitted for a nobler sphere of action; that he had but to change his course of life, and, in a legitimate career, the same courage and endowments which now made him an object of terror, would assure him the applause and admiration of society.

I had not mistaken my man; my discourse both touched and excited him. He seized my hand, pressed it, and replied with strong emotion—"You have guessed the truth; you have judged of me rightly." He remained for a moment silent; then with a kind of effort, he resumed—"I will tell you some particulars of my life and you will perceive that it was the oppression of others, rather than my own crimes, which drove me to the mountains. I sought to serve my fellow-men, and they have persecuted me from among them." We seated ourselves on the grass, and the robber gave me the following anecdotes of his history.

The Story of the Bandit Chieftain

I AM A NATIVE OF THE VILLAGE OF PROSSEDI. MY FATHER WAS EASY ENOUGH IN circumstances, and we lived peaceably and independently, cultivating our fields. All went on well with us until a new chief of the Sbirri was sent to our village to take command of the police. He was an arbitrary fellow, prying into every thing, and practising all sorts of vexations and oppressions in the discharge of his office. I was at that time eighteen years of age, and had a natural love of justice and good neighborhood. I had also a little education, and knew something of history, so as to be able to judge a little of men and their actions. All this inspired me with hatred for this paltry despot. My own family, also, became the object of his suspicion or dislike, and felt more than once the arbitrary abuse of his power. These things worked together in my mind, and I gasped after vengeance. My character was always ardent and energetic, and, acted upon by the love of justice, determined me, by one blow, to rid the country of the tyrant.

Full of my project, I rose one morning before peep of day, and concealing a stiletto under my waistcoat—here you see it!—(and he drew forth a long keen poniard) I lay in wait for him in the outskirts of the village. I knew all his haunts, and his habit of making his rounds and prowling about like a wolf in the gray of the morning. At length I met him, and attacked him with fury. He was armed, but I took him unawares, and was full of youth and vigor. I gave him repeated blows to make sure work, and laid him lifeless at my feet.

When I was satisfied that I had done for him, I returned with all haste to the village, but had the ill luck to meet two of the Sbirri as I entered it. They accosted me, and asked if I had seen their chief. I assumed an air of tranquillity, and told them I had not. They continued on their way, and within a few hours brought back the dead body to Prossedi. Their suspicions of me being already awakened, I was arrested and thrown into prison. Here I lay several weeks, when the Prince, who was Seigneur of Prossedi, directed judicial proceedings against me. I was brought to trial, and a witness was produced, who pretended to have seen me flying with precipitation not far from the bleeding body; and so I was condemned to the galleys for thirty years.

"Curse on such laws!" vociferated the bandit, foaming with rage: "Curse on such a government! and ten thousand curses on the Prince who caused me to be adjudged so rigorously, while so many other Roman princes harbor and protect assassins a thousand times more culpable! What had I done but what was inspired by a love of justice and my country? Why was my act more culpable than that of Brutus, when he sacrificed Caesar to the cause of liberty and justice?"

There was something at once both lofty and ludicrous in the rhapsody of this robber chief, thus associating himself with one of the great names of antiquity. It showed, however, that he had at least the merit of knowing the remarkable facts in the history of his country. He became more calm, and resumed his narrative.

I was conducted to Civita Vecchia in fetters. My heart was burning with rage. I had been married scarce six months to a woman whom I passionately loved, and who was pregnant. My family was in despair. For a long time I made unsuccessful efforts to break my chain. At length I found a morsel of iron, which I hid carefully, and endeavored, with a pointed flint, to fashion it into a kind of file. I occupied myself in this work during the night-time, and when it was finished, I made out, after a long time, to sever one of the rings of my chain. My flight was successful.

I wandered for several weeks in the mountains which surround Prossedi, and found means to inform my wife of the place where I was concealed. She came often to see me. I had determined to put myself at the head of an armed band. She endeavored, for a long time, to dissuade me, but finding my resolution fixed, she at length united in my project of vengeance, and brought me, herself, my poniard. By her means I communicated with several brave fellows of the neighboring villages, whom I knew to be ready to take to the mountains, and only panting for an opportunity to exercise their daring spirits. We soon formed a combination, procured arms, and we have had ample opportunities of revenging ourselves for the wrongs and injuries which most of us have suffered. Every thing has succeeded with us until now, and had it not been for our blunder in mistaking you for the Prince, our fortunes would have been made.

* * *

Here the robber concluded his story. He had talked himself into complete companionship, and assured me he no longer bore me any grudge for the error of which I had been the innocent cause. He even professed a kindness for me, and wished me to remain some time with them. He promised to give me a sight of certain grottos which they occupied beyond Villetri, and whither they resorted during the intervals of their expeditions.

He assured me that they led a jovial life there; had plenty of good cheer; slept on beds of moss; and were waited upon by young and beautiful females, whom I might take for models.

I confess I felt my curiosity roused by his descriptions of the grottos and their inhabitants: they realized those scenes in robber story which I had always looked upon as mere creations of the fancy. I should gladly have accepted his invitation, and paid a visit to these caverns, could I have felt more secure in my company.

I began to find my situation less painful. I had evidently propitiated the good will of the chieftain, and hoped that he might release me for a moderate ransom. A new alarm, however, awaited me. While the captain was looking out with impatience for the return of the messenger who had been sent to the Prince, the sentinel posted on the side of the mountain facing the plain of La Molara came running towards us. "We are betrayed!" exclaimed he. "The police of Frascati are after us. A party of carabineers have just stopped at the inn below the mountain." Then, laying his hand on his stiletto, he swore, with a terrible oath, that if they made the least movement towards the mountain, my life and the lives of my fellow-prisoners should answer for it

The chieftain resumed all his ferocity of demeanor, and approved of what his companion said; but when the latter had returned to his post, he turned to me with a softened air: "I must act as chief," said he, "and humor my dangerous subalterns. It is a law with us to kill our prisoners rather than suffer them to be rescued; but do not be alarmed. In case we are surprised, keep by me; fly with us, and I will consider myself responsible for your life."

There was nothing very consolatory in this arrangement, which would have placed me between two dangers. I scarcely knew, in case of flight, from which I should have the most to apprehend, the carbines of the pursuers, or the stilettos of the pursued. I remained silent, however, and endeavored to maintain a look of tranquillity.

For an hour was I kept in this state of peril and anxiety. The robbers, crouching among their leafy coverts, kept an eagle watch upon the carabineers below, as they loitered about the inn; sometimes lolling about the portal; sometimes disappearing for several minutes; then sallying out, examining their weapons, pointing in different directions, and apparently asking questions about the neighborhood. Not a movement, a gesture, was lost upon the keen eyes of the brigands. At length we were relieved from our apprehensions. The carabineers having finished their refreshment, seized their arms, continued along the valley towards the great road, and gradually left the mountain behind them. "I felt almost certain," said the chief, "that they could not be sent after us. They know too well how prisoners have fared in our hands on similar occasions. Our laws in this respect are inflexible, and are necessary for our safety. If we once flinched from them, there would no longer be such a thing as a ransom to be procured."

There were no signs yet of the messenger's return. I was preparing to resume my sketching, when the captain drew a quire of paper from his knapsack. "Come," said he, laughing, "you are a painter,—take my likeness. The leaves of your portfolio are small,—draw it on this." I gladly consented, for it was a study that seldom presents itself to a painter. I recollected that Salvator Rosa in his youth had voluntarily sojourned for a time among the banditti of Calabria, and had filled his mind with the savage scenery and savage associates by which he was surrounded. I seized my pencil with enthusiasm at the thought. I found the captain the most docile of subjects, and, after various shiftings of position, placed him in an attitude to my mind.

Picture to yourself a stern muscular figure, in fanciful bandit costume; with pistols and poniards in belt; his brawny neck bare; a handkerchief loosely thrown round it, and the two ends in front strung with rings of all kinds, the spoils of travellers; relics and medals hanging on his breast; his hat decorated with various colored ribands; his vest and short breeches of bright colors and finely embroidered; his legs in buskins or leggins. Fancy him on a mountain height, among wild rocks and rugged oaks, leaning on his carbine, as if meditating some exploit; while far below are beheld villages and villas, the scenes of his maraudings, with the wide Campagna dimly extending in the distance.

The robber was pleased with the sketch, and seemed to admire himself upon paper. I had scarcely finished, when the laborer arrived who had been sent for my ransom. He had reached Tusculum two hours after midnight. He brought me a letter from the Prince, who was in bed at the time of his arrival. As I had predicted, he treated the demand as extravagant, but offered five hundred dollars for my ransom. Having no money by him at the moment, he had sent a note for the amount, payable to whomsoever should conduct me safe and sound to Borne. I presented the note of hand to the chieftain; he received it with a shrug. "Of what use are notes of hand to us?" said he. "Who can we send with you to Rome to receive it? We are all marked men; known and described at every gate and military post and village church door. No; we must have gold and silver; let the sum be paid in cash, and you shall be restored to liberty."

The captain again placed a sheet of paper before me to communicate his determination to the Prince. When I had finished the letter, and took the sheet from the quire, I found on the opposite side of it the portrait which I had just been tracing. I was about to tear it off and give it to the chief.

"Hold!" said he, "let it go to Rome; let them see what kind of looking fellow I am. Perhaps the Prince and his friends may form as good an opinion of me from my face as you have done."

This was said sportively, yet it was evident there was vanity lurking at the bottom. Even this wary, distrustful chief of banditti forgot for a moment his usual foresight and precaution, in the common wish to be admired. He never reflected what use might be made of this portrait in his pursuit and conviction.

The letter was folded and directed, and the messenger departed again for Tusculum. It was now eleven o'clock in the morning, and as yet we had eaten nothing. In spite of all my anxiety, I began to feel a craving appetite. I was glad therefore to hear the captain talk something about eating. He observed that for three days and nights they had been lurking about among rocks and woods, meditating their expedition to Tusculum, during which time all their provisions had been exhausted. He should now take measures to procure a supply. Leaving me therefore in charge of his comrade, in whom he appeared to have implicit confidence, he departed, assuring me that in less than two hours we should make a good dinner. Where it was to come from was an enigma to me, though it was evident these beings had their secret friends and agents throughout the country.

Indeed, the inhabitants of these mountains, and of the valleys which they embosom, are a rude, half-civilized set. The towns and villages among the forests of the Abruzzi, shut up from the rest of the world, are almost like savage dens. It is wonderful that such rude abodes, so little known and visited, should be embosomed in the midst of one of the most travelled and civilized countries of Europe. Among these regions the robber prowls unmolested; not a mountaineer hesitates to give him secret harbor and assistance. The shepherds, however, who tend their flocks among the mountains, are the favorite emissaries of the robbers, when they would send messages down to the valleys either for ransom or supplies.

The shepherds of the Abruzzi are as wild as the scenes they frequent. They are clad in a rude garb of black or brown sheep-skin; they have high conical hats, and coarse sandals of cloth bound round their legs with thongs, similar to those worn by the robbers. They carry long staves, on which, as they lean, they form picturesque objects in the lonely landscape, and they are followed by their ever-constant companion, the dog. They are a curious, questioning set, glad at any time to relieve the monotony of their solitude by the conversation of the passer-by; and the dog will lend an attentive ear, and put on as sagacious and inquisitive a look as his master.

But I am wandering from my story. I was now left alone with one of the robbers, the confidential companion of the chief. He was the youngest and most vigorous of the band; and though his countenance had something of that dissolute fierceness which seems natural to this desperate, lawless mode of life, yet there were traces of manly beauty about it. As an artist I could not but admire it I had remarked in him an air of abstraction and reverie, and at times a movement of inward suffering and impatience. He now sat on the ground, his elbows on his knees, his head resting between his clinched fists, and his eyes fixed on the earth with an expression of sad and bitter rumination. I had grown familiar with him from repeated conversations, and had found him superior in mind to the rest of the band. I was anxious to seize any opportunity of sounding the feelings of these singular beings. I fancied I read in the countenance of this one traces of self-condemnation and remorse; and the ease with which I had drawn forth the confidence of the chieftain encouraged me to hope the same with his follower.

After a little preliminary conversation, I ventured to ask him if he did not feel regret at having abandoned his family, and taken to this dangerous profession. "I feel," replied he, "but one regret, and that will end only with my life."

As he said this, he pressed his clinched fists upon his bosom, drew his breath through his set teeth, and added, with a deep emotion, "I have something within here that stifles me; it is like a burning iron consuming my very heart. I could tell you a miserable story—but not now—another time."

He relapsed into his former position, and sat with his head between his hands, muttering to himself in broken ejaculations, and what appeared at times to be curses and maledictions. I saw he was not in a mood to be disturbed, so I left him to himself.

In a little while the exhaustion of his feelings, and probably the fatigues he had undergone in this expedition, began to produce drowsiness. He struggled with it for a time, but the warmth and stillness of mid-day made it irresistible, and he at length stretched himself upon the herbage and fell asleep.

I now beheld a chance of escape within my reach. My guard lay before me at my mercy. His vigorous limbs relaxed by sleep—his bosom open for the blow—his carbine slipped from his nerveless grasp, and lying by his side—his stiletto half out of the pocket in which it was usually carried. Two only of his comrades were in sight, and those at a considerable distance on the edge of the mountain, their backs turned to us, and their attention occupied in keeping a look-out upon the plain. Through a strip of intervening forest, and at the foot of a steep descent, I beheld the village of Rocca Priori. To have secured the carbine of the sleeping brigand; to have seized upon his poniard, and have plunged it in his heart, would have been the work of an instant. Should he die without noise, I might dart through the forest, and down to Rocca Priori before my flight might be discovered. In case of alarm, I should still have a fair start of the robbers, and a chance of getting beyond the reach of their shot.

Here then was an opportunity for both escape and vengeance; perilous indeed, but powerfully tempting. Had my situation been more critical I could not have resisted it. I reflected, however, for a moment. The attempt, if successful, would be followed by the sacrifice of my two fellow-prisoners, who were sleeping profoundly, and could not be awakened in time to escape. The laborer who had gone after the ransom might also fall a victim to the rage of the robbers, without the money which he brought being saved. Besides, the conduct of the chief towards me made me feel confident of speedy deliverance. These reflections overcame the first powerful impulse, and I calmed the turbulent agitation which it had awakened.

I again took out my materials for drawing, and amused my-self with sketching the magnificent prospect. It was now about noon, and every thing had sunk into repose, like the sleeping bandit before me. The noontide stillness that reigned over these mountains, the vast landscape below, gleaming with distant towns, and dotted with various habitations and signs of life, yet all so silent, had a powerful effect upon my mind. The intermediate valleys, too, which lie among the mountains, have a peculiar air of solitude. Few sounds are heard at mid-day to break the quiet of the scene. Sometimes the whistle of a solitary muleteer, lagging with his lazy animal along the road which winds through the centre of the valley; sometimes the faint piping of a shepherd's reed from the side of the mountain, or sometimes the bell of an ass slowly pacing along, followed by a monk with bare feet, and bare, shining head, and carrying provisions to his convent.

I had continued to sketch for some time among my sleeping companions, when at length I saw the captain of the band approaching, followed by a peasant leading a mule, on which was a well-filled sack. I at first apprehended that this was some new prey fallen into the hands of the robbers; but the contented look of the peasant soon relieved me, and I was rejoiced to hear that it was our promised repast. The brigands now came running from the three sides of the mountain, having the quick scent of vultures. Every one busied himself in unloading the mule, and relieving the sack of its contents.

The first thing that made its appearance was an enormous ham, of a color and plumpness that would have inspired the pencil of Teniers; it was followed by a large cheese, a bag of boiled chestnuts, a little barrel of wine, and a quantity of good household bread. Every thing was arranged on the grass with a degree of symmetry; and the captain, presenting me with his knife, requested me to help myself. We all seated ourselves round the viands, and nothing was heard for a time but the sound of vigorous mastication, or the gurgling of the barrel of wine as it revolved briskly about the circle. My long fasting, and the mountain air and exercise, had given me a keen appetite; and never did repast appear to me more excellent or picturesque.

From time to time one of the band was dispatched to keep a look-out upon the plain. No enemy was at hand, and the dinner was undisturbed. The peasant received nearly three times the value of his provisions, and set off down the mountain highly satisfied with his bargain. I felt invigorated by the hearty meal I had made, and notwithstanding that the wound I had received the evening before was painful, yet I could not but feel extremely interested and gratified by the singular scenes continually presented me. Every thing was picturesque about these wild beings and their haunts. Their bivouacs; their groups on guard; their indolent noontide repose on the mountain-brow; their rude repast on the herbage among rocks and trees; every thing presented a study for a painter: but it was towards the approach of evening that I felt the highest enthusiasm awakened.

The setting sun, declining beyond the vast Campagna, shed its rich yellow beams on the woody summit of the Abruzzi. Several mountains crowned with snow shone brilliantly in the distance, contrasting their brightness with others, which, thrown into shade, assumed deep tints of purple and violet. As the evening advanced, the landscape darkened into a sterner character. The immense solitude around; the wild mountains broken into rocks and precipices, intermingled with vast oaks, corks, and chestnuts; and the groups of banditti in the foreground, reminded me of the savage scenes of Salvator Rosa.

To beguile the time, the captain proposed to his comrades to spread before me their jewels and cameos, as I must doubtless be a judge of such articles, and able to form an estimate of their value. He set the example, the others followed it; and in a few moments I saw the grass before me sparkling with jewels and gems that would have delighted the eyes of an antiquary or a fine lady.

Among them were several precious jewels, and antique intaglios and cameos of great value; the spoils, doubtless, of travellers of distinction. I found that they were in the habit of selling their booty in the frontier towns; but as these in general were thinly and poorly peopled, and little frequented by travellers, they could offer no market for such valuable articles of taste and luxury. I suggested to them the certainty of their readily obtaining great prices for these gems among the rich strangers with whom Rome was thronged.

The impression made upon their greedy minds was immediately apparent. One of the band, a young man, and the least known, requested permission of the captain to depart the following day, in disguise, for Rome, for the purpose of traffic; promising, on the faith of a bandit, (a sacred pledge among them,) to return in two days to any place he might appoint. The captain consented, and a curious scene took place; the robbers crowded round him eagerly, confiding to him such of their jewels as they wished to dispose of, and giving him instructions what to demand. There was much bargaining and exchanging and selling of trinkets among them; and I beheld my watch, which had a chain and valuable seals, purchased by the young robber-merchant of the ruffian who had plundered me, for sixty dollars. I now conceived a faint hope, that if it went to Rome, I might somehow or other regain possession of it.[1]

In the meantime day declined, and no messenger returned from Tusculum. The idea of passing another night in the woods was extremely disheartening, for I began to

---

1. The hopes of the artist were not disappointed—the robber was stopped at one of the gates of Rome. Something in his looks or deportment had excited suspicion. He was searched, and the valuable trinkets found on him sufficiently evinced his character. On applying to the police, the artist's watch was returned to him.

be satisfied with what I had seen of robber-life. The chieftain now ordered his men to follow him that he might station them at their posts; adding, that if the messenger did not return before night, they must shift their quarters to some other place.

I was again left alone with the young bandit who had before guarded me; he had the same gloomy air and haggard eye, with now and then a bitter sardonic smile. I was determined to probe this ulcerated heart, and reminded him of a kind promise he had given me to tell me the cause of his suffering. It seemed to me as if these troubled spirits were glad of any opportunity to disburden themselves, and of having some fresh, undiseased mind, with which they could communicate. I had hardly made the request, when he seated himself by my side, and gave me his story in, as nearly as I can recollect, the following words.

The Story of the Young Robber

I WAS BORN IN THE LITTLE TOWN OF FROSINONE, WHICH LIES AT THE SKIRTS of the Abruzzi. My father had made a little property in trade, and gave me some education, as he intended me for the church; but I had kept gay company too much to relish the cowl, so I grew up a loiterer about the place. I was a heedless fellow, a little quarrelsome on occasion, but good-humored in the main; so I made my way very well for a time, until I fell in love. There lived in our town a surveyor or land-bailiff of the prince, who had a young daughter, a beautiful girl of sixteen; she was looked upon as something better than the common run of our townsfolk, and was kept almost entirely at home. I saw her occasionally, and became madly in love with her—she looked so fresh and tender, and so different from the sunburnt females to whom I had been accustomed.

As my father kept me in money, I always dressed well, and took all opportunities of showing myself off to advantage in the eyes of the little beauty. I used to see her at church; and as I could play a little upon the guitar, I gave a tune sometimes under her window of an evening; and I tried to have interviews with her in her father's vineyard, not far from the town, where she sometimes walked. She was evidently pleased with me, but she was young and shy; and her father kept a strict eye upon her, and took alarm at my attentions, for he had a bad opinion of me, and looked for a better match for his daughter. I became furious at the difficulties thrown in my way, having been accustomed always to easy success among the women, being considered one of the smartest young fellows of the place.

Her father brought home a suitor for her, a rich farmer from a neighboring town. The wedding-day was appointed, and preparations were making. I got sight of her at her window, and I thought she looked sadly at me. I determined the match should not take place, cost what it might I met her intended bridegroom in the market-place, and could not restrain the expression of my rage. A few hot words passed between us, when I drew my stiletto and stabbed him to the heart. I fled to a neighboring church for refuge, and with a little money I obtained absolution, but I did not dare to venture from my asylum.

At that time our captain was forming his troop. He had known me from boyhood; and hearing of my situation, came to me in secret, and made such offers, that I agreed to enroll myself among his followers. Indeed, I had more than once thought of taking to this mode of life, having known several brave fellows of the mountains, who used to spend their money freely among us youngsters of the town. I accordingly left my asylum late one night, repaired to the appointed place of meeting, took the oaths prescribed, and became one of the troop. We were for some time in a distant part of the mountains, and our wild adventurous kind of life hit my fancy wonderfully, and diverted my thoughts. At length they returned with all their violence to the recollection of Rosetta; the solitude in which I often found myself gave me time to brood over her image and, as I have kept watch at night over our sleeping camp in the mountains, my feelings have been roused almost to a fever.

At length we shifted our ground, and determined to make a descent upon the road between Terracina and Naples. In the course of our expedition we passed a day or two in the woody mountains which rise above Frosinone. I cannot tell you how I felt when I looked down upon the place, and distinguished the residence of Rosetta. I determined to have an interview with, her;—but to what purpose? I could not expect that she would quit her home, and accompany me in my hazardous life among the mountains. She had been brought up too tenderly for that; and when I looked upon the women who were associated with some of our troop, I could not have borne the thoughts of her being their companion. All return to my former life was likewise hopeless, for a price was set upon my head. Still I determined to see her; the very hazard and fruitlessness of the thing made me furious to accomplish it.

About three weeks since, I persuaded our captain to draw down to the vicinity of Frosinone, suggesting the chance of entrapping some of its principal inhabitants, and compelling them to a ransom. We were lying in ambush towards evening, not far from the vineyard of Rosetta's father. I stole quietly from my companions, and drew near to reconnoitre the place of her frequent walks. How my heart beat when among the vines I beheld the gleaming of a white dress! I knew it must be Rosetta's; it being rare for any female of the place to dress in white. I advanced secretly and without noise, until, putting aside the vines, I stood suddenly before her. She uttered a piercing shriek, but I seized her in my arms, put my hand upon her mouth, and conjured her to be silent. I poured out all the frenzy of my passion; offered to renounce my mode of life; to put my fate in her hands; to fly with her where we might live in safety together. All that I could say or do would not pacify her. Instead of love, horror and affright seemed to have taken possession of her beast She struggled partly from my grasp, and filled the air with her cries.

In an instant the captain and the rest of my companions were around us. I would have given any thing at that moment had she been safe out of our hands, and in her father's house. It was too late. The captain pronounced her a prize, and ordered that she should be borne to the mountains. I represented to him that she was my prize; that I had a previous claim to her; and I mentioned my former attachment. He sneered bitterly in reply; observed that brigands had no business with village intrigues, and that, according to the laws of the troop, all spoils of the kind were determined by lot. Love and jealousy were raging in my heart, but I had to choose between obedience and death. I surrendered her to the captain, and we made for the mountains.

She was overcome by affright, and her steps were so feeble and faltering that it was necessary to support her. I could not endure the idea that my comrades should touch her, and assuming a forced tranquillity, begged she might be confided to me, as one to whom she was more accustomed. The captain regarded me, for a moment, with a searching look, but I bore it without flinching, and he consented. I took her in my arms; she was almost senseless. Her head rested on my shoulder; I felt her breath on my face, and it seemed to fan the flame which devoured me. Oh God! to have this glowing treasure in my arms, and yet to think it was not mine!

We arrived at the foot of the mountain; I ascended it with difficulty, particularly where the woods were thick, but I would not relinquish my delicious burden. I reflected with rage, however, that I must soon do so. The thoughts that so delicate a creature must be abandoned to my rude companions maddened me. I felt tempted, the stiletto in my hand, to cut my way through them all, and bear her off in triumph. I scarcely conceived the idea before I saw its rashness; but my brain was fevered with the thought that any but myself should enjoy her charms. I endeavored to outstrip my companions by the quickness of my movements, and to get a little distance ahead, in case any favorable opportunity of escape should present. Vain effort! The voice of the captain suddenly ordered a halt. I trembled, but had to obey. The poor girl partly opened a languid eye, but was without strength or motion. I laid her upon the grass. The captain darted on me a terrible look of suspicion, and ordered me to scour the woods with my companions in search of some shepherd, who might be sent to her father's to demand a ransom.

I saw at once the peril To resist with violence was certain death—but to leave her alone, in the power of the captain!—I spoke out then with a fervor, inspired by my passion and my despair. I reminded the captain that I was the first to seize her; that she was my prize; and that my previous attachment to her ought to make her sacred among my companions. I insisted, therefore, that he should pledge me his word to respect her, otherwise I should refuse obedience to his orders. His only reply was to cock his carbine, and at the signal my comrades did the same. They laughed with cruelty at my impotent rage. What could I do? I felt the madness of resistance. I was menaced on all hands, and my companions obliged me to follow them. She remained alone with the chief—yes, alone—and almost lifeless!—

Here the robber paused in his recital, overpowered by his emotions. Great drops of sweat stood on his forehead; he panted rather than breathed; his brawny bosom rose and fell like the waves of the troubled sea. When he had become a little calm, he continued his recital.

I was not long in finding a shepherd, said he. I ran with the rapidity of a deer, eager, if possible, to get back before that I dreaded might take place. I had left my companions far behind, and I rejoined them before they had reached one half the distance I had made. I hurried them back to the place where we had left the captain. As we approached, I beheld him seated by the side of Rosetta. His triumphant look, and the desolate condition of the unfortunate girl, left me no doubt of her fate. I know not how I restrained my fury.

It was with extreme difficulty, and by guiding her hand, that she was made to trace a few characters, requesting her father to send three hundred dollars as her ransom. The letter was dispatched by the shepherd. When he was gone, the chief turned sternly to me. "You have set an example," said he, "of mutiny and self-will, which, if indulged, would be ruinous to the troop. Had I treated you as our laws require, this bullet would have been driven through your brain. But you are an old friend. I have borne patiently with your fury and your folly. I have even protected you from a foolish passion that would have unmanned you. As to this girl, the laws of our association must have their course." So saying, he gave his commands: lots were drawn, and the helpless girl was abandoned to the troop.

Here the robber paused again, panting with fury, and it was some moments before he could resume his story.

Hell, said he, was raging in my heart. I beheld the impossibility of avenging myself; and I felt that, according to the articles in which we stood bound to one another, the captain was in the right. I rushed with frenzy from the place; I threw myself upon the earth; tore up the grass with my hands; and beat my head and gnashed my teeth in agony and rage. When at length I returned, I beheld the wretched victim, pale, dishevelled, her dress torn and disordered. An emotion of pity, for a moment, subdued my fiercer feelings. I bore her to the foot of a tree, and leaned her gently against it. I took my gourd, which was filled with wine, and applying it to her lips, endeavored to make her swallow a little. To what a condition was she reduced! she, whom I had once seen the pride of Frosinone; who but a short time before I had beheld sporting in her father's vineyard, so fresh, and beautiful and happy! Her teeth were clinched; her eyes fixed on the ground; her form without motion, and in a state of absolute insensibility. I hung over her in an agony of recollection at all that she had been, and of anguish at what I now beheld her. I darted round a look of horror at my companions, who seemed like so many fiends exulting in the downfall of an angel; and I felt a horror at myself for being their accomplice.

The captain, always suspicious, saw, with his usual penetration, what was passing within me, and ordered me to go upon the ridge of the woods, to keep a look-out over the neighborhood, and await the return of the shepherd. I obeyed, of course, stifling the fury that raged within me, though I felt, for the moment, that he was my most deadly foe.

On my way, however, a ray of reflection came across my mind. I perceived that the captain was but following, with strictness, the terrible laws to which we had sworn fidelity. That the passion by which I had been blinded might, with justice, have been fatal to me, but for his forbearance; that he had penetrated my soul, and had taken precautions, by sending me out of the way, to prevent my committing any excess in my anger. From that instant I felt that I was capable of pardoning him.

Occupied with these thoughts, I arrived at the foot of the mountain. The country was solitary and secure, and in a short time I beheld the shepherd at a distance crossing the plain. I hastened to meet him. He had obtained nothing. He had found the father plunged in the deepest distress. He had read the letter with violent emotion, and then, calming himself with a sudden exertion, he had replied coldly: "My daughter has been dishonored by those wretches; let her be returned without ransom,—or let her die!"

I shuddered at this reply. I knew that, according to the laws of our troop, her death was inevitable. Our oaths required it. I felt, nevertheless, that not having been able to have her to myself, I could be her executioner!

The robber again paused with agitation. I sat musing upon his last frightful words, which proved to what excess the passions may be carried, when escaped from all moral restraint. There was a horrible verity in this story that reminded me of some of the tragic fictions of Dante.

We now come to a fatal moment, resumed he bandit. After the report of the shepherd, I returned with him, and the chieftain received from his lips the refusal of the father. At a signal which we all understood, we followed him to some distance from the victim. He there pronounced her sentence of death. Every one stood ready to execute his order, but I interfered. I observed that there was something due to pity as well as to justice. That I was as ready as any one to approve the implacable law, which was to serve as a warning to all those who hesitated to pay the ransoms demanded for our prisoners; but that though the sacrifice was proper, it ought to be made without cruelty. The night is approaching, continued I; she will soon be wrapped in sleep; let her then be dispatched. All I now claim on the score of former kindness is, let me strike the blow. I will do it as surely, though more tenderly than another. Several raised their voices against my proposition, but the captain imposed silence on them. He told me I might conduct her into a thicket at some distance, and he relied upon my promise.

I hastened to seize upon my prey. There was a forlorn kind of triumph at having at length become her exclusive possessor. I bore her off into the thickness of the forest. She remained in the same state of insensibility or stupor. I was thankful that she did not recollect me, for had she once murmured my name, I should have been overcome. She slept at length in the arms of him who was to poniard her. Many were the conflicts I underwent before I could bring myself to strike the blow. But my heart had become sore by the recent conflicts it had undergone, and I dreaded lest, by procrastination, some other should become her executioner. When her repose had continued for some time, I separated myself gently from her, that I might not disturb her sleep, and seizing suddenly my poniard plunged it into her bosom. A painful and concentrated murmur, but without any convulsive movement, accompanied her last sigh.—So perished this unfortunate!

He ceased to speak. I sat, horror-struck, covering my face with my hands, seeking, as it were, to hide from myself the frightful images he had presented to my mind. I was roused from this silence by the voice of the captain: "You sleep," said he, "and it is time to be off. Come, we must abandon this height, as night is setting in, and the messenger is not returned. I will post some one on the mountain edge to conduct him to the place where we shall pass the night."

This was no agreeable news to me. I was sick at heart with the dismal story I had heard. I was harassed and fatigued, and the sight of the banditti began to grow insupportable to me.

The captain assembled his comrades. We rapidly descended the forest, which we had mounted with so much difficulty in the morning, and soon arrived in what appeared to be a frequented road. The robbers proceeded with great caution, carrying their guns cocked, and looking on every side with wary and suspicious eyes. They were apprehensive of encountering the civic patrole. We left Rocca Priori behind us. There was a fountain near by, and as I was excessively thirsty, I begged permission to stop and drink. The captain himself went and brought me water in his hat. We pursued our route, when, at the extremity of an alley which crossed the road, I perceived a female on horseback, dressed in white. She was alone. I recollected the fate of the poor girl in the story, and trembled for her safety.

One of the brigands saw her at the same instant, and plunging into the bushes, he ran precipitately in the direction towards her. Stopping on the border of the alley, he put one knee to the ground, presented his carbine ready to menace her, or to shoot her horse if she attempted to fly, and in this way awaited her approach. I kept my eyes fixed on her with intense anxiety. I felt tempted to shout and warn her of her danger, though my own destruction would have been the consequence. It was awful to see this tiger crouching ready for a bound, and the poor innocent victim wandering unconsciously near him. Nothing but a mere chance could save her. To my joy the chance turned in her favor. She seemed almost accidentally to take an opposite path, which led outside of the wood, where the robber dared not venture. To this casual deviation she owed her safety.

I could not imagine why the captain of the band had ventured to such a distance from the height on which he had placed the sentinel to watch the return of the messenger. He seemed himself anxious at the risk to which he exposed himself. His movements were rapid and uneasy; I could scarce keep pace with him. At length, after three hours of what might be termed a forced march, we mounted the extremity of the same woods, the summit of which we had occupied during the day; and I learnt with satisfaction that we had reached our quarters for the night. "You must be fatigued," said the chieftain; "but it was necessary to survey the environs, so as not to be surprised during the night. Had we met with the famous civic guard of Rocca Priori, you would have seen fine sport." Such was the indefatigable precaution and forethought of this robber chief, who really gave continual evidence of military talent.

The night was magnificent. The moon, rising above the horizon in a cloudless sky, faintly lit up the grand features of the mountain; while lights twinkling here and there, like terrestrial stars in the wide dusky expanse of the landscape, betrayed the lonely cabins of the shepherds. Exhausted by fatigue, and by the many agitations I had experienced, I prepared to sleep, soothed by the hope of approaching deliverance. The captain ordered his companions to collect some dry moss; he arranged with his own hands a kind of mattress and pillow of it, and gave me his ample mantle as a covering. I could not but feel both surprised and gratified by such unexpected attentions on the part of this benevolent cut-throat; for there is nothing more striking than to find the ordinary charities, which are matters of course in common life, flourishing by the side of such stern and sterile crime. It is like finding the tender flowers and fresh herbage of the valley growing among the rocks and cinders of the volcano.

Before I fell asleep I had some further discourse with the captain, who seemed to feel great confidence in me. He referred to our previous conversation of the morning; told me he was weary of his hazardous profession; that he had acquired sufficient property, and was anxious to return to the world, and lead a peaceful life in the bosom of his family. He wished to know whether it was not in my power to procure for him a passport to the United States of America. I applauded his good intentions, and promised to do every thing in my power to promote its success. We then parted for the night I stretched myself upon my couch of moss, which, after my fatigues, felt like a bed of down; and, sheltered by the robber-mantle from all humidity, I slept soundly, without waking, until the signal to arise.

It was nearly six o'clock, and the day was just dawning. As the place where we had passed the night was too much exposed, we moved up into the thickness of the woods. A fire was kindled. While there was any flame, the mantles were again extended round it: but when nothing remained but glowing cinders, they were lowered, and the robbers seated themselves in a circle.

The scene before me reminded me of some of those described by Homer. There wanted only the victim on the coals, and the sacred knife to cut off the succulent parts, and distribute them around. My companions might have rivalled the grim warriors of Greece. In place of the noble repasts, however, of Achilles and Agamemnon, I beheld displayed on the grass the remains of the ham which had sustained so vigorous an attack on the preceding evening, accompanied by the relics of the bread, cheese, and wine. We had scarcely commenced our frugal breakfast, when I heard again an imitation of the bleating of sheep, similar to what I had heard the day before. The captain answered it in the same tone. Two men were soon after seen descending from the woody height, where we had passed the preceding evening. On nearer approach, they proved to be the sentinel and the messenger. The captain rose, and went to meet them. He made a signal for his comrades to join him. They had a short conference, and then returning to me with great eagerness, "Your ransom is paid," said he; "you are free!"

Though I had anticipated deliverance, I cannot tell you what a rush of delight these tidings gave me. I cared not to finish my repast, but prepared to depart. The captain took me by the hand, requested permission to write to me, and begged me not to forget the passport. I replied, that I hoped to be of effectual service to him, and that I relied on his honor to return the Prince's note for five hundred dollars, now that the cash was paid. He regarded me for a moment with surprise, then seeming to recollect himself, "*E giusto*," said he, "*eccolo—adio*!"[1] He delivered me the note, pressed my hand once more, and we separated. The laborers were permitted to follow me, and we resumed with joy our road toward Tusculum.

The Frenchman ceased to speak. The party continued, for a few moments, to pace the shore in silence. The story had made a deep impression, particularly on the Venetian lady. At that part which related to the young girl of Frosinone, she was violently affected. Sobs broke from her; she clung closer to her husband, and as she looked up to him as for protection, the moonbeams shining on her beautifully fair countenance, showed it paler than usual, while tears glittered in her fine dark eyes.

---

1. It is just—there it is—adieu!

"*Corragio, mia vita*!" said he, as he gently and fondly tapped the white hand that lay upon his arm.

The party now returned to the inn, and separated for the night. The fair Venetian, though of the sweetest temperament, was half out of humor with the Englishman, for a certain slowness of faith which he had evinced throughout the whole evening. She could not understand this dislike to "humbug," as he termed it, which held a kind of sway over him, and seemed to control his opinions and his very actions.

"I'll warrant," said she to her husband, as they retired for the night,—"I'll warrant, with all his affected indifference, this Englishman's heart would quake at the very sight of a bandit."

Her husband gently, and good-humoredly, checked her.

"I have no patience with these Englishmen," said she, as she got into bed—"they are so cold and insensible!"

The Adventure of the Englishman

IN THE MORNING ALL WAS BUSTLE IN THE INN AT TERRACINA. THE PROCACCIO had departed at daybreak on its route towards Rome, but the Englishman was yet to start, and the departure of an English equipage is always enough to keep an inn in a bustle. On this occasion there was more than usual stir, for the Englishman, having much property about him, and having been convinced of the real danger of the road, had applied to the police, and obtained, by dint of liberal pay, an escort of eight dragoons and twelve foot soldiers, as far as Fondi. Perhaps, too, there might have been a little ostentation at bottom, though, to say the truth, he had nothing of it in his manner. He moved about, taciturn and reserved as usual, among the gaping crowd; gave laconic orders to John, as he packed away the thousand and one indispensable conveniences of the night; double loaded his pistols with great *sang froid*, and deposited them in the pockets of the carriage; taking no notice of a pair of keen eyes gazing on him from among the herd of loitering idlers.

The fair Venetian now came up with a request, made in her dulcet tones, that he would permit their carriage to proceed under protection of his escort. The Englishman, who was busy loading another pair of pistols for his servant, and held the ramrod between his teeth, nodded assent, as a matter of course, but without lifting up his eyes. The fair Venetian was a little piqued at what she supposed indifference:—"O Dio!" ejaculated she softly as she retired; "Quanto sono insensibili questi Inglesi."

At length, off they set in gallant style. The eight dragoons prancing in front, the twelve foot soldiers marching in rear, and the carriage moving slowly in the centre, to enable the infantry to keep pace with them. They had proceeded but a few hundred yards, when it was discovered that some indispensable article had been left behind.

In fact, the Englishman's purse was missing, and John was dispatched to the inn to search for it. This occasioned a little delay, and the carriage of the Venetians drove slowly on. John came back out of breath and out of humor. The purse was not to be found. His master was irritated; he recollected the very place where it lay; he had not a doubt that the Italian servant had pocketed it. John was again sent back. He returned once more without the purse, but with the landlord and the whole household at his heels. A thousand ejaculations and protestations, accompanied by all sorts of grimaces and contortions—"No purse had been seen—his eccellenza must be mistaken."

"No—his eccellenza was not mistaken—the purse lay on the marble table, under the mirror, a green purse, half full of gold and silver." Again a thousand grimaces and contortions, and vows by San Gennaro, that no purse of the kind had been seen.

The Englishman became furious. "The waiter had pocketed it—the landlord was a knave—the inn a den of thieves—it was a vile country—he had been cheated and plundered from one end of it to the other—but he'd have satisfaction—he'd drive right off to the police."

He was on the point of ordering the postilions to turn back, when, on rising, he displaced the cushion of the carriage, and the purse of money fell chinking to the floor.

All the blood in his body seemed to rush into his face—"Curse the purse," said he, as he snatched it up. He dashed a handful of money on the ground before the pale cringing waiter—"There—be off!" cried he. "John, order the postilions to drive on."

Above half an hour had been exhausted in this altercation. The Venetian carriage had loitered along; its passengers looking out from time to time, and expecting the escort every moment to follow. They had gradually turned an angle of the road that shut them out of sight. The little army was again in motion, and made a very picturesque appearance as it wound along at the bottom of the rocks; the morning sunshine beaming upon the weapons of the soldiery.

The Englishman lolled back in his carriage, vexed with himself at what had passed, and consequently out of humor with all the world. As this, however, is no uncommon case with gentlemen who travel for their pleasure, it is hardly worthy of remark. They had wound up from the coast among the hills, and came to a part of the road that admitted of some prospect ahead.

"I see nothing of the lady's carriage, sir," said John, leaning down from the coach-box.

"Pish!" said the Englishman, testily—"don't plague me about the lady's carriage; must I be continually pestered with the concerns of strangers?" John said not another word, for he understood his master's mood.

The road grew more wild and lonely; they were slowly proceeding on a foot-pace up a hill; the dragoons were some distance ahead, and had just reached the summit of the hill, when they uttered an exclamation, or rather shout, and galloped forward. The Englishman was roused from his sulky reverie. He stretched his head from the carriage, which had attained the brow of the hill. Before him extended a long hollow defile, commanded on one side by rugged precipitous heights, covered with bushes of scanty forest. At some distance he beheld the carriage of the Venetians overturned. A numerous gang of desperadoes were rifling it; the young man and his servant were overpowered, and partly stripped; and the lady was in the hands of two of the ruffians. The Englishman seized his pistols, sprang from the carriage, and called upon John to follow him.

In the meantime, as the dragoons came forward, the robbers, who were busy with the carriage, quitted their spoil, formed themselves in the middle of the road, and taking a deliberate aim, fired. One of the dragoons fell, another was wounded, and the whole were for a moment checked and thrown into confusion. The robbers loaded again in an instant. The dragoons discharged their carbines, but without apparent effect. They received another volley, which, though none fell, threw them again into confusion. The robbers were loading a second time when they saw the foot soldiers at hand. "*Scampa via*!" was the word: they abandoned their prey, and retreated up the rocks, the soldiers after them. They fought from cliff to cliff and bush to bush, the robbers turning every now and then to fire upon their pursuers; the soldiers scrambling after them, and discharging their muskets whenever they could get a chance. Sometimes a soldier or a robber was shot down, and came tumbling among the cliffs. The dragoons kept firing from below, whenever a robber came in sight.

The Englishman had hastened to the scene of action, and the balls discharged at the dragoons had whistled past him as he advanced. One object, however, engrossed his attention. It was the beautiful Venetian lady in the hands of two of the robbers, who, during the confusion of the fight, carried her shrieking up the mountain. He saw her dress gleaming among the bushes, and he sprang up the rocks to intercept the robbers, as they bore off their prey. The ruggedness of the steep, and the entanglements of the bushes, delayed and impeded him. He lost sight of the lady, but was still guided by her cries, which grew fainter and fainter. They were off to the left, while the reports of muskets showed that the battle was raging to the right. At length he came upon what appeared to be a rugged footpath, faintly worn in a gully of the rocks, and beheld the ruffians at some distance hurrying the lady up the defile. One of them hearing his approach, let go his prey, advanced towards him, and levelling the carbine which had been slung on his back, fired. The ball whizzed through the Englishman's hat, and carried with it some of his hair. He returned the fire with one of his pistols, and the robber fell. The other brigand now dropped the lady, and drawing a long pistol from his belt, fired on his adversary with deliberate aim. The ball passed between his left arm and his side, slightly wounding the arm. The Englishman advanced, and discharged his remaining pistol, which wounded the robber, but not severely.

The brigand drew a stiletto and rushed upon his adversary, who eluded the blow, receiving merely a slight wound, and defended himself with his pistol, which had a spring bayonet. They closed with one another, and a desperate struggle ensued. The robber was a square-built, thick-set man, powerful, muscular, and active. The Englishman, though of larger frame and greater strength, was less active and less accustomed to athletic exercises and feats of hardihood, but he showed himself practised and skilled in the art of defence. They were on a craggy height, and the Englishman perceived that his antagonist was striving to press him to the edge. A side-glance showed him also the robber whom he had first wounded, scrambling up to the assistance of his comrade, stiletto in hand. He had in fact attained the summit of the cliff, he was within a few steps, and the Englishman felt that his case was desperate, when he heard suddenly the report of a pistol, and the ruffian fell. The shot came from John, who had arrived just in time to save his master.

The remaining robber, exhausted by loss of blood and the violence of the contest, showed signs of faltering. The Englishman pursued his advantage, pressed on him, and as his strength relaxed, dashed him headlong from the precipice. He looked after him, and saw him lying motionless among the rocks below.

The Englishman now sought the fair Venetian. He found her senseless on the ground. With his servant's assistance he bore her down to the road, where her husband was raving like one distracted. He had sought her in vain, and had given her over for lost; and when he beheld her thus brought back in safety, his joy was equally wild and ungovernable. He would have caught her insensible form to his bosom had not the Englishman restrained him. The latter, now really aroused, displayed a true tenderness and manly gallantry, which one would not have expected from his habitual phlegm. His kindness, however, was practical, not wasted in words. He dispatched John to the carriage for restoratives of all kinds, and, totally thoughtless of himself, was anxious only about his lovely charge. The occasional discharge of firearms along the height, showed that a retreating fight was still kept up by the robbers. The lady gave signs of reviving animation. The Englishman, eager to get her from this place of danger, conveyed her to his own carriage, and, committing her to the care of her husband, ordered the dragoons to escort them to Fondi. The Venetian would have insisted on the Englishman's getting into the carriage; but the latter refused. He poured forth a torrent of thanks and benedictions; but the Englishman beckoned to the postilions to drive on.

John now dressed his master's wounds, which were found not to be serious, though he was faint with loss of blood. The Venetian carriage had been righted, and the baggage replaced; and, getting into it, they set out on their way towards Fondi, leaving the foot-soldiers still engaged in ferreting out the banditti.

Before arriving at Fondi, the fair Venetian had completely recovered from her swoon. She made the usual question—

"Where was she?"

"In the Englishman's carriage."

"How had she escaped from the robbers?"

"The Englishman had rescued her."

Her transports were unbounded; and mingled with them were enthusiastic ejaculations of gratitude to her deliverer. A thousand times did she reproach herself for having accused him of coldness and insensibility. The moment she saw him she rushed into his arms with the vivacity of her nation, and hung about his neck in a speechless transport of gratitude. Never was man more embarrassed by the embraces of a fine woman.

"Tut! tut!" said the Englishman.

"You are wounded!" shrieked the fair Venetian, as she saw blood upon his clothes.

"Pooh! nothing at all!"

"My deliverer!—my angel!" exclaimed she, clasping him again round the neck, and sobbing on his bosom.

"Pish!" said the Englishman, with a good-humored tone, but looking somewhat foolish, this is all humbug."

The fair Venetian, however, has never since accused the English of insensibility.

PART IV

The Money-Diggers

Found Among the Papers of the Late Diedrich Knickerbocker

"Now I remember those old women's words,
Who in my youth would tell me winter's tales:
And speak of sprites and ghosts that glide by night
About the place where treasure hath been hid."

MARLOW'S *JEW OF MALTA*

Hell-gate

About six miles from the renowned city of the Manhattoes, in that Sound or arm of the sea which passes between the main-land and Nassau, or Long Island, there is a narrow strait, where the current is violently compressed between shouldering promontories, and horribly perplexed by rocks and shoals. Being at the best of times, a very violent, impetuous current, it takes these impediments in mighty dudgeon; boiling in whirlpools; brawling and fretting in ripples; raging and roaring in rapids and breakers; and, in short, indulging in all kinds of wrong-headed paroxysms. At such times, woe to any unlucky vessel that ventures within its clutches.

This termagant humor, however, prevails only at certain times of tide. At low water, for instance, it is as pacific a stream as you would wish to see; but as the tide rises, it begins to fret; at half-tide it roars with might and main, like a bull bellowing for more drink; but when the tide is full, it relapses into quiet, and, for a time, sleeps as soundly as an alderman after dinner. In fact, it may be compared to a quarrelsome toper, who is a peaceable fellow enough when he has no liquor at all, or when he has a skinfull, but who, when half-seas-over, plays the very devil.

This mighty blustering, bullying, hard-drinking little strait, was a place of great danger and perplexity to the Dutch navigators of ancient days; hectoring their tub-built barks in a most unruly style; whirling them about in a manner to make any but a Dutchman giddy, and not unfrequently stranding them upon rocks and reefs, as it did the famous squadron of Oloffe the Dreamer, when seeking a place to found the city of the Manhattoes. Whereupon, out of sheer spleen, they denominated it *Helle-gat*, and solemnly gave it over to the devil. This appellation has since been aptly rendered into English by the name of Hell-gate, and into nonsense by the name of *Hurl-gate*, according to certain foreign intruders, who neither understood Dutch nor English—may St. Nicholas confound them!

This strait of Hell-gate was a place of great awe and perilous enterprise to me in my boyhood; having been much of a navigator on those small seas, and having more than once run the risk of shipwreck and drowning in the course of certain holiday voyages, to which, in common with other Dutch urchins, I was rather prone. Indeed, partly from the name, and partly from various strange circumstances connected with it, this place had far more terrors in the eyes of my truant companions and myself than had Scylla and Charybdis for the navigators of yore.

In the midst of this strait, and hard by a group of rocks called the Hen and Chickens, there lay the wreck of a vessel which had been entangled in the whirlpools and stranded during a storm. There was a wild story told to us of this being the wreck of a pirate, and some tale of bloody murder which I cannot now recollect, but which made us regard it with great awe, and keep far from it in our cruisings. Indeed, the desolate look of the forlorn hulk, and the fearful place where it lay rotting, were enough to awaken strange notions. A row of timber-heads, blackened by time, just peered above the surface at high water; but at low tide a considerable part of the hull was bare, and its great ribs or timbers, partly stripped of their planks and dripping with sea-weeds, looked like the huge skeleton of some sea-monster. There was also the stump of a mast, with a few ropes and blocks swinging about and whistling in the wind, while the seagull wheeled and screamed around the melancholy carcass. I have a faint recollection of some hobgoblin tale of sailors' ghosts being seen about this wreck at night, with bare skulls, and blue lights in their sockets instead of eyes, but I have forgotten all the particulars.

In fact, the whole of this neighborhood was like the straits of Pelorus of yore, a region of fable and romance to me. From the strait to the Manhattoes the borders of the Sound are greatly diversified, being broken and indented by rocky nooks overhung with trees, which give them a wild and romantic look. In the time of my boyhood, they abounded with traditions about pirates, ghosts, smugglers, and buried money; which had a wonderful effect upon the young minds of my companions and myself.

As I grew to more mature years, I made diligent research after the truth of these strange traditions; for I have always been a curious investigator of the valuable but obscure branches of the history of my native province. I found infinite difficulty, however, in arriving at any precise information. In seeking to dig up one fact, it is incredible the number of fables that I unearthed. I will say nothing of the devil's stepping-stones, by which the arch fiend made his retreat from Connecticut to Long

Island, across the Sound; seeing the subject is likely to be learnedly treated by a worthy friend and contemporary historian, whom I have furnished with particulars thereof.[1] Neither will I say any thing of the black man in a three-cornered hat, seated in the stern of a jolly-boat, who used to be seen about Hell-gate in stormy weather, and who went by the name of the pirate's *spuke*, (i e. pirate's ghost,) and whom, it is said, old Governor Stuyvesant once shot with a silver bullet; because I never could meet with any person of stanch edibility who professed to have seen this spectrum, unless it were the widow of Manus Conklen, the blacksmith, of Frogsneck; but then, poor woman, she was a little purblind, and might have been mistaken; though they say she saw farther than other folks in the dark.

All this, however, was but little satisfactory in regard to the tales of pirates and their buried money, about which I was most curious; and the following is all that I could for a long time collect that had any thing like an air of authenticity.

---

1. For a very interesting and authentic account of the devil and his stepping-stones, see the valuable Memoir read before the New-York Historical Society, since the death of Mr. Knickerbocker, by his friend, an eminent jurist of the place.

Kidd the Pirate

In old times, just after the territory of the New-Netherlands had been wrested from the hands of their High Mightinesses, the Lords States-General of Holland, by King Charles the Second, and while it was as yet in an unquiet state, the province was a great resort of random adventurers, loose livers, and all that class of hap-hazard fellows who live by their wits, and dislike the old-fashioned restraint of law and gospel. Among these, the foremost were the buccaneers. These were rovers of the deep, who perhaps, in time of war had been educated in those schools of piracy, the privateers; but having once tasted the sweets of plunder, had ever retained a hankering after it. There is but a slight step from the privateersman to the pirate; both fight for the love of plunder; only that the latter is the bravest, as he dares both the enemy and the gallows.

But in whatever school they had been taught, the buccaneers that kept about the English colonies were daring fellows, and made sad work in times of peace among the Spanish settlements and Spanish merchantmen. The easy access to the harbor of the Manhattoes, the number of hiding-places about its waters, and the laxity of its scarcely-organized government, made it a great rendezvous of the pirates; where they might dispose of their booty, and concert new depredations. As they brought home with them wealthy lading of all kinds, the luxuries of the tropics, and the sumptuous spoils of the Spanish provinces, and disposed of them with the proverbial carelessness of freebooters, they were welcome visitors to the thrifty traders of the Manhattoes. Crews of these desperadoes, therefore, the runagates of every country and every clime, might be seen swaggering in open day about the streets of the little burgh, elbowing its quiet mynheers; trafficking away their rich outlandish plunder at half or quarter price to the wary merchant; and then squandering their prize-money in taverns, drinking, gambling, singing, swearing, shouting, and astounding the neighborhood with midnight brawl and ruffian revelry.

At length these excesses rose to such a height as to become a scandal to the provinces, and to call loudly for the interposition of government. Measures were accordingly taken to put a stop to the widely-extended evil, and to ferret this vermin brood out of the colonies.

Among the agents employed to execute this purpose was the notorious Captain Kidd. He had long been an equivocal character; one of those nondescript animals of the ocean that are neither fish, flesh, nor fowl. He was somewhat of a trader, something more of a smuggler, with a considerable dash of the picaroon. He had traded for many years among the pirates, in a little rakish, musquito-built vessel, that could run into all kinds of waters. He knew all their haunts and lurking-places; was always hooking about on mysterious voyages; and was as busy as a Mother Cary's chicken in a storm.

This nondescript personage was pitched upon by government as the very man to hunt the pirates by sea, upon the good old maxim of "setting a rogue to catch a rogue;" or as otters are sometimes used to catch their cousins-german, the fish.

Kidd accordingly sailed for New-York, in 1695, in a gallant vessel called the Adventure Galley, well armed and duly commissioned. On arriving at his old haunts, however, he shipped his crew on new terms; enlisted a number of his old comrades, lads of the knife and the pistol; and then set sail for the East. Instead of cruising against pirates, he turned pirate himself; steered to the Madeiras, to Bonavista, and Madagascar, and cruised about the entrance of the Red Sea. Here, among other maritime robberies, he captured a rich Quedah merchantman, manned by Moors, though commanded by an Englishman. Kidd would fain have passed this off for a worthy exploit, as being a kind of crusade against the infidels; but government had long since lost all relish for such Christian triumphs.

After roaming the seas, trafficking his prizes, and changing from ship to ship, Kidd had the hardihood to return to Boston, laden with booty, with a crew of swaggering companions at his heels.

Times, however, were changed. The buccaneers could no longer show a whisker in the colonies with impunity. The new governor, Lord Bellamont, had signalized himself by his zeal in extirpating these offenders; and was doubly exasperated against Kidd, having been instrumental in appointing him to the trust which he had betrayed. No sooner, therefore, did he show himself in Boston, than the alarm was given of his reappearance, and measures were taken to arrest this cutpurse of the ocean. The daring character which Kidd had acquired, however, and the desperate fellows who followed like bull-dogs at his heels, caused a little delay in his arrest. He took advantage of this, it is said, to bury the greater part of his treasures, and then carried a high head about the streets of Boston. He even attempted to defend himself when arrested, but was secured and thrown into prison, with his followers. Such was the formidable character of this pirate, and his crew, that it was thought advisable to dispatch a frigate to bring them to England. Great exertions were made to screen him from justice, but in vain; he and his comrades were tried, condemned, and hanged at Execution Dock in London. Kidd died hard, for the rope with which he was first tied up broke with his weight, and he tumbled to the ground. He was tied up a second time, and more effectually; hence came, doubtless, the story of Kidd's having a charmed life, and that he had to be twice hanged.

Such is the main outline of Kidd's history; but it has given birth to an innumerable progeny of traditions. The report of his having buried great treasures of gold and jewels before his arrest, set the brains of all the good people along the coast in a ferment. There were rumors on rumors of great sums of money found here and there, sometimes in one part of the country, sometimes in another; of coins with Moorish inscriptions, doubtless the spoils of his eastern prizes, but which the common people looked upon with superstitious awe, regarding the Moorish letters as diabolical or magical characters.

Some reported the treasure to have been buried in solitary, unsettled places about Plymouth and Cape Cod; but by degrees various other parts, not only on the eastern coast, but along the shores of the Sound, and even of Manhattan and Long Island, were gilded by these rumors. In fact, the rigorous measures of Lord Bellamont spread sudden consternation among the buccaneers in every part of the provinces: they secreted their money and jewels in lonely out-of-the-way places, about the wild shores of the rivers and sea-coast, and dispersed themselves over the face of the country. The hand of justice prevented many of them from ever returning to regain their buried treasures, which remained, and remain probably to this day, objects of enterprise for the money-digger.

This is the cause of those frequent reports of trees and rocks bearing mysterious marks, supposed to indicate the spots where treasure lay hidden; and many have been the ransackings after the pirate's booty. In all the stories which once abounded of these enterprises, the devil played a conspicuous part. Either he was conciliated by ceremonies and invocations, or some solemn compact was made with him. Still he was ever prone to play the money-diggers some slippery trick. Some would dig so far as to come to an iron chest, when some baffling circumstance was sure to take place. Either the earth would fall in and fill up the pit, or some direful noise or apparition would frighten the party from the place: sometimes the devil himself would appear, and bear off the prize when within their very grasp; and if they revisited the place the next day, not a trace would be found of their labors of the preceding night.

All these rumors, however, were extremely vague, and for a long time tantalized without gratifying my curiosity. There is nothing in this world so hard to get at as truth, and there is nothing in this world but truth that I care for. I sought among all my favorite sources of authentic information, the oldest inhabitants, and particularly the old Dutch wives of the province; but though I flatter myself that I am better versed than most men in the curious history of my native province, yet for a long time my inquiries were unattended with any substantial result.

At length it happened that, one calm day in the latter part of summer, I was relaxing myself from the toils of severe study, by a day's amusement in fishing in those waters which had been the favorite resort of my boyhood. I was in company with several worthy burghers of my native city, among whom were more than one illustrious member of the corporation, whose names, did I dare to mention them, would do honor to my humble page. Our sport was indifferent. The fish did not bite freely, and we frequently changed our fishing-ground without bettering our luck. We were at length anchored close under a ledge of rocky coasts on the eastern side of the island of Manhatta. It was a still, warm day. The stream whirled and dimpled by us, without a wave or even a ripple; and every thing was so calm and quiet, that it was almost startling when the kingfisher would pitch himself from the branch of some high tree, and after suspending himself for a moment in the air to take his aim, would souse into the smooth water after his prey. While we were lolling in our boat, half drowsy with the warm stillness of the day, and the dulness of our sport, one of our party, a worthy alderman, was overtaken by a slumber, and, as he dozed, suffered the sinker of his drop-line to lie upon the bottom of the river. On waking, he found he had caught something of importance from the weight. On drawing it to the surface, we were much surprised to find it a long pistol of very curious and outlandish fashion, which, from its rusted condition, and its stock being wormeaten and covered with barnacles, appeared to have lain a long time under water. His unexpected appearance of this document of warfare, occasioned much speculation among my pacific companions. One supposed it to have fallen there during the revolutionary war; another, from the peculiarity of its fashion, attributed it to the voyagers in the earliest days of the settlement; perchance to the renowned Adrian Block, who explored the Sound, and discovered Block Island, since so noted for its cheese. But a third, after regarding it for some time, pronounced it to be of veritable Spanish workmanship.

"I'll warrant," said he, "if this pistol could talk, it would tell strange stories of hard fights among the Spanish Dons. I've no doubt but it is a relic of the buccaneers of old times—who knows but it belonged to Kidd himself?"

"Ah! that Kidd was a resolute fellow," cried an old iron-faced Cape Cod whaler.—"There's a fine old song about him, all to the tune of—

My name is Captain Kidd,
As I sailed, as I sailed—

And then it tells about how he gained the devil's good graces by burying the Bible:

I had the Bible in my hand,
As I sailed, as I sailed.
And I buried it in the sand
As I sailed.—

"Odsfish, if I thought this pistol had belonged to Kidd, I should set great store by it, for curiosity's sake. By the way, I recollect a story about a fellow who once dug up Kidd's buried money, which was written by a neighbor of mine, and which I learnt by heart. As the fish don't bite just now, I'll tell it to you, by way of passing away the time."—And so saying, he gave us the following narration.

The Devil and Tom Walker

A FEW MILES FROM BOSTON IN MASSACHUSETTS, THERE IS A DEEP INLET, winding several miles into the interior of the country from Charles Bay, and terminating in a thickly-wooded swamp or morass. On one side of this inlet is a beautiful dark grove; on the opposite side the land rises abruptly from the water's edge into a high ridge, on which grow a few scattered oaks of great age and immense size. Under one of these gigantic trees, according to old stories, there was a great amount of treasure buried by Kidd the pirate. The inlet allowed a facility to bring the money in a boat secretly and at night to the very foot of the hill; the elevation of the place permitted a good look-out to be kept that no one was at hand; while the remarkable trees formed good landmarks by which the place might easily be found again. The old stories add, moreover, that the devil presided at the hiding of the money, and took it under his guardianship; but this it is well known he always does with buried treasure, particularly when it has been ill-gotten. Be that as it may, Kidd never returned to recover his wealth; being shortly after seized at Boston, sent out to England, and there hanged for a pirate.

About the year 1727, just at the time that earthquakes were prevalent in New-England, and shook many tall sinners down upon their knees, there lived near this place a meagre, miserly fellow of the name of Tom Walker. He had a wife as miserly as himself: they were so miserly that they even conspired to cheat each other. Whatever the woman could lay hands on, she hid away; a hen could not cackle but she was on the alert to secure the new-laid egg. Her husband was continually prying about to detect her secret hoards, and many and fierce were the conflicts that took place about what ought to have been common property. They lived in a forlorn-looking house that stood alone, and had an air of starvation. A few straggling savin-trees, emblems of sterility, grew near it; no smoke ever curled from its chimney; no traveller stopped at its door. A miserable horse, whose ribs were as articulate as the bars of a gridiron, stalked about a field, where a thin carpet of moss, scarcely covering the ragged beds of puddingstone, tantalized and balked his hunger; and sometimes he would lean his head over the fence, look piteously at the passer-by, and seem to petition deliverance from this land of famine.

The house and its inmates had altogether a bad name. Tom's wife was a tall termagant, fierce of temper, loud of tongue, and strong of arm. Her voice was often heard in wordy warfare with her husband; and his face sometimes showed signs that their conflicts were not confined to words. No one ventured, however, to interfere between them. The lonely wayfarer shrunk within himself at the horrid clamor and clapper-clawing; eyed the den of discord askance; and hurried on his way, rejoicing, if a bachelor, in his celibacy.

One day that Tom Walker had been to a distant part of the neighborhood, he took what he considered a short cut homeward, through the swamp. Like most short cuts, it was an ill-chosen route. The swamp was thickly grown with great gloomy pines and hemlocks, some of them ninety feet high, which made it dark at noonday, and a retreat for all the owls of the neighborhood. It was full of pits and quagmires, partly covered with weeds and mosses, where the green surface often betrayed the traveller into a gulf of black, smothering mud: there were also dark and stagnant pools, the abodes of the tadpole, the bull-frog, and the water-snake; where the trunks of pines and hemlocks lay half-drowned, half-rotting, looking like alligators sleeping in the mire.

Tom had long been picking his way cautiously through this treacherous forest; stepping from tuft to tuft of rushes and roots, which afforded precarious footholds among deep sloughs; or pacing carefully, like a cat, along the prostrate trunks of trees; startled now and then by the sudden screaming of the bittern, or the quacking of a wild duck, rising on the wing from some solitary pool. At length he arrived at a piece of firm ground, which ran out like a peninsula into the deep bosom of the swamp. It had been one of the strong-holds of the Indians during their wars with the first colonists. Here they had thrown up a kind of fort, which they had looked upon as almost impregnable, and had used as a place of refuge for their squaws and children. Nothing remained of the old Indian fort but a few embankments, gradually sinking to the level of the surrounding earth, and already overgrown in part by oaks and other forest trees, the foliage of which formed a contrast to the dark pines and hemlocks of the swamp.

It was late in the dusk of evening when Tom Walker reached the old fort, and he paused there awhile to rest himself. Any one but he would have felt unwilling to linger in this lonely, melancholy place, for the common people had a bad opinion of it, from the stories handed down from the time of the Indian wars; when it was asserted that the savages held incantations here, and made sacrifices to the evil spirit.

Tom Walker, however, was not a man to be troubled with any fears of the kind. He reposed himself for some time on the trunk of a fallen hemlock, listening to the boding cry of the tree toad, and delving with his walking staff into a mound of black mould at his feet. As he turned up the soil unconsciously, his staff struck against something hard. He raked it out of the vegetable mould, and lo! a cloven skull, with an Indian tomahawk buried deep in it, lay before him. The rust on the weapon showed the time that had elapsed since this death-blow had been given. It was a dreary memento of the fierce struggle that had taken place in this last foothold of the Indian warriors.

"Humph!" said Tom Walker, as he gave it a kick to shake the dirt from it.

"Let that skull alone!" said a gruff voice. Tom lifted up his eyes, and beheld a great black man seated directly opposite him, on the stump of a tree. He was exceedingly surprised, having neither heard nor seen any one approach; and he was still more perplexed on observing, as well as the gathering gloom would permit, that the stranger was neither negro nor Indian. It is true he was dressed in a rude half Indian garb, and had a red belt or sash swathed round his body; but his face was neither black nor copper-color, but swarthy and dingy, and begrimed with soot, as if he had been accustomed to toil among fires and forges. He had a shock of coarse black hair, that stood out from his head in all directions, and bore an axe on his shoulder.

He scowled for a moment at Tom with a pair of great red eyes.

"What are you doing on my grounds?" said the black man, with a hoarse growling voice.

"Your grounds!" said Tom with a sneer, "no more your grounds than mine; they belong to Deacon Peabody."

"Deacon Peabody be d——d," said the stranger, "as I flatter myself he will be, if he does not look more to his own sins and less to those of his neighbors. Look yonder, and see how Deacon Peabody is faring."

Tom looked in the direction that the strange pointed, and beheld one of the great trees, fair and flourishing without, but rotten at the core, and saw that it had been nearly hewn through, so that the first high wind was likely to blow it down. On the bark of the tree was scored the name of Deacon Peabody, an eminent man, who had waxed wealthy by driving shrewd bargains with the Indians. He now looked round, and found most of the tall trees marked with the name of some great man of the colony, and all more or less scored by the axe. The one on which he had been seated, and which had evidently just been hewn down, bore the name of Crowninshield; and he recollected a mighty rich man of that name, who made a vulgar display of wealth, which it was whispered he had acquired by buccaneering.

"He's just ready for burning!" said the black man, with a growl of triumph. "You see I am likely to have a good stock of firewood for winter."

"But what right have you," said Tom, "to cut down Deacon Peabody's timber?"

"The right of a prior claim." said the other. "This wood-land belonged to me long before one of your white-faced race put foot upon the soil."

"And pray, who are you, if I may be so bold?" said Tom.

"Oh, I go by various names. I am the wild huntsman in some countries; the black miner in others. In this neighborhood I am known by the name of the black woodsman. I am he to whom the red men consecrated this spot, and in honor of whom they now and then roasted a white man, by way of sweet-smelling sacrifice. Since the red men have been exterminated by you white savages, I amuse myself by presiding at the persecutions of Quakers and Anabaptists; I am the great patron and prompter of slave-dealers, and the grand-master of the Salem witches."

"The upshot of all which is, that, if I mistake not," said Tom sturdily, "you are he commonly called Old Scratch."

"The same, at your service!" replied the black man, with a half civil nod.

Such was the opening of this interview, according to the old story; though it has almost too familiar an air to be credited. One would think that to meet with such a singular personage, in this wild, lonely place, would have shaken any man's nerves; but Tom was a hard-minded fellow, not easily daunted, and he had lived so long with a termagant wife, that he did not even fear the devil.

It is said that after this commencement they had a long and earnest conversation together as Tom returned homeward. The black man told him of great sums of money buried by Kidd the pirate, under the oak-trees on the high ridge, not far from the morass. All these were under his command, and protected by his power, so that none could find them but such as propitiated his favor. These he offered to place within Tom Walker's reach, having conceived an especial kindness for him; but they were to be had only on certain conditions. What these conditions were may easily be surmised, though Tom never disclosed them publicly. They must have been very hard, for he required time to think of them, and he was not a man to stick at trifles where money was in view. When they had reached the edge of the swamp, the stranger paused—"What proof have I that all you have been telling me is true?" said Tom. "There is my signature," said the black man, pressing his finger on Tom's forehead. So saying, he turned off among the thickets of the swamp, and seemed, as Tom said, to go down, down, down, into the earth, until nothing but his head and shoulders could be seen, and so on, until he totally disappeared.

When Tom reached home, he found the black print of a finger, burnt, as it were, into his forehead, which nothing could obliterate.

The first news his wife had to tell him was the sudden death of Absalom Crowninshield, the rich buccaneer. It was announced in the papers with the usual flourish, that "A great man had fallen in Israel."

Tom recollected the tree which his black friend had just hewn down, and which was ready for burning, "Let the freebooter roast," said Tom, "who cares!" He now felt convinced that all he had heard and seen was no illusion.

He was not prone to let his wife into his confidence; but as this was an uneasy secret, he willingly shared it with her. All her avarice was awakened at the mention of hidden gold, and she urged her husband to comply with the black man's terms, and secure what would make them wealthy for life. However Tom might have felt disposed to sell himself to the Devil, he was determined not to do so to oblige his wife; so he flatly refused, out of the mere spirit of contradiction. Many and bitter were the quarrels they had on the subject, but the more she talked, the more resolute was Tom not to be damned to please her.

At length she determined to drive the bargain on her own account, and if she succeeded, to keep all the gain to herself. Being of the same fearless temper as her husband, she set off for the old Indian fort towards the close of a summer's day. She was many hours absent. When she came back, she was reserved and sullen in her replies. She spoke something of a black man, whom she had met about twilight, hewing at the root of a tall tree. He was sulky, however, and would not come to terms: she was to go again with a propitiatory offering, but what it was she forbore to say.

The next evening she sat off again for the swamp, with her apron heavily laden. Tom waited and waited for her, but in vain; midnight came, but she did not make her appearance: morning, noon, night returned, but still she did not come. Tom now grew uneasy for her safety, especially as he found she had carried off in her apron the silver teapot and spoons, and every portable article of value. Another night elapsed, another morning came; but no wife. In a word, she was never heard of more.

What was her real fate nobody knows, in consequence of so many pretending to know. It is one of those facts which have become confounded by a variety of historians. Some asserted that she lost her way among the tangled mazes of the swamp, and sank into some pit or slough; others, more uncharitable, hinted that she had eloped with the household booty, and made off to some other province; while others surmised that the tempter had decoyed her into a dismal quagmire, on the top of which her hat was found lying. In confirmation of this, it was said a great black man, with an axe on his shoulder, was seen late that very evening coming out of the swamp, carrying a bundle tied in a check apron, with an air of surly triumph.

The most current and probable story, however, observes, that Tom Walker grew so anxious about the fate of his wife and his property, that he set out at length to seek them both at the Indian fort. During a long summer afternoon he searched about the gloomy place, but no wife was to be seen. He called her name repeatedly, but she was nowhere to be heard. The bittern alone responded to his voice, as he flew screaming by; or the bull-frog croaked dolefully from a neighboring pool. At length, it is said, just in the brown hour of twilight, when the owls began to hoot, and the bats to flit about, his attention was attracted by the clamor of carrion crows hovering about a cypress-tree. He looked up, and beheld a bundle tied in a check apron, and hanging in the branches of the tree, with a great vulture perched hard by, as if keeping watch upon it. He leaped with joy; for he recognised his wife's apron, and supposed it to contain the household valuables.

"Let us get hold of the property," said he, consolingly to himself, "and we will endeavor to do without the woman."

As he scrambled up the tree, the vulture spread its wide wings, and sailed off screaming into the deep shadows of the forest. Tom seized the check apron, but woful sight! found nothing but a heart and liver tied up in it!

Such, according to the most authentic old story, was all that was to be found of Tom's wife. She had probably attempted to deal with the black man as she had been accustomed to deal with her husband; but though a female scold is generally considered a match for the devil, yet in this instance she appears to have had the worst of it. She must have died game, however; for it is said Tom noticed many prints of cloven feet deeply stamped about the tree, and found handfuls of hair, that locked as if they had been plucked from the coarse black shock of the woodman. Tom knew his wife's prowess by experience. He shrugged his shoulders, as he looked at the signs of a fierce clapper-clawing. "Egad," said he to himself, "Old Scratch must have had a tough time of it!"

Tom consoled himself for the loss of his property, with the loss of his wife, for he was a man of fortitude. He even felt something like gratitude towards the black woodman, who, he considered, had done him a kindness. He sought, therefore, to cultivate a further acquaintance with him, but for some time without success; the old black-legs played shy, for whatever people may think, he is not always to be had for calling for: he knows how to play his cards when pretty sure of his game.

At length, it is said, when delay had whetted Tom's eagerness to the quick, and prepared him to agree to any thing rather than not gain the promised treasure, he met the black man one evening in his usual woodman's dress, with his axe on his shoulder, sauntering along the swamp, and humming a tune. He affected to receive Tom's advances with great indifference, made brief replies, and went on humming his tune.

By degrees, however, Tom brought him to business, and they began to haggle about the terms on which the former was to have the pirate's treasure. There was one condition which need not be mentioned, being generally understood in all cases where the devil grants favors; but there were others about which, though of less importance, he was inflexibly obstinate. He insisted that the money found through his means should be employed in his service. He proposed, therefore, that Tom should employ it in the black traffick; that is to say, that he should fit out a slave-ship. This, however, Tom resolutely refused: he was bad enough in all conscience; but the devil himself could not tempt him to turn slave-trader.

Finding Tom so squeamish on this point, he did not insist upon it, but proposed, instead, that he should turn usurer; the devil being extremely anxious for the increase of usurers, looking upon them as his peculiar people.

To this no objections were made, for it was just to Tom's taste.

"You shall open a broker's shop in Boston next month," said the black man.

"I'll do it to-morrow, if you wish," said Tom Walker.

"You shall lend money at two per cent. a month."

"Egad, I'll charge four!" replied Tom Walker."

"You shall extort bonds, foreclose mortgages, drive the merchant to bankruptcy—"

"I'll drive him to the d——l," cried Tom Walker.

"You are the usurer for my money!" said the black-legs with delight. "When will you want the rhino?"

"This very night."

"Done!" said the devil.

"Done!" said Tom Walker.—So they shook hands and struck a bargain.

A few days' time saw Tom Walker seated behind his desk in a counting-house in Boston.

His reputation for a ready-moneyed man, who would lend money out for a good consideration, soon spread abroad. Every body remembers the time of Governor Belcher, when money was particularly scarce. It was a time of paper credit. The country had been deluged with government bills; the famous Land Bank had been established; there had been a rage for speculating; the people had run mad with schemes for new settlements; for building cities in the wilderness; land-jobbers went about with maps of grants, and townships, and Eldorados, lying nobody knew where, but which every body was ready to purchase. In a word, the great speculating fever which breaks out every now and then in the country, had raged to an alarming degree, and every body was dreaming of making sudden fortunes from nothing. As usual the fever had subsided; the dream had gone off, and the imaginary fortunes with it; the patients were left in doleful plight, and the whole country resounded with the consequent cry of "hard times."

At this propitious time of public distress did Tom Walker set up as usurer in Boston. His door was soon thronged by customers. The needy and adventurous; the gambling speculator; the dreaming land-jobber; the thriftless tradesman; the merchant with cracked credit; in short, every one driven to raise money by desperate means and desperate sacrifices, hurried to Tom Walker.

Thus Tom was the universal friend of the needy, and acted like a "friend in need;" that is to say, he always exacted good pay and good security. In proportion to the distress of the applicant was the hardness of his terms. He accumulated bonds and mortgages; gradually squeezed his customers closer and closer: and sent them at length, dry as a sponge, from his door.

In this way he made money hand over hand; became a rich and mighty man, and exalted his cocked hat upon 'Change. He built himself, as usual, a vast house, out of ostentation; but left the greater part of it unfinished and unfurnished, out of parsimony. He even set up a carriage in the fulness of his vainglory, though he nearly starved the horses which drew it; and as the ungreased wheels groaned and screeched on the axle-trees, you would have thought you heard the souls of the poor debtors he was squeezing.

As Tom waxed old, however, he grew thoughtful. Having secured the good things of this world, he began to feel anxious about those of the next. He thought with regret on the bargain he had made with his black friend, and set his wits to work to cheat him out of the conditions. He became, therefore, all of a sudden, a violent church-goer. He prayed loudly and strenuously, as if heaven were to be taken by force of lungs. Indeed, one might always tell when he had sinned most during the week, by the clamor of his Sunday devotion. The quiet Christians who had been modestly and steadfastly travelling Zionward, were struck with self-reproach at seeing themselves so suddenly out-stripped in their career by this new-made convert. Tom was as rigid in religious as in money matters; he was a stern supervisor and censurer of his neighbors, and seemed to think every sin entered up to their account became a credit on his own side of the page. He even talked of the expediency of reviving the persecution of Quakers and Anabaptists. In a word, Tom's zeal became as notorious as his riches.

Still, in spite of all this strenuous attention to forms, Tom had a lurking dread that the devil, after all, would have his due. That he might not be taken unawares, therefore, it is said he always carried a small Bible in his coat-pocket. He had also a great folio Bible on his counting-house desk, and would frequently be found reading it when people called on business; on such occasions he would lay his green spectacles in the book, to mark the place, while he turned round to drive some usurious bargain.

Some say that Tom grew a little crack-brained in his old days, and that fancying his end approaching, he had his horse new shod, saddled and bridled, and buried with his feet upper-most; because he supposed that at the last day the world would be turned upside down; in which case he should find his horse standing ready for mounting, and he was determined at the worst to give his old friend a run for it. This, however, is probably a mere old wives' fable. If he really did take such a precaution, it was totally superfluous; at least so says the authentic old legend, which closes his story in the following manner.

One hot summer afternoon in the dog-days, just as a terrible black thundergust was coming up, Tom sat in his counting-house in his white linen cap and India silk morning-gown. He was on the point of foreclosing a mortgage, by which he would complete the ruin of an unlucky land speculator for whom he had professed the greatest friendship. The poor land-jobber begged him to grant a few months' indulgence. Tom had grown testy and irritated, and refused another day.

"My family will be ruined and brought upon the parish," said the land-jobber. "Charity begins at home," replied Tom; "I must take care of myself in these hard times."

"You have made so much money out of me," said the speculator.

Tom lost his patience and his piety—"The devil take me," said he, "if I have made a farthing!"

Just then there were three loud knocks at the street door. He stepped out to see who was there. A black man was holding a black horse, which neighed and stamped with impatience.

"Tom, you're come for," said the black fellow, gruffly. Tom shrunk back, but too late. He had left his little Bible at the bottom of his coat-pocket, and his big Bible on the desk buried under the mortgage he was about to foreclose: never was sinner taken more unawares. The black man whisked him like a child into the saddle, gave the horse the lash, and away he galloped with Tom on his back, in the midst of the thunder-storm. The clerks stuck their pens behind their ears, and stared after him from the windows. Away went Tom Walker, dashing down the streets; his white cap bobbing up and down; his morning-gown fluttering in the wind, and his steed striking fire out of the pavement at every bound. When the clerks turned to look for the black man he had disappeared.

Tom Walker never returned to foreclose the mortgage. A countryman who lived on the border of the swamp, reported that in the height of the thundergust he had heard a great clattering of hoofs and a howling along the road, and running to the window caught sight of a figure, such as I have described, on a horse that galloped like mad across the fields, over the hills and down into the black hemlock swamp towards the old Indian fort; and that shortly after a thunderbolt falling in that direction seemed to set the whole forest in a blaze.

The good people of Boston shook their heads and shrugged their shoulders, but had been so much accustomed to witches and goblins and tricks of the devil, in all kind of shapes from the first settlement of the colony, that they were not so much horror-struck as might have been expected. Trustees were appointed to take charge of Tom's effects. There was nothing, however, to administer upon. On searching his coffers all his bonds and mortgages were found reduced to cinders. In place of gold and silver his iron chest was filled with chips and shavings; two skeletons lay in his stable instead of his half-starved horses, and the very next day his great house took fire and was burnt to the ground.

Such was the end of Tom Walker and his ill-gotten wealth. Let all griping money-brokers lay this story to heart. The truth of it is not to be doubted. The very hole under the oak-trees, whence he dug Kidd's money, is to be seen to this day; and the neighboring swamp and old Indian fort are often haunted in stormy nights by a figure on horseback, in morning-gown and white cap, which is doubtless the troubled spirit of the usurer. In fact, the story has resolved itself into a proverb, and is the origin of that popular saying, so prevalent throughout New England, of "The Devil and Tom Walker."

Such, as nearly as I can recollect, was the purport of the tale told by the Cape Cod whaler. There were divers trivial particulars which I have omitted, and which whiled away the morning very pleasantly, until the time of tide favorable to fishing being passed, it was proposed to land, and refresh ourselves under the trees, till the noontide heat should have abated.

We accordingly landed on a delectable part of the island of Mannahatta, in that shady and embowered tract formerly under the dominion of the ancient family of the Hardenbrooks. It was a spot well known to me in the course of the aquatic expeditions of my boyhood. Not far from where we landed, there was an old Dutch family vault, constructed in the side of a bank, which had been an object of great awe and fable among my schoolboy associates. We had peeped into it during one of our coasting voyages, and been startled by the sight of mouldering coffins and musty bones within; but what had given it the most fearful interest in our eyes, was its being in some way connected with the pirate wreck which lay rotting among the rocks of Hell-gate. There were stories also of smuggling connected with it, particularly relating to a time when this retired spot was owned by a noted burgher called Ready Money Provost; a man of whom it was whispered that he had many and mysterious dealings with parts beyond seas. All these things, however, had been jumbled together in our minds in that vague way in which such themes are mingled up in the tales of boyhood.

While I was pondering upon these matters, my companions had spread a repast, from the contents of our well-stored pannier, under a broad chestnut, on the green-sward which swept down to the water's edge. Here we solaced ourselves on the cool grassy carpet during the warm sunny hours of mid-day. While lolling on the grass, indulging in that kind of musing reverie of which I am fond, I summoned up the dusky recollections of my boyhood respecting this place, and repeated them like the imperfectly-remembered traces of a dream, for the amusement of my companions. When I had finished, a worthy old burgher, John Josse Vandermoere, the same who once related to me the adventures of Dolph Heyliger, broke silence and observed, that he recollected a story of money-digging which occurred in this very neighborhood, and might account for some of the traditions which I had heard in my boyhood. As we knew him to be one of the most authentic narrators in the province, we begged him to let us have the particulars, and accordingly, while we solaced ourselves with a clean long pipe of Blase Moore's best tobacco, the authentic John Josse Vandermoere related the following tale.

Wolfert Webber, or Golden Dreams

IN THE YEAR OF GRACE ONE THOUSAND SEVEN HUNDRED AND—BLANK—FOR I do not remember the precise date; however, it was somewhere in the early part of the last century, there lived in the ancient city of the Manhattoes a worthy burgher, Wolfert Webber by name. He was descended from old Cobus Webber of the Brille in Holland, one of the original settlers, famous for introducing the cultivation of cabbages, and who came over to the province during the protectorship of Oloffe Van Kortlandt, otherwise called the Dreamer.

The field in which Cobus Webber first planted himself and his cabbages had remained ever since in the family, who continued in the same line of husbandry, with that praiseworthy perseverance for which our Dutch burghers are noted. The whole family genius, during several generations, was devoted to the study and development of this one noble vegetable; and to this concentration of intellect may doubtless be ascribed the prodigious renown to which the Webber cabbages attained.

The Webber dynasty continued in uninterrupted succession; and never did a line give more unquestionable proofs of legitimacy. The eldest son succeeded to the looks, as well as the territory of his sire; and had the portraits of this line of tranquil potentates been taken, they would have presented a row of heads marvellously resembling in shape and magnitude the vegetables over which they reigned.

The seat of government continued unchanged in the family mansion:—a Dutch-built house, with a front, or rather gable-end of yellow brick, tapering to a point, with the customary iron weathercock at the top. Every thing about the building bore the air of long-settled ease and security. Flights of martins peopled the little coops nailed against its walls, and swallows built their nests under the eaves; and every one knows that these house-loving birds bring good luck to the dwelling where they take up their abode. In a bright sunny morning in early summer, it was delectable to hear their cheerful notes, as they sported about in the pure sweet air, chirping forth, as it were, the greatness and prosperity of the Webbers.

Thus quietly and comfortably did this excellent family vegetate under the shade of a mighty button-wood tree, which by little and little grew so great as entirely to overshadow their palace. The city gradually spread its suburbs round their domain. Houses sprang up to interrupt their prospects. The rural lanes in the vicinity began to grow into the bustle and populousness of streets; in short, with all the habits of rustic life they began to find themselves the inhabitants of a city. Still, however, they maintained their hereditary character, and hereditary possessions, with all the tenacity of petty German princes in the midst of the empire. Wolfert was the last of the line, and succeeded to the patriarchal bench at the door, under the family tree, and swayed the sceptre of his fathers, a kind of rural potentate in the midst of a metropolis.

To share the cares and sweets of sovereignty, he had taken unto himself a helpmate, one of that excellent kind, called stirring women; that is to say, she was one of those notable little housewives who are always busy when there is nothing to do. Her activity, however, took one particular direction; her whole life seemed devoted to intense knitting; whether at home or abroad, walking or sitting, her needles were continually in motion, and it is even affirmed that by her unwearied industry she very nearly supplied her household with stockings throughout the year. This worthy couple were blessed with one daughter, who was brought up with great tenderness and care; uncommon pains had been taken with her education, so that she could stitch in every variety of way; make all kinds of pickles and preserves, and mark her own name on a sampler. The influence of her taste was seen also in the family garden, where the ornamental began to mingle with the useful; whole rows of fiery marigolds and splendid hollyhocks bordered the cabbage beds; and gigantic sunflowers lolled their broad jolly faces over the fences, seeming to ogle most affectionately the passers-by.

Thus reigned and vegetated Wolfert Webber over his paternal acres, peacefully and contentedly. Not but that, like all other sovereigns, he had his occasional cares and vexations. The growth of his native city sometimes caused him annoyance. His little territory gradually became hemmed in by streets and houses, which intercepted air and sunshine. He was now and then subjected to the irruptions of the border population that infest the streets of a metropolis; who would make midnight forays into his dominions, and carry off captive whole platoons of his noblest subjects. Vagrant swine would make a descent, too, now and then, when the gate was left open, and lay all waste before them; and mischievous urchins would decapitate the illustrious sunflowers, the glory of the garden, as they lolled their heads so fondly over the walls. Still all these were petty grievances, which might now and then ruffle the surface of his mind, as a summer breeze will ruffle the surface of a mill-pond; but they could not disturb the deep-seated quiet of his soul. He would but seize a trusty staff, that stood behind the door, issue suddenly out, and anoint the back of the aggressor, whether pig or urchin, and then return within doors, marvellously refreshed and tranquillized.

The chief cause of anxiety to honest Wolfert, however, was the growing prosperity of the city. The expenses of living doubled and trebled; but he could not double and treble the magnitude of his cabbages; and the number of competitors prevented the increase of price; thus, therefore, while every one around him grew richer, Wolfert grew poorer, and he could not, for the life of him, perceive how the evil was to be remedied.

This growing care, which increased from day to day, had its gradual effect upon our worthy burgher; insomuch, that it at length implanted two or three wrinkles in his brow; things unknown before in the family of the Webbers; and it seemed to pinch up the corners of his cocked hat into an expression of anxiety, totally opposite to the tranquil, broad-brimmed, low-crowned beavers of his illustrious progenitors.

Perhaps even this would not have materially disturbed the serenity of his mind, had he had only himself and his wife to care for; but there was his daughter gradually growing to maturity; and all the world knows that when daughters begin to ripen no fruit nor flower requires so much looking after. I have no talent at describing female charms, else fain would I depict the progress of this little Dutch beauty. How her blue eyes grew deeper and deeper, and her cherry lips redder and redder; and how she ripened and ripened, and rounded and rounded in the opening breath of sixteen summers, until, in her seventeenth spring, she seemed ready to burst out of her bodice, like a half blown rose-bud.

Ah, well-a-day! could I but show her as she was then, tricked out on a Sunday morning, in the hereditary finery of the old Dutch clothes-press, of which her mother had confided to her the key. The wedding-dress of her grandmother, modernized for use, with sundry ornaments, handed down as heirlooms in the family. Her pale brown hair smoothed with buttermilk in flat waving lines on each side of her fair forehead. The chain of yellow virgin gold, that encircled her neck; the little cross, that just rested at the entrance of a soft valley of happiness, as if it would sanctify the place. The—but, pooh!—it is not for an old man like me to be prosing about female beauty; suffice it to say, Amy had attained her seventeenth year. Long since had her sampler exhibited hearts in couples desperately transfixed with arrows, and true lovers' knots worked in deep-blue silk; and it was evident she began to languish for some more interesting occupation than the rearing of sunflowers or pickling of cucumbers.

At this critical period of female existence, when the heart within a damsel's bosom, like its emblem, the miniature which hangs without, is apt to be engrossed by a single image, a new visitor began to make his appearance under the roof of Wolfert Webber. This was Dirk Waldron, the only son of a poor widow, but who could boast of more fathers than any lad in the province; for his mother had had four husbands, and this only child, so that though born in her last wedlock, he might fairly claim to be the tardy fruit of a long course of cultivation. This son of four others, united the merits and the vigor of all his sires. If he had not had a great family before him, he seemed likely to have a great one after him; for you had only to look at the fresh bucksome youth, to see that he was formed to be the founder of a mighty race.

This youngster gradually became an intimate visitor of the family. He talked little, but he sat long. He filled the father's pipe when it was empty, gathered up the mother's knitting-needle, or ball of worsted when it fell to the ground; stroked the sleek coat of the tortoise-shell cat, and replenished the teapot for the daughter from the bright copper kettle that sang before the fire. All these quiet little offices may seem of trifling import; but when true love is translated into Low Dutch, it is in this way that it eloquently expresses itself. They were not lost upon the Webber family. The winning youngster found marvellous favor in the eyes of the mother; the tortoise-shell cat, albeit the most staid and demure of her kind, gave indubitable signs of approbation of his visits, the teakettle seemed to sing out a cheering note of welcome at his approach, and if the sly glances of the daughter might be rightly read, as she sat bridling and dimpling, and sewing by her mother's side, she was not a whit behind Dame Webber, or grimalkin, or the teakettle, in good with.

Wolfert alone saw nothing of what was going on. Profoundly wrapt up in meditation on the growth of the city and his cabbages, he sat looking in the fire, and puffing his pipe in silence. One night, however, as the gentle Amy, according to custom, lighted her lover to the outer door, and he, according to custom, took his parting salute, the smack resounded so vigorously through the long, silent entry, as to startle even the dull ear of Wolfert. He was slowly roused to a new source of anxiety. It had never entered into his head that this mere child, who, as it seemed, but the other day had been climbing about his knees, and playing with dolls and baby-houses, could all at once be thinking of lovers and matrimony. He rubbed his eyes, examined into the fact, and really found that while he had been dreaming of other matters, she had actually grown to be a woman, and what was worse, had fallen in love. Here arose new cares for Wolfert. He was a kind father, but he was a prudent man. The young man was a lively, stirring lad; but then he had neither money nor land. Wolfert's ideas all ran in one channel; and he saw no alternative in case of a marriage, but to portion off the young couple with a corner of his cabbage garden, the whole of which was barely sufficient for the support of his family.

Like a prudent father, therefore, he determined to nip this passion in the bud, and forbade the youngster the house; though sorely did it go against his fatherly heart, and many a silent tear did it cause in the bright eye of his daughter. She showed herself, however, a pattern of filial piety and obedience. She never pouted and sulked; she never flew in the face of parental authority; she never flew into a passion, nor fell into hysterics, as many romantic novel-read young ladies would do. Not she, indeed! She was none such heroical rebellious trumpery, I'll warrant ye. On the contrary, she acquiesced like an obedient daughter, shut the street door in her lover's face, and if ever she did grant him an interview, it was either out of the kitchen window, or over the garden fence.

Wolfert was deeply cogitating these matters in his mind, and his brow wrinkled with unusual care, as he wended his way one Saturday afternoon to a rural inn, about two miles from the city. It was a favorite resort of the Dutch part of the community, from being always held by a Dutch line of landlords, and retaining an air and relish of the good old times. It was a Dutch-built house, that had probably been a country-seat of some opulent burgher in the early time of the settlement. It stood near a point of land, called Corlear's Hook, which stretches out into the Sound, and against which the tide, at its flux and reflux, sets with extraordinary rapidity. The venerable and somewhat crazy mansion was distinguished from afar, by a grove of elms and sycamores that seemed to wave a hospitable invitation, while a few weeping-willows, with their dank, drooping foliage, resembling fallen waters, gave an idea of coolness, that rendered it an attractive spot during the heats of summer.

Here, therefore, as I said, resorted many of the old inhabit-ants of the Manahattoes, where, while some played at shuffle-board and quoits and nine-pins, others smoked a deliberate pipe, and talked over public affairs.

It was on a blustering autumnal afternoon that Wolfert made his visit to the inn. The grove of elms and willows was stripped of its leaves, which whirled in rustling eddies about the fields. The nine-pin alley was deserted, for the premature chilliness of the day had driven the company within doors. As it was Saturday afternoon, the habitual club was in session, composed principally of regular Dutch burghers, though mingled occasionally with persons of various character and country, as is natural in a place of such motley population.

Beside the fireplace, in a huge leather-bottomed arm-chair, sat the dictator of this little world, the venerable Rem, or as it was pronounced, Ramm Rapelye. He was a man of Walloon race, and illustrious for the antiquity of his line; his great-grandmother having been the first white child born in the province. But he was still more illustrious for his wealth and dignity: he had long filled the noble office of alderman, and was a man to whom the governor himself took off his hat. He had maintained possession of the leather-bottomed chair from time immemorial; and had gradually waxed in bulk as he sat in his seat of government, until in the course of years he filled its whole magnitude, his word was decisive with his subjects; for he was so rich a man, that he was never expected to support any opinion by argument. The landlord waited on him with peculiar officiousness; not that he paid better than his neighbors, but then the coin of a rich man seems always to be so much more acceptable. The landlord had ever a pleasant word and a joke, to insinuate in the ear of the august Ramm. It is true, Ramm never laughed, and, indeed, ever maintained a mastiff-like gravity, and even surliness of aspect; yet he now and then rewarded mine host with a token of approbation; which though nothing more nor less than a kind of grunt, still delighted the landlord more than a broad laugh from a poorer man.

"This will be a rough night for the money-diggers," said mine host, as a gust of wind howled round the house, and rattled at the windows.

"What! are they at their works again?" said an English half-pay captain, with one eye, who was a very frequent attendant at the inn.

"Aye, are they," said the landlord, "and well may they be. They've had luck of late. They say a great pot of money has been dug up in the fields, just behind Stuyvesant's orchard. Folks think it must have been buried there in old times, by Peter Stuyvesant, the Dutch governor."

"Fudge!" said the one-eyed man of war, as he added a small portion of water to a bottom of brandy.

"Well, you may believe it, or not, as you please," said mine host, somewhat nettled; "but every body knows that the old governor buried a great deal of his money at the time of the Dutch troubles, when the English red-coats seized on the province. They say, too, the old gentleman walks; aye, and in the very same dress that he wears in the picture that hangs up in the family house."

"Fudge!" said the half-pay officer.

"Fudge, if you please!—But didn't Corney Van Zandt see him at midnight, stalking about in the meadow with his wooden leg, and a drawn sword in his hand, that flashed like fire? And what can he be walking for, but because people have been troubling the place where he buried his money in old times?"

Here the landlord was interrupted by several guttural sounds from Ramm Rapelye betokening that he was laboring with the unusual production of an idea. As he was too great a man to be slighted by a prudent publican, mine host respectfully paused until he should deliver himself. The corpulent frame of this mighty burgher now gave all the symptoms of a volcanic mountain on the point of an eruption. First, there was a certain heaving of the abdomen, not unlike an earthquake; then was emitted a cloud of tobacco-smoke from that crater, his mouth; then there was a kind of rattle in the throat, as if the idea were working its way up through a region of phlegm; then there were several disjointed members of a sentence thrown out, ending in a cough; at length his voice forced its way in the slow, but absolute tone of a man who feels the weight of his purse, if not of his ideas; every portion of his speech being marked by a testy puff of tobacco-smoke.

"Who talks of old Peter Stuyvesant's walking?—puff—Have people no respect for persons?—puff—puff—Peter Stuyvesant knew better what to do with his money than to bury it—puff—I know the Stuyvesant family—puff—every one of them—puff—not a more respectable family in the province—puff—old standards—puff—warm householders—puff—none of your upstarts—puff—puff—puff.—Don't talk to me of Peter Stuyvesant's walking—puff—puff—puff—puff."

Here the redoubtable Ramm contracted his brow, clasped up his mouth, till it wrinkled at each corner, and redoubled his smoking with such vehemence, that the cloudy volumes soon wreathed round his head, as the smoke envelopes the awful summit of Mount Etna.

A general silence followed the sudden rebuke of this very rich man. The subject, however, was too interesting to be readily abandoned. The conversation soon broke forth again from the lips of Peechy Prauw Van Hook, the chronicler of the club, one of those prosing, narrative old men who seem to be troubled with an incontinence of words, as they grow old.

Peechy could, at any time, tell as many stories in an evening as his hearers could digest in a month. He now resumed the conversation, by affirming that, to his knowledge, money had at different times been digged up in various parts of the island. The lucky persons who had discovered them had always dreamt of them three times beforehand, and what was worthy of remark those treasures had never been found but by some descendant of the good old Dutch families, which clearly proved that they had been buried by Dutchmen in the olden time.

"Fiddlestick with your Dutchmen!" cried the half-pay officer. "The Dutch had nothing to do with them. They were all buried by Kidd the pirate, and his crew."

Here a key-note was touched that roused the whole company. The name of Captain Kidd was like a talisman in those times, and was associated with a thousand marvellous stories.

The half-pay officer took the lead and in his narrations fathered upon Kidd all the plunderings and exploits of Morgan, Blackbeard, and the whole list of bloody buccaneers.

The officer was a man of great weight among the peaceable members of the club, by reason of his warlike character and gun-powder tales. All his golden stories of Kidd, however, and of the booty he had buried, were obstinately rivalled by the tales of Peechy Prauw, who, rather than suffer his Dutch progenitors to be eclipsed by a foreign freebooter, enriched every field and shore in the neighborhood with the hidden wealth of Peter Stuyvesant and his contemporaries.

Not a word of this conversation was lost upon Wolfert Webber. He returned pensively home, full of magnificent ideas. The soil of his native island seemed to be turned into gold dust; and every field to teem with treasure. His head almost reeled at the thought how often he must have heedlessly rambled over places where countless sums lay, scarcely covered by the turf beneath his feet. His mind was in an uproar with this whirl of new ideas. As he came in sight of the venerable mansion of his forefathers, and the little realm where the Webbers had so long, and so contentedly flourished, his gorge rose at the narrowness of his destiny.

"Unlucky Wolfert!" exclaimed he; "others can go to bed and dream themselves into whole mines of wealth; they have but to seize a spade in the morning, and turn up doubloons like potatoes; but thou must dream of hardships, and rise to poverty—must dig thy field from year's end to year's end, and yet raise nothing but cabbages!"

Wolfert Webber went to bed with a heavy heart; and it was long before the golden visions that disturbed his brain permitted him to sink into repose. The same visions, however, extended into his sleeping thoughts, and assumed a more definite form. He dreamt that he had discovered an immense treasure in the centre of his garden. At every stroke of the spade he laid bare a golden ingot; diamond crosses sparkled out of the dust; bags of money turned up their bellies, corpulent with pieces-of-eight, or venerable doubloons; and chests, wedged close with moidores, ducats, and pistareens, yawned before his ravished eyes, and vomited forth their glittering contents.

Wolfert awoke a poorer man than ever. He had no heart to go about his daily concerns, which appeared so paltry and profitless; but sat all day long in the chimney-corner, picturing to himself ingots and heaps of gold in the fire. The next night his dream was repeated. He was again in his garden, digging, and laying open stores of hidden wealth. There was something very singular in this repetition. He passed another day of reverie, and though it was cleaning-day, and the house, as usual in Dutch households, completely topsy-turvy, yet he sat unmoved amidst the general uproar.

The third night he went to bed with a palpitating heart. He put on his red night-cap wrong side outwards, for good luck. It was deep midnight before his anxious mind could settle itself into sleep. Again the golden dream was repeated, and again he saw his garden teeming with ingots and money bags.

Wolfert rose the next morning in complete bewilderment. A dream three times repeated was never known to lie; and if so, his fortune was made.

In his agitation he put on his waistcoat with the hind part before, and this was a corroboration of good luck. He no longer doubted that a huge store of money lay buried somewhere in his cabbage field, coyly waiting to be sought for; and he repined at having so long been scratching about the surface of the soil instead of digging to the centre.

He took his seat at the breakfast table full of these speculations; asked his daughter to put a lump of gold into his tea, and on handing his wife a plate of slap-jacks, begged her to help herself to a doubloon.

His grand care now was how to secure this immense treasure without its being known. Instead of working regularly in his grounds in the daytime, he now stole from his bed at night, and with spade and pickaxe, went to work to rip up and dig about his paternal acres, from one end to the other. In a little time the whole garden, which had presented such a goodly and regular appearance, with its phalanx of cabbages, like a vegetable army in battle array, was reduced to a scene of devastation; while the relentless Wolfert, with night-cap on head, and lantern and spade in hand, stalked through the slaughtered ranks, the destroying angel of his own vegetable world.

Every morning bore testimony to the ravages of the preceding night in cabbages of all ages and conditions, from the tender sprout to the full-grown head, piteously rooted from their quiet beds like worthless weeds, and left to wither in the sunshine. In vain Wolfert's wife remonstrated; in vain his darling daughter wept over the destruction of some favorite marigold. "Thou shalt have gold of another guess sort," he would cry, chucking her under the chin; "thou shalt have a string of crooked ducats for thy wedding necklace, my child." His family began really to fear that the poor man's wits were diseased. He muttered in his sleep at night about mines of wealth, about pearls and diamonds and bars of gold. In the daytime he was moody and abstracted, and walked about as if in a trance. Dame Webber held frequent councils with all the old women of the neighborhood; scarce an hour in the day but a knot of them might be seen wagging their white caps together round her door, while the poor woman made some piteous recital. The daughter too was fain to seek for more frequent consolation from the stolen interviews of her favored swain Dirk Waldron. The delectable little Dutch songs with which she used to dulcify the house grew less and less frequent, and she would forget her sewing and look wistfully in her father's face, as he sat pondering by the fireside. Wolfert caught her eye one day fixed on him thus anxiously, and for a moment was roused from his golden reveries.—"Cheer up, my girl," said he, exultingly, "why dost thou droop?—thou shalt hold up thy head one day with the Brinckerhoffs, and the Schermerhorns, the Van Hornes, and the Van Dams.—By Saint Nicholas, but the patroon himself shall be glad to get thee for his son!"

Amy shook her head at this vainglorious boast, and was more than ever in doubt of the soundness of the good man's intellect.

In the meantime Wolfert went on digging and digging; but the field was extensive, and as his dream had indicated no precise spot, he had to dig at random. The winter set in before one-tenth of the scene of promise had been explored.

The ground became frozen hard, and the nights too cold for the labors of the spade.

No sooner, however, did the returning warmth of spring loosen the soil, and the small frogs begin to pipe in the meadows, but Wolfert resumed his labors with renovated zeal. Still, however, the hours of industry were reversed.

Instead of working cheerily all day, planting and setting out his vegetables, he remained thoughtfully idle, until the shades of night summoned him to his secret labors. In this way he continued to dig from night to night, and week to week, and month to month, but not a stiver did he find. On the contrary, the more he digged, the poorer he grew. The rich soil of his garden was digged away, and the sand and gravel from beneath were thrown to the surface, until the whole field presented an aspect of sandy barrenness.

In the meantime the seasons gradually rolled on. The little frogs which had piped in the meadows in early spring, croaked as bull-frogs during the summer heats, and then sank into silence. The peach-tree budded, blossomed, and bore its fruit. The swallows and martins came, twittered about the roof, built their nests, reared their young, held their congress along the eaves, and then winged their flight in search of another spring. The caterpillar spun its winding-sheet, dangled in it from the great button-wood tree before the house; turned into a moth, fluttered with the last sunshine of summer, and disappeared; and finally the leaves of the button-wood tree turned yellow, then brown, then rustled one by one to the ground, and whirling about in little eddies of wind and dust, whispered that winter was at hand.

Wolfert gradually woke from his dream of wealth as the year declined. He had reared no crop for the supply of his household during the sterility of winter. The season was long and severe, and for the first time the family was really straitened in its comforts. By degrees a revulsion of thought took place in Wolfert's mind, common to those whose golden dreams have been disturbed by pinching realities. The idea gradually stole upon him that he should come to want. He already considered himself one of the most unfortunate men in the province, having lost such an incalculable amount of undiscovered treasure, and now, when thousands of pounds had eluded his search, to be perplexed for shillings and pence was cruel in the extreme.

Haggard care gathered about his brow; he went about with a money-seeking air, his eyes bent downwards into the dust, and carrying his hands in his pockets, as men are apt to do when they have nothing else to put into them. He could not even pass the city almshouse without giving it a rueful glance, as if destined to be his future abode.

The strangeness of his conduct and of his looks occasioned much speculation and remark. For a long time he was suspected of being crazy, and then every body pitied him; at length it began to be suspected that he was poor, and then every body avoided him.

The rich old burghers of his acquaintance met him outside of the door when he called, entertained him hospitably on the threshold, pressed him warmly by the hand at parting, shook their heads as he walked away, with the kind-hearted expression of "poor Wolfert," and turned a corner nimbly, if by chance they saw him approaching as they walked the streets. Even the barber and cobbler of the neighborhood, and a tattered tailor in an alley hard by, three of the poorest and merriest rogues in the world, eyed him with that abundant sympathy which usually attends a lack of means; and there is not a doubt but their pockets would have been at his command, only that they happened to be empty.

Thus every body deserted the Webber mansion, as if poverty were contagious, like the plague; every body but honest Dirk Waldron, who still kept up his stolen visits to the daughter, and indeed seemed to wax more affectionate as the fortunes of his mistress were in the wane.

Many months had elapsed since Wolfert had frequented his old resort, the rural inn. He was taking a long lonely walk one Saturday afternoon, musing over his wants and disappointments, when his feet took instinctively their wonted direction, and on awaking out of a reverie, he found himself before the door of the inn. For some moments he hesitated whether to enter, but his heart yearned for companionship; and where can a ruined man find better companionship than at a tavern, where there is neither sober example nor sober advice to put him out of countenance?

Wolfert found several of the old frequenters of the inn at their usual posts, and seated in their usual places; but one was missing, the great Ramm Rapelye, who for many years had filled the leather-bottomed chair of state. His place was supplied by a stranger, who seemed, however, completely at home in the chair and the tavern. He was rather under size, but deep chested, square, and muscular. His broad shoulders, double joints, and bow knees, gave tokens of prodigious strength. His face was dark and weather-beaten; a deep scar, as if from the slash of a cutlass, had almost divided his nose, and made a gash in his upper lip, through which his teeth shone like a bull-dog's. A mop of iron-gray hair gave a grisly finish to his hard-favored visage. His dress was of an amphibious character. He wore an old hat edged with tarnished lace, and cocked in martial style, on the side of his head; a rusty blue military coat with brass buttons, and a wide pair of short petticoat trowsers, or rather breeches, for they were gathered up at the knees. He ordered every body about him with an authoritative air; talked in a brattling voice, that sounded like the crackling of thorns under a pot; d——d the landlord and servants with perfect impunity, and was waited upon with greater obsequiousness than had ever been shown to the mighty Ramm himself.

Wolfert's curiosity was awakened to know who and what was this stranger, who had thus usurped absolute sway in this ancient domain. Peechy Prauw took him aside, into a remote corner of the hall, and there, in an under voice, and with great caution, imparted to him all that he knew on the subject. The inn had been aroused several months before, on a dark stormy night, by repeated long shouts, that seemed like the howlings of a wolf. They came from the water-side; and at length were distinguished to be hailing the house in the seafaring manner, "House-a-hoy!" The landlord turned out with his head waiter, tapster, hostler, and errand-boy—that is to say, with his old negro Cuff. On approaching the place whence the voice proceeded, they found this amphibious-looking personage at the water's edge, quite alone, and seated on a great oaken sea-chest. How he came there, whether he had been set on shore from some boat, or had floated to land on his chest, nobody could tell, for he did not seem disposed to answer questions; and there was something in his looks and manners that put a stop to all questioning. Suffice it to say, he took possession of a corner room of the inn, to which his chest was removed with great difficulty. Here he had remained ever since, keeping about the inn and its vicinity. Sometimes, it is true, he disappeared for one, two, or three days at a time, going and returning without giving any notice or account of his movements. He always appeared to have plenty of money, though often of a very strange outlandish coinage; and he regularly paid his bill every evening before turning in.

He had fitted up his room to his own fancy, having slung a hammock from the ceiling instead of a bed, and decorated the walls with rusty pistols and cutlasses of foreign workmanship. A great part of his time was passed in this room, seated by the window, which commanded a wide view of the Sound, a short old-fashioned pipe in his mouth, a glass of rum toddy at his elbow, and a pocket telescope in his hand, with which he reconnoitred every boat that moved upon the water. Large square-rigged vessels seemed to excite but little attention; but the moment he descried any thing with a shoulder-of-mutton sail, or that a barge, or yawl, or jolly-boat hove in sight, up went the telescope, and he examined it with the most scrupulous attention.

All this might have passed without much notice, for in those times the province was so much the resort of adventurers of all characters and climes, that any oddity in dress or behavior attracted but small attention. In a little while, however, this strange sea-monster, thus strangely cast upon dry land, began to encroach upon the long-established customs and customers of the place, and to interfere in a dictatorial manner in the affairs of the nine-pin alley and the bar-room, until in the end he usurped an absolute command over the whole inn. It was all in vain to attempt to withstand his authority. He was not exactly quarrelsome, but boisterous and peremptory, like one accustomed to tyrannize on a quarter-deck; and there was a dare-devil air about every thing he said and did, that inspired a wariness in all bystanders. Even the half-pay officer, so long the hero of the dub, was soon silenced by him; and the quiet burghers stared with wonder at seeing their inflammable man of war so readily and quietly extinguished.

And then the tales that he would tell were enough to make a peaceable man's hair stand on end. There was not a sea-fight nor marauding nor freebooting adventure that had happened within the last twenty years, but he seemed perfectly versed in it. He delighted to talk of the exploits of the buccaneers in the West Indies and on the Spanish Main. How his eyes would glisten as he described the waylaying of treasure ships, the desperate fights, yard-arm and yard-arm—broadside and broadside—the boarding and capturing of huge Spanish galleons! With what chuckling relish would he describe the descent upon some rich Spanish colony; the rifling of a church; the sacking of a convent! You would have thought you heard some gormandizer dilating upon the roasting of a savory goose at Michaelmas as he described the roasting of some Spanish Don to make him discover his treasure—a detail given with a minuteness that made every rich old burgher present turn uncomfortably in his chair. All this would be told with infinite glee, as if he considered it an excellent joke; and then he would give such a tyrannical leer in the face of his next neighbor, that the poor man would be fain to laugh out of sheer faint-heartedness. If any one, however, pretended to contradict him in any of his stories he was on fire in an instant. His very cocked hat assumed a momentary fierceness, and seemed to resent the contradiction. "How the devil should you know as well as I?—I tell you it was as I say"; and he would at the same time let slip a broadside of thundering oaths and tremendous sea-phrases, such as had never been heard before within these peaceful walls.

Indeed, the worthy burghers began to surmise that he knew more of those stories than mere hearsay. Day after day their conjectures concerning him grew more and more wild and fearful. The strangeness of his arrival, the strangeness of his manners, the mystery that surrounded him, all made him something incomprehensible in their eyes. He was a kind of monster of the deep to them—he was a merman—he was a behemoth—he was a leviathan—in short, they knew not what he was.

The domineering spirit of this boisterous sea-urchin at length grew quite intolerable. He was no respecter of persons; he contradicted the richest burghers without hesitation; he took possession of the sacred elbow-chair, which, time out of mind, had been the seat of sovereignty of the illustrious Ramm Rapelye. Nay, he even went so far in one of his rough jocular moods, as to slap that mighty burgher on the back, drink his toddy, and wink in his face, a thing scarcely to be believed. From this time Ramm Rapelye appeared no more at the inn; his example was followed by several of the most eminent customers, who were too rich to tolerate being bullied out of their opinions, or being obliged to laugh at another man's jokes. The landlord was almost in despair; but he knew not how to get rid of this sea-monster and his sea-chest, who seemed both to have grown like fixtures, or excrescences, on his establishment.

Such was the account whispered cautiously in Wolfert's ear, by the narrator, Peechy Prauw, as he held him by the button in a corner of the hall, casting a wary glance now and then towards the door of the bar-room, lest he should be overheard by the terrible hero of his tale.

Wolfert took his seat in a remote part of the room in silence; impressed with profound awe of this unknown, so versed in freebooting history. It was to him a wonderful instance of the revolutions of mighty empires, to find the venerable Ramm Rapelye thus ousted from the throne, and a rugged tarpawling dictating from his elbow-chair, hectoring the patriarchs, and filling this tranquil little realm with brawl and bravado.

The stranger was on this evening in a more than usually communicative mood, and was narrating a number of astounding stories of plunderings and burnings on the high seas. He dwelt upon them with peculiar relish, heightening the frightful particulars in proportion to their effect on his peaceful auditors. He gave a swaggering detail of the capture of a Spanish merchant-man. She was lying becalmed during a long summer's day, just off from an island which was one of the lurking-places of the pirates. They had reconnoitred her with their spy-glasses from the shore, and ascertained her character and force. At night a picked crew of daring fellows set off for her in a whaleboat. They approached with muffled oars, as she lay rocking idly with the undulations of the sea, and her sails flapping against the masts. They were close under her stern before the guard on deck was aware of their approach. The alarm was given; the pirates threw hand-grenades on deck, and sprang up the main chains sword in hand.

The crew flew to arms, but in great confusion; some were shot down, others took refuge in the tops; others were driven overboard and drowned, while others fought hand to hand from the main-deck to the quarter-deck, disputing gallantly every inch of ground. There were three Spanish gentlemen on board with their ladies, who made the most desperate resistance. They defended the companion-way, cut down several of their assailants, and fought like very devils, for they were maddened by the shrieks of the ladies from the cabin. One of the Dons was old, and soon dispatched. The other two kept their ground vigorously, even though the captain of the pirates was among their assailants. Just then there was a shout of victory from the main-deck. "The ship is ours!" cried the pirates.

One of the Dons immediately dropped his sword and surrendered; the other, who was a hot-headed youngster, and just married, gave the captain a slash in the face that laid all open. The captain just made out to articulate the words "no quarter."

"And what did they do with their prisoners?" said Peechy Prauw, eagerly.

"Threw them all overboard!" was the answer. A dead pause followed the reply. Peechy Prauw sunk quietly back, like a man who had unwarily stolen upon the lair of a sleeping lion. The honest burghers cast fearful glances at the deep scar slashed across the visage of the stranger, and moved their chairs a little farther off. The seaman, however, smoked on without moving a muscle, as though he either did not perceive or did not regard the unfavorable effect he had produced upon his hearers.

The half-pay officer was the first to break the silence; for he was continually tempted to make ineffectual head against this tyrant of the seas, and to regain his lost consequence in the eyes of his ancient companions. He now tried to match the gunpowder tales of the stranger by others equally tremendous. Kidd, as usual, was his hero, concerning whom he seemed to have picked up many of the floating traditions of the province. The seaman had always evinced a settled pique against the one-eyed warrior. On this occasion he listened with peculiar impatience. He sat with one arm akimbo, the other elbow on a table, the hand holding on to the small pipe he was pettishly puffing; his legs crossed; drumming with one foot on the ground, and casting every now and then the side-glance of a basilisk at the prosing captain. At length the latter spoke of Kidd's having ascended the Hudson with some of his crew, to land his plunder in secrecy.

"Kidd up the Hudson!" burst forth the seaman, with a tremendous oath—"Kidd never was up the Hudson!"

"I tell you he was," said the other. "Aye, and they say he buried a quantity of treasure on the little flat that runs out into the river, called the Devil's Dans Kammer."

"The Devil's Dans Kammer in your teeth!" cried the seaman. "I tell you Kidd never was up the Hudson. What a plague do you know of Kidd and his haunts?"

"What do I know?" echoed the half-pay officer. "Why, I was in London at the time of his trial; aye, and I had the pleasure of seeing him hanged at Execution Dock."

"Then, sir, let me tell you that you saw as pretty a fellow hanged as ever trod shoe-leather. Aye!" putting his face nearer to that of the officer, "and there was many a land-lubber looked on that might much better have swung in his stead."

The half-pay officer was silenced; but the indignation thus pent up in his bosom glowed with intense vehemence in his single eye, which kindled like a coal.

Peechy Prauw, who never could remain silent, observed that the gentleman certainly was in the right. Kidd never did bury money up the Hudson, nor indeed in any of those parts, though many affirmed such to be the fact. It was Bradish and others of the buccaneers who had buried money; some said in Turtle Bay, others on Long Island, others in the neighborhood of Hell-gate. Indeed, added he, I recollect an adventure of Sam, the negro fisherman, many years ago, which some think had something to do with the buccaneers. As we are all friends here, and as it will go no farther, I'll tell it to you.

"Upon a dark night many years ago, as Black Sam was returning from fishing in Hell-gate—"

Here the story was nipped in the bud by a sudden movement from the unknown, who laying his iron fist on die table, knuckles downward, with a quiet force that indented the very boards, and looking grimly over his shoulder, with the grin of an angry bear —"Heark'ee, neighbor," said he, with significant nodding of the head, "you'd better let the buccaneers and their money alone—they're not for old men and old women to meddle with. They fought hard for their money; they gave body and soul for it; and wherever it lies buried, depend upon it he must have a tug with the devil who gets it!"

This sudden explosion was succeeded by a blank silence throughout the room. Peechy Prauw shrunk within himself, and even the one-eyed officer turned pale. Wolfert, who from a dark corner of the room had listened with intense eagerness to all this talk about buried treasure, looked with mingled awe and reverence at this bold buccaneer, for such he really suspected him to be. There was a chinking of gold and a sparkling of jewels in all his stories about the Spanish Main that gave a value to every period; and Wolfert would have given any thing for the rummaging of the ponderous sea-chest, which his imagination crammed full of golden chalices, crucifixes, and jolly round bags of doubloons.

The dead stillness that had fallen upon the company was at length interrupted by the stranger, who pulled out a prodigious watch of curious and ancient workmanship, and which in Wolfert's eyes had a decidedly Spanish look. On touching a spring it struck ten o'clock; upon which the sailor called for his reckoning, and having paid it out of a handful of outlandish coin, he drank off the remainder of his beverage, and without taking leave of any one, rolled out of the room, muttering to himself, as he stamped up stairs to his chamber.

It was some time before the company could recover from the silence into which they had been thrown. The very footsteps of the stranger, which were heard now and then as he traversed his chamber, inspired awe.

Still the conversation in which they had been engaged was too interesting not to be resumed. A heavy thundergust had gathered up unnoticed while they were lost in talk, and the torrents of rain that fell forbade all thoughts of setting off for home until the storm should subside. They drew nearer together, therefore, and entreated the worthy Peechy Prauw to continue the tale which had been so discourteously interrupted. He readily complied, whispering, however, in a tone scarcely above his breath, and drowned occasionally by the rolling of the thunder; and he would pause every now and then, and listen with evident awe, as he heard the heavy footsteps of the stranger pacing overhead.

The following is the purport of his story.

The Adventure of the Black Fisherman

EVERY BODY KNOWS BLACK SAM, THE OLD NEGRO FISHERMAN, OR, AS HE is commonly called, Mud Sam, who has fished about the Sound for the last half century. It is now many years since Sam, who was then as active a young negro as any in the province, and worked on the farm of Killian Suydam on Long Island, having finished his day's work at an early hour, was fishing, one still summer evening, just about the neighborhood of Hell-gate.

He was in a light skiff, and being well acquainted with the currents and eddies, had shifted his station according to the shifting of the tide, from the Hen and Chickens to the Hog's Back, from the Hog's Back to the Pot, and from the Pot to the Frying-Pan; but in the eagerness of his sport he did not see that the tide was rapidly ebbing, until the roaring of the whirlpools and eddies warned him of his danger; and he had some difficulty in shooting his skiff from among the rocks and breakers, and getting to the point of Blackwell's Island. Here he cast anchor for some time, waiting the turn of the tide to enable him to return homewards. As the night set in, it grew blustering and gusty. Dark clouds came bundling up in the west; and now and then a growl of thunder or a flash of lightning told that a summer storm was at hand. Sam pulled over, therefore, under the lee of Manhattan Island, and coasting along, came to a snug nook, just under a steep beetling rock, where he fastened his skiff to the root of a tree that shot out from a deft, and spread its broad branches like a canopy over the water. The gust came scouring along; the wind threw up the river in white surges; the rain rattled among the leaves; the thunder bellowed worse than that which is now bellowing; the lightning seemed to lick up the surges of the stream; but Sam, snugly sheltered under rock and tree, lay crouching in his skiff, rocking upon the billows until he fell asleep. When he woke all was quiet. The gust had passed away, and only now and then a faint gleam of lightning in the east showed which way it had gone. The night was dark and moonless; and from the state of the tide Sam concluded it was near midnight. He was on the point of making loose his skiff to return homewards, when he saw a light gleaming along the water from a distance, which seemed rapidly approaching. As it drew near he perceived it came from a lantern in the bow of a boat gliding along under shadow of the land. It pulled up in a small cove, close to where he was. A man jumped on shore, and searching about with the lantern, exclaimed, "This is the place—here's the iron ring." The boat was then made fast, and the man returning on board, assisted his comrades in conveying something heavy on shore. As the light gleamed among them, Sam saw that they were five stout desperate-looking fellows, in red woollen caps, with a leader in a three-cornered hat, and that some of them were armed with dirks, or long knives, and pistols. They talked low to one another, and occasionally in some outlandish tongue which he could not understand.

On landing they made their way among the bushes, taking turns to relieve each other in lugging their burden up the rocky bank. Sam's curiosity was now fully aroused; so leaving his skiff he clambered silently up a ridge that overlooked their path. They had stopped to rest for a moment, and the leader was looking about among the bushes with his lantern. "Have you brought the spades?" said one. "They are here," replied another, who had them on his shoulder. "We must dig deep, where there will be no risk of discovery," said a third.

A cold chill ran through Sam's veins. He fancied he saw before him a gang of murderers, about to bury their victim. His knees smote together. In his agitation he shook the branch of a tree with which he was supporting himself as he looked over the edge of the cliff.

"What's that?" cried one of the gang. "Some one stirs among the bushes!"

The lantern was held up in the direction of the noise. One of the red-caps cocked a pistol, and pointed it towards the very place where Sam was standing. He stood motionless—breathless; expecting the next moment to be his last. Fortunately his dingy complexion was in his favor, and made no glare among the leaves.

"'Tis no one," said the man with the lantern. "What a plague! you would not fire off your pistol and alarm the country!"

The pistol was uncocked; the burden was resumed, and the party slowly toiled along the bank. Sam watched them as they went; the light sending back fitful gleams through the dripping bushes, and it was not till they were fairly out of sight that he ventured to draw breath freely. He now thought of getting back to his boat, and making his escape out of the reach of such dangerous neighbors; but curiosity was all-powerful. He hesitated and lingered and listened. By and by he heard the strokes of spades. "They are digging the grave!" said he to himself; and the cold sweat started upon his forehead. Every stroke of a spade, as it sounded through the silent groves, went to his heart; it was evident there was as little noise made as possible; every thing had an air of terrible mystery and secrecy. Sam had a great relish for the horrible,—a tale of murder was a treat for him; and he was a constant attendant at executions. He could not resist an impulse, in spite of every danger, to steal nearer to the scene of mystery, and overlook the midnight fellows at their work. He crawled along cautiously, therefore, inch by inch; stepping with the utmost care among the dry leaves, lest their rustling should betray him. He came at length to where a steep rock intervened between him and the gang; for he saw the light of their lantern shining up against the branches of the trees on the other side. Sam slowly and silently clambered up the surface of the rock, and raising his head above its naked edge, beheld the villains immediately below him, and so near, that though he dreaded discovery, he dared not withdraw lest the least movement should be heard. In this way he remained, with his round black face peering above the edge of the rock, like the sun just emerging above the edge of the horizon, or the round-cheeked moon on the dial of a clock.

The red-caps had nearly finished their work; the grave was filled up, and they were carefully replacing the turf. This done, they scattered dry leaves over the place. "And now," said the leader, "I defy the devil himself to find it out."

"The murderers!" exclaimed Sam, involuntarily.

The whole gang started, and looking up beheld the round black head of Sam just above them. His white eyes strained half out of their orbits; his white teeth chattering, and his whole visage shining with cold perspiration.

"We're discovered!" cried one.

"Down with him!" cried another.

Sam heard the cocking of a pistol, but did not pause for the report. He scrambled over rock and stone, through brash and brier; rolled down banks like a hedge-hog; scrambled up others like a catamount. In every direction he heard some one or other of the gang hemming him in. At length he reached the rocky ridge along the river; one of the red-caps was hard behind him. A steep rock like a wall rose directly in his way; it seemed to cut off all retreat, when fortunately he espied the strong cord-like branch of a grape-vine reaching half way down it. He sprang at it with the force of a desperate man, seized it with both hands, and being young and agile, succeeded in swinging himself to the summit of the cliff. Here he stood in full relief against the sky, when the red-cap cocked his pistol and fired. The ball whistled by Sam's head. With the lucky thought of a man in an emergency, he uttered a yell, fell to the ground, and detached at the same time a fragment of the rock, which tumbled with a loud splash into the river.

"I've done his business," said the red-cap to one or two of his comrades as they arrived panting. "He'll tell no tales, except to the fishes in the river."

His pursuers now turned to meet their companions. Sam sliding silently down the surface of the rock, let himself quietly into his skiff, cast loose the fastening, and abandoned himself to the rapid current, which in that place runs like a mill-stream, and soon swept him off from the neighborhood. It was not, however, until he had drifted a great distance that he ventured to ply his oars; when he made his skiff dart like an arrow through the strait of Hell-gate, never heeding the danger of Pot, Frying-Pan, nor Hog's Back itself: nor did he feel himself thoroughly secure until safely nestled in bed in the cockloft of the ancient farm-house of the Suydams.

Here the worthy Peechy Prauw paused to take breath, and to take a sip of the gossip tankard that stood at his elbow. His auditors remained with open mouths and outstretched necks, gaping like a nest of swallows for an additional mouthful.

"And is that all?" exclaimed the half-pay officer.

"That's all that belongs to the story," said Peechy Prauw.

"And did Sam never find out what was buried by the red-caps?" said Wolfert, eagerly, whose mind was haunted by nothing but ingots and doubloons.

"Not that I know of," said Peechy; "he had no time to spare from his work, and, to tell the truth, he did not like to run the risk of another race among the rocks. Besides, how should he recollect the spot where the grave had been digged? every thing would look so different by daylight. And then, where was the use of looking for a dead body, when there was no chance of hanging the murderers?"

"Aye, but are you sure it was a dead body they buried?" said Wolfert.

"To be sure," cried Peechy Prauw, exultingly. "Does it not haunt in the neighborhood to this very day?"

"Haunts!" exclaimed several of the party, opening their eyes still wider, and edging their chairs still closer.

"Aye, haunts," repeated Peechy; "have none of you heard of father Red-cap, who haunts the old burnt farm-house in the woods, on the border of the Sound, near Hell-gate?"

"Oh, to be sure, I've heard tell of something of the kind, but then I took it for some old wives' fable."

"Old wives' fable or not," said Peechy Prauw, "that farm-house stands hard by the very spot. It's been unoccupied time out of mind, and stands in a lonely part of the coast; but those who fish in the neighborhood have often heard strange noises there; and lights have been seen about the wood at night; and an old fallow in a red cap has been seen at the windows more than once, which people take to be the ghost of the body buried there. Once upon a time three soldiers took shelter in the building for the night, and rummaged it from top to bottom, when they found old father Red-cap astride of a cider-barrel in the cellar, with a jug in one band and a goblet in the other. He offered them a drink out of his goblet, but just as one of the soldiers was patting it to his mouth—whew!—a flash of fire blazed through the cellar, blinded every mother's son of them for several minutes, and when they recovered their eye-sight, jug, goblet, and Red-cap had vanished, and nothing but the empty cider-barrel remained."

Here the half-pay officer, who was growing very muzzy and sleepy, and nodding ever his liquor, with half-extinguished eye, suddenly gleamed up like an expiring rushlight.

"That's all fudge!" said he, as Peechy finished his last story.

"Well, I don't vouch for the truth of it myself," said Peechy Prauw, "though all the world knows that there's something strange about that house and grounds; but as to the story of Mud Sam, I believe it just as well as if it had happened to myself."

The deep interest taken in this conversation by the company had made them unconscious of the uproar abroad among the elements when suddenly they were electrified by a tremendous clap of thunder. A lumbering crash followed instantaneously, shaking the building to its very foundation. All started from their seats, imagining it the shock of an earthquake, or that old father Red-cap was coming among them in all his terrors. They listened for a moment, but only heard the rain pelting against the windows, and the wind howling among the trees. The explosion was soon explained by the apparition of an old negro's bald head thrust in at the door, his white goggle eyes contrasting with his jetty poll, which was wet with rain, and shone like a bottle. In a jargon but half intelligible, he announced that the kitchen chimney had been struck with lightning.

A sullen pause of the storm, which now rose and sunk in gusts, produced a momentary stillness. In this interval the report of a musket was heard, and a long shout, almost like a yell, resounded from the shores. Every one crowded to the window; another musket-shot was heard, and another long shout, mingled wildly with a rising blast of wind. It seemed as if the cry came up from the bosom of the waters; for though incessant flashes of lightning spread a light about the shore, no one was to be seen.

Suddenly the window of the room overhead was opened, and a loud halloo uttered by the mysterious stranger. Several hailings passed from one party to the other, but in a language which none of the company in the bar-room could understand; and presently they heard the window closed, and a great noise overhead, as if all the furniture were pulled and hauled about the room. The negro servant was summoned, and shortly afterwards was seen assisting the veteran to lug the ponderous sea-chest down stairs.

The landlord was in amazement. "What, you are not going on the water in such a storm?"

"Storm!" said the other, scornfully, "do you call such a sputter of weather a storm?"

"You'll get drenched to the skin—You'll catch your death!" said Peechy Prauw, affectionately.

"Thunder and lightning!" exclaimed the merman, "don't preach about weather to a man that has cruised in whirlwinds and tornadoes."

The obsequious Peechy was again struck dumb. The voice from the water was heard once more in a tone of impatience; the bystanders stared with redoubled awe at this man of storms, who seemed to have come up out of the deep, and to be summoned back to it again. As, with the assistance of the negro, he slowly bore his ponderous sea-chest towards the shore, they eyed it with a superstitious feeling; half doubting whether he were not really about to embark upon it and launch forth upon the wild waves. They followed him at a distance with a lantern.

"Dowse the light!" roared the hoarse voice from the water. "No one wants lights here!"

"Thunder and lightning!" exclaimed the veteran, turning short upon them; "back to the house with you!"

Wolfert and his companions shrunk back in dismay. Still their curiosity would not allow them entirely to withdraw. A long sheet of lightning now flickered across the waves, and discovered a boat, filled with men, just under a rocky point, rising and sinking with the heaving surges, and swashing the water at every heave. It was with difficulty held to the rocks by a boathook, for the current rushed furiously round the point. The veteran hoisted one end of the lumbering sea-chest on the gunwale of the boat, and seized the handle at the other end to lift it in, when the motion propelled the boat from the shore; the chest slipped off from the gunwale, and, sinking into the waves, pulled the veteran headlong after it. A loud shriek was uttered by all on shore, and a volley of execrations by those on board; but boat and man were hurried away by the rushing swiftness of the tide. A pitchy darkness succeeded; Wolfert Webber indeed fancied that he distinguished a cry for help, and that he beheld the drowning man beckoning for assistance; but when the lightning again gleamed along the water, all was void; neither man nor boat was to be seen; nothing but the dashing and weltering of the waves as they hurried past.

The company returned to the tavern to await the subsiding of the storm. They resumed their seats, and gazed on each other with dismay. The whole transaction had not occupied five minutes, and not a dozen words had been spoken. When they looked at the oaken chair, they could scarcely realize the fact that the strange being who had so lately tenanted it, full of life and Herculean vigor, should already be a corpse. There was the very glass he had just drunk from; there lay the ashes from the pipe which he had smoked, as it were, with his last breath. As the worthy burghers pondered on these things, they felt a terrible conviction of the uncertainty of existence, and each felt as if the ground on which he stood was rendered less stable by this awful example.

As, however, the most of the company were possessed of that valuable philosophy which enables a man to bear up with fortitude against the misfortunes of his neighbors, they soon managed to console themselves for the tragic end of the veteran. The landlord was particularly happy that the poor dear man had paid his reckoning before he went; and made a kind of farewell speech on the occasion.

"He came," said he, "in a storm, and he went in a storm; he came in the night, and he went in the night; he came nobody knows whence, and he has gone nobody knows where. For aught I know he has gone to sea once more on his chest, and may land to bother some people on the other side of the world! Though it's a thousand pities," added he, "if he has gone to Davy Jones' locker, that he had not left his own locker behind him."

"His locker! St Nicholas preserve us!" cried Peechy Prauw. "I'd not have had that sea-chest in the house for any money; I'll warrant he'd come racketing after it at nights, and making a haunted house of the inn. And, as to his going to sea in his chest, I recollect what happened to Skipper Onderdonk's ship on his voyage from Amsterdam.

"The boatswain died during a storm, so they wrapped him up in a sheet, and put him in his own sea-chest, and threw him overboard; but they neglected in their hurry-skurry to say prayers over him—and the storm raged and roared louder than ever, and they saw the dead man seated in his chest, with his shroud for a sail, coming hard after the ship; and the sea breaking before him in great sprays like fire; and there they kept scudding day after day, and night after night, expecting every moment to go to wreck; and every night they saw the dead boatswain in his sea-chest trying to get up with them, and they heard his whistle above the blasts of wind, and he seemed to send great seas mountain high after them, that would have swamped the ship if they had not put up the dead-lights. And so it went on till they lost sight of him in the fogs off Newfoundland, and supposed he had veered ship and stood for Dead Man's Isle. So much for burying a man at sea without saying prayers over him."

The thundergust which had hitherto detained the company was now at an end. The cuckoo clock in the hall told midnight; every one pressed to depart, for seldom was such a late hour of the night trespassed on by these quiet burghers. As they sallied forth, they found the heavens once more serene. The storm which had lately obscured them had rolled away, and lay piled up in fleecy masses on the horizon, lighted up by the bright crescent of the moon, which looked like a little silver lamp hung up in a palace of clouds.

The dismal occurrence of the night, and the dismal narrations they had made, had left a superstitious feeling in every mind. They cast a fearful glance at the spot where the buccaneer had disappeared, almost expecting to see him sailing on his chest in the cool moonshine. The trembling rays glittered along the waters, but all was placid; and the current dimpled over the spot where he had gone down. The party huddled together in a little crowd as they repaired homewards; particularly when they passed a lonely field where a man had been murdered; and even the sexton, who had to complete his journey alone, though accustomed, one would think, to ghosts and goblins, went a long way round, rather than pass by his own church-yard.

Wolfert Webber had now carried home a fresh stock of stories and notions to ruminate upon. These accounts of pots of money and Spanish treasures, buried here and there and every where, about the rocks and bays of these wild shores, made him almost dizzy. "Blessed St. Nicholas!" ejaculated he half aloud, "is it not possible to come upon one of these golden hoards, and to make one's self rich in a twinkling? How hard that I most go on, delving and delving, day in and day out, merely to make a morsel of bread, when one lucky stroke of a spade might enable me to ride in my carriage for the rest of my life?"

As he turned over in his thoughts all that had been told of the singular adventure of the negro fisherman, his imagination gave a totally different complexion to the tale. He saw in the gang of red-caps nothing but a crew of pirates burying their spoils, and his cupidity was once more awakened by the possibility of at length getting on the traces of some of this lurking wealth. Indeed, his infected fancy tinged every thing with gold. He felt like the greedy inhabitant of Bagdad, when his eyes, had been greased with the magic ointment of the dervish, that gave him to see all the treasures of the earth. Caskets of buried jewels, chests of ingots, and barrels of outlandish coins, seemed to court him from their concealments, and supplicate him to relieve them from their untimely graves.

On making private inquiries about the grounds said to be haunted by Father Red-cap, he was more and more confirmed in his surmise. He learned that the place had several times been visited by experienced money-diggers, who had heard black Sam's story, though none of them had met with success. On the contrary, they had always been dogged with ill-luck of some kind or other, in consequence, as Wolfert concluded, of not going to work at the proper time, and with the proper ceremonials. The last attempt had been made by Cobus Quackenbos, who dug for a whole night, and met with incredible difficulty, for as fast as he threw one shovel full of earth out of the hole, two were thrown in by invisible hands. He succeeded so far, however, as to uncover an iron chest, when there was a terrible roaring, ramping, and raging of uncouth figures about the hole, and at length a shower of blows, dealt by invisible cudgels, fairly belabored him off of the forbidden ground. This Cobus Quackenbos had declared on his death-bed, so that there could not be any doubt of it. He was a man that had devoted many years of his life to money-digging, and it was thought would have ultimately succeeded, had he not died recently of a brain-fever in the alms-house.

Wolfert Webber was now in a worry of trepidation and impatience; fearful lest some rival adventurer should get a scent of the buried gold. He determined privately to seek out the black fisherman, and get him to serve as guide to the place where he had witnessed the mysterious scene of interment. Sam was easily found; for he was one of those old habitual beings that live about a neighborhood until they wear themselves a place in the public mind, and become, in a manner, public characters. There was not an unlucky urchin about town that did not know Sam the fisherman, and think that he had a right to play his tricks upon the old negro. Sam had led an amphibious life for more than half a century, about the shores of the bay, and the fishing-grounds of the Sound. He passed the greater part of his time on and in the water, particularly about Hell-gate; and might have been taken, in bad weather, for one of the hobgoblins that used to haunt that strait. There would he be seen, at all times, and in all weathers; sometimes in his skiff, anchored among the eddies, or prowling, like a shark about some wreck, where the fish are supposed to be most abundant. Sometimes seated on a rock from hour to hour looking in the mist and drizzle, like a solitary heron watching for its prey. He was well acquainted with every hole and corner of the Sound; from the Wallabout to Hell-gate, and from Hell-gate even unto the Devil's Stepping-Stones; and it was even affirmed that he knew all the fish in the river by their Christian names.

Wolfert found him at his cabin, which was not much larger than a tolerable dog-house. It was rudely constructed of fragments of wrecks and drift-wood, and built on the rocky shore, at the foot of the old fort, just about what at present forms the point of the Battery. A "most ancient and fish-like smell" pervaded the place. Oars, paddles, and fishing-rods were leaning against the wall of the fort; a net was spread on the sands to dry; a skiff was drawn up on the beach, and at the door of his cabin was Mud Sam himself, indulging in the true negro luxury of sleeping in the sunshine.

Many years had passed away since the time of Sam's youthful adventure, and the snows of many a winter had grizzled the knotty wool upon his head. He perfectly recollected the circumstances, however, for he had often been called upon to relate them, though in his version of the story he differed in many points from Peechy Prauw; as is not unfrequently the case with authentic historians. As to the subsequent researches of money-diggers, Sam knew nothing about them; they were matters quite out of his line; neither did the cautious Wolfert care to disturb his thoughts on that point. His only wish was to secure the old fisherman as a pilot to the spot, and this was readily effected. The long time that had intervened since his nocturnal adventure had effaced all Sam's awe of the place, and the promise of a trifling reward roused him at once from his sleep and his sunshine.

The tide was adverse to making the expedition by water, and Wolfert was too impatient to get to the land of promise, to wait for its turning; they set off, therefore, by land. A walk of four or five miles brought them to the edge of a wood, which at that time covered the greater part of the eastern side of the island. It was just beyond the pleasant region of Bloomen-dael. Here they struck into a long lane, straggling among trees and bushes, very much overgrown with weeds and mullen-stalks, as if but seldom used, and so completely overshadowed as to enjoy but a kind of twilight. Wild vines entangled the trees and flaunted in their faces; brambles and briers caught their clothes as they passed; the garter-snake glided across their path; the spotted toad hopped and waddled before them, and the restless cat-bird mewed at them from every thicket. Had Wolfert Webber been deeply read in romantic legend, he might have fancied himself entering upon forbidden, enchanted ground; or that these were some of the guardians set to keep watch upon buried treasure. As it was, the loneliness of the place, and the wild stories connected with it, had their effect upon his mind.

On reaching the lower end of the lane, they found themselves near the shore of the Sound in a kind of amphitheatre, surrounded by forest trees. The area had once been a grassplot, but was now shagged with briers and rank weeds. At one end, and just on the river bank, was a ruined building, little better than a heap of rubbish, with a stack of chimneys rising like a solitary tower out of the centre. The current of the Sound rushed along just below it; with wildly grown trees drooping their branches into its waves.

Wolfert had not a doubt that this was the haunted house of Father Red-cap, and called to mind the story of Peechy Prauw. The evening was approaching, and the light falling dubiously among these woody places, gave a melancholy tone to the scene, well calculated to foster any lurking feeling of awe or superstition. The night-hawk, wheeling about in the highest regions of the air, emitted his peevish, boding cry. The woodpecker gave a lonely tap now and then on some hollow tree, and the fire-bird[1] streamed by them with his deep-red plumage.

They now came to an inclosure that had once been a garden. It extended along the foot of a rocky ridge, but was little better than a wilderness of weeds, with here and there a matted rose-bush, or a peach or plum-tree grown wild and ragged, and covered with moss. At the lower end of the garden they passed a kind of vault in the side of a bank, facing the water. It had the look of a root-house. The door, though decayed, was still strong, and appeared to have been recently patched up. Wolfert pushed it open.

---

1. Orchard Oriole.

It gave a harsh grating upon its hinges, and striking against something like a box, a rattling sound ensued, and a skull rolled on the floor. Wolfert drew back shuddering, but was reassured on being informed by the negro that this was a family-vault, belonging to one of the old Dutch families that owned this estate; an assertion corroborated by the sight of coffins of various sizes piled within. Sam had been familiar with all these scenes when a boy, and now knew that he could not be far from the place of which they were in quest.

They now made their way to the water's edge, scrambling along ledges of rocks that overhung the waves, and obliged often to hold by shrubs and grape-vines to avoid slipping into the deep and hurried stream. At length they came to a small cove, or rather indent of the shore. It was protected by steep rocks, and overshadowed by a thick copse of oaks and chestnuts, so as to be sheltered and almost concealed. The beach shelved gradually within the cove, but the current swept deep and black and rapid along its jutting points. The negro paused; raised his remnant of a hat, and scratched his grizzled poll for a moment, as he regarded this nook; then suddenly clapping his hands, he stepped exultingly forward, and pointed to a large iron ring, stapled firmly in the rock, just where a broad shelf of stone furnished a commodious landing-place. It was the very spot where the red-caps had landed. Tears had changed the more perishable features of the scene; but rock and iron yield slowly to the influence of time. On looking more closely, Wolfert remarked three crosses cut in the rock just above the ring, which had no doubt some mysterious signification. Old Sam now readily recognized the overhanging rock under which his skiff had been sheltered during the thundergust. To follow up the course which the midnight gang had taken, however, was a harder task. His mind had been so much taken up on that eventful occasion by the persons of the drama, as to pay but little attention to the scenes; and these places look so different by night and day. After wandering about for some time, however, they came to an opening among the trees which Sam thought resembled the place. There was a ledge of rock of moderate height like a wall on one side, which he thought might be the very ridge whence he had overlooked the diggers. Wolfert examined it narrowly, and at length discovered three crosses similar to those above the iron ring, cut deeply into the face of the rock, but nearly obliterated by moss that had grown over them. His heart leaped with joy, for he doubted not they were the private marks of the buccaneers. All now that remained was to ascertain the precise spot where the treasure lay buried; for otherwise he might dig at random in the neighborhood of the crosses, without coming upon the spoils, and he had already had enough of such profitless labor. Here, however, the old negro was perfectly at a loss, and indeed perplexed him by a variety of opinions; for his recollections were all confused. Sometimes he declared it must have been at the foot of a mulberry-tree hard by; then beside a great white stone; then under a small green knoll, a short distance from the ledge of rocks; until at length Wolfert became as bewildered as himself.

The shadows of evening were now spreading themselves over the woods, and rock and tree began to mingle together. It was evidently too late to attempt any thing farther at present; and, indeed, Wolfert had come unprovided with implements to prosecute his researches. Satisfied, therefore, with having ascertained the place, he took note of all its landmarks, that he might recognize it again, and set out on his return homewards, resolved to prosecute this golden enterprise without delay.

The leading anxiety which had hitherto absorbed every feeling, being now in some measure appeased, fancy began to wander, and to conjure up a thousand shapes and chimeras as he returned through this haunted region. Pirates hanging in chains seemed to swing from every tree, and he almost expected to see some Spanish Don, with his throat cut from ear to ear, rising slowly out of the ground, and shaking the ghost of a money-bag.

Their way back lay through the desolate garden, and Wolfert's nerves had arrived at so sensitive a state that the flitting of a bird, the rustling of a leaf, or the falling of a nut, was enough to startle him. As they entered the confines of the garden, they caught sight of a figure at a distance advancing slowly up one of the walks, and bending under the weight of a burden. They paused and regarded him attentively. He wore what appeared to be a woollen cap, and still more alarming, of a most sanguinary red.

The figure moved slowly on, ascended the bank, and stopped at the very door of the sepulchral vault. Just before entering it he looked around. What was the affright of Wolfert, when he recognized the grisly visage of the drowned buccaneer! He uttered an ejaculation of horror. The figure slowly raised his iron fist, and shook it with a terrible menace. Wolfert did not pause to see any more, but hurried off as fast as his legs could carry him, nor was Sam slow in following at his heels, having all his ancient terrors revived. Away, then, did they scramble through bush and brake, horribly frightened at every bramble that tugged at their skirts, nor did they pause to breathe, until they had blundered their way through this perilous wood, and fairly reached the high road to the city.

Several days elapsed before Wolfert could summon courage enough to prosecute the enterprise, so much had he been dismayed by the apparition, whether living or dead, of the grisly buccaneer. In the meantime, what a conflict of mind did he suffer! He neglected all his concerns, was moody and restless all day, lost his appetite, wandered in his thoughts and words, and committed a thousand blunders. His rest was broken; and when he fell asleep, the nightmare, in shape of a huge money-bag, sat squatted upon his breast. He babbled about incalculable sums; fancied himself engaged in money-digging; threw the bedclothes right and left, in the idea that he was shovelling away the dirt; groped under the bed in quest of the treasure, and lugged forth, as he supposed, an inestimable pot of gold.

Dame Webber and her daughter were in despair at what they conceived a returning touch of insanity. There are two family oracles, one or other of which Dutch housewives consult in all cases of great doubt and perplexity—the dominie and the doctor. In the present instance they repaired to the doctor. There was at that time a little dark mouldy man of medicine, famous among the old wives of the Manhattoes for his skill, not only in the healing art, but in all matters of strange and mysterious nature. His name was Dr. Knipperhausen, but he was more commonly known by the appellation of the High German Doctor.[2] To him did the poor women repair for counsel and assistance touching the mental vagaries of Wolfert Wehber.

They found the doctor seated in his little study, dad in his dark camlet robe of knowledge, with his black velvet cap; after the manner of Boorhaave, Van Helmont, and other medical sages; a pair of green spectacles set in black horn upon his clubbed nose, and poring over a German folio that reflected back the darkness of his physiognomy. The doctor listened to their statement of the symptoms of Wolfert's malady with profound attention; but when they came to mention his raving about buried money, the little man pricked up his ears. Alas, poor women! they little knew the aid they had called in.

Dr. Knipperhausen had been half his life engaged in seeking the short cuts to fortune, in quest of which so many a long lifetime is wasted. He had passed some years of his youth among the Harz mountains of Germany, and had derived much valuable instruction from the miners, touching the mode of seeking treasure buried in the earth.

---

2. The same, no doubt, of whom mention is made in the history of Dolph Heyliger.

He had prosecuted his studies also under a travelling sage who united the mysteries of medicine with magic and legerdemain. His mind therefore had become stored with all kinds of mystic lore; he had dabbled a little in astrology, alchemy, divination; knew how to detect stolen money, and to tell where springs of water lay hidden; in a word, by the dark nature of his knowledge he had acquired the name of the High German Doctor, which is pretty nearly equivalent to that of necromancer. The doctor had often heard rumors of treasure being buried in various parts of the island, and had long been anxious to get on the traces of it. No sooner were Wolfert's waking and sleeping vagaries confided to him, than he beheld in them the confirmed symptoms of a case of money-digging, and lost no time in probing it to the bottom. Wolfert had long been sorely oppressed in mind by the golden secret, and as a family physician is a kind of father confessor, he was glad of any opportunity of unburdening himself. So far from curing, the doctor caught the malady from his patient. The circumstances unfolded to him awakened all his cupidity; he had not a doubt of money being buried somewhere in the neighborhood of the mysterious crosses, and offered to join Wolfert in the search. He informed him that much secrecy and caution must be observed in enterprises of the kind; that money is only to be digged for at night; with certain forms and ceremonies; the burning of drugs; the repeating of mystic words, and above all, that the seekers must first be provided with a divining rod, which had the wonderful property of pointing to the very spot on the surface of the earth under which treasure lay hidden. As the doctor had given much of his mind to these matters, he charged himself with all the necessary preparations, and, as the quarter of the moon was propitious, he undertook to have the divining rod ready by a certain night.[3]

---

3. The following note was found appended to this passage in the hand-writing of Mr. Knickerbocker. "There has been much written against the divining rod by those light minds who are ever ready to scoff at the mysteries of nature; but I fully join with Dr. Knipperhausen in giving it my faith. I shall not insist upon its efficacy in discovering the concealment of stolen goods, the boundary stones of fields, the traces of robbers and murderers, or even the existence of subterraneous springs and streams of water: albeit, I think these properties not to be readily discredited; but of its potency in discovering veins of precious metal, and hidden sums of money and jewels, I have not the least doubt. Some said that the rod turned only in the hands of persons who had been born in particular months of the year; hence astrologers had recourse to planetary influence when they would procure a talisman. Others declared that the properties of the rod were either an effect of chance, or the fraud of the holder, or the work of the devil. Thus saith the reverend father Gaspard Serbett in his Treatise on Magic: 'Propter hæc et similia argumenta audacter ego promisero vim conversivam virgulæ bifurcatæ nequaquam naturalem esse, sed vel casu vel fhinde virgulam tractantis vel ope diaboli,' &c.

Wolfert's heart leaped with joy at having met with so learned and able a coadjutor. Every thing went on secretly, but swimmingly. The doctor had many consultations with his patient, and the good woman of the household landed the comforting effect of his visits. In the meantime the wonderful divining rod, that great key to nature's secrets, was duly prepared. The doctor had thumbed over all his books of knowledge for the occasion; and the black fisherman was engaged to take them in his skiff to the scene of enterprise; to work with spade and pickaxe in unearthing the treasure; and to freight his bark with the weighty spoils they were certain of finding.

At length the appointed night arrived for this perilous undertaking. Before Wolfert left his home he counselled his wife and daughter to go to bed and feel no alarm if he should not return during the night. Like reasonable women, on being told not to feel alarm they fell immediately into a panic. They saw at once by his manner that something unusual was in agitation; all their fears about the unsettled state of his mind were revived with ten-fold force: they hung about him, entreating him not to expose himself to the night air, but all in vain. When once Wolfert was mounted on his hobby, it was no easy matter to get him out of the saddle. It was a clear starlight night, when he issued out of the portal of the Webber palace. He wore a large flapped hat tied under the chin with a handkerchief of his daughter's, to secure him from the night damp, while Dame Webber threw her long red cloak about his shoulders, and fastened it round his neck.

The doctor had been no less carefully armed and accoutred by his housekeeper, the vigilant Frau Ilsy; and sallied forth in his camlet robe by way of surcoat; his black velvet cap under his cocked hat, a thick clasped book under his arm, a basket of drugs and dried herbs in one hand, and in the other the miraculous rod of divination.

"Georgius Agricola also was of opinion that it was a mere delusion of the devil to inveigle the avaricious and unwary into his clutches, and in his treatise 'de re Metallica,' lays particular stress on the mysterious words pronounced by those persons who employed the divining rod during his time. But I make not a doubt that the divining rod is one of those secrets of natural magic, the mystery of which is to be explained by the sympathies existing between physical things operated upon by the planets, and rendered efficacious by the strong faith of the individual. Let the divining rod be properly gathered at the proper time of the moon, cut into the proper form, used with the necessary ceremonies, and with a perfect faith in its efficacy, and I can confidently recommend it to my fellow-citizens as an infallible means of discovering the various places on the Island of the Manhattoes where treasure hath been buried in the olden time. D. K."

The great church clock struck ten as Wolfert and the doctor passed by the churchyard, and the watchman bawled in hoarse voice a long and doleful "all's well!" A deep sleep had already fallen upon this primitive little burgh: nothing disturbed this awful silence, excepting now and then the bark of some profligate night-walking dog, or the serenade of some romantic cat. It is true, Wolfert fancied more than once that he heard the sound of a stealthy footfall at a distance behind them; but it might have been merely the echo of their own steps along the quiet streets. He thought also at one time that he saw a tall figure skulking after them—stopping when they stopped, and moving on as they proceeded; but the dim and uncertain lamplight threw such vague gleams and shadows, that this might all have been mere fancy.

They found the old fisherman waiting for them, smoking his pipe in the stern of his skiff, which was moored just in front of his little cabin. A pickaxe and spade were lying in the bottom of the boat, with a dark lantern, and a stone bottle of good Dutch courage, in which honest Sam no doubt put even more faith than Dr. Knipperhausen in his drugs.

Thus then did these three worthies embark in their cockle-shell of a skiff upon this nocturnal expedition, with a wisdom and valor equalled only by the three wise men of Gotham, who adventured to sea in a bowl. The tide was rising and running rapidly up the Sound. The current bore them along, almost without the aid of an oar. The profile of the town lay all in shadow. Here and there a light feebly glimmered from some sick chamber, or from the cabin window of some vessel at anchor in the stream. Not a cloud obscured the deep starry firmament, the lights of which wavered on the surface of the placid river; and a shooting meteor, streaking its pale course in the very direction they were taking, was interpreted by the doctor into a most propitious omen.

In a little while they glided by the point of Corlaer's Hook with the rural inn which had been the scene of such night adventures. The family had retired to rest and the house was dark and still. Wolfert felt a chill pass over him as they passed the point where the buccaneer had disappeared. He pointed it out to Dr. Knipperhausen. While regarding it, they thought they saw a boat actually lurking at the very place; but the shore cast such a shadow over the border of the water that they could discern nothing distinctly. They had not proceeded far when they heard the low sounds of distant oars, as if cautiously pulled. Sam plied his oars with redoubled vigor, and knowing all the eddies and currents of the stream, soon left their followers, if such they were, far astern. In a little while they stretched across Turtle bay and Kip's bay, then shrouded themselves in the deep shadows of the Manhattan shore, and glided swiftly along, secure from observation. At length the negro shot his skiff into a little cove, darkly embowered by trees, and made it fast to the well-known iron ring. They now landed, and lighting the lantern, gathered their various implements and proceeded slowly through the bushes. Every sound startled them, even that of their own footsteps among the dry leaves; and the hooting of a screech-owl, from the shattered chimney of the neighboring ruin, made their blood run cold.

In spite of all Wolfert's caution in taking note of the land-marks, it was some time before they could find the open place among the trees, where the treasure was supposed to be buried. At length they came to the ledge of rock; and on examining its surface by the aid of the lantern, Wolfert recognized the three mystic crosses. Their hearts beat quick, for the momentous trial was at hand that was to determine their hopes.

The lantern was now held by Wolfert Webber, while the doctor produced the divining rod. It was a forked twig, one end of which was grasped firmly in each hand, while the centre, forming the stem, pointed perpendicularly upwards. The doctor moved this wand about, within a certain distance of the earth, from place to place, but for some time without any effect, while Wolfert kept the light of the lantern tamed full upon it, and watched it with the most breathless interest. At length the rod began slowly to turn. The doctor grasped it with greater earnestness, his hands trembling with the agitation of his mind. The wand continued to turn gradually, until at length the stem had reversed its position, and pointed perpendicularly downward, and remained pointing to one spot as fixedly as the needle to the pole.

"This is the spot!" said the doctor, in an almost inaudible tone.

Wolfert's heart was in his throat.

"Shall I dig?" said the negro, grasping the spade.

"*Pots tausends*, no!" replied the little doctor, hastily. He now ordered his companions to keep close by him, and to maintain the most inflexible silence. That certain precautions must be taken and ceremonies used to prevent the evil spirits which kept about buried treasure from doing them any harm. He then drew a circle about the place, enough to include the whole party. He next gathered dry twigs and leaves and made a fire, upon which he threw certain drugs and dried herbs which he had brought in his basket. A thick smoke rose, diffusing a potent odor, savoring marvellously of brimstone and asafœtida, which, however grateful it might be to the olfactory nerves of spirits, nearly strangled poor Wolfert, and produced a fit of coupling and wheezing that made the whole grove resound. Doctor Knipperhausen then unclasped the volume which he had brought under his arm, which was printed in red and black characters in German text. While Wolfert held the lantern, the doctor, by the aid of his spectacles, read off several forms of conjuration in Latin and German. He then ordered Sam to seize the pickaxe and proceed to work. The close-bound soil gave obstinate signs of not having been disturbed for many a year. After having picked his way through the surface, Sam came to a bed of sand and gravel, which he threw briskly to right and left with the spade.

"Hark!" said Wolfert, who fancied he heard a trampling among the dry leaves, and a rustling through the bushes. Sam paused for a moment, and they listened. No footstep was near. The bat flitted by them in silence; a bird, roused from its roost by the light which glared up among the trees, flew circling about the flame. In the profound stillness of the woodland, they could distinguish the current rippling along the rocky shore, and the distant murmuring and roaring of Hell-gate.

The negro continued his labors, and had already digged a considerable hole. The doctor stood on the edge, reading formulæ every now and then from his black-letter volume, or throwing more drugs and herbs upon the fire; while Wolfert bent anxiously over the pit, watching every stroke of the spade. Any one witnessing the scene thus lighted up by fire, lantern, and the reflection of Wolfert's red mantle, might have mistaken the little doctor for some foul magician, busied in his incantations, and the grizzly-headed negro for some swart goblin, obedient to his commands.

At length the spade of the fisherman struck upon something that sounded hollow. The sound vibrated to Wolfert's heart. He struck his spade again.—

"'Tis a chest," said Sam.

"Full of gold, I'll warrant it!" cried Wolfert, clasping his hands with rapture.

Scarcely had he uttered the words when a sound from above caught his ear. He cast up his eyes, and lo! by the expiring light of the fire he beheld, just over the disk of the rock, what appeared to be the grim visage of the drowned buccaneer, grinning hideously down upon him.

Wolfert gave a loud cry, and let fall the lantern. His panic communicated itself to his companions. The negro leaped out of the hole; the doctor dropped his book and basket and began to pray in German. All was horror and confusion. The fire was scattered about, the lantern extinguished. In their hurry-scurry they ran against and confounded one another. They fancied a legion of hobgoblins let loose upon them, and that they saw, by the fitful gleams of the scattered embers, strange figures, in red caps, gibbering and ramping around them. The doctor ran one way, the negro another, and Wolfert made for the water side. As he plunged struggling onwards through brush and brake, he heard the tread of some one in pursuit. He scrambled frantically forward. The footsteps gained upon him. He felt himself grasped by his cloak, when suddenly his pursuer was attacked in turn: a fierce fight and struggle ensued—a pistol was discharged that lit up rock and bush for a second, and showed two figures grappling together—all was then darker than ever. The contest continued—the combatants clinched each other, and panted, and groaned, and rolled among the rocks. There was snarling and growling as of a cur, mingled with curses, in which Wolfert fancied he could recognize the voice of the buccaneer. He would fain have fled, but he was on the brink of a precipice, and could go no farther.

Again the parties were on their feet; again there was a tugging and struggling, as if strength alone could decide the combat, until one was precipitated from the brow of the cliff, and sent headlong into the deep stream that whirled below. Wolfert heard the plunge, and a kind of strangling, bubbling murmur, but the darkness of the night hid every thing from him, and the swiftness of the current swept every thing instantly out of hearing. One of the combatants was disposed of, but whether friend or foe, Wolfert could not tell, nor whether they might not both be foes. He heard the survivor approach, and his terror revived. He saw, where the profile of the rocks rose against the horizon, a human form advancing. He could not be mistaken: it must be the buccaneer. Whither should he fly!—a precipice was on one aide—a murderer on the other. The enemy approached—he was close at hand. Wolfert attempted to let himself down the face of the cliff. His cloak caught in a thorn that grew on the edge. He was jerked from off his feet, and held dangling in the air, half-choked by the string with which his careful wife had fastened the garment round his neck. Wolfert thought his last moment was arrived; already had he committed his soul to St. Nicholas, when the string broke, and he tumbled down the bank, bumping from rock to rock, and bush to bush, and leaving the red cloak fluttering like a bloody banner in the air.

It was a long while before Wolfert came to himself. When he opened his eyes, the ruddy streaks of morning were already shooting up the sky. He found himself grievously battered, and lying in the bottom of a boat. He attempted to sit up, but was too sore and stiff to move. A voice requested him in friendly accents to lie still. He turned his eyes towards the speaker: it was Dirk Waldron. He had dogged the party, at the earnest request of Dame Webber and her daughter, who with the laudable curiosity of their sex, had pried into the secret consultations of Wolfert and the doctor. Dirk had been completely distanced in following the light skiff of the fisherman, and had just come in time to rescue the poor money-digger from his pursuer.

Thus ended this perilous enterprise. The doctor and Black Sam severally found their way back to the Manhattoes, each having some dreadful tale of peril to relate. As to poor Wolfert, instead of returning in triumph laden with bags of gold, he was borne home on a shutter, followed by a rabble-rout of curious urchins. His wife and daughter saw the dismal pageant from a distance, and alarmed the neighborhood with their cries: they thought the poor man had suddenly settled the great debt of nature in one of his wayward moods. Finding him, however, still living, they had him speedily to bed, and a jury of old matrons of the neighborhood assembled, to determine how he should be doctored. The whole town was in a buzz with the story of the money-diggers. Many repaired to the scene of the previous night's adventures: but though they found the very place of the digging, they discovered nothing that compensated them for their trouble. Some say they found the fragments of an oaken chest, and an iron pot-lid, which savored strongly of hidden money; and that in the old family vault there were traces of bales and boxes, but this is all very dubious.

In fact, the secret of all this story has never to this day been discovered: whether any treasure were ever actually buried at that place; whether, if so, it were carried off at night by those who had buried it; or whether it still remains there under the guardianship of gnomes and spirits until it shall be properly sought for, is all matter of conjecture. For my part I incline to the latter opinion; and make no doubt that great sums lie buried, both there and in other parts of this island and its neighborhood, ever since the times of the buccaneers and the Dutch colonists; and I would earnestly recommend the search after them to such of my fellow-citizens as are not engaged in any other speculations.

There were many conjectures formed, also, as to who and what was the strange man of the seas who had domineered over the little fraternity at Corlaer's Hook for a time; disappeared so strangely, and reappeared so fearfully. Some supposed him a smuggler stationed at that place to assist his comrades in landing their goods among the rocky coves of the island. Others that he was one of the ancient comrades of Kidd or Bradish, returned to convey away treasures formerly hidden in the vicinity. The only circumstance that throws any thing like a vague light on this mysterious matter, is a report which prevailed of a strange foreign-built shallop, with much the look of a picaroon, having been seen hovering about the Sound for several days without landing or reporting herself, though boats were seen going to and from her at night: and that she was seen standing out of the mouth of the harbor, in the gray of the dawn after the catastrophe of the money-diggers.

I must not omit to mention another report, also, which I confess is rather apocryphal, of the buccaneer, who was supposed to have been drowned, being seen before daybreak, with a lantern in his hand, seated astride of his great sea-chest, and sailing through Hell-gate, which just then began to roar and bellow with redoubled fury.

While all the gossip world was thus filled with talk and rumor, poor Wolfert lay sick and sorrowful in his bed, bruised in body and sorely beaten down in mind. His wife and daughter did all they could to bind up his wounds, both corporal and spiritual. The good old dame never stirred from his bedside, where she sat knitting from morning till night; while his daughter busied herself about him with the fondest care. Nor did they lack assistance from abroad. Whatever may be said of the desertion of friends in distress, they had no complaint of the kind to make. Not an old wife of the neighborhood but abandoned her work to crowd to the mansion of Wolfert Webber, inquire after his health, and the particulars of his story. Not one came moreover without her little pipkin of pennyroyal, sage, balm, or other herb tea, delighted at an opportunity of signalizing her kindness and her doctorship. What drenchings did not the poor Wolfert undergo, and all in vain! It was a moving sight to behold him wasting away day by day; growing thinner and thinner, and ghastlier and ghastlier, and staring with rueful visage from under an old patchwork counterpane, upon the jury of matrons kindly assembled to sigh and groan and look unhappy around him.

Dick Waldron was the only being that seemed to shed a ray of sunshine into this house of mourning. He came in with cheery look and manly spirit, and tried to reanimate the expiring heart of the poor money-digger, but it was all in vain. Wolfert was completely done over. If any thing was waiting to complete his despair, it was a notice served upon him in the midst of his distress, that the corporation were about to run a new street through the very centre of his cabbage-garden. He now saw nothing before him but poverty and ruin; his last reliance, the garden of his forefathers, was to be laid waste, and what then was to become of his poor wife and child?

His eyes filled with tears as they followed the dutiful Amy out of the room one morning. Dirk Waldron was seated beside him; Wolfert grasped his hand, pointed after his daughter, and for the first time since his illness, broke the silence he had maintained.

"I am going!" said he, shaking his head feebly, "and when I am gone—my poor daughter—"

"Leave her to me, father!" said Dirk, manfully—"I'll take care of her!"

Wolfert looked up in the face of the cheery, strapping youngster, and saw there was none better able to take care of a woman.

"Enough," said he—"she is yours!—and now fetch me a lawyer—let me make my will and die."

The lawyer was brought—a dapper, bustling, round-headed little man, Roorback (or Rollebuck as it was pronounced) by name. At the sight of him the women broke into loud lamentations, for they looked upon the signing of a will as the signing of a death-warrant. Wolfert made a feeble motion for them to be silent. Poor Amy buried her face and her grief in the bed-curtain. Dame Webber resumed her knitting to hide her distress, which betrayed itself however in a pellucid tear, which trickled silently down, and hung at the end of her peaked nose; while the cat, the only unconcerned member of the family, played with the good dame's ball of worsted, as it rolled about the floor.

Wolfert lay on his back, his night-cap drawn over his forehead; his eyes closed; his whole visage the picture of death. He begged the lawyer to be brief, for he felt his end approaching, and that be had no time to lose. The lawyer nibbed his pen, spread out his paper, and prepared to write.

"I give and bequeath," said Wolfert, faintly, "my small farm—"

"What—all!" exclaimed the lawyer.

Wolfert half opened his eyes and looked upon the lawyer.

"Yes—all," said he.

"What! all that great patch of land with cabbages and sunflowers, which the corporation is just going to run a main street through?"

"The same," said Wolfert, with a heavy sigh, and sinking back upon his pillow.

"I wish him joy that inherits it!" said the little lawyer, chuckling and rubbing his hands involuntarily.

"What do you mean?" said Wolfert, again opening his eyes.

"That he'll be one of the richest men in the place!" cried little Rollebuck.

The expiring Wolfert seemed to step back from the threshold of existence: his eyes again lighted up; he raised himself in his bed, shoved back his worsted red night-cap, and stared broadly at the lawyer.

"You don't say so!" exclaimed he.

"Faith, but I do!" rejoined the other. "Why, when that great field and that huge meadow come to be laid out in streets, and cut up into snug building lots—why, whoever owns it need not pull off his hat to the patroon!"

"Say you so?" cried Wolfert, half thrusting one leg out of bed, "why, then I think I'll not make my will yet!"

To the surprise of every body the dying man actually recovered. The vital spark, which had glimmered faintly in the socket, received fresh fuel from the oil of gladness, which the little lawyer poured into his soul. It once more burnt up into a flame.

Give physic to the heart, ye who would revive the body of a spirit-broken man! In a few days Wolfert left his room; in a few days more his table was covered with deeds, plans of streets, and building lots. Little Rollebuck was constantly with him, his right-hand man and adviser; and instead of making his will, assisted in the more agreeable task of making his fortune. In fact Wolfert Webber was one of those worthy Dutch burghers of the Manhattoes whose fortunes have been made, in a manner, in spite of themselves; who have tenaciously held on to their hereditary acres, raising turnips and cabbages about the skirts of the city, hardly able to make both ends meet, until the corporation has cruelly driven streets through their abodes, and they have suddenly awakened out of their lethargy, and, to their astonishment, found themselves rich men.

Before many months had elapsed, a great bustling street passed through the very centre of the Webber garden, just where Wolfert had dreamed of finding a treasure. His golden dream was accomplished; he did indeed find an unlooked-for source of wealth; for, when his paternal lands were distributed into building lots, and rented out to safe tenants, instead of producing a paltry crop of cabbages, they returned him an abundant crop of rents; insomuch that on quarter-day, it was a goodly sight to see his tenants knocking at his door, from morning till night, each with a little round-bellied bag of money, a golden produce of the soil.

The ancient mansion of his forefathers was still kept up; but instead of being a little yellow-fronted Dutch house in a garden, it now stood boldly in the midst of a street, the grand house of the neighborhood; for Wolfert enlarged it with a wing on each side, and a cupola or tea-room on top, where he might climb up and smoke his pipe in hot weather; and in the course of time the whole mansion was overrun by the chubby-faced progeny of Amy Webber and Dirk Waldron.

As Wolfert waxed old, and rich, and corpulent, he also set up a great gingerbread-colored carriage, drawn by a pair of black Flanders mares, with tails that swept the ground; and to commemorate the origin of his greatness, he had for his crest, a full-blown cabbage painted on the panels, with the pithy motto Alles Kopf, that is to say, ALL HEAD; meaning thereby that he had risen by sheer head-work.

To fill the measure of his greatness, in the fulness of time the renowned Ramm Rapelye slept with his fathers, and Wolfert Webber succeeded to the leather-bottomed arm-chair, in the inn parlor at Corlaer's Hook; where he long reigned greatly honored and respected, insomuch that he was never known to tell a story without its being believed, nor to utter a joke without its being laughed at.

WOLFERT'S ROOST AND OTHER PAPERS

Wolfert's Roost

CHRONICLE I

ABOUT FIVE-AND-TWENTY MILES FROM THE ANCIENT AND RENOWNED CITY of Manhattan, formerly called New-Amsterdam, and vulgarly called New-York, on the eastern bank of that expansion of the Hudson, known among Dutch mariners of yore, as the Tappan Zee, being in fact the great Mediterranean Sea of the New-Netherlands, stands a little old-fashioned stone mansion, all made up of gable-ends, and as full of angles and corners as an old cocked hat. It is said, in fact, to have been modelled after the cocked hat of Peter the Headstrong, as the Escurial was modelled after the gridiron of the blessed St. Lawrence. Though but of small dimensions, yet, like many small people, it is of mighty spirit, and values itself greatly on its antiquity, being one of the oldest edifices, for its size, in the whole country. It claims to be an ancient seat of empire, I may rather say an empire in itself, and like all empires, great and small, has had its grand historical epochs. In speaking of this doughty and valorous little pile, I shall call it by its usual appellation of "The Roost"; though that is a name given to it in modern days, since it became the abode of the white man.

Its origin, in truth, dates far back in that remote region commonly called the fabulous age, in which vulgar fact becomes mystified, and tinted up with delectable fiction. The eastern shore of the Tappan Sea was inhabited in those days by an unsophisticated race, existing in all the simplicity of nature; that is to say, they lived by hunting and fishing, and recreated themselves occasionally with a little tomahawking and scalping. Each stream that flows down from the hills into the Hudson, had its petty sachem, who ruled over a hand's breadth of forest on either side, and had his seat of government at its mouth. The chieftain who ruled at the Roost, was not merely a great warrior, but a medicine-man, or prophet, or conjurer, for they all mean the same thing in Indian parlance. Of his fighting propensities, evidences still remain, in various arrow-heads of flint, and stone battle-axes, occasionally digged up about the Roost: of his wizard powers, we have a token in a spring which wells up at the foot of the bank, on the very margin of the river, which, it is said, was gifted by him with rejuvenating powers, something like the renowned Fountain of Youth in the Floridas, so anxiously but vainly sought after by the veteran Ponce de Leon. This story, however, is stoutly contradicted by an old Dutch matter-of-fact tradition, which declares that the spring in question was smuggled over from Holland in a churn, by Femmetie Van Blarcom, wife of Goosen Garret Van Blarcom, one of the first settlers, and that she took it up by night, unknown to her husband, from beside their farm-house near Rotterdam; being sure she should find no water equal to it in the new country—and she was right.

The wizard sachem had a great passion for discussing territorial questions, and settling boundary lines, in other words, he had the spirit of annexation; this kept him in continual feud with the neighboring sachems, each of whom stood up stoutly for his handbreadth of territory; so that there is not a petty stream nor rugged hill in the neighborhood, that has not been the subject of long talks and hard battles. The sachem, however, as has been observed, was a medicine-man, as well as warrior, and vindicated his claims by arts as well as arms; so that, by dint of a little hard fighting here, and hocus pocus (or diplomacy) there, he managed to extend his boundary line from field to field and stream to stream, until it brought him into collision with the powerful sachem of Sing Sing.[1] Many were the sharp conflicts between these rival chieftains for the sovereignty of a winding valley, a favorite hunting ground watered by a beautiful stream called the Pocantico. Many were the ambuscades, surprisals, and deadly onslaughts that took place among its fastnesses, of which it grieves me much that I cannot pursue the details, for the gratification of those gentle but bloody-minded readers, of both sexes, who delight in the romance of the tomahawk and scalping-knife. Suffice it to say, that the wizard chieftain was at length victorious, though his victory is attributed, in Indian tradition, to a great medicine, or charm, by which he laid the sachem of Sing-Sing and his warriors asleep among the rocks and recesses of the valley, where they remain asleep to the present day, with their bows and war-clubs beside them. This was the origin of that potent and drowsy spell, which still prevails

---

1. A corruption of the Old Indian name, O-sin-sing. Some have rendered it, O-sin-song, or O-sing-song; in token of its being a great market town; where any thing may be had for a mere song. Its present melodious alteration to Sing Sing is said to have been made in compliment to a Yankee singing-master, who taught the inhabitants the art of singing through the nose.

over the valley of the Pocantico, and which has gained it the well-merited appellation of Sleepy Hollow. Often, in secluded and quiet parts of that valley, where the stream is overhung by dark woods and rocks, the ploughman, on some calm and sunny day, as he shouts to his oxen, is surprised at hearing faint shouts from the hill-sides in reply; being it is said, the spell-bound warriors, who half start from their rocky couches and grasp their weapons, but sink to sleep again.

The conquest of the Pocantico was the last triumph of the wizard sachem. Notwithstanding all his medicines and charms, he fell in battle, in attempting to extend his boundary line to the east, so as to take in the little wild valley of the Sprain, and his grave is still shown, near the banks of that pastoral stream. He left, however, a great empire to his successors, extending along the Tappan Sea, from Yonkers quite to Sleepy Hollow, and known in old records and maps by the Indian name of Wicquaes-Keck.

The wizard Sachem was succeeded by a line of chiefs of whom nothing remarkable remains on record. One of them was the very individual on whom master Hendrick Hudson and his mate Robert Juet made that sage experiment gravely recorded by the latter, in the narrative of the discovery.

"Our master and his mate determined to try some of the cheefe men of the country, whether they had any treacherie in them. So they took them down into the cabin, and gave them so much wine and aqua vitæ, that they were all very merrie; one of them had his wife with him, which sate so modestly as any of our countrywomen would do in a strange place. In the end, one of them was drunke; and that was strange to them, for they could not tell how to take it."[2]

How far master Hendrick Hudson and his worthy mate carried their experiment with the sachem's wife, is not recorded, neither does the curious Robert Juet make any mention of the after consequences of this grand moral test; tradition, however, affirms that the sachem, on landing, gave his modest spouse a hearty rib-roasting, according to the connubial discipline of the aboriginals; it farther affirms, that he remained a hard drinker to the day of his death, trading away all his lands, acre by acre, for aqua vitæ; by which means the Roost and all its domains, from Yonkers to Sleepy Hollow, came, in the regular course of trade, and by right of purchase, into the possession of the Dutchmen.

---

2. See Juet's Journal. Purchas' Pilgrams.

The worthy government of the New Netherlands was not suffered to enjoy this grand acquisition unmolested. In the year 1654, the losel Yankees of Connecticut, those swapping, bargaining, squatting enemies of the Manhattoes, made a daring inroad into this neighborhood, and founded a colony called Westchester, or, as the ancient Dutch records term it, Vest Dorp, in the right of one Thomas Pell, who pretended to have purchased the whole surrounding country of the Indians; and stood ready to argue their claims before any tribunal of Christendom.

This happened during the chivalrous reign of Peter Stuyvesant, and roused the ire of that gunpowder old hero. Without waiting to discuss claims and titles, he pounced at once upon the nest of nefarious squatters, carried off twenty-five of them in chains to the Manhattoes, nor did he stay his hand, nor give rest to his wooden leg, until he had driven the rest of the Yankees back into Connecticut, or obliged them to acknowledge allegiance to their High Mightinesses. In revenge, however, they introduced the plague of witchcraft into the province. This doleful malady broke out at Vest Dorp, and would have spread throughout the country had not the Dutch farmers nailed horse-shoes to the doors of their houses and barns, sure protections against witchcraft, many of which remain to the present day.

The seat of empire of the wizard sachem now came into the possession of Wolfert Acker, one of the privy counsellors of Peter Stuyvesant. He was a worthy, but ill-starred man, whose aim through life had been to live in peace and quiet. For this he had emigrated from Holland, driven abroad by family feuds and wrangling neighbors. He had warred for quiet through the fidgetting reign of William the Testy, and the fighting reign of Peter the Headstrong, sharing in every brawl and rib-roasting, in his eagerness to keep the peace and promote public tranquillity. It was his doom, in fact, to meet a head wind at every turn, and be kept in a constant fume and fret by the perverseness of mankind. Had he served on a modern jury he would have been sure to have eleven unreasonable men opposed to him.

At the time when the province of the New Netherlands was wrested from the domination of their High Mightinesses by the combined forces of Old and New England, Wolfert retired in high dudgeon to this fastness in the wilderness, with the bitter determination to bury himself from the world, and live here for the rest of his days in peace and quiet. In token of that fixed purpose he inscribed over his door (his teeth clenched at the time) his favorite Dutch motto, "Lust in Rust," (pleasure in quiet). The mansion was thence called Wolfert's Rust—(Wolfert's Rest), but by the uneducated, who did not understand Dutch, Wolfert's Roost; probably from its quaint cock-loft look, and from its having a weather-cock perched on every gable.

Wolfert's luck followed him into retirement. He had shut himself up from the world, but he had brought with him a wife, and it soon passed into a proverb throughout the neighborhood that the cock of the Roost was the most henpecked bird in the country. His house too was reputed to be harassed by Yankee witchcraft. When the weather was quiet every where else, the wind, it was said, would howl and whistle about the gables; witches and warlocks would whirl about upon the weather-cocks, and scream down the chimneys; nay it was even hinted that Wolfert's wife was in league with the enemy, and used to ride on a broomstick to a witches' sabbath in Sleepy Hollow. This, however, was all mere scandal, founded perhaps on her occasionally flourishing a broomstick in the course of a curtain lecture, or raising a storm within doors, as termagant wives are apt to do, and against which sorcery horse shoes are of no avail.

Wolfert Acker died and was buried, but found no quiet even in the grave: for if popular gossip be true, his ghost has occasionally been seen walking by moonlight among the old gray moss-grown trees of his apple orchard.

CHRONICLE II

THE NEXT PERIOD AT WHICH WE FIND THIS VENERABLE AND EVENTFUL PILE rising into importance, was during the dark and troublous time of the revolutionary war. It was the keep or stronghold of Jacob Van Tassel, a valiant Dutchman of the old stock of Van Tassels, who abound in Westchester County. The name, as originally written, was Van Texel, being derived from the Texel in Holland, which gave birth to that heroic line.

The Roost stood in the very heart of what at that time was called the debatable ground, lying between the British and American lines. The British held possession of the city and island of New York; while the Americans drew up towards the Highlands, holding their head-quarters at Peekskill. The intervening country from Croton River to Spiting Devil Creek was the debatable ground in question, liable to be harried by friend and foe, like the Scottish borders of yore.

It is a rugged region; full of fastnesses. A line of rocky hills extends through it like a backbone, sending out ribs on either side; but these rude hills are for the most part richly wooded, and inclose little fresh pastoral valleys watered by the Neperan, the

Pocantico,[3] and other beautiful streams, along which the Indians built their wigwams in the olden time.

In the fastnesses of these hills, and along these valleys existed, in the time of which I am treating, and indeed exist to the present day, a race of hard-headed, hard-handed, stout-hearted yeomen, descendants of the primitive Nederlanders. Men obstinately attached to the soil, and neither to be fought nor bought out of their paternal acres. Most of them were strong Whigs throughout the war; some, however, were Tories, or adherents to the old kingly rule; who considered the revolution a mere rebellion, soon to he put down by his majesty's forces. A number of these took refuge within the British lines, joined the military bands of refugees, and became pioneers or leaders to foraging parties sent out from New York to scour the country and sweep off supplies for the British army.

In a little while the debatable ground became infested by roving bands, claiming from either side, and all pretending to redress wrongs and punish political offences; but all prone in the exercise of their high functions, to sack hen-roosts, drive off cattle, and lay farm-houses under contribution: such was the origin of two great orders of border chivalry, the Skinners and the Cow Boys, famous in revolutionary story; the former fought, or rather marauded under the American, the latter under the British banner. In the zeal of service, both were apt to make blunders, and confound the property of friend and foe. Neither of them in the heat and hurry of a foray had time to ascertain the politics of a horse or cow, which they were driving off into captivity; nor, when they wrung the neck of a rooster, did they trouble their heads whether he crowed for Congress or King George.

To check these enormities, a confederacy was formed among the yeomanry who had suffered from these maraudings. It was composed for the most part of farmers' sons, bold, hard-riding lads, well armed, and well mounted, and undertook to clear the country round of Skinner and Cow Boy, and all other border vermin; as the Holy Brotherhood in old times cleared Spain of the banditti which infested her highways.

---

3. The Neperan, vulgarly called the Saw-Mill River, winds for many miles through a lovely valley, shrouded by groves, and dotted by Dutch farm-houses, and empties itself into the Hudson, at the ancient Dorp of Yonkers. The Pocantico, rising among woody hills, winds in many a wizard maze, through the sequestered haunts of Sleepy Hollow. We owe it to the indefatigable researches of Mr. Knickerbocker, that those beautiful streams are rescued from modern common-place, and reinvested with their ancient Indian names. The correctness of the venerable historian may be ascertained by reference to the records of the original Indian grants to the Herr Frederick Philipsen, preserved in the county clerk's office, at White Plains.

Wolfert's Roost was one of the rallying places of this confederacy, and Jacob Van Tassel one of its members. He was eminently fitted for the service: stout of frame, bold of heart, and like his predecessor, the warrior sachem of yore, delighting in daring enterprises. He had an Indian's sagacity in discovering when the enemy was on the maraud, and in hearing the distant tramp of cattle. It seemed as if he had a scout on every hill, and an ear as quick as that of Fine Ear in the fairy tale.

The foraging parties of tories and refugees had now to be secret and sudden in their forays into Westchester County; to make a hasty maraud among the farms, sweep the cattle into a drove, and hurry down to the lines along the river road, or the valley of the Neperan. Before they were half way down, Jacob Van Tassel, with the holy brotherhood of Tarrytown, Petticoat Lane, and Sleepy Hollow, would be clattering at their heels. And now there would be a general scamper for King's Bridge, the pass over Spiting Devil Creek into the British lines. Sometimes the moss-troopers would be overtaken, and eased of part of their booty. Sometimes the whole cavalgada would urge its headlong course across the bridge with thundering tramp and dusty whirlwind. At such times their pursuers would rein up their steeds, survey that perilous pass with wary eye and, wheeling about, indemnify themselves by foraging the refugee region of Morrisania.

While the debatable land was liable to be thus harried, the great Tappan Sea, along which it extends, was likewise domineered over by the foe. British ships of war were anchored here and there in the wide expanses of the river, mere floating castles to hold it in subjection. Stout galleys armed with eighteen pounders, and navigated with sails and oars, cruised about like hawks; while row-boats made descents upon the land, and foraged the country along shore.

It was a sore grievance to the yeomanry along the Tappan Sea to behold that little Mediterranean ploughed by hostile prows, and the noble river of which they were so proud, reduced to a state of thraldom. Councils of war were held by captains of market-boats and other river craft, to devise ways and means of dislodging the enemy. Here and there on a point of land extending into the Tappan Sea, a mud work would be thrown up, and an old field-piece mounted, with which a knot of rustic artillerymen would fire away for a long summer's day at some frigate dozing at anchor far out of reach; and reliques of such works may still be seen overgrown with weeds and brambles, with peradventure the half-buried fragment of a cannon which may have burst.

Jacob Van Tassel was a prominent man in these belligerent operations; but he was prone moroever, to carry on a petty warfare of his own for his individual recreation and refreshment. On a row of hooks above the fireplace of the Roost, reposed his great piece of ordnance; a duck, or rather goose gun of unparalleled longitude, with which it was said he could kill a wild goose half way across the Tappan Sea. Indeed there are as many wonders told of this renowned gun, as of the enchanted weapons of classic story. When the belligerent feeling was strong upon Jacob, he would take down his gun, sally forth alone, and prowl along shore, dodging behind rocks and trees, watching for hours together any ship or galley at anchor or becalmed; as a valorous mouser will watch a rat hole. So sure as a boat approached the shore, bang! went the great goose gun, sending on board a shower of slugs and buck shot; and away scuttled Jacob Van Tassel through some woody ravine. As the Roost stood in a lonely situation, and might be attacked, he guarded against surprise by making loop-holes in the stone walls, through which to fire upon an assailant. His wife was stout-hearted as himself, and could load as fast as he could fire, and his sister, Nochie Van Wurmer, a redoubtable widow, was a match, as he said, for the stoutest man in the country. Thus garrisoned, his little castle was fitted to stand a siege, and Jacob was the man to defend it to the last charge of powder.

In the process of time the Roost became one of the secret stations, or lurking places, of the Water Guard. This was an aquatic corps in the pay of government, organized to range the waters of the Hudson, and keep watch upon the movements of the enemy. It was composed of nautical men of the river and hardy youngsters of the adjacent country, expert at pulling an oar or handling a musket. They were provided with whale-boats, long and sharp, shaped like canoes, and formed to lie lightly on the water, and be rowed with great rapidity. In these they would lurk out of sight by day, in nooks and bays, and behind points of land; keeping a sharp look-out upon the British ships, and giving intelligence to head quarters of any extraordinary movement. At night they rowed about in pairs, pulling quietly along with muffled oars, under shadow of the land, or gliding like spectres about frigates and guard ships to cut off any boat that might be sent to shore. In this way they were a source of constant uneasiness and alarm to the enemy.

The Roost, as has been observed, was one of their lurking places; having a cove in front where their whale-boats could be drawn up out of sight, and Jacob Van Tassel being a vigilant ally, ready to take a part in any "scout or scrummage" by land or water. At this little warrior nest the hard-riding lads from the hills would hold consultations with the chivalry of the river, and here were concerted divers of those daring enterprises which resounded from Spiting Devil Creek even unto Anthony's Nose. Here was concocted the midnight invasion of New York Island, and the conflagration of Delancy's Tory mansion, which makes such a blaze in revolutionary history. Nay more, if the traditions of the Roost may be credited, here was meditated by Jacob Van Tassel and his compeers, a nocturnal foray into New York itself, to surprise and carry off the British commanders Howe and Clinton, and put a triumphant close to the war.

There is no knowing whether this notable scheme might not have been carried into effect, had not one of Jacob Van Tassel's egregious exploits along shore with his goose-gun, with which he thought himself a match for any thing, brought vengeance on his house.

It so happened, that in the course of one of his solitary prowls he descried a British transport aground; the stern swung toward shore within point-blank shot. The temptation was too great to be resisted. Bang! went the great goose-gun, from the covert of the trees, shivering the cabin windows and driving all hands forward. Bang! bang! the shots were repeated. The reports brought other of Jacob's fellow bush-fighters to the spot. Before the transport could bring a gun to bear, or land a boat to take revenge, she was soundly peppered, and the coast evacuated.

This was the last of Jacob's triumphs. He fared like some heroic spider that has unwittingly ensnared a hornet to the utter ruin of his web. It was not long after the above exploit that he fell into the hands of the enemy in the course of one of his forays, and was carried away prisoner to New York. The Roost itself, as a pestilent rebel nest, was marked out for signal punishment. The cock of the Roost being captive, there was none to garrison it but his stout-hearted spouse, his redoubtable sister, Nochie Van Wurmer, and Dinah, a strapping negro wench. An armed vessel came to anchor in front; a boat full of men pulled to shore. The garrison flew to arms; that is to say, to mops, broomsticks, shovels, tongs, and all kinds of domestic weapons; for unluckily, the great piece of ordnance, the goose-gun, was absent with its owner. Above all, a vigorous defence was made with that most potent of female weapons, the tongue. Never did invaded hen-roost make a more vociferous outcry. It was all in vain. The house was sacked and plundered, fire was set to each corner, and in a few moments its blaze shed a baleful light far over the Tappan Sea. The invaders then pounced upon the blooming Laney Van Tassel, the beauty of the Roost, and endeavored to bear her off to the boat. But here was the real tug of war. The mother, the aunt, and the strapping negro wench, all flew to the rescue. The struggle continued down to the very water's edge; when a voice from the armed vessel at anchor, ordered the spoilers to desist; they relinquished their prize, jumped into their boats, and pulled off, and the heroine of the Roost escaped with a mere rumpling of the feathers.

As to the stout Jacob himself, he was detained a prisoner in New York for the greater part of the war; in the mean time the Roost remained a melancholy ruin, its stone walls and brick chimneys alone standing, the resorts of bats and owls. Superstitious notions prevailed about it. None of the country people would venture alone at night down the rambling lane which led to it, overhung with trees and crossed here and there by a wild wandering brook. The story went that one of the victims of Jacob Van Tassel's great goose-gun had been buried there in unconsecrated ground.

Even the Tappan Sea in front was said to be haunted. Often in the still twilight of a summer evening, when the Sea would be as glass, and the opposite hills would throw their purple shadows half across it, a low sound would be heard as of the steady vigorous pull of oars, though not a boat was to be descried. Some might have supposed that a boat was rowed along unseen under the deep shadows of the opposite shores; but the ancient traditionists of the neighborhood knew better. Some said it was one of the whale-boats of the old water-guard, sunk by the British ships during the war, but now permitted to haunt its old cruising grounds; but the prevalent opinion connected it with the awful fate of Rambout Van Dam of graceless memory. He was a roystering Dutchman of Spiting Devil, who in times long past had navigated his boat alone one Saturday the whole length of the Tappan Sea, to attend a quilting frolic at Kakiat, on the western shore. Here he had danced, and drunk, until midnight, when he entered his boat to return home. He was warned that he was on the verge of Sunday morning; but he pulled off nevertheless, swearing he would not land until he reached Spiting Devil, if it took him a month of Sundays. He was never seen afterwards; but may be heard plying his oars, as above mentioned, being the Flying Dutchman of the Tappan Sea, doomed to ply between Kakiat and Spiting Devil until the day of judgment.

CHRONICLE III

THE REVOLUTIONARY WAR WAS OVER. THE DEBATABLE GROUND HAD ONCE MORE become a quiet agricultural region; the border chivalry had turned their swords into ploughshares, and their spears into pruning hooks, and hung up their guns, only to be taken down occasionally in a campaign against wild pigeons on the hills, or wild ducks upon the Hudson. Jacob Van Tassel, whilome carried captive to New York, a flagitious rebel, had come forth from captivity a "hero of seventy-six." In a little while he sought the scenes of his former triumphs and mishaps, rebuilt the Roost, restored his goose-gun to the hooks over the fireplace, and reared once more on high the glittering weathercocks.

Years and years passed over the time-honored little mansion. The honeysuckle and the sweetbrier crept up its walls; the wren and the phœbe bird built under the eaves; it gradually became almost hidden among trees, through which it looked forth, as with half-shut eyes, upon the Tappan Sea. The Indian spring, famous in the days of the wizard sachem, still welled up at the bottom of the green bank; and the wild brook, wild as ever, came babbling down the ravine, and threw itself into the little cove where of yore the water-guard harbored their whaleboats.

Such was the state of the Roost many years since, at the time when Diedrich Knickerbocker came into this neighborhood, in the course of his researches among the Dutch families for materials for his immortal history. The exterior of the eventful little pile seemed to him full of promise. The crow-step gables were of the primitive architecture of the province. The weathercocks which surmounted them had crowed in the glorious days of the New Netherlands. The one above the porch had actually glittered of yore on the great Vander Heyden palace at Albany.

The interior of the mansion fulfilled its external promise. Here were records of old times; documents of the Dutch dynasty, rescued from the profane hands of the English, by Wolfert Acker, when he retreated from New Amsterdam. Here he had treasured them up like buried gold, and here they had been miraculously preserved by St. Nicholas, at the time of the conflagration of the Roost.

Here then did old Diedrich Knickerbocker take up his abode for a time, and set to work with antiquarian zeal to decipher these precious documents, which, like the lost books of Livy, had baffled the research of former historians; and it is the facts drawn from these sources which give his work the preference, in point of accuracy, over every other history.

It was during his sojourn in this eventful neighborhood, that the historian is supposed to have picked up many of those legends, which have since been given by him to the world, or found among his papers. Such was the legend connected with the old Dutch church of Sleepy Hollow. The church itself was a monument of bygone days. It had been built in the early times of the province. A tablet over the portal bore the names of its founders: Frederick Filipson, a mighty man of yore, patroon of Yonkers, and his wife Katrina Van Courtland, of the Van Courtlands of Croton; a powerful family connexion, with one foot resting on Spiting Devil Creek, and the other on the Croton River.

Two weathercocks, with the initials of these illustrious personages, graced each end of the church, one perched over the belfry, the other over the chancel. As usual with ecclesiastical weathercocks, each pointed a different way; and there was a perpetual contradiction between them on all points of windy doctrine; emblematic, alas! of the Christian propensity to schism and controversy.

In the burying-ground adjacent to the church, reposed the earliest fathers of a wide rural neighborhood. Here families were garnered together, side by side, in long platoons, in this last gathering place of kindred. With pious hand would Diedrich Knickerbocker turn down the weeds and brambles which had overgrown the tombstones, to decipher inscriptions in Dutch and English, of the names and virtues of succeeding generations of Van Tassels, Van Warts, and other historical worthies, with their portraitures faithfully carved, all bearing the family likeness to cherubs.

The congregation in those days was of a truly rural character. City fashions had not as yet stole up to Sleepy Hollow. Dutch sun-bonnets and honest homespun still prevailed. Every thing was in primitive style, even to the bucket of water and tin cup near the door in summer, to assuage the thirst caused by the heat of the weather or the drouth of the sermon.

The pulpit, with its wide-spreading sounding board, and the communion table, curiously carved, had each come from Holland in the olden time, before the arts had sufficiently advanced in the colony for such achievements. Around these on Sundays would be gathered the elders of the church, gray-headed men who led the psalmody, and in whom it would be difficult to recognize the hard-riding lads of yore, who scoured the debatable land in the time of the revolution.

The drowsy influence of Sleepy Hollow was apt to breathe into this sacred edifice; and now and then an elder might be seen with his handkerchief over his face to keep off the flies, and apparently listening to the dominie; but really sunk into a summer slumber, lulled by the sultry notes of the locust from the neighboring trees.

And now a word or two about Sleepy Hollow, which many have rashly deemed a fanciful creation, like the Lubberland of mariners. It was probably the mystic and dreamy sound of the name which first tempted the historian of the Manhattoes into its spellbound mazes. As he entered, all nature seemed for the moment to awake from its slumbers and break forth in gratulations. The quail whistled a welcome from the corn field; the loquacious cat-bird flew from bush to bush with restless wing proclaiming his approach, or perked inquisitively into his face, as if to get a knowledge of his physiognomy. The woodpecker tapped a tattoo on the hollow apple tree, and then peered round the trunk, as if asking how he relished the salutation; while the squirrel scampered along the fence, whisking his tail over his head by way of a huzza.

Here reigned the golden mean extolled by poets, in which no gold was to be found and very little silver. The inhabitants of the Hollow were of the primitive stock, and had intermarried and bred in and in, from the earliest time of the province, never swarming far from the parent hive, but dividing and subdividing their paternal acres as they swarmed.

Here were small farms, each having its little portion of meadow and corn field; its orchard of gnarled and sprawling apple trees; its garden in which the rose, the marigold and hollyhock, grew sociably with the cabbage, the pea, and the pumpkin: each had its low-eaved mansion redundant with white-headed children; with an old hat nailed against the wall for the housekeeping wren, the coop on the grass-plot, where the motherly hen clucked round with her vagrant brood: each had its stone well, with a moss-covered bucket suspended to the long balancing pole, according to antediluvian hydraulics; while within doors resounded the eternal hum of the spinning wheel.

Many were the great historical facts which the worthy Diedrich collected in these lowly mansions, and patiently would he sit by the old Dutch housewives with a child on his knee, or a purring grimalkin on his lap, listing to endless ghost stories spun forth to the humming accompaniment of the wheel.

The delighted historian pursued his explorations far into the foldings of the hills where the Pocantico winds its wizard stream among the mazes of its old Indian haunts; sometimes running darkly in pieces of woodland beneath balancing sprays of beech and chestnut: sometimes sparkling between grassy borders in fresh green intervals; here and there receiving the tributes of silver rills which came whimpering down the hill sides from their parent springs.

In a remote part of the Hollow, where the Pocantico forced its way down rugged rocks, stood Carl's mill, the haunted house of the neighborhood. It was indeed a goblin-looking pile; shattered and time-worn; dismal with clanking wheels and rushing streams, and all kinds of uncouth noises. A horse shoe nailed to the door to keep off witches, seemed to have lost its power; for as Diedrich approached, an old negro thrust his head all dabbled with flour, out of a hole above the water wheel, and grinned and rolled his eyes, and appeared to be the very hobgoblin of the place. Yet this proved to be the great historic genius of the Hollow, abounding in that valuable information never to be acquired from books. Diedrich Knickerbocker soon discovered his merit. They had long talks together seated on a broken millstone, heedless of the water and the clatter of the mill; and to his conference with that African sage, many attribute the surprising, though true story of Ichabod Crane, and the Headless Horseman of Sleepy Hollow. We refrain, however, from giving farther researches of the historian of the Manhattoes, during his sojourn at the Roost; but may return to them in future pages.

Reader, the Roost still exists. Time, which changes all things, is slow in its operations on a Dutchman's dwelling. The stout Jacob Van Tassel, it is true, sleeps with his fathers; and his great goose-gun with him: yet his strong-hold still bears the impress of its Dutch origin. Odd rumors have gathered about it, as they are apt to do about old mansions, like moss and weather stains. The shade of Wolfert Acker still walks his unquiet rounds at night in the orchard; and a white figure has now and then been seen seated at a window and gazing at the moon, from a room in which a young lady is said to have died of love and green apples.

Mementoes of the sojourn of Diedrich Knickerbocker are still cherished at the Roost. His elbow chair and antique writing-desk maintain their place in the room he occupied, and his old cocked hat still hangs on a peg against the wall.

The Birds of Spring

My quiet residence in the country, aloof from fashion, politics, and the money market, leaves me rather at a loss for occupation, and drives me occasionally to the study of nature, and other low pursuits. Having few neighbors, also, on whom to keep a watch, and exercise my habits of observation, I am fain to amuse myself with prying into the domestic concerns and peculiarities of the animals around me; and, during the present season, have derived considerable entertainment from certain sociable little birds, almost the only visitors we have, during this early part of the year.

Those who have passed the winter in the country, are sensible of the delightful influences that accompany the earliest indications of spring; and of these, none are more delightful than the first notes of the birds. There is one modest little sad-colored bird, much resembling a wren, which came about the house just on the skirts of winter, when not a blade of grass was to be seen, and when a few prematurely warm days had given a flattering foretaste of soft weather. He sang early in the dawning, long before sun rise, and late in the evening, just before the closing in of night, his matin and his vesper hymns. It is true, he sang occasionally throughout the day; but at these still hours, his song was more remarked. He sat on a leafless tree, just before the window, and warbled forth his notes, few and simple, but singularly sweet, with something of a plaintive tone, that heightened their effect.

The first morning that he was heard, was a joyous one among the young folks of my household. The long, death-like sleep of winter was at an end; nature was once more awakening; they now promised themselves the immediate appearance of buds and blossoms. I was reminded of the tempest-tossed crew of Columbus, when, after their long dubious voyage, the field birds came singing round the ship, though still far at sea, rejoicing them with the belief of the immediate proximity of land. A sharp return of winter almost silenced my little songster, and dashed the hilarity of the household; yet still he poured forth, now and then, a few plaintive notes, between the frosty pipings of the breeze, like gleams of sunshine between wintry clouds.

I have consulted my book of ornithology in vain, to find out the name of this kindly little bird, who certainly deserves honor and favor far beyond his modest pretensions. He comes like the lowly violet, the most unpretending, but welcomest of flowers, breathing the sweet promise of the early year.

Another of our feathered visitors, who follow close upon the steps of winter, is the Pe-wit, or Pe-wee, or Phœbe-bird; for he is called by each of these names, from a fancied resemblance to the sound of his monotonous note. He is a sociable little being, and seeks the habitation of man. A pair of them have built beneath my porch, and have reared several broods there, for two years past, their nest being never disturbed. They arrive early in the spring, just when the crocus and the snow-drop begin to peep forth. Their first chirp spreads gladness through the house. "The Phœbe birds have come!" is heard on all sides; they are welcomed back like members of the family; and speculations are made upon where they have been, and what countries they have seen, during their long absence. Their arrival is the more cheering, as it is pronounced, by the old weather-wise people of the country, the sure sign that the severe frosts are at an end, and that the gardener may resume his labors with confidence.

About this time, too, arrives the blue-bird, so poetically yet truly described by Wilson. His appearance gladdens the whole landscape. You hear his soft warble in every field. He sociably approaches your habitation, and takes up his residence in your vicinity. But why should I attempt to describe him, when I have Wilson's own graphic verses, to place him before the reader?

When winter's cold tempests and snows are no more,
    Green meadows and brown furrowed fields rëappearing,
The fishermen hauling their shad to the shore,
    And cloud-cleaving geese to the lakes are a-steering;
When first the lone butterfly flits on the wing,
    When red glow the maples, so fresh and so pleasing,
O then comes the blue-bird, the herald of spring.
    And hails with his warblings the charms of the season.

The loud-piping frogs make the marshes to ring;
　　Then warm glows the sunshine, and warm grows the weather
The blue woodland flowers just beginning to spring,
　　And spice-wood and sassafras budding together;
O then to your gardens, ye housewives, repair,
　　Your walks border up, sow and plant at your leisure
The blue-bird will chant from his box such an air,
　　That all your hard toils will seem truly a pleasure!

He flits through the orchard, he visits each tree.
　　The red flowering peach, and the apple's sweet blossoms;
He snaps up destroyers, wherever they be,
　　And seizes the caitiffs that lurk in their bosoms;
He drags the vile grub from the corn it devours.
　　The worms from the webs where they riot and welter;
His song and his services freely are ours,
　　And all that he asks is, in summer a shelter.

The ploughman is pleased when he gleans in his train.
　　Now searching the furrows, now mounting to cheer him;
The gard'ner delights in his sweet simple strain.
　　And leans on his spade to survey and to hear him.
The slow lingering school-boys forget they'll be chid.
　　While gazing intent, as he warbles before them.
In mantle of sky-blue, and bosom so red.
　　That each little loiterer seems to adore him.

The happiest bird of our spring, however, and one that rivals the European lark in my estimation, is the Boblincon, or Boblink, as he is commonly called. He arrives at that choice portion of our year, which, in this latitude, answers to the description of the month of May, so often given by the poets. With us, it begins about the middle of May, and lasts until nearly the middle of June. Earlier than this, winter is apt to return on its traces, and to blight the opening beauties of the year; and later than this, begin the parching, and panting, and dissolving heats of summer. But in this genial interval, nature is in all her freshness and fragrance "the rains are over and gone, the flowers appear upon the earth, the time of the singing of birds is come, and the voice of the turtle is heard in the land." The trees are now in their fullest foliage and brightest verdure; the woods are gay with the clustered flowers of the laurel; the air is perfumed by the sweet-brier and the wild rose; the meadows are enamelled with clover-blossoms; while the young apple, the peach, and the plum, begin to swell, and the cherry to glow, among the green leaves.

This is the chosen season of revelry of the Boblink. He comes amidst the pomp and fragrance of the season; his life seems all sensibility and enjoyment, all song and sunshine. He is to be found in the soft bosoms of the freshest and sweetest meadows; and is most in song, when the clover is in blossom. He perches on the topmost twig of a tree, or on some long flaunting weed, and as he rises and sinks with the breeze, pours forth a succession of rich tinkling notes; crowding one upon another, like the outpouring melody of the skylark, and possessing the same rapturous character. Sometimes he pitches from the summit of a tree, begins his song as soon as he gets upon the wing, and flutters tremulously down to the earth, as if overcome with ecstasy at his own music. Sometimes he is in pursuit of his paramour always in full song, as if he would win her by his melody; and always with the same appearance of intoxication and delight.

Of all the birds of our groves and meadows, the Boblink was the envy of my boyhood. He crossed my path in the sweetest weather, and the sweetest season of the year, when all nature called to the fields, and the rural feeling throbbed in every bosom; but when I, luckless urchin! was doomed to be mewed up, during the livelong day, in that purgatory of boyhood, a school-room. It seemed as if the little varlet mocked at me, as he flew by in full song, and sought to taunt me with his happier lot. Oh, how I envied him! No lessons, no task, no hateful school; nothing but holiday, frolic, green fields, and fine weather. Had I been then more versed in poetry, I might have addressed him in the words of Logan to the cuckoo:

Sweet bird! thy bower is ever green,
Thy sky is ever clear
Thou hast no sorrow in thy note,
No winter in thy year.

Oh I could I fly, I'd fly with thee;
We'd make, on joyful wing,
Our annual visit round the globe.
Companions of the spring!

Further observation and experience have given me a different idea of this little feathered voluptuary, which I will venture to impart, for the benefit of my schoolboy readers, who may regard him with the same unqualified envy and admiration which I once indulged. I have shown him only as I saw him at first, in what I may call the poetical part of his career, when he in a manner devoted himself to elegant pursuits and enjoyments, and was a bird of music, and song, and taste, and sensibility, and refinement. While this lasted, he was sacred from injury; the very schoolboy would not fling a stone at him, and the merest rustic would pause to listen to his strain. But mark the difference. As the year advances, as the clover blossoms disappear, and the spring fade into summer, he gradually gives up his elegant tastes and habits, doffs his poetical suit of black, assumes a russet dusty garb, and sinks to the gross enjoyments of common vulgar birds. His notes no longer vibrate on the ear; he is stuffing himself with the seeds of the tall weeds on which he lately swung and chanted so melodiously. He has become a "bon vivant," a "gourmand;" with him now there is nothing like the "joys of the table." In a little while he grows tired of plain homely fare, and is off on a gastronomical tour in quest of foreign luxuries. We next hear of him with myriads of his kind, banqueting among the reeds of the Delaware; and grown corpulent with good feeding. He has changed his name in travelling. Boblincon no more—he is the *Reed-bird* now, the much sought for titbit of Pennsylvania epicures; the rival in unlucky fame of the ortolan! Wherever he goes, pop! pop! pop! every rusty firelock in the country is blazing away. He sees his companions falling by thousands around him.

Does he take warning and reform?—Alas not he! Incorrigible epicure! again he wings his flight. The rice swamps of the south invite him. He gorges himself among them almost to bursting; he can scarcely fly for corpulency. He has once more changed his name, and is now the famous *Rice-bird* of the Carolinas.

Last stage of his career; behold him spitted with dozens of his corpulent companions, and served up, a vaunted dish, on the table of some Southern gastronome.

Such is the story of the Boblink; once spiritual, musical, admired, the joy of the meadows, and the favorite bird of spring; finally, a gross little sensualist who expiates his sensuality in the larder, his story contains a moral, worthy the attention of all little birds and little boys; warning them to keep to those refined and intellectual pursuits, which raised him to so high a pitch of popularity during the early part of his career; but to eschew all tendency to that gross and dissipated indulgence, which brought this mistaken little bird to an untimely end.

Which is all at present, from the well-wisher of little boys and little birds,

GEOFFREY CRAYON GENT.

The Creole Village

A Sketch from a Steamboat

FIRST PUBLISHED IN 1837

IN TRAVELLING ABOUT OUR MOTLEY COUNTRY, I AM OFTEN REMINDED OF Ariosto's account of the moon, in which the good paladin Astolpho found every thing garnered up that had been lost on earth. So I am apt to imagine, that many things lost in the old world, are treasured up in the new; having been handed down from generation to generation, since the early days of the colonies. A European antiquary, therefore, curious in his researches after the ancient and almost obliterated customs and usages of his country, would do well to put himself upon the track of some early band of emigrants, follow them across the Atlantic, and rummage among their descendants on our shores.

In the phraseology of New England might be found many an old English provincial phrase, long since obsolete in the parent country; with some quaint relics of the roundheads; while Virginia cherishes peculiarities characteristic of the days of Elizabeth and Sir Walter Raleigh.

In the same way, the sturdy yeomanry of New Jersey and Pennsylvania keep up many usages fading away in ancient Germany; while many an honest, broad-bottomed custom, nearly extinct in venerable Holland, may be found flourishing in pristine vigor and luxuriance in Dutch villages, on the banks of the Mohawk and the Hudson.

In no part of our country, however, are the customs and peculiarities, imported from the old world by the earlier settlers, kept up with more fidelity than in the little, poverty-stricken villages of Spanish and French origin, which border the rivers of ancient Louisiana. Their population is generally made up of the descendants of those nations, married and interwoven together, since occasionally crossed with a slight dash of the Indian. The French character, however, floats on top, as, from its buoyant qualities, it is sure to do, whenever it forms a particle, however small, of an intermixture.

In these serene and dilapidated villages, art and nature stand still, and the world forgets to turn round. The revolutions that distract other parts of this mutable planet, reach not here, or pass over without leaving any trace. The fortunate inhabitants have none of that public spirit which extends its cares beyond its horizon, and imports trouble and perplexity from all quarters in newspapers. In fact, newspapers are almost unknown in these villages, and as French is the current language, the inhabitants have little community of opinion with their republican neighbors. They retain, therefore, their old habits of passive obedience to the decrees of government, as though they still lived under the absolute sway of colonial commandants, instead of being part and parcel of the sovereign people, and having a voice in public legislation.

A few aged men, who have grown gray on their hereditary acres, and are of the good old colonial stock, exert a patriarchal sway in all matters of public and private import; their opinions are considered oracular, and their word is law.

The inhabitants, moreover, have none of that eagerness for gain, and rage for improvement, which keep our people continually on the move, and our country towns incessantly in a state of transition. There the magic phrases, "town lots," "water privileges," "railroads," and other comprehensive and soul-stirring words, from the speculator's vocabulary, are never heard. The residents dwell in the houses built by their forefathers, without thinking of enlarging or modernizing them, or pulling them down and turning them into granite stores. The trees, under which they have been born, and have played in infancy, flourish undisturbed; though, by cutting them down, they might open new streets, and put money in their pockets. In a word, the almighty dollar, that great object of universal devotion throughout our land, seems to have no genuine devotees in these peculiar villages; and unless some of its missionaries penetrate there, and erect banking houses and other pious shrines, there is no knowing how long the inhabitants may remain in their present state of contented poverty.

In descending one of our great western rivers in a steamboat, I met with two worthies from one of these villages, who had been on a distant excursion, the longest they had ever made, as they seldom ventured far from home. One was the great man, or Grand Seigneur of the village; not that he enjoyed any legal privileges or power there, every thing of the kind having been done away when the province was ceded by France to the United States. His sway over his neighbors was merely one of custom and convention, out of deference to his family. Beside, he was worth full fifty thousand dollars, an amount almost equal, in the imaginations of the villagers, to the treasures of King Solomon.

This very substantial old gentleman, though of the fourth or fifth generation in this country, retained the true Gallic feature and deportment, and reminded me of one of those provincial potentates, that are to be met with in the remote parts of France. He was of a large frame, a ginger-bread complexion, strong features, eyes that stood out like glass knobs, and a prominent nose, which he frequently regaled from a gold snuff-box, and occasionally blew with a colored handkerchief, until it sounded like a trumpet.

He was attended by an old negro, as black as ebony, with a huge mouth, in a continual grin; evidently a privileged and favorite servant, who had grown up and grown old with him. He was dressed in Creole style—with white jacket and trousers, a stiff shirt collar, that threatened to cut off his ears, a bright madras handkerchief tied round his head, and large gold ear-rings. He was the politest negro I met with in a western tour; and that is saying a great deal, for, excepting the Indians, the negroes are the most gentlemanlike personages to be met with in those parts. It is true, they differ from the Indians in being a little extra polite and complimentary. He was also one of the merriest; and here, too, the negroes, however we may deplore their unhappy condition, have the advantage of their masters. The whites are, in general, too free and prosperous to be merry. The cares of maintaining their rights and liberties, adding to their wealth, and making presidents, engross all their thoughts, and dry up all the moisture of their souls. If you hear a broad, hearty, devil-may-care laugh, be assured it is a negro's.

Beside this African domestic, the seigneur of the village had another no less cherished and privileged attendant. This was a huge dog, of the mastiff breed, with a deep, hanging mouth, and a look of surly gravity. He walked about the cabin with the air of a dog perfectly at home, and who had paid for his passage. At dinner time he took his seat beside his master, giving him a glance now and then out of a corner of his eye, which bespoke perfect confidence that he would not be forgotten. Nor was he—every now and then a huge morsel would be thrown to him, peradventure the half-picked leg of a fowl, which he would receive with a snap like the springing of a steel-trap—one gulp, and all was down; and a glance of the eye told his master that he was ready for another consignment.

The other village worthy, travelling in company with the seigneur, was of a totally different stamp. Small, thin, and weazen-faced, as Frenchmen are apt to be represented in caricature, with a bright, squirrel-like eye, and a gold ring in his ear. His dress was flimsy, and sat loosely on his frame, and he had altogether the look of one with but little coin in his pocket. Yet, though one of the poorest, I was assured he was one of the merriest and most popular personages in his native village.

Compere Martin, as he was commonly called, was the factotum of the place—sportsman, schoolmaster, and land-surveyor. He could sing, dance, and, above all, play on the fiddle, an invaluable accomplishment in an old French Creole village, for the inhabitants have a hereditary love for balls and fêtes; if they work but little, they dance a great deal, and a fiddle is the joy of their heart.

What had sent Compere Martin travelling with the Grand Seigneur I could not learn; he evidently looked up to him with great deference, and was assiduous in rendering him petty attentions; from which I concluded that he lived at home upon the crumbs which fell from his table. He was gayest when out of his sight; and had his song and his joke when forward, among the deck passengers; but altogether Compere Martin was out of his element on board of a steamboat. He was quite another being, I am told, when at home, in his own village.

Like his opulent fellow-traveller, he too had his canine follower and retainer—and one suited to his different fortunes—one of the civilest, most unoffending little dogs in the world. Unlike the lordly mastiff, he seemed to think he had no right on board of the steamboat; if you did but look hard at him, he would throw himself upon his back, and lift up his legs, as if imploring mercy.

At table he took his seat a little distance from his master; not with the bluff, confident air of the mastiff, but quietly and diffidently; his head on one side, with one ear dubiously slouched, the other hopefully cocked up; his under teeth projecting beyond his black nose, and his eye wistfully following each morsel that went into his master's mouth.

If Compere Martin now and then should venture to abstract a morsel from his plate, to give to his humble companion, it was edifying to see with what diffidence the exemplary little animal would take hold of it, with the very tip of his teeth, as if he would almost rather not, or was fearful of taking too great a liberty. And then with what decorum would he eat it! How many efforts would he make in swallowing it, as if it stuck in his throat; with what daintiness would he lick his lips; and then with what an air of thankfulness would lie resume his seat, with his teeth once more projecting beyond his nose, and an eye of humble expectation fixed upon his master.

It was late in the afternoon when the steamboat stopped at the village which was the residence of these worthies. It stood on the high bank of the river, and bore traces of having been a frontier trading post. There were the remains of stockades that once protected it from the Indians, and the houses were in the ancient Spanish and French colonial taste, the place having been successively under the domination of both those nations prior to the cession of Louisiana to the United States.

The arrival of the seigneur of fifty thousand dollars, and his humble companion, Compere Martin, had evidently been looked forward to as an event in the village. Numbers of men, women, and children, white, yellow, and black, were collected on the river bank; most of them clad in old-fashioned French garments, and their heads decorated with colored handkerchiefs, or white nightcaps. The moment the steamboat came within sight and hearing, there was a waving of handkerchiefs, and a screaming and bawling of salutations, and felicitations, that baffle all description.

The old gentleman of fifty thousand dollars was received by a train of relatives, and friends, and children, and grandchildren, whom he kissed on each cheek, and who formed a procession in his rear, with a legion of domestics, of all ages, following him to a large, old-fashioned French house, that domineered over the village.

His black valet de chambre, in white jacket and trousers, and gold ear-rings, was met on the shore by a boon, though rustic companion, a tall negro fellow, with a long, good-humored face, and the profile of a horse, which stood out from beneath a narrow-rimmed straw hat, stuck on the back of his head. The explosions of laughter of these two varlets on meeting and exchanging compliments, were enough to electrify the country round.

The most hearty reception, however, was that given to Compere Martin. Every body, young and old, hailed him before he got to land. Every body had a joke for Compere Martin, and Compere Martin had a joke for every body. Even his little dog appeared, to partake of his popularity, and to be caressed by every hand. Indeed, he was quite a different animal the moment he touched the land. Here he was at home; here he was of consequence. He barked, he leaped, he frisked about his old friends, and then would skim round the place in a wide circle, as if mad.

I traced Compere Martin and his little dog to their home. It was an old ruinous Spanish house, of large dimensions, with verandas overshadowed by ancient elms.

The house had probably been the residence, in old times, of the Spanish commandant. In one wing of this crazy, but aristocratical abode, was nestled the family of my fellow-traveller; for poor devils are apt to be magnificently clad and lodged, in the cast-off clothes and abandoned palaces of the great and wealthy.

The arrival of Compere Martin was welcomed by a legion of women, children, and mongrel curs; and, as poverty and gayety generally go hand in hand among the French and their descendants, the crazy mansion soon resounded with loud gossip and lighthearted laughter.

As the steamboat paused a short time at the village, I took occasion to stroll about the place. Most of the houses were in the French taste, with casements and rickety verandas, but most of them in flimsy and ruinous condition. All the waggons, ploughs, and other utensils about the place were of ancient and inconvenient Gallic construction, such as had been brought from France in the primitive days of the colony. The very looks of the people reminded me of the villages of France.

From one of the houses came the hum of a spinning wheel, accompanied by a scrap of an old French chanson, which I have heard many a time among the peasantry of Languedoc, doubtless a traditional song, brought over by the first French emigrants, and handed down from generation to generation.

Half a dozen young lasses emerged from the adjacent dwellings, reminding me, by their light step and gay costume, of scenes in ancient France, where taste in dress comes natural to every class of females. The trim bodice and colored petticoat, and little apron, with its pockets to receive the hands when in an attitude for conversation; the colored kerchief wound tastefully round the head, with a coquettish knot perking above one ear; and the neat slipper and tight drawn stocking, with its braid of narrow ribbon embracing the ankle where it peeps from its mysterious curtain. It is from this ambush that Cupid sends his most inciting arrows.

While I was musing upon the recollections thus accidentally summoned up, I heard the sound of a fiddle from the mansion of Compere Martin, the signal, no doubt, for a joyous gathering. I was disposed to turn my steps thither, and witness the festivities of one of the very few villages I had met with in my wide tour, that was yet poor enough to be merry; but the bell of the steamboat summoned me to re-embark.

As we swept away from the shore, I cast back a wistful eye upon the moss-grown roofs and ancient elms of the village, and prayed that the inhabitants might long retain their happy ignorance, their absence of all enterprise and improvement, their respect for the fiddle, and their contempt for the almighty dollar.[1] I fear, however, my prayer is doomed to be of no avail. In a little while, the steamboat whirled me to an American town, just springing into bustling and prosperous existence.

The surrounding forest had been laid out in town lots; frames of wooden buildings were rising from among stumps and burnt trees. The place already boasted a court-house, a jail, and two banks, all built of pine boards, on the model of Grecian temples. There were rival hotels, rival churches, and rival newspapers; together with the usual number of judges, and generals, and governors; not to speak of doctors by the dozen, and lawyers by the score.

The place, I was told, was in an astonishing career of improvement, with a canal and two railroads in embryo. Lots doubled in price every week; every body was speculating in land; every body was rich; and every body was growing richer. The community, however, was torn to pieces by new doctrines in religion and in political economy; there were camp meetings, and agrarian meetings; and an election was at hand, which, it was expected would throw the whole country into a paroxysm.

Alas! with such an enterprising neighbor, what is to become of the poor little creole village!

---

1. This phrase used for the first time, in this sketch, has since passed into current circulation, and by some has been questioned as savoring of irreverence. The author, therefore, owes it to his orthodoxy to declare that no irreverence was intended even to the dollar itself; which he is aware is daily becoming more and more an object of worship.

Mountjoy:

or Some Passages Out of the Life of a Castle-Builder

I WAS BORN AMONG ROMANTIC SCENERY, IN ONE OF THE WILDEST PARTS OF THE Hudson, which at that time was not so thickly settled as at present. My father was descended from one of the old Huguenot families, that came over to this country on the revocation of the Edict of Nantz. He lived in a style of easy, rural independence, on a patrimonial estate that had been for two or three generations in the family. He was an indolent, good-natured man, took the world as it went, and had a kind of laughing philosophy, that parried all rubs and mishaps, and served him in the place of wisdom. This was the part of his character least to my taste; for I was of an enthusiastic, excitable temperament, prone to kindle up with new schemes and projects, and he was apt to dash my sallying enthusiasm by some unlucky joke; so that whenever I was in a glow with any sudden excitement, I stood in mortal dread of his good-humor.

Yet he indulged me in every vagary; for I was an only son, and of course a personage of importance in the household. I had two sisters older than myself, and one younger. The former were educated at New York, under the eye of a maiden aunt; the latter remained at home, and was my cherished playmate, the companion of my thoughts. We were two imaginative little beings, of quick susceptibility, and prone to see wonders and mysteries in every thing around us. Scarce had we learned to read, when our mother made us holiday presents of all the nursery literature of the day; which at that time consisted of little books covered with gilt paper, adorned with "cuts," and filled with tales of fairies, giants, and enchanters. What draughts of delightful fiction did we then inhale! My sister Sophy was of a soft and tender nature. She would weep over the woes of the Children in the Wood, or quake at the dark romance of Blue-Beard, and the terrible mysteries of the blue chamber. But I was all for enterprise and adventure. I burned to emulate the deeds of that heroic prince, who delivered the white cat from her enchantment; or he of no less royal blood, and doughty emprise, who broke the charmed slumber of the Beauty in the Wood!

The house in which we lived, was just the kind of place to foster such propensities. It was a venerable mansion, half villa, half farm-house. The oldest part was of stone, with loopholes for musketry, having served as a family fortress, in the time of the Indians. To this there had been made various additions, some of brick, some of wood, according to the exigencies of the moment; so that it was full of nooks and crooks, and chambers of all sorts and sizes. It was buried among willows, elms, and cherry trees, and surrounded with roses and hollyhocks, with honeysuckle and sweetbrier clambering about every window. A brood of hereditary pigeons sunned themselves upon the roof; hereditary swallows and martins built about the eaves and chimneys; and hereditary bees hummed about the flower-beds.

Under the influence of our story-books, every object around us now assumed a new character, and a charmed interest. The wild flowers were no longer the mere ornaments of the fields, or the resorts of the toilful bee; they were the lurking-places of fairies. We would watch the humming-bird, as it hovered around the trumpet creeper at our porch, and the butterfly as it flitted up into the blue air, above the sunny tree tops, and fancy them some of the tiny beings from fairy land. I would call to mind all that I had read of Robin Goodfellow, and his power of transformation. O how I envied him that power! How I longed to be able to compress my form into utter littleness; to ride the bold dragonfly; swing on the tall bearded grass; follow the ant into his subterraneous habitation, or dive into the cavernous depths of the honeysuckle!

While I was yet a mere child, I was sent to a daily school, about two miles distant. The school-house was on the edge of a wood, close by a brook overhung with birches, alders, and dwarf willows. We of the school who lived at some distance, came with our dinners put up in little baskets. In the intervals of school hours, we would gather round a spring, under a tuft of hazel-bushes, and have a kind of picnic; interchanging the rustic dainties with which our provident mothers had fitted us out. Then, when our joyous repast was over, and my companions were disposed for play, I would draw forth one of my cherished storybooks, stretch myself on the greensward, and soon lose myself in its bewitching contents.

I became an oracle among my school-mates, on account of my superior erudition, and soon imparted to them the contagion of my infected fancy. Often in the evening, after school hours, we would sit on the trunk of some fallen tree in the woods, and vie with each other in telling extravagant stories, until the whip-poor-will began his nightly moaning, and the fire-flies sparkled in the gloom. Then came the perilous journey homeward. What delight we would take in getting up wanton panics, in some dusky part of the wood; scampering like frightened deer; pausing to take breath; renewing the panic, and scampering off again, wild with fictitious terror!

Our greatest trial was to pass a dark, lonely pool, covered with pond-lilies, peopled with bull-frogs and water snakes, and haunted by two white cranes. Oh! the terrors of that pond! How our little hearts would beat, as we approached it; what fearful glances we would throw around! And if by chance a plash of a wild duck, or the guttural twang of a bull-frog, struck our ears, as we stole quietly by—away we sped, nor paused until completely out of the woods. Then, when I reached home, what a world of adventures, and imaginary terrors, would I have to relate to my sister Sophy!

As I advanced in years, this turn of mind increased upon me, and became more confirmed. I abandoned myself to the impulses of a romantic imagination, which controlled my studies, and gave a bias to all my habits. My father observed me continually with a book in my hand, and satisfied himself that I was a profound student; but what were my studies? Works of fiction; tales of chivalry; voyages of discovery; travels in the east; every thing, in short, that partook of adventure and romance. I well remember with what zest I entered upon that part of my studies which treated of the heathen mythology, and particularly of the sylvan deities. Then indeed my school-books became dear to me. The neighborhood was well calculated to foster the reveries of a mind like mine. It abounded with solitary retreats, wild streams, solemn forests, and silent valleys. I would ramble about for a whole day, with a volume of Ovid's Metamorphoses in my pocket, and work myself into a kind of self-delusion, so as to identify the surrounding scenes with those of which I had just been reading. I would loiter about a brook that glided through the shadowy depths of the forest, picturing it to myself the haunt of Naiades. I would steal round some bushy copse that opened upon a glade, as if I expected to come suddenly upon Diana and her nymphs; or to behold Pan and his satyrs bounding, with whoop and halloo, through the woodland. I would throw myself, during the panting heats of a summer noon, under the shade of some wide-spreading tree, and muse and dream away the hours, in a state of mental intoxication. I drank in the very light of day, as nectar, and my soul seemed to bathe with ecstasy in the deep blue of a summer sky.

In these wanderings, nothing occurred to jar my feelings, or bring me back to the realities of life. There is a repose in our mighty forests, that gives full scope to the imagination. Now and then I would hear the distant sound of the wood-cutter's axe, or the crash of some tree which he had laid low; but these noises, echoing along the quiet landscape, could easily be wrought by fancy into harmony with its illusions. In general, however, the woody recesses of the neighborhood were peculiarly wild and unfrequented. I could ramble for a whole day, without coming upon any traces of cultivation. The partridge of the wood scarcely seemed to shun my path, and the squirrel, from his nut-tree, would gaze at me for an instant, with sparkling eye, as if wondering at the unwonted intrusion.

I cannot help dwelling on this delicious period of my life; when as yet I had known no sorrow, nor experienced any worldly care. I have since studied much, both of books and men, and of course have grown too wise to be so easily pleased; yet with all my wisdom, I must confess I look back with a secret feeling of regret to the days of happy ignorance, before I had begun to be a philosopher.

It must be evident that I was in a hopeful training, for one who was to descend into the arena of life, and wrestle with this world. The tutor, also, who superintended my studies, in the more advanced stage of my education, was just fitted to complete the *fata morgana* which was forming in my mind. His name was Glencoe. He was a pale, melancholy-looking man, about forty years of age; a native of Scotland, liberally educated, and who had devoted himself to the instruction of youth, from taste rather than necessity; for, as he said, he loved the human heart, and delighted to study it in its earlier impulses. My two elder sisters, having returned home from a city boarding-school, were likewise placed under his care, to direct their reading in history and belles-lettres.

We all soon became attached to Glencoe. It is true, we were at first somewhat prepossessed against him. His meagre, pallid countenance, his broad pronunciation, his inattention to the little forms of society, and an awkward and embarrassed manner, on first acquaintance, were much against him; but we soon discovered that under this unpromising exterior existed the kindest urbanity; the warmest sympathies; the most enthusiastic benevolence. His mind was ingenious and acute. His reading had been various, but more abstruse than profound: his memory was stored, on all subjects, with facts, theories, and quotations, and crowded with crude materials for thinking. These, in a moment of excitement, would be, as it were, melted down, and poured forth in the lava of a heated imagination. At such moments, the change in the whole man was wonderful. His meagre form would acquire a dignity and grace; his long, pale visage would flash with a hectic glow; his eyes would beam with intense speculation; and there would be pathetic tones and deep modulations in his voice, that delighted the ear, and spoke movingly to the heart.

But what most endeared him to us, was the kindness and sympathy with which he entered into all our interests and wishes. Instead of curbing and checking our young imaginations with the reins of sober reason, be was a little too apt to catch the impulse, and be hurried away with us. He could not withstand the excitement of any sally of feeling or fancy; and was prone to lend heightening tints to the illusive coloring of youthful anticipation.

Under his guidance, my sisters and myself soon entered upon a more extended range of studies, but while they wandered, with delighted minds, through the wide field of history and belles-lettres, a nobler walk was opened to my superior intellect.

The mind of Glencoe presented a singular mixture of philosophy and poetry. He was fond of metaphysics, and prone to indulge in abstract speculations, though his metaphysics were somewhat fine spun and fanciful, and his speculations were apt to partake of what my father most irreverently termed "humbug." For my part, I delighted in them, and the more especially, because they set my father to sleep, and completely confounded my sisters. I entered, with my accustomed eagerness, into this new branch of study. Metaphysics were now my passion. My sisters attempted to accompany me, but they soon faltered, and gave out before they had got half way through Smith's Theory of Moral Sentiments. I, however, went on, exulting in my strength. Glencoe supplied me with books, and I devoured them with appetite, if not digestion. We walked and talked together under the trees before the house, or sat apart, like Milton's angels, and held high converse upon themes beyond the grasp of ordinary intellects. Glencoe possessed a kind of philosophic chivalry, in imitation of the old peripatetic sages, and was continually dreaming of romantic enterprises in morals, and splendid systems for the improvement of society. He had a fanciful mode of illustrating abstract subjects, peculiarly to my taste; clothing them with the language of poetry, and throwing round them almost the magic hues of fiction. "How charming," thought I, "is divine philosophy"; not harsh and crabbed, as dull fools suppose,

> But a perpetual feast of nectar'd sweets,
> Where no crude surfeit reigns.

I felt a wonderful self-complacency at being on such excellent terms with a man whom I considered on a parallel with the sages of antiquity, and looked down with a sentiment of pity on the feebler intellects of my sisters, who could comprehend nothing of metaphysics. It is true, when I attempted to study them by myself I was apt to get in a fog; but when Glencoe came to my aid, every thing was soon as clear to me as day. My ear drank in the beauty of his words; my imagination was dazzled with the splendor of his illustrations. It caught up the sparkling sands of poetry that glittered through his speculations, and mistook them for the golden ore of wisdom. Struck with the facility with which I seemed to imbibe and relish the most abstract doctrines, I conceived a still higher opinion of my mental powers, and was convinced that I also was a philosopher.

I was now verging toward man's estate, and though my education had been extremely irregular following the caprices of my humor, which I mistook for the impulses of my genius—yet I was regarded with wonder and delight by my mother and sisters, who considered me almost as wise and infallible as I considered myself. This high opinion of me was strengthened by a declamatory habit, which made me an oracle and orator at the domestic board. The time was now at hand, however, that was to put my philosophy to the test.

We had passed through a long winter, and the spring at length opened upon us, with unusual sweetness. The soft serenity of the weather; the beauty of the surrounding country; the joyous notes of the birds; the balmy breath of flower and blossom, all combined to fill my bosom with indistinct sensations, and nameless wishes. Amid the soft seductions of the season, I lapsed into a state of utter indolence, both of body and mind.

Philosophy had lost its charms for me. Metaphysics—faugh! I tried to study; took down volume after volume, ran my eye vacantly over a few pages, and threw them by with distaste. I loitered about the house, with my hands in my pockets, and an air of complete vacancy. Something was necessary to make me happy; but what was that something! I sauntered to the apartments of my sisters, hoping their conversation might amuse me. They had walked out, and the room was vacant. On the table lay a volume which they had been reading. It was a novel. I had never read a novel, having conceived a contempt for works of the kind, from hearing them universally condemned. It is true, I had remarked they were universally read; but I considered them beneath the attention of a philosopher, and never would venture to read them, lest I should lessen my mental superiority in the eyes of my sisters. Nay, I had taken up a work of the kind, now and then, when I knew my sisters were observing me, looked into it for a moment, and then laid it down, with a slight supercilious smile. On the present occasion, out of mere listlessness, I took up the volume, and turned over a few of the first pages. I thought I heard some one coming, and laid it down. I was mistaken; no one was near, and what I had read, tempted my curiosity to read a little farther. I leaned against a window-frame, and in a few minutes was completely lost in the story. How long I stood there reading, I know not, but I believe for nearly two hours. Suddenly I heard my sisters on the stairs, when I thrust the book into my bosom, and the two other volumes, which lay near, into my pockets, and hurried out of the house to my beloved woods. Here I remained all day beneath the trees, bewildered, bewitched; devouring the contents of these delicious volumes; and only returned to the house when it was too dark to peruse their pages.

This novel finished, I replaced it in my sister's apartment, and looked for others. Their stock was ample, for they had brought home all that were current in the city; but my appetite demanded an immense supply. All this course of reading was carried on clandestinely, for I was a little ashamed of it, and fearful that my wisdom might be called in question; but this very privacy gave it additional zest. It was "bread eaten in secret;" it had the charm of a private amour.

But think what must have been the effect of such a course of reading on a youth of my temperament and turn of mind; indulged, too, amidst romantic scenery, and in the romantic season of the year. It seemed as if I had entered upon a new scene of existence. A train of combustible feelings were lighted up in me, and my soul was all tenderness and passion. Never was youth more completely love sick, though as yet it was a mere general sentiment, and wanted a definite object. Unfortunately, our neighborhood was particularly deficient in female society, and I languished in vain for some divinity, to whom I might offer up this most uneasy burthen of affections. I was at one time seriously enamored of a lady whom I saw occasionally in my rides, reading at the window of a country-seat; and actually serenaded her with my flute; when, to my confusion, I discovered that she was old enough to be my mother. It was a sad damper to my romance; especially as my father heard of it, and made it the subject of one of those household jokes, which he was apt to serve up at every meal-time.

I soon recovered from this check, however, but it was only to relapse into a state of amorous excitement. I passed whole days in the fields, and along the brooks; for there is something in the tender passion that makes us alive to the beauties of nature. A soft sunshine morning infused a sort of rapture into my breast, I flung open my arms, like the Grecian youth in Ovid, as if I would take in and embrace the balmy atmosphere.[1] The song of the birds melted me to tenderness. I would lie by the side of some rivulet, for hours, and form garlands of the flowers on its banks, and muse on ideal beauties, and sigh from the crowd of undefined emotions that swelled my bosom.

In this state of amorous delirium, I was strolling one morning along a beautiful wild brook which I had discovered in a glen. There was one place where a small water-fall, leaping from among rocks into a natural basin, made a scene such as a poet might have chosen as the haunt of some shy Naiad. It was here I usually retired to banquet on my novels. In visiting the place this morning, I traced distinctly, on the margin of the basin, which was of fine clear sand, the prints of a female foot, of the most slender and delicate proportions. This was sufficient for an imagination like mine. Robinson Crusoe himself, when he discovered the print of a savage foot on the beach of his lonely island, could not have been more suddenly assailed with thick-coming fancies.

I endeavored to track the steps, but they only passed for a few paces along the fine sand, and then were lost among the herbage. I remained gazing in reverie upon this passing trace of loveliness. It evidently was not made by any of my sisters, for they knew nothing of this haunt; besides, the foot was smaller than theirs; it was remarkable for its beautiful delicacy.

My eye accidentally caught two or three half-withered wild flowers, lying on the ground. The unknown nymph had doubtless dropped them from her bosom! Here was a new document of taste and sentiment. I treasured them up as invaluable relics. The place, too, where I found them, was remarkably picturesque, and the most beautiful part of the brook. It was overhung with fine elm, entwined with grape-vines. She who could select such a spot, who could delight in wild brooks, and wild flowers, and silent solitudes, must have fancy, and feeling, and tenderness; and with all these qualities, she must be beautiful!

---

1. Ovid's Metamorphoses, Book vii.

But who could be this Unknown, that had thus passed by, as in a morning dream, leaving merely flowers and fairy footsteps, to tell of her loveliness! There was a mystery in it that bewildered me. It was so vague and disembodied, like those "airy tongues that syllable men's names" in solitude. Every attempt to solve the mystery was vain. I could hear of no being in the neighborhood to whom this trace could be ascribed. I haunted the spot, and became more and more enamored. Never, surely, was passion more pure and spiritual, and never lover in more dubious situation. My case could only be compared with that of the amorous prince, in the fairy tale of Cinderella; but he had a glass slipper on which to lavish his tenderness. I, alas! was in love with a footstep!

The imagination is alternately a cheat and a dupe; nay more, it is the most subtle of cheats, for it cheats itself, and becomes the dupe of its own delusions. It conjures up "airy nothings," gives to them a "local habitation and a name," and then bows to their control as implicitly as if they were realities. Such was now my case. The good Numa could not more thoroughly have persuaded himself that the nymph Egeria hovered about her sacred fountain, and communed with him in spirit, than I had deceived myself into a kind of visionary intercourse with the airy phantom fabricated in my brain. I constructed a rustic seat at the foot of the tree where I had discovered the footsteps. I made a kind of bower there, where I used to pass my mornings, reading poetry and romances. I carved hearts and darts on the tree, and hung it with garlands. My heart was full to overflowing, and wanted some faithful bosom into which it might relieve itself. What is a lover without a confidante? I thought at once of my sister Sophy, my early playmate, the sister of my affections. She was so reasonable, too, and of such correct feelings, always listening to my words as oracular sayings, and admiring my scraps of poetry, as the very inspirations of the muse. From such a devoted, such a rational being, what secrets could I have?

I accordingly took her, one morning, to my favorite retreat. She looked around, with delighted surprise, upon the rustic seat, the bower, the tree carved with emblems of the tender passion. She turned her eyes upon me to inquire the meaning.

"Oh, Sophy," exclaimed I, clasping both her hands in mine, and looking earnestly in her face, "I am in love!"

She started with surprise.

"Sit down," said I, "and I will tell you all."

She seated herself upon the rustic bench, and I went into a full history of the footstep, with all the associations of idea that had been conjured up by my imagination.

Sophy was enchanted; it was like a fairy tale: She had read of such mysterious visitations in books, and the loves thus conceived were always for beings of superior order, and were always happy. She caught the illusion, in all its force; her cheek glowed; her eye brightened.

"I dare say she's pretty," said Sophy.

"Pretty!" echoed I, "she is beautiful!" I went through all the reasoning by which I had logically proved the fact to my own satisfaction, I dwelt upon the evidences of her taste, her sensibility to the beauties of nature; her soft meditative habit, that delighted in solitude; "oh," said I, clasping my hands "to have such a companion to wander through these scenes; to sit with her by this murmuring stream; to wreathe garlands round her brows; to hear the music of her voice mingling with the whisperings of these groves;—"

"Delightful! delightful!" cried Sophy; "what a sweet creature she must be! She is just the friend I want. How I shall dote upon her! Oh, my dear brother! you must not keep her all to yourself. You must let me have some share of her!"

I caught her to my bosom: "You shall—you shall!" cried I, "my dear Sophy; we will all live for each other!"

The conversation with Sophy heightened the illusions of my mind; and the manner in which she had treated my day-dream, identified it with facts and persons, and gave it still more the stamp of reality. I walked about as one in a trance, heedless of the world around, and lapped in an elysium of the fancy.

In this mood I met, one morning, with Glencoe. He accosted me with his usual smile, and was proceeding with some general observations, but paused and fixed on me an inquiring eye.

"What is the matter with you? "said he; "you seem agitated; has any thing in particular happened?"

"Nothing," said I, hesitating; "at least nothing worth communicating to you."

"Nay, my dear young friend," said he, "whatever is of sufficient importance to agitate you, is worthy of being communicated to me."

"Well; but my thoughts are running on what you would think a frivolous subject."

"No subject is frivolous, that has the power to awaken strong feelings."

"What think you," said I, hesitating, "what think you of love?"

Glencoe almost started at the question. "Do you call that a frivolous subject?" replied he. "Believe me, there is none fraught with such deep, such vital interest. If you talk, indeed, of the capricious inclination awakened by the mere charm of perishable beauty, I grant it to be idle in the extreme; but that love which springs from the concordant sympathies of virtuous hearts; that love which is awakened by the perception of moral excellence, and fed by meditation on intellectual as well as personal beauty; that is a passion which refines and ennobles the human heart. Oh, where is there a sight more nearly approaching to the intercourse of angels, than that of two young beings, free from the sins and follies of the world, mingling pure thoughts, and looks, and feelings, and becoming as it were soul of one soul, and heart of one heart! How exquisite the silent converse that they hold; the soft devotion of the eye, that needs no words to make it eloquent! Yes, my friend, if there be any thing in this weary world worthy of heaven, it is the pure bliss of such a mutual affection!"

The words of my worthy tutor overcame all farther reserve. "Mr. Glencoe," cried I, blushing still deeper, "I am in love!"

"And is that what you were ashamed to tell me? Oh, never seek to conceal from your friend so important a secret. If your passion be unworthy, it is for the steady hand of friendship to pluck it forth; if honorable, none but an enemy would seek to stifle it. On nothing does the character and happiness so much depend, as on the first affection of the heart. Were you caught by some fleeting and superficial charm—a bright eye, a blooming cheek, a soft voice, or a voluptuous form—I would warn you to beware; I would tell you that beauty is but a passing gleam of the morning, a perishable flower; that accident may becloud and blight it, and that at best it must soon pass away. But were you in love with such a one as I could describe; young in years, but still younger in feelings; lovely in person, but as a type of the mind's beauty; soft in voice, in token of gentleness of spirit; blooming in countenance, like the rosy tints of morning kindling with the promise of a genial day; an eye beaming with the benignity of a happy heart; a cheerful temper, alive to all kind impulses, and frankly diffusing its own felicity; a self-poised mind, that needs not lean on others for support; an elegant taste, that can embellish solitude, and furnish out its own enjoyments—"

"My dear sir," cried I, for I could contain myself no longer, "you have described the very person!"

"Why then, my dear young friend," said he, affectionately pressing my hand, "in God's name, love on!"

* * *

For the remainder of the day, I was in some such state of dreamy beatitude as a Turk is said to enjoy, when under the influence of opium. It must be already manifest, how prone I was to bewilder myself with picturings of the fancy, so as to confound them with existing realities. In the present instance, Sophy and Glencoe had contributed to promote the transient delusion. Sophy, dear girl, had as usual joined with me in my castle-building, and indulged in the same train of imaginings, while Glencoe, duped by my enthusiasm, firmly believed that I spoke of a being I had seen and known. By their sympathy with my feelings, they in a manner became associated with the Unknown in my mind, and thus linked her with the circle of my intimacy.

In the evening, our family party was assembled in the hall, to enjoy the refreshing breeze. Sophy was playing some favorite Scotch airs on the piano, while Glencoe, seated apart, with his forehead resting on his hand, was buried in one of those pensive reveries, that made him so interesting to me.

"What a fortunate being I am!" thought I, "blessed with such a sister and such a friend! I have only to find out this amiable Unknown, to wed her, and be happy! What a paradise will be my home, graced with a partner of such exquisite refinement! It will be a perfect fairy bower, buried among sweets and roses. Sophy shall live with us, and be the companion of all our enjoyments. Glencoe, too, shall no more be the solitary being that he now appears. He shall have a home with us. He shall have his study, where, when he pleases, he may shut himself up from the world, and bury himself in his own reflections. His retreat shall be held sacred; no one shall intrude there; no one but myself, who will visit him now and then, in his seclusion, where we will devise grand schemes together for the improvement of mankind. How delightfully our days will pass, in a round of rational pleasures and elegant employments! Sometimes we will have music; sometimes we will read; sometimes we will wander through the flower-garden, when I will smile with complacency on every flower my wife has planted; while in the long winter evenings, the ladies will sit at their work and listen, with hushed attention, to Glencoe and myself, as we discuss the abstruse doctrines of metaphysics."

From this delectable reverie, I was startled by my father's slapping me on the shoulder: "What possesses the lad?" cried he: "here have I been speaking to you half a dozen times, without receiving an answer."

"Pardon me, sir," replied I; "I was so completely lost in thought, that I did not hear you."

"Lost in thought! And pray what were you thinking of? Some of your philosophy, I suppose."

"Upon my word," said my sister Charlotte, with an arch laugh, "I suspect Harry's in love again."

"And if I were in love, Charlotte," said I, somewhat nettled, and recollecting Glencoe's enthusiastic eulogy of the passion, "if I were in love, is that a matter of jest and laughter? Is the tenderest and most fervid affection that can animate the human breast, to be made a matter of cold-hearted ridicule?"

My sister colored. "Certainly not, brother!—nor did I mean to make it so, nor to say any thing that should wound your feelings. Had I really suspected that you bad formed some genuine attachment, it would have been sacred in my eyes; but—but," said she, smiling, as if at some whimsical recollection, "I thought that you—you might be indulging in another little freak of the imagination."

"I'll wager any money," cried my father, "he has fallen in love again with some old lady at a window!"

"Oh no!" cried my dear sister Sophy, with the most gracious warmth; "she is young and beautiful."

"From what I understand," said Glencoe, rousing himself, "she must be lovely in mind as in person."

I found my friends were getting me into a fine scrape. I began to perspire at every pore, and felt my ears tingle.

"Well, but," cried my father, "who is she?—what is she? Let us hear something about her."

This was no time to explain so delicate a matter. I caught up my hat, and vanished out of the house.

The moment I was in the open air, and alone, my heart upbraided me. Was this respectful treatment to my father—to such a father too—who had always regarded me as the pride of his age—the staff of his hopes? It is true, he was apt, sometimes, to laugh at my enthusiastic flights, and did not treat my philosophy with due respect; but when had he ever thwarted a wish of my heart? Was I then to act with reserve toward him, in a matter which might affect the whole current of my future life? "I have done wrong," thought I; "but it is not too late to remedy it. I will hasten back, and open my whole heart to my father!"

I returned accordingly, and was just on the point of entering the house, with my heart full of filial piety, and a contrite speech upon my lips, when I heard a burst of obstreperous laughter from my father, and a loud titter from my two elder sisters.

"A footstep!" shouted he, as soon as he could recover himself; "in love with a footstep! why, this beats the old lady at the window!" And then there was another appalling burst of laughter. Had it been a clap of thunder, it could hardly have astounded me more completely, Sophy, in the simplicity of het heart, had told all, and had set my father's risible propensities in full action.

Never was poor mortal so thoroughly crest-fallen as myself. The whole delusion was at an end. I drew off silently from the house, shrinking smaller and smaller at every fresh peal of laughter; and wandering about until the family had retired, stole quietly to my bed. Scarce any sleep, however, visited my eyes that night! I lay overwhelmed with mortification, and meditating how I might meet the family in the morning. The idea of ridicule was always intolerable to me; but to endure it on a subject by which my feelings had been so much excited, seemed worse than death. I almost determined, at one time, to get up, saddle my horse, and ride off, I knew not whither.

At length I came to a resolution. Before going down to breakfast, I sent for Sophy, and employed her as ambassador to treat formally in the matter. I insisted that the subject should be buried in oblivion; otherwise, I would net show my face at table. It was readily agreed to; for not one of the family would have given me pain for the world. They faithfully kept their promise. Not a word was said of the matter; but there were wry faces, and suppressed titters, that went to my soul; and whenever my father looked me in the face, it was with such a tragic-comical leer—such an attempt to pull down a serious brow upon a whimsical mouth—that I had a thousand times rather he had laughed outright.

For a day or two after the mortifying occurrence mentioned, I kept as much as possible out of the way of the family, and wandered about the fields and woods by myself. I was sadly out of tune: my feelings were all jarred and unstrung. The birds sang from every grove, but I took no pleasure in their melody; and the flowers of the field bloomed unheeded around me. To be crossed in love, is bad enough; but then one can fly to poetry for relief; and turn one's woes to account in soul-subduing stanzas. But to have one's whole passion, object and all, annihilated, dispelled, proved to be such stuff as dreams are made of—or, worse than all, to be turned into a proverb and a jest—what consolation is there in such a case?

I avoided the fatal brook where I had seen the footstep. My favorite resort was now the banks of the Hudson, where I sat upon the rocks, and mused upon the current that dimpled by, or the waves that laved the shore; or watched the bright mutations of the clouds, and the shifting lights and shadows of the distant mountain. By degrees, a returning serenity stole over my feelings; and a sigh now and then, gentle and easy, and unattended by pain, showed that my heart was recovering its susceptibility.

As I was sitting in this musing mood, my eye became gradually fixed upon an object that was borne along by the tide. It proved to be a little pinnace, beautifully modelled, and gaily painted and decorated. It was an unusual sight in this neighborhood, which was rather lonely: indeed, it was rare to see any pleasure-barks in this part of the river. As it drew nearer, I perceived that there was no one on board; it had apparently drifted from its anchorage. There was not a breath of air: the little bark came floating along on the glassy stream, wheeling about with the eddies. At length it ran aground, almost at the foot of the rock on which I was seated. I descended to the margin of the river, and drawing the bark to shore, admired its light and elegant proportions, and the taste with which it was fitted up. The benches were covered with cushions, and its long streamer was of silk. On one of the cushions lay a lady's glove, of delicate size and shape, with beautifully tapered fingers. I instantly seized it and thrust it in my bosom: it seemed a match for the fairy footstep that had so fascinated me.

In a moment, all the romance of my bosom was again in a glow. Here was one of the very incidents of fairy tale: a bark sent by some invisible power, some good genius, or benevolent fairy, to waft me to some delectable adventure. I recollected something of an enchanted bark, drawn by white swans, that conveyed a knight down the current of the Rhine, on some enterprise connected with love and beauty. The glove, too, showed that there was a lady fair concerned in the present adventure. It might be a gauntlet of defiance, to dare me to the enterprise.

In the spirit of romance, and the whim of the moment, I sprang on board, hoisted the light sail, and pushed from shore. As if breathed by some presiding power, a light breeze at that moment sprang up, swelled out the sail, and dallied with the silken streamer. For a time I glided along under steep umbrageous banks, or across deep sequestered bays; and then stood out over a wide expansion of the river, toward a high rocky promontory. It was a lovely evening: the sun was setting in a congregation of clouds that threw the whole heavens in a glow, and were reflected in the river. I delighted myself with all kinds of fantastic fancies, as to what enchanted island, or mystic bower, or necromantic palace, I was to be conveyed by the fairy bark.

In the revel of my fancy, I had not noticed that the gorgeous congregation of clouds which had so much delighted me, was in fact a gathering thunder-gust. I perceived the truth too late. The clouds came hurrying on, darkening as they advanced. The whole face of nature was suddenly changed, and assumed that baleful and livid tint, predictive of a storm. I tried to gain the shore, but before I could reach it, a blast of wind struck the water, and lashed it at once into foam. The next moment it overtook the boat. Alas! I was nothing of a sailor; and my protecting fairy forsook me in the moment of peril. I endeavored to lower the sail: but in so doing, I had to quit the helm; the bark was overturned in an instant, and I was thrown into the water. I endeavored to cling to the wreck, but missed my hold: being a poor swimmer, I soon found myself sinking, but grasped a light oar that was floating by me. It was not sufficient for my support: I again sank beneath the surface; there was a rushing and bubbling sound in my ears, and all sense forsook me.

How long I remained insensible, I know not. I had a confused notion of being moved and tossed about, and of hearing strange beings and strange voices around me; but all was like a hideous dream. When I at length recovered full consciousness and perception, I found myself in bed, in a spacious chamber, furnished with more taste than I had been accustomed to. The bright rays of a morning sun were intercepted by curtains of a delicate rose color, that gave a soft, voluptuous tinge to every object. Not far from my bed, on a classic tripod, was a basket of beautiful exotic flowers, breathing the sweetest fragrance.

"Where am I? How came I here?"

I tasked my mind to catch at some previous event, from which I might trace up the thread of existence to the present moment. By degrees I called to mind the fairy pinnace, my daring embarcation, my adventurous voyage, and my disastrous shipwreck. Beyond that, all was chaos. How came I here? What unknown region had I landed upon? The people that inhabited it must be gentle and amiable, and of elegant tastes, for they loved downy beds, fragrant flowers, and rose-colored curtains.

While I lay thus musing, the tones of a harp reached my ear. Presently, they were accompanied by a female voice. It came from the room below; but in the profound stillness of my chamber not a modulation was lost. My sisters were all considered good musicians, and sang very tolerably; but I had never heard a voice like this. There was no attempt at difficult execution, or striking effect; but there were exquisite inflexions, and tender turns, which art could not reach. Nothing but feeling and sentiment could produce them. It was soul breathed forth in sound. I was always alive to the influence of music: indeed, I was susceptible of voluptuous influences of every kind—sounds, colors, shapes, and fragrant odors. I was the very slave of sensation.

I lay mute and breathless, and drank in every note of this siren strain. It thrilled through my whole frame, and filled my soul with melody and love. I pictured to myself, with curious logic, the form of the unseen musician. Such melodious sounds and exquisite inflexions could only be produced by organs of the most delicate flexibility. Such organs do not belong to coarse, vulgar forms; they are the harmonious results of fair proportions and admirable symmetry. A being so organized, must be lovely.

Again my busy imagination was at work. I called to mind the Arabian story of a prince, borne away during sleep by a good genius, to the distant abode of a princess, of ravishing beauty. I do not pretend to say that I believed in having experienced a similar transportation; but it was my inveterate habit to cheat myself with fancies of the kind, and to give the tinge of illusion to surrounding realities.

The witching sound had ceased, but its vibrations still played round my heart, and filled it with a tumult of soft emotions. At this moment, a self-upbraiding pang shot through my bosom. "Ah, recreant!" a voice seemed to exclaim, "is this the stability of thine affections? What! hast thou so soon forgotten the nymph of the fountain? Has one song, idly piped in thine ear, been sufficient to charm away the cherished tenderness of a whole summer? "

The wise may smile—but I am in a confiding mood, and must confess my weakness. I felt a degree of compunction at this sudden infidelity, yet I could not resist the power of present fascination. My peace of mind was destroyed by conflicting claims. The nymph of the fountain came over my memory, with all the associations of fairy footsteps, shady groves, soft echoes, and wild streamlets; but this new passion was produced by a strain of soul-subduing melody, still lingering in my ear, aided by a downy bed, fragrant flowers, and rose-colored curtains. "Unhappy youth!" sighed I to myself, "distracted by such rival passions, and the empire of thy heart thus violently contested by the sound of a voice, and the print of a footstep!"

* * *

I had not remained long in this mood, when I heard the door of the room gently opened. I turned my head to see what inhabitant of this enchanted palace should appear; whether page in green, hideous dwarf, or haggard fairy. It was my own man Scipio. He advanced with cautious step, and was delighted, as he said, to find me so much myself again. My first questions were as to where I was, and how I came there? Scipio told me a long story of his having been fishing in a canoe, at the time of my hare-brained cruise; of his noticing the gathering squall, and my impending danger; of his hastening to join me, but arriving just in time to snatch me from a watery grave; of the great difficulty in restoring me to animation; and of my being subsequently conveyed, in a state of insensibility, to this mansion.

"But where am I?" was the reiterated demand.

"In the house of Mr. Somerville."

"Somerville—Somerville!" I recollected to have heard that a gentleman of that name had recently taken up his residence at some distance from my father's abode, on the opposite side of the Hudson. He was commonly known by the name of "French Somerville," from having passed part of his early life in France, and from his exhibiting traces of French taste in his mode of living, and the arrangements of his house. In fact, it was in his pleasure-boat, which had got adrift, that I had made my fanciful and disastrous cruise. All this was simple straight-forward matter of fact, and threatened to demolish all the cobweb romance I had been spinning, when fortunately I again heard the tinkling of a harp. I raised myself in bed, and listened.

"Scipio," said I, with some little hesitation, "I heard some one singing just now. Who was it?"

"Oh, that was Miss Julia."

"Julia! Julia! Delightful! what a name! And, Scipio—is she—is she pretty?"

Scipio grinned from ear to ear. "Except Miss Sophy, she was the most beautiful young lady he had ever seen."

I should observe, that my sister Sophia was considered by all the servants a paragon of perfection.

Scipio now offered to remove the basket of flowers; he was afraid their odor might be too powerful; but Miss Julia had given them that morning to be placed in my room.

These flowers, then, had been gathered by the fairy fingers of my unseen beauty; that sweet breath which had filled my ear with melody, had passed over them. I made Scipio hand them to me, culled several of the most delicate, and laid them on my bosom.

Mr. Somerville paid me a visit not long afterward. He was an interesting study for me, for he was the father of my unseen beauty, and probably resembled her. I scanned him closely. He was a tall and elegant man, with an open, affable manner, and an erect and graceful carriage. His eyes were bluish-gray, and, though not dark, yet at times were sparkling and expressive. His hair was dressed and powdered, and being lightly combed up from his forehead, added to the loftiness of his aspect. He was fluent in discourse, but his conversation had the quiet tone of polished society, without any of those bold flights of thought, and picturings of fancy, which I so much admired.

My imagination was a little puzzled, at first, to make out of this assemblage of personal and mental qualities, a picture that should harmonize with my previous idea of the fair unseen. By dint, however, of selecting what it liked, and rejecting what it did not like, and giving a touch here and a touch there, it soon finished out a satisfactory portrait.

"Julia must be tall," thought I, "and of exquisite grace and dignity. She is not quite so courtly as her father, for she has been brought up in the retirement of the country. Neither is she of such vivacious deportment; for the tones of her voice are soft and plaintive, and she loves pathetic music. She is rather pensive—yet not too pensive; just what is called interesting. Her eyes are like her father's, except that they are of a purer blue, and more tender and languishing. She has light hair—not exactly flaxen, for I do not like flaxen hair, but between that and auburn. In a word, she is a tall, elegant, imposing, languishing, blue-eyed, romantic-looking beauty." And having thus finished her picture, I felt ten times more in love with her than ever.

I felt so much recovered, that I would at once have left my room, but Mr. Somerville objected to it. He had sent early word to my family of my safety; and my father arrived in the course of the morning. He was shocked at learning the risk I had run, but rejoiced to find me so much restored, and was warm in his thanks to Mr. Somerville for his kindness. The other only required, in return, that I might remain two or three days as his guest, to give time for my recovery, and for our forming a closer acquaintance; a request which my father readily granted. Scipio accordingly accompanied my father home, and returned with a supply of clothes, and with affectionate letters from my mother and sisters.

The next morning, aided by Scipio, I made my toilet with rather more care than usual, and descended the stairs, with some trepidation, eager to see the original of the portrait which had been so completely pictured in my imagination.

On entering the parlor, I found it deserted. Like the rest of the house, it was furnished in a foreign style. The curtains were of French silk; there were Grecian couches, marble tables, pier-glasses, and chandeliers. What chiefly attracted my eye, were documents of female taste that I saw around me; a piano, with an ample stock of Italian music; a book of poetry lying on the sofa; a vase of fresh flowers on a table, and a portfolio open with a skilful and half-finished sketch of them. In the window was a Canary bird, in a gilt cage, and near by, the harp that had been in Julia's arms. Happy harp! But where was the being that reigned in this little empire of delicacies?—that breathed poetry and song, and dwelt among birds and flowers, and rose-colored curtains?

Suddenly I heard the hall door fly open, the quick pattering of light steps, a wild, capricious strain of music, and the shrill barking of a dog. A light frolic nymph of fifteen came tripping into the room, playing on a flageolet, with a little spaniel ramping after her. Her gypsy hat had fallen back upon her shoulders; a profusion of glossy brown hair was blown in rich ringlets about her face, which beamed through them with the brightness of smiles and dimples.

At sight of me, she stopped short, in the most beautiful confusion, stammered out a word or two about looking for her father, glided out of the door, and I heard her bounding up the staircase, like a frightened fawn, with the little dog barking after her.

When Miss Somerville returned to the parlor, she was quite a different being. She entered, stealing along by her mother's side with noiseless step, and sweet timidity: her hair was prettily adjusted, and a soft blush mantled on her damask cheek. Mr. Somerville accompanied the ladies, and introduced me regularly to them. There were many kind inquiries, and much sympathy expressed on the subject of my nautical accident, and some remarks upon the wild scenery of the neighborhood, with which the ladies seemed perfectly acquainted.

"You must know," said Mr. Somerville, "that we are great navigators, and delight in exploring every nook and corner of the river. My daughter, too, is a great hunter of the picturesque, and transfers every rock and glen to her portfolio. By the way, my dear, show Mr. Mountjoy that pretty scene you have lately sketched." Julia complied, blushing, and drew from her portfolio a colored sketch. I almost started at the sight. It was my favorite brook. A sudden thought darted across my mind. I glanced down my eye, and beheld the divinest little foot in the world. Oh, blissful conviction! The struggle of my affections was at an end. The voice and the footstep were no longer at variance. Julia Somerville was the nymph of the fountain!

What conversation passed during breakfast, I do not recollect, and hardly was conscious of at the time, for my thoughts were in complete confusion. I wished to gaze on Miss Somerville, but did not dare. Once, indeed, I ventured a glance. She was at that moment darting a similar one from under a covert of ringlets. Our eyes seemed shocked by the rencontre, and fell; hers through the natural modesty of her sex, mine through a bashfulness produced by the previous workings of my imagination. That glance, however, went like a sunbeam to my heart.

A convenient mirror favored my diffidence, and gave me the reflection of Miss Somerville's form. It is true it only presented the back of her head, but she had the merit of an ancient statue; contemplate her from any point of view, she was beautiful. And yet she was totally different from every thing I had before conceived of beauty. She was not the serene, meditative maid that I had pictured the nymph of the fountain; nor the tall, soft, languishing, blue-eyed, dignified being, that I had fancied the minstrel of the harp. There was nothing of dignity about her: she was girlish in her appearance, and scarcely of the middle size; but then there was the tenderness of budding youth; the sweetness of the half-blown rose, when not a tint or perfume has been withered or exhaled; there were smiles and dimples, and all the soft witcheries of ever-varying expression. I wondered that I could ever have admired any other style of beauty.

After breakfast, Mr. Somerville departed to attend to the concerns of his estate, and gave me in charge of the ladies. Mrs. Somerville also was called away by household cares, and I was left alone with Julia! Here then was the situation which of all others I had most coveted. I was in the presence of the lovely being that had so long been the desire of my heart. We were alone; propitious opportunity for a lover! Did I sieze upon it? Did I break out in one of my accustomed rhapsodies? No such thing! Never was being more awkwardly embarrassed.

"What can be the cause of this?" thought I. "Surely I cannot stand in awe of this young girl. I am of course her superior in intellect, and am never embarrassed in company with my tutor notwithstanding all his wisdom."

It was passing strange. I felt that if she were an old woman, I should be quite at my ease; if she were even an ugly woman, I should make out very well; it was her beauty that overpowered me. How little do lovely women know what awful beings they are, in the eyes of inexperienced youth! Young men brought up in the fashionable circles of our cities will smile at all this. Accustomed to mingle incessantly in female society, and to have the romance of the heart deadened by a thousand frivolous flirtations, women are nothing but women in their eyes; but to a susceptible youth like myself, brought up in the country, they are perfect divinities.

Miss Somerville was at first a little embarrassed herself; but, somehow or other, women have a natural adroitness in recovering their self-possession; they are more alert in their minds, and graceful in their manners. Besides, I was but an ordinary personage in Miss Somerville's eyes; she was not under the influence of such a singular course of imaginings as had surrounded her, in my eyes, with the illusions of romance. Perhaps, too, she saw the confusion in the opposite camp, and gained courage from the discovery. At any rate, she was the first to take the field.

Her conversation, however, was only on common-place topics, and in an easy, well-bred style. I endeavored to respond in the same manner; but I was strangely incompetent to the task. My ideas were frozen up; even words seemed to fail me. I was excessively vexed at myself, for I wished to be uncommonly elegant. I tried two or three times to turn a pretty thought, or to utter a fine sentiment; but it would come forth so trite, so forced, so mawkish, that I was ashamed of it. My very voice sounded discordantly, though I sought to modulate it into the softest tones. "The truth is," thought I to myself, "I cannot bring my mind down to the small talk necessary for young girls; it is too masculine and robust for the mincing measure of parlor gossip. I am a philosopher—and that accounts for it."

The entrance of Mrs. Somerville at length gave me relief. I at once breathed freely, and felt a vast deal of confidence come over me. "This is strange," thought I, "that the appearance of another woman should revive my courage; that I should be a better match for two women than one. However, since it is so, I will take advantage of the circumstance, and let this young lady see that I am not so great a simpleton as she probably thinks me."

I accordingly took up the book of poetry which lay upon the sofa. It was Milton's Paradise Lost. Nothing could have been more fortunate; it afforded a fine scope for my favorite vein of grandiloquence. I went largely into a discussion of its merits, or rather an enthusiastic eulogy of them. My observations were addressed to Mrs. Somerville, for I found I could talk to her with more ease than to her daughter. She appeared perfectly alive to the beauties of the poet, and disposed to meet me in the discussion; but it was not my object to hear her talk; it was to talk myself. I anticipated all she had to say, overpowered her with the copiousness of my ideas, and supported and illustrated them by long citations from the author.

While thus holding forth, I cast a side glance to see how Miss Somerville was affected. She had some embroidery stretched on a frame before her, but had paused in her labor, and was looking down as if lost in mute attention. I felt a glow of self-satisfaction, but I recollected, at the same time, with a kind of pique, the advantage she had enjoyed over me in our tête-à-tête. I determined to push my triumph, and accordingly kept on with redoubled ardor, until I had fairly exhausted my subject, or rather my thoughts.

I had scarce come to a full stop, when Miss Somerville raised her eyes from the work on which they had been fixed, and turning to her mother, observed: "I have been considering, mamma, whether to work these flowers plain, or in colors."

Had an ice-bolt been shot to my heart, it could not have chilled me more effectually. "What a fool," thought I, "have I been making myself—squandering away fine thoughts, and fine language upon a light mind, and an ignorant ear! This girl knows nothing of poetry. She has no soul, I fear, for its beauties. Can any one have real sensibility of heart, and not be alive to poetry? However, she is young: this part of her education has been neglected: there is time enough to remedy it. I will be her preceptor. I will kindle in her mind the sacred flame, and lead her through the fairy land of song. But after all, it is rather unfortunate that I should have fallen in love with a woman who knows nothing of poetry."

I passed a day not altogether satisfactory. I was a little disappointed that Miss Somerville did not show more poetical feeling. "I am afraid, after all," said I to myself, "she is light and girlish, and more fitted to pluck wild flowers, play on the flageolet, and romp with little dogs, than to converse with a man of my turn."

I believe, however, to tell the truth, I was more out of humor with myself. I thought I had made the worst first appearance that ever hero made, either in novel or fairy tale. I was out of all patience, when I called to mind my awkward attempts at ease and elegance, in the *tête-à-tête*. And then my intolerable long lecture about poetry, to catch the applause of a heedless auditor! But there I was not to blame. I had certainly been eloquent; it was her fault that the eloquence was wasted. To meditate upon the embroidery of a flower, when I was expatiating on the beauties of Milton! She might at least have admired the poetry, if she did not relish the manner in which it was delivered; though that was not despicable, for I had recited passages in my best style, which my mother and sisters had always considered equal to a play. "Oh, it is evident," thought I, "Miss Somerville has very little soul! "

Such were my fancies and cogitations, during the day, the greater part of which was spent in my chamber, for I was still languid. My evening was passed in the drawing-room, where I overlooked Miss Somerville's portfolio of sketches. They were executed with great taste, and showed a nice observation of the peculiarities of nature. They were all her own, and free from those cunning tints and touches of the drawing-master, by which young ladies' drawings, like their heads, are dressed up for company. There was no garish and vulgar trick of colors, either; all was executed with singular truth and simplicity.

"And yet," thought I, "this little being, who has so pure an eye to take in, as in a limpid brook, all the graceful forms and magic tints of nature, has no soul for poetry!"

Mr. Somerville toward the latter part of the evening, observing my eye to wander occasionally to the harp, interpreted and met my wishes with his accustomed civility.

"Julia, my dear," said he, "Mr. Mountjoy would like to hear a little music from your harp; let us hear, too, the sound of your voice."

Julia immediately complied, without any of that hesitation and difficulty, by which young ladies are apt to make the company pay dear for bad music. She sang a sprightly strain, in a brilliant style, that came trilling playfully over the ear; and the bright eye and dimpling smile showed that her little heart danced with the song. Her pet Canary bird, who hung close by, was wakened by the music, and burst forth into an emulating strain. Julia smiled with a pretty air of defiance, and played louder.

After some time, the music changed, and ran into a plaintive strain, in a minor key. Then it was, that all the former witchery of her voice came over me; then it was, that she seemed to sing from the heart and to the heart. Her fingers moved about the chords as if they scarcely touched them. Her whole manner and appearance changed; her eyes beamed with the softest expression; her countenance, her frame, all seemed subdued into tenderness. She rose from the harp, leaving it still vibrating, with sweet sounds, and moved toward her father, to bid him good night.

His eyes had been fixed on her intently, during her performance. As she came before him, he parted her shining ringlets with both his hands, and looked down with the fondness of a father on her innocent face. The music seemed still lingering in its lineaments, and the action of her father brought a moist gleam in her eye. He kissed her fair forehead, after the French mode of parental caressing: "Good night, and God bless you," said he, "my good little girl!"

Julia tripped away, with a tear in her eye, a dimple in her cheek, and a light heart in her bosom. I thought it the prettiest picture of paternal and filial affection I had ever seen.

When I retired to bed, a new train of thoughts crowded into my brain. "After all," said I to myself, "it is clear this girl has a soul, though she was not moved by my eloquence. She has all the outward signs and evidences of poetic feeling. She paints well, and has an eye for nature. She is a fine musician, and enters into the very soul of song. What a pity that she knows nothing of poetry! But we will see what is to be done. I am irretrievably in love with her; what then am I to do? Come down to the level of her mind, or endeavor to raise her to some kind of intellectual equality with myself? That is the most generous course. She will look up to me as a benefactor. I shall become associated in her mind with the lofty thoughts and harmonious graces of poetry. She is apparently docile: besides, the difference of our ages will give me an ascendency over her. She cannot be above sixteen years of age, and I am full turned of twenty." So, having built this most delectable of air-castles, I fell asleep.

The next morning, I was quite a different being. I no longer felt fearful of stealing a glance at Julia; on the contrary, I contemplated her steadily, with the benignant eye of a benefactor. Shortly after breakfast, I found myself alone with her, as I had on the preceding morning; but I felt nothing of the awkwardness of our previous tête-à-tête. I was elevated by the consciousness of my intellectual superiority, and should almost have felt a sentiment of pity for the ignorance of the lovely little being, if I had not felt also the assurance that I should be able to dispel it. "But it is time," thought I, "to open school."

Julia, was occupied in arranging some music on her piano. I looked over two or three songs; they were Moore's Irish melodies.

"These are pretty things," said I, flirting the leaves over lightly, and giving a slight shrug, by way of qualifying the opinion.

"Oh, I love them of all things!" said Julia, "they're so touching!"

"Then you like them for the poetry," said I, with an encouraging smile.

"Oh yes; she thought them charmingly written."

Now was my time. "Poetry," said I, assuming a didactic attitude and air, "poetry is one of the most pleasing studies that can occupy a youthful mind. It renders us susceptible of the gentle impulses of humanity, and cherishes a delicate perception of all that is virtuous and elevated in morals, and graceful and beautiful in physics. It—"

I was going on in a style that would have graced a professor of rhetoric, when I saw a light smile playing about Miss Somerville's mouth, and that she began to turn over the leaves of a music book. I recollected her inattention to my discourse of the preceding morning. "There is no fixing her light mind," thought I, "by abstract theory; we will proceed practically." As it happened, the identical volume of Milton's Paradise Lost was lying at hand.

"Let me recommend to you, my young friend," said I, in one of those tones of persuasive admonition, which I had so often loved in Glencoe—"let me recommend to you this admirable poem: you will find in it sources of intellectual enjoyment far superior to those songs which have delighted you." Julia looked at the book, and then at me, with a whimsically dubious air. "Milton's Paradise Lost?" said she; "oh, I know the greater part of that by heart."

I had not expected to find my pupil so far advanced; however, the Paradise Lost is a kind of school book, and its finest passages are given to young ladies as tasks.

"I find," said I to myself, "I must not treat her as so complete a novice; her inattention, yesterday, could not have proceeded from absolute ignorance, but merely from a want of poetic feeling. I'll try her again."

I now determined to dazzle her with my own erudition, and launched into a harangue that would have done honor to an institute. Pope, Spenser, Chaucer, and the old dramatic writers, were all dipped into, with the excursive flight of a swallow. I did not confine myself to English poets, but gave a glance at the French and Italian schools: I passed over Ariosto in full wing, but paused on Tasso's Jerusalem Delivered. I dwelt on the character of Clorinda: "There's a character," said I, "that you will find well worthy a woman's study. It shows to what exalted heights of heroism the sex can rise; how gloriously they may share even in the stern concerns of men."

"For my part," said Julia, gently taking advantage of a pause—"for my part, I prefer the character of Sophronia."

I was thunderstruck. She then had read Tasso! This girl that I had been treating as an ignoramus in poetry! She proceeded, with a slight glow of the cheek, summoned up perhaps by a casual glow of feeling:

"I do not admire those masculine heroines," said she, "who aim at the bold qualities of the opposite sex. Now Sophronia only exhibits the real qualities of a woman, wrought up to their highest excitement. She is modest, gentle, and retiring, as it becomes a woman to be; but she has all the strength of affection proper to a woman. She cannot fight for her people, as Clorinda does, but she can offer herself up, and die, to serve them. You may admire Clorinda, but you surely would be more apt to love Sophronia; at least," added she, suddenly appearing to recollect herself, and blushing at having launched into such a discussion, "at least, that is what papa observed, when we read the poem together."

"Indeed," said I, dryly, for I felt disconcerted and nettled at being unexpectedly lectured by my pupil—"indeed, I do not exactly recollect the passage."

"Oh," said Julia, "I can repeat it to you"; and she immediately gave it in Italian.

Heavens and earth!—here was a situation! I knew no more of Italian than I did of the language of Psalmanazar. What a dilemma for a would-be-wise man to be placed in! I saw Julia waited for my opinion.

"In fact," said I, hesitating, "I—I do not exactly understand Italian."

"Oh," said Julia, with the utmost naïveté, "I have no doubt it is very beautiful in the translation."

I was glad to break up school, and get back to my chamber, full of the mortification which a wise man in love experiences on finding his mistress wiser than himself. "Translation! translation!" muttered I to myself, as I jerked the door shut behind me. "I am surprised my father has never had me instructed in the modern languages. They are all-important. What is the use of Latin and Greek? No one speaks them; but here, the moment I make my appearance in the world, a little girl slaps Italian in my face. However, thank Heaven, a language is easily learned. The moment I return home, I'll set about studying Italian; and to prevent future surprise, I will study Spanish and German at the same time; and if any young lady attempts to quote Italian upon me again, I'll bury her under a heap of High Dutch poetry!"

I felt now like some mighty chieftain, who has carried the war into a weak country, with full confidence of success, and been repulsed and obliged to draw off his forces from before some inconsiderable fortress.

"However," thought I, "I have as yet brought only my light artillery into action; we shall see what is to be done with my heavy ordnance. Julia is evidently well versed in poetry; but it is natural she should be so; it is allied to painting and music, and is congenial to the light graces of the female character. We will try her on graver themes."

I felt all my pride awakened; it even for a time swelled higher than my love. I was determined completely to establish my mental superiority, and subdue the intellect of this little being: it would then be time to sway the sceptre of gentle empire, and win the affections of her heart.

Accordingly, at dinner I again took the field, *en potence*. I now addressed myself to Mr. Somerville, for I was about to enter upon topics in which a young girl like her could not be well versed. I led, or rather forced, the conversation into a vein of historical erudition, discussing several of the most prominent facts of ancient history and accompanying them with sound, indisputable apothegms.

Mr. Somerville listened to me with the air of a man receiving information. I was encouraged, and went on gloriously from theme to theme of school declamation. I sat with Marius on the ruins of Carthage; I defended the bridge with Horatius Cocles; thrust my hand into the flame with Martins Scævola, and plunged with Curtius into the yawning gulf; I fought side by side with Leonidas, at the straits of Thermopylæ; and was going full drive into the battle of Platsea, when my memory, which is the worst in the world, failed me, just as I wanted the name of the Lacedemonian commander.

"Julia, my dear," said Mr. Somerville, "perhaps you may recollect the name of which Mr. Mountjoy is in quest?"

Julia colored slightly: "I believe," said she, in a low voice,—"I believe it was Pausanias."

This unexpected sally, instead of reinforcing me, threw my whole scheme of battle into confusion, and the Athenians remained unmolested in the field.

I am half inclined, since, to think Mr. Somerville meant this as a sly hit at my school-boy pedantry; but he was too well bred not to seek to relieve me from my mortification. "Oh!" said he, "Julia is our family book of reference for names, dates, and distances, and has an excellent memory for history and geography."

I now became desperate; as a last resource, I turned to metaphysics. "If she is a philosopher in petticoats," thought I, "it is all over with me."

Here, however, I had the field to myself I gave chapter and verse of my tutor's lectures, heightened by all his poetical illustrations: I even went farther than he had ever ventured, and plunged into such depths of metaphysics, that I was in danger of sticking in the mire at the bottom. Fortunately, I had auditors who apparently could not detect my flounderings. Neither Mr. Somerville nor his daughter offered the least interruption.

When the ladies had retired, Mr. Somerville sat some time with me; and as I was no longer anxious to astonish, I permitted myself to listen, and found that he was really agreeable. He was quite communicative, and from his conversation I was enabled to form a juster idea of his daughter's character, and the mode in which she had been brought up. Mr. Somerville had mingled much with the world, and with what is termed fashionable society. He had experienced its cold elegancies, and gay insincerities; its dissipation of the spirits, and squanderings of the heart. Like many men of the world, though he had wandered too far from nature ever to return to it, yet he had the good taste and good feeling to look back fondly to its simple delights, and to determine that his child, if possible, should never leave them. He had superintended her education with scrupulous care, storing her mind with the graces of polite literature, and with such knowledge as would enable it to furnish its own amusement and occupation, and giving her all the accomplishments that sweeten and enliven the circle of domestic life. He had been particularly sedulous to exclude all fashionable affectations; all false sentiment, false sensibility, and false romance. "Whatever advantages she may possess," said he, "she is quite unconscious of them. She is a capricious little being, in every thing but her affections; she is, however, free from art: simple, ingenuous, innocent, amiable, and I thank God! happy."

Such was the eulogy of a fond father, delivered with a tenderness that touched me. I could not help making a casual inquiry whether, among the graces of polite literature, he had included a slight tincture of metaphysics. He smiled, and told me he had not.

On the whole, when, as usual, that night, I summed up the day's observations on my pillow, I was not altogether dissatisfied. "Miss Somerville," said I, "loves poetry, and I like her the better for it. She has the advantage of me in Italian: agreed; what is it to know a variety of languages, but merely to have a variety of sounds to express the same idea? Original thought is the ore of the mind; language is but the accidental stamp and coinage, by which it is put into circulation. If I can furnish an original idea, what care I how many languages she can translate it into? She may be able, also, to quote names, and dates, and latitudes, better than I; but that is a mere effort of the memory. I admit she is more accurate in history and geography than I; but then she knows nothing of metaphysics."

I had now sufficiently recovered, to return home; yet I could nob think of leaving Mr. Somerville's, without having a little farther conversation with him on the subject of his daughter's education.

"This Mr. Somerville," thought I, "is a very accomplished, elegant man; he has seen a good deal of the world, and, upon the whole, has profited by what he has seen. He is not without information, and, as far as he thinks, appears to think correctly; but after all, he is rather superficial, and does not think profoundly. He seems to take no delight in those metaphysical abstractions, that are the proper aliment of masculine minds. I called to mind various occasions in which I had indulged largely in metaphysical discussions, but could recollect no instance where I had been able to draw him out. He had listened, it is true, with attention, and smiled as if in acquiescence, but had always appeared to avoid reply. Besides, I had made several sad blunders in the glow of eloquent declamation; but he had never interrupted me, to notice and correct them, as he would have done had he been versed in the theme.

"Now it is really a great pity," resumed I, "that he should have the entire management of Miss Somerville's education. What a vast advantage it would be, if she could be put for a little time under the superintendence of Glencoe. He would throw some deeper shades of thought into her mind, which at present is all sunshine; not but that Mr. Somerville has done very well, as far as he has gone; but then he has merely prepared the soil for the strong plants of useful knowledge. She is well versed in the leading facts of history, and the general course of belles-lettres," said I; "a little more philosophy would do wonders."

I accordingly took occasion to ask Mr. Somerville for a few moments' conversation in his study, the morning I was to depart. When we were alone, I opened the matter fully to him. I commenced with the warmest eulogium of Glencoe's powers of mind, and vast acquirements, and ascribed to him all my proficiency in the higher branches of knowledge. I begged, therefore, to recommend him as a friend calculated to direct the studies of Miss Somerville; to lead her mind, by degrees to the contemplation of abstract principles, and to produce habits of philosophical analysis; "which," added I, gently smiling, "are not often cultivated by young ladies." I ventured to hint, in addition, that he would find Mr. Glencoe a most valuable and interesting acquaintance for himself; one who would stimulate and evolve the powers of his mind; and who might open to him tracts of inquiry and speculation, to which perhaps he had hitherto been a stranger.

Mr. Somerville listened with grave attention. When I had finished, he thanked me in the politest manner for the interest I took in the welfare of his daughter and himself. He observed that, as regarded himself, he was afraid he was too old to benefit by the instructions of Mr. Glencoe, and that as to his daughter, he was afraid her mind was but little fitted for the study of metaphysics. "I do not wish," continued he, "to strain her intellects with subjects they cannot grasp, but to make her familiarly acquainted with those that are within the limits of her capacity. I do not pretend to prescribe the boundaries of female genius, and am far from indulging the vulgar opinion, that women are unfitted by nature for the highest intellectual pursuits. I speak only with reference to my daughter's taste and talents. She will never make a learned woman; nor in truth do I desire it; for such is the jealousy of our sex, as to mental as well as physical ascendency, that a learned woman is not always the happiest. I do not wish my daughter to excite envy, nor to battle with the prejudices of the world; but to glide peaceably through life, on the good will and kind opinion of her friends. She has ample employment for her little head, in the course I have marked out for her; and is busy at present with some branches of natural history, calculated to awaken her perceptions to the beauties and wonders of nature, and to the inexhaustible volume of wisdom constantly spread open before her eyes. I consider that woman most likely to make an agreeable companion, who can draw topics of pleasing remark from every natural object; and most likely to be cheerful and contented, who is continually sensible of the order, the harmony, and the invariable beneficence, that reign throughout the beautiful world we inhabit."

"But," added he, smiling, "I am betraying myself into a lecture, instead of merely giving a reply to your kind offer. Permit me to take the liberty, in return, of inquiring a little about your own pursuits. You speak of having finished your education; but of course you have a line of private study and mental occupation marked out; for you must know the importance, both in point of interest and happiness, of keeping the mind employed. May I ask what system you observe in your intellectual exercises?"

"Oh, as to system," I observed, "I could never bring myself into any thing of the kind. I thought it best to let my genius take its own course, as it always acted the most vigorously when stimulated by inclination."

Mr. Somerville shook his head. "This same genius," said he, "is a wild quality, that runs away with our most promising young men. It has become so much the fashion, too, to give it the reins, that it is now thought an animal of too noble and generous a nature to be brought to the harness. But it is all a mistake. Nature never designed these high endowments to run riot through society, and throw the whole system into confusion. No, my dear sir: genius, unless it acts upon system, is very apt to be a useless quality to society; sometimes an injurious, and certainly a very uncomfortable one, to its possessor. I have had many opportunities of seeing the progress through life of young men who were accounted geniuses, and have found it too often end in early exhaustion and bitter disappointment; and have as often noticed that these effects might be traced to a total want of system. There were no habits of business, of steady purpose, and regular application, superinduced upon the mind; every thing was left to chance and impulse, and native luxuriance, and every thing of course ran to waste and wild entanglement. Excuse me, if I am tedious on this point, for I feel solicitous to impress it upon you, being an error extremely prevalent in our country, and one into which too many of our youth have fallen. I am happy, however, to observe the zeal which still appears to actuate you for the acquisition of knowledge, and augur every good from the elevated bent of your ambition. May I ask what has been your course of study for the last six months?"

Never was question more unluckily timed. For the last six months I had been absolutely buried in novels and romances.

Mr. Somerville perceived that the question was embarrassing, and with his invariable good breeding, immediately resumed the conversation, without waiting for a reply. He took care, however, to turn it in such a way as to draw from me an account of the whole manner in which I had been educated, and the various currents of reading into which my mind had run. He then went on to discuss briefly, but impressively, the different branches of knowledge most important to a young man in my situation; and to my surprise I found him a complete master of those studies on which I had supposed him ignorant, and on which I had been descanting so confidently.

He complimented me, however, very graciously, upon the progress I had made, but advised me for the present to turn my attention to the physical rather than the moral sciences. "These studies," said he, "store a man's mind with valuable facts, and at the same time repress self-confidence, by letting him know how boundless are the realms of knowledge, and how little we can possibly know. Whereas metaphysical studies, though of an ingenious order of intellectual employment, are apt to bewilder some minds with vague speculations. They never know how far they have advanced, or what may be the correctness of their favorite theory. They render many of our young men verbose and declamatory, and prone to mistake the aberrations of their fancy for the inspirations of divine philosophy."

I could not but interrupt him, to assent to the truth of these remarks, and to say that it had been my lot, in the course of my limited experience, to encounter young men of the kind, who had overwhelmed me by their verbosity.

Mr. Somerville smiled. "I trust," said he, kindly, "that you will guard against these errors. Avoid the eagerness with which a young man is apt to hurry into conversation, and to utter the crude and ill-digested notions which he has picked up in his recent studies. Be assured that extensive and accurate knowledge is the slow acquisition of a studious lifetime; that a young man, however pregnant his wit, and prompt his talent, can have mastered but the rudiments of learning, and, in a manner, attained the implements of study. Whatever may have been your past assiduity, you must be sensible that as yet you have but reached the threshold of true knowledge; but at the same time, you have the advantage that you are still very young, and have ample time to learn."

Here our conference ended. I walked out of the study, a very different being from what I was on entering it. I had gone in with the air of a professor about to deliver a lecture; I came out like a student, who had failed in his examination, and been degraded in his class.

"Very young," and "on the threshold of knowledge!" This was extremely flattering, to one who had considered himself an accomplished scholar, and profound philosopher!

"It is singular," thought I; "there seems to have been a spell upon my faculties, ever since I have been in this house. I certainly have not been able to do myself justice. Whenever I have undertaken to advise, I have had the tables turned upon me. It must be that I am strange and diffident among people I am not accustomed to. I wish they could hear me talk at home!"

"After all," added I, on farther reflection,—"after all, there is a great deal of force in what Mr. Somerville has said. Some how or other, these men of the world do now and then hit upon remarks that would do credit to a philosopher. Some of his general observations came so home, that I almost thought they were meant for myself. His advice about adopting a system of study, is very judicious. I will immediately put it in practice. My mind shall operate henceforward with the regularity of clockwork."

How far I succeeded in adopting this plan, how I fared in the farther pursuit of knowledge, and how I succeeded in my suit to Julia Somerville, may afford matter for a farther communication to the public, if this simple record of my early life is fortunate enough to excite any curiosity.

The Bermudas

A Shakspearian Research

> Who did not think, till within these foure yeares, but that these islands had been rather a habitation for Divells, than fit for men to dwell in? Who did not hate the name, when hee was on land, and shun the place when he was on the seas? But behold the misprision and conceits of the world! For true and large experience hath now told us, it is one of the sweetest paradises that be upon earth.
>
> A Plaine Descript. of the Barmudas: 1613

In the course of a voyage home from England, our ship had been struggling, for two or three weeks, with perverse head-winds, and a stormy sea. It was in the month of May, yet the weather had at times a wintry sharpness, and it was apprehended that we were in the neighborhood of floating islands of ice, which at that season of the year drift out of the Gulf of Saint Lawrence, and sometimes occasion the wreck of noble ships.

Wearied out by the continued opposition of the elements, our captain bore away to the south, in hopes of catching the expiring breath of the trade-winds, and making what is called the southern passage. A few days wrought, as it were, a magical "sea change" in every thing around us. We seemed to emerge into a different world. The late dark and angry sea, lashed up into roaring and swashing surges, became calm and sunny; the rude winds died away and gradually a light breeze sprang up directly aft, filling out every sail, and wafting us smoothly along on an even keel. The air softened into a bland and delightful temperature. Dolphins began to play about us; the nautilus came floating by, like a fairy ship, with its mimic sail and rainbow tints; and flying-fish, from time to time, made their short excursive flights, and occasionally fell upon the deck. The cloaks and overcoats in which we had hitherto wrapped ourselves, and moped about the vessel, were thrown aside; for a summer warmth had succeeded to the late wintry chills. Sails were stretched as awnings over the quarter-deck, to protect us from the mid-day sun. Under these we lounged away the day, in luxurious indolence, musing, with half-shut eyes, upon the quiet ocean. The night was scarcely less beautiful than the day. The rising moon sent a quivering column of silver along the undulating surface of the deep, and, gradually climbing the heaven, lit up our towering topsails and swelling mainsails, and spread a pale, mysterious light around. As our ship made her whispering way through this dreamy world of waters, every boisterous sound on board was charmed to silence; and the low whistle, or drowsy song, of a sailor from the forecastle, or the tinkling of a guitar, and the soft warbling of a female voice from the quarter-deck, seemed to derive a witching melody from the scene and hour. I was reminded of Oberon's exquisite description of music and moonlight on the ocean:

—Thou rememberest
Since once I sat upon a promontory,
And heard a mermaid on a dolphin's back,
Uttering such dulcet and harmonious breath,
That the rude sea grew civil at her song;
And certain stars shot madly from their spheres,
To hear the sea-maid's music.

Indeed, I was in the very mood to conjure up all the imaginary beings with which poetry has peopled old ocean, and almost ready to fancy I heard the distant song of the mermaid, or the mellow shell of the triton, and to picture to myself Neptune and Amphitrite with all their pageant sweeping along the dim horizon.

A day or two of such fanciful voyaging, brought us in sight of the Bermudas, which first looked like mere summer clouds, peering above the quiet ocean. All day we glided along in sight of them, with just wind enough to fill our sails; and never did land appear more lovely. They were clad in emerald verdure, beneath the serenest of skies: not an angry wave broke upon their quiet shores, and small fishing craft, riding on the crystal waves, seemed as if hung in air. It was such a scene that Fletcher pictured to himself, when he extolled the halcyon lot of the fisherman:

Ah I would thou knewest how much it better were
To bide among the simple fisher-swains:
No shrieking owl, no night-crow lodgeth here,
Nor is our simple pleasure mixed with pains.
Our sports begin with, the beginning year;
In calms, to pull the leaping fish to land,
In roughs, to sing and dance along the yellow sand.

In contemplating these beautiful islands, and the peaceful sea around them, I could hardly realize that these were the "still vexed Bermoothes" of Shakspeare, once the dread of mariners, and infamous in the narratives of the early discoverers, for the dangers and disasters which beset them. Such, however, was the case; and the islands derived additional interest in my eyes, from fancying that I could trace in their early history, and in the superstitious notions connected with them, some of the elements of Shakspeare's wild and beautiful drama of the Tempest. I shall take the liberty of citing a few historical facts, in support of this idea, which may claim some additional attention from the American reader, as being connected with the first settlement of Virginia.

At the time when Shakspeare was in the fulness of his talent, and seizing upon every thing that could furnish aliment to his imagination, the colonization of Virginia was a favorite object of enterprise among people of condition in England, and several of the courtiers of the court of Queen Elizabeth were personally engaged in it. In the year 1609, a noble armament of nine ships and five hundred men sailed for the relief of the colony. It was commanded by Sir George Somers, as admiral, a gallant and generous gentleman, above sixty years of age, and possessed of an ample fortune, yet still bent upon hardy enterprise, and ambitious of signalizing himself in the service of his country.

On board of his flag-ship, the Sea-Vulture, sailed also Sir Thomas Gates, lieutenant-general of the colony. The voyage was long and boisterous. On the twenty-fifth of July, the admiral's ship was separated from the rest in a hurricane. For several days she was driven about at the mercy of the elements, and so strained and racked, that her seams yawned open, and her hold was half filled with water. The storm subsided, but left her a mere foundering wreck. The crew stood in the hold to their waists in water, vainly endeavoring to bail her with kettles, buckets, and other vessels. The leaks rapidly gained on them, while their strength was as rapidly declining. They lost all hope of keeping the ship afloat, until they should reach the American coast; and wearied with fruitless toil, determined, in their despair, to give up all farther attempt, shut down the hatches, and abandon themselves to Providence. Some, who had spirituous liquors, or "comfortable waters," as the old record quaintly terms them, brought them forth, and shared them with their comrades, and they all drank a sad farewell to one another, as men who were soon to part company in this world.

In this moment of extremity, the worthy admiral, who kept sleepless watch from the high stern of the vessel, gave the thrilling cry of "land! "All rushed on deck, in a frenzy of joy, and nothing now was to be seen or heard on board, but the transports of men who felt as if rescued from the grave. It is true the land in sight would not, in ordinary circumstances, have inspired much self-gratulation. It could be nothing else but the group of islands called after their discoverer, one Juan Bermudas, a Spaniard, but stigmatized among the mariners of those days as "the islands of devils!" "For the islands of the Bermudas," says the old narrative of this voyage, "as every man knoweth that hath heard or read of them, were never inhabited by any christian or heathen people, but were ever esteemed and reputed a most prodigious and inchanted place, affording nothing but gusts, stormes, and foul weather, which made every navigator and mariner to avoide them as Scylla and Charybdis, or as they would shun the Divell himself."[1]

Sir George Somers and his tempest-tossed comrades, however, hailed them with rapture, as if they had been a terrestrial paradise. Every sail was spread, and every exertion made to urge the foundering ship to land. Before long, she struck upon a rock. Fortunately, the late stormy winds had subsided, and there was no surf. A swelling wave lifted her from off the rock, and bore her to another; and thus she was borne on from rock to rock, until she remained wedged between two, as firmly as if set upon the stocks. The boats were immediately lowered, and, though the shore was above a mile distant, the whole crew were lauded in safety.

Every one had now his task assigned him. Some made all haste to unload the ship, before she should go to pieces; some constructed wigwams of palmetto leaves, and others ranged the island in quest of wood and water. To their surprise and joy, they found it far different from the desolate and frightful place they had been taught by seamen's stories to expect. It was well wooded and fertile; there were birds of various

---

1. A Plaine Description of the Barmudas.

kinds, and herds of swine roaming about, the progeny of a number that had swum ashore, in former years, from a Spanish wreck. The island abounded with turtle, and great quantities of their eggs were to be found among the rocks. The bays and inlets were full of fish; so tame, that if any one stepped into the water, they would throng around him. Sir George Somers, in a little while, caught enough with hook and line to furnish a meal to his whole ship's company. Some of them were so large, that two were as much as a man could carry. Craw-fish, also, were taken in abundance. The air was soft and salubrious, and the sky beautifully serene. Waller, in his "Summer Islands," has given us a faithful picture of the climate:

> "For the kind spring, (which but salutes us here,)
> Inhabits these, and courts them all the year:
> Ripe fruits and blossoms on the same trees live;
> At once they promise, and at once they give:
> So sweet the air, so moderate the clime,
> None sickly lives, or dies before his time.
> Heaven sure has kept this spot of earth uncursed.
> To show how all things were created first."

We may imagine the feelings of the shipwrecked mariners, on finding themselves cast by stormy seas upon so happy a coast where abundance was to be had without labor; where what in other climes constituted the costly luxuries of the rich, were within every man's reach; and where life promised to be a mere holiday. Many of the common sailors, especially, declared they desired no better lot than to pass the rest of their lives on this favored island.

The commanders, however, were not so ready to console themselves with mere physical comforts, for the severance from the enjoyment of cultivated life, and all the objects of honorable ambition. Despairing of the arrival of any chance ship on these shunned and dreaded islands, they fitted out the long-boat, making a deck of the ship's hatches, and having manned her with eight picked men, despatched her, under the command of an able and hardy mariner, named Raven, to proceed to Virginia, and procure shipping to be sent to their relief.

While waiting in anxious idleness for the arrival of the looked for aid, dissensions arose between Sir George Somers and Sir Thomas Gates, originating, very probably, in jealousy of the lead which the nautical experience and professional station of the admiral gave him in the present emergency. Each commander of course had his adherents these dissensions ripened into a complete schism; and this handful of shipwrecked men, thus thrown together on an uninhabited island, separated into two parties, and lived asunder in bitter feud, as men rendered fickle by prosperity, instead of being brought into brotherhood by a common calamity.

Weeks and months elapsed, without bringing the looked-for aid from Virginia, though that colony was within but a few days sail. Fears were now entertained that the long-boat had been either swallowed up in the sea, or wrecked on some savage coast; one or other of which most probably was the case, as nothing was ever heard of Raven and his comrades.

Each party now set to work to build a vessel for itself out of the cedar with which the island abounded. The wreck of the Sea-Vulture furnished rigging, and various other articles; but they had no iron for bolts, and other fastenings; and for want of pitch and tar, they payed the seams of their vessels with lime and turtle's oil, which soon dried, and became as hard as stone.

On the tenth of May, 1610, they set sail, having been about nine months on the island. They reached Virginia without farther accident, but found the colony in great distress for provisions. The account that they gave of the abundance that reigned in the Bermudas, and especially of the herds of swine that roamed the island, determined Lord Delaware, the governor of Virginia, to send thither for supplies. Sir George Somers, with his wonted promptness and generosity, offered to undertake what was still considered a dangerous voyage. Accordingly on the nineteenth of June, he set sail, in his own cedar vessel of thirty tons, accompanied by another small vessel, commanded by Captain Argall.

The gallant Somers was doomed again to be tempest-tossed. His companion vessel was soon driven back to port, but he kept the sea; and, as usual, remained at his post on deck, in all weathers. His voyage was long and boisterous, and the fatigues and exposures which he underwent, were too much for a frame impaired by age, and by previous hardships. He arrived at Bermudas completely exhausted and broken down.

His nephew, Captain Matthew Somers, attended him in his illness with affectionate assiduity. Finding his end approaching, the veteran called his men together, and exhorted them to be true to the interests of Virginia; to procure provisions, with all possible despatch, and hasten back to the relief of the colony.

With this dying charge, he gave up the ghost, leaving his nephew and crew overwhelmed with grief and consternation. Their first thought was to pay honor to his remains. Opening the body, they took out the heart and entrails, and buried them, erecting a cross over the grave. They then embalmed the body, and set sail with it for England; thus, while paying empty honors to their deceased commander, neglecting his earnest wish and dying injunction, that they should return with relief to Virginia.

The little bark arrived safely at Whitechurch in Dorsetshire, with its melancholy freight. The body of the worthy Somers was interred with the military honors due to a brave soldier, and many volleys fired over his grave. The Bermudas have since received the name of the Somer Islands, as a tribute to his memory.

The accounts given by Captain Matthew Somers and his crew of the delightful climate, and the great beauty, fertility, and abundance of these islands, excited the zeal of enthusiasts, and the cupidity of speculators, and a plan was set on foot to colonize them. The Virginia company sold their right to the islands to one hundred and twenty of their own members, who erected themselves into a distinct corporation, under the name of the "Somer Island Society"; and Mr. Richard More was sent out, in 1612, as governor, with sixty men, to found a colony: and this leads me to the second branch of this research.

The Three Kings of Bermuda

And Their Treasure of Ambergris

At the time that Sir George Somers was preparing to launch his cedar-built bark, and sail for Virginia, there were three culprits among his men, who had been guilty of capital offences. One of them was shot; the others, named Christopher Carter and Edward Waters, escaped. Waters, indeed, made a very narrow escape, for he had actually been tied to a tree to be executed, but cut the rope with a knife, which he had concealed about his person, and fled to the woods, where he was joined by Carter. These two worthies kept themselves concealed in the secret parts of the island, until the departure of the two vessels. When Sir George Somers revisited the island, in quest of supplies for the Virginia colony, these culprits hovered about the landing-place, and succeeded in persuading another seaman, named Edward Chard, to join them, giving him the most seductive picture of the ease and abundance in which they revelled.

When the bark that bore Sir George's body to England had faded from the watery horizon, these three vagabonds walked forth in their majesty and might, the lords and sole inhabitants of these islands. For a time their little commonwealth went on prosperously and happily. They built a house, sowed corn, and the seeds of various fruits; and having plenty of hogs, wild fowl, and fish of all kinds, with turtle in abundance, carried on their tripartite sovereignty with great harmony and much feasting. All kingdoms, however, are doomed to revolution, convulsion, or decay; and so it fared with the empire of the three kings of Bermuda, albeit they were monarchs without subjects. In an evil hour, in their search after turtle, among the fissures of the rocks, they came upon a great treasure of ambergris, which had been cast on shore by the ocean. Besides a number of pieces of smaller dimensions, there was one great mass, the largest that had ever been known, weighing eighty pounds, and which of itself, according to the market value of ambergris in those days, was worth about nine or ten thousand pounds.

From that moment the happiness and harmony of the three kings of Bermuda were gone for ever. While poor devils, with nothing to share but the common blessings of the island, which administered to present enjoyment, but had nothing of convertible value, they were loving and united; but here was actual wealth, which would make them rich men, whenever they could transport it to market.

Adieu the delights of the island! They now became flat and insipid. Each pictured to himself the consequence he might now aspire to, in civilized life, could he once get there with this mass of ambergris. No longer a poor Jack Tar, frolicking in the low taverns of Wapping, he might roll through London in his coach, and perchance arrive, like Whittington, at the dignity of Lord Mayor.

With riches came envy and covetousness. Each was now for assuming the supreme power, and getting the monopoly of the ambergris. A civil war at length broke out: Chard and Waters defied each other to mortal combat, and the kingdom of the Bermudas was on the point of being deluged with royal blood. Fortunately, Carter took no part in the bloody feud. Ambition might have made him view it with secret exultation; for if either or both of his brother potentates were slain in the conflict, he would be a gainer in purse and ambergris. But he dreaded to be left alone in this uninhabited island, and to find himself the monarch of a solitude: so he secretly purloined and hid the weapons of the belligerent rivals, who, having no means of carrying on the war, gradually cooled down into a sullen armistice.

The arrival of Governor More, with an overpowering force of sixty men, put an end to the empire. He took possession of the kingdom, in the name of the Somer Island Company, and forthwith proceeded to make a settlement. The three kings tacitly relinquished their sway, but stood up stoutly for their treasure. It was determined, however, that they had been fitted out at the expense, and employed in the service, of the Virginia Company; that they had found the ambergris while in the service of that company, and on that company's land; that the ambergris therefore belonged to that company, or rather to the Somer Island Company, in consequence of their recent purchase of the island and all their appurtenances. Having thus legally established their right, and being moreover able to back it by might, the company laid the lion's paw upon the spoil; and nothing more remains on historic record of the Three Kings of Bermuda, and their treasure of ambergris.

The reader will now determine whether I am more extravagant than most of the commentators on Shakespeare, in my surmise that the story of Sir George Somers' shipwreck, and the subsequent occurrences that took place on the uninhabited island may have furnished the bard with some of the elements of his drama of the Tempest. The tidings of the shipwreck, and of the incidents connected with it, reached England not long before the production of this drama, and made a great sensation there. A narrative of the whole matter, from which most of the foregoing particulars are extracted, was published at the time in London, in a pamphlet form, and could not fail to be eagerly perused by Shakespeare, and to make a vivid impression on his fancy. His expression, in the Tempest, of "the still vext Bermoothes," accords exactly with the storm-beaten character of those islands. The enchantments, too, with which he has clothed the island of Prospero, may they not be traced to the wild and superstitious notions entertained about the Bermudas? I have already cited two passages from a pamphlet published at the time, showing that they were esteemed "a most *prodigious* and *inchanted* place," and the "habitation of divells"; and another pamphlet, published shortly afterward, observes: "And whereas it is reported that this land of the Barmudas, with the islands about, (which are many, at least an hundred), are inchanted, and kept with evil and wicked spirits, it is a most idle false report."[2]

The description, too, given in the same pamphlets, of the real beauty and fertility of the Bermudas, and of their serene and happy climate, so opposite to the dangerous and inhospitable character with which they had been stigmatized, accords with the eulogium of Sebastian on the island of Prospero.

2. "Newes from the Barmudas:" 1612.

> Though this island seem to be desert, uninhabitable, and almost inaccessible, it must needs be of subtle, tender, and delicate temperance. The air breathes upon us here most sweetly. Here is every thing advantageous to life. How lush and lusty the grass looks! how green!

I think too, in the exulting consciousness of ease, security, and abundance, felt by the late tempest-tossed mariners, while revelling in the plenteousness of the island, and their inclination to remain there, released from the labors, the cares, and the artificial restraints of civilized life, I can see something of the golden commonwealth of honest Gonzalo:

> Had I a plantation of this isle, my lord,
> And were the king of it, what would I do?
> I' the commonwealth I would by contraries
> Execute all things: for no kind of traffic
> Would I admit; no name of magistrate.
> Letters should not be known; riches, poverty.
> And use of service, none; contract, succession.
> Bourn, bound of land, tilth, vineyard, none:
> No use of metal, corn, or wine, or oil:
> No occupation; all men idle, all.
>
> * * * * *
>
> All things in common, nature should produce,
> Without sweat or endeavor: Treason, felony,
> Sword, pike, knife, gun, or need of any engine.
> Would I not have; but nature should bring forth,
> Of its own kind all foizon, all abundance,
> To feed my innocent people.

But above all, in the three fugitive vagabonds who remained in possession of the island of Bermuda, on the departure of their comrades, and in their squabbles about supremacy, on the finding of their treasure, I see typified Sebastian, Trinculo, and their worthy companion Caliban:

> Trinculo, the king and all our company being drowned, we will inherit here.
>
> Monster, I will kill this man; his daughter and I will be king and queen, (save our graces!) and Trinculo and thyself shall be viceroys.

I do not mean to hold up the incidents and characters in the narrative and in the play as parallel, or as being strikingly similar: neither would I insinuate that the narrative suggested the play; I would only suppose that Shakespeare, being occupied about that time on the drama of the Tempest, the main story of which, I believe, is of Italian origin, had many of the fanciful ideas of it suggested to his mind by the shipwreck of Sir George Somers on the "still vext Bermoothes," and by the popular superstitions connected with these islands, and suddenly put in circulation by that event.

The Widow's Ordeal,

or a Judicial Trial by Combat

THE WORLD IS DAILY GROWING OLDER AND WISER. ITS INSTITUTIONS vary with its years, and mark its growing wisdom; and none more so than its modes of investigating truth, and ascertaining guilt or innocence. In its nonage, when man was yet a fallible being, and doubted the accuracy of his own intellect, appeals were made to heaven in dark and doubtful eases of atrocious accusation.

The accused was required to plunge his hand in boiling oil, or to walk across red-hot ploughshares, or to maintain his innocence in armed fight and listed field, in person or by champion. If he passed these ordeals unscathed, he stood acquitted, and the result was regarded as a verdict from on high.

It is somewhat remarkable that, in the gallant age of chivalry, the gentler sex should have been most frequently the subjects of these rude trials and perilous ordeals; and that, too, when assailed in their most delicate and vulnerable part—their honor.

In the present very old and enlightened age of the world, when the human intellect is perfectly competent to the management of its own concerns, and needs no special interposition of heaven in its affairs, the trial by jury has superseded these superhuman ordeals; and the unanimity of twelve discordant minds is necessary to constitute a verdict. Such a unanimity would, at first sight, appear also to require a miracle from heaven; but it is produced by a simple device of human ingenuity. The twelve jurors are locked up in their box, there to fast until abstinence shall have so clarified their intellects that the whole jarring panel can discern the truth, and concur in a unanimous decision. One point is certain, that truth is one, and is immutable—until the jurors all agree, they cannot all be right.

It is not our intention, however, to discuss this great judicial point, or to question the avowed superiority of the mode of investigating truth, adopted in this antiquated and very sagacious era. It is our object merely to exhibit to the curious reader, one of the most memorable cases of judicial combat we find in the annals of Spain. It occurred at the bright commencement of the reign, and in the youthful, and, as yet, glorious days, of Roderick the Goth; who subsequently tarnished his fame at home by his misdeeds, and, finally, lost his kingdom and his life on the banks of the Guadalete, in that disastrous battle which gave up Spain a conquest to the Moors. The following is the story:—

There was once upon a time a certain duke of Lorraine, who was acknowledged throughout his domains to be one of the wisest princes that ever lived. In fact, there was no one measure adopted by him that did not astonish his privy counsellors and gentlemen in attendance; and he said such witty things, and made such sensible speeches, that the jaws of his high chamberlain were well nigh dislocated from laughing with delight at one, and gaping with wonder at the other:

This very witty and exceedingly wise potentate lived for half a century in single-blessedness; at length his courtiers began to think it a great pity so wise and wealthy a prince should not have a child after his own likeness, to inherit his talents and domains; so they urged him most respectfully to marry, for the good of his estate, and the welfare of his subjects.

He turned their advice over in his mind some four or five years, and then sent forth emissaries to summon to his court all the beautiful maidens in the land, who were ambitious of sharing a ducal crown. The court was soon crowded with beauties of all styles and complexions, from among whom he chose one in the earliest budding of her charms, and acknowledged by all the gentlemen to be unparalleled for grace and loveliness. The courtiers extolled the duke to the skies for making such a choice, and considered it another proof of his great wisdom. "The duke," said they, "is waxing a little too old, the damsel, on the other hand, is a little too young; if one is lacking in years, the other has a superabundance; thus a want on one side, is balanced by an excess on the other, and the result is a well-assorted marriage."

The duke, as is often the case with wise men who marry rather late, and take damsels rather youthful to their bosoms, became dotingly fond of his wife, and very properly indulged her in all things. He was, consequently, cried up by his subjects in general, and by the ladies in particular, as a pattern for husbands; and, in the end, from the wonderful docility with which he submitted to be reined and checked, acquired the amiable and enviable appellation of Duke Philibert the wife-ridden.

There was only one thing that disturbed the conjugal felicity of this paragon of husbands—though a considerable time elapsed after his marriage, there was still no prospect of an heir. The good duke left no means untried to propitiate Heaven. He made vows and pilgrimages, he fasted and he prayed, but all to no purpose. The courtiers were all astonished at the circumstance. They could not account for it. While the meanest peasant in the country had sturdy brats by dozens, without putting up a prayer, the duke wore himself to skin and bone with penances and fastings, yet seemed farther off from his object than ever.

At length, the worthy prince fell dangerously ill, and felt his end approaching. He looked sorrowfully and dubiously upon his young and tender spouse, who hung over him with tears and sobbings. "Alas!" said he, "tears are soon dried from youthful eyes, and sorrow lies lightly on a youthful heart. In a little while thou wilt forget in the arms of another husband him who has loved thee so tenderly."

"Never! never!" cried the duchess, "Never will I cleave to another! Alas, that my lord should think me capable of such inconstancy!"

The worthy and wife-ridden duke was soothed by her assurances; for he could not brook the thought of giving her up even after he should be dead. Still he wished to have some pledge of her enduring constancy:

"Far be it from me, my dearest wife," said he, "to control thee through a long life. A year and a day of strict fidelity will appease my troubled spirit. Promise to remain faithful to my memory for a year and a day, and I will die in peace."

The duchess made a solemn vow to that effect, but the uxorious feelings of the duke were not yet satisfied. "Safe bind, safe find," thought he; so he made a will, bequeathing to her all his domains, on condition of her remaining true to him for a year and a day after his decease; but, should it appear that, within that time, she had in anywise lapsed from her fidelity, the inheritance should go to his nephew, the lord of a neighboring territory.

Having made his will, the good duke died and was buried. Scarcely was he in his tomb, when his nephew came to take possession, thinking, as his uncle had died without issue, the domains would be devised to him of course. He was in a furious passion, when the will was produced, and the young widow declared inheritor of the dukedom. As he was a violent, highhanded man, and one of the sturdiest knights in the land, fears were entertained that he might attempt to seize on the territories by force. He had, however, two bachelor uncles for bosom counsellors,—swaggering rakehelly old cavaliers, who, having led loose and riotous lives, prided themselves upon knowing the world, and being deeply experienced in human nature. "Prithee, man, be of good cheer," said they, "the duchess is a young and buxom widow. She has just buried our brother, who, God rest his soul! was somewhat too much given to praying and fasting, and kept his pretty wife always tied to his girdle. She is now like a bird from a cage. Think you she will keep her vow? Pooh, pooh—impossible!—Take our words for it—we know mankind, and, above all, womankind. She cannot hold out for such a length of time; it is not in womanhood—it is not in widowhood—we know it, and that's enough. Keep a sharp look-out upon the widow, therefore, and within the twelvemonth you will catch her tripping—and then the dukedom is your own."

The nephew was pleased with this counsel, and immediately placed spies round the duchess, and bribed several of her servants to keep watch upon her, so that she could not take a single step, even from one apartment of her palace to another, without being observed. Never was young and beautiful widow exposed to so terrible an ordeal.

The duchess was aware of the watch thus kept upon her. Though confident of her own rectitude, she knew that it is not enough for a woman to be virtuous—she must be above the reach of slander. For the whole term of her probation, therefore, she proclaimed a strict non-intercourse with the other sex. She had females for cabinet ministers and chamberlains, through whom she transacted all her public and private concerns; and it is said that never were the affairs of the dukedom so adroitly administered.

All males were rigorously excluded from the palace; she never went out of its precincts, and whenever she moved about its courts and gardens, she surrounded herself with a body-guard of young maids of honor, commanded by dames renowned for discretion. She slept in a bed without curtains, placed in the centre of a room illuminated by innumerable wax tapers. Four ancient spinsters, virtuous as Virginia, perfect dragons of watchfulness, who only slept during the daytime, kept vigils throughout the night, seated in the four corners of the room on stools without backs or arms, and with seats cut in checkers of the hardest wood, to keep them from dozing.

Thus wisely and warily did the young duchess conduct herself for twelve long months, and slander almost bit her tongue off in despair, at finding no room even for a surmise. Never was ordeal more burdensome, or more enduringly sustained.

The year passed away. The last, odd day arrived, and a long, long day it was. It was the twenty-first of June, the longest day in the year. It seemed as if it would never come to an end. A thousand times did the duchess and her ladies watch the sun from the windows of the palace, as he slowly climbed the vault of heaven, and seemed still more slowly to roll down. They could not help expressing their wonder, now and then, why the duke should have tagged this supernumerary day to the end of the year, as if three hundred and sixty-five days were not sufficient to try and task the fidelity of any woman. It is the last grain that turns the scale—the last drop that overflows the goblet—and the last moment of delay that exhausts the patience. By the time the sun sank below the horizon, the duchess was in a fidget that passed all bounds, and, though several hours were yet to pass before the day regularly expired, she could not have remained those hours in durance to gain a royal crown, much less a ducal coronet. So she gave orders, and her palfrey, magnificently caparisoned, was brought into the court-yard of the castle, with palfreys for all her ladies in attendance. In this way she sallied forth, just as the sun had gone down. It was a mission of piety—a pilgrim cavalcade to a convent at the foot of a neighboring mountain—to return thanks to the blessed Virgin, for having sustained her through this fearful ordeal.

The orisons performed, the duchess and her ladies returned, ambling gently along the border of a forest. It was about that mellow hour of twilight when night and day are mingled, and all objects are indistinct. Suddenly, some monstrous animal sprang from out a thicket, with fearful howlings. The female body-guard was thrown into confusion, and fled different ways. It was some time before they recovered from their panic, and gathered once more together; but the duchess was not to be found. The greatest anxiety was felt for her safety. The hazy mist of twilight had prevented their distinguishing perfectly the animal which had affrighted them. Some thought it a wolf, others a bear, others a wild man of the woods. For upwards of an hour did they beleaguer the forest, without daring to venture in, and were on the point of giving up the duchess as torn to pieces and devoured, when, to their great joy, they beheld her advancing in the gloom, supported by a stately cavalier.

He was a stranger knight, whom nobody knew. It was impossible to distinguish his countenance in the dark; but all the ladies agreed that he was of noble presence and captivating address. He had rescued the duchess from the very fangs of the monster, which, he assured the ladies, was neither a wolf, nor a bear, nor yet a wild man of the woods, but a veritable fiery dragon, a species of monster peculiarly hostile to beautiful females in the days of chivalry, and which all the efforts of knight-errantry had not been able to extirpate.

The ladies crossed themselves when they heard of the danger from which they had escaped, and could not enough admire the gallantry of the cavalier. The duchess would fain have prevailed on her deliverer to accompany her to her court; but he had no time to spare, being a knight-errant, who had many adventures on hand, and many distressed damsels and afflicted widows to rescue and relieve in various parts of the country. Taking a respectful leave, therefore, he pursued his wayfaring, and the duchess and her train returned to the palace. Throughout the whole way, the ladies were unwearied in chanting the praises of the stranger knight; nay, many of them would willingly have incurred the danger of the dragon to have enjoyed the happy deliverance of the duchess. As to the latter, she rode pensively along, but said nothing.

No sooner was the adventure of the wood made public, than a whirlwind was raised about the ears of the beautiful duchess. The blustering nephew of the deceased duke went about, armed to the teeth, with a swaggering uncle at each shoulder, ready to back him, and swore the duchess had forfeited her domain. It was in vain that she called all the saints, and angels, and her ladies in attendance into the bargain, to witness that she had passed a year and a day of immaculate fidelity. One fatal hour remained to be accounted for; and into the space of one little hour sins enough may be conjured up by evil tongues, to blast the fame of a whole life of virtue.

The two graceless uncles, who had seen the world, were ever ready to bolster the matter through, and as they were brawny, broad-shouldered warriors, and veterans in brawl as well as debauch, they had great sway with the multitude. If any one pretended to assert the innocence of the duchess, they interrupted him with a loud ha! ha! of derision. "A pretty story, truly," would they cry, "about a wolf and a dragon, and a young widow rescued in the dark by a sturdy varlet, who dares not show his face in the daylight. You may tell that to those who do not know human nature; for our parts, we know the sex, and that's enough."

If, however, the other repeated his assertion, they would suddenly knit their brows, swell, look big, and put their hands upon their swords. As few people like to fight in a cause that does not touch their own interests, the nephew and the uncles were suffered to have their way, and swagger uncontradicted.

The matter was at length referred to a tribunal composed of all the dignitaries of the dukedom, and many and repeated consultations were held. The character of the duchess, throughout the year was as bright and spotless as the moon in a cloudless night; one fatal hour of darkness alone intervened to eclipse its brightness. Finding human sagacity incapable of dispelling the mystery, it was determined to leave the question to Heaven; or in other words, to decide it by the ordeal of the sword—a sage tribunal in the age of chivalry. The nephew and two bully uncles were to maintain their accusation in listed combat, and six months were allowed to the duchess to provide herself with three champions, to meet them in the field. Should she fail in this, or should her champions be vanquished, her honor would be considered as attainted, her fidelity as forfeit, and her dukedom would go to the nephew, as a matter of right.

With this determination the duchess was fain to comply. Proclamations were accordingly made, and heralds sent to various parts; but day after day, week after week, and month after month, elapsed, without any champion appearing to assert her loyalty throughout that darksome hour. The fair widow was reduced to despair, when tidings reached her of grand tournaments to be held at Toledo, in celebration of the nuptials of Don Roderick, the last of the Gothic kings, with the Morisco princess Exilona. As a last resort, the duchess repaired to the Spanish court, to implore the gallantry of its assembled chivalry.

The ancient city of Toledo was a scene of gorgeous revelry on the event of the royal nuptials. The youthful king, brave, ardent, and magnificent, and his lovely bride, beaming with all the radiant beauty of the east, were hailed with shouts and acclamations whenever they appeared. Their nobles vied with each other in the luxury of their attire, their prancing steeds, and splendid retinues; and the haughty dames of the court appeared in a blaze of jewels.

In the midst of all this pageantry, the beautiful, but afflicted Duchess of Lorraine made her approach to the throne. She was dressed in black, and closely veiled; four duennas of the most staid and severe aspect, and six beautiful demoiselles, formed her female attendants. She was guarded by several very ancient, withered, and grayheaded cavaliers; and her train was borne by one of the most deformed and diminutive dwarfs in existence.

Advancing to the foot of the throne, she knelt down, and, throwing up her veil, revealed a countenance so beautiful that half the courtiers present were ready to renounce wives and mistresses, and devote themselves to her service; but when she made known that she came in quest of champions to defend her fame, every cavalier pressed forward to offer his arm and sword, without inquiring into the merits of the case; for it seemed clear that so beauteous a lady could have done nothing but what was right; and that, at any rate, she ought to be championed in following the bent of her humors, whether right or wrong.

Encouraged by such gallant zeal, the duchess suffered herself to be raised from the ground, and related the whole story of her distress. When she concluded, the king remained for some time silent, charmed by the music of her voice. At length: "As I hope for salvation, most beautiful duchess," said he, "were I not a sovereign king, and bound in duty to my kingdom, I myself would put lance in rest to vindicate your cause; as it is, I here give full permission to my knights, and promise lists and a fair field, and that the contest shall take place before the walls of Toledo, in presence of my assembled court."

As soon as the pleasure of the king was known, there was a strife among the cavaliers present, for the honor of the contest. It was decided by lot, and the successful candidates were objects of great envy, for every one was ambitious of finding favor in the eyes of the beautiful widow.

Missives were sent, summoning the nephew and his two uncles to Toledo, to maintain their accusation, and a day was appointed for the combat. When the day arrived, all Toledo was in commotion at an early hour. The lists had been prepared in the usual place, just without the walls, at the foot of the rugged rocks on which the city is built, and on that beautiful meadow along the Tagus, known by the name of the king's garden. The populace had already assembled, each one eager to secure a favorable place; the balconies were filled with the ladies of the court, clad in their richest attire, and bands of youthful knights, splendidly armed and decorated with their ladies' devices, were managing their superbly caparisoned steeds about the field. The king at length came forth in state, accompanied by the queen Exilona. They took their seats in a raised balcony, under a canopy of rich damask; and, at sight of them, the people rent the air with acclamations.

The nephew and his uncles now rode into the field, armed *cap-a-pie*, and followed by a train of cavaliers of their own roystering cast, great swearers and carousers, arrant swashbucklers, with clanking armor and jingling spurs. When the people of Toledo beheld the vaunting and discourteous appearance of these knights, they were more anxious than ever for the success of the gentle duchess; but, at the same time, the sturdy and stalwart frames of these warriors, showed that whoever won the victory from them, must do it at the cost of many a bitter blow.

As the nephew and his riotous crew rode in at one side of the field, the fair widow appeared at the other, with her suite of grave grayheaded courtiers, her ancient duennas and dainty demoiselles, and the little dwarf toiling along under the weight of her train. Every one made way for her as she passed, and blessed her beautiful face, and prayed for success to her cause. She took her seat in a lower balcony, not far from the sovereigns; and her pale face, set off by her mourning weeds, was as the moon, shining forth from among the clouds of night.

The trumpets sounded for the combat. The warriors were just entering the lists, when a stranger knight, armed in panoply, and followed by two pages and an esquire, came galloping into the field, and, riding up to the royal balcony, claimed the combat as a matter of right.

"In me," cried he, "behold the cavalier who had the happiness to rescue the beautiful duchess from the peril of the forest, and the misfortune to bring on her this grievous calumny. It was but recently, in the course of my errantry, that tidings of her wrongs have reached my ears, and I have urged hither at all speed, to stand forth in her vindication."

No sooner did the duchess hear the accents of the knight than she recognized his voice, and joined her prayers with his that he might enter the lists. The difficulty was, to determine which of the three champions already appointed should yield his place, each insisting on the honor of the combat. The stranger knight would have settled the point, by taking the whole contest upon himself; but this the other knights would not permit. It was at length determined, as before, by lot, and the cavalier who lost the chance retired murmuring and disconsolate.

The trumpets again sounded—the lists were opened. The arrogant nephew and his two drawcansir uncles appeared so completely cased in steel, that they and their steeds were like moving masses of iron. When they understood the stranger knight to be the same that had rescued the duchess from her peril, they greeted him with the most boisterous derision:

"O ho! sir Knight of the Dragon," said they, "you who pretend to champion fair widows in the dark, come on, and vindicate your deeds of darkness in the open day."

The only reply of the cavalier was, to put lance in rest, and brace himself for the encounter. Needless is it to relate the particulars of a battle, which was like so many hundred combats that have been said and sung in prose and verse. Who is there but must have foreseen the event of a contest, where Heaven had to decide on the guilt or innocence of the most beautiful and immaculate of widows?

The sagacious reader, deeply read in this kind of judicial combats, can imagine the encounter of the graceless nephew and the stranger knight. He sees their concussion, man to man, and horse to horse, in mid career, and sir Graceless hurled to the ground, and slain. He will not wonder that the assailants of the brawny uncles were less successful in their rude encounter; but he will picture to himself the stout stranger spurring to their rescue, in the very critical moment; he will see him transfixing one with his lance, and cleaving the other to the chine with a back stroke of his sword, thus leaving the trio of accusers dead upon the field, and establishing the immaculate fidelity of the duchess, and her title to the dukedom, beyond the shadow of a doubt.

The air rang with acclamations; nothing was heard but praises of the beauty and virtue of the duchess, and of the prowess of the stranger knight; but the public joy was still more increased when the champion raised his visor, and revealed the countenance of one of the bravest cavaliers of Spain, renowned for his gallantry in the service of the sex, and who had been round the world in quest of similar adventures.

That worthy knight, however, was severely wounded, and remained for a long time ill of his wounds. The lovely duchess, grateful for having twice owed her protection to his arm, attended him daily during his illness; and finally rewarded his gallantry with her hand.

The king would fain have had the knight establish his title to such high advancement by farther deeds of arms; but his courtiers declared that he already merited the lady, by thus vindicating her fame and fortune in a deadly combat to outrance; and the lady herself hinted that she was perfectly satisfied of his prowess in arms, from the proofs she had received in his achievement in the forest.

Their nuptials were celebrated with great magnificence. The present husband of the duchess did not pray and fast like his predecessor, Philibert the wife-ridden; yet he found greater favor in the eyes of Heaven, for their union was blessed with a numerous progeny—the daughters chaste and beauteous as their mother the sons stout and valiant as their sire, and renowned, like him, for relieving disconsolate damsels and desolated widows.

The Knight of Malta

In the course of a tour in Sicily, in the days of my juvenility, I passed some little time at the ancient city of Catania, at the foot of Mount Ætna. Here I became acquainted with the Chevalier L——, an old knight of Malta. It was not many years after the time that Napoleon had dislodged the knights from their island, and he still wore the insignia of his order. He was not, however, one of those reliques of that once chivalrous body, who have been described as "a few worn-out old men, creeping about certain parts of Europe, with the Maltese cross on their breasts;" on the contrary, though advanced in life, his form was still light and vigorous: he had a pale, thin, intellectual visage, with a high forehead, and a bright, visionary eye. He seemed to take a fancy to me, as I certainly did to him, and we soon became intimate. I visited him occasionally, at his apartments, in the wing of an old palace, looking toward Mount Ætna. He was an antiquary, a virtuoso, and a connoisseur. His rooms were decorated with mutilated statues, dug up from Grecian and Roman ruins; old vases, lachrymals, and sepulchral lamps. He had astronomical and chemical instruments, and black-letter books, in various languages. I found that he had dipped a little in chimerical studies, and had a hankering after astrology and alchemy. He affected to believe in dreams and visions, and delighted in the fanciful Rosicrucian doctrines. I cannot persuade myself, however, that he really believed in all these; I rather think he loved to let his imagination carry him away into the boundless fairy land which they unfolded.

In company with the chevalier, I made several excursions on horseback about the environs of Catania, and the picturesque skirts of Mount Ætna. One of these led through a village, which had sprung up on the very track of an ancient eruption, the houses being built of lava. At one time we passed, for some distance, along a narrow lane, between two high dead convent walls. It was a cut-throat looking place, in a country where assassinations are frequent; and just about midway through it, we observed blood upon the pavement and the walls, as if a murder had actually been committed there.

The chevalier spurred on his horse, until he had extricated himself completely from this suspicious neighborhood. He then observed, that it reminded him of a similar blind alley in Malta, infamous on account of the many assassinations that had taken place there; concerning one of which, he related a long and tragical story, that lasted until we reached Catania. It involved various circumstances of a wild and supernatural character, but which he assured me were handed down in tradition, and generally credited by the old inhabitants of Malta.

As I like to pick up strange stories, and as I was particularly struck with several parts of this, I made a minute of it, on my return to my lodgings. The memorandum was lost, with several of my travelling papers, and the story had faded from my mind, when recently, on perusing a French memoir, I came suddenly upon it, dressed up, it is true, in a very different manner, but agreeing in the leading facts, and given upon the word of that famous adventurer, the Count Cagliostro.

I have amused myself, during a snowy day in the country, by rendering it roughly into English, for the entertainment of a youthful circle round the Christmas fire. It was well received by my auditors, who, however, are rather easily pleased. One proof of its merits is, that it sent some of the youngest of them quaking to their beds, and gave them very fearful dreams. Hoping that it may have the same effect upon the ghost-hunting reader, I subjoin it. I would observe, that wherever I have modified the French version of the story, it has been in conformity to some recollection of the narrative of my friend, the Knight of Malta.

The Grand Prior of Minorca

A Veritable Ghost Story.

"Keep my wits, heaven! They say spirits appear
To melancholy minds, and the graves open!"

Fletcher

About the middle of the last century, while the Knights of Saint John of Jerusalem still maintained something of their ancient state and sway in the island of Malta, a tragical event took place there, which is the groundwork of the following narrative.

It may be as well to premise, that at the time we are treating of, the Order of Saint John of Jerusalem, grown excessively wealthy, had degenerated from its originally devout and warlike character. Instead of being a hardy body of "monk-knights," sworn soldiers of the cross, fighting the Paynim in the Holy Land, or scouring the Mediterranean, and scourging the Barbary coasts with their galleys, or feeding the poor, and attending upon the sick at their hospitals, they led a life of luxury and libertinism, and were to be found in the most voluptuous courts of Europe. The order, in fact, had become a mode of providing for the needy branches of the Catholic aristocracy of Europe. "A commandery," we are told, was a splendid provision for a younger brother; and men of rank, however dissolute, provided they belonged to the highest aristocracy, became Knights of Malta, just as they did bishops, or colonels of regiments, or court chamberlains. After a brief residence at Malta, the knights passed the rest of their time in their own countries, or only made a visit now and then to the island. While there, having but little military duty to perform, they beguiled their idleness by paying attentions to the fair.

There was one circle of society, however, into which they could not obtain currency. This was composed of a few families of the old Maltese nobility, natives of the island. These families, not being permitted to enroll any of their members in the order, affected to hold no intercourse with its chevaliers; admitting none into their exclusive coteries, but the Grand Master, whom they acknowledged as their sovereign, and the members of the chapter which composed his council.

To indemnify themselves for this exclusion, the chevaliers carried their gallantries into the next class of society, composed of those who held civil, administrative, and judicial situations. The ladies of this class were called *honorate*, or honorables, to distinguish them from the inferior orders; and among them were many of superior grace, beauty and fascination.

Even in this more hospitable class, the chevaliers were not all equally favored. Those of Germany had the decided preference, owing to their fair and fresh complexions, and the kindliness of their manners: next to these, came the Spanish cavaliers, on account of their profound and courteous devotion, and most discreet secrecy. Singular as it may seem, the chevaliers of France fared the worst. The Maltese ladies dreaded their volatility, and their proneness to boast of their amours, and shunned all entanglement with them. They were forced, therefore, to content themselves with conquests among females of the lower orders. They revenged themselves, after the gay French manner, by making the "honorate" the objects of all kinds of jests and mystifications; by prying into their tender affairs with the more favored chevaliers and making them the theme of song and epigram.

About this time, a French vessel arrived at Malta, bringing out a distinguished personage of the Order of. Saint John of Jerusalem, the Commander de Foulquerre, who came to solicit the post of commander-in-chief of the galleys. He was descended from an old and warrior line of French nobility, his ancestors having long been seneschals of Poitou, and claiming descent from the first Counts of Angouleme.

The arrival of the commander caused a little uneasiness among the peaceably inclined, for he bore the character, in the island, of being fiery, arrogant, and quarrelsome. He had already been three times at Malta, and on each visit had signalized himself by some rash and deadly affray. As he was now thirty-five years of age, however, it was hoped that time might have taken off the fiery edge of his spirit, and that he might prove more quiet and sedate than formerly. The commander set up an establishment befitting his rank and pretensions; for he arrogated to himself an importance greater even than that of the Grand Master. His house immediately became the rallying place of all the young French chevaliers. They informed him of all the slights they had experienced or imagined, and indulged their petulant and satirical vein at the expense of the honorate and their admirers. The chevaliers of other nations soon found the topics and tone of conversation at the Commander's irksome and offensive, and gradually ceased to visit there. The commander remained at the head of a national *clique*, who looked up to him as their model. If he was not as boisterous and quarrelsome as formerly, he had become haughty and overbearing. He was fond of talking over his past affairs of punctilio and bloody duel. When walking the streets, he was generally attended by a ruffling train of young French chevaliers, who caught his own air of assumption and bravado. These he would conduct to the scenes of his deadly encounters, point out the very spot where each fatal lunge had been given, and dwell vaingloriously on every particular.

Under his tuition, the young French chevaliers began to add bluster and arrogance to their former petulance and levity; they fired up on the most trivial occasions, particularly with those who had been most successful with the fair; and would put on the most intolerable drawcansir airs. The other chevaliers conducted themselves with all possible forbearance and reserve; but they saw it would be impossible to keep on long, in this manner, without coming to an open rupture.

Among the Spanish cavaliers, was one named Don Luis de Lima Vasconcellos. He was distantly related to the Grand Master; and had been enrolled at an early age among his pages, but had been rapidly promoted by him, until, at the age of twenty-six, he had been given the richest Spanish commandery in the order. He had, moreover, been fortunate with the fair, with one of whom, the most beautiful honorata of Malta, he had long maintained the most tender correspondence.

The character, rank, and connections of Don Luis put him on a par with the imperious Commander de Foulquerre, and pointed him out as a leader and champion to his countrymen. The Spanish cavaliers repaired to him, therefore, in a body; represented all the grievances they had sustained, and the evils they apprehended, and urged him to use his influence with the commander and his adherents to put a stop to the growing abuses.

Don Luis was gratified by this mark of confidence and esteem, on the part of his countrymen, and promised to have an interview with the Commander de Foulquerre on the subject. He resolved to conduct himself with the utmost caution and delicacy on the occasion; to represent to the commander the evil consequences which might result from the inconsiderate conduct of the young French chevaliers, and to entreat him to exert the great influence he so deservedly possessed over them, to restrain their excesses. Don Luis was aware, however, of the peril that attended any interview of the kind with this imperious and fractious man, and apprehended, however it might commence, that it would terminate in a duel. Still, it was an affair of honor, in which Castilian dignity was concerned; beside, lie had a lurking disgust at the overbearing manners of De Foulquerre, and perhaps had been somewhat offended by certain intrusive attentions which he had presumed to pay to the beautiful honorata.

It was now Holy Week; a time too sacred for worldly feuds and passions, especially in a community under the dominion of a religious order: it was agreed, therefore, that the dangerous interview in question should not take place until after the Easter holydays. It is probable, from subsequent circumstances, that the Commander de Foulquerre had some information of this arrangement among the Spanish cavaliers, and was determined to be beforehand, and to mortify the pride of their champion, who was thus preparing to read him a lecture. He chose Good Friday for his purpose. On this sacred day, it is customary in Catholic countries to make a tour of all the churches, offering up prayers in each. In every Catholic church, as is well known, there is a vessel of holy water near the door. In this, every one, on entering, dips his fingers, and makes therewith the sign of the cross on his forehead and breast. An office of gallantry, among the young Spaniards, is to stand near the door, dip their hands in the holy vessel, and extend them courteously and respectfully to any lady of their acquaintance who may enter; who thus receives the sacred water at second hand, on the tips of her fingers, and proceeds to cross herself, with all due decorum. The Spaniards, who are the most jealous of lovers, are impatient when this piece of devotional gallantry is proffered to the object of their affections by any other hand: on Good Friday, therefore, when a lady makes a tour of the churches, it is the usage among them for the inamorato to follow her from church to church, so as to present her the holy water at the door of each; thus testifying his own devotion, and at the same time preventing the officious services of a rival.

On the day in question, Don Luis followed the beautiful honorata, to whom, as has already been observed, he had long been devoted. At the very first church she visited, the Commander de Foulquerre was stationed at the portal, with several of the young French chevaliers about him. Before Don Luis could offer her the holy water, he was anticipated by the commander, who thrust himself between them, and, while he performed the gallant office to the lady, rudely turned his back upon her admirer, and trod upon his feet. The insult was enjoyed by the young Frenchmen who were present: it was too deep and grave to be forgiven by Spanish pride; and at once put an end to all Don Luis's plans of caution and forbearance. He repressed his passion for the moment, however, and waited until all the parties left the church: then, accosting the commander with an air of coolness and unconcern, he inquired after his health, and asked to what church he proposed making his second visit. "To the Magisterial Church of Saint John." Don Luis offered to conduct him thither, by the shortest route. His offer was accepted, apparently without suspicion, and they proceeded together. After walking some distance, they entered a long, narrow lane, without door or window opening upon it, called the "Strada Stretta," or narrow street. It was a street in which duels were tacitly permitted, or connived at, in Malta, and were suffered to pass as accidental encounters. Every where else, they were prohibited. This restriction had been instituted to diminish the number of duels formerly so frequent in Malta. As a farther precaution to render these encounters less fatal, it was an offence, punishable with death, for any one to enter this street armed with either poniard or pistol. It was a lonely, dismal street, just wide enough for two men to stand upon their guard and cross their swords; few persons ever traversed it, unless with some sinister design; and on any preconcerted duello, the seconds posted themselves at each end, to stop all passengers, and prevent interruption.

In the present instance, the parties had scarce entered the street, when Don Luis drew his sword, and called upon the commander to defend himself.

De Foulquerre was evidently taken by surprise: he drew back, and attempted to expostulate; but Don Luis persisted in defying him to the combat.

After a second or two, he likewise drew his sword, but immediately lowered the point.

"Good Friday!" ejaculated he, shaking his head: "one word with you; it is full six years since I have been in a confessional: I am shocked at the state of my conscience; but within three days—that is to say, on Monday next—"

Don Luis would listen to nothing. Though naturally of a peaceable disposition, he had been stung to fury, and people of that character when once incensed, are deaf to reason. He compelled the commander to put himself on his guard. The latter, though a man accustomed to brawl and battle, was singularly dismayed, Terror was visible in all his features. He placed himself with his back to the wall, and the weapons were crossed. The contest was brief and fatal. At the very first thrust, the sword of Don Luis passed through the body of his antagonist. The commander staggered to the wall, and leaned against it.

"On Good Friday!" ejaculated he again, with a failing voice and despairing accents. "Heaven pardon you!" added he; "take my sword to Têtefoulques, and have a hundred masses performed in the chapel of the castle, for the repose of my soul!" With these words he expired.

The fury of Don Luis was at an end. He stood aghast, gazing at the bleeding body of the commander. He called to mind the prayer of the deceased for three days' respite, to make his peace with heaven; he had refused it; had sent him to the grave, with all his sins upon his head! His conscience smote him to the core; he gathered up the sword of the commander, which he had been enjoined to take to Têtefoulques, and hurried from the fatal Strada Stretta.

The duel of course made a great noise in Malta, but had no injurious effect on the worldly fortunes of Don Luis. He made a full declaration of the whole matter, before the proper authorities; the chapter of the order considered it one of those casual encounters of the Strada Stretta, which were mourned over, but tolerated; the public by whom the late commander had been generally detested, declared that he deserved his fate. It was but three days after the event, that Don Luis was advanced to one of the highest dignities of the order, being invested by the Grand Master with the Priorship of the kingdom of Minorca.

From that time forward, however, the whole character and conduct of Don Luis underwent a change. He became a prey to a dark melancholy, which nothing could assuage. The most austere piety, the severest penances, had no effect in allaying the horror which preyed upon his mind. He was absent for a long time from Malta; having gone, it was said, on remote pilgrimages: when he returned, lie was more haggard than ever. There seemed something mysterious and inexplicable in this disorder of his mind. The following is the revelation made by himself, of the horrible visions or chimeras by which he was haunted:

"When I had made my declaration before the chapter," said he, "my provocations were publicly known, I had made my peace with man; but it was not so with God, nor with my confessor, nor with my own conscience. My act was doubly criminal, from the day on which it was committed, and from my refusal to a delay of three days, for the victim of my resentment to receive the sacraments. His despairing ejaculation, 'Good Friday! Good Friday!' continually rang in my ears. 'Why did I not grant the respite!' cried I to myself; 'was it not enough to kill the body, but must I seek to kill the soul!'

"On the night following Friday, I started suddenly from my sleep. An unaccountable horror was upon me. I looked wildly around. It seemed as if I were not in my apartment, nor in my bed, but in the fatal Strada Stretta, lying on the pavement. I again saw the commander leaning against the wall; I again heard his dying words: 'Take my sword to Têtefoulques, and have a hundred masses performed in the chapel of the castle, for the repose of my soul!'

"On the following night, I caused one of my servants to sleep in the same room with me. I saw and heard nothing, either on that night or any of the nights following, until the next Friday; when I had again the same vision, with this difference, that my valet seemed to be lying some distance from me on the pavement of the Strada Stretta. The vision continued to be repeated on every Friday night, the commander always appearing in the same manner, and uttering the same words: 'Take my sword to Têtefoulques, and have a hundred masses performed in the chapel of the castle, for the repose of my soul!'

"On questioning my servant on the subject, he stated, that on these occasions he dreamed that he was lying in a very narrow street, but he neither saw nor heard any thing of the commander.

"I knew nothing of this Têtefoulques, whither the defunct was so urgent I should carry his sword. I made inquiries, therefore, concerning it, among the French chevaliers. They informed me that it was an old castle, situated about four leagues from Poitiers, in the midst of a forest. It had been built in old times, several centuries since by Foulques Taillefer, (or Fulke Hack-iron,) a redoubtable hard-fighting Count of Angouleme, who gave it to an illegitimate son, afterwards created Grand Seneschal of Poitou, which son became the progenitor of the Foulquerres of Têtefoulques, hereditary seneschals of Poitou. They farther informed me, that strange stories were told of this old castle, in the surrounding country, and that it contained many curious reliques. Among these, were the arms of Foulques Taillefer, together with those of the warriors he had slain; and that it was an immemorial usage with the Foulquerres to have the weapons deposited there which they had yielded either in war or single combat. This, then, was the reason of the dying injunction of the commander respecting his sword. I carried this weapon with me, wherever I went, but still I neglected to comply with his request.

"The vision still continued to harass me with undiminished horror. I repaired to Rome, where I confessed myself to the Grand Cardinal penitentiary, and informed him of the terrors with which I was haunted. He promised me absolution, after I should have performed certain acts of penance, the principal of which was to execute the dying request of the commander, by carrying his sword to Têtefoulques, and having the hundred masses performed in the chapel of the castle for the repose of his soul.

"I set out for France as speedily as possible, and made no delay in my journey. On arriving at Poitiers, I found that the tidings of the death of the commander had reached there, but had caused no more affliction than among the people of Malta, Leaving my equipage in the town, I put on the garb of a pilgrim, and taking a guide, set out on foot for Têtefoulques. Indeed the roads in this part of the country were impracticable for carriages.

"I found the castle of Têtefoulques a grand but gloomy and dilapidated pile. All the gates were closed, and there reigned over the whole place an air of almost savage loneliness and desertion. I had understood that its only inhabitants were the concierge, or warder, and a kind of hermit who had charge of the chapel. After ringing for some time at the gate, I at length succeeded in bringing forth the warder, who bowed with reverence to my pilgrim's garb. I begged him to conduct me to the chapel, that being the end of my pilgrimage. We found the hermit there, chanting the funeral service; a dismal sound to one who came to perform a penance for the death of a member of the family. When he had ceased to chant, I informed him that I came to accomplish an obligation of conscience, and that I wished him to perform a hundred masses for the repose of the soul of the commander. He replied that, not being in orders, he was not authorized to perform mass, but that he would willingly undertake to see that my debt of conscience was discharged. I laid my offering on the altar, and would have placed the sword of the commander there, likewise. 'Hold!' said the hermit, with a melancholy shake of the head, 'this is no place for so deadly a weapon, that has so often been bathed in Christian blood. Take it to the armory; you will find there trophies enough of like character. It is a place into which I never enter.'

"The warder here took up the theme abandoned by the peaceful man of God. He assured me that I would see in the armory the swords of all the warrior race of Foulquerres, together with those of the enemies over whom they had triumphed. This, he observed, had been a usage kept up since the time of Mellusine, and of her husband, Geoffrey à la Giand-dent, or Geoffrey with the Great-tooth.

"I followed the gossiping warder to the armory. It was a great dusty hall, hung round with Gothic-looking portraits, of a stark line of warriors, each with his weapon, and the weapons of those he had slain in battle, hung beside his picture. The most conspicuous portrait was that of Foulques Taillefer, (Fulke Hackiron,) Count of Angouleme, and founder of the castle. He was represented at full length, armed *cap-à-pie*, and grasping a huge buckler, on which were emblazoned three lions passant. The figure was so striking, that it seemed ready to start from the canvas: and I observed beneath this picture, a trophy composed of many weapons, proofs of the numerous triumphs of this hardfighting old cavalier. Beside the weapons connected with the portraits, there were swords of all shapes, sizes, and centuries, hung round the hall; with piles of armor, placed as it were in effigy.

"On each side of an immense chimney, were suspended the portraits of the first seneschal of Poitou (the illegitimate son of Foulques Taillefer) and his wife Isabella de Lusignan; the progenitors of the grim race of Foulquerres that frowned around. They had the look of being perfect likenesses; and as I gazed on them, I fancied I could trace in their antiquated features some family resemblance to their unfortunate descendant, whom I had slain! This was a dismal neighborhood, yet the armory was the only part of the castle that had a habitable air; so I asked the warder whether he could not make a fire, and give me something for supper there, and prepare me a bed in one corner.

" 'A fire and a supper you shall have, and that cheerfully, most worthy pilgrim,' said he; 'but as to a bed, I advise you to come and sleep in my chamber.'

" 'Why so?' inquired I; 'why shall I not sleep in this hall?'

" 'I have my reasons; I will make a bed for you close to mine.'

"I made no objections, for I recollected that it was Friday, and I dreaded the return of my vision. He brought in billets of wood, kindled a fire in the great overhanging chimney, and then went forth to prepare my supper. I drew a heavy chair before the fire, and seating myself in it, gazed musingly round upon the portraits of the Foulquerres, and the antiquated armor and weapons, the mementos of many a bloody deed. As the day declined, the smoky draperies of the hall gradually became confounded with the dark ground of the paintings, and the lurid gleams from the chimney only enabled me to see visages staring at me from the gathering darkness. All this was dismal in the extreme, and somewhat appalling: perhaps it was the state of my conscience that rendered me peculiarly sensitive, and prone to fearful imaginings.

"At length the warder brought in my supper. It consisted of a dish of trout, and some crawfish taken in the fosse of the castle. He procured also a bottle of wine, which he informed me was wine of Poitou. I requested him to invite the hermit to join me in my repast; but the holy man sent back word that he allowed himself nothing but roots and herbs, cooked with water. I took my meal, therefore, alone, but prolonged it as much as possible, and sought to cheer my drooping spirits by the wine of Poitou, which I found very tolerable.

"When supper was over, I prepared for my evening devotions. I have always been very punctual in reciting my breviary; it is the prescribed and bounden duty of all cavaliers of the religious orders; and I can answer for it, is faithfully performed by those of Spain. I accordingly drew forth from my pocket a small missal and a rosary, and told the warder he need only designate to me the way to his chamber, where I could come and rejoin him, when I had finished my prayers.

"He accordingly pointed out a winding stair-case, opening from the hall. 'You will descend this stair-case,' said he, 'until you come to the fourth landing-place, where you enter a vaulted passage, terminated by an arcade, with a statue of the blessed Jeanne of France: you cannot help finding my room, the door of which I will leave open; it is the sixth door from the landing place. I advise you not to remain in this hall after midnight. Before that hour, you will hear the hermit ring the bell, in going the rounds of the corridors. Do not linger here after that signal.'

"The warder retired, and I commenced my devotions. I continued at them earnestly; pausing from time to time to put wood upon the fire. I did not dare to look much around me, for I felt myself becoming a prey to fearful fancies. The pictures appeared to become animated. If I regarded one attentively, for any length of time, it seemed to move the eyes and lips. Above all, the portraits of the Grand Seneschal and his lady, which hung on each side of the great chimney, the progenitors of the Foulquerres of Têtefoulques, regarded me, I thought, with angry and baleful eyes: I even fancied they exchanged significant glances with each other. Just then a terrible blast of wind shook all the casements, and, rushing through the hall, made a fearful rattling and clashing among the armor. To my startled fancy, it seemed something supernatural.

"At length I heard the bell of the hermit, and hastened to quit the hall. Taking a solitary light, which stood on the upper table, I descended the winding stair-case; but before I had reached the vaulted passage, leading to the statue of the blessed Jeanne of France, a blast of wind extinguished my taper. I hastily remounted the stairs, to light it again at the chimney; but judge of my feelings, when, on arriving at the entrance to the armory, I beheld the Seneschal and his lady, who had descended from their frames, and seated themselves on each side of the fire-place!

"'Madam, my love,' said the Seneschal, with great formality, and in antiquated phrase, 'what think you of the presumption of this Castilian, who comes to harbor himself and make wassail in this our castle, after having slain our descendant, the commander, and that without granting him time for confession?'

"'Truly, my lord,' answered the female spectre, with no less stateliness of manner, and with great asperity of tone—'truly, my lord, I opine that this Castilian did a grievous wrong in this encounter; and he should never be suffered to depart hence, without your throwing him the gauntlet.' I paused to hear no more, but rushed again down stairs, to seek the chamber of the warder. It was impossible to find it in the darkness, and in the perturbation of my mind. After an hour and a half of fruitless search, and mortal horror and anxieties, I endeavored to persuade myself that the day was about to break, and listened impatiently for the crowing of the cock; for I thought if I could hear his cheerful note, I should be reassured; catching, in the disordered state of my nerves, at the popular notion that ghosts never appear after the first crowing of the cock.

"At length I rallied myself, and endeavored to shake off the vague terrors which haunted me. I tried to persuade myself that the two figures which I had seemed to see and hear, had existed only in my troubled imagination. I still had the end of a candle in my hand, and determined to make another effort to re-light it, and find my way to bed; for I was ready to sink with fatigue. I accordingly sprang up the stair-case, three steps at a time, stopped at the door of the armory, and peeped cautiously in. The two Gothic figures were no longer in the chimney corners, but I neglected to notice whether they had re-ascended to their frames. I entered, and made desperately for the fire-place, but scarce had I advanced three strides, when Messire Foulques Taillefer stood before me, in the centre of the hall, armed *cap-à-pie*, and standing in guard, with the point of his sword silently presented to me I would have retreated to the stair-case, but the door of it was occupied by the phantom figure of an esquire, who rudely flung a gauntlet in my face. Driven to fury, I snatched down a sword from the wall: by chance, it was that of the commander which I had placed there. I rushed upon my fantastic adversary, and seemed to pierce him through and through; but at the same time I felt as if something pierced my heart, burning like a red-hot iron. My blood inundated the hall, and I fell senseless.

"When I recovered consciousness, it was broad day, and I found myself in a small chamber, attended by the warder and the hermit. The former told me that on the previous night, he had awakened long after the midnight hour, and perceiving that I had not come to his chamber, he had furnished himself with a vase of holy water, and set out to seek me. He found me stretched senseless on the pavement of the armory, and bore me to his room. I spoke of my wound; and of the quantity of blood that I had lost. He shook his head, and knew nothing about it; and to my surprise, on examination, I found myself perfectly sound and unharmed. The wound and blood, therefore, had been all delusion. Neither the warder nor the hermit put any questions to me, but advised me to leave the castle as soon as possible. I lost no time in complying with their counsel, and felt my heart relieved from an oppressive weight, as I left the gloomy and fate-bound battlements of Têtefoulques behind me.

"I arrived at Bayonne, on my way to Spain, on the following Friday. At midnight I was startled from my sleep, as I had formerly been; but it was no longer by the vision of the dying commander. It wag old Foulques Taillefer who stood before me, armed *cap-à-pie,* and presenting the point of his sword. I made the sign of the cross, and the spectre vanished, but I received the same red-hot thrust in the heart which I had felt in the armory, and I seemed to be bathed in blood. I would have called out, or have risen from my bed and gone in quest of succor, but I could neither speak nor stir. This agony endured until the crowing of the cock, when I fell asleep again; but the next day I was ill, and in a most pitiable state. I have continued to be harassed by the same vision every Friday night; no acts of penitence and devotion have been able to relieve me from it; and it is only a lingering hope in divine mercy that sustains me, and enables me to support so lamentable a visitation."

The Grand Prior of Minorca wasted gradually away under this constant remorse of conscience, and this horrible incubus. He died some time after having revealed the preceding particulars of his case, evidently the victim of a diseased imagination.

The above relation has been rendered, in many parts literally, from the French memoir, in which it is given as a true story: if so, it is one of those instances in which truth is more romantic than fiction.

"A Time of Unexampled Prosperity"

In the course of a voyage from England, I once fell in with a convoy of merchant ships, bound for the West Indies. The weather was uncommonly bland; and the ships vied with each other in spreading sail to catch a light, favoring breeze, until their hulls were almost hidden beneath a cloud of canvas. The breeze went down with the sun, and his last yellow rays shone upon a thousand sails, idly flapping against the masts.

I exulted in the beauty of the scene, and augured a prosperous voyage; but the veteran master of the ship shook his head, and pronounced this halcyon calm a "weather-breeder." And so it proved. A storm burst forth in the night; the sea roared and raged; and when the day broke, I beheld the late gallant convoy scattered in every direction; some dismasted, others scudding tinder bare poles, and many firing signals of distress.

I have since been occasionally reminded of this scene, by those calm, sunny seasons in the commercial world, which are known by the name of "times of unexampled prosperity." They are the sure weather-breeders of traffic. Every now and then the world is visited by one of these delusive seasons, when "the credit system," as it is called, expands to full luxuriance: every body trusts every body; a bad debt is a thing unheard of; the broad way to certain and sudden wealth lies plain and open; and men are tempted to dash forward boldly, from the facility of borrowing.

Promissory notes, interchanged between scheming individuals, are liberally discounted at the banks, which become so many mints to coin words into cash; and as the supply of words is inexhaustible, it may readily be supposed what a vast amount of promissory capital is soon in circulation. Every one now talks in thousands; nothing is heard but gigantic operations in trade; great purchases and sales of real property, and immense sums made at every transfer. All, to be sure, as yet exists in promise; but the believer in promises calculates the aggregate as solid capital, and falls back in amazement at the amount of public wealth, the "unexampled state of public prosperity!"

Now is the time for speculative and dreaming or designing men. They relate their dreams and projects to the ignorant and credulous, dazzle them with golden visions, and set them maddening after shadows. The example of one stimulates another; speculation rises on speculation; bubble rises on bubble; every one helps with his breath to swell the windy superstructure, and admires and wonders at the magnitude of the inflation he has contributed to produce.

Speculation is the romance of trade, and casts contempt upon all its sober realities. It renders the stock-jobber a magician, and the exchange a region of enchantment. It elevates the merchant into a kind of knight-errant, or rather a commercial Quixote. The slow but sure gains of snug percentage become despicable in his eyes: no "operation" is thought worthy of attention, that does not double or treble the investment. No business is worth following, that does not promise an immediate fortune. As he sits musing over his ledger, with pen behind his ear, he is like La Mancha's hero in his study, dreaming over his books of chivalry. His dusty counting-house fades before his eyes, or changes into a Spanish mine: he gropes after diamonds, or dives after pearls. The subterranean garden of Aladdin is nothing to the realms of wealth that break upon his imagination.

Could this delusion always last, the life of a merchant would indeed be a golden dream; but it is as short as it is brilliant. Let but a doubt enter, and the "season of unexampled prosperity" is at end. The coinage of words is suddenly curtailed; the promissory capital begins to vanish into smoke; a panic succeeds, and the whole superstructure, built upon credit, and reared by speculation, crumbles to the ground, leaving scarce a wreck behind:

It is such stuff as dreams are made of.

When a man of business, therefore, hears on every side rumors of fortunes suddenly acquired; when he finds banks liberal, and brokers busy; when he sees adventurers flush of paper capital, and full of scheme and enterprise; when he perceives a greater disposition to buy than to sell; when trade overflows its accustomed channels, and deluges the country; when he hears of new regions of commercial adventure; of distant marts and distant mines, swallowing merchandise and disgorging gold; when he finds joint stock companies of all kinds forming; railroads, canals, and locomotive engines, springing up on every side; when idlers suddenly become men of business, and dash into the game of commerce as they would into the hazards of the faro table, when he beholds the streets glittering with new equipages, palaces conjured up by the magic of speculation; tradesmen flushed with sudden success, and vying with each other in ostentatious expense; in a word, when he hears the whole community joining in the theme of "unexampled prosperity," let him look upon the whole as a "weather-breeder," and prepare for the impending storm.

The foregoing remarks are intended merely as a prelude to a narrative I am about to lay before the public, of one of the most memorable instances of the infatuation of gain, to be found in the whole history of commerce. I allude to the famous Mississippi bubble. It is a matter that has passed into a proverb, and become a phrase in every one's mouth, yet of which not one merchant in ten has probably a distinct idea. I have therefore thought that an authentic account of it would be interesting and salutary, at the present moment, when we are suffering under the effects of a severe access of the credit system, and just recovering from one of its ruinous delusions.

The Great Mississippi Bubble

Before entering into the story of this famous chimera, it is proper to give a few particulars concerning the individual who engendered it. JOHN LAW was born in Edinburgh, in 1671. His father, William Law, was a rich goldsmith, and left his son an estate of considerable value, called Lauriston, situated about four miles from Edinburgh. Goldsmiths, in those days, acted occasionally as bankers, and his father's operations, under this character, may have originally turned the thoughts of the youth to the science of calculation, in which he became an adept; so that at an early age he excelled in playing at all games of combination.

In 1694, he appeared in London, where a handsome person, and an easy and insinuating address, gained him currency in the first circles, and the nickname of "Beau Law." The same personal advantages gave him success in the world of gallantry, until he became involved in a quarrel with Beau Wilson, his rival in fashion, whom he killed in a duel, and then fled to France to avoid prosecution.

He returned to Edinburgh in 1700, and remained there several years; during which time he first broached his great credit system, offering to supply the deficiency of coin by the establishment of a bank, which, according to his views, might emit a paper currency equivalent to the whole landed estate of the kingdom.

His scheme excited great astonishment in Edinburgh; but, though the government was not sufficiently advanced in financial knowledge to detect the fallacies upon which it was founded, Scottish caution and suspicion served in place of wisdom, and the project was rejected. Law met with no better success with the English parliament; and the fatal affair of the death of Wilson still hanging over him, for which he had never been able to procure a pardon, he again went to France.

The financial affairs of France were at this time in a deplorable condition. The wars, the pomp, and profusion, of Louis XIV, and his religious persecutions of whole classes of the most industrious of his subjects, had exhausted his treasury, and overwhelmed the nation with debt. The old monarch clung to his selfish magnificence, and could not be induced to diminish his enormous expenditure; and his minister of finance was driven to his wits' end to devise all kinds of disastrous expedients to keep up the royal state, and to extricate the nation from its embarrassments.

In this state of things, Law ventured to bring forward his financial project. It was founded on the plan of the Bank of England, which had already been in successful operation several years. He met with immediate patronage, and a congenial spirit, in the Duke of Orleans, who had married a natural daughter to the king. The duke had been astonished at the facility with which England had supported the burden of a public debt, created by the wars of Anne and William, and which exceeded in amount that under which France was groaning. The whole matter was soon explained by Law to his satisfaction. The latter maintained that England had stopped at the mere threshold of an art capable of creating unlimited sources of national wealth. The duke was dazzled with his splendid views and specious reasonings, and thought he clearly comprehended his system. Demarets, the Comptroller General of Finance, was not so easily deceived. He pronounced the plan of Law more pernicious than any of the disastrous expedients that the government had yet been driven to. The old king also, Louis XIV, detested all innovations, especially those which came from a rival nation: the project of a bank, therefore, was utterly rejected.

Law remained for a while in Paris, leading a gay and affluent existence, owing to his handsome person, easy manners, flexible temper, and a faro-bank which he had set up. His agreeable career was interrupted by a message from D'Argenson, Lieutenant General of Police, ordering him to quit Paris, alleging that he was "*rather too skilful at the game which he had introduced*!"

For several succeeding years, he shifted his residence from state to state of Italy and Germany; offering his scheme of finance to every court that he visited, but without success. The Duke of Savoy, Victor Amadeas, afterward King of Sardinia, was much struck with his project; but after considering it for a time, replied; "I am not sufficiently powerful to ruin myself."

The shifting, adventurous life of Law, and the equivocal means by which he appeared to live, playing high, and always with great success, threw a cloud of suspicion over him, wherever he went, and caused him to be expelled by the magistracy from the semi-commercial, semi-aristocratical cities of Venice and Genoa.

The events of 1715, brought Law back again to Paris. Louis XIV was dead. Louis XV was a mere child, and during his minority the Duke of Orleans held the reins of government as Regent. Law had at length found his man.

The Duke of Orleans has been differently represented by different contemporaries. He appears to have had excellent natural qualities, perverted by a bad education. He was of the middle size, easy and graceful, with an agreeable countenance, and open, affable demeanor. His mind was quick and sagacious, rather than profound; and his quickness of intellect and excellence of memory, supplied the lack of studious application. His wit was prompt and pungent; he expressed himself with vivacity and precision; his imagination was vivid, his temperament sanguine and joyous; his courage daring. His mother, the Duchess of Orleans, expressed his character in a jeu d'esprit. "The fairies," said she "were invited to be present at his birth, and each one conferring a talent on my son, be possesses them all. Unfortunately, we bad forgotten to invite an old fairy, who, arriving after all the others, exclaimed, 'He shall have all the talents, excepting that to make good use of them.'"

Under proper tuition, the duke might have risen to real greatness; but in his early years, he was put under the tutelage of the Abbé Dubois, one of the subtlest and basest spirits that ever intrigued its way into eminent place and power. The Abbé was of low origin and despicable exterior, totally destitute of morals, and perfidious in the extreme; but with a supple, insinuating address, and an accommodating spirit, tolerant of all kinds of profligacy in others. Conscious of his own inherent baseness, he sought to secure an influence over his pupil, by corrupting his principles, and fostering his vices: he debased him, to keep himself from being despised. Unfortunately he succeeded. To the early precepts of this infamous pander have been attributed those excesses that disgraced the manhood of the Regent, and gave a licentious character to his whole course of government. His love of pleasure, quickened and indulged by those who should have restrained it, led him into all kinds of sensual indulgence. He had been taught to think lightly of the most serious duties and sacred ties, to turn virtue into a jest, and consider religion mere hypocrisy. He was a gay misanthrope, that bad a sovereign but sportive contempt for mankind; believed that his most devoted servant would be his enemy, if interest prompted; and maintained that an honest man was he who had the art to conceal that he was the contrary.

He surrounded himself with a set of dissolute men like himself, who, let loose from the restraint under which they had been held, during the latter hypocritical days of Louis XIV, now gave way to every kind of debauchery. With these men the Regent used to shut himself up, after the hours of business, and excluding all graver persons and graver concerns, celebrate the most drunken and disgusting orgies, where obscenity and blasphemy formed the seasoning of conversation. For the profligate companions of these revels he invented the appellation of his *roués*, the literal meaning of which is, men broken on the wheel; intended, no doubt, to express their broken-down characters and dislocated fortunes; although a contemporary asserts that it designated the punishment that most of them merited. Madame de Labran, who was present at one of the Regent's suppers, was disgusted by the conduct and conversation of the host and his guests, and observed at table, that God, after he had created man, took the refuse clay that was left, and made of it the souls of lackeys and princes.

Such was the man that now ruled the destinies of France. Law found him full of perplexities, from the disastrous state of the finances. He had already tampered with the coinage, calling in the coin of the nation, re-stamping it, and issuing it at a nominal increase of one fifth; thus defrauding the nation out of twenty per cent, of its capital. He was not likely, therefore, to be scrupulous about any means likely to relieve him from financial difficulties: he had even been led to listen to the cruel alternative of a national bankruptcy.

Under these circumstances, Law confidently brought forward his scheme of a bank, that was to pay off the national debt, increase the revenue, and at the same time diminish the taxes. The following is stated as the theory by which he recommended his system to the Regent. The credit enjoyed by a banker or a merchant, he observed, increases his capital tenfold; that is to say, he who has a capital of one hundred thousand livres, may, if he possess sufficient credit, extend his operations to a million, and reap profits to that amount. In like manner, a state that can collect into a bank all the current coin of the kingdom, would be as powerful as if its capital were increased tenfold. The specie must be drawn into the bank, not by way of loan, or by taxations, but in the way of deposit. This might be effected in different modes, either by inspiring confidence, or by exerting authority. One mode, he observed, had already been in use. Each time that a state makes a re-coinage, it becomes momentarily the depository of all the money called in, belonging to the subjects of that state. His bank was to effect the same purpose; that is to say, to receive in deposit all the coin of the kingdom, but to give in exchange its bills, which, being of an invariable value, bearing an interest, and being payable on demand, would not only supply the place of coin, but prove a better and more profitable currency.

The Regent caught with avidity at the scheme. It suited his bold, reckless spirit, and his grasping extravagance. Not that he was altogether the dupe of Law's specious projects: still he was apt, like many other men, unskilled in the arcana of finance, to mistake the multiplication of money, for the multiplication of wealth; not understanding that it was a mere agent or instrument in the interchange of traffic, to represent the value of the various productions of industry; and that an increased circulation of coin or bank-bills, in the shape of currency, only adds a proportionably increased and fictitious value to such productions. Law enlisted the vanity of the Regent in his cause. He persuaded him that he saw more clearly than others into sublime theories of finance, which were quite above the ordinary apprehension. He used to declare that, excepting the Regent and the Duke of Savoy, no one had thoroughly comprehended his system.

It is certain that it met with strong opposition from the Regent's ministers, the Duke de Noailles and the Chancelloi d'Anguesseau; and it was no less strenuously opposed by the parliament of Paris. Law, however, had a potent though secret coadjutor in the Abbé Dubois, now rising, during the regency, into great political power, and who retained a baneful influence over the mind of the Regent. This wily priest, as avaricious as he was ambitious, drew large sums from Law as subsidies, and aided him greatly in many of his most pernicious operations. He aided him, in the present instance, to fortify the mind of the Regent against all the remonstrances of his ministers and the parliament.

Accordingly, on the 2d of May, 1716, letters patent were granted to Law, to establish a bank of deposit, discount, and circulation, under the firm of "Law and Company," to continue for twenty years. The capital was fixed at six millions of livres, divided into shares of five hundred livres each, which were to be sold for twenty-five per cent. of the regent's debased coin, and seventy-five per cent. of the public securities, which were then at a great reduction from their nominal value, and which then amounted to nineteen hundred millions. The ostensible object of the bank, as set forth in the patent, was to encourage the commerce and manufactures of France. The louis-d'ors, and crowns of the bank were always to retain the same standard of value, and its bills to be payable in them on demand.

At the outset, while the bank was limited in its operations, and while its paper really represented the specie in its vaults, it seemed to realize all that had been promised from it. It rapidly acquired public confidence, and an extended circulation, and produced an activity in commerce, unknown under the baneful government of Louis XIV. As the bills of the bank bore an interest, and as it was stipulated they would be of invariable value, and as hints had been artfully circulated that the coin would experience successive diminution, every body hastened to the bank to exchange gold and silver for paper. So great became the throng of depositors, and so intense their eagerness, that there was quite a press and struggle at the back door, and a ludicrous panic was awakened, as if there was danger of their not being admitted. An anecdote of the time relates, that one of the clerks, with an ominous smile, called out to the struggling multitude, "Have a little patience, my friends; we mean to take all your money;" an assertion disastrously verified in the sequel.

Thus by the simple establishment of a bank, Law and the Regent obtained pledges of confidence for the consummation of farther and more complicated schemes, as yet hidden from the public. In a little while the bank shares rose enormously, and the amount of its notes in circulation exceeded one hundred and ten millions of livres. A subtle stroke of policy had rendered it popular with the aristocracy. Louis XIV had several years previously imposed an income tax of a tenth, giving his royal word that it should cease in 1717. This tax had been exceedingly irksome to the privileged orders; and, in the present disastrous times, they had dreaded an augmentation of it. In consequence of the successful operation of Law's scheme, however, the tax was abolished, and now nothing was to be heard among the nobility and clergy but praises of the Regent and the bank.

Hitherto all had gone well, and all might have continued to go well, had not the paper system been farther expanded. But Law had yet the grandest part of his scheme to develop. He had to open his ideal world of speculation, his El Dorado of unbounded wealth. The English had brought the vast imaginary commerce of the South Seas in aid of their banking operations. Law sought to bring, as an immense auxiliary of his bank, the whole trade of the Mississippi. Under this name was included not merely the river so called, but the vast region known as Louisiana, extending from north latitude 29° up to Canada in north latitude 40°. This country had been granted by Louis XIV to the Sieur Crozat, but he had been induced to resign his patent. In conformity to the plea of Mr. Law, letters patent were granted in August, 1717, for the creation of a commercial company, which was to have the colonizing of this country, and the monopoly of its trade and resources, and of the beaver or fur trade with Canada. It was called the Western, but became better known as the Mississippi Company. The capital was fixed at one hundred millions of livres, divided into shares, bearing an interest of four per cent., which were subscribed for in the public securities. As the bank was to cooperate with the company, the Regent ordered that its bills should be received the same as coin, in all payments of the public revenue. Law was appointed chief director of this company, which was an exact copy of the Earl of Oxford's South Sea Company, set on foot in 1711, and which distracted all England with the frenzy of speculation. In like manner with the delusive picturings given in that memorable scheme of the sources of rich trade to be opened in the South Sea countries, Law held forth magnificent prospects of the fortunes to be made in colonizing Louisiana, which was represented as a veritable land of promise, capable of yielding every variety of the most precious produce. Reports, too, were artfully circulated, with great mystery, as if to the "chosen few," of mines of gold and silver recently discovered in Louisiana, and which would insure instant wealth to the early purchasers. These confidential whispers of course soon became public; and were confirmed by travellers fresh from the Mississippi, and doubtless bribed, who had seen the mines in question, and declared them superior in richness to those of Mexico and Peru. Nay more, ocular proof was furnished to public credulity, in ingots of gold, conveyed to the mint, as if just brought from the mines of Louisiana.

Extraordinary measures were adopted to force a colonization. An edict was issued to collect and transport settlers to the Mississippi. The police lent its aid. The streets and prisons of Paris, and of the provincial cities, were swept of mendicants and vagabonds of all kinds, who were conveyed to Havre de Grace. About six thousand were crowded into ships, where no precautions had been taken for their health or accommodation. Instruments of all kinds proper for the working of mines were ostentatiously paraded in public, and put on board the vessels; and the whole set sail for this fabled El Dorado, which was to prove the grave of the greater part of its wretched colonists.

D'Anguesseau, the chancellor, a man of probity and integrity, still lifted his voice against the paper system of Law, and his project of colonization, and was eloquent and prophetic in picturing the evils they were calculated to produce; the private distress and public degradation; the corruption of morals and manners; the triumph of knaves and schemers; the ruin of fortunes, and downfall of families. He was incited more and more to this opposition by the Duke de Noailles, the Minister of Finance, who was jealous of the growing ascendency of Law over the mind of the regent, but was less honest than the chancellor in his opposition. The Regent was excessively annoyed by the difficulties they conjured up in the way of his darling schemes of finance, and the countenance they gave to the opposition of parliament; which body, disgusted more and more with the abuses of the regency, and the system of Law, had gone so far as to carry its remonstrances to the very foot of the throne.

He determined to relieve himself from these two ministers, who, either through honesty or policy, interfered with all his plans. Accordingly, on the 28th of January, 1718, he dismissed the chancellor from office, and exiled him to his estate in the country; and shortly afterward removed the Duke de Noailles from the administration of the finance.

The opposition of parliament to the Regent and his measures was carried on with increasing violence. That body aspired to an equal authority with the Regent in the administration of affairs, and pretended, by its decree, to suspend an edict of the regency ordering a new coinage, and altering the value of the currency. But its chief hostility was levelled against Law, a foreigner and a heretic, and one who was considered by a majority of the members in the light of a malefactor. In fact, so far was this hostility carried, that secret measures were taken to investigate his malversations, and to collect evidence against him; and it was resolved in parliament that, should the testimony collected justify their suspicions, they would have him seized and brought before them; would give him a brief trial, and if convicted, would hang him in the court-yard of the palace, and throw open the gates after the execution, that the public might behold his corpse!

Law received intimation of the danger hanging over him, and was in terrible trepidation. He took refuge in the Palais Royal, the residence of the Regent, and implored his protection. The Regent himself was embarrassed by the sturdy opposition of parliament, which contemplated nothing less than a decree reversing most of his public measures, especially those of finance. His indecision kept Law for a time in an agony of terror and suspense. Finally, by assembling a board of justice, and bringing to his aid the absolute authority of the king, he triumphed over parliament, and relieved Law from his dread of being hanged.

The system now went on with flowing sail. The Western, or Mississippi Company, being identified with the bank, rapidly increased in power and privileges. One monopoly after another was granted to it; the trade of the Indian Seas; the slave trade with Senegal and Guinea; the farming of tobacco; the national coinage, etc. Each new privilege was made a pretext for issuing more bills, and caused an immense advance in the price of stock. At length, on the 4th of December, 1718, the Regent gave the establishment the imposing title of The Royal Bank, and proclaimed that he had effected the purchase of all the shares, the proceeds of which he had added to its capital. This measure seemed to shock the public feeling more than any other connected with the system, and roused the indignation of parliament. The French nation had been so accustomed to attach an idea of every thing noble, lofty, and magnificent, to the royal name and person, especially during the stately and sumptuous reign of Louis XIV, that they could not at first tolerate the idea of royalty being in any degree mingled with matters of traffic and finance, and the king being in a manner a banker. It was one of the downward steps, however, by which royalty lost its illusive splendor in France and became gradually cheapened in the public mind.

Arbitrary measures now began to be taken to force the bills of the bank into artificial currency. On the 27th of December, appeared an order in council, forbidding, under severe penalties, the payment of any sum above six hundred livres in gold or silver. This decree rendered bank bills necessary in all transactions of purchase and sale, and called for a new emission. The prohibition was occasionally evaded or opposed; confiscations were the consequence; informers were rewarded, and spies and traitors began to spring up in all the domestic walks of life.

The worst effect of this illusive system was the mania for gain, or rather for gambling in stocks, that now seized upon the whole nation. Under the exciting effects of lying reports, and the forcing effects of government decrees, the shares of the company went on rising in value, until they reached thirteen hundred per cent. Nothing was now spoken of but the price of shares, and the immense fortunes suddenly made by lucky speculators. Those whom Law had deluded used every means to delude others. The most extravagant dreams were indulged, concerning the wealth to flow in upon the company, from its colonies, its trade, and its various monopolies. It is true, nothing as yet had been realized, nor could in some time be realized, from these distant sources even if productive; but the imaginations of speculators are ever in the advance, and their conjectures are immediately converted into facts. Lying reports now flew from mouth to mouth, of sure avenues to fortune suddenly thrown open. The more extravagant the fable, the more readily was it believed. To doubt, was to awaken anger, or incur ridicule. In a time of public infatuation, it requires no small exercise of courage to doubt a popular fallacy.

Paris now became the centre of attraction for the adventurous and the avaricious, who flocked to it not merely from the provinces, but from neighboring countries. A stock exchange was established in a house in the Rue Quincampoix, and became immediately the gathering place of stock-jobbers. The exchange opened at seven o'clock with the beat of drum and sound of bell, and closed at night with the same signals. Guards were stationed at each end of the street, to maintain order and exclude carriages and horses. The whole street swarmed throughout the day like a bee-hive. Bargains of all kinds were seized upon with avidity. Shares of stock passed from hand to hand, mounting in value, one knew not why. Fortunes were made in a moment as if by magic; and every lucky bargain prompted those around to a more desperate throw of the die. The fever went on, increasing in intensity as the day declined; and when the drum beat, and the bell rang, at night, to close the exchange, there were exclamations of impatience and despair, as if the wheel of fortune had suddenly been stopped, when about to make its luckiest evolution.

To ingulf all classes in this ruinous vortex, Law now split the shares of fifty millions of stock each into one hundred shares; thus, as in the splitting of lottery tickets, accommodating the venture to the humblest purse. Society was thus stirred up to its very dregs, and adventurers of the lowest order hurried to the stock market. All honest, industrious pursuits, and modest gains, were now despised. Wealth was to be obtained instantly, without labor, and without stint. The upper classes were as base in their venality as the lower. The highest and most powerful nobles, abandoning all generous pursuits and lofty aims, engaged in the vile scuffle for gain. They were even baser than the lower classes; for some of them, who were members of the council of the regency, abused their station and their influence, and promoted measures by which shares arose while in their hands, and they made immense profits.

The Duke de Bourbon, the Prince of Conti, the Dukes de la Force and D'Antin, were among the foremost of these illustrious stock-jobbers. They were nicknamed the Mississippi Lords, and they smiled at the sneering title. In fact, the usual distinctions of society had lost their consequence, under the reign of this new passion. Rank, talent, military fame, no longer inspired deference. All respect for others, all self-respect, were forgotten in the mercenary struggle of the stock-market. Even prelates and ecclesiastical corporations, forgetting their true objects of devotion, mingled among the votaries of mammon. They were not behind those who wielded the civil power in fabricating ordinances suited to their avaricious purposes. Theological decisions forthwith appeared, in which the anathema launched by the church against usury, was conveniently construed as not extending to the traffic in bank shares!

The Abbé Dubois entered into the mysteries of stock-jobbing with all the zeal of an apostle, and enriched himself by the spoils of the credulous; and he continually drew large sums from Law, as considerations for his political influence. Faithless to his country, in the course of his gambling speculations he transferred to England a great amount of specie, which had been paid into the royal treasury; thus contributing to the subsequent dearth of the precious metals.

The female sex participated in this sordid frenzy. Princesses of the blood, and ladies of the highest nobility, were among the most rapacious of stock-jobbers. The Regent seemed to have the riches of Croesus at his command, and lavished money by hundreds of thousands upon his female relatives and favorites, as well as upon his *roués*, the dissolute companions of his debauches. "My son," writes the Regent's mother, in her correspondence, "gave me shares to the amount of two millions, which I distributed among my household. The king also took several millions for his own household. All the royal family have had them; all the children and grandchildren of France, and the princes of the blood."

Luxury and extravagance kept pace with this sudden inflation of fancied wealth. The hereditary palaces of nobles were pulled down, and rebuilt on a scale of augmented splendor. Entertainments were given, of incredible cost and magnificence. Never before had been such display in houses, furniture, equipages, and amusements. This was particularly the case among persons of the lower ranks, who had suddenly become possessed of millions. Ludicrous anecdotes are related of some of these upstarts. One, who had just launched a splendid carriage, when about to use it for the first time, instead of getting in at the door, mounted, through habitude, to his accustomed place behind. Some ladies of quality, seeing a well-dressed woman covered with diamonds, but whom nobody knew, alight from a very handsome carriage, inquired who she was, of the footman. He replied, with a sneer: "It is a lady who has recently tumbled from a garret into this carriage." Mr. Law's domestics were said to become in like manner suddenly enriched by the crumbs that fell from his table. His coachman, having made a fortune, retired from his service. Mr. Law requested him to procure a coachman in his place. He appeared the next day with two, whom he pronounced equally good, and told Mr. Law: "Take which of them you choose, and I will take the other!"

Nor were these *novi homini* treated with the distance and disdain they would formerly have experienced from the haughty aristocracy of France. The pride of the old noblesse had been stifled by the stronger instinct of avarice. They rather sought the intimacy and confidence of these lucky upstarts; and it has been observed that a nobleman would gladly take his seat at the table of the fortunate lackey of yesterday, in hopes of learning from him the secret of growing rich!

Law now went about with a countenance radiant with success, and apparently dispensing wealth on every side. "He is admirably skilled in all that relates to finance," writes the Duchess of Orleans, the Regent's mother, "and has put the affairs of the state in such good order, that all the king's debts have been paid. He is so much run after, that he has no repose night or day. A duchess even kissed his hand publicly. If a duchess can do this, what will other ladies do!"

Wherever he went, his path, we are told, was beset by a sordid throng, who waited to see him pass, and sought to obtain the favor of a word, a nod, or smile, as if a mere glance from him would bestow fortune. When at home, his house was absolutely besieged by furious candidates for fortune. "They forced the doors," says the Duke de St. Simon; "they scaled his windows from the garden; they made their way into his cabinet down the chimney!"

The same venal court was paid by all classes to his family. The highest ladies of the court vied with each other in meannesses, to purchase the lucrative friendship of Mrs. Law and her daughter. They waited upon them with as much assiduity and adulation as if they had been princesses of the blood. The Regent one day expressed a desire that some duchess should accompany his daughter to Genoa. "My Lord," said some one present, "if you would have a choice from among the duchesses, you need but send to Mrs. Law's; you will find them all assembled there."

The wealth of Law rapidly increased with the expansion of the bubble. In the course of a few months, he purchased fourteen titled estates, paying for them in paper; and the public hailed these sudden and vast acquisitions of landed property, as so many proofs of the soundness of his system. In one instance, he met with a shrewd bargainer, who had not the general faith in his paper money. The President de Novion insisted on being paid for an estate in hard coin. Law accordingly brought the amount, four hundred thousand livres, in specie, saying, with a sarcastic smile, that he preferred paying in money, as its weight rendered it a mere incumbrance. As it happened, the President could give no clear title to the land, and the money had to be refunded. He paid it back *in paper*, which Law dared not refuse? lest he should depreciate it in the market!

The course of illusory credit went on triumphantly for eighteen months. Law had nearly fulfilled one of his promises, for the greater part of the public debt had been paid off; but how paid? In bank shares, which had been trumped up several hundred per cent, above their value, and which were to vanish like smoke in the hands of the holders.

One of the most striking attributes of Law, was the imperturbable assurance and self-possession with which he replied to every objection, and found a solution for every problem. He had the dexterity of a juggler in evading difficulties; and what was peculiar, made figures themselves, which are the very elements of exact demonstration, the means to dazzle and bewilder.

Toward the latter end of 1719, the Mississippi scheme had reached its highest point of glory. Half a million of strangers had crowded into Paris, in quest of fortune. The hotels and lodging-houses were overflowing; lodgings were procured with excessive difficulty; granaries were turned into bedrooms; provisions had risen enormously in price; splendid houses were multiplying on every side; the streets were crowded with carriages; above a thousand new equipages had been launched.

On the eleventh of December, Law obtained another prohibitory decree, for the purpose of sweeping all the remaining specie in circulation into the bank. By this it was forbidden to make any payments in silver above ten livres, or in gold above three hundred.

The repeated decrees of this nature, the object of which was to depreciate the value of gold, and increase the illusive credit of paper, began to awaken doubts of a system which required such bolstering. Capitalists gradually awoke from their bewilderment. Sound and able financiers consulted together, and agreed to make common cause against this continual expansion of a paper system. The shares of the bank and of the company began to decline in value. Wary men took the alarm, and began to *realize*, a word now first brought into use, to express the conversion of *ideal* property into something *real*.

The Prince of Conti, one of the most prominent and grasping of the Mississippi lords, was the first to give a blow to the credit of the bank. There was a mixture of ingratitude in his conduct, that characterized the venal baseness of the times. He had received, from time to time, enormous sums from Law, as the price of his influence and patronage. His avarice had increased with every acquisition, until Law was compelled to refuse one of his exactions. In revenge, the prince immediately sent such an amount of paper to the bank to be cashed, that it required four waggons to bring away the silver, and he had the meanness to loll out of the window of his hotel, and jest and exult, as it was trundled into his port cochère.

This was the signal for other drains of like nature. The English and Dutch merchants, who had purchased a great amount of bank paper at low prices, cashed them at the bank, and carried the money out of the country. Other strangers did the like, thus draining the kingdom of its specie, and leaving paper in its place.

The Regent, perceiving these symptoms of decay in the system, sought to restore it to public confidence, by conferring marks of confidence upon its author. He accordingly resolved to make Law Comptroller General of the Finances of France. There was a material obstacle in the way. Law was a protestant, and the Regent, unscrupulous as he was himself, did not dare publicly to outrage the severe edicts which Louis XIV., in his bigot days; had fulminated against all heretics. Law soon let him know that there would be no difficulty on that head. He was ready at any moment to abjure his religion in the way of business. For decency's sake, however, it was judged proper he should previously be convinced and converted. A ghostly instructor was soon found ready to accomplish his conversion in the shortest possible time. This was the Abbé Tencin, a profligate creature of the profligate Dubois, and like him working his way to ecclesiastical promotion and temporal wealth, by the basest means.

Under the instructions of the Abbé Tencin, Law soon mastered the mysteries and dogmas of the Catholic doctrine; and, after a brief course of ghostly training, declared himself thoroughly convinced and converted. To avoid the sneers and jests of the Parisian public, the ceremony of abjuration took place at Melun. Law made a pious present of one hundred thousand livres to the Church of St. Roque, and the Abbé Tencin was rewarded for his edifying labors, by sundry shares and bank-bills, which he shrewdly took care to convert into cash, having as little faith in the system, as in the piety of his new convert. A more grave and moral community might have been outraged by this scandalous farce; but the Parisians laughed at it with their usual levity, and contented themselves with making it the subject of a number of songs and epigrams.

Law being now orthodox in his faith, took out letters of naturalization, and having thus surmounted the intervening obstacles, was elevated by the Regent to the post of

Comptroller General. So accustomed had the community become to all juggles and transmutations in this hero of finance, that no one seemed shocked or astonished at his sudden elevation. On the contrary, being now considered perfectly established in place and power, he became more than ever the object of venal adoration. Men of rank and dignity thronged his antechamber, waiting patiently their turn for an audience; and titled dames demeaned themselves to take the front seats of the carriages of his wife and daughter, as if they had been riding with princesses of the blood royal. Law's head grew giddy with his elevation, and he began to aspire after aristocratical distinction. There was to be a court ball, at which several of the young noblemen were to dance in a ballet with the youthful king. Law requested that his son might be admitted into the ballet, and the Regent consented. The young scions of nobility, however, were indignant, and scouted the "intruding upstart." Their more worldly parents, fearful of displeasing the modern Midas, reprimanded them in vain. The striplings had not yet imbibed the passion for gain, and still held to their high blood. The son of the banker received slights and annoyances on all sides, and the public applauded them for their spirit. A fit of illness came opportunely to relieve the youth from an honor which would have cost him a world of vexations and affronts.

In February, 1720, shortly after Law's instalment in office, a decree came out, uniting the bank to the India Company, by which last name the whole establishment was now known. The decree stated, that as the bank was royal, the king was bound to make good the value of its bills; that he committed to the company the government of the bank for fifty years, and sold to it fifty millions of stock belonging to him, for nine hundred millions, a simple advance of eighteen hundred per cent. The decree farther declared, in the king's name, that he would never draw on the bank, until the value of his drafts had first been lodged in it by his receivers general.

The bank, it was said, had by this time issued notes to the amount of one thousand millions; being more paper than all the banks of Europe were able to circulate. To aid its credit, the receivers of the revenue were directed to take bank-notes of the sub-receivers. All payments, also, of one hundred livres and upward, were ordered to be made in bank-notes. These compulsory measures for a short time gave a false credit to the hank, which proceeded to discount merchants' notes, to lend money on jewels, plate, and other valuables, as well as on mortgages.

Still farther to force on the system, an edict next appeared, forbidding any individual, or any corporate body, civil or religious, to hold in possession more than five hundred livres in current coin; that is to say, about seven louis-d'ors; the value of the louis-d'or in paper being, at the time, seventy-two livres. All the gold and silver they might have, above this pittance, was to be brought to the royal bank, and exchanged either for shares or bills.

As confiscation was the penalty of disobedience to this decree, and informers were assured a share of the forfeitures, a bounty was in a manner held out to domestic spies and traitors; and the most odious scrutiny was awakened into the pecuniary affairs of families and individuals. The very confidence between friends and relatives was impaired, and all the domestic ties and virtues of society were threatened, until a general sentiment of indignation broke forth, that compelled the Regent to rescind the odious decree. Lord Stairs, the British ambassador, speaking of the system of espionage encouraged by this edict, observed that it was impossible to doubt that Law was a thorough Catholic, since he had thus established the *inquisition*, after having already proved transubstantiation, by changing specie into paper.

Equal abuses had taken place under the colonizing project. In his thousand expedients to amass capital, Law had sold parcels of land in Mississippi, at the rate of three thousand livres for a league square. Many capitalists had purchased estates large enough to constitute almost a principality; the only evil was, Law had sold a property which he could not deliver. The agents of police, who aided in recruiting the ranks of the colonists, had been guilty of scandalous impositions. Under pretence of taking up mendicants and vagabonds, they had scoured the streets at night, seizing upon honest mechanics, or their sons, and hurrying them to their crimping-houses, for the sole purpose of extorting money from them as a ransom. The populace was roused to indignation by these abuses. The officers of police were mobbed in the exercise of their odious functions, and several of them were killed, which put an end to this flagrant abuse of power.

In March, a most extraordinary decree of the council fixed the price of shares of the India Company at nine thousand livres each. All ecclesiastical communities and hospitals were now prohibited from investing money at interest, in any thing but India stock. With all these props and stays, the system continued to totter. How could it be otherwise, under a despotic government, that could alter the value of property at every moment? The very compulsory measures that were adopted to establish the credit of the bank, hastened its fall: plainly showing there was a want of solid security. Law caused pamphlets to be published, setting forth, in eloquent language, the vast profits that must accrue to holders of the stock, and the impossibility of the king's ever doing it any harm. On the very back of these assertions, came forth an edict of the king, dated the 22d of May, wherein, under pretence of having reduced the value of his coin, it was declared necessary to reduce the value of his bank-notes one half, and of the India shares from nine thousand to five thousand livres!

This decree came like a clap of thunder upon shareholders. They found one half of the pretended value of the paper in their hands annihilated in an instant: and what certainty had they with respect to the other half? The rich considered themselves ruined; those in humbler circumstances looked forward to abject beggary.

The parliament seized the occasion to stand forth as the protector of the public, and refused to register the decree. It gained the credit of compelling the Regent to retrace his step, though it is more probable he yielded to the universal burst of public astonishment and reprobation. On the 27th of May, the edict was revoked, and bank-bills were restored to their previous value. But the fatal blow had been struck; the delusion was at an end. Government itself had lost all public confidence, equally with the bank it had engendered, and which its own arbitrary acts had brought into discredit. "All Paris," says the Regent's mother, in her letters, "has been mourning at the cursed decree which Law has persuaded my son to make. I have received anonymous letters, stating that I have nothing to fear on my own account, but that my son shall be pursued with fire and sword."

The Regent now endeavored to avert the odium of his ruinous schemes from himself. He affected to have suddenly lost confidence in Law, and on the 29th of May, discharged him from his employ, as Comptroller General, and stationed a Swiss guard of sixteen men in his house. He even refused to see him, when, on the following day, he applied at the portal of the Palais Royal for admission: but having played off this farce before the public, he admitted him secretly the same night, by a private door, and continued as before to co-operate with him in his financial schemes.

On the first of June, the Regent issued a decree, permitting persons to have as much money as they pleased in their possession. Few, however, were in a state to benefit by this permission. There was a run upon the bank, but a royal ordinance immediately suspended payment, until farther orders. To relieve the public mind, a city stock was created, of twenty-five millions, bearing an interest of two and a half per cent., for which banknotes were taken in exchange. The bank-notes thus withdrawn from circulation, were publicly burnt before the Hotel de Ville. The public, however, had lost confidence in every thing and every body, and suspected fraud and collusion in those who pretended to burn the bills.

A general confusion now took place in the financial world. Families who had lived in opulence, found themselves suddenly reduced to indigence. Schemers who had been revelling in the delusion of princely fortunes, found their estates vanishing into thin air. Those who had any property remaining, sought to secure it against reverses. Cautious persons found there was no safety for property in a country where the coin was continually shifting in value, and where a despotism was exercised over public securities, and even over the private purses of individuals. They began to send their effects into other countries; when lo! on the 20th of June, a royal edict commanded them to bring back their effects, under penalty of forfeiting twice their value; and forbade them, under like penalty, from investing their money in foreign stocks. This was soon followed by an another decree, forbidding any one to retain precious stones in his possession, or to sell them foreigners: all must be deposited in the bank, in exchange for depreciating paper!

Execrations were now poured out, on all sides, against Law, and menaces of vengeance. What a contrast, in a short time, to the venal incense once offered up to him! "This person," writes the Regent's mother, "who was formerly worshipped as a god, is now not sure of his life. It is astonishing how greatly terrified he is. He is as a dead man; he is pale as a sheet, and it is said he can never get over it. My son is not dismayed, though he is threatened on all sides, and is very much amused with Law's terrors."

About the middle of July, the last grand attempt was made by Law and the Regent, to keep up the system, and provide for the immense emission of paper. A decree was fabricated, giving the India Company the entire monopoly of commerce, on condition that it would, in the course of a year, reimburse six hundred millions of livres of its bills, at the rate of fifty millions per month.

On the 17th, this decree was sent to parliament to be registered. It at once raised a storm of opposition in that assembly; and a vehement discussion took place. While that was going on, a disastrous scene was passing out of doors.

The calamitous effects of the system had reached the humblest concerns of human life. Provisions had risen to an enormous price; paper money was refused at all the shops; the people had not wherewithal to buy bread. It had been found absolutely indispensable to relax a little from the suspension of specie payments, and to allow small sums to be scantily exchanged for paper. The doors of the bank and the neighboring street were immediately thronged with a famishing multitude, seeking cash for banknotes of ten livres. So great was the press and struggle, that several persons were stifled and crashed to death. The mob carried three of the bodies to the court-yard of the Palais Royal. Some cried for the Regent to come forth, and behold the effect of his system; others demanded the death of Law, the impostor, who had brought this misery and ruin upon the nation.

The moment was critical: the popular fury was rising to a tempest, when Le Blanc, the Secretary of State, stepped forth. He had previously sent for the military, and now only sought to gain time. Singling out six or seven stout fellows, who seemed to be the ringleaders of the mob; "My good fellows," said he, calmly, "carry away these bodies, and place them in some church, and then come back quickly to me for your pay." They immediately obeyed; a kind of funeral procession was formed; the arrival of troops dispersed those who lingered behind; and Paris was probably saved from an insurrection.

About ten o'clock in the morning, all being quiet. Law ventured to go in his carriage to the Palais Royal. He was saluted with cries and curses, as he passed along the streets; and he reached the Palais Royal in a terrible fright. The Regent amused himself with his fears, but retained him with him, and sent off his carriage, which was assailed by the mob, pelted with stones, and the glasses shivered. The news of this outrage was communicated to parliament in the midst of a furious discussion of the decree for the commercial monopoly. The first president, who had been absent for a short time, re-entered, and communicated the tidings in a whimsical couplet:

"Messieurs, Messieurs! bonne nouvelle!
Le carrosse de Law est reduite en carrelle."

"Gentlemen, Gentlemen! good news!
The carriage of Law is shivered to atoms!"

The members sprang up with joy; "And Law!" exclaimed they, "has he been torn to pieces?" The president was ignorant of the result of the tumult; whereupon the debate was cut short, the decree rejected, and the house adjourned; the members hurrying to learn the particulars. Such was the levity with which public affairs were treated, at that dissolute and disastrous period.

On the following day, there was an ordinance from the king, prohibiting all popular assemblages; and troops were stationed at various points, and in all public places. The regiment of guards was ordered to hold itself in readiness; and the musketeers to be at their hotels, with their horses ready saddled. A number of small offices were opened, where people might cash small notes, though with great delay and difficulty. An edict was also issued, declaring that whoever should refuse to take bank-notes in the course of trade, should forfeit double the amount!

The continued and vehement opposition of parliament to the whole delusive system of finance, had been a constant source of annoyance to the Regent; but this obstinate rejection of his last grand expedient of a commercial monopoly, was not to be tolerated. He determined to punish that intractable body. The Abbé Dubois and Law suggested a simple mode; it was to suppress the parliament altogether, being, as they observed, so far from useful, that it was a constant impediment to the march of public affairs. The Regent was half inclined to listen to their advice; but upon calmer consideration, and the advice of friends, he adopted a more moderate course. On the 20th of July, early in the morning, all the doors of the parliament-house were taken possession of by the troops. Others were sent to surround the house of the first president, and others to the houses of the various members; who were all at first in great alarm, until an order from the king was put into their hands, to render themselves at Pontoise, in the course of two days, to which place the parliament was thus suddenly and arbitrarily transferred.

This despotic act, says Voltaire, would at any other time have caused an insurrection; but one half of the Parisians were occupied by their ruin, and the other half by their fancied riches, which were soon to vanish. The president and members of parliament acquiesced in the mandate without a murmur; they even went as if on a party of pleasure, and made every preparation to lead a joyous life in their exile. The musketeers, who held possession of the vacated parliament-house, a gay corps of fashionable young fellows, amused themselves with making songs and pasquinades, at the expense of the exiled legislators; and at length, to pass away time, formed themselves into a mock parliament; elected their presidents, kings, ministers, and advocates; took their seats in due form; arraigned a cat at their bar, in place of the Sieur Law, and after giving it a "fair trial," condemned it to be hanged. In this manner, public affairs and public institutions were lightly turned to jest.

As to the exiled parliament, it lived gaily and luxuriously at Pontoise, at the public expense; for the Regent had furnished funds, as usual, with a lavish hand. The first president had the mansion of the Duke de Bouillon put at his disposal, all ready furnished, with a vast and delightful garden on the borders of a river. There he kept open house to all the members of parliament. Several tables were spread every day, all furnished luxuriously and splendidly; the most exquisite wines and liquors, the choicest fruits and refreshments of all kinds, abounded. A number of small chariots for one and two horses were always at hand, for such ladies and old gentlemen as wished to take an airing after dinner, and card and billiard tables for such as chose to amuse themselves in that way until supper. The sister and the daughter of the first president did the honors of his house, and he himself presided there with an air of great ease, hospitality, and magnificence. It became a party of pleasure to drive from Paris to Pontoise, which was six leagues distant, and partake of the amusements and festivities of the place. Business was openly slighted; nothing was thought of but amusement. The Regent and his government were laughed at, and made the subjects of continual pleasantries; while the enormous expenses incurred by this idle and lavish course of life, more than doubled the liberal sums provided. This was the way in which the parliament resented their exile.

During all this time, the system was getting more and more involved. The stock exchange had some time previously been removed to the Place Vendome; but the tumult and noise becoming intolerable to the residents of that polite quarter, and especially to the chancellor, whose hotel was there, the Prince and Princess Carignan, both deep gamblers in Mississippi stock, offered the extensive garden of their Hotel de Soissons as a rallying-place for the worshippers of mammon. The offer was accepted. A number of barracks were immediately erected in the garden, as offices for the stock-brokers, and an order was obtained from the Regent, under pretext of police regulations, that no bargain should be valid, unless concluded in these barracks. The rent of them immediately mounted to a hundred livres a month for each, and the whole yielded these noble proprietors an ignoble revenue of half a million of livres.

The mania for gain, however, was now at an end. A universal panic succeeded. "*Sauve qui peut*!" was the watchword. Every one was anxious to exchange falling paper for something of intrinsic and permanent value. Since money was not to be had, jewels, precious stones, plate, porcelain, trinkets of gold and silver, all commanded any price, in paper. Land was bought at fifty years' purchase, and he esteemed himself happy, who could get it even at this price. Monopolies now became the rage among the noble holders of paper. The Duke de la Force bought up nearly all the tallow, grease, and soap; others the coffee and spices; others hay and oats. Foreign exchanges were almost impracticable. The debts of Dutch and English merchants were paid in this fictitious money, all the coin of the realm having disappeared. All the relations of debtor and creditor were confounded. With one thousand crowns one might pay a debt of eighteen thousand livres.

The Regent's mother, who once exulted in the affluence of bank paper, now wrote in a very different tone: "I have often wished," said she, in her letters, "that these bank-notes were in the depths of the infernal regions. They have given my son more trouble than relief. Nobody in France has a penny. . . . My son was once popular, but since the arrival of this cursed Law, he is hated more and more. Not a week passes, without my receiving letters filled with frightful threats, and speaking of him as a tyrant. I have just received one, threatening him with poison. When I showed it to him, he did nothing but laugh."

In the mean time. Law was dismayed by the increasing troubles, and terrified at the tempest he had raised. He was not a man of real courage; and fearing for his personal safety, from popular tumult, or the despair of ruined individuals, he again took refuge in the palace of the Regent. The latter, as usual, amused himself with his terrors, and turned every new disaster into a jest; but he, too, began to think of his own security.

In pursuing the schemes of Law, he had no doubt calculated to carry through his term of government with ease and splendor; and to enrich himself, his connections, and his favorites; and had hoped that the catastrophe of the system would not take place until after the expiration of the regency.

He now saw his mistake; that it was impossible much longer to prevent an explosion; and he determined at once to get Law out of the way, and then to charge him with the whole tissue of delusions of this paper alchemy. He accordingly took occasion of the recall of parliament in December, 1720, to suggest to Law the policy of his avoiding an encounter with that hostile and exasperated body. Law needed no urging to the measure. His only desire was to escape from Paris and its tempestuous populace. Two days before the return of parliament, he took his sudden and secret departure. He travelled in a chaise bearing the arms of the Regent, and was escorted by a kind of safe-guard of servants, in the duke's livery. His first place of refuge was an estate of the Regent's, about six leagues from Paris, from whence he pushed forward to Bruxelles.

As soon as Law was fairly out of the way, the Duke of Orleans summoned a council of the regency, and informed them that they were assembled to deliberate on the state of the finances, and the affairs of the India Company. Accordingly La Houssaye, Comptroller-General, rendered a perfectly clear statement, by which it appeared that there were bank-bills in circulation to the amount of two milliards, seven hundred millions of livres, without any evidence that this enormous sum had been emitted in virtue of any ordinance from the general assembly of the India Company, which alone had the right to authorize such emissions.

The council was astonished at this disclosure, and looked to the Regent for explanation. Pushed to the extreme, the Regent avowed that Law had emitted bills to the amount of twelve hundred millions beyond what had been fixed by ordinances, and in contradiction to express prohibitions; that the thing being done, he, the Regent, had legalized or rather covered the transaction, by decrees ordering such emissions, which decrees he had *ante-dated.*

A stormy scene ensued between the Regent and the Duke de Bourbon, little to the credit of either, both having been deeply implicated in the cabalistic operations of the system. In fact, the several members of the council had been among the most venal "beneficiaries" of the scheme, and had interests at stake which they were anxious to secure. From all the circumstances of the case, I am inclined to think that others were more to blame than Law, for the disastrous effects of his financial projects. His bank, had it been confined to its original limits, and left to the control of its own internal regulations, might have gone on prosperously, and been of great benefit to the nation. It was an institution fitted for a free country; but unfortunately, it was subject to the control of a despotic government, that could, at its pleasure, alter the value of the specie within its vaults, and compel the most extravagant expansions of its paper circulation. The vital principle of a bank is security in the regularity of its operations, and the immediate convertibility of its paper into coin; and what confidence could be reposed in an institution, or its paper promises, when the sovereign could at any moment centuple those promises in the market, and seize upon all the money in the bank? The compulsory measures used, likewise, to force bank-notes into currency, against the judgment of the public, was fatal to the system; for credit must be free and uncontrolled as the common air. The Regent was the evil spirit of the system, that forced Law on to an expansion of his paper currency far beyond what he had ever dreamed of. He it was that in a manner compelled the unlucky projector to devise all kinds of collateral companies and monopolies, by which to raise funds to meet the constantly and enormously increasing emissions of shares and notes. Law was but like a poor conjuror in the hands of a potent spirit that he has evoked, and that obliges him to go on, desperately and ruinously, with his conjurations. He only thought at the outset to raise the wind, hut the Regent compelled him to raise the whirlwind.

The investigation of the affairs of the company by the council, resulted in nothing beneficial to the public. The princes and nobles who bad enriched themselves by all kinds of juggles and extortions, escaped unpunished, and retained the greater part of their spoils. Many of the "suddenly rich," who had risen from obscurity to a giddy height of imaginary prosperity, and had indulged in all kinds of vulgar and ridiculous excesses, awoke as but of a dream, in their original poverty, now made more galling and humiliating by their transient elevation.

The weight of the evil, however, fell on more valuable classes of society; honest tradesmen and artisans, who had been seduced away from the slow accumulations of industry, to the specious chances of speculation. Thousands of meritorious families, also, once opulent, had been reduced to indigence, by a too great confidence in government. There was a general derangement in the finances, that long exerted a baneful influence over the national prosperity; but the most disastrous effects of the system were upon the morals and manners of the nation. The faith of engagements, the sanctity of promises in affairs of business, were at an end. Every expedient to grasp present profit, or to evade present difficulty, was tolerated. While such deplorable laxity of principle was generated in the busy classes, the chivalry of France had soiled their pennons; and honor and glory, so long the idols of the Gallic nobility, had been tumbled to the earth, and trampled in the dirt of the stock-market.

As to Law, the originator of the system, he appears eventually to have profited but little by his schemes. "He was a quack," says Voltaire, "to whom the state was given to be cured, but who poisoned it with his drugs, and who poisoned himself." The effects which he left behind in France, were sold at a low rice, and the proceeds dissipated. His landed estates were confiscated. He carried away with him barely enough to maintain himself, his wife, and daughter, with decency. The chief relic of his immense fortune was a great diamond, which he was often obliged to pawn. He was in England in 1721, and was presented to George the First. He returned, shortly afterward, to the continent; shifting about from place to place, and died in Venice, in 1729. His wife and daughter, accustomed to live with the prodigality of princesses, could not conform to their altered fortunes, but dissipated the scanty means left to them, and sank into abject poverty. "I saw his wife," says Voltaire, "at Bruxelles, as much humiliated as she had been haughty and triumphant at Paris." An elder brother of Law remained in France, and was protected by the Duchess of Bourbon. His descendants acquitted themselves honorably, in various public employments; and one of them was the Marquis Lauriston, sometime Lieutenant General and Peer of France.

Sketches in Paris in 1825

From the Travelling Note-Book of Geoffrey Crayon, Gent.

The Parisian Hotel

A great hotel in Paris is a street set on end: the grand staircase is the highway, and every floor or apartment a separate habitation. The one in which I am lodged may serve as a specimen. It is a large quadrangular pile, built round a spacious paved court. The ground floor is occupied by shops, magazines, and domestic offices. Then comes the entre-sol, with low ceilings, short windows, and dwarf chambers; then succeed a succession of floors, or stories, rising one above the other, to the number of Mahomet's heavens. Each floor is a mansion, complete within itself, with ante-chamber, saloons, dining and sleeping rooms, kitchen and other conveniences. Some floors are divided into two or more suites of apartments. Each apartment has its main door of entrance, opening upon the staircase, or landing-places, and locked like a street door. Thus several families and numerous single persons live under the same roof, totally independent of each other, and may live so for years, without holding more intercourse than is kept up in other cities by residents in the same street.

Like the great world, this little microcosm has its gradations of rank and style and importance. The *Premier*, or first floor with its grand saloons, lofty ceilings, and splendid furniture, is decidedly the aristocratical part of the establishment. The second floor is scarcely less aristocratical and magnificent; the other floors go on lessening in splendor as they gain in altitude, and end with the attics, the region of petty tailors, clerks, and sewing girls. To make the filling up of the mansion complete, every odd nook and corner is fitted up as a *joli petit appartement à garcon*, (a pretty little bachelor's apartment,) that is to say, some little dark inconvenient nestling-place for a poor devil of a bachelor.

The whole domain is shut up from the street by a great *porte-cochère*, or portal, calculated for the admission of carriages. This consists of two massy folding doors, that swing heavily open upon a spacious entrance, passing under the front of the edifice into the court-yard. On one side is a grand staircase leading to the upper apartments. Immediately without the portal, is the porter's lodge, a small room with one or two bedrooms adjacent, for the accommodation of the concierge, or porter, and his family. This is one of the most important functionaries of the hotel. He is, in fact, the Cerberus of the establishment, and no one can pass in or out without his knowledge and consent. The *porte-cochère* in general is fastened by a sliding bolt, from which a cord or wire passes into the porter's lodge. Whoever wishes to go out must speak to the porter, who draws the bolt. A visitor from without gives a single rap with the massive knocker; the bolt is immediately drawn, as if by an invisible hand; the door stands ajar, the visitor pushes it open, and enters. A face presents itself at the glass door of the porter's little chamber: the stranger pronounces the name of the person he comes to seek. If the person or family is of importance, occupying the first or second floor, the porter sounds a bell once or twice, to give notice that a visitor is at hand. The stranger in the mean time ascends the great staircase, the highway common to all, and arrives at the outer door, equivalent to a street door, of the suite of rooms inhabited by his friends. Beside this hangs a bell-cord, with which he rings for admittance.

When the family or person inquired for is of less importance, or lives in some remote part of the mansion less easy to be apprised, no signal is given. The applicant pronounces the name at the porter's door, and is told, "*Montez au troisième, au quatrième; sonnez à la porte à droite, ou à gauche*"; ("Ascend to the third or fourth story; ring the bell on the right or left hand door,") as the case may be.

The porter and his wife act as domestics to such of the inmates of the mansion as do not keep servants; making their beds, arranging their rooms, lighting their fires, and doing other menial offices, for which they receive a monthly stipend. They are also in confidential intercourse with the servants of the other inmates, and, having an eye on all the incomers and outgoers, are thus enabled, by hook and by crook, to learn the secrets and the domestic history of every member of the little territory within the *porte-cochère*.

The porter's lodge is accordingly a great scene of gossip, where all the private affairs of this interior neighborhood are dismissed. The court-yard, also, is an assembling place in the evenings for the servants of the different families, and a sisterhood of sewing girls from the entre-sols and the attics, to play at various games, and dance to the music of their own songs, and the echoes of their feet; at which assemblages the porter's daughter takes the lead: a fresh, pretty, buxom girl, generally called "*La Petite*," though almost as tall as a grenadier. These little evening gatherings, so characteristic of this gay country, are countenanced by the various families of the mansion, who often look down from their windows and balconies, on moonlight evenings, and enjoy the simple revels of their domestics. I must observe, however, that the hotel I am describing is rather a quiet, retired one, where most of the inmates are permanent residents from year to year, so that there is more of the spirit of neighborhood, than in the bustling, fashionable hotels in the gay parts of Paris, which are continually changing their inhabitants.

My French Neighbor

I often amuse myself by watching from my window (which by the by is tolerably elevated) the movements of the teeming little world below me; and as I am on sociable terms with the porter and his wife, I gather from them, as they light my fire, or serve my breakfast, anecdotes of all my fellow-lodgers. I have been somewhat curious in studying a little antique Frenchman, who occupies one of the *jolie chambres à garçon* already mentioned. He is one of those superannuated veterans who flourished before the revolution, and have weathered all the storms of Paris, in consequence, very probably, of being fortunately too insignificant to attract attention. He has a small income, which he manages with the skill of a French economist: appropriating so much for his lodgings, so much for his meals, so much for his visits to St Cloud and Versailles, and so much for his seat at the theatre. He has resided at the hotel for years, and always in the same chamber, which he furnishes at his own expense. The decorations of the room mark his various ages. There are some gallant pictures, which he hung up in his younger days, with a portrait of a lady of rank, whom he speaks tenderly of, dressed in the old French taste, and a pretty opera dancer, pirouetting in a hoop petticoat, who lately died at a good old age. In a corner of this picture is stuck a prescription for rheumatism, and below it stands an easy-chair. He has a small parrot at the window, to amuse him when within doors, and a pug-dog to accompany him in his daily peregrinations. While I am writing, he is crossing the court to go out. He is attired in his best coat, of sky-blue, and is doubtless bound for the Tuileries. His hair is dressed in the old style, with powdered ear-locks and a pigtail. His little dog trips after him, sometimes on four legs, sometimes on three, and looking as if his leather small-clothes were too tight for him. Now the old gentleman stops to have a word with an old crony who lives in the entre-sol, and is just returning from his promenade. Now they take a pinch of snuff together; now they pull out huge red cotton handkerchiefs, (those "flags of abomination," as they have well been called,) and blow their noses most sonorously. Now they turn to make remarks upon their two little dogs, who are exchanging the morning's salutation; now they part, and my old gentleman stops to have a passing word with the porter's wife: and now he sallies forth, and is fairly launched upon the town for the day.

No man is so methodical as a complete idler, and none so scrupulous in measuring and portioning out his time as he whose time is worth nothing. The old gentleman in question has his exact hour for rising, and for shaving himself by a small mirror hung against his casement. He sallies forth at a certain hour every morning, to take his cup of coffee and his roll at a certain café, where he reads the papers. He has been a regular admirer of the lady who presides at the bar, and always stops to have a little badinage with her, en passant. He has his regular walks on the Boulevards and in the Palais Royal, where he sets his watch by the petard fired off by the sun at mid-day. He has his daily resort in the Garden of the Tuileries, to meet with a knot of veteran idlers like himself, who talk on pretty much the same subjects whenever they meet. He has been present at all the sights and shows and rejoicings of Paris for the last fifty years; has witnessed the great events of the revolution; the guillotining of the king and queen; the coronation of Bonaparte; the capture of Paris, and the restoration of the Bourbons. All these he speaks of with the coolness of a theatrical critic; and I question whether he has not been gratified by each in its turn; not from any inherent love of tumult, but from that insatiable appetite for spectacle, which prevails among the inhabitants of this metropolis. I have been amused with a farce, in which one of these systematic old triflers is represented. He sings a song detailing his whole day's round of insignificant occupations, and goes to bed delighted with the idea that his next day will be an exact repetition of the same routine:

Je me couche le soir,
Enchanté de pouvoir
Recommencer mon train
Le lendemain
Matin.

The Englishman at Paris

In another part of the hotel, a handsome suite of rooms is occupied by an old English gentleman, of great probity, some understanding, and very considerable crustiness, who has come to France to live economically. He has a very fair property, but his wife, being of that blessed kind compared in Scripture to the fruitful vine, has overwhelmed him with a family of buxom daughters, who hang clustering about him, ready to be gathered by any hand. He is seldom to be seen in public, without one hanging on each arm, and smiling on all the world, while his own mouth is drawn down at each corner like a mastiff's, with internal growling at every thing about him. He adheres rigidly to English fashion in dress, and trudges about in long gaiters and broad-brimmed hat; while his daughters almost overshadow him with feathers, flowers, and French bonnets.

He contrives to keep up an atmosphere of English habits, opinions, and prejudices, and to carry a semblance of London into the very heart of Paris. His mornings are spent at Galignani's newsroom, where he forms one of a knot of inveterate quidnuncs, who read the same articles over a dozen times in a dozen different papers. He generally dines in company with some of his own countrymen, and they have what is called a "comfortable sitting," after dinner, in the English fashion, drinking wine, discussing the news of the London papers, and canvassing the French character, the French metropolis, and the French revolution, ending with a unanimous admission of English courage, English morality, English cookery, English wealth, the magnitude of London, and the ingratitude of the French.

His evenings are chiefly spent at a club of his countrymen, where the London papers are taken. Sometimes his daughters entice him to the theatres, but not often. He abuses French tragedy, as all fustian and bombast, Talma as a ranter, and Duchesnois as a mere termagant. It is true his ear is not sufficiently familiar with the language to understand French verse, and he generally goes to sleep during the performance. The wit of the French comedy is flat and pointless to him. He would not give one of Munden's wry faces, or Liston's inexpressible looks, for the whole of it.

He will not admit that Paris has any advantage over London. The Seine is a muddy rivulet in comparison with the Thames; the West End of London surpasses the finest parts of the French capital; and on some one's observing that there was a very thick fog out of doors: "Pish!" said he, crustily, "it's nothing to the fogs we have in London!"

He has infinite trouble in bringing his table into any thing like conformity to English rule. With his liquors, it is true, he is tolerably successful. He procures London porter, and a stock of port and sherry, at considerable expense; for he observes that he cannot stand those cursed thin French wines: they dilute his blood so much as to give him the rheumatism. As to their white wines, he stigmatizes them as mere substitutes for cider; and as to claret, why "it would be port if it could." He has continual quarrels with his French cook, whom he renders wretched by insisting on his conforming to Mrs. Grass; for it is easier to convert a Frenchman from his religion than his cookery. The poor fellow, by dint of repeated efforts, once brought himself to serve up *ros bif* sufficiently raw to suit what he considered the cannibal taste of his master; but then he could not refrain, at the last moment, adding some exquisite sauce, that put the old gentleman in a fury.

He detests wood-fires, and has procured a quantity of coal; out not having a grate, he is obliged to burn it on the hearth. Here he sits poking and stirring the fire with one end of a tongs, while the room is as murky as a smithy; railing at French chimneys, French masons, and French architects; giving a poke, at the end of every sentence, as though he were stirring up the very bowels of the delinquents he is anathematizing. He lives in a state militant with inanimate objects around him; gets into high dudgeon with doors and casements, because they will not come under English law, and has implacable feuds with sundry refractory pieces of furniture. Among these is one in particular with which he is sure to have a high quarrel every time he goes to dress. It is a commode, one of those smooth, polished, plausible pieces of French furniture, that have the perversity of five hundred devils. Each drawer has a will of its own; will open or not, just as the whim takes it, and sets lock and key at defiance. Sometimes a drawer will refuse to yield to either persuasion or force, and will part with both handles rather than yield; another will come out in the most coy and coquettish manner imaginable; elbowing along, zigzag; one corner retreating as the other advances, making a thousand difficulties and objections at every move; until the old gentleman, out of all patience, gives a sudden jerk, and brings drawer and contents into the middle of the floor. His hostility to this unlucky piece of furniture increases every day, as if incensed that it does not grow better. He is like the fretful invalid, who cursed his bed, that the longer he lay, the harder it grew. The only benefit he has derived from the quarrel is, that it has furnished him with a crusty joke, which he utters on all occasions. He swears that a French *commode* is the most *incommodious* thing in existence, and that although the nation cannot make a joint-stool that will stand steady, yet they are always talking of every thing's being *perfectionée*.

His servants understand his humor, and avail themselves of it. He was one day disturbed by a pertinacious rattling and shaking at one of the doors, and bawled out in an angry tone to know the cause of the disturbance. "Sir," said the footman, testily, "it's this confounded French lock!" "Ah!" said the old gentleman, pacified by this hit at the nation, "I thought there was something French at the bottom of it!"

English and French Character

As I am a mere looker-on in Europe, and hold myself as much as possible aloof from its quarrels and prejudices, I feel something like one overlooking a game, who, without any great skill of his own, can occasionally perceive the blunders of much abler players. This neutrality of feeling enables me to enjoy the contrasts of character presented in this time of general peace; when the various people of Europe, who have so long been sundered by wars, are brought together, and placed side by side in this great gathering place of nations. No greater contrast, however, is exhibited, than that of the French and English. The peace has deluged this gay capital with English visitors, of all ranks and conditions. They throng every place of curiosity and amusement; fill the public gardens, the galleries, the cafés, saloons, theatres; always herding together, never associating with the French. The two nations are like two threads of different colors, tangled together, but never blended.

In fact, they present a continual antithesis, and seem to value themselves upon being unlike each other; yet each have their peculiar merits, which should entitle them to each other's esteem. The French intellect is quick and active, It flashes its way into a subject with the rapidity of lightning; seizes upon remote conclusions with a sudden bound, and its deductions are almost intuitive. The English intellect is less rapid, but more persevering; less sudden, but more sure in its deductions. The quickness and mobility of the French enable them to find enjoyment in the multiplicity of sensations. They speak and act more from immediate impressions than from reflection and meditation. They are therefore more social and communicative; more fond of society, and of places of public resort and amusement. An Englishman is more reflective in his habits. He lives in the world of his own thoughts, and seems more self-existent and self-dependent. He loves the quiet of his own apartment; even when abroad, he in a manner, makes a little solitude around him, by his silence and reserve: he moves about shy and solitary, and as it were, buttoned up, body and soul.

The French are great optimists: they seize upon every good as it flies, and revel in the passing pleasure. The Englishman is too apt to neglect the present good, in preparing against the possible evil. However adversities may lower, let the sun shine but for a moment, and forth sallies the mercurial Frenchman, in holiday dress and holiday spirits, gay as a butterfly, as though his sunshine were perpetual; but let the sun beam never so brightly so there be but a cloud in the horizon, the wary Englishman ventures forth distrustfully, with his umbrella in his hand.

The Frenchman has a wonderful facility at turning small things to advantage. No one can be gay and luxurious on smaller means; no one requires less expense to be happy. He practises a kind of gilding in his style of living, and hammers out every guinea into gold leaf. The Englishman, on the contrary, is expensive in his habits, and expensive in his enjoyments. He values every thing, whether useful or ornamental, by what it costs. He has no satisfaction in show, unless it be solid and complete. Every thing goes with him by the square foot. Whatever display he makes, the depth is sure to equal the surface.

The Frenchman's habitation, like himself, is open, cheerful, bustling, and noisy. He lives in a part of a great hotel, with wide portal, paved court, a spacious dirty stone staircase, and a family on every floor. All is clatter and chatter. He is good-humored and talkative with his servants, sociable with his neighbors, and complaisant to all the world. Any body has access to himself and his apartments; his very bedroom is open to visitors, whatever may be its state of confusion; and all this not from any peculiarly hospitable feeling, but from that communicative habit which predominates over his character.

The Englishman, on the contrary, ensconces himself in a snug brick mansion, which he has all to himself; locks the front door, puts broken bottles along his walls, and spring-guns and man-traps in his gardens; shrouds himself with trees and window-curtains; exults in his quiet and privacy, and seems disposed to keep out noise, daylight, and company. His house, like himself, has a reserved, inhospitable exterior; yet whoever gains admittance, is apt to find a warm heart and warm fireside within.

The French excel in wit; the English in humor: the French have gayer fancy, the English richer imaginations. The former are full of sensibility; easily moved, and prone to sudden and great excitement; but their excitement is not durable: the English are more phlegmatic; not so readily affected; but capable of being aroused to great enthusiasm. The faults of these opposite temperaments are, that the vivacity of the French is apt to sparkle up and be frothy, the gravity of the English to settle down and grow muddy. When the two characters can be fixed in a medium, the French kept from effervescence and the English from stagnation, both will be found excellent.

This contrast of character may also be noticed in the great concerns of the two nations. The ardent Frenchman is all for military renown; he fights for glory, that is to say, for success in arms. For, provided the national flag be victorious, he cares little about the expense, the injustice, or the inutility of the war. It is wonderful how the poorest Frenchman will revel on a triumphant bulletin; a great victory is meat and drink to him; and at the sight of a military sovereign, bringing home captured cannon and captured standards, he throws up his greasy cap in the air and is ready to jump out of his wooden shoes for joy.

John Bull, on the contrary, is a reasoning, considerate person. If he does wrong, it is in the most rational way imaginable. He fights because the good of the world requires it. He is a moral person, and makes war upon his neighbor for the maintenance of peace and good order, and sound principles. He is a money-making personage, and fights for the prosperity of commerce and manufactures. Thus the two nations have been fighting, time out of mind, for glory and good. The French, in pursuit of glory, have had their capital twice taken; and John, in pursuit of good, has run himself over head and ears in debt.

The Tuileries and Windsor Castle

I have sometimes fancied I could discover national characteristics in national edifices. In the Chateau of the Tuileries, for instance, I perceive the same jumble of contrarieties that marks the French character; the same whimsical mixture of the great and the little; the splendid and the paltry, the sublime and the grotesque. On visiting this famous pile, the first thing that strikes both eye and ear, is military display. The courts glitter with steel-clad soldiery, and resound with tramp of horse, the roll of drum, and the bray of trumpet. Dismounted guardsmen patrol its arcades, with loaded carbines, jingling spurs, and clanking sabres. Gigantic grenadiers are posted about its staircases, young officers of the guards loll from the balconies, or lounge in groups upon, the terraces: and the gleam of bayonet from window to window, shows that sentinels are pacing up and down the corridors and ante-chambers. The first floor is brilliant with the splendors of a court. French taste has tasked itself in adorning the sumptuous suites of apartments; nor are the gilded chapel and splendid theatre forgotten, where Piety and Pleasure are next-door neighbors, and harmonize together with perfect French *bienseance*.

Mingled up with all this regal and military magnificence, is a world of whimsical and make-shift detail. A great part of the huge edifice is cut up into little chambers and nestling-places for retainers of the court, dependants on retainers, and hangers-on of dependants. Some are squeezed into narrow entre-sols, those low, dark, intermediate slices of apartments between floors, the inhabitants of which seem shoved in edgeways, like books between narrow shelves; others are perched, like swallows, under the eaves; the high roofs, too, which are as tall and steep as a French cocked hat, have rows of little dormer windows, tier above tier, just large enough to admit light and air for some dormitory, and to enable its occupant to peep out at the sky. Even to the very ridge of the roof, may be seen, here and there, one of these air-holes, with a stove-pipe beside it, to carry off the smoke from the handful of fuel with which its weasen-faced tenant simmers his *demi-tasse* of coffee.

On approaching the palace from the Pont Royal, you take in at a glance all the various strata of inhabitants; the garreteer in the roof; the retainer in the entre-sol; the courtiers at the casements of the royal apartments; while on the ground-floor a steam of savory odors, and a score or two of cooks, in white caps, bobbing their heads about the windows, betray that scientific and all-important laboratory, the royal kitchen.

Go into the grand ante-chamber of the royal apartments on Sunday, and see the mixture of Old and New France: the old emigrés, returned with the Bourbons; little withered, spindle-shanked old noblemen, clad in court dresses, that figured in these saloons before the revolution, and have been carefully treasured up during their exile; with the solitaires and *ailes de pigeon* of former days: and the court swords strutting out behind, like pins stuck through dry beetles. See them haunting the scenes of their former splendor, in hopes of a restitution of estates, like ghosts haunting the vicinity of buried treasure: while around them you see Young France, grown up in the fighting school of Napoleon; equipped *en militaire*: tall, hardy, frank, vigorous, sunburnt, fierce-whiskered; with tramping boots, towering crests, and glittering breastplates.

It is incredible the number of ancient and hereditary feeders on royalty said to be housed in this establishment. Indeed all the royal palaces abound with noble families returned from exile, and who have nestling-places allotted them while they await the restoration of their estates, or the much-talked-of law, indemnity. Some of them have fine quarters, but poor living. Some families have but five or six hundred francs a year, and all their retinue consists of a servant woman. With all this, they maintain their old aristocratical *hauteur*, look down with vast contempt upon the opulent families which have risen since the revolution; stigmatize them all as *parvenus*, or upstarts, and refuse to visit them.

In regarding the exterior of the Tuileries, with all its outward signs of internal populousness, I have often thought what a rare sight it would be to see it suddenly unroofed, and all its nooks and corners laid open to the day. It would be like turning up the stump of an old tree, and dislodging the world of grubs, and ants, and beetles lodged beneath. Indeed there is a scandalous anecdote current, that in the time of one of the petty plots, when petards were exploded under the windows of the Tuileries, the police made a sudden investigation of the palace at four o'clock in the morning, when a scene of the most whimsical confusion ensued. Hosts of supernumerary inhabitants were found foisted into the huge edifice: every rat-hole had its occupant; and places which had been considered as tenanted only by spiders, were found crowded with a surreptitious population. It is added, that many ludicrous accidents occurred; great scampering and slamming of doors, and whisking away in night-gowns and slippers; and several persons, who were found by accident in their neighbors' chambers, evinced indubitable astonishment at the circumstance.

As I have fancied I could read the French character in the national palace of the Tuileries, so I have pictured to myself some of the traits of John Bull in his royal abode of Windsor Castle. The Tuileries, outwardly a peaceful palace, is in effect a swaggering military hold; while the old castle, on the contrary, in spite of its bullying look, is completely under petticoat government. Every corner and nook is built up into some snug, cosy nestling-place, some "procreant cradle," not tenanted by meagre expectants or whiskered warriors, but by sleek placemen; knowing realizers of present pay and present pudding; who seem placed there not to kill and destroy, but to breed and multiply. Nursery maids and children shine with rosy faces at the windows, and swarm about the courts and terraces. The very soldiery have a pacific look, and when off duty, may be seen loitering about the place with the nursery-maids; not making love to them in the gay gallant style of the French soldiery, but with infinite bonhommie aiding them to take care of the broods of children.

Though the old castle is in decay, every thing about it thrives; the very crevices of the walls are tenanted by swallows, rooks, and pigeons, all sure of quiet lodgment: the ivy strikes its roots deep in the fissures, and flourishes about the mouldering tower.[1] Thus it is with honest John: according to his own account, he is ever going to ruin, yet every thing that lives on him, thrives and waxes fat. He would fain be a soldier, and swagger like his neighbors; but his domestic, quiet-loving, uxorious nature continually gets the upper hand; and though he may mount his helmet and gird on his sword, yet he is apt to sink into the plodding, painstaking father of a family; with a troop of children at his heels, and his womenkind hanging on each arm.

The Field of Waterloo

I have spoken heretofore with some levity of the contrast that exists between the English and French character; but it deserves more serious consideration. They are the two great nations of modern times most diametrically opposed, and most worthy of each other's rivalry; essentially distinct in their characters, excelling in opposite qualities, and reflecting lustre on each other by their very opposition. In nothing is this contrast more strikingly evinced than in their military conduct. For ages have they been contending, and for ages have they crowded each other's history with acts of splendid heroism. Take the Battle of Waterloo, for instance, the last and most memorable trial of their rival prowess. Nothing could surpass the brilliant daring on the one side, and the steadfast enduring on the other. The French cavalry broke like waves on the compact squares of English infantry. They were seen galloping round those serried walls of men, seeking in vain for an entrance; tossing their arms in the air, in the heat of their enthusiasm, and braving the whole front of battle. The British troops, on the other hand, forbidden to move or fire, stood firm and enduring. Their columns were ripped up by cannonry; whole rows were swept down at a shot: the survivors closed their ranks, and stood firm. In this way many columns stood through the pelting of the iron tempest without firing a shot; without any action to stir their blood, or excite their spirits. Death thinned their ranks, but could not shake their souls.

A beautiful instance of the quick and generous impulses to which the French are prone, is given in the case of a French cavalier, in the hottest of the action, charging furiously upon a British officer, but perceiving in the moment of assault that his

1. The above sketch was written before the thorough repairs and magnificent additions made of late years to Windsor Castle.

adversary had lost his sword-arm, dropping the point of his sabre, and courteously riding on. Peace be with that generous warrior, whatever were his fate! If he went down in the storm of battle, with the foundering fortunes of his chieftain, may the turf of Waterloo grow green above his grave!—and happier far would be the fate of such a spirit, to sink amidst the tempest, unconscious of defeat, than to survive, and mourn over the blighted laurels of his country.

In this way the two armies fought through a long and bloody day. The French with enthusiastic valor, the English with cool-inflexible courage, until Fate, as if to leave the question of superiority still undecided between two such adversaries, brought up the Prussians to decide the fortunes of the field.

It was several years afterward, that I visited the field of Waterloo. The ploughshare had been busy with its oblivious labors, and the frequent harvest had nearly obliterated the vestiges of war. Still the blackened ruins of Hoguemont stood, a monumental pile, to mark the violence of this vehement struggle. Its broken walls, pierced by bullets, and shattered by explosions, showed the deadly strife that had taken place within; when Gaul and Briton, hemmed in between narrow walls, hand to hand and foot to foot, fought from garden to court-yard, from court-yard to chamber, with intense and concentrated rivalship. Columns of smoke towered from this vortex of battle as from a volcano: "it was," said my guide, "like a little hell upon earth." Not far off, two or three broad spots of rank, unwholesome green still marked the places where these rival warriors, after their fierce and fitful struggle, slept quietly together in the lap of their common mother earth. Over all the rest of the field, peace had resumed its sway. The thoughtless whistle of the peasant floated on the air, instead of the trumpet's clangor; the team slowly labored up the hill-side, once shaken by the hoofs of rushing squadrons; and wide fields of corn waved peacefully over the soldiers' grave, as summer seas dimple over the place where the tall ship lies buried.

To the foregoing desultory notes on the French military character, let me append a few traits which I picked up verbally in one of the French provinces. They may have already appeared in print, but I have never met with them.

At the breaking out of the revolution, when so many of the old families emigrated, a descendant of the great Tuvenne, by the name of De Latour D'Auvergne, refused to accompany his relations, and entered into the republican army. He served in all the campaigns of the revolution, distinguished himself by his valor, his accomplishments, and his generous spirit, and might have risen to fortune and to the highest honors. He refused, however, all rank in the army, above that of captain, and would receive no recompense for his achievements but a sword of honor. Napoleon, in testimony of his merits, gave him the title of Premier Grenadier de France (First Grenadier of France), which was the only title he would ever bear. He was killed in Germany, at the battle of Neuburg. To honor his memory, his place was always retained in his regiment, as if he still occupied it; and whenever the regiment was mustered, and the name of De Latour D'Auvergne was called out, the reply was: "Dead on the field of honor!"

Paris at the Restoration

Paris presented a singular aspect just after the downfall of Napoleon, and the restoration of the Bourbons. It was filled with a restless, roaming population; a dark, sallow race, with fierce moustaches, black cravats, and feverish, menacing looks; men suddenly thrown out of employ by the return of peace; officers cut short in their career, and cast loose with scanty means, many of them in utter indigence, upon the world; the broken elements of armies. They haunted the places of public resort, like restless, unhappy spirits, taking no pleasure; hanging about, like lowering clouds that linger after a storm, and giving a singular air of gloom to this otherwise gay metropolis.

The vaunted courtesy of the old school, the smooth urbanity that prevailed in former days of settled government and long-established aristocracy, had disappeared amidst the savage republicanism of the revolution and the military furor of the empire: recent reverses had stung the national vanity to the quick; and English travellers, who crowded to Paris on the return of peace, expecting to meet with a gay, good-humored, complaisant populace, such as existed in the time of the "Sentimental Journey," were surprised at finding them irritable and fractious, quick at fancying affronts, and not unapt to offer insults. They accordingly inveighed with heat and bitterness at the rudeness they experienced in the French metropolis: yet what better had they to expect? Had Charles II been reinstated in his kingdom by the valor of French troops; had he been wheeled triumphantly to London over the trampled bodies and trampled standards of England's bravest sons; had a French general dictated to the English capital, and a French army been quartered in Hyde-Park; had Paris poured forth its motley population, and the wealthy bourgeoisie of every French trading town swarmed to London; crowding its squares; filling its streets with their equipages; thronging its fashionable hotels, and places of amusements; elbowing its impoverished nobility out of their palaces and opera boxes, and looking down on the humiliated inhabitants as a conquered people; in such a reverse of the case, what degree of courtesy would the populace of London have been apt to exercise toward their visitors?[2]

On the contrary, I have always admired the degree of magnanimity exhibited by the French on the occupation of their capital by the English. When we consider the military ambition of this nation, its love of glory, the splendid height to which its renown in arms had recently been carried, and with these, the tremendous reverses it had just undergone, its armies shattered, annihilated, its capital captured, garrisoned, and overrun, and that too by its ancient rival, the English, toward whom it had cherished for centuries a jealous and almost religious hostility; could we have wondered, if the tiger spirit of this fiery people had broken out in bloody feuds and deadly quarrels; and that they had sought to rid themselves in any way, of their invaders? But it is cowardly nations only, those who dare not wield the sword, that revenge themselves with the lurking dagger. There were no assassinations in Paris. The French had fought valiantly, desperately, in the field; but, when valor was no longer of avail, they submitted like gallant men to a fate they could not withstand. Some instances of insult from the populace were experienced by their English visitors; some personal rencontres, which led to duels, did take place; but these smacked of open and honorable hostility. No instances of lurking and perfidious revenge occurred, and the British soldier patrolled the streets of Paris safe from treacherous assault.

If the English met with harshness and repulse in social intercourse, it was in some degree a proof that the people are more sincere than has been represented. The emigrants who had just returned, were not yet reinstated. Society was constituted of those who had flourished under the late régime; the newly ennobled, the recently enriched, who felt their prosperity and their consequence endangered by this change of things. The broken-down officer, who saw his glory tarnished, his fortune ruined, his occupation gone, could not be expected to look with complacency upon the authors of his downfall. The English visitor, flushed with health, and wealth, and victory, could little enter into the feelings of the blighted warrior, scarred with a hundred battles, an

---

2. The above remarks were suggested by a conversation with the late Mr. Canning, whom the author met in Paris, and who expressed himself in the most liberal way concerning the magnanimity of the French on the occupation of their capital by strangers.

exile from the camp, broken in constitution by the wars, impoverished by the peace, and cast back, a needy stranger in the splendid but captured metropolis of his country.

Oh! who can tell what heroes feel
When all but life and honor's lost!

And here let me notice the conduct of the French soldiery on the dismemberment of the Army of the Loire, when two hundred thousand men were suddenly thrown out of employ; men who had been brought up to the camp, and scarce knew any other home. Few in civil, peaceful life, are aware of the severe trial to the feelings that takes place on the dissolution of a regiment. There is a fraternity in arms. The community of dangers, hardships, enjoyments; the participation in battles and victories, the companionship in adventures, at a time of life when men's feelings are most fresh, susceptible, and ardent, all these bind the members of a regiment strongly together. To them the regiment is friends, family, home. They identify themselves with his fortunes, its glories, its disgraces. Imagine this romantic tie suddenly dissolved; the regiment broken up; the occupation of its members gone; their military pride mortified; the career of glory closed behind them; that of obscurity, dependence, want, neglect, perhaps beggary, before them. Such was the case with the soldiers of the Army of the Loire. They were sent off in squads, with officers, to the principal towns where they were to be disarmed and discharged. In this way they passed through the country with arms in their hands, often exposed to slights and scoffs, to hunger and various hardships and privations; but they conducted themselves magnanimously, without any of those outbreaks of violence and wrong that so often attend the dismemberment of armies.

The few years that have elapsed since the time above alluded to, have already had their effect. The proud and angry spirits which then roamed about Paris unemployed, have cooled down, and found occupation. The national character begins to recover its old channels, though worn deeper by recent torrents. The natural urbanity of the French begins to find its way, like oil, to the surface, though there still remains a degree of roughness and bluntness of manner, partly real, and partly affected, by such as imagine it to indicate force and frankness. The events of the last thirty years have rendered the French a more reflecting people. They have acquired greater independence of mind and strength of judgment, together with a portion of that prudence which results from experiencing the dangerous consequences of excesses. However that period may have been stained by crimes, and filled with extravagances, the French have certainly come out of it a greater nation than before. One of their own philosophers observes, that in one or two generations the nation will probably combine the ease and elegance of the old character with force and solidity. They were light, he says, before the revolution; then wild and savage; they have become more thoughtful and reflective. It is only old Frenchmen, now-a-days, that are gay and trivial the young are very serious personages.

P.S. In the course of a morning's walk, about the time the above remarks were written, I observed the Duke of Wellington, who was on a brief visit to Paris. He was alone, simply attired in a blue frock; with an umbrella under his arm, and his hat drawn over his eyes, and sauntering across the Place Vendome, close by the column of Napoleon. He gave a glance up at the column as he passed, and continued his loitering way up the Rue de la Paix; stopping occasionally to gaze in at the shop-windows; elbowed now and then by other gazers, who little suspected that the quiet, lounging individual they were jostling so unceremoniously, was the conqueror who had twice entered their capital victoriously; had controlled the destinies of the nation, and eclipsed the glory of the military idol, at the base of whose column he was thus negligently sauntering.

Some years afterwards I was at an evening's entertainment given by the Duke at Apsley House, to William IV. The Duke had manifested his admiration of his great adversary, by having portraits of him in different parts of the house. At the bottom of the grand staircase, stood the colossal statue of the Emperor by Canova. It was of marble, in the antique style, with one arm partly extended, holding a figure of victory. Over this arm the ladies, in tripping up stairs to the ball, had thrown their shawls. It was a singular office for the statue of Napoleon to perform it the mansion of the Duke of Wellington!

Imperial Cæsar dead, and turned to clay, etc., etc.

A Contented Man

In the garden of the Tuileries there is a sunny corner under the wall of a terrace which fronts the south. Along the wall is a range of benches commanding a view of the walks and avenues of the garden. This genial nook is a place of great resort in the latter part of autumn, and in fine days in winter, as it seems to retain the flavor of departed summer. On a calm, bright morning it is quite alive with nursery-maids and their playful little charges. Hither also resort a number of ancient ladies and gentlemen, who, with laudable thrift in small pleasures and small expenses, for which the French are to be noted, come here to enjoy sunshine and save firewood. Here may often be seen some cavalier of the old school, when the sunbeams have warmed his blood into something like a glow, fluttering about like a frostbitten moth thawed before the fire, putting forth a feeble show of gallantry among the antiquated dames, and now and then eyeing the buxom nursery-maids with what might almost be mistaken for an air of libertinism.

Among the habitual frequenters of this place, I had often remarked an old gentleman, whose dress was decidedly anti-revolutional. He wore the three-cornered cocked hat of the *ancien régime*; his hair was frizzed over each ear into *ailes de pigeon*, a style strongly savoring of Bourbonism; and a queue stuck out behind, the loyalty of which was not to be disputed. His dress, though ancient, had an air of decayed gentility, and I observed that he took his snuff out of an elegant though old-fashioned gold box. He appeared to be the most popular man on the walk. He had a compliment for every old lady, he kissed every child, and he patted every little dog on the head; for children and little dogs are very important members of society in France. I must observe, however, that he seldom kissed a child without, at the same time, pinching the nursery-maid's cheek; a Frenchman of the old school never forgets his devoirs to the sex.

I had taken a liking to this old gentleman. There was an habitual expression of benevolence in his face, which I have very frequently remarked in these relics of the politer days of France. The constant interchange of those thousand little courtesies which imperceptibly sweeten life, have a happy effect upon the features, and spread a mellow evening charm over the wrinkles of old age.

Where there is a favorable predisposition, one soon forms a kind of tacit intimacy by often meeting on the same walks. Once or twice I accommodated him with a bench, after which we touched hats on passing each other; at length we got so far as to take a pinch of snuff together out of his box, which is equivalent to eating salt together in the East; from that time our acquaintance was established.

I now became his frequent companion in his morning promenades, and derived much amusement from his good-humored remarks on men and manners. One morning, as we were strolling through an alley of the Tuileries, with the autumnal breeze whirling the yellow leaves about our path, my companion fell into a peculiarly communicative vein, and gave me several particulars of his history. He had once been wealthy, and possessed of a fine estate in the country, and a noble hotel in Paris; but the revolution, which effected so many disastrous changes, stripped him of every thing. He was secretly denounced by his own steward during a sanguinary period of the revolution, and a number of the bloodhounds of the Convention were sent to arrest him. He received private intelligence of their approach in time to effect his escape. He landed in England without money or friends, but considered himself singularly fortunate in having his head upon his shoulders; several of his neighbors having been guillotined as a punishment for being rich.

When he reached London he had but a louis in his pocket, and no prospect of getting another. He ate a solitary dinner on beefsteak, and was almost poisoned by port wine, which from its color he had mistaken for claret. The dingy look of the chop-house, and of the little mahogany-colored box in which he ate his dinner, contrasted sadly with the gay saloons of Paris. Every thing looked gloomy and disheartening. Poverty stared him in the face; he turned over the few shillings he had of change; did not know what was to become of him; and—went to the theatre!

He took his seat in the pit, listened attentively to a tragedy of which he did not understand a word, and which seemed made up of fighting, and stabbing, and scene-shifting, and began to feel his spirits sinking within him; when, casting his eyes into the orchestra, what was his surprise to recognize an old friend and neighbor in the very act of extorting music from a huge violon cello.

As soon as the evening's performance was over he tapped his friend on the shoulder; they kissed each other on each cheek, and the musician took him home, and shared his lodgings with him. He had learned music as an accomplishment; by his friend's advice he now turned to it as a mean of support. He procured a violin, offered himself for the orchestra, was received, and again considered himself one of the most fortunate men upon earth.

Here therefore he lived for many years during the ascendency of the terrible Napoleon. He found several emigrants living like himself, by the exercise of their talents. They associated together, talked of France and of old times, and endeavored to keep up a semblance of Parisian life in the centre of London.

They dined at a miserable cheap French restaurateur in the neighborhood of Leicester-square, where they were served with a caricature of French cookery. They took their promenade in St. James's Park, and endeavored to fancy it the Tuileries; in short, they made shift to accommodate themselves to every thing but an English Sunday. Indeed the old gentleman seemed to have nothing to say against the English, whom he affirmed to be braves gens; and he mingled so much among them, that at the end of twenty years he could speak their language almost well enough to be understood.

The downfall of Napoleon was another epoch in his life. He had considered himself a fortunate man to make his escape penniless out of France, and he considered himself fortunate to be able to return penniless into it. It is true that he found his Parisian hotel had passed through several hands during the vicissitudes of the times, so as to be beyond the reach of recovery; but then he had been noticed benignantly by government, and had a pension of several hundred francs, upon which, with careful management, he lived independently, and, as far as I could judge, happily.

As his once splendid hotel was now occupied as a *hôtel garni*, he hired a small chamber in the attic; it was but, as he said, changing his bedroom up two pair of stairs—he was still in his own house. His room was decorated with pictures of several beauties of former times, with whom he professed to have been on favorable terms: among them was a favorite opera-dancer, who had been the admiration of Paris at the breaking out of the revolution. She had been a *protegée* of my friend, and one of the few of his youthful favorites who had survived the lapse of time and its various vicissitudes. They had renewed their acquaintance, and she now and then visited him; but the beautiful Psyche, once the fashion of the day and the idol of the *parterre*, was now a shrivelled, little old woman, warped in the back, and with a hooked nose.

The old gentleman was a devout attendant upon levees: he was most zealous in his loyalty, and could not speak of the royal family without a burst of enthusiasm, for he still felt towards them as his companions in exile. As to his poverty he made light of it, and indeed had a good-humored way of consoling himself for every cross and privation. If he had lost his chateau in the country, he had half a dozen royal palaces, as it were, at his command. He had Versailles and St. Cloud for his country resorts, and the shady alleys of the Tuileries and the Luxembourg or his town recreation. Thus all his promenades and relaxations were magnificent, yet cost nothing. When I walk through these fine gardens, said he, I have only to fancy myself the owner of them, and they are mine. All these gay crowds are my visitors, and I defy the grand seignior himself to display a greater variety of beauty. Nay, what is better, I have not the trouble of entertaining them. My estate is a perfect *Sans Souci*, where every one does as he pleases, and no one troubles the owner. All Paris is my theatre, and presents me with a continual spectacle. I have a table spread for me in every street, and thousands of waiters ready to fly at my bidding. When my servants have waited upon me I pay them, discharge them, and there's an end: I have no fears of their wronging or pilfering me when my back is turned. Upon the whole, said the old gentleman, with a smile of infinite good humor, when I think upon the various risks I have run, and the manner in which I have escaped them; when I recollect all that I have suffered, and consider all that I at present enjoy, I cannot but look upon myself as a man of singular good fortune.

Such was the brief history of this practical philosopher, and it is a picture of many a Frenchman ruined by the revolution. The French appear to have a greater facility than most men in accommodating themselves to the reverses of life, and of extracting honey out of the bitter things of this world. The first shock of calamity is apt to overwhelm them, but when it is once past, their natural buoyancy of feeling soon brings them to the surface. This may be called the result of levity of character, but it answers the end of reconciling us to misfortune, and if it be not true philosophy, it is something almost as efficacious. Ever since I have heard the story of my little Frenchman, I have treasured it up in my heart: and I thank my stars I have at length found, what I had long considered as not to be found on earth—a contented man.

* * *

P.S. There is no calculating on human happiness. Since writing the foregoing, the law of indemnity has been passed, and my friend restored to a great part of his fortune. I was absent from Paris at the time, but on my return hastened to congratulate him. I found him magnificently lodged on the first floor of his hotel. I was ushered, by a servant in livery, through splendid saloons, to a cabinet richly furnished, where I found my little Frenchman reclining on a couch. He received me with his usual cordiality; but I saw the gayety and benevolence of his countenance had fled; he had an eye full of care and anxiety.

I congratulated him on his good fortune. "Good fortune?" echoed he; "bah! I have been plundered of a princely fortune, and they give me a pittance as an indemnity."

Alas! I found my late poor and contented friend one of the richest and most miserable men in Paris. Instead of rejoicing in the ample competency restored to him, he is daily repining at the superfluity withheld. He no longer wanders in happy idleness about Paris, but is a repining attendant in the ante-chambers of ministers. His loyalty has evaporated with his gayety; he screws his mouth when the Bourbons are mentioned, and even shrugs his shoulders when he hears the praises of the king. In a word, he is one of the many philosophers undone by the law of indemnity, and his case is desperate, for I doubt whether even another reverse of fortune, which should restore him to poverty, could make him again a happy man.

Broek: or the Dutch Paradise

IT HAS LONG BEEN A MATTER OF DISCUSSION AND CONTROVERSY AMONG THE pious and the learned, as to the situation of the terrestrial paradise whence our first parents were exiled. This question has been put to rest by certain of the faithful in Holland, who have decided in favor of the vilage of BROEK, about six miles from Amsterdam. It may not, they observe, correspond in all respects to the description of the garden of Eden, handed down from days of yore, but it comes nearer to their ideas of a perfect paradise than any other place on earth.

This eulogium induced me to make some inquiries as to this favored spot, in the course of a sojourn at the city of Amsterdam, and the information I procured fully justified the enthusiastic praises I had heard. The village of Broek is situated in Waterland, in the midst of the greenest and richest pastures of Holland, I may say, of Europe. These pastures are the source of its wealth, for it is famous for its dairies, and for those oval cheeses which regale and perfume the whole civilized world. The population consists of about six hundred persons, comprising several families which have inhabited the place since time immemorial, and have waxed rich on the products of their meadows. They keep all their wealth among themselves; intermarrying, and keeping all strangers at a wary distance. They are a "hard money" people, and remarkable for turning the penny the right way. It is said to have been an old rule, established by one of the primitive financiers and legislators of Broek, that no one should leave the village with more than six guilders in his pocket, or return with less than ten; a shrewd regulation, well worthy the attention of modern political economists, who are so anxious to fix the balance of trade.

What, however, renders Broek so perfect an elysium, in the eyes of all true Hollanders, is the matchless height to which the spirit of cleanliness is carried there. It amounts almost to a religion among the inhabitants, who pass the greater part of their time rubbing and scrubbing, and painting and varnishing: each housewife vies with her neighbor in her devotion to the scrubbing brush, as zealous Catholics do in their devotion to the cross; and it is said, a notable housewife of the place in days of yore, is held in pious remembrance, and almost canonized as a saint, for having died of pure exhaustion and chagrin, in an ineffectual attempt to scour a black man white.

These particulars awakened my ardent curiosity to see a place which I pictured to myself the very fountain-head of certain hereditary habits and customs prevalent among the descendants of the original Dutch settlers of my native state. I accordingly lost no time in performing a pilgrimage to Broek.

Before I reached the place, I beheld symptoms of the tranquil character of its inhabitants. A little clump-built boat was in full sail along the lazy bosom of a canal, but its sail consisted of the blades of two paddles stood on end, while the navigator sat steering with a third paddle in the stern, crouched down like a toad, with a slouched hat drawn over his eyes. I presumed him to be some nautical lover, on the way to his mistress. After proceeding a little farther, I came in sight of the harbor or port of destination of this drowsy navigator. This was the Broeken-Meer, an artificial basin, or sheet of olive-green water, tranquil as a millpond. On this the village of Broek is situated, and the borders are laboriously decorated with flower-beds, box-trees clipped into all kinds of ingenious shapes and fancies, and little "lust" houses or pavilions.

I alighted outside of the village, for no horse nor vehicle is permitted to enter its precincts, lest it should cause defilement of the well-scoured pavements. Shaking the dust off my feet, therefore, I prepared to enter, with due reverence and circumspection, this sanctum sanctorum of Dutch cleanliness. I entered by a narrow street, paved with yellow bricks, laid edgewise, and so clean that one might eat from them. Indeed, they were actually worn deep, not by the tread of feet, but by the friction of the scrubbing-brush.

The houses were built of wood, and all appeared to have been freshly painted, of green, yellow, and other bright colors. They were separated from each other by gardens and orchards, and stood at some little distance from the street, with wide areas or courtyards, paved in mosaic, with variegated stones, polished by frequent rubbing. The areas were divided from the street by curiously-wrought railings, or balustrades, of iron, surmounted with brass and copper balls, scoured into dazzling effulgence. The very trunks of the trees in front of the houses were by the same process made to look as if they had been varnished. The porches, doors, and window-frames of the houses were of exotic woods, curiously carved, and polished like costly furniture. The front doors are never opened, excepting on christenings, marriages, or funerals: on all ordinary occasions, visitors enter by the back door. In former times, persons when admitted had to put on slippers, but this oriental ceremony is no longer insisted upon.

A poor devil Frenchman, who attended upon me as cicerone, boasted with some degree of exultation, of a triumph of his countrymen over the stern regulations of the place. During the time that Holland was overrun by the armies of the French republic, a French general, surrounded by his whole état major, who had come from Amsterdam to view the wonders of Broek, applied for admission at one of these taboo'd portals. The reply was, that the owner never received any one who did not come introduced by some friend. "Very well," said the general; "take my compliments to your master, and tell him I will return here to-morrow with a company of soldiers, *pour parler raison avec mon ami Hollandais*." Terrified at the idea of having a company of soldiers billeted upon him, the owner threw open his house, entertained the general and his retinue with unwonted hospitality; though it is said it cost the family a month's scrubbing and scouring, to restore all things to exact order, after this military invasion. My vagabond informant seemed to consider this one of the greatest victories of the republic.

I walked about the place in mute wonder and admiration. A dead stillness prevailed around, like that in the deserted streets of Pompeii. No sign of life was to be seen, excepting now and then a hand, and a long pipe, and an occasional puff of smoke, out of the window of some "lust-haus" overhanging a miniature canal; and on approaching a little nearer, the periphery in profile of some robustious burgher.

Among the grand houses pointed out to me, were those of Claes Bakker, and Cornelius Bakker, richly carved and gilded, with flower-gardens and clipped shrubberies; and that of the Great Ditmus, who, my poor devil cicerone informed me, in a whisper, was worth two millions; all these were mansions shut up from the world, and only kept to be cleaned. After having been conducted from one wonder to another of the village, I was ushered by my guide into the grounds and gardens of Mynheer Broekker, another mighty cheese-manufacturer, worth eighty thousand guilders a year. I had repeatedly been struck with the similarity of all that I had seen in this amphibious little village, to the buildings and landscapes on Chinese platters and tea-pots; but here I found the similarity complete; for I was told that these gardens were modelled upon Van Bramm's description of those of Yuen min Yuen, in China.

Here were serpentine walks, with trellised borders; winding canals, with fanciful Chinese bridges; flower beds resembling huge baskets, with the flower of "love lies bleeding" falling over to the ground. But mostly had the fancy of Mynheer Broekker been displayed about a stagnant little lake, on which a corpulent like pinnace lay at anchor. On the border was a cottage, within which were a wooden man and woman seated at table, and a wooden dog beneath, all the size of life: on pressing a spring, the woman commenced spinning, and the dog barked furiously. On the lake were wooden swans, painted to the life: some floating, others on the nest among the rushes; while a wooden sportsman, crouched among the bushes, was preparing his gun to take deadly aim. In another part of the garden was a dominie in his clerical robes, with wig, pipe, and cocked hat; and mandarins with nodding heads, amid red lions, green tigers, and blue hares. Last of all, the heathen deities, in wood and plaster, male and female, naked and barefaced as usual, and seeming to stare with wonder at finding themselves in such strange company.

My shabby French guide, while he pointed out all these mechanical marvels of the garden, was anxious to let me see that he had too polite a taste to be pleased by them. At every new nick-nack he would screw down his mouth, shrug up his shoulders, take a pinch of snuff, and exclaim: "*Ma foi, Monsieur, ces Hollandais sont forts pour ces betises la*!"

To attempt to gain admission to any of these stately abodes was out of the question, having no company of soldiers to enforce a solicitation. I was fortunate enough, however, through the aid of my guide, to make my way into the kitchen of the illustrious Ditmus, and I question whether the parlor would have proved more worthy of observation. The cook, a little wiry, hook-nosed woman, worn thin by incessant action and friction, was bustling about among her kettles and sauce-pans, with the scullion at her heels, both clattering in wooden shoes, which were as clean and white as the milk-pails; rows of vessels, of brass and copper, regiments of pewter dishes, and portly porringers, gave resplendent evidence of the intensity of their cleanliness; the very trammels and hangers in the fire-place were highly scoured, and the burnished face of the good Saint Nicholas shone forth from the iron plate of the chimney-back.

Among the decorations of the kitchen, was a printed sheet of wood-cuts, representing the various holiday customs of Holland, with explanatory rhymes. Here I was delighted to recognize the jollities of New-Year's day; the festivities of Paäs and Pinkster, and all the other merrymakings handed down in my native place from the earliest times of New-Amsterdam, and which had been such bright spots in the year, in my childhood. I eagerly made myself master of this precious document, for a trifling consideration, and bore it off as a memento of the place; though I question if, in so doing, I did not carry off with me the whole current literature of Broek.

I must not omit to mention, that this village is the paradise of cows as well as men: indeed you would almost suppose the cow to be as much an object of worship here, as the bull was among the ancient Egyptians; and well does she merit it, for she is in fact the patroness of the place. The same scrupulous cleanliness, however, which pervades every thing else, is manifested in the treatment of this venerated animal. She is not permitted to perambulate the place, but in winter, when she forsakes the rich pasture, a well-built house is provided for her, well painted, and maintained in the most perfect order. Her stall is of ample dimensions; the floor is scrubbed and polished; her hide is daily curried and brushed, and sponged to her heart's content, and her tail is daintily tucked up to the ceiling, and decorated with a ribbon!

On my way back through the village, I passed the house of the prediger, or preacher; a very comfortable mansion, which led me to augur well of the state of religion in the village. On inquiry, I was told that for a long time the inhabitants lived in a great state of indifference as to religious matters: it was in vain that their preachers endeavored to arouse their thoughts as to a future state: the joys of heaven, as commonly depicted, were but little to their taste. At length a dominie appeared among them, who struck out in a different vein. He depicted the New Jerusalem as a place all smooth and level; with beautiful dykes, and ditches, and canals; and houses all shining with paint and varnish, and glazed tiles; and where there should never come horse, nor ass, nor cat, nor dog, nor any thing that could make noise or dirt; but there should be nothing but rubbing and scrubbing, and washing and painting, and gilding and varnishing, for ever and ever, amen! Since that time, the good housewives of Broek have all turned their faces Zionward.

Guests from Gibbet-Island

A Legend of Communipaw
Found Among the Knickerbocker Papers at Wolfert's Roost.

WHOEVER HAS VISITED THE ANCIENT AND RENOWNED VILLAGE OF Communipaw, may have noticed an old stone building, of most ruinous and sinister appearance. The doors and window-shutters are ready to drop from their hinges; old clothes are stuffed in the broken panes of glass, while legions of half-starved dogs prowl about the premises, and rush out and bark at every passer by; for your beggarly house in a village is most apt to swarm with profligate and ill-conditioned dogs. What adds to the sinister appearance of this mansion, is a tall frame in front, not a little resembling a gallows, and which looks as if waiting to accommodate some of the inhabitants with a well-merited airing. It is not a gallows, however, but an ancient sign-post; for this dwelling in the golden days of Communipaw, was one of the most orderly and peaceful of village taverns, where public affairs were talked and smoked over. In fact, it was in this very building that Oloffe the Dreamer, and his companions, concerted that great voyage of discovery and colonization, in which they explored Buttermilk Channel, were nearly shipwrecked in the strait of Hell-gate, and finally landed on the island of Manhattan, and founded the great city of New-Amsterdam.

Even after the province had been cruelly wrested from the sway of their High Mightinesses, by the combined forces of the British and the Yankees, this tavern continued its ancient loyalty. It is true, the head of the Prince of Orange disappeared from the sign, a strange bird being painted over it, with the explanatory legend of "DIE WILDE GANS," or, The Wild Goose; but this all the world knew to be a sly riddle of the landlord, the worthy Teunis Van Grieson, a knowing man, in a small way, who laid his finger beside his nose and winked, when any one studied the signification of his sign, and observed that his goose was hatching, but would join the flock whenever they flew over the water; an enigma which was the perpetual recreation and delight of the loyal but fat-headed burghers of Communipaw.

Under the sway of this patriotic, though discreet and quiet publican, the tavern continued to flourish in primeval tranquillity, and was the resort of true-hearted Nederlanders, from all parts of Pavonia; who met here quietly and secretly, to smoke and drink the downfall of Briton and Yankee, and success to Admiral Van Tromp.

The only drawback on the comfort of the establishment, was a nephew of mine host, a sister's son, Yan Yost Vanderscamp by name, and a real scamp by nature. This unlucky whipster showed an early propensity to mischief, which he gratified in a small way, by playing tricks upon the frequenters of the Wild Goose; putting gunpowder in their pipes, or squibs in their pockets, and astonishing them with an explosion, while they sat nodding round the fireplace in the bar-room; and if perchance a worthy burgher from some distant part of Pavonia lingered until dark over his potation, it was odds but young Vanderscamp would slip a brier under his horse's tail, as he mounted, and send him clattering along the road, in neck-or-nothing style, to the infinite astonishment and discomfiture of the rider.

It may be wondered at, that mine host of the Wild Goose did not turn such a graceless varlet out of doors; but Teunis Van Gieson was an easy-tempered man, and having no child of his own, looked upon his nephew with almost parental indulgence. His patience and good nature were doomed to be tried by another inmate of his mansion. This was a cross-grained curmudgeon of a negro, named Pluto, who was a kind of enigma in Communipaw. Where he came from, nobody knew. He was found one morning, after a storm, cast like a sea-monster on the strand, in front of the Wild Goose, and lay there, more dead than alive. The neighbors gathered round, and speculated on this production of the deep; whether it were fish or flesh, or a compound of both, commonly yclept a merman. The kind-hearted Teunis Van Gieson, seeing that he wore the human form, took him into his house, and warmed him into life. By degrees, he showed signs of intelligence, and even uttered sounds very much like language, but which no one in Communipaw could understand. Some thought him a negro just from Guinea, who had either fallen overboard, or escaped from a slave-ship. Nothing, however, could ever draw from him any account of his origin. When questioned on the subject, he merely pointed to Gibbet-Island, a small rocky islet, which lies in the open bay, just opposite Communipaw, as if that were his native place, though every body knew it had never been inhabited.

In the process of time, he acquired something of the Dutch language, that is to say, he learnt all its vocabulary of oaths and maledictions, with just words sufficient to string them together. "Donder en blicksem!" (thunder and lightning), was the gentlest of his ejaculations. For years he kept about the Wild Goose, more like one of those familiar spirits, or household goblins, we read of, than like a human being. He acknowledged allegiance to no one, but performed various domestic offices, when it suited his humor; waiting occasionally on the guests; grooming the horses, cutting wood, drawing water; and all this without being ordered. Lay any command on him, and the stubborn sea urchin was sure to rebel. He was never so much at home, however, as when on the water, plying about in skiff or canoe, entirely alone, fishing, crabbing, or grabbing for oysters, and would bring home quantities for the larder of the Wild Goose, which he would throw down at the kitchen door, with a growl. No wind nor weather deterred him from launching forth on his favorite element: indeed, the wilder the weather, the more he seemed to enjoy it. If a storm was brewing, he was sure to put off from shore; and would be seen far out in the bay, his light skiff dancing like a feather on the waves, when sea and sky were in a turmoil, and the stoutest ships were fain to lower their sails. Sometimes on such occasions he would be absent for days together. How he weathered the tempest, and how and where he subsisted, no one could divine, nor did any one venture to ask, for all had an almost superstitious awe of him. Some of the Communipaw oystermen declared they had more than once seen him suddenly disappear, canoe and all, as if plunged beneath the waves, and after a while come up again, in quite a different part of the bay; whence they concluded that he could live under water like that notable species of wild duck, commonly called the hell-diver. All began to consider him in the light of a foul-weather bird, like the Mother Carey's Chicken, or stormy petrel; and whenever they saw him putting far out in his skiff, in cloudy weather, made up their minds for a storm.

The only being for whom he seemed to have any liking, was Yan Yost Vanderscamp, and him he liked for his very wickedness. He in a manner took the boy under his tutelage, prompted him to all kinds of mischief, aided him in every wild harum-scarum freak, until the lad became the complete scape-grace of the village; a pest to his uncle, and to every one else. Nor were his pranks confined to the land; he soon learned to accompany old Pluto on the water. Together these worthies would cruise about the broad bay, and all the neighboring straits and rivers; poking around in skiffs and canoes; robbing the set nets of the fishermen; landing on remote coasts, and laying waste orchards and water-melon patches; in short, carrying on a complete system of piracy, on a small scale. Piloted by Pluto, the youthful Vanderscamp soon became acquainted with all the bays, rivers, creeks, and inlets of the watery world around him; could navigate from the Hook to Spiting-devil on the darkest night, and learned to set even the terrors of Hell-gate at defiance.

At length, negro and boy suddenly disappeared, and days and weeks elapsed, but without tidings of them. Some said they must have run away and gone to sea; others jocosely hinted, that old Pluto, being no other than his namesake in disguise, had spirited away the boy to the nether regions. All, however, agreed in one thing, that the village was well rid of them.

In the process of time, the good Tennis Van Gieson slept with his fathers, and the tavern remained shut up, waiting for a claimant, for the next heir was Yan Yost Vanderscamp, and he had not been heard of for years. At length, one day, a boat was seen pulling for shore, from a long, black, rakish-looking schooner, that lay at anchor in the bay. The boat's crew seemed worthy of the craft from which they debarked. Never had such a set of noisy, roistering, swaggering varlets landed in peaceful Communipaw. They were outlandish in garb and demeanor, and were headed by a rough, burly, bully ruffian, with fiery whiskers, a copper nose, a scar across his face, and a great Flaunderish beaver slouched on one side of his head, in whom, to their dismay, the quiet inhabitants were made to recognise their early pest, Yan Yost Vanderscamp. The rear of this hopeful gang was brought up by old Pluto, who had lost an eye, grown grizzly-headed, and looked more like a devil than ever. Vanderscamp renewed his acquaintance with the old burghers, much against their will, and in a manner not at all to their taste. He slapped them familiarly on the back, gave them an iron grip of the hand, and was hail fellow well met. According to his own account, he had been all the world over; had made money by bags full; had ships in every sea, and now meant to turn the Wild Goose into a country-seat, where he and his comrades, all rich merchants from foreign parts, might enjoy themselves in the interval of their voyages.

Sure enough, in a little while there was a complete metamorphose of the Wild Goose. From being a quiet, peaceful Dutch public house, it became a most riotous, uproarious private dwelling; a complete rendezvous for boisterous men of the seas, who came here to have what they called a "blow out" on dry land, and might be seen at all hours, lounging about the door, or lolling out of the windows; swearing among themselves, and cracking rough jokes on every passer by. The house was fitted up, too, in so strange a manner: hammocks slung to the walls, instead of bedsteads; odd kinds of furniture, of foreign fashion; bamboo couches, Spanish chairs; pistols, cutlasses, and blunderbusses, suspended on every peg; silver crucifixes on the mantelpieces, silver candlesticks and porringers on the tables, contrasting oddly with the pewter and Delf ware of the original establishment. And then the strange amusements of these sea-monsters! Pitching Spanish dollars, instead of quoits; firing blunderbusses out of the window; shooting at a mark, or at any unhappy dog, or cat, or pig, or barn-door fowl, that might happen to come within reach.

The only being who seemed to relish their rough waggery was old Pluto; and yet he led but a dog's life of it; for they practised all kinds of manual jokes upon him; kicked him about like a football; shook him by his grizzly mop of wool, and never spoke to him without coupling a curse by way of adjective to his name, and consigning him to the infernal regions. The old fellow, however, seemed to like them the better, the more they cursed him, though his utmost expression of pleasure never amounted to more than the growl of a petted bear, when his ears are rubbed.

Old Pluto was the ministering spirit at the orgies of the Wild Goose; and such orgies as took place there! Such drinking, singing, whooping, swearing; with an occasional interlude of quarrelling and fighting. The noisier grew the revel, the more old Pluto plied the potations, until the guests would become frantic in their merriment, smashing every thing to pieces, and throwing the house out of the windows. Sometimes, after a drinking bout, they sallied forth and scoured the village, to the dismay of the worthy burghers, who gathered their women within doors, and would have shut up the house. Vanderscamp, however, was not to be rebuffed. He insisted on renewing acquaintance with his old neighbors, and on introducing his friends, the merchants, to their families; swore he was on the look-out for a wife, and meant, before he stopped, to find husbands for all their daughters. So, will-ye, nill-ye, sociable he was; swaggered about their best parlors, with his hat on one side of his head; sat on the good wife's nicely-waxed mahogany table, kicking his heels against the carved and polished legs; kissed and tousled the young vrouws; and, if they frowned and pouted, gave them a gold rosary, or a sparkling cross, to put them in good humor again.

Sometimes nothing would satisfy him, but he must have some of his old neighbors to dinner at the Wild Goose. There was no refusing him, for he had the complete upper hand of the community, and the peaceful burghers all stood in awe of him. But what a time would the quiet, worthy men have, among these rake-hells, who would delight to astound them with the most extravagant gunpowder tales, embroidered with all kinds of foreign oaths; clink the can with them; pledge them in deep potations; bawl drinking songs in their ears; and occasionally fire pistols over their heads, or under the table, and then laugh in their faces, and ask them how they liked the smell of gunpowder.

Thus was the little village of Communipaw for a time like the unfortunate wight possessed with devils; until Vanderscamp and his brother merchants would sail on another trading voyage, when the Wild Goose would be shut up, and every thing relapse into quiet, only to be disturbed by his next visitation.

The mystery of all these proceedings gradually dawned upon the tardy intellects of Communipaw. These were the times of the notorious Captain Kidd, when the American harbors were the resorts of piratical adventurers of all kinds, who, under pretext of mercantile voyages, scoured the West Indies, made plundering descents upon the Spanish Main, visited even the remote Indian Seas, and then came to dispose of their booty, have their revels, and fit out new expeditions, in the English colonies.

Vanderscamp had served in this hopeful school, and having risen to importance among the buccaneers, had pitched upon his native village and early home, as a quiet, out-of-the way, unsuspected place, where he and his comrades, while anchored at New York, might have their feasts, and concert their plans, without molestation.

At length the attention of the British government was called to these piratical enterprises, that were becoming so frequent and outrageous. Vigorous measures were taken to check and punish them. Several of the most noted freebooters were caught and executed, and three of Vanderscamp's chosen comrades, the most riotous swashbucklers of the Wild Goose, were hanged in chains on Gibbet-Island, in full sight of their favorite resort. As to Vanderscamp himself, he and his man Pluto again disappeared, and it was hoped by the people of Communipaw that he had fallen in some foreign brawl, or been swung on some foreign gallows.

For a time, therefore, the tranquillity of the village was restored; the worthy Dutchmen once more smoked their pipes in peace, eyeing, with peculiar complacency, their old pests and terrors, the pirates, dangling and drying in the sun, on Gibbet-Island.

This perfect calm was doomed at length to be ruffled. The fiery persecution of the pirates gradually subsided. Justice was satisfied with the examples that had been made, and there was no more talk of Kidd, and the other heroes of like kidney. On a calm summer evening, a boat, somewhat heavily laden, was seen pulling into Communipaw. What was the surprise and disquiet of the inhabitants, to see Yan Yost Vanderscamp seated at the helm, and his man Pluto tugging at the oar! Vanderscamp, however, was apparently an altered man. He brought home with him a wife, who seemed to be a shrew, and to have the upper hand of him. He no longer was the swaggering, bully ruffian, but affected the regular merchant, and talked of retiring from business, and settling down quietly, to pass the rest of his days in his native place.

The Wild Goose mansion was again opened, but with diminished splendor, and no riot. It is true, Vanderscamp had frequent nautical visitors, and the sound of revelry was occasionally overheard in his house; but every thing seemed to be done under the rose; and old Pluto was the only servant that officiated at these orgies. The visitors, indeed, were by no means of the turbulent tamp of their predecessors; but quiet, mysterious traders, full of nods, and winks, and hieroglyphic signs, with whom, to use their cant phrase, "every thing was smug." Their ships came to anchor at night, in the lower bay; and, on a private signal, Vanderscamp would launch his boat, and accompanied solely by his man Pluto, would make them mysterious visits. Sometimes boats pulled in at night, in front of the Wild Goose, and various articles of merchandise were landed in the dark, and spirited away, nobody knew whither. One of the more curious of the inhabitants kept watch, and caught a glimpse of the features of some of these night visitors, by the casual glance of a lantern, and declared that he recognized more than one of the freebooting frequenters of the Wild Goose, in former times; whence he concluded that Vanderscamp was at his old game, and that this mysterious merchandise was nothing more nor less than piratical plunder. The more charitable opinion, however, was, that Vanderscamp and his comrades, having been driven from their old line of business, by the "oppressions of government," had resorted to smuggling to make both ends meet.

Be that as it may: I come now to the extraordinary fact, which is the butt-end of this story. It happened late one night, that Yan Yost Vanderscamp was returning across the broad bay, in his light skiff, rowed by his man Pluto. He had been carousing on board of a vessel, newly arrived, and was somewhat obfuscated in intellect, by the liquor he had imbibed. It was a still, sultry night; a heavy mass of lurid clouds was rising in the west, with the low muttering of distant thunder. Vanderscamp called on Pluto to pull lustily, that they might get home before the gathering storm. The old negro made no reply, but shaped his course so as to skirt the rocky shores of Gibbet-Island. A faint creaking overhead caused Vanderscamp to cast up his eyes, when, to his horror, he beheld the bodies of his three pot companions and brothers in iniquity dangling in the moonlight, their rags fluttering, and their chains creaking, as they were slowly swung backward and forward by the rising breeze.

"What do you mean, you blockhead!" cried Vanderscamp, "by pulling so close to the island?"

"I thought you'd be glad to see your old friends once more," growled the negro: "you were never afraid of a living man, what do you fear from the dead?"

"Who's afraid?" hiccupped Vanderscamp, partly heated by liquor, partly nettled by the jeer of the negro; "who's afraid! Hang me, but I would be glad to see them once more, alive or dead, at the Wild Goose. Come, my lads in the wind!" continued he, taking a draught, and flourishing the bottle above his head, "here's fair weather to you in the other world; and if you should be walking the rounds to-night, odds fish! but I'll be happy if you will drop in to supper."

A dismal creaking was the only reply. The wind blew loud and shrill, and as it whistled round the gallows, and among the bones, sounded as if they were laughing and gibbering in the air. Old Pluto chuckled to himself, and now pulled for home. The storm burst over the voyagers, while they were yet far from shore. The rain fell in torrents, the thunder crashed and pealed, and the lightning kept up an incessant blaze. It was stark midnight before they landed at Communipaw.

Dripping and shivering, Vanderscamp crawled homeward. He was completely sobered by the storm; the water soaked from without, having diluted and cooled the liquor within. Arrived at the Wild Goose, he knocked timidly and dubiously at the door, for he dreaded the reception he was to experience from his wife He had reason to do so. She met him at the threshold, in a precious ill-humor.

"Is this a time," said she, "to keep people cut of their beds, and to bring home company, to turn the house upside down?"

"Company?" said Vanderscamp, meekly; "I have brought no company with me, wife."

"No indeed! they have got here before you, but by your invitation; and blessed-looking company they are, truly!"

Vanderscamp's knees smote together. "For the love of heaven, where are they, wife?"

"Where?—why in the blue room up stairs, making themselves as much at home as if the house were their own."

Vanderscamp made a desperate effort, scrambled up to the room, and threw open the door. Sure enough, there at a table, on which burned a light as blue as brimstone, sat the three guests from Gibbet-Island, with halters round their necks, and bobbing their cups together, as if they were hob-or-nobbing, and trolling the old Dutch freebooter's glee, since translated into English:

> For three merry lads be we,
> And three merry lads be we;
> I on the land, and thou on the sand,
> And Jack on the gallows-tree.

Vanderscamp saw and heard no more. Starting back with horror, he missed his footing on the landing place, and fell from the top of the stairs to the bottom. He was taken up speechless, and, either from the fall or the fright, was buried in the yard of the little Dutch church at Bergen, on the following Sunday.

From that day forward, the fate of the Wild Goose was sealed. It was pronounced a haunted house, and avoided accordingly. No one inhabited it but Vanderscamp's shrew of a widow, and old Pluto, and they were considered but little better than its hobgoblin visitors. Pluto grew more and more haggard and morose, and looked more like an imp of darkness than a human being. He spoke to no one, but went about muttering to himself; or, as some hinted, talking with the devil, who, though unseen, was ever at his elbow. Now and then he was seen pulling about the bay alone, in his skiff, in dark weather, or at the approach of nightfall; nobody could tell why, unless on an errand to invite more guests from the gallows. Indeed it was affirmed that the Wild Goose still continued to be a house of entertainment for such guests, and that on stormy nights, the blue chamber was occasionally illuminated, and sounds of diabolical merriment were overheard, mingling with the howling of the tempest. Some treated these as idle stories, until on one such night, it was about the time of the equinox, there was a horrible uproar in the Wild Goose, that could not be mistaken. It was not so much the sound of revelry, however, as strife, with two or three piercing shrieks, that pervaded every part of the village. Nevertheless, no one thought of hastening to the spot. On the contrary, the honest burghers of Communipaw drew their nightcaps over their ears, and buried their heads under the bed-clothes, at the thoughts of Vanderscamp and his gallows companions.

The next morning, some of the bolder and more curious undertook to reconnoitre. All was quiet and lifeless at the Wild Goose. The door yawned wide open, and had evidently been open all night, for the storm had beaten into the house. Gathering more courage from the silence and apparent desertion, they gradually ventured over the threshold. The house had indeed the air of having been possessed by devils. Every thing was topsy-turvy; trunks had been broken open, and chests of drawers and corner cupboards turned inside out, as in a time of general sack and pillage; but the most woeful sight was the widow of Yan Yost Vanderscamp, extended a corpse on the floor of the blue chamber, with the marks of a deadly gripe on the windpipe.

All now was conjecture and dismay at Communipaw; and the disappearance of old Pluto, who was nowhere to be found, gave rise to all kinds of wild surmises. Some suggested that the negro had betrayed the house to some of Vanderscamp's buccaneering associates, and that they had decamped together with the booty; others surmised that the negro was nothing more nor less than a devil incarnate, who had now accomplished his ends, and made off with his dues.

Events, however, vindicated the negro from this last imputation. His skiff was picked up, drifting about the bay, bottom upward, as if wrecked in a tempest; and his body was found, shortly afterward, by some Communipaw fishermen, stranded among the rocks of Gibbet-Island, near the foot of the pirates' gallows. The fishermen shook their heads, and observed that old Pluto had ventured once too often to invite Guests from Gibbet-Island.

The Early Experiences of Ralph Ringwood

Noted Down From His Conversations: by Geoffrey Crayon, Gent.[1]

I AM A KENTUCKIAN BY RESIDENCE AND CHOICE, BUT A VIRGINIAN BY BIRTH. The cause of my first leaving the 'Ancient Dominion,' and emigrating to Kentucky, was a jackass! You stare, but have a little patience, and I'll soon show you how it came to pass. My father, who was of one of the old Virginian families, resided in Richmond. He was a widower, and his domestic affairs were managed by a housekeeper of the old school, such as used to administer the concerns of opulent Virginian households. She was a dignitary that almost rivalled my father in importance, and seemed to think every thing belonged to her; in fact she was so considerate in her economy, and so careful of expense, as sometimes to vex my father; who would swear she was disgracing him by her meanness. She always appeared with that ancient insignia of housekeeping trust and authority, a great bunch of keys jingling at her girdle. She superintended the arrangements of the table at every meal, and saw that the dishes were all placed according to her primitive notions of symmetry. In the evening she took her stand and served out tea with a mingled respectfulness and pride of station, truly exemplary. Her great ambition was to have every thing in order, and

---

1. Ralph Ringwood, though a fictitious name, is a real personage—the late Governor Duval of Florida. I have given some anecdotes of his early and eccentric career in, as nearly as I can recollect, the very words in which he related them. They certainly afford strong temptations to the embellishments of fiction; but I thought them so strikingly characteristic of the individual, and of the scenes and society into which his peculiar humors carried him, that I preferred giving them in their original simplicity. G. C.

that the establishment under her sway should be cited as a model of good housekeeping. If any thing went wrong, poor old Barbara would take it to heart, and sit in her room and cry; until a few chapters in the Bible would quiet her spirits, and make all calm again. The Bible, in fact, was her constant resort in time of trouble. She opened it indiscriminately, and whether she chanced among the Lamentations of Jeremiah, the Canticles of Solomon, or the rough enumeration of the tribes in Deuteronomy, a chapter was a chapter, and operated like balm to her soul. Such was our good old housekeeper Barbara; who was destined, unwittingly, to have a most important effect upon my destiny.

"It came to pass, during the days of my juvenility, while I was yet what is termed 'an unlucky boy,' that a gentleman of our neighborhood, a great advocate for experiments and improvements of all kinds, took it into his head that it would be an immense public advantage to introduce a breed of mules, and accordingly imported three jacks to stock the neighborhood. This in a part of the country where the people cared for nothing but blood horses! Why, sir! they would have considered their mares disgraced, and their whole stud dishonored, by such a misalliance. The whole matter was a town-talk, and a town scandal. The worthy amalgamator of quadrupeds found himself in a dismal scrape; so he backed out in time, abjured the whole doctrine of amalgamation, and turned his jacks loose to shift for themselves upon the town common. There they used to run about and lead an idle, good-for-nothing, holiday life, the happiest animals in the country.

"It so happened, that my way to school lay across the common. The first time that I saw one of these animals, it set up a braying and frightened me confoundedly. However, I soon got over my fright, and seeing that it had something of a horse look, my Virginian love for any thing of the equestrian species predominated, and I determined to back it. I accordingly applied at a grocer's shop, procured a cord that had been round a loaf of sugar, and made a kind of halter; then summoning some of my schoolfellows, we drove master Jack about the common until we hemmed him in an angle of a 'worm fence.' After some difficulty, we fixed the halter round his muzzle, and I mounted. Up flew his heels, away I went over his head, and off he scampered. However, I was on my legs in a twinkling, gave chase, caught him, and remounted. By dint of repeated tumbles I soon learned to stick to his back, so that he could no more cast me than he could his own skin. From that time, master Jack and his companions had a scampering life of it, for we all rode them between school hours, and on holiday afternoons; and you may be sure school-boys' nags are never permitted to suffer the grass to grow under their feet. They soon became so knowing, that they took to their heels at sight of a school-boy; and we were generally much longer in chasing than we were in riding them.

"Sunday approached, on which I projected an equestrian excursion on one of these long-eared steeds. As I knew the jacks, would be in great demand on Sunday morning, I secured one over night, and conducted him home, to be ready for an early outset. But where was I to quarter him for the night? I could not put him in the stable; our old black groom George was as absolute in that domain as Barbara was within doors, and would have thought his stable, his horses, and himself disgraced, by the introduction of a jackass. I recollected the smoke-house; an out-building appended to all Virginian establishments for the smoking of hams, and other kinds of meat. So I got the key, put master. Jack in, locked the door, returned the key to its place, and went to bed, intending to release my prisoner at an early hour, before any of the family were awake. I was so tired, however, by the exertions I had made in catching the donkey, that I fell into a sound sleep, and the morning broke without my waking.

"Not so with dame Barbara, the housekeeper. As usual, to use her own phrase, 'she was up before the crow put his shoes on,' and bustled about to get things in order for breakfast. Her first resort was to the smoke-house. Scarce had she opened the door, when master Jack, tired of his confinement, and glad to be released from darkness, gave a loud bray, and rushed forth. Down dropped old Barbara; the animal trampled over her, and made off for the common. Poor Barbara! She had never before seen a donkey, and having read in the Bible that the Devil went about like a roaring lion, seeking whom he might devour, she took it for granted that this was Beelzebub himself. The kitchen was soon in a hubbub; the servants hurried to the spot. There lay old Barbara in fits; as fast as she got out of one, the thoughts of the Devil came over her, and she fell into another, for the good soul was devoutly superstitious.

"As ill luck would have it, among those attracted by the noise, was a little cursed fidgetty, crabbed uncle of mine; one of those uneasy spirits that cannot rest quietly in their beds in the morning, but must be up early, to bother the household. He was only a kind of half uncle, after all, for he had married my father's sister: yet he assumed great authority on the strength of this left-handed relationship, and was a universal inter-meddler, and family pest. This prying little busy-body soon ferreted out the truth of the story, and discovered, by hook and by crook, that I was at the bottom of the affair, and had locked up the donkey in the smoke-house. He stopped to inquire no farther, for he was one of those testy curmudgeons, with whom unlucky boys are always in the wrong. Leaving old Barbara to wrestle in imagination with the Devil, he made for my bed-chamber, where I still lay wrapped in rosy slumbers, little dreaming of the mischief I had done, and the storm about to break over me.

"In an instant, I was awakened by a shower of thwacks, and started up in wild amazement. I demanded the meaning of this attack, but received no other reply than that I had murdered the housekeeper; while my uncle continued whacking away during my confusion. I seized a poker, and put myself on the defensive. I was a stout boy for my years, while my uncle was a little wiffet of a man; one that in Kentucky we would not call even an 'individual;' nothing more than a 'remote circumstance.' I soon, therefore, brought him to a parley, and learned the whole extent of the charge brought against me. I confessed to the donkey and the smoke-house, but pleaded not guilty of the murder of the housekeeper. I soon found out that old Barbara was still alive. She continued under the doctor's hands, however, for several days; and whenever she had an ill turn, my uncle would seek to give me another flogging. I appealed to my father, but got no redress. I was considered an 'unlucky boy,' prone to all kinds of mischief; so that prepossessions were against me, in all cases of appeal,

"I felt stung to the soul at all this. I had been beaten, degraded, and treated with slighting when I complained. I lost my usual good spirits and good humor; and, being out of temper with every body, fancied every body out of temper with me. A certain wild, roving spirit of freedom, which I believe is as inherent in me as it is in the partridge, was brought into sudden activity by the checks and restraints I suffered. 'I'll go from home,' thought I, 'and shift for myself.' Perhaps this notion was quickened by the rage for emigrating to Kentucky, which was at that time prevalent in Virginia. I had heard such stories of the romantic beauties of the country; of the abundance of game of all kinds, and of the glorious independent life of the hunters who ranged its noble forests, and lived by the rifle, that I was as much agog to get there, as boys who live in sea-ports are to launch themselves among the wonders and adventures of the ocean.

"After a time, old Barbara got better in mind and body, and matters were explained to her; and she became gradually convinced that it was not the Devil she had encountered. When she heard how harshly I had been treated on her account, the good old soul was extremely grieved, and spoke warmly to my father in my behalf. He had himself remarked the change in my behavior, and thought punishment might have been carried too far. He sought, therefore, to have some conversation with me, and to soothe my feelings; but it was too late. I frankly told him the course of mortification that I had experienced, and the fixed determination I had made to go from home.

" 'And where do you mean to go?'

" 'To Kentucky.'

" 'To Kentucky! Why, you know nobody there.'

" 'No matter: I can soon make acquaintances.'

" 'And what will you do when you get there?'

" 'Hunt!'

"My father gave a long, low whistle, and looked in my face with a serio-comic expression. I was not far in my teens, and to talk of setting off alone for Kentucky, to turn hunter, seemed doubtless the idle prattle of a boy. He was little aware of the dogged resolution of my character; and his smile of incredulity but fixed me more obstinately in my purpose. I assured him I was serious in what I said, and would certainly set off for Kentucky in the spring.

"Month after month passed away. My father now and then adverted slightly to what had passed between us; doubtless for the purpose of sounding me. I always expressed the same grave and fixed determination. By degrees he spoke to me more directly on the subject; endeavoring earnestly but kindly to dissuade me. My only reply was, 'I had made up my mind.'

"Accordingly, as soon as the spring had fairly opened, I sought him one day in his study, and informed him I was about to set out for Kentucky, and had come to take my leave. He made no objection, for he had exhausted persuasion and remonstrance, and doubtless thought it best to give way to my humor, trusting that a little rough experience would soon bring me home again. I asked money for my journey. He went to a chest, took out a long green silk purse, well filled, and laid it on the table. I now asked for a horse and servant.

" 'A horse!' said my father, sneeringly: 'why, you would not go a mile without racing him, and breaking your neck; and as to a servant, you cannot take care of yourself, much less of him.'

" 'How am I to travel, then?'

" 'Why, I suppose you are man enough to travel on foot.'

"He spoke jestingly, little thinking I would take him at his word; but I was thoroughly piqued in respect to my enterprise; so I pocketed the purse; went to my room, tied up three or four shirts in a pocket-handkerchief, put a dirk in my bosom, girt a couple of pistols round my waist, and felt like a knight-errant armed cap-à-pie, and ready to rove the world in quest of adventures.

"My sister (I had but one) hung round me and wept, and entreated me to stay. I felt my heart swell in my throat: but I gulped it back to its place, and straightened myself up: I would not suffer myself to cry. I at length disengaged myself from her, and got to the door.

" 'When will you come back?' cried she.

" 'Never, by heavens!' cried I, 'until I come back a member of Congress from Kentucky. I am determined to show that I am not the tail-end of the family.'

"Such was my first outset from home. You may suppose what a green-horn I was, and how little I knew of the world I was launching into.

"I do not recollect any incident of importance, until I reached the borders of Pennsylvania. I had stopped at an inn to get some refreshment; as I was eating in a back-room, I overheard two men in the bar-room conjecture who and what I could be. One determined, at length, that I was a runaway apprentice, and ought to be stopped, to which the other assented. When I had finished my meal, and paid for it, I went out at the back door, lest I should be stopped by my supervisors. Scorning, however, to steal off like a culprit, I walked round to the front of the house. One of the men advanced to the front door. He wore his hat on one side, and had a consequential air that nettled me.

" 'Where are you going, youngster?' demanded he.

" 'That's none of your business!' replied I, rather pertly.

" 'Yes, but it is though! You have run away from home, and must give an account of yourself.'

"He advanced to seize me, when I drew forth a pistol. 'If you advance another step, I'll shoot you!'

"He sprang back as if he had trodden upon a rattlesnake, and his hat fell off in the movement.

" 'Let him alone!' cried his companion; 'he's a foolish, mad-headed boy, and don't know what he's about. He'll shoot you, you may rely on it.'

"He did not need any caution in the matter; he was afraid even to pick up his hat: so I pushed forward on my way, without molestation. This incident, however, had its effect upon me. I became fearful of sleeping in any house at night, lest I should be stopped. I took my meals in the houses, in the course of the day, but would turn aside at night, into some wood or ravine, make a fire, and sleep before it. This I considered was true hunter's style, and I wished to inure myself to it.

"At length I arrived at Brownsville, leg-weary and way-worn, and in a shabby plight, as you may suppose, having been 'camping out' for some nights past. I applied at some of the inferior inns, but could gain no admission. I was regarded for a moment with a dubious eye, and then informed they did not receive foot-passengers. At last I went boldly to the principal inn. The landlord appeared as unwilling as the rest to receive a vagrant boy beneath his roof; but his wife interfered, in the midst of his excuses, and half elbowing him aside:

" 'Where are you going, my lad?' said she.

" 'To Kentucky.'

" 'What are you going there for?'

" 'To hunt.'

"She looked earnestly at me for a moment or two. 'Have you a mother living?' said she, at length.

" 'No, madam: she has been dead for some time.'

" 'I thought so!' cried she, warmly. 'I knew if you had a mother living, you would not be here.' From that moment the good woman treated me with a mother's kindness.

I remained several days beneath her roof, recovering from the fatigue of my journey. While here, I purchased a rifle, and practised daily at a mark, to prepare myself for a hunter's life. When sufficiently recruited in strength, I took leave of my kind host and hostess, and resumed my journey.

"At Wheeling I embarked in a flat-bottomed family boat, technically called a broad-horn, a prime river conveyance in those days. In this ark for two weeks I floated down the Ohio. The river was as yet in all its wild beauty. Its loftiest trees had not been thinned out. The forest overhung the water's edge, and was occasionally skirted by immense canebrakes. Wild animals of all kinds abounded. We heard them rushing through the thickets, and plashing in the water. Deer and bears would frequently swim across the river; others would come down to the bank, and gaze at the boat as it passed. I was incessantly on the alert with my rifle; but somehow or other, the game was never within shot. Sometimes I got a chance to land and try my skill on shore. I shot squirrels, and small birds, and even wild turkeys; but though I caught glimpses of deer bounding away through the woods, I never could get a fair shot at them.

"In this way we glided in our broad-horn past Cincinnati, the 'Queen of the West,' as she is now called; then a mere group of log cabins; and the site of the bustling city of Louisville, then designated by a solitary house. As I said before, the Ohio was as yet a wild river; all was forest, forest, forest! Near the confluence of Green River with the Ohio, I landed, bade adieu to the broad-horn, and struck for the interior of Kentucky. I had no precise plan; my only idea was to make for one of the wildest parts of the country. I had relatives in Lexington, and other settled places, to whom I thought it probable my father would write concerning me: so as I was full of manhood and independence, and resolutely bent on making my way in the world without assistance or control, I resolved to keep clear of them all.

"In the course of my first day's trudge, I shot a wild turkey, and slung it on my back for provisions. The forest was open and clear from underwood. I saw deer in abundance, but always running, running. It seemed to me as if these animals never stood still.

"At length I came to where a gang of half-starved wolves were feasting on the carcass of a deer which they had run down; and snarling and snapping, and fighting like so many dogs. They were all so ravenous and intent upon their prey, that they did not notice me, and I had time to make my observations. One, larger and fiercer than the rest, seemed to claim the larger share, and to keep the others in awe. If any one came too near him while eating, he would fly off, seize and shake him, and then return to his repast. 'This,' thought I, 'must be the captain; if I can kill him, I shall defeat the whole army.' I accordingly took aim, fired, and down dropped the old fellow. He might be only shamming dead; so I loaded and put a second ball through him. He never budged; all the rest ran off, and my victory was complete.

"It would not be easy to describe my triumphant feelings on this great achievement. I marched on with renovated spirit, regarding myself as absolute lord of the forest. As night drew near, I prepared for camping. My first care was to collect dry wood and make a roaring fire to cook and sleep by, and to frighten off wolves, and bears, and panthers. I then began to pluck my turkey for supper. I had camped out several times in the early part of my expedition; but that was in comparatively more settled and civilized regions; where there were no wild animals of consequence in the forest. This was my first camping out in the real wilderness; and I was soon made sensible of the loneliness and wildness of my situation.

"In a little while, a concert of wolves commenced: there might have been a dozen or two, but it seemed to me as if there were thousands. I never heard such howling and whining. Having prepared my turkey, I divided it into two parts, thrust two sticks into one of the halves, and planted them on end before the fire, the hunter's mode of roasting. The smell of roast meat quickened the appetites of the wolves, and their concert became truly infernal. They seemed to be all around me, but I could only now and then get a glimpse of one of them, as he came within the glare of the light.

"I did not much care for the wolves, who I knew to be a cowardly race, but I had heard terrible stories of panthers, and began to fear their stealthy prowlings in the surrounding darkness. I was thirsty, and heard a brook bubbling and tinkling along at no great distance, but absolutely dared not go there, lest some panther might lie in wait, and spring upon me. By and by a deer whistled. I had never heard one before, and thought it must be a panther. I now felt uneasy lest he might climb the trees, crawl along the branches over head, and plump down upon me; so I kept my eyes fixed on the branches, until my head ached. I more than once thought I saw fiery eyes glaring down from among the leaves. At length I thought of my supper, and turned to see if my half turkey was cooked. In crowding so near the fire, I had pressed the meat into the flames, and it was consumed. I had nothing to do but toast the other half, and take better care of it. On that half I made my supper, without salt or bread. I was still so possessed with the dread of panthers, that I could not close my eyes all night, but lay watching the trees until daybreak, when all my fears were dispelled with the darkness; and as I saw the morning sun sparkling down through the branches of the trees, I smiled to think how I suffered myself to be dismayed by sounds and shadows: but I was a young woodsman, and a stranger in Kentucky.

"Having breakfasted on the remainder of my turkey, and slaked my thirst at the bubbling stream, without farther dread of panthers, I resumed my wayfaring with buoyant feelings. I again saw deer, but as usual running, running! I tried in vain to get a shot at them, and began to fear I never should. I was gazing with vexation after a herd in full scamper, when I was startled by a human voice. Turning round, I saw a man at a short distance from me, in a hunting-dress.

" 'What are you after, my lad?' cried he.

" 'Those deer;' replied I, pettishly; 'but it seems as if they never stand still.'

"Upon that he burst out laughing. 'Where are you from?' said he.

" 'From Richmond.'

" 'What! In old Virginny?'

" 'The same.'

"'And how on earth did you get here?'

"'I landed at Green River from a broad-horn,'

"'And where are your companions?'

"'I have none.'

"'What?—all alone!'

"'Yes.'

"'Where are you going?'

"'Any where.'

"'And what have you come here for?'

"'To hunt.'

"'Well,' said he, laughingly, 'you'll make a real hunter; there's no mistaking that!'

"'Have you killed any thing?'

"'Nothing but a turkey; I can't get within shot of a deer: they are always running.'

"'Oh, I'll tell you the secret of that. You're always pushing forward, and starting the deer at a distance, and gazing at those that are scampering; but you must step as slow, and silent, and cautious as a cat, and keep your eyes close around you, and lurk from tree to tree, if you wish to get a chance at deer. But come, go home with me. My name is Bill Smithers; I live not far off: stay with me a little while, and I'll teach you how to hunt.'

"I gladly accepted the invitation of honest Bill Smithers. We soon reached his habitation; a mere log hut, with a square hole for a window, and a chimney made of sticks and clay. Here he lived, with a wife and child. He had 'girdled' the trees for an acre or two around, preparatory to clearing a space for corn and potatoes. In the mean time he maintained his family entirely by his rifle, and I soon found him to be a first-rate huntsman. Under his tutelage I received my first effective lessons in 'woodcraft.'

"The more I knew of a hunter's life, the more I relished it. The country, too, which had been the promised land of my boyhood, did not, like most promised lands, disappoint me. No wilderness could be more beautiful than this part of Kentucky, in these times. The forests were open and spacious, with noble trees, some of which looked as if they had stood for centuries. There were beautiful prairies, too, diversified with groves and clumps of trees, which looked like vast parks, and in which you could see the deer running, at a great distance. In the proper season, these prairies would be covered in many places with wild strawberries, where your horse's hoofs would be dyed to the fetlock. I thought there could not be another place in the world equal to Kentucky—and I think so still.

"After I had passed ten or twelve days with Bill Smithers, I thought it time to shift my quarters, for his house was scarce large enough for his own family, and I had no idea of being an encumbrance to any one. I accordingly made up my bundle, shouldered my rifle, took a friendly leave of Smithers and his wife, and set out in quest of a Nimrod of the wilderness, one John Miller, who lived alone, nearly forty miles off, and who I hoped would be well pleased to have a hunting companion.

"I soon found out that one of the most important items in woodcraft, in a new country, was the skill to find one's way in the wilderness. There were no regular roads in the forests, but they were cut up and perplexed by paths leading in all directions. Some of these were made by the cattle of the settlers, and were called 'stock-tracks,' but others had been made by the immense droves of buffaloes which roamed about the country, from the flood until recent times. These were called buffalo-tracks, and traversed Kentucky from end to end, like highways. Traces of them may still be seen in uncultivated parts, or deeply worn in the rocks where they crossed the mountains. I was a young woodsman, and sorely puzzled to distinguish one kind of track from the other, or to make out my course through this tangled labyrinth. While thus perplexed, I heard a distant roaring and rushing sound; a gloom stole over the forest: on looking up, when I could catch a stray glimpse of the sky, I beheld the clouds rolled up like balls, the lower part as black as ink. There was now and then an explosion, like a burst of cannonry afar off, and the crash of a falling tree. I had heard of hurricanes in the woods, and surmised that one was at hand. It soon came crashing its way; the forest writhing, and twisting, and groaning before it. The hurricane did not extend far on either side, but in a manner ploughed a furrow through the woodland; snapping off or uprooting trees that had stood for centuries, and filling the air with whirling branches. I was directly in its course, and took my stand behind an immense poplar, six feet in diameter. It bore for a time the full fury of the blast, but at length began to yield. Seeing it falling, I scrambled nimbly round the trunk like a squirrel. Down it went bearing down another tree with it. I crept under the trunk as a shelter, and was protected from other trees which fell around me, but was sore all over, from the twigs and branches driven against me by the blast.

"This was the only incident of consequence that occurred on my way to John Miller's, where I arrived on the following day, and was received by the veteran with the rough kindness of a backwoodsman. He was a gray-haired man, hardy and weather-beaten, with a blue wart, like a great bead, over one eye, whence he was nicknamed by the hunters, 'Blue-bead Miller.' He had been in these parts from the earliest settlements, and had signalized himself in the hard conflicts with the Indians, which gained Kentucky the appellation of 'the Bloody Ground.' In one of these fights he had had an arm broken; in another he had narrowly escaped, when hotly pursued, by jumping from a precipice, thirty feet high into a river.

"Miller willingly received me into his house as an inmate, and seemed pleased with the idea of making a hunter of me. His dwelling was a small log-house, with a loft or garret of boards, so that there was ample room for both of us. Under his instruction, I soon made a tolerable proficiency in hunting. My first exploit of any consequence was killing a bear. I was hunting in company with two brothers, when we came upon the track of Bruin, in a wood where there was an undergrowth of canes and grape-vines. He was scrambling up a tree, when I shot him through the breast: he fell to the ground, and lay motionless. The brothers sent in their dog, who seized the bear by the throat. Bruin raised one arm, and gave the dog a hug that crushed his ribs. One yell, and all was over. I don't know which was first dead, the dog or the bear. The two brothers sat down and cried like children over their unfortunate dog. Yet they were mere rough huntsmen almost as wild and untamable as Indians: but they were fine fellows.

"By degrees I became known, and somewhat of a favorite among the hunters of the neighborhood; that is to say, men who lived within a circle of thirty or forty miles, and came occasionally to see John Miller, who was a patriarch among them. They lived widely apart, in log-huts and wigwams, almost with the simplicity of Indians, and well-nigh as destitute of the comforts and inventions of civilized life. They seldom saw each other; weeks, and even months would elapse, without their visiting. When they did meet, it was very much after the manner of Indians; loitering about all day, without having much to say, but becoming communicative as evening advanced, and sitting up half the night before the fire, telling hunting stories, and terrible tales of the fights of the Bloody Ground.

"Sometimes several would join in a distant hunting expedition, or rather campaign. Expeditions of this kind lasted from November until April; during which we laid up our stock of summer provisions. We shifted our hunting camps from place to place, according as we found the game. They were generally pitched near a run of water, and close by a canebrake, to screen us from the wind. One side of our lodge was open towards the fire. Our horses were hoppled and turned loose in the canebrakes, with bells round their necks. One of the party staid at home to watch the camp, prepare the meals, and keep off the wolves; the others hunted. When a hunter killed a deer at a distance from the camp, he would open it and take out the entrails; then climbing a sapling, he would bend it down, tie the deer to the top, and let it spring up again so as to suspend the carcass out of reach of the wolves. At night he would return to the camp, and give an account of his luck. The next morning early he would get a horse out of the canebrake and bring home his game. That day he would stay at home to cut up the carcass, while the others hunted.

"Our days were thus spent in silent and lonely occupations. It was only at night that we would gather together before the fire, and be sociable. I was a novice, and used to listen with open eyes and ears to the strange and wild stories told by the old hunters, and believed every thing I heard. Some of their stories bordered upon the supernatural. They believed that their rifles might be spellbound, so as not to be able to kill a buffalo, even at arm's length. This superstition they had derived from the Indians, who often think the white hunters have laid a spell upon their rifles. Miller partook of this superstition, and used to tell of his rifle's having a spell upon it; but it often seemed to me to be a shuffling way of accounting for a bad shot. If a hunter grossly missed his aim, he would ask, 'Who shot last with his rifle?'—and hint that he must have charmed it. The sure mode to disenchant the gun was to shoot a silver bullet out of it.

"By the opening of spring we would generally have quantities of bear's meat and venison salted, dried, and smoked, and numerous packs of skins. We would then make the best of our way home from our distant hunting-grounds; transporting our spoils, sometimes in canoes along the rivers, sometimes on horseback over land, and our return would often be celebrated by feasting and dancing, in true backwoods style. I have given you some idea of our hunting; let me now give you a sketch of our frolicking.

"It was on our return from a winter's hunting in the neighborhood of Green River, when we received notice that there was to be a grand frolic at Bob Mosely's, to greet the hunters. This Bob Mosely was a prime fellow throughout the country. He was an indifferent hunter, it is true, and rather lazy, to boot; but then he could play the fiddle, and that was enough to make him of consequence. There was no other man within a hundred miles that could play the fiddle, so there was no having a regular frolic without Bob Mosely. The hunters, therefore, were always ready to give him a share of their game in exchange for his music, and Bob was always ready to get up a carousal, whenever there was a party returning from a hunting expedition. The present frolic was to take place at Bob Mosely's own house, which was on the Pigeon-Roost Fork of the Muddy, which is a branch of Rough Creek, which is a branch of Green River.

"Every body was agog for the revel at Bob Mosely's; and as all the fashion of the neighborhood was to be there, I thought I must brush up for the occasion. My leathern hunting-dress, which was the only one I had, was somewhat the worse for wear, it is true, and considerably japanned with blood and grease; but I was up to hunting expedients. Getting into a periogue, I paddled off to a part of the Green River where there was sand and clay, that might serve for soap; then taking off my dress, I scrubbed and scoured it, until I thought it looked very well. I then put it on the end of a stick, and hung it out of the periogue to dry, while I stretched myself very comfortably on the green bank of the river. Unluckily a flaw struck the periogue, and tipped over the stick: down went my dress to the bottom of the river, and I never saw it more. Here was I, left almost in a state of nature I managed to make a kind of Robinson Crusoe garb of undressed skins, with the hair on, which enabled me to get home with decency; but my dream of gayety and fashion was at an end; for how could I think of figuring in high life at the Pigeon-Roost, equipped like a mere Orson?

"Old Miller, who really began to take some pride in me, was confounded when he understood that I did not intend to go to Bob Mosely's; but when I told him my misfortune, and that I had no dress: 'By the powers,' cried he, 'but you *shall* go, and you shall be the best dressed and the best mounted lad there!'

"He immediately set to work to cut out and make up a hunting-shirt, of dressed deer-skin, gaily fringed at the shoulders, and leggins of the same, fringed from hip to heel. He then made me a rakish raccoon-cap, with a flaunting tail to it; mounted me on his best horse; and I may say, without vanity, that I was one of the smartest fellows that figured on that occasion, at the Pigeon-Boost Fork of the Muddy.

"It was no small occasion, either, let me tell you. Bob Mosely's house was a tolerably large bark shanty, with a clapboard roof; and there were assembled all the young hunters and pretty girls of the country, for many a mile round. The young men were in their best hunting-dresses, but not one could compare with mine; and my raccoon-cap, with its flowing tail, was the admiration of every body. The girls were mostly in doe-skin dresses; for there was no spinning and weaving as yet in the woods; nor any need of it. I never saw girls that seemed to me better dressed; and I was somewhat of a judge, having seen fashions at Richmond. We had a hearty dinner, and a merry one;

for there was Jemmy Kiel, famous for raccoon-hunting, and Bob Tarleton, and Wesley Pigman, and Joe Taylor, and several other prime fellows for a frolic, that made all ring again, and laughed that you might have heard them a mile.

"After dinner, we began dancing, and were hard at it, when, about three o'clock in the afternoon, there was a new arrival—the two daughters of old Simon Schultz; two young ladies that affected fashion and late hours. Their arrival had nearly put an end to all our merriment. I must go a little round about in my story, to explain to you how that happened.

"As old Schultz, the father, was one day looking in the canebrakes for his cattle, he came upon the track of horses. He knew they were none of his, and that none of his neighbors had horses about that place. They must be stray horses; or must belong to some traveller who had lost his way, as the track led nowhere. He accordingly followed it up, until he came to an unlucky peddler, with two or three packhorses, who had been bewildered among the cattle-tracks, and had wandered for two or three days among woods and canebrakes, until he was almost famished.

"Old Schultz brought him to his house; fed him on venison, bear's meat, and hominy, and at the end of a week put him in prime condition. The peddler could not sufficiently express his thankfulness; and when about to depart, inquired what he had to pay? Old Schultz stepped back, with surprise. 'Stranger,' said he, 'you have been welcome under my roof. I've given you nothing but wild meat and hominy, because I had no better, but have been glad of your company. You are welcome to stay as long as you please; but by Zounds! if any one offers to pay Simon Schultz for food, be affronts him!' So saying, he walked out in a huff.

"The peddler admired the hospitality of his host, but could not reconcile it to his conscience to go away without making some recompense. There were honest Simon's two daughters, two strapping, red-haired girls. He opened his packs and displayed riches before them of which they had no conception; for in those days there were no country stores in those parts, with their artificial finery and trinketry; and this was the first peddler that had wandered into that part of the wilderness. The girls were for a time completely dazzled, and knew not what to choose: but what caught their eyes most, were two looking-glasses, about the size of a dollar, set in gilt tin. They had never seen the like before, having used no other mirror than a pail of water. The peddler presented them these jewels, without the least hesitation: nay, he gallantly hung them round their necks by red ribbons, almost as fine as the glasses themselves.

This done, he took his departure, leaving them as much astonished as two princesses in a fairy tale, that have received a magic gift from an enchanter.

"It was with these looking-glasses, hung round their necks as lockets, by red ribbons, that old Schultz's daughters made their appearance at three o'clock in the afternoon, at the frolic at Bob Mosely's on the Pigeon-Roost Fork of the Muddy.

"By the powers, but it was an event! Such a thing had never before been seen in Kentucky. Bob Tarleton, a strapping fellow, with a head like a chestnut-burr, and a look like a boar in an apple orchard, stepped up, caught hold of the looking-glass of one of the girls, and gazing at it for a moment, cried out; 'Joe Taylor, come here! come here! I'll be darn'd if Patty Schultz aint got a locket that you can see your face in, as clear as in a spring of water!'

"In a twinkling all the young hunters gathered round old Schultz's daughters. I, who knew what looking-glasses were did not budge. Some of the girls who sat near me were excessively mortified at finding themselves thus deserted. I heard Peggy Pugh say to Sally Pigman, 'Goodness knows, it's well Schultz's daughters is got them things round their necks, for it's the first time the young men crowded round them!'

"I saw immediately the danger of the case. We were a small community, and could not afford to be split up by feuds. So I stepped up to the girls, and whispered to them: 'Polly,' said I, 'those lockets are powerful fine, and become you amazingly; but you don't consider that the country is not advanced enough in these parts for such things. You and I understand these matters, but these people don't. Fine things like these may do very well in the old settlements, but they won't answer at the Pigeon-Roost Pork of the Muddy. You had better lay them aside for the present, or we shall have no peace.'

"Polly and her sister luckily saw their error; they took off the lockets, laid them aside, and harmony was restored: otherwise, I verily believe there would have been an end of our community. Indeed, notwithstanding the great sacrifice they made on this occasion, I do not think old Schultz's daughters were ever much liked afterwards among the young women.

"This was the first time that looking-glasses were ever seen in the Green River part of Kentucky.

"I had now lived some time with old Miller, and had become a tolerably expert hunter. Game, however, began to grow scarce. The buffalo had gathered together, as if by universal understanding, and had crossed the Mississippi never to return. Strangers kept pouring into the country, clearing away the forests, and building in all directions. The hunters began to grow restive. Jemmy Kiel, the same of whom I have already spoken, for his skill in raccoon catching, came to me one day: 'I can't stand this any longer,' said he; 'we're getting too thick here. Simon Schultz crowds me so, that I have no comfort of my life.'

" 'Why, how you talk!' said I; 'Simon Schultz lives twelve miles off.'

" 'No matter; his cattle run with mine, and I've no idea of living where another man's cattle-can run with mine. That's too close neighborhood; I want elbow-room. This country, too, is growing too poor to live in; there's no game: so two or three of us have made up our minds to follow the buffalo to the Missouri, and we should like to have you of the party.' Other hunters of my acquaintance talked in the same manner. This set me thinking: but the more I thought, the more I was perplexed. I had no one to advise with: old Miller and his associates knew of but one mode of life, and I had no experience in any other: but I had a wider scope of thought. When out hunting alone, I used to forget the sport, and sit for hours together on the trunk of a tree, with rifle in hand, buried in thought, and debating with myself; 'Shall I go with Jemmy Kiel and his company, or shall I remain here? If I remain here, there will soon be nothing left to hunt. But am I to be a hunter all my life? Have not I something more in me, than to be carrying a rifle on my shoulder, day after day, and dodging about after bears, and deer, and other brute beasts?' My vanity told me I had; and I called to mind my boyish boast to my sister, that I would never return home, until I returned a member of Congress from Kentucky; but was this the way to fit myself for such a station?

"Various plans passed through my mind, but they were abandoned almost as soon as formed. At length I determined on becoming a lawyer. True it is, I knew almost nothing. I had left school before I had learnt beyond the 'rule of three.' 'Never mind,' said I to myself, resolutely; 'I am a terrible fellow for hanging on to any thing, when I've once made up my mind; and if a man has but ordinary capacity, and will set to work with heart and soul, and stick to it, he can do almost any thing.' With this maxim, which has been pretty much my main stay throughout life, I fortified myself in my determination to attempt the law. But how was I to set about it? I must quit this forest life, and go to one or other of the towns, where I might be able to study, and to attend the courts. This too required funds. I examined into the state of my finances. The purse given me by my father had remained untouched, in the bottom of an old chest up in the loft, for money was scarcely needed in these parts. I had bargained away the skins acquired in hunting, for a horse and various other matters, on which, in case of need, I could raise funds. I therefore thought I could make shift to maintain myself until I was fitted for the bar.

"I informed my worthy host and patron, old Miller, of my plan. He shook his head at my turning my back upon the woods, when I was in a fair way of making a first-rate hunter; but he made no effort to dissuade me. I accordingly set off in September, on horseback, intending to visit Lexington, Frankfort, and other of the principal towns, in search of a favorable place to prosecute my studies. My choice was made sooner than I expected. I had put up one night at Bardstown, and found, on inquiry that I could get comfortable board and accommodation in a private family for a dollar and a half a week. I liked the place, and resolved to look no farther. So the next morning I prepared to turn my face homeward, and take my final leave of forest life.

"I had taken my breakfast, and was waiting for my horse, when, in pacing up and down the piazza, I saw a young girl seated near a window, evidently a visitor. She was very pretty; with auburn hair, and blue eyes, and was dressed in white. I had seen nothing of the kind since I had left Richmond; and at that time I was too much of a boy to be much struck by female charms. She was so delicate and dainty-looking, so different from the hale, buxom, brown girls of the woods; and then her white dress!—it was perfectly dazzling! Never was poor youth more taken by surprise, and suddenly bewitched. My heart yearned to know her; but how was I to accost her? I had grown wild in the woods, and had none of the habitudes of polite life. Had she been like Peggy Pugh, or Sally Pigman, or any other of my leathern-dressed belles of the Pigeon-Roost, I should have approached her without dread; nay, had she been as fair as Schultz's daughters, with their looking-glass lockets, I should not have hesitated: but that white dress, and those auburn ringlets, and blue eyes, and delicate looks, quite daunted, while they fascinated me. I don't know what put it into my head, but I thought, all at once, that I would kiss her! It would take a long acquaintance to arrive at such a boon, but I might seize upon it by sheer robbery. Nobody knew me here. I would just step in, snatch a kiss, mount my horse, and ride off. She would not be the worse for it; and that kiss—oh! I should die if I did not get it!

"I gave no time for the thought to cool, but entered the house, and stepped lightly into the room. She was seated with her back to the door, looking out at the window, and did not hear my approach. I tapped her chair, and as she turned and looked up, I snatched as sweet a kiss as ever was stolen, and vanished in a twinkling. The next moment I was on horseback, galloping homeward; my very ears tingling at what I had done.

"On my return home, I sold my horse, and turned every thing to cash, and found, with the remains of the paternal purse, that I had nearly four hundred dollars; a little capital, which I resolved to manage with the strictest economy.

"It was hard parting with old Miller, who had been like a father to me: it cost me, too, something of a struggle to give up the free, independent wild-wood life I had hitherto led; but I had marked out my course, and have never been one to flinch or turn back.

"I footed it sturdily to Bardstown; took possession of the quarters for which I had bargained, shut myself up, and set to work with might and main, to study. But what a task I had before me! I had every thing to learn; not merely law, but all the elementary branches of knowledge. I read and read, for sixteen hours out of the four-and-twenty; but the more I read, the more I became aware of my own ignorance, and shed bitter tears over my deficiency. It seemed as if the wilderness of knowledge expanded and grew more perplexed as I advanced. Every height gained, only revealed a wider region to be traversed, and nearly filled me with despair. I grew moody, silent, and unsocial, but studied on doggedly and incessantly. The only person with whom I held any conversation, was the worthy man in whose house I was quartered. He was honest and well-meaning, but perfectly ignorant, and I believe would have liked me much better, if I had not been so much addicted to reading. He considered all books filled with lies and impositions, and seldom could look into one, without finding something to rouse his spleen. Nothing put him into a greater passion, than the assertion that the world turned on its own axis every four-and-twenty hours. He swore it was an outrage upon common sense. 'Why, if it did,' said he, 'there would not be a drop of water in the well, by morning, and all the milk and cream in the dairy would be turned topsy-turvy!' And then to talk of the earth going round the sun! 'How do they know it? I've seen the sun rise every morning, and set every evening for more than thirty years. They must not talk to one about the earth's going round the sun!'

"At another time he was in a perfect fret at being told the distance between the sun and moon. 'How can any one tell the distance?' cried he. 'Who surveyed it? who carried the chain? By Jupiter! they only talk this way before me to annoy me. But then there's some people of sense who give in to this cursed humbug! There's Judge Broadnax, now, one of the best lawyers we have; isn't it surprising he should believe in such stuff. Why, sir, the other day I heard him talk of the distance from a star he called Mars to the sun! He must have got it out of one or other of those confounded books he's so fond of reading; a book some impudent fellow has written, who knew nobody could swear the distance was more or less.'

"For my own part, feeling my own deficiency in scientific lore, I never ventured to unsettle his conviction that the sun made his daily circuit round the earth; and for aught I said to the contrary, he lived and died in that belief.

"I had been about a year at Bardstown, living thus studiously and reclusely, when, as I was one day walking the street, I met two young girls, in one of whom I immediately recalled the little beauty whom I had kissed so impudently. She blushed up to the eyes, and so did I; but we both passed on without farther sign of recognition. This second glimpse of her, however, caused an odd fluttering about my heart. I could not get her out of my thoughts for days. She quite interfered with my studies. I tried to think of her as a mere child, but it would not do: she had improved in beauty, and was tending toward womanhood; and then I myself was but little better than a stripling. However, I did not attempt to seek after her, or even to find out who she was, but returned doggedly to my books. By degrees she faded from my thoughts, or if she did cross them occasionally, it was only to increase my despondency; for I feared that with all my exertions, I should never be able to fit myself for the bar, or enable myself to support a wife.

"One cold stormy evening I was seated, in dumpish mood, in the bar-room of the inn, looking into the fire, and turning over uncomfortable thoughts, when I was accosted by some one who had entered the room without my perceiving it, I looked up, and saw before me a tall and, as I thought, pompous-looking man, arrayed in small-clothes and knee-buckles, with powdered head, and shoes nicely blacked and polished; a style of dress unparalleled in those days, in that rough country. I took a pique against him from the very portliness of his appearance, and stateliness of his manner, and bristled up as he accosted me. He demanded if my name was not Ringwood.

"I was startled, for I supposed myself perfectly incog.; but I answered in the affirmative.

"'Your family, I believe, lives in Richmond.'

"My gorge began to rise. 'Yes, sir,' replied I, sulkily, 'my family does live in Richmond.'

"'And what, may I ask, has brought you into this part of the country?'

"'Zounds, sir! ' cried I, starting on my feet, 'what business is it of yours? How dare you to question me in this manner?'

"The entrance of some persons prevented a reply; but I walked up and down the bar-room, fuming with conscious independence and insulted dignity, while the pompous-looking personage, who had thus trespassed upon my spleen, retired without proffering another word.

"The next day, while seated in my room, some one tapped at the door, and, on being bid to enter, the stranger in the powdered head, small-clothes, and shining shoes and buckles, walked in with ceremonious courtesy.

"My boyish pride was again in arms; but he subdued me. He was formal, but kind and friendly. He knew my family and understood my situation, and the dogged struggle I was making. A little conversation, when my jealous pride was once put to rest, drew every thing from me. He was a lawyer of experience, and of extensive practice, and offered at once to take me with him, and direct my studies. The offer was too advantageous and gratifying not to be immediately accepted. From that time I began to look up. I was put into a proper track, and was enabled to study to a proper purpose. I made acquaintance, too, with some of the young men of the place, who were in the same pursuit, and was encouraged at finding that I could 'hold my own' in argument with them. We instituted a debating club, in which I soon became prominent and popular. Men of talents, engaged in other pursuits, joined it, and this diversified our subjects, and put me on various tracks of inquiry. Ladies, too, attended some of our discussions, and this gave them a polite tone, and had an influence on the manners of the debaters. My legal patron also may have had a favorable effect in correcting any roughness contracted in my hunter's life. He was calculated to bend me in an opposite direction, for he was of the old school; quoted Chesterfield on all occasions, and talked of Sir Charles Grandison, who was his beau-ideal. It was Sir Charles Grandison, however, Kentuckyized.

"I had always been fond of female society. My experience, however, had hitherto been among the rough daughters of the backwoodsmen; and I felt an awe of young ladies in 'store clothes,' and delicately brought up. Two or three of the married ladies of Bardstown, who had heard me at the debating club, determined that I was a genius, and undertook to bring me out. I believe I really improved under their hands; became quiet where I had been shy or sulky, and easy where I had been impudent.

I called to take tea one evening with one of these ladies, when to my surprise, and somewhat to my confusion, I found with her the identical blue-eyed little beauty whom I had so audaciously kissed. I was formally introduced to her, but neither of us betrayed any sign of previous acquaintance, except by blushing to the eyes. While tea was getting ready, the lady of the house went out of the room to give some directions, and left us alone.

"Heavens and earth, what a situation! I would have given all the pittance I was worth, to have been in the deepest dell of the forest. I felt the necessity of saying something in excuse of my former rudeness, but I could not conjure up an idea, nor utter a word. Every moment matters were growing worse I felt at one time tempted to do as I had done when I robbed her of the kiss: bolt from the room, and take to flight; but I was chained to the spot, for I really longed to gain her good will.

"At length I plucked up courage, on seeing that she was equally confused with myself, and walking desperately up to her, I exclaimed:

" 'I have been trying to muster up something to say to you, but I cannot. I feel that I am in a horrible scrape. Do have pity on me, and help me out of it!'

"A smile dimpled about her mouth, and played among the blushes of her cheek. She looked up with a shy but arch glance of the eye, that expressed a volume of comic recollection; we both broke into a laugh, and from that moment all went on well.

"A few evenings afterward, I met her at a dance, and prosecuted the acquaintance. I soon became deeply attached to her; paid my court regularly; and before I was nineteen years of age, had engaged myself to marry her. I spoke to her mother, a widow lady, to ask her consent. She seemed to demur; upon which, with my customary haste, I told her there would be no use in opposing the match, for if her daughter chose to have me, I would take her, in defiance of her family, and the whole world.

"She laughed, and told me I need not give myself any uneasiness; there would be no unreasonable opposition. She knew my family, and all about me. The only obstacle was, that I had no means of supporting a wife, and she had nothing to give with her daughter.

"No matter; at that moment every thing was bright before me. I was in one of my sanguine moods. I feared nothing, doubted nothing. So it was agreed that I should prosecute my studies, obtain a license, and as soon as I should be fairly launched in business, we would be married.

"I now prosecuted my studies with redoubled ardor, and was up to my ears in law, when I received a letter from my father, who had heard of me and my whereabouts. He applauded the course I had taken, but advised me to lay a foundation of general knowledge, and offered to defray my expenses, if I would go to college. I felt the want of a general education, and was staggered with this offer. It militated somewhat against the self-dependent course I had so proudly, or rather conceitedly, marked out for myself, but it would enable me to enter more advantageously upon my legal career. I talked over the matter with the lovely girl to whom I was engaged. She sided in opinion with my father, and talked so disinterestedly, yet tenderly, that if possible, I loved her more than ever. I reluctantly, therefore, agreed to go to college for a couple of years, though it must necessarily postpone our union.

"Scarcely had I formed this resolution, when her mother was taken ill, and died, leaving her without a protector. This again altered all my plans. I felt as if I could protect her. I gave up all idea of collegiate studies; persuaded myself that by dint of industry and application I might overcome the deficiencies of education, and resolved to take out a license as soon as possible.

"That very autumn I was admitted to the bar, and within a month afterward, was married. We were a young couple; she not much above sixteen, I not quite twenty; and both almost without a dollar in the world. The establishment which we set up was suited to our circumstances: a log-house, with two small rooms; a bed, a table, a half dozen chairs, a half dozen knives and forks, a half dozen spoons; every thing by half dozens; a little delft ware; every thing in a small way: we were so poor, but then so happy!

"We had not been married many days, when court was held at a county town, about twenty-five miles distant. It was necessary for me to go there, and put myself in the way of business: but how was I to go? I had expended all my means on our establishment; and then, it was hard parting with my wife so soon after marriage. However, go I must. Money must be made, or we should soon have the wolf at the door. I accordingly borrowed a horse, and borrowed a little cash, and rode off from my door, leaving my wife standing at it, and waving her hand after me. Her last look, so sweet and beaming, went to my heart. I felt as if I could go through fire and water for her.

"I arrived at the county town, on a cool October evening. The inn was crowded, for the court was to commence on the following day. I knew no one, and wondered how I, a stranger, and a mere youngster, was to make my way in such a crowd, and to get business. The public room was thronged with the idlers of the country, who gather together on such occasions. There was some drinking going forward, with much noise, and a little altercation. Just as I entered the room, I saw a rough bully of a fellow, who was partly intoxicated, strike an old man. He came swaggering by me, and elbowed me as he passed. I immediately knocked him down, and kicked him into the street. I needed no better introduction. In a moment I had a dozen rough shakes of the hand, and invitations to drink, and found myself quite a personage in this rough assembly.

"The next morning the court opened. I took my seat among the lawyers, but felt as a mere spectator, not having a suit in progress or prospect, nor having any idea where business was to come from. In the course of the morning, a man was put at the bar charged with passing counterfeit money, and was asked if he was ready for trial. He answered in the negative. He had been confined in a place where there were no lawyers, and had not had an opportunity of consulting any. He was told to choose counsel from the lawyers present, and to be ready for trial on the following day. He looked round the court, and selected me. I was thunderstruck. I could not tell why he should make such a choice. I, a beardless youngster; unpractised at the bar; perfectly unknown. I felt diffident yet delighted, and could have hugged the rascal.

"Before leaving the court, he gave me one hundred dollars in a bag, as a retaining fee. I could scarcely believe my senses; it seemed like a dream. The heaviness of the fee spoke but lightly in favor of his innocence, but that was no affair of mine. I was to be advocate, not judge, nor jury. I followed him to jail, and learned from him all the particulars of his case: thence I went to the clerk's office, and took minutes of the indictment. I then examined the law on the subject, and prepared my brief in my room. All this occupied me until midnight, when I went to bed, and tried to sleep. It was all in vain. Never in my life was I more wide awake. A host of thoughts and fancies kept rushing through my mind: the shower of gold that bad so unexpectedly fallen into my lap; the idea of my poor little wife at home, that I was to astonish with my good fortune! But then the awful responsibility I had undertaken!—to speak for the first time in a strange court; the expectations the culprit bad evidently formed of my talents; all these, and a crowd of similar notions, kept whirling through my mind. I tossed about all night, fearing the morning would find me exhausted and incompetent; in a word, the day dawned on me, a miserable fellow!

"I got up feverish and nervous. I walked out before breakfast, striving to collect my thoughts, and tranquillize my feelings. It was a bright morning; the air was pure and frosty. I bathed my forehead and my bands in a beautiful running stream; but I could not allay the fever beat that raged within. I returned to breakfast, but could not eat. A single cup of coffee formed my repast. It was time to go to court, and I went there with a throbbing heart. I believe if it had not been for the thoughts of my little wife, in her lonely log-house I should have given back to the man his hundred dollars, and relinquished the cause. I took my seat, looking, I am convinced, more like a culprit than the rogue I was to defend.

"When the time came for me to speak, my heart died within me. I rose embarrassed and dismayed, and stammered in opening my cause. I went on from bad to worse, and felt as if I was going down hill. Just then the public prosecutor, a man of talents, but somewhat rough in his practice, made a sarcastic remark on something I had said. It was like an electric spark, and ran tingling through every vein in my body. In an instant my diffidence was gone. My whole spirit was in arms. I answered with promptness and bitterness, for I felt the cruelty of such an attack upon a novice in my situation. The public prosecutor made a kind of apology; this, from a man of his redoubted powers, was a vast concession. I renewed my argument with a fearless glow; carried the case through triumphantly, and the man was acquitted.

"This was the making of me. Every body was curious to know who this new lawyer was, that had thus suddenly risen among them, and bearded the attorney-general at the very outset. The story of my debut at the inn, on the preceding evening, when I had knocked down a bully, and kicked him out of doors, for striking an old man, was circulated, with favorable exaggerations. Even my very beardless chin and juvenile countenance were in my favor, for people gave me far more credit than I really deserved. The chance business which occurs in our country courts came thronging upon me. I was repeatedly employed in other causes; and by Saturday night, when the court closed, and I had paid my bill at the inn, I found myself with a hundred and fifty dollars in silver, three hundred dollars in notes, and a horse that I afterward sold for two hundred dollars more.

"Never did miser gloat on his money with more delight. I locked the door of my room; piled the money In a heap upon the table; walked round it; sat with my elbows on the table, and my chin upon my hands, and gazed upon it. Was I thinking of the money? No! I was thinking of my little wife at home. Another sleepless night ensued; but what a night of golden fancies, and splendid air castles! As soon as morning dawned, I was up, mounted the borrowed horse with which I had come to court, and led the other, which I had received as a fee. All the way I was delighting myself with the thoughts of the surprise I had in store for my little wife; for both of us had expected nothing but that I should spend all the money I had borrowed, and should return in debt.

"Our meeting was joyous, as you may suppose: but I played the part of the Indian hunter, who, when he returns from the chase, never for a time speaks of his success.

She had prepared a snug little rustic meal for me, and while it was getting ready, I seated myself at an old-fashioned desk in one corner, and began to count over my money, and put it away. She came to me before I had finished, and asked who I had collected the money for.

" 'For myself, to be sure,' replied I, with affected coolness; 'I made it at court.'

"She looked me for a moment in the face, incredulously. I tried to keep my countenance, and to play Indian, but it would not do. My muscles began to twitch; my feelings all at once gave way, I caught her in my arms; laughed, cried, and danced about the room, like a crazy man. From that time forward, we never wanted for money,

"I had not been long in successful practice, when I was surprised one day by a visit from my woodland patron, old Miller. The tidings of my prosperity had reached him in the wilderness and he had walked one hundred and fifty miles on foot to see me. By that time I had improved my domestic establishment, and had all things comfortable about me. He looked around him with a wondering eye, at what he considered luxuries and superfluities; but supposed they were all right, in my altered circumstances. He said he did not know, upon the whole, but that I had acted for the best. It is true, if game had continued plenty, it would have been a folly for me to quit a hunter's life; but hunting was pretty nigh done up in Kentucky. The buffalo had gone to Missouri; the elk were nearly gone also; deer, too, were growing scarce; they might last out his time, as he was growing old, but they were not worth setting up life upon. He had once lived on the borders of Virginia. Game grew scarce there; he followed it up across Kentucky, and now it was again giving him the slip; but he was too old to follow it farther.

"He remained with us three days. My wife did every thing in her power to make him comfortable; but at the end of that time, he said he must be off again to the woods. He was tired of the village, and of having so many people about him. He accordingly returned to the wilderness, and to hunting life. But I fear he did not make a good end of it; for I understand that a few years before his death, he married Sukey Thomas, who lived at the White Oak Run."

The Seminoles

FROM THE TIME OF THE CHIMERICAL CRUISINGS OF OLD PONCE DE LEON in search of the Fountain of Youth; the avaricious expedition of Pamphilo de Narvaez in quest of gold; and the chivalrous enterprise of Hernando de Soto, to discover and conquer a second Mexico, the natives of Florida have been continually subjected to the invasions and encroachments of white men. They have resisted them perseveringly but fruitlessly, and are now battling amidst swamps and morasses, for the last foothold of their native soil, with all the ferocity of despair. Can we wonder at the bitterness of a hostility that has been handed down from father to son, for upward of three centuries, and exasperated by the wrongs and miseries of each succeeding generation! The very name of the savages with whom we are fighting, betokens their fallen and homeless condition. Formed of the wrecks of once powerful tribes, and driven from their ancient seats of prosperity and dominion, they are known by the name of the Seminoles, or "Wanderers."

Bartram, who travelled through Florida in the latter part of the last century, speaks of passing through a great extent of ancient Indian fields, now silent and deserted, overgrown with forests, orange groves, and rank vegetation, the site of the ancient Alachua, the capital of a famous and powerful tribe, who in days of old could assemble thousands at bull-play and other athletic exercises "over these then happy fields and green plains." "Almost every step we take," adds he, "over these fertile heights, discovers the remains and traces of ancient human habitations and cultivation."

We are told that about the year 1763, when Florida was ceded by the Spaniards to the English, the Indians generally retired from the towns and the neighborhood of the whites, and burying themselves in the deep forests, intricate swamps and hommocks, and vast savannahs of the interior, devoted themselves to a pastoral life, and the rearing of horses and cattle. These are the people that received the name of the Seminoles, or Wanderers, which they still retain.

Bartram gives a pleasing picture of them at the time he visited them in their wilderness; where their distance from the abodes of the white man gave them a transient quiet and security. "This handful of people," says he, "possesses a vast territory, all East and the greatest part of West Florida, which being naturally cut and divided into thousands of islets, knolls, and eminences, by the innumerable rivers, lakes, swamps, vast savannahs, and ponds, form so many secure retreats and temporary dwelling-places that effectually guard them from any sudden invasions or attacks from their enemies; and being such a swampy, hommocky country, furnishes such a plenty and variety of supplies for the nourishment of varieties of animals, that I can venture to assert, that no part of the globe so abounds with wild game, or creatures fit for the food of man.

"Thus they enjoy a superabundance of the necessaries and conveniences of life, with the security of person and property, the two great concerns of mankind. The hides of deer, bears, tigers, and wolves, together with honey, wax, and other productions of the country, purchase their clothing equipage, and domestic utensils from the whites. They seem to be free from want or desires. No cruel enemy to dread; nothing to give them disquietude, but the gradual encroachments of the white people. Thus contented and undisturbed, they appear as blithe and free as the birds of the air, and like them as volatile and active, tuneful and vociferous. The visage, action, and deportment of the Seminoles form the most striking picture of happiness in this life; joy, contentment, love, and friendship, without guile or affectation, seem inherent in them, or predominant in their vital principle, for it leaves them with but the last breath of life. . . . They are fond of games and gambling, and amuse themselves like children, in relating extravagant stories, to cause surprise and mirth."[1]

The same writer gives an engaging picture of his treatment by these savages:

"Soon after entering the forests, we were met in the path by a small company of Indians, smiling and beckoning to us long before we joined them. This was a family of Talahasochte, who had been out on a hunt and were returning home loaded with barbecued meat, hides, and honey. Their company consisted of the man, his wife and children, well mounted on fine horses, with a number of pack-horses. The man offered us a fawn skin of honey, which I accepted, and at parting presented him with some fishhooks, sewing-needles, etc.

---

1. Bartram's Travels in North America.

"On our return to camp in the evening, we were saluted by a party of young Indian warriors, who had pitched their tents on a green eminence near the lake, at a small distance from our camp under a little grove of oaks and palms. This company consisted of seven young Seminoles, under the conduct of a young prince or chief of Talahasochte, a town southward in the Isthmus. They were all dressed and painted with singular elegance, and richly ornamented with silver plates, chains, etc., after the Seminole mode, with waving plumes of feathers on their crests. On our coming up to them, they arose and shook hands; we alighted and sat a while with them by their cheerful fire.

"The young prince informed our chief that he was in pursuit of a young fellow who had fled from the town, carrying of with him one of his favorite young wives. He said, merrily, he would have the ears of both of them before he returned. He was rather above the middle stature, and the most perfect human figure I ever saw; of an amiable, engaging countenance, air, and deportment; free and familiar in conversation, yet retaining a becoming gracefulness and dignity. We arose, took leave of them, and crossed a little vale, covered with a charming green turf, already illuminated by the soft light of the full moon.

"Soon after joining our companions at camp, our neighbors, the prince and his associates, paid us a visit. We treated them with the best fare we had, having till this time preserved our spirituous liquors. They left us with perfect cordiality and cheerfulness, wishing us a good repose, and retired to their own camp. Having a band of music with them, consisting of a drum, flutes, and a rattle-gourd, they entertained us during the night with their music, vocal and instrumental.

"There is a languishing softness and melancholy air in the Indian convivial songs, especially of the amorous class, irresistibly moving attention, and exquisitely pleasing, especially in their solitary recesses, when all nature is silent."

Travellers who have been among them, in more recent times, before they had embarked in their present desperate struggle, represent them in much the same light; as leading a pleasant, indolent life, in a climate that required little shelter or clothing, and where the spontaneous fruits of the earth furnished subsistence without toil. A cleanly race, delighting in bathing, passing much of their time under the shade of their trees, with heaps of oranges and other fine fruits for their refreshment; talking, laughing, dancing and sleeping. Every chief had a fan hanging to his side, made of feathers of the wild turkey, the beautiful pink-colored crane, or the scarlet flamingo. With this he would sit and fan himself with great stateliness, while the young people danced before him. The women joined in the dances with the men, excepting the war-dances. They wore strings of tortoise-shells and pebbles round their legs, which rattled in cadence to the music. They were treated with more attention among the Seminoles than among most Indian tribes.

Origin of the White, the Red, and the Black Men

A Seminole Tradition

When the Floridas were erected into a territory of the United States, one of the earliest cares of the Governor, William P. Duval, was directed to the instruction and civilization of the natives. For this purpose he called a meeting of the chiefs, in which he informed them of the wish of their Great Father at Washington that they should have schools and teachers among them, and that their children should be instructed like the children of white men. The chiefs listened with their customary silence and decorum to a long speech, setting forth the advantages that would accrue to them from this measure, and when he had concluded, begged the interval of a day to deliberate on it.

On the following day, a solemn convocation was held, at which one of the chiefs addressed the governor in the name of all the rest. "My brother," said he, "we have been thinking over the proposition of our Great Father at Washington, to send teachers and set up schools among us. We are very thankful for the interest he takes in our welfare; but after much deliberation, have concluded to decline his offer. What will do very well for white men, will not do for red men. I know you white men say we all come from the same father and mother, but you are mistaken. We have a tradition handed down from our forefathers, and we believe it, that the Great Spirit, when he undertook to make men, made the black man; it was his first attempt, and pretty well for a beginning; but he soon saw he had bungled; so he determined to try his hand again. He did so, and made the red man. He liked him much better than the black man, but still he was not exactly what he wanted. So he tried once more, and made the white man; and then he was satisfied. You see, therefore, that you were made last, and that is the reason I call you my youngest brother.

"When the Great Spirit had made the three men, he called them together and showed them three boxes. The first was filled with books, and maps, and papers; the second with bows and arrows, knives and tomahawks; the third with spades, axes, hoes, and hammers. 'These, my sons,' said he, 'are the means by which you are to live; choose among them according to your fancy.'

"The white man, being the favorite, had the first choice. He passed by the box of working-tools without notice; but when he came to the weapons for war and hunting, he stopped and looked hard at them. The red man trembled, for he had set his heart upon that box. The white man, however, after looking upon it for a moment, passed on, and chose the box of books and papers. The red man's turn came next; and you may be sure he seized with joy upon the bows and arrows, and tomahawks. As to the black man, he had no choice left, but to put up with the box of tools.

"From this it is clear that the Great Spirit intended the white man should learn to read and write; to understand all about the moon and stars; and to make every thing, even rum and whiskey. That the red man should be a first-rate hunter, and a mighty warrior, but he was not to learn any thing from books, as the Great Spirit had not given him any: nor was he to make rum and whiskey, lest he should kill himself with drinking. As to the black man, as he had nothing but working-tools, it was clear he was to work for the white and red man, which he has continued to do.

"We must go according to the wishes of the Great Spirit, or we shall get into trouble. To know how to read and write, is very good for white men, but very bad for red men. It makes white men better, but red men worse. Some of the Creeks and Cherokees learnt to read and write, and they are the greatest rascals among all the Indians. They went on to Washington, and said they were going to see their Great Father, to talk about the good of the nation. And when they got there, they all wrote upon a little piece of paper, without the nation at home knowing any thing about it. And the first thing the nation at home knew of the matter, they were called together by the Indian agent, who showed them a little piece of paper, which he told them was a treaty, which, their brethren had made in their name, with their Great Father at Washington. And as they knew not what a treaty was, he held up the little piece of paper, and they looked under it, and lo! it covered a great extent of country, and they found that their brethren, by knowing how to read and write, had sold their houses, and their lands, and the graves of their fathers; and that the white man, by knowing how to read and write, had gained them. Tell our Great Father at Washington, therefore, that we are very sorry we cannot receive teachers among us; for reading and writing, though very good for white men, is very bad for Indians."

The Conspiracy of Neamathla

An Authentic Sketch

In the autumn of 1823, Governor Duval, and other commissioners on the part of the United States, concluded a treaty with the chiefs and warriors of the Florida Indians, by which the latter, for certain considerations, ceded all claims to the whole territory, excepting a district in the eastern part, to which they were to remove, and within which they were to reside for twenty years. Several of the chiefs signed the treaty with great reluctance; but none opposed it more strongly than Neamathla, principal chief of the Mickasookies, a fierce and warlike people, many of them Creeks by origin, who lived about the Mickasookie lake. Neamathla had always been active in those depredations on the frontiers of Georgia, which had brought vengeance and ruin on the Seminoles. He was a remarkable man; upward of sixty years of age, about six feet high, with a fine eye, and a strongly-marked countenance, over which he possessed great command. His hatred of the white men appeared to be mixed with contempt: on the common people he looked down with infinite scorn. He seemed unwilling to acknowledge any superiority of rank or dignity in Governor Duval, claiming to associate with him on terms of equality, as two great chieftains. Though he had been prevailed upon to sign the treaty, his heart revolted at it. In one of his frank conversations with Governor Duval, he observed: "This country belongs to the red man; and if I had the number of warriors at my command that this nation once had, I would not leave a white man on my lands. I would exterminate the whole. I can say this to you, for you can understand me: you are a man; but I would not say it to your people. They'd cry out I was a savage, and would take my life. They cannot appreciate the feelings of a man that loves his country."

As Florida had but recently been erected into a territory, every thing as yet was in rude and simple style. The Governor, to make himself acquainted with the Indians, and to be near at hand to keep an eye upon them, fixed his residence at Tallahassee, near the Fowel towns, inhabited by the Mickasookies. His government palace for a time was a mere log-house, and he lived on hunters' fare. The village of Neamathla was but about three miles off, and thither the governor occasionally rode, to visit the old chieftain. In one of these visits, he found Neamathla seated in his wigwam, in the centre of the village, surrounded by his warriors. The governor had brought him some liquor as a present, but it mounted quickly into his brain, and rendered him quite boastful and belligerent.

The theme ever uppermost in his mind, was the treaty with the whites. "It was true," he said, "the red men had made such a treaty, but the white men had not acted up to it. The red men had received none of the money and the cattle that had been promised them; the treaty, therefore, was at an end, and they did not mean to be bound by it."

Governor Duval calmly represented to him that the time appointed in the treaty for the payment and delivery of the money and the cattle had not yet arrived. This the old chieftain knew full well, but he chose, for the moment, to pretend ignorance. He kept on drinking and talking, his voice growing louder and louder, until it resounded all over the village. He held in his hand a long knife, with which he had been rasping tobacco; this he kept flourishing backward and forward, as he talked, by way of giving effect to his words, brandishing it at times within an inch of the governor's throat. He concluded his tirade by repeating, that the country belonged to the red men, and that sooner than give it up, his bones and the bones of his people should bleach upon its soil.

Duval knew that the object of all this bluster was to see whether he could be intimidated. He kept his eye, therefore, fixed steadily on the chief, and the moment he concluded with his menace, seized him by the bosom of his hunting-shirt, and clinching his other fist:

"I've heard what you have said," replied he. "You have made a treaty, yet you say your bones shall bleach before you comply with it. As sure as there is a sun in heaven, your bones *shall* bleach, if you do not fulfil every article of that treaty! I'll let you know that I am *first* here, and will see that you do your duty!"

Upon this the old chieftain threw himself back, burst into a fit of laughing, and declared that all he had said was in joke. The governor suspected, however, that there was a grave meaning at the bottom of this jocularity.

For two months, every thing went on smoothly: the Indians repaired daily to the log-cabin palace of the governor, at Tallahassee, and appeared perfectly contented. All at once they ceased their visits, and for three or four days not one was to be seen. Governor Duval began to apprehend that some mischief was brewing. On the evening of the fourth day, a chief named Yellow-Hair, a resolute, intelligent fellow, who had always evinced an attachment for the governor, entered his cabin about twelve o'clock at night, and informed him, that between four and five hundred warriors, painted and decorated, were assembled to hold a secret war-talk at Neamathla's town. He had slipped off to give intelligence, at the risk of his life, and hastened back lest his absence should be discovered.

Governor Duval passed an anxious night after this intelligence. He knew the talent and the daring character of Neamathla; he recollected the threats he had thrown out; he reflected that about eighty white families were scattered widely apart, over a great extent of country, and might be swept away at once, should the Indians, as he feared, determine to clear the country, That he did not exaggerate the dangers of the case, has been proved by the horrid scenes of Indian warfare which have since desolated that devoted region. After a night of sleepless cogitation Duval determined on a measure suited to his prompt and resolute character. Knowing the admiration of the savages for personal courage, he determined, by a sudden surprise, to endeavor to overawe and check them. It was hazarding much; but where so many lives were in jeopardy, he felt bound to incur the hazard.

Accordingly, on the next morning, he set off on horseback, attended merely by a white man, who had been reared among the Seminoles, and understood their language and manners, and who acted as interpreter. They struck into an Indian "trail," leading to Neamathla's village. After proceeding about half a mile, Governor Duval informed the interpreter of the object of his expedition. The latter, though a bold man, paused and remonstrated. The Indians among whom they were going were among the most desperate and discontented of the nation. Many of them were veteran warriors, impoverished and exasperated by defeat, and ready to set their lives at any hazard. He said that if they were holding a war council, it must be with desperate intent, and it would be certain death to intrude among them.

Duval made light of his apprehensions: he said he was perfectly well acquainted with the Indian character, and should certainly proceed. So saying, he rode on. When within half a mile of the village, the interpreter addressed him again, in such a tremulous tone, that Duval turned and looked him in the face. He was deadly pale, and once more urged the governor to return, as they would certainly be massacred if they proceeded.

Duval repeated his determination to go on, but advised the other to return, lest his pale face should betray fear to the Indians, and they might take advantage of it. The interpreter replied that he would rather die a thousand deaths, than have it said he had deserted his leader when in peril.

Duval then told him he must translate faithfully all he should say to the Indians, without softening a word. The interpreter promised faithfully to do so, adding that he well knew, when they were once in the town, nothing but boldness could save them.

They now rode into the village and advanced to the council-house. This was rather a group of four houses, forming a square, in the centre of which was a great council-fire. The houses were open in front, toward the fire, and closed in the rear. At each corner of the square, there was an interval between the houses, for ingress and egress. In these houses sat the old men and the chiefs; the young men were gathered round the fire. Neamathla presided at the council, elevated on a higher seat than the rest.

Governor Duval entered by one of the corner intervals, and rode boldly into the centre of the square. The young men made way for him; an old man who was speaking, paused in the midst of his harangue. In an instant thirty or forty rifles were cocked and levelled. Never had Duval heard so loud a click of triggers; it seemed to strike to his heart. He gave one glance at the Indians, and turned off with an air of contempt. He did not dare, he says, to look again, lest it might affect his nerves, and on the firmness of his nerves every thing depended.

The chief threw up his arm. The rifles were lowered. Duval breathed more freely; he felt disposed to leap from his horse, but restrained himself, and dismounted leisurely. He then walked deliberately up to Neamathla, and demanded, in an authoritative tone, what were his motives for holding that council. The moment he made this demand, the orator sat down. The chief made no reply, but hung his head in apparent confusion. After a moment's pause, Duval proceeded:

"I am well aware of the meaning of this war-council; and deem it my duty to warn you against prosecuting the schemes you have been devising. If a single hair of a white man in this country falls to the ground, I will hang you and your chiefs on the trees around your council-house! You cannot pretend to withstand the power of the white men. You are in the palm of the hand of your Great Father at Washington, who can crush you like an egg-shell! You may kill me; I am but one man; but recollect, white men are numerous as the leaves on the trees. Remember the fate of your warriors whose bones are whitening in battle-fields. Remember your wives and children who perished my swamps. Do you want to provoke more hostilities? Another war with the white men, and there will not be a Seminole left to tell the story of his race."

Seeing the effect of his words, he concluded by appointing a day for the Indians to meet him at St. Marks, and give an account of their conduct. He then rode off, without giving them time to recover from their surprise. That night he rode forty miles to Apalachicola River, to the tribe of the same name, who were in feud with the Seminoles. They promptly put two hundred and fifty warriors at his disposal, whom he ordered to be at St. Marks at the appointed day. He sent out runners, also, and mustered one hundred of the militia to repair to the same place, together with a number of regulars from the army. All his arrangements were successful.

Having taken these measures, he returned to Tallahassee, to the neighborhood of the conspirators, to show them that he was not afraid. Here he ascertained, through Yellow-Hair, that nine towns were disaffected, and had been concerned in the conspiracy. He was careful to inform himself, from the same source, of the names of the warriors in each of those towns who were most popular, though poor, and destitute of rank and command.

When the appointed day was at hand for the meeting at St. Marks, Governor Duval set off with Neamathla, who was at the head of eight or nine hundred warriors, but who feared to venture into the fort without him. As they entered the fort, and saw troops and militia drawn up there, and a force of Apalachicola soldiers stationed on the opposite bank of the river, they thought they were betrayed, and were about to fly; but Duval assured them they were safe, and that when the talk was over, they might go home unmolested.

A grand talk was now held, in which the late conspiracy was discussed. As he had foreseen, Neamathla and the other old chiefs threw all the blame upon the young men. "Well," replied Duval, "with us white men, when we find a man incompetent to govern those under him, we put him down, and appoint another in his place. Now, as you all acknowledge you cannot manage your young men, we must put chiefs over them who can."

So saying, he deposed Neamathla first; appointing another in his place; and so on with all the rest; taking care to substitute the warriors who bad been pointed out to him as poor and popular; putting medals round their necks, and investing them with great ceremony. The Indians were surprised and delighted at finding the appointments fall upon the very men they would themselves have chosen, and hailed them with acclamations. The warriors thus unexpectedly elevated to command, and clothed with dignity, were secured to the interests of the governor, and sure to keep an eye on the disaffected. As to the great chief Neamathla, he left the country in disgust, and returned to the Creek Nation, who elected him a chief of one of their towns. Thus by the resolute spirit and prompt sagacity of one man, a dangerous conspiracy was completely defeated.

Governor Duval was afterwards enabled to remove the whole nation, through his own personal influence, without the aid of the General Government.

NOTE.—The foregoing anecdotes concerning the Seminoles, were gathered in conversation with Governor Duval (the original of Ralph Ringwood).

The Count Van Horn

During the minority of Louis XV, while the Duke of Orleans was Regent of Franco, a young Flemish nobleman, the Count Antoine Joseph Van Horn, made his sudden appearance in Paris, and by his character, conduct, and the subsequent disasters in which he became involved, created a great sensation in the high circles of the proud aristocracy. He was about twenty-two years of age, tall, finely formed, with a pale, romantic countenance, and eyes of remarkable brilliancy and wildness.

He was one of the most ancient and highly-esteemed families of European nobility, being of the line of the Princes of Horn and Overique, sovereign Counts of Hautekerke, and hereditary Grand Veneurs of the empire.

The family took its name from the little town and seigneurie of Horn, in Brabant; and was known as early as the eleventh century among the little dynasties of the Netherlands, and since that time, by a long line of illustrious generations. At the peace of Utrecht, when the Netherlands passed under subjection to Austria, the house of Van Horn came under the domination of the emperor. At the time we treat of, two of the branches of this ancient house were extinct; the third and only surviving branch was represented by the reigning prince, Maximilian Emanuel Van Horn, twenty-four years of age, who resided in honorable and courtly style on his hereditary domains at Baussigny, in the Netherlands, and his brother the Count Antoine Joseph, who is the subject of this memoir.

The ancient house of Van Horn, by the intermarriage of its various branches with the noble families of the continent, had become widely connected and interwoven with the high aristocracy of Europe. The Count Antoine, therefore, could claim relationship to many of the proudest names in Paris. In fact, he was grandson, by the mother's side, of the Prince de Ligne, and even might boast of affinity to the Regent (the Duke of Orleans) himself. There were circumstances, however, connected with his sudden appearance in Paris, and his previous story, that placed him in what is termed "a false position;" a word of baleful significance in the fashionable vocabulary of France.

The young Count had been a captain in the service of Austria, but had been cashiered for irregular conduct, and for disrespect to Prince Louis of Baden, commander-in-chief. To check him in his wild career, and bring him to sober reflection, his brother the Prince caused him to be arrested, and sent to the old castle of Van Wert, in the domains of Horn. This was the same castle in which, in former times, John Van Horn, Statholder of Gueldres, had imprisoned his father; a circumstance which has furnished Rembrandt with the subject of an admirable painting. The governor of the castle was one Van Wert, grandson of the famous John Van Wert, the hero of many a popular song and legend. It was the intention of the Prince that his brother should be held in honorable durance, for his object was to sober and improve, not to punish and afflict him. Van Wert, however, was a stern, harsh man, of violent passions. He treated the youth in a manner that prisoners and offenders were treated in the strongholds of the robber counts of Germany, in old times; confined him in a dungeon, and inflicted on him such hardships and indignities, that the irritable temperament of the young count was roused to continual fury, which ended in insanity. For six months was the unfortunate youth kept in this horrible state, without his brother the Prince being informed of his melancholy condition, or of the cruel treatment to which he was subjected. At length, one day, in a paroxysm of frenzy, the Count knocked down two of his gaolers with a beetle, escaped from the castle of Van Wert, and eluded all pursuit: and after roving about in a state of distraction, made his way to Baussigny, and appeared like a spectre before his brother.

The Prince was shocked at his wretched, emaciated appearance, and his lamentable state of mental alienation. He received him with the most compassionate tenderness; lodged him in his own room; appointed three servants to attend and watch over him day and night; and endeavored, by the most soothing and affectionate assiduity, to atone for the past act of rigor with which he reproached himself. When he learned, however, the manner in which his unfortunate brother had been treated in confinement, and the course of brutalities that had led to his mental malady, he was aroused to indignation. His first step was to cashier Van Wert from his command. That violent man set the Prince at defiance, and attempted to maintain himself in his government and his castle, by instigating the peasants, for several leagues round, to revolt. His insurrection might have been formidable against the power of a petty prince; but he was put under the ban of the empire, and seized as a state prisoner. The memory of his grandfather, the oft-sung John Van Wert, alone saved him from a gibbet; but he was imprisoned in the strong tower of Horn-op-Zee. There he remained until he was eighty-two years of age, savage, violent, and unconquered to the last; for we are told that he never ceased fighting and thumping, as long as he could close a fist or wield a cudgel.

In the mean time, a course of kind and gentle treatment and wholesome regimen, and above all, the tender and affectionate assiduity of his brother, the Prince, produced the most salutary effects upon Count Antoine. He gradually recovered his reason; but a degree of violence seemed always lurking at the bottom of his character, and he required to be treated with the greatest caution and mildness, for the least contradiction exasperated him.

In this state of mental convalescence, he began to find the supervision and restraints of brotherly affection insupportable; so he left the Netherlands furtively, and repaired to Paris, whither, in fact, it is said he was called by motives of interest, to make arrangements concerning a valuable estate which he inherited from his relative the Princess d'Epinay.

On his arrival in Paris, he called upon the Marquis of Créqui, and other of the high nobility with whom he was connected. He was received with great courtesy; but, as he brought no letters from his elder brother, the Prince, and as various circumstances of his previous history had transpired, they did not receive him into their families, nor introduce him to their ladies. Still they fêted him in bachelor style, gave him gay and elegant suppers at their separate apartments, and took him to their boxes at the theatres. He was often noticed, too, at the doors of the most fashionable churches, taking his stand among the young men of fashion; and at such times, his tall, elegant figure, his pale but handsome countenance, and his flashing eyes, distinguished him from among the crowd; and the ladies declared that it was almost impossible to support his ardent gaze.

The Count did not afflict himself much at his limited circulation in the fastidious circles of the high aristocracy. He relished society of a wilder and less ceremonious cast; and meeting with loose companions to his taste, soon ran into all the excesses of the capital, in that most licentious period. It is said that, in the course of his wild career, he had an intrigue with a lady of quality, a favorite of the Regent; that he was surprised by that prince in one of his interviews; that sharp words passed between them; and that the jealousy and vengeance thus awakened, ended only with his life.

About this time, the famous Mississippi scheme of Law was at its height, or rather it began to threaten that disastrous catastrophe which convulsed the whole financial world. Every effort was making to keep the bubble inflated. The vagrant population of France was swept off from the streets at night, and conveyed to Havré de Grace, to be shipped to the projected colonies; even laboring people and mechanics were thus crimped and spirited away. As Count Antoine was in the habit of sallying forth at night, in disguise, in pursuit of his pleasures, he came near being carried off by a gang of crimps; it seemed, in fact, as if they had been lying in wait for him, as he had experienced very rough treatment at their hands Complaint was made of his case by his relation, the Marquis de Créqui, who took much interest in the youth; but the Marquis received mysterious intimations not to interfere in the matter, but to advise the Count to quit Paris immediately: "If he lingers, he is lost!" This has been cited as a proof that vengeance was dogging at the heels of the unfortunate youth, and only watching for an opportunity to destroy him.

Such opportunity occurred but too soon. Among the loose companions with whom the Count had become intimate, were two who lodged in the same hotel with him. One was a youth only twenty years of age, who passed himself off as the Chevalier d'Etampes, but whose real name was Lestang, the prodigal son of a Flemish banker. The other, named Laurent de Mille, a Piedmontese, was a cashiered captain, and at the time an esquire in the service of the dissolute Princess de Carignan, who kept gambling-tables in her palace. It is probable that gambling propensities had brought these young men together, and that their losses had driven them to desperate measures; certain it is, that all Paris was suddenly astounded by a murder which they were said to have committed. What made the crime more startling, was, that it seemed connected with the great Mississippi scheme, at that time the fruitful source of all kinds of panics and agitations. A Jew, a stockbroker, who dealt largely in shares of the bank of Law, founded on the Mississippi scheme, was the victim. The story of his death is variously related. The darkest account states, that the Jew was decoyed by these young men into an obscure tavern, under pretext of negotiating with him for bank shares, to the amount of one hundred thousand crowns, which he had with him in his pocket-book. Lestang kept watch upon the stairs. The Count and De Mille entered with the Jew into a chamber. In a little while there were heard cries and struggles from within. A waiter passing by the room, looked in, and seeing the Jew weltering in his blood, shut the door again, double-locked it, and alarmed the house. Lestang rushed down stairs, made his way to the hotel, secured his most portable effects, and fled the country. The Count and De Mille endeavored to escape by the window, but were both taken, and conducted to prison.

A circumstance which occurs in this part of the Count's story, seems to point him out as a fated man. His mother, and his brother, the Prince Van Horn, had received intelligence some time before at Baussigny, of the dissolute life the Count was leading at Paris, and of his losses at play. They despatched a gentleman of the Prince's household to Paris, to pay the debts of the Count, and persuade him to return to Flanders; or, if he should refuse, to obtain an order from the Regent for him to quit the capital. Unfortunately the gentleman did not arrive at Paris until the day after the murder.

The news of the Count's arrest and imprisonment, on a charge of murder, caused a violent sensation among the high aristocracy. All those connected with him, who had treated him hitherto with indifference, found their dignity deeply involved in the question of his guilt or innocence. A general convocation was held at the hotel of the Marquis de Créqui, of all the relatives and allies of the house of Horn. It was an assemblage of the most proud and aristocratic personages of Paris. Inquiries were made into the circumstances of the affair. It was ascertained, beyond a doubt, that the Jew was dead, and that he had been killed by several stabs of a poniard. In escaping by the window, it was said that the Count had fallen, and been immediately taken; but that De Mille had fled through the streets, pursued by the populace, and had been arrested at some distance from the scene of the murder; that the Count had declared himself innocent of the death of the Jew, and that he had risked his own life in endeavoring to protect him; but that De Mille on being brought back to the tavern, confessed to a plot to murder the broker, and rob him of his pocket-book, and inculpated the Count in the crime.

Another version of the story was, that the Count Van Horn had deposited with the broker bank shares to the amount of eighty-eight thousand livres; that he had sought him in this tavern, which was one of his resorts, and had demanded the shares; that the Jew had denied the deposit; that a quarrel had ensued, in the course of which the Jew struck the Count in the face; that the latter, transported with rage, had snatched up a knife from a table, and wounded the Jew in the shoulder; and that thereupon De Mille, who was present, and who had likewise been defrauded by the broker, fell on him, and despatched him with blows of a poniard, and seized upon his pocket-book: that he had offered to divide the contents of the latter with the Count, *pro rata*, of what the usurer had defrauded them; that the latter had refused the proposition with disdain, and that, at a noise of persons approaching, both had attempted to escape from the premises, but had been taken.

Regard the story in any way they might, appearances were terribly against the Count, and the noble assemblage was in great consternation. What was to be done to ward off so foul a disgrace and to save their illustrious escutcheons from this murderous stain of blood? Their first attempt was to prevent the affair from going to trial, and their relative from being dragged before a criminal tribunal, on so horrible and degrading a charge. They applied, therefore, to the Regent, to intervene his power; to treat the Count as having acted under an access of his mental malady; and to shut him up in a madhouse. The Regent was deaf to their solicitations. He replied, coldly, that if the Count was a madman, one could not get rid too quickly of madmen who were furious in their insanity. The crime was too public and atrocious to be hushed up, or slurred over; justice must take its course.

Seeing there was no avoiding the humiliating scene of a public trial, the noble relatives of the Count endeavored to predispose the minds of the magistrates before whom he was to be arraigned. They accordingly made urgent and eloquent representations of the high descent, and noble and powerful connections of the Count; set forth the circumstances of his early history; his mental malady; the nervous irritability to which he was subject, and his extreme sensitiveness to insult or contradiction. By these means, they sought to prepare the judges to interpret every thing in favor of the Count, and, even if it should prove that he had inflicted the mortal blow on the usurer, to attribute it to access of insanity provoked by insult.

To give full effect to these representations, the noble conclave determined to bring upon the judges the dazzling rays of the whole assembled aristocracy. Accordingly, on the day that the trial took place, the relations of the Count, to the number of fifty-seven persons, of both sexes, and of the highest rank, repaired in a body to the Palace of Justice, and took their stations, in a long corridor which led to the court-room. Here, as the judges entered, they had to pass in review this array of lofty and noble personages, who saluted them mournfully and significantly, as they passed. Ally one conversant with the stately pride and jealous dignity of the French noblesse of that day, may imagine the extreme state of sensitiveness that produced this self-abasement. It was confidently presumed, however, by the noble suppliants, that having once brought themselves to this measure, their influence over the tribunal would be irresistible.

There was one lady present, however, Madame de Beauffremont, who was affected with the Scottish gift of second sight, and related such dismal and sinister apparitions as passing before her eyes, that many of her female companions were filled with doleful presentiments.

Unfortunately for the Count, there was another interest at work, more powerful even than the high aristocracy. The infamous but all-potent Abbé Dubois, the grand favorite and bosom counsellor of the Regent, was deeply interested in the scheme of Law, and the prosperity of his bank, and of course in the security of the stock-brokers. Indeed, the Regent himself is said to have dipped deep in the Mississippi scheme. Dubois and Law, therefore, exerted their influence to the utmost to have the tragic affair pushed to the extremity of the law, and the murder of the broker punished in the most signal and appalling manner. Certain it is, the trial was neither long nor intricate. The Count and his fellow-prisoner were equally inculpated in the crime, and both were condemned to a death the most horrible and ignominious—to be broken alive on the wheel!

As soon as the sentence of the court was made public, all the nobility, in any degree related to the house of Van Horn, went into mourning. Another grand aristocratical assemblage was held, and a petition to the Regent, on behalf of the Count, was drawn out and left with the Marquis de Créqui for signature. This petition set forth the previous insanity of the Count, and showed that it was an hereditary malady in his family. It stated various circumstances in mitigation of his offence, and implored that his sentence might be commuted to perpetual imprisonment.

Upward of fifty names of the highest nobility, beginning with the Prince de Ligne, and including cardinals, archbishops, dukes, marquises, etc. together with ladies of equal rank, were signed to this petition. By one of the caprices of human pride and vanity, it became an object of ambition to get enrolled among the illustrious suppliants; a kind of testimonial of noble blood, to prove relationship to a murderer! The Marquis de Créqui was absolutely besieged by applicants to sign, and had to refer their claims to this singular honor, to the Prince de Ligne, the grandfather of the Count. Many who were excluded were highly incensed, and numerous feuds took place. Nay, the affronts thus given to the morbid pride of some aristocratical families, passed from generation to generation; for, fifty years afterward, the Duchess of Mazarin complained of a slight which her father had received from the Marquis de Créqui; which proved to be something connected with the signature of this petition.

This important document being completed, the illustrious body of petitioners, male and female, on Saturday evening, the eve of Palm Sunday, repaired to the Palais Royal, the residence of the Regent, and were ushered, with great ceremony, but profound silence, into his hall of council. They had appointed four of their number as deputies, to present the petition, viz.: the Cardinal de Rohan, the Duke de Havré, the Prince de Ligne, and the Marquis de Créqui. After a little while, the deputies were summoned to the cabinet of the Regent. They entered, leaving the assembled petitioners in a state of the greatest anxiety. As time slowly wore away, and the evening advanced, the gloom of the company increased. Several of the ladies prayed devoutly; the good Princess of Armagnac told her beads.

The petition was received by the Regent with a most unpropitious aspect. "In asking the pardon of the criminal," said he, "you display more zeal for the house of Van Horn, than for the service of the king." The noble deputies enforced the petition by every argument in their power. They supplicated the Regent to consider that the infamous punishment in question would reach not merely the person of the condemned, not merely the house of Van Horn, but also the genealogies of princely and illustrious families, in whose armorial bearings might be found quarterings of this dishonored name.

"Gentlemen," replied the Regent, "it appears to me the disgrace consists in the crime, rather than in the punishment."

The Prince de Ligne spoke with warmth: "I have in my genealogical standard," said he, "four escutcheons of Van Horn, and of course have four ancestors of that house. I must have them erased and effaced, and there would be so many blank spaces, like holes, in my heraldic ensigns. There is not a sovereign family which would not suffer, through the rigor of your Royal Highness; nay, all the world knows, that in the thirty-two quarterings of Madame, your Mother, there is an escutcheon of Van Horn."

"Very well," replied the Regent, "I will share the disgrace with you, gentlemen."

Seeing that a pardon could not be obtained, the Cardinal de Rohan and the Marquis de Créqui left the cabinet; but the Prince de Ligne and the Duke de Havré remained behind. The honor of their houses, more than the life of the unhappy Count, was the great object of their solicitude. They now endeavored to obtain a minor grace. They represented, that in the Netherlands, and in Germany, there was an important difference in the public mind as to the mode of inflicting the punishment of death upon persons of quality. That decapitation had no influence on the fortunes of the family of the executed, but that the punishment of the wheel was such an infamy, that the uncles, aunts, brothers, and sisters, of the criminal, and his whole family, for three succeeding generations, were excluded from all noble chapters, princely abbeys, sovereign bishoprics, and even Teutonic commanderies of the Order of Malta. They showed how this would operate immediately upon the fortunes of a sister of the Count, who was on the point of being received as a canoness into one of the noble chapters.

While this scene was going on in the cabinet of the Regent, the illustrious assemblage of petitioners remained in the hall of council, in the most gloomy state of suspense. The reentrance from the cabinet of the Cardinal de Rohan and the Marquis de Créqui, with pale downcast countenances, had struck a chill into every heart. Still they lingered until near midnight, to learn the result of the after application. At length the cabinet conference was at an end. The Regent came forth, and saluted the high personages of the assemblage in a courtly manner. One old lady of quality, Madame de Guyon, whom he had known in his infancy, he kissed on the cheek, calling her his "good aunt." He made a most ceremonious salutation to the stately Marchioness de Créqui, telling her he was charmed to see her at the Palais Royal; "a compliment very ill-timed," said the Marchioness, "considering the circumstance which brought me there." He then conducted the ladies to the door of the second saloon, and there dismissed them, with the most ceremonious politeness.

The application of the Prince de Ligne and the Duke de Havré, for a change of the mode of punishment, had, after much difficulty, been successful. The Regent had promised solemnly to send a letter of commutation to the attorney-general on Holy Monday the 25th of March, at five o'clock in the morning. According to the same promise, a scaffold would be arranged in the cloister of the Conciergerie, or prison, where the Count would be beheaded on the same morning, immediately after having received absolution. This mitigation of the form of punishment gave but little consolation to the great body of petitioners, who had been anxious for the pardon of the youth: it was looked upon as all important, however, by the Prince de Ligne, who, as has been before observed, was exquisitely alive to the dignity of his family.

The Bishop of Bayeux and the Marquis de Créqui visited the unfortunate youth in prison. He had just received the communion in the chapel of the Conciergerie, and was kneeling before the altar, listening to a mass for the dead, which was performed at his request. He protested his innocence of any intention to murder the Jew, but did not deign to allude to the accusation of robbery. He made the Bishop and the Marquis promise to see his brother the Prince, and inform him of this his dying asseveration.

Two other of his relations, the Prince Rebecq-Montmorency and the Marshal Van Isenghien, visited him secretly, and offered him poison, as a means of evading the disgrace of a public execution. On his refusing to take it, they left him with high indignation. "Miserable man!" said they, "you are fit only to perish by the hand of the executioner!"

The Marquis de Créqui sought the executioner of Paris, to bespeak an easy and decent death for the unfortunate youth, "Do not make him suffer," said he; "uncover no part of him but the neck; and have his body placed in a coffin before you deliver it to his family." The executioner promised all that was requested, but declined a rouleau of a hundred louis-d'ors which the Marquis would have put into his hand. "I am paid by the King for fulfilling my office," said he; and added, that he had already refused a like sum, offered by another relation of the Marquis.

The Marquis de Créqui returned home in a state of deep affliction. There he found a letter from the Duke de St. Simon, the familiar friend of the Regent, repeating the promise of that Prince, that the punishment of the wheel should be commuted to decapitation.

"Imagine," says the Marchioness de Créqui, who in her memoirs gives a detailed account of this affair, "imagine what we experienced, and what was our astonishment, our grief, and indignation, when, on Tuesday the 26th of March, an hour after midday, word was brought us that the Count Van Horn had been exposed on the wheel, in the Place de Grève, since half-past six in the morning, on the same scaffold with the Piedmontese, De Mille, and that he had been tortured previous to execution!"

One more scene of aristocratic pride closed this tragic story. The Marquis de Créqui, on receiving this astounding news, immediately arrayed himself in the uniform of a general officer, with his cordon of nobility on the coat. He ordered six valets to attend him in grand livery, and two of his carriages, each with six horses, to be brought forth. In this sumptuous state, he set off for the Palace de Gréve, where he had been preceded by the Princes de Ligne, de Rohan, de Croüy, and the Duke de Havré.

The Count Van Horn was already dead, and it was believed that the executioner had had the charity to give him the coup de grace, or "death blow," at eight o'clock in the morning. At five o'clock in the evening, when the Judge Commissary left his post at the Hotel de Ville, these noblemen, with their own hands, aided to detach the mutilated remains of their relation; the Marquis de Créqui placed them in one of his carriages, and bore them off to his hotel, to receive the last sad obsequies.

The conduct of the Regent in this affair excited general indignation. His needless severity was attributed by some to vindictive jealousy; by others to the persevering machinations of Law and the Abbé Dubois. The house of Van Horn, and the high nobility of Flanders and Germany, considered themselves flagrantly outraged: many schemes of vengeance were talked of, and a hatred engendered against the Regent, that followed him through life, and was wreaked with bitterness upon his memory after his death.

The following letter is said to have been written to the Regent by the Prince Van Horn, to whom the former had adjudged the confiscated effects of the Count:

"I do not complain, sir, of the death of my brother, but I complain that your Royal Highness has violated in his person the rights of the kingdom, the nobility, and the nation. I thank you for the confiscation of his effects; but I should think myself as much disgraced as he, should I accept any favor at your hands. *I hope that God and the King may render to you as strict justice as you have rendered to my unfortunate brother.*"

Don Juan: A Spectral Research

> I have heard of spirits walking with aërial bodies, and have been wondered at by others; but I must only wonder at myself, for, if they be not mad, I'me come to my own buriall.
>
> SHIRLEY'S "WITTY FAIRIE ONE"

EVERY BODY HAS HEARD OF THE FATE OF DON JUAN, THE FAMOUS LIBERTINE of Seville, who for his sins against the fair sex, and other minor peccadilloes, was hurried away to the internal regions. His story has been illustrated in play, in pantomime, and farce, on every stage in Christendom, until at length it has been rendered the theme of the opera of operas, and embalmed to endless duration in the glorious music of Mozart. I well recollect the effect of this story upon my feelings in my boyish days, though represented in grotesque pantomime; the awe with which I contemplated the monumental statue on horseback of the murdered commander, gleaming by pale moonlight in the convent cemetery: how my heart quaked as he bowed his marble head, and accepted the impious invitation of Don Juan: how each foot-fall of the statue smote upon my heart, as I heard it approach, step by step, through the echoing corridor, and beheld it enter, and advance, a moving figure of stone, to the supper table! But then the convivial scene in the charnel house, where Don Juan returned the visit of the statue; was offered a banquet of sculls and bones and on refusing to partake, was hurled into a yawning gulf under a tremendous shower of fire! These were accumulated horrors enough to shake the nerves of the most pantomime-loving schoolboy. Many have supposed the story of Don Juan a mere fable, I myself thought so once; but "seeing is believing." I have since beheld the very scene where it took place, and now to indulge any doubt on the subject, would be preposterous.

I was one night perambulating the streets of Seville, in company with a Spanish friend, a curious investigator of the popular traditions and other good-for-nothing lore of the city, and who was kind enough to imagine he had met, in me, with a congenial spirit. In the course of our rambles, we were passing by a heavy dark gateway, opening into the court-yard of a convent, when he laid his hand upon my arm: "Stop!" said he; "this is the convent of San Francisco; there is a story connected with it, which I am sure must be known to you. You cannot but have heard of Don Juan and the marble statue."

"Undoubtedly," replied I; "it has been familiar to me from childhood."

"Well, then, it was in the cemetery of this very convent that the event took place."

"Why, you do not mean to say that the story is founded on fact?"

"Undoubtedly it is. The circumstances of the case are said to have occurred during the reign of Alfonso XI, Don Juan was of the noble family of Tenorio, one of the most illustrious houses of Andalusia. His father, Don Diégo Tenorio, was a favorite of the king, and his family ranked among the *veintecuatros*, or magistrates, of the city. Presuming on his high descent and powerful connections, Don Juan set no bounds to his excesses: no female, high or low, was sacred from his pursuit; and he soon became the scandal of Seville. One of his most daring outrages was, to penetrate by night into the palace of Don Gonzalo de Ulloa, Commander of the Order of Calatrava, and attempt to carry off his daughter. The household was alarmed; a scuffle in the dark took place; Don Juan escaped, but the unfortunate commander was found weltering in his blood, and expired without being able to name his murderer. Suspicions attached to Don Juan; he did not stop to meet the investigations of justice and the vengeance of the powerful family of Ulloa, but fled from Seville, and took refuge with his uncle, Don Pedro Tenorio, at that time ambassador at the court of Naples. Here he remained until the agitation occasioned by the murder of Don Gonzalo had time to subside; and the scandal which the affair might cause to both the families of Ulloa and Tenorio had induced them to hush it up. Don Juan, however, continued his libertine career at Naples, until at length his excesses forfeited the protection of his uncle the ambassador, and obliged him again to flee. He had made his way back to Seville, trusting that his past misdeeds were forgotten, or rather trusting to his dare-devil spirit and the power of his family, to carry him through all difficulties.

"It was shortly after his return, and while in the height of his arrogance, that on visiting this very convent of Francisco, he beheld on a monument the equestrian statue of the murdered commander, who had been buried within the walls of this sacred edifice, where the family of Ulloa had a chapel. It was on this occasion that Don Juan, in a moment of impious levity, invited the statue to the banquet, the awful catastrophe of which has given such celebrity to his story."

"And pray how much of this story," said I, "is believed in Seville?"

"The whole of it by the populace; with whom it has been a favorite tradition since time immemorial, and who crowd to the theatres to see it represented in dramas written long since by Tyrso de Molina, and another of our popular writers. Many in our higher ranks also, accustomed from childhood to this story, would feel somewhat indignant at hearing it treated with contempt. An attempt has been made to explain the whole, by asserting that, to put an end to the extravagances of Don Juan, and to pacify the family of Ulloa, without exposing the delinquent to the degrading penalties of justice, he was decoyed into this. convent under false pretext, and either plunged into a perpetual dungeon, or privately hurried out of existence; while the story of the statue was circulated by the monks, to account for his sudden disappearance. The populace, however, are not to be cajoled out of a ghost story by any of these plausible explanations; and the marble statue still strides the stage, and Don Juan is still plunged into the infernal regions, as an awful warning to all rake-helly youngsters, in like case offending."

While my companion was relating these anecdotes, we had traversed the exterior court-yard of the convent, and made our way into a great interior court; partly surrounded by cloisters and dormitories, partly by chapels, and having a large fountain in the centre. The pile had evidently once been extensive and magnificent; but it was for the greater part in ruins. By the light of the stars, and of twinkling lamps placed here and there in the chapels and corridors, I could see that many of the columns and arches were broken; the walls were rent and riven; while burnt beams and rafters showed the destructive effects of fire. The whole place had a desolate air; the night breeze rustled through grass and weeds flaunting out of the crevices of the walls, or from the shattered columns; the bat flitted about the vaulted passages, and the owl hooted from the ruined belfry. Never was any scene more completely fitted for a ghost story.

While I was indulging in picturings of the fancy, proper to such a place, the deep chant of the monks from the convent church came swelling upon the ear. "It is the vesper service," said my companion; "follow me."

Leading the way across the court of the cloisters, and through one or two ruined passages, he reached the portal of the church, and pushing open a wicket, cut in the folding-doors, we found ourselves in the deep arched vestibule of the sacred edifice.

To our left was the choir, forming one end of the church, and having a low vaulted ceiling, which gave it the look of a cavern. About this were ranged the monks, seated on stools, and chanting from immense books placed on music stands, and having the notes scored in such gigantic characters as to be legible from every part of the choir. A few lights on these music stands dimly illumined the choir, gleamed on the shaven heads of the monks, and threw their shadows on the walls. They were gross, blue-bearded, bullet-headed men, with bass voices, of deep metallic tone, that reverberated out of the cavernous choir.

To our right extended the great body of the church. It was spacious and lofty; some of the side chapels had gilded grates, and were decorated with images and paintings, representing the sufferings of our Saviour. Aloft was a great painting by Murillo, but too much in the dark to be distinguished. The gloom of the whole church was but faintly relieved by the reflected light from the choir, and the glimmering here and there of a votive lamp before the shrine of the saint.

As my eye roamed about the shadowy pile, it was struck with the dimly seen figure of a man on horseback, near a distant altar. I touched my companion, and pointed to it: "The spectre statue!" said I.

"No," replied he; "it is the statue of the blessed St. Iago; the statue of the commander was in the cemetery of the convent, and was destroyed at the time of the conflagration. But," added he, "as I see you take a proper interest in these kind of stories, come with me to the other end of the church, where our whisperings will not disturb these holy fathers at their devotions, and I will tell you another story, that has been current for some generations in our city, by which you will find that Don Juan is not the only libertine that has been the object of supernatural castigation in Seville."

I accordingly followed him with noiseless tread to the farther part of the church, where we took our seats on the steps of an altar opposite to the suspicious-looking figure on horseback, and there, in a low mysterious voice, he related to me the following narrative:—

"There was once in Seville a gay young fellow, Don Manuel de Manara by name, who having come to a great estate by the death of his father, gave the reins to his passions, and plunged into all kinds of dissipation. Like Don Juan, whom he seemed to have taken for a model, he became famous for his enterprises among the fair sex, and was the cause of doors being barred and windows grated with more than usual strictness. All in vain. No balcony was too high for him to scale: no bolt nor bar was proof against his efforts: and his very name was a word of terror to all the jealous husbands and cautious fathers of Seville. His exploits extended to country as well as city; and in the village dependent on his castle, scarce a rural beauty was safe from his arts and enterprises.

"As he was one day ranging the streets of Seville, with several of his dissolute companions, he beheld a procession, about to enter the gate of a convent. In the centre was a young female, arrayed in the dress of a bride; it was a novice, who, having accomplished her year of probation, was about to take the black veil, and consecrate herself to heaven. The companions of Don Manuel drew back, out of respect to the sacred pageant; but he pressed forward, with his usual impetuosity, to gain a near view of the novice. He almost jostled her, in passing through the portal of the church, when, on her turning round, he beheld the countenance of a beautiful village girl, who had been the object of his ardent pursuit, but who had been spirited secretly out of his reach by her relatives. She recognized him at the same moment, and fainted: but was borne within the grate of the chapel. It was supposed the agitation of the ceremony and the heat of the throng had overcome her. After some time, the curtain which hung within the grate was drawn up: there stood the novice, pale and trembling, surrounded by the abbess and the nuns. The ceremony proceeded; the crown of flowers was taken from her head, she was shorn of her silken tresses, received the black veil, and went passively through the remainder of the ceremony.

"Don Manuel de Manara, on the contrary, was roused to fury at the sight of this sacrifice. His passion, which had almost faded away in the absence of the object, now glowed with tenfold ardor, being inflamed by the difficulties placed in his way, and piqued by the measures which had been taken to defeat him. Never had the object of his pursuit appeared so lovely and desirable as when within the grate of the convent; and he swore to have her, in defiance of heaven and earth. By dint of bribing a female servant of the convent, he contrived to convey letters to her, pleading his passion in the most eloquent and seductive terms. How successful they were, is only matter of conjecture; certain it is, he undertook one night to scale the garden wall of the convent, either to carry off the nun, or gain admission to her cell. Just as he was mounting the wall, he was suddenly plucked back, and a stranger, muffled in a cloak, stood before him.

" 'Rash man, forbear!' cried he: 'is it not enough to have violated all human ties? Wouldst thou steal a bride from heaven!'

"The sword of Don Manuel had been drawn on the instant, and furious at this interruption, he passed it through the body of the stranger, who fell dead at his feet. Hearing approaching footsteps, he fled the fatal spot, and mounting his horse, which was at hand, retreated to his estate in the country, at no great distance from Seville. Here he remained throughout the next day, full of horror and remorse; dreading lest he should be known as the murderer of the deceased, and fearing each moment the arrival of the officers of justice.

"The day passed, however, without molestation; and, as the evening advanced, unable any longer to endure this state of uncertainty and apprehension, he ventured back to Seville. Irresistibly his footsteps took the direction of the convent; but he paused and hovered at a distance from the scene of blood. Several persons were gathered round the place, one of whom was busy nailing something against the convent wall. After a while they dispersed, and one passed near to Don Manuel. The latter addressed him, with hesitating voice.

" 'Señor,' said he, 'may I ask the reason of yonder throng?'

" 'A cavalier,' replied the other, 'has been murdered.'

" 'Murdered!' echoed Don Manuel; 'and can you tell me his name?'

" 'Don Manuel de Manara,' replied the stranger, and passed on.

" 'Don Manuel was startled at this mention of his own name; especially when applied to the murdered man. He ventured, when it was entirely deserted, to approach the fatal spot. A small cross had been nailed against the wall, as is customary in Spain, to mark the place where a murder has been committed; and just below it he read, by the twinkling light of a lamp; 'Here was murdered Don Manuel de Manara. Pray to God for his soul!'

"Still more confounded and perplexed by this inscription, he wandered about the streets until the night was far advanced, and all was still and lonely. As he entered the principal square, the light of torches suddenly broke on him, and he beheld a grand funeral procession moving across it. There was a great train of priests, and many persons of dignified appearance, in ancient Spanish dresses, attending as mourners, none of whom he knew. Accosting a servant who followed in the train, he demanded the name of the defunct.

" 'Don Manuel de Manara,' was the reply; and it went cold to his heart. He looked, and indeed beheld the armorial bearings of his family emblazoned on the funeral escutcheons. Yet not one of his family was to be seen among the mourners. The mystery was more and more incomprehensible.

"He followed the procession as it moved on to the cathedral. The bier was deposited before the high altar; the funeral service was commenced, and the grand organ began to peal through the vaulted aisles.

"Again the youth ventured to question this awful pageant. 'Father,' said he, with trembling voice, to one of the priests, 'who is this you are about to inter?'

" 'Don Manuel de Manara!' replied the priest.

" 'Father,' cried Don Manuel, impatiently, 'you are deceived. This is some imposture. Know that Don Manuel de Manara is alive and well, and now stands before you. *I* am Don Manuel de Manara!'

" 'Avaunt, rash youth!' cried the priest; 'know that Don Manuel de Manara is dead!—is dead!—is dead!—and we are all souls from purgatory, his deceased relatives and ancestors, and others that have been aided by masses from his family, who are permitted to come here and pray for the repose of his soul!'

"Don Manuel cast round a fearful glance upon the assemblage, in antiquated Spanish garbs, and recognized in their pale and ghastly countenances the portraits of many an ancestor that hung in the family picture-gallery. He now lost all self-command, rushed up to the bier, and beheld the counterpart of himself, but in the fixed and livid lineaments of death. Just at that moment the whole choir burst forth with a '*Requiescat in pace,*' that shook the vaults of the cathedral. Don Manuel sank senseless on the pavement. He was found there early the next morning by the sacristan, and conveyed to his home. When sufficiently recovered, he sent for a friar, and made a full confession of all that had happened.

" 'My son,' said the friar, 'all this is a miracle and a mystery intended for thy conversion and salvation. The corpse thou hast seen was a token that thou hadst died to sin and the world; take warning by it, and henceforth live to righteousness and heaven!'

"Don Manuel did take warning by it. Guided by the councils of the worthy friar, he disposed of all his temporal affairs; dedicated the greater part of his wealth to pious uses, especially to the performance of masses for souls in purgatory; and finally, entering a convent, became one of the most zealous and exemplary monks in Seville."

While my companion was relating this story, my eyes wandered, from time to time, about the dusky church. Methought the burly countenances of the monks in the distant choir assumed a pallid, ghastly hue, and their deep metallic voices a sepulchral sound.

By the time the story was ended, they had ended their chant; and, extinguishing their lights, glided one by one, like shadows, through a small door in the side of the choir. A deeper gloom prevailed over the church; the figure opposite me on horseback grew more and more spectral; and I almost expected to see it bow its head.

"It is time to be off," said my companion, "unless we intend to sup with the statue."

"I have no relish for such fare nor such company," replied I; and following my companion, we groped our way through the mouldering cloisters. As we passed by the ruined cemetery, keeping up a casual conversation, by way of dispelling the loneliness of the scene, I called to mind the words of the poet:

> —The tombs
> And monumental caves of death look cold,
> And shoot a chillness to my trembling heart!
> Give me thy hand, and let me hear thy voice;
> Nay, speak—and let me hear thy voice;
> Mine own affrights me with its echoes.

There wanted nothing but the marble statue of the commander, striding along the echoing cloisters, to complete the haunted scene.

Since that time, I never fail to attend the theatre whenever the story of Don Juan is represented, whether in pantomime or opera. In the sepulchral scene, I feel myself quite at home; and when the statue makes his appearance, I greet him as an old acquaintance. When the audience applaud, I look round upon them with a degree of compassion; "Poor souls!" I say to myself, "they think they are pleased; they think they enjoy this piece, and yet they consider the whole as a fiction! How much more would they enjoy it, if, like me, they knew it to be true—*and had seen the very place*!"

Legend of the Engulphed Convent

At the dark and melancholy period when Don Roderick the Goth and his chivalry were overthrown on the banks of the Guadalete, and all Spain was overrun by the Moors, great was the devastation of churches and convents throughout that pious kingdom. The miraculous fate of one of those holy piles is thus recorded in an authentic legend of those days.

On the summit of a hill, not very distant from the capital city of Toledo, stood an ancient convent and chapel, dedicated to the invocation of Saint Benedict, and inhabited by a sisterhood of Benedictine nuns. This holy asylum was confined to females of noble lineage. The younger sisters of the highest families were here given in religious marriage to their Saviour, in order that the portions of their elder sisters might be increased, and they enabled to make suitable matches on earth; or that the family wealth might go undivided to elder brothers, and the dignity of their ancient houses be protected from decay. The convent was renowned, therefore, for enshrining within its walls a sisterhood of the purest blood, the most immaculate virtue, and most resplendent beauty, of all Gothic Spain.

When the Moors overran the kingdom, there was nothing that more excited their hostility, than these virgin asylums. The very sight of a convent-spire was sufficient to set their Moslem blood in a foment, and they sacked it with as fierce a zeal as though the sacking of a nunnery were a sure passport to Elysium.

Tidings of such outrages, committed in various parts of the kingdom, reached this noble sanctuary, and filled it with dismay. The danger came nearer and nearer; the infidel hosts were spreading all over the country; Toledo itself was captured; there was no flying from the convent, and no security within its walls.

In the midst of this agitation, the alarm was given one day, that a great band of Saracens were spurring across the plain. In an instant the whole convent was a scene of confusion. Some of the nuns wrung their fair hands at the windows; others waved their veils, and uttered shrieks, from the tops of the towers, vainly hoping to draw relief from a country overrun by the foe. The sight of these innocent doves thus fluttering about their dove-cote, but increased the zealot fury of the whiskered Moors. They thundered at the portal, and at every blow the ponderous gates trembled on their hinges.

The nuns now crowded round the abbess. They had been accustomed to look up to her as all-powerful, and they now implored her protection. The mother abbess looked with a rueful eye upon the treasures of beauty and vestal virtue exposed to such imminent peril. Alas! how was she to protect them from the spoiler! She had, it is true, experienced many signal interpositions of Providence in her individual favor. Her early days had been passed amid the temptations of a court, where her virtue had been purified by repeated trials, from none of which had she escaped but by miracle. But were miracles never to cease? Could she hope that the marvellous protection shown to herself, would be extended to a whole sisterhood? There was no other resource. The Moors were at the threshold; a few moments more, and the convent would be at their mercy. Summoning her nuns to follow her, she hurried into the chapel, and throwing herself on her knees before the image of the blessed Mary, "Oh, holy Lady!" exclaimed she, "oh, most pure and immaculate of virgins! thou seest our extremity. The ravager is at the gate, and there is none on earth to help us! Look down with pity, and grant that the earth may gape and swallow us, rather than that our cloister vows should suffer violation!"

The Moors redoubled their assault upon the portal; the gates gave way, with a tremendous crash; a savage yell of exultation arose; when of a sudden the earth yawned; down sank the convent, with its cloisters, its dormitories, and all its nuns. The chapel tower was the last that sank, the bell ringing forth a peal of triumph in the very teeth of the infidels.

Forty years had passed and gone, since the period of this miracle. The subjugation of Spain was complete. The Moors lorded it over city and country; and such of the Christian population as remained, and were permitted to exercise their religion, did it in humble resignation to the Moslem sway.

At this time, a Christian cavalier, of Cordova, hearing that a patriotic band of his countrymen had raised the standard of the cross in the mountains of the Asturias, resolved to join them, and unite in breaking the yoke of bondage. Secretly arming himself, and caparisoning his steed, he set forth from Cordova, and pursued his course by unfrequented mule-paths, and along the dry channels made by winter torrents. His spirit burned with indignation, whenever, on commanding a view over a long sweeping plain, he beheld the mosque swelling in the distance, and the Arab horsemen careering about, as if the rightful lords of the soil. Many a deep-drawn sigh, and heavy groan, also, did the good cavalier utter, on passing the ruins of churches and convents desolated by the conquerors.

It was on a sultry midsummer evening, that this wandering cavalier, in skirting a hill thickly covered with forest, heard the faint tones of a vesper bell sounding melodiously in the air, and seeming to come from the summit of the hill. The cavalier crossed himself with wonder, at this unwonted and Christian sound. He supposed it to proceed from one of those humble chapels and hermitages permitted to exist through the indulgence of the Moslem conquerors. Turning his steed up a narrow path of the forest, he sought this sanctuary, in hopes of finding a hospitable shelter for the night. As he advanced, the trees threw a deep gloom around him, and the bat flitted across his path. The bell ceased to toll, and all was silence.

Presently a choir of female voices came stealing sweetly through the forest, chanting the evening service, to the solemn accompaniment of an organ. The heart of the good cavalier melted at the sound, for it recalled the happier days of his country. Urging forward his weary steed, he at length arrived at a broad grassy area, on the summit of the hill, surrounded by the forest. Here the melodious voices rose in full chorus, like the swelling of the breeze; but whence they came, he could not tell. Sometimes they were before, sometimes behind him; sometimes in the air, sometimes as if from within the bosom of the earth. At length they died away, and a holy stillness settled on the place.

The cavalier gazed around with bewildered eye. There was neither chapel nor convent, nor humble hermitage, to be seen; nothing but a moss-grown stone pinnacle, rising out of the centre of the area, surmounted by a cross. The green sward appeared to have been sacred from the tread of man or beast, and the surrounding trees bent toward the cross, as if in adoration.

The cavalier felt a sensation of holy awe. He alighted, and tethered his steed on the skirts of the forest, where he might crop the tender herbage; then approaching the cross, he knelt and poured forth his evening prayers before this relic of the Christian days of Spain. His orisons being concluded, he laid himself down at the foot of the pinnacle, and reclining his head against one of its stones, fell into a deep sleep.

About midnight, he was awakened by the tolling of a bell, and found himself lying before the gate of an ancient convent. A train of nuns passed by, each bearing a taper. He rose and followed them into the chapel; in the centre was a bier, on which lay the corpse of an aged nun. The organ performed a solemn requiem, the nuns joining in chorus. When the funeral service was finished, a melodious voice chanted, "*Requiescat in pace!*"—"May she rest in peace!" The lights immediately vanished: the whole passed away as a dream; and the cavalier found himself at the foot of the cross, and beheld, by the faint rays of the rising moon, his steed quietly grazing near him.

When the day dawned, he descended the hill, and following the course of a small brook, came to a cave, at the entrance of which was seated an ancient man, in hermit's garb, with rosary and cross, and a beard that descended to his girdle. He was one of those holy anchorites permitted by the Moors to live unmolested in the dens and caves, and humble hermitages, and even to practise the rites of their religion. The cavalier, dismounting, knelt and craved a benediction. He then related all that had befallen him in the night, and besought the hermit to explain the mystery.

"What thou hast heard and seen, my son," replied the other, "is but a type and shadow of the woes of Spain."

He then related the foregoing story of the miraculous deliverance of the convent.

"Forty years," added the holy man, "have elapsed since this event, yet the bells of that sacred edifice are still heard, from time to time, sounding from underground, together with the pealing of the organ, and the chanting of the choir. The Moors avoid this neighborhood, as haunted ground, and the whole place, as thou mayest perceive, has become covered with a thick and lonely forest."

The cavalier listened with wonder to the story. For three days and nights did he keep vigils with the holy man beside the cross; but nothing more was to be seen of nun or convent. It is supposed that, forty years having elapsed, the natural lives of all the nuns were finished, and the cavalier had beheld the obsequies of the last. Certain it is, that from that time, bell, and organ, and choral chant, have never more been heard.

The mouldering pinnacle, surmounted by the cross, remains an object of pious pilgrimage. Some say that it anciently stood in front of the convent, but others that it was the spire which remained above ground, when the main body of the building sank, like the topmast of some tall ship that has foundered. These pious believers maintain, that the convent is miraculously preserved entire in the centre of the mountain, where, if proper excavations were made, it would be found, with all its treasures, and monuments, and shrines, and relics, and the tombs of its virgin nuns.

Should any one doubt the truth of this marvellous interposition of the Virgin, to protect the vestal purity of her votaries let him read the excellent work entitled "España Triumphante," written by Fray Antonio de Sancta Maria, a barefoot friar of the Carmelite order, and he will doubt no longer.

The Phantom Island

Break, Phantsie, from thy cave of cloud,
And wave thy purple wings,
Now all thy figures are allowed,
And various shapes of things.
Create of airy forms a stream;
It must have blood and naught of phlegm;
And though it he a walking dream,
Yet let it like an odor rise
To all the senses here,
And fall like sleep upon their eyes,
Op music on their ear.

—Ben Jonson

There are more things in heaven and earth than are dreamed of in our philosophy," and among these may he placed that marvel and mystery of the seas, the Island of St. Brandan. Those who have read the history of the Canaries, the fortunate islands of the ancients, may remember the wonders told of this enigmatical island. Occasionally it would be visible from their shores, stretching away in the clear bright west, to all appearance substantial like themselves, and still more beautiful. Expeditions would launch forth from the Canaries to explore this land of promise. For a time its sun-gilt peaks and long, shadowy promontories would remain distinctly visible, but in proportion as the voyagers approached, peak and promontory would gradually fade away until nothing would remain but blue sky above, and deep blue water below. Hence this mysterious isle was stigmatized by ancient cosmographers with the name of Aprositus or the Inaccessible. The failure of numerous expeditions sent in quest of it, both in ancient and modern days, have at length caused its very existence to be called in question, and it has been rashly pronounced a mere optical illusion, like the Fata Morgana of the Straits of Messina, or has been classed with those unsubstantial regions known to mariners as Cape Fly Away and the coast of Cloud Land.

Let us not permit, however, the doubts of worldly-wise skeptics to rob us of all the glorious realms owned by happy credulity in days of yore. Be assured, reader of easy faith!—thou for whom it is my delight to labor—be assured that such an island actually exists, and has from time to time, been revealed to the gaze, and trodden by the feet, of favored mortals. Historians and philosophers may have their doubts, but its existence has been fully attested by that inspired race, the poets; who, being gifted with a kind of second sight, are enabled to discern those mysteries of nature hidden from the eyes of ordinary men. To this gifted race it has ever been a kind of wonder-land. Here once bloomed, and perhaps still blooms, the famous garden of the Hesperides, with its golden fruit. Here, too, the sorceress Armida had her enchanted garden, in which she held the Christian paladin, Rinaldo, in delicious but inglorious thraldom, as set forth in the immortal lay of Tasso. It was in this island that Sycorax the witch held sway, when the good Prospero and his infant daughter Miranda, were wafted to its shores. Who does not know the tale as told in the magic page of Shakspeare? The isle was then

—full of noises,
Sounds, and sweet airs, that give delight, and hurt not.

The island, in fact at different times, has been under the sway of different powers, genii of earth, and air, and ocean, who have made it their shadowy abode. Hither have retired many classic but broken-down deities, shorn of almost all their attributes, but who once ruled the poetic world. Here Neptune and Amphitrite hold a diminished court; sovereigns in exile. Their ocean chariot, almost a wreck, lies bottom upward in some sea-beaten cavern; their pursy Tritons and haggard Nereids bask listlessly like seals about the rocks. Sometimes those deities assume, it is said, a shadow of their ancient pomp, and glide in state about a summer sea; and then, as some tall Indiaman lies becalmed with idly flapping sail, her drowsy crew may hear the mellow note of the Triton's shell swelling upon the ear as the invisible pageant sweeps by.

On the shores of this wondrous isle the kraken heaves its unwieldy bulk and wallows many a rood. Here the sea-serpent, that mighty but much contested reptile, lies coiled up during the intervals of its revelations to the eyes of true believers. Here even the Flying Dutchman finds a port, and casts his anchor, and furls his shadowy sail, and takes a brief repose from his eternal cruisings.

In the deep bays and harbors of the island lies many a spellbound ship, long since given up as lost by the ruined merchant. Here too its crew, long, long bewailed in vain, lie sleeping from age to age, in mossy grottoes, or wander about in pleasing oblivion of all things. Here in caverns are garnered up the priceless treasures lost in the ocean. Here sparkles in vain the diamond and flames the carbuncle. Here are piled up rich bales of Oriental silks, boxes of pearls, and piles of golden ingots.

Such are some of the marvels related of this island, which may serve to throw light upon the following legend, of unquestionable truth, which I recommend to the implicit belief of the reader.

The Adalantado of the Seven Cities

A Legend of St. Brandan

In the early part of the fifteenth century, when Prince Henry of Portugal, of worthy memory, was pushing the career of discovery along the western coast of Africa, and the world was resounding with reports of golden regions on the mainland, and new-found islands in the ocean, there arrived at Lisbon an old bewildered pilot of the seas, who had been driven by tempests, he knew not whither, and raved about an island far in the deep, upon which he had landed, and which he had found peopled with Christians, and adorned with noble cities.

The inhabitants, he said, having never before been visited by a ship, gathered round, and regarded him with surprise. They told him they were descendants of a band of Christians, who fled from Spain when that country was conquered by the Moslems. They were curious about the state of their fatherland, and grieved to hear that the Moslems still held possession of the kingdom of Granada. They would have taken the old navigator to church, to convince him of their orthodoxy; but, either through lack of devotion, or lack of faith in their words, he declined their invitation, and preferred to return on board of his ship. He was properly punished. A furious storm arose, drove him from his anchorage, hurried him out to sea, and he saw no more of the unknown island.

This strange story caused great marvel in Lisbon and elsewhere. Those versed in history, remembered to have read, in an ancient chronicle, that, at the time of the conquest of Spain, in the eighth century, when the blessed cross was cast down, and the crescent erected in its place, and when Christian churches were turned into Moslem mosques, seven bishops, at the head of seven bands of pious exiles, had fled from the peninsula, and embarked in quest of some ocean island, or distant land, where they might found seven Christian cities, and enjoy their faith unmolested.

The fate of these saints errant had hitherto remained a mystery, and their story had faded from memory; the report of the old tempest-tossed pilot, however, revived this long-forgotten theme; and it was determined by the pious and enthusiastic, that the island thus accidentally discovered, was the identical place of refuge, whither the wandering bishops had been guided by a protecting Providence, and where they had folded their flocks.

This most excitable of worlds has always some darling object of chimerical enterprise; the "Island of the Seven Cities" now awakened as much interest and longing among zealous Christians, as has the renowned city of Timbuctoo among adventurous travellers, or the Northeast passage among hardy navigators; and it was a frequent prayer of the devout, that these scattered and lost portions of the Christian family might be discovered, and reunited to the great body of Christendom.

No one, however, entered into the matter with half the zeal of Don Fernando de Ulmo, a young cavalier, of high standing in the Portuguese court, and of most sanguine and romantic temperament. He had recently come to his estate, and had run the round of all kinds of pleasures and excitements, when this new theme of popular talk and wonder presented itself. The Island of the Seven Cities became now the constant subject of his thoughts by day, and his dreams by night: it even rivalled his passion for a beautiful girl, one of the greatest belles of Lisbon, to whom he was betrothed. At length, his imagination became so inflamed on the subject, that he determined to fit out an expedition, at his own expense, and set sail in quest of this sainted island. It could not be a cruise of any great extent; for, according to the calculations of the tempest-tossed pilot, it must be somewhere in the latitude of the Canaries; which at that time, when the new world was as yet undiscovered, formed the frontier of ocean enterprise. Don Fernando applied to the crown for countenance and protection. As he was a favorite at court, the usual patronage was readily extended to him; that is to say, he received a commission from the king, Don Ioam II, constituting him Adalantado, or military governor, of any country he might discover, with the single proviso, that he should bear all the expenses of the discovery, and pay a tenth of the profits to the crown.

Don Fernando now set to work in the true spirit of a projector. He sold acre after acre of solid land, and invested the proceeds in ships, guns, ammunition, and sea-stores. Even his old family mansion, in Lisbon, was mortgaged without scruple, for he looked forward to a palace in one of the Seven Cities, of which he was to be Adalantado. This was the age of nautical romance, when the thoughts of all speculative dreamers were turned to-the ocean. The scheme of Don Fernando, therefore, drew adventurers of every kind. The merchant promised himself new marts of opulent traffic; the soldier hoped to sack and plunder some one or other of those Seven Cities; even the fat monk shook off the sleep and sloth of the cloister, to join in a crusade which promised such increase to the possessions of the church.

One person alone regarded the whole project with sovereign contempt and growling hostility. This was Don Ramiro Alvarez, the father of the beautiful Serafina, to whom Don Fernando was betrothed. He was one of those perverse, matter-of-fact old men, who are prone to oppose every thing speculative and romantic. He had no faith in the Island of the Seven Cities; regarded the projected cruise as a crack-brained freak; looked with angry eye and internal heart-burning on the conduct of his intended son-in-law, chaffering away solid lands for lands in the moon; and scoffingly dubbed him Adalantado of Cloud Land. In fact, he had never really relished the intended match, to which his consent had been slowly extorted, by the tears and entreaties of his daughter. It is true he could have no reasonable objections to the youth, for Don Fernando was the very flower of Portuguese chivalry. No one could excel him at the tilting match, or the riding at the ring; none was more bold and dexterous in the bull fight; none composed more gallant madigrals in praise of his lady's charms, or sang them with sweeter tones to the accompaniment of her guitar; nor could any one handle the castanets and dance the bolero with more captivating grace. All these admirable qualities and endowments, however, though they had been sufficient to win the heart of Serafina, were nothing in the eyes of her unreasonable father. Oh Cupid, god of Love! why will fathers always be so unreasonable?

The engagement to Serafina had threatened at first to throw an obstacle in the way of the expedition of Don Fernando, and for a time perplexed him in the extreme. He was passionately attached to the young lady; but he was also passionately bent on this romantic enterprise. How should he reconcile the two passionate inclinations? A simple and obvious arrangement at length presented itself: marry Serafina, enjoy a portion of the honeymoon at once, and defer the rest until his return from the discovery of the Seven Cities!

He hastened to make known this most excellent arrangement to Don Ramiro, when the long-smothered wrath of the old cavalier burst forth. He reproached him with being the dupe of wandering vagabonds and wild schemers, and with squandering all his real possessions, in pursuit of empty bubbles. Don Fernando was too sanguine a projector, and too young a man, to listen tamely to such language. He acted with what is technically called "becoming spirit." A high quarrel ensued; Don Ramiro pronounced him a madman, and forbade all farther intercourse with his daughter, until he should give proof of returning sanity, by abandoning this madcap enterprise; while Don Fernando flung out of the house, more bent than ever on the expedition, from the idea of triumphing over the incredulity of the graybeard, when he should return successful. Don Ramiro's heart misgave him. Who knows, thought he, but this crack-brained visionary may persuade my daughter to elope with him, and share his throne in this unknown paradise of fools? If I could only keep her safe until his ships are fairly out at sea!

He repaired to her apartment, represented to her the sanguine, unsteady character of her lover and the chimerical value of his schemes, and urged the propriety of suspending all intercourse with him until he should recover from his present hallucination. She bowed her head as if in filial acquiescence, whereupon he folded her to his bosom with parental fondness and kissed away a tear that was stealing over her cheek, but as he left the chamber quietly turned the key on the lock; for though he was a fond father and had a high opinion of the submissive temper of his child, he had a still higher opinion of the conservative virtues of lock and key, and determined to trust to them until the caravels should sail. Whether the damsel had been in any wise shaken in her faith as to the schemes of her lover by her father's eloquence, tradition does not say; but certain it is, that, the moment she heard the key turn in the lock, she became a firm believer in the Island of the Seven Cities.

The door was locked; but her will was unconfined. A window of the chamber opened into one of those stone balconies, secured by iron bars, which project like huge cages from Portuguese and Spanish houses. Within this balcony the beautiful Serafina had her birds and flowers, and here she was accustomed to sit on moonlight nights as in a bower, and touch her guitar and sing like a wakeful nightingale. From this balcony an intercourse was now maintained between the lovers, against which the lock and key of

Don Ramiro were of no avail. All day would Fernando be occupied hurrying the equipments of his ships, but evening found him in sweet discourse beneath his lady's window.

At length the preparations were completed. Two gallant caravels lay at anchor in the Tagus ready to sail at sunrise. Late at night by the pale light of a waning moon the lover had his last interview. The beautiful Serafina was sad at heart and full of dark forebodings; her lover full of hope and confidence. "A few short months," said he, "and I shall return in triumph. Thy father will then blush at his incredulity, and hasten to welcome to his house the Adalantado of the Seven Cities."

The gentle lady shook her head. It was not on this point she felt distrust. She was a thorough believer in the Island of the Seven Cities, and so sure of the success of the enterprise that she might have been tempted to join it had not the balcony been high and the grating strong. Other considerations induced that dubious shaking of the head. She had heard of the inconstancy of the seas, and the inconstancy of those who roam them. Might not Fernando meet with other loves in foreign ports? Might not some peerless beauty in one or other of those Seven Cities efface the image of Serafina from his mind? Now let the truth be spoken, the beautiful Serafina had reason for her disquiet. If Don Fernando had any fault in the world, it was that of being rather inflammable and apt to take fire from every sparkling eye. He had been somewhat of a rover among the sex on shore, what might he be on sea?

She ventured to express her doubt, but he spurned at the very idea. "What! he false to Serafina! He bow at the shrine of another beauty? Never! never!" Repeatedly did he bend his knee, and smite his breast, and call upon the silver moon to witness his sincerity and truth.

He retorted the doubt, "Might not Serafina herself forget her plighted faith? Might not some wealthier rival present himself while he was tossing on the sea; and, backed by her father's wishes, win the treasure of her hand!"

The beautiful Serafina raised her white arms between the iron bars of the balcony, and, like her lover, invoked the moon to testify her vows. Alas! how little did Fernando know her heart. The more her father should oppose, the more would she be fixed in faith. Though years should intervene, Fernando on his return would find her true. Even should the salt sea swallow him up (and her eyes shed salt tears at the very thought), never would she be the wife of another! Never, *never*, NEVER! She drew from her finger a ring gemmed with a ruby heart, and dropped it from the balcony, a parting pledge of constancy.

Thus the lovers parted with many a tender word and plighted vow. But will they keep those vows? Perish the doubt! Have they not called the constant moon to witness?

With the morning dawn the caravels dropped down the Tagus, and put to sea. They steered for the Canaries, in those days the regions of nautical discovery and romance, and the outposts of the known world, for as yet Columbus had not steered his daring barks across the ocean. Scarce had they reached those latitudes when they were separated by a violent tempest. For many days was the caravel of Don Fernando driven about at the mercy of the elements; all seamanship was baffled, destruction seemed inevitable and the crew were in despair. All at once the storm subsided; the ocean sank into a calm; the clouds which had veiled the face of heaven were suddenly withdrawn, and the tempest-tossed mariners beheld a fair and mountainous island, emerging as if by enchantment from the murky gloom. They rubbed their eyes and gazed for a time almost incredulously, yet there lay the island spread out in lovely landscapes, with the late stormy sea laving its shores with peaceful billows.

The pilot of the caravel consulted his maps and charts; no island like the one before him was laid down as existing in those parts; it is true he had lost his reckoning in the late storm, but, according to his calculations, he could not be far from the Canaries; and this was not one of that group of islands. The caravel now lay perfectly becalmed off the mouth of a river, on the banks of which, about a league from the sea, was descried a noble city, with lofty walls and towers, and a protecting castle.

After a time, a stately barge with sixteen oars was seen emerging from the river, and approaching the caravel. It was quaintly carved and gilt; the oarsmen were clad in antique garb, their oars painted of a bright crimson, and they came slowly and solemnly, keeping time as they rowed to the cadence of an old Spanish ditty. Under a silken canopy in the stern, sat a cavalier richly clad, and over his head was a banner bearing the sacred emblem of the cross.

When the barge reached the caravel, the cavalier stepped on board. He was tall and gaunt; with a long Spanish visage, moustaches that curled up to his eyes, and a forked beard. He wore gauntlets reaching to his elbows, a Toledo blade strutting out behind, with a basket hilt, in which he carried his handkerchief. His air was lofty and precise, and bespoke indisputably the hidalgo. Thrusting out a long spindle leg, he took off a huge sombrero, and swaying it until the feather swept the ground, accosted Don Fernando in the old Castilian language and with the old Castilian courtesy, welcoming him to the Island of the Seven Cities.

Don Fernando was overwhelmed with astonishment. Could this be true? Had he really been tempest-driven to the very land of which he was in quest?

It was even so. That very day the inhabitants were holding high festival in commemoration of the escape of their ancestors from the Moors. The arrival of the caravel at such a juncture was considered a good omen, the accomplishment of an ancient prophecy through which the island was to be restored to the great community of Christendom. The cavalier before him was grand-chamberlain, sent by the alcayde to invite him to the festivities of the capital.

Don Fernando could scarce believe that this was not all a dream. He made known his name, and the object of his voyage. The grand chamberlain declared that all was in perfect accordance with the ancient prophecy, and that the moment his credentials were presented, he would be acknowledged as the Adalantado of the Seven Cities. In the mean time the day was waning; the barge was ready to convey him to the land, and would as assuredly bring him back.

Don Fernando's pilot, a veteran of the seas, drew him aside and expostulated against his venturing, on the mere word of a stranger, to land in a strange barge on an unknown shore. "Who knows, Señor, what land this is, or what people inhabit it?"

Don Fernando was not to be dissuaded. Had he not believed in this island when all the world doubted? Had he not sought it in defiance of storm and tempest, and was he now to shrink from its shores when they lay before him in calm weather? In a word, was not faith the very corner-stone of his enterprise?

Having arrayed himself, therefore, in gala dress befitting the occasion, he took his seat in the barge. The grand chamberlain seated himself opposite. The rowers plied their oars, and renewed the mournful old ditty, and the gorgeous but unwieldy barge moved slowly through the water.

The night closed in before they entered the river, and swept along past rock and promontory, each guarded by its tower. At every post they were challenged by the sentinel.

"Who goes there?"

"The Adalantado of the Seven Cities."

"Welcome, Señor Adalantado. Pass on."

Entering the harbor they rowed close by an armed galley of ancient form. Soldiers with crossbows patrolled the deck.

"Who goes there?"

"The Adalantado of the Seven Cities."

"Welcome, Señor Adalantado. Pass on."

They landed at a broad flight of stone steps, leading up between two massive towers, and knocked at the water-gate. A sentinel, in ancient steel casque, looked from the barbecan.

"Who is there?"

"The Adalantado of the Seven Cities."

"Welcome, Señor Adalantado."

The gate swung open, grating upon rusty hinges. They entered between two rows of warriors in Gothic armor, with cross-bows, maces, battle-axes, and faces old-fashioned as their armor. There were processions through the streets, in commemoration of the landing of the seven Bishops and their followers, and bonfires, at which effigies of losel Moors expiated their invasion of Christendom by a kind of auto-da-fé. The groups round the fires, uncouth in their attire, looked like the fantastic figures that roam the streets in Carnival time. Even the dames who gazed down from Gothic balconies hung with antique tapestry, resembled effigies dressed up in Christmas mummeries. Every thing, in short, bore the stamp of former ages, as if the world had suddenly rolled back for several centuries. Nor was this to be wondered at. Had not the Island of the Seven Cities been cut off from the rest of the world for several hundred years; and were not these the modes and customs of Gothic Spain before it was conquered by the Moors?

Arrived at the palace of the alcayde, the grand chamberlain knocked at the portal. The porter looked through a wicket, and demanded who was there.

"The Adalantado of the Seven Cities."

The portal was thrown wide open. The grand chamberlain led the way up a vast, heavily-moulded, marble staircase, and into a hall of ceremony, where was the alcayde with several of the principal dignitaries of the city, who had a marvellous resemblance, in form and feature, to the quaint figures in old illuminated manuscripts.

The grand chamberlain stepped forward and announced the name and title of the stranger guest, and the extraordinary nature of his mission. The announcement appeared to create no extraordinary emotion or surprise, but to be received as the anticipated fulfilment of a prophecy.

The reception of Don Fernando, however, was profoundly gracious, though in the same style of stately courtesy which every where prevailed. He would have produced his credentials, but this was courteously declined. The evening was devoted to high festivity; the following day, when he should enter the port with his caravel, would be devoted to business, when the credentials would be received in due form, and he inducted into office as Adalantado of the Seven Cities.

Don Fernando was now conducted through one of those interminable suites of apartments, the pride of Spanish palaces, all furnished in a style of obsolete magnificence. In a vast saloon blazing with tapers was assembled all the aristocracy and fashion of the city; stately dames and cavaliers, the very counterpart of the figures in the tapestry which decorated the walls. Fernando gazed in silent marvel. It was a reflex of the proud aristocracy of Spain in the time of Roderick the Goth.

The festivities of the evening were all in the style of solemn and antiquated ceremonial. There was a dance, but it was as if the old tapestry were put in motion, and all the figures moving in stately measure about the floor. There was one exception, and one that told powerfully upon the susceptible Adalantado. The alcayde's daughter—such a ripe, melting beauty! Her dress, it is true, like the dresses of her neighbors, might have been worn before the flood, but she had the black Andalusian eye, a glance of which, through its long dark lashes, is irresistible. Her voice, too, her manner, her undulating movements, all smacked of Andalusia, and showed how female charms may be transmitted from age to age, and clime to clime, without ever going out of fashion. Those who know the witchery of the sex, in that most amorous part of amorous old Spain, may judge of the fascination to which Don Fernando was exposed, as he joined in the dance with one of its most captivating descendants.

He sat beside her at the banquet! such an old world feast! such obsolete dainties! At the head of the table the peacock, that bird of state and ceremony, was served up in full plumage on a golden dish. As Don Fernando cast his eyes down the glittering board, what a vista presented itself of odd heads and head-dresses; of formal bearded dignitaries and stately dames, with castellated locks and towering plumes! Is it to be wondered at that he should turn with delight from these antiquated figures to the alcayde's daughter, all smiles and dimples, and melting looks and melting accents? Beside, for I wish to give him every excuse in my power, he was in a particularly excitable mood from the novelty of the scene before him, from this realization of all his hopes and fancies, and from frequent draughts of the wine cup presented to him at every moment by officious pages during the banquet.

In a word—there is no concealing the matter—before the evening was over, Don Fernando was making love outright to the alcayde's daughter. They had wandered together to a moon-lit balcony of the palace, and he was charming her ear with one of those love ditties with which, in a like balcony, he had serenaded the beautiful Serafina.

The damsel hung her head coyly. "Ah! Señor, these are flattering words; but you cavaliers, who roam the seas, are unsteady as its waves. To-morrow you will be throned in state, Adalantado of the Seven Cities; and will think no more of the alcayde's daughter."

Don Fernando in the intoxication of the moment called the moon to witness his sincerity. As he raised his hand in adjuration, the chaste moon cast a ray upon the ring that sparkled on his finger. It caught the damsel's eye. "Signor Adalantado," said she archly, "I have no great faith in the moon, but give me that ring upon your finger in pledge of the truth of what you profess."

The gallant Adalantado was taken by surprise; there was no parrying this sudden appeal. before he had time to reflect, the ring of the beautiful Serafina glittered on the finger of the alcayde's daughter.

At this eventful moment the chamberlain approached with lofty demeanor, and announced that the barge was waiting to bear him back to the caravel. I forbear to relate the ceremonious partings with the alcayde and his dignitaries, and the tender farewell of the alcayde's daughter. He took his seat in the barge opposite the grand chamberlain. The rowers plied their crimson oars in the same slow and stately manner to the cadence of the same mournful old ditty. His brain was in a whirl with all that he had seen, and his heart now and then gave him a twinge as he thought of his temporary infidelity to the beautiful Serafina. The barge sallied out into the sea, but no caravel was to be seen; doubtless she had been carried to a distance by the current of the river. The oarsmen rowed on; their monotonous chant had a lulling effect. A drowsy influence crept over Don Fernando. Objects swam before his eyes. The oarsmen assumed odd shapes as in a dream. The grand chamberlain grew larger and larger, and taller and taller. He took off his huge sombrero, and held it over the head of Don Fernando, like an extinguisher over a candle. The latter cowered beneath it; he felt himself sinking in the socket.

"Good night! Señor Adalantado of the Seven Cities!" said the grand chamberlain.

The sombrero slowly descended—Don Fernando was extinguished!

How long he remained extinct no mortal man can tell. When he returned to consciousness, he found himself in a strange cabin, surrounded by strangers. He rubbed his eyes, and looked round him wildly. Where was he?—On board of a Portuguese ship, bound to Lisbon. How came he there?—He had been taken senseless from a wreck drifting about the ocean.

Don Fernando was more and more confounded and perplexed. He recalled, one by one, every thing that had happened to him in the Island of the Seven Cities, until he had been extinguished by the sombrero of the grand chamberlain. But what had happened to him since? What had become of his caravel? Was it the wreck of her on which he had been found floating?

The people about him could give no information on the subject. He entreated them to take him to the Island of the Seven Cities, which could not be far off. Told them all that had befallen him there. That he had but to land to be received as Adalantado; when he would reward them magnificently for their services.

They regarded his words as the ravings of delirium, and in their honest solicitude for the restoration of his reason, administered such rough remedies that he was fain to drop the subject and observe a cautious taciturnity.

At length they arrived in the Tagus, and anchored before the famous city of Lisbon. Don Fernando sprang joyfully on shore, and hastened to his ancestral mansion, A strange porter opened the door, who knew nothing of him or of his family; no people of the name had inhabited the house for many a year.

He sought the mansion of Don Ramiro. He approached the balcony beneath which he had bidden farewell to Serafina. Did his eyes deceive him? No! There was Serafina herself among the flowers in the balcony. He raised his arms toward her with an exclamation of rapture. She east upon him a look of indignation, and, hastily retiring, closed the casement with a slam that testified her displeasure.

Could she have heard of his flirtation with the alcayde's daughter? But that was mere transient gallantry. A moment's interview would dispel every doubt of his constancy.

He rang at the door; as it was opened by the porter he rushed up stairs; sought the well known chamber, and threw himself at the feet of Serafina. She started back with affright, and took refuge in the arms of a youthful cavalier.

"What mean you, Señor," cried the latter, "by this intrusion?"

"What right have you to ask the question?" demanded Don Fernando fiercely.

"The right of an affianced suitor!"

Don Fernando started and turned pale. "Oh, Serafina! Serafina!" cried he, in a tone of agony; "is this thy plighted constancy?"

"Serafina? What mean you by Serafina, Señor? If this be the lady you intend, her name is Maria."

"May I not believe my senses? May I not believe my heart?" cried Don Fernando. "Is not this Serafina Alvarez, the original of yon portrait, which, less fickle than herself, still smiles on me from the wall?"

"Holy Virgin!" cried the young lady, casting her eyes upon the portrait. "He is talking of my great-grandmother!"

An explanation ensued, if that could be called an explanation, which plunged the unfortunate Fernando into tenfold perplexity. If he might believe his eyes, he saw before him his beloved Serafina; if he might believe his ears, it was merely her hereditary form and features, perpetuated in the person of her great-granddaughter.

His brain began to spin. He sought the office of the Minister of Marine, and made a report of his expedition, and of the Island of the Seven Cities, which he had so fortunately discovered. Nobody knew any thing of such an expedition, or such an island. He declared that he had undertaken the enterprise under a formal contract with the crown, and had received a regular commission, constituting him Adalantado. This must be matter of record, and he insisted loudly, that the books of the department should be consulted. The wordy strife at length attracted the attention of an old gray-headed clerk, who sat perched on a high stool, at a high desk, with iron-rimmed spectacles on the top of a thin, pinched nose, copying records into an enormous folio. He had wintered and summered in the department for a great part of a century, until he had almost grown to be a piece of the desk at which he sat; his memory was a mere index of official facts and documents, and his brain was little better than red tape and parchment. After peering down for a time from his lofty perch, and ascertaining the matter in controversy, he put his pen behind his ear, and descended. He remembered to have heard something from his predecessor about an expedition of the kind in question, but then it had sailed during the reign of Dom Ioam II., and he had been dead at least a hundred years. To put the matter beyond dispute, however, the archives of the Torre do Tombo, that sepulchre of old Portuguese documents, were diligently searched, and a record was found of a contract between the crown and one Fernando do Ulmo, for the discovery of the Island of the Seven Cities, and of a commission secured to him as Adalantado of the country he might discover.

"There!" cried Don Fernando, triumphantly, "there you have proof, before your own eyes, of what I have said. I am the Fernando de Ulmo specified in that record.

I have discovered the Island of the Seven Cities, and am entitled to be Adalantado, according to contract."

The story of Don Fernando had certainly, what is pronounced the best of historical foundation, documentary evidence; but when a man, in the bloom of youth, talked of events that had taken place above a century previously, as having happened to himself, it is no wonder that he was set down for a madman.

The old clerk looked at him from above and below his spectacles, shrugged his shoulders, stroked his chin, reascended his lofty stool, took the pen from behind his ears, and resumed his daily and eternal task, copying records into the fiftieth volume of a series of gigantic folios. The other clerks winked at each other shrewdly, and dispersed to their several places, and poor Don Fernando, thus left to himself, flung out of the office, almost driven wild by these repeated perplexities.

In the confusion of his mind, he instinctively repaired to the mansion of Alvarez, but it was barred against him. To break the delusion under which the youth apparently labored, and to convince him that the Serafina about whom he raved was really dead, he was conducted to her tomb. There she lay, a stately matron, cut out in alabaster; and there lay her husband beside her; a portly cavalier, in armor; and there knelt, on each side, the effigies of a numerous progeny, proving that she had been a fruitful vine. Even the very monument gave evidence of the lapse of time; the hands of her husband, folded as if in prayer, had lost their fingers, and the face of the once lovely Serafina was without a nose.

Don Fernando felt a transient glow of indignation at beholding this monumental proof of the inconstancy of his mistress; but who could expect a mistress to remain constant during a whole century of absence? And what right had he to rail about constancy, after what had passed between himself and the alcayde's daughter? The unfortunate cavalier performed one pious act of tender devotion; he had the alabaster nose of Serafina restored by a skilful statuary, and then tore himself from the tomb.

He could now no longer doubt the fact that, somehow or other, he had skipped over a whole century, during the night he had spent at the Island of the Seven Cities; and he was now as complete a stranger in his native city, as if he had never been there. A thousand times did he wish himself back to that wonderful island, with its antiquated banquet halls, where he had been so courteously received; and now that the once young and beautiful Serafina was nothing but a great-grandmother in marble, with generations of descendants, a thousand times would he recall the melting black eyes of the alcayde's daughter, who doubtless, like himself, was still flourishing in fresh juvenility, and breathe a secret wish that he were seated by her side.

He would at once have set on foot another expedition, at his own expense, to cruise in search of the sainted island, but his means were exhausted. He endeavored to rouse others to the enterprise, setting forth the certainty of profitable results, of which his own experience furnished such unquestionable proof. Alas! no one would give faith to his tale; but looked upon it as the feverish dream of a shipwrecked man. He persisted in his efforts; holding forth in all places and all companies, until he became an object of jest and jeer to the light-minded, who mistook his earnest enthusiasm for a proof of insanity; and the very children in the streets bantered him with the title of "The Adalantado of the Seven Cities."

Finding all efforts in vain, in his native city of Lisbon, he took shipping for the Canaries, as being nearer the latitude of his former cruise, and inhabited by people given to nautical adventure. Here he found ready listeners to his story; for the old pilots and mariners of those parts were notorious island-hunters, and devout believers in all the wonders of the seas. Indeed, one and all treated his adventure as a common occurrence, and turning to each other, with a sagacious nod of the head, observed, "He has been at the Island of St. Brandan."

They then went on to inform him of that great marvel and enigma of the ocean; of its repeated appearance to the inhabitants of their islands; and of the many but ineffectual expeditious that had been made in search of it. They took him to a promontory of the island of Palma, whence the shadowy St. Brandan had oftenest been descried, and they pointed out the very tract in the west where its mountains had been seen.

Don Fernando listened with rapt attention. He had no longer a doubt that this mysterious and fugacious island must be the same with that of the Seven Cities; and that some supernatural influence connected with it had operated upon himself, and made the events of a night occupy the space of a century.

He endeavored, but in vain, to rouse the islanders to another attempt at discovery; they had given up the phantom island as indeed inaccessible. Fernando, however, was not to be discouraged. The idea wore itself deeper and deeper in his mind, until it became the engrossing subject of his thoughts and object of his being. Every morning he would repair to the promontory of Palma, and sit there throughout the livelong day, in hopes of seeing the fairy mountains of St. Brandan peering above the horizon;

every evening he returned to his home, a disappointed man, but ready to resume his post on the following morning.

His assiduity was all in vain. He grew gray in his ineffectual attempt: and was at length found dead at his post. His grave is still shown in the island of Palma, and a cross is erected on the spot where he used to sit and look out upon the sea, in hopes of the reappearance of the phantom island.

NOTE.—For various particulars concerning the *Island of St. Brandan* and the *Island of the Seven Cities*, those ancient problems of the ocean, the curious reader is referred to articles under those heads in the Appendix to the Life of Columbus.

Recollections of the Alhambra

I HAVE ALREADY GIVEN TO THE WORLD SOME ANECDOTES OF A SUMMER'S residence in the old Moorish palace of the Alhambra. It was a dreamy sojourn, during which I lived, as it were, in the midst of an Arabian tale, and shut my eyes as much as possible to every thing that should call me back to every day life. If there is any country in Europe where one can do so, it is among these magnificent but semi-barbaric ruins of poor, wild, legendary, romantic Spain. In the silent and deserted halls of the Alhambra, surrounded with the insignia of regal sway, and the vivid, though dilapidated traces of Oriental luxury, I was in the stronghold of Moorish story, where every thing spoke of the palmy days of Granada when under the dominion of the crescent.

Much of the literature of Spain turns upon the wars of the Moors and Christians, and consists of traditional ballads and tales or romances, about the "buenas andanzas," and "grandes hechos," the "lucky adventures," and "great exploits" of the warriors of yore. It is worthy of remark, that many of these lays which sing of prowess and magnanimity in war, and tenderness and fidelity in love, relate as well to Moorish as to Spanish cavaliers. The lapse of peaceful centuries has extinguished the rancor of ancient hostility; and the warriors of Granada, once the objects of bigot detestation, are now often held up by Spanish poets as mirrors of chivalric virtue.

None have been the theme of higher eulogy than the illustrious line of the Abencerrages, who in the proud days of Moslem domination were the soul of every thing noble and chivalric. The veterans of the family sat in the royal council, and were foremost in devising heroic enterprises to carry dismay into the Christian territories; and what the veterans devised the young men of the name were foremost to execute. In all adventures, enterprises, and hair-breadth hazards, the Abencerrages were sure to win the brightest laurels. In the tilt and tourney, in the riding at the ring, the daring bull fight, and all other recreations which bore an affinity to war, the Abencerrages carried off the palm. None equalled them for splendor of array, for noble bearing, and glorious horsemanship. Their open-handed munificence made them the idols of the people; their magnanimity and perfect faith gained the admiration of the high-minded. Never did they decry the merits of a rival, nor betray the confidings of a friend; and the word of an Abencerrage was a guarantee never to be doubted.

And then their devotion to the fair! Never did Moorish beauty consider the fame of her charms established, until she had an Abencerrage for a lover; and never did an Abencerrage prove recreant to his vows. Lovely Granada! City of delights! Who ever bore the favors of thy dames more proudly on their casques, or championed them more gallantly in the chivalrous tilts of the Vivarambla? Or who ever made thy moon-lit balconies, thy gardens of myrtles and roses, of oranges, citrons, and pomegranates, respond to more tender serenades?

Such were the fancies I used to conjure up as I sat in the beautiful hall of the Abencerrages, celebrated in the tragic story of that devoted race, where thirty-six of its bravest cavaliers were treacherously sacrificed to appease the jealous fears of a tyrant. The fountain which once ran red with their blood, throws up a sparkling jet, and spreads a dewy freshness through the hall; but a deep stain on the marble pavement is still pointed out as a sanguinary record of the massacre. The truth of the record has been called in question, but I regarded it with the same determined faith with which I contemplated the stains of Rizzio's blood on the floor of the palace of Holyrood. I thank no one for enlightening my credulity on points of poetical belief. It is like robbing the statue of Memnon of its mysterious music. Dispel historical illusions, and there is an end to half the charms of travelling.

The hall of the Abencerrages is connected moreover with the recollection of one of the sweetest evenings and sweetest scenes I ever enjoyed in Spain. It was a beautiful summer evening, when the moon shone down into the Court of Lions, lighting up its sparkling fountain. I was seated with a few companions in the hall in question, listening to those traditional ballads and romances in which the Spaniards delight. They were sung to the accompaniment of the guitar, by one of the most gifted and fascinating beings that I ever met with even among the fascinating daughters of Spain. She was young and beautiful; and light and ethereal; full of fire, and spirit, and pure enthusiasm. She wore the fanciful Andalusian dress; touched the guitar with speaking eloquence; improvised with wonderful facility; and, as she became excited by her theme, or by the rapt attention of her auditors, would pour forth in the richest and most melodious strains, a succession of couplets, full of striking description, or stirring narrative, and composed, as I was assured, at the moment. Most of these were suggested by the place, and related to the ancient glories of Granada, and the prowess of her chivalry. The Abencerrages were her favorite heroes; she felt a woman's admiration of their gallant courtesy, and high-souled honor; and it was touching and inspiring to hear the praises of that generous but devoted race, chanted in this fated ball of their calamity, by the lips of Spanish beauty.

Among the subjects of which she treated, was a tale of Moslem honor, and old-fashioned Spanish courtesy, which made a strong impression on me. She disclaimed all merit of invention, however, and said she had merely dilated into verse a popular tradition; and, indeed, I have since found the main facts inserted at the end of Conde's History of the Domination of the Arabs, and the story itself embodied in the form of an episode in the Diana of Montemayor. From these sources I have drawn it forth, and endeavored to shape it according to my recollection of the version of the beautiful minstrel; but alas! what can supply the want of that voice, that look, that form, that action, which gave magical effect to her chant, and held every one rapt in breathless admiration! Should this mere travestie of her inspired numbers ever meet her eye, in her stately abode at Granada, may it meet with that indulgence which belongs to her benignant nature. Happy should I be, if it could awaken in her bosom one kind recollection of the stranger, for whose gratification she did not think it beneath her to exert those fascinating powers, in the moon-lit halls of the Alhambra.

The Abencerrage

On the summit of a craggy hill, a spur of the mountains of Ronda, stands the castle of Allora; now a mere ruin, infested by bats and owlets; but in old times, a strong border-hold which kept watch upon the warlike kingdom of Granada, and held the Moors in check. It was a post always confided to some well-tried commander, and at the time of which we treat, was held by Roderigo de Narvaez, alcayde, or military governor of Antiquera. It was a frontier post of his command; but he passed most of his time there, because its situation on the borders gave frequent opportunity for those adventurous exploits in which the Spanish chivalry delighted.

He was a veteran, famed among both Moors and Christians, not only for deeds of arms, but for that magnanimous courtesy which should ever be entwined with the stern virtues of the soldier.

His garrison consisted of fifty chosen men, well appointed and well-mounted, with which he maintained such vigilant watch that nothing could escape his eye. While some remained on guard in the castle, he would sally forth with others, prowling about the highways, the paths and defiles of the mountains by day and night, and now and then making a daring foray into the very Vega of Granada.

On a fair and beautiful night in summer, when the moon was in the full, and the freshness of the evening breeze had tempered the heat of day, the alcayde, with nine of his cavaliers, was going the rounds of the mountains in quest of adventures. They rode silently and cautiously, for it was a night to tempt others abroad, and they might be overheard by Moorish scout or traveller; they kept along ravines and hollow ways, moreover, lest they should be betrayed by the glittering of the moon upon their armor. Coming to a fork in the road, the alcayde ordered five of his cavaliers to take one of the branches, while he, with the remaining four, would take the other. Should either party be in danger, the blast of a horn was to be the signal for succor. The party of five had not proceeded far, when, in passing through a defile, they heard the voice of a man singing. Concealing themselves among trees, they awaited his approach. The moon, which left the grove in shadow, shone full upon his person, as he slowly advanced, mounted on a dapple gray steed of powerful frame and generous spirit, and magnificently caparisoned. He was a Moorish cavalier of noble demeanor and graceful carriage, arrayed in a marlota, or tunic, and an albornoz of crimson damask fringed with gold. His Tunisian turban, of many folds, was of striped silk and cotton, bordered with a golden fringe; at his girdle hung a Damascus scimitar, with loops and tassels of silk and gold. On his left arm he bore an ample target, and his right hand grasped a long double-pointed lance. Apparently dreaming of no danger he sat negligently on his steed, gazing on the moon, and singing, with a sweet and manly voice, a Moorish love ditty.

Just opposite the grove where the cavaliers were concealed, the horse turned aside to drink at a small fountain in a rock beside the road. His rider threw the reins on his neck to let him drink at his ease, and continued his song.

The cavaliers whispered with each other. Charmed with the gallant and gentle appearance of the Moor, they determined not to harm, but capture him; an easy task, as they supposed, in his negligent mood. Rushing forth, therefore, they thought to surround, and take him by surprise. Never were men more mistaken. To gather up his reins, wheel round his steed, brace his buckler, and couch his lance, was the work of an instant, and there he sat, fixed like a castle in his saddle.

The cavaliers checked their steeds, and reconnoitred him warily, loth to come to an encounter which must prove fatal to him.

The Moor now held a parley. "If ye be true knights, and seek for honorable fame, come on singly, and I will meet each in succession; if ye be mere lurkers of the road, intent on spoil, come all at once, and do your worst."

The cavaliers communed together for a moment, when one parting from the others, advanced. "Although no law of chivalry," said he, "obliges us to risk the loss of a prize, when fairly in our power, yet we willingly grant as a courtesy what we might refuse as a right. Valiant Moor, defend thyself!"

So saying, he wheeled, took proper distance, couched his lance, and putting spurs to his horse, made at the stranger. The latter met him in mid career, transpierced him with his lance, and threw him from his saddle. A second and a third succeeded, but were unhorsed with equal facility, and thrown to the earth, severely wounded. The remaining two, seeing their comrades thus roughly treated, forgot all compact of courtesy, and charged both at once upon the Moor. He parried the thrust of one, but was wounded by the other in the thigh, and in the shock and confusion dropped his lance. Thus disarmed, and closely pressed, he pretended to fly, and was hotly pursued. Having drawn the two cavaliers some distance from the spot, he wheeled short about, with one of those dexterous movements for which the Moorish horsemen were renowned; passed swiftly between them, swung himself down from his saddle, so as to catch up his lance, then, lightly replacing himself, turned to renew the combat.

Seeing him thus fresh for the encounter, as if just issued from his tent, one of the cavaliers put his lips to his horn, and blew a blast, that soon brought the Alcayde and his four companions to the spot.

Narvaez, seeing three of his cavaliers extended on the earth, and two others hotly engaged with the Moor, was struck with admiration, and coveted a contest with so accomplished a warrior. Interfering in the fight, he called upon his followers to desist, and with courteous words invited the Moor to a more equal combat. The challenge was readily accepted. For some time the contest was doubtful, and the Alcayde had need of all his skill and strength to ward off the blows of his antagonist. The Moor, however, exhausted by previous fighting, and by loss of blood, no longer sat his horse firmly, nor managed him with his wonted skill. Collecting all his strength for a last assault, he rose in his stirrups, and made a violent thrust with his lance; the Alcayde received it upon his shield, and at the same time wounded the Moor in the right arm; then closing, in the shock, grasped him in his arms, dragged him from his saddle, and fell with him to the earth: when putting his knee upon his breast, and his dagger to his throat, "Cavalier," exclaimed he, "render thyself my prisoner, for thy life is in my hands!"

"Kill me, rather," replied the Moor, "for death would be less grievous than loss of liberty."

The Alcayde, however, with the clemency of the truly brave, assisted him to rise, ministered to his wounds with his own hands, and had him conveyed with great care to the castle of Allora. His wounds in a few days were nearly cured; but the deepest had been inflicted on his spirit. He was constantly buried in a profound melancholy.

The Alcayde, who had conceived a great regard for him, treated him more as a friend than a captive, and tried in every way to cheer him, but in vain; he was always sad and moody, and, when on the battlements of the castle, would keep his eyes turned to the south, with a fixed and wistful gaze.

"How is this?" exclaimed the Alcayde, reproachfully, "that you, who were so hardy and fearless in the field, should lose all spirit when a captive. If any secret grief preys on your heart, confide it to me, as to a friend, and I promise on the faith of a cavalier, that you shall have no cause to repent the disclosure."

The Moorish knight kissed the hand of the Alcayde. "Noble cavalier," said he, "that I am cast down in spirit, is not from my wounds, which are slight, nor from my captivity, for your kindness has robbed it of all gloom; nor from my defeat, for to be conquered by so accomplished and renowned a cavalier, is no disgrace. But to explain the cause of my grief, it is necessary to give some particulars of my story; and this I am moved to do by the sympathy you have manifested toward me, and the magnanimity that shines through all your actions.

"Know, then, that my name is Abendavaez, and that I am of the noble but unfortunate line of the Abencerrages. You have doubtless heard of the destruction that fell upon our race. Charged with treasonable designs, of which they were entirely innocent, many of them were beheaded, the rest banished; so that not an Abencerrage was permitted to remain in Granada, excepting my father and my uncle, whose innocence was proved, even to the satisfaction of their persecutors. It was decreed, however, that, should they have children, the sons should be educated at a distance from Granada, and the daughters should be married out of the kingdom.

"Conformably to this decree, I was sent, while yet an infant, to be reared in the fortress of Cartama, the Alcayde of which was an ancient friend of my father. He had no children, and received me into his family as his own child, treating me with the kindness and affection of a father; and I grew up in the belief that he really was such. A few years afterward, his wife gave birth to a daughter, but his tenderness toward me continued undiminished. I thus grew up with Xarisa, for so the infant daughter of the Alcayde was called, as her own brother. I beheld her charms unfolding, as it were, leaf by leaf, like the morning rose, each moment disclosing fresh sweetness and beauty, and thought the growing passion which I felt for her was mere fraternal affection.

"At length one day I accidentally overheard a conversation between the Alcayde and his confidential domestic, of which I found myself the subject.

"In this I learnt the secret of my real parentage, which the Alcayde had withheld from me as long as possible, through reluctance to inform me of my being of a proscribed and unlucky race. It was time now, he thought, to apprise me of the truth, that I might adopt a career in life.

"I retired without letting it be perceived that I had overheard the conversation. The intelligence it conveyed, would have overwhelmed me at an earlier period; but now the intimation that Xarisa was not my sister, operated like magic. In an instant the brotherly affection with which my heart at times had throbbed almost to excess, was transformed into ardent love.

"I sought Xarisa in the garden, where I found her in a bower of jessamines, arranging her beautiful hair in the mirror of a crystal fountain. I ran to her with open arms, and was received with a sister's embraces; upbraiding me for leaving her so long alone.

"We seated ourselves by the fountain, and I hastened to reveal the secret conversation I had overheard.

"'Alas!' cried she, 'then our happiness is at an end!'

"'How!' cried I, 'wilt thou cease to love me because I am not thy brother?'

"'Alas, no!' replied she, gently withdrawing from my embrace, 'but when it is once made known we are not brother and sister, we shall no longer be permitted to be thus 'always together.'

"In fact, from that moment our intercourse took a new character. We met often at the fountain among the jessamines, but Xarisa no longer advanced with open arms to meet me. She became reserved and silent, and would blush, and cast down her eyes, when I seated myself beside her. My heart became a prey to the thousand doubts and fears that ever attend upon true love. Restless and uneasy, I looked back with regret to our unreserved intercourse when we supposed ourselves brother and sister; yet I would not have had the relationship true, for the world.

"While matters were in this state between us, an order came from the King of Granada for the Alcayde to take command of the fortress of Coyn, on the Christian frontier. He prepared to remove, with all his family, but signified that I should remain at Cartama. I declared that I could not be parted from Xarisa. 'That is the very cause,' said he, 'why I leave thee behind. It is time, Abendaraez, thou shouldst know the secret of thy birth. Thou art no son of mine, neither is Xarisa thy sister.' 'I know it all,' exclaimed I, 'and I love her with tenfold the affection of a brother. You have brought us up together; you have made us necessary to each other's happiness; our hearts have entwined themselves with our growth; do not now tear them asunder. Fill up the measure of your kindness; be indeed a father to me, by giving me Xarisa for my wife.'

"The brow of the Alcayde darkened as I spoke. 'Have I then been deceived?' said he. 'Have those nurtured in my very bosom, been conspiring against me? Is this your return for my paternal tenderness?—to beguile the affections of my child, and teach her to deceive her father? It would have been cause enough to refuse thee the hand of my daughter, that thou wert of a proscribed race, who can never approach the walls of Granada; this, however, I might have passed over; but never will I give my daughter to a man who has endeavored to win her from me by deception.'

"All my attempts to vindicate myself and Xarisa were unavailing. I retired in anguish from his presence, and seeking Xarisa, told her of this blow, which was worse than death to me.

'Xarisa,' said I, 'we part for ever! I shall never see thee more! Thy father will guard thee rigidly. Thy beauty and his wealth will soon attract some happier rival, and I shall be forgotten!'

"Xarisa reproached my want of faith, and promised eternal constancy. I still doubted and desponded, until, moved by my anguish and despair, she agreed to a secret union. Our espousals made, we parted, with a promise on her part to send me word from Coyn, should her father absent himself from the fortress. The very day after our secret nuptials, I beheld the whole train of the Alcayde depart from Cartama, nor would he admit me to his presence, nor permit me to bid farewell to Xarisa. I remained at Cartama, somewhat pacified in spirit by our secret bond of union; but every thing around fed my passion, and reminded me of Xarisa. I saw the window at which I had so often beheld her. I wandered through the apartment she had inhabited; the chamber in which she had slept. I visited the bower of jessamines, and lingered beside the fountain in which she had delighted. Every thing recalled her to my imagination, and filled my heart with melancholy.

"At length, a confidential servant arrived with a letter from her, informing me, that her father was to depart that day for Granada, on a short absence, inviting me to hasten to Coyn, describing a secret portal at which I should apply, and the signal by which I would obtain admittance.

"If ever you have loved, most valiant Alcayde, you may judge of my transport. That very night I arrayed myself in gallant attire, to pay due honor to my bride; and arming myself against any casual attack, issued forth privately from Cartama. You know the rest, and by what sad fortune of war I find myself instead of a happy bridegroom in the nuptial bower of Coyn, vanquished, wounded, and a prisoner within the walls of Allora. The term of absence of the father of Xarisa is nearly expired. Within three days he will return to Coyn, and our meeting will no longer be possible. Judge, then, whether I grieve without cause and whether I may not well be excused for showing impatience under confinement."

Don Rodrigo was greatly moved by this recital; for, though more used to rugged war than scenes of amorous softness, he was of a kind and generous nature.

"Abendaraez," said he, "I did not seek thy confidence to gratify an idle curiosity. It grieves me much that the good fortune which delivered thee into my hands, should have marred so fair an enterprise. Give me thy faith, as a true knight, to return prisoner to my castle, within three days, and I will grant thee permission to accomplish thy nuptials."

The Abencerrage, in a transport of gratitude, would have thrown himself at his feet, but the Alcayde prevented him. Calling in his cavaliers, he took Abendaraez by the right hand, in their presence, exclaiming solemnly, "You promise, on the faith of a cavalier, to return to my castle of Allora within three days, and render yourself my prisoner?" And the Abencerrage said, "I promise."

Then said the Alcayde, "Go! and may good fortune attend you. If you require any safeguard, I and my cavaliers are ready to be your companions."

The Abencerrage kissed the hand of the Alcayde, in grateful acknowledgment. "Give me," said he, "my own armor, and my steed, and I require no guard. It is not likely that I shall again meet with so valorous a foe."

The shades of night had fallen, when the tramp of the dapple gray steed resounded over the drawbridge, and immediately afterwards, the light clatter of hoofs along the road bespoke the fleetness with which the youthful lover hastened to his bride. It was deep night when the Moor arrived at the castle of Coyn. He silently and cautiously walked his panting steed under its dark walls, and having nearly passed round them, came to the portal denoted by Xarisa. He paused, looked round to see that he was not observed, and knocked three times with the butt of his lance. In a little while the portal was timidly unclosed by the duenna of Xarisa. "Alas! Señor," said she, "what has detained you thus long? Every night have I watched for you; and my lady is sick at heart with doubt and anxiety."

The Abencerrage hung his lance, and shield, and scimitar against the wall, and followed the duenna, with silent steps, up a winding staircase, to the apartment of Xarisa. Vain would be the attempt to describe the raptures of that meeting. Time flew too swiftly, and the Abencerrage had nearly forgotten, until too late, his promise to return a prisoner to the Alcayde of Allora. The recollection of it came to him with a pang, and woke him from his dream of bliss. Xarisa saw his altered looks, and heard with alarm his stifled sighs; but her countenance brightened when she heard the cause. "Let not thy spirit be cast down," said she, throwing her white arms around him. "I have the keys of my father's treasures; send ransom more than enough to satisfy the Christian, and remain with me."

"No," said Abendaraez, "I have given my word to return in person, and like a true knight, must fulfil my promise. After that, fortune must do with me as it pleases."

"Then," said Xarisa, "I will accompany thee. Never shalt thou return a prisoner, and I remain at liberty."

The Abencerrage was transported with joy at this new proof of devotion in his beautiful bride. All preparations were speedily made for their departure. Xarisa mounted behind the Moor, on his powerful steed; they left the castle walls before daybreak, nor did they pause, until they arrived at the gate of the castle of Allora.

Alighting in the court, the Abencerrage supported the steps of his trembling bride, who remained closely veiled, into the presence of Rodrigo de Narvaez. "Behold, valiant Alcayde!" said he, "the way in which an Abencerrage keeps his word. I promised to return to thee a prisoner, but I deliver two captives into thy power. Behold Xarisa, and judge whether I grieved without reason, over the loss of such a treasure. Receive us as thine own, for I confide my life and her honor to thy hands."

The Alcayde was lost in admiration of the beauty of the lady, and the noble spirit of the Moor. "I know not," said he, "which of you surpasses the other; but I know that my castle is graced and honored by your presence. Consider it your own, while you deign to reside with me."

For several days, the lovers remained at Allora, happy in each other's love, and in the friendship of the Alcayde. The latter wrote a letter to the Moorish king of Granada, relating the whole event, extolling the valor and good faith of the Abencerrage, and craving for him the royal countenance.

The king was moved by the story, and pleased with an opportunity of showing attention to the wishes of a gallant and chivalrous enemy; for though he had often suffered from the prowess of Don Rodrigo de Narvaez, he admired his heroic character. Calling the Alcayde of Coyn into his presence, he gave him the letter to read. The Alcayde turned pale, and trembled with rage, on the perusal. "Restrain thine anger," said the king; "there is nothing that the Alcayde of Allora could ask, that I would not grant, if in my power. Go thou to Allora; pardon thy children; take them to thy home. I receive this Abencerrage into my favor, and it will be my delight to heap benefits upon you all."

The kindling ire of the Alcayde was suddenly appeased. He hastened to Allora; and folded his children to his bosom, who would have fallen at his feet Rodrigo de Narvaez gave liberty to his prisoner without ransom, demanding merely a promise of his friendship. He accompanied the youthful couple and their father to Coyn, where their nuptials were celebrated with great rejoicings. When the festivities were over, Don Rodrigo returned to his fortress of Allora.

After his departure, the Alcayde of Coyn addressed his children: "To your hands," said he, "I confide the disposition of my wealth. One of the first things I charge you, is not to forget the ransom you owe to the Alcayde of Allora. His magnanimity you can never repay, but you can prevent it from wronging him of his just dues. Give him, moreover, your entire friendship, for he merits it fully, though of a different faith."

The Abencerrage thanked him for his proposition, which so truly accorded with his own wishes. He took a large sum of gold, and inclosed it in a rich coffer; and, on his own part, sent six beautiful horses, superbly caparisoned; with six shields and lances, mounted and embossed with gold. The beautiful Xarisa, at the same time, wrote a letter to the Alcayde, filled with expressions of gratitude and friendship, and sent him a box of fragrant cypress wood, containing linen, of the finest quality, for his person.

The Alcayde disposed of the present in a characteristic manner. The horses and armor he shared among the cavaliers who had accompanied him on the night of the skirmish. The box of cypress wood and its contents he retained, for the sake of the beautiful Xarisa; and sent her, by the hands of the messenger, the sum of gold paid as a ransom, entreating her to receive it as a wedding present. This courtesy and magnanimity raised the character of the Alcayde Rodrigo de Narvaez still higher in the estimation of the Moors, who extolled him as a perfect mirror of chivalric virtue; and from that time forward, there was a continual exchange of good offices between them.

Those who would read the foregoing story decked out with poetic grace in the pure Castilian, let them seek it in the Diana of Montemayor.